VISIONS OF
WONDER
The Science Fiction Research Association
Anthology

VISIONS OF
WONDER

The Science Fiction Research Association
Anthology

Edited by

DAVID G. HARTWELL
AND MILTON T. WOLF

TOR

A TOM DOHERTY ASSOCIATES BOOK / NEW YORK

A Tor Book
Published by Tom Doherty Associates, Inc.
175 Fifth Avenue
New York, NY 10010

Tor Books on the World Wide Web:
http://www.tor.com

Tor® is a registered trademark of Tom Doherty Associates, Inc.

Design by Lynn Newmark

Library of Congress Cataloging-in-Publication Data

Visions of wonder : the Science Fiction Research Association
    anthology/edited by David G. Hartwell & Milton T. Wolf.—
    1st ed.
        p.   cm.
    "A Tom Doherty Associates book."
    Includes bibliographical references.
    ISBN 0-312-86224-5(hc)
    ISBN 0-312-85287-8(pb)
        1. Science fiction, American.   2. Science fiction, English.
    I. Hartwell, David G.   II. Wolf, Milton T.   III. Science Fiction
    Research Association.
    PS648.S3V57   1996
    813'.0876208—dc20   96-24524
                                                                    CIP

First Edition: November 1996

Printed in the United States of America

0 9 8 7 6 5 4 3 2 1

COPYRIGHT ACKNOWLEDGMENTS

Introduction © 1996 by David G. Hartwell and Milton T. Wolf.

"Credo" © 1956, 1967 by Damon Knight. Reprinted by permission of the author.

"The Ship Who Sang" © 1961, 1989 by Anne McCaffrey; first appeared in *The Magazine of Fantasy and Science Fiction;* reprinted by permission of the author and the author's agent, Virginia Kidd.

"Blood Music" © 1982 by Greg Bear. Used by permission of the author and the author's agent, Richard Curtis.

"Paperjack" © 1991 by Charles de Lint. Reprinted by permission of the author.

"Forever Yours, Anna" © 1989 by Omni Publications International, Ltd. Reprinted by permission of the author.

"The Golden Age of SF Is Twelve" © 1984 by David G. Hartwell. From the book *Age of Wonders,* first published by Walker and Company. Reprinted by permission of the author and the author's agent, Susan Ann Protter.

"Mr. Boy" © 1990 by Davis Publications. First published in *Asimov's Science Fiction,* June 1990. Reprinted by permission of the author.

"Jamboree" © 1969 by Universal Publishing Company, © 1970 by Jack Williamson. Reprinted by permission of the author.

"The Death of Doctor Island" © 1973 by Gene Wolfe. First published in *Universe 3.* Reprinted by permission of the author and the author's agent, Virginia Kidd.

"Ender's Game" © 1977 by Orson Scott Card. Reprinted by permission of the author.

"What Do You Mean . . . Human?" © 1959 by John W. Campbell, Jr. Reprinted by permission of the author's estates and their agents, Scott Meredith Literary Agency, L.P., 845 Third Avenue, New York, New York 10022.

"Bears Discover Fire" © 1990 by Davis Publications, Inc. First published in *Isaac Asimov's Science Fiction Magazine,* January 1990. Reprinted by permission of the author and the author's agent, Susan Ann Protter.

"One Down, One to Go" © 1990 by Philip José Farmer. Reprinted by permission of the author.

"Sur" © 1982 by Ursula K. Le Guin; first appeared in *The New Yorker;* reprinted by permission of the author and the author's agent, Virginia Kidd.

Introduction to *England Swings SF* © 1968, 1996 by Judith Merril; first appeared in *England Swings SF;* reprinted by permission of the author and the author's agent, Virginia Kidd.

"Doing Lennon" © 1976 by Abbenford Associates. Reprinted by permission of the author.

"A Tupolev Too Far" © 1989 by Brian W. Aldiss. Reprinted by permission of the author and his agent, Robin Straus Agency, Inc.

To:

Isaac Asimov
James Blish
Ray Bradbury
Arthur C. Clarke
Robert A. Heinlein
Damon Knight
Fritz Leiber, Jr.
Theodore Sturgeon
A. E. Van Vogt
sine qua non

CONTENTS

INTRODUCTION

This is the third anthology of science fiction to bear the imprimatur of the Science Fiction Research Association (SFRA), the international organization of teachers and scholars devoted to science fiction. The first two, in the 1970s and 1980s, each used by a generation of teachers, reflected the current concerns of SF and the SF field in those decades. Now, in the 1990s, a new book is needed, this time mixing fantasy and science fiction and using essays to illuminate the fiction.

If there is one point we wish to make with this book, it is that SF is a living literature still in the 1990s, and a lively one to boot. There is more blurring of genre boundaries than ever before, and new subgenres such as "Alternate History" SF and "cyberpunk" have come to prominence, gained, and waned in influence in the recent decade past. To manifest all this ferment and change, we felt we had to refrain from smoothing the rough edges off the genre and present a sense of where the action is in the 1990s, with only a few pieces more than ten years old.

We wanted to construct an anthology that was fresh and new, and at the same time address a broad spectrum of the concerns of SF readers today (such as the human impact of new technologies; the social problems and social forces creating possible futures—and possible pasts; the promise and threat of new science, especially biological science; the future in space; gender issues). We also went out of our way to include stories of varied excellences that have not as yet made their way into the accepted canon, and writers whose reputations are in the early stages of formation, whose works are influencing the evolution of the field now.

Also, we chose to make the book unusual in another way, by including pieces by Anne McCaffrey, Andre Norton, and Robert Jordan, three of the most popular and influential writers working in SF and fantasy whose works are rarely anthologized (certainly, at least, rarely in a teaching anthology). Among the three of them, they may have introduced more younger readers to fantastic genre literature than any other writers of recent decades.

In making the selections for this book, we consulted a number of teachers with a longtime interest and expertise in the field, including especially Samuel R. Delany and Gary K. Wolfe, both of whom went over our tentative tables of contents and made useful suggestions. The essays were added, for instance, at their behest, and many of the essays are ones Delany and Wolfe described as both very useful and illuminating, and difficult to obtain for classroom use.

A more difficult decision was to eliminate from consideration the classics of the 1940s–1960s, including the stories of the masters to whom this book is dedicated. Those stories and writers are the core of every other anthology and we wanted to do something different and more contemporary. So when we have chosen to include a story by Farmer, Le Guin, Aldiss, or Pohl, it is a recent story, showing the author as a challenging contemporary rather than an old master showing off old medals.

Visions of Wonder is, then, an unusual anthology of SF, a bit quirky, full of juxtapositions, intentionally off-center. We feel that by doing it this way, we are more true to the reality of the field, and that that reality is worthwhile and interesting.

It may seem surprising to some, but the underlying purpose of this anthology is that it was created to be fun to read. Science fiction has many virtues and uses, is often provocative and engaging, but the primary intent is to entertain. We believe that *Visions of Wonder* represents SF in the 1990s.

—David G. Hartwell and Milton T. Wolf

CRITICS

Damon Knight

This essay is the first chapter of the first mature book of science fiction criticism, Damon Knight's *In Search of Wonder* (1956, revised 1967). Damon Knight was the most influential book reviewer and critical essayist in the SF field from the late 1940s to the early 1960s, when he ceased reviewing to concentrate on his many other involvements in SF. He is also an important editor of anthologies, the founder of the Science Fiction Writers of America, and one of the finest living SF writers. This essay, which has never been superseded, sums up the standards to which SF holds itself.

This credo appeared in my first review column for Lester del Rey's *Science Fiction Adventures* (November 1952); I have stuck to it ever since, and I think it introduces this book as well as the column.

Some readers (not to mention writers, editors and publishers) may be unpleasantly surprised by the pugnacious tone of the reviews that follow. I won't apologize—not very often, anyhow—but I will explain. As a critic, I operate under certain basic assumptions, all eccentric, to wit:

1. That the term "science fiction" is a misnomer, that trying to get two enthusiasts to agree on a definition of it leads only to bloody knuckles; that better labels have been devised (Heinlein's suggestion, "speculative fiction," is the best, I think), but that we're stuck with this one; and that it will do us no particular harm if we remember that, like "The Saturday Evening Post," it means what we point to when we say it.

2. That a publisher's jacket blurb and a book review are two different things, and should be composed accordingly.

3. That science fiction is a field of literature worth taking seriously, and that ordinary critical standards can be meaningfully applied to it: e.g., originality, sincerity, style, construction, logic, coherence, sanity, garden-variety grammar.

4. That a bad book hurts science fiction more than ten bad notices.

The publishers disclaim all responsibility; angry readers please apply to me.

* * *

Nowadays, we like to think, everybody loves science-fantasy, from Artie Shaw to Clifton Fadiman; but occasionally we are reminded that not all the world's respectable literary parlors are yet open to us. Such a reminder is Arthur Koestler's short essay, "The Boredom of Fantasy," in the August, 1953 issue of *Harper's Bazaar.*

After a burst of good-humored laughter at the expense of one of A. E. van Vogt's wilder novels (the hero of which Koestler identifies as "Robert Headrock"), Koestler admits that he is partially addicted to the stuff himself, deals briefly and penetratingly with the history of the field, and then gets down to his major point: He likes it, but it isn't art.

> . . . Swift's *Gulliver,* Huxley's *Brave New World,* Orwell's *Nineteen Eighty-Four* are great works of literature because in them the oddities of alien worlds serve merely as a background or pretext for a social message. In other words, they are literature precisely to the extent to which they are not science fiction, to which they are works of disciplined imagination and not of unlimited fantasy.

This criticism is less than we might have expected from one of the most brilliant of all living novelists. All that Koestler says here is inarguably true, and perfectly irrelevant.

"A similar rule holds for the detective story," he goes on. Just so; and for the historical story, the realistic story, the story of protest, the story of ideas, the story of manners, the story of adventure; in short, for all fiction. Science-fantasy is a form: what matters is what you put into it.

Again: "This is why the historical novel is practically dead today. The life of an Egyptian civil servant under the Eighteenth Dynasty, or even of a soldier in Cromwell's army, is only imaginable to us in a dim outline; we are unable to identify ourselves with the strange figure moving in a strange world." Koestler should have added, "unless the writer has genius"; in science-fantasy as elsewhere, this is not a true statement of a limitation but only of an obstacle. We have not been to Mars; neither have we been to Elsinore, nor to ancient Rome, nor, most of us, to a Russian prison, to a penthouse, to a sweatshop, to a DP camp.

This obstacle was brilliantly surmounted in Koestler's own first novel, *The Gladiators;* and what is *Darkness at Noon* but a masterful exercise in speculative imagination?

If science-fantasy has to date failed to produce much great literature, don't blame the writers who have worked in the field: blame those who, out of snobbery, haven't.

This question of the respectability, or respectable value of science fiction has vexed a lot of the people who read it. Thousands, I suppose, have torn off the covers of science fiction magazines before taking them home, and many must have felt guiltily doubtful about the contents even then. Science fiction has long had, still has a dubious aura: we read it for a certain special kind of satisfaction, but we are frequently aware that according to ordinary standards of taste we ought not to like it.

Dozens of scholarly articles have been written to demonstrate the special nature of science fiction ("the *genre*") and why it really is (or isn't) a scare litera-ture for adolescents. Most of these have been produced by people with only a superficial acquaintance with the field, but even knowledgeable critics often add to the confusion.

To see what may be at the bottom of all this argument, suppose we try ask-ing two questions:

1. What is reputable fiction?
2. What is special about science fiction?

Reputable fiction—meaning fiction that the critics and the librarians like—has many distinguishing characteristics, but two of them appear to be central: it is fiction laid against familiar backgrounds (familiar, at least, to readers of rep-utable fiction—as far as the reader's personal experience goes, a Dakota wheat farm may be as exotic as the moons of Mars); and it tries to deal honestly with the tragic and poetic theme of love-and-death.

The disreputable forms, the Western, science fiction, sports story and so on are defined by their backgrounds; but please note that this is a convention. You could define all of fiction in this way, piecemeal—"New York stories," "Dakota wheat farm stories" and so on, but it isn't convenient or necessary to do so. What really distinguishes the disreputable forms is their reduction of love and death to perfunctory gestures, formalized almost like ideographs. (The villain falls over a cliff; the heroine falls into the hero's arms; neither event takes more than a paragraph.)

Detective fiction, a half-reputable form, owes its half-acceptance to its partial honesty with death. The popular forms, the slick short story, TV serial and so on, suppress both love and death (substituting "romance" and "menace"); that's why they are popular.

Now, what is special about science fiction?

It might be more appropriate to ask what is special about "mainstream" fic-tion. The latter is restricted to a small number of conventional times-and-places. Science fiction includes all these, and all others that a writer of our time-and-place can imagine.

Science fiction is speculative; but so is every work of fiction, to some degree; historical and exotic fiction particularly so.

These are convenient standards, and it's inevitable that librarians and critics will use them—but there must have been a time when stories about India or Alaska or the South Seas were "outlandish," "weird," "unbelievable," "unheard of" and so on. Such stories have gained mass acceptance simply by being around long enough to become familiar; and we may expect that science fiction will do the same.

What we get from science fiction—what keeps us reading it, in spite of our doubts and occasional disgust—is not different from the thing that makes main-stream stories rewarding, but only expressed differently. We live on a minute is-land of known things. Our undiminished wonder at the mystery which surrounds us is what makes us human. In science fiction we can approach that mystery, not in small, everyday symbols, but in the big ones of space and time.

That's all—or nearly all.

Science fiction is already moving out of the realm of disreputable forms, just as the Western is, and just as, to a considerable degree, the detective story is moving upward from its half-reputable status. It can't, I'm afraid, ever become a popular form—it won't stand the suppression. But it can be wholly respectable, and in such stories as C. L. Moore's "No Woman Born" (*Astounding,* December, 1944), Philip Farmer's "The Lovers" (*Startling,* August, 1952) and many more, it's already well on the way.

The librarians are already on our side; give the critics time.

THE SHIP WHO SANG

Anne McCaffrey

Anne McCaffrey is most famous for her immensely popular novels of Pern—*Dragonflight, The White Dragon,* etc.—but has written many other SF stories and novels of widespread popular appeal. Her dragon novels, although they are SF, have the feel of fantasy and embody the same appeal as the Witch World stories of Andre Norton or the *Darkover* series of Marion Zimmer Bradley. Perhaps her most important other SF work is "The Ship Who Sang," which developed into a series of stories, then a series of books.

She was born a thing and as such would be condemned if she failed to pass the encephalograph test required of all newborn babies. There was always the possibility that though the limbs were twisted, the mind was not, that though the ears would hear only dimly, the eyes see vaguely, the mind behind them was receptive and alert.

The electro-encephalogram was entirely favorable, unexpectedly so, and the news was brought to the waiting, grieving parents. There was the final, harsh decision: to give their child euthanasia or permit it to become an encapsulated "brain," a guiding mechanism in any one of a number of curious professions. As such, their offspring would suffer no pain, live a comfortable existence in a metal shell for several centuries, performing unusual service to Central Worlds.

She lived and was given a name, Helva. For her first three vegetable months she waved her crabbed claws, kicked weakly with her clubbed feet and enjoyed the usual routine of the infant. She was not alone, for there were three other such children in the big city's special nursery. Soon they all were removed to Central Laboratory School, where their delicate transformation began.

One of the babies died in the initial transferral, but of Helva's "class," seventeen thrived in the metal shells. Instead of kicking feet, Helva's neural responses started her wheels; instead of grabbing with hands, she manipulated mechanical extensions. As she matured, more and more neural synapses would be adjusted to operate other mechanisms that went into the maintenance and running of a spaceship. For Helva was destined to be the "brain" half of a scout ship, partnered with a man or a woman, whichever she chose, as the mobile half. She would be among the elite of her kind. Her initial intelligence tests registered above normal and her adaptation index was unusually high. As long as her development within her shell lived up to expectations, and there were no side effects from the pituitary tinkering, Helva would live a rewarding, rich and unusual life, a far cry from what she would have faced as an ordinary, "normal" being.

However, no diagram of her brain patterns, no early I.Q. tests recorded certain essential facts about Helva that Central must eventually learn. They would have to bide their official time and see, trusting that the massive doses of shell psychology would suffice her, too, as the necessary bulwark against her unusual confinement and the pressures of her profession. A ship run by a human brain could not run rogue or insane with the power and resources Central had to build into their scout ships. Brain ships were, of course, long past the experimental stages. Most babies survived the perfected techniques of pituitary manipulation that kept their bodies small, eliminating the necessity of transfers from smaller to larger shells. And very, very few were lost when the final connection was made to the control panels of ship or industrial combine. Shell-people resembled mature dwarfs in size whatever their natal deformities were, but the well-oriented brain would not have changed places with the most perfect body in the Universe.

So, for happy years, Helva scooted around in her shell with her classmates, playing such games as Stall, Power-Seek, studying her lessons in trajectory, propulsion techniques, computation, logistics, mental hygiene, basic alien psychology, philology, space history, law, traffic, codes: all the et ceteras that eventually became compounded into a reasoning, logical, informed citizen. Not so obvious to her, but of more importance to her teachers, Helva ingested the precepts of her conditioning as easily as she absorbed her nutrient fluid. She would one day be grateful to the patient drone of the subconscious-level instruction.

Helva's civilization was not without busy, do-good associations, exploring possible inhumanities to terrestrial as well as extraterrestrial citizens. One such group—Society for the Preservation of the Rights of Intelligent Minorities—got all incensed over shelled "children" when Helva was just turning fourteen. When they were forced to, Central Worlds shrugged its shoulders, arranged a tour of the Laboratory Schools and set the tour off to a big start by showing the members case histories, complete with photographs. Very few committees ever looked past the first few photos. Most of their original objections about "shells" were overridden by the relief that these hideous (to them) bodies *were* mercifully concealed.

Helva's class was doing fine arts, a selective subject in her crowded program. She had activated one of her microscopic tools which she would later use for minute repairs to various parts of her control panel. Her subject was large—a copy of "The Last Supper"—and her canvas, small—the head of a tiny screw. She had tuned her sight to the proper degree. As she worked she absentmindedly crooned, producing a curious sound. Shell-people used their own vocal cords and diaphragms, but sound issued through microphones rather than mouths. Helva's hum, then, had a curious vibrancy, a warm, dulcet quality even in its aimless chromatic wanderings.

"Why, what a lovely voice you have," said one of the female visitors.

Helva "looked" up and caught a fascinating panorama of regular, dirty craters on a flaky pink surface. Her hum became a gurgle of surprise. She instinctively regulated her "sight" until the skin lost its cratered look and the pores assumed normal proportions.

"Yes, we have quite a few years of voice training, madam," remarked Helva calmly. "Vocal peculiarities often become excessively irritating during prolonged intrastellar distances and must be eliminated. I enjoyed my lessons."

Although this was the first time that Helva had seen unshelled people, she took this experience calmly. Any other reaction would have been reported instantly.

"I meant that you have a nice singing voice . . . dear," the lady said.

"Thank you. Would you like to see my work?" Helva asked, politely. She instinctively sheered away from personal discussions, but she filed the comment away for further meditation.

"Work?" asked the lady.

"I am currently reproducing the 'Last Supper' on the head of a screw."

"Oh, I say," the lady twittered.

Helva turned her vision back to magnification and surveyed her copy critically.

"Of course, some of my color values do not match the Old Master's and the perspective is faulty, but I believe it to be a fair copy."

The lady's eyes, unmagnified, bugged out.

"Oh, I forget," and Helva's voice was really contrite. If she could have blushed, she would have. "You people don't have adjustable vision."

The monitor of this discourse grinned with pride and amusement as Helva's tone indicated pity for the unfortunate.

"Here, this will help," said Helva, substituting a magnifying device in one extension and holding it over the picture.

In a kind of shock, the ladies and gentlemen of the committee bent to observe the incredibly copied and brilliantly executed "Last Supper" on the head of a screw.

"Well," remarked one gentleman who had been forced to accompany his wife, "the good Lord can eat where angels fear to tread."

"Are you referring, sir," asked Helva politely, "to the Dark Age discussions of the number of angels who could stand on the head of a pin?"

"I had that in mind."

"If you substitute 'atom' for 'angel,' the problem is not insoluble, given the metallic content of the pin in question."

"Which you are programmed to compute?"

"Of course."

"Did they remember to program a sense of humor, as well, young lady?"

"We are directed to develop a sense of proportion, sir, which contributes the same effect."

The good man chortled appreciatively and decided the trip was worth his time.

If the investigation committee spent months digesting the thoughtful food served them at the Laboratory School, they left Helva with a morsel as well.

"Singing" as applicable to herself required research. She had, of course, been exposed to and enjoyed a music appreciation course that had included the better known classical works such as "Tristan und Isolde," "Candide," "Oklahoma," and "Le Nozze di Figaro," along with the atomic age singers, Birgit

Nilsson, Bob Dylan, and Geraldine Todd, as well as the curious rhythmic progressions of the Venusians, Capellan visual chromatics, the sonic concerti of the Altairians and Reticulan croons. But "singing" for any shell-person posed considerable technical difficulties. Shell-people were schooled to examine every aspect of a problem or situation before making a prognosis. Balanced properly between optimism and practicality, the nondefeatist attitude of the shell-people led them to extricate themselves, their ships, and personnel from bizarre situations. Therefore, to Helva, the problem that she couldn't open her mouth to sing, among other restrictions, did not bother her. She would work out a method, bypassing her limitations, whereby she could sing.

She approached the problem by investigating the methods of sound reproduction through the centuries, human and instrumental. Her own sound production equipment was essentially more instrumental than vocal. Breath control and the proper enunciation of vowel sounds within the oral cavity appeared to require the most development and practice. Shell-people did not, strictly speaking, breathe. For their purposes, oxygen and other gases were not drawn from the surrounding atmosphere through the medium of lungs but sustained artificially by solution in their shells. After experimentation, Helva discovered that she could manipulate her diaphragmic unit to sustain tone. By relaxing the throat muscles and expanding the oral cavity well into the frontal sinuses, she could direct the vowel sounds into the most felicitous position for proper reproduction through her throat microphone. She compared the results with tape recordings of modern singers and was not unpleased, although her own tapes had a peculiar quality about them, not at all unharmonious, merely unique. Acquiring a repertoire from the Laboratory library was no problem to one trained to perfect recall. She found herself able to sing any role and any song which struck her fancy. It would not have occurred to her that it was curious for a female to sing bass, baritone, tenor, mezzo, suprano, and coloratura as she pleased. It was, to Helva, only a matter of the correct reproduction and diaphragmic control required by the music attempted.

If the authorities remarked on her curious avocation, they did so among themselves. Shell-people were encouraged to develop a hobby so long as they maintained proficiency in their technical work.

On the anniversary of her sixteenth year, Helva was unconditionally graduated and installed in her ship, the XH-834. Her permanent titanium shell was recessed behind an even more indestructible barrier in the central shaft of the scout ship. The neural, audio, visual, and sensory connections were made and sealed. Her extendibles were diverted, connected, or augmented, and the final, delicate-beyond-description brain taps were completed while Helva remained anesthetically unaware of the proceedings. When she woke, she *was* the ship. Her brain and intelligence controlled every function from navigation to such loading as a scout ship of her class needed. She could take care of herself, and her ambulatory half, in any situation already recorded in the annals of Central Worlds and any situation its most fertile minds could imagine.

Her first actual flight, for she and her kind had made mock flights on dummy panels since they were eight, showed her to be a complete master of the techniques of her profession. She was ready for her great adventures and the arrival of her mobile partner.

There were nine qualified scouts sitting around collecting base pay the day

Helva reported for active duty. There were several missions that demanded instant attention, but Helva had been of interest to several department heads in Central for some time and each bureau chief was determined to have her assigned to *his* section. No one had remembered to introduce Helva to the prospective partners. The ship always chose its own partner. Had there been another brain ship at the base at the moment, Helva would have been guided to make the first move. As it was, while Central wrangled among itself, Robert Tanner sneaked out of the pilots' barracks, out of the field and over to Helva's slim metal hull.

"Hello, anyone at home?" Tanner said.

"Of course," replied Helva, activating her outside scanners. "Are you my partner?" she asked hopefully, as she recognized the Scout Service uniform.

"All you have to do is ask," he retorted in a wistful tone.

"No one has come. I thought perhaps there were no partners available and I've had no directives from Central."

Even to herself Helva sounded a little self-pitying, but the truth was she was lonely, sitting on the darkened field. She had always had the company of other shells and, more recently, technicians by the score. The sudden solitude had lost its momentary charm and become oppressive.

"No directives from Central is scarcely a cause for regret, but there happen to be eight other guys biting their fingernails to the quick just waiting for an invitation to board you, you beautiful thing."

Tanner was inside the central cabin as he said this, running appreciative fingers over her panel, the scout's gravity-chair, poking his head into the cabins, the galley, the head, the pressured-storage compartments.

"Now, if you want to goose Central and do *us* a favor all in one, call up the barracks and let's have a ship-warming partner-picking party. Hmmmm?"

Helva chuckled to herself. He was so completely different from the occasional visitor or the various Laboratory technicians she had encountered. He was so gay, so assured, and she was delighted by his suggestion of a partner-picking party. Certainly it was not against anything in her understanding of regulations.

"Cencom, this is XH-834. Connect me with Pilot Barracks."

"Visual?"

"Please."

A picture of lounging men in various attitudes of boredom came on her screen.

"This is XH-834. Would the unassigned scouts do me the favor of coming aboard?"

Eight figures galvanized into action, grabbing pieces of wearing apparel, disengaging tape mechanisms, disentangling themselves from bedsheet and towels.

Helva dissolved the connection while Tanner chuckled gleefully and settled down to await their arrival.

Helva was engulfed in an unshell-like flurry of anticipation. No actress on her opening night could have been more apprehensive, fearful, or breathless. Unlike the actress, she could throw no hysterics, china objets d'art, or grease paint to relieve her tension. She could, of course, check her stores for edibles and drinks, which she did, serving Tanner from the virgin selection of her commissary.

Scouts were colloquially known as "brawns" as opposed to their ship "brains." They had to pass as rigorous a training program as the brains and only the top one percent of each contributory world's highest scholars were admitted to Central Worlds Scout Training Program. Consequently the eight young men who came pounding up the gantry into Helva's hospitable lock were unusually fine-looking, intelligent, well-coordinated and adjusted young men, looking forward to a slightly drunken evening, Helva permitting, and all quite willing to do each other dirt to get possession of her.

Such a human invasion left Helva mentally breathless, a luxury she thoroughly enjoyed for the brief time she felt she should permit it.

She sorted out the young men. Tanner's opportunism amused but did not specifically attract her; the blond Nordsen seemed too simple; darkhaired Alatpay had a kind of obstinacy with which she felt no compassion; Mir-Ahnin's bitterness hinted an inner darkness she did not wish to lighten, although he made the biggest outward play for her attention. Hers was a curious courtship—this would be only the first of several marriages for her, for brawns retired after seventy-five years of service, or earlier if they were unlucky. Brains, their bodies safe from any deterioration, were indestructible. In theory, once a shell-person had paid off the massive debt of early care, surgical adaptation, and maintenance charges, he or she was free to seek employment elsewhere. In practice, shell-people remained in the service until they chose to self-destruct or died in line of duty. Helva had actually spoken to one shell-person 322 years old. She had been so awed by the contact she hadn't presumed to ask the personal questions she had wanted to.

Her choice of a brawn did not stand out from the others until Tanner started to sing a scout ditty, recounting the misadventures of the bold, dense, painfully inept Billy Brawn. An attempt at harmony resulted in cacophony and Tanner wagged his arms wildly for silence.

"What we need is a roaring good lead tenor. Jennan, besides palming aces, what do you sing?"

"Sharp," Jennan replied with easy good humor.

"If a tenor is absolutely necessary, I'll attempt it," Helva volunteered.

"My good *woman*," Tanner protested.

"Sound your 'A,'" laughed Jennan.

Into the stunned silence that followed the rich, clear, high "A," Jennan remarked quietly, "Such an A Caruso would have given the rest of his notes to sing."

It did not take them long to discover her full range.

"All Tanner asked for was one roaring good lead tenor," Jennan said jokingly, "and our sweet mistress supplied us an entire repertory company. The boy who gets this ship will go far, far, far."

"To the Horsehead Nebula?" asked Nordsen, quoting an old Central saw.

"To the Horsehead Nebula and back, we shall make beautiful music," said Helva, chuckling.

"Together," Jennan said. "Only you'd better make the music and, with my voice, I'd better listen."

"I rather imagined it would be I who listened," suggested Helva.

Jennan executed a stately bow with an intricate flourish of his crush-brimmed hat. He directed his bow toward the central control pillar where Helva *was.* Her own personal preference crystallized at that precise moment and for that particular reason: Jennan, alone of the men, had addressed his remarks directly at her physical presence, regardless of the fact that he knew she could pick up his image wherever he was in the ship and regardless of the fact that her body was behind massive metal walls. Throughout their partnership, Jennan never failed to turn his head in her direction no matter where he was in relation to her. In response to this personalization, Helva at that moment and from then on always spoke to Jennan only through her central mike, even though that was not always the most efficient method.

Helva didn't know that she fell in love with Jennan that evening. As she had never been exposed to love or affection, only the drier cousins, respect and admiration, she could scarcely have recognized her reaction to the warmth of his personality and thoughtfulness. As a shell-person, she considered herself remote from emotions largely connected with physical desires.

"Well, Helva, it's been swell meeting you," said Tanner suddenly as she and Jennan were arguing about the baroque quality of "Come All Ye Sons of Art." "See you in space some time, you lucky dog, Jennan. Thanks for the party, Helva."

"You don't have to go so soon?" asked Helva, realizing belatedly that she and Jennan had been excluding the others from this discussion.

"Best man won," Tanner said, wryly. "Guess I'd better go get a tape on love ditties. Might need 'em for the next ship, if there're any more at home like you."

Helva and Jennan watched them leave, both a little confused.

"Perhaps Tanner's jumping to conclusions?" Jennan asked.

Helva regarded him as he slouched against the console, facing her shell directly. His arms were crossed on his chest and the glass he held had been empty for some time. He was handsome, they all were; but his watchful eyes were unwary, his mouth assumed a smile easily, his voice (to which Helva was particularly drawn) was resonant, deep, and without unpleasant overtones or accent.

"Sleep on it, at any rate, Helva. Call me in the morning if it's your opt."

She called him at breakfast, after she had checked her choice through Central. Jennan moved his things aboard, received their joint commission, had his personality and experience file locked into her reviewer, gave her the coordinates of their first mission. The XH-834 officially became the JH-834.

Their first mission was a dull but necessary crash priority (Medical got Helva), rushing a vaccine to a distant system plagued with a virulent spore disease. They had only to get to Spica as fast as possible.

After the initial, thrilling forward surge at her maximum speed, Helva realized her muscles were to be given less of a workout than her brawn on this tedious mission. But they did have plenty of time for exploring each other's personalities. Jennan, of course, knew what Helva was capable of as a ship and partner, just as she knew what she could expect from him. But these were only facts and Helva looked forward eagerly to learning that human side of her partner which could not be reduced to a series of symbols. Nor could the give and take of two personalities be learned from a book. It had to be experienced.

"My father was a scout, too, or is that programmed?" began Jennan their third day out.

"Naturally."

"Unfair, you know. You've got all my family history and I don't know one blamed thing about yours."

"I've never known either," Helva said. "Until I read yours, it hadn't occurred to me I must have one, too, someplace in Central's files."

Jennan snorted. "Shell psychology!"

Helva laughed. "Yes, and I'm even programmed against curiosity about it. You'd better be, too."

Jennan ordered a drink, slouched into the gravity couch opposite her, put his feet on the bumpers, turning himself idly from side to side on the gimbals.

"Helva—a made-up name . . ."

"With a Scandinavian sound."

"You aren't blond," Jennan said positively.

"Well, then, there're dark Swedes."

"And blond Turks and this one's harem is limited to one."

"Your woman in purdah, yes, but you can comb the pleasure houses—" Helva found herself aghast at the edge to her carefully trained voice.

"You know," Jennan interrupted her, deep in some thought of his own, "my father gave me the impression he was a lot more married to his ship, the Silvia, than to my mother. I know I used to think Silvia was my grandmother. She was a low number so she must have been a great-great-grandmother at least. I used to talk to her for hours."

"Her registry?" asked Helva, unwittingly jealous of everyone and anyone who had shared his hours.

"422. I think she's TS now. I ran into Tom Burgess once."

Jennan's father had died of a planetary disease, the vaccine for which his ship had used up in curing the local citizens.

"Tom said she'd got mighty tough and salty. You lose your sweetness and I'll come back and haunt you, girl," Jennan threatened.

Helva laughed. He startled her by stamping up to the column panel, touching it with light, tender fingers.

"I *wonder* what you look like," he said softly, wistfully.

Helva had been briefed about this natural curiosity of scouts. She didn't know anything about herself and none of them ever would or could.

"Pick any form, shape, and shade and I'll be yours obliging," she countered, as training suggested.

"Iron Maiden, I fancy blondes with long tresses," and Jennan pantomined Lady Godiva-like tresses. "Since you're immolated in titanium, I'll call you Brunhilde, my dear," and he made his bow.

With a chortle, Helva launched into the appropriate aria just as Spica made contact.

"What'n'ell's that yelling about? Who are you? And unless you're Central Worlds Medical, go away. We've got a plague. No visiting privileges."

"My ship is singing, we're the JH-834 of Worlds and we've got your vaccine. What are our landing coordinates?"

"Your *ship* is singing?"

"The greatest S.A.T.B. in organized space. Any requests?"

The JH-834 delivered the vaccine but no more arias and received immediate orders to proceed to Leviticus IV. By the time they got there, Jennan found a reputation awaiting him and was forced to defend the 834's virgin honor.

"I'll stop singing," murmured Helva contritely as she ordered up poultices for this third black eye in a week.

"You will not," Jennan said through gritted teeth. "If I have to black eyes from here to the Horsehead to keep the snicker out of the title, we'll be the ship who sings."

After the "ship who sings" tangled with a minor but vicious narcotic ring in the Lesser Magellanics, the title became definitely respectful. Central was aware of each episode and punched out a "special interest" key on JH-834's file. A first-rate team was shaking down well.

Jennan and Helva considered themselves a first-rate team, too, after their tidy arrest.

"Of all the vices in the universe, I *hate* drug addiction," Jennan remarked as they headed back to Central Base. "People can go to hell quick enough without that kind of help."

"Is that why you volunteered for Scout Service? To redirect traffic?"

"I'll bet my official answer's on your review."

"In far too flowery wording. 'Carrying on the traditions of my family, which has been proud of four generations in Service,' if I may quote you your own words."

Jennan groaned. "I was *very* young when I wrote that. I certainly hadn't been through Final Training. And once I was in Final Training, my pride wouldn't let me fail. . . .

"As I mentioned, I used to visit Dad on board the Silvia and I've a very good idea she might have had her eye on me as a replacement for my father because I had had massive doses of scout-oriented propaganda. It took. From the time I was seven, I was going to be a scout or else." He shrugged as if deprecating a youthful determination that had taken a great deal of mature application to bring to fruition.

"Ah, so? Scout Sahir Silan on the JS-44 penetrating into the Horsehead Nebulae?"

Jennan chose to ignore her sarcasm.

"With *you*, I may even get that far. But even with Silvia's nudging *I* never daydreamed myself *that* kind of glory in my wildest flights of fancy. I'll leave the whoppers to your agile brain henceforth. I have in mind a smaller contribution to space history."

"So modest?"

"No. Practical. We also serve, et cetera." He placed a dramatic hand on his heart.

"Glory hound!" scoffed Helva.

"Look who's talking, my Nebula-bound friend. At least I'm not greedy. There'll only be one hero like my dad at Parsaea, but I *would* like to be remembered for some kudo. Everyone does. Why else do or die?"

"Your father died on his way back from Parsaea, if I may point out a few cogent facts. So he could never have known he was a hero for damming the flood with his ship. Which kept Parsaean colony from being abandoned. Which gave them a chance to discover the antiparalytic qualities of Parsaea. Which *he* never knew."

"I know," said Jennan softly.

Helva was immediately sorry for the tone of her rebuttal. She knew very well how deep Jennan's attachment to his father had been. On his review a note was made that he had rationalized his father's loss with the unexpected and welcome outcome of the Affair at Parsaea.

"Facts are not human, Helva. My father was and so am I. And *basically,* so are you. Check over your dial, 834. Amid all the wires attached to you is a heart, an underdeveloped human heart. Obviously!"

"I apologize, Jennan," she said.

Jennan hesitated a moment, threw out his hands in acceptance, and then tapped her shell affectionately.

"If they ever take us off the milkruns, we'll make a stab at the Nebula, huh?"

As so frequently happened in the Scout Service, within the next hour they had orders to change course, not to the Nebula, but to a recently colonized system with two habitable planets, one tropical, one glacial. The sun, named Ravel, had become unstable; the spectrum was that of a rapidly expanding shell, with absorption lines rapidly displacing toward violet. The augmented heat of the primary had already forced evacuation of the nearer world, Daphnis. The pattern of spectral emissions gave indication that the sun would sear Chloe as well. All ships in the immediate spatial vicinity were to report to Disaster Headquarters on Chloe to effect removal of the remaining colonists.

The JH-834 obediently presented itself and was sent to outlying areas on Chloe to pick up scattered settlers, who did not appear to appreciate the urgency of the situation. Chloe, indeed, was enjoying the first temperatures above freezing since it had been flung out of its parent. Since many of the colonists were religious fanatics who had settled on rigorous Chloe to fit themselves for a life of pious reflection, Chloe's abrupt thaw was attributed to sources other than a rampaging sun.

Jennan had to spend so much time countering specious arguments that he and Helva were behind schedule on their way to the fourth and last settlement.

Helva jumped over the high range of jagged peaks that surrounded and sheltered the valley from the former raging snows as well as the present heat. The violent sun with its flaring corona was just beginning to brighten the deep valley as Helva dropped down to a landing.

"They'd better grab their toothbrushes and hop aboard," Helva said. "HQ says speed it up."

"All women," remarked Jennan in surprise as he walked down to meet them. "Unless the men on Chloe wear furred skirts."

"Charm 'em but pare the routine to the bare essentials. And turn on your two-way private."

Jennan advanced smiling, but his explanation of his mission was met with absolute incredulity and considerable doubt as to his authenticity. He groaned inwardly as the matriarch paraphrased previous explanations of the warming sun.

"Revered mother, there's been an overload on that prayer circuit and the sun is blowing itself up in one obliging burst. I'm here to take you to the spaceport at Rosary—"

"That Sodom?" The worthy woman glowered and shuddered disdainfully at his suggestion. "We thank you for your warning but we have no wish to leave our cloister for the rude world. We must go about our morning meditation which has been interrupted—"

"It'll be permanently interrupted when that sun starts broiling you. You must come now," Jennan said firmly.

"Madame," said Helva, realizing that perhaps a female voice might carry more weight in this instance than Jennan's very masculine charm.

"Who spoke?" cried the nun, startled by the bodiless voice.

"I, Helva, the ship. Under my protection you and your sisters-in-faith may enter safely and be unprofaned by association with a male. I will guard you and take you safely to a place prepared for you."

The matriarch peered cautiously into the ship's open port.

"Since only Central Worlds is permitted the use of such ships, I acknowledge that you are not trifling with us, young man. However, we are in no danger here."

"The temperature at Rosary is now ninety-nine degrees," said Helva. "As soon as the sun's rays penetrate directly into this valley, it will also be ninety-nine degrees, and it is due to climb to approximately one-hundred-and-eighty degrees today. I notice your buildings are made of wood with moss chinking. Dry moss. It should fire around noontime."

The sunlight was beginning to slant into the valley through the peaks and the fierce rays warmed the restless group behind the matriarch. Several opened the throats of their furry parkas.

"Jennan," said Helva privately to him, "our time is very short."

"I can't leave them, Helva. Some of those girls are barely out of the teens."

"Pretty, too. No wonder the matriarch doesn't want to get in."

"Helva."

"It will be the Lord's will," said the matriarch stoutly and turned her back squarely on rescue.

"To burn to death?" shouted Jennan as she threaded her way through her murmuring disciples.

"They want to be martyrs? Their opt, Jennan," said Helva dispassionately. "We must leave and that is no longer a matter of option."

"How can I leave, Helva?"

"Parsaea?" Helva asked tauntingly as he stepped forward to grab one of the women. "You can't drag them *all* aboard and we don't have time to fight it out. Get on board, Jennan, or I'll have you on report."

"They'll die," muttered Jennan dejectedly as he reluctantly turned to climb on board.

"You can risk only so much," Helva said sympathetically. "As it is we'll just have time to make a rendezvous. Lab reports a critical speedup in spectral evolution."

Jennan was already in the airlock when one of the younger women, screaming, rushed to squeeze in the closing port. Her action set off the others. They stampeded through the narrow opening. Even crammed back to breast, there was not enough room inside for all the women. Jennan broke out spacesuits to the three who would have to remain with him in the airlock. He wasted valuable time explaining to the matriarch that she must put on the suit because the airlock had no independent oxygen or cooling units.

"We'll be caught," said Helva in a grim tone to Jennan on their private connection. "We've lost eighteen minutes in this last-minute rush. I am now overloaded for maximum speed and I must attain maximum speed to outrun the heat wave."

"Can you lift? We're suited."

"Lift? Yes," she said, doing so. "Run? I stagger."

Jennan, bracing himself and the women, could feel her sluggishness as she blasted upward. Heartlessly, Helva applied thrust as long as she could, despite the fact that the gravitational force mashed her cabin passengers brutally and crushed two fatally. It was a question of saving as many as possible. The only one for whom she had any concern was Jennan and she was in desperate terror about his safety. Airless and uncooled, protected by only one layer of metal, not three, the airlock was not going to be safe for the four trapped there, despite their spacesuits. These were only the standard models, not built to withstand the excessive heat to which the ship would be subjected.

Helva ran as fast as she could but the incredible wave of heat from the explosive sun caught them halfway to cold safety.

She paid no heed to the cries, moans, pleas, and prayers in her cabin. She listened only to Jennan's tortured breathing, to the missing throb in his suit's purifying system and the sucking of the overloaded cooling unit. Helpless, she heard the hysterical screams of his three companions as they writhed in the awful heat. Vainly, Jennan tried to calm them, tried to explain they would soon be safe and cool if they could be still and endure the heat. Undisciplined by their terror and torment, they tried to strike out at him despite the close quarters. One flailing arm became entangled in the leads to his power pack and the damage was quickly done. A connection, weakened by heat and the dead weight of the arm, broke.

For all the power at her disposal, Helva was helpless. She watched as Jennan fought for his breath, as he turned his head beseechingly toward *her*, and died.

Only the iron conditioning of her training prevented Helva from swinging around and plunging back into the cleansing heart of the exploding sun. Numbly she made rendezvous with the refugee convoy. She obediently transferred her burned, heat-prostrated passengers to the assigned transport.

"I will retain the body of my scout and proceed to the nearest base for burial," she informed Central dully.

"You will be provided escort," was the reply.

"I have no need of escort."

"Escort is provided, XH-834," she was told curtly. The shock of hearing Jennan's initial severed from her call number cut off her half-formed protest. Stunned, she waited by the transport until her screens showed the arrival of two other slim brain ships. The cortege proceeded homeward at unfunereal speeds.

"834? The ship who sings?"

"I have no more songs."

"Your scout was Jennan."

"I do not wish to communicate."

"I'm 422."

"Silvia?"

"Silvia died a long time ago. I'm 422. Currently MS," the ship rejoined curtly. "AH-640 is our other friend, but Henry's not listening in. Just as well—he wouldn't understand it if you wanted to turn rogue. But I'd stop *him* if he tried to deter you."

"Rogue?" The term snapped Helva out of her apathy.

"Sure. You're young. You've got power for years. Skip. Others have done it.

732 went rogue twenty years ago after she lost her scout on a mission to that white dwarf. Hasn't been seen since."

"I never heard about rogues."

"As it's exactly the thing we're conditioned against, you sure wouldn't hear about it in school, my dear," 422 said.

"Break conditioning?" cried Helva, anguished, thinking longingly of the white, white furious hot heat of the sun she had just left.

"For you I don't think it would be hard at the moment," 422 said quietly, her voice devoid of her earlier cynicism. "The stars are out there, winking."

"Alone?" cried Helva from her heart.

"Alone!" 422 confirmed bleakly.

Alone with all of space and time. Even the Horsehead Nebula would not be far enough away to daunt her. Alone with a hundred years to live with her memories and nothing . . . nothing more.

"Was Parsaea worth it?" she asked 422 softly.

"Parsaea?" 422 repeated, surprised. "With his father? Yes. We were there, at Parsaea, when we were needed. Just as you . . . and his son . . . were at Chloe. When you were needed. The crime is not knowing where need is and not being there."

"But *I* need *him*. Who will supply my need?" said Helva bitterly. . . .

"834," said 422 after a day's silent speeding. "Central wishes your report. A replacement awaits your opt at Regulus Base. Change course accordingly."

"A replacement?" That was certainly not what she needed . . . a reminder inadequately filling the void Jennan left. Why, her hull was barely cool of Chloe's heat. Atavistically, Helva wanted time to mourn Jennan.

"Oh, none of them are impossible if *you're* a good ship," 422 remarked philosophically. "And it is just what you need. The sooner the better."

"You told them I wouldn't go rogue, didn't you?" Helva said.

"The moment passed you even as it passed me after Parsaea, and before that, after Glen Arhur, and Betelgeuse."

"We're conditioned to go on, aren't we? We *can't* go rogue. You were testing."

"Had to. Orders. Not even Psych knows why a rogue occurs. Central's very worried, and so, daughter, are your sister ships. I asked to be your escort. I . . . I don't want to lose you both."

In her emotional nadir, Helva could feel a flood of gratitude for Silvia's rough sympathy.

"We've all known this grief, Helva. It's no consolation, but if we couldn't feel with our scouts, we'd only be machines wired for sound."

Helva looked at Jennan's still form stretched before her in its shroud and heard the echo of his rich voice in the quiet cabin.

"Silvia, I *couldn't* help him," she cried from her soul.

"Yes, dear, I know," 422 murmured gently and then was quiet.

The three ships sped on, wordless, to the great Central Worlds base at Regulus. Helva broke silence to acknowledge landing instructions and the officially tendered regrets.

The three ships set down simultaneously at the wooded edge where Regulus's gigantic blue trees stood sentinel over the sleeping dead in the small Service cemetery. The entire Base complement approached with measured step and formed an aisle from Helva to the burial ground. The honor detail, out of step, walked slowly into her cabin. Reverently they placed the body of her dead love on the wheeled bier, covered it honorably with the deep blue, star-splashed flag of the Service. She watched as it was driven slowly down the living aisle which closed in behind the bier in late escort.

Then, as the simple words of interment were spoken, as the atmosphere planes dipped in tribute over the open grave, Helva found voice for her lonely farewell.

Softly, barely audible at first, the strains of the ancient song of evening and requiem swelled to the final poignant measure until black space itself echoed back the sound of the song the ship sang.

BLOOD MUSIC

Greg Bear

Greg Bear is one of the leading writers of hard SF, that branch of science fiction that is most concerned with science and technology and with rigorous speculation. Although he entered the SF field as an artist in the 1970s, he rapidly changed his focus to writing. He has produced a number of novels and stories, including *Eon* and "Hardfought," that brought him, by the early 1980s, to the forefront of the ranks of SF writers. Though commonly identified as a vocal defender of hard SF (the killer Bs—Benford, Brin, and Bear—attacked cyberpunk [see the note on William Gibson] in the mid-1980s), Bear was included in the definitive cyberpunk anthology, *Mirrorshades*. "Blood Music" is the award-winning story that became part of Bear's novel of the same name.

There is a principle in nature I don't think anyone has pointed out before. Each hour, a myriad of trillions of little live things—bacteria, microbes, "animalcules"—are born and die, not counting for much except in the bulk of their existence and the accumulation of their tiny effects. They do not perceive deeply. They do not suffer much. A hundred billion, dying, would not begin to have the same importance as a single human death.

Within the ranks of magnitude of all creatures, small as microbes or great as humans, there is an equality of "elan," just as the branches of a tall tree, gathered together, equal the bulk of the limbs below, and all the limbs equal the bulk of the trunk.

That, at least, is the principle. I believe Vergil Ulam was the first to violate it.

It had been two years since I'd last seen Vergil. My memory of him hardly matched the tan, smiling, well-dressed gentleman standing before me. We had made a lunch appointment over the phone the day before, and now faced each other in the wide double doors of the employees' cafeteria at the Mount Freedom Medical Center.

"Vergil?" I asked. "My God, Vergil!"

"Good to see you, Edward." He shook my hand firmly. He had lost ten or twelve kilos and what remained seemed tighter, better proportioned. At university, Vergil had been the pudgy, shock-haired, snaggle-toothed whiz kid who hot-wired doorknobs, gave us punch that turned our piss blue, and never got a date except with Eileen Termagent, who shared many of his physical character-istics.

"You look fantastic," I said. "Spend a summer in Cabo San Lucas?"

We stood in line at the counter and chose our food. "The tan," he said, pick-ing out a carton of chocolate milk, "is from spending three months under a sun-lamp. My teeth were straightened just after I last saw you. I'll explain the rest, but we need a place to talk where no one will listen close."

I steered him to the smoker's corner, where three diehard puffers were scat-tered among six tables.

"Listen, I mean it," I said as we unloaded our trays. "You've changed. You're looking good."

"I've changed more than you know." His tone was motion-picture ominous, and he delivered the line with a theatrical lift of his brows. "How's Gail?"

Gail was doing well, I told him, teaching nursery school. We'd married the year before. His gaze shifted down to his food—pineapple slice and cottage cheese, piece of banana cream pie—and he said, his voice almost cracking, "No-tice something else?"

I squinted in concentration. "Uh."

"Look closer."

"I'm not sure. Well, yes, you're not wearing glasses. Contacts?"

"No. I don't need them anymore."

"And you're a snappy dresser. Who's dressing you now? I hope she's as sexy as she is tasteful."

"Candice isn't—wasn't responsible for the improvement in my clothes," he said. "I just got a better job, more money to throw around. My taste in clothes is better than my taste in food, as it happens." He grinned the old Vergil self-deprecating grin, but ended it with a peculiar leer. "At any rate, she's left me; I've been fired from my job. I'm living on savings."

"Hold it," I said. "That's a bit crowded. Why not do a linear breakdown? You got a job. Where?"

"Genetron Corp.," he said. "Sixteen months ago."

"I haven't heard of them."

"You will. They're putting out common stock in the next month. It'll shoot off the board. They've broken through with MABs. Medical—"

"I know what MABs are," I interrupted. "At least in theory. Medically Ap-plicable Biochips."

"They have some that work."

"What?" It was my turn to lift my brows.

"Microscopic logic circuits. You inject them into the human body, they set up shop where they're told and troubleshoot. With Dr. Michael Bernard's ap-proval."

That was quite impressive. Bernard's reputation was spotless. Not only was he associated with the genetic engineering biggies, but he had made news at least once a year in his practice as a neurosurgeon before retiring. Covers on *Time, Mega, Rolling Stone.*

"That's supposed to be secret—stock, breakthrough, Bernard, everything." He looked around and lowered his voice. "But you do whatever the hell you want. I'm through with the bastards."

I whistled. "Make me rich, huh?"

"If that's what you want. Or you can spend some time with me before rushing off to your broker."

"Of course." He hadn't touched the cottage cheese or pie. He had, however, eaten the pineapple slice and drunk the chocolate milk. "So tell me more."

"Well, in med school I was training for lab work. Biochemical research. I've always had a bent for computers, too. So I put myself through my last two years—"

"By selling software packages to Westinghouse," I said.

"It's good my friends remember. That's how I got involved with Genetron, just when they were starting out. They had big money backers, all the lab facilities I thought anyone would ever need. They hired me, and I advanced rapidly.

"Four months and I was doing my own work. I made some breakthroughs"—he tossed his hand nonchalantly—"then I went off on tangents they thought were premature. I persisted and they took away my lab, handed it over to a certifiable flatworm. I managed to save part of the experiment before they fired me. But I haven't exactly been cautious . . . or judicious. So now it's going on outside the lab."

I'd always regarded Vergil as ambitious, a trifle cracked, and not terribly sensitive. His relations with authority figures had never been smooth. Science, for him, was like the woman you couldn't possibly have, who suddenly opens her arms to you, long before you're ready for mature love—leaving you afraid you'll forever blow the chance, lose the prize. Apparently, he did. "Outside the lab? I don't get you."

"Edward, I want you to examine me. Give me a thorough physical. Maybe a cancer diagnostic. Then I'll explain more."

"You want a five-thousand-dollar exam?"

"Whatever you can do. Ultrasound, NMR, thermogram, everything."

"I don't know if I can get access to all that equipment. NMR full-scan has only been here a month or two. Hell, you couldn't pick a more expensive way—"

"Then ultrasound. That's all you'll need."

"Vergil, I'm an obstetrician, not a glamour-boy lab-tech. OB-GYN, butt of all jokes. If you're turning into a woman, maybe I can help you."

He leaned forward, almost putting his elbow into the pie, but swinging wide at the last instant by scant millimeters. The old Vergil would have hit it square. "Examine me closely and you'll . . ." He narrowed his eyes. "Just examine me."

"So I make an appointment for ultrasound. Who's going to pay?"

"I'm on Blue Shield." He smiled and held up a medical credit card. "I messed with the personnel files at Genetron. Anything up to a hundred thousand dollars medical, they'll never check, never suspect."

He wanted secrecy, so I made arrangements. I filled out his forms myself. As long as everything was billed properly, most of the examination could take place without official notice. I didn't charge for my services. After all, Vergil had turned my piss blue. We were friends.

He came in late at night. I wasn't normally on duty then, but I stayed late, waiting for him on the third floor of what the nurses called the Frankenstein wing. I sat on an orange plastic chair. He arrived, looking olive-colored under the fluorescent lights.

He stripped, and I arranged him on the table. I noticed, first off, that his ankles looked swollen. But they weren't puffy. I felt them several times. They seemed healthy but looked odd. "Hm," I said.

I ran the paddles over him, picking up areas difficult for the big unit to hit, and programmed the data into the imaging system. Then I swung the table around and inserted it into the enameled orifice of the ultrasound diagnostic unit, the hum-hole, so-called by the nurses.

I integrated the data from the hum-hole with that from the paddle sweeps and rolled Vergil out, then set up a video frame. The image took a second to integrate, then flowed into a pattern showing Vergil's skeleton. My jaw fell.

Three seconds of that and it switched to his thoracic organs, then his musculature, and, finally, vascular system and skin.

"How long since the accident?" I asked, trying to take the quiver out of my voice.

"I haven't been in an accident," he said. "It was deliberate."

"Jesus, they beat you to keep secrets?"

"You don't understand me, Edward. Look at the images again. I'm not damaged."

"Look, there's thickening here"—I indicated the ankles—"and your ribs—that crazy zigzag pattern of interlocks. Broken sometime, obviously. And—"

"Look at my spine," he said. I rotated the image in the video frame.

Buckminster Fuller, I thought. It was fantastic. A cage of triangular projections, all interlocking in ways I couldn't begin to follow, much less understand. I reached around and tried to feel his spine with my fingers. He lifted his arms and looked off at the ceiling.

"I can't find it," I said. "It's all smooth back there." I let go of him and looked at his chest, then prodded his ribs. They were sheathed in something tough and flexible. The harder I pressed, the tougher it became. Then I noticed another change.

"Hey," I said. "You don't have any nipples." There were tiny pigment patches, but no nipple formations at all.

"See?" Vergil asked, shrugging on the white robe, "I'm being rebuilt from the inside out."

In my reconstruction of those hours, I fancy myself saying, "So tell me about it." Perhaps mercifully, I don't remember what I actually said.

He explained with his characteristic circumlocutions. Listening was like trying to get to the meat of a newspaper article through a forest of sidebars and graphic embellishments.

I simplify and condense.

Genetron had assigned him to manufacturing prototype biochips, tiny circuits made out of protein molecules. Some were hooked up to silicon chips little more than a micrometer in size, then went through rat arteries to chemically keyed locations, to make connections with the rat tissue and attempt to monitor and even control lab-induced pathologies.

"*That* was something," he said.

"We recovered the most complex microchip by sacrificing the rat, then debriefed it—hooked the silicon portion up to an imaging system. The computer gave us bar graphs, then a diagram of the chemical characteristics of about eleven centimeters of blood vessel . . . then put it all together to make a picture. We zoomed down eleven centimeters of rat artery. You never saw so many scientists jumping up and down, hugging each other, drinking buckets of bug juice." But juice was lab ethanol mixed with Dr Pepper.

Eventually, the silicon elements were eliminated completely in favor of nucleoproteins. He seemed reluctant to explain in detail, but I gathered they found ways to make huge molecules—as large as DNA, and even more complex—into electrochemical computers, using ribosomelike structures as "encoders" and "readers" and RNA as "tape." Vergil was able to mimic reproductive separation and reassembly in his nucleoproteins, incorporating program changes at key points by switching nucleotide pairs. "Genetron wanted me to switch over to supergene engineering, since that was the coming thing everywhere else. Make all kinds of critters, some out of our imagination. But I had different ideas." He twiddled his finger around his ear and made theremin sounds. "Mad scientist time, right?" He laughed, then sobered. "I injected my best nucleoproteins into bacteria to make duplication and compounding easier. Then I started to leave them inside, so the circuits could interact with the cells. They were heuristically programmed; they taught themselves. The cells fed chemically coded information to the computers, the computers processed it and made decisions, the cells became smart. I mean, smart as planaria, for starters. Imagine an *E. coli* as smart as a planarian worm!"

I nodded. "I'm imagining."

"Then I really went off on my own. We had the equipment, the techniques; and I knew the molecular language. I could make really dense, really complicated biochips by compounding the nucleoproteins, making them into little brains. I did some research into how far I could go, theoretically. Sticking with bacteria, I could make a biochip with the computing capacity of a sparrow's brain. Imagine how jazzed I was! Then I saw a way to increase the complexity a thousandfold, by using something we regarded as a nuisance—quantum chit-chat between the fixed elements of the circuits. Down that small, even the slightest change could bomb a biochip. But I developed a program that actually predicted and took advantage of electron tunneling. Emphasized the heuristic aspects of the computer, used the chit-chat as a method of increasing complexity."

"You're losing me," I said.

"I took advantage of randomness. The circuits could repair themselves, compare memories, and correct faulty elements. I gave them basic instructions: Go forth and multiply. Improve. By God, you should have seen some of the cultures a week later! It was amazing. They were evolving all on their own, like little cities. I destroyed them all. I think one of the petri dishes would have grown legs and walked out of the incubator if I'd kept feeding it."

"You're kidding." I looked at him. "You're not kidding."

"Man, they *knew* what it was like to improve! They knew where they had to go, but they were just so limited, being in bacteria bodies, with so few resources."

"How smart were they?"

"I couldn't be sure. They were associating in clusters of a hundred to two hundred cells, each cluster behaving like an autonomous unit. Each cluster might have been as smart as a rhesus monkey. They exchanged information through their pili, passed on bits of memory, and compared notes. Their organization was obviously different from a group of monkeys. Their world was so much simpler, for one thing. With their abilities, they were masters of the petri dishes. I put phages in with them; the phages didn't have a chance. They used every option available to change and grow."

"How is that possible?"

"What?" He seemed surprised I wasn't accepting everything at face value.

"Cramming so much into so little. A rhesus monkey is not your simple little calculator, Vergil."

"I haven't made myself clear," he said, obviously irritated. "I was using nucleoprotein computers. They're like DNA, but all the information can interact. Do you know how many nucleotide pairs there are in the DNA of a single bacteria?"

It had been a long time since my last biochemistry lesson. I shook my head.

"About two million. Add in the modified ribosome structures—fifteen thousand of them, each with a molecular weight of about three million—and consider the combinations and permutations. The RNA is arranged like a continuous loop paper tape, surrounded by ribosomes ticking off instructions and manufacturing protein chains. . . ." His eyes were bright and slightly moist. "Besides, I'm not saying every cell was a distinct entity. They cooperated."

"How many bacteria in the dishes you destroyed?"

"Billions. I don't know." He smirked. "You got it, Edward. Whole planetsful of *E. coli*."

"But Genetron didn't fire you then?"

"No. They didn't know what was going on, for one thing. I kept compounding the molecules, increasing their size and complexity. When bacteria were too limited, I took blood from myself, separated out white cells, and injected them with the new biochips. I watched them, put them through mazes and little chemical problems. They were whizzes. Time is a lot faster at that level—so little distance for the messages to cross, and the environment is much simpler. Then I forgot to store a file under my secret code in the lab computers. Some managers found it and guessed what I was up to. Everybody panicked. They thought we'd have every social watchdog in the country on our backs because of what I'd done. They started to destroy my work and wipe my programs. Ordered me to sterilize my white cells. Christ." He pulled the white robe off and started to get dressed. "I only had a day or two. I separated out the most complex cells—"

"How complex?"

"They were clustering in hundred-cell groups, like the bacteria. Each group as smart as a four-year-old kid, maybe." He studied my face for a moment. "Still doubting? Want me to run through how many nucleotide pairs there are in a mammalian cell? I tailored my computers to take advantage of the white cells' capacity. Four billion nucleotide pairs, Edward. And they don't have a huge body to worry about, taking up most of their thinking time."

"Okay," I said. "I'm convinced. What did you do?"

"I mixed the cells back into a cylinder of whole blood and injected myself with it." He buttoned the top of his shirt and smiled thinly at me. "I'd programmed them with every drive I could, talked as high a level as I could using just enzymes and such. After that, they were on their own."

"You programmed them to go forth and multiply, improve?" I repeated.

"I think they developed some characteristics picked up by the biochips in their *E. coli* phases. The white cells could talk to each other with extruded memories. They found ways to ingest other types of cells and alter them without killing them."

"You're crazy."

"You can see the screen! Edward, I haven't been sick since. I used to get colds all the time. I've never felt better."

"They're inside you, finding things, changing them."

"And by now, each cluster is as smart as you or I."

"You're absolutely nuts."

He shrugged. "Genetron fired me. They thought I was going to take revenge for what they did to my work. They ordered me out of the labs, and I haven't had a real chance to see what's been going on inside me until now. Three months."

"So . . ." My mind was racing. "You lost weight because they improved your fat metabolism. Your bones are stronger; your spine has been completely rebuilt—"

"No more backaches even if I sleep on my old mattress."

"Your heart looks different."

"I didn't know about the heart," he said, examining the frame image more closely. "As for the fat—I was thinking about that. They could increase my brown cells, fix up the metabolism. I haven't been as hungry lately. I haven't changed my eating habits that much—I still want the same old junk—but somehow I get around to eating only what I need. I don't think they know what my brain is yet. Sure, they've got all the glandular stuff—but they don't have the *big* picture, if you see what I mean. They don't know *I'm* in here. But boy, they sure did figure out what my reproductive organs are."

I glanced at the image and shifted my eyes away.

"Oh, they look pretty normal," he said, hefting his scrotum obscenely. He snickered. "But how else do you think I'd land a real looker like Candice? She was just after a one-night stand with a techie. I looked okay then, no tan but trim, with good clothes. She'd never screwed a techie before. Joke time, right? But my little geniuses kept us up half the night. I think they made improvements each time. I felt like I had a goddamned fever."

His smile vanished. "But then one night my skin started to crawl. It really scared me. I thought things were getting out of hand. I wondered what they'd do when they crossed the blood-brain barrier and found out about *me*—about the brain's real function. So I began a campaign to keep them under control. I figured, the reason they wanted to get into the skin was the simplicity of running circuits across a surface. Much easier than trying to maintain chains of communication in and around muscles, organs, vessels. The skin was much more direct. So I bought a quartz lamp." He caught my puzzled expression. "In the lab, we'd break down the protein in biochip cells by exposing them to ultraviolet light. I alternated sunlamp with quartz treatments. Keeps them out of my skin and gives me a nice tan."

"Give you skin cancer, too," I commented.

"They'll probably take care of that. Like police."

"Okay. I've examined you; you've told me a story I still find hard to believe. . . . What do you want me to do?"

"I'm not as nonchalant as I act, Edward. I'm worried. I'd like to find some way to control them before they find out about my brain. I mean, think of it, they're in the trillions by now, each one smart. They're cooperating to some extent. I'm probably the smartest thing on the planet, and they haven't even begun to get their act together. I don't really want them to take over." He laughed unpleasantly. "Steal my soul, you know? So think of some treatment to block them. Maybe we can starve the little buggers. Just think on it." He buttoned his shirt. "Give me a call." He handed me a slip of paper with his address and phone number. Then he went to the keyboard and erased the image on the frame, dumping the memory of the examination. "Just you," he said. "Nobody else for now. And please . . . hurry."

It was three o'clock in the morning when Vergil walked out of the examination room. He'd allowed me to take blood samples, then shaken my hand—his palm was damp, nervous—and cautioned me against ingesting anything from the specimens.

Before I went home, I put the blood through a series of tests. The results were ready the next day.

I picked them up during my lunch break in the afternoon, then destroyed all of the samples. I did it like a robot. It took me five days and nearly sleepless nights to accept what I'd seen. His blood was normal enough, though the machines diagnosed the patient as having an infection. High levels of leukocytes—white blood cells—and histamines. On the fifth day, I believed.

Gail came home before I did, but it was my turn to fix dinner. She slipped one of the school's disks into the home system and showed me video art her nursery kids had been creating. I watched quietly, ate with her in silence.

I had two dreams, part of my final acceptance. In the first, that evening, I witnessed the destruction of the planet Krypton, Superman's home world. Billions of superhuman geniuses went screaming off in walls of fire. I related the destruction to my sterilizing the samples of Vergil's blood.

The second dream was worse. I dreamed that New York City was raping a woman. By the end of the dream, she gave birth to little embryo cities, all wrapped up in translucent sacs, soaked with blood from the difficult labor.

I called him on the morning of the sixth day. He answered on the fourth ring. "I have some results," I said. "Nothing conclusive. But I want to talk with you. In person."

"Sure," he said. "I'm staying inside for the time being." His voice was strained; he sounded tired.

Vergil's apartment was in a fancy high-rise near the lake shore. I took the elevator up, listening to little advertising jingles and watching dancing holograms display products, empty apartments for rent, the building's hostess discussing social activities for the week.

Vergil opened the door and motioned me in. He wore a checked robe with long sleeves and carpet slippers. He clutched an unlit pipe in one hand, his fingers twisting it back and forth as he walked away from me and sat down, saying nothing.

"You have an infection," I said.

"Oh?"

"That's all the blood analyses tell me. I don't have access to the electron microscopes."

"I don't think it's really an infection," he said. "After all, they're my own cells. Probably something else . . . some sign of their presence, of the change. We can't expect to understand everything that's happening."

I removed my coat. "Listen," I said, "you really have me worried now." The expression on his face stopped me: a kind of frantic beatitude. He squinted at the ceiling and pursed his lips.

"Are you stoned?" I asked.

He shook his head, then nodded once, very slowly. "Listening," he said.

"To what?"

"I don't know. Not sounds . . . exactly. Like music. The heart, all the blood vessels, friction of blood along the arteries, veins. Activity. Music in the blood." He looked at me plaintively. "Why aren't you at work?"

"My day off. Gail's working."

"Can you stay?"

I shrugged. "I suppose." I sounded suspicious. I glanced around the apartment, looking for ashtrays, packs of papers.

"I'm not stoned, Edward," he said. "I may be wrong, but I think something big is happening. I think they're finding out who I am."

I sat down across from Vergil, staring at him intently. He didn't seem to notice. Some inner process involved him. When I asked for a cup of coffee, he motioned to the kitchen. I boiled a pot of water and took a jar of instant from the cabinet. With cup in hand, I returned to my seat. He twisted his head back and forth, eyes open. "You always knew what you wanted to be, didn't you?" he asked.

"More or less."

"A gynecologist. Smart moves. Never false moves. I was different. I had goals, but no direction. Like a map without roads, just places to be. I didn't give a shit for anything, anyone but myself. Even science. Just a means. I'm surprised I got so far. I even hated my folks."

He gripped his chair arms.

"Something wrong?" I asked.

"They're talking to me," he said. He shut his eyes.

For an hour he seemed to be asleep. I checked his pulse, which was strong and steady, felt his forehead—slightly cool—and made myself more coffee. I was looking through a magazine, at a loss what to do, when he opened his eyes again. "Hard to figure exactly what time is like for them," he said. "It's taken them maybe three, four days to figure out language, key human concepts. Now they're on to it. On to me. Right now."

"How's that?"

He claimed there were thousands of researchers hooked up to his neurons. He couldn't give details. "They're damned efficient, you know," he said. "They haven't screwed me up yet."

"We should get you into the hospital now."

"What in hell could other doctors do? Did *you* figure out any way to control them? I mean, they're my own cells."

"I've been thinking. We could starve them. Find out what metabolic differences—"

"I'm not sure I want to be rid of them," Vergil said. "They're not doing any harm."

"How do you know?"

He shook his head and held up one finger. "Wait. They're trying to figure out what space is. That's tough for them: They break distances down into concentrations of chemicals. For them, space is like intensity of taste."

"Vergil—"

"Listen! Think, Edward!" His tone was excited but even. "Something big is happening inside me. They talk to each other across the fluid, through membranes. They tailor something—viruses?—to carry data stored in nucleic acid chains. I think they're saying 'RNA.' That makes sense. That's one way I programmed them. But plasmidlike structures, too. Maybe that's what your machines think is a sign of infection—all their chattering in my blood, packets of data. Tastes of other individuals. Peers. Superiors. Subordinates."

"Vergil, I still think you should be in a hospital."

"This is my show, Edward," he said. "I'm their universe. They're amazed by the new scale." He was quiet again for a time. I squatted by his chair and pulled up the sleeve to his robe. His arm was crisscrossed with white lines. I was about to go to the phone when he stood and stretched. "Do you realize," he said, "how many blood cells we kill each time we move?"

"I'm going to call for an ambulance," I said.

"No, you aren't." His tone stopped me. "I told you, I'm not sick, this is my show. Do you know what they'd do to me in a hospital? They'd be like cavemen trying to fix a computer. It would be a farce."

"Then what the hell am I doing here?" I asked, getting angry. "I can't do anything. I'm one of those cavemen."

"You're a friend," Vergil said, fixing his eyes on me. I had the impression I was being watched by more than just Vergil. "I want you here to keep me company." He laughed. "But I'm not exactly alone."

He walked around the apartment for two hours, fingering things, looking out windows, slowly and methodically fixing himself lunch. "You know, they can actually feel their own thoughts," he said about noon. "I mean, the cytoplasm seems to have a will of its own, a kind of subconscious life counter to the rationality they've only recently acquired. They hear the chemical 'noise' of the molecules fitting and uniftting inside."

At two o'clock, I called Gail to tell her I would be late. I was almost sick with tension, but I tried to keep my voice level. "Remember Vergil Ulam? I'm talking with him right now."

"Everything okay?" she asked.

Was it? Decidedly not. "Fine," I said.

"Culture!" Vergil said, peering around the kitchen wall at me. I said goodbye and hung up the phone. "They're always swimming in that bath of information. Contributing to it. It's a kind of gestalt thing. The hierarchy is absolute. They send tailored phages after cells that don't interact properly. Viruses specified to individuals or groups. No escape. A rogue cell gets pierced by the virus, the cell blebs outward, it explodes and dissolves. But it's not just a dictatorship. I think they effectively have more freedom than in a democracy. I mean, they vary so differently from individual to individual. Does that make sense? They vary in different ways than we do."

"Hold it," I said, gripping his shoulders. "Vergil, you're pushing me to the edge. I can't take this much longer. I don't understand; I'm not sure I believe—"

"Not even now?"

"Okay, let's say you're giving me the right interpretation. Giving it to me straight. Have you bothered to figure out the consequences yet? What all this means, where it might lead?"

He walked into the kitchen and drew a glass of water from the tap then returned and stood next to me. His expression had changed from childish absorption to sober concern. "I've never been very good at that."

"Are you afraid?"

"I was. Now, I'm not sure." He fingered the tie of his robe. "Look, I don't want you to think I went around you, over your head or something. But I met with Michael Bernard yesterday. He put me through his private clinic, took specimens. Told me to quit the lamp treatments. He called this morning, just before you did. He says it all checks out. And he asked me not to tell anybody." He paused and his expression became dreary again. "Cities of cells," he continued. "Edward, they push tubes through the tissues, spread information—"

"Stop it!" I shouted. "Checks out? What checks out?"

"As Bernard puts it, I have 'severely enlarged macrophages' throughout my system. And he concurs on the anatomical changes."

"What does he plan to do?"

"I don't know. I think he'll probably convince Genetron to reopen the lab."

"Is that what you want?"

"It's not just having the lab again. I want to show you. Since I stopped the lamp treatments, I'm still changing." He undid his robe and let it slide to the floor. All over his body, his skin was crisscrossed with white lines. Along his back, the lines were starting to form ridges.

"My God," I said.

"I'm not going to be much good anywhere else but the lab soon. I won't be able to go out in public. Hospitals wouldn't know what to do, as I said."

"You're . . . you can talk to them, tell them to slow down," I said, aware how ridiculous that sounded.

"Yes, indeed I can, but they don't necessarily listen."

"I thought you were their god or something."

"The ones hooked up to my neurons aren't the big wheels. They're researchers, or at least serve the same function. They know I'm here, what I am, but that doesn't mean they've convinced the upper levels of the heirarchy."

"They're disputing?"

"Something like that. It's not all that bad, anyway. If the lab is reopened, I have a home, a place to work." He glanced out the window, as if looking for someone. "I don't have anything left but them. They aren't afraid, Edward. I've never felt so close to anything before." The beatific smile again. "I'm responsible for them. Mother to them all."

"You have no way of knowing what they're going to do."

He shook his head.

"No, I mean it. You say they're like a civilization—"

"Like a thousand civilizations."

"Yes, and civilizations have been known to screw up. Warfare, the environment—"

I was grasping at straws, trying to restrain a growing panic. I wasn't competent to handle the enormity of what was happening. Neither was Vergil. He was the last person I would have called insightful and wise about large issues.

"But I'm the only one at risk."

"You don't know that. Jesus, Vergil, look what they're *doing* to you!"

"To me, all to me!" he said. "Nobody else."

I shook my head and held up my hands in a gesture of defeat. "Okay, so Bernard gets them to reopen the lab, you move in, become a guinea pig. What then?"

"They treat me right. I'm more than just good old Vergil Ulam now. I'm a goddamned galaxy, a super-mother."

"Super-host, you mean." He conceded the point with a shrug.

I couldn't take any more. I made my exit with a few flimsy excuses, then sat in the lobby of the apartment building, trying to calm down. Somebody had to talk some sense into him. Who would he listen to? He had gone to Bernard . . .

And it sounded as if Bernard was not only convinced, but very interested. People of Bernard's stature didn't coax the Vergil Ulams of the world along unless they felt it was to their advantage.

I had a hunch, and I decided to play it. I went to a pay phone, slipped in my credit card, and called Genetron.

"I'd like you to page Dr. Michael Bernard," I told the receptionist.

"Who's calling, please?"

"This is his answering service. We have an emergency call and his beeper doesn't seem to be working."

A few anxious minutes later, Bernard came on the line. "Who the hell is this?" he asked. "I don't have an answering service."

"My name is Edward Milligan. I'm a friend of Vergil Ulams's. I think we have some problems to discuss."

We made an appointment to talk the next morning.

I went home and tried to think of excuses to keep me off the next day's hospital shift. I couldn't concentrate on medicine, couldn't give my patients anywhere near the attention they deserved.

Guilty, angry, afraid.

That was how Gail found me. I slipped on a mask of calm and we fixed dinner together. After eating, holding onto each other, we watched the city lights come on in late twilight through the bayside window. Winter starlings pecked at the yellow lawn in the last few minutes of light, then flew away with a rising wind which made the windows rattle.

"Something's wrong," Gail said softly. "Are you going to tell me, or just act like everything's normal?"

"It's just me," I said. "Nervous. Work at the hospital."

"Oh, lord," she said, sitting up. "You're going to divorce me for that Baker woman." Mrs. Baker weighed three hundred and sixty pounds and hadn't known she was pregnant until her fifth month.

"No," I said, listless.

"Rapturous relief," Gail said, touching my forehead lightly. "You know this kind of introspection drives me crazy."

"Well, it's nothing I can talk about yet, so . . ." I patted her hand.

"That's disgustingly patronizing," she said, getting up. "I'm going to make some tea. Want some?" Now she was miffed, and I was tense with not telling.

Why not just reveal all? I asked myself. An old friend was turning himself into a galaxy.

I cleared away the table instead. That night, unable to sleep, I looked down on Gail in bed from my sitting position, pillow against the wall, and tried to determine what I knew was real, and what wasn't.

I'm a doctor, I told myself. A technical, scientific profession. I'm supposed to be immune to things like future shock.

Vergil Ulam was turning into a galaxy.

How would it feel to be topped off with a trillion Chinese? I grinned in the dark and almost cried at the same time. What Vergil had inside him was unimaginably stranger than Chinese. Stranger than anything I—or Vergil—could easily understand. Perhaps ever understand.

But I knew what was real. The bedroom, the city lights faint through gauze curtains. Gail sleeping. Very important. Gail in bed, sleeping.

The dream returned. This time the city came in through the window and attacked Gail. It was a great, spiky, lighted-up prowler, and it growled in a language I couldn't understand, made up of auto horns, crowd noises, construction bedlam. I tried to fight it off, but it got to her—and turned into a drift of stars, sprinkling all over the bed, all over everything. I jerked awake and stayed up until dawn, dressed with Gail, kissed her, savored the reality of her human, unviolated lips.

I went to meet with Bernard. He had been loaned a suite in a big downtown hospital; I rode the elevator to the sixth floor, and saw what fame and fortune could mean.

The suite was tastefully furnished, fine serigraphs on wood-paneled walls, chrome and glass furniture, cream-colored carpet, Chinese brass, and wormwood-grain cabinets and tables.

He offered me a cup of coffee, and I accepted. He took a seat in the breakfast nook, and I sat across from him, cradling my cup in moist palms. He wore a dapper gray suit and had graying hair and a sharp profile. He was in his mid sixties and he looked quite a bit like Leonard Bernstein.

"About our mutual acquaintance," he said. "Mr. Ulam. Brilliant. And, I won't hesitate to say, courageous."

"He's my friend. I'm worried about him."

Bernard held up one finger. "Courageous—and a bloody damned fool. What's happening to him should never have been allowed. He may have done it under duress, but that's no excuse. Still, what's done is done. He's talked to you, I take it."

I nodded. "He wants to return to Genetron."

"Of course. That's where all his equipment is. Where his home probably will be while we sort this out."

"Sort it out—how? Why?" I wasn't thinking too clearly. I had a slight headache.

"I can think of a large number of uses for small, superdense computer elements with a biological base. Can't you? Genetron has already made break-throughs, but this is something else again."

"What do you envision?"

Bernard smiled. "I'm not really at liberty to say. It'll be revolutionary. We'll have to get him in lab conditions. Animal experiments have to be conducted. We'll start from scratch, of course. Vergil's . . . um . . . colonies can't be transferred. They're based on his own white blood cells. So we have to develop colonies that won't trigger immune reactions in other animals."

"Like an infection?" I asked.

"I suppose there are comparisons. But Vergil is not infected."

"My tests indicate he is."

"That's probably the bits of data floating around in his blood, don't you think?"

"I don't know."

"Listen, I'd like you to come down to the lab after Vergil is settled in. Your expertise might be useful to us."

Us. He was working with Genetron hand in glove. Could he be objective? "How will you benefit from all this?"

"Edward, I have always been at the forefront of my profession. I see no reason why I shouldn't be helping here. With my knowledge of brain and nerve functions, and the research I've been conducting in neurophysiology—"

"You could help Genetron hold off an investigation by the government," I said.

"That's being very blunt. Too blunt, and unfair."

"Perhaps. Anyway, yes: I'd like to visit the lab when Vergil's settled in. If I'm still welcome, bluntness and all." He looked at me sharply. I wouldn't be playing on *his* team; for a moment, his thoughts were almost nakedly apparent.

"Of course," Bernard said, rising with me. He reached out to shake my hand. His palm was damp. He was as nervous as I was, even if he didn't look it.

I returned to my apartment and stayed there until noon, reading, trying to sort things out. Reach a decision. What was real, what I needed to protect.

There is only so much change anyone can stand: innovation, yes, but slow application. Don't force. Everyone has the right to stay the same until they decide otherwise.

The greatest thing in science since . . .

And Bernard would force it. Genetron would force it. I couldn't handle the thought. "Neo-Luddite," I said to myself. A filthy accusation.

When I pressed Vergil's number on the building security panel, Vergil answered almost immediately. "Yeah," he said. He sounded exhilarated. "Come on up. I'll be in the bathroom. Door's unlocked."

I entered his apartment and walked through the hallway to the bathroom. Vergil lay in the tub, up to his neck in pinkish water. He smiled vaguely and splashed his hands. "Looks like I slit my wrists, doesn't it?" he said softly. "Don't worry. Everything's fine now. Genetron's going to take me back. Bernard just called." He pointed to the bathroom phone and intercom.

I sat on the toilet and noticed the sunlamp fixture standing unplugged next to the linen cabinets. The bulbs sat in a row on the edge of the sink counter. "You're sure that's what you want," I said, my shoulders slumping.

"Yeah, I think so," he said. "They can take better care of me. I'm getting cleaned up, going over there this evening. Bernard's picking me up in his limo. Style. From here on in, everything's style."

The pinkish color in the water didn't look like soap. "Is that bubble bath?" I asked. Some of it came to me in a rush then and I felt a little weaker; what had occurred to me was just one more obvious and necessary insanity.

"No," Vergil said. I knew that already.

"No," he repeated, "it's coming from my skin. They're not telling me everything, but I think they're sending out scouts. Astronauts." He looked at me with an expression that didn't quite equal concern; more like curiosity as to how I'd take it.

The confirmation made my stomach muscles tighten as if waiting for a punch. I had never even considered the possibility until now, perhaps because I had been concentrating on other aspects. "Is this the first time?" I asked.

"Yeah," he said. He laughed. "I've half a mind to let the little buggers down the drain. Let them find out what the world's really about."

"They'd go everywhere," I said.

"Sure enough."

"How . . . how are you feeling?"

"I'm feeling pretty good now. Must be billions of them." More splashing with his hands. "What do you think? Should I let the buggers out?"

Quickly, hardly thinking, I knelt down beside the tub. My fingers went for the cord on the sunlamp and I plugged it in. He had hot-wired doorknobs, turned my piss blue, played a thousand dumb practical jokes and never grown up, never grown mature enough to understand that he was sufficiently brilliant to transform the world; he would never learn caution.

He reached for the drain knob. "You know, Edward, I—"

He never finished. I picked up the fixture and dropped it into the tub, jumping back at the flash of steam and sparks. Vergil screamed and thrashed and jerked and then everything was still, except for the low, steady sizzle and the smoke wafting from his hair.

I lifted the toilet lid and vomited. Then I clenched my nose and went into the living room. My legs went out from under me and I sat abruptly on the couch.

After an hour, I searched through Vergil's kitchen and found bleach, ammonia, and a bottle of Jack Daniel's. I returned to the bathroom, keeping the center of my gaze away from Vergil. I poured first the booze, then the bleach, then the ammonia into the water. Chlorine started bubbling up and I left, closing the door behind me.

The phone was ringing when I got home. I didn't answer. It could have been the hospital. It could have been Bernard. Or the police. I could envision having to explain everything to the police. Genetron would stonewall; Bernard would be unavailable.

I was exhausted, all my muscles knotted with tension and whatever name one can give to the feelings one has after—

Committing genocide?

That certainly didn't seem real. I could not believe I had just murdered a hundred trillion intelligent beings. Snuffed a galaxy. It was laughable. But I didn't laugh.

It was easy to believe that I had just killed one human being, a friend. The smoke, the melted lamp rods, the drooping electrical outlet and smoking cord.

Vergil.

I had dunked the lamp into the tub with Vergil.

I felt sick. Dreams, cities raping Gail (and what about his girlfriend, Candice?). Letting the water filled with them out. Galaxies sprinkling over us all. What horror. Then again, what potential beauty—a new kind of life, symbiosis and transformation.

Had I been thorough enough to kill them all? I had a moment of panic. Tomorrow, I thought, I will sterilize his apartment. Somehow, I didn't even think of Bernard.

When Gail came in the door, I was asleep on the couch. I came to, groggy, and she looked down at me.

"You feeling okay?" she asked, perching on the edge of the couch. I nodded.

"What are you planning for dinner?" My mouth didn't work properly. The words were mushy. She felt my forehead.

"Edward, you have a fever," she said. "A very high fever."

I stumbled into the bathroom and looked in the mirror. Gail was close behind me. "What is it?" she asked.

There were lines under my collar, around my neck. White lines, like freeways. They had already been in me a long time, days.

"Damp palms," I said. So obvious.

I think we nearly died. I struggled at first, but in minutes I was too weak to move. Gail was just as sick within an hour.

I lay on the carpet in the living room, drenched in sweat. Gail lay on the couch, her face the color of talcum, eyes closed, like a corpse in an embalming parlor. For a time I thought she was dead. Sick as I was, I raged—hated, felt tremendous guilt at my weakness, my slowness to understand all the possibilities. Then I no longer cared. I was too weak to blink, so I closed my eyes and waited.

There was a rhythm in my arms, my legs. With each pulse of blood, a kind of sound welled up within me, like an orchestra thousands strong, but not playing in unison; playing whole seasons of symphonies at once. Music in the blood. The sound became harsher, but more coordinated, wave-trains finally canceling into silence, then separating into harmonic beats.

The beats seemed to melt into me, into the sound of my own heart.

First, they subdued our immune responses. The war—and it was a war, on a scale never before known on Earth, with trillions of combatants—lasted perhaps two days.

By the time I regained enough strength to get to the kitchen faucet, I could feel them working on my brain, trying to crack the code and find the god within the protoplasm. I drank until I was sick, then drank more moderately and took a glass to Gail. She sipped at it. Her lips were cracked, her eyes bloodshot and ringed with yellowish crumbs. There was some color in her skin. Minutes later, we were eating feebly in the kitchen.

"What in hell is happening?" was the first thing she asked. I didn't have the strength to explain. I peeled an orange and shared it with her. "We should call a doctor," she said. But I knew we wouldn't. I was already receiving messages; it was becoming apparent that any sensation of freedom we experienced was illusory.

The messages were simple at first. Memories of commands, rather than the commands themselves, manifested themselves in my thoughts. We were not to leave the apartment—a concept which seemed quite abstract to those in control, even if undesirable—and we were not to have contact with others. We would be allowed to eat certain foods and drink tap water for the time being.

With the subsidence of the fevers, the transformations were quick and drastic. Almost simultaneously, Gail and I were immobilized. She was sitting at the table, I was kneeling on the floor. I was able barely to see her in the corner of my eye.

Her arm developed pronounced ridges.

They had learned inside Vergil; their tactics within the two of us were very different. I itched all over for about two hours—two hours in hell—before they made the breakthrough and found me. The effort of ages on their timescale paid off and they communicated smoothly and directly with this great, clumsy intelligence who had once controlled their universe.

They were not cruel. When the concept of discomfort and its undesirability was made clear, they worked to alleviate it. They worked too effectively. For another hour, I was in a sea of bliss, out of all contact with them.

With dawn the next day, they gave us freedom to move again; specifically, to go to the bathroom. There were certain waste products they could not deal with. I voided those—my urine was purple—and Gail followed suit. We looked at each other vacantly in the bathroom. Then she managed a slight smile. "Are they talking to you?" she said. I nodded. "Then I'm not crazy."

For the next twelve hours, control seemed to loosen on some levels. I suspect there was another kind of war going on in me. Gail was capable of limited motion, but no more.

When full control resumed, we were instructed to hold each other. We did not hesitate.

"Eddie . . ." she whispered. My name was the last sound I ever heard from outside.

Standing, we grew together. In hours, our legs expanded and spread out. Then extensions grew to the windows to take in sunlight, and to the kitchen to take water from the sink. Filaments soon reached to all corners of the room, stripping paint and plaster from the walls, fabric and stuffing from the furniture.

By the next dawn, the transformation was complete.

I no longer have any clear view of what we look like. I suspect we resemble cells—large, flat, and filamented cells, draped purposefully across most of the apartment. The great shall mimic the small.

Our intelligence fluctuates daily as we are absorbed into the minds within. Each day, our individuality declines. We are, indeed, great clumsy dinosaurs. Our memories have been taken over by billions of them, and our personalities have been spread through the transformed blood.

Soon there will be no need for centralization.

Already the plumbing has been invaded. People throughout the building are undergoing transformation.

Within the old time frame of weeks, we will reach the lakes, rivers, and seas in force.

I can barely begin to guess the results. Every square inch of the planet will teem with thought. Years from now, perhaps much sooner, they will subdue their own individuality—what there is of it.

New creatures will come, then. The immensity of their capacity for thought will be inconceivable.

All my hatred and fear is gone now.

I leave them—us—with only one question.

How many times has this happened, elsewhere? Travelers never came through space to visit the Earth. They had no need.

They had found universes in grains of sand.

PAPERJACK

Charles de Lint

Charles de Lint is a fantasist who has made his specialty "urban fantasy," fantasy set in the real world rather than an invented otherworld. He is in fact one of the founders of that subgenre that evolved out of the *Unknown Worlds* group of magazine writers in the early 1940s (Robert A. Heinlein, Eric Frank Russell, L. Ron Hubbard, Theodore Sturgeon, and particularly Fritz Leiber—for more information, see the Budrys essay) and grew into a major part of genre fantasy in the 1980s.

> *If you think education is*
> *expensive, try ignorance.*
> —Derek Bok

Churches aren't havens of spiritual enlightenment; they enclose the spirit. The way Jilly explains it, organizing Mystery tends to undermine its essence. I'm not so sure I agree, but then I don't really know enough about it. When it comes to things that can't be logically explained, I take a step back and leave them to Jilly or my brother Christy—they thrive on that kind of thing. If I had to describe myself as belonging to any church or mystical order, it'd be one devoted to secular humanism. My concerns are for real people and the here and now; the possible existence of God, faeries, or some metaphysical Otherworld just doesn't fit into my worldview.

Except . . .

You knew there'd be an "except," didn't you, or else why would I be writing this down?

It's not like I don't have anything to say. I'm all for creative expression, but my medium's music. I'm not an artist like Jilly, or a writer like Christy. But the kinds of things that have been happening to me can't really be expressed in a fiddle tune—no, that's not entirely true. I can express them, but the medium is such I can't be assured that, when I'm playing, listeners hear what I mean them to hear.

That's how it works with instrumental music, and it's probably why the best of it is so enduring: the listener takes away whatever he or she wants from it. Say the composer was trying to tell us about the aftermath of some great battle. When we hear it, the music might speak to us of a parent we've lost, a friend's struggle with some debilitating disease, a doe standing at the edge of a forest at twilight, or any of a thousand other unrelated things.

Realistic art like Jilly does—or at least it's realistically rendered; her subject matter's right out of some urban update of those Andrew Lang color-coded fairy tale books that most of us read when we were kids—and the collections of urban legends and stories that my brother writes don't have that same leeway. What goes down on the canvas or on paper, no matter how skillfully drawn or written, doesn't allow for much in the way in an alternate interpretation.

So that's why I'm writing this down: to lay it all out in black and white where maybe I can understand it myself.

For the past week, every afternoon after busking up by the Williamson Street Mall for the lunchtime crowds, I've packed up my fiddlecase and headed across town to come here to St. Paul's Cathedral. Once I get here, I sit on the steps about halfway up, take out this notebook, and try to write. The trouble is, I haven't been able to figure out where to start.

I like it out here on the steps. I've played inside the cathedral—just once, for a friend's wedding. The wedding was okay, but I remember coming in on my own to test the acoustics an hour or so before the rehearsal; ever since then I've been a little unsure about how Jilly views this kind of place. My fiddling didn't feel enclosed. Instead the walls seemed to open the music right up; the cathedral gave the reel I was playing a stately grace—a spiritual grace—that it had never held for me before. I suppose it had more to do with the architect's design than the presence of God, still I could've played there all night only—

But I'm rambling again. I've filled a couple of pages now, which is more than I've done all week, except after just rereading what I've written so far, I don't know if any of it's relevant.

Maybe I should just tell you about Paperjack. I don't know that it starts with him exactly, but it's probably as good a place as any to begin.

It was a glorious day, made all the more precious because the weather had been so weird that spring. One day I'd be bundled up in a jacket and scarf, cloth cap on my head, with fingerless gloves to keep the cold from my finger joints while I was out busking, the next I'd be in a T-shirt, breaking into a sweat just thinking about standing out on some street corner to play tunes.

There wasn't a cloud in the sky, the sun was halfway home from noon to the western horizon, and Jilly and I were just soaking up the rays on the steps of St. Paul's. I was slouched on the steps, leaning on one elbow, my fiddlecase propped up beside me, wishing I had worn shorts because my jeans felt like leaden weights on my legs. Sitting beside me, perched like a cat about to pounce on something terribly interesting that only it could see, Jilly was her usual scruffy self. There were flecks of paint on her loose cotton pants and her short-sleeved blouse, more under her fingernails, and still more half-lost in the tangles of her hair. She turned to look at me, her face miraculously untouched by her morning's work, and gave me one of her patented smiles.

"Did you ever wonder where he's from?" Jilly asked.

That was one of her favorite phrases: "Did you ever wonder . . . ?" It could take you from considering if and when fish slept, or why people look up when they're thinking, to more arcane questions about ghosts, little people living behind wallboards, and the like. And she loved guessing about people's origins. Sometimes when I was busking she'd tag along and sit by the wall at my back, sketching the people who were listening to me play. Invariably, she'd come up behind me and whisper in my ear—usually when I was in the middle of a complicated tune that needed all my attention—something alone the lines of, "The guy in the polyester suit? Ten to one he rides a big chopper on the weekends, complete with a jean vest."

So I was used to it.

Today she wasn't picking out some nameless stranger from a crowd. Instead her attention was on Paperjack, sitting on the steps far enough below us that he couldn't hear what we were saying.

Paperjack had the darkest skin I'd ever seen on a man—an amazing ebony that seemed to swallow light. He was in his mid-sixties, I'd guess, short corkscrew hair all gone grey. The dark suits he wore were threadbare and out of fashion, but always clean. Under his suit jacket he usually wore a white T-shirt that flashed so brightly in the sun it almost hurt your eyes—just like his teeth did when he gave you that lopsided grin of his.

Nobody knew his real name and he never talked. I don't know if he was mute, or if he just didn't have anything to say, but the only sounds I ever heard him make were a chuckle or a laugh. People started calling him Paperjack because he worked an origami gig on the streets.

He was a master at folding paper into shapes. He kept a bag of different colored paper by his knee; people would pick their color and then tell him what they wanted, and he'd make it—no cuts, just folding. And he could make anything. From simple flower and animal shapes to things so complex it didn't seem possible for him to capture their essence in a piece of folded paper. So far as I know, he'd never disappointed a single customer.

I'd seen some of the old men come down from Little Japan to sit and watch him work. They called him *sensei,* a term of respect that they didn't exactly bandy around.

But origami was only the most visible side of his gig. He also told fortunes. He had one of those little folded paper Chinese fortune-telling devices that we all played around with when we were kids. You know the kind: you fold the corners in to the center, turn it over, then fold them in again. When you're done you can stick your index fingers and thumbs inside the little flaps of the folds and open it up so that it looks like a flower. You move your fingers back and forth, and it looks like the flower's talking to you.

Paperjack's fortune-teller was just like that. It had the names of four colors on the outside and eight different numbers inside. First you picked a color—say, red. The fortune-teller would seem to talk soundlessly as his fingers moved back and forth to spell the word, R-E-D, opening and closing until there'd be a choice from four of the numbers. Then you picked a number, and he counted it out until the fortune-teller was open with another or the same set of numbers revealed. Under the number you choose at that point was your fortune.

Paperjack didn't read it out—he just showed it to the person, then stowed the fortune-teller back into the inside pocket of his jacket from which he'd taken it earlier. I'd never had my fortune read by him, but Jilly'd had it done for her a whole bunch of times.

"The fortunes are always different," she told me once. "I sat behind him while he was doing one for a customer, and I read the fortune over her shoulder. When she'd paid him, I got mine done. I picked the same number she did, but when he opened it, there was a different fortune there."

"He's just got more than one of those paper fortune-tellers in his pocket," I said, but she shook her head.

"He never put it away," she said. "It was the same fortune-teller, the same number, but some time between the woman's reading and mine, it changed."

I knew there could be any number of logical explanations for how that could have happened, starting with plain sleight of hand, but I'd long ago given up continuing arguments with Jilly when it comes to that kind of thing.

Was Paperjack magic? Not in my book, at least not the way Jilly thought he was. But there was a magic about him, the magic that always hangs like an aura about someone who's as good an artist as Paperjack was. He also made me feel good. Around him, an overcast day didn't seem half so gloomy, and when the sun shone, it always seemed brighter. He just exuded a glad feeling that you couldn't help but pick up on. So in that sense, he was magic.

I'd also wondered where he'd come from, how he'd ended up on the street. Street people seemed pretty well evenly divided between those who had no choice but to be there, and those who chose to live there like I do. But even then there's a difference. I had a little apartment not far from Jilly's. I could get a job when I wanted one, usually in the winter when the busking was bad and club gigs were slow.

Not many street people have that choice, but I thought that Paperjack might be one of them.

"He's such an interesting guy," Jilly was saying.

I nodded.

"But I'm worried about him," she went on.

"How so?"

Jilly's brow wrinkled with a frown. "He seems to be getting thinner, and he doesn't get around as easily as he once did. You weren't here when he showed up today—he walked as though gravity had suddenly doubled its pull on him."

"Well, he's an old guy, Jilly."

"That's exactly it. Where does he live? Does he have someone to look out for him?"

That was Jilly for you. She had a heart as big as a city, with room in it for everyone and everything. She was forever taking in strays, be they dogs, cats, or people.

I'd been one of her strays once, but that was a long time ago.

"Maybe we should ask him," I said.

"He can't talk," she reminded me.

"Maybe he just doesn't *want* to talk."

Jilly shook her head. "I've tried a zillion times. He hears what I'm saying, and somehow he manages to answer with a smile or a raised eyebrow or whatever, but he doesn't talk." The wrinkles in her brow deepened until I wanted to reach over and smooth them out. "These days," she added, "he seems haunted to me."

If someone else had said that, I'd know that they meant Paperjack had something troubling him. With Jilly though, you often had to take that kind of a statement literally.

"Are we talking ghosts now?" I asked.

I tried to keep the skepticism out of my voice, but from the flash of disappointment that touched Jilly's eyes, I knew I hadn't done a very good job.

"Oh, Geordie," she said. "Why can't you just *believe* what happened to us?"

Here's one version of what happened that night, some three years ago now, to which Jilly was referring:

We saw a ghost. He stepped out of the past on a rainy night and stole away the woman I loved. At least that's the way I remember it. Except for Jilly, no one else does.

Her name was Samantha Rey. She worked at Gypsy Records and had an apartment on Stanton Street, except after that night, when the past came up to steal her away, no one at Gypsy Records remembered her anymore, and the landlady of her Stanton Street apartment had never heard of her. The ghost hadn't just stolen her, he'd stolen all memory of her existence.

All I had left of her was an old photograph that Jilly and I found in Moore's Antiques a little while later. It had a photographer's date on the back: 1912. It was Sam in the picture, Sam with a group of strangers standing on the front porch of some old house.

I remembered her, but she'd never existed. That's what I had to believe. Because nothing else made sense. I had all these feelings and memories of her, but they had to be what my brother called *jamais vu*. That's like *déjà vu*, except instead of having felt you'd been somewhere before, you remembered something that had never happened. I'd never heard the expression before—he got it from a David Morrell thriller that he'd been reading—but it had an authentic ring about it.

Jamais vu.

But Jilly remembered Sam, too.

Thinking about Sam always brought a tightness to my chest; it made my head hurt trying to figure it out. I felt as if I were betraying Sam by trying to convince myself she'd never existed, but I had to convince myself of that, because believing that it really *had* happened was even scarier. How do you live in a world where anything can happen?

"You'll get used to it," Jilly told me. "There's a whole invisible world out there, lying side by side with our own. Once you get a peek into it, the window doesn't close. You're always going to be *aware* of it."

"I don't want to be," I said.

She just shook her head. "You don't really get a lot of choice in this kind of thing," she said.

You always have a choice—that's what I believe. And I chose to not get caught up in some invisible world of ghosts and spirits and who knew what. But I still dreamed of Sam, as if she'd been real. I still kept her photo in my fiddlecase.

I could feel its presence right now, glimmering through the leather, whispering to me.

Remember me . . .

I couldn't forget. *Jamais vu.* But I wanted to.

Jilly scooted a little closer to me on the step and laid a hand on my knee.

"Denying it just makes things worse," she said, continuing an old ongoing argument that I don't think we'll ever resolve. "Until you accept that it really happened, the memory's always going to haunt you, undermining everything that makes you who you are."

"Haunted like Paperjack?" I asked, trying to turn the subject back onto more comfortable ground, or at least focus the attention onto someone other than myself. "Is that what you think's happened to him?"

Jilly sighed. "Memories can be just like ghosts," she said.

Didn't I know it.

I looked down the steps to where Paperjack had been sitting, but he was gone, and now a couple of pigeons were waddling across the steps. The wind blew a candy bar wrapper up against a riser. I laid my hand on Jilly's and gave it a squeeze, then picked up my fiddlecase and stood up.

"I've got to go," I told her.

"I didn't mean to upset you. . . ."

"I know. I've just got to walk for a bit and think."

She didn't offer to accompany me and for that I was glad. Jilly was my best friend, but right then I had to be alone.

I went rambling; just let my feet take me wherever they felt like going, south from St. Paul's and down Battersfield Road, all the way to the Pier, my fiddlecase banging against my thigh as I walked. When I got to the waterfront, I leaned up against the fieldstone wall where the Pier met the beach. I stood and watched the fishermen work their lines farther out over the lake. Fat gulls wheeled above, crying like they hadn't been fed in months. Down on the sand, a couple was having an animated discussion, but they were too far away for me to make out what they were arguing about. They looked like figures in some old silent movie; caricatures, their movements larger than life, rather than real people.

I don't know what I was thinking about; I was trying *not* to think, I suppose, but I wasn't having much luck. The arguing couple depressed me.

Hang on to what you've got, I wanted to tell them, but it wasn't any of my business. I thought about heading across town to Fitzhenry Park—there was a part of it called the Silenus Gardens filled with some benches and statuary where I always felt better—when I spied a familiar figure sitting down by the river west of the Pier: Paperjack.

The Kickaha River was named after that branch of the Algonquin language family that originally lived in this area before the white men came and took it all away from them. All the tribe had left now was a reservation north of the city and this river named after them. The Kickaha had its source north of the reserve and cut through the city on its way to the lake. In this part of town it separated the business section and commercial waterfront from the Beaches where the money lives.

There are houses in the Beaches that make the old stately homes in Lower Crowsea look like tenements, but you can't see them from here. Looking west, all you see is green—first the City Commission's manicured lawns on either side of the river, then the treed hills that hide the homes of the wealthy from the rest of us plebes. On the waterfront itself are a couple of country clubs and the private beaches of the *really* wealthy whose estates back right onto the water.

Paperjack was sitting on this side of the river, doing I don't know what. From where I stood, I couldn't tell. He seemed to be just sitting there on the riverbank, watching the slow water move past. I watched him for awhile, then hoisted my fiddlecase from where I'd leaned it against the wall and hopped down to the sand. When I got to where he was sitting, he looked up and gave me an easy, welcoming grin, as if he'd been expecting me to show up.

Running into him like this was fate, Jilly would say. I'll stick to calling it co-incidence. It's a big city, but it isn't that big.

Paperjack made a motion with his hand, indicating I should pull up a bit of lawn beside him. I hesitated for a moment—right up until then, I realized later, everything could have worked out differently. But I made the choice and sat be-side him.

There was a low wall, right down by the water, with rushes and lilies grow-ing up against it. Among the lilies was a family of ducks—mother and a paddling of ducklings—and that was what Paperjack had been watching. He had an empty plastic bag in his hand, and the breadcrumbs that remained in the bot-tom told me he'd been feeding the ducks until his bread ran out.

He made another motion with his hand, touching the bag, then pointing to the ducks.

I shook my head. "I wasn't planning on coming down," I said, "so I didn't bring anything to feed them."

He nodded, understanding.

We sat quietly awhile longer. The ducks finally gave up on us and paddled farther up the river, looking for better pickings. Once they were gone, Paperjack turned to me again. He laid his hand against his heart, then raised his eyebrows questioningly.

Looking at that slim black hand with its long narrow fingers lying against his dark suit, I marveled again at the sheer depth of his ebony coloring. Even with the bit of a tan I'd picked up busking the last few weeks, I felt absolutely pallid beside him. Then I lifted my gaze to his eyes. If his skin swallowed light, I knew where it went: into his eyes. They were dark, so dark you could barely tell the difference between pupil and cornea, but inside their darkness was a kind of glow—a shine that resonated inside me like the deep hum that comes from my fiddle's bass strings whenever I play one of those wild Shetland reels in A minor.

I suppose it's odd, describing something visual in terms of sound, but right then, right at that moment, I *heard* the shine of his eyes, singing inside me. And I understood immediately what he'd meant by his gesture.

"Yeah," I said. "I'm feeling a little low."

He touched his chest again, but it was a different, lighter gesture this time. I knew what that meant as well.

"There's not much anybody can do about it," I said.

Except Sam. She could come back. Or maybe if I just knew she'd been *real* . . . But that opened a whole other line of thinking that I wasn't sure I wanted to get into again. I wanted her to have been real, I wanted her to come back, but if I accepted that, I also had to accept that ghosts were real and that the past could sneak up and steal someone from the present, taking them back into a time that had already been and gone.

Paperjack took his fortune-telling device out of the breast pocket of his jacket and gave me a questioning look. I started to shake my head, but before I could think about what I was doing, I just said, "What the hell," and let him do his stuff.

I chose blue from the colors, because that was the closest to how I was feeling; he didn't have any colors like confused or lost or foolish. I watched his fingers move the paper to spell out the color, then chose four from the numbers, because that's how many strings my fiddle has. When his fingers stopped moving the second time, I picked seven for no particular reason at all.

He folded back the paper flap so I could read my fortune. All it said was: "Swallow the past."

I didn't get it. I thought it'd say something like that Bobby McFerrin song, "Don't Worry, Be Happy." What it did say didn't make any sense at all.

"I don't understand," I told Paperjack. "What's it supposed to mean?"

He just shrugged. Folding up the fortune-teller, he put it back in his pocket.

Swallow the past. Did that mean I was supposed to forget about it? Or . . . well, swallow could also mean believe or accept. Was that what he was trying to tell me? Was he echoing Jilly's argument?

I thought about that photo in my fiddlecase, and then an idea came to me. I don't know why I'd never thought of it before. I grabbed my fiddlecase and stood up.

"I . . ." I wanted to thank him, but somehow the words just escaped me. All that came out was, "I've gotta run."

But I could tell he understood my gratitude. I wasn't exactly sure what he'd done, except that that little message on his fortune-teller had put together a connection for me that I'd never seen before.

Fate, I could hear Jilly saying.

Paperjack smiled and waved me off.

I followed coincidence away from Paperjack and the riverbank and back up Battersfield Road to the Newford Public Library in Lower Crowsea.

Time does more than erode a riverbank or wear mountains down into tired hills. It takes the edge from our memories as well, overlaying everything with a soft focus so that it all blurs together. What really happened gets all jumbled up with the hopes and dreams we once had and what we wish had really happened. Did you ever run into someone you went to school with—someone you never really hung around with, but just passed in the halls, or had a class with—and they act like you were the best of buddies, because that's how they remember it? For that matter, maybe you *were* buddies, and it's you that's remembering it wrong. . . .

Starting some solid detective work on what happened to Sam took the blur from my memories and brought her back into focus for me. The concepts of ghosts or people disappearing into the past just got pushed to one side, and all I thought about was Sam and tracking her down; if not the Sam I had known, then the woman she'd become in the past.

My friend Amy Scallan works at the library. She's a tall, angular woman with russet hair and long fingers that would have stood her in good stead at a piano keyboard. Instead she took up the Uillean pipes, and we play together in an on-again, off-again band called Johnny Jump Up. Matt Casey, our third member, is the reason we're not that regular a band.

Matt's a brilliant bouzouki and guitar player and a fabulous singer, but he's not got much in the way of social skills, and he's way too cynical for my liking. Since he and I don't really get along well, it makes rehearsals kind of tense at times. On the other hand, I love playing with Amy. She's the kind of musician who has such a good time playing that you can't help but enjoy yourself as well. Whenever I think of Amy, the first image that always comes to mind is of her rangy frame folded around her pipes, right elbow moving back and forth on the bellows to fill the bag under her left arm, those long fingers just dancing on the chanter, foot tapping, head bobbing, a grin on her face.

She always makes sure that the gig goes well, and we have a lot of fun, so it balances out, I guess.

I showed her the picture I had of Sam. There was a street number on the porch's support pillar to the right of the steps and enough of the house in the picture that I'd be able to match it up to the real thing. If I could find out what street it was on. If the house still existed.

"This could take forever," Amy said as she laid the photo down on the desk.

"I've got the time."

Amy laughed. "I suppose you do. I don't know how you do it, Geordie. Everyone else in the world has to bust their buns to make a living, but you just cruise on through."

"The trick's having a low overhead," I said.

Amy just rolled her eyes. She'd been to my apartment, and there wasn't much to see: a spare fiddle hanging on the wall with a couple of Jilly's paintings; some tune books with tattered covers and some changes of clothing; one of those old-fashioned record players that had the turntable and speakers all in one unit and a few albums leaning against the side of the apple crate it sat on; a couple of bows that desperately needed rehairing; the handful of used paperbacks I'd picked up for the week's reading from Duffy's Used Books over on Walker Street; and a little beat-up old cassette machine with a handful of tapes.

And that was it. I got by.

I waited at the desk while Amy got the books we needed. She came back with an armload. Most had Newford in the title, but a few also covered that period of time when the city was still called Yoors, after the Dutchman Diederick van Yoors, who first settled the area in the early 1800s. It got changed to Newford back around the turn of the century, so all that's left now to remind the city of its original founding father is a street name.

Setting the books down before me on the desk, Amy went off into the stacks to look for some more obscure titles. I didn't wait for her to get back, but went ahead and started flipping through the first book on the pile, looking carefully at the pictures.

I started off having a good time. There's a certain magic in old photos, especially when they're of the place where you grew up. They cast a spell over you. Dirt roads where now there was pavement, sided by office complexes. The old Brewster Theatre in its heyday—I remembered it as the place where I first saw Phil Ochs and Bob Dylan, and later all-night movie festivals, but the Williamson Street Mall stood there now. Boating parties on the river. Old City Hall—it was a youth hostel these days.

But my enthusiasm waned with the afternoon. By the time the library closed, I was no closer to getting a street name for the house in Sam's photo than I had been when I came in. Amy gave me a sympathetic "I told you so" look when we separated on the front steps of the library. I just told her I'd see her tomorrow.

I had something to eat at Kathryn's Cafe. I'd gone there hoping to see Jilly, only I'd forgotten it was her night off. I tried calling her when I'd finished eating, but she was out. So I took my fiddle over to the theatre district and worked the crowds waiting in line there for an hour or so before I headed off for home, my pockets heavy with change.

That night, just before I fell asleep, I felt like a hole sort of opened in the air above my bed. Lying there, I found myself touring Newford—just floating through its streets. Though the time was the present, there was no color. Everything appeared in the same sepia tones as in my photo of Sam.

I don't remember when I finally did fall asleep.

The next morning I was at the library right when it opened, carrying two cups of take-out coffee in a paper bag, one of which I offered to Amy when I got to her desk. Amy muttered something like, "when owls prowl the day, they shouldn't look so bloody cheerful about it," but she accepted the coffee and cleared a corner of her desk so that I could get back to the books.

In the photo I had of Sam there was just the edge of a bay window visible beside the porch, with fairly unique rounded gingerbread trim running off from either side of its keystone. I'd thought it would be the clue to tracking down the place. It looked almost familiar, but I was no longer sure if that was because I'd actually seen the house at some time, or it was just from looking at the photo so much.

Unfortunately, those details weren't helping at all.

"You know, there's no guarantee you're going to find a picture of the house you're looking for in those books," Amy said around midmorning when she was taking her coffee break. "They didn't exactly go around taking pictures of everything."

I was at the last page of *Walks Through Old Crowsea*. Closing the book, I set it on the finished pile beside my chair and then leaned back, lacing my fingers behind my head. My shoulders were stiff from sitting hunched over a desk all morning.

"I know. I'm going to give Jack a call when I'm done here to see if I can borrow his bike this afternoon."

"You're going to pedal all around town looking for this house?"

"What else can I do?"

"There's always the archives at the main library."

I nodded, feeling depressed. It had seemed like such a good idea yesterday. It was still a good idea. I just hadn't realized how long it would take.

"Or you could go someplace like the Market and show the photo around to some of the older folks. Maybe one of them will remember the place."

"I suppose."

I picked up the next book, *The Architectural Heritage of Old Yoors*, and went back to work.

And there it was, on page thirty-eight. The house. There were three buildings in a row in the photo; the one I'd been looking for was the middle one. I checked the caption: "Grasso Street, circa 1920."

"I don't believe it," Amy said. I must have made some kind of a noise, because she was looking up at me from her own work. "You found it, didn't you?" she added.

"I think so. Have you got a magnifying glass?"

She passed it over, and I checked out the street number of the middle house. One-forty-two. The same as in my photo.

Amy took over then. She phoned a friend who worked in the land registry office. He called back a half hour later and gave us the name of the owner in 1912, when my photo had been taken: Edward Dickenson. The house had changed hands a number of times since the Dickensons had sold it in the forties.

We checked the phone book, but there were over a hundred Dickensons listed, twelve with just an initial "E" and one Ed. None of the addresses were on Grasso Street.

"Which makes sense," Amy said, "since they sold the place fifty years ago."

I wanted to run by that block on Grasso where the house was—I'd passed it I don't know how many times, and never paid much attention to it or any of its neighbors—but I needed more background on the Dickensons first. Amy showed me how to run the microfiche, and soon I was going through back issues of *The Newford Star* and *The Daily Journal,* concentrating on the local news sections and the gossip columns.

The first photo of Edward Dickenson that came up was in *The Daily Journal,* the June 21st, 1913 issue. He was standing with the Dean of Butler University at some opening ceremony. I compared him to the people with Sam in my photo and found him standing behind her to her left.

Now that I was on the right track, I began to work in a kind of frenzy. I whipped through the microfiche, making notes of every mention of the Dickensons. Edward turned out to have been a stockbroker, one of the few who didn't lose his shirt in subsequent market crashes. Back then the money lived in Lower Crowsea, mostly on McKennitt, Grasso, and Stanton Streets. Edward made the papers about once a month—business deals, society galas, fund-raising events, political dinners, and the like. It wasn't until I hit the October 29, 1915, issue of *The Newford Star* that I had the wind knocked out of my sails.

It was a picture that got to me: Sam and a man who was no stranger. I'd seen him before. He was the ghost that had stepped out of the past and stolen her away. Under the photo was a caption announcing the engagement of Thomas Edward Dickenson, son of the well-known local businessman, to Samantha Rey.

In the picture of Sam that I had, Dickenson wasn't there with the rest of the people—he'd probably taken it. But here he was. Real. With Sam. I couldn't ignore it.

Back then they didn't have the technology to make a photograph lie.

There was a weird buzzing in my ears as that picture burned its imprint onto my retinas. It was hard to breathe, and my T-shirt suddenly seemed too tight.

I don't know what I'd been expecting, but I knew it wasn't this. I suppose I thought I'd track down the people in the picture and find out that the woman who looked like Sam was actually named Gertrude something-or-other, and she'd lived her whole life with that family. I didn't expect to find Sam. I didn't expect the ghost to have been real.

I was in a daze as I put away the microfiche and shut down the machine.

"Geordie?" Amy asked as I walked by her desk. "Are you okay?"

I remember nodding and muttering something about needing a break. I picked up my fiddle and headed for the front door. The next thing I remember is standing in front of the address on Grasso Street and looking at the Dickensons' house.

I had no idea who owned it now; I hadn't been paying much attention to Amy after she told me that the Dickensons had sold it. Someone had renovated it fairly recently, so it didn't look at all the same as in the photos, but under its trendy additions, I could see the lines of the old house.

I sat down on the curb with my fiddlecase across my knees and just stared at the building. The buzzing was back in my head. My shirt still felt too tight.

I didn't know what to do anymore, so I just sat there, trying to make sense out of what couldn't be reasoned away. I no longer had any doubt that Sam had been real, or that a ghost had stolen her away. The feeling of loss came back all over again, as if it had happened just now, not three years ago. And what scared me was, if she and the ghost were real, then what else might be?

I closed my eyes, and headlines of supermarket tabloids flashed across my eyes, a strobing flicker of bizarre images and words. That was the world Jilly lived in—one in which anything was possible. I didn't know if I could handle living in that kind of world. I neded rules and boundaries. Patterns.

It was a long time before I got up and headed for Kathryn's Cafe.

The first thing Jilly asked when I got in the door was, "Have you seen Paper-jack?"

It took me a few moments to push back the clamor of my own thoughts to register what she'd asked. Finally I just shook my head.

"He wasn't at St. Paul's today," Jilly went on, "and he's always there, rain or shine, winter or summer. I didn't think he was looking well yesterday, and now . . ."

I tuned her out and took a seat at an empty table before I could fall down. That feeling of dislocation that had started up in me when I first saw Sam's photo in the microfiche kept coming and going in waves. It was cresting right now, and I found it hard to just sit in the chair, let alone listen to what Jilly was saying. I tuned her back in when the spaciness finally started to recede.

". . . heart attack, who would he call? He can't *speak*."

"I saw him yesterday," I said, surprised that my voice sounded so calm. "Around midafternoon. He seemed fine."

"He did?"

I nodded. "He was down by the Pier, sitting on the riverbank, feeding the ducks. He read my fortune."

"He *did?*"

"You're beginning to sound like a broken record, Jilly."

For some reason, I was starting to feel better. That sense of being on the verge of a panic attack faded and then disappeared completely. Jilly pulled up a chair and leaned across the table, elbows propped up, chin cupped in her hands.

"So tell me," she said. "What made you do it? What was your fortune?"

I told her everything that had happened since I had seen Paperjack. That sense of dislocation came and went again a few times while I talked, but mostly I was holding firm.

"Holy shit!" Jilly said when I was done.

She put her hand to her mouth and looked quickly around, but none of the customers seemed to have noticed. She reached a hand across the table and caught one of mine.

"So now you believe?" she asked.

"I don't have a whole lot of choice, do I?"

"What are you going to do?"

I shrugged. "What's to do? I found out what I needed to know—now I've got to learn to live with it and all the other baggage that comes with it."

Jilly didn't say anything for a long moment. She just held my hand and exuded comfort as only Jilly can.

"You could find her," she said finally.

"Who? Sam?"

"Who else?"

"She's probably—" I stumbled over the word dead and settled for "—not even alive anymore."

"Maybe not," Jilly said. "She'd definitely be old. But don't you think you should find out?"

"I . . ."

I wasn't sure I wanted to know. And if she were alive, I wasn't sure I wanted to meet her. What could we say to each other?

"Think about it, anyway," Jilly said.

That was Jilly; she never took no for an answer.

"I'm off at eight," she said. "Do you want to meet me then?"

"What's up?" I asked, halfheartedly.

"I thought maybe you'd help me find Paperjack."

I might as well, I thought. I was becoming a bit of an expert in tracking people down by this point. Maybe I should get a card printed: Geordie Riddell, Private Investigations and Fiddle Tunes.

"Sure," I told her.

"Great," Jilly said.

She bounced up from her seat as a couple of new customers came into the cafe. I ordered a coffee from her after she'd gotten them seated, then stared out the window at the traffic going by on Battersfield. I tried not to think of Sam—trapped in the past, making a new life for herself there—but I might as well have tried to jump to the moon.

By the time Jilly came off shift I was feeling almost myself again, but instead of being relieved, I had this great load of guilt hanging over me. It all centered around Sam and the ghost. I'd denied her once. Now I felt as though I was betraying her all over again. Knowing what I knew—the photo accompanying the engagement notice in that old issue of *The Newford Star* flashed across my mind—the way I was feeling at the moment didn't seem right. I felt too normal; and so the guilt.

"I don't get it," I said to Jilly as we walked down Battersfield towards the Pier. "This afternoon I was falling to pieces, but now I just feel . . ."

"Calm?"

"Yeah."

"That's because you've finally stopped fighting yourself and accepted that what you saw—what you remember—really happened. It was denial that was screwing you up."

She didn't add, "I told you so," but she didn't have to. It echoed in my head anyway, joining the rest of the guilt I was carrying around with me. If I'd only listened to her with an open mind, then . . . what?

I wouldn't be going through this all over again?

We crossed Lakeside Drive and made our way through the closed concession and souvenir stands to the beach. When we reached the Pier, I led her westward to where I'd last seen Paperjack, but he wasn't sitting by the river anymore. A lone duck regarded us hopefully, but neither of us had thought to bring any bread.

"So I track down Sam," I said, still more caught up in my personal quest than in looking for Paperjack. "If she's not dead, she'll be an old lady. If I find her—then what?"

"You'll complete the circle," Jilly said. She looked away from the river and faced me, her pixie features serious. "It's like the Kickaha say: everything is on a wheel. You stepped off the one that represents your relationship with Sam before it came full circle. Until you complete your turn on it, you'll never have peace of mind."

"When do you know you've come full circle?" I asked.

"You'll know."

She turned away before I could go on and started back towards the Pier. By day the place was crowded and full of noise, alive with tourists and people out relaxing, just looking to have a good time; by night, its occupancy was turned over to gangs of kids, fooling around on skateboards or simply hanging out, and the homeless: winos, bag ladies, hoboes, and the like.

Jilly worked the crowd, asking after Paperjack, while I followed in her wake. Everybody knew him, or had seen him in the past week, but no one knew where he was now, or where he lived. We were about to give up and head over to Fitzhenry Park to start over again with the people hanging out there, when we heard the sound of a harmonica. It was playing the blues, a soft, mournful sound that drifted up from the beach.

We made for the nearest stairs and then walked back across the sand to find the Bossman sitting under the boardwalk, hands cupped around his instrument, head bowed down, eyes closed. There was no one listening to him except us. The people with money to throw in his old cloth cap were having dinner now in the fancy restaurants across Lakeside Drive or over in the theatre district. He was just playing for himself.

When he was busking, he stuck to popular pieces—whatever was playing on the radio mixed with old show tunes, jazz favorites, and that kind of thing. The music that came from his harmonica now was pure magic. It transformed him, making him larger than life. The blues he played held all the world's sorrows in its long sliding notes and didn't so much change it, as make it bearable.

My fingers itched to pull out my fiddle and join him, but we hadn't come to jam. So we waited until he was done. The last note hung in the air for far longer than seemed possible, then he brought his hands away from his mouth and cradled the harmonica on his lap. He looked up at us from under drooping eyelids, the magic disappearing now that he'd stopped playing. He was just an old, homeless black man now, with the faint trace of a smile touching his lips.

"Hey, Jill—Geordie," he said. "What's doin'?"

"We're looking for Paperjack," Jilly told him.

The Bossman nodded. "Jack's the man for paperwork, all right."

"I've been worried about him," Jilly said. "About his health."

"You a doctor now, Jill?"

She shook her head.

"Anybody got a smoke?"

This time we both shook our heads.

From his pocket he pulled a half-smoked butt that he must have picked up off the boardwalk earlier, then lit it with a wooden match that he struck on the zipper of his jeans. He took a long drag and let it out so that the blue-grey smoke wreathed his head, studying us all the while.

"You care too much, you just get hurt," he said finally.

Jilly nodded. "I know. But I can't help it. Do you know where we can find him?"

"Well now. Come winter, he lives with a Mex family down in the Barrio."

"And in the summer?"

The Bossman shrugged. "I heard once he's got himself a camp up behind the Beaches."

"Thanks," Jilly said.

"He might not take to uninvited guests," the Bossman added. "Body gets himself an out-of-the-way squat like that, I'd think he be lookin' for privacy."

"I don't want to intrude," Jilly assured him. "I just want to make sure he's okay."

The Bossman nodded. "You're a stand-up kind of lady, Jill. I'll trust you to do what's right. I've been thinkin' old Jack's lookin' a little peaked myself. It's somethin' in his eyes—like just makin' do is gettin' to be a chore. But you take care, goin' back up in there. Some of the 'boes, they're not real accommodatin' to havin' strangers on their turf."

"We'll be careful," Jilly said.

The Bossman gave us both another long, thoughtful look, then lifted his harmonica and started to play again. Its mournful sound followed us back up to the boardwalk and seemed to trail us all the way to Lakeside Drive where we walked across the bridge to get to the other side of the Kickaha.

I don't know what Jilly was thinking about, but I was going over what she'd told me earlier. I kept thinking about wheels and how they turned.

Once past the City Commission's lawns on the far side of the river, the land starts to climb. It's just a lot of rough scrub on this side of the hills that make up the Beaches and every summer some of the hoboes and other homeless people camp out in it. The cops roust them from time to time, but mostly they're left alone, and they keep to themselves.

Going in there I was more nervous than Jilly; I don't think she's scared of anything. The sun had gone down behind the hills, and while it was twilight in the city, here it was already dark. I know a lot of the street people and get along with them better than most—everyone likes a good fiddle tune—but some of them could look pretty rough, and I kept anticipating that we'd run into some big wild-eyed hillbilly who'd take exception to our being there.

Well, we did run into one, but—like ninety percent of the street people in Newford—he was somebody that Jilly knew. He seemed pleased, if a little surprised to find her here, grinning at us in the fading light. He was a tall, big-shouldered man, dressed in dirty jeans and a flannel shirt, with big hobnailed boots on his feet and a shock of red hair that fell to his neck and stood up on top of his head in matted tangles. His name, appropriately enough, was Red. The smell that emanated from him made me want to shift position until I was standing upwind.

He not only knew where Paperjack's camp was, but took us there, only Paperjack wasn't home.

The place had Paperjack stamped all over it. There was a neatly rolled bedroll pushed up against a knapsack which probably held his changes of clothing. We didn't check it out, because we weren't there to go through his stuff. Behind the pack was a food cooler with a Coleman stove sitting on top of it, and everywhere you could see small origami stars that hung from the tree branches. There must have been over a hundred of them. I felt as if I were standing in the middle of space with stars all around me.

Jilly left a note for Paperjack, then we followed Red back out to Lakeside Drive. He didn't wait for our thanks. He just drifted away as soon as we reached the mown lawns that bordered the bush.

We split up then. Jilly had work to do—some art for Newford's entertainment weekly, *In the City*—and I didn't feel like tagging along to watch her work at her studio. She took the subway, but I decided to walk. I was bone-tired by then, but the night was one of those perfect ones when the city seems to be smiling. You can't see the dirt or the grime for the sparkle over everything. After all I'd been through today, I didn't want to be cooped up inside anywhere. I just wanted to enjoy the night.

I remember thinking about how Sam would've loved to be out walking with me on a night like this—the old Sam I'd lost, not necessarily the one she'd become. I didn't know that Sam at all, and I still wasn't sure I wanted to, even if I could track her down.

When I reached St. Paul's, I paused by the steps. Even though it was a perfect night to be out walking, something drew me inside. I tried the door, and it opened soundlessly at my touch. I paused just inside the door, one hand resting on the back pew, when I heard a cough.

I froze, ready to take flight. I wasn't sure how churches worked. Maybe my creeping around here at this time of night was . . . I don't know, sacrilegious or something.

I looked up to the front and saw that someone was sitting in the foremost pew. The cough was repeated, and I started down the aisle.

Intuitively, I guess I knew I'd find him here. Why else had I come inside?

Paperjack nodded to me as I sat down beside him on the pew. I laid my fiddlecase by my feet and leaned back. I wanted to ask after his health, to tell him how worried Jill was about him, but my day caught up with me in a rush. Before I knew it, I was nodding off.

I knew I was dreaming when I heard the voice. I had to be dreaming, because there was only Paperjack and I sitting on the pew, and Paperjack was mute. But the voice had the sound that I'd always imagined Paperjack's would have if he could speak. It was like the movement of his fingers when he was folding origami—quick, but measured and certain. Resonant, like his finished paper sculptures that always seemed to have more substance to them than just their folds and shapes.

"No one in this world views it the same," the voice said. "I believe that is what amazes me the most about it. Each person has his or her own vision of the world, and whatever lies outside that worldview becomes invisible. The rich ignore the poor. The happy can't see those who are hurting."

"Paperjack . . . ?" I asked.

There was only silence in reply.

"I . . . I thought you couldn't talk."

"So a man who has nothing he wishes to articulate is considered mute," the voice went on as though I hadn't interrupted. "It makes me weary."

"Who . . . who are you?" I asked.

"A mirror into which no one will look. A fortune that remains forever unread. My time here is done."

The voice fell silent again.

"Paperjack?"

Still silence.

It was just a dream, I told myself. I tried to wake myself from it. I told myself that the pew was made of hard, unyielding wood, and far too uncomfortable to sleep on. And Paperjack needed help. I remembered the cough and Jilly's worries.

But I couldn't wake up.

"The giving itself is the gift," the voice said suddenly. It sounded as though it came from the back of the church, or even farther away. "The longer I remain here, the more I forget."

Then the voice went away for good. I lost it in a dreamless sleep.

I woke early, and all my muscles were stiff. My watch said it was ten to six. I had a moment's disorientation—where the hell *was* I?—and then I remembered. Paperjack. And the dream.

I sat up straighter in the pew, and something fell from my lap to the floor. A piece of folded paper. I bent stiffly to retrieve it, turning it over and over in my hands, holding it up to the dim grey light that was creeping in through the windows. It was one of Paperjack's Chinese fortune-tellers.

After awhile I fit my fingers into the folds of the paper and looked down at the colors. I chose blue, same as I had the last time, and spelled it out, my fingers moving the paper back and forth so that it looked like a flower speaking soundlessly to me. I picked numbers at random, then unfolded the flap to read what it had to say.

"The question is more important than the answer," it said.

I frowned, puzzling over it, then looked at what I would have gotten if I'd picked another number, but all the other folds were blank when I turned them over. I stared at it, then folded the whole thing back up and stuck in my pocket. I was starting to get a serious case of the creeps.

Picking up my fiddlecase, I left St. Paul's and wandered over to Chinatown. I had breakfast in an all-night diner, sharing the place with a bunch of blue-collar workers who were all talking about some baseball game they'd watched the night before. I thought of calling Jilly, but knew that if she'd been working all night on that *In the City* assignment, she'd be crashed out now and wouldn't appreciate a phone call.

I dawdled over breakfast, then slowly made my way up to that part of Foxville that's call the Rosses. That's where the Irish immigrants all lived in the forties and fifties. The place started changing in the sixties when a lot of hippies who couldn't afford the rents in Crowsea moved in, and it changed again with a new wave of immigrants from Vietnam and the Caribbean in the following decades. But the area, for all its changes, was still called the Rosses. My apartment was in the heart of it, right where Kelly Street meets Lee and crosses the Kickaha River. It's two doors down from The Harp, the only real Irish pub in town, which makes it convenient for me to get to the Irish music sessions on Sunday afternoons.

My phone was ringing when I got home. I was half-expecting it to be Jilly, even though it was only going on eight, but found myself talking to a reporter from *The Daily Journal* instead. His name was Ian Begley, and it turned out he was a friend of Jilly's. She'd asked him to run down what information he could on the Dickensons in the paper's morgue.

"Old man Dickenson was the last real businessman of the family," Begley told me. "Their fortunes started to decline when his son Tom took over—he's the one who married the woman that Jilly said you were interested in tracking down. He died in 1976. I don't have an obit on his widow, but that doesn't necessarily mean she's still alive. If she moved out of town, the paper wouldn't have an obit for her unless the family put one in."

He told me a lot of other stuff, but I was only half listening. The business with Paperjack last night and the fortune-telling device this morning were still eating away at me. I did take down the address of Sam's granddaughter when it came up. Begley ran out of steam after anther five minutes or so.

"You got enough there?" he asked.

I nodded, then realized he couldn't see me. "Yeah. Thanks a lot."

"Say hello to Jilly for me and tell her she owes me one."

After I hung up, I looked out the window for a long time. I managed to shift gears from Paperjack to thinking about what Begley had told me, about wheels, about Sam. Finally I got up and took a shower and shaved. I put on my cleanest jeans and shirt and shrugged on a sports jacket that had seen better days before I bought it in a retro fashion shop. I thought about leaving my fiddle behind, but knew I'd feel naked without it—I couldn't remember the last time I'd gone somewhere without it. The leather handle felt comforting in my hand as I hefted the case and went out the door.

All the way over to the address Begley had given me I tried to think of what I was going to say when I met Sam's granddaughter. The truth would make me sound like I was crazy, but I couldn't seem to concoct a story that would make sense.

I remember wondering—where was my brother when I needed him? Christy was never at a loss for words, no matter what the situation.

It wasn't until I was standing on the sidewalk in front of the house that I decided to stick as close to the truth as I could—I was an old friend of her grandmother's, could she put me in touch with her?—and take it from there. But even my vague plans went out the door when I rang the bell and stood face-to-face with Sam's granddaughter.

Maybe you saw this coming, but it was the last thing I'd expected. The woman had Sam's hair, Sam's eyes, Sam's face . . . to all intents and purposes it *was* Sam standing there, looking at me with that vaguely uncertain expression that most of us wear when we open the door to a stranger standing on our steps.

My chest grew so tight I could barely breathe, and suddenly I could hear the sound of rain in my memory—it was always raining when Sam saw the ghost; it was raining the night he stole her away into the past.

Ghosts. *I* was looking at a ghost.

The woman's expression was starting to change, the uncertainty turning into nervousness. There was no recognition in her eyes. As she began to step back—in a moment she'd close the door in my face, probably call the cops—I found my voice. I knew what I was going to say—I was going to ask about her grandmother—but all that came out was her name: "Sam."

"Yes?" she said. She looked at me a little more carefully. "Do I know you?"

Jesus, even the name was the same.

A hundred thoughts were going through my head, but they all spiraled down into one mad hope: this was Sam. We could be together again. Then a child appeared behind the woman. She was a little girl no more than five, blond-haired, blue-eyed, just like her mother—just like her *mother's* grandmother. Reality came crashing down around me.

This Sam wasn't the woman I knew. She was married, she had children, she had a life.

"I . . . I knew your grandmother," I said. "We were . . . we used to be friends."

It sounded so inane to my ears, almost crazy. What would her grandmother—a woman maybe three times my age if she was still alive—have to do with a guy like me?

The woman's gaze traveled down to my fiddlecase. "Is your name Geordie? Geordie Riddell?"

I blinked in surprise, then nodded slowly.

The woman smiled a little sadly, mostly with her eyes.

"Granny said you'd come by," she said. "She didn't know when, but she said you'd come by one day." She stepped away from the door, shooing her daughter down the hall. "Would you like to come in?"

"I . . . uh, sure."

She led me into a living room that was furnished in mismatched antiques that, taken all together, shouldn't have worked, but did. The little girl perched in a Morris chair and watched me curiously as I sat down and set my fiddlecase down by my feet. Her mother pushed back a stray lock with a mannerism so like Sam's that my chest tightened up even more.

"Would you like some coffee or tea?" she asked.

I shook my head. "I don't want to intrude. I . . ." Words escaped me again.

"You're not intruding," she said. She sat down on the couch in front of me, that sad look back in her eyes. "My grandmother died a few years ago—she'd moved to New England in the late seventies, and she died there in her sleep. Because she loved it so much, we buried her there in a small graveyard overlooking the sea."

I could see it in my mind as she spoke. I could hear the sound of the waves breaking on the shore below, the spray falling on the rocks like rain.

"She and I were very close, a lot closer than I ever felt to my mother." She gave me a rueful look. "You know how it is."

She didn't seem to be expecting a response, but I nodded anyway.

"When her estate was settled, most of her personal effects came to me. I . . ." She paused, then stood up. "Excuse me for a moment, would you?"

I nodded again. She'd looked sad, talking about Sam. I hoped that bringing it all up hadn't made her cry.

The little girl and I sat in silence, looking at each other until her mother returned. She was such a serious kid, her big eyes taking everything in; she sat quietly, not running around or acting up like most kids do when there's someone new in the house that they can show off to. I didn't think she was shy; she was just . . . well, serious.

Her mother had a package wrapped in brown paper and twine in her hands when she came back. She sat down across from me again and laid the package on the table between us.

"Granny told me a story once," she said, "about her first and only real true love. It was an odd story, a kind of ghost story, about how she'd once lived in the future until granddad's love stole her away from her own time and brought her to his." She gave me an apologetic smile. "I knew it was just a story because, when I was growing up, I'd met people she'd gone to school with, friends from her past before she met granddad. Besides, it was too much like some science fiction story.

"But it was true, wasn't it?"

I could only nod. I didn't understand how Sam and everything about her except my memories of her could vanish into the past, how she could have a whole new set of memories when she got back there, but I knew it was true.

I accepted it now, just as Jilly had been trying to get me to do for years. When I looked at Sam's granddaughter, I saw that she accepted it as well.

"When her effects were sent to me," she went on, "I found this package in them. It's addressed to you."

I had seen my name on it, written in a familiar hand. My own hand trembled as I reached over to pick it up.

"You don't have to open it now," she said.

I was grateful for that.

"I . . . I'd better go," I said and stood up. "Thank you for taking the time to see me."

That sad smile was back as she saw me to the door.

"I'm glad I got the chance to meet you," she said when I stepped out onto the porch.

I wasn't sure I could say the same. She looked so much like Sam, *sounded* so much like Sam, that it hurt.

"I don't think we'll be seeing each other again," she added.

No. She had her husband, her family. I had my ghosts.

"Thanks," I said again and started off down the walk, fiddlecase in one hand, the brown paper package in the other.

I didn't open the package until I was sitting in the Silenus Gardens in Fitzhenry Park, a place that always made me feel good; I figured I was going to need all the help I could get. Inside there was a book with a short letter. The book I recognized. It was the small J. M. Dent & Sons edition of Shakespeare's *A Mid-*

summer Night's Dream that I'd given Sam because I'd known it was one of her favorite stories.

There was nothing special about the edition, other than its size—it was small enough for her to carry around in her purse, which she did. The inscription I'd written to her was inside, but the book was far more worn than it had been when I'd first given it to her. I didn't have to open the book to remember that famous quotation from Puck's final lines:

> *If we shadows have offended,*
> *Think but this, and all is mended,*
> *That you have but slumber'd here,*
> *While these visions did appear.*
> *And this weak and idle theme,*
> *No more yielding but a dream . . .*

But it hadn't been a dream—not for me, and not for Sam. I set the book down beside me on the stone bench and unfolded the letter.

"Dear Geordie," it said. "I know you'll read this one day, and I hope you can forgive me for not seeing you in person, but I wanted you to remember me as I was, not as I've become. I've had a full and mostly happy life; you know my only regret. I can look back on our time together with the wisdom of an old woman now and truly know that all things have their time. Our was short—too short, my heart—but we did have it.

"Who was it that said, 'better to have loved and lost, than never to have loved at all'? We loved and lost each other, but I would rather cherish the memory than rail against the unfairness. I hope you will do the same."

I sat there and cried. I didn't care about the looks I was getting from people walking by, I just let it all out. Some of my tears were for what I'd lost, some were for Sam and her bravery, and some were for my own stupidity at denying her memory for so long.

I don't know how long I sat there like that, holding her letter, but the tears finally dried on my cheeks. I heard the scuff of feet on the path and wasn't surprised to look up and find Jilly standing in front of me.

"Oh Geordie, me lad," she said.

She sat down at my side and leaned against me. I can't tell you how comforting it was to have her there. I handed her the letter and book and sat quietly while she read the first and looked at the latter. Slowly she folded up the letter and slipped it inside the book.

"How do you feel now?" she asked finally. "Better or worse?"

"Both."

She raised her eyebrows in a silent question.

"Well, it's like what they say funerals are for," I tried to explain. "It gives you the chance to say good-bye, to settle things, like taking a"—I looked at her and managed to find a small smile—"final turn on a wheel. But I feel depressed about Sam. I know what we had was real, and I know how it felt for me, losing her. But I only had to deal with it for a few years. She carried it for a lifetime."

"Still, she carried on."

I nodded. "Thank god for that."

Neither of us spoke for awhile, but then I remembered Paperjack. I told her what I thought had happened last night, then showed her the fortune-telling device that he'd left with me in St. Paul's. She read my fortune with pursed lips and the start of a wrinkle on her forehead, but didn't seem particularly surprised by it.

"What do you think?" I asked her.

She shrugged. "Everybody makes the same mistake. Fortune-telling doesn't reveal the future; it mirrors the present. It resonates against what your subconscious already knows and hauls it up out of the darkness so that you can get a good look at it."

"I meant about Paperjack."

"I think he's gone—back to wherever it was that he came from."

She was beginning to exasperate me in that way that only she could.

"But who was he?" I asked. "No, better yet, *what* was he?"

"I don't know," Jilly said. "I just know it's like your fortune said. It's the questions we ask, the journey we take to get where we're going that's more important than the actual answer. It's good to have mysteries. It reminds us that there's more to the world than just making do and having a bit of fun."

I sighed, knowing I wasn't going to get much more sense out of her than that.

It wasn't until the next day that I made my way alone to Paperjack's camp in back of the Beaches. All his gear was gone, but the paper stars still hung from the trees. I wondered again about who he was. Some oracular spirit, a kind of guardian angel, drifting around, trying to help people see themselves? Or an old homeless black man with a gift for folding paper? I understood then that my fortune made a certain kind of sense, but I didn't entirely agree with it.

Still, in Sam's case, knowing the answer had brought me peace.

I took Paperjack's fortune-teller from my pocket and strung it with a piece of string I'd brought along for that purpose. Then I hung it on the branch of a tree so that it could swing there, in among all those paper stars, and I walked away.

FOREVER YOURS, ANNA

Kate Wilhelm

Kate Wilhelm is one of the most admired writers in science fiction, an eminent writer of novels and stories since the 1950s. Along with her husband, Damon Knight, she has been particularly influential in improving the literary standards of SF writing, through the Milford SF Writing Conferences from 1958 onward and through teaching at the Clarion SF Writing Workshops from the late 1960s through the mid-1990s. She is also prominent as a writer of mystery novels. This is one of her recent award-winning stories.

Anna entered his life on a spring afternoon, not invited, not even wanted. Gordon opened his office door that day to a client who was expected and found a second man also in the hallway. The second man brought him Anna, although Gordon did not yet know this. At the moment, he simply said, "Yes?"

"Gordon Sills? I don't have an appointment, but . . . may I wait?"

"Afraid I don't have a waiting room."

"Out here's fine."

He was about fifty, and he was prosperous. It showed in his charcoal-colored suit, a discreet blue-gray silk tie, a silk shirtfront. Gordon assumed the rest of the shirt was also silk. He also assumed the stone on his finger was a real emerald of at least three carats. Ostentatious touch, that.

"Sure," Gordon said and ushered his client inside. They passed through a foyer to his office-workroom. The office section was partitioned from the rest of the room by three rice-paper screens with beautiful Chinese calligraphy. In the office area were his desk and two chairs for visitors, his chair, and an overwhelmed bookcase, with books on the floor in front of it.

Their business only took half an hour; when the client left, the hall was empty. Gordon shrugged and returned to his office. He pulled his telephone across the desk and dialed his former wife's number, let it ring a dozen times, hung up.

He leaned back in his chair and rubbed his eyes. Late afternoon sunlight streamed through the slats in the venetian blinds, zebra light. He should go away for a while, he thought. Just close shop and walk away from it all until he started getting overdraft notices. Three weeks, he told himself, that was about as long as it would take.

Gordon Sills was thirty-five, a foremost expert in graphology, and could have been rich, his former wife had reminded him quite often. If you don't make it before forty, she had also said, too often, you simply won't make it, and he did not care, simply did not care about money, security, the future, the children's future. . . .

Abruptly he pushed himself away from the desk and left the office, went into his living room. Like the office, it was messy, with several days' worth of newspapers, half a dozen books, magazines scattered haphazardly. To his eyes it was comfortable looking, comfort giving; he distrusted neatness in homes. Karen had most of the furniture; he had picked up only a chair, a couch, a single lamp, a scarred oak coffee table that he could put his feet on, a card table and several chairs for the kitchen. And a very good radio. It was sufficient. Some fine Japanese landscapes were on the walls.

The buzzer sounded. When he opened the door, the prosperous, uninvited client was there. He was carrying a brushed suede briefcase.

"Hi," Gordon said. "I thought you'd left."

"I did, and came back."

Gordon admitted him and led him through the foyer into the office, where he motioned toward a chair and went behind his desk and sat down. The sunlight was gone, eclipsed by the building across Amsterdam.

"I apologize for not making an appointment," his visitor said. He withdrew a wallet from his breast pocket, took out a card, and slid it across the desk. "I'm Avery Roda. On behalf of my company I should like to consult with you regarding some correspondence in our possession."

"That's my business," Gordon said. "And what is your company, Mr. Roda?"

"Draper Fawcett."

Gordon nodded slowly. "And your position?"

Roda looked unhappy. "I am vice-president in charge of research and development, but right now I am in charge of an investigation we have undertaken. My first duty in connection with this was to find someone with your expertise. You come very highly recommended, Mr. Sills."

"Before we go on any further," Gordon said, "I should tell you that there are a number of areas where I'm not interested in working. I don't do paternity suits, for example. Or employer-employee pilferage cases."

Roda flushed.

"Or blackmail," Gordon finished equably. "That's why I'm not rich, but that's how it is."

"The matter I want to discuss is none of the above," Roda snapped. "Did you read about the explosion we had at our plant on Long Island two months ago?" He did not wait for Gordon's response. "We lost a very good scientist, one of the best in the country. And we cannot locate some of his paperwork, his notes. He was involved with a woman who may have them in her possession. We want to find her, recover them."

Gordon shook his head. "You need the police then, private detectives, your own security force."

"Mr. Sills, don't underestimate our resolve or our resources. We have set all that in operation, and no one has been able to locate the woman. Last week we had a conference during which we decided to try this route. What we want from you is as complete an analysis of the woman as you can give us, based on her handwriting. That may prove fruitful." His tone said he doubted it very much.

"I assume the text has not helped."

"You assume correctly," Roda said with some bitterness. He opened his briefcase and withdrew a sheaf of papers and laid them on the desk.

From the other side Gordon could see that they were not the originals, but photocopies. He let his gaze roam over the upside-down letters and then shook his head. "I have to have the actual letters to work with."

"That's impossible. They are being kept under lock and key."

"Would you offer a wine taster colored water?" Gordon's voice was bland, but he could not stop his gaze. He reached across the desk and turned the top letter right side up to study the signature. Anna. Beautifully written; even in the heavy black copy it was delicate, as artful as any of the Chinese calligraphy on his screens. He looked up to find Roda watching him intently. "I can tell you a few things from just this, but I have to have the originals. Let me show you my security system."

He led the way to the other side of the room. Here he had a long worktable, an oversized light table, a copy camera, enlarger, files. There was a computer and printer on a second desk. It was all fastidiously neat and clean.

"The files are fireproof," he said dryly, "and the safe is also. Mr. Roda, if you've investigated me, you know I've handled some priceless documents. And I've kept them right here in the shop. Leave the copies. I can start with them, but tomorrow I'll want the originals."

"Where's the safe?"

Gordon shrugged and went to the computer, keyed in his code, and then moved to the wall behind the worktable and pushed aside a panel to reveal a safe front. "I don't intend to open it for you. You can see enough without that."

"Computer security?"

"Yes."

"Very well. Tomorrow I'll send you the originals. You said you can already tell us something."

They returned to the office space. "First you," Gordon said, pointing to the top letter. "Who censored them?"

The letters had been cut off just above the greeting, and there were rectangles of white throughout.

"That's how they were when we found them," Roda said heavily. "Mercer must have done it himself. One of the detectives said the holes were cut with a razor blade."

Gordon nodded. "Curiouser and curiouser. Well, for what it's worth at this point, she's an artist more than likely. Painter would be my first guess."

"Are you sure?"

"Don't be a bloody fool. Of course I'm not sure, not with copies to work with. It's a guess. Everything I report will be a guess. Educated guesswork, Mr. Roda, that's all I can guarantee."

Roda sank down into his chair and expelled a long breath. "How long will it take?"

"How many letters?"

"Nine."

"Two, three weeks."

Very slowly Roda shook his head. "We are desperate, Mr. Sills. We will double your usual fee if you can give this your undivided attention."

"And how about your cooperation?"

"What do you mean?"

"His handwriting also. I want to see at least four pages of his writing."

Roda looked blank.

"It will help to know her if I know her correspondent."

"Very well," Roda said.

"How old was he?"

"Thirty."

"Okay. Anything else you can tell me?"

Roda seemed deep in thought, his eyes narrowed, a stillness about him that suggested concentration. With a visible start he looked up, nodded. "What you said about her could be important already. She mentions a show in one of the letters. We assumed a showgirl, a dancer, something like that. I'll put someone on it immediately. An artist. That could be right."

"Mr. Roda, can you tell me anything else? How important are those papers? Are they salable? Would anyone outside your company have an idea of their value?"

"They are quite valuable," he said with such a lack of tone that Gordon's ears almost pricked to attention. "If we don't recover them in a relatively short time, we will have to bring in the FBI. National security may be at stake. We want to handle it ourselves, obviously." He finished in the same monotone. "The Russians would pay millions for them, I'm certain. And we will pay whatever we have to. She has them. She says so in one of the letters. We have to find that woman."

For a moment Gordon considered turning down the job. Trouble, he thought. Real trouble. He glanced at the topmost letter again, the signature *Anna,* and he said, "Okay. I have a contract I use routinely . . ."

After Roda left he studied the one letter for several minutes, not reading it, in fact examining it upside down again, and he said softly, "Hello, Anna."

Then he gathered up all the letters and put them in a file which he deposited in his safe. He had no intention of starting until he had the originals. But it would comfort Roda to believe he was already at work.

Roda sent the originals and a few samples of Mercer's writing before noon the next day, and for three hours Gordon studied them all. He arranged hers on the worktable under the gooseneck lamp and turned them this way and that, not yet reading them, making notes now and then. As he suspected, her script was fine, delicate, with beautiful shading. She used a real pen with real ink, not a felt-tip or a ballpoint. Each stroke was visually satisfying, artistic in itself. One letter was three pages long, four were two pages, the others were single sheets. None of them had a date, an address, a complete name. He cursed the person who had mutilated them. One by one he turned them over to examine the backs and jotted: "Pressure—light to medium." His other notes were equally brief: "Fluid, rapid, not conventional; proportions, 1:5." That was European and he did not think she was, but it would bear close examination. Each note was simply a direction marker, a first impression. He was whistling tunelessly as he worked and was startled when the telephone rang.

It was Karen, finally returning his many calls. The children would arrive by six, and he must return them by seven Sunday night. Her voice was cool, as if she were giving orders about laundry. He said okay and hung up, surprised at how little he felt about the matter. Before, it had given him a wrench every time they talked; he had asked questions: How was she? Was she working? Was the house all right? She had the house on Long Island, and that was fine with him, he had spent more and more time in town anyway over the past few years; but still, they had bought it together, he had repaired this and that, put up screens, taken them down, struggled with plumbing.

That night he took the two children to a Greek restaurant. Buster, eight years old, said it was yucky; Dana, ten, called him a baby and Gordon headed off the fight by saying he had bought a new Monopoly game. Dana said Buster was into winning. Dana looked very much like her mother, but Buster was her true genetic heir. Karen was into winning too.

They went to the Cloisters and fantasized medieval scenarios; they played monopoly again, and on Sunday he took them to a puppet show at the Met and then drove them home. He was exhausted. When he got back he looked about, deeply depressed. There were dirty dishes in the sink, on the table, in the living room. Buster had slept on the couch and his bedclothes and covers were draped over it. Karen said they were getting too old to share a room any longer. Dana's bedroom was also a mess. She had left her pajamas and slippers. Swiftly he gathered up the bedding from the living room and tossed it all onto the bed in Dana's room and closed the door. He overfilled the dishwasher and turned it on and finally went into his workroom and opened the safe.

"Hello, Anna," he said softly, and tension seeped from him; the ache that had settled in behind his eyes vanished; he forgot the traffic jams coming home from Long Island, forgot the bickering his children seemed unable to stop.

He took the letters to the living room and sat down to read them through for the first time.

Love letters, passionate letters, humorous in places, perceptive, intelligent. Without dates it was hard to put them in chronological order, but the story emerged. She had met Mercer in the city; they had walked and talked and he had left. He had come back and this time they were together for a weekend and became lovers. She sent her letters to a post office box; he did not write to her, although he left papers covered with incomprehensible scribbles in her care. She was married to someone, whose name had been cut out with a razor blade every time she referred to him. Mercer knew him, visited him, apparently. They were even friends, and had long serious talks from which she was excluded. She was afraid; Mercer was involved in something very dangerous, and no one told her what it was, although her husband knew. She called Mercer her mystery man and speculated about his secret life, his family, his insane wife, or tyrannical father, or his own lapses into lycanthropy. Gordon smiled. Anna was not a whiner or a weeper, but she was hopelessly in love with Mercer and did not even know where he lived, where he worked, what danger threatened him, anything about him except that when he was with her, she was alive and happy. That was enough. Her husband understood and wanted only her happiness, and it was destroying her, knowing she was hurting him so much, but she was helpless.

He pursed his lips and reread one. "My darling, I can't stand it. I really can't stand it any longer. I dream of you, see you in every stranger on the street, hear your voice every time I answer the phone. My palms become wet and I tingle all over, thinking it's your footsteps I hear. You are my dreams. So, I told myself today, that is how it is? No way! Am I a silly schoolgirl mooning over a television star? At twenty-six? I gathered all your papers and put them in a carton and addressed it, and as I wrote the box number, I found myself giggling. You can't send a Dear John to a post office box number. What if you failed to pick it up and an inspector opened it finally? I should entertain such a person? They're all gray and desiccated, you know, those inspectors. Let them find their own entertainment! What if they could read your mysterious squiggles and discover the secret of the universe? Do any of them deserve such enlightenment? No. I put everything back in [excised] safe—" Mercer was not the mystery man, Gordon thought then; the mystery was the other man, the nameless one whose safe hid Mercer's papers. Who was he? He shook his head over the arrangement of two men and a woman, and continued to read: "—and [excised] came in and let me cry on his shoulder. Then we went to dinner. I was starved."

Gordon laughed out loud and put the letters down on the coffee table, leaned back with his hands behind his head and contemplated the ceiling. It needed paint.

For the next two weeks he worked on the letters, and the few pages of Mercer's handwriting. He photographed everything, made enlargements, and searched for signs of weakness, illness. He keystroked the letters into his computer and ran the program he had developed, looking for usages, foreign or regional combinations, anything unusual or revealing. Mercer, he decided, had been born in a test tube and never left school and the laboratory until the day he met Anna. She was from the Midwest, not a big city, somewhere around one of the Great Lakes. The name that had been consistently cut out had six letters. She had gone to an opening and the artist's name had been cut out also. It had nine letters. Even without her testimony about the artist, it was apparent that she had been excited by his work. It showed in the writing. He measured the spaces between the words, the size of individual letters, the angle of her slant, the proportions of everything. Every movement she made was graceful, rhythmic. Her connections were garlands, open and trusting; that meant she was honest herself. Her threadlike connections that strung her words together indicated her speed in writing, her intuition, which she trusted.

As the work went on he made more complete notes, drawing conclusions more and more often. The picture of Anna was becoming real.

He paid less attention to Mercer's writing after making an initial assessment of him. A scientist, technologist, precise, angular, a genius, inhibited, excessively secretive, a loner. He was a familiar type.

When Roda returned, Gordon felt he could tell him more about those two people than their own mothers knew about them.

What he could not tell was what they looked like, or where Anna was now, or where the papers were that she had put in her husband's safe.

He watched Roda skim through the report on Anna. Today, rain was falling in gray curtains of water; the air felt thick and clammy.

"That's all?" Roda demanded when he finished.

"That's it."

"We checked every art show in the state," Roda said, scowling at him. "We didn't find her. And we have proof that Mercer couldn't have spent as much time with her as she claimed in the letters. We've been set up. You've been set up. You say she's honest, ethical, and we say she's an agent or worse. She got her hooks in him and got those papers, and these letters are fakes, every one of them is a fake!"

Gordon shook his head. "There's not a lie in those letters."

"Then why didn't she come forward when he died? There was enough publicity at the time. We saw to that. I tell you he never spent any real time with her. We found him in a talent hunt when he was a graduate student, and he stayed in that damn lab ever since, seven days a week for four years. He never had time for a relationship of the sort she talks about. It's a lie through and through. A fantasy." He slumped in his chair. Today his face was almost as gray as his very good suit. He looked years older than he had the last time he had been in the office. "They're going to win," he said in a low voice. "The woman and her partner, they're probably out of the country already. Probably left the day after the accident, with the papers, their job done. Well done. That stupid, besotted fool!" He stared at the floor for several more seconds, then straightened. His voice was hard, clipped. "I was against consulting you from the start. A waste of time and money. Voodoo crap, that's all this is. Well, we've done what we can. Send in your bill. Where are her letters?"

Silently Gordon slid a folder across the desk. Roda went through it carefully, then put it in his briefcase and stood up. "If I were you, I would not give our firm as reference in the future, Sills." He pushed Gordon's report away from him. "We can do without that. Good day."

It should have ended there, Gordon knew, but it did not end. Where are you, Anna? he thought, gazing at the world swamped in cold rain. Why hadn't she come forward, attended the funeral, turned in the papers? He had no answers. She was out there, painting, living with a man who loved her very much, enough to give her the freedom to fall in love with someone else. Take good care of her, he thought at that other man. Be gentle with her, be patient while she heals. She's very precious, you know. He leaned his head against the window, let the coolness soothe him. He said aloud, "She's very precious."

"Gordon, are you all right?" Karen asked on the phone. It was his weekend for the children again.

"Sure. Why?"

"I just wondered. You sound strange. Do you have a girlfriend?"

"What do you want, Karen?"

The ice returned to her voice, and they made arrangements for the children's arrival, when he was to return them. Library books, he thought distantly. Just like library books.

When he hung up he looked at the apartment and was dismayed by the dinginess, the disregard for the barest amenities. Another lamp, he thought. He needed a second lamp, at the very least. Maybe even two. Anna loved light. A girlfriend? He wanted to laugh, and to cry also. He had a signature, some love letters written to another man, a woman who came to his dreams and spoke to him in the phrases from her letters. A girlfriend! He closed his eyes and saw the name: Anna. The capital *A* was a flaring volcano, high up into the stratosphere, then the even, graceful *n*'s, the funny little final *a* that had trouble staying on the base line, that wanted to fly away. And a beautiful sweeping line that flew out from it, circled above the entire name, came down to cross the first letter, turn it into an *A,* and in doing so formed a perfect palette. A graphic representation of Anna, soaring into the heavens, painting, creating art with every breath, every motion. Forever yours, Anna. Forever yours.

He took a deep breath and tried to make plans for the children's weekend, for the rest of the month, the summer, the rest of his life.

The next day he bought a lamp, and on his way home stopped in a florist shop and bought half a dozen flowering plants. She had written that the sunlight turned the flowers on the sill into jewels. He put them on the sill and raised the blind; the sunlight turned the blossoms into jewels. His hands were clenched; abruptly he turned away.

He went back to work; spring became summer, hot and humid as only New York could be, and he found himself going from one art show to another. He mocked himself, and cursed himself for it, but he attended openings, examined new artists' work, signatures, again and again and again. If the investigators trained in this couldn't find her, he told himself firmly, and the FBI couldn't find her, he was a fool to think he had even a remote chance. But he went to the shows. He was lonely, he told himself, and tried to become interested in other women, any other woman, and continued to attend openings.

In the fall he went to the opening of yet another new artist, out of an art school, a teacher. And he cursed himself for not thinking of that before. She could be an art teacher. He made a list of schools and started down the list, perfecting a story as he worked down it one by one. He was collecting signatures of artists for an article he planned to write. It was a passable story. It got him nothing.

She might be ugly, he told himself. What kind of woman would have fallen in love with Mercer? He had been inhibited, constricted, without grace, brilliant, eccentric, and full of wonder. It was the wonder that she had sensed, he knew. She had been attracted to that in Mercer, and had got through his many defenses, had found a boy-man who was truly appealing. And he had adored her. That was apparent from her letters; it had been mutual. Why had he lied to her? Why hadn't he simply told her who he was, what he was doing? The other man in her life had not been an obstacle, that had been made clear also. The two men had liked each other, and both loved her. Gordon brooded about her, about Mercer, the other man, and he haunted openings, became a recognized figure at the various studios and schools where he collected signatures. It was an obsession, he told himself, unhealthy, maybe even a sign of neurosis—or worse. It was insane to fall in love with someone's signature, love letters to another man.

And he could be wrong, he told himself. Maybe Roda had been right, after all. The doubts were always short-lived.

The cold October rains had come. Karen was engaged to a wealthy man. The children's visits had become easier because he no longer was trying to entertain them every minute; he had given in and bought a television and video games for them. He dropped by the Art Academy to meet Rick Henderson, who had become a friend over the past few months. Rick taught watercolors.

Gordon was in his office waiting for him to finish with a class critique session when he saw the *A*, Anna's capital *A*.

He felt his arms prickle, and sweat form on his hands, and a tightening in the pit of his stomach as he stared at an envelope on Rick's desk. Almost fearfully he turned it around to study the handwriting. The *A*'s in Art Academy were like volcanoes, reaching up into the stratosphere, crossed with a quirky, insouciant line, like a sombrero at a rakish angle. Anna's *A*. It did not soar and make a palette, but it wouldn't, not in an address. That was her personal sign.

He let himself sink into Rick's chair and drew in a deep breath. He did not touch the envelope again. When Rick finally joined him, he nodded toward it.

"Would you mind telling me who wrote that?" His voice sounded hoarse, but Rick seemed not to notice. He opened the envelope and scanned a note, then handed it over. Her handwriting. Not exactly the same, but it was hers. He was certain it was hers, even with the changes. The way the writing was positioned on the page, the sweep of the letters, the fluid grace . . . But it was not the same. The *A* in her name, Anna, was different. He felt bewildered by the differences, and knew it was hers in spite of them. Finally, he actually read the words. She would be out of class for a few days. It was dated four days ago.

"Just a kid," Rick said. "Fresh in from Ohio, thinks she has to be excused from class. I'm surprised it's not signed by her mother."

"Can I meet her?"

Now Rick looked interested. "Why?"

"I want her signature."

Rick laughed. "You're a real nut, you know. Sure. She's in the studio, making up for time off. Come on."

He stopped at the doorway and gazed at the young woman painting. She was no more than twenty, almost painfully thin, hungry looking. She wore scruffy sneakers, very old, faded blue jeans, a man's plaid shirt. Not the Anna of the letters. Not yet.

Gordon felt dizzy and held on to the door frame for a moment, and he knew what it was that Mercer had worked on, what he had discovered. He felt as if he had slipped out of time himself as his thoughts raced, explanations formed, his next few years shaped themselves in his mind. Understanding came the way a memory comes, a gestalt of the entire event or series of events, all accessible at once. Mercer's notes had shown him to be brilliant, obsessional, obsessed with time, secretive. Roda had assumed Mercer failed because he had blown himself up. Everyone must have assumed that. But he had not failed. He had gone forward five years, six at the most, to the time when Anna would be twenty-six. He had slipped out of time to the future.

Gordon knew with certainty that it was his own name that had been excised from Anna's letters. Phrases from her letters tumbled through his mind. She had mentioned a Japanese bridge, from his painting, the flowers on the sill, even the way the sun failed when it sank behind the building across the street. He thought of Roda and the hordes of agents searching for the papers that were to be hidden, had been hidden in the safest place in the world—the future. The safe Anna would put the papers in would be his, Gordon's, safe. He closed his eyes hard, already feeling the pain he knew would come when Mercer realized that he was to die, that he had died. For Mercer there could not be a love strong enough to make him abandon his work.

Gordon knew he would be with Anna, watch her mature, become the Anna of the letters, watch her soar into the stratosphere, and when Mercer walked through his time door, Gordon would still love her, and wait for her, help her heal afterward.

Rick cleared his throat and Gordon released his grasp of the door frame, took the next step into the studio. Anna's concentration was broken; she looked up at him. Her eyes were dark blue.

Hello, Anna.

THE GOLDEN AGE OF SCIENCE FICTION IS TWELVE

David G. Hartwell

This essay is the opening chapter of *Age of Wonders*. It is included as an introduction to SF as a literature (body of texts) that emerges from a field of living, interacting readers and writers. It has recently become fashionable in criticism to view literary genres as conversations among texts. In science fiction this is inadequate, because the readers and writers talk and argue outside, as well as through, the texts, immeasurably enriching the dialogue.

> *The golden age of science fiction is twelve.*
> —Peter Graham

Immersed in science fiction. Bathing in it, drowning in it; for the adolescent who leans this way it can be better than sex. More accessible, more compelling. And the outsider can only wonder, What's the matter with him? What is he into, what's the attraction, why is it so intense?

Grown men and women, sixty years old, twenty-five years old, sit around and talk about "the golden age of science fiction," remembering when every story in every magazine was a masterwork of daring, original thought. Some say the golden age was circa 1928; some say 1939; some favor 1953, or 1970 or 1984. The arguments rage till the small of the morning, and nothing is ever resolved.

Because the real golden age of science fiction is twelve.

This is a book about the science fiction field and that body of contemporary writing known as science fiction, or SF. Over the years there have been a number of books on the writing the field has produced, its artwork and illustration, histories, memoirs, even books devoted to the amateur publications of the fans. But no general attempt to describe both the literature and the specific subculture out of which the literature flows has ever been presented to the world at large. Donald A. Wollheim, in *The Universe Makers*, and Lester del Rey, in *The World of Science Fiction 1926–1976*, come closer than any others and you might try them, though both are dated. Damon Knight's *The Futurians* gives some perspective on the SF world as it grew up and on one particularly influential circle (and is full of great gossip). Theodore Cogswell's *P.I.T.F.C.S.* captures another moment. Various autobiographies such as Samuel R. Delany's *The Motion of Light in Water*, Frederik Pohl's *The Way the Future Was*, and Jack Williamson's

Wonder's Child present other pieces of the puzzle. But never one book for the whole.

For one thing, the world at large, especially all who do not read and do not wish to read SF, couldn't have cared less. "Everyone" knows that science fiction is not serious literature and that since the word "science" occurs in the name you wouldn't be interested or able to understand if you did try to read it—so why try?

Despite the fact that twelve-year-olds who read it understand it perfectly, and that millions of readers over the years have found it great fun (it is supposed to be fun), the majority of educated readers in the English-speaking world spurn SF without reading it or knowing any more about it than what "everyone" knows. Well, this book is not an attempt to convert anyone (although later on I do recommend some SF for people who have not read in the field before). What I do intend is to offer a book that informs you about an amusing and significant phenomenon that reaches into every home and family in the country and influences the way we all see the world around us.

This is an outsider's guidebook and road map through the world of science fiction, pointing out the historical monuments, backyard follies, highways, and back streets of the SF community—a tour of main events and sideshows and a running commentary on why the SF world is the way it is. I hope it will be particularly useful for the casually curious, the neophyte reader, and of course the person who knows people in SF and wonders why they are that way. Is your child threatened by this strange stuff, or by the companionship of lovers of science fiction? Does SF rot the mind and ruin the character? Just how wild and crazy are those SF people and what do they really do, where do they come from, why do they stay in the SF world? This tour, if successful, should take you not only through the nooks and crannies of the SF world, but into some unsuspected aspects of the everyday world as well.

Written science fiction, like cooking, mathematics, or rock 'n' roll, is a whole bunch of things that some people can understand or do and some cannot. We all know people who love cooking, math, or rock (perhaps all three), and others who can hardly boil water, add two plus two, or distinguish music from noise. Your present tour guide stopped trying to convert people to instant appreciation of science fiction years ago when he finally understood that most new readers have to go through a process of SF education and familiarization before they can love it. Just because someone can read does not mean that he necessarily can read SF, just as the ability to write Arabic numerals and add and subtract doesn't mean you necessarily can or want to perform long division.

So I have set out to describe science fiction without assuming that you have read any or would even know what to do if you were faced with the text of an SF story. I will discuss as clearly as possible all the barriers you might have against understanding SF and all the barriers that SF has erected to keep from being understood by outsiders—for, like the world of the circus and the carny, the SF world only wants insiders behind the scenes. And more, the SF world does not want an audience (such as the "mass audience") who won't take the time to learn the rules and conventions of the game. SF is special within its community, which has built complex fortifications and groundworks surrounding its treasures; and for most people, the rewards of reading SF or being an SF-type person are worthless or pernicious or even a bit scary. To one who is comfortable and has adjusted to the compromises of our culture, being or becoming something of an outsider has no advantages.

Wait for a moment, though, before you make up your mind that you don't really have to become acquainted with what is going on in this other reality. The underground world of SF interpenetrates your daily world so thoroughly in so many ways that finding out what those relatively few people who live in the SF world are like may let you understand a lot more about how your own world operates. Besides, as Thomas Pynchon so amusingly posited in his eccentric novella *The Crying of Lot 49*, if you begin to look beneath the surface of everyday life, almost everyone is involved in some sort of underground or underground activity. This kind of activity is so much a part of what everyone does (without ever seeing the big picture) that if you pull back and look at it all, the real world seems very different. That is, in one very real sense, what this book is about.

When you spot a science fiction devotee on a bus, in a library, or on lunch break in the cafeteria, she or he is identifiable only by a display of some kind: she is reading a flashy paperback that says "Science Fiction" on the cover; he is wearing a "Star Trek Lives!" T-shirt over his bathing trunks at the beach; she is quietly asking the bookseller if there is a copy of *Women of Wonder* in the store; he is arguing loudly with a friend that Terry Pratchett is much better than Piers Anthony (who is not truly funny) while munching a sandwich and sipping Coke.

Otherwise, there are no reliable outward signs, unless you happen to stop over at a hotel or motel anywhere in the U.S. where one of the at-least-weekly science fiction conventions is being held—after one look, you switch accommodations, because the whole place is filled with people in costumes, Bacchanalian howls, teenagers in capes and swords, normally dressed adults wearing garish name tags that identify them as Gork or Kalinga Joe or Conan or David G. Hartwell or Beardsley Trunion. Your immediate perception of this social situation is either "Feh!" or "Let me back off and view these weirdos from a safe distance, say at the end of tomorrow's newscast!"

The science fiction person, you see, always lives in the SF world, but under cover of normality most of the time—except while attending a gathering of like minds such as the SF conventions given in understated flashes above. The science fiction reader may be your attorney, your dentist, your children's schoolteachers, the film projectionist at your local theater, your wife or husband or child, happily living in two worlds at once, the real world of science fiction and the only apparent reality of everyday life.

If you have lived with or worked with a science fiction person, you will have noticed how intensely she seems to be involved in science fiction, how much she reads it, watches it, recommends to those around her that they try it, because it is her special kind of fun. And if you examine her behavior in everyday life, you may well notice an impatience with the way things are, an ironic, sometimes sarcastic attitude toward everyday things (particularly imposed tasks of a wearisome nature), a desire for change. This complex of attitudes is closely congruent to the complex of attitudes found in the normal human teenager.

In fact, a majority of all science fiction is read by readers who are under the age of twenty-one. The great change in the last twenty years is that most of the stuff popular with younger readers in large numbers is generally thought of as trash by adult SF readers—film and gaming tie-ins, series novels—really no change at all if you squint at it. The question is not how they got that way but why it should surprise anyone that they are. Teenagers are not fully integrated into the tedium of adult life and tend to view such everyday life with healthy suspicion. Quite logical. The science fiction reader preserves this attitude as long in life as his association with science fiction continues, more often these days into full maturity. (Today, the majority of readers of SF are adults who read fewer books a month than teenagers but keep at it for life.) It makes him act strangely sometimes. But mostly he feeds his head with more science fiction and continues to get the job done, whatever it is.

Nearly a thousand readers of *Locus*, the newspaper of the science fiction field (a semiprofessional monthly published by California fan Charles N. Brown), responded to a survey in the early 1980s that indicated that the initial involvement in science fiction of almost every respondent happened between the ages of ten and fourteen. After decades of word-of-mouth evidence, this survey simply confirmed what everyone in the SF field already knew, so no one has bothered to conduct another one since. This lends substance to the tradition in the science fiction world that active involvement starts early and lasts at least until the early twenties. Science fiction is an addiction (or habit) so reasonable in any teenager who can read (and many who can't very well, in this age of *Star Trek* and fantasy gaming) that it is superficially a curiosity that it doesn't always last. But it doesn't, and most of us do end up well-adjusted more or less, resigned to life as it is known to be beyond 1984 (and soon will be beyond 2001).

The science fiction drug is available everywhere to kids—in superhero comics, on TV, in the movies, in books and magazines. It is impossible to avoid exposure, to avoid the least hint of excitement at Marvel Comics superheroes and *Star Trek* reruns and *Star Wars*, impossible not to become habituated even before kindergarten to the language, clichés, basic concepts of science fiction. Children's culture in the contemporary U.S. is a supersaturated SF environment. By the time a kid can read comic books and attend a movie unaccompanied by an adult, his mind is a fertile environment for the harder stuff. Even the cardboard monsters on TV reruns feed the excitement. The science fiction habit is established early.

In some cases, accompanied by the hosannas of proud parents, a bright kid focuses his excitement on the science part and goes on to construct winning exhibits in school science fairs, avoids being arrested for computer hacking, obtains scholarships, and supports proud parents in their old age with his honorable gains as a career corporate technologist. Most often, a kid freezes at the gosh-wow TV/comics/movies stage and carries an infatuation with fantastic and absurd adventure into later life. But sometimes, usually by the age of twelve, a kid progresses to reading science fiction in paperback, in magazines, book club editions—wherever he can find it, because written SF offers more concentrated excitement. This is the beginning of addiction; he buys, borrows, even steals all the science fiction he can get his hands on and reads omnivorously for months or even years, sometimes until the end of high school years, sometimes a book or more a day. But the classic symptom is intense immersion in written SF for at least six months around age twelve.

Publishers adore this phenomenon, akin to the addiction to mystery and detective fiction that flourished in the decades prior to the mid-sixties. One major publisher of SF remarked to me in the 1980s that his books are supported by twelve-year-olds of all ages. Every professional writer, editor, and publisher in the science fiction field knows that the structure of science fiction publishing is founded on the large teenage audience, which guarantees a minimally acceptable market for almost every paperback book or magazine published—it requires extreme ignorance and determination akin to constipating oneself by an act of will to be unsuccessful when selling science fiction to the omnivorous teenage audience of smart, alienated readers. Yet some have failed. And in the 1990s there has finally been established a large enough population of adult readers to support a regular hardcover publishing industry in science fiction—and no one believes the average hardcover is being bought by a teenager. More about this later.

What happens to science fiction omnivores? Well, obviously, most of them discover the compulsive excitement of the opposite (or same) sex, and stop reading much of anything for pleasure, most of them permanently. However, once you have been an omnivore, your life has been permanently altered, if only in minor ways. Years later, you may experience an irrational desire to watch *Battlestar Galactica* reruns on TV, even though you know it's dumb stuff. You tend not to forbid your kids or kid your friends if they want a little toke of science fiction from time to time. A news report on solar energy possibilities in the near future doesn't seem like total balderdash, just, perhaps, a bit optimistic in the short run. A front-page newspaper article on the U.S. space probe to Jupiter doesn't read like Sanskrit or form associations with gufflike spirit-rapping. Surprise! Your life has been altered and you didn't even notice.

Discovering sex (or competitive sports or evangelical Christianity or demon rum) is not always a total diversion, though. You can, of course, read with one hand. And there are further activities open to the fan in the omnivorous stage: hundreds, often thousands, of fans gather at conventions every weekend throughout Western civilization (the World Science Fiction Convention—generically called the "Worldcon"—was in Glasgow, Scotland, in 1995; the 1999 Worldcon may be in Australia, for the third time in thirty years) to act strangely together. To a teenage omnivore, such a weekend of license to be maladjusted in the company of and in harmony with the covertly alienated of all ages can be golden. No one much notices how you dress or act as long as you do not injure yourself or others.

Swords and capes (Ah! Romance!) are particularly favored among the fat and pimply population, male and female. One wag counted seventy-two Princess Leias at the World SF Convention of 1978 in Phoenix! Star Trek costumes still abound in the mid-nineties. My favorite moment at the Worldcon in Winnipeg, Manitoba, in 1994 was seeing the fully costumed Klingon Butt Massage team enter a late-night party. Or you can hang out in your everyday slacks and jacket or torn jeans and T-shirt with like minds.

And right there among the crowd (at least at the Worldcon—the traditional gathering of the cliques) are all the big-name professionals, from Aldiss and Anderson to Zahn and Zindell, by tradition and in fact approachable for conversation and frivolity. Although this ideal is seldom approached at large SF conventions any longer—two decades of SF media cons, at which the stars are the pros and the fans are merely consumers, have split the psyche of the whole community. My own opinion is that the growth of the consumer/producer split in the SF community has been generally a bad thing for fandom and a good thing for commerce. My advice: seek out smaller conventions and avoid the large Northeast and West Coast ones at first. Just being there makes you a potentially permanent member of the SF family.

It's a really big clique, you see—or rather a band of several cliques. Just like the ones you are cut out of in the local junior high or whatever, only now you are automatically a member of one until you do something beyond the pale. You might be so shy as to be tongue-tied for your first ten conventions; still, when I was younger I could walk into a room party, sit on the floor, and listen to Isaac Asimov and Anne McCaffrey sing Gilbert and Sullivan—and join in. And go home and tell my friends that I spent time with Asimov last weekend. You can still find similar events today. Just so you don't feel lonely in the arid stretches between conventions you can afford to attend, there are approximately a thousand fan magazines produced by individuals and written by themselves and/or other fans to keep you in communication with the SF world day to day. And there is the Internet.

Today, no matter how isolated or young and ignorant or just plain shy you are, if you have access to a computer and a modem, you can visit the SF forums on the commercial services such as Compuserve, GEnie, or America Online, or the "newsgroups" of the Internet, or surf the World Wide Web, or lurk like an invisible shade watching while Mike Resnick and George Alec Effinger chat online, until you feel like joining in the SF world.

As you might have gathered, the great family aspect of SF is, in the long run, only for the most ardent—maybe ten thousand active fans in the U.S. at any time, and a few thousand more in Europe, Japan, Australia. Most often, fans mature socially enough to adjust to their home environment and just read the stuff off and on, attending, perhaps, a Worldcon every year or two to keep contact with a few friends. This is the chronic stage of addiction, following the active omnivore phase. And this stage can last for life.

If you grew up in isolation from movies, TV, and comics and have never read a work of science fiction (or if you tried one once, and found it dumb, incomprehensible, or both), you might ask at this point, Why the fuss? The answer is that even if you have kept yourself in pristine separation from the material, you are interacting daily with people who have progressed to at least a stage-one involvement in science fiction and who have altered your environment because of it.

Science fiction as written and published during the last twenty years is so diverse in every aspect that no reader except at the height of the omnivorous stage can expect to be attracted to all of it. And more science fiction has been published in the 1980s and 1990s than ever before: fifty or sixty new paperbacks every month, several magazines, even a number of hardbounds—too much even for the most dedicated omnivore to read. The quality of the individual book or story varies from advanced literary craftsmanship to hack trash, from precise and intellectual visions of the future to ignorant swordsmen hacking their way through to beautiful damsels (less than one-quarter clad) across an absurd environment. There are enough varieties of science fiction and fantasy to confuse anybody.

If you look at a wide spectrum of covers in your local SF paperback section, you begin to notice a lot of categories of science fiction. How do the advanced omnivores and chronics select what to read? By this very process: as in any other kind of book, you can tell the importance of the author of a science fiction book by the size of the author's name on the cover. Another reliable indicator of commercial importance, or at least popularity, is how many copies of an individual title by an author the store has and how many (and how many inches) of the author's titles are on the shelf. Martin Harry Greenberg, the prolific anthologist, has kept records of such measurements (inches of shelf space) in one store for years, and swears by this as a gauge of growth and decline in popularity.

But popularity and importance aside, how do you identify whether this is the kind of SF you are looking for? By the complex symbology of the cover. Not always, of course, because the paperback industry (never mind hardcover publishers, who tend to be indeterminate) is guilty of lack of confidence, or ignorance, leading to fairly regular mispackaging—but in the huge majority of cases, science fiction is quite precisely marketed and packaged.

The images on science fiction covers range from futuristic mechanical devices (which connote a story heavily into SF ideas, or perhaps just science fictional clichés) to covers with recognizable computer art, perhaps a human body part, and a dark background (which connotes cyberpunk, about which more later), to covers featuring humans against a futuristic setting, with or without machines (which connote adventure SF), to covers with humans carrying swords or other anachronistic weapons (which connote fantasy or fantastic adventure against a cardboard or clichéd SF background), to hypermuscled males carrying big swords and adorned with clinging hyperzaftig females, both scant-clad against a threateningly monstrous background (which connote sword-&-sorcery or heroic-fantasy adventures, with perhaps some SF elements), to covers representing several varieties of pure fantasy (from rich romantic flowery quests to freaky supernatural horror). Every SF omnivore has sampled all the varieties of SF, from Lovecraftian supernatural horror to the swashbuckling adventure tales of Poul Anderson to the technical and literary conundrums of Samuel R. Delany. Chronic readers usually center their interests in one limited area and read everything packaged to their taste.

The net effect is that there is a rather large number of SF audiences with focused interests, all of which interlock and overlap to form the inchoate SF reading audience. Most individual books reach their targeted audience and prosper from overlap into other related audiences. Occasionally, an SF work satisfies several of these overlapping audiences at once (for example, *Dune* by Frank Herbert, *Dhalgren* by Samuel R. Delany, or *Neuromancer* by William Gibson) and reaches what the publishing industry calls the mass audience (truly humongous numbers of readers)—and then extends for a decade or more in sales into the audience that consists of normal people who decide to try the stuff and have heard three or four big names (like Robert A. Heinlein's *Stranger in a Strange Land*, which paid most of the light bills in the period 1961 to 1981 for its publisher and allowed Mr. and Mrs. Heinlein to visit opera festivals in Europe on whim—and is still in print today).

The situation is exceedingly complex. Some say that the whole SF audience (the market) is composed of teenagers, for all practical purposes, and turns over almost completely every three to five years. This theory, the omnivore theory, eliminates all chronic readers (the actual majority) from consideration. It has the virtue of practicality from the publishing point of view, though it means you can recycle individual books endlessly and can publish practically anything, no matter how crippled, and reach a basic, dependable, supposedly profitable (though small) audience.

The most successful variant on this in recent decades is the *Star Trek* novel series (which indeed reaches a very large audience, with nearly every title a national best-seller), but it is also the unspoken theory behind the *Dragonlance* books, the *Star Wars* novels, and many other such series. One does not seek out the one great *Star Trek* novel, as one does not search for the one great Pontiac or can of Snow's Clam Chowder. One buys, one consumes.

The combined, or omnivore/chronic theory, which is the unarticulated basis behind most SF publishing, would sound something like a classier version of the omnivore theory—keep the good books in print for omnivores who pass into the chronic state and for the non-SF reader who wishes to sample the field through books or authors he has heard of, and scatter the rest of your publishing program among the three spectra (fantasy/science fantasy/science fiction) in hopes of discovering chronic sellers—works that everyone who reads SF must sooner or later hear about and read. At its best, this philosophy (if we may so dignify a marketing strategy) leads to the publishing of soaring works of the speculative imagination—but mostly it leads to carefully marketed crap. But even that is okay. Both omnivores and chronics are patient and have long memories. They are willing to wade through a fair amount of swamp to find islands of rationality and the real thing—wonderful SF.

It's a kind of quixotic quest, you see, admirable in its way. The SF reader is willing to keep trying, reading through rather large numbers of half-cooked ideas, brutal clichés, and cardboard characters and settings in search of the truly original and exciting and good. How many of us outside the SF field could be so determined? The SF reader has fun along the way that is not often visible to outsiders.

The SF reader sneers at fake SF, artificially produced film tie-in novels and stories, most SF films, most TV SF. This he calls sci-fi (or "skiffy")—junk no right-thinking omnivore or chronic should read, watch, or support. But with beatific inconsistency he will pursue his own quest—through endless hours of films, cable specials, and TV reruns, like *Space: 1999, Twilight Zone, Battlestar Galactica, Mork and Mindy, My Favorite Martian,* and some truly horrendous paperbacks and magazines—in search of something as good as he remembers finding during his initial omnivore excitement. It is not only the media fans who support the Sci-Fi channel. SF readers do too. This quest through the rubble is not without its rewards.

Consider: the aforementioned conventions are broken down into discrete areas of programming and many conventions have a general or even quite limited theme. Aside from the World Science Fiction Convention, which is a general gathering of the clans, there is a World Fantasy Convention, numerous Star Trek conventions, a pulp-magazine convention (Pulpcon), Darkovercon (devoted to the *Darkover* novels of Marion Zimmer Bradley), an SF film convention, and numerous "relaxacons" (at which there is no programming—chronics and omnivores gather to party with like minds for a weekend). There are also literally dozens of localized conventions, ranging from hundreds to thousands of attendees: Armadillocon (Austin), Boskone (Boston), Lunacon (New York City), Westercon (West Coast), Ad Astra (Toronto), Philcon (Philadelphia),

Balticon (Baltimore), Disclave (Washington, DC). The list is extensive, each with a guest of honor, films, panels, speeches, a roomful of booksellers, an art show, and many special events (often including a masquerade, gaming room, computer room) and parties (pretty dependably twenty-four hours a day). Besides general saturnalia, these conventions build audiences for name authors (guests of honor and other featured guests) and reflect audience fascination with discrete kinds of SF.

The World Science Fiction Convention, a six-day bash, has nearly five twenty-four-hour days of programming. Conadian (Worldcon '94), named patriotically for its northern setting in Winnipeg, had attendees who came from Japan to present the annual Japanese party after the awards and a healthy European contingent, including Russian fans selling souvenirs to raise hard cash; feminists and those interested in women writers who came for the several Women in Science Fiction events; film fans who came for the twenty-four-hour-a-day film programs (a bargain); Georgette Heyer fans who came for the Regency Dress Dance (yes, at a science fiction convention); some who came to see and hear their favorite big-name authors—fantasy readers to see Guy Gavriel Kay and L. Sprague de Camp, *Darkover* fans to see Marion Zimmer Bradley, *Amber* fans to see Roger Zelazny—and even L-5 fans who came to proselytize for space industrial colonies.

Of the almost five thousand attendees, a variety of audiences were represented, often recognizable from the individual package. Aside from the general run of jeaned teenagers and suited publishing types, the Star Trek fans often wore costumes from the show (Klingons were definitely "in" in 1994); the regency fans dressed regency; the heroic fantasy fans sported swords and capes; the medieval fans and Society for Creative Anachronism members dressed in a variety of medieval costumes; Spider Robinson, Canadian immigrant, played his guitar and sang well in the main corridor to a crowd of enthusiastic fans for hours at night. These people filled more than four hotels. Sponsoring similar events, INTERSECTION, the 1995 Worldcon in Glasgow, Scotland, had about six thousand attendees in more than ten hotels. Each reader discovers his or her special fun at conventions.

Omnivores tend to form preferences early on in their reading spree, and chronics are usually fixed for life. This is a quick rundown of the main possibilities an omnivore might fix on: classic fantasy (ghost stories, legends, tales); supernatural horror (two categories: classic, from Le Fanu, Blackwood, and Machen to Stephen King and *Rosemary's Baby;* and Lovecraftian, the school of H. P. Lovecraft and his followers); Tolkienesque fantasy (in the manner of *The Lord of the Rings*—carefully constructed fantasy worlds as the setting for a heroic guest, now typified by Robert Jordan's works); heroic fantasy (the descendents of Robert E. Howard's Conan the Barbarian stories, barely repressed sex fantasy in which a muscular, macho, sword-bearing male overcomes monsters, magicians, racial inferiors, and effete courtiers by cleverness and brute force, then services every willing woman in sight—and they are all willing); Burroughsian science fantasy (adventure on another planet or thinly rationalized SF setting in which fantasy and anachronism—sword fighting among the stars—are essentials); space opera (the Western genre paradigm of heroic action on the frontier, with clear good-guys-versus-bad-guys action, but set in space and using the traditional trappings of SF); hard science fiction (the SF idea is the center of attention, usually involving chemistry or physics or astronomy); soft science fiction (two alternate types, one in which the character is more important than the SF idea, the other focusing on any science other than physics or chemistry); experimental science fiction (stylistically, that is); fine writing science fiction (may include a work from any of the above categories, hard though that may be to accept); single author (reads all published stories of H. P. Lovecraft, his nonfiction, the five volumes of collected letters, the volumes of posthumous collaborations, all pastiches, and so on—archetypal fan behavior). You can begin to see the enormous variety available.

The most significant development of the last decade for the future of SF is that by about the mid-sixties, enough "fine writing" had been done in the SF field so that a chronic might fixate on that aspect of SF without running out of reading matter before running out of patience. There has always been excellent writing in the SF field, but now there is an actual audience looking for it— before the sixties, literate prose was fine when it was found, but was generally irrelevant to the SF omnivores and most chronics.

The increased volume of the fine-writing category has had its effect on outsiders' evaluation of the medium. In the seventies, the academic appraisal of SF moved from "it's trash" to "it's interesting trash" to "some of it is important and worth attention, even study." Oh, sigh. Already there are dissertations written by Ph.D.s on science fiction. In the eighties that "some of it" was reduced to "that part that can be called postmodern" (for which read "cyberpunk") and most of the rest of SF was thrown back into the gutter or became "character-driven," about which more later.

But SF is alive and still growing—not literary history—and most of the Ph.D. work is a waste of good dissertation paper because many advanced omnivores have read more SF than almost all of the Ph.D.s, and, given the categories presented above, no one has yet been able to define SF well enough so that non-SF readers can figure it out. SF readers know it when they see it, what is real and what is sci-fi (which has come to denote, among the chronics, what is probably admissible as SF but is extremely bad—able to fool some of the people some of the time).

SF people know, for instance, that Superman is real SF. In his book *Seekers of Tomorrow*, Sam Moskowitz tells the story of the teenage fans associated with the creation of the character and its early publication in *Action Comics* in 1938—and if the first generation of science fiction people had produced nothing more than Superman and Buck Rogers, the effect of science fiction on American culture still would have been profound. Because to the science fiction devotee, the attitude of SF is naturally carried over into every area of everyday life. She tends to solve problems at work with science fictional solutions or by using the creative methodology learned through reading SF. He tends to see visions of alternative futures that can be influenced by right actions in the present. She tends to be good at extrapolating trends, and especially good at puncturing the inflated predictions of others by pointing out complexities and alternatives. He tends to be optimistic about ecology through technology, has no fear of machines, and tends to be a loner.

The science fiction person never agrees with anybody else in conversation just to be friendly. Ideas are too important to be betrayed. Science fiction people, among their own kind, are almost always contentious—after all, a favorite activity is to point to an unlabeled work that may be considered SF and argue about whether or not it is, really, SF.

At that time when involvement is at its peak for the science fiction person, SF is what holds the world together. It is important, exciting, and gives the science fiction person a basis for feeling superior to the rest of humanity, those who don't know. The early fans, the generation of the thirties many of whom (Forrest J. Ackerman, Ray Bradbury, Isaac Asimov, Frederik Pohl, Donald A. Wollheim, and a host of others) are among the major writers, publishers, and editors of recent decades, evolved a theory to justify the superiority of science fiction people, then a persecuted, mainly teenage, minority. At the Third Annual World Science Fiction Convention in Denver in 1941, Robert A. Heinlein—then, as now, the most respected author in the field—gave a speech intended to define the science fiction field for its readers and authors. The theme of the speech was change, and it examined the concept and problem of "future shock" nearly thirty years before Alvin Toffler wrote his famous book.

"I think," said Heinlein, "that science fiction, even the corniest of it, even the most outlandish of it, no matter how badly it's written, has a distinct therapeutic value because all of it has as its primary postulate that the world does change." He then went on to tell the fascinated audience, in this speech that is legendary even after five decades, that he believed them to be way above average in intelligence and sensitivity—a special group.

Science fiction fans differ from most of the rest of the race by thinking in terms of racial magnitude—not even centuries but thousands of years. . . . Most human beings, and those who laugh at us for reading science fiction, time-bind, make their plans, make their predictions, only within the limits of their immediate personal affairs. . . . In fact, most people, as compared with science fiction fans, have no conception whatsoever of the fact that the culture they live in does change, that it can change.

We can only imagine the impact of such a coherent articulation of alienation and superiority on a bunch of mostly late-adolescent men at the end of the Great Depression. Though the inferior mass of humanity laughs at us, we are the ones who know; we are the wave of the future, the next evolutionary step in the human race. If only our pimples would clear up, we could get on with changing the world. Fans are Slans! (*Slan,* a novel by A. E. Van Vogt serialized in *Astounding Science Fiction* about a superior race living in secret among normal humans, was an instant classic in 1941.)

Adults ignore lousy technique when they are being deceived (in literature or elsewhere) if the deception supports the view of reality they have chosen to embrace. Adults stand to lose their sense of security if they don't cling to everyday reality. Teenagers (and the other groups of people described above) have no sense of security as a rule. They are searching for something—change, a future—and unconvincing, mundane reality does not satisfy. Oddly, then, the assumptions made in a science fiction story, which are transparent assumptions and which the young social reject of any age can share as an intellectual exercise, are more acceptable to him than the everyday assumptions made in a "serious" work of fiction about real (mundane adult) life in which he cannot or does not wish to participate.

Science fiction is preeminently the literature of the bright child, the kid who is brighter perhaps than her teachers. This is the reader to whom SF comes naturally, like the air, and becomes a refuge promising hope for the future, giving radical scenarios of difference and change.

Thus the science fiction novel or story is generally aimed at the person who has not embraced a particular set of assumptions about the way things are—this helps to explain both SF's appeal to the young and its seeming shallowness to most "mature" readers. Science fiction is still in the 1990s often shallow in its presentation of adult human relations (most often the sole concern of most other literature), but it is profound in the opportunities it offers the reader to question his most basic assumptions, even if you have to ignore lousy technique a lot of the time to participate in the illusion. This last is easy for the omnivore and chronic reader—in fact, the minute you overcome the suspension-of-disbelief problem, admittedly much easier in the early teenage years than in later life, you tend to enter your omnivore stage. Make no mistake—you don't lose your critical ability or literary education when you begin to read science fiction. You just have to learn the trick of putting all your preconceptions aside every time you sit down to read. Hah! You were right, this is just another piece of hack work. But the next one, or the story after that may be the real thing, innovative, well written, surprising, exciting.

Throughout the past decade or more, there has been a growing number of adults who have discovered science fiction as a tool without discovering the thing itself. There are now many new uses for SF in the mundane world: it can be used to combat future shock; to teach religion, political science, physics, and astronomy; to promote ecology; to support the U.S. space program; to provide an index to pop cultural attitudes toward science; and to advance academic careers and make profits for publishers, film producers, even toy makers. But the business of science fiction itself is to provide escape from the mundane world, to get at what is real by denying all of the assumptions that enforce quotidian reality for the duration of the work.

This is reflected in what really goes on at science fiction conventions. Beneath the surface frivolity, cliquishness, costumery, beneath the Libertarian or just plan licentious anarchism of the all-night carousing, beyond the author worship, the serious panel discussions, and the family of hail-fellow-fan-well-met, the true core of being a science fiction person is that the convention is abnormal and alienated from daily life. Not just separated in time and space—different! There is no parallel more apt than the underground movements of the last two hundred years in Western civilization: the Romantics in England, Baudelaire and his circle in France, the Modernists, the Beats. (Note to literary historians: this would make an interesting study.) The difference is that to an outsider, it just looks like fun and games, since many of these people go home after a convention, go back to work, school, housewifery, unemployment, mundane reality. Or so it seems.

While they are spending time in the science fiction world, though, things are really different. How different? Let's circle around this for a moment. For instance, at a convention you can almost certainly talk to people there who, in normal life, are removed from you by taboos or social barriers. No matter how obnoxious you are, people will talk to you unless you insult them directly, and the chances are excellent that you can find one or more people willing to engage in serious, extended, knowledgeable conversation about some of the things that interest you most, whether it is the stock market or macrame, clothing design or conservative politics, science or literature or rock 'n' roll. This is now just as true of the SF bulletin boards of the Internet and the online services such as GEnie, America Online, and Compuserve, where the conversations take place every hour of every day. Science fiction people tend not to be well rounded but rather multiple specialists; the only thing that holds them and the whole SF world together is science fiction. Actually you spend a minority of your time at a convention talking about science fiction, but the reality of science fiction underlies the whole experience and is its basis. For the duration of the science fiction experience, you agree to set aside the assumptions and preconceptions that rule your ordinary behavior and to live free in a kind of personal utopian space. A science fiction convention, like a work of science fiction, is an escape into an alternate possibility that you can test, when it is over, against mundane reality. Even the bad ones provide this context.

Harlan Ellison, writer and science fiction personality, has spoken of his first encounter with science fiction as a kid in a dentist's office, where he discovered a copy of a science fiction magazine. On the cover, Captain Future was battling Krag the robot for possession of a scantily clad woman; the picture filled his young mind with awe, wonder, and excitement. His life was changed. He wanted more. The reason science fiction creates such chronic addicts as Harlan Ellison is that once you admit the possibility that reality is not as solid and fixed as it used to seem, you feel the need for repeated doses of science fictional realities. Today that moment of transformation may occur while watching a film or TV, or even reading a comic book, but it still happens and creates fans who then have the urgent desire to find others like themselves.

Of course, sometimes what you discover in the science fiction field that attracts you is not the thing itself but one of its associates. A chronic reader may actually read almost entirely classical fantasy and Lovecraftian supernatural horror, or a writer such as Fritz Leiber may spend a career writing in every variety of fantasy and science fiction, and yet always be "in the field." There is an interesting investigation to be done someday on why the classical fantasy, a main tradition of Western literature for several millennia, is now part of the science fiction field. In the latter half of the twentieth century, with certain best-selling exceptions, fantasy is often produced by writers of science fiction and fantasy, edited by editors of science fiction, illustrated by SF and fantasy artists, read by omnivore fantasy and SF addicts who support the market. Fantasy is no longer in the 1990s just a subdivision of SF, but is related to the phenomenon that confronts us in an unpredictably evolving way in the 1990s, since being established in the 1980s as a separate marketing category.

Since the 1930s, science fiction has been an umbrella under which any kind of estrangement from mundane reality is welcome (though some works, such as the John Norman *Gor* series in the 1970s and '80s, or the gaming tie-in novels of the eighties and nineties, both of which began life under the SF umbrella, are admitted but generally despised and generally believed to sell mostly to an audience outside any other SF audience). To present the broad, general context of the SF field, let us consider in more detail the main areas and relationships as they have evolved over the past several decades.

The general question of fantasy has been dealt with frequently, from Freud's well-known essay on the uncanny, through recent structuralist works such as Todorov's *The Fantastic*, and is not central to our concern with science fiction.

Several things need to be said, however, about fantasy literature before we move on to varieties of science fiction. Fantasy, through its close association with science fiction since the 1920s in America, has developed a complex interaction with science fiction that has changed much of what is written as fantasy today.

H. P. Lovecraft, the greatest writer of supernatural horror of the century, a literary theoretician, and mentor, through correspondence and personal contact, to Frank Belknap Long, Robert E. Howard, Robert Bloch, Fritz Leiber, Clark Ashton Smith, August Derleth, Donald and Howard Wandrei, and a number of others, was an agnostic, a rationalist, and a believer in science. His work was published both in *Weird Tales*, the great fantasy magazine, between the twenties and the early fifties, and in *Astounding Stories*, the great science fiction magazine of its day. Almost all his acolytes followed the same pattern of commercial and literary ties to both areas.

In 1939, after the greatest SF editor of modern times, John W. Campbell, took the helm at *Astounding*, he proceeded to found the second great fantasy magazine, *Unknown*, encouraging all his newly discovered writing talents— Robert A. Heinlein, Theodore Sturgeon, L. Sprague de Camp, L. Rob Hubbard, Anthony Boucher, Alfred Bester, H. L. Gold, Fredric Brown, Eric Frank Russell, as well as Henry Kuttner, Jack Williamson, C. L. Moore, and Fritz Leiber—to create a new kind of fantasy, one with modern settings and contemporary atmosphere, as highly rationalized and consistent as the science fiction he wanted them to write for *Astounding*. Through Lovecraft and Campbell a strong link was forged not only commercially but also aesthetically between fantasy and science fiction.

Today, and for the last three decades, the most distinguished and consistently brilliant publication in the field has been the *Magazine of Fantasy and Science Fiction* (Anthony Boucher, from Campbell's *Unknown*, was a founding editor and set the aesthetic tone), required reading for all who wish to discover the field at its best and broadest—though it has never been the most popular magazine in the field, always surpassed in circulation by more focused magazines. Its most serious competitor for top honors is *Asimov's SF Magazine*, embodying the same broad and modern aesthetic position since the advent of editors Shawna McCarthy and then Gardner R. Dozois in the mid-eighties. In some years *Asimov's* has unquestionably dominated the field, publishing as much fantasy and unclassifiable fiction as SF.

After Lovecraft and Campbell, the third towering figure in fantasy so far in the twentieth century is J. R. R. Tolkien, whose *Lord of the Rings* trilogy is both a classic of contemporary literature and an example of the dominant position of the science fiction field as stated above. Tolkien's works, although hardcovers at first, were popularized in paperback through SF publishers and have spawned an entire marketing substructure to support works of world-building fantasy in the Tolkien tradition. More books appear every month featuring the quest of a single heroic figure across a detailed and rationalized fantasy world, accompanied by a group of major and minor fantasy characters and ending in a confrontation between Good and Evil, in which after a tough battle, Good always wins.

The fourth towering figure is not one person, but is a posthumous collaboration between the artist Frank Frazetta, formerly a comic illustrator, and the author Robert E. Howard, a pulp fantasy adventure hack who committed suicide in 1936 on the day his mother died and who created a number of fantastic heroes, the best-known of whom is Conan the Barbarian. Howard's works had been mostly out of print since his death, except for several small press editions and a few paperbacks, until the early 1960s. Then L. Sprague de Camp obtained the rights from Howard's estate to arrange and anthologize the whole Conan series for the first time in paperback, and to write additions and sequels himself and with others. Through a stroke of marketing genius, comics artist Frazetta was hired to illustrate the paperback covers, which seized the imagination of the audience enough to sell in millions of copies, established the Howard name, and made Frazetta wealthy and famous. Howard now has nearly fifty books in print in the sixth decade following his death, and a sword-swinging barbarian hero brutishly adventuring across a fantasy/historic landscape (inside a book with an imitation Frazetta cover—Frazetta's originals from the 1960s and '70s now sell at auction for six figures) is the principal reading focus of a large number of chronic SF readers. This category, which was formerly called sword-&-sorcery fiction, is now referred to more accurately as heroic fantasy. If Mickey Spillane wrote SF, it would be heroic fantasy. In fact, a hundred years from now SF may have acquired Spillane's works under this rubric.

But terminology remains slippery. Robert Jordan wrote Conan sequels before he wrote his epic Wheel of Time sequence. Since he was a heroic fantasy writer when writing the Conans, people continued to refer to his work as heroic fantasy and now, given Jordan's great popularity, have begun to apply the phrase backward to all Tolkienesque fantasy (since Jordan's Wheel of Time is in the tradition of Tolkien). Where this will end in the short run is confusion for all concerned. Maybe usages will become clear again in the next century.

Two areas of fantasy that are not presently annexed under the SF umbrella, or published with a fantasy logo in that marketing category, perhaps because these two areas are not presently in popular (middle-class) disrepute, are Arthurian romances and the occult horror best-seller. There are indications that these two areas may remain separate and independent—both types tend to be written by authors who have no desire to associate themselves and their works with low-class, nonliterary, low-paying (until recently) stuff. On the other hand, there are intimate links between horror and SF from *Unknown* and *Weird Tales* to the present. There are even horror conventions and fantasy conventions spawned by the SF conventions, and the writers often write and socialize across the genre boundaries. Category (non-bestseller) horror and fantasy is and always has been published for the last six decades along with SF by the SF publishers.

The only science in all the areas of fantasy is either straw-man science (which cannot cope) or black science (used by the evil sorcerer). Amoral science is a recent addition to some heroic fantasy (especially noticeable in the works of Michael Moorcock). The idea of magic as a scientific discipline was a contribution of the Campbell era. And I can generalize without fear of contradiction by saying that except in a tiny minority of cases, technology is associated with evil in fantasy literature. So it is particularly curious that the element of estrangement from everyday reality has come to yoke by itself the two separates, fantasy and science fiction, even though SF was invented to exclude "mere" fantasy. This complex of seeming contradiction will be investigated in more depth shortly. For the moment we will move on to a consideration of the subdivisions of the center of the field, science fiction.

Hugo Gernsback, who invented modern science fiction in April, 1926, knew what he meant by "scientifiction" (as he named it) and assumed it would be evident to others: all that work Wells and Verne and Poe wrote ("charming romance intermingled with scientific fact and prophetic vision," as Gernsback says in the editorial in the first issue of the first magazine, *Amazing Stories*). In addition to this confusion, Gernsback, an eccentric immigrant and technological visionary, was tone-deaf to the English language, printing barely literate stories, often by enthusiastic teenagers, about new inventions and the promise of a wondrous technological future cheek by jowl with fiction by H. G. Wells, Poe, Edgar Rice Burroughs, and a growing number of professional pulp writers who wanted to break into the new market. The new thing was amorphous, formed and reformed over the decades by major editors and writers, and all the chronic readers, into the diversity that is science fiction today.

It is a source of both amusement and frustration to SF people that public consciousness of science fiction has almost never penetrated beyond the first decade of the field's development. Sure, *Star Wars* is wonderful, but in precisely the same way and at the same level of consciousness and sophistication that SF from the late twenties and early thirties was: fast, almost plotless stories of zipping through the ether in spaceships, meeting aliens, using futuristic devices, and fighting the bad guys (and winning).

By now it should be obvious that we are dealing not with a limited thing but with a segment of reality. More than an alternate literary form or an alternate lifestyle, science fiction informs the lives of thousands and affects the lives of millions, is a fact of life more intimate than inflation, whose influence is so all-pervasive that it is traceable daily in every home through the artifacts and ideas that represent all possible futures and all possible change.

MR. BOY

James Patrick Kelly

James Patrick Kelly has emerged in the last decade as a leading SF writer and this
story is perhaps the most famous piece to date. It is also the first section of his
novel *Wildlife*. Like Greg Bear, Kelly was represented in the important anthology,
Mirrorshades, with a cyberpunk story, although he was a member of the group of SF
writers known as the Humanists (along with John Kessel, Karen Joy Fowler, Kim Stanley
Robinson, and others associated with the Sycamore Hill annual writers workshop)—a
group devoted to emphasizing characterization in their fiction, especially to the inner life
of characters in their stories, their thoughts and feelings rather than their actions. Consequently, they often describe their fiction as "character-driven."

I was already twitching by the time they strapped me down. Nasty pleasure and
beautiful pain crackled through me, branching and rebranching like lightning.
Extreme feelings are hard to tell apart when you have endorphins spilling across
your brain. Another spasm shot down my legs and curled my toes. I moaned.
The stiffs wore surgical masks that hid their mouths, but I knew that they were
smiling. They hated me because my mom could afford to have me stunted.
When I really was just a kid I did not understand that. Now I hated them back;
it helped me get through the therapy. We had a very clean transaction going
here. No secrets between us.

Even though it hurts, getting stunted is still the ultimate flash. As I unlived
my life, I overdosed on dying feelings and experiences. My body was not big
enough to hold them all; I thought I was going to explode. I must have
screamed because I could see the laugh lines crinkling around the stiffs' eyes.
You do not have to worry about laugh lines after they twank your genes and reset your mitotic limits. My face was smooth and I was going to be twelve years
old forever, or at least as long as Mom kept paying for my rejuvenation.

I giggled as the short one leaned over me and pricked her catheter into my
neck. Even through the mask, I could smell her breath. She reeked of dead
meat.

*   *   *

Getting stunted always left me wobbly and thick, but this time I felt like last Tuesday's pizza. One of the stiffs had to roll me out of recovery in a wheelchair.

The lobby looked like a furniture showroom. Even the plants had been newly waxed. There was nothing to remind the clients that they were bags of blood and piss. You are all biological machines now, said the lobby, clean as space station lettuce. A scattering of people sat on the hard chairs. Stennie and Comrade were fidgeting by the elevators. They looked as if they were thinking of rearranging the furniture—like maybe into a pile in the middle of the room. Even before they waved, the stiff seemed to know that they were waiting for me.

Comrade smiled. *"Zdrast'ye."*

"You okay, Mr. Boy?" said Stennie. Stennie was a grapefruit yellow stenonychosaurus with a brown underbelly. His razor-clawed toes clicked against the slate floor as he walked.

"He's still a little weak," said the stiff, as he set the chair's parking brake. He strained to act nonchalant, not realizing that Stennie enjoys being stared at. "He needs rest. Are you his brother?" he said to Comrade.

Comrade appeared to be a teenaged spike neck with a head of silky black hair that hung to his waist. He wore a window coat of which twenty-three different talking heads chattered. He could pass for human, even though he was really a Panasonic. *"Nyet,"* said Comrade. "I'm just another one of his hallucinations."

The poor stiff gave him a dry nervous cough that might have been meant as a chuckle. He was probably wondering whether Stennie wanted to take me home to eat me for lunch. I always thought that the way Stennie got reshaped was more funny looking than fierce—a python that had rear-ended an ostrich. But even though he was a head shorter than me, he did have enormous eyes and a mouthful of serrated teeth. He stopped next to the wheelchair and rose up to his full height. "I appreciate everything you've done." Stennie offered the stiff his spindly three-fingered hand to shake. "Sorry if he caused any trouble."

The stiff took it gingerly, then shrieked and flew backwards. I mean, he jumped almost a meter off the floor. Everyone in the lobby turned and Stennie opened his hand and waved the joy buzzer. He slapped his tail against the slate in triumph. Stennie's sense of humor was extreme, but then he was only thirteen years old.

Stennie's parents had given him the Nissan Alpha for his twelfth birthday and we had been customizing it ever since. We installed blue mirror glass and Stennie painted scenes from the Late Cretaceous on the exterior body armor. We ripped out all the seats, put in a wall-to-wall gel mat and a fridge and a microwave and a screen and a mini-dish. Comrade had even done an illegal operation on the carbrain so that we could override in an emergency and actually steer the Alpha ourselves with a joystick. It would have been cramped, but we would have lived in Stennie's car if our parents had let us.

"You okay there, Mr. Boy?" said Stennie.

"Mmm." As I watched the trees whoosh past in the rain, I pretended that the car was standing still and the world was passing me by.

"Think of something to do, okay?" Stennie had the car and all and he was fun to play with, but ideas were not his specialty. He was probably smart for a dinosaur. "I'm bored."

"Leave him alone, will you?" Comrade said.

"He hasn't said anything yet." Stennie stretched and nudged me with his foot. "Say something." He had legs like a horse; yellow skin stretched tight over long bones and stringy muscle.

"*Prosrees!* He just had his genes twanked, you jack." Comrade always took good care of me. Or tried to. "Remember what that's like? He's in damage control."

"Maybe I should go to socialization," Stennie said. "Aren't they having a dance this afternoon?"

"You're talking to me?" said the Alpha. "You haven't earned enough learning credits to socialize. You're a quiz behind and forty-five minutes short of E-class. You haven't linked since . . ."

"Just shut up and drive me over." Stennie and the Alpha did not get along. He thought the car was too strict. "I'll make up the plugging quiz, okay?" He probed a mess of empty juice boxes and snack wrappers with his foot. "Anyone see my comm anywhere?"

Stennie's schoolcomm was wedged behind my cushion. "You know," I said, "I can't take much more of this." I leaned forward, wriggled it free and handed it over.

"Of what, *poputchik?*" said Comrade. "Joyriding? Listening to the lizard here?"

"Being stunted."

Stennie flipped up the screen of his comm and went on line with the school's computer. "You guys help me, okay?" He retracted his claws and tapped at the oversized keyboard.

"It's extreme while you're on the table," I said, "but now I feel empty. Like I've lost myself."

"You'll get over it," said Stennie. "First question: Brand name of the first wiseguys sold for home use?"

"NEC-Bots, of course," said Comrade.

"Geneva? It got nuked, right?"

"*Da.*"

"Haile Selassie was that king of Egypt who the Marleys claim is god, right? Name the Cold Wars: Nicaragua, Angola . . . Korea was the first." Typing was hard work for Stennie; he did not have enough fingers for it. "One was something like Venezuela. Or something."

"Sure it wasn't Venice?"

"Or Venus?" I said, but Stennie was not paying attention.

"All right, I know that one. And that. The Sovs built the first space station. Ronald Reagan—he was the president who dropped the bomb?"

Comrade reached inside of his coat and pulled out an envelope. "I got you something, Mr. Boy. A get-well present for your collection."

I opened it and scoped a picture of a naked dead fat man on a stainless steel table. The print had a DI verification grid on it, which meant this was the real thing, not a composite. Just above the corpse's left eye there was a neat hole. It was rimmed with purple which had faded to bruise blue. He had curly gray hair on his head and chest, skin the color of dried mayonnaise and a wonderfully complicated penis graft. He looked relieved to be dead. "Who was he?" I liked Comrade's present. It was extreme.

"CEO of Infoline. He had the wife, you know, the one who stole all the money so she could download herself into a computer."

I shivered as I stared at the dead man. I could hear myself breathing and feel the blood squirting through my arteries. "Didn't they turn her off?" I said. This was the kind of stuff we were not even supposed to imagine, much less look at. Too bad they had cleaned him up. "How much did this cost me?"

"You don't want to know."

"Hey!" Stennie thumped his tail against the side of the car. "I'm taking a quiz here and you guys are drooling over porn. When was the First World Depression?"

"Who cares?" I slipped the picture back into the envelope and grinned at Comrade.

"Well, let me see then," Stennie snatched the envelope. "You know what I think, Mr. Boy? I think this corpse jag you're on is kind of sick. Besides, you're going to get in trouble if you let Comrade keep breaking laws. Isn't this picture private?"

"Privacy is twentieth century thinking. It's all information, Stennie, and information should be accessible." I held out my hand. "But if *glasnost* bothers you, give it up." I wiggled my fingers.

Comrade snickered. Stennie pulled out the picture, glanced at it and hissed. "You're scaring me, Mr. Boy."

His schoolcomm beeped as it posted his score on the quiz and he sailed the envelope back across the car at me. "Not Venezuela, Viet Nam. Hey, *Truman* dropped the plugging bomb. Reagan was the one who spent all the money. What's wrong with you dumbscuts? Now I owe school another fifteen minutes."

"Hey, if you don't make it look good, they'll know you had help." Comrade laughed.

"What's with this dance anyway? You don't dance." I picked Comrade's present up and tucked it into my shirt pocket. "You find yourself a cush or something, lizard boy?"

"Maybe." Stennie could not blush but sometimes when he was embarrassed the loose skin under his jaw quivered. Even though he had been reshaped into a dinosaur, he was still growing up. "Maybe I am getting a little. What's it to you?"

"If you're getting it," I said, "it's got to be microscopic." This was a bad sign. I was losing him to his dick, just like all the other pals. No way I wanted to start over with someone new. I had been alive for twenty-five years now. I was running out of things to say to thirteen-year-olds.

As the Alpha pulled up to the school, I scoped the crowd waiting for the doors to open for third shift. Although there were a handful of stunted kids, and a pair of gorilla brothers who were football stars and Freddy the Teddy, a bear who had furry hands instead of real paws, the majority of students at New Canaan High looked more or less normal. Most working stiffs thought that people who had their genes twanked were freaks.

"Come get me at 5:15," Stennie told the Alpha. "In the meantime, take these guys wherever they want to go." He opened the door. "You rest up, Mr. Boy, okay?"

"What?" I was not paying attention. "Sure." I had just seen the most beautiful girl in the world.

She leaned against one of the concrete columns of the portico, chatting with a couple other kids. Her hair was long and nut-colored and the ends twinkled. She was wearing a loose black robe over mirror skintights. Her schoolcomm dangled from a strap around her waist. She appeared to be seventeen, maybe eighteen. But of course, appearances could be deceiving.

Girls had never interested me much, but I could not help but admire this one. "Wait, Stennie! Who's that?" She saw me point at her. "With the hair?"

"She's new—has one of those names you can't pronounce." He showed me his teeth as he got out. "Hey Mr. Boy, you're *stunted*. You haven't got what she wants."

He kicked the door shut, lowered his head and crossed in front of the car. When he walked he looked like he was trying to squash a bug with each step. His snaky tail curled high behind him for balance, his twiggy little arms dangled. When the new girl saw him, she pointed and smiled. Or maybe she was pointing at me.

"Where to?" said the car.

"I don't know." I sank low into my seat and pulled out Comrade's present again. "Home, I guess."

I was not the only one in my family with twanked genes. My mom was a three-quarters scale replica of the Statue of Liberty. Originally she wanted to be fullsized, but then she would have been the tallest thing in New Canaan, Connecticut. The town turned her down when she applied for a zoning variance. Her lawyers and their lawyers sued and countersued for almost two years. Mom's claim was that since she was born human, her freedom of form was protected by the Thirtieth Amendment. However, the form she wanted was a curtain of reshaped cells which would hang on a forty-two meter high ferroplastic skeleton. Her structure, said the planning board, was clearly subject to building codes and zoning laws. Eventually they reached an out-of-court settlement, which was why Mom was only as tall as an eleven story building.

She complied with the town's request for a setback of five hundred meters from Route 123. As Stennie's Alpha drove us down the long driveway, Comrade broadcast the recognition code which told the robot sentries that we were okay. One thing Mom and the town agreed on from the start: no tourists. Sure, she loved publicity, but she was also very fragile. In some places her skin was only a centimeter thick. Chunks of ice falling from her crown could punch holes in her.

The end of our driveway cut straight across the lawn to Mom's granite-paved foundation pad. To the west of the plaza, directly behind her, was a utility building faced in ashlar that housed her support systems. Mom had been bioengineered to be pretty much self-sufficient. She was green not only to match the real Statue of Liberty but also because she was photosynthetic. All she needed was a yearly truckload of fertilizer, water from the well, and a hundred and fifty kilowatts of electricity a day. Except for emergency surgery, the only time she required maintenance was in the fall, when her outer cells tended to flake off and had to be swept up and carted away.

Stennie's Alpha dropped us off by the doorbone in the right heel and then drove off to do whatever cars do when nobody is using them. Mom's greeter was waiting in the reception area inside the foot.

"Peter." She tried to hug me but I dodged out of her grasp. "How are you, Peter?"

"Tired." Even though Mom knew I did not like to be called that, I kissed the air near her cheek. Peter Cage was her name for me; I had given it up years ago.

"You poor boy. Here, let me see you." She held me at arm's length and brushed her fingers against my cheek. "You don't look a day over twelve. Oh, they do such good work—don't you think?" She squeezed my shoulder. "Are you happy with it?"

I think my mom meant well, but she never did understand me. Especially when she talked to me with her greeter remote. I wormed out of her grip and fell back onto one of the couches. "What's to eat?"

"Doboys, noodles, fries—whatever you want." She beamed at me and then bent over impulsively and gave me a kiss that I did not want. I never paid much attention to the greeter; she was lighter than air. She was always smiling and asking five questions in a row without waiting for an answer and flitting around the room. It wore me out just watching her. Naturally everything I said or did was cute, even if I was trying to be obnoxious. It was no fun being cute. Today Mom had her greeter wearing a dark blue dress and a very dumb white apron. The greeter's umbilical was too short to stretch up to the kitchen. So why was she wearing an apron? "I'm really, really glad you're home," she said.

"I'll take some cinnamon doboys." I kicked off my shoes and rubbed my bare feet through the dense black hair on the floor. "And a beer."

All of Mom's remotes had different personalities. I liked Nanny all right; she was simple but at least she listened. The lovers were a challenge because they were usually too busy looking into mirrors to notice me. Cook was as pretentious as a four-star menu; the housekeeper had all the charm of a vacuum cleaner. I had always wondered what it would be like to talk directly to Mom's main brain up in the head, because then she would not be filtered through a remote. She would be herself.

"Cook is making you some nice broth to go with your doboys," said the greeter. "Nanny says you shouldn't be eating dessert all the time."

"Hey, did I ask for broth?"

At first Comrade had hung back while the greeter was fussing over me. Then he slid along the wrinkled pink walls of the reception room toward the plug where the greeter's umbilical was attached. When she started in about the broth I saw him lean against the plug. Carelessly, you know? At the same time he stepped on the greeter's umbilical, crimping the furry black cord. She gasped and the smile flattened horribly on her face as if her lips were two ropes someone had suddenly yanked taut. Her head jerked toward the umbilical plug.

"E-Excuse me." She was twitching.

"What?" Comrade glanced down at his foot as if it belonged to a stranger. "Oh, sorry." He pushed away from the wall and strolled across the room toward us. Although he seemed apologetic, about half the heads on his window coat were laughing.

The greeter flexed her cheek muscles. "You'd better watch out for your toy, Peter," she said. "It's going to get you in trouble someday."

Mom did not like Comrade much, even though she had given him to me when I was first stunted. She got mad when I snuck him down to Manhattan a couple of years ago to have a chop job done on his behavioral regulators. For a while after the operation, he used to ask me before he broke the law. Now he was on his own. He got caught once and she warned me he was out of control. But she still threw money at the people until they went away.

"Trouble?" I said. "Sounds like fun." I thought we were too rich for trouble. I was the trust baby of a trust baby; we had vintage money and lots of it. I stood and Comrade picked up my shoes for me. "And he's not a toy; he's my best friend." I put my arms around his shoulder. "Tell Cook I'll eat in my rooms."

I was tired after the long climb up the circular stairs to Mom's chest. When the roombrain sensed I had come in, it turned on all the electronic windows and blinked my message indicator. One reason I still lived in my mom was that she kept out of my rooms. She had promised me total security and I believed her. Actually I doubted that she cared enough to pry, although she could easily have tapped my windows. I was safe from her remotes up here, even the housekeeper. Comrade did everything for me.

I sent him for supper, perched on the edge of the bed, and cleared the nearest window of army ants foraging for meat through some Angolan jungle. The first message in the queue was from a gray-haired stiff wearing a navy blue corporate uniform. "Hello, Mr. Cage. My name is Weldon Montross and I'm with Datasafe. I'd like to arrange a meeting with you at your convenience. Call my DI number, 408-966-3286. I hope to hear from you soon."

"What the hell is Datasafe?"

The roombrain ran a search. "Datasafe offers services in encryption and information security. It was incorporated in the state of Delaware in 2013. Estimated billings last year were 340 million dollars. Headquarters are in San Jose, California, with branch offices in White Plains, New York, and Chevy Chase, Maryland. Foreign offices . . ."

"Are they trying to sell me something or what?"

The room did not offer an answer. "Delete," I said. "Next?"

Weldon Montross was back again, looking exactly as he had before. I wondered if he were using a virtual image. "Hello, Mr. Cage. I've just discovered that you've been admitted to the Thayer Clinic for rejuvenation therapy. Believe me when I say that I very much regret having to bother you during your convalescence and I would not do so if this were not a matter of importance. Would you please contact Department of Identification number 408-966-3286 as soon as you're able?"

"You're a pro, Weldon, I'll say that for you." Prying client information out of the Thayer Clinic was not easy, but then the guy was no doubt some kind of op. He was way too polite to be a salesman. What did Datasafe want with me? "Any more messages from him?"

"No," said the roombrain.

"Well, delete this one too and if he calls back tell him I'm too busy unless he wants to tell me what he's after." I stretched out on my bed. "Next?" The gel mattress shivered as it took my weight.

Happy Lurdane was having a smash party on the twentieth but Happy was a boring cush and there was a bill from the pet store for the iguanas that I paid and a warning from the SPCA that I deleted and a special offer for preferred customers from my favorite fireworks company that I saved to look at later and my dad was about to ask for another loan when I paused him and deleted and last of all there was a message from Stennie, time stamped ten minutes ago.

"Hey Mr. Boy, if you're feeling better I've lined up a VR party for tonight." He did not quite fit into the school's telelink booth; all I could see was his toothy face and the long yellow curve of his neck. "Bunch of us have reserved some time on Playroom. Come in disguise. That new kid said she'd link, so scope her yourself if you're so hot. I found out her name but it's kind of unpronounceable. Tree-something Joplin. Anyway it's at seven, meet on channel 17, password is warhead. Hey, did you send my car back yet? Later." He faded.

"Sounds like fun." Comrade kicked the doorbone open and backed through, balancing a tray loaded with soup and fresh doboys and a mug of cold beer. "Are we going?" He set it onto the nightstand next to my bed.

"Maybe." I yawned. It felt good to be in my own bed. "Flush the damn soup, would you?" I reached over for a doboy and felt something crinkle in my jacket pocket. I pulled out the picture of the dead CEO. About the only thing I did not like about it was that the eyes were shut. You feel dirtier when the corpse stares back. "This is one sweet hunk of meat, Comrade." I propped the picture beside the tray. "How did you get it, anyway? Must have taken some operating."

"Three days worth. Encryption wasn't all that tough but there was lots of it." Comrade admired the picture with me as he picked up the bowl of soup. "I ended up buying about ten hours from IBM to crack the file. Kind of pricey but since you were getting stunted, I had nothing else to do."

"You see the messages from that security op?" I bit into a doboy. "Maybe you were a little sloppy." The hot cinnamon scent tickled my nose.

"Ya v'rot ego ebal!" He laughed. "So some stiff is cranky? Plug him if he can't take a joke."

I said nothing. Comrade could be a pain sometimes. Of course I loved the picture, but he really should have been more careful. He had made a mess and left it for me to clean up. Just what I needed. I knew I would only get mad if I thought about it, so I changed the subject. "Well, do you think she's cute?"

"What's-her-face Joplin?" Comrade turned abruptly toward the bathroom. "Sure, for a *perdunya*," he said over his shoulder. "Why not?" Talking about girls made him snippy. I think he was afraid of them.

I brought my army ants back onto the window; they were swarming over a lump with brown fur. Thinking about him hanging on my elbow when I met this Tree-something Joplin made me feel weird. I listened as he poured the soup down the toilet. I was not myself at all. Getting stunted changes you; no one can predict how. I chugged the beer and rolled over to take a nap. It was the first time I had ever thought of leaving Comrade behind.

"VR party, Mr. Boy." Comrade nudged me awake. "Are we going or not?"

"Huh?" My gut still ached from the rejuvenation and I woke up mean enough to chew glass. "What do you mean *we?*"

"Nothing." Comrade had that blank look he always put on so I would not know what he was thinking. Still I could tell he was disappointed. "Are you going then?" he said.

I stretched—*ouch!* "Yeah, sure, get my joysuit." My bones felt brittle as candy. "And stop acting sorry for yourself." This nasty mood had momentum; it swept me past any regrets. "No way I'm going to lie here all night watching you pretend you have feelings to hurt."

"Tak tochno." He saluted and went straight to the closet. I got out of bed and hobbled to the bathroom.

"This is a costume party, remember," Comrade called. "What are you wearing?"

"Whatever." Even his efficiency irked me; sometimes he did too much. "You decide." I needed to get away from him for a while.

Playroom was a new virtual reality service on our local net. If you wanted to throw an electronic party at Versailles or Monticello or San Simeon, all you had to do was link—if you could get a reservation.

I came back to the bedroom and Comrade stepped up behind me, holding the joysuit. I shrugged into it, velcroed the front seam and eyed myself in the nearest window. He had synthesized some kid-sized armor in the German Gothic style. My favorite. It was made of polished silver, with great fluting and scalloping. He had even programmed a little glow into the image so that on the window I looked like a walking night-light. There was an armet helmet with a red ostrich plume; the visor was tipped up so I could see my face. I raised my arm and the joysuit translated the movement to the window so that my armored image waved back.

"Try a few steps," he said.

Although I could move easily in the lightweight joysuit, the motion interpreter made walking in the video armor seem realistically awkward. Comrade had scored the sound effects, too. Metal hinges rasped, chain mail rattled softly, and there was a satisfying *clunk* whenever my foot hit the floor.

"Great." I clenched my fist in approval. I was awake now and in control of my temper. I wanted to make up but Comrade was not taking the hint. I could never quite figure out whether he was just acting like a machine or whether he really did not care how I treated him.

"They're starting." All the windows in the room lit up with Playroom's welcome screen. "You want privacy, so I'm leaving. No one with bother you."

"Hey Comrade, you don't have to go . . ."

But he had already left the room. Playroom prompted me to identify myself. "Mr. Boy," I said, "Department of Identification number 203-966-2445. I'm looking for channel 17; the password is warhead."

A brass band started playing "Hail to the Chief" as the title screen lit the windows:

The White House
1600 Pennsylvania Avenue
Washington, DC, USA
copyright 2096, Playroom Presentations
REPRODUCTION OR REUSE STRICTLY PROHIBITED

and then I was looking at a wraparound view of a VR ballroom. A caption bar opened at the top of the windows and a message scrolled across. *This is the famous East Room, the largest room in the main house. It is used for press conferences, public receptions, and entertainments.* I lowered my visor and entered the simulation.

The East Room was decorated in bone white and gold; three chandeliers hung like cut glass mushrooms above the huge parquet floor. A band played skitter at one end of the room but no one was dancing yet. The band was War-head, according to their drum set. I had never heard of them. Someone's dis-guise? I turned and the joysuit changed the view on the windows. Just ahead Satan was chatting with a forklift and a rhinoceros. Beyond some blue cartoons were teasing Johnny America. There was not much furniture in the room, a cou-ple of benches, an ugly piano, and some life-sized paintings of George and Martha. George looked like he had just been peeled off a cash card. I stared at him too long and the closed caption bar informed me that the painting had been painted by Gilbert Stuart and was the only White House object dating from the mansion's first occupancy in 1800.

"Hey," I said to a girl who was on fire. "How do I get rid of the plugging tour guide?"

"Can't," she said. "When Playroom found out we were kids they turned on all their educational crap and there's no override. I kind of don't think they want us back."

"Dumbscuts." I scoped the room for something that might be Stennie. No luck. "I like the way your hair is burning." Now that it was too late, I was sorry I had to make idle party chat.

"Thanks." When she tossed her head, sparks flared and crackled. "My mom helped me program it."

"So, I've never been to the White House. Is there more than this?"

"Sure," she said. "We're supposed to have pretty much the whole first floor. Unless they shorted us. You wouldn't be Stone Kinkaid in there, would you?"

"No, not really." Even though the voice was disguised, I could tell this was Happy Lurdane. I edged away from her. "I'm going to check the other rooms now. Later."

"If you run into Stone, tell him I'm looking for him."

I left the East Room and found myself in a long marble passageway with a red carpet. A dog skeleton trotted toward me. Or maybe it was supposed to be a sheep. I waved and went through a door on the other side.

Everyone in the Red Room was standing on the ceiling; I knew I had found Stennie. Even though what they see is only a simulation, most people lock into the perceptual field of a VR as if it were real. Stand on your head long enough—even if only in your imagination—and you get airsick. It took kilohours of prac-tice to learn to compensate. Upside down was one of Stennie's trademark ways of showing off.

The Red Room is an intimate parlor in the American Empire style of 1815–20 . . .

"Hi," I said. I hopped over the wainscotting and walked up the silk-covered wall to join the three of them.

"You're wearing German armor." When the boy in blue grinned at me, his cheeks dimpled. He was wearing shorts and white knee socks, a navy sweater over a white shirt. "Augsburg?" said Little Boy Blue. Fine blond hair drooped from beneath his tweed cap.

"Try Wolf of Landshut," I said. Stennie and I had spent a lot of time fight-ing VR wars in full armor. "Nice shorts." Stennie's costume reminded me of Christopher Robin. Terminally cute.

"It's not fair," said the snowman, who I did not recognize. "He says this is what he actually looks like." The snowman was standing in a puddle which was dripping onto the rug below us. Great effect.

"No," said Stennie, "what I said was I would like this if I hadn't done something about it, okay?"

I had not known Stennie before he was a dinosaur. "No wonder you got twanked." I wished I could have saved this image, but Playroom was copy-protected.

"You've been twanked? No joke?" The great horned owl ruffled in alarm. She had a girl's voice. "I know it's none of my business, but I don't understand why anyone would do it. Especially a kid. I mean, what's wrong with good old-fashioned surgery? And you can be whoever you want in a VR." She paused, waiting for someone to agree with her. No help. "Okay, so I don't understand. But when you mess with your genes, you change who you are. I mean, don't you like who you are? *I* do."

"We're so happy for you." Stennie scowled. "What is this, mental health week?"

"We're rich," I said. "We can afford to hate ourselves."

"This may sound rude . . ." The owl's big blunt head swiveled from Stennie to me. ". . . but I think that's sad."

"Yeah well, we'll try to work up some tears for you, birdie," Stennie said.

Silence. In the East Room, the band turned the volume up.

"Anyway, I've got to be going." The owl shook herself. "Hanging upside-down is fine for bats, but not for me. Later." She let go of her perch and swooped out into the hall. The snowman turned to watch her go.

"You're driving them off, young man." I patted Stennie on the head. "Come on now, be nice."

"Nice makes me puke."

"You *do* have a bit of an edge tonight." I had trouble imagining this dainty little brat as my best friend. "Better watch out you don't cut someone."

The dog skeleton came to the doorway and called up to us. "We're supposed to dance now."

"About time." Stennie fell off the ceiling like a drop of water and splashed headfirst onto the beige Persian rug. His image went all muddy for a moment and then he re-formed, upright and unharmed. "Going to skitter, tin man?"

"I need to talk to you for a moment," the snowman murmured.

"You *need* to?" I said.

"Dance, dance, dance," sang Stennie. "Later." He swerved after the skeleton out of the room.

The snowman said, "It's about a possible theft of information."

Right then was when I should have slammed it into reverse. Caught up with Stennie or maybe faded from Playroom altogether. But all I did was raise my hands over my head. "You got me, snowman; I confess. But society is to blame, too, isn't it? You will tell the judge to go easy on me? I've had a tough life."

"This is serious."

"You're Weldon—what's your name?" Down the hall, I could hear the thud of Warhead's bass line. "Montross."

"I'll come to the point, Peter." The only acknowledgment he made was to drop the kid voice. "The firm I represent provides information security services. Last week someone operated on the protected database of one of our clients. We have reason to believe that a certified photograph was accessed and copied. What can you tell me about this?"

"Not bad, Mr. Montross sir. But if you were as good as you think you are, you'd know my name isn't Peter. It's Mr. Boy. And since nobody invited you to this party, maybe you'd better tell me now why I shouldn't just go ahead and have you deleted?"

"I know that you were undergoing genetic therapy at the time of the theft so you could not have been directly responsible. That's in your favor. However, I also know that you can help me clear this matter up. And you need to do that, son, just as quickly as you can. Otherwise there's big trouble coming."

"What are you going to do, tell my mommy?" My blood started to pump; I was coming back to life.

"This is my offer. It's not negotiable. You let me sweep your files for this image. You turn over any hardcopies you've made and you instruct your wiseguy to let me do a spot reprogramming, during which I will erase his memory of this incident. After that, we'll consider the matter closed."

"Why don't I just drop my pants and bend over while I'm at it?"

"Look, you can pretend if you want, but you're not a kid anymore. You're twenty-five years old. I don't believe for a minute that you're as thick as your friends out there. If you think about it, you'll realize that you can't fight us. The fact that I'm here and I know what I know means that all your personal information systems are already tapped. I'm an op, son. I could wipe your files clean any time and I will, if it comes to that. However, my orders are to be thorough. The only way I can be sure I have everything is if you cooperate."

"You're not even real, are you, Montross? I'll bet you're nothing but cheesy old code. I've talked to elevators with more personality."

"The offer is on the table."

"Stick it!"

The owl flew back into the room, braked with outstretched wings and caught onto the armrest of the Dolley Madison sofa. "Oh, you're still here," she said, noticing us. "I didn't mean to interrupt. . . ."

"Wait there," I said. "I'm coming right down."

"I'll be in touch," said the snowman. "Let me know just as soon as you change your mind." He faded.

I flipped backward off the ceiling and landed in front of her; my video armor rang from the impact. "Owl, you just saved the evening." I knew I was showing off, but just then I was willing to forgive myself. "Thanks."

"You're welcome, I guess." She edged away from me, moving with precise little birdlike steps toward the top of the couch. "But all I was trying to do was escape the band."

"Bad?"

"And loud." Her ear tufts flattened. "Do you think shutting the door would help?"

"Sure. Follow me. We can shut lots of doors." When she hesitated, I flapped my arms like silver wings. Actually, Montross had done me a favor; when he threatened me some inner clock had begun an adrenaline tick. If this was trouble, I wanted more. I felt twisted and dangerous and I did not care what happened next. Maybe that was why the owl flitted after me as I walked into the next room.

The sumptuous State Dining Room can seat about 130 for formal dinners. The white and gold decor dates from the administration of Theodore Roosevelt.

The owl glided over to the banquet table. I shut the door behind me. "Better?" Warhead still pounded on the walls.

"A little." She settled on a huge bronze doré centerpiece with a mirrored surface. "I'm going soon anyway."

"Why?"

"The band stinks. I don't know anyone and I hate these stupid disguises."

"I'm Mr. Boy." I raised my visor and grinned at her. "All right? Now you know someone."

She tucked her wings into place and fixed me with her owlish stare. "I don't like VRs much."

"They take some getting used to."

"Why bother?" she said. "I mean, if anything can happen in a simulation, nothing matters. And I feel dumb standing in a room all alone jumping up and down and flapping my arms. Besides, this joysuit is hot and I'm renting it by the hour."

"The trick is not to look at yourself," I said. "Just watch the screens and use your imagination."

"Reality is less work. You look like a little kid."

"Is that a problem?"

"Mr. Boy? What kind of name is that anyway?"

I wished she would blink. "A made-up name. But then all names are made up, aren't they?"

"Didn't I see you at school Wednesday? You were the one who dropped off the dinosaur."

"My friend Stennie." I pulled out a chair and sat facing her. "Who you probably hate because he's twanked."

"That was him on the ceiling, wasn't it? Listen, I'm sorry about what I said. I'm new here. I'd never met anyone like him before I came to New Canaan. I mean, I'd heard of reshaping and all—getting twanked. But where I used to live, everybody was pretty much the same."

"Where was that, Squirrel Crossing, Nebraska?"

"Close." She laughed. "Elkhart; it's in Indiana."

The reckless ticking in my head slowed. Talking to her made it easy to forget about Montross. "You want to leave the party?" I said. "We could go into discreet."

"Just us?" She sounded doubtful. "Right now?"

"Why not? You said you weren't staying. We could get rid of these disguises. And the music."

She was silent for a moment. Maybe people in Elkhart, Indiana, did not ask one another into discreet unless they had met in Sunday school or the Four H Club.

"Okay," she said finally, "but I'll enable. What's your DI?"

I gave her my number.

"Be back in a minute."

I cleared Playroom from my screens. The message *Enabling discreet mode* flashed. I decided not to change out of the joysuit; instead I called up my wardrobe menu and chose an image of myself wearing black baggies. The loose folds and padded shoulders helped hide the scrawny little boy's body.

The message changed. *Discreet mode enabled. Do you accept, yes/no?*
"Sure," I said.

She was sitting naked in the middle of a room filled with tropical plants. Her skin was the color of cinnamon. She had freckles on her shoulders and across her breasts. Her hair tumbled down the curve of her spine; the ends glowed like embers in a breeze. She clutched her legs close to her and gave me a curious smile. Teenage still life. We were alone and secure. No one could tap us while we were in discreet. We could say anything we wanted. I was too croggled to speak.

"You *are* a little kid," she said.

I did not tell her that what she was watching was an enhanced image, a virtual me. "Uh . . . well, not really." I was glad Stennie could not see me. Mr. Boy at a loss—a first. "Sometimes I'm not sure what I am. I guess you're not going to like me either. I've been stunted a couple of times. I'm really twenty-five years old."

She frowned. "You keep deciding I won't like people. Why?"

"Most people are against genetic surgery. Probably because they haven't got the money."

"Myself, I wouldn't do it. Still, just because you did doesn't mean I hate you." She gestured for me to sit. "But my parents would probably be horrified. They're realists, you know."

"No fooling?" I could not help but chuckle. "That explains a lot." Like why she had an attitude about twanking. And why she thought VRs were dumb. And why she was naked and did not seem to care. According to hardcore realists, first came clothes, then jewelry, fashion, makeup, plastic surgery, skin tints, and *hey jack,* here we are up to our eyeballs in the delusions of 2096. Gene twanking, VR addicts, people downloading themselves into computers—better never to have started. They wanted to turn back to wornout twentieth-century modes. "But you're no realist," I said. "Look at your hair."

She shook her head and the ends twinkled. "You like it?"

"It's extreme. But realists don't decorate!"

"Then maybe I'm not a realist. My parents let me try lots of stuff they wouldn't do themselves, like buying hairworks or linking to VRs. They're afraid I'd leave otherwise."

"Would you?"

She shrugged. "So what's it like to get stunted? I've heard it hurts."

I told her how sometimes I felt as if there were broken glass in my joints and how my bones ached and—more showing off—about the blood I would find on the toilet paper. Then I mentioned something about Mom. She had heard of Mom, of course. She asked about my dad and I explained how Mom paid him to stay away but that he kept running out of money. She wanted to know if I was working or still going to school and I made up some stuff about courses in history I was taking from Yale. Actually I had faded after my first semester. Couple of years ago. I did not have time to link to some boring college; I was too busy playing with Comrade and Stennie. But I still had an account at Yale.

"So that's who I am." I was amazed at how little I had lied. "Who are you?"

She told me that her name was Treemonisha but her friends called her Tree. It was an old family name; her great-great-grand-something-or-other had been a composer named Scott Joplin. Treemonisha was the name of his opera.

I had to force myself not to stare at her breasts when she talked. "You like *opera?*" I said.

"My dad says I'll grow into it." She made a face. "I hope not."

The Joplins were a franchise family; her mom and dad had just been transferred to the Green Dream, a plant shop in the Elm Street Mall. To hear her talk, you would think she had ordered them from the Good Fairy. They had been married for twenty-two years and were still together. She had a brother, Fidel, who was twelve. They all lived in the greenhouse next to the shop where they grew most of their food and where flowers were always in bloom and where everybody loved everyone else. Nice life for a bunch of mall drones. So why was she thinking of leaving?

"You should stop by sometime," she said.

"Sometime," I said. "Sure."

For hours after we faded, I kept remembering things about her I had not realized I had noticed. The fine hair on her legs. The curve of her eyebrows. The way her hands moved when she was excited.

It was Stennie's fault: after the Playroom party he started going to school almost every day. Not just linking to E-class with his comm, but actually showing up. We knew he had more than remedial reading on his mind, but no matter how much we teased, he would not talk about his mysterious new cush. Before he fell in love we used to joyride in his Alpha afternoons. Now Comrade and I had the call all to ourselves. Not as much fun.

We had already dropped Stennie off when I spotted Treemonisha waiting for the bus. I waved, she came over. The next thing I knew we had another passenger on the road to nowhere. Comrade stared vacantly out the window as we pulled onto South Street; he did not seem pleased with the company.

"Have you been out to the reservoir?" I said. "There are some extreme houses out there. Or we could drive over to Greenwich and look at yachts."

"I haven't been anywhere yet, so I don't care," she said. "By the way, you don't go to college." She was not accusing me or even asking—merely stating a fact.

"Why do you say that?" I said.

"Fidel told me."

I wondered how her twelve-year-old brother could know anything at all about me. Rumors maybe, or just guessing. Since she did not seem mad, I decided to tell the truth.

"He's right," I said, "I lied. I have an account at Yale but I haven't linked for months. Hey, you can't live without telling a few lies. At least I don't discriminate. I'll lie to anyone, even myself."

"You're bad." A smile twitched at the corners of her mouth. "So what *do* you do then?"

"I drive around a lot." I waved at the interior of Stennie's car. "Let's see . . . I go to parties. I buy stuff and use it."

"Fidel says you're rich."

"I'm going to have to meet this Fidel. Does money make a difference?"

When she nodded, her hairworks twinkled. Comrade gave me a knowing glance but I paid no attention. I was trying to figure out how she could make insults sound like compliments when I realized we were flirting. The idea took me by surprise. *Flirting.*

"Do you have any music?" Treemonisha said.

The Alpha asked what groups she liked and so we listened to some mindless dance hits as we took the circle route around the Laurel Reservoir. Treemonisha told me about how she was sick of her parents' store and rude customers and especially the dumb Green Dream uniform. "Back in Elkhart, Daddy used to make me wear it to school. Can you believe that? He said it was good advertising. When we moved, I told him either the khakis went or I did."

She had a yellow and orange dashiki over midnight blue skintights. "I like your clothes," I said. "You have taste."

"Thanks." She bobbed her head in time to the music. "I can't afford much because I can't get an outside job because I have to work for my parents. It makes me mad, sometimes. I mean, franchise life is fine for Mom and Dad; they're happy being tucked in every night by GD, Inc. But I want more. Thrills, chills—you know, adventure. No one has adventures in the mall."

As we drove, I showed her the log castle, the pyramids, the private train that pulled sleeping cars endlessly around a two-mile track and the marble bunker where Sullivan, the assassinated president, still lived on in computer memory. Comrade kept busy acting bored.

"Can we go see your mom?" said Treemonisha. "All the kids at school tell me she's awesome."

Suddenly Comrade was interested in the conversation. I was not sure what the kids at school were talking about. Probably they wished they had seen Mom but I had never asked any of them over—except for Stennie.

"Not a good idea." I shook my head. "She's more flimsy than she looks, you know, and she gets real nervous if strangers just drop by. Or even friends."

"I just want to look. I won't get out of the car."

"Well," said Comrade, "if she doesn't get out of the car, who could she hurt?"

I scowled at him. He knew how paranoid Mom was. She was not going to like Treemonisha anyway, but certainly not if I brought her home without warning. "Let me work on her, okay?" I said to Treemonisha. "One of these days. I promise."

She pouted for about five seconds and then laughed at my expression. When I saw Comrade's smirk, I got angry. He was just sitting there watching us. Looking to cause trouble. Later there would be wisecracks. I had had about enough of him and his attitude.

By that time the Alpha was heading up High Ridge Road toward Stamford. "I'm hungry," I said. "Stop at the Seven-Eleven up ahead." I pulled a cash card out and flipped it at him. "Go buy us some doboys."

I waited until he disappeared into the store and then ordered Stennie's car to drive on.

"Hey!" Treemonisha twisted in her seat and looked back at the store. "What are you doing?"

"Ditching him."

"Why? Won't he be mad?"

"He's got my card; he'll call a cab."

"But that's mean."

"So?"

Treemonisha thought about it. "He doesn't say much, does he?" She did not seem to know what to make of me—which I suppose was what I wanted. "At first I thought he was kind of like your teddy bear. Have you seen those big ones that keep little kids out of trouble?"

"He's just a wiseguy."

"Have you had him long?"

"Maybe too long."

I could not think of anything to say after that so we sat quietly listening to the music. Even though he was gone, Comrade was still aggravating me.

"Were you really hungry?" Treemonisha said finally. "Because I was. Think there's something in the fridge?"

I waited for the Alpha to tell us but it said nothing. I slid across the seat and opened the refrigerator door. Inside was a sheet of paper. "Dear Mr. Boy," it said. "If this was a bomb you and Comrade would be dead and the problem would be solved. Let's talk soon. Weldon Montross."

"What's that?"

I felt the warm flush that I always got from good corpse porn and for a moment I could not speak. "Practical joke," I said, crumpling the paper. "Too bad he doesn't have a sense of humor."

Push-ups. *Ten, eleven.*

"Uh-oh. Look at this," said Comrade.

"I'm busy!" *Twelve, thirteen, fourteen, fifteen . . . sixteen . . . seven . . .* Dizzy, I slumped and rested my cheek against the warm floor. I could feel Mom's pulse beneath the tough skin. It was no good. I would never get muscles this way. There was only one fix for my skinny arms and bony shoulders. Grow up, Mr. Boy.

"*Ya yebou!* You really should scope this," said Comrade. "Very spooky."

I pulled myself onto the bed to see why he was bothering me; he had been pretty tame since I had stranded him at the 7-Eleven. Most of the windows showed the usual: army ants next to old war movies next to feeding time from the Bronx Zoo's reptile house. But Firenet, which provided twenty-four-hour coverage of killer fires from around the world, had been replaced with a picture of a morgue. There were three naked bodies, shrouds pulled back for identification: a fat gray-haired CEO with a purple hole over his left eye, Comrade, and me.

"You look kind of dead," said Comrade.

My tongue felt thick. "Where's it coming from?"

"Viruses all over the system," he said. "Probably Montross."

"You know about him?" The image on the window changed back to a *barridas* fire in Lima.

"He's been in touch." Comrade shrugged. "Made his offer."

Crying women watched as the straw walls of their huts peeled into flame and floated away.

"Oh." I did not know what to say. I wanted to reassure him, but this was serious. Montross was invading my life and I had no idea how to fight back. "Well, don't talk to him anymore."

"Okay," Comrade grinned. "He's dull as a spoon anyway."

"I bet he's a simulation. What else would a company like Datasafe use? You can't trust real people." I was still thinking about what I would look like dead. "Whatever, he's kind of scary." I shivered, worried and aroused at the same time. "He's slick enough to operate on Playroom. And now he's hijacking windows right here in my own mom." I should probably have told Comrade then about the note in the fridge, but we were still not talking about that day.

"He tapped into Playroom?" Comrade fitted input clips to the spikes on his neck, linked and played back the house files. "*Zayebees.* He was already here then. He piggybacked on with you." Comrade slapped his leg. "I can't understand how he beat my security so easily."

The roombrain flicked the message indicator. "Stennie's calling," it said.

"Pick up," I said.

"Hi, it's that time again." Stennie was alone in his car. "I'm on my way over to give you jacks a thrill." He pushed his triangular snout up to the camera and licked at the lens. "Doing anything?"

"Not really. Sitting around."

"I'll fix that. Five minutes." He faded.

Comrade was staring at nothing.

"Look Comrade, you did your best," I said. "I'm not mad at you."

"Too plugging easy." He shook his head as if I had missed the point.

"What I don't understand is why Montross is so cranky anyway. It's just a picture of meat."

"Maybe he's not really dead."

"Sure he is," I said. "You can't fake a verification grid."

"No, but you can fake a corpse."

"You know something?"

"If I did I wouldn't tell you," said Comrade. "You have enough problems already. Like how do we explain this to your mom?"

"We don't. Not yet. Let's wait him out. Sooner or later he's got to realize that we're not going to use his picture for anything. I mean if he's that nervous, I'll even give it back. I don't care anymore. You hear that Montross, you dumbscut? We're harmless. Get out of our lives!"

"It's more than the picture now," said Comrade. "It's me. I found the way in." He was careful to keep his expression blank.

I did not know what to say to him. No way Montross would be satisfied erasing only the memory of the operation. He would probably reconnect Comrade's regulators to bring him back under control. Turn him into pudding. He would be just another wiseguy, like anyone else could own. I was surprised that Comrade did not ask me to promise not to hand him over. Maybe he just assumed I would stand by him.

We did not hear Stennie coming until he sprang into the room.

"Have fun or die!" He was clutching a plastic gun in his spindly hand which he aimed at my head.

"Stennie, *no.*"

He fired as I rolled across the bed. The jellybee buzzed by me and squished against one of the windows. It was a purple and immediately I smelled the tang of artificial grape flavor. The splatter on the wrinkled wall pulsed and split in two, emitting a second burst of grapeness. The two halves oozed in opposite directions, shivered and divided again.

"Fun extremist!" He shot Comrade with a cherry as he dove for the closet. "Dance!"

I bounced up and down on the bed, timing my move. He fired a green at me that missed. Comrade, meanwhile, gathered himself up as zits of red jellybee squirmed across his window coat. He barreled out of the closet into Stennie, knocking him sideways. I sprang on top of them and wrestled the gun away. Stennie was paralyzed with laughter. I had to giggle too, in part because now I could put off talking to Comrade about Montross.

By the time we untangled ourselves, the jellybees had faded. "Set for twelve generations before they all die out," Stennie said as he settled himself on the bed. "So what's this my car tells me, you've been giving free rides? Is this the cush with the name?"

"None of your business. You never tell me about your cush."

"Okay. Her name is Janet Hoyt."

"Is it?" He caught me off guard again. Twice in one day, a record. "Comrade, let's see this prize."

Comrade linked to the roombrain and ran a search. "Got her." He called Janet Hoyt's DI file to screen and her face ballooned across an entire window. She was a tanned blue-eyed blond with the kind of off-the-shelf looks that med students slapped onto rabbits in genoplasty courses. Nothing on her face said she was different from any other ornamental moron fresh from the OR—not a dimple or a mole, not even a freckle. "You're ditching me for her?" It took all the imagination of a potato chip to be as pretty as Janet Hoyt. "Stennie, she's generic."

"Now wait a minute," said Stennie. "If we're going to play critic, let's scope your cush, too."

Without asking, Comrade put Tree's DI photo next to Janet's. I realized he was still mad at me because of her; he was only pretending not to care. "She's not my cush," I said, but no one was listening.

Stennie leered at her for a moment. "She's stiff, isn't she?" he said. "She has that hungry look."

Seeing him standing there in front of the two huge faces on the wall, I felt like I was peeping on a stranger—that I was a stranger, too. I could not imagine how the two of us had come to this: Stennie and Mr. Boy with cushes. We were growing up. A frightening thought. Maybe next Stennie would get himself untwanked and really look like he had on Playroom. Then where would I be?

"Janet wants me to plug her," Stennie said.

"Right, and I'm the queen of Brooklyn."

"I'm old enough, you know." He thumped his tail against the floor.

"You're a dinosaur!"

"Hey, just because I got twanked doesn't mean *my* dick fell off."

"So do it then."

"I'm going to. I will, okay? But . . . this is no good." Stennie waved impatiently at Comrade. "I can't think with them watching me." He nodded at the windows. "Turn them off already."

"*N'ye pizdi!*" Comrade wiped the two faces from the windows, cleared all the screens in the room to blood red, yanked the input clips from his neck spikes, and left them dangling from the roombrain's terminal. His expression empty, he walked from the room without asking permission or saying anything at all.

"What's his problem?" Stennie said.

"Who knows?" Comrade had left the door open; I shut it. "Maybe he doesn't like girls."

"Look, I want to ask a favor." I could tell Stennie was nervous; his head kept swaying. "This is kind of embarrassing but . . . okay, do you think maybe your mom would maybe let me practice on her lovers? I don't want Janet to know I've never done it before and there's some stuff I've got to figure out."

"I don't know," I said. "Ask her."

But I did know. She would be amused.

People claimed my mom did not have a sense of humor. Lovey was huge, an ocean of a woman. Her umbilical was as big around as my thigh. When she walked waves of flesh heaved and rolled. She had beautiful skin, flawless and moist. It did not take much to make her sweat. Peeling a banana would do it. Lovey was as oral as a baby; she would put anything into her mouth. And when she did not have a mouthful, she would babble on about whatever came into Mom's head. Dear hardly ever talked, although he could moan and growl and laugh. He touched Lovey whenever he could and shot her long smouldering looks. He was not furry, exactly, but he was covered with fine silver hair. Dear was a little guy, about my size. Although he had one of Upjohn's finest penises, elastic and overloaded with neurons, he was one of the least convincing males I had ever met. I doubt Mom herself believed in him all that much.

Big chatty woman, squirrelly tongue-tied little man. It *was* funny in a bent sort of way to watch the two of them go at each other. Kind of like a tug churning against a supertanker. They did not get the chance that often. It was dangerous; Dear had to worry about getting crushed and poor Lovey's heart had stopped two or three times. Besides, I think Mom liked building up the pressure. Sometimes, as the days without sex stretched, you could almost feel lust sparkling off them like static electricity.

That was how they were when I brought Stennie up. Their suite took up the entire floor at the hips, Mom's widest part. Lovey was lolling in a tub of warm oil. She liked it flowery and laced with pheromones. Dear was prowling around her with a desperate expression, like he might jam his plug into a wall socket if he did not get taken care of soon. Stennie's timing was perfect.

"Look who's come to visit, Dear," said Lovey. "Peter and Stennie. How nice of you boys to stop by." She let Dear mop her forehead with a towel. "What can we do for you?"

The skin under Stennie's jaw quivered. He glanced at me, then at Dear and then at the thick red lips that served as the bathroom door. Never even looked at her. He was losing his nerve.

"Oh my, isn't this exciting, Dear? There's something going on." She sank into the bath until her chin touched the water. "It's a secret, isn't it, Peter? Share it with Lovey."

"No secret," I said, "he wants to ask a favor." And then I told her.

She giggled and sat up. "I love it." Honey-colored oil ran from her hair and slopped between her breasts. "Were you thinking of both of us, Stennie? Or just me?"

"Well, I . . ." Stennie's tail switched. "Maybe we just ought to forget it."

"No, no." She waved a hand at him. "Come here, Stennie. Come close, my pretty little monster."

He hesitated, then approached the tub. She reached for his right leg and touched him just above the heelknob. "You know, I've always wondered what scales would feel like." Her hand climbed; the oil made his yellow hide glisten. His eyes were the size of eggs.

The bedroom was all mattress. Beneath the transparent skin was a screen implant, so that Mom could project images not only on the walls but on the surface of the bed itself. Under the window was a layer of heavily vascular flesh, which could be stiffened with blood or drained until it was soft as raw steak. A window dome arched over everything and could show slo-mo or thermographic fx across its span. The air was warm and wet and smelled like a chemical engineer's idea of a rose garden.

I settled by the lips. Dear ghosted along the edges of the room, dragging his umbilical like a chain, never coming quite near enough to touch anyone. I heard him humming as he passed me, a low moaning singsong, as if to block out what was happening. Stennie and Lovey were too busy with each other to care. As Lovey knelt in front of Stennie, Dear gave a mocking laugh. I did not understand how he could be jealous. He was with her, part of it. Lovey and Dear were Mom's remotes, two nodes of her nervous system. Yet his pain was as obvious as her pleasure. At last he squatted and rocked back and forth on his heels. I glanced up at the fx dome; yellow scales slid across oily rolls of flushed skin.

I yawned. I had always found sex kind of dull. Besides, this was all on the record. I could have Comrade replay it for me any time. Lovey stopped breathing—then came four or five shuddering gasps in a row. I wondered where Comrade had gone. I felt sorry for him. Stennie said something to her about rolling over. "Okay?" Feathery skin sounds. A grunt. The soft wet slap of flesh against flesh. I thought of my mother's brain, up there in the head where no one ever went. I had no idea how much attention she was paying. Was she quivering with Lovey and at the same time calculating insolation rates on her chloroplasts? Investing in soy futures on the Chicago Board of Trade? Fending off Weldon Montross's latest attack? *Plug Montross.* I needed to think about something fun. My collection. I started piling bodies up in my mind. The hangings and the open casket funerals and the stacks of dead at the camps and all those muddy soldiers. I shivered as I remembered the empty rigid faces. I liked it when their teeth showed. "Oh, oh, *oh!*" My greatest hits dated from the late twentieth century. The dead were everywhere back then, in vids and the news and even on T-shirts. They were not shy. That was what made Comrade's photo worth having; it was hard to find modern stuff that dirty. Dear brushed by me, his erection bobbing in front of him. It was as big around as my wrist. As he passed I could see Stennie's leg scratch across the mattress skin, which glowed with blood blue light. Lovey giggled beneath him and her umbilical twitched and suddenly I found myself wondering whether Tree was a virgin.

I came into the mall through the Main Street entrance and hopped the west-bound slidewalk headed up Elm Street toward the train station. If I caught the

3:36 to Grand Central, I could eat dinner in Manhattan, far from my problems with Montross and Comrade. Running away had always worked for me before. Let someone else clean up the mess while I was gone.

The slidewalk carried me past a real estate agency, a flash bar, a jewelry store, and a Baskin-Robbins. I thought about where I wanted to go after New York. San Francisco? Montreal? Maybe I should try Elkhart, Indiana—no one would think to look for me there. Just ahead, between a drugstore and a take-out Russian restaurant, was the wiseguy dealership where Mom had bought Comrade.

I did not want to think about Comrade waiting for me to come home, so I stepped into the drugstore and bought a dose of Carefree for $4.29. Normally I did not bother with drugs. I had been stunted; no over-the-counter flash could compare to that. But the propyl dicarbamates were all right. I fished the cash card out of my pocket and handed it to the stiff behind the counter. He did a doubletake when he saw the denomination, then carefully inserted the card into the reader to deduct the cost of the Carefree. It had my mom's name on it; he must have expected it would trip some alarm for counterfeit plastic or stolen credit. He stared at me for a moment, as if trying to remember my face so he could describe me to a cop, and then gave the cash card back. The denomination readout said it was still good for $16,381.18.

I picked out a bench in front of a specialty shop called The Happy Hippo, hiked up my shorts and poked Carefree into the widest part of my thigh. I took a short dreamy swim in the sea of tranquility and when I came back to myself, my guilt had been washed away. But so had my energy. I sat for a while and scoped the display of glass hippos and plastic hippos and fuzzy stuffed hippos, hippo vids and sheets and candles. Down the bench from me a homeless woman dozed. It was still pretty early in the season for a weather gypsy to have come this far north. She wore red shorts and droopy red socks with plastic sandals and four long-sleeved shirts, all unbuttoned, over a Funny Honey halter top. Her hair needed vacuuming and she smelled old. All grownups smelled that way to me; it was something I had never gotten used to. No perfume or deodorant could cover up the leathery stink of adulthood. Kids could smell bad, too, but usually from something they got on them. It did not come from a rotting body. I rubbed a finger in the dampness under my arm, slicked it and sniffed. There was a sweetness to kid sweat. I touched the drying finger to my tongue. You could even taste it. If I gave up getting stunted, stopped being Mr. Boy, I would smell like the woman at the end of the bench. I would start to die. I had never understood how grownups could live with that.

The gypsy woke up, stretched and smiled at me with gummy teeth. "You left Comrade behind?" she said.

I was startled. "What did you say?"

"You know what this is?" She twitched her sleeve and a penlight appeared in her hand.

My throat tightened. "I know what it looks like."

She gave me a wicked smile, aimed the penlight and burned a pinhole through the bench a few centimeters from my leg. "Maybe I could interest you in some free laser surgery?"

I could smell scorched plastic. "You're going to needle me here, in the middle of the Elm Street Mall?" I thought she was bluffing. Probably. I hoped.

"If that's the way you want it. Mr. Montross wants to know when you're delivering the wiseguy to us."

"Get away from me."

"Not until you do what needs to be done."

When I saw Happy Lurdane come out of The Happy Hippo, I waved. A desperation move, but then it was easy to be brave with a head full of Carefree.

"Mr. Boy." She veered over to us. "Hi!"

I scooted farther down the bench to make room for her between me and the gypsy. I knew she would stay to chat. Happy Lurdane was one of those chirpy lightweights who seemed to want lots of friends but did not really try to be one. We tolerated her because she did not mind being snubbed and she threw great parties.

"Where have you been?" She settled beside me. "Haven't seen you in ages." The penlight disappeared and the gypsy fell back into drowsy character.

"Around."

"Want to see what I just bought?"

I nodded. My heart was hammering.

She opened the bag and took out a fist-sized bundle covered with shipping plastic. She unwrapped a statue of a blue hippopotamus. "Be careful." She handed it to me.

"Cute." The hippo had crude flower designs drawn on its body; it was chipped and cracked.

"Ancient Egyptian. That means it's even *before* antique." She pulled a slip from the bag and read. "Twelfth Dynasty, 1991–1786 B.C. Can you believe you can just buy something like that here in the mall? I mean it must be like a thousand years old or something."

"Try four thousand."

"No wonder it cost so much. He wasn't going to sell it to me, so I had to spend some of next month's allowance." She took it from me and rewrapped it. "It's for the smash party tomorrow. You're coming, aren't you?"

"Maybe."

"Is something wrong?"

I ignored that.

"Hey, where's Comrade? I don't think I've ever seen you two apart before."

I decided to take a chance. "Want to get some doboys?"

"*Sure.*" She glanced at me with delighted astonishment. "Are you sure you're all right?"

I took her arm, maneuvering to keep her between me and the gypsy. If Happy got needled it would be no great loss to western civilization. She babbled on about her party as we stepped onto the westbound slidewalk. I turned to look back. The gypsy waved as she hopped the eastbound.

"Look Happy," I said, "I'm sorry, but I changed my mind. Later, okay?"

"But . . ."

I did not stop for an argument. I darted off the slidewalk and sprinted through the mall to the station. I went straight to a ticket window, shoved the cash card under the grille and asked the agent for a one way to Grand Central. Forty thousand people live in New Canaan; most of them had heard of me because of my mom. Nine million strangers jammed New York City; it was a good place to disappear. The agent had my ticket in her hand when the reader beeped and spat the card out.

"No!" I slammed my fist on the counter. "Try it again." The cash card was guaranteed by AmEx to be secure. And it had just worked at the drugstore.

She glanced at the card, then slid it back under the grille. "No use." The denomination readout flashed alternating messages: *Voided* and *Bank recall.* "You've got trouble, son."

She was right. As I left the station, I felt the Carefree struggle one last time with my dread—and lose. I did not even have the money to call home. I wandered around for a while, dazed, and then I was standing in front of the flower shop in the Elm Street Mall.

GREEN DREAM

CONTEMPORARY AND CONVENTIONAL PLANTS

I had telelinked with Tree every day since our drive and every day she had asked me over. But I was not ready to meet her family; I suppose I was still trying to pretend she was not a stiff. I wavered at the door now, breathing the cool scent of damp soil in clay pots. The gypsy could come after me again; I might be putting these people in danger. Using Happy as a shield was one thing, but I liked Tree. A lot. I backed away and peered through a window fringed with sweat and teeming with bizarre plants with flame-colored tongues. Someone wearing khaki moved. I could not tell if it was Tree or not. I thought of what she had said about no one having adventures in the mall.

The front of the showroom was a green cave, darker than I had expected. Baskets dripping with bright flowers hung like stalactites; leathery-leaved understory plants formed stalagmites. As I threaded my way toward the back I came upon the kid I had seen wearing the Green Dream uniform, a khaki nightmare of pleats and flaps and brass buttons and about six too many pockets. He was misting leaves with a pump bottle filled with blue liquid. I decided he must be the brother.

"Hi," I said. "I'm looking for Treemonisha."

Fidel was shorter than me and darker than his sister. He had a wiry plush of beautiful black hair that I was immediately tempted to touch.

"Are you?" He eyed me as if deciding how hard I would be to beat up, then he smiled. He had crooked teeth. "You don't look like yourself."

"No?"

"What are you, scared? You're whiter than rice, cashman. Don't worry, the stiffs won't hurt you." Laughing, he feinted a punch at my arm; I was not reassured.

"You're Fidel."

"I've seen your DI files," he said. "I asked around. I know about you. So don't be telling my sister any more lies, understand?" He snapped his fingers in my face. "Behave yourself, cashman, and we'll be fine." He still had the boyish excitability I had lost after the first stunting. "She's out back, so first you have to get by the old man."

The rear of the store was brighter; sunlight streamed through the clear krylac roof. There was a counter and behind it a glass-doored refrigerator filled with cut flowers. A side entrance opened to the greenhouse. Mrs. Schlieman, one of Mom's lawyers who had an office in the mall, was deciding what to buy. She was shopping with her wiseguy secretary, who looked like he had just stepped out of a vodka ad.

"Wait." Fidel rested a hand on my shoulder. "I'll tell her you're here."

"But how long will they last?" Mrs. Schlieman sniffed a frilly yellow flower. "I should probably get the duraroses."

"Whatever you want, Mrs. Schlieman. Duraroses are a good product; I sell them by the truckload," said Mr. Joplin with a chuckle. "But these carnations are real flowers, raised here in my greenhouse. So maybe you can't stick them in your dishwasher, but put some where people can touch and smell them and I guarantee you'll get compliments."

"Why Peter Cage," said Mrs. Schlieman. "Is that you? I haven't seen you since the picnic. How's your mother?" She did not introduce her wiseguy.

"Extreme," I said.

She nodded absently. "That's nice. All right then, Mr. Joplin, give me a dozen of your carnations—and two dozen yellow duraroses."

Mrs. Schlieman chatted politely at me while Tree's father wrapped the order. He was a short, rumpled, balding man who smiled too much. He seemed to like wearing the corporate uniform. Anyone else would have fixed the hair and the wrinkles. Not Mr. Joplin; he was a museum-quality throwback. As he took Mrs. Schlieman's cash card from the wiseguy, he beamed at me over his glasses. Glasses!

When Mrs. Schlieman left, so did the smile. "Peter Cage?" he said. "Is that your name?"

"Mr. Boy is my name, sir."

"You're Tree's new friend." He nodded. "She's told us about you. She's doing chores just now. You know, we have to work for a living here."

Sure, and I knew what he left unsaid: *unlike you, you spoiled little freak.* It was always the same with these stiffs. I walked in the door and already they hated me. At least he was not pretending, like Mrs. Schlieman. I gave him two points for honesty and kept my mouth shut.

"What is it you want here, Peter?"

"Nothing, sir." If he was going to "Peter" me, I was going to "sir" him right back. "I just stopped by to say hello. Treemonisha did invite me, sir, but if you'd rather I left . . ."

"No, no. Tree warned us you might come."

She and Fidel raced into the room as if they were afraid their father and I would already be at each other's throats. "Oh hi, Mr. Boy," she said.

Her father snorted at the sound of my name.

"Hi." I grinned at her. It was the easiest thing I had done that day.

She was wearing her uniform. When she saw that I had noticed, she blushed. "Well, you asked for it." She tugged self-consciously at the waist of her fatigues. "You want to come in?"

"Just a minute." Mr. Joplin stepped in front of the door, blocking our escape. "You finished E-class?"

"Yes."

"Checked the flats?"

"I'm almost done."

"After that you'd better pick some dinner and get it started. Your mama called and said she wouldn't be home until six-fifteen."

"Sure."

"And you'll take orders for me on line two?"

She leaned against the counter and sighed. "Do I have a choice?"

He backed away and waved us through. "Sorry, sweetheart. I don't know how we would get along without you." He caught her brother by the shirt. "Not you, Fidel. You're misting, remember?"

A short tunnel ran from their mall storefront to the rehabbed furniture warehouse build over the Amtrack rails. Green Dream had installed a krylac roof and fans and a grolighting system; the Joplins squeezed themselves into the left-over spaces not filled with inventory. The air in the greenhouse was heavy and warm and it smelled like rain. No walls, no privacy other than that provided by the plants.

"Here's where I sleep." Tree sat on her unmade bed. Her space was formed by a cinder block wall painted yellow and a screen of palms. "Chinese fan, bamboo, lady, date, kentia," she said, naming them for me like they were her pets. "I grow them myself for spending money." Her schoolcomm was on top of her dresser. Several drawers hung open; pink skintights trailed from one. Clothes were scattered like piles of leaves across the floor. "I guess I'm kind of a slob," she said as she stripped off the uniform, wadded it and then banked it off the dresser into the top drawer. I could see her bare back in the mirror plastic taped to the wall. "Take your things off if you want."

I hesitated.

"Or not. But it's kind of muggy to stay dressed. You'll sweat."

I unvelcroed my shirt. I did not mind seeing Tree without clothes. But I did not undress for anyone except the stiffs at the clinic. I stepped out of my pants. Being naked somehow had got connected with being helpless. I had this puckery feeling in my dick, like it was going to curl up and die. I could imagine the gypsy popping out from behind a palm and laughing at me. No, I was not going to think about *that*. Not here.

"Comfortable?" said Tree.

"Sure." My voice was turning to dust in my throat. "Do all Green Dream employees run around the back room in the nude?"

"I doubt it." She smiled as if the thought tickled her. "We're not exactly your average mall drones. Come help me finish the chores."

I was glad to let her lead so that she was not looking at me, although I could still watch her. I was fascinated by the sweep of her buttocks, the curve of her spine. She strolled, flatfooted and at ease, through her private jungle. At first I scuttled along on the balls of my feet, ready to dart behind a plant if anyone came. But after a while I decided to stop being so skittish. I realized I would probably survive being naked.

Tree stopped in front of a workbench covered with potted seedlings in plastic trays and picked up a hose from the floor.

"What's this stuff?" I kept to the opposite side of the bench, using it to cover myself.

"Greens." She lifted a seedling to check the water level in the tray beneath.

"What are greens?"

"It's too boring." She squirted some water in and replaced the seedling.

"Tell me, I'm interested."

"In greens? You liar." She glanced at me and shook her head. "Okay." She pointed as she said the names. "Lettuce, spinach, pak choi, chard, kale, rocket—got that? And a few tomatoes over there. Peppers, too. GD is trying to break into the food business. They think people will grow more of their own if they find out how easy it is."

"Is it?"

"Greens are." She inspected the next tray. "Just add water."

"Yeah, sure."

"It's because they've been photosynthetically enhanced. Bigger leaves arranged better, low respiration rates. They teach us this stuff at GD Family Camp. It's what we do instead of vacation." She squashed something between her thumb and forefinger. "They mix all these bacteria that make their own fertilizer into the soil—fix nitrogen right out of the air. And then there's this other stuff that sticks to the roots, rhizobacteria and mycorrhizae." She finished the last tray and coiled the hose. "These flats will produce under candlelight in a closet. Bored yet?"

"How do they taste?"

"Pretty bland, most of them. Some stink, like kale and rocket. But we have to eat them for the good of the corporation." She stuck her tongue out. "You want to stay for dinner?"

Mrs. Joplin made me call home before she would feed me; she refused to understand that my mom did not care. So I linked, asked Mom to send a car to the back door at eight-thirty, and faded. No time to discuss the missing sixteen thousand.

Dinner was from the cookbook Tree had been issued at camp: a bowl of cold bean soup, fresh corn bread, and chard and cheese loaf. She let me help her make it, even though I had never cooked before. I was amazed at how simple corn bread was. Six ingredients: flour, corn meal, baking powder, milk, oil, and ovobinder. Mix and pour into a greased pan. Bake twenty minutes at 220 Celsius and serve! There is nothing magic or even very mysterious about home-made corn bread, except for the way its smell held me spellbound.

Supper was the Joplins' daily meal together. They ate in front of security windows near the tunnel to the store; when a customer came, someone ran out front. According to contract, they had to stay open twenty-four hours a day. Many of the suburban malls had gone to all-night operation; the competition from New York City was deadly. Mr. Joplin stood duty most of the time, but since they were a franchise family everybody took turns. Even Mrs. Joplin, who also worked part-time as a factfinder at the mall's DataStop.

Tree's mother was plump and graying and she had a smile that was almost bright enough to distract me from her naked body. She seemed harmless, except that she knew how to ask questions. After all, her job was finding out stuff for DataShop customers. She had this way of locking onto you as you talked; the longer the conversation, the greater her intensity. It was hard to lie to her. Normally that kind of aggressiveness in grownups made me jumpy.

No doubt she had run a search on me; I wondered just what she had turned up. Factfinders had to obey the law, so they only accessed public domain information—unlike Comrade, who would cheerfully operate on whatever I set him to. The Joplins' bank records, for instance. I knew that Mrs. Joplin had made about $11,000 last year at the Infomat in the Elkhart Mall, that the family borrowed $135,000 at 9.78 percent interest to move to their new franchise and that they lost $213 in their first two months in New Canaan.

I kept my research a secret, of course, and they acted innocent, too. I let them pump me about Mom as we ate. I was used to being asked; after all, Mom was famous. Fidel wanted to know how much it had cost her to get twanked, how big she was, what she looked like on the inside and what she ate, if she got cold in the winter. Stuff like that. The others asked more personal questions. Tree wondered if Mom ever got lonely and whether she was going to be the Statue of Liberty for the rest of her life. Mrs. Joplin was interested in Mom's re-motes, of all things. Which ones I got along with, which ones I could not stand, whether I thought any of them was really her. Mr. Joplin asked if she liked be-ing what she was. How was I supposed to know?

After dinner, I helped Fidel clear the table. While we were alone in the kitchen, he complained. "You think they eat this shit at GD headquarters?" He scraped his untouched chard loaf into the composter.

"I kind of liked the corn bread."

"If only he'd buy meat once in a while, but he's too cheap. Or doboys. Tree says you bought her doboys."

I told him to skip school some time and we would go out for lunch; he thought that was a great idea.

When we came back out, Mr. Joplin actually smiled at me. He had been los-ing his edge all during dinner. Maybe chard agreed with him. He pulled a pipe from his pocket, began stuffing something into it and asked me if I followed baseball. I told him no. Paintball? No. Basketball? I said I watched dino fights sometimes.

"His pal is the dinosaur that goes to our school," said Fidel.

"He may look like a dinosaur, but he's really a boy," said Mr. Joplin, as if making an important distinction. "The dinosaurs died out millions of years ago."

"Humans aren't allowed in dino fights," I said, just to keep the conversation going. "Only twanked dogs and horses and elephants."

Silence. Mr. Joplin puffed on his pipe and then passed it to his wife. She watched the glow in the bowl through half-lidded eyes as she inhaled. Fidel caught me staring.

"What's the matter? Don't you get twisted?" He took the pipe in his turn.

I was so croggled I did not know what to say. Even the Marleys had switched to THC inhalers. "But smoking is bad for you." It smelled like a dirty sock had caught fire.

"Hemp is ancient. Natural." Mr. Joplin spoke in a clipped voice as if swal-lowing his words. "Opens the mind to what's real." When he sighed, smoke poured out of his nose. "We grow it ourselves, you know."

I took the pipe when Tree offered it. Even before I brought the stem to my mouth, the world tilted and I watched myself slide into what seemed very much like an hallucination. Here I was sitting around naked, in the mall, with a bunch of stiffs, smoking antique drugs. And I was enjoying myself. Incredible. I in-haled and immediately the flash hit me; it was as if my brain were an enormous bud, blooming inside my head.

"Good stuff." I laughed smoke and then began coughing.

Fidel refilled my glass with ice water. "Have a sip, cashman."

"Customer." Tree pointed at the window.

"Leave!" Jr. Joplin waved impatiently at him. "Go away." The man on the screen knelt and turned over the price tag on a fern. "Damn." He jerked his uniform from the hook by the door, pulled on the khaki pants and was slithering into the shirt as he disappeared down the tunnel.

"So is Green Dream trying to break into the flash market, too?" I handed the pipe to Mrs. Joplin. There was a fleck of ash on her left breast.

"What we do back here is our business," she said. "We work hard so we can live the way we want." Tree was studying her fingerprints. I realized I had said the wrong thing so I shut up. Obviously, the Joplins were drifting from the lifestyle taught at Green Dream Family Camp.

Fidel announced he was going to school tomorrow and Mrs. Joplin told him no, he could link to E-class as usual, and Fidel claimed he could not concentrate at home, and Mrs. Joplin said he was trying to get out of his chores. While they were arguing, Tree nudged my leg and shot me a *let's leave* look. I nodded.

"Excuse us." She pushed back her chair. "Mr. Boy has got to go home soon."

Mrs. Joplin pointed for her to stay. "You wait until your father gets back," she said. "Tell me, Mr. Boy, have you lived in New Canaan long?"

"All my life," I said.

"How old did you say you were?"

"Mama, he's twenty-five," said Tree. "I told you."

"And what do you do for a living?"

"*Mama,* you promised."

"Nothing," I said. "I'm lucky, I guess. I don't need to worry about money. If you didn't need to work, would you?"

"Everybody needs work to do," Mrs. Joplin said. "Work makes us real. Unless you have work to do and people who love you, you don't exist."

Talk about twentieth-century humanist goop! At another time in another place, I probably would have snapped, but now the words would not come. My brain had turned into a flower; all I could think were daisy thoughts. The Joplins were such a strange combination of fast-forward and rewind. I could not tell what they wanted from me.

"Seventeen dollars and ninety-nine cents," said Mr. Joplin, returning from the storefront. "What's going on in here?" He glanced at his wife and some signal which I did not catch passed between them. He circled the table, came up behind me, and laid his heavy hands on my shoulders. I shuddered; I thought for a moment he meant to strangle me.

"I'm not going to hurt you, Peter," he said. "Before you go I have something to say."

"*Daddy.*" Tree squirmed in her chair. Fidel looked uncomfortable, too, as if he guessed what was coming.

"Sure." I did not have much choice.

The weight on my shoulders eased but did not entirely go away. "You should feel the ache in this boy, Ladonna."

"I know," said Mrs. Joplin.

"Hard as plastic." Mr. Joplin touched the muscles corded along my neck. "You get too hard, you snap." He set his thumbs at the base of my skull and kneaded with an easy circular motion. "Your body isn't some machine that you've downloaded into. It's alive. Real. You have to learn to listen to it. That's why we smoke. Hear these muscles? They're screaming." He let his hand slide down my shoulders. "Now listen." His fingertips probed along my upper spine. "Hear that? Your muscles stay tense because you don't trust anyone. You always have to be ready to take a hit and you can't tell where it's coming from. You're rigid and angry and scared. Reality . . . your body is speaking to you."

His voice was as big and warm as his hands. Tree was giving him a look that could boil water but the way he touched me made too much sense to resist.

"We don't mind helping you ease the strain. That's the way Mrs. Joplin and I are. That's the way we brought the kids up. But first you have to admit you're hurting. And then you have to respect us enough to take what we have to give. I don't feel that in you, Peter. You're not ready to give up your pain. You just want us poor stiffs to admire how hard it's made you. We haven't got time for that kind of shit, okay? You learn to listen to yourself and you'll be welcome around here. We'll even call you Mr. Boy, even though it's a damn stupid name."

No one spoke for a moment.

"Sorry, Tree," he said. "We've embarrassed you again. But we love you, so you're stuck with us." I could feel it in his hands when he chuckled. "I suppose I do get carried away sometimes."

"*Sometimes?*" said Fidel. Tree just smouldered.

"It's late," said Mrs. Joplin. "Let him go now, Jamaal. His mama's sending a car over."

Mr. Joplin stepped back and I almost fell off my chair from leaning back against him. I stood, shakily. "Thanks for dinner."

Tree stalked through the greenhouse to the rear exit, her hairworks glittering against her bare back. I had to trot to keep up with her. There was no car in sight so we waited at the doorway and I put on my clothes.

"I can't take much more of this." She stared through the little wire glass window in the door, like a prisoner plotting her escape. "I mean, he's *not* a psychologist or a great philosopher or whatever the hell he thinks he is. He's just a pompous mall drone."

"He's not that bad." Actually, I understood what her father had said to me; it was scary. "I like your family."

"You don't have to live with them!" She kept watching at the door. "They promised they'd behave with you; I should have known better. This happens every time I bring someone home." She puffed an imaginary pipe, imitating her father. "Think what you're doing to yourself, you poor fool, and say, isn't it just too bad about modern life? Love, love, love—*fuck!*" She turned to me. "I'm sick of it. People are going to think I'm as sappy and thickheaded as my parents."

"I don't."

"You're lucky. You're rich and your mom leaves you alone. You're New Canaan. My folks are Elkhart, Indiana."

"Being New Canaan is nothing to brag about. So what are you?"

"Not a Joplin." She shook her head. "Not much longer, anyway; I'm eighteen in February. I think your car's here." She held out her arms and hugged me good-bye. "Sorry you had to sit through that. Don't drop me, okay? I like you, Mr. Boy." She did not let go for a while.

Dropping her had never occurred to me; I was not thinking of anything at all except the silkiness of her skin, the warmth of her body. Her breath whispered through my hair and her nipples brushed my ribs and then she kissed me. Just on the cheek but the damage was done. I was stunted. I was not supposed to feel this way about anyone.

Comrade was waiting in the backseat. We rode home in silence; I had nothing to say to him. He would not understand—none of my friends would. They would warn me that all she wanted was to spend some of my money. Or they would make bad jokes about the nudity or the Joplins' mushy realism. No way I could explain the innocence of the way they touched one another. *The old man did what to you?* Yeah, and if I wanted a hug at home who was I supposed to ask? Comrade? Lovey? The greeter? Was I supposed to climb up to the head and fall asleep against Mom's doorbone, waiting for it to open, like I used to do when I was really a kid?

The greeter was her usual nonstick self when I got home. She was so glad to see me and she wanted to know where I had been and if I had a good time and if I wanted Cook to make me a snack? Around. Yes. No.

She said the bank had called about some problem with one of the cash cards she had given me, a security glitch which they had taken care of and were very sorry about. Did I know about it and did I need a new card and would twenty thousand be enough? Yes. Please. Thanks.

And that was it. I found myself resenting Mom because she did not have to care about losing sixteen or twenty or fifty thousand dollars. And she had reminded me of my problems when all I wanted to think of was Tree. She was no help to me, never had been. I had things so twisted around that I almost told her about Montross myself, just to get a reaction. Here some guy had tapped our files and threatened my life and she asked if I wanted a snack. Why keep me around if she was going to pay so little attention? I wanted to shock her, to make her take me seriously.

But I did not know how.

The roombrain woke me. "Stennie's calling."

"Mmm."

"Talk to me, Mr. Party Boy." A window opened; he was in his car. "You dead or alive?"

"Asleep." I rolled over. "Time is it?"

"Ten-thirty and I'm bored. Want me to come get you now or should I meet you there?"

"Wha . . . ?"

"Happy's. Don't tell me you forgot. They're doing a *piano*."

"Who cares?" I crawled out of bed and dropped into the bathroom.

"She says she's asking Tree Joplin," Stennie called after me.

"Asking her what?" I came out.

"To the party."

"Is she going?"

"She's your cush." He gave me a toothy smile. "Call back when you're ready. Later." He faded.

"She left a message," said the roombrain. "Half hour ago."

"Tree? You got me up for Stennie and not for her?"

"He's on the list, she's not. Happy called, too."

"Comrade should've told you. Where is he?" Now I was grouchy. "She's on the list, okay? Give me playback."

Tree seemed pleased with herself. "Hi, this is me. I got myself invited to a smash party this afternoon. You want to go?" She faded.

"That's all? Call her!"

"Both her numbers are busy; I'll set redial. I found Comrade; he's on another line. You want Happy's message?"

"No. Yes."

"You promised, Mr. Boy." Happy giggled. "Look, you really, really don't want to miss this. Stennie's coming and he said I should ask Joplin if I wanted you here. So you've got no excuse."

Someone tugged at her. "Stop that! Sorry, I'm being molested by a thick . . ." She batted at her assailant. "Mr. Boy, did I tell you that this Japanese reporter is coming to shoot a vid? What?" She turned off camera. "Sure, just like on the nature channel. Wildlife of America. We're all going to be famous. In Japan! This is history, Mr. Boy. And you're . . ."

Her face froze as the redial program finally linked to the Green Dream. The roombrain brought Tree up in a new window. "Oh hi," she said. "You rich boys sleep late."

"What's this about Happy's?"

"She invited me." Tree was recharging her hairworks with a red brush. "I said yes. Something wrong?"

Comrade slipped into the room; I shushed him. "You sure you want to go to a smash party? Sometimes they get a little crazy."

She aimed the brush at me. "You've been to smash parties before. You survived."

"Sure, but . . ."

"Well, I haven't. All I know is that everybody at school is talking about this one and I want to see what it's about."

"You tell your parents you're going?"

"Are you kidding? They'd just say it was too dangerous. What's the matter, Mr. Boy, are you scared? Come on, it'll be extreme."

"She's right. You *should* go," said Comrade.

"Is that Comrade?" Tree said. "You tell him, Comrade!"

I glared at him. "Okay, okay, I guess I'm outnumbered. Stennie said he'd drive. You want us to pick you up?"

She did.

I flew at Comrade as soon as Tree faded. "Don't you ever do that again!" I shoved him and he bumped up against the wall. "I ought to throw you to Montross."

"You know, I just finished chatting with him." Comrade stayed calm and made no move to defend himself. "He wants to meet—the three of us, face to face. He suggested Happy's."

"He suggested . . . I told you not to talk to him."

"I know." He shrugged. "Anyway, I think we should do it."

"Who gave you permission to think?"

"You did. What if we give him the picture back and open our files and then

I grovel, say I'm sorry, it'll never happen again, blah, blah, blah. Maybe we can even buy him off. What have we got to lose?"

"You can't bribe software. And what if he decides to snatch us?" I told Comrade about the gypsy with the penlight. "You want Tree mixed up in this?"

All the expression drained from his face. He did not say anything at first but I had watched his subroutines long enough to know that when he looked this blank, he was shaken. "So we take a risk, maybe we can get it over with," he said. "He's not interested in Tree and I won't let anything happen to you. Why do you think your mom bought me?"

Happy Lurdane lived on the former estate of Philip Johnson, a notorious twentieth-century architect. In his will Johnson had arranged to turn his compound into the Philip Johnson Memorial Museum, but after he died his work went out of fashion. The glass skyscrapers in the cities did not age well; they started to fall apart or were torn down because they wasted energy. Nobody visited the museum and it went bankrupt. The Lurdanes had bought the property and made some changes.

Johnson had designed all the odd little buildings on the estate himself. The main house was a shoebox of glass with no inside walls; near it stood a windowless brick guest house. On a pond below was a dock that looked like a Greek temple. Past the circular swimming pool near the houses were two galleries which had once held Johnson's art collection, long since sold off. In Johnson's day, the scattered buildings had been connected only by paths, which made the compound impossible in the frosty Connecticut winters. The Lurdanes had enclosed the paths in clear tubes and commuted in a golf cart.

Stennie told his Alpha not to wait, since the lot was already full and cars were parked well down the driveway. Five of us squeezed out of the car: me, Tree, Comrade, Stennie, and Janet Hoyt. Janet wore a Yankees jersey over pinstriped shorts, Tree was a little overdressed in her silver jaunts, I had on baggies padded to make me seem bigger, and Comrade wore his usual window coat. Stennie lugged a box with his swag for the party.

Freddy the Teddy let us in. "Stennie and Mr. Boy!" He reared back on his hindquarters and roared. "Glad I'm not going to be the only beastie here. Hi, Janet. Hi, I'm Freddy," he said to Tree. His pink tongue lolled. "Come in, this way. Fun starts right here. Some kids are swimming and there's sex in the guest house. Everybody else is with Happy having lunch in the sculpture gallery."

The interior of the Glass House was bright and hard. Dark wood block floor, some unfriendly furniture, huge panes of glass framed in black painted steel. The few kids in the kitchen were passing an inhaler around and watching a microwave fill up with popcorn.

"I'm hot." Janet stuck the inhaler into her face and pressed. "Anybody want to swim? Tree?"

"Okay." Tree breathed in a polite dose and breathed out a giggle. "You?" she asked me.

"I don't think so." I was too nervous: I kept expecting someone to jump out and throw a net over me. "I'll watch."

"I'd swim with you," said Stennie, "but I promised Happy I'd bring her these party favors as soon as I arrived." He nudged the box with his foot. "Can you wait a few minutes?"

"Comrade and I will take them over." I grabbed the box and headed for the door, glad for the excuse to leave Tree behind while I went to find Montross. "Meet you at the pool."

The golf cart was gone so we walked through the tube toward the sculpture gallery. "You have the picture?" I said.

Comrade patted the pocket of his window coat.

The tube was not air-conditioned and the afternoon sun pounded us through the optical plastic. There was no sound inside; even our footsteps were swallowed by the astroturf. The box got heavier. We passed the entrance to the old painting gallery, which looked like a bomb shelter. Finally I had to break the silence. "I feel strange, being here," I said. "Not just because of the thing with Montross. I really think I lost myself last time I got stunted. Not sure who I am anymore, but I don't think I belong with these kids."

"People change, *tovarisch,*" said Comrade. "Even you."

"Have I changed?"

He smiled. "Now that you've got a cush, your own mother wouldn't recognize you."

"You know what your problem is?" I grinned and bumped up against him on purpose. "You're jealous of Tree."

"Shouldn't I be?"

"Oh, I don't know. I can't tell if Tree likes who I was or who I might be. She's changing, too. She's so hot to break away from her parents, become part of this town. Except that what she's headed for probably isn't worth the trip. I feel like I should protect her, but that means guarding her from people like me, except I don't think I'm Mom's Mr. Boy anymore. Does that make sense?"

"Sure." He gazed straight ahead but all the heads on his window coat were scoping me. "Maybe when you're finished changing, you won't need me."

The thought had occurred to me. For years he had been the only one I could talk to but, as we closed on the gallery, I did not know what to say. I shook my head. "I just feel strange."

And then we arrived. The sculpture gallery was designed for showoffs: short flights of steps and a series of stagy balconies descended around the white brick exterior walls to the central exhibition area. The space was open so you could chat with your little knot of friends and, at the same time, spy on everyone else. About thirty kids were eating pizza and Crispex off paper plates. At the bottom of the stairs, as advertised, was a black upright piano. Piled beside it was the rest of the swag. A Boston rocker, a case of green Coke bottles, a Virgin Mary in half a blue bathtub, a huge conch shell, china and crystal and assorted smaller treasures, including a four-thousand-year-old ceramic hippo. There were real animals, too, in cages near the gun rack: a turkey, some stray dogs and cats, turtles, frogs, assorted rodents.

I was threading my way across the first balcony when I was stopped by the Japanese reporter, who was wearing microcam eyes.

"Excuse me, please," he said. "I am Matsuo Shikibu and I will be recording this event today for Nippon Hoso Kyokai. Public telelink of Japan." He smiled and bowed. When his head came up the red light between his lenses was on. "You are . . . ?"

"Raskolnikov," said Comrade, edging between me and the camera. "Rodeo Raskolnikov." He took Shikibu's hand and pumped it. "And my associate here,

Mr. Peter Pan." He turned as if to introduce me but we had long since choreo-
graphed this dodge. As I sidestepped past, he kept shielding me from the reporter with his body. "We're friends of the bride," Comrade said, "and we're
really excited to be making new friends in your country. Banzai, Nippon!"

I slipped by them and scooted downstairs. Happy was basking by the piano;
she spotted me as I reached the middle landing.

"Mr. Boy!" It was not so much a greeting as an announcement. She was
wearing a body mike and her voice boomed over the sound system. "You made
it."

The stream of conversation rippled momentarily, a few heads turned and
then the party flowed on. Shikibu rushed to the edge of the upper balcony and
caught me with a long shot.

I set the box on the Steinway. "Stennie brought this."

She opened it eagerly. "Look everyone!" She held up a stack of square cardboard albums, about thirty centimeters on a side. There were pictures of musicians on the front, words on the back. "What are they?" she asked me.

"Phonograph records," said the kid next to Happy. "It's how they used to
play music before digital."

"Erroll Garner *Soliloquy*," she read aloud. "What's this? D-j-a-n-g-o Rein-
hardt and the American Jazz Giants. Sounds scary." She giggled as she pawed
through the other albums. Handy, Ellington, Hawkins, Parker, three Arm-
strongs. One was *Piano Rags by Scott Joplin*. Stennie's bent idea of a joke?
Maybe the lizard was smarter than he looked. Happy pulled a black plastic
record out of one sleeve and scratched a fingernail across the ridges. "Oh, a non-
slip surface."

The party had a limited attention span. When she realized she had lost her
audience, she shut off the mike and put the box with the rest of the swag. "We
have to start at four, no matter what. There's so much stuff." The kid who knew
about records wormed into our conversation; Happy put her hand on his shoulder. "Mr. Boy, do you know my friend, Weldon?" she said. "He's new."

Montross grinned. "We met on Playroom."

"Where *is* Stennie, anyway?" said Happy.

"Swimming," I said. Montross appeared to be in his late teens. Bigger than
me—everyone was bigger than me. He wore green shorts and a window shirt of
surfers at Waimea. He looked like everybody; there was nothing about him to
remember. I considered bashing the smirk off his face but it was a bad idea. If
he was software he could not feel anything and I would probably break my hand
on his temporary chassis. "Got to go. I promised Stennie I'd meet him back at
the pool. Hey Weldon, want to tag along?"

"You come right back," said Happy. "We're starting at four. Tell everyone."

We avoided the tube and cut across the lawn for privacy. Comrade handed Montross the envelope. He slid the photograph out and I had one last glimpse. This
time the dead man left me cold. In fact, I was embarrassed. Although he kept a
straight face, I knew what Montross was thinking about me. Maybe he was
right. I wished he would put the picture away. He was not one of us; he could
not understand. I wondered if Tree had come far enough yet to appreciate
corpse porn.

"It's the only copy," Comrade said.

"All right." Finally Montross crammed it into the pocket of his shorts.

"You tapped our files; you know it's true."

"So?"

"So enough!" I said. "You have what you wanted."

"I've already explained." Montross was being patient. "Getting this back doesn't close the case. I have to take preventive measures."

"Meaning you turn Comrade into a carrot."

"Meaning I repair him. You're the one who took him to the chop shop. Deregulated wiseguys are dangerous. Maybe not to you, but certainly to property and probably to other people. It's a straightforward procedure. He'll be fully functional afterward."

"Plug your procedure, jack. We're leaving."

Both wiseguys stopped. "I thought you agreed," said Montross.

"Let's go, Comrade." I grabbed his arm but he shook me off.

"Where?" he said.

"Anywhere! Just so I never have to listen to this again." I pulled again, angry at Comrade for stalling. Your wiseguy is supposed to anticipate your needs, do whatever you want.

"But we haven't even tried to . . ."

"Forget it then. I give up." I pushed him toward Montross. "You want to chat, fine, go right ahead. Let him rip the top of your head off while you're at it, but I'm not sticking around to watch."

I checked the pool but Tree, Stennie, and Janet had already gone. I went through the Glass House and caught up with them in the tube to the sculpture gallery.

"Can I talk to you?" I put my arm around Tree's waist, just like I had seen grownups do. "In private." I could tell she was annoyed to be separated from Janet. "We'll catch up." I waved Stennie on. "See you over there."

She waited until they were gone. "What?" Her hair, slick from swimming, left dark spots where it brushed her silver jaunts.

"I want to leave. We'll call my mom's car." She did not look happy. "I'll take you anywhere you want to go."

"But we just got here. Give it a chance."

"I've been to too many of these things."

"Then you shouldn't have come."

Silence. I wanted to tell her about Montross—everything—but not here. Anyone could come along and the tube was so hot. I was desperate to get her away, so I lied. "Believe me, you're not going to like this. I know." I tugged at her waist. "Sometimes even I think smash parties are too much."

"We've had this discussion before," she said. "Obviously you weren't listening. I don't need you to decide for me whether I'm going to like something, Mr. Boy. I have two parents too many; I don't need another." She stepped away from me. "Hey, I'm sorry if you're having a bad time. But do you really need to spoil it for me?" She turned and strode down the tube toward the gallery, her beautiful hair slapping against her back. I watched her go.

"But I'm in trouble," I muttered to the empty tube—and then was disgusted with myself because I did not have the guts to say it to Tree. I was too scared she would not care. I stood there, sweating. For a moment the stink of doubt filled my nostrils. Then I followed her in. I could not abandon her to the extremists.

The gallery was jammed now; maybe a hundred kids swarmed across the balconies and down the stairs. Some perched along the edges, their feet scuffing the white brick. Happy had turned up the volume.

". . . according to Guinness, was set at the University of Oklahoma in Norman, Oklahoma, in 2012. Three minutes and fourteen seconds." The crowd rumbled in disbelief. "The challenge states each piece must be small enough to pass through a hole thirty centimeters in diameter."

I worked my way to an opening beside a rubber tree. Happy posed on the keyboard of the piano. Freddy the Teddy and the gorilla brothers, Mike and Bubba, lined up beside her. "No mechanical tools are allowed." She gestured at an armory of axes, sledgehammers, spikes, and crowbars laid out on the floor. A paper plate spun across the room. I could not see Tree.

"This piano is over two hundred years old," Happy continued, "which means the white keys are ivory." She plunked a note. "Dead elephants!" Everybody heaved a sympathetic *awww*. "The blacks are ebony, hacked from the rain forest." Another note, less reaction. "It deserves to die."

Applause. Comrade and I spotted each other at almost the same time. He and Montross stood toward the rear of the lower balcony. He gestured for me to come down; I ignored him.

"Do you boys have anything to say?" Happy said.

"Yeah." Freddy hefted an ax. "Let's make landfill."

I ducked around the rubber tree and heard the *crack* of splitting wood, the iron groan of a piano frame yielding its last music. The spectators hooted approval. As I bumped past kids, searching for Tree, the instrument's death cry made me think of taking a hammer to Montross. If fights broke out, no one would care if Comrade and I dragged him outside. I wanted to beat him until he shuddered and came unstrung and his works glinted in the thudding August light. It would make me feel extreme again. *Crunch!* Kids shrieked, "Go, go, go!" The party was lifting off and taking me with it.

"You are Mr. Boy Cage." Abruptly Shikibu's microcam eyes were in my face. "We know your famous mother." He had to shout to be heard. "I have a question."

"Go away."

"Thirty seconds." A girl's voice boomed over the speakers.

"U.S. and Japan are very different, yes?" He pressed closer. "We honor ancestors, our past. You seem to hate so much." He gestured at the gallery. "Why?"

"Maybe we're spoiled." I barged past him.

I saw Freddy swing a sledgehammer at the exposed frame. *Clang!* A chunk of twisted iron clattered across the brick floor, trailing broken strings. Happy scooped the mess up and shoved it through a thirty-centimeter hole drilled in an upright sheet of particle board.

The timekeeper called out again. *"One minute."* I had come far enough around the curve of the stairs to see her.

"Treemonisha!"

She glanced up, her face alight with pleasure, and waved. I was frightened for her. She was climbing into the same box I needed to break out of. So I rushed down the stairs to rescue her—little boy knight in shining armor—and ran right into Comrade's arms.

"I've decided," he said. *"Mnye vcyaw ostoyeblo."*

"Great." I had to get to Tree. "Later, okay?" When I tried to go by, he picked me up. I started thrashing. It was the first fight of the afternoon and I lost. He carried me over to Montross. The gallery was in an uproar.

"All set," said Montross. "I'll have to borrow him for a while. I'll drop him off tonight at your mom's. Then we're done."

"Done?" I kept trying to get free but Comrade crushed me against him.

"It's what you want." His body was so hard. "And what your mom wants."

"Mom? She doesn't even know."

"She knows everything," Comrade said. "She watches you constantly. What else does she have to do all day?" He let me go. "Remember you said I was sloppy getting the picture? I wasn't; it was a clean operation. Only someone tipped Datasafe off."

"But she promised. Besides, that makes no . . ."

"Two minutes," Tree called.

". . . but he threatened me," I said. "He was going to blow me up. Needle me in the mall."

"We wouldn't do that." Montross spread his hands innocently. "It's against the law."

"Yeah? Well, then drop dead, jack." I poked a finger at him. "Deal's off."

"No, it's not," said Comrade. "It's too late. This isn't about the picture anymore, Mr. Boy; it's about you. You weren't supposed to change but you did. Maybe they botched the last stunting, maybe it's Treemonisha. Whatever, you've outgrown me, the way I am now. So I have to change, too, or else I'll keep getting in your way."

He always had everything under control; it made me crazy. He was too good at running my life. "You should have told me Mom turned you in." *Crash!* I felt like the crowd was inside my head, screaming.

"You could've figured it out, if you wanted to. Besides, if I had said anything, your mom wouldn't have bothered to be subtle. She would've squashed me. She still might, even though I'm being fixed. Only by then I won't care. *Rosproyebi tvayou mat!"*

I heard Tree finishing the count. ". . . *twelve, thirteen, fourteen!"* No record today. Some kids began to boo, others laughed. "Time's up, you losers!"

I glared at the two wiseguys. Montross was busy emulating sincerity. Comrade found a way to grin for me, the same smirk he always wore when he tortured the greeter. "It's easier this way."

Easier. My life was too plugging easy. I had never done anything important by myself. Not even grown up. I wanted to smash something.

"Okay," I said. "You asked for it."

Comrade turned to Montross and they shook hands, I thought next they might clap one another on the shoulder and whistle as they strolled off into the sunset together. I felt like puking. "Have fun," said Comrade. *"Da svedanya."*

"Sure." Betraying Comrade, my best friend, brought me both pain and pleasure at once—but not enough to satisfy the shrieking wildness within me. The party was just starting.

Happy stood beaming beside the ruins of the Steinway. Although nothing of what was left was more than half a meter tall, Freddy, Mike, and Bubba had given up now that the challenge was lost. Kids were already surging down the stairs to claim their share of the swag. I went along with them.

"Don't worry," announced Happy. "Plenty for everyone. Come take what you like. Remember, guns and animals outside, if you want to hunt. The safeties won't release unless you go through the door. Watch out for one another, people; we don't want anyone shot."

A bunch of kids were wrestling over the turkey cage; one of them staggered backwards and knocked into me. "Gobble, gobble," she said. I shoved her back.

"Mr. Boy! Over here." Tree, Stennie, and Janet were waiting on the far side of the gallery. As I crossed to them, Happy gave the sign and Stone Kinkaid hurled the four-thousand-year-old ceramic hippo against the wall. It shattered. Everybody cheered. In the upper balconies, they were playing catch with a frog.

"You see who kept time?" said Janet.

"Didn't need to see," I said. "I could hear. They probably heard in Elkhart. So you like it, Tree?"

"It's about what I expected: dumb but fun. I don't think they . . ." The frog sailed from the top balcony and splatted at our feet. Its legs twitched and guts spilled from its open mouth. I watched Tree's smile turn brittle. She seemed slightly embarrassed, as if she had just been told the price of something she could not afford.

"This is going to be a war zone soon," Stennie said.

"Yeah, let's fade." Janet towed Stennie to the stairs, swerving around the three boys lugging Our Lady of the Bathtub out to the firing range.

"Wait." I blocked Tree. "You're here, so you have to destroy something. Get with the program."

"I have to?" She seemed doubtful. "Oh all right—but no animals."

A hail of antique Coke bottles crashed around Happy as she directed traffic at the dwindling swag heap. "Hey people, please be very careful where you throw things." Her amplified voice blasted us as we approached. The first floor was a graveyard of broken glass and piano bones and bloody feathers. Most of the good stuff was already gone.

"Any records left?" I said.

Happy wobbled closer to me. "What?" She seemed punchy, as if stunned by the success of her own party.

"The box I gave you. From Stennie." She pointed; I spotted it under some cages and grabbed it. Tree and the others were on the stairs. Outside I could hear the crackle of small arms fire. I caught up.

"Sir! Mr. Dinosaur, please," The press still lurked on the upper balcony. "Matsuo Shikibu, Japanese telelink NHK. Could I speak with you for a moment?"

"Excuse me, but this jack and I have some unfinished business." I handed Stennie the records and cut in front. He swayed and lashed his tail upward to counterbalance their weight.

"Remember me?" I bowed to Shikibu.

"My apologies if I offended . . ."

"Hey, Matsuo—can I call you Matsuo? This is your first smash party, right? Please, eyes on me. I want to explain why I was rude before. Help you understand the local customs. You see, we're kind of self-conscious here in the U.S. We don't like it when someone just watches while we play. You either join in or you're not one of us."

My little speech drew a crowd. "What's he talking about?" said Janet. She was shushed.

"So if you drop by our party and don't have fun, people resent you," I told him. "No one came here today to put on a show. This is who we are. What we believe in."

"Yeah!" Stennie was cheerleading for the extreme Mr. Boy of old. "Tell him." Too bad he did not realize it was his final appearance. What was Mr. Boy without his Comrade? "Make him feel some pain."

I snatched an album from the top of the stack, slipped the record out and held it close to Shikibu's microcam eyes. "What does this say?"

He craned his neck to read the label. "John Coltrane, *Giant Steps.*"

"Very good." I grasped the record with both hands, and raised it over my head for all to see. "We're not picky, Matsuo. We welcome everyone. Therefore today it is my honor to initiate you—and the home audience back on NHK. If you're still watching, you're part of this too." I broke the record over his head.

He yelped and staggered backward and almost tripped over a dead cat. Stone Kinkaid caught him and propped him up. "Congratulations," said Stennie, as he waved his claws at Japan. "You're all extremists now."

Shikibu gaped at me, his microcam eyes askew. A couple of kids clapped.

"There's someone else here who has not yet joined us." I turned on Tree. "Another spectator." Her smile faded.

"You leave her alone," said Janet. "What are you, crazy?"

"I'm not going to touch her." I held up empty hands. "No, I just want her to ruin something. That's why you came, isn't it, Tree? To get a taste?" I rifled through the box until I found what I wanted. "How about this?" I thrust it at her.

"Oh yeah," said Stennie, "I meant to tell you . . ."

She took the record and scoped it briefly. When she glanced up at me, I almost lost my nerve.

"Matsuo Shikibu, meet Treemonisha Joplin." I clasped my hands behind my back so no one could see me tremble. "The great-great-great-granddaughter of the famous American composer, Scott Joplin. Yes, Japan, we're all celebrities here in New Canaan. Now please observe." I read the record for him. "*Piano Rags by Scott Joplin,* Volume III. Who knows, this might be the last copy. We can only hope. So, what are you waiting for, Tree? You don't want to be a Joplin anymore? Just wait until your folks get a peek at this. We'll even send GD a copy. Go ahead, enjoy."

"Smash it!" The kids around us took up the chant. "Smash it!" Shikibu adjusted his lenses.

"You think I won't?" Tree pulled out the disc and threw the sleeve off the balcony. "This is a piece of junk, Mr. Boy." She laughed and then shattered the album against the wall. She held onto a shard. "It doesn't mean anything to me."

I heard Janet whisper. "What's going on?"

"I think they're having an argument."

"You want me to be your little dream cush." Tree tucked the piece of broken plastic into the pocket of my baggies. "The stiff from nowhere who knows nobody and does nothing without Mr. Boy. So you try to scare me off. You tell me you're so rich, you can afford to hate yourself. Stay home, you say, it's too dangerous, we're all crazy. Well, if you're so sure this is poison, how come you've still got your wiseguy and your cash cards? Are you going to move out of your mom, leave town, stop getting stunted? You're not giving it up, Mr. Boy, so why should I?"

Shikibu turned his camera eyes on me. No one spoke.

"You're right," I said. "She's right." I could not save anyone until I saved myself. I felt the wildness lifting me to it. I leapt onto the balcony wall and shouted for everyone to hear. "Shut up and listen everybody! You're all invited to my place, okay?"

There was one last thing to smash.

"Stop this, Peter." The greeter no longer thought I was cute. "What're you doing?" She trembled as if the kids spilling into her were an infection.

"I thought you'd like to meet my friends," I said. A few had stayed behind with Happy, who had decided to sulk after I hijacked her guests. The rest had followed me home in a caravan so I could warn off the sentry robots. It was already a hall-of-fame bash. "Treemonisha Joplin, this is my mom. Sort of."

"Hi," Tree held out her hand uncertainly.

The greeter was no longer the human doormat. "Get them out of me." She was too jumpy to be polite. "Right now!"

Someone turned up a boombox. Skitter music filled the room like a siren. Tree said something I could not hear. When I put a hand to my ear, she leaned close and said, "Don't be so mean, Mr. Boy. I think she's really frightened."

I grinned and nodded. "I'll tell Cook to make us some snacks."

Bubba and Mike carried boxes filled with the last of the swag and set them on the coffee table. Kids fanned out, running their hands along her wrinkled blood-hot walls, bouncing on the furniture. Stennie waved at me as he led a bunch upstairs for a tour. A leftover cat had gotten loose and was hissing and scratching underfoot. Some twisted kids had already stripped and were rolling in the floor hair, getting ready to have sex.

"Get dressed, you." The greeter kicked at them as she coiled her umbilical to keep it from being trampled. She retreated to her wall plug. "You're *hurting* me." Although her voice rose to a scream, only half a dozen kids heard her. She went limp and sagged to the floor.

The whole room seemed to throb, as if to some great heartbeat, and the lights went out. It took a while for someone to kill the sound on the boombox. "What's wrong?" Voices called out. "Mr. Boy? Lights."

Both doorbones swung open and I saw a bughead silhouetted against the twilit sky. Shikibu in his microcams. "Party's over," Mom said over her speaker system. There was nervous laughter. "Leave before I call the cops. Peter, go to your room right now. I want to speak to you."

As the stampede began, I found Tree's hand. "Wait for me?" I pulled her close. "I'll only be a minute."

"What are you going to do?" She sounded frightened. It felt good to be taken so seriously.

"I'm moving out, chucking all this. I'm going to be a working stiff." I chuckled. "Think your dad would give me a job?"

"Look out, dumbscut! Hey, *hey*. Don't push!"

Tree dragged me out of the way. "You're crazy."

"I know. That's why I have to get out of Mom."

"Listen," she said, "you've never been poor, you have no idea. . . . Only a rich kid would think it's easy being a stiff. Just go up, apologize, tell her it won't happen again. Then change things later on, if you want. Believe me, life will be a lot simpler if you hang onto the money."

"I can't. Will you wait?"

"You want me to tell you it's okay to be stupid, is that it? Well, I've *been* poor, Mr. Boy, and still am, and I don't recommend it. So don't expect me to stand around and clap while you throw away something I've always wanted." She spun away from me and I lost her in the darkness. I wanted to catch up with her but I knew I had to do Mom now or I would lose my nerve.

As I was fumbling my way upstairs I heard stragglers coming down. "On your right," I called. Bodies nudged by me.

"Mr. Boy, is that you?" I recognized Stennie's voice.

"He's gone," I said.

Seven flights up, the lights were on. Nanny waited on the landing outside my rooms, her umbilical stretched nearly to its limit. She was the only remote which was physically able to get to my floor and this was as close as she could come.

It had been a while since I had seen her; Mom did not use her much anymore and I rarely visited, even though the nursery was only one flight down. But this was the remote who used to pick me up when I cried and who had changed my diapers and who taught me how to turn on my roombrain. She had skin so pale you could almost see veins and long black hair piled high on her head. I never thought of her as having a body because she always wore dark turtlenecks and long woolen skirts and silky panty hose. Nanny was a smile and warm hands and the smell of fresh pillowcases. Once upon a time I thought her the most beautiful creature in the world. Back then I would have done anything she said.

She was not smiling now. "I don't know how you expect me to trust you anymore, Peter." Nanny had never been a very good scold. "Those brats were out of control. I can't let you put me in danger this way."

"If you wanted someone to trust, maybe you shouldn't have had me stunted. You got exactly what you ordered, the neverending kid. Well, kids don't have to be responsible."

"What do you mean, what I ordered? It's what you wanted, too."

"Is it? Did you ever ask? I was only ten, the first time, too young to know better. For a long time I did it to please you. Getting stunted was the only thing I did that seemed important to you. But *you* never explained. You never sat me down and said, 'This is the life you'll have and this is what you'll miss and this is how you'll feel about it.'"

"You want to grow up, is that it?" She was trying to threaten me. "You want to work and worry and get old and die someday?" She had no idea what we were talking about.

"I can't live this way anymore, Nanny."

At first she acted stunned, as if I had spoken in Albanian. Then her expression hardened when she realized she had lost her hold on me. She was ugly when she was angry. "They put you up to this." Her gaze narrowed in accusation. "That little black cush you've been seeing. Those realists!"

I had always managed to hide my anger from Mom. Right up until then. "How do you know about her?" I had never told her about Tree.

"Peter, they live in a mall!"

Comrade was right. "You've been spying on me." When she did not deny it, I went berserk. "You liar." I slammed my fist into her belly. "You said you wouldn't watch." She staggered and fell onto her umbilical, crimping it. As she twitched on the floor, I pounced. "You promised." I slapped her face. "Promised." I hit her again. Her hair had come undone and her eyes rolled back in their sockets and her face was slack. She made no effort to protect herself. Mom was retreating from this remote, too, but I was not going to let her get away.

"Mom!" I rolled off Nanny. "I'm coming up, Mom! You hear? Get ready." I was crying; it had been a long time since I had cried. Not something Mr. Boy did.

I scrambled up to the long landing at the shoulders. At one end another circular stairway wound up into the torch; in the middle four steps led into the neck. It was the only doorbone I had never seen open; I had no idea how to get through.

"Mom, I'm here." I pounded. "Mom! You hear me?"

Silence.

"Let me in, Mom." I smashed myself against the doorbone. Pain branched through my shoulder like lightning but it felt great because Mom shuddered from the impact. I backed up and, in a frenzy, hurled myself again. Something warm dripped on my cheek. She was bleeding from the hinges. I aimed a vicious kick at the doorbone and it banged open. I went through.

For years I had imagined that if only I could get into the head I could meet my real mother. Touch her. I had always wondered what she looked like; she got reshaped just after I was born. When I was little I used to think of her as a magic princess glowing with fairy light. Later I pictured her as one or another of my friends' moms, only better dressed. After I had started getting twanked, I was afraid she might be just a brain floating in nutrient solution, like in some pricey memory bank. All wrong.

The interior of the head was dark and absolutely freezing. There was no sound except for the hum of refrigeration units. "Mom?" My voice echoed in the empty space. I stumbled and caught myself against a smooth wall. Not skin, like everywhere else in Mom—metal. The tears froze on my face.

"There's nothing for you here," she said. "This is a clean room. You're compromising it. You must leave immediately."

Sterile environment, metal walls, the bitter cold that superconductors needed. I did not need to see. No one lived there. It had never occurred to me that there was no Mom to touch. She had downloaded, become an electron ghost tripping icy logic gates. "How long have you been dead?"

"This isn't where you belong," she said.

I shivered. "How long?"

"Go away," she said.

So I did. I had to. I could not stay very long in her secret place or I would die of the cold.

As I reeled down the stairs, Mom herself seemed to shift beneath my feet and

I saw her as if she were a stranger. Dead—and I had been living in a tomb. I ran past Nanny; she still sprawled where I had left her. All those years I had loved her, I had been in love with death. Mom had been sucking life from me the way her refrigerators stole the warmth from my body.

Now I knew there was no way I could stay, no matter what anyone said. I knew it was not going to be easy leaving, and not just because of the money. For a long time Mom had been my entire world. But I could not let her use me to pretend she was alive, or I would end up like her.

I realized now that the door had always stayed locked because Mom had to hide what she had become. If I wanted, I could have destroyed her. Downloaded intelligences have no more rights than cars or wiseguys. Mom was legally dead and I was her only heir. I could have had her shut off, her body razed. But somehow it was enough to go, to walk away from my inheritance. I was scared and yet with every step I felt lighter. Happier. Extremely free.

I had not expected to find Tree waiting at the doorbone, chatting with Comrade as if nothing had happened. "I just had to see if you were really the biggest fool in the world," she said.

"Out." I pulled her through the door. "Before I change my mind."

Comrade started to follow us. "No, not you." I turned and stared back at the heads on his window coat. I had not intended to see him again; I had wanted to be gone before Montross returned him. "Look, I'm giving you back to Mom. She needs you more than I do."

If he had argued, I might have given in. The old, unregulated Comrade would have said something. But he just slumped a little and nodded and I knew that he was dead, too. The thing in front of me was another ghost. He and Mom were two of a kind. "Pretend you're her kid, maybe she'll like that." I patted his shoulder.

"*Prekrassnaya ideya,*" he said. "*Spaceba.*"

"You're welcome," I said.

Tree and I trotted down the long driveway. Robot sentries crossed the lawn and turned their spotlights on us. I wanted to tell her she was right. I had probably just done the single most irresponsible thing of my life—and I had high standards. Still, I could not imagine how being poor could be worse than being rich and hating yourself. I had seen enough of what it was like to be dead. It was time to try living.

"Are we going someplace, Mr. Boy?" Tree squeezed my hand. "Or are we just wandering around in the dark?"

"Mr. Boy is a damn stupid name, don't you think?" I laughed. "Call me Pete." I felt like a kid again.

JAMBOREE

by Jack Williamson

Jack Williamson is the grand old man of science fiction. He has been writing and publishing SF in every decade since the 1920s and is still going strong, with a new novel nearly every year. He won a Hugo Award in the 1980s for his autobiography, *Wonder's Child*. Nowadays, he is writing fewer short stories and traveling to fewer conventions, but his long and impressive career is not over yet. "Jamboree" is one of his later stories, showing the seemingly effortless craft of an accomplished master of SF.

The scoutmaster slipped into the camp on black plastic tracks. Its slick yellow hood shone in the cold early light like the shell of a bug. It paused in the door, listening for boys not asleep. Then its glaring eyes began to swivel, darting red beams into every corner, looking for boys out of bed.

"Rise and smile!" Its loud merry voice bounced off the gray iron walls. "Fox Troop rise and smile! Hop for old Pop! Mother says today is Jamboree!"

The Nuke Patrol, next to the door, was mostly tenderfeet, still in their autonomic prams. They all began squalling, because they hadn't learned to love old Pop. The machine's happy voice rose louder than their howling, and it came fast down the narrow aisle to the cubs in the Anthrax Patrol.

"Hop for Pop! Mother says it's Jamboree!"

The cubs jumped up to attention, squealing with delight. Jamboree was bright gold stars to paste on their faces. Jamboree was a whole scoop of pink ice milk and maybe a natural apple. Jamboree was a visit to Mother's.

The older scouts in the Scavanger Patrol and the Skull Patrol were not so noisy, because they knew Mother wouldn't have many more Jamborees for them. Up at the end of the camp, three boys sat up without a sound and looked at Joey's empty pallet.

"Joey's late," Ratbait whispered. He was a pale, scrawny, wise-eyed scout who looked too old for twelve. "We oughta save his hide. We oughta fix a dummy and fool old Pop."

"Naw!" muttered Butch. "He'll get us all in bad."

"But we oughta—" Blinkie wheezed. "We oughta help—"

Ratbait began wadding up a pillow to be the dummy's head, but he dropped flat when he saw the scoutmaster rushing down with a noise like wind, red lamps stabbing at the empty bed.

"Now, now, scouts!" Its voice fluttered like a hurt bird. "You can't play pranks on poor old Pop. Not today. You'll make us late for Jamboree."

Ratbait felt a steel whip twitch the blanket from over his head and saw red light burning through his tight-shut lids.

"Better wake up, Scout R-8." Its smooth, sad voice dripped over him like warm oil. "Better tell old Pop where J-0 went."

He squirmed under that terrible blaze. He couldn't see and he couldn't breathe and he couldn't think what to say. He gulped at the terror in his throat and tried to shake his head. At last the red glare went on to Blinkie.

"Scout Q-2, you're a twenty-badger." The low, slow voice licked at Blinkie like a friendly pup. "You like to help old Pop keep a tidy camp for Mother. You'll tell us where J-0 went."

Blinkie was a fattish boy. His puffy face was toadstool-pale, and his pallet had a sour smell from being wet. He sat up and ducked back from the steel whip over him.

"Please d-d-d-d-d—" His wheezy stammer stalled his voice, and he couldn't dodge the bright whip that looped around him and dragged him up to the heat and the hum and the hot oil smell of Pop's yellow hood.

"Well, Scout Q-2?"

Blinkie gasped and stuttered and finally sagged against the plastic tracks like gray jelly. The shining coils rippled around him like thin snakes, constricting. His breath wheezed out and his fat arm jerked up, pointing at a black sign on the wall:

DANGER!
Power Access
ROBOTS ONLY!

The whips tossed him back on his sour pallet. He lay there, panting and blinking and dodging, even after the whips were gone. The scoutmaster's eyes flashed to the sign and the square grating under it, and swiveled back to Butch.

Butch was a slow, stocky, bug-eyed boy, young enough to come back from another Jamboree. He had always been afraid of Pop, but he wanted to be the new leader of Skull Patrol in Joey's place, and now he thought he saw his chance.

"Don't hit me, Pop!" His voice squeaked and his face turned red, but he scrambled off his pallet without waiting for the whips. "I'll tell on Joey. I been wantin' all along to tell, but I was afraid they'd beat me."

"Good boy!" the scoutmaster's loud words swelled out like big soap-bubbles bursting in the sun. "Mother wants to know all about Scout J-0."

"He pries that grating—" His voice quavered and caught when he saw the look on Ratbait's face, but when he turned to Pop it came back loud. "Does it every night. Since three Jamborees ago. Sneaks down in the pits where the robots work. I dunno why, except he sees somebody there. An' brings things back. Things he shouldn't have. Things like this!"

He fumbled in his uniform and held up a metal tag.

"This is your good turn today, Scout X-6." The thin tip of a whip took the tag and dangled it close to the hot red lamps. "Whose tag is this?"

"Lookit the number—"

Butch's voice dried up when he saw Ratbait's pale lips making words without a sound. "What's so much about an ID tag?" Ratbait asked. "Anyhow, what were you doing in Joey's bed."

"It's odd!" Butch looked away and squeaked at Pop. "A girl's number!"

The silent shock of that bounced off the iron walls, louder than old Pop's boom. Most of the scouts had never seen a girl. After a long time, the cubs near the door began to whisper and titter.

"Shhhhh!" Pop roared like steam. "Now we can all do a good turn for Mother. And play a little joke on Scout J-0! He didn't know today would be Jamboree, but he'll find out." Pop laughed like a heavy chain clanking. "Back to bed! Quiet as robots!"

Pop rolled close to the wall near the power-pit grating, and the boys lay back on their pallets. Once Ratbait caught his breath to yell, but he saw Butch's bug-eyes watching. Pop's hum sank, and even the tenderfeet in their prams were quiet as robots.

Ratbait heard the grating creak. He saw Joey's head, tangled yellow hair streaked with oil and dust. He frowned and shook his head and saw Joey's sky-blue eyes go wide.

Joey tried to duck, but the quick whips caught his neck. They dragged him out of the square black pit and swung him like a puppet toward old Pop's eyes.

"Well, Scout J-0!" Pop laughed like thick oil bubbling. "Mother wants to know where you've been."

Joey fell on his face when the whip uncoiled, but he scrambled to his feet. He gave Ratbait a pale grin before he looked up at Pop, but he didn't say anything.

"Better tell old Pop the truth." The slick whips drew back like lean snakes about to strike. "Or else we'll have to punish you, Scout J-0."

Joey shook his head, and the whips went to work. Still he didn't speak. He didn't even scream. But something fell out of his torn uniform. The whip-tips snatched it off the floor.

"What's this thing, Scout J-0?" The whip-fingers turned it delicately under the furious eyes and nearly dropped it again. "Scout J-0, this is a book!"

Silence echoed in the iron camp.

"Scout J-0, you've stolen a book." Pop's shocked voice changed into a toneless buzz, reading the title. *Operator's Handbook, Nuclear Reactor, Series 9-Z.*

Quiet sparks of fear crackled through the camp. Two or three tenderfeet began sobbing in their prams. When they were quiet, old Pop made an ominous, throat-clearing sound.

"Scout J-0, what are you doing with a book?"

Joey gulped and bit his under lip till blood seeped down his chin, but he made no sound. Old Pop rolled closer, while the busy whips were stowing the book in a dark compartment under the yellow hood.

"Mother won't like this." Each word clinked hard, like iron on iron. "Books aren't for boys. Books are for robots only. Don't you know that?"

Joey stood still.

"This hurts me, Scout J-0." Pop's voice turned downy soft, the slow words like tears of sadness now. "It hurts your poor Mother. More than anything can ever hurt you."

The whips cracked and cracked and cracked. At last they picked him up and shook him and dropped him like a red-streaked rag on the floor. Old Pop backed away and wheeled around.

"Fox Troop rise and smile!" Its roaring voice turned jolly again, as if it had forgotten Joey. "Hop for Pop. Today is Jamboree, and we're on our way to visit Mother. Fall out in marching order."

The cubs twittered with excitement until their leaders threatened to keep them home from Jamboree, but at last old Pop led the troop out of camp and down the paved trail toward Mother's. Joey limped from the whips, but he set his teeth and kept his place at the head of his patrol.

Marching through boy territory, they passed the scattered camps of troops whose Jamborees came on other days. A few scouts were out with their masters, but nobody waved or even looked straight at them.

The spring sun was hot and Pop's pace was too fast for the cubs. Some of them began to whimper and fall out of line. Pop rumbled back to warn them that Mother would give no gold stars if they were late for Jamboree. When Pop was gone, Joey glanced at Ratbait and beckoned with his head.

"I gotta get away!" he whispered low and fast. "I gotta get back to the pits—"

Butch ran out of his place, leaning to listen. Ratbait shoved him off the trail.

"You gotta help!" Joey gasped. "There's a thing we gotta do—an' we gotta do it now. 'Cause this will be the last Jamboree for most of us. We'll never get another chance."

Butch came panting along the edge of the trail, trying to hear, but Blinkie got in his way.

"What's all this?" Ratbait breathed. "What you gonna do?"

"It's all in the book," Joey said. "Something called manual override. There's a dusty room, down under Mother's, back of a people-only sign. Two red buttons. Two big levers. With a glass wall between. It takes two people."

"Who? One of us?"

Joey shook his head, waiting for Blinkie to elbow Butch. "I got a friend. We been working together, down in the pits. Watching the robots. Reading the books. Learning what we gotta do—"

He glanced back. Blinkie was scuffling with Butch to keep him busy, but how the scoutmaster came clattering back from the rear, booming merrily, "Hop for Pop! Hop a lot for Pop!"

"How you gonna work it?" Alarm took Ratbait's breath. "Now the robots will be watching—"

"We got a back door," Joey's whisper raced. "A drainage tunnel. Hot water out of the reactor. Comes out under Black Creek bridge. My friend'll be there. If I can dive off this end of the bridge—"

"Hey, Pop!" Butch was screaming. "Ratbait's talking! Blinkie pushed me! Joey's planning something bad!"

"Good boy, Scout X-6!" Pop slowed beside him. "Mother wants to know if they're plotting more mischief."

When Pop rolled on ahead of the troop, Ratbait wanted to ask what would happen when Joey and his friend pushed the two red buttons and pulled the two big levers, but Butch stuck so close they couldn't speak again. He thought it must be something about the reactor. Power was the life of Mother and the robots. If Joey could cut the power off—

Would they die? The idea frightened him. If the prams stopped, who would care for the tenderfeet? Who would make chow? Who would tell anybody what to do? Perhaps the books would help, he thought. Maybe Joey and his friend would know.

With Pop rolling fast in the lead, they climbed a long hill and came in sight of Mother's. Old gray walls that had no windows. Two tall stacks of dun-colored brick. A shimmer of heat in the pale sky.

The trail sloped down. Ratbait saw the crinkled ribbon of green brush along Black Creek, and then the concrete bridge. He watched Butch watching Joey, and listened to Blinkie panting, and tried to think how to help.

The cubs stopped whimpering when they saw Mother's mysterious walls and stacks, and the troop marched fast down the hill. Ratbait slogged along, staring at the yellow sun-dazzle on old Pop's hood. He couldn't think of anything to do.

"I got it!" Blinkie was breathing, close to his ear. "I'll take care of Pop."

"You?" Ratbait scowled. "You were telling on Joey—"

"That's why," Blinkie gasped. "I wanta make it up. I'll handle Pop. You stop Butch—an' give the sign to Joey."

They came to the bridge and Pop started across.

"Wait, Pop!" Blinkie darted out of line, toward the brushy slope above the trail. "I saw a girl! Hiding in the bushes to watch us go by."

Pop roared back off the bridge.

"A girl in boy territory!" Its shocked voice splashed them like cold rain. "What would Mother say?" Black tracks spurting gravel, it lurched past Blinkie and crashed into the brush.

"Listen, Pop!" Butch started after it, waving and squealing. "They ain't no girl—"

Ratbait tripped him and turned to give Joey the sign, but Joey was already gone. Something splashed under the bridge and Ratbait saw a yellow head sliding under the steam that drifted out of a black tunnel-mouth.

"Pop! Pop!" Butch rubbed gravel out of his mouth and danced on the pavement. "Come back, Pop. Joey's in the creek! Ratbait and Blinkie—they helped him get away."

The scoutmaster swung back down the slope, empty whips waving. It skidded across the trail and down the bank to the hot creek. Its yellow hood faded into the steam.

"Tattletale!" Blinkie clenched his fat fists. "You told on Joey."

"An' you'll catch it!" Murky eyes bugging, Butch edged away. "You just wait till Pop gets back."

They waited. The tired cubs sat down to rest and the tenderfeet fretted in their hot prams. Breathing hard, Blinkie kept close to Butch. Ratbait watched till Pop swam back out of the drain.

The whips were wrapped around two small bundles that dripped pink water. Unwinding, the whips dropped Joey and his friend on the trail. They crumpled down like rag dolls, but the whips set them up again.

"How's this, scouts?" Old Pop laughed like steel gears clashing. "We've caught ourselves a real live girl!"

In a bird-quick way, she shook the water out of her sand-colored hair. Standing straight, without the whips to hold her, she faced Pop's glaring lamps. She looked tall for twelve.

Joey was sick when the whips let him go. He leaned off the bridge to heave, and limped back to the girl. She wiped his face with her wet hair. They caught hands and smiled at each other as if they were all alone.

"They tripped me, Pop." Braver now, Butch thumbed his nose at Blinkie and ran toward the machine. "They tried to stop me telling you—"

"Leave them to Mother," Pop sang happily. "Let them try their silly tricks on her." It wheeled toward the bridge, and the whips pushed Joey and the girl ahead of the crunching tracks. "Now hop with Pop to Jamboree!"

They climbed that last hill to a tall iron door in Mother's old gray wall. The floors beyond were naked steel, alive with machinery underneath. They filed into a dim round room that echoed to the grating squeal of Pop's hard tracks.

"Fox Troop, here we are for Jamboree!" Pop's jolly voice made a hollow booming on the curved steel wall, and its red lights danced in tall reflections there. "Mother wants you to know why we celebrate this happy time each year."

The machine was rolling to the center of a wide black circle in the middle of the floor. Something drummed far below like a monster heart, and Ratbait saw that the circle was the top of a black steel piston. It slid slowly up, lifting Pop. The drumming died, and Pop's eyes blazed down on the cubs in the Anthrax Patrol to stop their awed murmuring.

"Once there wasn't any Mother." The shock of that crashed and throbbed and faded. "There wasn't any yearly Jamboree. There wasn't even any Pop, to love and care for little boys."

The cubs were afraid to whisper, but a stir of troubled wonder spread among them.

"You won't believe how tenderfeet were made." There was a breathless hush. "In those bad old days, boys and girls were allowed to change like queer insects. They changed into creatures called adults—"

The whips writhed and the red lamps glared and the black cleats creaked on the steel platform.

"Adults!" Pop spewed the word. "They malfunctioned and wore out and ran down. Their defective logic circuits programmed them to damage one another. In a kind of strange group malfunction called war, they systematically destroyed one another. But their worst malfunction was in making new tenderfeet."

Pop turned slowly on the high platform, sweeping the silent troop with blood-red beams that stopped on Joey and his girl. All the scouts but Ratbait and Blinkie had edged away from them. Her face white and desperate, she was whispering in Joey's ear. Listening with his arm around her, he scowled at Pop.

"Once adults made tenderfeet, strange as that may seem to you. They used a weird natural process we won't go into. It finally broke down, because they had damaged their genes in war. The last adults couldn't make new boys and girls at all."

The red beams darted to freeze a startled cub.

"Fox Troop, that's why we have Mother. Her job is to collect undamaged genes and build them into whole cells with which she can assemble whole boys and girls. She has been doing that a long time now, and she does it better than those adults ever did.

"And that's why we have Jamboree! To fill the world with well-made boys and girls like you, and to keep you happy in the best time of life—even those old adults always said childhood was the happy time. Scouts, clap for Jamboree!" The cubs clapped, the echo like a spatter of hail on the high iron ceiling.

"Now, Scouts, those bad old days are gone forever," Pop burbled merrily. "Mother has a cozy place for each one of you, and old Pop watched over you, and you'll never be adult—"

"Pop! Pop!" Butch squealed. "Lookit Joey an' his girl!"

Pop spun around on the high platform. Its blinding beams picked up Joey and the girl, sprinting toward a bright sky-slice where the door had opened for the last of the prams.

"Wake up, guys!" Joey's scream shivered against the red steel wall. "That's all wrong. Mother's just a runaway machine. Pop's a crazy robot—"

"Stop for Pop!" The scoutmaster was trapped on top of that huge piston, but its blazing lamps raced after Joey and the girl. "Catch 'em, cubs! Hold 'em tight. Or there'll be no Jamboree!"

"I told you, Pop!" Butch scuttled after them. "Don't forget I'm the one that told—"

Ratbait dived at his heels, and they skidded together on the floor.

"Come on, scouts!" Joey was shouting. "Run away with us. Our own genes are good enough."

The floor shuddered under him and that bright sky-slice grew thinner. Lurching on their little tracks, the prams formed a line to guard it. Joey jumped the shrieking tenderfeet, but the girl stumbled. He stopped to pick her up.

"Help us, scouts!" he gasped. "We gotta get away—"

"Catch 'em for Pop!" that metal bellow belted them. "Or there'll be no gold stars for anybody!"

Screeching cubs swarmed around them. The door clanged shut. Pop plunged off the sinking piston, almost too soon. It crunched down on the yellow hood. Hot oil splashed and smoked, but the whips hauled it upright again.

"Don't mess around with M-M-M-M-Mother!" Its anvil voice came back with a stuttering croak. "She knows best!"

The quivering whips dragged Joey and the girl away from the clutching cubs and pushed them into a shallow black pit, where now that great black piston had dropped below the level of the floor.

"Sing for your Mother!" old Pop chortled. "Sing for the Jamboree!"

The cubs howled out their official song, and the Jamboree went on. There were Pop-shaped balloons for the tenderfeet, and double scoops of pink ice milk for the cubs, and gold stars for nearly everybody.

"But Mother wants a few of you." Old Pop was a fat cat purring.

When a pointing whip picked Blinkie out, he jumped into the pit without waiting to be dragged. But Butch turned white and tried to run when it struck at him.

"Pop! Not m-m-m-m-me!" he squeaked. "Don't forget I told on Joey. I'm only going on eleven, and I'm in line for leader, and I'll tell on everybody—"

"That's why Mother wants you." Old Pop laughed like a pneumatic hammer. "You're getting too adult."

The whip snaked Butch into the pit, dull eyes bulging more than ever. He slumped down on the slick black piston and struggled like a squashed bug and then lay moaning in a puddle of terror.

Ratbait stood sweating, as the whip came back to him. His stomach felt cold and strange, and the tall red wall spun like a crazy wheel around him, and he couldn't move till the whip pulled him to the rim of the pit.

But there Blinkie took his hand. He shook the whip off, and stepped down into the pit. Joey nodded, and the girl gave him a white, tiny smile. They all closed around her, arms linked tight, as the piston dropped.

"Now hop along for Pop! You've had your Jamboree—"

That hooting voice died away far above, and the pit's round mouth shrank into a blood-colored moon. The hot dark drummed like thunder all around them, and the slick floor tilted. It spilled them all into Mother's red steel jaws.

THE DEATH OF DOCTOR ISLAND

Gene Wolfe

Gene Wolfe has been called the finest writer in SF today. He is the author of the classic four-volume *The Book of the New Sun*, of *The Fifth Head of Cerberus*, of many strange and wonderful short stories, collected in such volumes as *Endangered Species* and *The Island of Doctor Death and Other Stories and Other Stories*. He is equally a master of fantasy, as evidenced in such novels as *Soldier of the Mist*, *There Are Doors*, and *Castleview*.

> *I have desired to go*
> *Where springs not fail,*
> *To fields where flies no sharp and sided hail*
> *And a few lilies blow.*
>
> *And I have asked to be*
> *Where no storms come,*
> *Where the green swell is in the heavens dumb,*
> *And out of the swing of the sea.*
> —Gerard Manley Hopkins

A grain of sand, teetering on the brink of the pit, trembled and fell in; the ant lion at the bottom angrily flung it out again. For a moment there was quiet. Then the entire pit, and a square meter of sand around it, shifted drunkenly while two coconut palms bent to watch. The sand rose, pivoting at one edge, and the scarred head of a boy appeared—a stubble of brown hair threatened to erase the marks of the sutures; with dilated eyes hypnotically dark he paused, his neck just where the ant lion's had been; then, as though goaded from below, he vaulted up and onto the beach, turned, and kicked sand into the dark hatchway from which he had emerged. It slammed shut. The boy was about fourteen.

For a time he squatted, pushing the sand aside and trying to find the door. A few centimeters down, his hands met a gritty, solid material which, though neither concrete nor sandstone, shared the qualities of both—a sand-filled organic plastic. On it he scraped his fingers raw, but he could not locate the edges of the hatch.

Then he stood and looked about him, his head moving continually as the heads of certain reptiles do—back and forth, with no pauses at the terminations of the movements. He did this constantly, ceaselessly—always—and for that reason it will not often be described again, just as it will not be mentioned that he breathed. He did; and as he did, his head, like a rearing snake's, turned from side to side. The boy was thin, and naked as a frog.

Ahead of him the sand sloped gently down toward sapphire water; there were coconuts on the beach, and sea shells, and a scuttling crab that played with the finger-high edge of each dying wave. Behind him there were only palms and sand for a long distance, the palms growing ever closer together as they moved away from the water until the forest of their columniated trunks seemed architectural; like some palace maze becoming as it progressed more and more draped with creepers and lianas with green, scarlet and yellow leaves, the palms interspersed with bamboo and deciduous trees dotted with flaming orchids until almost at the limit of his sight the whole ended in a spangled wall whose predominant color was black-green.

The boy walked toward the beach, then down the beach until he stood in knee-deep water as warm as blood. He dipped his fingers and tasted it—it was fresh, with no hint of the disinfectants to which he was accustomed. He waded out again and sat on the sand about five meters up from the high-water mark, and after ten minutes, during which he heard no sound but the wind and the murmuring of the surf, he threw back his head and began to scream. His screaming was high-pitched, and each breath ended in a gibbering, ululant note, after which came the hollow, iron gasp of the next indrawn breath. On one occasion he had screamed in this way, without cessation, for fourteen hours and twenty-two minutes, at the end of which a nursing nun with an exemplary record stretching back seventeen years had administered an injection without the permission of the attending physician.

After a time the boy paused—not because he was tired, but in order to listen better. There was, still, only the sound of the wind in the palm fronds and the murmuring surf, yet he felt that he had heard a voice. The boy could be quiet as well as noisy, and he was quiet now, his left hand sifting white sand as clean as salt between its fingers while his right tossed tiny pebbles like beachglass beads into the surf.

"*Hear me,*" said the surf. "*Hear me. Hear me.*"

"I hear you," the boy said.

"Good," said the surf, and it faintly echoed itself: "*Good, good, good.*"

The boy shrugged.

"What shall I call you?" asked the surf.

"My name is Nicholas Kenneth de Vore."

"Nick, *Nick . . . Nick?*"

The boy stood, and turning his back on the sea, walked inland. When he was out of sight of the water he found a coconut palm growing sloped and angled, leaning and weaving among its companions like the plume of an ascending jet blown by the wind. After feeling its rough exterior with both hands, the boy began to climb; he was inexpert and climbed slowly and a little clumsily, but his body was light and he was strong. In time he reached the top, and disturbed the little brown plush monkeys there, who fled chattering into other palms, leaving him to nestle alone among the stems of the fronds and the green coconuts. "I am here also," said a voice from the palm.

"Ah," said the boy, who was watching the tossing, sapphire sky far over his head.

"I will call you Nicholas."

The boy said, "I can see the sea."

"Do you know my name?"

The boy did not reply. Under him the long, long stem of the twisted palm swayed faintly.

"My friends all call me Dr. Island."

"I will not call you that," the boy said.

"You mean that you are not my friend."

A gull screamed.

"But you see, I take you for my friend. You may say that I am not yours, but I say that you are mine. I like you, Nicholas, and I will treat you as a friend."

"Are you a machine or a person or a committee?" the boy asked.

"I am all those things and more. I am the spirit of this island, the tutelary genius."

"Bullshit."

"Now that we have met, would you rather I leave you alone?"

Again the boy did not reply.

"You may wish to be alone with your thoughts. I would like to say that we have made much more progress today than I anticipated. I feel that we will get along together very well."

After fifteen minutes or more, the boy asked, "Where does the light come from?" There was no answer. The boy waited for a time, then climbed back down the trunk, dropping the last five meters and rolling as he hit the soft sand.

He walked to the beach again and stood staring out at the water. Far off he could see it curving up and up, the distant combers breaking in white foam until the sea became white-flecked sky. To his left and his right the beach curved away, bending almost infinitesimally until it disappeared. He began to walk, then saw, almost at the point where perception was lost, a human figure. He broke into a run; a moment later, he halted and turned around. Far ahead another walker, almost invisible, strode the beach; Nicholas ignored him; he found a coconut and tried to open it, then threw it aside and walked on. From time to time fish jumped, and occasionally he saw a wheeling sea bird dive. The light grew dimmer. He was aware that he had not eaten for some time, but he was not in the strict sense hungry—or rather, he enjoyed his hunger now in the same way that he might, at another time, have gashed his arm to watch himself bleed. Once he said, "Dr. Island!" loudly as he passed a coconut palm, and then later began to chant "Dr. Island, Dr. Island, Dr. Island" as he walked until the words had lost all meaning. He swam in the sea as he had been taught to swim in the great quartanary treatment tanks on Callisto to improve his coordination, and spluttered and snorted until he learned to deal with the waves. When it was so dark he could see only the white sand and the white foam of the breakers, he drank from the sea and fell asleep on the beach, the right side of his taut, ugly face relaxing first, so that it seemed asleep even while the left eye was open and staring; his head rolling from side to side; the left corner of his mouth preserving, like a death mask, his characteristic expression—angry, remote, tinged with that inhuman quality which is found nowhere but in certain human faces.

When he woke it was not yet light, but the night was fading to a gentle gray. Headless, the palms stood like tall ghosts up and down the beach, their tops lost in fog and the lingering dark. He was cold. His hands rubbed his sides; he danced on the sand and sprinted down the edge of the lapping water in an effort to get warm; ahead of him a pinpoint of red light became a fire, and he slowed.

A man who looked about twenty-five crouched over the fire. Tangled black hair hung over this man's shoulders, and he had a sparse beard; otherwise he was as naked as Nicholas himself. His eyes were dark, and large and empty, like the ends of broken pipes; he poked at his fire, and the smell of roasting fish came with the smoke. For a time Nicholas stood at a distance, watching.

Saliva ran from a corner of the man's mouth, and he wiped it away with one hand, leaving a smear of ash on his face. Nicholas edged closer until he stood on the opposite side of the fire. The fish had been wrapped in broad leaves and mud, and lay in the center of the coals. "I'm Nicholas," Nicholas said. "Who are you?" The young man did not look at him, had never looked at him.

"Hey, I'd like a piece of your fish. Not much. All right?"

The young man raised his head, looking not at Nicholas but at some point far beyond him; he dropped his eyes again. Nicholas smiled. The smile emphasized the disjointed quality of his expression, his mouth's uneven curve.

"Just a little piece? Is it about done?" Nicholas crouched, imitating the young man, and as though this were a signal, the young man sprang for him across the fire. Nicholas jumped backward, but the jump was too late—the young man's body struck his and sent him sprawling on the sand; fingers clawed for his throat. Screaming, Nicholas rolled free, into the water; the young man splashed after him; Nicholas dove.

He swam underwater, his belly almost grazing the wave-rippled sand until he found deeper water; then he surfaced, gasping for breath, and saw the young man, who saw him as well. He dove again, this time surfacing far off, in deep water. Treading water, he could see the fire on the beach, and the young man when he returned to it, stamping out of the sea in the early light. Nicholas then swam until he was five hundred meters or more down the beach, then waded in to shore and began walking back toward the fire.

The young man saw him when he was still some distance off, but he continued to sit, eating pink-tinted tidbits from his fish, watching Nicholas. "What's the matter?" Nicholas said while he was still a safe distance away. "Are you mad at me?"

From the forest, birds warned, "Be careful, Nicholas."

"I won't hurt you," the young man said. He stood up, wiping his oily hands on his chest, and gestured toward the fish at his feet. "You want some?"

Nicholas nodded, smiling his crippled smile.

"Come then."

Nicholas waited, hoping the young man would move away from the fish, but he did not; neither did he smile in return.

"Nicholas," the little waves at his feet whispered, "this is Ignacio."

"Listen," Nicholas said, "is it really all right for me to have some?"

Ignacio nodded, unsmiling.

Cautiously Nicholas came forward; as he was bending to pick up the fish, Ignacio's strong hands took him; he tried to wrench free but was thrown down, Ignacio on top of him. "Please!" he yelled. "Please!" Tears started into his eyes.

He tried to yell again, but he had no breath; the tongue was being forced, thicker than his wrist, from his throat.

Then Ignacio let go and struck him in the face with his clenched fist. Nicholas had been slapped and pummeled before, had been beaten, had fought, sometimes savagely, with other boys; but he had never been struck by a man as men fight. Ignacio hit him again and his lips gushed blood.

He lay a long time on the sand beside the dying fire. Consciousness returned slowly; he blinked, drifted back into the dark, blinked again. His mouth was full of blood, and when at last he spit it out onto the sand, it seemed a soft flesh, dark and polymerized in strange shapes; his left cheek was hugely swollen, and he could scarcely see out of his left eye. After a time he crawled to the water; a long time after that, he left it and walked shakily back to the ashes of the fire. Ignacio was gone, and there was nothing left of the fish but bones.

"Ignacio is gone," Dr. Island said with lips of waves.

Nicholas sat on the sand, cross-legged.

"You handled him very well."

"You saw us fight?"

"I saw you; I see everything, Nicholas."

"This is the worst place," Nicholas said; he was talking to his lap.

"What do you mean by that?"

"I've been in bad places before—places where they hit you or squirted big hoses of ice water that knocked you down. But not where they would let someone else—"

"Another patient?" asked a wheeling gull.

"—do it."

"You were lucky, Nicholas. Ignacio is homicidal."

"You could have stopped him."

"No, I could not. All this world is my eye, Nicholas, my ear and my tongue; but I have no hands."

"I thought you did all this."

"Men did all this."

"I mean, I thought you kept it going."

"It keeps itself going, and you—all the people here—direct it."

Nicholas looked at the water. "What makes the waves?"

"The wind and the tide."

"Are we on Earth?"

"Would you feel more comfortable on Earth?"

"I've never been there; I'd like to know."

"I am more like Earth than Earth now is, Nicholas. If you were to take the best of all the best beaches of Earth, and clear them of all the poisons and all the dirt of the last three centuries, you would have me."

"But this isn't Earth?"

There was no answer. Nicholas walked around the ashes of the fire until he found Ignacio's footprints. He was no tracker, but the depressions in the soft beach sand required none; he followed them, his head swaying from side to side as he walked, like the sensor of a mine detector.

For several kilometers Ignacio's trail kept to the beach; then, abruptly, the footprints swerved, wandered among the coconut palms, and at last were lost on the firmer soil inland. Nicholas lifted his head and shouted, "Ignacio? Ignacio!" After a moment he heard a stick snap, and the sound of someone pushing aside leafy branches. He waited.

"Mum?"

A girl was coming toward him, stepping out of the thicker growth of the interior. She was pretty, though too thin, and appeared to be about nineteen; her hair was blond where it had been most exposed to sunlight, darker elsewhere. "You've scratched yourself," Nicholas said. "You're bleeding."

"I thought you were my mother," the girl said. She was a head taller than Nicholas. "Been fighting, haven't you. Have you come to get me?"

Nicholas had been in similar conversations before and normally would have preferred to ignore the remark, but he was lonely now. He said, "Do you want to go home?"

"Well, I think I should, you know."

"But do you want to?"

"My mum always says if you've got something on the stove you don't want to burn—she's quite a good cook. She really is. Do you like cabbage with bacon?"

"Have you got anything to eat?"

"Not now. I had a thing a while ago."

"What kind of thing?"

"A bird." The girl made a vague little gesture, not looking at Nicholas. "I'm a memory that has swallowed a bird."

"Do you want to walk down by the water?" They were moving in the direction of the beach already.

"I was just going to get a drink. You're a nice tot."

Nicholas did not like being called a "tot." He said, "I set fire to places."

"You won't set fire to this place; it's been nice the last couple of days, but when everyone is sad, it rains."

Nicholas was silent for a time. When they reached the sea, the girl dropped to her knees and bent forward to drink, her long hair falling over her face until the ends trailed in the water, her nipples, then half of each breast, in the water. "Not there," Nicholas said. "It's sandy, because it washes the beach so close. Come on out here." He waded out into the sea until the lapping waves nearly reached his armpits, then bent his head and drank.

"I never thought of that," the girl said. "Mum says I'm stupid. So does Dad. Do you think I'm stupid?"

Nicholas shook his head.

"What's your name?"

"Nicholas Kenneth de Vore. What's yours?"

"Diane. I'm going to call you Nicky. Do you mind?"

"I'll hurt you while you sleep," Nicholas said.

"You wouldn't."

"Yes I would. At St. John's where I used to be, it was zero G most of the time, and a girl there called me something I didn't like, and I got loose one night and came into her cubical while she was asleep and nulled her restraints, and then she floated around until she banged into something, and that woke her up and she tried to grab, and then that made her bounce all around inside and she broke two fingers and her nose and got blood all over. The attendants came, and one told me—they didn't know then I did it—when he came out his white suit was, like, polka-dot red all over because wherever the blood drops had touched him they soaked right in."

The girl smiled at him, dimpling her thin face. "How did they find out it was you?"

"I told someone and he told them."

"I bet you told them yourself."

"I bet I didn't!" Angry, he waded away, but when he had stalked a short way up the beach he sat down on the sand, his back toward her.

"I didn't mean to make you mad, Mr. de Vore."

"I'm not mad!"

She was not sure for a moment what he meant. She sat down beside and a trifle behind him, and began idly piling sand in her lap.

Dr. Island said, "I see you've met."

Nicholas turned, looking for the voice. "I thought you saw everything."

"Only the important things, and I have been busy on another part of myself. I am happy to see that you two know one another; do you find you interact well?"

Neither of them answered.

"You should be interacting with Ignacio; he needs you."

"We can't find him," Nicholas said.

"Down the beach to your left until you see the big stone, then turn inland. Above five hundred meters."

Nicholas stood up, and turning to his right, began to walk away. Diane followed him, trotting until she caught up.

"I don't like," Nicholas said, jerking a shoulder to indicate something behind him.

"Ignacio?"

"The doctor."

"Why do you move your head like that?"

"Didn't they tell you?"

"No one told me anything about you."

"They opened it up"—Nicholas touched his scars—"and took this knife and cut all the way through my corpus . . . corpus . . ."

"Corpus callosum," muttered a dry palm frond.

"—corpus callosum," finished Nicholas. "See, your brain is like a walnut inside. There are the two halves, and then right down in the middle a kind of thick connection of meat from one to the other. Well, they cut that."

"You're having a bit of fun with me, aren't you?"

"No, he isn't," a monkey who had come to the water line to look for shellfish told her. "His cerebrum has been surgically divided; it's in his file." It was a young monkey, with a trusting face full of small, ugly beauties.

Nicholas snapped, "It's in my head."

Diane said, "I'd think it would kill you, or make you an idiot or something."

"They say each half of me is about as smart as both of us were together. Anyway, this half is . . . the half . . . the *me* that talks."

"There are two of you now?"

"If you cut a worm in half and both parts are still alive, that's two, isn't it? What else would you call us? We can't ever come together again."

"But I'm talking to just one of you?"

"We both can hear you."

"Which one answers?"

Nicholas touched the right side of his chest with his right hand. "Me; I do. They told me it was the left side of my brain, that one has the speech centers, but it doesn't feel that way; the nerves cross over coming out, and it's just the right side of me, I talk. Both my ears hear for both of us, but out of each eye we only see half and half—I mean, I only see what's on the right of what I'm look- ing at, and the other side, I guess, only sees the left, so that's why I keep mov- ing my head. I guess it's like being a little bit blind; you get used to it."

The girl was still thinking of his divided body. She said, "If you're only half, I don't see how you can walk."

"I can move the left side a little bit, and we're not mad at each other. We're not supposed to be able to come together at all, but we do: down through the legs and at the ends of the fingers and then back up. Only I can't talk with my other side because he can't, but he understands."

"Why did they do it?"

Behind them the monkey, who had been following them, said, "He had un- controllable seizures."

"Did you?" the girl asked. She was watching a sea bird swooping low over the water and did not seem to care.

Nicholas picked up a shell and shied it at the monkey, who skipped out of the way. After half a minute's silence he said, "I had visions."

"Ooh, did you?"

"They didn't like that. They said I would fall down and jerk around horrible, and sometimes I guess I would hurt myself when I fell, and sometimes I'd bite my tongue and it would bleed. But that wasn't what it felt like to me; I wouldn't know about any of those things until afterward. To me it was like I had gone way far ahead, and I had to come back. I didn't want to."

The wind swayed Diane's hair, and she pushed it back from her face. "Did you see things that were going to happen?" she asked.

"Sometimes."

"Really? Did you?"

"Sometimes."

"Tell me about it. When you saw what was going to happen."

"I saw myself dead. I was all black and shrunk up like the dead stuff they cut off in the pontic gardens; and I was floating and turning, like in water but it wasn't water—just floating and turning out in space, in nothing. And there were lights on both sides of me, so both sides were bright but black, and I could see my teeth because the stuff"—he pulled at his cheeks—"had fallen off there, and they were really white."

"That hasn't happened yet."

"Not here."

"Tell me something you saw that happened."

"You mean, like somebody's sister was going to get married, don't you? That's what the girls where I was mostly wanted to know. Or were they going to go home; mostly it wasn't like that."

"But sometimes it was?"

"I guess."

"Tell me one."

Nicholas shook his head. "You wouldn't like it, and anyway it wasn't like that. Mostly it was lights like I never saw anyplace else, and voices like I never heard any other time, telling me things there aren't any words for; stuff like that, only now I can't ever go back. Listen, I wanted to ask you about Ignacio."

"He isn't anybody," the girl said.

"What do you mean, he isn't anybody? Is there anybody here besides you and me and Ignacio and Dr. Island?"

"Not that we can see or touch."

The monkey called, "There are other patients, but for the present, Nicholas, for your own well-being as well as theirs, it is best for you to remain by yourselves." It was a long sentence for a monkey.

"What's that about?"

"If I tell you, will you tell me about something you saw that really happened?"

"All right."

"Tell me first."

"There was this girl where I was—her name was Maya. They had, you know, boys' and girls' dorms, but you saw everybody in the rec room and the dining hall and so on, and she was in my psychodrama group." Her hair had been black, and shiny as the lacquered furniture in Dr. Hong's rooms, her skin white like the mother-of-pearl, her eyes long and narrow (making him think of cats' eyes) and darkly blue. She was fifteen, or so Nicholas believed—maybe sixteen. "*I'm going home,*" she told him. It was psychodrama, and he was her brother, younger than she, and she was already at home; but when she said this the floating ring of light that gave them the necessary separation from the small doctor-and-patient audience, ceased, by instant agreement, to be Maya's mother's living room and became a visiting lounge. Nicholas/Jerry said: "Hey, that's great! Hey, I got a new bike—when you come home you want to ride it?"

Maureen/Maya's mother said, "Maya, don't. You'll run into something and break your teeth, and you know how much they cost."

"You don't want me to have any fun."

"We do, dear, but *nice* fun. A girl has to be so much more careful—oh, Maya, I wish I could make you understand, really, how careful a girl has to be."

Nobody said anything, so Nicholas/Jerry filled in with, "It has a three-bladed prop, and I'm going to tape streamers to them with little weights at the ends, an' when I go down old thirty-seven B passageway, look out, here comes that old coleslaw grater!"

"Like this," Maya said, and held her legs together and extended her arms, to make a three-bladed bike prop or a crucifix. She had thrown herself into a spin as she made the movement, and revolved slowly, stage center—red shorts, white blouse, red shorts, white blouse, red shorts, no shoes.

Diane asked, "And you saw that she was never going home, she was going to hospital instead, she was going to cut her wrist there, she was going to die?"

Nicholas nodded.

"Did you tell her?"

"Yes," Nicholas said. "No."

"Make up your mind. Didn't you tell her? Now, don't get mad."

"Is it telling, when the one you tell doesn't understand?"

Diane thought about that for a few steps while Nicholas dashed water on the hot bruises Ignacio had left upon his face. "If it was plain and clear and she ought to have understood—that's the trouble I have with my family."

"What is?"

"They won't say things—do you know what I mean? I just say look, just tell me, just tell me what I'm supposed to do, tell me what it is you want, but it's different all the time. My mother says, 'Diane, you ought to meet some boys, you can't go out with him, your father and I have never met him, we don't even know his family at all, Douglas, there's something I think you ought to know about Diane, she gets confused sometimes, we've had her to doctors, she's been in a hospital, try—'"

"Not to get her excited," Nicholas finished for her.

"Were you listening? I mean, are you from the Trojan Planets? Do you know my mother?"

"I only live in these places," Nicholas said, "that's for a long time. But you talk like other people."

"I feel better now that I'm with you; you're really nice. I wish you were older."

"I'm not sure I'm going to get much older."

"It's going to rain—feel it?"

Nicholas shook his head.

"Look." Diane jumped, bunnyrabbit-clumsy, three meters into the air. "See how high I can jump? That means people are sad and it's going to rain. I told you."

"No, you didn't."

"Yes, I did, Nicholas."

He waved the argument away, struck by a sudden thought. "You ever been to Callisto?"

The girl shook her head, and Nicholas said, "I have; that's where they did the operation. It's so big the gravity's mostly from natural mass, and it's all domed in, with a whole lot of air in it."

"So?"

"And when I was there it rained. There was a big trouble at one of the generating piles, and they shut it down and it got colder and colder until everybody in the hospital wore their blankets, just like Amerinds in books, and they locked the switches off on the heaters in the bathrooms, and the nurses and the com screen told you all the time it wasn't dangerous, they were just rationing power to keep from blacking out the important stuff that was still running. And then it rained, just like on Earth. They said it got so cold the water condensed in the air, and it was like the whole hospital was right under a shower bath. Everybody on the top floor had to come down because it rained right on their beds, and for two nights I had a man in my room with me that had his arm cut off in a machine. But we couldn't jump any higher, and it got kind of dark."

"It doesn't always get dark here," Diane said. "Sometimes the rain sparkles. I think Dr. Island must do it to cheer everyone up."

"No," the waves explained, "or at least not in the way you mean, Diane."

Nicholas was hungry and started to ask them for something to eat, then turned his hunger in against itself, spat on the sand, and was still.

"It rains here when most of you are sad," the waves were saying, "because rain is a sad thing, to the human psyche. It is that, that sadness, perhaps because it recalls to unhappy people their own tears, that palliates melancholy."

Diane said, "Well, I know sometimes I feel better when it rains."

"That should help you to understand yourself. Most people are soothed when their environment is in harmony with their emotions, and anxious when it is not. An angry person becomes less angry in a red room, and unhappy people are only exasperated by sunshine and birdsong. Do you remember:

> *And, missing thee, I walk unseen*
> *On the dry smooth-shaven green*
> *To behold the wandering moon,*
> *Riding near her highest noon,*
> *Like one that had been led astray*
> *Through the heaven's wide pathless way?*

The girl shook her head.

Nicholas said, "No. Did somebody write that?" and then "You said you couldn't do anything."

The waves replied, "I can't—except talk to you."

"You make it rain."

"Your heart beats; I sense its pumping even as I speak—do you control the beating of your heart?"

"I can stop my breath."

"Can you stop your heart? Honestly, Nicholas?"

"I guess not."

"No more can I control the weather of my world, stop anyone from doing what he wishes, or feed you if you are hungry; with no need of volition on my part your emotions are monitored and averaged, and our weather responds. Calm and sunshine for tranquility, rain for melancholy, storms for rage, and so on. This is what mankind has always wanted."

Diane asked, "What is?"

"That the environment should respond to human thought. That is the core of magic and the oldest dream of mankind; and here, on me, it is fact."

"So that we'll be well?"

Nicholas said angrily, "You're not sick!"

Dr. Island said, "So that some of you, at least, can return to society."

Nicholas threw a sea shell into the water as though to strike the mouth that spoke. "Why are we talking to this thing?"

"Wait, tot, I think it's interesting."

"Lies and lies."

Dr. Island said, "How do I lie, Nicholas?"

"You said it was magic—"

"No, I said that when humankind has dreamed of magic, the wish behind that dream has been the omnipotence of thought. Have you never wanted to be a magician, Nicholas, making palaces spring up overnight, or riding an enchanted horse of ebony to battle with the demons of the air?"

"I am a magician—I have preternatural powers, and before they cut us in two—"

Diane interrupted him. "You said you averaged emotions. When you made it rain."

"Yes."

"Doesn't that mean that if one person was really, terribly sad, he'd move the average so much he could make it rain all by himself? Or whatever? That doesn't seem fair."

The waves might have smiled. "That has never happened. But if it did, Diane, if one person felt such deep emotion, think how great her need would be. Don't you think we should answer it?"

Diane looked at Nicholas, but he was walking again, his head swinging, ignoring her as well as the voice of the waves. "Wait," she called. "You said I wasn't sick; I am, you know."

"No, you're not."

She hurried after him. "Everyone says so, and sometimes I'm so confused, and other times I'm boiling inside, just boiling. Mum says if you've got something on the stove you don't want to have burn, you just have to keep one finger on the handle of the pan and it won't, but I can't, I can't always find the handle or remember."

Without looking back the boy said, "Your mother is probably sick; maybe your father too, I don't know. But you're not. If they'd just let you alone you'd be all right. Why shouldn't you get upset, having to live with two crazy people?"

"Nicholas!" She grabbed his thin shoulders. "That's not true!"

"Yes, it is."

"I am sick. Everyone says so."

"I don't; so 'everyone' just means the ones that do—isn't that right? And if you don't either, that will be two; it can't be everyone then."

The girl called, "Doctor? Dr. Island?"

Nicholas said, "You aren't going to believe that, are you?"

"Dr. Island, is it true?"

"Is what true, Diane?"

"What he said. Am I sick?"

"Sickness—even physical illness—is relative, Diane; and complete health is an idealization, an abstraction, even if the other end of the scale is not."

"You know what I mean."

"You are not physically ill." A long, blue comber curled into a line of hissing spray reaching infinitely along the sea to their left and right. "As you said yourself a moment ago, you are sometimes confused, and sometimes disturbed."

"He said if it weren't for other people, if it weren't for my mother and father, I wouldn't have to be here."

"Diane . . ."

"Well, is that true or isn't it?"

"Most emotional illness would not exist, Diane, if it were possible in every case to separate oneself—in thought as well as circumstance—if only for a time."

"Separate oneself?"

"Did you ever think of going away, at least for a time?"

The girl nodded, then as though she were not certain Dr. Island could see her, said, "Often, I suppose; leaving the school and getting my own compartment somewhere—going to Achilles. Sometimes I wanted to so badly."

"Why didn't you?"

"They would have worried. And anyway, they would have found me, and made me come home."

"Would it have done any good if I—or a human doctor—had told them not to?"

When the girl said nothing Nicholas snapped, "You could have locked them up."

"They were functioning, Nicholas. They bought and sold; they worked, and paid their taxes—"

Diane said softly, "It wouldn't have done any good anyway, Nicholas; they are inside me."

"Diane was no longer functioning: she was failing every subject at the university she attended, and her presence in her classes, when she came, disturbed the instructors and the other students. You were not functioning either, and people of your own age were afraid of you."

"That's what counts with you, then. Functioning."

"If I were different from the world, would that help you when you got back into the world?"

"You are different." Nicholas kicked the sand. "Nobody ever saw a place like this."

"You mean that reality to you is metal corridors, rooms without windows, noise."

"Yes."

"That is the unreality, Nicholas. Most people have never had to endure such things. Even now, this—my beach, my sea, my trees—is more in harmony with most human lives than your metal corridors; and here, I am your social environment—what individuals call 'they.' You see, sometimes if we take people who are troubled back to something like me, to an idealized natural setting, it helps them."

"Come on," Nicholas told the girl. He took her arm, acutely conscious of being so much shorter than she.

"A question," murmured the waves. "If Diane's parents had been taken here instead of Diane, do you think it would have helped them?"

Nicholas did not reply.

"We have treatments for disturbed persons, Nicholas. But, at least for the time being, we have no treatment for disturbing persons." Diane and the boy had turned away, and the waves' hissing and slapping ceased to be speech. Gulls wheeled overhead, and once a red-and-yellow parrot fluttered from one palm to another. A monkey running on all fours like a little dog approached them, and Nicholas chased it, but it escaped.

"I'm going to take one of those things apart someday," he said, "and pull the wires out."

"Are we going to walk all the way 'round?" Diane asked. She might have been talking to herself.

"Can you do that?"

"Oh, you can't walk all around Dr. Island; it would be too long, and you can't get there anyway. But we could walk until we get back to where we started—we're probably more than halfway now."

"Are there other islands you can't see from here?"

The girl shook her head. "I don't think so; there's just this one big island in his satellite, and all the rest is water."

"Then if there's only the one island, we're going to have to walk all around it to get back to where we started. What are you laughing at?"

"Look down the beach, as far as you can. Never mind how it slips off to the side—pretend it's straight."

"I don't see anything."

"Don't you? Watch." Diane leaped into the air, six meters or more this time, and waved her arms.

"It looks like there's somebody ahead of us, way down the beach."

"Uh-huh. Now look behind."

"Okay, there's somebody there too. Come to think of it, I saw someone on the beach when I first got here. It seemed funny to see so far, but I guess I thought they were other patients. Now I see two people."

"They're us. That was probably yourself you saw the other time, too. There are just so many of us to each strip of beach, and Dr. Island only wants certain ones to mix. So the space bends around. When we get to one end of our strip and try to step over, we'll be at the other end."

"How did you find out?"

"Dr. Island told me about it when I first came here." The girl was silent for a moment, and her smile vanished. "Listen, Nicholas, do you want to see something really funny?"

Nicholas asked, "What?" As he spoke, a drop of rain struck his face.

"You'll see. Come on, though. We have to go into the middle instead of following the beach, and it will give us a chance to get under the trees and out of the rain."

When they had left the sand and the sound of the surf, and were walking on solid ground under green-leaved trees, Nicholas said, "Maybe we can find some fruit." They were so light now that he had to be careful not to bound into the air with each step. The rain fell slowly around them, in crystal spheres.

"Maybe," the girl said doubtfully. "Wait, let's stop here." She sat down where a huge tree sent twenty-meter wooden arches over dark, mossy ground. "Want to climb up there and see if you can find us something?"

"All right," Nicholas agreed. He jumped, and easily caught hold of a branch far above the girl's head. In a moment he was climbing in a green world, with the rain pattering all around him; he followed narrowing limbs into leafy wildernesses where the cool water ran from every twig he touched, and twice found the empty nests of birds, and once a slender snake, green as any leaf with a head as long as his thumb; but there was no fruit. "Nothing," he said, when he dropped down beside the girl once more.

"That's all right, we'll find something."

He said, "I hope so," and noticed that she was looking at him oddly, then realized that his left hand had lifted itself to touch her right breast. It dropped as he looked, and he felt his face grow hot. He said, "I'm sorry."

"That's all right."

"We like you. He—over there—he can't talk, you see. I guess I can't talk either."

"I think it's just you—in two pieces. I don't care."

"Thanks." He had picked up a leaf, dead and damp, and was tearing it to shreds; first his right hand tearing while the left held the leaf, then turnabout. "Where does the rain come from?" The dirty flakes clung to the fingers of both

"Hmm?"

"Where does the rain come from? I mean, it isn't because it's colder here now, like on Callisto; it's because the gravity's turned down some way, isn't it?"

"From the sea. Don't you know how this place is built?"

Nicholas shook his head.

"Didn't they show it to you from the ship when you came? It's beautiful. They showed it to me—I just sat there and looked at it, and I wouldn't talk to them, and the nurse thought I wasn't paying any attention, but I heard everything. I just didn't want to talk to her. It wasn't any use."

"I know how you felt."

"But they didn't show it to you?"

"No, on my ship they kept me locked up because I burned some stuff. They thought I couldn't start a fire without an igniter, but if you have electricity in the wall sockets it's easy. They had a thing on me—you know?" He clasped his arms to his body to show how he had been restrained. "I bit one of them, too— I guess I didn't tell you that yet: I bite people. They locked me up, and for a long time I had nothing to do, and then I could feel us dock with something, and they came and got me and pulled me down a regular companionway for a long time, and it just seemed like a regular place. Then they stuck me full of Tranquil-C—I guess they didn't know it doesn't hardly work on me at all—with a pneumogun, and lifted a kind of door thing and shoved me up."

"Didn't they make you undress?"

"I already was. When they put the ties on me I did things in my clothes and they had to take them off me. It made them mad." He grinned unevenly. "Does Tranquil-C work on you? Or any of that other stuff?"

"I suppose they would, but then I never do the sort of thing you do anyway."

"Maybe you ought to."

"Sometimes they used to give me medication that was supposed to cheer me up; then I couldn't sleep, and I walked and walked, you know, and ran into things and made a lot of trouble for everyone; but what good does it do?"

Nicholas shrugged. "Not doing it doesn't do any good either—I mean, we're both here. My way, I know I've made them jump; they shoot that stuff in me and I'm not mad anymore, but I know what it is and I just think what I would do if I *were* mad, and I do it, and when it wears off I'm glad I did."

"I think you're still angry somewhere, deep down."

Nicholas was already thinking of something else. "This island says Ignacio kills people." He paused. "What does it look like?"

"Ignacio?"

"No, I've seen him. Dr. Island."

"Oh, you mean when I was in the ship. The satellite's round of course, and all clear except where Dr. Island is, so that's a dark spot. The rest of it's temperglass, and from space you can't even see the water."

"That *is* the sea up there, isn't it?" Nicholas asked, trying to look up at it through the tree leaves and the rain. "I thought it was when I first came."

"Sure. It's like a glass ball, and we're inside, and the water's inside too, and just goes all around up the curve."

"That's why I could see so far out on the beach, isn't it? Instead of dropping down from you like on Callisto it bends up so you can see it."

The girl nodded. "And the water lets the light through, but filters out the ultraviolet. Besides, it gives us thermal mass, so we don't heat up too much when we're between the sun and the Bright Spot."

"Is that what keeps us warm? The Bright Spot?"

Diane nodded again. "We go around in ten hours, you see, and that holds us over it all the time."

"Why can't I see it, then? It ought to look like Sol does from the Belt, only bigger; but there's just a shimmer in the sky, even when it's not raining."

"The waves diffract the light and break up the image. You'd see the Focus, though, if the air weren't so clear. Do you know what the Focus is?"

Nicholas shook his head.

"We'll get to it pretty soon, after this rain stops. Then I'll tell you."

"I still don't understand about the rain."

Unexpectedly Diane giggled. "I just thought—do you know what I was supposed to be? While I was going to school?"

"Quiet," Nicholas said.

"No, silly. I mean what I was being trained to do, if I graduated and all that. I was going to be a teacher, with all those cameras on me and tots from everywhere watching and popping questions on the two-way. Jolly time. Now I'm doing it here, only there's no one but you."

"You mind?"

"No, I suppose I enjoy it." There was a black-and-blue mark on Diane's thigh, and she rubbed it pensively with one hand as she spoke. "Anyway, there are three ways to make gravity. Do you know them? Answer, clerk."

"Sure; acceleration, mass, and synthesis."

"That's right; motion and mass are both bendings of space, of course, which is why Zeno's paradox doesn't work out that way, and why masses move toward each other—what we call falling—or at least try to; and if they're held apart it produces the tension we perceive as a force and call weight and all that rot. So naturally if you bend the space direct, you synthesize a gravity effect, and that's what holds all that water up against the translucent shell—there's nothing like enough mass to do it by itself."

"You mean"—Nicholas held out his hand to catch a slow-moving globe of rain—"that this is water from the sea?"

"Right-o, up on top. Do you see, the temperature differences in the air make the winds, and the winds make the waves and surf you saw when we were walking along the shore. When the waves break they throw up these little drops, and if you watch you'll see that even when it's clear they go up a long way sometimes. Then if the gravity is less they can get away altogether, and if we were on the outside they'd fly off into space; but we aren't, we're inside, so all they can do is go across the center, more or less, until they hit the water again, or Dr. Island."

"Dr. Island said they had storms sometimes, when people got mad."

"Yes. Lots of wind, and so there's lots of rain too. Only the rain then is because the wind tears the tops off the waves, and you don't get light like you do in a normal rain."

"What makes so much wind?"

"I don't know. It happens somehow."

They sat in silence, Nicholas listening to the dripping of the leaves. He remembered then that they had spun the hospital module, finally, to get the little spheres of clotting blood out of the air; Maya's blood was building up on the grills of the purification intake ducts, spotting them black, and someone had been afraid they would decay there and smell. He had not been there when they did it, but he could imagine the droplets settling, like this, in the slow spin. The old psychodrama group had already been broken up, and when he saw Maureen or any of the others in the rec room they talked about Good Old Days. It has not seemed like Good Old Days then except that Maya had been there.

Diane said, "It's going to stop."

"It looks just as bad to me."

"No, it's going to stop—see, they're falling a little faster now, and I feel heavier."

Nicholas stood up. "You rested enough yet? You want to go on?"

"We'll get wet."

He shrugged.

"I don't want to get my hair wet, Nicholas. It'll be over in a minute."

He sat down again. "How long have you been here?"

"I'm not sure."

"Don't you count the days?"

"I lose track a lot."

"Longer than a week?"

"Nicholas, don't ask me, all right?"

"Isn't there anybody on this piece of Dr. Island except you and me and Ignacio?"

"I don't think there was anyone but Ignacio before you came."

"Who is he?"

She looked at him.

"Well, who is he? You know me—us—Nicholas Kenneth de Vore; and you're Diane who?"

"Phillips."

"And you're from the Trojan Planets, and I was from the Outer Belt, I guess, to start with. What about Ignacio? You talk to him sometimes, don't you? Who is he?"

"I don't know. He's important."

For an instant, Nicholas froze. "What does that mean?"

"Important." The girl was feeling her knees, running her hands back and forth across them.

"Maybe everybody's important."

"I know you're just a tot, Nicholas, but don't be so stupid. Come on, you wanted to go, let's go now. It's pretty well stopped." She stood, stretching her thin body, her arms over her head. "My knees are rough—you made me think of that. When I came here they were still so smooth, I think. I used to put a certain lotion on them. Because my Dad would feel them, and my hands and elbows too, and he'd say if they weren't smooth nobody'd ever want me; Mum wouldn't say anything, but she'd be cross after, and they used to come and visit, and so I kept a bottle in my room and I used to put it on. Once I drank some."

Nicholas was silent.

"Aren't you going to ask me if I died?" She stepped ahead of him, pulling aside the dripping branches. "See here, I'm sorry I said you were stupid."

"I'm just thinking," Nicholas said. "I'm not mad at you. Do you really know anything about him?"

"No, but look at it." She gestured. "Look around you; someone *built* all this."

"You mean it cost a lot."

"It's automated, of course, but still . . . well, the other places where you were before—how much space was there for each patient? Take the total volume and divide it by the number of people there."

"Okay, this is a whole lot bigger, but maybe they think we're worth it."

"Nicholas . . ." She paused. "Nicholas, Ignacio is homicidal. Didn't Dr. Island tell you?"

"Yes."

"And you're fourteen and not very big for it, and I'm a girl. Who are they worried about?"

The look on Nicholas's face startled her.

After an hour or more of walking they came to it. It was a band of withered vegetation, brown and black and tumbling, and as straight as if it had been drawn with a ruler. "I was afraid it wasn't going to be here," Diane said. "It moves around whenever there's a storm. It might not have been in our sector anymore at all."

Nicholas asked, "What is it?"

"The Focus. It's been all over, but mostly the plants grow back quickly when it's gone."

"It smells funny—like the kitchen in a place where they wanted me to work in the kitchen once."

"Vegetables rotting, that's what that is. What did you do?"

"Nothing—put detergent in the stuff they were cooking. What makes this?"

"The Bright Spot. See, when it's just about overhead the curve of the sky and the water up there make a lens. It isn't a very good lens—a lot of the light scatters. But enough is focused to do this. It wouldn't fry us if it came past right now, if that's what you're wondering, because it's not that hot. I've stood right in it, but you want to get out in a minute."

"I thought it was going to be about seeing ourselves down the beach."

Diane seated herself on the trunk of a fallen tree. "It was, really. The last time I was here it was further from the water, and I suppose it had been there a long time, because it had cleared out a lot of the dead stuff. The sides of the sector are nearer here, you see; the whole sector narrows down like a piece of pie. So you could look down the Focus either way and see yourself nearer than you could on the beach. It was almost as if you were in a big, big room, with a looking-glass on each wall, or as if you could stand behind yourself. I thought you might like it."

"I'm going to try it here," Nicholas announced, and he clambered up one of the dead trees while the girl waited below, but the dry limbs creaked and snapped beneath his feet, and he could not get high enough to see himself in either direction. When he dropped to the ground beside her again, he said, "There's nothing to eat here either, is there?"

"I haven't found anything."

"They—I mean, Dr. Island wouldn't just let us starve, would he?"

"I don't think he could do anything; that's the way this place is built. Sometimes you find things, and I've tried to catch fish, but I never could. A couple of times Ignacio gave me part of what he had, though; he's good at it. I bet you think I'm skinny, don't you? But I was a lot fatter when I came here."

"What are we going to do now?"

"Keep walking, I suppose, Nicholas. Maybe go back to the water."

"Do you think we'll find anything?"

From a decaying log, insect stridulations called, "Wait."

Nicholas asked, "Do *you* know where anything is?"

"Something for you to eat? Not at present. But I can show you something much more interesting, not far from here, than this clutter of dying trees. Would you like to see it?"

Diane said, "Don't go, Nicholas."

"What is it?"

"Diane, who calls this 'the Focus,' calls what I wish to show you 'the Point.' "

Nicholas asked Diane, "Why shouldn't I go?"

"I'm not going. I went there once anyway."

"I took her," Dr. Island said. "And I'll take you. I wouldn't take you if I didn't think it might help you."

"I don't think Diane liked it."

"Diane may not wish to be helped—help may be painful, and often people do not. But it is my business to help them if I can, whether or not they wish it."

"Suppose I don't want to go?"

"Then I cannot compel you; you know that. But you will be the only patient in this sector who has not seen it, Nicholas, as well as the youngest; both Diane and Ignacio have, and Ignacio goes there often."

"Is it dangerous?"

"No. Are you afraid?"

Nicholas looked questioningly at Diane. "What is it? What will I see?"

She had walked away while he was talking to Dr. Island, and was now sitting cross-legged on the ground about five meters from where Nicholas stood, staring at her hands. Nicholas repeated, "What will I see, Diane?" He did not think she would answer.

She said, "A glass. A mirror."

"Just a mirror?"

"You know how I told you to climb the tree here? The Point is where the edges come together. You can see yourself—like on the beach—but closer."

Nicholas was disappointed. "I've seen myself in mirrors lots of times."

Dr. Island, whose voice was now in the sighing of the dead leaves, whispered, "Did you have a mirror in your room, Nicholas, before you came here?"

"A steel one."

"So that you could not break it?"

"I guess so. I threw things at it sometimes, but it just got puckers in it." Remembering dimpled reflections, Nicholas laughed.

"You can't break this one either."

"It doesn't sound like it's worth going to see."

"I think it is."

"Diane, do you still think I shouldn't go?"

There was no reply. The girl sat staring at the ground in front of her.

Nicholas walked over to look at her and found a tear had washed a damp trail down each thin cheek, but she did not move when he touched her. "She's catatonic, isn't she," he said.

A green limb just outside the Focus nodded. "Catatonic schizophrenia."

"I had a doctor once that said those names—like that. They didn't mean anything." (The doctor had been a therapy robot, but a human doctor gave more status. Robots' patients sat in doorless booths—two and a half hours a day for Nicholas: an hour and a half in the morning, an hour in the afternoon—and talked to something that appeared to be a small, friendly food freezer. Some people sat every day in silence, while other talked continually, and for such patients as these the attendants seldom troubled to turn the machines on.)

"He meant cause and treatment. He was correct."

Nicholas stood looking down at the girl's streaked, brown-blond head. "What *is* the cause? I mean for her."

"I don't know."

"And what's the treatment?"

"You are seeing it."

"Will it help her?"

"Probably not."

"Listen, she can hear you, don't you know that? She hears everything we say."

"If my answer disturbs you, Nicholas, I can change it. It will help her if she wants to be helped; if she insists on clasping her illness to her it will not."

"We ought to go away from here," Nicholas said uneasily.

"To your left you will see a little path, a very faint one. Between the twisted tree and the bush with the yellow flowers."

Nicholas nodded and began to walk, looking back at Diane several times. The flowers were butterflies, who fled in a cloud of color when he approached them, and he wondered if Dr. Island had known. When he had gone a hundred paces and was well away from the brown and rotting vegetation, he said, "She was sitting in the Focus."

"Yes."

"Is she still there?"

"Yes."

"What will happen when the Bright Spot comes?"

"Diane will become uncomfortable and move, if she is still there."

"Once in one of the places I was in there was a man who was like that, and they said he wouldn't get anything to eat if he didn't get up and get it, they weren't going to feed him with the nose tube anymore; and they didn't, and he died. We told them about it and they wouldn't do anything and he starved to death right there, and when he was dead they rolled him off onto a stretcher and changed the bed and put somebody else there."

"I know, Nicholas. You told the doctors at St. John's about all that, and it is in your file; but think: well men have starved themselves—yes, to death—to protest what they felt were political injustices. Is it so surprising that your friend killed himself in the same way to protest what he felt as a psychic injustice?"

"He wasn't my friend. Listen, did you really mean it when you said the treatment she was getting here would help Diane if she wanted to be helped?"

"No."

Nicholas halted in mid-stride. "You didn't mean it? You don't think it's true?"

"No, I doubt that anything will help her."

"I don't think you ought to lie to us."

"Why not? If by chance you become well you will be released, and if you are released you will have to deal with your society, which will lie to you frequently. Here, where there are so few individuals, I must take the place of society. I have explained that."

"Is that what you are?"

"Society's surrogate? Of course. Who do you imagine built me? What else could I be?"

"The doctor."

"You have had many doctors, and so has she. Not one of them has benefited you much."

"I'm not sure you even want to help us."

"Do you wish to see what Diane calls 'the Point'?"

"I guess so."

"Then you must walk. You will not see it standing here."

Nicholas walked, thrusting aside leafy branches and dangling creepers wet with rain. The jungle smelled of the life of green things; there were ants on the tree trunks, and the dragonflies with hot, red bodies and wings as long as his hands. "Do you want to help us?" he asked after a time.

"My feelings toward you are ambivalent. But when you wish to be helped, I wish to help you."

The ground sloped gently upward, and as it rose became somewhat more clear, the big trees a trifle farther apart, the underbrush spent in grass and fern. Occasionally there were stone outcrops to be climbed, and clearings open to the tumbling sky. Nicholas asked, "Who made this trail?"

"Ignacio. He comes here often."

"He's not afraid, then? Diane's afraid."

"Ignacio is afraid too, but he comes."

"Diane says Ignacio is important."

"Yes."

"What do you mean by that? Is he important? More important than we are?"

"Do you remember that I told you I was the surrogate of society? What do you think society wants, Nicholas?"

"Everybody to do what it says."

"You mean conformity. Yes, there must be conformity, but something else too—consciousness."

"I don't want to hear about it."

"Without consciousness, which you may call sensitivity if you are careful not to allow yourself to be confused by the term, there is no progress. A century ago, Nicholas, mankind was suffocating on Earth; now it is suffocating again. About half of the people who have contributed substantially to the advance of humanity have shown signs of emotional disturbance."

"I told you, I don't want to hear about it. I asked you an easy question—is Ignacio more important than Diane and me—and you won't tell me. I've heard all this you're saying. I've heard it fifty, maybe a hundred times from everybody, and it's lies; it's the regular thing, and you've got it written down on a card somewhere to read out when anybody asks. Those people you talk about that went crazy, they went crazy because while they were 'advancing humanity,' or whatever you call it, people kicked them out of their rooms because they couldn't pay, and while they were getting thrown out you were making other people rich that had never done anything in their whole lives except think about how to get that way."

"Sometimes it is hard, Nicholas, to determine before the fact—or even at the time—just who should be honored."

"How do you know if you've never tried?"

"You asked if Ignacio was more important than Diane or yourself. I can only say that Ignacio seems to me to hold a brighter promise of a full recovery coupled with a substantial contribution to human progress."

"If he's so good, why did he crack up?"

"Many do, Nicholas. Even among the inner planets space is not a kind environment for mankind; and our space, trans-Martian space, is worse. Any young person here, anyone like yourself or Diane who would seem to have a better-than-average chance of adapting to the conditions we face, is precious."

"Or Ignacio."

"Yes, or Ignacio. Ignacio has a tested IQ of two hundred and ten, Nicholas. Diane's is one hundred and twenty. Your own is ninety-five."

"They never took mine."

"It's on your records, Nicholas."

"They tried to and I threw down the helmet and it broke; Sister Carmela— she was the nurse—just wrote down something on the paper and sent me back."

"I see. I will ask for a complete investigation of this, Nicholas."

"Sure."

"Don't you believe me?"

"I don't think you believe me."

"Nicholas, Nicholas . . ." The long tongues of grass now beginning to appear beneath the immense trees sighed. "Can't you see that a certain measure of trust between the two of us is essential?"

"Did you believe me?"

"Why do you ask? Suppose I were to say I did; would you believe that?"

"When you told me I had been reclassified."

"You would have to be retested, for which there are no facilities here."

"If you believed me, why did you say retested? I told you I haven't ever been tested at all—but anyway you could cross out the ninety-five."

"It is impossible for me to plan your therapy without some estimate of your intelligence, Nicholas, and I have nothing with which to replace it."

The ground was sloping up more sharply now, and in a clearing the boy halted and turned to look back at the leafy film, like algae over a pool, beneath which he had climbed, and at the sea beyond. To his right and left his view was still hemmed with foliage, and ahead of him a meadow on edge (like the square of sand through which he had come, though he did not think of that), dotted still with trees, stretched steeply toward an invisible summit. It seemed to him that under his feet the mountainside swayed ever so slightly. Abruptly he demanded of the wind, "Where's Ignacio?"

"Not here. Much closer to the beach."

"And Diane?"

"Where you left her. Do you enjoy the panorama?"

"It's pretty, but it feels like we're rocking."

"We are. I am moored to the temperglass exterior of our satellite by two hundred cables, but the tide and the currents none the less impart a slight motion to my body. Naturally this movement is magnified as you go higher."

"I thought you were fastened right onto the hull; if there's water under you, how do people get in and out?"

"I am linked to the main air lock by a communication tube. To you when you came, it probably seemed an ordinary companionway."

Nicholas nodded and turned his back on leaves and sea and began to climb again.

"You are in a beautiful spot, Nicholas; do you open your heart to beauty?" After waiting for an answer that did not come, the wind sang:

> The mountain wooded to the peak, the lawns
> And winding glades high up like ways to Heaven,
> The slender coco's drooping crown of plumes,
> The lightning flash of insect and of bird,
> The lustre of the long convolvuluses
> That coil'd around the stately stems, and ran
> Ev'n to the limit of the land, the glows
> And glories of the broad belt of the world,
> All these he saw.

"Does this mean nothing to you, Nicholas?"

"You read a lot, don't you?"

"Often, when it is dark, everyone else is asleep and there is very little else for me to do."

"You talk like a woman; are you a woman?"

"How could I be a woman?"

"You know what I mean. Except, when you were talking mostly to Diane, you sounded more like a man."

"You haven't yet said you think me beautiful."

"You're an Easter egg."

"What do you mean by that, Nicholas?"

"Never mind." He saw the egg as it had hung in the air before him, shining with gold and covered with flowers.

"Eggs are dyed with pretty colors for Easter, and my colors are beautiful—is that what you mean, Nicholas?"

His mother had brought the egg on visiting day, but she could never have made it. Nicholas knew who must have made it. The gold was that very pure gold used for shielding delicate instruments; the clear flakes of crystallized carbon that dotted the egg's surface with tiny stars could only have come from a laboratory high-pressure furnace. How angry he must have been when she told him she was going to give it to him.

"It's pretty, isn't it, Nicky?"

It hung in the weightlessness between them, turning very slowly with the memory of her scented gloves.

"The flowers are meadowsweet, fraxinella, lily of the valley, and moss rose—though I wouldn't expect you to recognize them, darling." His mother had never been below the orbit of Mars, but she pretended to have spent her girlhood on Earth; each reference to the lie filled Nicholas with inexpressible fury and shame. The egg was about twenty centimeters long and it revolved, end over end, in some small fraction more than eight of the pulse beats he felt in his cheeks. Visiting time had twenty-three minutes to go.

"Aren't you going to look at it?"

"I can see it from here." He tried to make her understand. "I can see every part of it. The little red things are aluminum oxide crystals, right?"

"I mean, look *inside*, Nicky."

He saw then that there was a lens at one end, disguised as a dewdrop in the throat of an asphodel. Gently he took the egg in his hands, closed one eye, and looked. The light of the interior was not, as he had half expected, gold tinted, but brilliantly white, deriving from some concealed source. A world surely meant for Earth shone within, as though seen from below the orbit of the moon—indigo sea and emerald land. Rivers brown and clear as tea ran down long plains.

His mother said, "Isn't it pretty?"

Night hung at the corners in funereal purple, and sent long shadows like cold and lovely arms to caress the day; and while he watched and it fell, long-necked birds of so dark a pink that they were nearly red trailed stilt legs across the sky, their wings making crosses.

"They are called flamingos," Dr. Island said, following the direction of his eyes. "Isn't it a pretty word? For a pretty bird, but I don't think we'd like them as much if we called them sparrows, would we?"

His mother said, "I'm going to take it home and keep it for you. It's too nice to leave with a little boy, but if you ever come home again it will be waiting for you. On your dresser, beside your hairbrushes."

Nicholas said, "Words just mix you up."

"You shouldn't despise them, Nicholas. Besides having great beauty of their own, they are useful in reducing tension. You might benefit from that."

"You mean you walk yourself out of it."

"I mean that a person's ability to verbalize his feelings, if only to himself, may prevent them from destroying him. Evolution teaches us, Nicholas, that the original purpose of language was to ritualize men's threats and curses, his spells to compel the gods; communication came later. Words can be a safety valve."

Nicholas said, "I want to be a bomb; a bomb doesn't need a safety valve." To his mother, "Is that South America, Mama?"

"No, dear, India. The Malabar Coast on your left, the Coromandel Coast on your right, and Ceylon below." Words.

"A bomb destroys itself, Nicholas."

"A bomb doesn't care."

He was climbing resolutely now, his toes grabbing at tree roots and the soft, mossy soil; his physician was no longer the wind but a small brown monkey that followed a stone's throw behind him. "I hear someone coming," he said.

"Yes."

"Is it Ignacio?"

The Death of Doctor Island   173

"No, it is Nicholas. You are close now."

"Close to the Point?"

"Yes."

He stopped and looked around him. The sounds he had heard, the naked feet padding on soft ground, stopped as well. Nothing seemed strange; the land still rose, and there were large trees, widely spaced, with moss growing in their deepest shade, grass where there was more light. "The three big trees," Nicholas said, "they're just alike. Is that how you know where we are?"

"Yes."

In his mind he called the one before him "Ceylon"; the others were "Coromandel" and "Malabar." He walked toward Ceylon, studying its massive, twisted limbs; a boy naked as himself walked out of the forest to his left, toward Malabar—this boy was not looking at Nicholas, who shouted and ran toward him.

The boy disappeared. Only Malabar, solid and real, stood before Nicholas; he ran to it, touched its rough bark with his hand, and then saw beyond it a fourth tree, similar too to the Ceylon tree, around which a boy peered with averted head. Nicholas watched him for a moment, then said, "I see."

"Do you?" the monkey chattered.

"It's like a mirror, only backwards. The light from the front of me goes out and hits the edge, and comes in the other side, only I can't see it because I'm not looking that way. What I see is the light from my back, sort of, because it comes back this way. When I ran, did I get turned around?"

"Yes, you ran out the left side of the segment, and of course returned immediately from the right."

"I'm not scared. It's kind of fun." He picked up a stick and threw it as hard as he could toward the Malabar tree. It vanished, whizzed over his head, vanished again, slapped the back of his legs. "Did this scare Diane?"

There was no answer. He strode farther, palely naked boys walking to his left and right, but always looking away from him, gradually coming closer.

"Don't go farther," Dr. Island said behind him. "It can be dangerous if you try to pass through the Point itself."

"I see it," Nicholas said. He saw three more trees, growing very close together, just ahead of him; their branches seemed strangely intertwined as they danced together in the wind, and beyond them there was nothing at all.

"You can't actually go through the Point," Dr. Island Monkey said. "The tree covers it."

"Then why did you warn me about it?" Limping and scarred, the boys to his right and left were no more than two meters away now; he had discovered that if he looked straight ahead he could sometimes glimpse their bruised profiles.

"That's far enough, Nicholas."

"I want to touch the tree."

He took another step, and another, then turned. The Malabar boy turned too, presenting his narrow back, on which the ribs and spine seemed welts. Nicholas reached out both arms and laid his hands on the thin shoulders, and as he did, felt other hands—the cool, unfeeling hands of a stranger, dry hands too small—touch his own shoulders and creep upward toward his neck.

"Nicholas!"

He jumped sidewise away from the tree and looked at his hands, his head swaying. "It wasn't me."

"Yes, it was, Nicholas," the monkey said.

"It was one of them."

"You are all of them."

In one quick motion Nicholas snatched up an arm-long section of fallen limb and hurled it at the monkey. It struck the little creature, knocking it down, but the monkey sprang up and fled on three legs. Nicholas sprinted after it.

He had nearly caught it when it darted to one side; as quickly, he turned toward the other, springing for the monkey he saw running toward him there. In an instant it was in his grip, feebly trying to bite. He slammed its head against the ground, then catching it by the ankles swung it against the Ceylon tree until at the third impact he heard the skull crack, and stopped.

He had expected wires, but there were none. Blood oozed from the battered little face, and the furry body was warm and limp in his hands. Leaves above his head said, "You haven't killed me, Nicholas. You never will."

"How does it work?" He was still searching for wires, tiny circuit cards holding micro-logic. He looked about for a sharp stone with which to open the monkey's body, but could find none.

"It is just a monkey," the leaves said. "If you had asked, I would have told you."

"How did you make him talk?" He dropped the monkey, stared at it for a moment, then kicked it. His fingers were bloody, and he wiped them on the leaves of the tree.

"Only my mind speaks to yours, Nicholas."

"Oh," he said. And then, "I've heard of that. I didn't think it would be like this. I thought it would be in my head."

"Your record shows no auditory hallucinations, but haven't you ever known someone who had them?"

"I knew a girl once . . ." He paused.

"Yes?"

"She twisted noises—you know?"

"Yes."

"Like, it would just be a service cart out in the corridor, but she'd hear the fan, and think . . ."

"What?"

"Oh, different things. That it was somebody talking, calling her."

"Hear them?"

"What?" He sat up in his bunk. "Maya?"

"They're coming after me."

"Maya?"

Dr. Island, through the leaves, said, "When I talk to you, Nicholas, your mind makes any sound you hear the vehicle for my thoughts' content. You may hear me softly in the patter of rain, or joyfully in the singing of a bird—but if I wished I could amplify what I say until every idea and suggestion I wished to give would be driven like a nail into your consciousness. Then you would do whatever I wished you to."

"I don't believe it," Nicholas said. "If you can do that, why don't you tell Diane not to be catatonic?"

"First, because she might retreat more deeply into her disease in an effort to escape me; and second, because ending her catatonia in that way would not remove its cause."

"And thirdly?"

"I did not say 'thirdly,' Nicholas."

"I thought I heard it—when two leaves touched."

"Thirdly, Nicholas, because both you and she have been chosen for your effect on someone else; if I were to change her—or you—so abruptly, that effect would be lost." Dr. Island was a monkey again now, a new monkey that chattered from the protection of a tree twenty meters away. Nicholas threw a stick at him.

"The monkeys are only little animals, Nicholas; they like to follow people, and they chatter."

"I bet Ingacio kills them."

"No, he likes them; he only kills fish to eat."

Nicholas was suddenly aware of his hunger. He began to walk.

He found Ignacio on the beach, praying. For an hour or more, Nicholas hid behind the trunk of a palm watching him, but for a long time he could not decide to whom Ignacio prayed. He was kneeling just where the lacy edges of the breakers died, looking out toward the water; and from time to time he bowed, touching his forehead to the damp sand; then Nicholas could hear his voice, faintly, over the crashing and hissing of the waves. In general, Nicholas approved of prayer, having observed that those who prayed were usually more interesting companions than those who did not; but he had also noticed that though it made no difference what name the devotee gave the object of his devotions, it was important to discover how the god was conceived. Ignacio did not seem to be praying to Dr. Island—he would, Nicholas thought, have been facing the other way for that—and for a time he wondered if he were not praying to the waves. From his position behind him he followed Ignacio's line of vision out and out, wave upon wave into the bright, confused sky, up and up until at last it curved completely around and came to rest on Ignacio's back again; and then it occurred to him that Ignacio might be praying to himself. He left the palm trunk then and walked about halfway to the place where Ignacio knelt, and sat down. Above the sounds of the sea and the murmuring of Ignacio's voice hung a silence so immense and fragile that it seemed that at any moment the entire crystal satellite might ring like a gong.

After a time Nicholas felt his left side trembling. With his right hand he began to stroke it, running his fingers down his left arm, and from his left shoulder to the thigh. It worried him that his left side should be so frightened, and he wondered if perhaps that other half of his brain, from which he was forever severed, could hear what Ignacio was saying to the waves. He began to pray himself, so that the other (and perhaps Ignacio too) could hear, saying not quite beneath his breath, "Don't worry, don't be afraid, he's not going to hurt us, he's nice, and if he does we'll get him; we're only going to get something to eat, maybe he'll show us how to catch fish, I think he'll be nice this time." But he knew, or at least felt he knew, that Ignacio would not be nice this time.

Eventually Ignacio stood up; he did not turn to face Nicholas, but waded out to sea; then, as though he had known Nicholas was behind him all the time (though Nicholas was not sure he had been heard—perhaps, so he thought, Dr.

Island had told Ignacio), he gestured to indicate that Nicholas should follow him.

The water was colder than he remembered, the sand coarse and gritty between his toes. He thought of what Dr. Island had told him—about floating—and that a part of her must be this sand, under the water, reaching out (how far?) into the sea; when she ended there would be nothing but the clear temperglass of the satellite itself, far down.

"Come," Ignacio said. "Can you swim?" Just as though he had forgotten the night before. Nicholas said yes, he could, wondering if Ignacio would look around at him when he spoke. He did not.

"And do you know why you are here?"

"You told me to come."

"Ignacio means *here*. Does this not remind you of any place you have seen before, little one?"

Nicholas thought of the crystal gong and the Easter egg, then of the micro-thin globes of perfumed vapor that, at home, were sometimes sent floating down the corridors at Christmas to explode in clean dust and a cold smell of pine forests when the children stuck them with their hoppingcanes; but he said nothing.

Ignacio continued. "Let Ignacio tell you a story. Once there was a man—a boy, actually—on the Earth, who—"

Nicholas wondered why it was always men (most often doctors and clinical psychologists, in his experience) who wanted to tell you stories. Jesus, he recalled, was always telling everyone stories, and the Virgin Mary almost never, though a woman he had once known who thought she was the Virgin Mary had always been talking about her son. He thought Ignacio looked a little like Jesus. He tried to remember if his mother had ever told him stories when he was at home, and decided that she had not; she just turned on the comscreen to the cartoons.

"—wanted to—"

"—tell a story," Nicholas finished for him.

"How did you know?" Angry and surprised.

"It was you, wasn't it? And you want to tell me one now."

"What you said was not what Ignacio would have said. He was going to tell you about a fish."

"Where is it?" Nicholas asked, thinking of the fish Ignacio had been eating the night before, and imagining another such fish, caught while he had been coming back, perhaps, from the Point, and now concealed somewhere, waiting the fire. "Is it a big one?"

"It is gone now," Ignacio said, "but it was only as long as a man's hand. I caught it in the big river."

Huckleberry—"I know, the Mississippi; it was a catfish. Or a sunfish."—*Finn.*

"Possibly that is what you call them; for a time he was as the sun to a certain one." The light from nowhere danced on the water. "In any event he was kept on that table in the salon in the house where life was lived. In a tank, but not the old kind in which one sees the glass, with metal at the corner. But the new kind in which the glass is so strong, but very thin, and curved so that it does not reflect, and there are no corners, and a clever device holds the water clear." He dipped up a handful of sparkling water, still not meeting Nicholas's eyes. "As clear even as this, and there were no ripples, and so you could not see it at all. My fish floated in the center of my table above a few stones."

Nicholas asked, "Did you float on the river on a raft?"

"No, we had a little boat. Ignacio caught this fish in a net, of which he almost bit through the strands before he could be landed; he possessed wonderful teeth. There was no one in the house but him and the other, and the robots; but each morning someone would go to the pool in the patio and catch a goldfish for him. Ignacio would see this goldfish there when he came down for his breakfast, and would think, 'Brave goldfish, you have been cast to the monster, will you be the one to destroy him? Destroy him and you shall have his diamond house forever.' And then the fish, who had a little spot of red beneath his wonderful teeth, a spot like a cherry, would rush upon that young goldfish, and for an instant the water would be all clouded with blood."

"And then what?" Nicholas asked.

"And then the clever machine would make the water clear once more, and the fish would be floating above the stones as before, the fish with the wonderful teeth, and Ignacio would touch the little switch on the table, and ask for more bread, and more fruit."

"Are you hungry now?"

"No, I am tired and lazy now; if I pursue you I will not catch you, and if I catch you—through your own slowness and clumsiness—I will not kill you, and if I kill you I will not eat you."

Nicholas had begun to back away, and at the last words, realizing that they were a signal, he turned and began to run, splashing through the shallow water. Ignacio ran after him, much helped by his longer legs, his hair flying behind his dark young face, his square teeth—each white as a bone and as big as Nicholas's thumbnail—showing like spectators who lined the railings of his lips.

"Don't run, Nicholas," Dr. Island said with the voice of a wave. "It only makes him angry that you run." Nicholas did not answer, but cut to his left, up the beach and among the trunks of the palms, sprinting all the way because he had no way of knowing Ignacio was not right behind him, about to grab him by the neck. When he stopped it was in the thick jungle, among the boles of the hardwoods, where he leaned, out of breath, the thumping of his own heart the only sound in an atmosphere silent and unwaked as Earth's long, prehuman day. For a time he listened for any sound Ignacio might make searching for him; there was none. He drew a deep breath then and said, "Well, that's over," expecting Dr. Island to answer from somewhere; there was only the green hush.

The light was still bright and strong and nearly shadowless, but some interior sense told him the day was nearly over, and he noticed that such faint shades as he could see stretched long, horizontal distortions of their objects. He felt no hunger, but he had fasted before and knew on which side of hunger he stood; he was not as strong as he had been only a day past, and by this time next day he would probably be unable to outrun Ignacio. He should, he now realized, have eaten the monkey he had killed; but his stomach revolted at the thought of the raw flesh, and he did not know how he might build a fire, although Ignacio seemed to have done so the night before. Raw fish, even if he were able to catch a fish, would be as bad, or worse, than raw monkey; he remembered his effort to open a coconut—he had failed, but it was surely not impossible. His mind was hazy as to what a coconut might contain, but there had to be an edible core, because they were eaten in books. He decided to make a wide sweep through the jungle that would bring him back to the beach well away from Ignacio; he had several times seen coconuts lying in the sand under the trees.

He moved quietly, still a little afraid, trying to think of ways to open the coconut when he found it. He imagined himself standing before a large and raggedly faceted stone, holding the coconut in both hands. He raised it and smashed it down, but when it struck it was no longer a coconut but Maya's head; he heard her nose cartilage break with a distinct, rubbery snap. Her eyes, as blue as the sky above Madhya Pradesh, the sparkling blue sky of the egg, looked up at him, but he could no longer look into them, they retreated from his own, and it came to him quite suddenly that Lucifer, in falling, must have fallen up, into the fires and the coldness of space, never again to see the warm blues and browns and greens of Earth: *I was watching Satan fall as lightning from heaven.* He had heard that on tape somewhere, but he could not remember where. He had read that on Earth lightning did not come down from the clouds, but leaped up from the planetary surface toward them, never to return.

"Nicholas."

He listened, but did not hear his name again. Faintly water was babbling; had Dr. Island used that sound to speak to him? He walked toward it and found a little rill that threaded a way among the trees, and followed it. In a hundred steps it grew broader, slowed, and ended in a long blind pool under a dome of leaves. Diane was sitting on moss on the side opposite him; she looked up as she saw him, and smiled.

"Hello," he said.

"Hello, Nicholas. I thought I heard you. I wasn't mistaken after all, was I?"

"I didn't think I said anything." He tested the dark water with his foot and found that it was very cold.

"You gave a little gasp, I fancy. I heard it, and I said to myself, *that's Nicholas,* and I called you. Then I thought I might be wrong, or that it might be Ignacio."

"Ignacio was chasing me. Maybe he still is, but I think he's probably given up by now."

The girl nodded, looking into the dark waters of the pool, but did not seem to have heard him. He began to work his way around to her, climbing across the snakelike roots of the crowding trees. "Why does Ignacio want to kill me, Diane?"

"Sometimes he wants to kill me too," the girl said.

"But why?"

"I think he's a bit frightened of us. Have you ever talked to him, Nicholas?"

"Today I did a little. He told me a story about a pet fish he used to have."

"Ignacio grew up all alone; did he tell you that? On Earth. On a plantation in Brazil, way up the Amazon—Dr. Island told me."

"I thought it was crowded on Earth."

"The cities are crowded, and the countryside closest to the cities. But there are places where it's emptier than it used to be. Where Ignacio was, there would have been Red Indian hunters two or three hundred years ago; when he was there, there wasn't anyone, just the machines. Now he doesn't want to be looked at, doesn't want anyone around him."

Nicholas said slowly, "Dr. Island said lots of people wouldn't be sick if only there weren't other people around all the time. Remember that?"

"Only there are other people around all the time; that's how the world is."

"Not in Brazil, maybe," Nicholas said. He was trying to remember something about Brazil, but the only thing he could think of was a parrot singing in a straw hat from the comview cartoons; and then a turtle and a hedgehog that turned into armadillos for the love of God, Montressor. He said, "Why didn't he stay here?"

"Did I tell you about the bird, Nicholas?" She had been not-listening again.

"What bird?"

"I have a bird. Inside." She patted the flat stomach below her small breasts, and for a moment Nicholas thought she had really found food. "She sits in here. She has tangled a nest in my entrails, where she sits and tears at my breath with her beak. I look healthy to you, don't I? But inside I'm hollow and rotten and turning brown, dirt and old feathers, oozing away. Her beak will break through soon."

"Okay." Nicholas turned to go.

"I've been drinking water here, trying to drown her. I think I've swallowed so much I couldn't stand up now if I tried, but she isn't even wet, and do you know something, Nicholas? I've found out I'm not really me, I'm her."

Turning back Nicholas asked, "When was the last time you had anything to eat?"

"I don't know. Two, three days ago. Ignacio gave me something."

"I'm going to try to open a coconut. If I can I'll bring you back some."

When he reached the beach, Nicholas turned and walked slowly back in the direction of the dead fire, this time along the rim of dampened sand between the sea and the palms. He was thinking about machines.

There were hundreds of thousands, perhaps millions, of machines out beyond the belt, but few or none of the sophisticated servant robots of Earth—those were luxuries. Would Ignacio, in Brazil (whatever that was like), have had such luxuries? Nicholas thought not; those robots were almost like people, and living with them would be like living with people. Nicholas wished that he could speak Brazilian.

There had been the therapy robots at St. John's; Nicholas had not liked them, and he did not think Ignacio would have liked them either. If he had liked his therapy robot he probably would not have had to be sent here. He thought of the chipped and rusted old machine that had cleaned the corridors—Maya had called it Corradora, but no one else ever called it anything but *Hey!* It could not (or at least did not) speak, and Nicholas doubted that it had emotions, except possibly a sort of love of cleanness that did not extend to its own person. "You will understand," someone was saying inside his head, "that motives of all sorts can be divided into two sorts." A doctor? A therapy robot? It did not matter. "Extrinsic and intrinsic. An extrinsic motive has always some further end in view, and that end we call an intrinsic motive. Thus when we have reduced motivation to intrinsic motivation we have reduced it to its simplest parts. Take that machine over there."

What machine?

"Freud would have said that it was fixated at the latter anal stage, perhaps due to the care its builders exercised in seeing that the dirt it collects is not released again. Because of its fixation it is, as you see, obsessed with cleanliness and order; compulsive sweeping and scrubbing palliate its anxieties. It is a strength

of Freud's theory, and not a weakness, that it serves to explain many of the ac
tivities of machines as well as the acts of persons."

Hello there, Corradora.

And hello, Ignacio.

*My head, moving from side to side, must remind you of a radar scanner. My
steps are measured, slow, and precise. I emit a scarcely audible humming as I walk
and my eyes are fixed, as I swing my head, not on you, Ignacio, but on the waves at
the edge of sight, where they curve up into the sky. I stop ten meters short of you, and
I stand.*

You go, I follow, ten meters behind. What do I want? Nothing.

Yes, I will pick up the sticks, and I will follow—five meters behind.

"Break them, and put them on the fire. Not all of them, just a few."

Yes.

"Ignacio keeps the fire here burning all the time. Sometimes he takes the
coals of fire from it to start others, but here, under the big palm log, he has a fire
always. The rain does not strike it here. Always the fire. Do you know how he
made it the first time? Reply to him!"

"No."

"No, *Patrão!*"

"'No, *Patrão*.'"

"Ignacio stole it from the gods, from Poseidon. Now Poseidon is dead, ly
ing at the bottom of the water. Which is the top. Would you like to see him?"

"If you wish it, *Patrão*."

"It will soon be dark, and that is the time to fish; do you have a spear?"

"No, *Patrão*."

"Then Ignacio will get you one."

Ignacio took a handful of the sticks and thrust the ends into the fire, blow
ing on them. After a moment Nicholas leaned over and blew too, until all the
sticks were blazing.

"Now we must find you some bamboo, and there is some back here. Follow
me."

The light, still nearly shadowless, was dimming now, so that it seemed to
Nicholas that they walked on insubstantial soil, though he could feel it beneath
his feet. Ignacio stalked ahead, holding up the burning sticks until the fire
seemed about to die, then pointing the ends down, allowing it to lick upward
toward his hand and come to life again. There was a gentle wind blowing out
toward the sea, carrying away the sound of the surf and bringing a damp cool
ness; and when they had been walking for several minutes, Nicholas heard in it
a faint, dry, almost rhythmic rattle.

Ignacio looked back at him and said, "The music. The big stems talking
hear it?"

They found a cane a little thinner than Nicholas's wrist and piled the burning
sticks around its base, then added more. When it fell, Ignacio burned through
the upper end too, making a pole about as long as Nicholas was tall, and with the
edge of a seashell scraped the larger end to a point. "Now you are a fisherman,"
he said. Nicholas said, "Yes, *Patrão*," still careful not to meet his eyes.

"You are hungry?"

"Yes, *Patrão*."

"Then let me tell you something. Whatever you get is Ignacio's, you under stand? And what he catches, that is his too. But when he has eaten what he wants, what is left is yours. Come on now, and Ignacio will teach you to fish or drown you."

Ignacio's own spear was buried in the sand not far from the fire; it was much bigger than the one he had made for Nicholas. With it held across his chest he went down to the water, wading until it was waist high, then swimming, not looking to see if Nicholas was following. Nicholas found that he could swim with the spear by putting all his effort into the motion of his legs, holding the spear in his left hand and stroking only occasionally with his right. "You breathe," he said softly, "and watch the spear," and after that he had only to allow his head to lift from time to time.

He had thought Ignacio would begin to look for fish as soon as they were well out from the beach, but the Brazilian continued to swim, slowly but steadily, until it seemed to Nicholas that they must be a kilometer or more from land. Suddenly, as though the lights in a room had responded to a switch, the dark sea around them became an opalescent blue. Ignacio stopped, treading water and using his spear to buoy himself.

"Here," he said. "Get them between yourself and the light."

Open-eyed, he bent his face to the water, raised it again to breathe deeply, and dove. Nicholas followed his example, floating belly-down with open eyes.

All the world of dancing glitter and dark island vanished as though he had plunged his face into a dream. Far, far below him Jupiter displayed its broad, striped disk, marred with the spreading Bright Spot where man-made silicone enzymes had stripped the hydrogen from methane for kindled fusion: a cancer and a burning infant sun. Between that sun and his eyes lay invisible a hundred thousand kilometers of space, and the temperglass shell of the satellite; hundreds of meters of illuminated water, and in it the spread body of Ignacio, dark against the light, still kicking downward, his spear a pencil line of blackness in his hand.

Involuntarily Nicholas's head came up, returning to the universe of sparkling waves, aware now that what he had called "night" was only the shadow cast by Dr. Island when Jupiter and the Bright Spot slid beneath her. That shadow line, indetectable in air, now lay sharp across the water behind him. He took breath and plunged.

Almost at once a fish darted somewhere below, and his left arm thrust the spear forward, but it was far out of reach. He swam after it, then saw another, larger, fish farther down and dove for that, passing Ignacio surfacing for air. The fish was too deep, and he had used up his oxygen; his lungs aching for air, he swam up, wanting to let go of his spear, then realizing at the last moment that he could, that it would only bob to the surface if he released it. His head broke water and he gasped, his heart thumping; water struck his face and he knew again, suddenly, as though they had ceased to exist while he was gone, the pulse-beat pounding of the waves.

Ignacio was waiting for him. He shouted, "This time you will come with Ignacio, and he will show you the dead sea god. Then we will fish."

Unable to speak, Nicholas nodded. He was allowed three more breaths; then Ignacio dove and Nicholas had to follow, kicking down until the pressure rang in his ears. Then through blue water he saw, looming at the edge of the light, a huge mass of metal anchored to the temperglass hull of the satellite itself; above it, hanging lifelessly like the stem of a great vine severed from the root, a cable twice as thick as a man's body; and on the bottom, sprawled beside the mighty anchor, a legged god that might have been a dead insect save that it was at least six meters long. Ignacio turned and looked back at Nicholas to see if he understood; he did not, but he nodded, and with the strength draining from his arms, surfaced again.

After Ignacio brought up the first fish, they took turns on the surface guarding their catch, and while the Bright Spot crept beneath the shelving rim of Dr Island, they speared two more, one of them quite large. Then when Nicholas was so exhausted he could scarcely lift his arms, they made their way back to shore, and Ignacio showed him how to gut the fish with a thorn and the edge of a shell, and reclose them and pack them in mud and leaves to be roasted by the fire. After Ignacio had begun to eat the largest fish, Nicholas timidly drew out the smallest, and ate for the first time since coming to Dr. Island. Only when he had finished did he remember Diane.

He did not dare to take the last fish to her, but he looked covertly at Ignacio, and began edging away from the fire. The Brazilian seemed not to have noticed him. When he was well into the shadows he stood, backed a few steps, then—slowly, as his instincts warned him—walked away, not beginning to trot until the distance between them was nearly a hundred meters.

He found Diane sitting apathetic and silent at the margin of the cold pool, and had some difficulty persuading her to stand. At last he lifted her, his hands under her arms pressing against her thin ribs. Once on her feet she stood steadily enough, and followed him when he took her by the hand. He talked to her knowing that although she gave no sign of hearing she heard him, and that the right words might wake her to response. "We went fishing—Ignacio showed me how. And he's got a fire, Diane, he got it from a kind of robot that was supposed to be fixing one of the cables that holds Dr. Island, I don't know how. Anyway, listen, we caught three big fish, and I ate one and Ignacio ate a great big one and I don't think he'd mind if you had the other one, only say, 'Yes, *Patrão*,' and 'No, *Patrão*,' to him—he likes that, and he's only used to machines. You don' have to smile at him or anything—just look at the fire, that's what I do, just look at the fire."

To Ignacio, perhaps wisely, he at first said nothing at all, leading Diane to the place where he had been sitting himself a few minutes before and placing some scraps from his fish in her lap. When she did not eat he found a sliver of the tender, roasted flesh and thrust it into her mouth. Ignacio said, "Ignacio believed that one dead," and Nicholas answered, "No, *Patrão*."

"There is another fish. Give it to her."

Nicholas did, raking the gob of baked mud from the coals to crack with the heel of his hand, and peeling the broken and steaming fillets from the skins and bones to give to her when they had cooled enough to eat; after the fish had lain in her mouth for perhaps half a minute she began to chew and swallow, and after the third mouthful she fed herself, though without looking at either of them.

"Ignacio believed that one dead," Ignacio said again.

"No, *Patrão*," Nicholas answered, and then added, "Like you can see, she's alive."

"She is a pretty creature, with the firelight on her face—no?"

"Yes, *Patrão*, very pretty."

"But too thin." Ignacio moved around the fire until he was sitting almost beside Diane, then reached for the fish Nicholas had given her. Her hands closed on it, though she still did not look at him.

"You see, she knows us after all," Ignacio said. "We are not ghosts."

Nicholas whispered urgently, "Let him have it."

Slowly Diane's fingers relaxed, but Ignacio did not take the fish. "I was only joking, little one," he said. "And I think not such a good joke after all." Then when she did not reply, he turned away from her, his eyes reaching out across the dark, tossing water for something Nicholas could not see.

"She likes you, *Patrão*," Nicholas said. The words were like swallowing filth, but he thought of the bird ready to tear through Diane's skin, and Maya's blood soaking in little round dots in the white cloth, and continued. "She is only shy. It is better that way."

"You. What do you know?"

At least Ignacio was no longer looking at the sea. Nicholas said, "Isn't it true, *Patrão?*"

"Yes, it is true."

Diane was picking at the fish again, conveying tiny flakes to her mouth with delicate fingers; distinctly but almost absently she said, "Go, Nicholas."

He looked at Ignacio, but the Brazilian's eyes did not turn toward the girl, nor did he speak.

"Nicholas, go away. Please."

In a voice he hoped was pitched too low for Ignacio to hear, Nicholas said, "I'll see you in the morning. All right?"

Her head moved a fraction of a centimeter.

Once he was out of sight of the fire, one part of the beach was as good to sleep on as another; he wished he had taken a piece of wood from the fire to start one of his own and tried to cover his legs with sand to keep off the cool wind, but the sand fell away whenever he moved, and his legs and his left hand moved without volition on his part.

The surf, lapping at the rippled shore, said, "That was well done, Nicholas."

"I can feel you move," Nicholas said. "I don't think I ever could before except when I was high up."

"I doubt that you can now; my roll is less than one one-hundredth of a degree."

"Yes, I can. You wanted me to do that, didn't you? About Ignacio."

"Do you know what the Harlow effect is, Nicholas?"

Nicholas shook his head.

"About a hundred years ago Dr. Harlow experimented with monkeys who had been raised in complete isolation—no mothers, no other monkeys at all."

"Lucky monkeys."

"When the monkeys were mature he put them into cages with normal ones; they fought with any that came near them, and sometimes they killed them."

"Psychologists always put things in cages; did he ever think of turning them loose in the jungle instead?"

"No, Nicholas, though we have . . . aren't you going to say anything?"

"I guess not."

"Dr. Harlow tried, you see, to get the isolate monkeys to breed—sex is the primary social function—but they wouldn't. Whenever another monkey of either sex approached they displayed aggressiveness, which the other monkeys returned. He cured them finally by introducing immature monkeys—monkey children—in place of the mature, socialized ones. These needed the isolate adults so badly that they kept on making approaches no matter how often or how violently they were rejected, and in the end they were accepted, and the isolates socialized. It's interesting to note that the founder of Christianity seems to have had an intuitive grasp of the principle—but it was almost two thousands years before it was demonstrated scientifically."

"I don't think it worked here," Nicholas said. "It was more complicated than that."

"Human beings are complicated monkeys, Nicholas."

"That's about the first time I ever heard you make a joke. You like not being human, don't you?"

"Of course. Wouldn't you?"

"I always thought I would, but now I'm not sure. You said that to help me, didn't you? I don't like that."

A wave higher than the others splashed chill foam over Nicholas's legs, and for a moment he wondered if this were Dr. Island's reply. Half a minute later another wave wet him, and another, and he moved farther up the beach to avoid them. The wind was stronger, but he slept despite it, and was awakened only for a moment by a flash of light from the direction from which he had come; he tried to guess what might have caused it, thought of Diane and Ignacio throwing the burning sticks into the air to see the arcs of fire, smiled—too sleepy now to be angry—and slept again.

Morning came cold and sullen; Nicholas ran up and down the beach, rubbing himself with his hands. A thin rain, or spume (it was hard to tell which), was blowing in the wind, clouding the light to gray radiance. He wondered if Diane and Ignacio would mind if he came back now and decided to wait, then thought of fishing so that he would have something to bring when he came; but the sea was very cold and the waves so high they tumbled him, wrenching his bamboo spear from his hand. Ignacio found him dripping with water, sitting with his back to a palm trunk and staring out toward the lifting curve of the sea.

"Hello, you," Ignacio said.

"Good morning, *Patrão*."

Ignacio sat down. "What is your name? You told me, I think, when we first met, but I have forgotten. I am sorry."

"Nicholas."

"Yes."

"*Patrão*, I am very cold. Would it be possible for us to go to your fire?"

"My name is Ignacio; call me that."

Nicholas nodded, frightened.

"But we cannot go to my fire, because the fire is out."

"Can't you make another one, *Patrão*?"

"You do not trust me, do you? I do not blame you. No, I cannot make another—you may use what I had, if you wish, and make one after I have gone. I came only to say good-bye."

"You're leaving?"

The wind in the palm fronds said, "Ignacio is much better now. He will be going to another place, Nicholas."

"A hospital?"

"Yes, a hospital, but I don't think he will have to stay there long."

"But . . ." Nicholas tried to think of something appropriate. At St. John's and the other places where he had been confined, when people left, they simply left, and usually were hardly spoken of once it was learned that they were going and thus were already tainted by whatever it was that froze the smiles and dried the tears of those outside. At last he said, "Thanks for teaching me how to fish."

"That was all right," Ignacio said. He stood up and put a hand on Nicholas's shoulder, then turned away. Four meters to his left the damp sand was beginning to lift and crack. While Nicholas watched, it opened on a brightly lit companionway walled with white. Ignacio pushed his curly black hair back from his eyes and went down, and the sand closed with a thump.

"He won't be coming back, will he?" Nicholas said.

"No."

"He said I could use his stuff to start another fire, but I don't even know what it is."

Dr. Island did not answer. Nicholas got up and began to walk back to where the fire had been, thinking about Diane and wondering if she was hungry; he was hungry himself.

He found her beside the dead fire. Her chest had been burned away, and lying close by, near the hole in the sand where Ignacio must have kept it hidden, was a bulky nuclear welder. The power pack was too heavy for Nicholas to lift, but he picked up the welding gun on its short cord and touched the trigger, producing a two-meter plasma discharge which he played along the sand until Diane's body was ash. By the time he had finished the wind was whipping the palms and sending stinging rain into his eyes, but he collected a supply of wood and built another fire, bigger and bigger until it roared like a forge in the wind. "He killed her!" he shouted to the waves.

"YES." Dr. Island's voice was big and wild.

"You said he was better."

"HE IS," howled the wind. "YOU KILLED THE MONKEY THAT WANTED TO PLAY WITH YOU, NICHOLAS, AS I BELIEVED IGNACIO WOULD EVENTUALLY KILL YOU, WHO ARE SO EASILY HATED, SO DIFFERENT FROM WHAT IT IS THOUGHT A BOY SHOULD BE. BUT KILLING THE MONKEY HELPED YOU, REMEMBER? MADE YOU BETTER. IGNACIO WAS FRIGHTENED BY WOMEN; NOW HE KNOWS THAT THEY ARE REALLY VERY WEAK, AND HE HAS ACTED UPON CERTAIN FANTASIES AND FINDS THEM BITTER."

"You're rocking," Nicholas said. "Am I doing that?"

"YOUR THOUGHT."

A palm snapped in the storm; instead of falling, it flew crashing among the others, its fronded head catching the wind like a sail. "I'm killing you," Nicholas said. "Destroying you." The left side of his face was so contorted with grief and rage that he could scarcely speak.

Dr. Island heaved beneath his feet. "NO."

"One of your cables is already broken—I saw that. Maybe more than one.

You'll pull loose. I'm turning this world, isn't that right? The attitude rockets are tuned to my emotions, and they're spinning us around, and the slippage is the wind and the high sea, and when you come loose nothing will balance anymore."

"NO."

"What's the stress on your cables? Don't you know?"

"THEY ARE VERY STRONG."

"What kind of talk is that? You ought to say something like: 'The D-twelve cable tension is twenty-billion kilograms' force. WARNING! WARNING! Expected time to failure is ninety-seven seconds! WARNING!' *Don't you even know how a machine is supposed to talk?*" Nicholas was screaming now, and every wave reached farther up the beach than the last, so that the bases of the most seaward palms were awash.

"GET BACK, NICHOLAS. FIND HIGHER GROUND. GO INTO THE JUNGLE." It was the crashing waves themselves that spoke.

"I won't."

A long serpent of water reached for the fire, which hissed and sputtered.

"GET BACK!"

"I won't!"

A second wave came, striking Nicholas calf-high and nearly extinguishing the fire.

"ALL THIS WILL BE UNDER WATER SOON. GET BACK!"

Nicholas picked up some of the still-burning sticks and tried to carry them, but the wind blew them out as soon as he lifted them from the fire. He tugged at the welder, but it was too heavy for him to lift.

"GET BACK!"

He went into the jungle, where the trees lashed themselves to leafy rubbish in the wind and broken branches flew through the air like debris from an explosion; for a while he heard Diane's voice crying in the wind; it became Maya's, then his mother's or Sister Carmela's, and a hundred others; in time the wind grew less, and he could no longer feel the ground rocking. He felt tired. He said, "I didn't kill you after all, did I?" but there was no answer. On the beach, when he returned to it, he found the welder half buried in sand. No trace of Diane's ashes, nor of his fire. He gathered more wood and built another, lighting it with the welder.

"Now," he said. He scooped aside the sand around the welder until he reached the rough understone beneath it, and turned the flame of the welder on that; it blackened and bubbled.

"No," Dr. Island said.

"Yes." He was bending intently over the flame, both hands locked on the welder's trigger.

"Nicholas, stop that." When he did not reply, "Look behind you." There was a splashing louder than the crashing of the waves, and a groaning of metal. He whirled and saw the great, beetlelike robot Ignacio had shown him on the sea floor. Tiny shellfish clung to its metal skin, and water, faintly green, still poured from its body. Before he could turn the welding gun toward it, it shot forward hands like clamps and wrenched it from him. All up and down the beach similar machines were smoothing the sand and repairing the damage of the storm.

"That thing was dead," Nicholas said. "Ignacio killed it."

It picked up the power pack, shook it clean of sand, and turning, stalked back toward the sea.

"That is what Ignacio believed, and it was better that he believed so."

"And you said you couldn't do anything, you had no hands."

"I also told you that I would treat you as society will when you are released, that that was my nature. After that, did you still believe all I told you? Nicholas, you are upset now because Diane is dead—"

"You could have protected her!"

"—but by dying she made someone else—someone very important—well. Her prognosis was bad; she really wanted only death, and this was the death I chose for her. You could call it the death of Dr. Island, a death that would help someone else. Now you are alone, but soon there will be more patients in this segment, and you will help them, too—if you can—and perhaps they will help you. Do you understand?"

"No," Nicholas said. He flung himself down on the sand. The wind had dropped, but it was raining hard. He thought of the vision he had once had, and of describing it to Diane the day before. "This isn't ending the way I thought," he whispered. It was only a squeak of sound far down in his throat. "Nothing ever turns out right."

The waves, the wind, the rustling palm fronds and the pattering rain, the monkeys who had come down to the beach to search for food washed ashore, answered, "Go away—go back—don't move."

Nicholas pressed his scarred head against his knees, rocking back and forth. "Don't move."

For a long time he sat still while the rain lashed his shoulders and the dripping monkeys frolicked and fought around him. When at last he lifted his face, there was in it some element of personality which had been only potentially present before, and with this an emptiness and an expression of surprise. His lips moved, and the sounds were the sounds made by a deaf-mute who tries to speak.

"Nicholas is gone," the waves said. "Nicholas, who was the right side of your body, the left half of your brain, I have forced into catatonia; for the remainder of your life he will be to you only what you once were to him—or less. Do you understand?"

The boy nodded.

"We will call you Kenneth, silent one. And if Nicholas tries to come again, Kenneth, you must drive him back—or return to what you have been."

The boy nodded a second time, and a moment afterward began to collect sticks for the dying fire. As though to themselves the waves chanted:

"Seas are wild tonight . . .
Stretching over Sado island
Silent clouds of stars."

There was no reply.

ENDER'S GAME

Orson Scott Card

Orson Scott Card entered SF in the 1970s and became a dominant figure in the 1980s. A man of enormous determination and incredible energy, he has been a reviewer, anthology editor, public figure, and most important, a writer of some of the most popular and powerful SF of the decade. His novel *Ender's Game* and its sequel remain his major work to date in SF, while his *Alvin Maker* series of fantasy novels is perhaps even better. This story is the original piece that was the genesis for later works in the *Ender* series.

"**W**hatever your gravity is when you get to the door, remember—the enemy' gate is *down*. If you step through your own door like you're out for a stroll you're a big target and you deserve to get hit. With more than a flasher." Ender Wiggin paused and looked over the group. Most were just watching him nervously. A few understanding. A few sullen and resisting.

First day with this army, all fresh from the teacher squads, and Ender had forgotten how young new kids could be. He'd been in it for three years, they'd had six months—nobody over nine years old in the whole bunch. But they were his. At eleven, he was half a year early to be a commander. He'd had a toon of his own and knew a few tricks but there were forty in his new army. Green. All marksmen with a flasher, all in top shape, or they wouldn't be here—but they were all just as likely as not to get wiped out first time into battle.

"Remember," he went on, "they can't see you till you get through that door. But the second you're out, they'll be on you. So hit that door the way you want to be when they shoot at you. Legs up under you, going straight *down*. He pointed at a sullen kid who looked like he was only seven, the smallest of them all. "Which way is down, greenoh!"

"Toward the enemy door." The answer was quick. It was also surly, saying "yeah, yeah, now get on with the important stuff."

"Name, kid?"

"Bean."

"Get that for size or for brains?"

Bean didn't answer. The rest laughed a little. Ender had chosen right. This kid *was* younger than the rest, must have been advanced because he was sharp.

The others didn't like him much, they were happy to see him taken down a little. Like Ender's first commander had taken him down.

"Well, Bean, you're right onto things. Now I tell you this, nobody's gonna get through that door without a good chance of getting hit. A lot of you are going to be turned into cement somewhere. Make sure it's your legs. Right? If only your legs get hit, then only your legs get frozen, and in nullo that's no sweat." Ender turned to one of the dazed ones. "What're legs for? Hmmm?"

Blank stare. Confusion. Stammer.

"Forget it. Guess I'll have to ask Bean here."

"Legs are for pushing off walls." Still bored.

"Thanks, Bean. Get that, everybody?" They all got it, and didn't like getting it from Bean. "Right. You can't *see* with legs, you can't *shoot* with legs, and most of the time they just get in the way. If they get frozen sticking straight out you've turned yourself into a blimp. No way to hide. So how do legs go?"

A few answered this time, to prove that Bean wasn't the only one who knew anything. "Under you. Tucked up under."

"Right. A shield. You're kneeling on a shield, and the shield is your own legs. And there's a trick to the suits. Even when your legs are flashed you can *still* kick off. I've never seen anybody do it but me—but you're all gonna learn it."

Ender Wiggin turned on his flasher. It glowed faintly green in his hand. Then he let himself rise in the weightless workout room, pulled his legs under him as though he were kneeling, and flashed both of them. Immediately his suit stiffened at the knees and ankles, so that he couldn't bend at all.

"Okay, I'm frozen, see?"

He was floating a meter above them. They all looked up at him, puzzled. He leaned back and caught one of the handholds on the wall behind him, and pulled himself flush against the wall.

"I'm stuck at a wall. If I had legs, I'd use legs, and string myself out like a string *bean*, right?"

They laughed.

"But I don't have legs, and that's *better*, got it? Because of this." Ender jackknifed at the waist, then straightened out violently. He was across the workout room in only a moment. From the other side he called to them. "Got that? I didn't use hands, so I still had use of my flasher. *And* I didn't have my legs floating five feet behind me. Now watch it again."

He repeated the jackknife, and caught a handhold on the wall near them. "Now, I don't just want you to do that when they've flashed your legs. I want you to do that when you've still got legs, because it's better. And because they'll never be expecting it. All right now, everybody up in the air and kneeling."

Most were up in a few seconds. Ender flashed the stragglers, and they dangled, helplessly frozen, while the others laughed. "When I give an order, you move. Got it? When we're at a door and they clear it, I'll be giving you orders in two seconds, as soon as I see the setup. And when I give the order you better be out there, because whoever's out there first is going to win, unless he's a fool. I'm not. And you better not be, or I'll have you back in the teacher squads." He saw more than a few of them gulp, and the frozen ones looked at him with fear. "You guys who are hanging there. You watch. You'll thaw out in about fifteen minutes, and let's see if you can catch up to the others."

For the next half hour Ender had then jackknifing off walls. He called a stop when he saw that they all had the basic idea. They were a good group, maybe They'd get better.

"Now you're warmed up," he said to them, "we'll start working."

Ender was the last one out after practice, since he stayed to help some of the slower ones improve on technique. They'd had good teachers, but like all armies they were uneven, and some of them could be a real drawback in battle. Their first battle might be weeks away. It might be tomorrow. A schedule was never printed. The commander just woke up and found a note by his bunk, giving him the time of his battle and the name of his opponent. So for the first while he was going to drive his boys until they were in top shape—all of them. Ready for any thing, at any time. Strategy was nice, but it was worth nothing if the soldiers couldn't hold up under the strain.

He turned the corner into the residence wing and found himself face to face with Bean, the seven-year-old he had picked on all through practice that day. Problems. Ender didn't want problems right now.

"Ho, Bean."

"Ho, Ender."

Pause.

"Sir," Ender said softly.

"We're not on duty."

"In my army, Bean, we're always on duty." Ender brushed past him.

Bean's high voice piped up behind him. "I know what you're doing, Ender sir, and I'm warning you."

Ender turned slowly and looked at him. "Warning me?"

"I'm the best man you've got. But I'd better be treated like it."

"Or what?" Ender smiled menacingly.

"Or I'll be the worst man you've got. One or the other."

"And what do you want? Love and kisses?" Ender was getting angry.

Bean was unworried. "I want a toon."

Ender walked back to him and stood looking down into his eyes. "I'll give a toon," he said, "to the boys who prove they're worth something. They've got to be good soldiers, they've got to know how to take orders, they've got to be able to think for themselves in a pinch, and they've got to be able to keep re spect. That's how I got to be a commander. That's how you'll get to be a toon leader."

Bean smiled. "That's fair. If you actually work that way, I'll be a toon leader in a month."

Ender reached down and grabbed the front of his uniform and shoved him into the wall. "When I say I work a certain way, Bean, then that's the way I work."

Bean just smiled. Ender let go of him and walked away, and didn't look back. He was sure, without looking, that Bean was still watching, still smiling, still just a little contemptuous. He might make a good toon leader at that. Ender would keep an eye on him.

Captain Graff, six foot two and a little chubby, stroked his belly as he leaned back in his chair. Across his desk sat Lieutenant Anderson, who was earnestly pointing out high points on a chart.

"Here it is, Captain," Anderson said. "Ender's already got them doing a tactic that's going to throw off everyone who meets it. Doubled their speed."

Graff nodded.

"And you know his test scores. He thinks well, too."

Graff smiled. "All true, all true, Anderson, he's a fine student, shows real promise."

They waited.

Graff sighed. "So what do you want me to do?"

"Ender's the one. He's got to be."

"He'll never be ready in time, Lieutenant. He's eleven, for heaven's sake, man, what do you want, a miracle?"

"I want him into battles, every day starting tomorrow. I want him to have a year's worth of battles in a month."

Graff shook his head. "That would have his army in the hospital."

"No sir. He's getting them into form. And we need Ender."

"All right, I think it's Ender. Which of the commanders if it isn't him?"

"I don't know, Lieutenant." Graff ran his hands over his slightly fuzzy bald head. "These are children, Anderson. Do you realize that? Ender's army is nine years old. Are we going to put them against the older kids? Are we going to put them through hell for a month like that?"

Lieutenant Anderson leaned even further over Graff's desk.

"Ender's test scores, Captain!"

"I've seen his bloody test scores! I've watched him in battle, I've listened to tapes of his training sessions, I've watched his sleep patterns, I've heard tapes of his conversations in the corridors and in the bathrooms, I'm more aware of Ender Wiggins than you could possibly imagine! And against all the arguments, against his obvious qualities, I'm weighing one thing. I have this picture of Ender a year from now, if you have your way. I see him completely useless, worn down, a failure, because he was pushed farther than he or any living person could go. But it doesn't weigh enough, does it, Lieutenant, because there's a war on, and our best talent is gone, and the biggest battles are ahead. So give Ender a battle every day this week. And then bring me a report."

Anderson stood and saluted. "Thank you, sir."

He had almost reached the door when Graff called his name. He turned and faced the captain.

"Anderson," Captain Graff said. "Have you been outside, lately I mean?"

"Not since last leave, six months ago."

"I didn't think so. Not that it makes any difference. But have you ever been to Beaman Park, there in the city? Hmm? Beautiful park. Trees. Grass. No nullo, no battles, no worries. Do you know what else there is in Beaman Park?"

"What, sir?" Lieutenant Anderson asked.

"Children," Graff answered.

"Of course children," said Anderson.

"I mean children. I mean kids who get up in the morning when their mothers call them and they go to school and then in the afternoons they go to Beaman Park and play. They're happy, they smile a lot, they laugh, they have fun. Hmmm?"

"I'm sure they do, sir."

"Is that all you can say, Anderson?"

Anderson cleared his throat. "It's good for children to have fun, I think, sir. I know I did when I was a boy. But right now the world needs soldiers. And this is the way to get them."

Graff nodded and closed his eyes. "Oh, indeed, you're right, by statistical proof and by all the important theories, and dammit they work and the system is right but all the same Ender's older than I am. He's not a child. He's barely a person."

"If that's true, sir, then at least we all know that Ender is making it possible for the others of his age to be playing in the park."

"And Jesus died to save all men, of course." Graff sat up and looked at Anderson almost sadly. "But we're the ones," Graff said, "we're the ones who are driving in the nails."

Ender Wiggins lay on his bed staring at the ceiling. He never slept more than five hours a night—but the lights went off at 2200 and didn't come on again until 0600. So he stared at the ceiling and thought. He'd had his army for three and a half weeks. Dragon Army. The name was assigned, and it wasn't a lucky one. Oh, the charts said that about nine years ago a Dragon Army had done fairly well. But for the next six years the name had been attached to inferior armies, and finally, because of the superstition that was beginning to play about the name, Dragon Army was retired. Until now. And now, Ender thought smiling, Dragon Army was going to take them by surprise.

The door opened softly. Ender did not turn his head. Someone stepped softly into his room, then left with the quiet sound of the door shutting. When soft steps died away Ender rolled over and saw a white slip of paper lying on the floor. He reached down and picked it up.

"Dragon Army against Rabbit Army, Ender Wiggins and Carn Carby, 0700."

The first battle. Ender got out of bed and quickly dressed. He went rapidly to the rooms of each of his toon leaders and told them to rouse their boys. In five minutes they were all gathered in the corridor, sleepy and slow. Ender spoke softly.

"First battle, 0700 against Rabbit Army. I've fought them twice before but they've got a new commander. Never heard of him. They're an older group, though, and I know a few of their old tricks. Now wake up. Run, doublefast warmup in workroom three."

For an hour and a half they worked out, with three mockbattles and calisthenics in the corridor out of the nullo. Then for fifteen minutes they all lay up in the air, totally relaxing in the weightlessness. At 0650 Ender roused them and they hurried into the corridor. Ender led them down the corridor, running again, and occasionally leaping to touch a light panel on the ceiling. The boys all touched the same light panel. And at 0658 they reached their gate to the battleroom.

The members of Toons C and D grabbed the first eight handholds in the ceiling of the corridor. Toons A, B, and E crouched on the floor. Ender hooked his feet into two handholds in the middle of the ceiling, so he was out of everyone's way.

"Which way is the enemy's door?" he hissed.

"Down!" they whispered back, and laughed.

"Flashers on." The boxes in their hands glowed green. They waited for a few seconds more, and then the gray wall in front of them disappeared and the battleroom was visible.

Ender sized it up immediately. The familiar open grid of the most early games, like the monkey bars at the park, with seven or eight boxes scattered through the grid. They called the boxes *stars*. There were enough of them, and in forward enough positions, that they were worth going for. Ender decided this in a second, and he hissed, "Spread to near stars. E hold!"

The four groups in the corners plunged through the forcefield at the doorway and fell down into the battleroom. Before the enemy even appeared through the opposite gate Ender's army had spread from the door to the nearest stars.

Then the enemy soldiers came through the door. From their stance Ender knew they had been in a different gravity, and didn't know enough to disorient themselves from it. They came through standing up, their entire bodies spread and defenseless.

"Kill 'em, E!" Ender hissed, and threw himself out the door knees first, with his flasher between his legs and firing. While Ender's group flew across the room the rest of Dragon Army lay down a protecting fire, so that E group reached a forward position with only one boy frozen completely, though they had all lost the use of their legs—which didn't impair them in the least. There was a lull as Ender and his opponent, Carn Carby, assessed their positions. Aside from Rabbit Army's losses at the gate, there had been few casualties, and both armies were near full strength. But Carn had no originality—he was in a four-corner spread that any five-year-old in the teacher squads might have thought of. And Ender knew how to defeat it.

He called out, loudly, "E covers A, C down. B, D angle east wall." Under E toon's cover, B and D toons lunged away from their stars. While they were still exposed, A and C toons left their stars and drifted toward the near wall. They reached it together, and together jackknifed off the wall. At double the normal speed they appeared behind the enemy's stars, and opened fire. In a few seconds the battle was over, with the enemy almost entirely frozen, including the commander, and the rest scattered to the corners. For the next five minutes, in squads of four, Dragon Army cleaned out the dark corners of the battleroom and shepherded the enemy into the center, where their bodies, frozen at impossible angles, jostled each other. Then Ender took three of his boys to the enemy gate and went through the formality of reversing the one-way field by simultaneously touching a Dragon Army helmet at each corner. Then Ender assembled his army in vertical files near the knot of frozen Rabbit Army soldiers.

Only three of Dragon Army's soldiers were immobile. Their victory margin—38 to 0—was ridiculously high, and Ender began to laugh. Dragon Army joined him, laughing long and loud. They were still laughing when Lieutenant Anderson and Lieutenant Morris came in from the teachergate at the south end of the battleroom.

Lieutenant Anderson kept his face stiff and unsmiling, but Ender saw him wink as he held out his hand and offered the stiff, formal congratulations that were ritually given to the victor in the game.

Morris found Carn Carby and unfroze him, and the thirteen-year-old came and presented himself to Ender, who laughed without malice and held out his hand. Carn graciously took Ender's hand and bowed his head over it. It was that or be flashed again.

Lieutenant Anderson dismissed Dragon Army, and they silently left the battleroom through the enemy's door—again part of the ritual. A light was blinking on the north side of the square door, indicating where the gravity was in that corridor. Ender, leading his soldiers, changed his orientation and went through the forcefield and into gravity on his feet. His army followed him at a brisk run back to the workroom. When they got there they formed up into squads, and Ender hung in the air, watching them.

"Good first battle," he said, which was excuse enough for a cheer, which he quieted. "Dragon Army did all right against Rabbits. But the enemy isn't always going to be that bad. And if that had been a good army we would have been smashed. We still would have won, but we would have been smashed. Now let me see B and D toons out here. Your takeoff from the stars was way too slow. If Rabbit Army knew how to aim a flasher, you all would have been frozen solid before A and C even got to the wall."

They worked out for the rest of the day.

That night Ender went for the first time to the commanders' mess hall. No one was allowed there until he had won at least one battle, and Ender was the youngest commander ever to make it. There was no great stir when he came in. But when some of the other boys saw the Dragon on his breast pocket, they stared at him openly, and by the time he got his tray and sat at an empty table, the entire room was silent, with the other commanders watching him. Intensely self-conscious, Ender wondered how they all knew, and why they all looked so hostile.

Then he looked above the door he had just come through. There was a huge scoreboard across the entire wall. It showed the win/loss record for the commander of every army; that day's battles were lit in red. Only four of them. The other three winners had barely made it—the best of them had only two men whole and eleven mobile at the end of the game. Dragon Army's score of thirty-eight mobile was embarrassingly better.

Other new commanders had been admitted to the commanders' mess hall with cheers and congratulations. Other new commanders hadn't won thirty-eight to zero.

Ender looked for Rabbit Army on the scoreboard. He was surprised to find that Carn Carby's score to date was eight wins and three losses. Was he that good? Or had he only fought against inferior armies? Whichever, there was still a zero in Carn's mobile and whole columns, and Ender looked down from the scoreboard grinning. No one smiled back, and Ender knew that they were afraid of him, which meant that they would hate him, which meant that anyone who went into battle against Dragon Army would be scared and angry and incompetent. Ender looked for Carn Carby in the crowd, and found him not too far away. He stared at Carby until one of the other boys nudged the Rabbit commander and pointed to Ender. Ender smiled again and waved slightly. Carby turned red, and Ender, satisfied, leaned over his dinner and began to eat.

At the end of the week Dragon Army had fought seven battles in seven days. The score stood 7 wins and 0 losses. Ender had never had more than five boys frozen in any game. It was no longer possible for the other commanders to ignore Ender. A few of them sat with him and quietly conversed about game strategies that Ender's opponents had used. Other much larger groups were talking with the commanders that Ender had defeated, trying to find out what Ender had done to beat them.

In the middle of the meal the teacher door opened and the groups fell silent as Lieutenant Anderson stepped in and looked over the group. When he located Ender he strode quickly across the room and whispered in Ender's ear. Ender nodded, finished his glass of water, and left with the lieutenant. On the way out, Anderson handed a slip of paper to one of the older boys. The room became very noisy with conversation as Anderson and Ender left.

Ender was escorted down corridors he had never seen before. They didn't have the blue glow of the soldier corridors. Most were wood paneled, and the floors were carpeted. The doors were wood, with nameplates on them, and they stopped at one that said, "Captain Graff, supervisor." Anderson knocked softly, and a low voice said, "Come in."

They went in. Captain Graff was seated behind a desk, his hands folded across his pot belly. He nodded, and Anderson sat. Ender also sat down. Graff cleared his throat and spoke.

"Seven days since your first battle, Ender."

Ender did not reply.

"Won seven battles, one every day."

Ender nodded.

"Scores unusually high, too."

Ender blinked.

"Why?" Graff asked him.

Ender glanced at Anderson, and then spoke to the captain behind the desk. "Two new tactics, sir. Legs doubled up as a shield, so that a flash doesn't immobilize. Jackknife takeoffs from the walls. Superior strategy, as Lieutenant Anderson taught, think places, not spaces. Five toons of eight instead of four of ten. Incompetent opponents. Excellent toon leaders, good soldiers."

Graff looked at Ender without expression. Waiting for what, Ender thought. Lieutenant Anderson spoke.

"Ender, what's the condition of your army."

"A little tired, in peak condition, morale high, learning fast. Anxious for the next battle."

Anderson looked at Graff, and Graff shrugged slightly. Then he nodded, and Anderson smiled. Graff turned to Ender.

"Is there anything you want to know?"

Ender held his hands loosely in his lap. "When are you going to put us up against a good army?"

Anderson was surprised, and Graff laughed out loud. The laughter rang in the room, and when it stopped, Graff handed a piece of paper to Ender. "Now," the Captain said, and Ender read the paper.

"Dragon Army against Leopard Army, Ender Wiggins and Pol Slattery, 2000."

Ender looked up at Captain Graff. "That's ten minutes from now, sir."

Graff smiled. "Better hurry, then, boy."

As Ender left he realized Pol Slattery was the boy who had been handed his orders as Ender left the mess hall.

He got to his army five minutes later. Three toon leaders were already undressed and lying naked on their beds. He sent them all flying down the corridors to rouse their toons, and gathered up their suits himself. As all his boys were assembled in the corridor, most of them still getting dressed, Ender spoke to them.

"This one's hot and there's no time. We'll be late to the door, and the enemy'll be deployed right outside our gate. Ambush, and I've never heard of it happening before. So we'll take our time at the door. E toon, keep your belts loose, and give your flashers to the leaders and seconds of the other toons."

Puzzled, E toon complied. By then all were dressed, and Ender led them at a trot to the gate. When they reached it the forcefield was already on one-way, and some of his soldiers were panting. They had had one battle that day and a full workout. They were tired.

Ender stopped at the entrance and looked at the placement of the enemy soldiers. Most of them were grouped not more than twenty feet out from the gate. There was no grid, there were no stars. A big empty space. Where were the other enemy soldiers? There should have been ten more.

"They're flat against this wall," Ender said, "where we can't see them."

He thought for a moment, then took two of the toons and made them kneel, their hands on their hips. Then he flashed them, so that their bodies were frozen rigid.

"You're shields," Ender said, and then had boys from two other toons kneel on their legs, and hook both arms under the frozen boys' shoulders. Each boy was holding two flashers. Then Ender and the members of the last toon picked up the duos, three at a time, and threw them out the door.

Of course, the enemy opened fire immediately. But they only hit the boys who were already flashed, and in a few moments pandemonium broke out in the battleroom. All the soldiers of Leopard Army were easy targets as they lay pressed flat against the wall, and Ender's soldiers, armed with two flashers each, carved them up easily. Pol Slattery reacted quickly, ordering his men away from the wall, but not quickly enough—only a few were able to move, and they were flashed before they could get a quarter of the way across the battleroom.

When the battle was over Dragon Army had only twelve boys whole, the lowest score they had ever had. But Ender was satisfied. And during the ritual of surrender Pol Slattery broke form by shaking hands and asking, "Why did you wait so long getting out of the gate?"

Ender glanced at Anderson, who was floating nearby. "I was informed late," he said. "It was an ambush."

Slattery grinned, and gripped Ender's hand again. "Good game."

Ender didn't smile at Anderson this time. He knew that now the games would be arranged against him, to even up the odds. He didn't like it.

It was 2150, nearly time for lights out, when Ender knocked at the door of the room shared by Bean and three other soldiers. One of the others opened the door, then stepped back and held it wide. Ender stood for a moment, then asked if he could come in. They answered, of course, of course, come in, and he walked to the upper bunk, where Bean had set down his book and was leaning on one elbow to look at Ender.

"Bean, can you give me twenty minutes?"

"Near lights out," Bean answered.

"My room," Ender answered. "I'll cover for you." Bean sat up and slid off his bed. Together he and Ender padded silently down the corridor to Ender's room. Bean entered first, and Ender closed the door behind them.

"Sit down," Ender said, and they both sat on the edge of the bed, looking at each other.

"Remember four weeks ago, Bean? When you told me to make you a toon leader?"

"Yeah."

"I've made five toon leaders since then, haven't I? And none of them was you."

Bean looked at him calmly.

"Was I right?" Ender asked.

"Yes, sir," Bean answered.

Ender nodded. "How have you done in these battles?"

Bean cocked his head to one side. "I've never been immobilized, sir, and I've immobilized forty-three of the enemy. I've obeyed orders quickly, and I've commanded a squad in mop-up and never lost a soldier."

"Then you'll understand this." Ender paused, then decided to back up and say something else first.

"You know you're early, Bean, by a good half year. I was, too, and I've been made a commander six months early. Now they've put me into battles after only three weeks of training with my army. They've given me eight battles in seven days. I've already had more battles than boys who were made commander four months ago. I've won more battles than many who've been commanders for a year. And then tonight. You know what happened tonight."

Bean nodded. "They told you late."

"I don't know what the teachers are doing. But my army is getting tired, and I'm getting tired, and now they're changing the rules of the game. You see, Bean, I've looked in the old charts. No one has ever destroyed so many enemies and kept so many of his own soldiers whole in the history of the game. I'm unique—and I'm getting unique treatment."

Bean smiled. "You're the best, Ender."

Ender shook his head. "Maybe. But it was no accident that I got the soldiers I got. My worst soldier could be a toon leader in another army. I've got the best. They've loaded things my way—but now they're loading it against me. I don't know why. But I know I have to be ready for it. I need your help."

"Why mine?"

"Because even though there are some better soldiers than you in Dragon Army—not many, but some—there's nobody who can think better and faster than you." Bean said nothing. They both knew it was true.

Ender continued. "I need to be ready, but I can't retrain the whole army. So I'm going to cut every toon down by one, including you—and you and four others will be a special squad under me. And you'll learn to do some new things. Most of the time you'll be in the regular toons just like you are now. But when I need you. See?"

Bean smiled and nodded. "That's right, that's good, can I pick them myself?"

"One from each toon except your own, and you can't take any toon leaders."

"What do you want us to do?"

"Bean, I don't know. I don't know what they'll throw at us. What would you do if suddenly our flashers didn't work, and the enemy's did? What would you do if we had to face two armies at once? The only thing I know is—we're not going for score anymore. We're going for the enemy's gate. That's when the battle is technically won—four helmets at the corners of the gate. I'm going for quick kills, battles ended even when we're outnumbered. Got it? You take them for two hours during regular workout. Then you and I and your soldiers, we'll work at night after dinner."

"We'll get tired."

"I have a feeling we don't know what tired is."

Ender reached out and took Bean's hand, and gripped it. "Even when it's rigged against us, Bean. We'll win."

Bean left in silence and padded down the corridor.

Dragon Army wasn't the only army working out after hours now. The other commanders finally realized they had some catching up to do. From early morning to lights out soldiers all over Training and Command Center, none of them over fourteen years old, were learning to jackknife off walls and use each other as living shields.

But while other commanders mastered the techniques that Ender had used to defeat them, Ender and Bean worked on solutions to problems that had never come up.

There were still battles every day, but for a while they were normal, with grids and stars and sudden plunges through the gate. And after the battles, Ender and Bean and four other soldiers would leave the main group and practice strange maneuvers. Attacks without flashers, using feet to physically disarm or disorient an enemy. Using four frozen soldiers to reverse the enemy's gate in less than two seconds. And one day Bean came to workout with a 300-meter cord.

"What's that for?"

"I don't know yet." Absently Bean spun one end of the cord. It wasn't more than an eighth of an inch thick, but it could have lifted ten adults without breaking.

"Where did you get it?"

"Commissary. They asked what for. I said to practice tying knots."

Bean tied a loop in the end of the rope and slid it over his shoulders.

"Here, you two, hang onto the wall here. Now don't let go of the rope. Give me about fifty yards of slack." They complied, and Bean moved about ten feet from them along the wall. As soon as he was sure they were ready, he jackknifed off the wall and flew straight out, fifty meters. Then the rope snapped taut. It was so fine that it was virtually invisible, but it was strong enough to force Bean to veer off at almost a right angle. It happened so suddenly that he had inscribed a perfect arc and hit the wall before most of the other soldiers knew what had happened. Bean did a perfect rebound and drifted quickly back where Ender and the others waited for him.

Many of the soldiers in the five regular squads hadn't noticed the rope, and were demanding to know how it was done. It was impossible to change direction that abruptly in nullo. Bean just laughed.

"Wait till the next game without a grid! They'll never know what hit them."

They never did. The next game was only two hours later, but Bean and two others had become pretty good at aiming and shooting while they flew at ridiculous speeds at the end of the rope. The slip of paper was delivered, and Dragon Army trotted off to the gate, to battle with Griffin Army. Bean coiled the rope all the way.

When the gate opened, all they could see was a large brown star only fifteen feet away, completely blocking their view of the enemy's gate.

Ender didn't pause. "Bean, give yourself fifty feet of rope and go around the star." Bean and his four soldiers dropped through the gate and in a moment Bean was launched sideways away from the star. The rope snapped taut, and Bean flew forward. As the rope was stopped by each edge of the star in turn, his arc became tighter and his speed greater, until when he hit the wall only a few feet away from the gate he was barely able to control his rebound to end up behind the star. But he immediately moved all his arms and legs so that those waiting inside the gate would know that the enemy hadn't flashed him anywhere.

Ender dropped through the gate, and Bean quickly told him how Griffin Army was situated. "They've got two squares of stars, all the way around the gate. All their soldiers are under cover, and there's no way to hit any of them until we're clear to the bottom wall. Even with shields, we'd get there at half strength and we wouldn't have a chance."

"They moving?" Ender asked.

"Do they need to?"

Ender thought for a moment. "That one's tough. We'll go for the gate, Bean."

Griffin Army began to call out to them.

"Hey, is anybody there!"

"Wake up, there's a war on!"

"We wanna join the picnic!"

They were still calling when Ender's army came out from behind their star with a shield of fourteen frozen soldiers. William Bee, Griffin Army's commander, waited patiently as the screen approached, his men waiting at the fringes of their stars for the moment when whatever was behind the screen became visible. About ten meters away the screen exploded as the soldiers behind it shoved the screen north. The momentum carried them south twice as fast, and at the same moment the rest of Dragon Army burst from behind their star at the opposite end of the room, firing rapidly.

William Bee's boys joined battle immediately, of course, but William Bee was far more interested in what had been left behind when the shield disappeared. A formation of four frozen Dragon Army soldiers were moving headfirst toward the Griffin Army gate, held together by another frozen soldier whose feet and hands were hooked through their belts. A sixth soldier hung to his wrist and trailed like the tail of a kite. Griffin Army was winning the battle easily, and William Bee concentrated on the formation as it approached the gate. Suddenly the soldier trailing in back moved—he wasn't frozen at all! And even though William Bee flashed him immediately, the damage was done. The formation drifted to the Griffin Army gate, and their helmets touched all four corners simultaneously. A buzzer sounded, the gate reversed, and the frozen soldier in the middle was carried by momentum right through the gate. All the flashers stopped working, and the game was over.

The teacher door opened and Lieutenant Anderson came in. Anderson stopped himself with a slight movement of his hands when he reached the center of the battleroom. "Ender," he called, breaking protocol. One of the frozen Dragon soldiers near the south wall tried to call through jaws that were clamped shut by the suit. Anderson drifted to him and unfroze him.

Ender was smiling.

"I beat you again, sir," Ender said. Anderson didn't smile.

"That's nonsense, Ender," Anderson said softly. "Your battle was with William Bee of Griffin Army."

Ender raised an eyebrow.

"After that maneuver," Anderson said, "the rules are being revised to require that all of the enemy's soldiers must be immobilized before the gate can be reversed."

"That's all right," Ender said. "It could only work once, anyway." Anderson nodded, and was turning away when Ender added, "Is there going to be a new rule that armies be given equal positions to fight from?"

Anderson turned back around. "If you're in one of the positions, Ender, you can hardly call them equal, whatever they are."

William Bee counted carefully and wondered how in the world he had lost when not one of his soldiers had been flashed, and only four of Ender's soldiers were even mobile.

And that night as Ender came into the commanders' mess hall, he was greeted with applause and cheers, and his table was crowded with respectful commanders, many of them two or three years older than he was. He was friendly, but while he ate he wondered what the teachers would do to him in his next battle. He didn't need to worry. His next two battles were easy victories, and after that he never saw the battleroom again.

It was 2100 and Ender was a little irritated to hear someone knock at his door. His army was exhausted, and he had ordered them all to be in bed after 2030. The last two days had been regular battles, and Ender was expecting the worst in the morning.

It was Bean. He came in sheepishly, and saluted.

Ender returned his salute and snapped, "Bean, I wanted everybody in bed."

Bean nodded but didn't leave. Ender considered ordering him out. But as he looked at Bean it occurred to him for the first time in weeks just how young Bean was. He had turned eight a week before, and he was still small and—no, Ender thought, he wasn't young. Nobody was young. Bean had been in battle, and with a whole army depending on him he had come through and won. And even though he was small, Ender could never think of him as young again.

Ender shrugged and Bean came over and sat on the edge of the bed. The younger boy looked at his hands for a while, and finally Ender grew impatient and asked, "Well, what is it?"

"I'm transferred. Got orders just a few minutes ago."

Ender closed his eyes for a moment. "I knew they'd pull something new. Now they're taking—where are you going?"

"Rabbit Army."

"How can they put you under an idiot like Carn Carby!"

"Carn was graduated. Support squads."

Ender looked up. "Well, who's commanding Rabbit then?"

Bean held his hands out helplessly.

"Me," he said.

Ender nodded, and then smiled. "Of course. After all, you're only four years younger than the regular age."

"It isn't funny," Bean said. "I don't know what's going on here. First all the changes in the game. And now this. I wasn't the only one transferred, either, Ender. Ren, Peder, Wins, Younger, Paul. All commanders now."

Ender stood up angrily and strode to the wall. "Every damn toon leader I've got!" he said, and whirled to face Bean. "If they're going to break up my army, Bean, why did they bother making me a commander at all?"

Bean shook his head. "I don't know. You're the best, Ender. Nobody's ever done what you've done. Nineteen battles in fifteen days, sir, and you won every one of them, no matter what they did to you."

"And now you and the others are commanders. You know every trick I've got, I trained you, and who am I supposed to replace you with? Are they going to stick me with six greenohs?"

"It stinks, Ender, but you know that if they gave you five crippled midgets and armed you with a roll of toilet paper you'd win."

They both laughed, and then they noticed that the door was open.

Lieutenant Anderson stepped in. He was followed by Captain Graff.

"Ender Wiggins," Graff said, holding his hands across his stomach.

"Yes, sir," Ender answered.

"Orders."

Anderson extended a slip of paper. Ender read it quickly, then crumpled it, still looking at the air where the paper had been. After a few moments he asked, "Can I tell my army?"

"They'll find out," Graff answered. "It's better not to talk to them after orders. It makes it easier."

"For you or for me?" Ender asked. He didn't wait for an answer. He turned to Bean, took his hand for a moment, and headed for the door.

"Wait," Bean said. "Where are you going? Tactical or Support School?"

"Command School," Ender answered, and then he was gone and Anderson closed the door.

Command School, Bean thought. Nobody went to Command School until they had gone through three years of Tactical. But then, nobody went to Tactical until they had been through at least five years of Battle School. Ender had only had three.

The system was breaking up. No doubt about it, Bean thought. Either somebody at the top was going crazy, or something was going wrong with the war—the real war, the one they were training to fight in. Why else would they break down the training system, advance somebody—even somebody as good as Ender—straight to Command School? Why else would they have an eight-year-old greenoh like Bean command an army?

Bean wondered about it for a long time, and then he finally lay down on Ender's bed and realized that he'd never see Ender again, probably. For some reason that made him want to cry. But he didn't cry, of course. Training in the preschools had taught him how to force down emotions like that. He remembered how his first teacher, when he was three, would have been upset to see his lip quivering and his eyes full of tears.

Bean went through the relaxing routine until he didn't feel like crying any more. Then he drifted off to sleep. His hand was near his mouth. It lay on his pillow hesitantly, as if Bean couldn't decide whether to bite his nails or suck on his fingertips. His forehead was creased and furrowed. His breathing was quick and light. He was a soldier, and if anyone had asked him what he wanted to be when he grew up, he wouldn't have known what they meant.

There's a war on, they said, and that was excuse enough for all the hurry in the world. They said it like a password and flashed a little card at every ticket counter and customs check and guard station. It got them to the head of every line.

Ender Wiggin was rushed from place to place so quickly he had no time to examine anything. But he did see trees for the first time. He saw men who were not in uniform. He saw women. He saw strange animals that didn't speak, but that followed docilely behind women and small children. He saw suitcases and conveyor belts and signs that said words he had never heard of. He would have asked someone what the words meant, except that purpose and authority surrounded him in the persons of four very high officers who never spoke to each other and never spoke to him.

Ender Wiggin was a stranger to the world he was being trained to save. He did not remember ever leaving Battle School before. His earliest memories were of childish war games under the direction of a teacher, of meals with other boys in the gray and green uniforms of the armed forces of his world. He did not know that the gray represented the sky and the green represented the great forests of his planet. All he knew of the world was from vague references to "outside."

And before he could make any sense of the strange world he was seeing for the first time, they enclosed him again within the shell of the military, where nobody had to say there's a war on anymore because nobody in the shell of the military forgot it for a single instant in a single day.

They put him in a spaceship and launched him to a large artificial satellite that circled the world.

This space station was called Command School. It held the ansible.

On his first day Ender Wiggin was taught about the ansible and what it meant to warfare. It meant that even though the starships of today's battles were launched a hundred years ago, the commanders of the starships were men of today, who used the ansible to send messages to the computers and the few men on each ship. The ansible sent words as they were spoken, orders as they were made. Battleplans as they were fought. Light was a pedestrian.

For two months Ender Wiggin didn't meet a single person. They came to him namelessly, taught him what they knew, and left him to other teachers. He had no time to miss his friends at Battle School. He only had time to learn how to operate the simulator, which flashed battle patterns around him as if he were in a starship at the center of the battle. How to command mock ships in mock battles by manipulating the keys on the simulator and speaking words into the ansible. How to recognize instantly every enemy ship and the weapons it carried by the pattern that the simulator showed. How to transfer all that he learned in the nullo battles at Battle School to the starship battles at Command School.

He had thought the game was taken seriously before. Here they hurried him through every step, were angry and worried beyond reason every time he forgot something or made a mistake. But he worked as he had always worked, and learned as he had always learned. After a while he didn't make any more mistakes. He used the simulator as if it were a part of himself. Then they stopped being worried and they gave him a teacher. The teacher was a person at last, and his name was Maezr Rackham.

Maezr Rackham was sitting cross-legged on the floor when Ender awoke. He said nothing as Ender got up and showered and dressed, and Ender did not bother to ask him anything. He had long since learned that when something unusual was going on, he would find out more information faster by waiting than by asking.

Maezr still hadn't spoken when Ender was ready and went to the door to leave the room. The door didn't open. Ender turned to face the man sitting on the floor. Maezr was at least forty, which made him the oldest man Ender had ever seen close up. He had a day's growth of black and white whiskers that grizzled his face only slightly less than his close-cut hair. His face sagged a little and his eyes were surrounded by creases and lines. He looked at Ender without interest.

Ender turned back to the door and tried again to open it.

"All right," he said, giving up. "Why's the door locked?"

Maezr continued to look at him blankly.

Ender became impatient. "I'm going to be late. If I'm not supposed to be there until later, then tell me so I can go back to bed." No answer. "Is it a guessing game?" Ender asked. No answer. Ender decided that maybe the man was trying to make him angry, so he went through a relaxing exercise as he leaned on the door, and soon he was calm again. Maezr didn't take his eyes off Ender.

For the next two hours the silence endured, Maezr watching Ender constantly, Ender trying to pretend he didn't notice the old man. The boy became more and more nervous, and finally ended up walking from one end of the room to the other in a sporadic pattern.

He walked by Maezr as he had several times before, and Maezr's hand shot out and pushed Ender's left leg into his right in the middle of a step. Ender fell flat on the floor.

He leaped to his feet immediately, furious. He found Maezr sitting calmly, cross-legged, as if he had never moved. Ender stood poised to fight. But the other's immobility made it impossible for Ender to attack, and he found himself wondering if he had only imagined the old man's hand tripping him up.

The pacing continued for another hour, with Ender Wiggin trying the door every now and then. At last he gave up and took off his uniform and walked to his bed.

As he leaned over to pull the covers back, he felt a hand jab roughly between his thighs and another hand grab his hair. In a moment he had been turned upside down. His face and shoulders were being pressed into the floor by the old man's knee, while his back was excruciatingly bent and his legs were pinioned by

Maezr's arm. Ender was helpless to use his arms, and he couldn't bend his back to gain slack so he could use his legs. In less than two seconds the old man had completely defeated Ender Wiggin.

"All right," Ender gasped. "You win."

Maezr's knee thrust painfully downward.

"Since when," Maezr asked in a soft, rasping voice, "do you have to tell the enemy when he has won?"

Ender remained silent.

"I surprised you once, Ender Wiggin. Why didn't you destroy me immediately afterward? Just because I looked peaceful? You turned your back on me. Stupid. You have learned nothing. You have never had a teacher."

Ender was angry now. "I've had too many damned teachers, how was I supposed to know you'd turn out to be a—" Ender hunted for a word. Maezr supplied one.

"An enemy, Ender Wiggin," Maezr whispered. "I am your enemy, the first one you've ever had who was smarter than you. There is no teacher but the enemy, Ender Wiggin. No one but the enemy will ever tell you what the enemy is going to do. No one but the enemy will ever teach you how to destroy and conquer. I am your enemy, from now on. From now on I am your teacher."

Then Maezr let Ender's legs fall to the floor. Because the old man still held Ender's head to the floor, the boy couldn't use his arms to compensate, and his legs hit the plastic surface with a loud crack and a sickening pain that made Ender wince. Then Maezr stood and let Ender rise.

Slowly the boy pulled his legs under him, with a faint groan of pain, and he knelt on all fours for a moment, recovering. Then his right arm flashed out. Maezr quickly danced back and Ender's hand closed on air as his teacher's foot shot forward to catch Ender on the chin.

Ender's chin wasn't there. He was lying flat on his back, spinning on the floor, and during the moment that Maezr was off balance from his kick Ender's feet smashed into Maezr's other leg. The old man fell on the ground in a heap.

What seemed to be a heap was really a hornet's nest. Ender couldn't find an arm or a leg that held still long enough to be grabbed, and in the meantime blows were landing on his back and arms. Ender was smaller—he couldn't reach past the old man's flailing limbs.

So he leaped back out of the way and stood poised near the door.

The old man stopped thrashing about and sat up, cross-legged again, laughing. "Better, this time, boy. But slow. You will have to be better with a fleet than you are with your body or no one will be safe with you in command. Lesson learned?"

Ender nodded slowly.

Maezr smiled. "Good. Then we'll never have such a battle again. All the rest with the simulator. I will program your battles, I will devise the strategy of your enemy, and you will learn to be quick and discover what tricks the enemy has for you. Remember, boy. From now on the enemy is more clever than you. From now on the enemy is stronger than you. From now on you are always about to lose."

Then Maezr's face became serious again. "You will be about to lose, Ender, but you will win. You will learn to defeat the enemy. He will teach you how."

Maezr got up and walked toward the door. Ender stepped back out of the way. As the old man touched the handle of the door, Ender leaped into the air and kicked Maezr in the small of the back with both feet. He hit hard enough that he rebounded onto his feet, as Maezr cried out and collapsed on the floor.

Maezr got up slowly, holding onto the door handle, his face contorted with pain. He seemed disabled, but Ender didn't trust him. He waited warily. And yet in spite of his suspicion he was caught off guard by Maezr's speed. In a moment he found himself on the floor near the opposite wall, his nose and lip bleeding where his face had hit the bed. He was able to turn enough to see Maezr open the door and leave. The old man was limping and walking slowly.

Ender smiled in spite of the pain, then rolled over onto his back and laughed until his mouth filled with blood and he started to gag. Then he got up and painfully made his way to the bed. He lay down and in a few minutes a medic came and took care of his injuries.

As the drug had its effect and Ender drifted off to sleep he remembered the way Maezr limped out of his room and laughed again. He was still laughing softly as his mind went blank and the medic pulled the blanket over him and snapped off the light. He slept until pain woke him in the morning. He dreamed of defeating Maezr.

The next day Ender went to the simulator room with his nose bandaged and his lip still puffy. Maezr was not there. Instead a captain who had worked with him before showed him an addition that had been made. The captain pointed to a tube with a loop at one end. "Radio. Primitive, I know, but it loops over your ear and we tuck the other end into your mouth with this piece here . . ."

"Watch it," Ender said as the captain pushed the end of the tube into his swollen lip.

"Sorry. Now you just talk."

"Good. Who to?"

The captain smiled. "Ask and see."

Ender shrugged and turned to the simulator. As he did a voice reverberated through his skull. It was too loud for him to understand, and he ripped the radio off his ear.

"What are you trying to do, make me deaf?"

The captain shook his head and turned a dial on a small box on a nearby table. Ender put the radio back on.

"Commander," the radio said in a familiar voice.

Ender answered, "Yes."

"Instructions, sir?"

The voice was definitely familiar. "Bean?" Ender asked.

"Yes sir."

"Bean, this is Ender."

Silence. And then a burst of laughter from the other side. Then six or seven more voices laughing, and Ender waited for silence to return. When it did, he asked, "Who else?" A few voices spoke at once, but Bean drowned them out. "Me, I'm Bean, and Peder, Wins, Younger, Lee, and Vlad."

Ender thought for a moment. Then asked what the hell was going on. They laughed again.

"They can't break up the group," Bean said. "We were commanders for maybe two weeks, and here we are at Command School, training with the simulator, and all of a sudden they told us they were going to form a fleet with a new commander. And that's you."

Ender smiled. "Are you boys any good?"

"If we aren't, you'll let us know."

Ender chuckled a little. "Might work out. A fleet."

For the next ten days Ender trained his toon leaders until they could maneuver their ships like precision dancers. It was like being back in the battleroom again, except that Ender could always see everything, and could speak to his toon leaders and change their orders at any time.

One day as Ender sat down at the control board and switched on the simulator, harsh green lights appeared in the space—the enemy.

"This is it," Ender said. "X, Y, bullet, C, D, reserve screen, E, south loop, Bean, angle north."

The enemy was grouped in a globe, and outnumbered Ender two to one. Half of Ender's force was grouped in a tight, bulletlike formation, with the rest in a flat circular screen—except for a tiny force under Bean that moved off the simulator, heading behind the enemy's formation. Ender quickly learned the enemy's strategy: whenever Ender's bullet formation came close, the enemy would give way, hoping to draw Ender inside the globe where he would be surrounded. So Ender obligingly fell into the trap, bringing his bullet to the center of the globe.

The enemy began to contract slowly, not wanting to come within range until all their weapons could be brought to bear at once. Then Ender began to work in earnest. His reserve screen approached the outside of the globe, and the enemy began to concentrate his forces there. Then Bean's force appeared on the opposite side, and the enemy again deployed ships on that side.

Which left most of the globe only thinly defended. Ender's bullet attacked, and since at the point of attack it outnumbered the enemy overwhelmingly, he tore a hole in the formation. The enemy reacted to try to plug the gap, but in the confusion the reserve force and Bean's small force attacked simultaneously, while the bullet moved to another part of the globe. In a few more minutes the formation was shattered, most of the enemy ships destroyed, and the few survivors rushing away as fast as they could go.

Ender switched the simulator off. All the lights faded. Maezr was standing beside Ender, his hands in his pockets, his body tense. Ender looked up at him.

"I thought you said the enemy would be smart," Ender said.

Maezr's face remained expressionless. "What did you learn?"

"I learned that a sphere only works if your enemy's a fool. He had his forces so spread out that I outnumbered him whenever I engaged him."

"And?"

"And," Ender said, "you can't stay committed to one pattern. It makes you too easy to predict."

"Is that all?" Maezr asked quietly.

Ender took off his radio. "The enemy could have defeated me by breaking the sphere earlier."

Maezr nodded. "You had an unfair advantage."

Ender looked up at him coldly. "I was outnumbered two to one."

Maezr shook his head. "You have the ansible. The enemy doesn't. We include that in the mock battles. Their messages travel at the speed of light."

Ender glanced toward the simulator. "Is there enough space to make a difference?"

"Don't you know?" Maezr asked. "None of the ships was ever closer than thirty thousand kilometers to another."

Ender tried to figure the size of the enemy's sphere. Astronomy was beyond him. But now his curiosity was stirred.

"What kind of weapons are on those ships? To be able to strike so fast and so far apart?"

Maezr shook his head. "The science is too much for you. You'd have to study many more years than you've lived to understand even the basics. All you need to know is that the weapons work."

"Why do we have to come so close to be in range?"

"The ships are all protected by force fields. A certain distance away the weapons are weaker, and can't get through. Closer in the weapons are stronger than the shields. But the computers take care of all that. They're constantly firing in any direction that won't hurt one of our ships. The computers pick targets, aim, they do all the detail work. You just tell them when and get them in a position to win. All right?"

"No." Ender twisted the tube of the radio around his fingers. "I have to know how the weapons work."

"I told you, it would take—"

"I can't command a fleet—not even on the simulator—unless I know." Ender waited a moment, then added, "Just the rough idea."

Maezr stood up and walked a few steps away. "All right, Ender. It won't make any sense, but I'll try. As simply as I can." He shoved his hands into his pockets. "It's this way, Ender. Everything is made up of atoms, little particles so small you can't see them with your eyes. These atoms, there are only a few different types, and they're all made up of even smaller particles that are pretty much the same. These atoms can be broken, so that they stop being atoms. So that this metal doesn't hold together anymore. Or the plastic floor. Or your body. Or even the air. They just seem to disappear, if you break the atoms. All that's left is the pieces. And they fly around and break more atoms. The weapons on the ships set up an area where it's impossible for atoms of anything to stay together. They all break down. So things in that area—they disappear."

Ender nodded. "You're right, I don't understand it. Can it be blocked?"

"No. But it gets wider and weaker the farther it goes from the ship, so that after a while a force field will block it. Okay? And to make it strong at all, it has to be focused, so that a ship can only fire effectively in maybe three or four directions at once."

Ender nodded again. Maezr wondered if the boy really understood it at all.

"If the pieces of the broken atoms go breaking more atoms, why doesn't it just make everything disappear?"

"Space. Those thousands of kilometers between the ships, they're empty. Almost no atoms. The pieces don't hit anything, and when they finally do hit something, they're so spread out they can't do any harm." Maezr cocked his head quizzically. "Anything else . . . ?"

Ender nodded. "Do the weapons on the ships—do they work against anything besides ships?"

Maezr moved in close to Ender and said firmly, "We only use them against ships. Never anything else. If we used them against anything else, the enemy would use them against us. Got it?"

Maezr walked away, and was nearly out the door when Ender called to him.
"I don't know your name yet," Ender said blandly.

"Maezr Rackham."

"Maezr Rackham," Ender said. "I defeated you."

Maezr laughed.

"Ender, you weren't fighting me today," he said. "You were fighting the stupidest computer in the Command School, set on a ten-year-old program. You don't think I'd use a sphere, do you?" He shook his head. "Ender, my dear little fellow, when you fight me you'll know it. Because you'll lose." And Maezr left the room.

Ender still practiced ten hours a day with his toon leaders. He never saw them, though, only heard their voices on the radio. Battles came every two or three days. The enemy had something new every time, something harder—but Ender coped with it. And won every time. And after every battle Maezr would point out mistakes and show Ender had really lost. Maezr only let Ender finish so that he would learn to handle the end of the game.

Until finally Maezr came in and solemnly shook Ender's hand and said, "That, boy, was a good battle."

Because the praise was so long in coming, it pleased Ender more than praise had ever pleased him before. And because it was so condescending, he resented it.

"So from now on," Maezr said, "we can give you hard ones."

From then on Ender's life was a slow nervous breakdown.

He began fighting two battles a day, with problems that steadily grew more difficult. He had been trained in nothing but the game all his life—but now the game began to consume him. He woke in the morning with new strategies for the simulator, and went fitfully to sleep at night with the mistakes of the day preying on him. Sometimes he would wake up in the middle of the night crying for a reason he didn't remember. Sometimes he woke with his knuckles bloody from biting them. But every day he went impassively to the simulator and drilled his toon leaders until the battles, and drilled his toon leaders after the battles, and endured and studied the harsh criticism that Maezr Rackham piled on him. He noted that Rackham perversely criticized him more after his hardest battles. He noted that every time he thought of a new strategy the enemy was using it within a few days. And he noted that while his fleet always stayed the same size, the enemy increased in numbers every day.

He asked his teacher.

"We are showing you what it will be like when you really command. The ratios of enemy to us."

"Why does the enemy always outnumber us in these battles?"

Maezr bowed his gray head for a moment, as if deciding whether to answer. Finally he looked up and reached out his hand and touched Ender on the shoulder. "I will tell you, even though the information is secret. You see, the enemy attacked us first. He had good reason to attack us, but that is a matter for politicians, and whether the fault was ours or his, we could not let him win. So when the enemy came to our worlds, we fought back, hard, and spent the finest of our young men in the fleets. But we won, and the enemy retreated."

Maezr smiled ruefully. "But the enemy was not through, boy. The enemy would never be through. They came again, with more numbers, and it was harder to beat them. And another generation of young men was spent. Only a few survived. So we came up with a plan—the big men came up with the plan. We knew that we had to destroy the enemy once and for all, totally, eliminate his ability to make war against us. To do that we had to go to his home worlds—his home world, really, since the enemy's empire is all tied to his capital world."

"And so?" Ender asked.

"And so we made a fleet. We made more ships than the enemy ever had. We made a hundred ships for every ship he had sent against us. And we launched them against his twenty-eight worlds. They left a hundred years ago. And they carried on them the ansible, and only a few men. So that someday a commander could sit on a planet somewhere far from the battle and command the fleet. So that our best minds would not be destroyed by the enemy."

Ender's question had still not been answered.

"Why do they outnumber us?"

Maezr laughed. "Because it took a hundred years for our ships to get there. They've had a hundred years to prepare for us. They'd be fools, don't you think, boy, if they waited in old tugboats to defend their harbors. They have new ships, great ships, hundreds of ships. All we have is the ansible, that and the face that they have to put a commander with every fleet, and when they lose—and they will lose—they lose one of their best minds every time."

Ender started to ask another question.

"No more, Ender Wiggin. I've told you more than you ought to know as it is."

Ender stood angrily and turned away. "I have a right to know. Do you think this can go on forever, pushing me through one school and another and never telling me what my life is for? You use me and the others as a tool; someday we'll command your ships, someday maybe we'll save your lives, but I'm not a computer, and I have to *know!*"

"Ask me a question, then, boy," Maezr said, "and if I can answer, I will."

"If you use your best minds to command the fleets, and you never lose any, then what do you need me for? Who am I replacing, if they're all still there?"

Maezr shook his head. "I can't tell you the answer to that, Ender. Be content that we will need you, soon. It's late. Go to bed. You have a battle in the morning."

Ender walked out of the simulator room. But when Maezr left by the same door a few moments later, the boy was waiting in the hall.

"All right, boy," Maezr said impatiently, "what is it? I don't have all night and you need to sleep."

Ender stayed silent, but Maezr waited. Finally the boy asked softly, "Do they live?"

"Does who live?"

"The other commanders. The ones now. And before me."

Maezr snorted. "Live. Of course they live. He wonders if they live." Still chuckling the old man walked off down the hall. Ender stood in the corridor for a while, but at last he was tired and he went off to bed. They live, he thought. They live, but he can't tell me what happens to them.

That night Ender didn't wake up crying. But he did wake up with blood on his hands.

*   *   *

Months wore on with battles every day, until at last Ender settled into the routine of the destruction of himself. He slept less every night, dreamed more, and he began to have terrible pains in his stomach. They put him on a very bland diet, but soon he didn't even have an appetite for that. "Eat," Maezr said, and Ender would mechanically put food in his mouth. But if nobody told him to eat he didn't eat.

One day as he was drilling his toon leaders the room went black and he woke up on the floor with his face bloody where he had hit the controls.

They put him to bed then, and for three days he was very ill. He remembered seeing faces in his dreams, but they weren't real faces, and he knew it even while he thought he saw them. He thought he saw Bean, sometimes, and sometimes he thought he saw Lieutenant Anderson and Captain Graff. And then he woke up and it was only his enemy, Maezr Rackham.

"I'm awake," he said to Maezr.

"So I see," Maezr answered. "Took you long enough. You have a battle today."

So Ender got up and fought the battle and he won it. But there was no second battle that day, and they let him go to bed earlier. His hands were shaking as he undressed.

During the night he thought he felt hands touching him gently, and he dreamed he heard voices, saying, "How long can he go on?"

"Long enough."

"So soon?"

"In a few days, then he's through."

"How will he do?"

"Fine. Even today, he was better than ever."

Ender recognized the last voice as Maezr Rackham's. He resented Rackham's intruding even in his sleep.

He woke up and fought another battle and won.

Then he went to bed.

He woke up and won again.

And the next day was his last day in Command School, though he didn't know it. He got up and went to the simulator for the battle.

Maezr was waiting for him. Ender walked slowly into the simulator room. His step was slightly shuffling, and he seemed tired and dull. Maezr frowned.

"Are you awake, boy?" If Ender had been alert, he would have noticed the concern in his teacher's voice. Instead, he simply went to the controls and sat down. Maezr spoke to him.

"Today's game needs a little explanation, Ender Wiggin. Please turn around and pay strict attention."

Ender turned around, and for the first time he noticed that there were people at the back of the room. He recognized Graff and Anderson from Battle School, and vaguely remembered a few of the men from Command School—teachers for a few hours at some time or another. But most of the people he didn't know at all.

"Who are they?"

Maezr shook his head and answered, "Observers. Every now and then we let observers come in to watch the battle. If you don't want them, we'll send them out."

Ender shrugged. Maezr began his explanation. "Today's game, boy, has a new element. We're staging this battle around a planet. This will complicate things in two ways. The planet isn't large, on the scale we're using, but the ansible can't detect anything on the other side of it—so there's a blind spot. Also, it's against the rules to use weapons against the planet itself. All right?"

"Why, don't the weapons work against planets?"

Maezr answered coldly, "There are rules of war, Ender, that apply even in training games."

Ender shook his head slowly. "Can the planet attack?"

Maezr looked nonplussed for a moment, then smiled. "I guess you'll have to find that one out, boy. And one more thing. Today, Ender, your opponent isn't the computer. I am your enemy today, and today I won't be letting you off so easily. Today is a battle to the end. And I'll use any means I can to defeat you."

Then Maezr was gone, and Ender expressionlessly led his toon leaders through maneuvers. Ender was doing well, of course, but several of the observers shook their heads, and Graff kept clasping and unclasping his hands, crossing and uncrossing his legs. Ender would be slow today, and today Ender couldn't afford to be slow.

A warning buzzer sounded, and Ender cleared the simulator board, waiting for today's game to appear. He felt muddled today, and wondered why people were there watching. Were they going to judge him today? Decide if he was good enough for something else? For another two years of grueling training, another two years of struggling to exceed his best? Ender was twelve. He felt very old. And as he waited for the game to appear, he wished he could simply lose it, lose the battle badly and completely so that they would remove him from the program, punish him however they wanted, he didn't care, just so he could sleep.

Then the enemy formation appeared, and Ender's weariness turned to desperation.

The enemy outnumbered him a thousand to one, the simulator glowed green with them, and Ender knew that he couldn't win.

And the enemy was not stupid. There was no formation that Ender could study and attack. Instead the vast swarms of ships were constantly moving, constantly shifting from one momentary formation to another, so that a space that for one moment was empty was immediately filled with a formidable enemy force. And even though Ender's fleet was the largest he had ever had, there was no place he could deploy it where he would outnumber the enemy long enough to accomplish anything.

And behind the enemy was the planet. The planet, which Maezr had warned him about. What difference did a planet make, when Ender couldn't hope to get near it? Ender waited, waited for the flash of insight that would tell him what to do, how to destroy the enemy. And as he waited, he heard the observers behind him begin to shift in their seats, wondering what Ender was doing, what plan he would follow. And finally it was obvious to everybody that Ender didn't know what to do, that there was nothing to do, and a few of the men at the back of the room made quiet little sounds in their throats.

Then Ender heard Bean's voice in his ear. Bean chuckled and said, "Remember, the enemy's gate is *down*." A few of the other leaders laughed, and Ender thought back to the simple games he had played and won in Battle School. They had put him against hopeless odds there, too. And he had beaten them. And he'd be damned if he'd let Maezr Rackham beat him with a cheap trick like outnumbering him a thousand to one. He had won a game in Battle School by going for something the enemy didn't expect, something against the rules—he had won by going against the enemy's gate.

And the enemy's gate was down.

Ender smiled, and realized that if he broke this rule they'd probably kick him out of school, and that way he'd win for sure; he would never have to play a game again.

He whispered into the microphone. His six commanders each took part of the fleet and launched themselves against the enemy. They pursued erratic courses, darting off in one direction and then another. The enemy immediately stopped his aimless maneuvering and began to group around Ender's six fleets.

Ender took off his microphone, leaned back in his chair, and watched. The observers murmured out loud, now. Ender was doing nothing—he had thrown the game away.

But a pattern began to emerge from the quick confrontations with the enemy. Ender's six groups lost ships constantly as they brushed with each enemy force—but they never stopped for a fight, even when for a moment they could have won a small tactical victory. Instead they continued on their erratic course that led, eventually, down. Toward the enemy planet.

And because of their seemingly random course the enemy didn't realize it until the same time that the observers did. By then it was too late, just as it had been too late for William Bee to stop Ender's soldiers from activating the gate. More of Ender's ships could be hit and destroyed, so that of the six fleets only two were able to get to the planet, and those were decimated. But those tiny groups *did* get through, and they opened fire on the planet.

Ender leaned forward now, anxious to see if his guess would pay off. He half expected a buzzer to sound and the game to be stopped, because he had broken the rule. But he was betting on the accuracy of the simulator. If it could simulate a planet, it could simulate what would happen to a planet under attack.

It did.

The weapons that blew up little ships didn't blow up the entire planet at first. But they did cause terrible explosions. And on the planet there was no space to dissipate the chain reaction. On the planet the chain reaction found more and more fuel to feed it.

The planet's surface seemed to be moving back and forth, but soon the surface gave way in an immense explosion that sent light flashing in all directions. It swallowed up Ender's entire fleet. And then it reached the enemy ships.

The first simply vanished in the explosion. Then, as the explosion spread and became less bright, it was clear what happened to each ship. As the light reached them they flashed brightly for a moment and disappeared. They were all fuel for the fire of the planet.

It took more than three minutes for the explosion to reach the limits of the simulator, and by then it was much fainter. All the ships were gone, and if any had escaped before the explosion reached them, they were few and not worth worrying about. Where the planet had been there was nothing. The simulator was empty.

Ender had destroyed the enemy by sacrificing his entire fleet and breaking the rule against destroying the planet. He wasn't sure whether to feel triumphant at his victory or defiant at the rebuke he was certain would come. So instead he felt nothing. He was tired. He wanted to go to bed and sleep.

He switched off the simulator, and finally heard the noise behind him.

There were no longer two rows of dignified military observers. Instead there was chaos. Some of them were slapping each other on the back, some of them were bowed with their head in their hands, others were openly weeping. Captain Graff detached himself from the group and came to Ender. Tears streamed down his face, but he was smiling. He reached out his arms, and to Ender's surprise he embraced the boy, held him tightly, and whispered, "Thank you, thank you, thank you, Ender."

Soon all the observers were gathered around the bewildered child, thanking him and cheering him and patting him on the shoulder and shaking his hand. Ender tried to make sense of what they were saying. He had passed the test after all? Why did it matter so much to them?

Then the crowd parted and Maezr Rackham walked through. He came straight up to Ender Wiggin and held out his hand.

"You made the hard choice, boy. But heaven knows there was no other way you could have done it. Congratulations. You beat them, and it's all over."

All over. Beat them. "I beat *you,* Maezr Rackham."

Maezr laughed, a loud laugh that filled the room. "Ender Wiggin, you never played me. You never played a *game* since I was your teacher."

Ender didn't get the joke. He had played a great many games, at a terrible cost to himself. He began to get angry.

Maezr reached out and touched his shoulder. Ender shrugged him off. Maezr then grew serious and said, "Ender Wiggin, for the last months you have been the commander of our fleets. There were no games. The battles were real. Your only enemy was *the* enemy. You won every battle. And finally today you fought them at their home world, and you destroyed their world, their fleet, you destroyed them completely, and they'll never come against us again. You did it. You."

Real. Not a game. Ender's mind was too tired to cope with it all. He walked away from Maezr, walked silently through the crowd that still whispered thanks and congratulations to the boy, walked out of the simulator room and finally arrived in his bedroom and closed the door.

He was asleep when Graff and Maezr Rackham found him. They came in quietly and roused him. He woke slowly, and when he recognized them he turned away to go back to sleep.

"Ender," Graff said. "We need to talk to you."

Ender rolled back to face them. He said nothing.

Graff smiled. "It was a shock to you yesterday, I know. But it must make you feel good to know you won the war."

Ender nodded slowly.

"Maezr Rackham here, he never played against you. He only analyzed your battles to find out your weak spots, to help you improve. It worked, didn't it?"

Ender closed his eyes tightly. They waited. He said, "Why didn't you tell me?"

Maezr smiled. "A hundred years ago, Ender, we found out some things. That when a commander's life is in danger he becomes afraid, and fear slows down his thinking. When a commander knows that he's killing people, he becomes cautious or insane, and neither of those help him do well. And when he is mature, when he has responsibilities and an understanding of the world, he becomes cautious and sluggish and can't do his job. So we trained children, who didn't know anything but the game, and never knew when it would become real. That was the theory, and you proved that the theory worked."

Graff reached out and touched Ender's shoulder. "We launched the ships so that they would all arrive at their destination during these few months. We knew that we'd probably only have one good commander, if we were lucky. In history it's been very rare to have more than one genius in a war. So we planned on having a genius. We were gambling. And you came along and we won."

Ender opened his eyes again and they realized he was angry. "Yes, you won."

Graff and Maezr Rackham looked at each other. "He doesn't understand," Graff whispered.

"I understand," Ender said. "You needed a weapon, and you got it, and it was me."

"That's right," Maezr answered.

"So tell me," Ender went on. "How many people lived on that planet that I destroyed?"

They didn't answer him. They waited a while in silence, and then Graff spoke. "Weapons don't need to understand what they're pointed at, Ender. We did the pointing, and so we're responsible. You just did your job."

Maezr smiled. "Of course, Ender, you'll be taken care of. The government will never forget you. You served us all very well."

Ender rolled over and faced the wall, and even though they tried to talk to him, he didn't answer them. Finally they left.

Ender lay in his bed for a long time before anyone disturbed him again. The door opened softly. Ender didn't turn to see who it was. Then a hand touched him softly.

"Ender, it's me, Bean."

Ender turned over and looked at the little boy who was standing by his bed.

"Sit down," Ender said.

Bean sat. "That last battle, Ender. I didn't know how you'd get us out of it."

Ender smiled. "I didn't. I cheated. I thought they'd kick me out."

"Can you believe it! We won the war. The whole war's over, and we thought we'd have to wait till we grew up to fight in it, and it was us fighting it all the time. I mean, Ender, we're little kids. I'm a little kid, anyway." Bean laughed and Ender smiled. Then they were silent for a little while, Bean sitting on the edge of the bed, and Ender watching him out of half-closed eyes.

Finally Bean thought of something else to say.

"What will we do now that the war's over?" he said.

Ender closed his eyes and said, "I need some sleep, Bean."

Bean got up and left and Ender slept.

Graff and Anderson walked through the gates into the park. There was a breeze but the sun was hot on their shoulders.

"Abba Technics? In the capital?" Graff asked.

"No, in Biggock County. Training division," Anderson replied. "They think my work with children is good preparation. And you?"

Graff smiled and shook his head. "No plans. I'll be here for a few more months. Reports, winding down. I've had offers. Personnel development for DCIA, executive vice-president for U and P, but I said no. Publisher wants me to do memoirs of the war. I don't know."

They sat on a bench and watched leaves shivering in the breeze. Children on the monkey bars were laughing and yelling, but the wind and the distance swallowed their words. "Look," Graff said, pointing. A little boy jumped from the bars and ran near the bench where the two men sat. Another boy followed him, and holding his hands like a gun he made an explosive sound. The child he was shooting at didn't stop. He fired again.

"I got you! Come back here!"

The other little boy ran on out of sight.

"Don't you know when you're dead?" The boy shoved his hands in his pockets and kicked a rock back to the monkey bars.

Anderson smiled and shook his head. "Kids," he said. Then he and Graff stood up and walked on out of the park.

"WHAT DO YOU MEAN . . . HUMAN?"

John W. Campbell, Jr.

John W. Campbell, Jr., who was the editor of *Astounding* (later *Analog*) magazine, was the single most powerful force behind the development and evolution of Modern SF. (See the Budrys essay for a fuller consideration of Campbell's importance to the field.) This is one of Campbell's editorials from the time when he was a primary influence on what writers wrote and what short fiction was perceived as significant in SF. His editorials were famous and writers flocked to incorporate Campbell's ideas in fiction, which they could then sell to him.

There are some questions that only small children and very great philosophers are supposed to ask—questions like "What is Death?" and "Where is God?"

And then there are some questions that, apparently, no one is supposed to ask at all; largely, I think, because people have gotten so many wrong answers down through the centuries, that it's been agreed-by-default not to ask the questions at all.

Science fiction, however, by its very existence, has been asking one question that belongs in the "Let's agree not to discuss it at all" category—of course, simply by implication, but nevertheless very persistently. To wit: "What do you mean by the term 'human being'?"

It asks the question in a number of ways; the question of "What is a super-man?" requires that we first define the limits of "normal man." The problem of "What's a robot?" asks the question in another way.

Some years ago now, Dr. Asimov introduced the Three Laws of Robotics into science fiction:

1. A robot cannot harm, nor allow harm to come to, a human being.
2. A robot must obey the orders of human beings.
3. A robot must, within those limits, protect itself against damage.

The crucial one is, of course, the First Law. The point that science fiction has elided very deftly is . . . how do you tell a robot what a human being is?

Look . . . I'll play robot; you tell me what you mean by "human being." What is this entity-type that I'm required to leave immune, and defend? How am I, Robot, to distinguish between the following entities: 1. A human idiot. 2. Another robot. 3. A baby. 4. A chimpanzee.

We might, quite legitimately, include a humanoid alien—or even Tregonsee, E. E. Smith's Rigellian Lensman, and Worsel, the Velantian—which we, as science-fictioneers, have agreed fulfill what we *really* mean by "human"! But let's not make the problem that tough just yet.

We do, however, have to consider the brilliant question Dr. W. Ross Ashby raised: If a mechanic with an artificial arm is working on an engine, is the mechanical arm part of the organism struggling with the environment, or part of the environment the organism is struggling with? If I, Robot, am to be instructed properly, we must consider human beings with prosthetic attachments. And, if I am a really functional robot, then that implies a level of technology that could turn up some very fancy prosthetic devices. Henry Kuttner some years back had a story about a man who had, through an accident, been reduced to a brain in a box; the box, however, had plug-in connections whereby it could be coupled to allow the brain in the box to "be" a whole spaceship, or a power-excavator, or any other appropriate machine.

Is this to be regarded as "a robot" or "a human being"? Intuitively we feel that, no matter how many prosthetic devices may be installed as replacements, the human being remains.

The theologians used to have a very handy answer to most of those questions; a human being, unlike animals or machines, has a soul. If that is to be included in the discussion, however, we must also include the associated problems of distinguishing between human beings and incubi, succubi, demons, and angels. The problem then takes on certain other aspects . . . but the problem remains. History indicates that it was just as difficult to distinguish between humans and demons as it is, currently, to distinguish between humans and robots.

Let's try a little "truth-table" of the order that logicians sometimes use, and that advertisers are becoming fond of. We can try various suggested tests, and check off how the various entities we're trying to distinguish compare.

You can, of course, continue to extend this, with all the tests you care to think of. I believe you'll find that you can find no test within the entire scope of permissible-in-our-society-evaluations that will permit a clear distinction between the five entities in the table.

Note, too, that that robot you want to follow the Three Laws is to modify the Second Law—obedience—rather extensively with respect to children and idiots, after you've told it how to distinguish between humanoids and chimpanzees.

There have been a good many wars fought over the question "What do you mean . . . human?" To the Greeks, the peoples of other lands didn't really speak languages—which meant Greek—but made mumbling noises that sounded like *bar-bar-bar,* which proved they were *barbarians,* and not really human.

The law should treat all human beings alike; that's been held as a concept for a long, long time. The Athenians subscribed to that concept. Of course, barbarians weren't really human, so the Law didn't apply to them, and slaves weren't; in fact only Athenian citizens were.

The easy way to make the law apply equally to all men is to so define "men" that the thing actually works. "Equal Justice for All! (All who are equal, of course.)"

Test	Idiot	Robot	Baby	Chimp	Man with prosthetic aids
1. Capable of logical thought.	No	Yes	No	No	Yes.
2. "Do I not bleed?" (Merchant of Venice test.)	Yes	No	Yes	Yes	Depends.
3. Capable of speech.	Yes	Yes	No	No	Yes.
4. "Rational animal"; this must be divided into					
a. Rational	No	Yes	No	No	Yes.
b. Animal	Yes	No	Yes	Yes	Partly.
5. Humanoid form & size.	Yes	Yes	No	Yes	Maybe.
6. Lack of fur or hair.	*	Yes	Yes	Yes	Maybe partly.
7. A living being.	Yes	No	Yes	Yes	Depends on what test you use for "living."

*A visit to a beach in summer will convince you that some adult male humans have a thicker pelt than some gorillas.

This problem of defining what you mean by "human being" appears to be at least as prolific a source of conflict as religion—and may, in fact, be why religion, that being the relationship between Man and God, has been so violent a ferment.

The law never has and never will apply equally to all; there are inferiors and superiors, whether we like it or not, and Justice does not stem from applying the same laws equally to different levels of being. Before blowing your stack on that one, look again and notice that every human culture has recognized that you could *not* have the same set of laws for children and adults—not since the saurians lost dominance on the planet has that concept been workable. (Reptilian forms are hatched from the egg with all the wisdom they're ever going to have; among reptiles of one species, there is only a difference of size and physical strength.)

Not only is there a difference on a vertical scale, but there's displacement horizontally—i.e., different-but-equal, also exists. A woman may be equal to a man, but she's not the same as a man.

This, also, makes for complications when trying to decide "what is a human being"; there have been many cultures in history that definitely held that women weren't human.

I have a slight suspicion that the basic difficulty is that we can't get anything even approximating a workable concept of Justice so long as we consider equality a necessary, inherent part of it. The Law of Gravity applies equally to all bodies in the Universe—but that doesn't mean that the *force* of gravity is the same for all! Gravity—the universal law—is the same on Mars and a white dwarf star as it is on Earth. That doesn't mean that the *force* of gravity is the same.

But it takes considerable genius to come up with a Universal Law of Gravity for sheer, inanimate mass. What it takes to discover the equivalent for intelligent entities . . . the human race hasn't achieved as yet! Not even once has an individual reached that level!

This makes defining "human" a somewhat explosive subject.

Now the essence of humanity most commonly discussed by philosophers has been Man, the Rational Animal. The ability to think logically; to have ideas, and be conscious of having those ideas. The implied intent in "defining humanness" is to define the unique, highest-level attribute that sets man apart from all other entities.

That "rational animal" gimmick worked pretty well for a long time; the development of electronic computers, and the clear implication of robots calls it into question. That, plus the fact that psychological experiments have shown that logical thought isn't quite so unique-to-Man as philosophers thought.

The thing that is unique to human beings is something the philosophers have sputtered at, rejected, damned, and loudly forsworn throughout history. Man is the only known entity that laughs, weeps, grieves, and yearns. There's been considerable effort made to prove that those are the result of simple biochemical changes of endocrine balance. That is, that you feel angry because there is adrenaline in the bloodstream, released from the suprarenal glands. Yes, and the horse moves because the cart keeps pushing him. Why did the gland start secreting that extra charge of adrenaline?

The essence of our actual definition of humanness is "I am human; any entity that *feels* as I feel is human also. But any entity that merely thinks, and *feels* differently is not human."

The "inhuman scientist" is so called because he doesn't appear to *feel* as the speaker does. While we were discussing possible theological ramifications of the humanness question, we might have included the zombie. Why isn't a zombie "human" any longer? Because he has become the logical philosopher's ideal; a purely rational, nonemotional entity.

Why aren't Tregonsee, the Rigellian, and Worsel, the Velantian, to be compared with animals and/or robots?

Because, as defined in E. E. Smith's stories, they *feel* as we do.

Now it's long since been observed that an individual will find his logical thinking subtly biased in the direction of his emotional feelings. His actions will be controlled not by his logic and reason but, in the end, by his emotional pulls. If a man is my loyal friend—i.e., if he *feels* favorable-to-me—then whatever powers of physical force or mental brilliance he may have are no menace to me, but are a menace to my enemies. If he *feels* about things as I do, I need not concern myself with how he *thinks* about them, or what he does. He is "human"—my kind of human.

But . . . if he can *choose* his feelings, if his emotions are subject to his conscious, judicious, volitional choice . . . ? What then? If his emotional biases are not as rigidly unalterable as his bones? If he can exercise judgment and vary his feelings, can I trust him to remain "human"?

Could an entity who felt differently about things—whose emotions were different—be "human"?

That question may be somewhat important to us. Someone, sooner or later, is going to meet an alien, a really *alien* alien, not just a member of Homo sapiens from a divergent breed and culture.

Now it's true that all things are relative. Einstein proved the relativity of even the purely physical level of reality. But be it noted that Einstein proved that *Law* of Relativity; things aren't "purely relative" in the sense that's usually used—"I can take any system of relationships I choose!" There are laws of relativity.

The emotional biases a culture induces in its citizens vary widely. Mores is a matter of cultural relativity.

That doesn't mean that ethics is; there are laws of relativity, and it's not true that any arbitrary system of relationships is just as good as any other.

Can we humans-who-define-humanness-in-emotional-terms—despite what we theoretically say!—meet an equally wise race with different emotions—and know them for fellow humans?

A man who thinks differently we can tolerate and understand, but our history shows we don't know how to understand a man who feels differently.

The most frightening thing about a man who feels differently is this; his feelings might be contagious. We might learn to feel *his* way—and then, of course, we wouldn't be human any more.

The wiser and sounder his different feelings are, the greater the awful danger of learning to feel that way. And that would make us inhuman, of course

How do you suppose an Athenian Greek of Pericles's time would have felt if threatened with a change of feelings such that he would not feel disturbed if someone denied the reality of the Gods, or suggested that the Latins had a sounder culture? Why—only a nonhuman barbarian could feel that way!

The interesting thing is that the implication of "inhuman" is invariably *sub*human.

I suspect one of the most repugnant aspects of Darwin's concept of evolution was—not that we descended from monkeys—but its implication that something was apt to descend from us! Something that wasn't human . . . *and wasn't subhuman.*

The only perfect correlation is auto-correlation; "I am exactly what I am." Any difference whatever makes the correlation less perfect.

Then if what I feel is human—anything different is less perfectly correlated with humanness. Hence any entity not identical is more or less subhuman; there can't possibly be something more like me than I am.

Anybody want to try for a workable definition of "human"? One warning before you get started too openly; logical discussion doesn't lead to violence—until it enters the area of emotion.

As of now, we'd have to tell that robot: "A human being is an entity having an emotional structure, as well as a physical and mental structure. Never mind what kind of emotional structure—good, indifferent, or insane. It's the fact of its existence that distinguishes the human."

Of course, that does lead to the problem of giving the robot emotion-perceptors so he can detect the existence of an emotion-structure.

And that, of course, gets almost as tough as the problem of distinguishing a masquerading demon from a man. You know . . . maybe they are the same problem?

It's always puzzled me that in the old days they detected so many demons, and so few angels, too. It always looked as though the Legions of Hell greatly outnumbered the Host of Heaven, or else were far more diligent on Earth.

But then . . . the subhuman is so much more acceptable than the superhuman.

BEARS DISCOVER FIRE

Terry Bisson

In the 1980s Terry Bisson built a reputation as a fantasy and SF writer to watch with three novels. He burst into prominence in the 1990s with his best SF novel to date, *Voyage to the Red Planet* (1990), and a sudden spate of excellent short stories, later collected in *Bears Discover Fire*. He is unquestionably a major figure in SF today. The moral concerns of his fiction speak to an audience larger than the genre.

I was driving with my brother, the preacher, and my nephew, the preacher's son on I-65 just north of Bowling Green when we got a flat. It was Sunday night and we had been to visit Mother at the Home. We were in my car. The flat caused what you might call knowing groans since, as the old-fashioned one in my family (so they tell me), I fix my own tires, and my brother is always telling me to get radials and quit buying old tires.

But if you know how to mount and fix tires yourself, you can pick them up for almost nothing.

Since it was a left rear tire, I pulled over left, onto the median grass. The way my Caddy stumbled to a stop, I figured the tire was ruined. "I guess there's no need asking if you have any of that *FlatFix* in the trunk," said Wallace.

"Here, son, hold the light," I said to Wallace Jr. He's old enough to want to help and not old enough (yet) to think he knows it all. If I'd married and had kids, he's the kind I'd have wanted.

An old Caddy has a big trunk that tends to fill up like a shed. Mine's a '56 Wallace was wearing his Sunday shirt, so he didn't offer to help while I pulled magazines, fishing tackle, a wooden tool box, some old clothes, a comealong wrapped in a grass sack, and a tobacco sprayer out of the way, looking for my jack. The spare looked a little soft.

The light went out. "Shake it, son," I said.

It went back on. The bumper jack was long gone, but I carry a little ¼ ton hydraulic. I finally found it under Mother's old *Southern Livings*, 1978–1986. had been meaning to drop them at the dump. If Wallace hadn't been along, I'd have let Wallace Jr. position the jack under the axle, but I got on my knees and did it myself. There's nothing wrong with a boy learning to change a tire. Even if you're not going to fix and mount them, you're still going to have to change a few in this life. The light went off again before I had the wheel off the ground. I was surprised at how dark the night was already. It was late October and beginning to get cool. "Shake it again, son," I said.

It went back on but it was weak. Flickery.

"With radials you just don't *have* flats," Wallace explained in that voice he uses when he's talking to a number of people at once; in this case, Wallace Jr. and myself. "And even when you *do*, you just squirt them with this stuff called *FlatFix* and you just drive on. $3.95 the can."

"Uncle Bobby can fix a tire hisself," said Wallace Jr., out of loyalty I presume.

"*Him*self," I said from halfway under the car. If it was up to Wallace, the boy would talk like what Mother used to call "a helock from the gorges of the mountains." But drive on radials.

"Shake that light again," I said. It was about gone. I spun the lugs off into the hubcap and pulled the wheel. The tire had blown out along the sidewall. "Won't be fixing this one," I said. Not that I cared. I have a pile as tall as a man out by the barn.

The light went out again, then came back better than ever as I was fitting the spare over the lugs. "Much better," I said. There was a flood of dim orange flickery light. But when I turned to find the lug nuts, I was surprised to see that the flashlight the boy was holding was dead. The light was coming from two bears at the edge of the trees, holding torches. They were big, three-hundred-pounders, standing about five feet tall. Wallace Jr. and his father had seen them and were standing perfectly still. It's best not to alarm bears.

I fished the lug nuts out of the hubcap and spun them on. I usually like to put a little oil on them, but this time I let it go. I reached under the car and let the jack down and pulled it out. I was relieved to see that the spare was high enough to drive on. I put the jack and the lug wrench and the flat into the trunk. Instead of replacing the hubcap, I put it in there too. All this time, the bears never made a move. They just held the torches up, whether out of curiosity or helpfulness, there was no way of knowing. It looked like there may have been more bears behind them, in the trees.

Opening three doors at once, we got into the car and drove off. Wallace was the first to speak. "Looks like bears have discovered fire," he said.

When we first took Mother to the Home, almost four years (forty-seven months) ago, she told Wallace and me she was ready to die. "Don't worry about me, boys," she whispered, pulling us both down so the nurse wouldn't hear. "I've drove a million miles and I'm ready to pass over to the other shore. I won't have long to linger here." She drove a consolidated school bus for thirty-nine years. Later, after Wallace left, she told me about her dream. A bunch of doctors were sitting around in a circle discussing her case. One said, "We've done all we can for her, boys, let's let her go." They all turned their hands up and smiled. When she didn't die that fall, she seemed disappointed, though as spring came she forgot about it, as old people will.

In addition to taking Wallace and Wallace Jr. to see Mother on Sunday nights, I go myself on Tuesdays and Thursdays. I usually find her sitting in front of the TV, even though she doesn't watch it. The nurses keep it on all the time. They say the old folks like the flickering. It soothes them down.

"What's this I hear about bears discovering fire?" she said on Tuesday.

"It's true," I told her as I combed her long white hair with the shell comb Wallace had brought her from Florida. Monday there had been a story in the Louisville *Courier-Journal,* and Tuesday one on NBC or CBS Nightly News. People were seeing bears all over the state, and in Virginia as well. They had quit hibernating, and were apparently planning to spend the winter in the medians of the interstates. There have always been bears in the mountains of Virginia, but not here in western Kentucky, not for almost a hundred years. The last one was killed when Mother was a girl. The theory in the *Courier-Journal* was that they were following I-65 down from the forests of Michigan and Canada, but one old man from Allen County (interviewed on nationwide TV) said that there had always been a few bears left back in the hills, and they had come out to join the others now that they had discovered fire.

"They don't hibernate anymore," I said. "They make a fire and keep it going all winter."

"I declare," Mother said. "What'll they think of next!" The nurse came to take her tobacco away, which is the signal for bedtime.

Every October, Wallace Jr. stays with me while his parents go to camp. I realize how backward that sounds, but there it is. My brother is a minister (House of the Righteous Way, Reformed), but he makes two-thirds of his living in real estate. He and Elizabeth go to a Christian Success Retreat in South Carolina where people from all over the country practice selling things to one another. I know what it's like not because they've ever bothered to tell me, but because I've seen the Revolving Equity Success Plan ads late at night on TV.

The schoolbus let Wallace Jr. off at my house on Wednesday, the day they left. The boy doesn't have to pack much of a bag when he stays with me. He has his own room here. As the eldest of our family, I hung onto the old home place near Smiths Grove. It's getting run down, but Wallace Jr. and I don't mind. He has his own room in Bowling Green, too, but since Wallace and Elizabeth move to a different house every three months (part of the Plan), he keeps his .22 and his comics, the stuff that's important to a boy his age, in his room here at the home place. It's the room his dad and I used to share.

Wallace Jr. is twelve. I found him sitting on the back porch that overlooks the interstate when I got home from work. I sell crop insurance.

After I changed clothes, I showed him how to break the bead on a tire two ways, with a hammer and by backing a car over it. Like making sorghum, fixing tires by hand is a dying art. The boy caught on fast, though. "Tomorrow I'll show you how to mount your tire with the hammer and a tire iron," I said.

"What I wish is I could see the bears," he said. He was looking across the field to I-65, where the northbound lanes cut off the corner of our field. From the house at night, sometimes the traffic sounds like a waterfall.

"Can't see their fire in the daytime," I said. "But wait till tonight." That night CBS or NBC (I forget which is which) did a special on the bears, which were becoming a story of nationwide interest. They were seen in Kentucky, West Virginia, Missouri, Illinois (southern), and, of course, Virginia. There have always been bears in Virginia. Some characters there were even talking about hunting them. A scientist said they were heading into the states where there is some snow but not too much, and where there is enough timber in the medians for firewood. He had gone in with a video camera, but his shots were just blurry figures sitting around a fire. Another scientist said the bears were attracted by the berries on a new bush that grew only in the medians of the interstates. He claimed this berry was the first new species in recent history, brought about by the mixing of seeds along the highway. He ate one on TV, making a face, and called it a "newberry." A climatic ecologist said that the warm winters (there was no snow last winter in Nashville, and only one flurry in Louisville) had changed the bears' hibernation cycle, and now they were able to remember things from year to year. "Bears may have discovered fire centuries ago," he said, "but forgot it." Another theory was that they had discovered (or remembered) fire when Yellowstone burned, several years ago.

The TV showed more guys talking about bears than it showed bears, and Wallace Jr. and I lost interest. After the supper dishes were done I took the boy out behind the house and down to our fence. Across the interstate and through the trees, we could see the light of the bears' fire. Wallace Jr. wanted to go back to the house and get his .22 and go shoot one, and I explained why that would be wrong. "Besides," I said, "a twenty-two wouldn't do much more to a bear than make it mad.

"Besides," I added, "it's illegal to hunt in the medians."

The only trick to mounting a tire by hand, once you have beaten or pried it onto the rim, is setting the bead. You do this by setting the tire upright, sitting on it, and bouncing it up and down between your legs while the air goes in. When the bead sets on the rim, it makes a satisfying "pop." On Thursday, I kept Wallace Jr. home from school and showed him how to do this until he got it right. Then we climbed our fence and crossed the field to get a look at the bears.

In northern Virginia, according to "Good Morning America," the bears were keeping their fires going all day long. Here in western Kentucky, though, it was still warm for late October and they only stayed around the fires at night. Where they went and what they did in the daytime, I don't know. Maybe they were watching from the newberry bushes as Wallace Jr. and I climbed the government fence and crossed the northbound lanes. I carried an axe and Wallace Jr. brought his .22, not because he wanted to kill a bear but because a boy likes to carry some kind of a gun. The median was all tangled with brush and vines under the maples, oaks, and sycamores. Even though we were only a hundred yards from the house, I had never been there, and neither had anyone else that I knew of. It was like a created country. We found a path in the center and followed it down across a slow, short stream that flowed out of one grate and into another. The tracks in the gray mud were the first bear signs we saw. There was a musty but not really unpleasant smell. In a clearing under a big hollow beech, where the fire had been, we found nothing but ashes. Logs were drawn up in a rough circle and the smell was stronger. I stirred the ashes and found enough coals left to start a new flame, so I banked them back the way they had been left.

I cut a little firewood and stacked it to one side, just to be neighborly.

Maybe the bears were watching us from the bushes even then. There's no way to know. I tasted one of the newberries and spit it out. It was so sweet it was sour, just the sort of thing you would imagine a bear would like.

*   *   *

That evening after supper, I asked Wallace Jr. if he might want to go with me to visit Mother. I wasn't surprised when he said "yes." Kids have more consideration than folks give them credit for. We found her sitting on the concrete front porch of the Home, watching the cars go by on I-65. The nurse said she had been agitated all day. I wasn't surprised by that, either. Every fall as the leaves change, she gets restless, maybe the word is hopeful, again. I brought her into the dayroom and combed her long white hair. "Nothing but bears on TV anymore," the nurse complained, flipping the channels. Wallace Jr. picked up the remote after the nurse left, and we watched a CBS or NBC Special Report about some hunters in Virginia who had gotten their houses torched. The TV interviewed a hunter and his wife whose $117,500 Shenandoah Valley home had burned. She blamed the bears. He didn't blame the bears, but he was suing for compensation from the state since he had a valid hunting license. The state hunting commissioner came on and said that possession of a hunting license didn't prohibit (*enjoin*, I think, was the word he used) *the hunted* from striking back. I thought that was a pretty liberal view for a state commissioner. Of course, he had a vested interest in not paying off. I'm not a hunter myself.

"Don't bother coming on Sunday," Mother told Wallace Jr. with a wink. "I've drove a million miles and I've got one hand on the gate." I'm used to her saying stuff like that, especially in the fall, but I was afraid it would upset the boy. In fact, he looked worried after we left and I asked him what was wrong.

"How could she have drove a million miles?" he asked. She had told him forty-eight miles a day for thirty-nine years, and he had worked it out on his calculator to be 336,960 miles.

"Have *driven*," I said. "And it's forty-eight in the morning and forty-eight in the afternoon. Plus there were the football trips. Plus, old folks exaggerate a little." Mother was the first woman school bus driver in the state. She did it every day and raised a family, too. Dad just farmed.

I usually get off the interstate at Smiths Grove, but that night I drove north all the way to Horse Cave and doubled back so Wallace Jr. and I could see the bears' fires. There were not as many as you would think from the TV—one every six or seven miles, hidden back in a clump of trees or under a rocky ledge. Probably they look for water as well as wood. Wallace Jr. wanted to stop, but it's against the law to stop on the interstate and I was afraid the state police would run us off.

There was a card from Wallace in the mailbox. He and Elizabeth were doing fine and having a wonderful time. Not a word about Wallace Jr., but the boy didn't seem to mind. Like most kids his age, he doesn't really enjoy going places with his parents.

On Saturday afternoon, the Home called my office (Burley Belt Drought & Hail) and left word that Mother was gone. I was on the road. I work Saturdays. It's the only day a lot of part-time farmers are home. My heart literally skipped a beat when I called in and got the message, but only a beat. I had long been prepared. "It's a blessing," I said when I got the nurse on the phone.

"You don't understand," the nurse said. "Not *passed* away, gone. *Ran* away, gone. Your mother has escaped." Mother had gone through the door at the end of the corridor when no one was looking, wedging the door with her comb and taking a bedspread which belonged to the Home. What about her tobacco? I asked. It was gone. That was a sure sign she was planning to stay away. I was in Franklin, and it took me less than an hour to get to the Home on I-65. The nurse told me that Mother had been acting more and more confused lately. Of course they are going to say that. We looked around the grounds, which is only an acre with no trees between the interstate and a soybean field. Then they had me leave a message at the sheriff's office. I would have to keep paying for her care until she was officially listed as Missing, which would be Monday.

It was dark by the time I got back to the house, and Wallace Jr. was fixing supper. This just involves opening a few cans, already selected and grouped together with a rubber band. I told him his grandmother had gone, and he nodded, saying, "She told us she would be." I called Florida and left a message. There was nothing more to be done. I sat down and tried to watch TV, but there was nothing on. Then, I looked out the back door, and saw the firelight twinkling through the trees across the northbound lane of I-65, and realized I just might know where to find her.

It was definitely getting colder, so I got my jacket. I told the boy to wait by the phone in case the sheriff called, but when I looked back, halfway across the field, there he was behind me. He didn't have a jacket. I let him catch up. He was carrying his .22, and I made him leave it leaning against our fence. It was harder climbing the government fence in the dark, at my age, than it had been in the daylight. I am sixty-one. The highway was busy with cars heading south and trucks heading north.

Crossing the shoulder, I got my pants cuffs wet on the long grass, already wet with dew. It is actually bluegrass.

The first few feet into the trees it was pitch black and the boy grabbed my hand. Then it got lighter. At first I thought it was the moon, but it was the high beams shining like moonlight into the treetops, allowing Wallace Jr. and me to pick our way through the brush. We soon found the path and its familiar bear smell.

I was wary of approaching the bears at night. If we stayed on the path we might run into one in the dark, but if we went through the bushes we might be seen as intruders. I wondered if maybe we shouldn't have brought the gun.

We stayed on the path. The light seemed to drip down from the canopy of the woods like rain. The going was easy, especially if we didn't try to look at the path but let our feet find their own way.

Then through the trees I saw their fire.

The fire was mostly of sycamore and beech branches, the kind of fire that puts out very little heat or light and lots of smoke. The bears hadn't learned the ins and outs of wood yet. They did okay at tending it, though. A large cinnamon brown northern-looking bear was poking the fire with a stick, adding a branch now and then from a pile at his side. The others sat around in a loose circle on the logs. Most were smaller black or honey bears, one was a mother with cubs. Some were eating berries from a hubcap. Not eating, but just watching the fire, my mother sat among them with the bedspread from the Home around her shoulders.

If the bears noticed us, they didn't let on. Mother patted a spot right next to her on the log and I sat down. A bear moved over to let Wallace Jr. sit on her other side.

The bear smell is rank but not unpleasant, once you get used to it. It's not like a barn smell, but wilder. I leaned over to whisper something to Mother and she shook her head. *It would be rude to whisper around these creatures that don't possess the power of speech,* she let me know without speaking. Wallace Jr. was silent too. Mother shared the bedspread with us and we sat for what seemed hours, looking into the fire.

The big bear tended the fire, breaking up the dry branches by holding one end and stepping on them, like people do. He was good at keeping it going at the same level. Another bear poked the fire from time to time, but the others left it alone. It looked like only a few of the bears knew how to use fire, and were carrying the others along. But isn't that how it is with everything? Every once in a while, a smaller bear walked into the circle of firelight with an armload of wood and dropped it onto the pile. Median wood had a silvery cast, like driftwood.

Wallace Jr. isn't fidgety like a lot of kids. I found it pleasant to sit and stare into the fire. I took a little piece of Mother's *Red Man,* though I don't generally chew. It was no different from visiting her at the Home, only more interesting, because of the bears. There were about eight or ten of them. Inside the fire itself, things weren't so dull, either: little dramas were being played out as fiery chambers were created and then destroyed in a crashing of sparks. My imagination ran wild. I looked around the circle at the bears and wondered what *they* saw. Some had their eyes closed. Though they were gathered together, their spirits still seemed solitary, as if each bear was sitting alone in front of its own fire.

The hubcap came around and we all took some newberries. I don't know about Mother, but I just pretended to eat mine. Wallace Jr. made a face and spit his out. When he went to sleep, I wrapped the bedspread around all three of us. It was getting colder and we were provided, like the bears, with fur. I was ready to go home, but not Mother. She pointed up toward the canopy of trees, where a light was spreading, and then pointed to herself. Did she think it was angels approaching from on high? It was only the high beams of some southbound truck, but she seemed mighty pleased. Holding her hand, I felt it grow colder and colder in mine.

Wallace Jr. woke me up by tapping on my knee. It was past dawn, and his grandmother had died sitting on the log between us. The fire was banked up and the bears were gone and someone was crashing straight through the woods, ignoring the path. It was Wallace. Two state troopers were right behind him. He was wearing a white shirt, and I realized it was Sunday morning. Underneath his sadness on learning of Mother's death, he looked peeved.

The troopers were sniffing the air and nodding. The bear smell was still strong. Wallace and I wrapped Mother in the bedspread and started with her body back out to the highway. The troopers stayed behind and scattered the bears' fire ashes and flung their firewood away into the bushes. It seemed a petty thing to do. They were like bears themselves, each one solitary in his own uniform.

There was Wallace's Olds 98 on the median, with its radial tires looking squashed on the grass. In front of it there was a police car with a trooper standing beside it, and behind it a funeral home hearse, also an Olds 98.

"First report we've had of them bothering old folks," the trooper said to Wallace. "That's not hardly what happened at all," I said, but nobody asked me to explain. They have their own procedures. Two men in suits got out of the hearse and opened the rear door. That to me was the point at which Mother departed this life. After we put her in, I put my arms around the boy. He was shivering even though it wasn't that cold. Sometimes death will do that, especially at dawn, with the police around and the grass wet, even when it comes as a friend.

We stood for a minute watching the cars pass. "It's a blessing," Wallace said. It's surprising how much traffic there is at 6:22 A.M.

That afternoon, I went back to the median and cut a little firewood to replace what the troopers had flung away. I could see the fire through the trees that night.

I went back two nights later, after the funeral. The fire was going and it was the same bunch of bears, as far as I could tell. I sat around with them a while but it seemed to make them nervous, so I went home. I had taken a handful of newberries from the hubcap, and on Sunday I went with the boy and arranged them on Mother's grave. I tried again, but it's no use, you can't eat them.

Unless you're a bear.

ONE DOWN, ONE TO GO

Philip José Farmer

Philip José Farmer began writing SF in the 1940s and rose to prominence in the 1950s and '60s, becoming in the opinion of critic Leslie Fiedler "the greatest science fiction writer ever." In the 1970s he became one of the most popular SF writers in the world with his *Riverworld* series, which begins with *To Your Scattered Bodies Go*. His wild imagination has always been a hallmark of his popular series novels (he has written a number of series). But throughout the last five decades he has produced powerful short stories that are among the finest in all SF. "One Down, One to Go" is a recent example.

This day, for Charlie Roth, would always be the Day of the Locust.

Twenty-nine years old, a Welfare Department employee, he was now an agent of its new branch, the General Office of Special Restitution. Every workday had been a bad day since he had entered the WD. But in times to come, he would liken today to the destruction wrought in a few hours by the sky-blackening and all-devouring swarms of the desert locust, *Schistocerca gregaria*.

Charlie Roth, attaché case filled with sterilization authorization forms, walked up a staircase in Building 13 of the Newstreet Housing Authority. He was headed toward the apartment of Riches Dott, unmarried mother of many. For the moment, his guilt and tension were gone. His mind was on Laura, the seventh child of Riches Dott. Laura was the only one of the fifteen children for whom he now had any hope. An older brother who had a high IQ and an intense but low ambition was a lifer in Joliet Penitentiary. An older sister had had a remarkable mathematical talent, long ago whisked away in the smoke of crack and snark.

Advising and aiding Laura was not part of his official mission. But perhaps he could be someone to talk to who really cared about her. He would give her money out of his own shallow pocket if that would make firmer a resolve that must be shaking despite her strong will.

Yet he himself might need help soon. Big help.

Ever since his wife, five months pregnant, had left him, he had been getting more and more easily angered. But their separation was only a lesser part of the steam-hot wrath he could just barely control. The larger part troubled him whether he was sleeping or awake.

His mind was like a water strider. One of those bugs (family Gerridae) that walked on the still waters of ponds. Its specially modified back legs skimmed the surface tension, that single layer of molecules that was a skin on the pond to the strider. The legs of his mind, an arthopod Jesus that had suddenly lost its faith in its powers, were poking now and then through the skin.

"I'm going to sink and then drown! I wanted to save all these wretches because I loved them! Now I hate them!"

Here he was, God help him, a would-be entomologist who could not master chemistry and mathematics. He had given up his goal before he even got his M.A. A man who loves the study of bugs, what does he do when he can't do that? He becomes a social worker.

As he turned onto the landing, he heard quick-paced footsteps above him. He paused, and Laura Dott appeared. She smiled when she saw him, said, "Hello, Mr. Roth," and clattered down the steps toward him. She was in the uniform of a waitress at a local fast-food restaurant. Just turned eighteen, Laura had been removed from her mother's welfare dependency roll. Though still living with her mother, she was making straight A's in high school and working five days a week from 4:00 P.M. to midnight, minimum wage.

She had always been an honor student. How she could have done that while living in the pressure-cooker pandemonium of her mother's apartment, Charlie did not understand. Equally mysterious was how she had managed to stay unpregnant, drug-free, and sane. Some other youths in this area had done the same, but their mother wasn't Riches.

"Hi, Laura," he said. "I'd like to talk to you."

She went past him, her head turned toward him. She was slim and long-legged, and her skin was as close to black as brown could get. She flashed a beautiful smile with teeth white and regular but long and thick.

"Busy, busy, busy, Mr. Roth. If it's important, see me during my midbreak, eight o'clock. Sorry."

She was gone. Charlies sighed and went on up the steps. At the top he saw Amin Ketcher coming down the hall from the staircase at the opposite end. He reached the door of Mrs. Dott's apartment before Charlie got there, and leaned against the wall by the door.

If he was waiting for Laura, he was too late. Probably held up completing a deal: crack, zoomers, blasters, and snark. The bastard. She's told him time and again to get lost. He's street-smart and shadow-elusive, but a loser: at twenty, the known father of twelve children, boasting of it, yet not giving a penny to support them.

So far he had refused to sign the form authorizing his sterilization. Why should he? He had the cash for a fleet of new cars. Moreover, the ability to knock up a horde of teenager was, to him, one of the main proofs of his manhood. But they had been pushovers. He wanted Laura Dott because she had only contempt and disgust for him, though she knew better than to insult him verbally.

Charlie strode down the hall. "Hey, a Charlie Charlie," Ketcher said. "The General Office of Special Reestituutiion man. The white gooser."

He inclined his handsome copper-colored face to look down on Charlie's six feet from his six feet six inches. His oil-dripping kinky hair was cut in the current "castle" style: high crenellated walls and six-inch-high turrets. A silver-banded plastic nosebone, huge gold earrings, and a ticktacktoe diagram, the symbol of his gang, cut by a razor into each cheek, gave him the barbaric appearance he desired. He wore a sequined purple jacket and jeans overlaid with battery-powered electric lights and neon-tube rock slogans. These flashed on and off while the yang-n-yin music of the EAT SHIT AND LIVE band played from a hundred microphone-buttons on his garments.

The enormous pupils of his glistening black eyes could have been caused by belladonna, used by many youths. But his faint gunpowdery odor told Charlie that he was on snark. The latest designer drug, its effects and chemical traces vanished within five minutes after being used. The narcs had to test a suspect on the spot to get the evidence to convict the user. That was possible only if a van carrying the heavy and intricate test equipment was at once available.

Also, every tiny bag of snark held two easily breakable vials. If the carrier was caught by the police and he had enough time, he threw the bag against anything hard. Bag, snark, and vials went up in a microexplosion. No drug residue was left.

Charlie passed by Ketcher and stopped in front of the door. He could hear the blast of the TV set and the yelling of children through the door. Something crashed loudly, and Riches's high-pitched voice drilled through the plastic.

"I swear, Milton, you knock that chair over again, I slap you sillier'n you already be!"

The doorbell had long been out of order. Charlie knocked hard three times on the door.

"Old fat-ass Riches ain't going to sign," Ketcher said. "You wasting your breath. Or you waiting till Laura come home from school? You wasting your time there, too, Charlie. She ain't interested in no small white dongs."

"You paleolithic atavism!" Charlie said, snarling. "You've been harassing Laura long enough to know she'd sooner screw an ape with diarrhea than you. Anyway, you mush-brained snarker, she isn't going to be around much longer. She'll be getting out of this shithole and away from corpse worms like you. Very very soon, I promise you."

Ketcher stepped closer to Charlie. His enormous eyes were as empty of intelligence as a wasp's.

"What that mean, paley . . . whatever? You making a racial remark, you blue-eyed shithead? I turn your skinny ass in to the Gooser Office. And what you mean, Laura gonna be gone?"

Charlie regretted losing his cool, and so warning Ketcher that Laura would soon be out of his reach.

The door started to swing open. The TV roared, and the children's voices shrilled like a horde of cicadas.

"You're extinct," Charlie said. "A fly in amber still kicking because you don't know you're dead. Laura'd sooner eat a live cockroach than let you get into her pants."

He stepped through the doorway and closed it while Ketcher yelled, "I'll cut you when you come out, you white motherfucker!"

Sure you'll cut me, Charlie thought. You know I just have to use Riches's phone, and the troops stationed down on the corner will be up here. If they find he knife on you, you go straight to a prison work camp.

Though often in the family room, Charlie had now been admitted only be-ause Riches had not heard his knock. One of the ten children living there had happened to be close to the door. He was optimist enough at the age of six to ake the chocolate bar Charlie offered and not wonder what it was going to cost him later. But he slid the bar inside his urine-yellowed jockey shorts, his only garment, before his siblings caught sight of it.

Mrs. Dott answered his greeting with a scowl, and then stared straight at the creen.

Charlie, sighing, pulled three stapled sheets from his attaché case. This visit, he was required only to read to her Paragraph 3 from Form WD-GOSSR C-392-T. Though he knew that Riches probably could not hear his voice above he blaring commercial or the shouting and screaming children, he did not care.

" '. . . available to all American citizens (see Paragraph 5 for age, mental, and physical exceptions and restrictions) REGARDLESS OF RACE, GENDER OR RELIGION. Guaranteed free: any new 100% American-made automobile, mo-orcycle, or pickup truck with 100 gallons of gasoline or diesel oil or alcohol, ten quarts of motor oil, a year's license plate, one year's warranty (see Paragraph 4.d or exceptions) and casualty insurance (see Paragraph 4.e for exceptions and re-trictions). . . .' "

Before he could get to the section dealing with the freedom of the govern-ment from lawsuits, Riches shrilled, "I told you time and again! Ain't nobody gonna mess around with my body!"

She settled back in the stained, torn, and broken-springed sofa. Riches looks like a huge queen bee swollen with eggs, Charlie thought.

Despite the anger twisting her face, her gaze was fixed on the soap opera unfolding its story as slowly as the wings of a just-molted dragonfly.

Holy humping Jesus! Charlie thought. She's borne sixteen children. Had lap three times. Syph twice. It's a miracle she's escaped AIDS. She doesn't re-lly understand the connection between sexual intercourse and venereal disease, hough it's often been explained to her. All those babies have drained the cal-ium from her bones, spiders sucking out the juice, leaving her toothless and with a widow's hump.

Don't mess around with her body?

Though he wasn't going to change her mind, he had to make his request this nal time, then report the failure. The big praying-mantis eyes of Junkers, his oss, would get deadlier and colder. He'd shout, "How you expect this office to eep up its quotas if you piss out on me?"

"Mrs. Dott," Charlie said, "all but six in this building have signed up, and m sure most of those will eventually come through. You're forty-five. The cut-ff date is forty-six. Why throw all that money away? Chances are high you can't ave any more babies, anyway."

Suddenly she looked smug and sly. Patting her anthill stomach, she said, You think I be too old to have any more? Wrong, Charlie. Got me another. She ot one, too."

She pointed at thirteen-year-old Crystal, watching TV.

Her smile became even slier. "The law say Crystal can't sign up with you oosers 'less I say she can till she fifteen. No way!"

She did not look at him as he walked away. Nor did she seem to notice that he was lingering by the door. The dusty wall mirror showed his light red hair and pale and grim face. The dark circles around his eyes looked like Sioux smoke rings signaling for help. His guts hurt as if wasp larvae had hatched inside him and were eating their way out.

Why? What he was doing was rational and humanitarian. It was not just for the good of the people as a whole, though it was that, too. It was also for the good of the people at whom the missions were directed, and it involved no force or cruelty, none that was apparent, anyway.

He saw a cockroach, *Blatta orientalis,* inevitable companion of dirt and colleague of poverty, scuttle out from beneath an end of Riches's sofa. It seized a potato-chip fragment and shot back into the darkness under the sofa.

The piece contained an antifertility drug harmless to humans. Charlie thought that 99.9 percent of the cockroaches might be made infertile. But 0.1 percent would survive because they had mutated to resist the drug. From that would come billions.

He went into the hallway. Ketcher was alone with a youth, an obvious customer. Seeing Charlie, both went down the stairs. A faint acrid odor like battlefield smoke hung in the hall. Charlie felt as if he had gone through a firefight. He was trembling slightly. The hallway with its garbage cans, its dusty light bulbs, and its hot, unmoving air seemed to shift a little. Somewhat dizzy, he leaned against the scabrous, once-green wall for support.

What he was doing was for the best. How many times had he told himself that? The welfare recipients were in an economic-social elevator, its cables cut, falling faster and faster, nothing but disaster at the bottom for them—and for all citizens, since what happens to a part always affects the whole. At the same time their numbers were increasing geometrically, far out of proportion to the rest of the population. Misery, hopelessness, disease, malnutrition, violence, and deep ignorance were also expanding.

The Ronn-Eagan legislation had not passed without vehement, and even violent, opposition, especially from some religious groups. But the nonreligious reaction to the excesses of the last three decades of the previous century was very strong. And though the law had made already burdensome taxes much heavier, it did promise an eventual lightening of the tax load and a large reduction in the welfare populations. But the vehicle-making, insurance, and petroleum industries, and the businesses dependent on these, were booming.

Someday the welfare problem (which also encompassed a part of the crime-drug problem) would be a small one. Why, then, did he have these dreams in which he strode down a very narrow and twilit hallway with no end? The doors ahead of him were open, but he slammed them shut as he passed.

"Charlie Roth! A ghost among spooks!"

Only Rex Bessey used that greeting. He climbed up from the staircase on which Charlie ascended. His face was a full, dark moon. Then another moon, checked black and white, the vest covering his huge paunch, rose above the steps. He smiled as he limped toward Charlie.

"I got more than today's quota. Those rednecks go apeshit over pickups. How you doing, Charlie?"

"Wasted too much time on Riches Dott, a hopeless case."

"That asshole Junkers thought he was screwing us when he gave me the white area and you the black," Rex said. "But when I remind those Neanderthal rednecks I played tackle for the Bears until I wrecked my leg, they get friendly. That makes me one of the good old boys even if I am a fucking nigger. What helps, I give them a few beers to soften them up."

His attaché case clinked when he shook it.

"Why don't you carry some beer, too?"

"Principles," Charlie said.

Rex laughed loudly. "Sure! You practicing genocide, and you got principles?"

Charlie did not get angry. Once, when drunk, Rex had admitted that he fully agreed with the sterilization policy. He hated his job, but he wouldn't like any work unless it brought in big money.

"This Laura Dott you'd like to rescue," he had once said. "She might make it, but only because she's very smart and strong. What about her brothers and sisters? They were born not so smart or so strong. Why should they have to live in the bottom of the shitpool just because they aren't superhuman? If they were given the environment your average upper-level poor people have . . . well, why go on? We've been through this before. End of lecture. Have another drink?"

Now he said, "Let's hoist a few at Big Pete's."

"The quota."

"That's Junkers's, not the GOOSR's. Why should we sweat and grunt and crap golden turds so that black-assed bastard can get promotion faster? I knew him when he was extorting lunch money from the little kids in sixth grade. He tried that once with me, and I kicked him in the balls. He hates my guts for that, but he isn't going to fire me. He knows I'll tell how he got his job, which he isn't qualified for, and he'll be out on his ass. Forget his quota."

Charlie had heard all this before. He said, "O.K."

Shortly before five, their eyes tending toward the glassy, they walked into the office. Junkers was not there. Charlie faxed his reports and went home to his apartment on High Street. It was one of seven semisleazy units in a once-magnificent mansion built by a whiskey baron in 1910. He could look down from his bathroom window at his domain of work, that part of Hell that did not border on the Styx, but on the Illinois River.

The small, dead-aired, and close-pressing apartment rooms rang with his footsteps as if they were great high-ceilinged palace halls. After his wife left him, he had been able to endure the apartment only when he was asleep. Now nightmares swarmed over him like carrion flies.

While his CD player poured out Mahler's *The Song of the Earth*, he ate a TV dinner. Then, sitting on the sofa, staring at the blank set, he slowly drank a tall glassful of medium-priced bourbon. Before he drowsed away, he set the alarm. Its loud ring startled him from—thank God!—a dreamless sleep. Beethoven's *Fifth* was just starting its loud knocking at the door of destiny.

After a shower he looked out the window. The darkness was thick enough that lights were beginning to be turned on. For him, there was only one glow in the Southside of the city: Laura's, a firefly (family Lampyridae) winking above a night-struck meadow.

Twenty minutes later, his hangover only slowly receding, he drove away in his beat-up and run-down car. (Maybe he should get sterilized and have a new car for the first time in his life.) Ten minutes later he was in the Newstreet HPA area. He would not have ventured there alone after dark, but the green-capped Special Police and steel-helmeted Emergency Reserve troops stationed on various street corners ensured a sort of safety. An FDA-unit van passed Charlie on the other side of the street. Black, mournful faces looked out from behind the barred windows.

The shiny new cars were bumper to bumper in the streets, parked on the sidewalks and jammed into open lots between houses.

Charlie's car turned into the alley back of Tchaka's Fast Food Emporium. A young black, his neon-tubed garments glowing, leaned against the wall by the side entrance. When he saw Charlie's car, he shut the door and stepped inside. He was "Slick" Ramsey, one of Ketcher's gang. He looked furtive, but that did not mean much down here.

Unable to find a parking space in the alley, Charlie drove slowly around the block. Before he was halfway, he realized—he jumped as if stung by a bee—that the kids on their work break always stood in the alley, talking and horsing around. But they had not been there.

He brought the car screeching around the corner and into the alley. His headlights spotlighted Ramsey's shiny, sweaty face sticking out from the doorway. Ramsey quickly shut the door. Charlie stopped the car by the door and was out of the car before it had quit rocking. He knew, he just knew, that Ketcher, inflamed with snark, his cool burned away when he found out that Laura would soon be out of his reach, was no longer waiting to get what he just had to have.

Ramsey and another youth caught Charlie by the arms as he burst into the dimly lit hallway. A third, John "Welcome Wagon" Penney, came toward him with a knife in his hand. Charlies screamed and kicked out. His foot slammed into Penney's hand, and the blade dropped. Twisting and turning, stomping on the feet of the two holding him, he broke loose and was down the hall and through the doorway from which Penney had come. Still screaming, he plunged into a large, well-lit storeroom. The workers were huddled in a corner, four of the gang standing guard, holding knives. One worker was down on her knees, vomiting, but several of her fellows were grinning and cheering Ketcher.

At the opposite corner, Laura, naked, was on her back on the floor with Ketcher, fully dressed, on top of her. Charlie saw her face, bloodied, her mouth fallen open like a corpse's, her eyes wide and glazed. Her outspread arms were pinned to the ground by the heavy feet of two gang members.

Silent, all stared at Charlie except Ketcher and Laura. He was savagely biting her nose while pumping away.

Charlie got to Ketcher before the others unfroze. No longer yelling, the others silent, the only sounds the slap of his shoes and those of the pursuers from the hall, he charged. No one got in his way, and he slammed his hands against the pockets of Ketcher's jacket. The vials within the bags broke; the two chemicals mingled; the bags popped like firecrackers; the brief spurts of flame from them looked like flaming gas jets.

Ketcher screamed while struggling to tear off his jacket.

The two standing on Laura's arms jumped at Charlie and grabbed him. Still silent, Charlie slapped at their pockets. There was more popping, and they let loose of him and tried to get rid of the clothes before they burned to death.

The workers ran yelling out of the storeroom. Some of the gang followed them. Two ran at Charlie, their knives waving. By then Ketcher's jacket was on the floor, but he was rolling in agony on the concrete, and seemingly unaware as yet that Charlie was here. Charlie snatched up the smoking and flaming jacket and thrust it into the face of the nearest knife fighter.

He had become a fire in a wind, whirling, slapping jacket pockets, staggering back when a blade went through his left biceps, grabbing a wrist when his cheek was sliced, and twisting the wrist until it cracked. Only because he acted like a crazy man and was as elusive as a gnat did he escape death.

When he saw Ketcher—his ribs, his shoulders, the front of his thighs, and one side of his face bright red with burns, again on top of Laura, but now slamming her head repeatedly into the concrete floor, blood spreading out below her, her mouth slack and open, her eyes shattered glass—Charlie truly became crazy.

Ketcher's only thought now seemed to be to kill Laura. It was as if he blamed her for the burns.

The rest of his gang had run out of the storeroom. They knew that the cops and the troops would soon be here.

Coughing from the smoke, Charlie ran toward Ketcher and Laura. Suddenly Ketcher sat back. His breath cracked. His chest heaved. But he looked at his work with what seemed to be satisfaction. Where the blood on Laura's face did not conceal it, her deep brown skin was underlayered with gray.

Ketcher rose, and Charlie turned. Ketcher started, and his eyes widened.

"You, you done this?" he said. "The white gooser?"

He half-turned and looked down at Laura.

"The uppity bitch is dead. I had her; she ain't gonna get away."

Charlie stopped and picked up a knife.

Ketcher turned back toward him. "I killed the bitch. I'll kill you, too, Charlie Charlie."

Charlie screamed. According to what he was told, he was still screaming when the cops came. He did not remember.

If he was screaming until his throat was raw for days afterward, it was because he was giving vent to all the futility and despair and suffering and the sense of being imprisoned, straitjacketed, chained, which he felt for himself and which the cesspool dwellers he worked for felt far more keenly than he. And it was for Laura, whose drive and brains might have freed her, given her some freedom, anyway. No one raised here ever really got free of it.

He did not remember stabbing Ketcher many times. Vaguely, he did recall a blurred vision of Ketcher on his back, his arms and legs up in the air and kicking like a dying water beetle. Charlie was told that blood had covered him, Ketcher, and Laura like liquid shrouds. His informant, a black cop, had not been trying to impress him. Born here, she had seen worse when she was in diapers.

When discharged from the mental ward of the hospital five months later, Charlie had no job and did not look for one. In what seemed a short time, he was on welfare.

The irony was doubled when Rex Bessey came to ask him if he wished to sign up for sterilization.

"I'm really embarrassed," Rex said. "But it's my job."

Charlie smiled. "Don't I know. But I'm not going to sign. My wife—you know Blanche—called me yesterday. She just had a baby girl. We're going to get together again. It may not work out, but we're trying for the sake of the baby, for ours, too. I got hope now, Rex. I'm on welfare, but I won't be forever. My situation's different. I wasn't raised on public aid, handicapped by my environment from birth, and I don't have two strikes against me because I'm black. I can make it. I will make it."

Rex got a beer and sat down. He said, "You've been so sunk in hopeless apathy, your friends just gave up. You know I was the last to quit coming around. You just wouldn't stop your dismal talk about Laura. I did my best, but I couldn't cheer you up. I'm sorry, I just couldn't take you anymore."

Charlie waved his hand. "I don't blame you. But I'm better. I know I'll make it. My wife's phone call, well, soon as I hung up, something seemed to turn over. How can I describe it? I'll try. Listen, insects thrive as a species mainly because they breed so wondrously. Kill all but two, and in less than a year, there are ten billion. It's nature's way; God's, if you prefer. People aren't insects, but nature doesn't seem to care about the individual human or insect being killed, or even millions being wiped out. Laura Dott was one of the unlucky ones, and that's the way it is.

"But I'm human. I do what insects can't do. I care; I hurt; I mourn; I grieve. But I wasn't doing what most humans do. Healing, getting over the hurt as time did its work, accepting this world for what it is. Nor was I trying to do my little bit to make the world just a little better. I gave up even that after Laura died."

Charlie feel silent until Rex said, "And?"

"Blanche and I were discussing what to name the baby. Blanche's mother was named Laura, and she wanted to name the baby Laura. I was so struck with the coincidence, I couldn't talk for a minute."

Rex leaned forward in the chair, his huge hand squeezing the sides of the beer can together.

"You mean?"

"One Laura down, one Laura to go."

SUR
A Summary Report of the Yelcho Expedition to the Antarctic, 1909-10

Ursula K. Le Guin

Ursula K. Le Guin is another of the most distinguished writers in fantasy and science fiction of recent decades, read by many outside the field. Her *Earthsea* books are classics of contemporary fantasy, and *The Left Hand of Darkness* and *The Dispossessed*, classics of contemporary SF. She is a poet and critic, and has published a number of books outside SF. She is the editor (with Brian Attebery and Karen Joy Fowler) of the *Norton Book of Science Fiction*. She is also a master of the short story and has had periodic bursts of writing short fantasy and SF throughout her career, which still continues. "Sur" is one of the many fine Le Guin stories from the last decade.

Although I have no intention of publishing this report, I think it would be nice if a grandchild of mine, or somebody's grandchild, happened to find it someday; so I shall keep it in the leather trunk in the attic, along with Rosita's christening dress and Juanito's silver rattle and my wedding shoes and finneskos.

The first requisite for mounting an expedition—money—is normally the hardest to come by. I grieve that even in a report destined for a trunk in the attic of a house in a very quiet suburb of Lima I dare not write the name of the generous benefactor, the great soul without whose unstinting liberality the Yelcho Expedition would never have been more than the idlest excursion into daydream. That our equipment was the best and most modern—that our provisions were plentiful and fine—that a ship of the Chilean government, with her brave officers and gallant crew, was twice sent halfway round the world for our convenience: all this is due to that benefactor whose name, alas!, I must not say, but whose happiest debtor I shall be till death.

When I was little more than a child, my imagination was caught by a newspaper account of the voyage of the *Belgica*, which, sailing south from Tierra del Fuego, was beset by ice in the Bellingshausen Sea and drifted a whole year with the floe, the men aboard her suffering a great deal from want of food and from the terror of the unending winter darkness. I read and reread that account, and later followed with excitement the reports of the rescue of Dr. Nordenskjöld from the South Shetland Islands by the dashing Captain Irizar of the *Uruguay,* and the adventures of the *Scotia* in the Weddell Sea. But all these exploits were to me but forerunners of the British National Antarctic Expedition of 1901–04, in the *Discovery,* and the wonderful account of that expedition by Captain Scott. This book, which I ordered from London and reread a thousand times, filled me with longing to see with my own eyes that strange continent, last Thule of the South, which lies on our maps and globes like a white cloud, a void, fringed here and there with scraps of coastline, dubious capes, supposititious islands, headlands that may or may not be there: Antarctica. And the desire was as pure as the polar snows: to go, to see—no more, no less. I deeply respect the scientific accomplishments of Captain Scott's expedition, and have read with passionate interest the findings of physicists, meteorologists, biologists, etc.; but having had no training in any science, nor any opportunity for such training, my ignorance obliged me to forgo any thought of adding to the body of scientific knowledge concerning Antarctica, and the same is true for all the members of my expedition. It seems a pity; but there was nothing we could do about it. Our goal was limited to observation and exploration. We hoped to go a little farther, perhaps, and see a little more; if not, simply to go and to see. A simple ambition, I think, and essentially a modest one.

Yet it would have remained less than an ambition, no more than a longing, but for the support and encouragement of my dear cousin and friend Juana ————. (I use no surnames, lest this report fall into strangers' hands at last, and embarrassment or unpleasant notoriety thus be brought upon unsuspecting husbands, sons, etc.) I had lent Juana my copy of *The Voyage of the "Discovery,"* and it was she who, as we strolled beneath our parasols across the Plaza de Armas after Mass one Sunday in 1908, said, "Well, if Captain Scott can do it, why can't we?"

It was Juana who proposed that we write Carlota ———— in Valparaíso. Through Carlota we met our benefactor, and so obtained our money, our ship, and even the plausible pretext of going on retreat in a Bolivian convent, which some of us were forced to employ (while the rest of us said we were going to Paris for the winter season). And it was my Juana who in the darkest moments remained resolute, unshaken in her determination to achieve our goal.

And there were dark moments, especially in the spring of 1909—times when I did not see how the Expedition would ever become more than a quarter ton of pemmican gone to waste and lifelong regret. It was so very hard to gather our expeditionary force together! So few of those we asked even knew what we were talking about—so many thought we were mad, or wicked, or both! And of those few who shared our folly, still fewer were able, when it came to the point, to leave their daily duties and commit themselves to a voyage of at least six months, attended with not inconsiderable uncertainty and danger. An ailing parent; an anxious husband beset by business cares; a child at home with only ignorant or incompetent servants to look after it: these are not responsibilities lightly to be set aside. And those who wished to evade such claims were not the companions we wanted in hard work, risk, and privation.

But since success crowned our efforts, why dwell on the setbacks and delays, or the wretched contrivances and downright lies that we all had to employ? I look back with regret only to those friends who wished to come with us but could not, by any contrivance, get free—those we had to leave behind to a life without danger, without uncertainty, without hope.

On the seventeenth of August, 1909, in Punta Arenas, Chile, all the members of the Expedition met for the first time: Juana and I, the two Peruvians; from Argentina, Zoe, Berta, and Teresa; and our Chileans, Carlota and her friends Eva, Pepita, and Dolores. At the last moment I had received word that María's husband, in Quito, was ill and she must stay to nurse him, so we were nine, not ten. Indeed, we had resigned ourselves to being but eight when, just as night fell, the indomitable Zoe arrived in a tiny pirogue manned by Indians, her yacht having sprung a leak just as it entered the Straits of Magellan.

That night before we sailed we began to get to know one another, and we agreed, as we enjoyed our abominable supper in the abominable seaport inn of Punta Arenas, that if a situation arose of such urgent danger that one voice must be obeyed without present question, the unenviable honor of speaking with that voice should fall first upon myself; if I were incapacitated, upon Carlota; if she, then upon Berta. We three were then toasted as "Supreme Inca," "La Araucana," and "The Third Mate," amid a lot of laughter and cheering. As it came out, to my very great pleasure and relief, my qualities as a "leader" were never tested; the nine of us worked things out amongst us from beginning to end without any orders being given by anybody, and only two or three times with recourse to a vote by voice or show of hands. To be sure, we argued a good deal. But then, we had time to argue. And one way or another the arguments always ended up in a decision, upon which action could be taken. Usually at least one person grumbled about the decision, sometimes bitterly. But what is life without grumbling and the occasional opportunity to say "I told you so"? How could one bear housework, or looking after babies, let alone the rigors of sledge-hauling in Antarctica, without grumbling? Officers—as we came to understand aboard the *Yelcho*—are forbidden to grumble; but we nine were, and are, by birth and upbringing, unequivocally and irrevocably, all crew.

Though our shortest course to the southern continent, and that originally urged upon us by the captain of our good ship, was to the South Shetlands and the Bellingshausen Sea, or else by the South Orkneys into the Weddell Sea, we planned to sail west to the Ross Sea, which Captain Scott had explored and described, and from which the brave Ernest Shackleton had returned only the previous autumn. More was known about this region than any other portion of the coast of Antarctica, and though that more was not much, yet it served as some insurance of the safety of the ship, which we felt we had no right to imperil. Captain Pardo had fully agreed with us after studying the charts and our planned itinerary; and so it was westward that we took our course out of the Straits the next morning.

Our journey half round the globe was attended by fortune. The little *Yelcho* steamed cheerily along through gale and gleam, climbing up and down those seas of the Southern Ocean that run unbroken round the world. Juana, who had fought bulls and the far more dangerous cows on her family's *estancia*, called the ship *la vaca valiente*, because she always returned to the charge. Once we got over being seasick, we all enjoyed the sea voyage, though oppressed at times by the kindly but officious protectiveness of the captain and his officers, who felt that we were only "safe" when huddled up in the three tiny cabins that they had chivalrously vacated for our use.

We saw our first iceberg much farther south than we had looked for it, and saluted it with Veuve Clicquot at dinner. The next day we entered the ice pack, the belt of floes and bergs broken loose from the land ice and winter-frozen seas of Antarctica which drifts northward in the spring. Fortune still smiled on us: our little steamer, incapable, with her unreinforced metal hull, of forcing a way into the ice, picked her way from lane to lane without hesitation, and on the third day we were through the pack, in which ships have sometimes struggled for weeks and been obliged to turn back at last. Ahead of us now lay the dark-gray waters of the Ross Sea, and beyond that, on the horizon, the remote glimmer, the cloud-reflected whiteness of the Great Ice Barrier.

Entering the Ross Sea a little east of Longitude West 160°, we came in sight of the Barrier at the place where Captain Scott's party, finding a bight in the vast wall of ice, had gone ashore and sent up their hydrogen-gas balloon for reconnaissance and photography. The towering face of the Barrier, its sheer cliffs and azure and violet waterworn caves, all were as described, but the location had changed: instead of a narrow bight, there was a considerable bay, full of the beautiful and terrific orca whales playing and spouting in the sunshine of that brilliant southern spring.

Evidently masses of ice many acres in extent had broken away from the Barrier (which—at least for most of its vast extent—does not rest on land but floats on water) since the *Discovery's* passage in 1902. This put our plan to set up camp on the Barrier itself in a new light; and while we were discussing alternatives, we asked Captain Pardo to take the ship west along the Barrier face toward Ross Island and McMurdo Sound. As the sea was clear of ice and quite calm, he was happy to do so and, when we sighted the smoke plume of Mt. Erebus, to share in our celebration—another half case of Veuve Clicquot.

The *Yelcho* anchored in Arrival Bay, and we went ashore in the ship's boat. I cannot describe my emotions when I set foot on the earth, on that earth, the barren, cold gravel at the foot of the long volcanic slope. I felt elation, impatience, gratitude, awe, familiarity. I felt that I was home at last. Eight Adélie penguins immediately came to greet us with many exclamations of interest not unmixed with disapproval. "Where on earth have you been? What took you so long? The Hut is around this way. Please come this way. Mind the rocks!" They insisted on our going to visit Hut Point, where the large structure built by Captain Scott's party stood, looking just as in the photographs and drawings that illustrate his book. The area about it, however, was disgusting—a kind of graveyard of seal skins, seal bones, penguin bones, and rubbish, presided over by the mad, screaming skua gulls. Our escorts waddled past the slaughterhouse in all tranquillity, and one showed me personally to the door, though it would not go in.

The interior of the hut was less offensive but very dreary. Boxes of supplies had been stacked up into a kind of room within the room; it did not look as I had imagined it when the *Discovery* party put on their melodramas and minstrel shows in the long winter night. (Much later, we learned that Sir Ernest had rearranged it a good deal when he was there just a year before us.) It was dirty, and had about it a mean disorder. A pound tin of tea was standing open. Empty meat tins lay about; biscuits were spilled on the floor; a lot of dog turds were underfoot—frozen, of course, but not a great deal improved by that. No doubt the last occupants had had to leave in a hurry, perhaps even in a blizzard. All the same, they could have closed the tea tin. But housekeeping, the art of the infinite, is no game for amateurs.

Teresa proposed that we use the hut as our camp. Zoe counterproposed that we set fire to it. We finally shut the door and left it as we had found it. The penguins appeared to approve, and cheered us all the way to the boat.

McMurdo Sound was free of ice, and Captain Pardo now proposed to take us off Ross Island and across the Victoria Land, where we might camp at the foot of the Western Mountains, on dry and solid earth. But those mountains, with their storm-darkened peaks and hanging cirques and glaciers, looked as awful as Captain Scott had found them on his western journey, and none of us felt much inclined to seek shelter among them.

Aboard the ship that night we decided to go back and set up our base as we had originally planned, on the Barrier itself. For all available reports indicated that the clear way south was across the level Barrier surface until one could ascend one of the confluent glaciers to the high plateau that appears to form the whole interior of the continent. Captain Pardo argued strongly against this plan, asking what would become of us if the Barrier "calved"—if our particular acre of ice broke away and started to drift northward. "Well," said Zoe, "then you won't have to come so far to meet us." But he was so persuasive on this theme that he persuaded himself into leaving one of the *Yelcho*'s boats with us when we camped, as a means of escape. We found it useful for fishing, later on.

My first steps on Antarctic soil, my only visit to Ross Island, had not been pleasure unalloyed. I thought of the words of the English poet,

> *Though every prospect pleases,*
> *And only Man is vile.*

But then, the backside of the heroism is often rather sad; women and servants know that. They know also that the heroism may be no less real for that But achievement is smaller than men think. What is large is the sky, the earth, the sea, the soul. I looked back as the ship sailed east again that evening. We were well into September now, with eight hours or more of daylight. The spring sunset lingered on the twelve-thousand-foot peak of Erebus and shone rosygold on her long plume of steam. The steam from our own small funnel faded blue on the twilit water as we crept along under the towering pale wall of ice.

On our return to "Orca Bay"—Sir Ernest, we learned years later, had named it the Bay of Whales—we found a sheltered nook where the Barrier edge was low enough to provide fairly easy access from the ship. The *Yelcho* put out her ice anchor, and the next long, hard days were spent in unloading our supplies and setting up our camp on the ice, a half kilometer in from the edge: a task in which the *Yelcho*'s crew lent us invaluable aid and interminable advice. We took all the aid gratefully, and most of the advice with salt.

The weather so far had been extraordinarily mild for spring in this latitude; the temperature had not yet gone below—20°F, and there was only one blizzard while we were setting up camp. But Captain Scott had spoken feelingly of the bitter south winds on the Barrier, and we had planned accordingly. Exposed as our camp was to every wind, we built no rigid structures aboveground. We set up tents to shelter in while we dug out a series of cubicles in the ice itself, lined them with hay insulation and pine boarding, and roofed them with canvas over bamboo poles, covered with snow for weight and insulation. The big central room was instantly named Buenos Aires by our Argentineans, to whom the center, wherever one is, is always Buenos Aires. The heating and cooking stove was in Buenos Aires. The storage tunnels and the privy (called Punta Arenas) got some back heat from the stove. The sleeping cubicles opened off Buenos Aires, and were very small, mere tubes into which one crawled feet first; they were lined deeply with hay and soon warmed by one's body warmth. The sailors called them coffins and wormholes, and looked with horror on our burrows in the ice. But our little warren or prairie-dog village served us well, permitting us as much warmth and privacy as one could reasonably expect under the circumstances. If the *Yelcho* was unable to get through the ice in February and we had to spend the winter in Antarctica, we certainly could do so, though on very limited rations. For this coming summer, our base—Sudamérica del Sur, South South America, but we generally called it the Base—was intended merely as a place to sleep, to store our provisions, and to give shelter from blizzards.

To Berta and Eva, however, it was more than that. They were its chief architect-designers, its most ingenious builder-excavators, and its most diligent and contented occupants, forever inventing an improvement in ventilation, or learning how to make skylights, or revealing to us a new addition to our suite of rooms, dug in the living ice. It was thanks to them that our stores were stowed so handily, that our stove drew and heated so efficiently, and that Buenos Aires, where nine people cooked, ate, worked, conversed, argued, grumbled, painted, played the guitar and banjo, and kept the Expedition's library of books and maps, was a marvel of comfort and convenience. We lived there in real amity; and if you simply had to be alone for a while, you crawled into your sleeping hole headfirst.

Berta went a little farther. When she had done all she could to make South South America livable, she dug out one more cell just under the ice surface, leaving a nearly transparent sheet of ice like a greenhouse roof; and there, alone, she worked at sculptures. They were beautiful forms, some like a blending of the reclining human figure with the subtle curves and volumes of the Weddell seal, others like the fantastic shapes of ice cornices and ice caves. Perhaps they are there still, under the snow, in the bubble in the Great Barrier. There where she made them, they might last as long as stone. But she could not bring them north. That is the penalty for carving in water.

Captain Pardo was reluctant to leave us, but his orders did not permit him to hang about the Ross Sea indefinitely, and so at last, with many earnest injunctions to us to stay put—make no journeys—take no risks—beware of frostbite—don't use edge tools—look out for cracks in the ice—and a heartfelt promise to return to Orca Bay on February 20th, or as near that date as wind and ice would permit, the good man bade us farewell, and his crew shouted us a great good-bye cheer as they weighed anchor. That evening, in the long orange twilight of October, we saw the topmast of the *Yelcho* go down the north horizon, over the edge of the world, leaving us to ice, and silence, and the Pole.

That night we began to plan the Southern Journey.

*   *   *

The ensuing month passed in short practice trips and depot-laying. The life we had led at home, though in its own way strenuous, had not fitted any of us for the kind of strain met with in sledge-hauling at ten or twenty degrees below freezing. We all needed as much working out as possible before we dared undertake a long haul.

My longest exploratory trip, made with Dolores and Carlota, was southwest toward Mt. Markham, and it was a nightmare—blizzards and pressure ice all the way out, crevasses and no view of the mountains when we got there, and white weather and sastrugi all the way back. The trip was useful, however, in that we could begin to estimate our capacities; and also in that we had started out with a very heavy load of provisions, which we depoted at a hundred and a hundred and thirty miles south-southwest of Base. Thereafter other parties pushed on farther, till we had a line of snow cairns and depots right down to Latitude 80° 43', where Juana and Zoe, on an exploring trip, had found a kind of stone gateway opening on a great glacier leading south. We established these depots to avoid, if possible, the hunger that had bedevilled Captain Scott's Southern Party, and the consequent misery and weakness. And we also established to our own satisfaction—intense satisfaction—that we were sledge-haulers at least as good as Captain Scott's husky dogs. Of course we could not have expected to pull as much or as fast as his men. That we did so was because we were favored by much better weather than Captain Scott's party ever met on the Barrier; and also the quantity and quality of our food made a very considerable difference. I am sure that the fifteen percent of dried fruits in our pemmican helped prevent scurvy; and the potatoes, frozen and dried according to an ancient Andean Indian method, were very nourishing yet very light and compact—perfect sledding rations. In any case, it was the considerable confidence in our capacities that we made ready at last for the Southern Journey.

The Southern Party consisted of two sledge teams: Juana, Dolores, and myself; Carlota, Pepita, and Zoe. The support team of Berta, Eva, and Teresa set out before us with a heavy load of supplies, going right up onto the glacier to prospect routes and leave depots of supplies for our return journey. We followed five days behind them, and met them returning between Depot Ercilla and Depot Miranda. That "night"—of course, there was no real darkness—we were all nine together in the heart of the level plain of ice. It was November 15th, Dolores's birthday. We celebrated by putting eight ounces of pisco in the hot chocolate, and became very merry. We sang. It is strange now to remember how thin our voices sounded in that great silence. It was overcast, white weather, without shadows and without visible horizon or any feature to break the level; there was nothing to see at all. We had come to that white place on the map, that void, and there we flew and sang like sparrows.

After sleep and a good breakfast the Base Party continued north and the Southern Party sledged on. The sky cleared presently. High up, thin clouds passed over very rapidly from southwest to northeast, but down on the Barrier it was calm and just cold enough, five or ten degrees below freezing, to give a firm surface for hauling.

On the level ice we never pulled less than eleven miles (seventeen kilometers) a day, and generally fifteen or sixteen miles (twenty-five kilometers). (Our instruments, being British-made, were calibrated in feet, miles, degrees Fahrenheit, etc., but we often converted miles to kilometers, because the larger numbers sounded more encouraging.) At the time we left South America, we knew only that Mr. Ernest Shackleton had mounted another expedition to the Antarctic in 1907, had tried to attain the Pole but failed, and had returned to England in June of the current year, 1909. No coherent report of his explorations had yet reached South America when we left; we did not know what route he had gone, or how far he had got. But we were not altogether taken by surprise when, far across the featureless white plain, tiny beneath the mountain peaks and the strange silent flight of the rainbow-fringed cloud wisps, we saw a fluttering dot of black. We turned west from our course to visit it: a snow heap nearly buried by the winter's storms—a flag on a bamboo pole, a mere shred of threadbare cloth, an empty oilcan—and a few footprints standing some inches above the ice. In some conditions of weather the snow compressed under one's weight remains when the surrounding soft snow melts or is scoured away by the wind; and so these reversed footprints had been left standing all these months, like rows of cobbler's lasts—a queer sight.

We met no other such traces on our way. In general I believe our course was somewhat east of Mr. Shackleton's. Juana, our surveyor, had trained herself well and was faithful and methodical in her sightings and readings, but our equipment was minimal—a theodolite on tripod legs, a sextant with artificial horizon, two compasses, and chronometers. We had only the wheel meter on the sledge to give distance actually travelled.

In any case, it was the day after passing Mr. Shackleton's waymark that I first saw clearly the great glacier among the mountains to the southwest, which was to give us a pathway from the sea level of the Barrier up to the altiplano, ten thousand feet above. The approach was magnificent: a gateway formed by immense vertical domes and pillars of rock. Zoe and Juana had called the vast ice river that flowed through that gateway the Florence Nightingale Glacier, wishing to honor the British, who had been the inspiration and guide of our Expedition; that very brave and very peculiar lady seemed to represent so much that is best, and strangest, in the island race. On maps, of course, this glacier bears the name Mr. Shackleton gave it: the Beardmore.

The ascent of the Nightingale was not easy. The way was open at first, and well marked by our support party, but after some days we came among terrible crevasses, a maze of hidden cracks, from a foot to thirty feet wide and from thirty to a thousand feet deep. Step by step we went, and step by step, and the way always upward now. We were fifteen days on the glacier. At first the weather was hot—up to 20°F—and the hot nights without darkness were wretchedly uncomfortable in our small tents. And all of us suffered more or less from snow blindness just at the time when we wanted clear eyesight to pick our way among the ridges and crevasses of the tortured ice, and to see the wonders about and before us. For at every day's advance more great, nameless peaks came into view in the west and southwest, summit beyond summit, range beyond range, stark rock and snow in the unending noon.

We gave names to these peaks, not very seriously, since we did not expect our discoveries to come to the attention of geographers. Zoe had a gift for naming, and it is thanks to her that certain sketch maps in various suburban South American attics bear such curious features as "Bolívar's Big Nose," "I Am General Rosas," "The Cloudmaker," "Whose Toe?," and "Throne of Our Lady of the Southern Cross." And when at last we got up onto the altiplano, the great interior plateau, it was Zoe who called it the pampa, and maintained that we walked there among vast herds of invisible cattle, transparent cattle pastured on the spindrift snow, their gauchos the restless, merciless winds. We were by then all a little crazy with exhaustion and the great altitude—twelve thousand feet—and the cold and the wind blowing and the luminous circles and crosses surrounding the suns, for often there were three or four suns in the sky, up there.

That is not a place where people have any business to be. We should have turned back; but since we had worked so hard to get there, it seemed that we should go on, at least for a while.

A blizzard came, with very low temperatures, so we had to stay in the tents, in our sleeping bags, for thirty hours—a rest we all needed, though it was warmth we needed most, and there was no warmth on that terrible plain anywhere at all but in our veins. We huddled close together all that time. The ice we lay on is two miles thick.

It cleared suddenly and became, for the plateau, good weather: twelve below zero and the wind not very strong. We three crawled out of our tent and met the others crawling out of theirs. Carlota told us then that her group wished to turn back. Pepita had been feeling very ill; even after the rest during the blizzard, her temperature would not rise above 94°. Carlota was having trouble breathing. Zoe was perfectly fit, but much preferred staying with her friends and lending them a hand in difficulties to pushing on toward the Pole. So we put the four ounces of pisco that we had been keeping for Christmas into the breakfast cocoa, and dug out our tents, and loaded our sledges, and parted there in the white daylight on the bitter plain.

Our sledge was fairly light by now. We pulled on to the south. Juana calculated our position daily. On the twenty-second of December, 1909, we reached the South Pole. The weather was, as always, very cruel. Nothing of any kind marked the dreary whiteness. We discussed leaving some kind of mark or monument, a snow cairn, a tent pole and flag; but there seemed no particular reason to do so. Anything we could do, anything we were, was insignificant, in that awful place. We put up the tent for shelter for an hour and made a cup of tea, and then struck "90° Camp."

Dolores, standing patient as ever in her sledging harness, looked at the snow; it was so hard frozen that it showed no trace of our footprints coming, and she said, "Which way?"

"North," said Juana.

It was a joke, because at that particular place there is no other direction. But we did not laugh. Our lips were cracked with frostbite and hurt too much to let us laugh. So we started back, and the wind at our backs pushed us along, and dulled the knife edges of the waves of frozen snow.

All that week the blizzard wind pursued us like a pack of mad dogs. I cannot describe it. I wished we had not gone to the Pole. I think I wish it even now. But I was glad even then that we had left no sign there, for some man longing to be first might come some day, and find it, and know then what a fool he had been, and break his heart.

We talked, when we could talk, of catching up to Carlota's party, since they might be going slower than we. In fact they used their tent as a sail to catch the following wind and had got far ahead of us. But in many places they had built snow cairns or left some sign for us; once, Zoe had written on the lee side of a ten-foot sastruga, just as children write on the sand of the beach at Miraflores, "This Way Out!" The wind blowing over the frozen ridge had left the words perfectly distinct.

In the very hour that we began to descend the glacier, the weather turned warmer, and the mad dogs were left to howl forever tethered to the Pole. The distance that had taken us fifteen days going up we covered in only eight days going down. But the good weather that had aided us descending the Nightingale became a curse down on the Barrier ice, where we had looked forward to a kind of royal progress from depot to depot, eating our fill and taking our time for the last three hundred-odd miles. In a tight place on the glacier I lost my goggles—I was swinging from my harness at the time in a crevasse—and then Juana broke hers when we had to do some rock-climbing coming down to the Gateway. After two days in bright sunlight with only one pair of snow goggles to pass amongst us, we were all suffering badly from snow blindness. It became acutely painful to keep lookout for landmarks or depot flags, to take sightings, even to study the compass, which had to be laid down on the snow to steady the needle. At Concolorcorvo Depot, where there was a particularly good supply of food and fuel, we gave up, crawled into our sleeping bags and bandaged eyes, and slowly boiled alive like lobsters in the tent exposed to the relentless sun. The voices of Berta and Zoe were the sweetest sound I ever heard. A little concerned about us, they had skied south to meet us. They led us home to Base.

We recovered quite swiftly, but the altiplano left its mark. When she was very little, Rosita asked if a dog "had bitten Mama's toes." I told her yes—a great, white, mad dog named Blizzard! My Rosita and my Juanito heard many stories when they were little, about that fearful dog and how it howled, and the transparent cattle of the invisible gauchos, and a river of ice eight thousand feet high called Nightingale, and how Cousin Juana drank a cup of tea standing on the bottom of the world under seven suns, and other fairy tales.

We were in for one severe shock when we reached Base at last. Teresa was pregnant. I must admit that my first response to the poor girl's big belly and sheepish look was anger—rage—fury. That one of us should have concealed anything, and such a thing, from the others! But Teresa had done nothing of the sort. Only those who had concealed from her what she most needed to know were to blame. Brought up by servants, with four years' schooling in a convent, and married at sixteen, the poor girl was still so ignorant at twenty years of age that she had thought it was "the cold weather" that made her miss her periods. Even this was not entirely stupid, for all of us on the Southern Journey had seen our periods change or stop altogether as we experienced increasing cold, hunger, and fatigue. Teresa's appetite had begun to draw general attention; and then she had begun, as she said pathetically, "to get fat." The others were worried at the thought of all the sledge-hauling she had done, but she flourished, and the only problem was her positively insatiable appetite. As well as could be determined from her shy references to her last night on the hacienda with her husband, the baby was due at just about the same time as the *Yelcho*, February

20th. But we had not been back from the Southern Journey two weeks when, on February 14th, she went into labor.

Several of us had borne children and had helped with deliveries, and anyhow most of what needs to be done is fairly self-evident; but a first labor can be long and trying, and we were all anxious, while Teresa was frightened out of her wits. She kept calling for her José till she was as hoarse as a skua. Zoe lost all patience at last and said, "By God, Teresa, if you say 'José!' once more, I hope you have a penguin!" But what she had, after twenty long hours, was a pretty little red-faced girl.

Many were the suggestions for that child's name from her eight proud mid-wife aunts: Polita, Penguina, McMurdo, Victoria . . . but Teresa announced, after she had had a good sleep and a large serving of pemmican, "I shall name her Rosa—Rosa del Sur," Rose of the South. That night we drank the last two bottles of Veuve Clicquot (having finished the pisco at 88° 60' South) in toasts to our little Rose.

On the nineteenth of February, a day early, my Juana came down into Buenos Aires in a hurry. "The ship," she said, "the ship has come," and she burst into tears—she who had never wept in all our weeks of pain and weariness on the long haul.

Of the return voyage there is nothing to tell. We came back safe.

In 1912 all the world learned that the brave Norwegian Amundsen had reached the South Pole; and then, much later, we heard the accounts of how Captain Scott and his men had come there after him but did not come home again.

Just this year, Juana and I wrote to the captain of the *Yelcho*, for the newspapers have been full of the story of his gallant dash to rescue Sir Ernest Shackleton's men from Elephant Island, and we wished to congratulate him, and once more to thank him. Never one word has he breathed of our secret. He is a man of honor, Luis Pardo.

I add this last note in 1929. Over the years we have lost touch with one another. It is very difficult for women to meet, when they live as far apart as we do. Since Juana died, I have seen none of my old sledgemates, though sometimes we write. Our little Rosa del Sur died of the scarlet fever when she was five years old. Teresa had many other children. Carlota took the veil in Santiago ten years ago. We are old women now, with old husbands, and grown children, and grandchildren who might someday like to read about the Expedition. Even if they are rather ashamed of having such a crazy grandmother, they may enjoy sharing in the secret. But they must not let Mr. Amundsen know! He would be terribly embarrassed and disappointed. There is no need for him or anyone else outside the family to know. We left no footprints, even.

INTRODUCTION TO *ENGLAND SWINGS SF*

Judith Merril

This essay is the Introduction to Judith Merril's groundbreaking anthology, *England Swings SF* (1968), the book that introduced the emerging generation of ambitious young SF writers (the British "New Wave") of the 1960s to the American SF audience. It is a fine example of the stylistic exuberance of the time. Merril was a leading SF writer and a powerful advocate of changing the name of science fiction to speculative fiction to acknowledge the literary maturity of the best SF. She promoted this effectively through the twelve impressive volumes of *Year's Best SF*, which she edited between 1956 and 1968, and through criticism and other anthologies during that period. She was perhaps the most important anthologist in SF for more than a decade.

Picture yourself on a boat in the river with
tangerine trees and marmalade skies . . .

You have never read a book like this before, and the next time you read one anything like it, it won't be *much* like it at all.

. . . It's getting better all the time . . .

It's an action-photo, a record of process-in-change,

. . . with kaleidoscope eyes . . .

a look through the perspex porthole at the

Plasticine porters with looking glass ties . . .

momentarily stilled bodies in a scout ship boosting

. . . filling the cracks that ran through the
door and kept my mind from wandering
where it will go . . .

fast, and heading out of sight into the multiplex mystery of inner/outer space.

Within you without you we were talking
about the space between us all . . .

I can't tell you where they're going, but

. . . there I will go and it doesn't really mat-
ter if I'm wrong I'm right where I belong I'm
right . . .

maybe that's why I keep wanting to read
what they write. The next time someone assembles the work of the writers in this—
well, "school" is too formal

. . . you're holding me down, turning me
round filling me up with your rules . . .

. . . and "movement" sound pretentious . . .

. . . wants you all to sing along so let me in-
troduce you to the one and only . . .

and "British sf" is ludicrously limiting—

. . . you're really only very small and life flows
on within you and without you . . .

so let's just say, the work of these writers
and/or others now setting out to work in
this way,

The colorful way and when my mind is wan-
dering there I will go . . .

it will probably have about as much resemblance to this anthology as this one does to
any other collection of science fiction, social
criticism,

. . . taking the time for a number of things
that weren't important yesterday . . .

surrealism—BEMs, Beats, Beatles, what-
have-you—

...rocking horse people eat marshmallow
pies...

you have ever read or heard before. Meanwhile,

With a little help from my friends...

I think this trip should be a good one.

...at the turnstile the girl with kaleidoscope
eyes and it doesn't really matter if I'm wrong
I'm right where I belong it's getting better all
the time...

Excerpts quoted above are from *Sgt. Pepper's Lonely Hearts Club Band,* by the Beatles; Capitol
Records, Inc., 1967

DOING LENNON

Gregory Benford

Gregory Benford is a physicist and writer whose work has always shown a concern with working scientists. He is the author of the contemporary SF masterpiece *Timescape* and many other novels and stories. He is particularly adept at evoking meaning from the details of everyday life in his fiction. He is perhaps the most articulate advocate of the rigorous use of science in SF, and one of the most accomplished stylists in SF as well. He was a great fan of John Lennon.

> *Sanity calms, but madness*
> *is more interesting.*
> —John Russell

As the hideous cold seeps from him he feels everything becoming sharp and clear again. He decides he can do it, he can make it work. He opens his eyes. "Hello." His voice rasps. "Bet you aren't expecting me. I'm John Lennon." "What?" the face above him says. "You know. John Lennon. The Beatles."

Professori Hermann—the name attached to the face which loomed over him as he drifted up, up from the Long Sleep—is vague about the precise date. It is either 2108 or 2180. Hermann makes a little joke about inversion of positional notation; it has something to do with nondenumerable set theory, which is all the rage. The ceiling glows with a smooth green phosphorescence and Fielding lies there letting them prick him with needles, unwrap his organiform nutrient webbing, poke and adjust and massage as he listens to a hollow *pock-pocketa*. He knows this is the crucial moment, he must hit them with it now.

"I'm glad it worked," Fielding says with a Liverpool accent. He has got it just right, the rising pitch at the end and the nasal tones.

"No doubt there is an error in our log," Hermann says pedantically. "You are listed as Henry Fielding."

Fielding smiles. "Ah, that's the ruse, you see."

Hermann blinks owlishly. "Deceiving Immortality Incorporated is—"

"I was fleeing political persecution, y'dig. Coming out for the workers and all. Writing songs about persecution and pollution and the working-class hero. Snarky stuff. So when the jackboot skinheads came in I decided to check out."

Fielding slips easily into the story he has memorized, all plotted and paced with major characters and minor characters and bits of incident, all of it sounding very real. He wrote it himself; he has it down. He continues talking while Hermann and some white-smocked assistants help him sit up, flex his legs, test his reflexes. Around them are vats and baths and tanks. A fog billows from a hole in the floor; a liquid nitrogen immersion bath.

Hermann listens intently to the story, nodding now and then, and summons other officials. Fielding tells his story again while the attendants work on him. He is careful to give the events in different order, with different details each time. His accent is standing up though there is mucus in his sinuses that makes the high singsong bits hard to get out. They give him something to eat; it tastes like chicken-flavored ice cream. After a while he sees he has them convinced. After all, the late twentieth was a turbulent time, crammed with gaudy events, lurid people. Fielding makes it seem reasonable that an aging rock star, seeing his public slip away and the government closing in, would corpsicle himself.

The officials nod and gesture and Fielding is wheeled out on a carry table. Immortality Incorporated is more like a church than a business. There is a ghostly hush in the hallways, the attendants are distant and reserved. Scientific servants in the temple of life.

They take him to an elaborate display, punch a button. A voice begins to drone a welcome to the year 2108 (or 2180). The voice tells him he is one of the few from his benighted age who saw the slender hope science held out to the diseased and dying. His vision has been rewarded. He has survived the unfreezing. There is some nondenominational talk about God and death and the eternal rhythm and balance of life, ending with a retouched holographic photograph of the Founding Fathers. They are a small knot of biotechnicians and engineers clustered around an immersion tank. Close-cropped hair, white shirts with ballpoint pens clipped in the pockets. They wear glasses and smile weakly at the camera, as though they have just been shaken awake.

"I'm hungry," Fielding says.

News that Lennon is revived spreads quickly. The Society for Dissipative Anachronisms holds a press conference for him. As he strides into the room Fielding clenches his fists so no one can see his hands shaking. This is the start. He has to make it here.

"How do you find the future, Mr. Lennon?"

"Turn right at Greenland." Maybe they will recognize it from *A Hard Day's Night*. This is before his name impacts fully, before many remember who John Lennon was. A fat man asks Fielding why he elected for the Long Sleep before he really needed it and Fielding says enigmatically, "The role of boredom in human history is underrated." This makes the evening news and the weekly topical roundup a few days later.

A fan of the twentieth asks him about the breakup with Paul, whether Ringo's death was a suicide, what about Allan Klein, how about the missing lines from *Abbey Road*? Did he like Dylan? What does he think of the Aarons theory that the Beatles could have stopped Vietnam?

Fielding parries a few questions, answers others. He does not tell them, of course, that in the early sixties he worked in a bank and wore granny glasses. Then he became a broker with Harcum, Brandels and Son and his take in 1969 was 57,803 dollars, not counting the money siphoned off into the two conealed accounts in Switzerland. But he read *Rolling Stone* religiously, collected Beatles memorabilia, had all the albums and books and could quote any verse from any song. He saw Paul once at a distance, coming out of a recording session. And he had a friend into Buddhism, who met Harrison one weekend in Surrey. Fielding did not mention his vacation spent wandering around Liverpool, picking up the accent and visiting all the old places, the cellars where they played and the narrow dark little houses their families owned in the early days. And as the years dribbled on and Fielding's money piled up, he lived increasingly in those golden days of the sixties, imagined himself playing side man along with Paul or George or John and crooning those same notes into the microphones, practically kissing the metal. And Fielding did not speak of his dreams.

t is the antiseptic Stanley Kubrick future. They are very adept at hardware. Population is stabilized at half a billion. Everywhere there are white hard decorator chairs in vaguely Danish modern. There seems no shortage of electrical power or oil or copper or zinc. Everyone has a hobby. Entertainment is a huge enterprise, with stress on ritual violence. Fielding watches a few games of Combat Golf, takes in a public execution or two. He goes to witness an electrical man short-circuit himself. The flash is visible over the curve of the Earth.

Genetic manipulants—*manips,* Hermann explains—are thin, stringy people, all bones and knobby joints where they connect directly into machine linkages. They are designed for some indecipherable purpose. Hermann, his guide, launches into an explanation but Fielding interrupts him to say, "Do you know where I can get a guitar?"

Fielding views the era 1950–1980:

"Astrology wasn't rational, nobody really believed it, you've got to realize that. It was *boogie woogie.* On the other hand, science and rationalism were progressive jazz."

He smiles as he says it. The 3D snout closes in. Fielding has purchased well and his plastic surgery, to lengthen the nose and give him that wry Lennonesque smirk, holds up well. Even the technicians at Immortality Incorporated missed it.

Fielding suffers odd moments of blackout. He loses the rub of rough cloth at a cuff on his shirt, the chill of air-conditioned breeze along his neck. The world dwindles away and sinks into inky black, but in a moment it is all back and he hears the distant murmur of traffic, and convulsively, by reflex, he squeezes the bulb in his hand and the orange vapor rises around him. He breathes deeply, sighs. Visions float into his mind and the sour tang of the mist reassures him.

Every age is known by its pleasures, Fielding reads from the library readout. The twentieth introduced two: high speed and hallucinogenic drugs. Both proved dangerous in the long run, which made them even more interesting. The twenty-first developed weightlessness, which worked out well except for the re-entry problems if one overindulged. In the twenty-second there were aquaform and something Fielding could not pronounce or understand.

He thumbs away the readout and calls Hermann for advice.

*   *   *

Translational difficulties:

They give him a sort of pasty suet when he goes to the counter to get his food. He shoves it back at them.

"Gah! Don't you have a hamburger someplace?" The stunted man behind the counter flexes his arms, makes a rude sign with his four fingers and goes away. The wiry woman next to Fielding rubs her thumbnail along the hideous scar at her side and peers at him. She wears only orange shorts and boots, but he can see the concealed dagger in her armpit.

"Hamburger?" she says severely. "That is the name of a citizen of the German city of Hamburg. Were you a cannibal then?"

Fielding does not know the proper response, which could be dangerous. When he pauses she massages her brown scar with new energy and makes a sign of sexual invitation. Fielding backs away. He is glad he did not mention French fries.

On 3D he makes a mistake about the recording date of *Sergeant Pepper's Lonely Hearts Club Band*. A ferret-eyed history student lunges in for the point but Fielding leans back casually, getting the accent just right, and says, "I zonk my brow with heel of hand, consterned!" and the audience laughs and he is away, free

Hermann has become his friend. The library readout says this is a common phenomenon among Immortality Incorporated employees who are fascinated by the past to begin with (or otherwise would not be in the business), and anyway Hermann and Fielding are about the same age, forty-seven. Hermann is not surprised that Fielding is practicing his chords and touching up his act.

"You want to get out on the road again, is that it?" Hermann says. "You want to be getting popular."

"It's my business."

"But your songs, they are old."

"Oldies but goldies," Fielding says solemnly.

"Perhaps you are right," Hermann sighs. "We are starved for variety. The people, no matter how educated—anything tickles their nose they think is champagne."

Fielding flicks on the tape input and launches into the hard-driving opening of "Eight Days a Week." He goes through all the chords, getting them right the first time. His fingers dance among the humming copper wires.

Hermann frowns but Fielding feels elated. He decides to celebrate. Precious reserves of cash are dwindling, even considering how much he made in the international bond market of '83; there is not much left. He decides to splurge. He orders an alcoholic vapor and a baked pigeon. Hermann is still worried but he eats the mottled pigeon with relish, licking his fingers. The spiced crust snaps crisply. Hermann asks to take the bones home to his family.

"You have drawn the rank-scented many," Hermann says heavily as the announcer begins his introduction. The air sparkles with anticipation.

"Ah, but they're *my* many," Fielding says. The applause begins, the background music comes up, and Fielding trots out onto the stage, puffing slightly

"One, two, three—" and he is into it, catching the chords just right, belting out a number from *Magical Mystery Tour*. He is right, he is on, he is John Lennon just as he always wanted to be. The music picks him up and carries him along. When he finishes, a river of applause bursts over the stage from the vast amphitheater and Fielding grins crazily to himself. It feels exactly the way he always thought it would. His heart pounds.

He goes directly into a slow ballad from the *Imagine* album to calm them down. He is swimming in the lights and the 3D snouts zoom in and out, bracketing his image from every conceivable direction. At the end of the number somebody yells from the audience, "You're radiating on all your eigenfrequencies!" And Fielding nods, grins, feels the warmth of it all wash over him.

"Thrilled to the gills," he says into the microphone.

The crowd chuckles and stirs.

When he does one of the last Lennon numbers, "The Ego-Bird Flies," the augmented sound seeps out from the stage and explodes over the audience. Fielding is euphoric. He dances as though someone is firing pistols at his feet.

He does cuts from *Beatles '65, Help!, Rubber Soul, Let It Be*—all with technical backing spliced in from the original tracks, Fielding providing only Lennon's vocals and instrumentals. Classical scholars have pored over the original material, deciding who did which guitar riff, which tenor line was McCartney's, dissecting the works as though they were salamanders under a knife. But Fielding doesn't care, as long as they let him play and sing. He does another number, then another, and finally they must carry him from the stage. It is the happiest moment he has ever known.

"But I don't understand what Boss 30 radio means," Hermann says.

"Thirty most popular songs."

"But why today?"

"Me."

"They call you a 'sonic boom sensation'—that is another phrase from your time?"

"Dead on. Fellow is following me around now, picking my brains for details. Part of his thesis, he says."

"But it is such noise—"

"Why, that's a crock, Hermann. Look, you chaps have such a small population, so bloody few creative people. What do you expect? Anybody with energy and drive can make it in this world. And I come from a time that was dynamic, that really got off."

"Barbarians at the gates," Hermann says.

"That's what *Reader's Digest* said, too," Fielding murmurs.

After one of his concerts in Australia, Fielding finds a girl waiting for him outside. He goes home with her—it seems the thing to do, considering—and finds there have been few technical advances, if any, in this field either. It is the standard, ten-toes-up, ten-toes-down position she prefers, nothing unusual, noting *à la carte*. But he likes her legs, he relishes her beehive hair and heavy mouth. He takes her along; she has nothing else to do.

On an off day, in what is left of India, she takes him to a museum. She shows him the first airplane (a piper cub), the original manuscript of the great collaboration between Buckminster Fuller and Hemingway, a delicate print of *The Fifty-Three Stations of the Takaido Road* from Japan.

"Oh yes," Fielding says. "We won that war, you know."

(He should not seem to be more than he is.)

Fielding hopes they don't discover, with all this burrowing in the old records, that he had the original Lennon killed. He argues with himself that it really was necessary. He couldn't possibly cover his story in the future if Lennon kept on living. The historical facts would not jibe. It was hard enough to convince Immortality Incorporated that even someone as rich as Lennon would be able to forge records and change fingerprints—they had checked that to escape the authorities. Well, Fielding thinks, Lennon was no loss by 1988 anyway. It was pure accident that Fielding and Lennon had been born in the same year, but that didn't mean that Fielding couldn't take advantage of the circumstances. He wasn't worth over ten million fixed 1985 dollars for nothing.

At one of his concerts he says to the audience between numbers, "Don't look back—you'll just see your mistakes." It sounds like something Lennon would have said. The audience seems to like it.

Press Conference.

"And why did you take a second wife, Mr. Lennon, and then a third?" In 2180 (or 2108) divorce is frowned upon. Yoko Ono is still the Beatle nemesis.

Fielding pauses and then says, "Adultery is the application of democracy to love." He does not tell them the line is from H. L. Mencken.

He has gotten used to the women now. "Just cast them aside like sucked oranges," Fielding mutters to himself. It is a delicious moment. He had never been very successful with women before, even with all his money.

He strides through the yellow curved streets, walking lightly on the earth. A young girl passes, winks.

Fielding calls after her, "Sic transit, Gloria!"

It is his own line, not a copy from Lennon. He feels a heady rush of joy. He is into it, the ideas flash through his mind spontaneously. He is doing Lennon.

Thus, when Hermann comes to tell him that Paul McCartney has been revived by the Society for Dissipative Anachronisms, the body discovered in a private vault in England, at first it does not register with Fielding. Lines of postcoital depression flicker across his otherwise untroubled brow. He rolls out of bed and stands watching a wave turn to white foam on the beach at La Jolla. He is in Nanking. It is midnight.

"Me old bud, then?" he manages to say, getting the lilt into the voice still. He adjusts his granny glasses. Rising anxiety stirs in this throat. "My, my . . ."

It takes weeks to defrost McCartney. He had died much later than Lennon, plump and prosperous, the greatest pop star of all time—or at least the biggest moneymaker. "Same thing," Fielding mutters to himself.

When Paul's cancer is sponged away and the sluggish organs palped to life, the world media press for a meeting.

"For what?" Fielding is nonchalant. "It's not as though we were ever reconciled, y'know. We got a *divorce*, Hermann."

"Can't you put that aside?"

"For a fat old slug who pro'bly danced on me grave?"

"No such thing occurred. There are videotapes, and Mr. McCartney was most polite."

"God, a future where everyone's literal! I *told* you I was a nasty type, why can't you simply accept—"

"It is arranged," Hermann says firmly. "You must go. Overcome your antagonism."

Fear clutches at Fielding.

McCartney is puffy, jowly, but his eyes crackle with intelligence. The years have not fogged his quickness. Fielding has arranged the meeting away from crowds, at a forest resort. Attendants help McCartney into the hushed room. An expectant pause.

"You want to join me band?" Fielding says brightly. It is the only quotation he can remember that seems to fit; Lennon had said that when they first met.

McCartney blinks, peers nearsightedly at him. "D'you really need another guitar?"

"Whatever noisemaker's your fancy."

"Okay."

"You're hired, lad."

They shake hands with mock seriousness. The spectators—who have paid dearly for their tickets—applaud loudly. McCartney smiles, embraces Fielding and then sneezes.

"Been cold lately," Fielding says. A ripple of laughter.

McCartney is offhand, bemused by the world he has entered. His manner is confident, interested. He seems to accept Fielding automatically. He makes a few jokes, as light and inconsequential as his post-Beatles music.

Fielding watches him closely, feeling an awe he had not expected. *That's him. Paul. The real thing.* He starts to ask something and realizes that it is a dumb, out-of-character, fan-type question. He is being betrayed by his instincts. He will have to be careful.

Later, they go for a walk in the woods. The attendants hover a hundred meters behind, portable med units at the ready. They are worried about McCartney's cold. This is the first moment they have been beyond earshot of others. Fielding feels his pulse rising. "You okay?" he asks the puffing McCartney.

"Still a bit dizzy, I am. Never thought it'd work, really."

"The freezing, it gets into your bones."

"Strange place. Clean, like Switzerland."

"Yeah. Peaceful. They're mad for us here."

"You meant that about your band?"

"Sure. Your fingers'll thaw out. Fat as they are, they'll still get around a guitar string."

"Ummm. Wonder if George is tucked away in an ice cube somewhere?"

"Hadn't thought." The idea fills Fielding with terror.

"Could ask about Ringo, too."

"Recreate the whole thing? I was against that. Dunno if I still am." Best to be noncommittal. He would love to meet them, sure, but his chances of bringing this off day by day, in the company of all three of them . . . He frowns.

McCartney's pink cheeks glow from the exercise. The eyes are bright, active, studying Fielding. "Did you think it would work? Really?"

"The freezing? Well, what's to lose? I said to Yoko, I said—"

"No, not the freezing. I mean this impersonation you're carrying off."

Fielding reels away, smacks into a pine tree. "What? What?"

"C'mon, you're not John."

A strangled cry erupts from Fielding's throat. "But . . . how . . ."

"Just not the same, is all."

Fielding's mouth opens, but he can say nothing. He has failed. Tripped up by some nuance, some trick phrase he should've responded to—

"Of course," McCartney says urbanely, "you don't know for sure if I'm the real one either, do you?"

Fielding stutters, "If, if, what're you saying, I—"

"Or I could even be a ringer planted by Hermann, eh? To test you out? In that case, you've responded the wrong way. Should've stayed in character, John."

"Could be this, could be that—what the hell you saying? Who *are* you?" Anger flashes through him. A trick, a maze of choices, possibilities that he had not considered. The forest whirls around him, McCartney leers at his confusion, bright spokes of sunlight pierce his eyes, he feels himself falling, collapsing, the pine trees wither, colors drain away, blue to pink to gray—

He is watching a blank dark wall, smelling nothing, no tremor through his skin, no wet touch of damp air. Sliding infinite silence. The world is black.

—Flat black, Fielding adds, like we used to say in Liverpool.

—Liverpool? He was never in Liverpool. That was a lie, too—

—And he knows instantly what he is. The truth skewers him.

Hello, you still operable?

Fielding rummages through shards of cold electrical memory and finds himself. He is not Fielding, he is a simulation. He is Fielding Prime.

Hey, you in there. It's me, the real Fielding. Don't worry about security, I'm the only one here.

Fielding Prime feels through his circuits and discovers a way to talk. "Yes, yes, I hear."

I made the computer people go away. We can talk.

"I—I see." Fielding Prime sends out feelers, searching for his sensory receptors. He finds a dim red light and wills it to grow brighter. The image swells and ripples, then forms into a picture of a sour-faced man in his middle fifties. It is Fielding Real.

Ah, Fielding Prime thinks to himself in the metallic vastness, he's older than I am. Maybe making me younger was some sort of self-flattery, either by him or his programmers. But the older man had gotten someone to work on his face. It was very much like Lennon's but with heavy jowls, a thicker mustache and balding some. The gray sideburns didn't look quite right but perhaps that is the style now.

The McCartney thing, you couldn't handle it.

"I got confused. It never occurred to me there'd be anyone I knew revived. I hadn't a clue what to say."

Well, no matter. The earlier simulations, the ones before you, they didn't even get that far. I had my men throw in that McCartney thing as a test. Not much chance it would occur, anyway, but I wanted to allow for it.

"Why?"

What? Oh, you don't know, do you? I'm sinking all this money into psychoanalytical computer models so I can see if this plan of mine would work. I mean whether I could cope with the problems and deceive Immortality Incorporated.

Fielding Prime felt a shiver of fear. He needed to stall for time, to think this through. "Wouldn't it be easier to bribe enough people now? You could have your body frozen and listed as John Lennon from the start."

No, their security is too good. I tried that.

"There's something I noticed," Fielding Prime said, his mind racing. "Nobody ever mentioned why I was unfrozen."

Oh, yes, that's right. Minor detail. I'll make a note about that—maybe cancer or congestive heart failure, something that won't be too hard to fix up within a few decades.

"Do you want it that soon? There would still be a lot of people who knew Lennon."

Oh, that's a good point. I'll talk to the doctor about it.

"You really care that much about being John Lennon?"

Why sure. Fielding Real's voice carried a note of surprise. *Don't you feel it too? If you're a true simulation you've got to feel that.*

"I do have a touch of it, yes."

They took the graphs and traces right out of my subcortical.

"It was great, magnificent. Really a lark. What came through was the music, doing it out. It sweeps up and takes hold of you."

Yeah, really? Damn, you know, I think it's going to work.

"With more planning—"

Planning, hell. I'm going. Fielding Real's face crinkled with anticipation.

"You're going to need help."

Hell, that's the whole point of having you, to check it out beforehand. I'll be all alone up there.

"Not if you take me with you."

Take you? You're just a bunch of germanium and copper.

"Leave me here. Pay for my files and memory to stay active."

For what?

"Hook me into a news service. Give me access to libraries. When you're unfrozen I can give you backup information and advice as soon as you can reach a terminal. With your money, that wouldn't be too hard. Hell, I could even take care of your money. Do some trading, maybe move your accounts out of countries before they fold up."

Fielding Real pursed his lips. He thought for a moment and looked shrewdly at the visual receptor. *That sort of makes sense. I could trust your judgment—it's mine, after all. I can believe myself, right? Yes, yes . . .*

"You're going to need company." Fielding Prime says nothing more. Best to stand pat with his hand and not push him too hard.

I think I'll do it. Fielding Real's face brightens. His eyes take on a fanatic gleam. *You and me. I know it's going to work, now!*

Fielding Real burbles on and Fielding Prime listens dutifully to him, making the right responses without effort. After all, he knows the other man's mind. It is easy to manipulate him, to play the game of ice and steel.

Far back, away from where Fielding Real's programmers could sense it, Fielding Prime smiles inwardly (the only way he could). It will be a century, at least. He will sit here monitoring data, input and output, the infinite dance of electrons. Better than death, far better. And there may be new developments, a way to transfer computer constructs to real bodies. Hell, anything could happen.

Boy, it's cost me a fortune to do this. A bundle. Bribing people to keep it secret, shifting the accounts so the Feds wouldn't know—and you cost the most. You're the best simulation ever developed, you realize that? Full consciousness, they say.

"Quite so."

Let him worry about his money—just so there was some left. The poor simple bastard thought he could trust Fielding Prime. He thought they were the same person. But Fielding Prime had played the chords, smelled the future, lived a vivid life of his own. He was older, wiser. He had felt the love of the crowd wash over him, been at the focal point of time. To him Fielding Real was just somebody else, and all his knife-sharp instincts could come to bear.

How was it? What was it like? I can see how you responded by running your tapes for a few sigmas. But I can't order a complete scan without wiping your personality matrix. Can't you tell me? How did it feel?

Fielding Prime tells him something, anything, whatever will keep the older man's attention. He speaks of ample-thighed girls, of being at the center of it all.

Did you really? God!

Fielding Prime spins him a tale.

He is running cool and smooth. He is radiating on all his eigenfrequencies. *Ah* and *ah.*

Yes, that is a good idea. After Fielding Real is gone, his accountants will suddenly discover a large sum left for scientific research into man-machine linkages. With a century to work, Fielding Prime can find a way out of this computer prison. He can become somebody else.

Not Lennon, no. He owed that much to Fielding Real.

Anyway, he had already lived through that. The Beatles' music was quite all right, but doing it once had made it seem less enticing. Hermann was right. The music was too simple-minded, it lacked depth.

He is ready for something more. He has access to information storage, tapes, consultant help from outside, all the libraries of the planet. He will study. He will train. In a century he can be anything. Ah, he will echo down the infinite reeling halls of time.

John Lennon, hell. He will become Wolfgang Amadeus Mozart.

A TUPOLEV TOO FAR

Brian W. Aldiss

Brian W. Aldiss has been one of the giants of SF from the 1950s to the present. His classic stature depends on such novels as *Hothouse*, the *Helliconia* trilogy, *Frankenstein Unbound*, and such fine critical works as *Billion Year Spree* and (cowritten with David Wingrove) *Trillion Year Spree*. He continues to produce lively new stories that stretch the boundaries of SF in each decade.

I know you want fiction for this anthology, but perhaps for once you would consider a true story. I offer a thought in extenuation for what is to follow: that this story is so fantastic and unbelievable it might as well be science fiction.

Well, it would be SF except for the fact that there is no scientific explanation for the bizarre central occurrence—or none beyond the way bizarre events occur with regularity, as vouched for by Charles Fort, Arthur Koestler, Carl Jung, Jesus Christ, and other historic figures.

Unfortunately, the story is not only bizarre but raunchy. It is the sort of tale men tell each other late at night, in a bar in Helsinki or somewhere similar. It has no moral and precious little morality.

Sex and lust come into it. And murder and incest and brigandage of the worst sort. There are some insights to be gleaned regarding the differing natures of men and women, if that is any consolation.

Another thing I have to add. This is not my story. I heard it from a friend. One of those friends you know off and on throughout life. He always enjoyed talking about the bad times.

We'll call him Ron Wallace. And this is what he told me.

This helping of agony took place in 1989, which had turned out to be a better year for Ron that he expected—and for much of Europe. He had been unemployed for a while. Now he had a good job with a West Country firm who made safes and security equipment employing the latest electronic devices. Ron was their overseas salesman. The Russians approached his company, who were sending Ron out to Moscow as a result. The managing director, who was a good guy, briefed Ron before he left, and he set off on the flight from Penge Airport in good fettle. His wife, Stephanie, saw him off.

Ron flew Royal Russian Airlines. Which, after TransAm, is regarded as the world's best airline. Plenty of leg room, little engine noise, pretty hostesses.

It was a brief flight. On the way, he picked up an in-flight magazine which had an illustrated article on the Russian Commonwealth and on modern Moscow in particular. There were photographs of Czar Nicholas III with the Czarina opening the grand new Governance of Nations building, designed by Richard Rogers, on White Square, and of the redecorated Metro in St. Petersburg. Ron dozed off while leafing through such commonplaces and was woken by a terrific bang.

The aircraft was passing through a ferocious storm, or so it seemed. Lightning flashed outside and the airliner began to fall. It shook violently as it fell.

Ron sat tight. He remembered his grandfather's account of the terrible firestorm which had partially destroyed Berlin in July 1914. His grandfather had been working in Berlin at the time and always talked about the experience. The old man claimed that was the first occasion on which all Europe had united in a major rescue operation; it had changed history, he claimed.

These thoughts and less pleasant ones ran through Ron's mind as the plane fell earthwards.

"I'll never screw Steff again—or any other woman," he said aloud. To his mind, that was the biggest bugbear regarding death: no screwing.

For an instant the plane was bathed in unnatural light. Then all became calm, as if nothing had happened.

The plane pulled from its dive. Cabin staff in their white uniforms moved down the aisles, soothing the passengers and bringing them drinks.

Everyone started talking to each other. But only for a few minutes. After which, a silence fell over them; they became uncannily quiet as they tried to digest their narrow escape from disaster.

Twenty minutes later, they landed at Sheremeteivo Airport.

Ron was surprised to find how drab and small everything was. He was surprised, too, to see how many men were in uniform—unfamiliar uniforms, too, with mysterious red stars on their caps. He had no idea what the stars stood for, unless for Mars, on which planet the Russians had just landed.

Of course, Ron had got down as much whisky as he could, following the alarming incident on the plane. His perceptions were possibly a little awry. All the same, he could not help noticing that most of the planes on the ground belonged to an airline called Aeroflot, of which he had never heard. There were no Royal Russian Airline planes to be seen.

When, at the luggage carousel, he asked a fellow passenger about Aeroflot, the man replied, "You ask too many questions round here, you find yourself in the gulag."

Ron began to feel rather cold and shaky. Something had happened. He did not know what.

The whole airport, the reception area, the customs area, gave no sign of the high-tech sheen for which Russia was renowned. He felt a sense of disorientation, which was calmed slightly when he was met by his Russian contact, Vassili Rugorsky, who made him welcome.

As they passed out through the foyer of the building, Ron observed a large framed portrait dominating the exits where he might have expected to see a picture of the graceful young Czar. Instead, the portrait showed a thick-set, almost neckless man with glittering eyes, a mottled complexion, and an unpleasant expression.

"Who's that?" he asked.

Vassili looked curiously at Ron, as if expecting him to be joking.

"Comrade Leonid Brezhnev, of course," he said.

Ron dared ask nothing more, but his sense of unease deepened. Who was Brezhnev?

He was shown to a black car. Soon they were driving through the city. Ron could hardly believe what he saw. Moscow was always billed as one of Europe's great pleasure cities, with smart people, and a vivid nightlife staged amid elegant buildings—fruit of Russia's great renaissance in the early 1940s, when the Czarina Elizabeta Ship Canal had linked Baltic and Black Sea. Here Parisian panache thrived among Parisian-type boulevards. Or so the legend had it. As they wound through a dreary suburb, he saw lines of dowdy people queueing at shops hardly worthy of the name. The buildings themselves were gray and grubby.

Red flags and banners flew everywhere. He could not understand. It was as if the whole place had been hit by revolution.

But the men he dealt with were agreeable enough. Ron prided himself on his powers of negotiation; his opposite numbers were cautious but amiable. He gathered to his mild astonishment that they regarded British technology to be in advance of their own.

"Of course, the KGB have all latest Western equipment," one man said jokingly as the contracts were signed. Ron did not like to ask what KGB stood for; he was clearly expected to know. It was all peculiar. He wondered if the electric storm he had flown through had affected his mind in some way.

It was on his second day that the contracts were signed. The first day was given over to discussion, when Ron often felt that the Russians were pumping him. At one point, when he had occasion to mention the Czarina Elizabeta Ship Canal, they all looked blank.

Even more disconcertingly, the Russians asked him how he liked being in the Soviet Union, and similar remarks. Ron belonged to an electronics union himself, but had never heard of a Soviet Union. He could almost fancy he had arrived in the wrong country.

Nevertheless, the contracts were signed on the second day, on terms favorable to Ron's company. They were witnessed in the ministry at three in the afternoon, following which the parties involved got down to some serious drinking. As well as Russian champagne there were vodka, wine, and a good Georgian brandy. Ron was an experienced drinker. He arrived back at the Hotel Moskva, contract in briefcase, just after 6:30, still more or less in control of his wits.

'm trying to tell you this story as Ron Wallace told it to me. When he came to describe the Hotel Moskva I had to interrupt him. I've stayed in that hotel a couple of times. Once I took the Camberwell–Moscow Trans-Continent Express on a package tour which included three nights in that very hotel. It was the pleasantest place in which I have ever stayed, light and airy, and full of elegant people. In fact, a few too many of the Russian aristocracy for my simple tastes.

It was not the dowdiness and gloom of the hotel about which Ron chiefly complained, or the uninteresting food, but the lack of beautiful women. Ron was always rather a ladies' man.

An old-fashioned band was playing old-fashioned music in the hotel restaurant. It was a period piece, like the hotel itself. He could not credit it. The dining room was cavernous, with stained-glass windows at one end, and a faded style of furnishing. The band lurched from Beatles' hits to the "Destiny" waltz. The place, he said, was a cross between the Café Royal in the 1920s and Salisbury Cathedral in the 1420s.

As Ron told his tale, I kept thinking about the concept of alternative worlds. Although the idea is at first fantastic, there is, after all, a well-attested theory which says that whatever is imagined moves nearer to reality. Edmund Husserl, in his pioneering work on phenomenology, *Investigations in Logic*, shows how little the psychological nature of historical processes are understood. Turning points in history—generatives, in Husserl's term—occur in greater or lesser modes related to quantal thought impulses which are themselves subject to random factors. The logical structures on which such points depend exist independently of their psychological correlates, so that we can expect subjective experiences to generate a multiplicity of effects, each of which bears equivalent objective reality; thus, whether or not signatures are appended to a treaty, for example, is dependent on various epistemological assumptions of transient nature, while the results of signing or non-signing may be multiplex generatives, giving rise to a spectrum of alternative objectivities, varying from slight to immense, affecting the lives of many people over considerable areas of space and time. I know this to be so because I read it in a book.

So it seemed clear to me—though not to Ron, who is no intellectual and consequently does not believe in variant subjective realities—that the electric storm which hit the Tupolev had been a Husserl's generative, causing Ron to switch objectivities, and materialize in a parallel version of objectivity along the spectrum, where history had at some point taken a decided turn for the worse.

Feeling a little weary, Ron decided not to go up to his room immediately, but to eat and then retreat to bed, in preparation for his early flight home the following morning.

Diners were few. They could scarcely be distinguished from the diners in a provincial Pan-European town, Belgrade, say, or Boheimkirchen, or Bergen. There was none of the glitter he had expected. And the service was terribly slow.

The maître d' had shown Ron to a small table, rather distant from the nearest light globe. From this vantage point, he looked the clientele over while awaiting his soup.

At the table nearest to him, two orientals sat drinking champagne. Their mood was subdued. He judged them to be Korean. Ron spared hardly a glance for the man. As he told me, "I could hardly take my eyes off the woman. Mainly I saw her in half-profile. A real beauty, clear-cut features, hawkish nose, dark eyes, red lips . . . Terrific."

When she smiled at her partner and raised her glass to her lips she was a vision of seduction. Ron dropped his napkin on the floor in order to take a look at her legs. She was wearing a long black evening dress.

He said his one thought was, "If only her husband would get lost . . ."

His desires turned naturally to sex. But he had sworn an oath to his wife Steff, on the subject of fidelity. As he was averting his eyes from the Korean cou ple, the woman turned to look at him. Even across the space between their tables, the stare was strong and disturbing. Ron could not tell what was in that stare. It made him curious, while at the same time repelling him.

He took a paperback book of crossword puzzles from his briefcase and tried to study a puzzle he had already started, but could not concentrate.

A memory came back to him of his first love. Then, how innocent had been her gaze. He could recall it perfectly. It had been a gaze of love and trust; all the sweetness of youth, of innocence, was in it. It could not be recovered. No one would ever look at him in that fashion again.

The Korean couple had decided something between them. The Korean man rose from the table, laid down his napkin, and came across to Ron.

"My God," Ron thought, "the little bugger's going to tell me not to ogle his wife. . . ."

The Korean was short and sturdy. Perhaps he was in his midthirties. His face was solemn, his eyes dark, his whole body held rigidly, and it was a rigid bow he made to Ron Wallace.

"You are English?" he asked, speaking in English with a heavy accent. "We saw you dining here last night and made enquiries. I am on official duties in the Soviet Union, a diplomat from the Democratic People's Republic of North Korea." He gave his name.

"What do you want? I'm having dinner."

"Meals are a source of fear to me. I can never rid my mind of one dinner in particular when I was a child of five. Someone from political motives poisoned my father. A servant was held responsible, but we never found out who was paying the servant. The servant did not tell, despite severe torture. My father rose from his place, screamed like a wounded horse, spun about, and fell headfirst into a dish—well, in our dialect it's *pruang hai,* I suppose a sort of kedgeree, though with little green chilies. He struggled a moment, sending rice all over us frightened children. Then he was still, and naturally the meal was ruined."

Ron Wallace took a sip of mineral water. Although the Korean was white and trembling, Ron would not ask him to sit down.

The Korean continued. "I should explain that there were four of us children. Three of us were triplets, and there was a younger sibling. My mother was demoralized by my father's death. I have to confess she was of the bourgeois class. Never a very stable personality, for she was an actress, she suffered illusions. One starry night, she jumped from a tall window through the glass roof of the conservatory to the ground. A theory was that she had seen the stars reflected in the glass and thought the conservatory was the Yalu River. This was never proved.

"We children were handed over into the care of an uncle and aunt who ran a rather poor pig and sorghum farm in the mountainous area of our land. My uncle was a bully, given to drink and criminality. He committed sexual atrocities on us poor defenseless children, and even on his farm animals. You can imagine how we suffered."

He looked fixedly at Ron, but Ron made no reply. Ron was aware of the avid gaze of the Korean's partner, back at the table, smiling yet not smiling in his direction.

"Our one consolation was the school to which we were sent. It was a long walk away, down the mountain, a cruel trial for us in winter months when the snow was deep. But the school was run by a remarkable Englishman, a Mr.

Holmberg. I have been told that Holmberg is not an English name. I cannot explain how that came about. In the world struggle, there are many anomalies.

"Mr. Holmberg had many skills and was unfailingly kind. He taught us something of the world. He also explained to us the mysteries of sex, and kindly drew pictures of the female sexual organs on the blackboard, with the fallopian tubes in red, despite a shortage of chalk.

"The day came when the ninth birthday approached for us three poor orphans. There we sat in the little classroom, stinking of sorghum and pigs, and this wonderful Englishman presented us with a marvelous gift, a kite he had made himself. It was such a kite as Koreans made in dynastic times to carry the spirits of the dead, very strong, very large and well decorated. It was, for us, the first gift we had received since our father was poisoned. You can imagine our delight."

He paused.

"Where's my bloody boeuf stroganoff?" asked Ron, looking round for a waitress.

Greatly though he desired something to eat, he desired much more the absence of this little man who stood by his table, telling his awful life story unbidden. Ron had never heard of the Democratic People's Republic of North Korea, and did not much want to. It was another department of the terrible world into which he had fallen.

He tried to think of pleasant English things—Ovaltine, Bob Monkhouse, cream teas, Southend, the National Anthem, Agatha Christie, the *Sun*, Saxby's pork pies—but they were drowned out by the Korean's doomed narrative.

"We had a problem. We feared that our cruel uncle would steal the kite from us. We resolved to fly it on the way home from school, to enjoy that pleasure at least once. Halfway up the mountain was a good eminence, with a view of the distant ocean and a strong updraught. The three of us hung on to the string and up went the grand kite, sailing into the sky. How we cheered. Just for a moment, we had no cares.

"Our little brother begged to be allowed to hold the kite. As we handed him the string, we heard the sound of shots being fired farther up the mountain. Our anxieties were easily awoken. In those lawless times, bandits were everywhere. Alas, one can pay for one moment's carelessness with a lifetime's regret. We turned to find that the kite was carrying away our little brother. His hand was caught in the loop in the string and up he was going. He cried. We cried. We waved.

"Helpless, we watched him about to be dashed against the rocks. Fortunately, he cleared them as the kite gained height. It drifted towards the northeast, and the ocean and southeastern coast of the Soviet Union. That was the last we saw of him. It is not impossible that even now he lives, and speaks and thinks in the Russian language."

The Korean bowed his head for a moment, while Ron tried to attract the attention of a distant waitress, who had lapsed into immobility, as if also overcome by the tragic tale.

"We were upset by this incident. We had lost our valued gift, and a rather annoying little brother as well. We fell to punching each other, each claiming the other two were to blame. Then we went home, up the rest of the mountain track.

"My uncle was in his favorite apple tree, quiet for once and not swearing at us. He hung head down, a rope round his ankles securing him to one of the branches of the tree. His hands were tied and he was fiercely gagged. His face was so red that we burst out laughing.

"Since he was still alive, we had a splendid time spinning him round. He could not cry out but he looked pretty funny. Then we got rakes and spades from the shed and battered him to death.

"Our aunt had been thrown in the pond. Many and dreadful were the atrocities committed on her body. We dragged her from the water but, so near to death was she, we put her back where we had found her.

"The house had been looted by the bandits whose firing we had heard. Those were lawless days before our great leader, Kim Il Sung, took over control of our destinies. We were happy to have the place to ourselves, especially since my uncle's two huge sons had been shot, bayoneted and beheaded by the bandits.

"Unfortunately, the bandits returned in the night, since it had begun to rain. They came for shelter. They found us asleep, tied the three of us up, put us in a foul dung cart, and promised to sell us for slaves to a foreign power in the market of Yuman-dong. Next morning, down the mountain we bumped. More rain fell. The monsoon came on in full force. We were crossing a wooden bridge over a river when a great rush of water struck the bridge.

"The bandits were thrown into confusion or drowned. We were better off in the cart, which floated, and we managed to get free.

"We ran to Yuman-dong for safety, since we had another uncle there. He took us in with protestations of affection, and his elder daughter fed us. Unfortunately, the town was the headquarters of the brigands, as we soon discovered. My uncle was the biggest brigand. The three of us children were made to work at the degrading business of carting night soil from the village and spreading it on the fields. You can imagine our humiliation."

The Korean shook his head sadly and searched Ron's face for signs of compassion.

"Where's my bloody food?" Ron asked.

"But fortune was as ever on our side. It was then that our great leader, Kim Il Sung, became President of our people's republic. My uncle was awarded the post of local commissar, since in his career of bandit he had harassed rich oppressor landlords such as my late uncle and aunt up in the mountain. Much celebration followed this event and everyone in the village remained totally drunk for twenty-one days, including the dogs. Three died. Maybe four. It was during this period of joy that a dog bit off the left ear of one of my brothers.

"Those were happy times. Under my uncle we marched from farm to farm along the valley, beating up the farmers, threatening and exhorting the workers. There was nothing we would not do for the Cause. Unfortunately, much misery was to follow."

"Don't tell me—let me guess," murmured Ron Wallace.

"But you cannot guess what befell us triplets. It was discovered after many years that the brother who had lost an ear was a capitalist running dog and had been associating secretly with the enemies of the state, who varied from time to time. Sometimes the enemies were Chinese, sometimes Russians. My brother had associated with all of them. I felt bound to denounce him myself, and his wife. A terrible vendetta of blood then started—"

In desperation, Ron stood up, waving his book and crossword puzzles. "Sorry," he said. "I have to finish this page. It is a secret code. I am employed by MI_5."

"I appreciate your feelings," said the Korean, standing rigid. "We must all exercise our duties. However, I tell you something of my history for a reason. The remarkable Englishman, Mr. Holmberg, who taught me at school, stays ever in my mind as an example of decency, morality, fairness, and liberalism. It is no less than the truth to say that I have modeled my life on him.

"Unfortunately, however, during the revolutionary times of the Flying Horse movement, it was necessary to have Mr. Holmberg shot. A tribunal convicted him of being a foreigner in wartime. To me befell the honor of carrying out the execution with my own hands. I have a small souvenir for his family back in England which I wish you to carry home to present to them. Please come to my table and I shall give it to you, concealed in a copy of *Pravda*."

Ron Wallace hesitated only for a moment. All he wanted was his dinner. But if he went over to this madman's table, he would be able to snatch a closer look at his companion. He rose.

At the Korean table sat the remarkable person with the bright-red lips and shoulder-length black hair. The full-length gown swept to the floor. Diamonds sparkled at the smooth neck. A cigarette in a holder sent a trail of smoke ceilingwards from a bejewelled right hand. A look of black intensity was fixed on Ron. He bowed.

"I'm pleased to meet your wife," he said to the North Korean.

"My brother." The Korean corrected him. "My sole surviving brother. Here is the souvenir for the Holmberg family—in fact for the small daughter of the son of the man I knew, who was convicted of the crime against the state. Her address is enclosed. Please take it, deliver it faithfully."

Ron had been expecting to receive the head of the late Mr. Holmberg, but it was a smaller object which the Korean passed over, easily rolled inside a copy of *Pravda*. He bowed again, shook hands with the Korean, smiled at his brother, who gave him a winning smile in return, and returned to his table. A waitress was delivering a boeuf stroganoff to his place.

"Thank you," he said. "Bring me another bottle of wine and a bottle of mineral water."

"Immediately," she said. But she paused for a second before leaving the table.

Setting the newspaper between his stomach and the table, Ron unrolled it. Inside lay a wooden doll with plaits, a savage grin painted on its wooden face. It wore traditional dress of red and white. Tied round its neck was a label on which was written the name Doreen Holmberg and an address in Surrey. He rolled it up in the paper again and shut it in his briefcase.

He began to eat without appetite the dish the waitress had brought, forking mouthfuls slowly between his lips, staring over the bleak reaches of the restaurant permeated by the strains of "Yesterday," and avoiding any glance towards the Korean table. He sighed. It would be a relief to get home to his wife, although he had some problems there.

The waitress returned with the two bottles of wine and mineral water on a tray. She could be sighted first behind a carved wooden screen which partly hid the entrance to the kitchens. Then she was observed behind a large aspidistra. Then she hove into full view, walking towards Ron's table, a thin middle-aged woman with straggling dyed hair.

He had been too preoccupied with the Koreans to pay the waitress any attention. As he scrutinized her in the way he scrutinized anything female, he saw that her gaze was fixed on him, not with the usual weary indifference characteristic of a waitress towards diners, but in a curious and not unfriendly fashion. He straightened slightly in his chair.

She set the bottles down on the table. Was there something suggestive in the way she fingered the neck of the wine bottle before uncorking it? She poured him a glass of the wine and a glass of the mineral water in slow motion. He caught a whiff of her underarm odor as she came near. Her hip brushed against his arm.

"You're imagining things," he said to himself.

He raised the wine glass to his lips and looked at her.

"Enjoy it please," she said in English, and turned away.

She was tired and in her late thirties, he judged. Not much of a bottom. Not really an attractive proposition. Besides, a waitress in a Russian hotel restaurant . . .

However, after a few more mouthfuls of the stroganoff, he summoned her across the room on the pretext of ordering a bread roll. She came readily enough, but he saw in the language of her angular body an independence of mind not yet eroded of all geniality. A spark of intent lit in his brain. He knew that spark. It could so easily be fanned into flame.

She did look worn. Her face was weathered, the flesh lifeless and dry, with strong lines moving downwards on either side of thin lips. Nothing to recommend her. Yet the expression on her face, the light gray eyes—somehow, he liked what he saw. Out of that ugly dress, those hideous shoes, she would be more attractive. His imagination ran ahead of him. He felt an erection stirring in his trousers.

Her breasts were not very noticeable as she bent to place the bread by Ron's side. No doubt she ate scraps in the kitchen off people's plates. A fatty diet. No doubt she had taken orders all her life. It was a matter of speculation as to what her private life could be.

He asked her if she ever did crosswords.

The shake of her head was contemptuous. Again the whiff of body odor. Possibly she did not understand what he said. She smiled a little. Her teeth were irregular, but it was an appealing smile.

Watching her hips, her legs, her ugly shoes, as she retreated, he told himself to relax and to think of something that a candle did in a low place, in six letters.

But a long dull evening stretched before him. He hated his own company.

Over the sweet, he extracted a few words from the waitress. She spoke a little German, a little English. She had worked in this hotel for five years. No, she cared nothing about the work. The lipstick she wore was not expertly applied. But there was no doubt that in some measure she was interested in him.

When she brought him a cup of bitter coffee, he said, "Will you come up to my room?"

The waitress shook her head, almost regretfully, as if she had anticipated the question. It did not surprise her; probably she had often been asked the same question by drunken clients.

Her glance went to where the impassive maître d'hotel stood, guardian of his underlings' Soviet morality. No doubt he had awful powers over them. She left Ron's table, to disappear into the kitchens.

Ron looked down at his puzzle.

When she came to pour him a second cup of coffee, he suggested that they went back to her place.

The waitress gave him a long hard look, weighing him up. The look disconcerted him, inasmuch as he felt himself judged. He saw himself sitting there, secure and decently dressed, possessor of foreign currency, about to return to the strange capitalist world from which he had come. Not bad looking. And yet—yet another man out of thousands, with a vacant evening before him, just wanting a bit of fun.

"There is difficulties," she said.

The words told him he was halfway to his desire.

Elation ran through him, not unmixed with a tinge of apprehension. Again, the stirrings of an erection. He told her she was wonderful. He would do anything. He smiled. She frowned. She made a small gesture with her hand: Be quiet. Or, Be patient.

As if she already had her regrets, she left the table hastily, clutching the coffeepot to her chest. Ron observed that she said something to an older waitress as they passed on the way to the kitchens.

Now he had to wait. He tried to think of an uncomplicated curative plant in six letters.

The waitress had disappeared. Perhaps he had, after all, been mistaken. When his impatience got the better of him, he rose to his feet. She appeared and came over. He had a sterling note ready—of a modest denomination, so as not to offend her.

"Where and when?"

Their faces were close. Her foreignness excited him, nor was he repelled by her body odor. She barely responded, barely moved her lips.

"Rear door by the wood hut. Midnight."

"I'll be there."

"Will you?"

He nodded a curt good night to the North Koreans, and retreated with his case to the bar. He sat alone, apart from a group of what he guessed were Swedes, getting heavily drunk in one corner. He had three hours to wait.

Idly, he picked up a newspaper printed in English and started to glance through it. It bewildered him utterly. For a while he entertained the thought that his company was playing an elaborate joke on him.

According to the newspaper, there was no Liberal government in power in Britain. Nor was there any mention of Bernard Mattingly. The Prime Minister, it was said, was a Mrs. Thatcher, head of a Conservative government. This piece of information disturbed him more than anything he had encountered so far. It seemed that the President of the United States was not Alan Stevenson but someone called Ronald Reagan.

In a medical column, he read that the whole world was being ravaged by a sexually transmitted disease called AIDS. Ron had never heard of it. Yet the column claimed that thousands of people were dying of it, in Africa, Europe, and the United States. No cure had been found.

Just as disturbingly, an editorial on disarmament moves appeared to be saying that there had been two wars involving the whole world during the twentieth century.

Ron knew this could not have happened. There was no way in which Albania and Italy or England and Germany—to take two instances—could possibly attempt to destroy each other. What it all meant he did not know.

With a sudden uneasy inspiration, he checked on the date of the newspaper. It read September 1989 clearly enough. The idea had entered his head that he had been caught in a time warp and was back in the early years of the twentieth century, before the days of the reforming Czars. Such was not the case.

He hid the newspaper under the table and clutched his head.

He was going mad. The sooner he got home the better.

After an hour, the Korean couple entered the bar. They ignored him and sat with their backs to him.

He thought of his wife. Their marriage had been a good one. Both had ruined it by their infidelity. Both nourished hurt feelings and a desire to get their own back. One of them was always an infidelity ahead of the other. Yet Steff had remained with him, had put up with all his drunkenness and bullying and failures. Now they had a little place of their own, heavily mortgaged, it was true, and were trying to build a better relationship. Ron had vowed never to hit her again.

The best advice he could give himself was to forget about that slut of a waitress and enjoy a good night's sleep in his comfortless single room. He had to catch the early flight from Moscow's Sheremeteivo Airport, to be in time for an important meeting with Bob Butler, his boss, tomorrow afternoon in Slough. He might get promoted. Steff would be pleased about that. She would also ask if he had been fucking other women.

He could lie his way out of this one, particularly if the promotion to sales manager came through.

Besides, this creature might give him some insight into what was happening. Perhaps she could tell him who Brezhnev was and what KGB stood for.

By this time, Ron—not an imaginative man—began to realize he had somehow got on an alternative possibility track. The shabby city that surrounded him felt heavy with sin—no, with sinfulness. It was as if some terrible crime had been committed which everyone had conspired not to discuss. And this secret had weighed the population down, so that the cheerful Moscow of his own time had sunk down into the earth from human view.

God knows what weird versions of clap the waitress might be carrying round with her. He had no idea what he was getting into.

Still, the thought of a woman's company in this miserable place was greatly attractive.

He tried to look at it all as a great stunt, a caper. How his pals would laugh when he told them. If he ever got back to them.

He smoked cigarettes and eked out a beer. The Swedes grew louder.

Came 11:30, Ron put on his coat, grabbed his case, and went out into the streets. Everywhere seemed dark and depressing. It was as if he had somehow crossed a border between day and night, between yin and yang, between positive and negative.

As he walked along by the Moskva he observed there was none of the cheerful riverside restaurants, no floating pleasure-boats, which he had heard were the center of the city's nightlife. No music, no wine, no women. The river flowed dark between high concrete banks, unloved, neglected, isolated from the life of Moscow, rushing on its secretive dark way. What if I am stuck here alone forever? he asked himself. Isn't there a science of Chaos, and haven't I fallen into it?

It was impossible to know whether the waitress was an escape from or an embodiment of the unreason into which he had fallen.

He turned on his heel and made his way warily down a back alley to the rear of the hotel. A rat scampered, but there were no humans about. He came to an area of broken pavements covered with litter, which he waded through in the dark, cursing as he trod in something soft and deep. He could not see. From a small barred window came an orange fragment of light. Spreading a hand out before him, he arrived against a barrier. Searching carefully with his fingers, he found he was touching wood. Most probably this was the hut the waitress had designated.

Feeling his way, staggering and tripping, he finally reassured himself that he was waiting in the right place. He located the back door of the hotel, tried it, found it locked.

He stood in the dark, cold and uneasy. No stars shone overhead.

Following the sound of tumblers turning in a lock, the hotel door opened. A man emerged and walked off briskly into the night. The door was locked again from the inside; he heard the sound of a bolt being shot. The Russians had a mania for secrecy. So did Ron. He understood.

Several staff emerged from the door in pairs or alone. Worried in case his waitress missed him, Ron stood out from the sheltering hut. Nobody looked in his direction.

A lorry with one headlight jolted along the alley and wheezed to a halt. Two men got out. As Ron shrank back, he saw that one of the men was old and bent, moving painfully as he climbed from the cab. They both began to sort among the rubbish outside the hotel, occasionally throwing something into the back of their vehicle.

The door of the building opened again. Ron's waitress came out. It was ten minutes past midnight. She paused to get her night vision and then walked over to him. He pressed himself against her, feeling her hard body. Neither of them spoke.

With a gesture of caution to Ron, she went over and talked to the men by the lorry. The old man gave a wheezing laugh. There was a brief conversation, during which all three lit cigarettes the waitress distributed. Ron waited impatiently until she returned to his side.

"What's going on?" he asked.

She did not reply, puffing at her cigarette.

After a while, the men were finished with the rubbish. The younger one gave a whistle. The waitress returned the whistle and went forward. Ron followed as

she climbed into the back of the lorry. He had misgivings but he went. They settled themselves down among the trash as the lorry started forward with a lurch.

Once through the maze of back streets, they were driving along a wide thor-
oughfare lit by sodium street lamps. Ron and the waitress stared at each other,
their faces made anonymous in the orange glow. Her face was a mask, centuries
old, her hair hung streakily over her temples. He felt in her a life of hard work,
without pride. The perception warmed him towards her and he put an arm
round her shoulders. He had always loved the downtrodden more than the
proud and beautiful. It accorded with his poor image of himself.

She was slow to return his gesture of affection. Languidly, she moved a leg
against his. He stared down the vanishing street, as once more they turned into
a dark quarter. The excitement of the adventure on which he was now embarked
dulled his apprehension, although he wondered about her relationship with the
two lorry men, speculating whether they would beat him up and rob him at
journey's end. He clutched his briefcase between his knees; it was metal and
would be a useful weapon in a fight.

Here at least he was on familiar ground. Ron was no stranger to fights over
women, and was used to giving a good account of himself. Whatever else had
gone wrong with the universe, some constants remained: the art of getting the
leg over, the swift knee in a rival's goolies. He sang a familiar little song in her
ear:

> *"With moonlight and romance*
> *If you don't seize the chance*
> *To get it on the sly*
> *Your archetype will be awry*
> *As time goes by."*

The waitress gave every appearance of not knowing the words, and silenced
him with a hand over his mouth. They bumped on in silence and discomfort for
a while.

"How far to go?"

"*Ein* kilometer." Holding up one finger.

He tried to observe the route in case he had to walk back. Where would he
turn for help in case of trouble? He did not want to end up in the Moskva. He
had a mad pal in Leeds who had been beaten up and thrown into the canal.

The depressing suburbs through which they passed, where hardly a light
showed, were without visible feature. Flat, closed, bleak, Asiatic façades. At one
point, on a corner, they passed a fight, where half a dozen men were hitting each
other with what might have been pick-helves.

The rumpus vanished into the night. Moscow slept like an ill-fed gourmet,
full of undigested secrets. The lorry stopped abruptly, sending its passengers
sliding among the filth. Ron climbed out fast, ready for trouble, the waitress following. They stood on a broken road surface. Immediately, the lorry bucked
and moved off.

They were isolated in an area of desolation. It was possible to make out an
immense pile of splintered wood, crowned by a bulldozer, where some rough-
looking men sat by the machine, perhaps guarding it, warming themselves
round a wood fire. To Ron's other hand, where a solitary lamp shone, a row of

small concrete houses stood, ending in a shuttered box of a shop which advertised beer. Further away, black against the night sky, silhouettes of tall apartment blocks could be seen. It was towards these blocks that the waitress now led Ron.

The heap of wood and beams was more extensive than he had thought. There were figures standing in it at intervals. It seemed to him that a complete old-fashioned village had been bulldozed to make way for Moscow's sprawl. Homes had been reduced to matchwood.

Someone called out to them, but the waitress made no answer. She led him down a side lane, where the way underfoot was unpaved.

To encourage Ron, she pointed ahead to a looming block of jagged outline. They skirted a low wall and reached the building. She went to a side door, knocked and waited. Ron stood there, staring about him, clutching his case and feeling that he needed a drink.

After a long delay, the door was unbolted, unlocked and dragged open. They went in, and the waitress passed a small package from her coat to a dumpy matron in black. Without changing her expression, the dumpy woman locked and bolted the door behind them and retreated into a small fortified office.

The smell of the place hit Ron as soon as he stepped into the passage. It reminded him of his term in jail. This institution was similar to prison. The smell was a compound of underprivilege, mixing disinfectant, polish, urine, dirt, fatty foods, and general staleness, bred by too many people being confined in an old building.

The waitress led him past noticeboards, battered lockers, and a broken armchair to another corridor, and on to a stairwell. The odors became sharper. They ascended the stairs.

The steps were of pre-cast concrete, the rail of cold metal, and the staircase cared nothing for human frailty. It was carpeted only as far as the first floor. As the waitress ascended beside him, Ron saw the weariness in her step. "Some night this is going to be," he told himself. He placed a hand encouragingly in the small of her back. She grimaced a smile without turning her head.

Smells of laundry, damp sheets, overworked heating appliances came and went. On the upper floors, he listened to a low stratum of noise issuing from behind locked doors. Despite the late hour, several women were wandering about the corridors. None took any notice of Ron and the waitress.

In a side passage the waitress pulled a large key from her coat pocket, unlocked a door, and motioned Ron to go in. As he entered, he saw how scratched and bruised the panels of the door were, almost as if it had been attacked by animals.

The same sense of something under duress was apparent in her room. The furnishings crowded together as if for protection. Every surface was fingered and stained, their overused appearance reinforced by the dim luminance of a forty-watt bulb shining overhead. The murkiest corner was filled by a cupboard on which stood a tin basin; this was the washing alcove. Close by was a one-ring electric stove, much rusted. The greater part of the room was occupied by a bed, covered by a patchwork peasant quilt which provided the one note of color in the room. A crucifix hung by a chain from one of the bedposts. Beside the bed, encroaching on it for lack of space, was a cupboard on top of which cardboard boxes were piled. The only other furniture—there was scarcely room for more—

consisted of a table standing under a narrow and grimy window letting in the dark of the night.

The waitress locked her door and bolted it before crossing to the window and dragging a heavy curtain over it. By the window and under the bed were piled old cigarette cartons, all foreign, from Germany, France, England, China, and the States. He knew instinctively they were empty—probably saved from the hotel refuse bins. Perhaps she liked the foreign names, Philip Morris and the rest. Well. He was up to his neck in the unknown now, and no mistake. Still. Nothing was ever going to be a greater shock than his first day at the orphanage, when he was four.

He was beginning to enjoy the adventure. He said to himself, "Now then, Ronnie, if you can't fight your way out of trouble, you'd better fuck your way out."

He set his case down and pulled off his coat. She hung the coat with hers on a hook behind the door, then went to the cupboard and brought out an unlabelled bottle with two small glasses. She poured clear liquid and passed him a glass. He sniffed. Vodka.

They toasted each other and drank.

He offered her an English cigarette, then handed her the pack. As they lit up, she gave him a smile, looking rather timid. Turning abruptly as if to hide weakness, she recorked her bottle and put it back in the cupboard. That was all he was getting in the way of alcohol.

"An instinctive liking," he said. "I mean, this is how it should be, eh? Friends on sight, right?" They sat side by side on the bed, puffing at their cigarettes; he laid a hand on her meager thigh.

Two cheap reproductions hung on the walls facing them, one of birch forests lost in mist, one of a woman looking out of a deep-set window into a well-lit street. He pointed to it, saying he liked it.

"Frank-land," she said. "Franzosisch."

She threw down her vodka, rose, pulled out a stained and tattered nightdress from under her bolster. It was or had been blue. She smoothed the wrinkles with one hand, while looking at him interrogatively.

"You won't need that," he said, and laughed.

She paused, then threw the garment down on the end of the bed.

Suddenly, in her hesitation, he saw that she considered saying no to him and throwing him out. He dropped his gaze. The decision was hers. He never forced a woman.

Thoughts of Steff came back to him. He remembered the bitterness they went through after his trip a few weeks ago to Lyons in France. Steff had discovered that he had gone with a prostitute. A row had followed, which rumbled on for days. She had poured out hatred, had made the house almost unlivable. In the first throes of her fury, she had coshed him with a frying pan when he was asleep on the sofa. He had become terrified of her and of what she might do next. Finally, he swore that he would never go with other women again.

Yet here he was, settling in with this strange creature with the disgusting nightdress. The little whore in Lyons had been pernickety clean, a beauty in every way. Steff was always clean, always having a shower, washing her hair. This poor bitch had no shower. Her hair looked as if it had never seen shampoo.

Stubbing out her cigarette, the waitress paused by the light, then switched it off. The room was plunged into darkness. She had made up her mind to let him stay. He heard the sounds of her getting undressed, and began to do the same.

As his eyes accustomed themselves to the dark, he saw her clearly by the corridor light shining under the bottom of the door. She pulled off soiled undergarments and threw them on the table. Fanning out, the light shone most strongly on her feet. They were gray and heavily veined, the toes splayed, their nails curved and long like bird claws. He saw they were filthy. They disappeared from view as she threw herself naked on the bed and pulled the quilt over herself.

An icy draught blew under the door. Ron put his clothes neatly on the table, trying to avoid her dirty undergarments, and climbed under the quilt beside her. She lifted her arms and wrapped them round his neck.

A rank odor assailed him, ancient and indecent. It caught in his throat. He almost gagged. It wafted from her, from all parts. She was settling back, opening her legs. He could scarcely breathe.

He sat up. "You'll have to wash yourself," he said. "I can't bear it."

He climbed off the bed again, fanning the air, rather than have her climb over him.

"You not like?" she asked.

When he did not reply, she got up and went on her gray feet over to the basin. Her toenails clicked on the floor covering. She poured water in the basin and commenced washing. He pulled open her cupboard, to drink from her vodka bottle, tipping the stuff down his throat. The waitress made no comment.

She rinsed her armpits and her sexual quarters with a dripping rag, drying herself on a square of towel.

"And the feet," he ordered, pointing.

Meekly, she washed her feet, dragging each up in turn to reach nearer the basin.

This is Ron's story, not mine. But I had to ask myself if there wasn't, in this sordid lie he was telling me, something I deeply envied. I mean, not just the tacky woman, the foul room, the filthy fantasy world of "Brezhnev's Russia," whatever that meant, but the whole desperate situation, something that took a man up wholly. This wish to be consumed. The whole romantic and absurd involvement. A hell. Oh yes, a hell all right.

And yet—we work away to build our security, to get a little roof and pay the rates. Still there's that thing unappeased. Don't we all secretly long, in our safe Britain, to take a Tupolev too far, to some godforsaken somewhere, where everything's to play for . . . ?

I only ask it.

At length she came back to the bed, standing looking at Ron in the deep gloom, as if asking his permission to re-enter.

At this point in the proceedings, he was again tempted to call the whole thing off. As he struggled with his feelings, to his reluctance to pass by any willing woman was added his kind of perpetual good humor with the other sex, quite different from his aggressive manner with men, which urged him not to disappoint this unlucky creature who had so far exhibited nothing but good will.

The waitress had started all this by encouraging him at the dinner table. He did not know if there was danger involved in this escapade but, if so, then she probably had more to lose than he. Men might not be allowed in this—lodging house, or whatever it was. He would hardly be sent to the gulag if he was caught, but no one could say what might happen to the waitress. He supposed that at the least she might lose her job; which would bring with it a whole train of difficulties in Brezhnev's Russia.

I should explain where I was when my friend Ron was telling me this story, just to give you a little background.

We met by accident on Paddington Station. We had not seen each other for about a year. I had come up on the train from Bournemouth to consult my parent company in Islington, and was crossing the forecourt when someone called my name.

There was Ron Wallace, grinning. He looked much as usual in a rather shabby gray suit with a cream shirt and a floppy tie—the picture, you might say, of an unprofessional professional man working for some down-at-heel outfit.

We were pleased to see each other, and went into the station bar for a pint or two of beer and a chat. I asked him where he was off to. This is what he said: "I'm off to Glastonbury to see a wise old man who will tell me where my life's going. With any luck."

It was an answer I liked. Of course, I had some knowledge of how his life had been, and the hard times he had seen. I asked after his wife, Stephanie, and it was then that he started telling me this story I repeat to you. Just don't let it go any further.

So there he was stuck in this poky little room with the waitress. Torn between compassion, lust, boredom, and exasperation. The way one always is, really.

He lay in the bed. She stood naked before him in the half-light, looking helpless.

"You ought to look after yourself better," he said, raising the quilt to let her in.

A sickly smell still pursued him. Concluding it came from the bed itself, he ignored it. She laid her head beside him on the patterned bolster. She smoothed dull hair back to gaze at him through the dim curdled light.

He stroked her cheek. When she buried her face suddenly in his chest, in a gesture of dependence, he caught the aroma of greasy kitchens, but he snuggled against her, feeling her still damp body. The waitress sniffed at him and sighed, rubbing against his thighs, perhaps excited by talc and deodorant scents, stigmata of the prosperous capitalist class. Prosperous! If only she knew! Ron and Steff had all manner of debts.

She opened her legs. As Ron groped in her moist pubic hair, he thought—a flash of humor—that he had his hand on the one thing that made life in the Soviet Union endurable. The Soviet Union and elsewhere . . . He penetrated her and she went almost immediately into orgasm, clutching him fiercely, bringing out a cry from the back of her throat. He thrust into her with savage glee.

Only afterwards, as they lay against each other, she clutching his limp penis, did her story start. She began to tell it in a low voice. He was idle, not really listening, comfortable with her against him, half-wanting a cigarette.

What she was saying became more important. She sat up, clutching a corner of the quilt over her naked breasts, addressing him fiercely. Her supply of English and German words was running out. He gathered this was something about her childhood. Yet maybe it wasn't. A horse was dying. It had to be shot. Or it had been shot. This was somewhere on a farm. The name Vladimir was repeated, but he was not sure if she referred to the town or a man. He tried to question her, to make things clear, but she was intent on pouring out her misery.

Now it was about an infant—"*eine kleine kind,*" and the waitress was acting out her drama, dropping the quilt to gesticulate. The baby had been seized and banged against a wall—this demonstrated by a violent banging of her own head against the wall behind her. He could not understand if she was talking about herself or about a baby of hers. But the pain came through.

The waitress was sobbing and crying aloud, waving her arms, frequently calling the word *smert*, which he knew meant "death." Her body shook with the grief of it all.

It reached a melancholy conclusion. The story, incomprehensible and disturbing, ended with her coming alone to Moscow to work.

"To work here in this place. *Arbeit. Nur Arbeit.* Work alone. *Abschliessen.*"

"There, there." He comforted her as he once used to comfort Steff's and his only child, wrapping her in his arms, rocking her. He was shaken by the agony of her outburst, angry with himself for failing to understand.

Of course there was no misunderstanding her misery. He felt it in his stomach, having known misery himself. Even in the pretty comfortable world he had left—to which he hoped to return on the morrow—personal tragedy was no rarity; some people always held the wrong cards. But he had fallen by accident into a shadow world, the world labeled "Brezhnev's Russia" or "Soviet Union," a world racked by terrible world wars and diseases. It was safe to say that whatever woes the poor waitress suffered, she represented millions who labored under similar burdens.

He gave her a cigarette. A simple human gesture. He could think of nothing else to do.

She cried a little in a resigned fashion and wiped her tears on the quilt. Then she began to make love to him in a tender and provocative way. For a while paradise existed in the squalid room.

Ron Wallace woke. A full bladder had roused him. The waitress lay beside him, asleep and breathing softly. In the dim light, her face was young, even childlike.

Disengaging his arms from under her neck, Ron sat up and looked at his watch. Next moment, he was out of bed. The time was 5:50 A.M. A suspicion of daylight showed round the curtains, and his flight was due to leave at 9:30. His check-in time at Sheremeteivo Airport was 8:00 A.M. He had two hours in which to get to the airport, and no idea of where he was.

He listened at the door. All was quiet in the building. He had to return to the hotel and collect his suitcase. And first he had to have a pee.

His impulse was to awaken the waitress. Capable though she had shown herself to be, she might be less reliable this morning. She would find herself in a difficult situation to which perhaps she had given no thought on the previous evening; the entertaining of foreigners in one's apartment was surely a crime in Brezhnev's Russia.

Since she did not stir, he decided to leave her sleeping. Keeping his gaze on her face, he dressed fast and quietly. He stood for a moment looking down at her, then unstrapped his watch from his wrist and laid it by the bedside as a parting present.

As noiselessly as possible, he slipped into his coat and unbolted and unlocked the door. In the corridor, he closed the door behind him. Thought of the tragic life he left behind came to him; damn it, that was none of his business. It was urgent that he got to a toilet. There must be one on this floor.

All the doors were locked. He ran from one to another in increasing agony. There seemed to be no toilet. He was sweating. He must piss outside, fast.

He went quickly down the stairs, alert for other people. He heard voices but saw no one.

His penis tingled. "Oh God," he thought, "have I caught a dose off that bitch? I must have been mad. How can I tell Steff? She'll leave me this time. Steff, I love you, I'm sorry, I'm a right bastard, I know it."

He rushed to the front door, which had a narrow fanlight above it, admitting wan signs of dawn. The door was double-locked, with a mortice lock and a large padlocked bar across it. Next to the door stood a cramped concierge's office, firmly closed. Everyone had been locked in for the night.

He ran about the ground floor rather haphazardly, gasping, and came on the side door by which, he believed, he had entered the previous evening. That too was securely locked. He gasped a prayer. At any moment his bladder would burst.

At this point in Ron's story, I broke into heartless laughter.

He stared at me halfway between anger and amusement.

"It's no fun, going off your head for want of a piss," he said.

I controlled my laughter. Ron is not a guy you like to offend. What amused me was the thought of a man who had been inside for GBH and done a stretch for breaking and entering in a situation where he was attempting breaking and exiting.

After trying and failing to kick in a panel on the side door, Ron ran about almost at random looking for a way of escape.

Two steps at the end of the main corridor led down to another locked door, a boiler room in all probability. Next to the door was a broom cupboard and an alcove containing a mop, a brass tap, and a drain.

With a groan of relief, Ron unzipped his trousers and pissed violently into the drain. The relief almost made him faint.

By now it must be almost half-past six.

As the urine drained from his body, he heard a door open along the corridor and a woman coughing. Her footsteps led away from where he stood. He heard her mount the stairs. Other doors were opening, female voices sounded, a snatch of song floated down; the noise level in the building was rising.

At last he was finished. He zipped his trousers, wondering what he should do to escape.

Two men were coming towards him. Although he saw them only in silhouette along the dark corridor, he recognized that they were old. They walked slowly, slack-kneed, and one jangled a bunch of keys. Ron sank back into the alcove.

The men passed within eighteen inches of him, talking to each other, not noticing him in the gloom. They unlocked the boiler-room door and went in.

Immediately they were gone. Ron came out of his hiding place and hurried back to the main door. As he went, he tried each handle in the corridor in turn. All were locked.

At the front door, he was looking up at the narrow fanlight, wondering if it would open, when he heard faint sounds from the concierge's nook. Impelled by urgency, he pushed the office door open and looked in.

A plump old woman with her hair in a bun was just leaving the main room to enter a cubbyhole which served as a kitchen. She began to rattle a coffeepot.

In the room lay three men, sleeping in ungainly attitudes. Two were huddled on a sturdy table pushed against the far wall, the third lay under the table, his head resting peacefully on a pair of boots. A cluster of empty bottles and full ashtrays suggested that they had had a good night of it.

The room, in considerable disarray, had five sides. It served regularly as a bedroom as well as an office; against the left-hand wall a bed stood under a shelf bulging with files. Timetables and keys hung from the walls.

The loud and labored breathing of the men reinforced the stuffy atmosphere. Where two of the walls came to a point was a window which the old woman had evidently opened to let air into the room.

Without hesitation, Ron crossed over to the window. In doing so, he kicked one of the empty vodka bottles. It rattled against its companions. He did not look round to see if the woman had caught sight of him.

One pane of the window had been repaired with brown paper. Taking little care not to injure himself, he forced himself through the opening feet first. The ground was further down than he had expected. He landed on concrete with a painful bump. Above him, an angry old woman stuck her head out and yelled at him. Ron got up and ran round the corner. At least he was free of that damned prison, where women were locked in every night.

Then came the thought.

"My bloody briefcase!"

He had left it standing by the waitress's bed.

Cursing furiously, he marched round the outside of the fortress. It was built of gray stone. All of its windows were barred.

A pile of rubbish, including the burnt-out carcass of a vehicle, stood against one wall. Even if he climbed up that way, it led only to a barred window. He prowled about, searching for the window of the boiler room, assuming there was one; he might be able to bribe the two old men to let him in that way.

He was frantic, and mad to know how the time was slipping away—what a fool to leave his watch with that bitch. He had to catch his plane, otherwise there would be trouble with his company and with Steff, not to mention all the difficulties with the airline—whatever it was called now . . . Aeroflot. And he could not leave without the briefcase. In it were his precious contracts.

Struggling to deal with his anxiety levels, he kept from his mind the more dreadful and nebulous fear: that the airliner would deliver him not to his lovely

Steff and the England he knew but to some other England ruled over not by Queen Margaret and PM Bernard Mattingly but by—whoever the lady was as mentioned in the newspaper—he had forgotten her name. He would perish if he was trapped forever in a dreadful shadow world where history had taken a wrong turn.

Despite his frenzy, he remembered something else. The damned doll the North Korean had given him. He was convinced it was packed with heroin or some other illegal substance. He had not believed the Korean's unlikely story about Mr. Holmberg for one moment, and had intended to throw away the doll as soon as he was outside the hotel. Sexual pursuit had made him forget.

Ron became really frightened.

Running round the building, isolated on its wasteland, he could find no low boiler-room window. He stood back, frustrated, when a stocky female figure in a black coat emerged from the building and walked off rapidly in the direction of the gigantic piles of broken wood Ron recalled from the previous night.

She had emerged from a side door. He ran to it, only to find it already locked. But even as he stood against it cursing, he heard the key turn from within, and it opened again. As another woman emerged, Ron dashed in. When an old man standing inside, key in hand, moved to stop him, Ron pushed him brutally in the chest. Other women were pressing to leave the building for the day's work, stern of face, burly of shoulder. He ran into the main corridor and hastened upstairs.

But which floor?

Which bloody floor?

He had seen from outside there were five floors.

Which floor was the waitress on?

Not the ground or first floors. Not the top . . .

Christ!

The scene was changed from a few minutes earlier. Everyone was now up and about, and women in states of undress were wandering the corridors. They yelled at him and tried to grab him. In a few minutes, they would get themselves organized. Then he would be arrested.

He tried the second floor. He ran down the side passage. First door on right. He remembered that. As soon as he faced the door, he remembered the markings on the waitress's door, the savage scratches as if an animal had been there. This was not it.

He ran up to the third floor, causing more disturbance, and to the side passage. God, this nightmare! He was furious with himself. Now he faced the door with the deep scratch marks, and hammered on it. The door opened.

Ron took a swift look back. No one saw him, though he heard sounds of pursuit. He went in.

The waitress stood there, half-dressed, hand up to mouth in an attitude of misgiving.

One reason for that misgiving was clear. On the bed—that bed!—on top of the quilt and the dirty blue nightdress, the contents of Ron's briefcase had been spread, a dirty shirt, a pair of socks, a pair of underpants, some aspirins, the crossword book, the Korean doll, a copy of the *Daily Express* from a week ago, the precious contracts, and other belonging. The case lay with a screwdriver beside it. She had managed to prise the lock open.

"Get dressed," he said. "*Schnell*. I need you to get me out of here."

"And to get me back to that sodding hotel," he thought.

The waitress tried to make some apology. She had not expected him back. She thought the case was a present. He barked at her. She hurried to put on yesterday's dress and fit her gray feet into her heavy working shoes, whimpering as she did so.

He hardly looked to see what he was doing as he pushed everything into the briefcase, shouting to her to move. She was now his guarantee. She could get him out of the lodging house. She knew the way back to the Hotel Moskva.

"*Schnell,*" he growled, deliberately scaring her as he forced the case shut.

She offered him his watch back but he shook his head.

"Let's go. Fast. *Vite. Schnell.*"

"OK, OK," she said.

Together they hurried down the corridor and down the stone stairs, Ron with a firm grasp on her arm. Several women gathered. They called to the waitress, but when she snapped back at them they stood aside and let her pass. A younger woman began to laugh. Others took it up. Soon there was general laughter. This was not the first time a woman had had a lodger for the night. Probably, Ron reflected, this was not the first time the waitress had had a lodger for the night.

The old man unlocked the side door and they were out with a stream of other workers into the chill air. Great was his relief. He had a chance with Steff yet.

"The hotel," he said. "*Schnell*. I must catch that bloody plane."

Ron Wallace caught the bloody plane. He rang his office from Penge. The managing director had had to go up to Halifax, so happily he was not wanted till the following morning. The day was his. He was able to go back to Steff, preparing as he went to be innocent. After all, she meant far more to him than any of these stray bitches. He would serve another stretch for Steff. He told himself he had learnt a lesson. He would never go with another woman.

Sitting on the coach going home, he was relieved to find everything was as normal. The *Daily Express* he picked up at the airport carried a photograph of Bernard Mattingly, Britain's popular Prime Minister, opening the first stretch of a new motorway that would run between London and Birmingham. He searched for a reference to Russia. A small paragraph announced that Russia had a record wheat surplus, which they were shipping to the Third World. And the Pope had returned to Rome from his tour of Siberia.

Everything was normal. He thought again of the strange electric storm which had bathed his plane on the flight out. Perhaps that had all been subjective, a major ischaemic event in the brain stem. He had been working too hard recently.

Nothing had happened. He had imagined that whole dark world, Brezhnev, the waitress and all.

Steff was amiable and credulous and listened to all he had to say about the boredom of Moscow. While he was showering, she even went to unpack his things for him.

He stepped naked from the shower. She had opened the briefcase. She was holding up for his inspection a dirty blue nightdress.

THEM OLD HYANNIS BLUES

Judith Tarr

Judith Tarr is more known for her fantasy novels and her historical fiction than for her SF, but she is equally adept at all the genres she has tried. This story is a work of alternate history SF, a subgenre that has flowered in the last decade. It is also a successful attempt to go "over the top" in that subgenre. The Kennedy boys as a rock group? Read on.

Jack was late again. "Who is it this time?" Marilyn wanted to know. She still had that voice, all breathy and sweetsy-nice. That body, too. She swore it didn't owe a thing to modern medical science. As far as Bobby knew, she was telling the truth.

He was dead bone-tired of running this road show. Jack late. Young Joe toked out in a corner. Sometimes he giggled. Most of the time he just let the makeup maven take off the last ten years or so of living high, Kennedy Brothers style. Teddy made great stone-faces in the dressing-room mirror. Sweet Tammy was home with the kids, singing hymns by the fire and waiting for Daddy and Uncle Joe and Uncle Jack and Uncle Bobby to show up on TV—Live from the Valens Center for the Performing Arts: The Inaugural Gala.

Marilyn was looking particularly voluptuous in a Halston silk suit. It was her new look, she'd informed Bobby last year, along about the time she passed the bar. She'd had it with being a sex object. She was going to realize the power of her femininity, burst out of the patriarchal power structures, and become a new woman.

She was certainly bursting out of that suit.

"Bobby, you're not listening to me," she said. Breathy. Sweet. Iron underneath. "I want a divorce."

"Ten minutes!" from outside.

"Later," said Bobby.

"I said," she said, "I want a divorce."

Bobby ran through the checklist. Secret Service codes all over it. Times down to the minute: "1800 hours, arrive Valens Center. 1806, pass checkpoint. 1820, secure dressing room. 1833, order dinner. 1854, consume dinner." Right up to "2200, arrive backstage" and "2216, begin rendition: 'Hail to the Chief.'"

They should have added, "2143, Jack still missing." Jack did what Jack damned well pleased.

"If he doesn't show up," Bobby said, "Joe, you take keyboard."

Joe stopped giggling. "Jack always shows up."

"One of these days he won't," Teddy said. He was all ready, every sequin in place. He'd called Sweet Tammy precisely at 2135, and talked to her for precisely two minutes and fifty-nine seconds, doling out twenty seconds apiece to each of the offspring. "I'll take over for him. I have the parts down."

Bobby's teeth hurt. "You stay at bass. We need that line. You know Joe can't play bass and sing at the same time."

"Can," said Joe.

"I want a divorce," said Marilyn. "I've done the paperwork. I'm filing tomorrow. Lee says it should be final just in time for me to matriculate at Yale."

Bobby jerked around. "Yale? What the hell do you think—"

"International law," she said. "I'm going for the doctorate. I'm thinking that with the new administration and the New Direction President Presley has promised, there should be room for a few good women."

"A doctorate," said Teddy, "takes at least four years. More like eight. Or ten. He'll be out of office before you get the degree. And you'll be almost sixt—"

She flashed the smile. Like the body, it hadn't dimmed much with age. "I'll do it in four. When he comes up for his second term, I'll be ready for him."

"God," said Bobby. "Yale."

She wouldn't divorce him. She'd threatened before. He'd always got her to come around. But this looked serious. The law degree had been bad enough. "What's wrong with Harvard?"

"You went there," she said sweetly. She touched up her lips—none of this no-makeup, no-bra, hairy-legs crap for her, he gave her that much—and shut her compact with a sharp click. "I'm going out now. Break a leg, boys."

"That's for stage actors," Teddy said, as usual.

"Shut up," Joe said, also as usual.

"Am I late?" Jack asked.

The forecast had been for sleet. It must be falling: it was in the famous hair. The famous smile was turned up to max. A blond hung on the famous arm.

Forty years of voice lessons and he still couldn't sing. The girls didn't care. They collected the old albums. They swooned over the old movies. They bought every single one of his hack best-sellers, even his "serious" shtick, *Profiles in Charisma*. They screamed when he went by.

Hiding him behind a piano hadn't worked when the Kennedy Brothers were the big band to end all big bands. When Bobby saw the future in a pounding beat and switched the act to rock and roll, Jack got himself a keyboard and taught himself some moves, and it was his name they screamed, even with Joe at lead vocals. Joe had It, said *Tiger Beat* and *Groovy* and *Rolling Stone*, but Jack had It cubed.

Jack and Marilyn together were death on the synapses. The blond on his arm pouted, dulled to dishwater and knowing it. Marilyn patted her on the shoulder. "There," she said. "You realize of course that you're succumbing to the lies of the patriarchal system? Come on now, they're due onstage and we have some talking to do."

"We do?" the blond asked.

"Of course we do." Marilyn got a grip on her arm. They hadn't got past the door before she started talking. "You think that there's no way to obtain power in this society except through a man. But if you consider—"

Jack laughed. "She said she wanted to meet Marilyn," he said. He looked around. "I thought we were going formal tonight. What's with the attack sequins? Are we trying to upstage Liberace?"

"We are trying," Bobby said through gritted teeth, "to perform at President Presley's inaugural ball."

"One of them," said Teddy. No one paid any attention.

The makeup maven started on Jack. He was moving stiffly, Bobby noticed. The back was out again. That meant he'd try something stupid in the performance, soldier through it with the famous bravery, and end up in the hospital. Bobby had figured it in. They weren't playing Vegas till March, and the filming wouldn't start till May. *The Road to Saigon.* Joe was the war hero this time. Jack got to be the handsome good-for-nothing who discovered himself in the last ten minutes, and saved the world for rock and roll.

"One minute!" from outside.

"Let's boogie," said Jack.

The Ritchie Valens Center for the Performing Arts smelled like a new car. Looked like one, too, shiny and new and every piece in its place, not even threatening to fall off. This was its first major gala, not that they got much bigger than the main inaugural ball. What Bobby saw was mostly glitter. Glitter hanging in sheets from the ceiling. Glitter inset in the floor. Glitter on the people packed as tight as fans at a rockfest. There were globes floating everywhere, glowing pearlily. "Alabaster," sighed Joe. "Alabaster globes." He wasn't looking up. A woman waited backstage—one of the acts, Bobby supposed; he didn't recognize her offhand. She was wearing a square yard, just about, of silver lamé, and a lot of pearls. They went nicely with her endowments, which were considerable.

Jack was over there already, flashing the grin. Joe was content to giggle. Teddy pursed his lips and disapproved. Bobby sighed.

"Time!" from the curtain.

They leaped into place: Bobby at drums, Joe at the mike, Teddy at bass. Jack sauntered. He inspected the keyboard. He frowned. "I'm not sure—"

The curtain sank through the floor. Crowd-roar rocked them back. A chord thundered out of the keyboard. The bass howled a split second late. Then they were into it: "Hail to the Chief," as arranged and performed by the Kennedy Brothers in honor of the thirty-seventh President of the United States.

"El-vis! El-vis! El-vis!"

He came in waving and smiling, looking just a little sultry in white tie and tails. The First Lady was radiant in clouds of white tulle, with her platinum hair done up just this side of extravagant, and a spray of orchids for a tiara. His nibs had lost some lard, Bobby noticed, and her FirstLadyship had gone ahead and got that breast-reduction surgery. Too bad. In her heyday she'd have outdone the bosom in the wings by a good six inches. She was still magnificent. There'd been a few nights, and that weekend in Malibu . . .

He'd forgotten it, of course. Until he needed it.

They ended the old standby with a new riff that took all of Bobby's concentration. Then they swung into something light and easy, mill-and-swill music for the President's ball. Joe crooned into the mike. "Them blues, them old Hyannis blues . . ."

They'd cover the country tonight, from Hyannis to Malibu, Grosse Pointe to Galveston, and end up with the President's own personal theme, "Graceland on My Mind." Teddy was back on track after doing half the first number a half-note behind. Joe was in good voice, for once. Jack hadn't missed any notes yet. Bobby let the rhythm play through him and, for the first time in months, thought he might relax.

Vice President King came backstage at the break, towing a nicely integrated pair of teenage gigglers. The redhead would be something when she was a few years older. The Veep's daughter already was. Took after her mother, Bobby noticed. "And how's Coretta?" Teddy was asking.

"Glowing," said the Veep. "Just glowing."

"Alabaster," crooned Joe. "Alabaster globes."

"New song," Bobby said quickly. He slashed a hand behind his back. One of the roadies boxed Joe in and got him talking about, as far as Bobby could tell, the High Sierras.

Jack had wandered off again. He wasn't interested in potential. He wanted his beauties ripe, and now. After a while he wandered back. Teddy and the Veep were swapping road stories—the campaign trail wasn't much different from the rock circuit. The gigglers were giggling and sliding eyes at Jack, who made their year with a grin and a platitude. They'd never know they'd had the brushoff. "Take a look at this," he said to Bobby.

Bobby started to snap back, but Jack had pulled him over to the edge of the stage. There was a gap in the curtain. Bobby got a wide angle on the audience, milling and swilling as frantically as ever. The President was in the middle, and the First Lady's platinum 'do glowed as brightly as one of those damned ambulating beach balls.

"Look over there," said Jack.

Marilyn still had the blond in tow, but they'd picked up a third weird sister. This one looked like a very genteel horse.

"She's British," Jack said. "Amazing how a woman can look like hell in chiffon."

"The dress isn't bad," said Bobby. "The hat is the problem."

"The hat is always the problem," Jack said. "Just ask the Queen." He paused. He wasn't grinning as much as usual. "You know, it's funny. Remember that crazy we had to ask Frankie to help us get rid of, back in L.A.? She looks like that."

"That crazy was male, filthy, and wouldn't know chiffon if you wrapped him in it."

"Not that, damn it," said Jack. "Look at her eyes."

Jack couldn't read a newspaper at less than three feet, but give him a hundred yards of packed ballroom and he could count the sequins on Liberace's cummerbund. Bobby squinted. Marilyn was holding forth. The blond was either rapt or shell-shocked. The woman in chiffon—God, a face like that and she wanted ruffles—wasn't looking at either of them. Marilyn was about twenty feet from the President, just outside the security perimeter. The President would be standing, from the woman's angle, just behind Marilyn's right shoulder.

Bobby didn't shiver often. "Tough," he said, "and mean. What's she got against him?"

"The Revolutionary War?" Jack shrugged. "Maybe the War of 1812, though we've got grudges of our own, there."

Bobby curled his lip. "Egghead," he said.

Jack punched Bobby on the shoulder. It was nicely calculated. Just hard enough to bruise, not hard enough to knock him sideways. Smiling all the while. "She does look like old dad, doesn't she?" He crossed himself devoutly. "May he rest in peace, if there's peace in downtown hell."

"Downtown," Joe twanged behind them. "Downtown hell."

There was one good thing about Joe's getting loose. The Veep wasn't there anymore to hear him.

Outside, onstage, Secretary of State Lennon was going on about New Directions and Brave New Worlds and When It's '84. He'd smoothed out his accent for the occasion.

Bobby happened to glance toward Marilyn. She hadn't moved. Hadn't stopped talking, either. But if the Brit in chiffon had looked mean when she looked at the President, she looked murderous as she listened to the Secretary of State.

Bobby shrugged. She wasn't his problem. Keeping this show on the road was.

They got through the medley—"Rocky Mountain Sighs," "California Babes," and the wall-thumping, teeth-rattling crescendos of "Niagara Falls." Then, while the floor was still rocking and the crowd still rolling, Jack grabbed the bass right out of Teddy's hands and leaped off the stage.

Bobby had been in between chords somewhere. He came out of it with a snap. Teddy goggling and empty-handed. Joe at the mike, starting in on "Manhattan Lovers." Blurs out beyond the stage, with smudges for eyes. Jack bounding through with Teddy's custom axe high over his head, heading right for President Presley.

People goggling. His nibs looking sultry. Suits closing in. Over on the edge, winter-white Halston and dishwater blonde and too damned much pink chiffon.

The chiffon had a gun.

So did the tux heading for the President.

The axe caught the tux's hand. Bobby didn't hear the gun go off. Too many screamers. Teddy's bass came back around and lobbed the tux right into the oncoming suits. Jack was grinning like a maniac. He might have been singing, too. Bobby didn't envy anybody who could hear him.

The chiffon braced her wrist with her other hand. Bobby's eye followed the line of her aim. Vice President King was somewhere in the muddle, suits all over, women shrieking, men hitting the floor. Secretary Lennon hadn't moved. His silly little glasses gleamed. His long egghead face looked more interested than anything else. Even when the red flower bloomed all over the front of his clean white shirt.

Halston tackled chiffon. Marilyn's timing was just a little off. It did keep the second shot from hitting anything but one of those damned globes. It shattered. The shrieking hit banshee volume.

Bobby slammed the cymbal. It brought Teddy around. Bobby jerked his head toward the keyboard. Teddy did a fish-take, but he went where Bobby told him. On the way by, he pulled at Joe's arm. Bobby signaled. Joe, bless his pickled brains, wrapped his hands around the mike. Teddy kicked a chord out of the board. Bobby set the beat. Joe started to wail. He had lungs on him, and the amps were cranked just short of feedback. Without the bass line it wasn't the gut-buster it could have been, but it outhowled anything the crowd could come up with. "Bay-*beeeeeee,* you just kill me, baby, do . . ."

Jack landed himself in the hospital. It wasn't the backhand that did it, though it finished off Teddy's bass. It was the pileup afterward, with the tux on the bottom and Jack on top of him and the Secret Service six deep on top of that.

The tux was Brit, too. "Name of Jagger," said President Presley in his best corn-pone drawl. "Front man for the Unified United Kingdom Front."

"The one that wants to take over Free Ireland and make it safe for tea and crumpets?" asked the hero of the hour. He was flat in the hospital bed and white as the sheets, but it didn't stop him from turning on the grin.

"That one," the President said. "The other bastard, though, who got John Lennon—God rest him—" he said, looking more sultry than usual, damn near smoldering, "that was their fearless leader herself."

"Iron Maggie," said Marilyn. Makeup just about hid the black eye, and she didn't limp when she thought anyone was noticing, but she carried herself with a certain air she hadn't had before. Satisfaction. "The Friedrich Engels of the underground. She'll take over Britain, she says, and make it a world power again."

"You've been talking to her?" Even Jack sounded surprised.

"She's supremely wrongheaded," Marilyn said, "and she's convinced herself that the only way to overcome male power structures is to dominate them and then destroy them, but she does agree that violence was not exactly the best way to go about it. I've sent her Betty's book, and Gloria is going to see her tomorrow."

"She'll be deported," said Teddy from where he sat by the window. His voice seemed to be coming out of a basket of gardenias. "If she's lucky, she'll get out of prison in about sixty years."

"Oh," said Marilyn, "I don't know. She did feel that she was executing a traitor. He was, if you look at things that way. He should have dedicated his genius to the cause of his own country, not to a pack of jumped-up rebels."

Bobby rolled his eyes. The President looked a bit glazed. Marilyn had that effect on people.

His nibs mustered up a smile. "You certainly saved us from a very unfortunate situation," he said. "We'd have lost more than John, without the two of you."

"And the boys, too," said Marilyn. "They kept the crowd calm."

"They certainly did," said the President, shaking hands all around. Joe wiped his hand on his pants. People pretended not to notice.

Jack traded grins with the President. "You know, Jack," his nibs said, "with a little help from your friends, you'd be a smash in politics."

"I'd need help?" Jack asked.

Everybody laughed. Jack just kept smiling.

"Think about it," the President said. "You saved my life—and the Veep's, too. You know how to work a crowd. I can just see the ads: Mad Jack with his bass guitar, saving the world for democracy."

Bobby's face hurt. So did his stomach.

"What do you say?" said the President in the fast patter of politicians and used-car salesmen everywhere. "There'll be a House seat vacant, you wait and see. Then maybe the Senate."

"I don't know," said Jack.

"It's the least I can do," said the President, "for the man who saved my life."

"What about the woman?"

Maybe no one heard that one but Bobby. Marilyn was smiling as sweet and empty as a pile of cotton candy. Until you saw her eyes. Bobby wondered just how much she'd been teaching Iron Maggie, and how much she'd been learning.

"Oh," Jack said again, "I don't know. I'm not much on speechifying, or on keeping my nose clean. Now, if you wanted to ask Teddy . . ."

Not Bobby, Bobby noticed. Teddy was already blustering, the old I'm-not-worthy shtick. The presidential focus turned on him. A minute more and they were an act, his nibs leaning, his purity protesting, and everybody else closed out.

"Clever," said Bobby.

Jack grinned. He looked gray under it. Soldiering on. Bloody fool.

"I wonder sometimes," Bobby said, "if politics might not have been the way to go after all."

"Not me," said Jack. "Not till hell freezes over."

"Downtown," Joe sang to himself from among the gardenias. "Downtown hell. Hot time, hot time in downtown, downtown, downtown hell."

"Washington," Jack sang in his just-off-key tenor. "Washington blues. So hot in August, we can't—you can't— Hell," he said. "I never could get a line to come out straight."

"Straight down," sang Joe, "straight down, go down, to downtown hell."

"I sent the papers in," said Marilyn, "yesterday. For the divorce."

Bobby grabbed a piece of paper. It was part of Jack's chart. He flipped it over and fished out a pen.

"You can keep the house," she said. "I've rented a cottage in Westport—Katherine was so sweet about it, she even threw in the maid and gardener. I'll commute to Yale from there."

"Hell," sang Joe, "hell so hot, so hot . . ."

Jack fingered imaginary keys on the tight white sheet. Joe sang nonsense, but nonsense with a beat. Bobby pulled it all together. Arrangements—bigger group for this one. Backups. Chicks in red, devil babes, lots of glitz. Teddy needed a new axe, got to get that straightened out, and Vegas, and the *Stone* interview, and maybe Jack should do the hero in the *Road* movie, after all, the ads for that, now, what his nibs said about Mad Jack wasn't a bad idea at all.

"I may even," she said, "now that I think of it, try politics myself."

Politics, Bobby thought, scribbling words and music. Who needs politics? We've got a song to write.

PARADISE CHARTED

Algis Budrys

This is a long excerpt of a still longer essay originally published in *Triquarterly*. Algis Budrys, an important SF writer (author of *Rogue Moon, Michelmas,* and *Hard Landing*) and critic, has accomplished the remarkable task of summarizing the literary history of Modern SF in a most thorough and accessible form. The lively biographical vignettes of major figures add special interest. His distinction between Modern SF and contemporary SF is now widely accepted in the field.

Neither earnest academic inquiry nor reader enthusiasm has yet served at all well to define the shape and nature of science fiction. The actual writers espouse whatever views best serve them, and because all views, to date, are fragmented and idiosyncratic, there is serious danger that any clear conception of this energetic and potentially important kind of literature will be buried in nonsense.

The case is not helped by the very high proportion of workaday and primitive writing that co-exists with the genuinely meritorious and accessible work also found in the commercial publications over the past half century. Nor by a tendency on the part of some litterateurs to base all discussion on the assumption that nothing in the popular media can possibly be relevant to the evolution of general literature.

The thrust of this essay is to present one coherent viewpoint in which commercial science fiction is related to literature as a whole. It is an example of what one practitioner perceives to be the history of his field, the essential nature of his mode, and its potential. In this essay, I casually use the term science fiction even when speaking of events and works occurring prior to the invention of the term. I use "science fiction," in quotes, whenever I wish to cast doubt on the actual propriety of using the term at that particular point of the discussion.

1

Science fiction's vaunted and highly visible preoccupation with the future is arguably the result of a transient cultural phenomenon: the as yet short-lived idea that the future is full of evolved technologies. This orientation, which barely goes back to the eighteenth century and did not gain a major toehold on Western thinking until the nineteenth, offers a perfect beast of dramatic burden to the author in search of fresh situational appurtenances. A similar artistic role had previously been fulfilled by undiscovered continents and imaginary Atlantean civilizations on behalf of social allegorists, from classical Sumerian, Egyptian, Greek, and Roman times on up through Bergerac, Swift, and Defoe.*

2

Rather early in the nineteenth century Percy Shelley's young wife, Mary Wollstonecraft, published *Frankenstein,* an instant best-seller that caused her to immediately overshadow her father's reputation as a novelist, if not her late mother's as a doyenne of the intellectual salon.

Frankenstein grew out of a challenge to write a modern ghost story. What did this mean? What in the decade after the invention of the steamship was a "ghost story"? What existing and implicitly familiar literary effect was being redefined by the modifier "modern" at a time when the 1815 invention of the Davy lamp made coal production more efficient? What was a best-seller in an England which had seen technocratic Napoleonic rule supplant the divinely righteous monarchies of Europe?

There was nothing overtly like Banquo's ghost in *Frankenstein,* nor anything like the later apparitions in Henry or M. R. James. *Frankenstein* resulted from what was an editorial market conference among Byron, his clever companion Doctor Polidori, Shelley, and Wollstonecraft at a villa one dark and stormy night on a European jaunt. It seems clear that these individuals were aware that the intrusion of technology into Western cultures was creating species of uneasy hope, analogous to that of participants at a séance who tap into omniscience while dreading its agents.

This potent little circle of litterateurs had no name for the new thing, but they knew what they meant when they pointed to it, and they expected it to create in audiences feelings analogous to those aroused by classical tales of traffic with the worlds beyond. It had to be called *something.* Thus, "modern ghost story," for better or taxonomic worse.

Although *Frankenstein* was allegorical in the same sense that *Crusoe* was allegorical, and similarly addressed itself to the relationship between a sentient, emotional creature and its creator, it called upon the furniture of contemporary technological thinking to create its story situation. For Defoe, God had sufficed.†

Frankenstein, however, lacked any overt uplifting purpose, distinguishing it from the ready interpretations available in *Crusoe.* By these various measure-

---

*Defoe's *Robinson Crusoe* can be seen as the last ripple of imaginary voyage tale, and as the prototype for *Frankenstein,* the first clear-cut "science fiction" novel. Mary Wollstonecraft Shelley's monster, calling in anguish on its creator, strongly evokes the solitary castaway's parrot incessantly mimicking, "Poor Crusoe! Poor Crusoe!"

†Actually, of course, Defoe was a rather sly fellow. Eventually, he was author of *A Journal of the Plague Year,* precursor, with a similar, mature work by Wollstonecraft, of all disaster "science fiction" to come. In showing Crusoe calling Job-like on his Maker for answers while hewing down entire trees to produce one plank, Defoe was saying more about the beginnings of the Age of Reason than Walt Disney ever gave him credit for.

ments it was not a tract; it was a work of prose drama, and today presents ready credentials as "science fiction."

Late in the nineteenth century, Rudyard Kipling dabbled in a few science fiction and fantasy works, among his other short stories, but these of course were overshadowed by the stories of the French adventure-tale writer, Jules Verne. Verne, like Michael Crichton or Martin Caidin today, occasionally borrowed some topic of contemporary interest on the "popular science" level and converted it into a prop for his fiction.

Often honored today as the Father of Science Fiction, Verne was rather the Bard of Steam—the romanticizer of larger, swifter engines and of decisive, adventurous men who seized issues by the throat. He took satisfaction from his enormous popularity and from the fact that every invention he described was, without exception, founded on some prototype already available on some drawing board in his day.

At his father's insistence, Verne had received professional legal training. Leaving his native port of Nantes for the Parisian intellectual community, he quickly began indulging literary avocations that reflected his broad taste for melodrama—which may have arisen as a reaction to the constraints of his almost totally sedentary, albeit materially pleasant, life. In *Jules Verne: A Biography*, his grandson Jean Jules-Verne, retired chief justice of the port of Toulon, describes the genesis of an early work, the novella *Martin Paz* about native uprising and anticolonial revolution in Peru: ". . . *Martin Paz* reveals one of Verne's major attributes as a writer: his visual approach to narrative. It seems that Verne wrote this story from a series of watercolors by the Peruvian painter Merino. . . ."

The watercolors were still lifes of Peruvian topography. On these Verne, the armchair traveler, superimposed star-crossed lovers, bands of Indians firing poison arrows, and a climactic plunge over a waterfall. This was Verne's method. Although he was wont to say in letters, "I'm on the eightieth parallel and it's eighty below zero . . . I'm catching cold . . ." or "I'm in New Zealand . . . ," he never actually strayed far from his writing desk in his metropolitan residences, or, at most, the tillers of the solitary sailboats in which he explored the estuaries of France in his early and middle years, before purchasing yachts that also never roamed very far.

He was apparently a man easy to like, or at least Dumas and Victor Hugo found him companionable; and as his fame grew, his access to the famous and the efficacious was not impaired by any terminal social idiosyncrasies, in contrast to H. G. Wells. He knew how to be a great man graciously. But there is no foundation whatever for conferring on him the gift of genuine technological prophecy. He took care to include the latest scientific advances within his purview, and he hobnobbed with science academicians. Thus he heard more swiftly about developments and would often be the first to aggrandize and popularize these to the general public.* Verne's literary impulses were saved for his poetry, plays, and

---

*This appears to be the same thing that twentieth-century "science fiction" preceptors such as John W. Campbell, Jr., did for their readers. But it is only what Campbell *claimed* to be principally engaged in. Campbell, technologically schooled like many of his writers for *Astounding Science Fiction* magazine, was actually doing something else. The claimed resemblance to Campbellian science fiction is a resemblance to Verne's popular image, not his substance. The actual resemblance of Campbell to Wells is to his substance, not his image. See further.

libretti, none of which survive as living things. When Wells appeared at the turn of the century, M. Verne characterized him as a fantasizer and demanded to be shown how any of Mr. Wells's inventions could possibly work. Significantly, a reply on Wells's behalf can be made to even that level of criticism.

Wells was the first writer in eight decades who felt required to apply some generic term to his kind of creation.* Those early novels are called "scientific romances," and were sharply distinguished in Wells's own mind from his later, truly respectable oeuvres, all of which are as abandoned by readers today as Verne's verse dramas.

As a descriptive term, "scientific romance" is not bad at all. Wells dealt with the condition of humans as other thinkers dealt with the exploration of Nature in disciplines called chemistry, physics, and biology, and he experimented by transposing the human condition into believable but, at least ostensibly, nonexistent social milieus. Unlike Verne, he was not particularly concerned with one central individual. Like Wollstonecraft, he preferred archetype. He was the first prominent writer to directly ask the question, "What will happen to society in general if this goes on?" and he asked it systematically, of any number of social conditions, long enough and in sufficient volume to deserve credit for creating a new sort of literature, while in fact giving a new cut of clothes to a very old one.

A curious fallout resulted from his approach. Thinking in terms of massive social effects, as typified by the segregation of the human race into Morlock troglodytes and Eloi cattle in the far future, he was forced by logic to fantasize enabling devices for his protagonists. Thus the English gentleman who observes human social devolution must have a device which will carry him forward in time. The good folk of rural England, faced with an allegorical individual embodying the overwhelming revolutionizing power of technology, must be given an invisible antagonist. To convey Victorian morality to a fabulous alternate society, Wells had to create the antigravity metal, Cavorite, for the *First Men in the Moon*. All are fantasy machines—impossibilities in the light of known science then and now.

But to properly arm the Martians, who must call the Age of Steam into question with *The War of the Worlds*, he conjured up the laser-like heat ray. Similarly, in contemplating the nature of Victorian warfare, he foresaw the need for and (not quite exactly) "invented" the armored tank in "The Land Ironclads." In looking at the farflung works of man, the densities of population, and the limitations of naval and military power in breaking down national boundaries—and assuming correctly that the need to exercise power must soon force into being a device to overcome the obstacles of geography—he, like Kipling, foresaw the natural future of aviation. But Kipling wrote a short story or two on that theme, whereas Wells wrote a number of them, as well as *The Shape of Things to Come*.

Thus it was Wells the social philosopher, at least as well as Verne the popularizer of contemporary science, who sometimes called into being devices which were not, but would become. The fact that he was almost totally indifferent to the details of their construction—and was concerned primarily with their utility

---

*Possibly because he expected it to be popularly identified as "Vernian"—something manifestly different from the truly literate.

as bits of business that made his suppositional social manipulations possible—does not detract. Recent history is also the tale of powerful entities treating technology only as a source of stage props.*

A peculiar consequence of this frequent appearance of suppositional hardware in what were actually social speculations was that a major segment of the English literary establishment—Chesterton, C. S. Lewis, Aldous Huxley—was able to assail him for being a crass technologist while they were really reacting badly to his unfortunate personality, social class, behavior at parties, and elitism.

An issue that should have been joined on loftier grounds degenerated into name calling, character assassination, and extensive use of the "technologist" red herring. The controversy served to further identify "scientific romances" with technology, and, in the shadow of Verne's reputation, began forging increasingly strong links in the popular mind among speculation, hardware, space travel, and the future as a milieu.

Nevertheless, "scientific romances" were still marginally, at least, part of general literature, as distinguished from the popular pap of the contemporaneous western and detective dime novel. Then Hugo Gernsback came along.

3

From the viewpoint of serious litterateurs, the late Hugo Gernsback was a totally insignificant person in his day—just another commercial publishing entrepreneur, doing whatever it is entrepreneurs do while the serious thinking of the world proceeds elsewhere. But from the viewpoint of the science-fiction community, Gernsback is a transcendent figure. The major annual community award for science-fiction writing accomplishment is called the Hugo, and no doubt always will be.

While Wollstonecraft and Wells were the parents of "science fiction" and John W. Campbell its stern uncle, Gernsback is the father of the "science fiction" community. Or ghetto, as some took to calling it and as some have not left off calling it.

It should be understood that by the 1920s, the social development that had stirred to create *Frankenstein,* that had made Verne a prophet in the sense that Billy Graham is a prophet, and that had cast a disproportionate emphasis on one feature of Wells's work, was paying off as never before or after. Technology has grown subtler since then, and carried us farther, but it has never moved at the pace or with the expansiveness of scale that it enjoyed after the First World War.

Bigger dams, more high tension lines, longer railroads, faster trains, sleeker cars, higher flights, deeper dives, taller buildings sprang up every day. Thomas Edison was reeling off fresh technological applications every week. Basements, barns, and garrets abounded with earnest young men winding coils.

They were, in large part, earnest young men without university educations: inconsiderable folk, far from the mainstream of what was important to academe or deep thinking, gripped by the fact that a few months' reading of elementary

*Which may be why one might prefer a Vernian universe. Captain Nemo can always be tracked down and personally punched in the nose.

tech manuals sufficed to bring a bright lad up to date on everything known about electricity or aerodynamics. At that point, the same lad had as good a chance as anyone to build the first practical rocket, the better auto engine, the radio any housewife could operate, the prototypical television set, the sound motion picture in color. What, in fact, was not possible? To anyone who kept his wits about him in the age of Ford, Marconi, Tesla, and all those other people no one had heard of before their names hit the newspaper headlines, anything was almost as likely as anything else.

Hugo Gernsback is the man who named television. And who thought of the newspaper facsimile receiver, the sleep-teaching machine (he called it the hypnobioscope), and scores of other likely sounding devices, some of which came to something and many of which did not. Gernsback was the publisher, in the 1920s and until his death in the 1960s, of a variety of popular science magazines, all essentially named either *Sexology* or *The Electrical Experimenter.*

An immigrant Luxemburger, Gernsback was a man who thought coil-winding was science. There is some possibility that, having learned English as an adult, he literally never understood the exact verbal distinction between technology and science. Part of what we have inherited may be a language difficulty. Certainly, like many other intelligent, multilingual persons, he used English in a cavalier but highly creative way, being not only a tireless neologist but an inveterate punster. It seems reasonable to suppose that a certain failure to grasp exactitudes of denotation would be the inverse result.

So it's quite possible that this at least partially explains why the fiction of technology is today called what it is, although there are steps between Gernsback and Robert A. Heinlein. It's even more certain that the same sort of thing was operating when the first magazine to put technology fiction on the pulp newsstands as a homogeneous category was named.

Publishing his magazines for the coil-winders of America, Gernsback hit upon a device that was still being used recently by *Popular Mechanics* magazine with its Gus Wilson's Model Garage "stories." Filling each issues with scores of articles such as how to build your own television signal decoder from three sheets of plywood and an electric fan motor,* editors tended to want to break up the pacing just a bit. Gernsback may have been the first to publish little inserted "fictions" that, still centered on the technology at hand, featured transient tech japes, or made a hero of a young lad whose quick thinking with spare wires and batteries created a device that solved some serious oncoming problem.

Fueled by his idiosyncratic sense of humor, his vast tech optimism, and his (probably accurate) high estimate of the range of his mind, Gernsback wrote almost all of these himself; their tone derives from his 1911 novel, *Ralph 124C41+* (one to foresee for one, plus). Ralph, a scientist of the ultratechnological future, had a series of naive adventures whose essential purpose was to furnish the reader with a travelogue through the marvels of the coming age.

These were in a sense rather modest marvels based only, and strictly, on something that could clearly be seen coming if the need to have it were to manifest itself. This constraint is essential to Gernsbackian fiction; the jape, whether

---

*It could be done: pre-iconoscope TV used a motor-rotated "scanning disc."

overtly humorous or more soberly "stimulating" of thought, had to have a base in reality in order to operate properly.

This is true even of locales. Outré alien beings might come to visit the precincts of the solar system, but Gernsbackian humans did not, as a rule, travel of their own volition beyond the margins described, with some confidence of essential factuality, by human astronomers peering through real human instruments. Nor were the aliens generally equipped with devices that could not be rationalized quite tightly in terms of human scientific theory. When exceptions occurred, they were usually kept in the background, and the story concentrated on the familiar, made glossier and more proficient, but retained within easy human reach.*

When readers expressed enthusiasm, Gernsback implemented the publication of a magazine containing nothing but such fictions. What to call it? Well, the fictions did not intend to imply that the devices described in them could actually be built with hardware *immediately* on one's shelf. Many of them were inside jokes—think of the diversion if you were an electrical engineer and the author, winking at you, offered a sober tale about what happens when you've wound a coil with zero resistance. Possibly while groping toward a synonym for "diverting" or "grandiloquent," Gernsback hit on "amazing," and brought out the first issue of *Amazing Stories* in 1926. The cover format was in the mode of popular science journals, featuring some eye-catching mechanical device under a logo that leapt off the magazine rack at potential readers, with a few human figures thrown in for scale, displaying their reaction to the device.

Naturally enough, it was mistaken for a pulp magazine by other publishers. With intelligences cold, remote, and unsympathetic, they began to take cognizance of this new thing, which Gernsback, looking for a category label, had called scienti*fic*tion.

With no significant exception in this context, *Amazing* has never done particularly well as a property. Throughout its history it has usually been marginal,

---

*The following quote is from a 1928 episode in Gernsback's long-running Baron Munchhausen's Scientific Adventures series. The narrator is in contact by radio with Munchhausen, who has gone from Earth to Mars on the spaceship *Interstellar* [*sic*] to see if Percival Lowell was right in his telescopic observations of canals, etc., and in his guesses that there might be a high-technology culture extant there. The tale is devoted largely to outright in-group jokes "explaining" possible difficulties in Lowell: e.g., the Martian are found to use "ion currents" to neutralize the weight of the necessarily huge volume of canal water, so that it may be "pushed along more easily." At this point, Sir Isaac Newton is erupting wroth from his grave, and all the coil-winders are grinning. But when it comes to explaining how the Baron's messages reach Earth, Gernsback feels constrained to describe a feasible system, making sure we understand thoroughly. The Baron has a "radiotomatic" relay station on the Moon, which records the signals from Mars and amplifies them so they can penetrate the radio-reflecting layers in the Earth's outer atmosphere:

> *Thus every night I took down the Baron's messages and everything ran along like clock-work, for many days. Munchhausen, of course, knew exactly whether the messages reached me or not, as he could readily check them. The Radiotomatic plant on the moon, as will be remembered, recorded the message, but did not send out the amplified message itself until several hours later, being regulated by clockwork to do this. The impulses never were sent out until 11 P.M., Eastern terrestrial time. Thus the Baron, who, of course, had a very fine radio plant of his own on Mars, could hear his own message, as well as I could. For, if the radio waves were powerful enough to travel from Mars to the moon, naturally they could travel from the moon to Mars, because the sending plant on the moon was even more powerful than the first one which Munchhausen had on Mars. It was just like an echo. Thus the Baron heard his own message every day, just as well as I did.*

is frequently sold, metamorphoses at intervals, but never dies; it is the longest-lived science fiction magazine.*

Gernsback lost *Amazing Stories* almost immediately for a variety of commercial reasons, and went on to found other magazines based on his original concept, which never prospered. There were not quite enough coil-winders, and Gernsback may never have netted a nickel out of "scientifiction." But his competitors did.

They were not precisely imitators, for few fictioneers have ever had the Gernsback way with a story. The Gernsback *Amazing Stories* itself was forced to pad its content with reprints of Verne and Wells, and with folks like Edgar Rice Burroughs, because it proved simply impossible to generate enough Gus Wilson–like wordage. Gernsback tried. He recruited for "writers" among various technologists of his acquaintance, sponsored "amateur writing" contests in his magazine, and ended by insistently pointing to the "science" content in conventionally written material.

In due course, grasping for readers and not too sure he wanted some of the readers he had, he founded the Science Fiction League. In editorials and with offers of membership cards and badges, he encouraged readers to get together, by mail or preferably in person, to further the interests of science, to discuss science, and, incidentally, to read the Gernsback fiction publications, which chartered various League chapters scattered sparsely around the country. It all came to nothing for him, but he had created the nucleus of what is today called Fandom: that is, the core of the community which at this point could probably exist and even prosper independently of science fiction, so intertwined and vociferous are its interpersonal concerns. If one of its aspects, Fandom continues to be *the* source of successful new writers, illustrators, and editors.

It is impossible to overstate Fandom's importance to stefnism. While tens or perhaps hundreds of thousands of "science fiction" readers have never heard of it, everyone who publishes, edits, writes, or illustrates in the field must take its articulations into account. It is the repository of the amorphous oral tradition; almost all professionals who are now adults were imbued with its preconceptions as children.

Thus Gernsback's major accomplishment, among other accomplishments, was to trigger the formation of a pocket universe—an enclave inside literature, equipped with its own readers and, in due course, its own writers, proceeding on its own evolutionary track as if the rest of the world's prose barely existed.

There is no parallel. True genre fiction finds overt models in reality. The western, crime, sports, air war, jungle adventure, pulp romance, and railroad

---

*"Scientifiction" as a term quickly developed variations. "Science-fiction," followed by "science fiction," came into tentative use in the 1930s through Gernsback. (Perhaps because he had surrendered proprietary right to "scientifiction" when he sold *Amazing Stories* prior to launching *Wonder Stories*.) Even in the 1940s, however, "stf" was still a common abbreviation analogous to today's "sf," and there was a short-lived effort by a prominent stf amateur named Jack Speer to institutionalize the neologism "stef," with declensions such as "stefnism," "stefnal," and "Stefnist." (I rather wish the idea had stuck. It saves a great number of syllables.)

In addition, "science fiction" has become a catchall. Fantasy and sometimes even occult fiction are reviewed by "science fiction" critics in many media, and the "science fiction" community contains many individuals with strong and sometimes paramount interests in fantasy as distinguished from technology fiction.

genres—to name the most prominent categories extant before mass TV—operate with direct, if not realistic, reference to observable phenomena. "Science fiction" does not and did not. Genres have aficionados; "science fiction" has fanatics.

Detective fiction has scion societies, and from time to time the Baker Street Irregulars hold a convention and a banquet, with guest speakers who discuss the literature of their field. "Science fiction" has hundreds, perhaps thousands, of amateur publications; at least one convention of some size nearly every weekend, culminating in an annual world convention with attendance approaching five thousand; innumerable subgroups founded on special interests within the special interest, particularly heroic fantasy; art shows; costume balls; its own repertoire of folk ("filk") songs; a well-developed jargon sufficient for good communication without more than passing reference to English; and guest speakers whose utterances are least well attended when they refer to the literature. "Science fiction" has all that, among other things.*

The question one might ask is just what enormous Word it was that Gernsback had uttered.

The short answer is that Fandom is the refuge of the bright, socially inept young intellectual seeking peers and an alternative to mundane reality. This conclusion is accurate but greatly invidious; many Fannish institutions conserve juvenile interests and behavior, but many others offer role rehearsals for high-level mundane careers within and without technology, or beneficial recreation for such careerists after they have matured.

One common factor cuts through all of Fandom's diversities, however. It is a quality of thought which Sercon Fandom—serious, constructive Fandom—long ago labeled "time-binding." Time-binding appears to be an innate quality, with Fandom attracting those time-binders who chance upon it. Fans as a class are spontaneously and instinctively aware that their own particular lifetimes represent only an infinitesimally thin section of the chronography of the Universe. This is expressed as a certain detachment from mundane concerns, interrupted by manifestations of a quite intense awareness that intellections and skills are tools for conveying betterment to the future, in stewardship of a gift from the past. By implication, too, there is a linked analogous quality of "locale-binding"; as a result, any human deed ever performed anywhere is potentially useful as a model, and nothing in the properly nouned Universe, past or future, is foreign.†

These qualities are of course consciously self-perceived and expressed according to the abilities and personalities of given individuals. The depth of genuine meaning or benefit in any one instance will vary considerably from the next. In a population which is otherwise quite heterogeneous, most sercon Fan-

---

*Recently, one of the other things was *Star Trek* fandom, nurtured in part by merchandisers from outside and by segments of the extensive merchandising establishment within the community. Trekkies outnumber Trufans. Some Trufans are also Trekkies, or ex-Trekkies. Never mind. Recalcitrant Trekkies will gafiate, and Trufandom will endure.

†I am not enamored of "time-binding" as a term, but there it is: there is no better, once one understands its Fannish connotations. "Binding" is used in the sense of gathering into sheaves—of being able to see correspondences and congruities across very broad diversions of data. The quality is not necessarily related to I.Q. or any other measure or description of intelligence level: there are *idiots savants* in stef as there are in mathematics. Yet inevitably there is a sense of being special, rein-

nish expressions cancel each other out. A movement was once initiated to declare Fandom the nucleus of a super race. ("Fans are Slans!" The model is a superman novel, called *Slan,* by A. E. van Vogt.) It was laughed to death. Nevertheless, clearly the Word uttered in all its deepest meanings by Gernsback was Shelter.

Fandom is markedly conservative of its own institutions. There is no paradox in this; so are all other human groupings centered on a common quality, no matter how outlandish their expressions might seem when viewed from within any other grouping.

Having affiliated itself in its beginning with a prose form whose only expressed concern was play with technological ideas, Fandom continued to assume that this prose was nonliterary at best, or literary in a very narrow sense. Though "scientifiction" was a Mayfly, dying even at the height of its existence, that underlying assumption still persists, not sufficiently attenuated to be at all in accord with the objective nature of "science fiction" as it is now written.

This is an important aspect of the stefnal culture. Adult members of the community tend to articulate and act in ways they saw and learned as children. Because these people have an unusually limited capacity for boredom, they in fact produce constant evolutions in the form. But those evolutions almost invariably proceed from trusted bases, and are labeled with the least possible variations from the labels of childhood.

The phenomenon is not unknown outside the community. Fans at one time had to stop and seriously puzzle out why mundane types tend to titter when overhearing a reference to *Astounding Science Fiction* as a serious medium. But does the *Saturday Evening Post* come out on Saturday evenings?

The evanescent nature of true scientifiction is easy to see. As a form, it is dependent for its attractions on a very short-lived condition—the eye blink in which technologies have been discovered but have not yet been institutionalized. Further, in order for scientifiction to offer any diversity at all, there is a requirement that several varying technologies arrive at this stage simultaneously. There must be a fiction of technology, not merely a fiction of high-tension electricity transmission or of auto mechanics. Otherwise, no even quasi-viable periodical medium could emerge. In addition, scientifiction's very existence, with its penchant for naming things and suggesting directions for technological inquiry, hastens consolidation into the everyday.

Furthermore, it is not possible for even the most nonliterary writer to do scientifiction without imposing *some* semblance of dramatic values recalled from other forms, and once that rot has set in, the rest is foredoomed. Gernsback himself, having corrupted his creation from the outset by juxtaposing it with the

---

forced frequently when mundane types react with wonder to what are actually very obvious and subjectively matter-of-fact analyses produced by time-binder minds. We notice, in fact, that we arouse the loudest exclamations of delight—and the least unease—when we are most like Ralph the Wonder Horse and least likely to be calling truly fundamental social precepts into question. "Mundane" is, by the way, the Fannish term for anything non-Fannish. It is used as a neutral descriptive term, and nothing scornful or derogatory is implied in the overwhelming majority of such uses. But we are aware that mundanes ovehearing us will at times take umbrage, and there are such occasions in which some of us have been known not to feel particularly embarrassed. Well, the Benevolent *Improved* Order of Elks had a bone to pick with the Benevolent Protective Order of Elks, too.

reprinted work of known writers, could not sustain the métier. His last stefnal magazine, *Science Fiction +*, published in the 1950s, was barely recognizable as a descendant of *Amazing*, although it was still quite different from what *Amazing* had become in the meantime.

Fandom in the 1920s was, by modern standards, so slight and primitive that it is best recognizable in hindsight. But Fandom grows by accretion, rather than by undergoing metamorphosis and leaving some elements behind. Its nature is self-directed, with each additional feature incorporated only on the basis of compatibility with all prior features. Every feature it has ever had is still in there. Meanwhile, technology fiction as a commodity was evolving according to the outside dictates of the marketplace, which are trendy, often revolutionary, and treat readers as an array of interchangeable numbers. The processes of the marketplace can and usually do ignore Fandom, whose numbers are no better than any similar set of numbers.

Fandom in a sense reciprocates the attitude. It is indeed capable of sustaining itself and proceeding without overt reference to "science fiction," since the time-binding quality of its members preexists as the core feature, independent of media. Amateurs and semiprofessionals emerging from Fandom to take up positions as purveyors of "science fiction," however, do necessarily metamorphose into professionals.*

4

By 1930 scientifiction was in fact dead, and a dual process of dancing on the remains was well under way.

Classical literary elements, usually perverted and attenuated but nevertheless present, were entering the "science fiction" market via commercial writers brought in from older genre periodical media, and by outside editors and publishers originating in the same talent pool. By this same token, "science fiction" was being defined *as* a genre, with no essential distinction from the preexisting genres, for the purely commercial purposes of its marketers.

A number of rather good mass-fiction magazines—notably *Argosy*—had been publishing fantasy and recognizable science fiction to the mass audience since the turn of the century. For that matter, the nineteenth-century dime novel is not free of imitation Verne, and a healthy body of *Frankenstein*-like poplit existed in Imperial Russia. Nor were any of these forms exclusive to only a few nations, thanks to innumerable foreign translations of Wollstonecraft, Poe, Verne, and Wells. Each country seeded its own pocket of local imitators (as, for instance, in Japan). But there were no generic or pseudogeneric pulp media.

The Mars and Pellucidar novels of Burroughs were originally serialized cheek-by-jowl with his premier creation, Tarzan, with his rivals in mass literature

---

*The metamorphosis is rarely complete. As previously noted, the recognized cadre of "science fiction" professionals contains almost no individuals who do not preserve some Fannish attitudes and activities throughout their lives. The extent of this symbiosis with what is, after all, only a fraction of the readership is yet another of the many and revelatory differences between commercial "science fiction" and all other forms of literature, popular or "serious," *and* every form of "science fiction" originating outside the community.

by Talbot Mundy and Rider Haggard, and a host of other adventure creations. The short fiction was modeled on "literary" short fiction, and its writers tended to share the cultural orientations of contemporaries who were being invited to literary teas on the respectable side of Publishers' Row. The principal distinction between a *Thrill Book* writer and a potential Hemingway or Fitzgerald was often simply one of talent and sometimes nonexistent. Certainly it was nothing like the gulf between a *Thrill Book* writer and some of the awful hacks who were following assiduously in the footsteps of dime novelist Ned Buntline,* writing pulp to strict formula and dreaming of someday breaking into *Argosy*.

Amazing, which except for page size was indistinguishable from other pulp magazines, changed all this in stef. In a society without portable radios, and without television series stocked by hacks writing to strict formula and treating rule-of-thumb ideas as merchandise, the pulp magazines dominated popular entertainment. Fortunes were made in their publication, a dime and fifteen cents at a time each month or every two weeks, and the genius who could invent a new genre had best hold on to it tight. Gernsback failed in the latter half of that proposition, but the exploiters of his apparent idea did not.

The important thing, as the pulp impresarios understood it, was to publish something with a rocket ship or a Martian on the cover, and fill it with stories that had some kind of hardware in them. Lacking writers who could do it the way *Amazing* tried to do it, they simply searched their stables of house hacks for individuals who could translate westerns and jungle stories into ray-gun drama set on an imaginary planet called Venus. Edgar Rice Burroughs and his near-equivalent, Otis Adelbert Kline, had already pointed that way.

Amazing, on the other hand, had created or found a handful of writers who could do the hardware with some verisimilitude, but who couldn't plot an entertaining story very well. Cobbling issues together, groping for an audience, such publications as *Astounding Stories of Super-Science* and eventually such other developments as *Thrilling Wonder Stories, Impossible Stories, Astonishing Stories*, and *Startling Stories*—to say nothing of *Cosmic, Dynamic*, and *Planet Stories*, or *Captain Future*—established a pseudo-generic market based on the work of born nobodies. Some of those people could write action, some of them may have had some grasp of science or technology, and a small number of them combined those abilities. Few of their media did as well as the average genre

---

*E. Z. C. Judson, otherwise "Ned Buntline," was the first person of consequence to realize what the late-nineteenth-century high-speed printing press meant. What it meant was communication on a scale hitherto undreamed of. There is room to doubt whether even consumer television, proportionally, had a greater ability to make articulation plain to the masses. Buntline is commonly known as the inventor of the dime novel, which these days is dimly seen as the prototype for the pulp magazine, and then for *Starsky and Hutch*. There is a long of it in which a redan of Ph.D. theses rests. The short of it is that more people were exposed to Buntline's propositions in a single summer than had ever been exposed to Shakespeare in all the centuries since Elizabeth I; that Buntline tested his powers by naming a charismatic hero of a smelly, colorless buffalo hunter named Bill, which says something for the transferability of Buntline's innate charisma; and that he ended by founding the major American conservative terrorist political party—the "Know Nothings"—of the nineteenth century. Which means he founded the major terrorist party of all human time, up to and including his time. The little bit of his insight into what made people dance, which crept into publishing, sufficed to build fortunes commensurate with Xanadu. One such beneficiary was the Street & Smith Publishing Company, which in due course would publish *Astounding Science Fiction* magazine.

magazine, but the economics of chain publishing, and a judicious leavening of illustrations featuring Martian priestesses with large breasts, kept them well enough afloat. Rates running to half a cent per word after publication also were a factor in profitability.

Yet if you scratch around among enough coil-winders, you will find some who have a perceptivity for the human condition and a way with words, and if you shuffle through enough pulp manuscripts, you will find some people who are not terminally stuporous to the impulses of art. What they need is an editor.

John W. Campbell, Jr., had found a way to help out his budget as an undergraduate at MIT and Duke University, and subsequently as an apprentice engineer without a decent job in the depths of the Depression. A hobbyist named Edward E. Smith, Ph.D., who was a chemist in sugars, had rewritten a manuscript by a lady acquaintance and hit upon a new style—superscience fiction—which proved wildly popular by stef standards. Campbell discovered he could write it as well as the master could.* In terms of pure prose technique, that was no difficult job, but superscience fiction proceeds at a blindingly swift pace of ideation, and few are equipped to maintain it.

The most interesting thing about it, literarily, is its obvious combination of the pulp Little Tailor plot with scientifiction tags.

Briefly put, superscience goes as follows:

At 9:00 A.M. Monday, a bright young Anglo-Saxon technist notices a peculiar effect on the instruments in his laboratory. By noon he has a workbench model of a device which applies that effect, usually as a means of traveling a good deal faster than light. At 2:00 P.M. his hidebound superiors refuse to recognize the importance of his discovery. Quitting, he sits down on the bus next to another young Anglo-Saxon male who proves to be technologically bright and the heir to an industrial fortune. By midnight they are in the second lad's giant workshops, contemplating a full-scale version of the device. First thing Tuesday, they fly to the Andromeda galaxy. There they identify a whitish civilization being oppressed by a blackish one. Utilizing a development of the original effect, combined with another observation they have noted and discussed while in flight, they build an irresistible energy-beam weapon out of materials at hand, and by dinnertime have wiped out the oppressor. Wednesday morning they make additional improvements on their vessel, including a totally impervi-

---

*In "The Battery of Hate," (*Amazing*, 1933, T. O'Conor Sloane, editor), Campbell depicts the adventures of Bruce Kennedy and Bob Donovan, who have installed a fuel battery in an airplane and are using it to drive an electric motor. They are pursued by gangster representatives of the long-line power transmission utilities:

> He pulled the rheostat control back smoothly, and the gentle hum of the motor mounted swiftly to a driving, tearing whine as the controller reached its limit. The heavy plane tugged forward with a sudden acceleration, and the entire fabric of the all-metal plane creaked under the strain of the great power.
>
> ... The plane below was falling behind now, as the larger plane pulled viciously under the great motor. The speed was still rising, though the power from the batteries remained the same: the hum rose to a scream as the motor ran swifter.
>
> Kennedy listened critically. "Bob—that propeller! It's all right for one thousand [horsepower] gas or internal combustion power, but remember an electric motor can, like a man or a steam engine, dig in its toes and heave, so to speak. A gas engine, like any explosive power, works the first time or not at all. . . ."

ous energy screen which allows them to pass unharmed through solid matter. They flit home, ready to star in the next novel, sharing brief memories of an incidental glimpse of a whitish maiden with the social attributes of a Swarthmore undergraduate.

The appeal of this story to unemployed technologists in the 1930s is obvious. Superscience fiction was the first version of technology fiction to make commercial sense. It was a kind of yard goods, but it isolated a viable audience out of the ruck of pulp readers, and added others.

First of all, with the strong superficial resemblance between superscience and scientifiction, the evolution in the prose carried with it a successful accretion upon Fandom, which accepted the new form readily.

It was in fact a radically new form. Scientifiction features one jape at a time; a scientifiction novel strings a series of scientifiction short-story situations together, like beads, to the number desired.* A superscience story, on the other hand, whether a novel or some shorter work, is made by pyramiding ideas.

In superscience, each notion is more exciting than the last. Whereas the milieus of scientifiction are givens—stable societies with a Chinese menu of plausible artifacts, each about as fundamental to that society as the next—the milieus of superscience are unstable and also usually forced into being, in the sense that the heroes plunge into them at distances so remote they might as well otherwise not exist, and are not directly modeled on known places.

This is a subtle distinction. To scientifiction readers, Percival Lowell had made Mars familiar—even if subsequent astronomers later exploded nearly every supposition which for a time had been gospel. But a planet in Andromeda can be anything; it is understood by the reader from the beginning that the detail of such a world must be a reflection of an auctorial fantasy, although that understanding does not necessarily occur on the conscious level.

What is more, the machines in superscience are introduced in the order Mighty, Mightier, Mightiest. And they, too, are vastly more suppositional than anything in scientifiction, if only because their scope and puissance are so far above everyday norms that it becomes rather more difficult to believe one could really—*really*, now—hope to hit upon one in one's own basement. The superscience reader who thinks about his attraction to the form must, if rational, admit that he is a bit farther off the ground than a scientifiction reader is. But, after all, this admission can be made in the privacy of one's own home, with the shades drawn, and many of us do that sort of thing. Many of us did.

This meant some reshuffling within Fandom. A bitter controversy raged for years between Gernsbackian adherents to "real science fiction" and all other forms, which were "fantasy." But the Gernsbackians were almost at once in a distinct minority-proportion, in part because so many new people came into Fandom. One assumes a parallel evolution, on a larger scale, within the general

---

*Ralph 124C41+ originally appeared in 1911 as twelve episodes in Gernsback's first magazine, *Modern Electrics*. The first nine episodes were written as isolated features; only the last three introduce any combining plot, in which Ralph, a villain, and a figure invariably described as "a lovesick Martian," vie for the hand(?) of a maiden who doubtless was just contemplating a transition from hoopskirts into bloomers, at least while watching television and plugging herself into her hypnobioscope in the privacy of her own automapartment.

readership. Once again, Monsieur Verne was losing the argument with Mister Wells.

The parallel is fairly close, if difficult to see except at a safe distance. There was not—or rather, there ostensibly was not—an individual to represent the Wellsian view in the same sense that Gernsback stood in for Verne. But superscience defends itself by its very nature, viz.: If the machines are fantastic, utilizing totally unknown forms of energy to controvert all the limitations imposed by the known physical laws, then the appeal is not to educated rationality but to something far more emotional and far less constrained by education. Not only does this automatically qualify more readers to participate; it touches compellingly upon the area from whence rise questions on the potential of the individual, on the responsibility of individuals and society toward each other, and on the extent of the set of all permissible social interactions. Those, of course, are questions of vast interest to time-binders, but they are also the questions all children and artists must immediately set about dealing with if they are to survive with their integrity essentially preserved.

So superscience is not simply scientifiction made more of, although it was arrived at by commercial pressure to find something that would sell bigger. Scientifiction is a cool, intellectual form; superscience is hot, and, despite all naiveté, fundamentally artistic. But, once again, because they appear to share the same furniture, no one at the time, as far as I know, was able to consciously realize that there is a class difference between a chair technologically elaborated with wheels and buttons to make its occupant more capable and a chair so large that a human figure upon it is a figure in a landscape. Or a human also made so large as to be a landscape.

Edward E. Smith, Ph.D., to the end of his days was a superscience writer, an attractive, stand-up gent who in his elder years was still wont to turn up at conventions in his motorcycle leathers.* He became in time the object of much fond editorial attention from John W. Campbell, Jr., who attempted to get Smith to bring his approach up to date.

In the late 1930s, Campbell left E. E. Smith behind, although that was not clearly visible because Campbell left superscience behind—I think not consciously at first, and certainly not at first visibly at all.

Also by the late 1930s Gernsback had already been cut off from the main line of development, but, more important, a glance at any newsstand would prove beyond doubt that the thing he had put on the market was trash. It was displayed with trash, packaged like trash, published by trash merchandisers using trash methods, and there was absolutely no hope that any practitioner of writing for those media could possibly hope to find his work in a Carnegie library.

Anyone committing himself to work in the field had to agree, either brokenly or defiantly, that his byline was cut off from respectability, from "litera-

---

*At costume balls such as the one at Seacon I (the world science-fiction convention in Seattle, 1961), I hasten to clarify. The rest of the time he favored solid brown pants, a brown-and-yellow checked sport coat, and a bow tie. But the leathers were his own and well worn-in, aviator helmet, goggles, and all.

ture"—that is, from anything written that was openly distributed in some way other than the way the pulps were brought to their audience.

One major factor ensured that the professionals' attitude would be not only defiant, often proudly defiant, but proprietary. The survivors of the competition to sell to the media were largely people weaned on scientifiction, who felt that their innate qualities had enabled them to beat the outside professionals at their own game. In a matter of a few years, only L. Ron Hubbard, Henry Kuttner (with his multiple pseudonyms), and most especially "Murray Leinster," who was a sweet gentlemanly genius named Will F. Jenkins, carried the flag for pulp generalists; and all three of them rapidly abandoned doing much work outside the field. All the other contributors were homegrown.*

Let us go back to the young John W. Campbell, Jr., superscience writer, 1932 B. S. graduate of Duke University after transferring out of MIT. Newly wed, employed marginally as a salaried junior technician at the height of the Depression, he was constrained to make every additional dollar out of every ability he could pummel out from among his resources.

He was physically impressive: a bulky, sharp-eyed, laughing man (who preferred to decide for himself what was funny), usually described as bearlike, even by myself. But I think if you look at him in still or motion pictures, and cling to the practice of finding the essential animal, you will see a lot of physical moves, particularly in the act of laughing or otherwise asserting a point, which bring to mind the fox. He was not some one thing; no one can yet say what he was in toto.

As a direct result of the prominence of his commercial by-line, Campbell accepted the editorship of *Astounding Stories of Super-Science* in late 1937. He almost immediately stopped writing fiction. This was, paradoxically, to have enormously fruitful consequences.

Campbell was a prodigious ideator. The conventional wisdom is that he sought out new writers with a similar bent, passed on to them his unused ideas, and thus initiated the Golden Age. It was virtually only a matter of months before nearly all the established by-lines were gone from *Astounding,* replaced by an almost entirely new group that housed such names as Heinlein, Asimov, Clement, del Rey, Sturgeon, de Camp, van Vogt, several pseudonyms of Henry Kuttner and Catherine L. Moore writing in concert, ad infinitum. Of all the names that still constitute the greater pantheon of contemporary science fiction,

---

*This continued to be true indefinitely. Fredric Brown, in the later 1940s and afterward, wrote many detective novels and simultaneously made himself famous as the master of the trick-ending supershort story in "science fiction," as well as the author of a few rather good stef novels. Almost all science-fiction writers have at one time or another sold something to commercially equivalent markets, when they existed—but not ambitiously. Some writers now famous elsewhere—John D. MacDonald, Donald Westlake, "Evan Hunter," for three—tried science fiction and left it as youths.

During boom times, a measurable number of writers for equivalent markets have dropped in for a story or two—William Campbell Gault, Leslie Charteris, Walt Sheldon. (Charteris's 1940s piece for *Startling Stories,* "The Darker Drink," featuring the Saint, is, however, by oral tradition a piece of ghostwriting from Kuttner. I'm thinking rather of "The Newdick Helicopter" and "The Man Who Liked Ants.") At any rate, it was not until "Cordwainer Smith" burst on the scene in the 1950s that a major "science fiction" writer appeared from "outside," if you don't count A. E. van Vogt, as you shouldn't in this context.

Campbell totally missed out only on Frederik Pohl, Ray Bradbury, and Alfred Bester at the height of his powers.*

It's not given to every editor to sow such a row of dragon's teeth. With a few exceptions, the elder giants of today were chivvied through their first efforts by Campbell, even though they may have sold some of that work to competitors after he finally rejected it. Or so the oral tradition goes, and in this case is closely in accord with verifiable facts.

In short order, there were no exact competitors. The Campbellian touch in ideation and in author recruitment produced a unique product. It did not get a distinctive name until after the first flush of creativity had passed and there was time to draw breath. It was propelled by group elan of such intense energy that a usually inarticulate sense of elitism sufficed to hold the cadre together.

Campbell did change the magazine title to indicate that something new was happening. It became *Astounding Science Fiction*. Thus, that term was lent enormous prestige, and "superscience" was dealt a death blow that even the general public could see.

"Science fiction" was of course a misnomer. But it had the advantage of conveying a sense of institution and respectability, in contrast to neologism or hyperbole. Campbell over the years devoted a variety of efforts to shaking loose from the "Astounding," since the full desired effect could hardly take place until this was accomplished. He wanted to call his publication just plain *Science Fiction;* unfortunately another publisher had already registered that title and, though sorely misusing it, was keeping it current.

So ASF's logo went through a series of gyrations, with the "Astounding" at times in thin, difficult script and the SCIENCE FICTION in block capitals, and at other times with the adjective in minuscule lettering. It always came back, however, probably at the urgent behest of the circulation manager. Not until long after the Golden Age was a sweet memory did Campbell succeed in getting the title changed to *Analog Science Fact-Science Fiction;* by then he was no longer the kingmaker in any case.†

But while he fulfilled that role, he was a titan. What would, in 1946, be dubbed Modern Science Fiction was *the* science fiction. Between 1938 and 1948, he ruled the roost, unquestioned and unquestionably. Until 1950 when, on a signal from Fritz Leiber, the community modified its perception of him nearly overnight, it was impossible to focus on him objectively because he sat in such a big chair. Even so, all that happened was that he became another sort of legend. It's still not possible to speak of him with impunity, so hard held are the opinions.

There's still not a "science fiction" writer working in the English language who can escape tracing his lineage from Modern Science Fiction. A similar degree of influence is visible on most writers in other portions of the world. Stanislaw Lem has to vilify what Campbell did. The Soviets are barely emerging from a mock-Modern period in the 1960s. Even such iconoclastic movements as the English "New Wave" of the early 1960s are conscious reactions, which

---

*And Cyril Kornbluth, until the last decade of their lives. But few today fully perceive just how important a career was truncated by Kornbluth's early death, so he is not much recalled except in certain quiet quarters.

†It is now ANALOG SCIENCE FICTION-*science fact.* Stand by for further mutations.

have been absorbed and which mingle with the effects of other conscious reactions to produce a contemporary "science fiction" whose more recent practitioners look back on Campbell as a dim figure. But we are all still in the same room with him. No one has been neutral toward him, then or now.

The question becomes, Who really was the late John Wood Campbell, Jr., that such a role was vouchsafed him?

5

Campbell (1910–1971), even more than Gernsback, wrapped himself in complexity. There were stories he would not publish even though he loved them, and things in stories that he would edit out or have rewritten even though organically they belonged there. The annual Fannism award for the most promising new writer is named after him, and, fittingly, it is consistently won by persons whose work he would have rejected out of hand, not for lack of talent but for eschewing the disciplines of pragmatic hypocrisy.

He was a fearless, rigorous thinker who prized logical honesty as navigators prize the North Star. But in writing for ASF, he saw euphemism and genteel obfuscation as essential attributes. He much resembled someone who'd read a lot of Kipling while young and found the bath of sensuality in which Victorianism laved itself. The legend is that his assistant, Miss Catherine Tarrant, was placed in his office by Street and Smith to guard its family image. Perhaps. But I think that, having her there, Campbell let her take the credit for verbal—not ideational—censorship that originated with him. There was nothing he wouldn't let you say. What you had to do was find some way of saying it to the vicar's mother.

Most observers now agree that he was a Calvinist conservative,* an authoritarian figure carefully self-cultivated in that guise; and young observers call him a stultifier. Authoritarian he was. There are many indications that he became extremely self-reliant while still quite young—this would be consistent with the profiles of most time-binders—but, not too typically, his energies were biased toward pragmatism rather than intellection.

There is no definitive Campbell biography. There probably never will be, since all the primary sources are dead and Campbell, though a voluminous correspondent and tireless conversationalist avoided all but fleeting references to his earliest years. A few capsule biographies published in his lifetime hint at a childhood containing a number of events that puzzled and troubled him, forcing him to cast about for resolutions of serious conflicts between the ideals expressed to him by authority figures and the observational data of his own senses. This, too, would not be unusual in the special sense that, although it is a universal experience, it seems to occur with particular intensity among time-binders and may be the cause of their nature.

Turning away toward pragmatic action, while retaining an interest in speculative philosophizing, is less common in the community than the opposite bias, but it certainly is seen fairly often. What distinguishes Campbell is the extent of his capacity.

*He was a professing atheist, but only in church.

Perceiving engineering as something that offers a physical hold on the Universe, he opted for the Massachusetts Institute of Technology. In an anecdote he related to me in the early 1950s, he created a picture of a tough, nerveless young man, trafficking between the university and his New Jersey family home over the icy and indifferent surfaces of the Boston Post Road, hurtling back and forth from holiday visits at the wheel of a Ford Model A. This was a thoroughly secondhand vehicle he had resurrected and rebuilt himself.*

He had to pay all or most of his tuition himself. Eventually he turned to superscience writing. His style was workmanlike, tinged by Victorian constructions picked up from youthful reading. His spelling and punctuation were idiosyncratic to the end, but in those days there were copy editors to smooth that away.

As a superscience writer and as an editor, he declared ideas to be components in a mechanism whose purpose was to entertain its selected audience—a sort of whirligig for the mind. Not only did all his public utterances reflect such a view, but when he abruptly stopped writing (they say because his bosses forced him to; then why did he stay in the job?) with several completed or nearly completed novellas on hand, he simply handed one of them as a scenario to Robert A. Heinlein like passing him a trayful of eggs. He was correctly confident that they would produce an effective omelet no matter which set of words embodied them.

(The Campbell version was published eventually as the novella "All," in the posthumous collection *The Space Beyond* [Pyramid Books, 1976, edited by Roger Elwood and George Zebrowski]. The Heinlein version was *Sixth Column*, a landmark Golden Age ASF serial by "Anson MacDonald.")

Campbell explicitly stated that producing stories was just *one* of the things you could do with ideas. Again and again—with his original cadre and then at subsequent times with others—he created or tried to create informal or formal clubs of "gentleman amateurs" whose first interest was in playing with ideas—technological ideas, ostensibly—for their own sake, or perhaps even for actual contemporaneous applicability.

Further than that, he said he preferred his writers to be hobbyists, to support themselves on other resources, such as salaries, and to produce work for him as a means of obtaining luxuries not otherwise budgeted for. The preference was not always expressed calmly.

One hypothesis is that he had reached a reasoned decision that hobbyist writing created a desirable effect in the work, and his intensity stemmed from defining that turf. I like the other hypothesis better: that at some level he was in conflict with the whole gestalt of an articulate, intelligent man's having to write at word-rates in order to live at all—with all its implications of having to write in ways editors could immediately see an audience for—of voluntarily putting on the cuffs so the jailer will have to take you in and give you your statutory bologna sandwich. Of course, he was himself the mightiest editor.

The two hypotheses are not mutually exclusive. What's interesting is that they can exist side-by-side. Campbell's reputation now is of the incisive story-

---

*After graduation, he worked for a brief time in the engineering test shops of the White Truck Company, winning out over other Depression applicants, one presumes, because he could show old wrench scars on his knuckles.

doctor, passing out capsule thumb rules to would-be contributors: a man who could "put his finger on it."

But this is not how it was. The famous letters to young writers were often vague, bumpy things; they were interminabilities in which he strained to make his meaning clear to both the addressee and himself, over and over again, until enough collisions with useful notions had occurred. His rejection notes were marvels of cryptic imprecision, as distinguished from polite obfuscation. His hortatory methods failed far more often then they succeeded: Alfred Bester and Damon Knight were specifically driven away by them, and who knows how many scores of lesser known or neophyte individuals, even of talent, could not accommodate to what were in fact seat-of-the-pants methods. The survivors, of course, praised his name.

This is not to denigrate him. Any editor would gladly wish to show results on anything like the Campbellian scale. It is to indicate that however articulate he might be when given a chance to prepare his statements, and however one-two-three those statements might go when thus prepared, there was very much another side to him.

There was a lot of the poet in Campbell and, with just a bit of extra twist, he would have been a superb comedian. He had some of the two essential ingredients: a great insight into the human heart and a willingness to stumble. But he didn't think people would approve of him unless he called the stumbling something else—freewheeling but practical speculation, by preference.

I think, in short, that Campbell spent a lot of time paying attention to what he ought to say and do in his role, and that, more than some people, he controlled what he would let himself realize about himself.

This business of ideas, for example. Most people assume his were tech ideas. He expressed a very casual attitude toward ideas, in the sense that the only interest he never professed was the proprietary one. He liked to give the impression of a man juggling them happily, caring little whence they came, sometimes half-seriously suggesting that there was some mystical source continually putting them "in the air" for ideators to catch. He habitually and deftly tossed the same new idea to half a dozen different writers, confident it would sometimes return within stories, certain that no two stories would be sufficiently alike to disturb his readers. And, in fact, one can find the story "All" both in *Sixth Column* and in Fritz Leiber's ASF serial, *Gather, Darkness,* but without the key it would be impossible to recognize the similarity.

Actually, the ideas of Modern Science Fiction *are* founded on ideas in super-science, and one can trace them back to that source. For instance, in Campbell's "Brain Stealers of Mars," Penton and Blake—two very well-received series characters—are sent into the "funny animal" subgenre founded by Stanley G. Weinbaum's "A Martian Odyssey" in the late 1930s.* Martian flora prove to be telempathetic and mimetic; perfect vegetable duplicates of Penton and Blake begin clumping around, conversing with them in their voices, but exhibiting nasty

---

*Weinbaum came and went like a meteor, and persists as a legend. He wrote a series of excellent stories, mostly founded in biological science, often as lighthearted tours through exotic flora and fauna on other planets—and then died young. The late thirties–early forties are dangerous years in the lives of stefnists; if they survive these years, they usually live to a ripe age in which most of them continue to produce.

intentions. Campbell explained this capability in biotech terms, and the problem was solved. But it came up again in Campbell's much later "Who Goes There?" commonly considered the best stef-suspense novella ever written, in which the ability is displayed by an extraterrestrial being found by an Antarctic expedition.

What's interesting to note is that Campbell didn't really favor any one particular "scientific" rationale for the mimesis; it was the mimesis itself, and its effect on his protagonists' equanimity, that returned him to the theme. One can readily see why, by examining what one knows of Campbell's childhood—but one can see it too readily. Campbell did not actually originate the idea, even if he played on it best. It involves all the common human apprehensions evoked by the classic doppelgänger theme in literature, which turns up repeatedly in "stories of identity" by such litterateurs as Kafka and Muriel Spark, as well as franker variations by newsstand stef writers before and since Campbell. The point is that in newsstand stef it is established as one of the master ideas, and the game is to find new enabling devices through which to exploit it.

If that were not the game, how could Campbell feel safe in giving the same "idea" to several different writers? So is it the tech furniture or the "idea" which is paramount, and is the "idea" technological or an expression of common human psychology? Is the "story" in how Penton and Blake dispose of the brain stealers? Or is it in how Penton and Blake, two friends bonded by many shared triumphant gambles on their mental and physical alertness, must cope with the sudden apprehension and suspicion that arise catastrophically when their social ability to rely on each other is destroyed? Is "Brain Stealers" about brain stealing or about one of the fundamental props of human social interaction? Which of those levels, do you suppose, is of greater interest to the reader, who is located about 60,000,000 miles from Mars but has to function in society every minute of his life? Particularly when he is characteristically someone to whom society presents unusually emphatic problems?

Modern Science Fiction established a catalogue of such "master ideas," drawing on superscience, and beyond it to scientifiction and classical sources for prototypes. It funneled them through Campbell, and the inner cadres which responded most readily to Campbell, and then dispersed them irrevocably into all subsequent stef, in all its subgeneric forms, and also into modes commercially identified as fantasy and its subgrenres.

Along the way, stef has thoroughly explored such subquestions as "Yes, it's obvious social responsibilities are incumbent, but what are they, exactly?" "What is 'superior' in this context?" "What is 'skill'?" "What is 'less advantaged'?" "What is 'worth'?" etc. Each newly broken-into level furnishes a fresh input of cash to its author, but the readers are simultaneously quick to question and expose meretricious thinking and false propositions, while they reward speculatively solid advances in what is essentially sociological philosophy.* Reader approval translates into additional sales; therefore, the commercial format positively reinforces genuinely useful thinking and tends to winnow conclusions with general applicability to actual human situations.

---

*In Campbell's own "Forgetfulness," from the late 1930s, the civilizing expedition is from Alpha Centauri, whose natives, just capable of interstellar travel, find Earth. The home of mankind abounds with enigmatic, unused high technology from a time, millennia past, when humans roamed the Galaxy and disposed of enormous physical power. The remaining humans live in little huts out-

Another master idea is that an individual obsessed with a particular form of technological advance, working in isolation and tossing despised scraps heedlessly over his shoulder, may find that humankind has meanwhile taken those by-products, found vast uses for them, and transformed its society into a configuration that makes his eventual success meaningless to him. ("Blindness," by Don A. Stuart, late 1930s; "Far Centaurus," by A. E. van Vogt, middle 1940s.)

Yet another is that technological dictatorships inevitably must fall to technologically superior rebels because the surviving undergrounders have automatic access to all science that is suppressed for "unorthodoxy." They are, thus, the only persons who continue to research those areas. ("Frictional Losses," Don A. Stuart, late 1930s; "When the Rockets Come," Robert Abernathy, middle 1940s, in which Abernathy, in Wellsian fashion, exactly predicts the feelings aroused by the Vietnam war.)

Obviously, such ideas are freighted with increasingly subtle possibilities for extrapolation; they also yield to successive abstractions. In a community that incessantly reinforces the value of developmental thinking, this process of combining successively deep intellections with geometrically broadening perspectives normally yields very rapid evolutions, each marked by an "idea," which is an extrapolation of a more primitive "idea" and only incidentally tied to fresh developments in mundane technology—which proceeds at a much slower pace even at its swiftest.

The speed with which such ideation can supersede its roots is seen in the archetypal case of "Don A. Stuart."

This was a writer who came unheralded upon the scene in a 1934 issue of *Astounding,* edited by F. Orlin Tremaine and blurbing the appearance next issue of a Campbell superscience serial, *The Mightiest Machine.* This first appearance, with the quiet, moody, totally revolutionary story "Twilight," places the actual foreshadowing of Modern Science Fiction some years ahead of its perceived chronology and was, as you might guess, by Campbell, who used a slight variation of his then-wife's maiden name.

"Twilight" caused a sensation, which subsequent Don A. Stuart stories reinforced. Campbell always declared that "Twilight" was inspired by a passage in a nonfiction book by C. E. Scoggins entitled *The Red Gods Call.* The passage depicts modern South American Indians assisting an archeologist in digging Inca ruins, totally ignorant of who might have erected those lost cities, oblivious to their own ancestry. That was the "idea" on which Campbell based a story about a time-traveler who encounters the listless remains of humanity in a future millions of years beyond his own.

But two things become obvious when the Stuart story is examined. One is its intricate, multilevel allegory of repeatedly failed communication, for which the "idea" was more of a spark than an underpinning. The other is the writing style, which is markedly different from that of John W. Campbell, Jr. It was by

---

side their abandoned cities, and cannot explain the forgotten machines. Their visitors' pity and condescension turn to something else when their ship is ultra swiftly returned home by the Earthmen's mentally marshaled powers alone. "Why couldn't you teach us your technology?" the visitors demand. "Neither can we remember how to chip flint for arrowheads," the Earthmen reply.

Campbell, without question, but it came from a different sector of Campbell's mind.

This style became generic in Modern Science Fiction. It is a broody murmur, occasionally rising toward shrillness. Others have described it as a "high whine," which is fair enough but implies more monotone than was actually there. Individual writers, of course, varied from it in their own perceived tones, but one major characteristic runs throughout, and that is melancholy.

There is no question that the author of "Twilight" had read and assimilated *The Time Machine.** The mood produced by "Twilight" was the mood of a man like Campbell, substituted for his ostensible protagonist Ares Sen Kenlin, finding himself in the penultimate Wellsian future, confronted by moth and rust, having no choice but to *do* something about it, galled because his best efforts might very well not suffice, frustrated because he would never be able to see the conclusion of them. The story was written years before it was sold.

It was, it is, the definitive Modern Science Fiction statement, ultimately distilled in a 1949 ASF short story, "To Watch the Watchers," by Walter Macfarlane: "It is a proud and lonely thing to be a man."†

Compared to all previous stories in the genre media (during the initial eight-year history of that commercial field), "Twilight" was essentially without precedent. Its effect depended not upon its plot, not upon its central technological supposition, not even so much on the arrangement of its primary and supporting ideas, but on its "mood"—that is, on what it evoked in the psyches, rather than in the intellects, of its readers. And that effect was literary. It transcended the mere building blocks of its words and sentences, and belied Campbell's assertion that it was simply a deployment of ideas to be speculated upon as ideas. It was a direct lineal descendant of the work of H. G. Wells, the would-be Mainstream author, as evolved to enwrap a philosophical statement. It does not matter that this quality apparently resulted from the merely intuitive creativity of a

---

*Wells's protagonist has just escaped from the Morlocks, but lost Weena, the Eloi girl. Catching his breath on a hillside, he contemplates the condition into which humanity has descended:

I grieved to think how brief the dream of the human intellect had been. It had committed suicide. It had set itself steadfastly toward comfort and ease, a balanced society with security and permanency as its watchword, it had attained its hopes—to come to this at last. Once, life and property must have reached almost absolute safety. The rich had been assured of his wealth and comfort, the toiler assured of his life and work. No doubt in that perfect world there had been no unemployed problem, no social question left unresolved. And a great quiet had followed.

It is a law of nature we overlook, that intellectual versatility is a compensation for change, danger, and trouble. An animal perfectly in harmony with its environment is a perfect mechanism. Nature never appeals to intelligence until habit and instinct are useless. There is no intelligence where there is no change. Only those animals partake of intelligence that have to meet a huge variety of needs and dangers.

So much for Wells as a rabid proponent of technocracy. And so much for Campbell, too. Though Ares Sen Kenlin in the far future turned at last to the machines, having given up on mankind, what he set the machines to attempt to do is a passing on of the torch: he set them to the task of developing curiosity.

†The melancholy Modern Science Fiction signature finds precedent in the climactic scenes of *The Time Machine,* but is otherwise at variance with the wittiness frequently seen in Wells, dry or lyrical. Modern Science Fiction—except conspicuously in the work of L. Sprague deCamp and Fritz Leiber—does not have a particularly broad range of moods. This distinguishes it from post-Modern stef, which began to take all forms of prose expression for its province. I think Campbell set the tone, in his work and conversation, but it's noteworthy that so many of his writers readily adopted it.

man who made a passable living as a rock-steady genre writer and who had never read a book from a liberal arts viewpoint in his life.

There is something to be made of the fact that as a genre businessman, Campbell must have realized, imprimis, that in "Twilight" he was producing the unsalable, and was compelled to go ahead and do it anyway. There was no place for it in the generic media; this was confirmed by its repeated failure to sell to anyone publishing "science fiction."

This is a famous failure; the oral tradition of the field refers to it often. The story was rejected for years, everywhere, until Tremaine eventually took it. There is reason to believe that he accepted it in part because he never had a very sure grasp of what "science fiction" was. Had he been more confident of what was expected in the field, he might never have run it. Campbell's own feeling was that it was so far out of line it required a pseudonym to protect John W. Campbell, Jr.'s, established reputation for knowing what the pure quill was, and supplying it.

What I am asserting is that there really is such a thing as literature, that it exists as a genuine entity generated by universal human aesthetics, and that its imperatives can under certain circumstances force themselves even upon prose salesmen with a vested interest in denying them. I believe that, for all practical purposes, "Twilight" represents the first incursion into original genre "science fiction" of art as something beyond mere craftsmanship.

It is necessary to think of literature as a quality, rather than the result of a writer's conscious abilities, in order to explain the revolutionary consequences of what resulted from "Twilight"'s eventual publication. The story is not all that well written, word for word, or free of cliché phrasing, didactic scene construction, or wan characterization. Putting it another way, it appears hamhanded. But somewhere in it is a taint different from other apparently similar collections of words in its contemporary media.

There is no nondramatic way to put this: "Twilight" struck the science fiction community like a thunderclap. It has no "science" in it. The technological descriptions are nearly as cursory as those in *The Time Machine;* the most detail is devoted to a womblike vehicle that takes its reclining passenger everywhere in perfect safety, managing his route until he has puzzled out of controls and taken them over for himself. It contains no physical conflict between the representatives of good and the representatives of evil. Rather, two—make it three— divergent cultures are seen reasonably and tragically disagreeing on the nature of the proper use of intelligence.§

In 1938 Campbell, doyen of the superscience story, was made editor of ASF, and quickly created "Modern Science Fiction." Is Modern Science Fiction based on *The Mightiest Machine?* Except in clinging to the Little Tailor, it is not. Were

---

This is a good time to lay to rest any speculation that stefnists as a class are an underground intellectual movement consciously out to lead the world away from error toward truth. One eavesdrop on any social gathering of "science fiction" writers will suffice to confirm their infinite variety on such points. But this is not to say there are no crusading individuals, and it seems likely that Campbell gathered around him a fairly high proportion of persons especially conscious of their burden and its demands.

§The third is our own time. The story ostensibly has its "frame" set in the present social context. The "frame" is artistically vital to the emotional functions of the story.

the new writers, produced in wholesale lots by Campbell, promulgators of the highly successful superscience flavor? They were not. He got rid of all but one of those as fast as possible. "Twilight" and Don A. Stuart—a diffident work of art, and an obscure artist—are the seminal precursors. E. E. Smith and John W. Campbell, Jr., are today the authors of curiosa.

The rhetoric of "science fiction" continued to be essentially the rhetoric of scientifiction and of superscience. Campbell insisted to his dying day that the worth of science fiction rested in its ability to "predict" the future, and that the worth of stef writers was quantifiable. He ran an "Analytical Laboratory" monthly feature which "rated" the "merit" of stories in previous issues, ostensibly on the basis of how many tech ideas they contained and elaborated. Everyone fell in with this unconscious conspiracy, intended to further the illusion that the principal preoccupation of ASF was with the promulgating and testing of tech speculations. Some of the effect of ASF was exactly that. But in hindsight it is ludicrous to suggest that this is what ASF was doing the greater part of the time.

A notable, central fact regarding Campbell is rarely placed in its proper perspective. After inheriting the editorial direction of ASF, he promptly created a sister magazine devoted to fantasy. It is the only publication Campbell ever founded. Called *Unknown*, and later *Unknown Worlds*, its format was identical with ASF's, and its core writers were shared between the two media. *Unknown* died in World War II paper shortages. Many Campbell writers promptly began selling some of their total production to *Weird Tales* and *Fantastic Adventures*, which paid badly. Campbell made several postwar efforts to revive *Unknown*. In other words, the editor and the writers now cited as hardheaded scientophiles were just as ready to practice magic under other hats.

So to what extent does stef *artistically* separate "science fiction" from "fantasy" or other forms of speculative fiction?

Among the few details available from Campbell's childhood is the anecdote relating that his mother and aunt, being identical twins, often exchanged clothes and roles in order to prankishly confuse the youngster. Wherever the truth and full extent of this Freudian nightmare might lie, observation declares that Campbell was himself a twinned person (and also hyperconscious of what it can meant to be a "junior").* While the articulate, public personality was busy generating verbal formulae intended to deny the brooding, anxious artist, the raw creative genius was getting his licks in by the very nature of the ideas that the public Campbell dispensed to his amanuenses—as if he were a genuine story-computational machine instead of a Maelzel's "mechanical" chess player with a hidden person inside. (Cf. "Poor Superman," by Fritz Leiber, the writer whose own art punctured more Campbell myths more precisely than the oral tradition yet recognizes.)

The universal quality shared by those ideas, again, is that they were not technological; they were sociological. The idea of "All," for instance, is that

---

* *Dianetics, the Modern Science of Mental Health* goes to obsessive lengths on the inescapable psychic damage resulting from being named for one's parent. See further passages relating to Campbell vis-à-vis Dianetics and Scientology.

technology might supply devices whose discreet use would support a new miraculous religion, which then would constitute an overwhelming political force. The specific hardware is totally optional, and differs among the Campbell, Heinlein, and Leiber versions.

If one seeks to make "science fiction" fit a definition that calls technology science, the hardware is assuredly there to find. So is the future, employed as a setting. But the very fact that it can differ from story to story, without impairing the essential emotional loading, clearly indicates that the hardware is not what the story is "about," and that the "future"—whichever enabling social setting is invented by whichever particular author—is relied on only because we "know" such methods have never been employed in the past. Although there are rumors about mechanical Egyptian idols with built-in voice boxes, and sly whispers about the Delphic oracle, as well as Greek ceramic-and-asphalt storage batteries the size of golf bags. These latter devices were never put to industrial use, but the priesthood must have had some purpose for them.*

I evoke these parallels, first, to call strongly into question any absolute *literary* need to futurize the essential story of "All," or any of its many variants among which the Heinlein and Leiber novels are only the most prominent. Second, what would be the viability, do you suppose, of a 1940s newsstand pulp raising such questions as: Where was the galvanic Jesus during the unchronicled decades of His life; and what did that Artisan bring back with Him from wherever He had gone on His fishing boat? Would it jerk life into dead fish?

You see my point. In *Adventures in Time and Space* (1946 et seq.), you'll see it again. This is the definitive anthology—still in print—of the Golden Age, unquestioningly and enthusiastically cited as such within the community. In it, Raymond J. Healy and J. Francis McComas not only selected the bellwether work of Campbellian stef but identified it as a "sub-genre," which they referred to as modern science fiction. This they implicitly define as being all science fiction that is not non-modern science fiction. They knew what they meant; only time has required critics to give it capitalized initials.

The first edition has 995 text pages, containing two ASF articles, three stories chosen from among the dozen alternative sources, and thirty ASF stories with copyright dates from 1937 to 1945. Almost all of them issue from bylines that still shake the gloaming beyond the nighted cookout fire at the summer stef-teaching seminar.

A few are time-travel paradox stories, Modern Science Fiction's version of the tech jape. Robert Heinlein, among others, still adores elaborating on it. Even "By His Bootstraps," from the early part of his career, derived its underlying salacity from the implicit truth that many of the enabling "technologies" of Modern Science Fiction are only storytelling conventions, and scientifically absurd conventions.

---

*It *is* hard to credit. But such artifacts have been found by archeologists, and there's no doubt what they were. Classical Mediterranean antiquity abounded with high technology, but not mass technology. Muscle power was cheaper and easier to generate, sufficed for almost all purposes, and fit in better with the prevailing social convictions. The future we represent to Pericles is not an advance by his standards.

A few more of the stories here are jabs at any middle-class complacency on technology as a servant. These are either symbolist slapstick comedy or Gothic grue unredeemed by worthwhile hope. All but one, significantly, are by "Lewis Padgett," a very specialized avatar of Henry Kuttner. The other is by Alfred Bester, and boils down to a statement that it might take no more than several billion years to bring the Earth back up to the point where a technologist could reduce it to cinders again. These are among the "best" and "most memorable" stories from what we all agree is the flowering of tech optimism in the most stringently technological of the media.

The overwhelming balance are stories based on the model "If this goes on . . ." from Wells via Stuart.* They work no matter what their hardware. In Cleve Cartmill's "The Link," set in a prehistoric milieu, the hardware is a found broken-off tree limb.† The story takes the reciprocal model "If this goes back. . . ." It is the best short example of a populous body of stef unaccounted for by any definition with a reliance on future as setting, and gives new meaning to any implicit reliance on "the scientific method."§

In this volume, the famous "ideas" of Modern Science Fiction are explicitly sociophilosophical ideas on the nature of humankind's relation to Nature. Compare "Forgetfulness" to "The Link." The various technisms are secondary plot-winding devices, or tertiary local color. Why, after all, would a person enshrine conspicuous gentility if all he were proposing to the world was literally only a better mousetrap?

If this is true at the fountainhead, it is true enough everywhere. "Science fiction" has no fundamental connection with the recently named, delimited disciplines of inquiry that result in white-coated figures peering into apparatus, or in coveralled individuals moving mountains. In the philological sense, of course, "science" is simply the summation of all humankind's observations on Nature and on the likelihood of making accurate observations, and of proposed schemata. This broader sense does, yes, apply to Modern Science Fiction, and by extension to all "science fiction," or all "literature," or all "art." At some

---

*Not included in this volume is a famous early Heinlein, "If This Goes On. . . ."

†The protagonist is a weak, pink-skinned mutation born into a tribe of properly hairy, bipedal scavengers of roots and grubs. Driven out, he wanders, then discovers that a club will extend his leverage to the point where he can even kill a "big head"—a sabertoothed tiger—and that dead carnivores are better sources of protein than things found in rotting logs. Infused with Promethean enthusiasm, he goes back to the tribe. Finding it in a clearing, he confronts and kills its leader, as well as several of his henchmen, expecting to be acclaimed and obeyed. But the surviving bipeds, including his mother, scorn and despise him nevertheless. He kills more, but wearies of it. Wandering again, he encounters a wounded abandoned female, succors her, and attempts to explain himself to her.

"I have killed a big head and"—he hesitated, searching his brain for a term to describe the dead he had strewn over the clearing —"and other animals," he concluded.

§Properly, just "scientific method," in which method is the main referent and "scientific" is a modifier, recognizing that there are many "non-scientific" systems of thought whose rigor is equally strict. It was originally proposed in the thirteenth century by Friar Roger Bacon, who attempted to circumvent contemporaneous suppression of the axioms of Aristotle; he sincerely offered it as a means of determining to what extent God permitted knowing the details of His handiwork. For more on what is a not inconsiderable distinction, see James Blish's long historical novel on Bacon, *Doctor Mirabilis.* Blish thought it would by itself collapse most stef definitions. Few noticed.

point in this area where C. P. Snow's "two cultures" merge, we encounter individuals who differ from one another in that the "scientist" tends to say "I have discovered. . . ." where the "artist" says "I have created. . . ." But anyone who has spent much time with either sort knows by observation that even this distinction is hardly clear-cut.

Throughout his career, Campbell fostered the idea that he and his domain were somehow primarily concerned with actual technology. There's no point speculating on how much he consciously saw the fallacy in this. Some of his writers saw it clearly, then or shortly thereafter, and consequently, with deliberation, created further profound effects on the evolution of the "genre." Others may simply have found their work developing fresh attributes. In looking back from a 1950 story to a 1940 story written in exactly the same feeling for what was "good" and "right," they might have wondered how they had gotten to where they were. If Campbell had inside processes that the top of his mind did not monitor, he was not, in that sense, unusual for either a scientist or an artist.

Campbell did have the idea that in the world's eyes, only the quantifiable is respectable. For instance, in the late 1940s L. Ron Hubbard* somehow hit on the idea that neurosis-processing could be described in cybernetic terms. He worked closely on this idea with Campbell, who for some time thereafter moonlighted his ASF job while heading a Dianetics Institute in New Jersey. The Institutes occurred as sparse scatterings of chapters across the land, including one in Los Angeles staffed by A. E. van Vogt. These beleaguered outposts eventually coalesced into the politically active Church of Scientology.

In Scientology today, progress beyond total retrieval and rationalization of all childhood traumas has been made. Now there is communication with past selves, and considerable use of hardware. Campbell would have liked to have a microphone and headset with which to sort out what had been said and done to him back past the fuzzy edge of conscious memory. But which is more important about a man: that he would speak with the Beyond, or the details of how he would go about doing that?

Campbell was an artist, a profound mystic, and, in the confabulatory as well as the genre sense, a fantasist seeking refuge within the fascia of technology.

It's conclusively revelatory that for *Dianetics* he chose to give the general public an impression of credentials and a work history he didn't possess. This, of course, runs completely counter to the Calvinistic basis of true Technocracy. Also, it was done where Campbell knew the knowledgeable community would see him doing it.

In the experience of all who knew him, Campbell was obsessively, stuffily—literally—honest in all respects. In what he did for *Dianetics* as a publishing property, it seems certain he believed he was serving a "higher truth." That is

---

*Campell doted on Hubbard, a former pulp adventure writer who could sell Florida oceanfront to Eskimos. No one now knows the truth of Hubbard's background or many reliable details of his life. During the Golden Age Hubbard wrote with blinding speed, on a specially geared electric typewriter—some say—and was capable of turning out a novel in 24 hours or less. It was invariably a flawed novel, but it might take several days after reading it for that realization to sink in. Many of his works founder on scientific and/or logical absurdities, but no one, not even Campbell, cared except in extreme cases.

the only circumstance under which our good acquaintance and great preceptor would have "lied," as distinguished from "made pleasant." But it does declare which was the "lesser" imperative.

6

Time-binders are unusually sensitive to doctrinaire honesty in highly intelligent individuals. It can be a signal of elaborated and invincible sincere error. By 1950, many of Campbell's stars had edged away from him, either totally or almost so. They gave a variety of post-factum reasons in later years; philosophical disagreement was the major one.

A few writers—Heinlein for one, Bester for another—had moved into markets such as the slick magazines or TV, and had adjusted their rates accordingly. Heinlein also began doing a series of juvenile novels in which he explored the potential of the newly emerging market for book rights, and which have done so much to bring intelligent new readers into the field.

But most Modern Science Fiction writers simply took a vacation, depending either on their salaried jobs or on writing of other kinds for other word-rate markets. Marginal semiprofessional book publishers began marketing adult-level reprints of Golden Age magazine serials and story collections or anthologies, at very slim recompense to the writers. James Blish, Gordon R. Dickson, and Poul Anderson, almost alone, began to supply ASF with work up to Golden Age standards, being a few years younger than the first generation of major contributors.

A variety of brand new or refreshed pulp titles had begun to appear after World War II, to no one's great excitement although there had been flurries. *Amazing* for a brief time had set circulation records that still stand—250,000 copies per month—by essentially abandoning stef and substituting occult fiction with the trappings of stef and of sadomasochism.* In a much more traditional development, a new editor for *Startling Stories,* Sam Merwin, Jr., unexpectedly brought literacy and strong storytelling values to that ragged sister of *Thrilling Wonder Stories* and *Captain Future.*

Merwin attracted sporadic contributions from such ex-Campbell writers as Sturgeon, A. Bertram Chandler, and George O. Smith, who had married Dona Stuart Campbell. Merwin also took the stories Ray Bradbury had not sold to *Planet Stories* or *Weird Tales.* He found mordant joy in publishing one of them under a house pseudonym, then standing back for outraged

---

*The editor was Raymond A. Palmer, an idiosyncratic ex-Fan employed by Ziff-Davis Publications when it was a pulp chain operating, atypically, from Chicago. An extremely shrewd marketer of stef raygun drama, Palmer hit on the new formula, rode it pyrotechnically, and was shortly dismissed, as a cause or more likely an effect of Z-D's moving to New York and rearranging itself into a publisher of popular avocational magazines. *Amazing* and its sister, *Fantastic,* went digest-sized and very slick in the early fifties, then languished, and have since been sold twice. Palmer died as the self-publisher of *Flying Saucers from Other Worlds.* B. G. Davis separated from William Ziff and purchased *Ellery Queen's Mystery Magazine.* His son, Joel, was the publisher of both *Asimov's Science Fiction Magazine,* and of *Analog* until they were sold to Dell in the 1980s, and then Penny in the 1990s.

reader reaction to the new "sentimentality and incomprehensibility" suddenly displayed by Brett Sterling, author of *Captain Future*.* Eventually, he edged up on Campbell's 90,000-copy monthly circulation, then handed it over to Samuel Mines, who briefly exceeded it just before TV terminated the pulps.

What this period represented to the readers was a hiatus far more pervasive than the one Campbell claimed had been created by the wartime service of so many of his best writers. In hindsight, a study of the bylines in immediately postwar publications reveals the persistence of a totally separate cadre of writers who had rarely, if ever, worked for Campbell: Pohl, Kornbluth, Knight, and Blish were the most prominent, alone or in pseudonymous concert. Blish did go to Campbell briefly at this time, but, like his peers, was essentially a Futurian.

The self-labeled Futurians were a Brooklyn group of street geniuses living on the edge not of poverty but of starvation. They had entered stef as teenagers before the war, selling to extremely marginal markets edited by Futurians Donald A. Wollheim, Robert A. W. Lowndes, Pohl, Knight, et al. They were marked by desperate precocity and the shrewdness cultivated while dining on ketchup stolen from cafeterias, as well as a radical world view commensurate with their milieu. Their writing was marked by a notably casual use of tech conventions, concentrating instead on the foibles of human nature.

They had a preceptor in the slightly older John B. Michel, a charismatic countercultural theorist. But their voice was the voice of the bitter, hair-triggered Cyril Kornbluth, who seemed constantly on the verge of tears for the world's condition and expressed them as scorn.

For an immediate insight into Futurian stef, there is the very brief "The Rocket of 1955," published in 1941, written by Kornbluth at the age of seventeen or eighteen. (For copious further detail, see the books *The Futurians*, by Damon Knight [John Day, 1977] and *The Way the Future Was*, Frederik Pohl [Del Rey, 1978].)

Germane here is that every Fan worthy of the name at that time made it a point to obtain and read every bit of stef published everywhere, and the Futurian media were no exception. But ASF's prestige then was so great that in most community schemata, Futurian authors and stories simply were not fitted in.

In hindsight, the Futurian publications are mined by anthologists, and critics can readily point to the fact that during the entire period in which ASF was presumed to be *the* source of stef's pocket Mainstream, a powerful and energetic school of (even) less technistic material was rehearsing its authors, recruiting highly talented fresh adherents, and in some cases producing finished work fully as effective as anything on the market. These were, furthermore, frank intellec-

---

*The *Future* "Sterling" had been Edmond Hamilton, until he was drafted. Wartime *Futures* were written by Manly Wade Wellman, now far better known as an author of regional fantasies. Hamilton, back from the war, suddenly unveiled a post-Modernist humanism in stories such as "Home Run" and the famous "What's It Like Out There?"

tuals, who were broadly conversant with the entire domain of the arts, widely read considering the circumstances, and prized intellectuality as ASF's writers ostensibly or actually did not.

In 1949 the first noteworthy tap into this potential occurred with the publication of *The Magazine of Fantasy*, which with its second issue became *The Magazine of Fantasy and Science Fiction*.

F&SF was then a sister to *Ellery Queen's Mystery Magazine*, and thus cousin to the *American Mercury*, formerly edited by H. L. Mencken, latterly by William Bradford Huie. It consequently was stef's first entree into the market for American intellectual diversionary fiction, quickly picking up the back-cover endorsements of Book-of-the-Month Club editor Basil Davenport, of Spring Byington, doyenne of the Hollywood intellectual establishment, of Hugo Gernsback(!), and of Mortimer Adler. It published poetry, cartoons, and spot art but no illustrations, used page-width columns, and for its fiction displayed a mix of "classic" reprints by "Mainstream" short story writers and very similarly oriented new pieces by stef names.

The readership was also mixed. Some readers were amenable individuals already within the existing stef magazine pool. Others were the sort of people who will read Huxley, Wells, Stapledon, and perhaps Franz Werfel's Book-of-the-Month-Club selection *Star of the Unborn*, but would never crack the pages of something called *Astounding* to find Leiber's *Destiny Times Three* or Catherine Moore's "No Woman Born."

The editors were J. Francis McComas and Anthony Boucher. Boucher had been a significant contributor to *Unknown*. A few of his stories had appeared in ASF. He was more at home in the milieu of the Agatha Christie school of 'tec fiction, and showed a predilection for the intellectual jape—the charming, rather than the powerful. In 1942, under a pseudonym,* H. H. Holmes, he had published a *roman à clef* called *Rocket to the Morgue*, a straight-line detection novel, whose cast featured lightly disguised Modern Science Fiction writers, as writers of this interesting new genre. To at least some extent, Boucher's intention clearly was to attract his sort of person to stef as an alternative form of permissible light reading.

For quite some time, there was a persistent distance between F&SF and some notable members of the stef community. Some of the reasons for this were partly mechanical. It was a long time before F&SF published a serial, or the sort of compressed novel which is the class stef "novelette," as distinguished from a long short story. This automatically eliminated some specialists from that market, but is in itself also a social statement implying aspersions on the prose format of the traditional media. It implies the same sort of distancing that occurred between *Ellery Queen's* and *Black Mask*,† home of Hammett, Chandler, and—*touché*—Erle Stanley Gardner.

---

*"Boucher" was actually one of the scores of people named White who abound in popular and semi-popular literature of the twentieth century. (If something began the 1900s by collecting Ambroses, to cite Charles Fort, did something then begin producing Whites?) In the case of our William Anthony Parker White, "Boucher" was more a *nom de guerre* than a true pseudonym.

†*Black Mask*, would you believe, had been founded by H. L. Mencken as an attempt to introduce profitability into the corporation that was publishing his *Smart Set*, at the time the premier vehicle

F&SF did not actively offend the community, taken as a whole, even thirty or twenty-five years ago, but it was a while before those who liked it achieved a majority, and a while before the magazine met them part way. Its history has been one of steady growth in popularity, under a succession of editors, with brief flirtings with conventional "genre" visuals, the steady receipt of Hugo and other awards as best magazine of the year, and increasingly frequent periods of publishing work at the cutting edge of whatever newsstand stef was doing at the time.

Stories of that sort first came from persons such as Theodore Sturgeon and Alfred Bester, with later inclusions from Knight and Pohl, Walter M. Miller, Jr., Harlan Ellison, and Avram Davidson.*

Robert P. Mills, in tenure 1958–1963, was F&SF's most stefnistic editor during this period, experimenting with interior illustration and other genre signatures, running Heinlein serials including some made from his juvenile novels, and in other ways making a conscious effort to improve contact with the stef community. He was actually a stranger to it, having come in via jobs at the other Mercury Press publications, but was an outstanding success at quickly familiarizing himself with its ways.

He was also the founding editor of *Venture Science Fiction*, F&SF's short-lived sister, which consisted of ten bimonthly issues beginning January, 1957. (There was an abortive, quarterly, second run which does not count in stef history.) *Venture* was planned as a "science adventure"† magazine, paying low rates.

Instead, it quickly became the most exciting stef medium of the time, featuring what were perceived as daringly excursionary experiments in full-fledged stef by most of the topflight and topflight-aspirant writers of the day. What it published were the stories F&SF would have gotten if it had begun differently. Writers for it were not conscious of any editorial dicta: they were instead en-

---

of American conscious intellection as well as of the essays which made Mencken famous as a commentator on manners and foibles. As soon as he could, Mencken sold out at a substantial profit to another company, which hired "Cap" Shaw as editor. Shaw is the Campbell of crime; he discovered the destitute, frustrated Hammett, and the suave, confident Raymond Chandler whose private and semiprivate articulations reveal him to have been a bewildered, misled bourgeois genius. But, at any rate, if you wish to build a case for how well conscious intellection actually represents the currents of general human thought, here is a good place to start.

*Davidson, who is, flatly, one of the outstanding American short-story writers of our time, was an early F&SF discovery who later matured, and who was for a time its editor. Ellison, in his teens editor-publisher of the fanzine *Dimensions*, justifiably also claims a (vociferous) place in general American letters.

†This is a term probably coined by Malcolm Reiss at Love Romances Publishing Company in aid of *Planet Stories*. It is the polite name for space opera. Reiss, a forgotten gentlemanly force in stef, knew better than anyone else in our history how to walk the line between the rousing tale rousingly told and simpleton thud-and-blunder. Under his supervision, a succession of editors were able to publish a number of literate pieces, epitomized by Paul L. Payne's winning hunch that his readers would respond wildly to the Ray Bradbury stories that have since become *The Martian Chronicles*.

Other subgeneric coinages include "science-fantasy"; all such terms refer not to science but to science fiction, from which these genres borrow such trappings as, for instance, the spaceships that enabled Northwest Smith to meet female vampires on other planets.

couraged to try anything that came to mind, and consequently were not afraid to fail, thus producing a notable ratio of success.*

Its history belies any thought that money is what matters to newsstand stef writers as a class. Mills at *Venture* was offered stories ahead of Mills at F&SF, and those stories include a great deal of work that is still integral to "Best of . . ." collections of its authors' work.

It did fail as a commercial property. It was a very bad time in the history of U.S. newsstand magazine distribution to attempt viability for a new stef magazine. It may, of course, also be that to some extent the public is reluctant to support what writers will do under these conditions. But it buys reprints of those stories now.

F&SF survived. Among other Mills contributions to stef was his willingness to take a chance on the *Long Afternoon of Earth* stories by England's hot new writer of the time, Brian Aldiss. Mills agonized over the propriety of running, in a "science fiction magazine," tales based on the enabling device of a massive spiderweb extending from the Earth to the Moon, but took the chance and the heavens did not fall.

F&SF gradually separated from the *Ellery Queen's* empirelette, which sent most of its ancillary titles to rest after selling off its flagships. Publisher Lawrence Spivak concentrated on producing *Meet the Press* for TV; successor publisher Joseph Ferman eventually turned F&SF over to his son, Edward. Edward Ferman, now editor-publisher, produces it from a remote Connecticut farmhouse—in Cornwall, where James Thurber and other New Yorkerites were wont to summer. It sustains itself admirably as stef's "little magazine," and, in precisely the same way that "little magazines" once swung great weight in the community of letters, hoes an influential row.

At the turn of the 1940s and into the 1950s, however, straight-line developmental science fiction history passed through *Galaxy Science Fiction*. (At various times in the late 1950s, it would attempt to market itself as *Galaxy Magazine*.) Excepting the "New Wave" centering on England's *New Worlds* magazine in the 1960s, *Galaxy* embodied the last great milestone in newsstand stef.

7

With the recent exception of *Omni* magazine, *Galaxy* represents the most thoroughly prepared, best funded attempt to capture top status overnight. It was planned to have a stefnally meaningful but publicly neutral title, a modern, design-ey cover format, a contemporary style in interior illustration, a reprint series of monthly "*Galaxy* Novels" which would serve as a substantial anchor to profit windward, and the highest rates of payment in the field. A major participant in the planning was Frederik Pohl, who had become proprietor of the

---

*No bones about it, it was the happiest time of my life as a writer, hurtling over the indifferent surfaces of the New Jersey Turnpike to stuff manuscript into Mills's Connecticut mailbox at three A.M. Sturgeon met deadlines by typing with a portable in his lap while his wife steered down the Merritt Parkway. Kornbluth commuted in from Long Island, and would have gone to work for Mills if he had lived. Other enthusiastic contributors were Asimov, Davidson, Del Rey, Leigh Brackett, Walter M. Miller, Jr., Judith Merril, and Anne McCaffrey with her first published story, as well as Poul Anderson, Clifford D. Simak, and A. Bertram Chandler.

most effective literary agency in stef, disposing of the works of all but a few top writers.

Almost every one of those plans went awry almost at once. While the first issues were appearing, beginning with October 1950, the original publisher was collapsing, the experimental new cover printing method had to be abandoned, the interior printing proved execrable, Street and Smith closed off the entire pool of Modern Science Fiction serials as sources of reprint novels, the payment rates and the cover format were imitated, and some of the earliest contributors began grumbling almost at once that the editor was rewriting their material capriciously.

None of this made visible difference to a three-year explosion in popularity and a general sense that those first thirty-six issues contain more concentrated good work than even the Golden Age could show. Furthermore, while it was perceptibly tinged with the attributes of Modern Science Fiction, they were Modern Science Fiction somehow made broader and more penetrating.

Backstage disasters made no difference to the audience, nor did the temporary disruption of the editor's ultimate intentions. It seems clear that *Galaxy* had greatness thrust upon it by forces too headlong to be baffled.

Actually, three waves of writers passed through *Galaxy* at that time, overlapping to a sufficient extent so that an appearance of homogeneity resulted. First were the Modern Science Fiction writers who had been appearing less and less in ASF. They were represented by material of whose themes Campbell would have been leery, or by an outspoken use of words and images that, by 1950 standards, were notably "daring."

The first six tables of contents comprise work from Clifford D. Simak, Theodore Sturgeon, Fritz Leiber, Isaac Asimov, James H. Schmitz, Raymond F. Jones, Lester del Rey, and "Murray Leinster," reading down the pages from top to bottom and looking for front-line ASF authors. A regular science column by Willy Ley represented the acquisition of the major ASF nonfiction byline.* A regular book review column by Groff Conklin represented the premier Modern Science Fiction anthologist, Healy and McComas having essentially retired from that métier after their one shot.

Among writers having lesser association with the grand days in ASF, but nevertheless with good ASF credentials, were Katherine MacLean, Fredric Brown, Anthony Boucher, and Frank M. Robinson. Other major bylines belonged to Richard Matheson, a contemporaneous spectacular F&SF discovery; to Sam Merwin, Jr.; to Ross Rocklynne (a man criticized by some *Planet* readers for putting too much deep thinking into his pulp productions); to William Campbell Gault and John D. MacDonald; to Mack Reynolds collaborating with Brown; and to "John Christopher." The last-named would in a few years write the famous *No Blade of Grass*, a worthy successor to *A Journal of the Plague Year*. He was effectively the only neophyte in that first set.

The November 1950 issue, we should note, contained Leiber's "Coming Attraction," the story that put "paid" to Modern Science Fiction as the leading subgenre. It exists with difficulty in the same universe of discourse with "Twi-

---

*Except for Campbell himself.

light." Its hero is set up to appear as a typical Campbellian prototype, who by its end is a gulled fool in tearful flight.*

What Leiber proposed was that the Swarthmore girl might have a hidden side, and thus that there might be serious vacancies in the sophistication of the Golden Age hero, and thus that Golden Ages might be founded on vacancies of perception. Quotation of specific prose passages also does not do justice to the totally controlled flavor of the story, masterfully sustained by someone hitherto presumed an archetypical Campbell writer. It argued that Leiber might be the most broadly insightful, most truly literate writer yet discovered in the magazines. It certainly opened doors.

For the merely clever, it offered a license to explore further into "taboo-breaking" words and situations for their own sake. Stef periodically discovers the thrill of spraying dirty words on fences, after which some people, encountering them, develop stories essentially about why people do such things, and thus reincorporate graffiti into the arts.

For those who already knew all that when Leiber first flashed it at them—and the last thing you want to believe in this context is that Leiber did it without great care for his target, or chose his mode on tittering impulse—the intervening steps did not have to wait to be taken. For them, the door opened on an entire universe of neglected aspects of nature which had been foreclosed by the sentimental humanisms of Modern Science Fiction. The effect of "Coming At-

---

*An Englishman has been sent on a commercial mission to post-WW III New York; the U.S. is recovering, but it has been wounded psychically by its near-disaster. The women go veiled. Here are excerpts from the first three hundred words:

The coupe with the fishhooks welded to the fender shouldered up over the curb like the nose of a nightmare. The girl in its path stood frozen, her face probably stiff with fright under her mask. For once my reflexes weren't shy. I took a fast step toward her, grabbed her elbow, yanked her back. Her black skirt swirled out.

The big coupe shot by, its turbine humming. I glimpsed three faces. Something ripped . . . the big coupe swerved back into the street . . . while from the fishhooks flew a black shimmering rag.

"Did they get you?" I asked the girl.

She had twisted around to look where the side of her skirt was torn away. She was wearing nylon tights.

"The hooks didn't touch me," she said shakily. . . . "Are you English? . . . You have an English accent."

Her voice came shudderingly from behind the sleek black satin mask. . . . "Will you come to my place tonight?" she asked rapidly. "I can't thank you now. And there's something you can help me about." . . . She gave me an address south of Inferno, an apartment number and a time.

But the lady in question proves to be not quite a damsel in distress, and not ready to follow through on her impulsive attempt to persuade the upright, gentlemanly Anglo-Saxon to take her away from all this. Her boyfriend is one of the male wrestlers who, in public spectacles, consistently lose to bigger, good-looking females. Jealousy over Zirk, the boyfriend, was the cause of the fishhook attack by three of his male hangers-on. Zirk encounters the "hero" and the girl in a saloon to which the girl has brought them. The hero of course punches him out. Here is the essence of the ending:

. . . as he crumpled back, I felt a slap and four stabs of pain in my cheek. I clapped my hand to it. I could feel the four gashes made by her dagger finger caps, and the warm blood oozing out from them.

She didn't look at me. She was bending over little Zirk and cuddling her mask to his cheek and crooning: "There, there, don't feel bad, you'll be able to hurt me afterward."

. . . I leaned forward and ripped the mask from her face. . . . Have you ever lifted a rock from damp soil?

traction" on many of Leiber's equally matured contemporaries was precisely the sort of effect "Twilight" had had on them as near-adolescents.

Inadvertently or otherwise, Leiber then shortly went on to underscore its effect with "Poor Superman," a much more overt heart-stab *à clef* at Hubbard and Campbell. Never let an artist grow to doubt you.

Even for those who did not possess the key, Leiber's work was genuinely powerful; so was the work of his contemporaries in *Galaxy*. Simak's leading serial would become the superb, popularly underrated *Time and Again,* a book which calls religiosity into question with a gentle implacability. Isaac Asimov's serial, *Tyrann,* which became *The Stars, like Dust,* was of ASF's Foundation series universe, yet tighter, more angular than anything done for ASF, which had rejected Asimov's first novel, *Pebble in the Sky.** *Tyrann* was the first Asimov magazine appearance with something longer than two installments, and not finding it in ASF was also a form of signal.

The second wave were Futurians: Kornbluth, Pohl, Knight, Blish, and Richard Wilson. Their increased maturity so much resembled the Modern stefnists' new liberty that the two separate origins produced something very much like one resultant.

The third wave were new writers. These were of two kinds. One kind were people attracted to *Galaxy* on its merits: Floyd L. Wallace, Wyman Guinn, "Boyd Ellenby," and to some extent J. T. MacIntosh and James E. Gunn—who would do excellent work for the magazine, persist for a few years, and never appear much elsewhere or elsewhen, except transformed. A man with a foot in both camps would be Michael Shaara, who belongs in a second category but also wrote stef only briefly and almost only for *Galaxy,* emerging in the literary world some years later with a Civil War novel, *Killer Angels,* which won the Pulitzer.

Shaara, like Robert Sheckley, Algis Budrys, Philip K. Dick, and several others, was a member of what might be called the Class of 1951: young men fresh from fragmentary careers in universities where a major purpose of their studies had been to qualify them for writing stef. Sheckley was old enough to have spent time in Korea, Shaara had been a Florida police patrolman, Dick had conducted a classical music program over a Berkeley radio station, and Budrys had been a travelers' check refund claims investigations clerk for American Express.

They had also played at other stopgaps—four-string guitar chords in a dance band, ditch digging, managing a record store, short-order cooking—but they had all come into terminal contact with Modern Science Fiction in their teens, and there was little doubt what they wanted to do with their lives. Not at all the same in their origins as most ASF writers, they were the first across-the-board line of ASF products.

Interestingly enough, they all attempted to confine their early appearances to *Galaxy*. Only one, Budrys, actually gravitated to ASF as a frequent contribu-

---

*A very early Doubleday stef novel, later condensed in *Two Complete Science-Adventure Books,* a pulp companion to *Planet,* and later still as a *Galaxy* Novel reprint, ostensibly not condensed but actually cut and slightly rewritten by Algis Budrys. It is best in Asimov's original, where it is very good. It's interesting that Campbell would not take it; the hero is a little tailor, perhaps too literally so.

tor, while becoming *Galaxy*'s earliest assistant editor for a brief spell truncated by acute claustrophobia, James Gunn having turned down the job.

Budrys excepted, this was the spine and nervous system of *Galaxy* for the first years. After that the magazine shook down, the earliest bylines began to disappear, except for Pohl, and fresh names, most of which are sunk without trace, began to dominate the contents. What seems to have happened is that the editor had finally gotten the situation under control, and headed in the direction he had originally intended. It seems quite clear the original plan had been to get the community's attention with familiar names, then gradually extend pseudopods into the general reading public with a new sort of stef that nearly wasn't stef, then retract out of the community altogether, or almost so.

The editor was H. L. Gold, once a frequent contributor to *Unknown* under his own name, to the Tremaine *Astounding* as Clyde Crane Campbell, and a veteran of mass-market publishing. He was the first editor of significance in stef to have thought of magazines as media rather than institutions, and of writers as instruments of policy with their work subject to policy dicta.

A charming, personable man face-to-face, and fully equipped with the ego required of a topflight editor, he was trapped, I think, inside his own concepts of professionalism, finding it imperative to produce a magazine which would gather readers by giving them the feeling they were included in the pop-intellectual community bounded on the north by the east sixties, on the south by Greenwich Village, and by the East River and Fifth Avenue.

To gain this objective, he saw nothing wrong in taking his pencil to manuscripts and making them increasingly bland and unsubtle, reducing classical concepts to catch phrases or to nothing, trying to get stef to fit the mode of the slick mass magazines. His potential audience rewarded him by ignoring him, his earliest writers tired of fighting his changes, and in due course he lost his edge.

He would visibly have lost it sooner but for the increasing ghost-editing of Frederik Pohl, to whom the magazine was eventually turned over officially. Pohl immediately reverted *Galaxy* to its 1950s configuration, then built it up into an evolved contemporary editorial format and, in the decade of the 1960s, gave it its only extended period of reliability combined with leadership.

Gold's direct accomplishments had been considerable. He created the possibility of Asimov's writing *The Caves of Steel*. Pohl and Kornbluth felt enabled to write the serial that became *The Space Merchants*. Alfred Bester gives him credit for leading him step by step through the writing of *The Demolished Man*, which institutionalized pyrotechnics in stef. He published Ray Bradbury's "The Fireman," which became *Fahrenheit 451*, and Damon Knight's most concentrated body of good work was done for him. William Tenn—who, like Dick, now recalls the *Galaxy* years with some bitterness—nevertheless was able to publish some of the best humorous stef ever written, a particularly good thing in a field which lacks numerous examples of something above the sophomoric along those lines.

Galaxy also furnished the last major market for Asimov's stef, which also included a brilliant series of novelettes. Although it's notable that just before he almost stopped writing fiction altogether, Asimov went back to Campbell.

What's most significant about the early history of *Galaxy* is that it illustrates both the excellences inherent in Golden Age writing and the degree of rising frustration imposed on its writers by ASF. As a class, they are clearly shown to be people who were too various to be constricted. Again as a class, they were people ready to abandon technism at the first opportunity, in favor of some other expressive wellspring in the mode.

They poured into *Galaxy* in a freshet. It cannot have been so much the money, because Campbell quickly brought his rates up to par and did not steal added time by demanding thematically trivial rewrites. It cannot have been so much the existence of a fresh market; there was a short-lived boom on, and it was hardly possible not to place anything one wrote. These were writers with ready access to old friends at many new or revived magazines, such as Lester del Rey's *Space Science Fiction* or Robert A. W. Lowndes's *Future Science Fiction*, where the community language was spoken fluently, rates were adjustable, and writers with good names were treated as valuable.

What *Galaxy* offered was not any one thing ostensibly, but what appeared to be a gestalt of factors: decent pay, halfway decent physical presentation, and blurbs describing them as literarily potent ("For Adults Only," said the headline over *Galaxy*'s first editorial). It offered them dignity.*

It was one thing, comprising those subsidiary features. When their dignity was affronted by Horace Gold's fits-all pencil, they left.

Some had found that there was no further need for a writer to tie himself to a particular market; they could be their own preceptors. Arthur C. Clarke and Asimov had clearly joined Heinlein and Bester in this discovery.† They found themselves moving into roles and income levels which permanently supported attitudes similar to those of any other sort of writer who has graduated into becoming a public figure.

Others had not made that particular breakthrough, but performed roughly analogous evolutions nevertheless. Shaara, Sheckley, Dick, and Tenn went various ways, into academe or into other fields of popular writing. Dick, always an original, produced several deliberately van Vogtian exploratory stef novels for Ace Books; then, in the early 1960s, *The Man in the High Castle;* and was off on his career as a novelist without further reference to the magainzes. Sheckley, in the spy-novel vogue of the day, did an interesting series around a low-key hero for Bantam, then began spending more and more time in Europe and writing slowly.

The great majority of Gold's short-lived stable of top names went to *Venture,* under the conditions previously described. Mills had only one recruitment ploy. His approach to stef writers was to express matter-of-fact faith that they had a great deal as yet unexplored within them, and that it was good. When he said such a thing, he was welcoming them into the entire literary establishment standing (shadowy) behind what was a still-flourishing Mercury Press. He also permanently disabused them of any lingering idea that there was some particu-

*1948 literary tea conversation: "And where does *your* work appear, Doctor Clarke?" "In *Astounding Science Fiction* Monthly, madam."
†Bester's contemporary novel about the New York TV industry, *Who He?*, had appeared. There had also been some sort of monumental hassle arising from Boucher's announcing his second stef novel, *The Burning Spear,* as an F&SF serial. It eventually ran in *Galaxy* as *The Stars My Destination,* but Bester's reconnection with magazine stef, and Gold's tutorial role, had obviously waned swiftly.

lar philosophical orientation it was their duty to serve excellently. Not all, but some, needed to be shown that.

Stef had, after all, spent a quarter century in the hands of a series of magazine editors who dominated their writers. Rough or smooth, they had been in a position to enforce their prejudices, and for some writers it did not come easily to realize there were other possible situations.

With the book market expanding rapidly—and, barring short cycles of adversity, it has continued to expand steadily since 1953—and with any number of other media beginning to take steady cognizance of genre-born stef, some time in the middle 1950s the pocket universe assumed its present diversity, in which there is hardly anything for which a decently skilled writer cannot find his or her own audience.

The ghetto attitude still exists in some quarters, at amateur, professional, and academic levels, expressed from inside and outside stefnism; nevertheless, functionally for many writers there has long been no distinction between their work and Mainstream work and work attitudes. Hindsight in some near future will make it possible to see that what Gernsback had done to institutionalize parochialism in 1926 was essentially undone by 1956, while the enthusiasm he had also introduced was continuing to proliferate, arguably to the benefit of all literature.

8

The drive to excellence has taken many forms in the stef universe, fueled by a sometimes unarticulated and unexamined, but highly energetic source. We are near to having established enough data and common vocabulary here to be able to reach some hard-edged conclusions about what that source might be, and how it relates to the impulses of art in general. But we should first examine some typical cases of writers who, to outside eyes, might be said to have been begun as purely commercial suppliers of product, but ended or have continued quite differently.

The conventional picture of Campbell's cadre as being nothing more than a group of semi-literate engineers flanging out plain tales plainly told shows even further defects.

Clifford Simak was a newspaperman writing fiction on the side, before and after the Golden Age. Jack Williamson and Will Jenkins were professional writers by first intention, before and after the Golden Age. Jenkins had been writing it before there were any stef media—almost as early as Gernsback.

In the core that Campbell is credited with having personally discovered and developed, the remaining great names, in no particular order, are L. Sprague de Camp, Hal Clement, Isaac Asimov, Hubbard, Sturgeon, George O. Smith, A. E. van Vogt, Eric Frank Russell, A. Bertram Chandler, and Lester del Rey. Of these, several are engineers, and several write like engineers, which does not mean they write badly. They are otherwise as various and variously sophisticated as any group of artists one could hope to find anywhere: a former sea captain, a former president of the Fortean Society, a former bulldozer operator, a former aircraft riveter, and the most urbane of the lot: L. Sprague de Camp. He did do much of the engineering that led to practical space suits but is impossible to picture holding any artifact harder-edged than a canape.

De Camp is the author of books on paleontology, natural history, and a host of other subjects; of historical novels on ancient Mediterranean cultures; and of ASF's *Viagens Interplanetarias* series, in which he displays not only a lively wit but an ability to slip straight-facedly into a steady increment of Portuguese obscenities. This is not a man created by any other man, and the same is true of all the rest. It is much easier to read their names as a list of very wide-ranging persons who happened to be able to talk tech, among other things (except van Vogt, who is ludicrously illiterate at it but whose readers—and whose editor— never cared).

Of course, there is Robert Anson Henlein. Heinlein may be the man Hubbard wanted to be. In a career that has included a host of nonliterary activities at home and overseas, this Annapolis graduate has found time since 1939 to incorporate a stefnal identity so much like the Campbellian archetype that some observers have wondered who invented whom. If there is a Mister Modern Science Fiction, it is Heinlein.

With the exception of 1966's *The Moon Is a Harsh Mistress*—one of the most subtle post-Modern novels, because ostensibly so perfectly Modern—readers' eyes are opened wide by Heinlein's work since the 1961 *Stranger in a Strange Land*. Half of *Stranger* reads as if written by the popularly conceived Heinlein and half by someone else who has dominated Heinlein's career since then.

Discussion can center on how much of this dramatic change is conscious, but it cannot make a Campbellian out of Heinlein through more than slightly half his career to date. It can gnaw at his motives, but it cannot change the fact that inside Heinlein all along there has been something more than Golden Age rhetoric can encompass. And a case can be made that, whatever those motives may be in detail, they amount to a repudiation of the Modern Science Fiction technical signatures: techniques that in large part were pioneered by Heinlein, or else were perfected by him.

I cannot think of a more plausible reason for this than a conscious decision at some level to do something "more important"—to live up to being the Grand Old Man, to display artistry, if only by jettisoning what others say is "not art." And that, for whatever it's ultimately worth as accomplishment in art, is at least the impulse of art.

If this is true here at the fountainhead, then . . . but that point has been made.

Knight was the man within the community who first began acting in ways that would turn this up.

Like Blish, Damon Knight (born in 1922), was not a native New Yorker. He had been invited to join the Futurians as the result of amateur work published from his home in Oregon. He and Blish were closely associated for many years, on a wide range of projects.

At first concentrating on his graphics talent, Knight gradually began doing more writing, and now uses his drawings professionally only as an occasional guide to illustrators of some of the more outré alien life forms in his stories. From writing he followed Frederik Pohl into editing stef, and after the war was the editor of *Worlds Beyond,* an F&SF-like magazine which was killed by its publisher as soon as the first issue caught his attention. Since then Knight's editing has been largely confined to anthologies of fiction, including the *Orbit* series of new stories, often by new and highly original writers. He is also, however, the editor of *Turning Points,* an anthology of critical essays on stef.

Knight's fiction is marked by a preference for short forms, some presented quite seriously and with vicious impact; at other times he is witty and even punsterish, but often with similar power. It seems clear from his work and from various statements that he would like to be John Collier. He comes close enough often enough to flatter his model.

His principal interests over the years, however, have been didactic and taxonomic. His book reviews began appearing in a variety of stef media in the early 1950s and were then collected as part of his *In Search of Wonder* (Advent: Publishers, Chicago, 1956; revised, 1967).

Catching the stef book market on the rise, Knight was the first critic to consistently treat book reviewing as something more than an opportunity to repeat the PR handouts of the publishers. His initial reputation was made in a fanzine essay demolishing van Vogt—up to that time a demigod—and he took some almost equally sharp looks at others in the pantheon.* His best work, however, was done in filleting the offerings of almost good writers: persons who produced something which appeared to be perfectly acceptable stef on the surface, but which was somehow troublesomely not quite right, and fell apart at the touch of Knight's scalpel. That is, he had standards; they were visibly useful, and they were now all available in one volume.

Most codified or institutionalized views of stef from within the field are Knight-influenced. The presumption that magazine-born stef was subject to general standards of literacy and logic is certainly his, as developed in concert with Blish. (Advent: Publishers also brought out *The Issue at Hand* and *More Issues at Hand,* 1964 and 1970—the collected reviews and essays of "William Atheling, Jr.")

Eye-catchingly deft, Knight was the perfect media critic at the exact best time. It was not so much what he said on any given occasion; it was the fact that he consistently operated from the position that it was time to take the field seriously, and that he refused to accept alternative views.

With Blish, and with former Futurian Judith Merril, Knight then announced the first professional stef writers' workshop, at Milford, Pennsylvania, where all three then resided with their families. The announcement was made at the 1956 New York world convention, where *In Search of Wonder* had just been awarded the first and only Hugo ever given a critical work, and the conference was scheduled for the week after the convention. Milford was within easy travel distance from New York, and the first of what was to become an annual series of Milford conferences was heavily attended.

Most of the writers would have willingly traveled farther to be one of a group taken seriously. Furthermore, editors and other publishers' representa-

---

*It's an excellent essay, its impact now stolen by the fact that van Vogt has had to devote the last twenty-five years to climbing back up from it, and so is not perceived as the giant he was. A converted writer of "true" confessions, van Vogt is sui generis, still obviously vulnerable to academic criticisms but fully capable of entertaining his readers inordinately. Others, Knight included, have experimented with some of his technical inventions, but he remains the master.

tives were permitted to attend—on a restricted basis—and some did choose to attend under those conditions: an even more gratifying experience for writers who discovered that under the circumstances they could be the bullies.

Out of Milford grew the Science Fiction Writers of America, a long-running series of Milford conferences at various sites, and a tradition of no-nonsense workshop sessions based on two presumptions: that the participants knew what they were doing, but that they could be brought to do it better.

Gradually, novices or comparative novices were cautiously let in. One of them, Robin Scott Wilson, then founded the Clarion SF Writers' Workshop for novices, initially at Clarion State Teachers' College in Pennsylvania, now both at Michigan State University and in Seattle as an expensive, high-standard, total-immersion six weeks' seminar staffed by six topflight visiting writers and a university supervisor.

Almost all of the many stef workshops now offered around the country and elsewhere are modeled on Milford via Clarion, and most of them were founded or are staffed by Clarion graduates.* It is now beginning to be true, for the first time, that most new stef writers have passed through such workshops as an alternative to, or a shortcut through, the seat-of-the-pants, trial-and-error methods of the past. The returns are not in on which method is the more successful in producing work that is both professional and individual, but the existence of the alternative is crucial to the present diversity of approaches in stef.

In the now-classic method as founded by Knight, students are accepted from among applicants furnishing examples of their work, and are then subjected to intense demands to produce work at the workshop. They are given nuts-and-bolts tips on everything from spelling and paragraphing to manuscript marketing; and the rotation of instructors as various in their own precepts as Wilson, Knight, Wilhelm, Samuel R. Delany, Thomas M. Disch, Gene Wolfe, and Ursula K. Le Guin—as well as Sturgeon, Ellison, Davidson, Pohl, Robert Silverberg, Carol Emshwiller, Kit Reed, and a small army of other practitioners over the years—ensures a minimum of channeling.

General litterateurs will of course see similarities to such institutions as the Breadloaf Writers' Conference and other respected sources of similar input for beginning general writers. There are also differences, founded on the special needs of stef writing as an art emerging from a variety of now inappropriate commercial strictures and as an art typically practiced by persons with highly individual views of the world. Knight is an adapter, not an inventor.

Still, he seems to have been exactly the right person at the right time in a succession of right places. It's noteworthy that the emergence of what amounts to a seminary system for the field came about in exact coincidence with the flourishing of a stef market for forms of fiction which the U.S. literary tradition has always defined as noncommercial and the province of the "little magazine." They have proved perfectly commercial in the contemporary stef marketplace, right alongside Brak the Barbarian and, if not Captain Future of fond-ish memory, then Cap Kennedy or Perry Rhodan, his more recent equivalent. In fact,

---

*Knight and his wife, Kate Wilhelm, anchor the last two weeks of Clarion. She is the multiple-award-winning stef writer who, among a number of others, now refuses to acknowledge the categorization.

stef is now one of the last refuges of the academic writer, and a number of the newer practitioners have come into it mostly for that reason.

The effect of Knight, working with Blish, Merril, or alone, was further compounded by the role of novelist Kingsley Amis, a person no one in America knew had any interest in stef. He is now widely credited with bringing on the revolution.

9

Actually the revolution grafted itself into the already accelerated evolutionary process. The revolution was the "New Wave" from England, where many of its outstanding participants deny the label, or, if accepting it, deny it applies to them.

In the 1950s, Princeton University invited Amis to give a series of lectures on anything he pleased, not realizing that he, like many Britons, was deeply involved in stef. Perhaps it would not have made any difference to the invitation. At any rate, Amis delivered a series on contemporary science fiction—its roots, characteristics, and purpose. The lectures were subsequently collected and published as *New Maps of Hell* (Ballantine, 1960), and academe's present involvement with stef dates from then.

U.S. stefnal establishmentarians were stunned to discover that Amis considered Frederik Pohl—the sometime editor of *Astonishing* and *Super Science;* former literary agent; emerging (and surely junior) collaborator with Cyril Kornbluth; and sometime hack of pseudonymous space opera—the most noteworthy stef writer on the scene because stef was essentially a satirical medium for holding up a sardonic mirror to contemporary society.

Coining the term "comic inferno," Amis imputed to the genre an uncommon power to affect the mass consciousness specifically because it was pop lit. Citing such recent Pohl works as the broadly satirical "Happy Birthday, Dear Jesus," as well as *The Space Merchants* (with its fish-in-a-barrel caricature of mass advertising and its simple chase plot in which the bedeviled hero eventually brings down the entire house of cards while striving to get society to take him back in), Amis conferred the laurel, packed his bags, and went home to enjoy the consequent tumult from across the water.

Whatever its merits as a construct of reasoning—and time has shown them to be considerable, if circumscribed—*New Maps* was at the very least totally anti-Campbellian, and in this respect reflected a general quarrel with U.S. stef that had been nurtured in the English academic community.

Up to that time, English commercial stef writers had been divided into two kinds: the hopeless and those who sold to the American media, such as Eric Frank Russell, A. Bertram Chandler, and, of course, Arthur C. Clarke, who had come late to ASF as the last Golden Age author. There were native British media; it was assumed on this side of the Atlantic that their essentially 1933 level more or less accurately reflected the degree of native intellection on stef.

In reasonably short order, a complete school of new English stef writers, headed by J. G. Ballard, Brian Aldiss, and Michael Moorcock, had end-run the older British establishment, by 1963 had gained control of *New Worlds* magazine under Moorcock's direction and set about producing large blocs of heavily intellectual, sometimes deliberately anti-Modern stef without reference to the U.S. establishment. In fact, they rapidly attracted a number of the newer U.S. writers, most notably Thomas M. Disch and Norman Spinrad, who for a while wrote very little for other media. In addition, they created a hospitable climate which—spiritually in the case of Judith Merril, actually in the case of James Blish and Harry Harrison—brought several established U.S. bylines to permanent or extended residence on their shores.

There are still pulp writers in England, as well as writers who aim primarily for the U.S. market with straightforward Modernistic stef. But the original cadre of New Wave individuals persists, has accreted second and third waves, and now sells quite freely in America, since the definition of what is "good" and "right" stef has expanded to include work like theirs.

To a visible extent, the shock of encountering such a talented cadre of people speaking what was at first a private language has accelerated the proliferation of modes within commercial stef. A writer such as Edward Bryant, for instance, ostensibly a purely American product of the early 1970s, would never have gotten the acceptance he did if the New Wave had never existed. Much the same is true of Craig Strete. Disch, who went to England a clumsy nihilist, would probably never have become the complex artists and subtle master of style he is now. Samuel R. Delany might never have written *Dhalgren*.* He would very likely not have embarked on the subsidiary critical and teaching career which has created a powerful second reputation for him and resulted in the publication of his collected essays, *The Jewel-Hinged Jaw.*

And there you have it. Genre labels are blatantly transient—convenient, utilitarian, and applicable only in short-run situations. If you want to call an aspect of speculative fiction "science fiction" so you can handle it as a commodity, nothing in Heaven or on Earth prevents it. But it does not arise from a specific impulse to do science fiction. Or genre fantasy. Or science fantasy or science adventure. It arises from the broad compulsion to speculate: an imperative as old as the day the second intelligent individual on this planet opened his or her eyes and found the first intelligent individual standing there in possession of reality and in command of the rules of behavior.

All the rest—the future, the imaginary island, the machine, the incantation, the demon, the Universe, the Mainstream which somehow does not contain an analogous stream displaying just as much breadth and depth—all the rest is detail.

---

*And there's room to wonder if the protean Frederik Pohl, stef editor for Bantam Books at the crucial moment, would have purchased it in reliance on a vast college undergraduate market for it. Pohl would not have touched it in earlier years. He is a very straightline, nonexperimental writer who has now emerged as well above the ordinary with such novels as *Gateway,* a genuine, nonbathetically moving work done in his middle fifties. You cannot catch a stefnist in a bottle . . . well, not most of them anyway, and certainly not Fred.

A Science fiction glossary*

ASF   *Astounding Stories of Super-Science* magazine; later, in its most fruitful period, *Astounding Science Fiction;* now *Analog.*

Fantasy   A commercial genre, identified by magazine titles such as *Unknown, Weird Tales, Fantasy Fiction,* and *The Avon Fantasy Reader.* Also *The Magazine of Fantasy and Science Fiction (F&SF).* Even in magazines with frank fantasy titles, some stories may be science fiction, set in milieus where temporal power derives from manipulations of physical laws rather than obedient concatenation of mystic symbols. Work in fantasy magazines must be examined story by story for such differences; many authors fluently cross back and forth between commercial science fiction and commercial fantasy. So do editors. Publishers insist that everything in such a magazine be labeled in accordance with the main title, whether it actually "belongs" or not.

Hugo   Annual award for excellence, given by members of the World Science Fiction Convention in categories such as Best Novel, Best Novelette, Best Short Story, Best Magazine. Winners are determined by vote of the Fannish community.

Fan   (with Fandom, Fannish, etc.) A person active in the large subculture loosely based on science fiction and fantasy reading. Differs from "reader" in that Fannish activity, which may or may not include reading, is the determinant.

Science adventure   Subgenre of science fiction; space opera. *Star Wars* is science adventure.

Science fantasy   Subgenre of science fiction. Identified by introduction of fantasy elements into milieus where such science fiction signatures as rocketships and ray guns also occur. The blend is usually one of fantasy and science adventure.

Science fiction   Commercial genre, identified by magazine titles. Stories are set in milieus where physical laws are held inviolate, although the stories themselves may err, or may deliberately elide such laws in order to function as stories. *Also:* A body of general literature, including commercial science fiction, commonly identified as science fiction by Fans.

SF   (or sf) Increasingly popular catchall term with various interpretations and applications. May stand for science fiction, science fantasy, speculative fiction, depending on user.

scientifiction   Obsolete term, originally coined by Hugo Gernsback, founder of magazine SF. Denotes science fiction with a primary emphasis on specific technological devices proposed in the story. Connotes Gernsback-styled science fiction; implies primitive writing style and "travelogue" plot construction.

---

*Not in alphabetical order.

Stef   (derived form stf, scientifiction) With *stefnal, stefnist,* etc. Proposed circa 1945 by Jack Speer, publisher of *Stefnews* community newsletter, as a flexible alternative to "science fiction-al," "pertaining to science fiction," and similar awkward constructions. Not adopted, but used as a nonce-word throughout the present essay in order to avoid such awkward constructions based on conventional terminology. Connotes anything having to do with Fannish activity and Fannish reading and writing, amateur or professional; a broad catchall.

Superscience   Originally "super-science" or "super science." A genre magazine label adopted to denote 1930–1938 stef based on manipulations of frankly fictional physical phenomena. Implies melodramatic writing style and "idea-pyramiding" plot construction.

Modern Science Fiction   Specifically, stories in the style of ASF fiction 1938–1950. Derives from references in the 1946 anthology, *Adventures in Time and Space,* which segregated such stories from all other sorts of stef. In current critical writing, sometimes "'Modern' science fiction."

post-Modern science fiction   Stef from 1950 to 1960, as typified by work published in *Galaxy* magazine 1950 and later. A term coined by Algis Budrys to denote evolved Modern work by former ASF writers. The edges of this category are quite fuzzy and subjective.

contemporary science fiction   Literally, any stef published in contemporary times. Purely a description, without limitation except by chronology.

New Wave   Circa-1960 school of stefnism centering on *New Worlds* magazine in England, exported to the U.S. community. Marked by conscious revulsion against Modern and post-Modern stef concepts and prose techniques. In spirit, closer to Huxleyan skepticism than to the commonly held picture of H. G. Wells as a technological optimist; thus, anti-Modern. Now incorporated as an influence within contemporary stef.

Nebula   The professional award given annually by the Science Fiction Writers of America, the writers' guild which includes overseas members.

novel   Prior to approximately 1955, a long stef story written multiclimactically for publication as a magazine serial. Since that time, usually a conventionally novelistic work written for book publication with possible editing into segments for magazine publication. *Also:* twentieth-century stef novels not written for publication in the genre magazines.

novella   Stef story 20,000 to 45,000 words long, often marketed as "A Novel Complete in This Issue."

novelette   A compressed novel, classically 10,000 to 20,000 words long, expandable into a novella by attaching scenes digressing from the main plot line. Later a matter of table-of-contents labeling in the dying pulp media circa 1950, when some "novelettes" might be 7,000 words long and might have been submitted as short stories. Classically, a story in which the protagonist undergoes an extended process of experiences (see short story).

short story   A depiction of one decisive experience in the protagonist's lifetime, often expressed in "O. Henry" structural tricks most especially in scientifiction; persisting as a waning major technique in superscience, Modern Science Fiction, and post-Modern stef. Since the New Wave, much less structured and closely akin to the general literature short story.

MASQUE OF THE RED SHIFT

Fred Saberhagen

In the 1960s Fred Saberhagen initiated one of the most popular and enduring of all SF series, now comprising many volumes of stories and novels and still growing: the *Berserker* series. Highlights include *The Berserker Wars, Berserker's Planet,* and *Berserker Kill.* The *Berserker* books are about a future universe in which human life is threatened by killer machines, and the stories are colorful and filled with action. "Masque of the Red Shift" is one of the earliest, and still one of the best, of the stories.

Finding himself alone and unoccupied, Felipe Nogara chose to spend a free moment in looking at the thing that had brought him out here beyond the last fringe of the galaxy. From the luxury of his quarters he stepped up into his private observation bubble. There, in a raised dome of invisible glass, he seemed to be standing outside the hull of his flagship *Nirvana.*

Under that hull, "below" the *Nirvana*'s artificial gravity, there slanted the bright disk of the galaxy, including in one of its arms all the star systems the Earth-descended man had yet explored. But in whatever direction Nogara looked, bright spots and points of light were plentiful. They were other galaxies, marching away at their recessional velocities of tens of thousands of miles per second, marching on out to the optical horizon of the universe.

Nogara had not come here to look at galaxies, however; he had come to look at something new, at a phenomenon never before seen by men at such close range.

It was made visible to him by the apparent pinching-together of the galaxies beyond it, and by the clouds and streamers of dust cascading into it. The star that formed the center of the phenomenon was itself held beyond human sight by the strength of its own gravity. Its mass, perhaps a billion times that of Sol, so bent spacetime around itself that not a photon of light could escape it with a visible wavelength.

The dusty debris of deep space tumbled and churned, falling into the grip of the hypermass. The falling dust built up static charges until lightning turned it into luminescent thunderclouds, and the flicker of the vast lightning shifted into the red before it vanished, near the bottom of the gravitational hill. Probably not even a neutrino could escape this sun. And no ship would dare approach much closer than *Nirvana* now rode.

Nogara had come out here to judge for himself if the recently discovered phenomenon might soon present any danger to inhabited planets; ordinary suns would go down like chips of wood into a whirlpool if the hypermass found them in its path. But it seemed that another thousand years would pass before any planets had to be evacuated; and before then the hypermass might have gorged itself on dust until its core imploded, whereupon most of its substance could be expected to reenter the universe in a most spectacular but less dangerous form.

Anyway, in another thousand years, it would be someone else's problem. Right now it might be said to be Nogara's—for men said that he ran the galaxy, if they said it of anyone.

A communicator sounded, calling him back to the enclosed luxury of his quarters, and he walked down quickly, glad of a reason to get out from under the galaxies.

He touched a plate with one finger. "What is it?"

"My lord, a courier ship has arrived. From the Flamland system. They are bringing . . ."

"Speak plainly. They are bringing my brother's body?"

"Yes, my lord. The launch bearing the coffin is already approaching *Nirvana*."

"I will meet the courier captain, alone, in the Great Hall. I want no ceremony. Have the robots at the airlock test the escort and the outside of the coffin for infection."

"Yes, my lord."

The mention of disease was a bit of misdirection. It was not the Flamland plague that had put Johann Karlsen into a box, though that was the official story. The doctors were supposed to have frozen the hero of the Stone Place as a last resort, to prevent his irreversible death.

An official lie was necessary because not even High Lord Nogara could lightly put out of the way the one man who had made the difference at the Stone Place. Since that battle it seemed that life in the galaxy would survive, though the fighting against the berserkers was still bitter.

The Great Hall was where Nogara met daily for feasting and pleasure with the forty or fifty people who were with him on *Nirvana*, as aides or crewmen or entertainers. But when he entered the Hall now he found it empty, save for one man who stood at attention beside a coffin.

Johann Karlsen's body and whatever remained of his life were sealed under the glass top of the heavy casket, which contained its own refrigeration and revival systems, controlled by a fiber-optic key theoretically impossible to duplicate. This key Nogara now demanded, with a gesture, from the courier captain.

The captain had the key hung around his neck, and it took him a moment to pull the golden chain over his head and hand it to Nogara. It was another moment before he remembered to bow; he was a spaceman and not a courtier. Nogara ignored the lapse of courtesy; it was his governors and admirals who were reinstituting ceremonies of rank; he himself cared nothing about how subordinates gestured and postured, so long as they obeyed intelligently.

Only now, with the key in his own hand, did Nogara look down at his frozen half brother. The plotting doctors had shaved away Johann's short beard and his hair. His lips were marble pale, and his sightless open eyes were ice. But still the face above the folds of the draped and frozen sheet was undoubtedly Johann's. There was something that would not freeze.

"Leave me for a time," Nogara said. He turned to face the end of the Great Hall and waited, looking out through the wide viewport to where the hypermass blurred space like a bad lens.

When he heard the door ease shut behind the courier captain he turned back—and found himself facing the short figure of Oliver Mical, the man he had selected to replace Johann as governor of Flamland. Mical must have entered as the spaceman left, which Nogara thought might be taken as symbolic of something.

Resting his hand familiarly on the coffin, Mical raised one graying eyebrow in his habitual expression of weary amusement. His rather puffy face twitched in an overcivilized smile.

"How does Browning's line go?" Mical mused, glancing down at Karlsen. "'Doing the king's work all the dim day long'—and now, this reward of virtue."

"Leave me," said Nogara.

Mical was in on the plot, as was hardly anyone else except the Flamland doctors. "I thought it best to appear to share your grief," he said. Then he looked at Nogara and ceased to argue. He made a bow that was mild mockery when the two of them were alone, and walked briskly to the door. Again it closed.

So, Johann. If you had plotted against me, I would have had you killed outright. But you were never a plotter, it was just that you served me too successfully, my enemies and friends alike began to love you too well. So here you are, my frozen conscience, the last conscience I'll ever have. Sooner or later you would have become ambitious, so it was either do this to you or kill you.

Now I'll put you away safely, and maybe someday you'll have another chance at life. It's a strange thought that someday you may stand musing over my coffin as I now stand over yours. No doubt you'll pray for what you think is my soul. . . . I can't do that for you, but I wish you sweet dreams. Dream of your Believers' heaven, not of your hell.

Nogara imagined a brain at absolute zero, its neurons superconducting, repeating one dream on and on and on. But that was nonsense.

"I cannot risk my power, Johann." This time he whispered the words aloud. "It was either this or have you killed." He turned again to the wide viewport.

"I suppose Thirty-three's gotten the body to Nogara already," said the Second Officer of Esteeler Courier Thirty-four, looking at the bridge chronometer. "It must be nice to declare yourself an emperor or whatever, and have people hurl themselves all over the galaxy to do everything for you."

"Can't be nice to have someone bring you your brother's corpse," said Captain Thurman Holt, studying his astrogational sphere. His ship's C-plus drive was rapidly stretching a lot of timelike interval between itself and the Flamland system. Even if Holt was not enthusiastic about his mission, he was glad to be away from Flamland, where Mical's political police were taking over.

"I wonder," said the Second, and chuckled.

"What's that mean?"

The Second looked over both shoulders, out of habit formed on Flamland. "Have you heard this one?" he asked. "Nogara is God—but half of his spacemen are atheists."

Holt smiled, but only faintly. "He's no mad tyrant, you know. Esteel's not the worst-run government in the galaxy. Nice guys don't put down rebellions."

"Karlsen did all right."

"That's right, he did."

The Second grimaced. "Oh, sure, Nogara could be worse, if you want to be serious about it. He's a politician. But I just can't stand that crew that's accumulated around him in the last few years. We've got an example on board now of what they do. If you want to know the truth I'm a little scared now that Karlsen's dead."

"Well, we'll soon see them." Holt sighed and stretched. "I'm going to look in on the prisoners. The bridge is yours, Second."

"I relieve you, sir. Do the man a favor and kill him, Thurm."

A minute later, looking through the spy-plate into the courier's small brig, Holt could wish with honest compassion that his male prisoner was dead.

He was an outlaw chieftain named Janda, and his capture had been the last success of Karlsen's Flamland service, putting a virtual end to the rebellion. Janda had been a tall man, a brave rebel, and a brutal bandit. He had raided and fought against Nogara's Esteeler empire until there was no hope left, and then he had surrendered to Karlsen.

"My pride commands me to conquer my enemy," Karlsen had written once, in what he thought was to be a private letter. "My honor forbids me to humble or hate my enemy." But Mical's political police operated with a different philosophy.

The outlaw might still be long-boned, but Holt had never seen him stand tall. The manacles still binding his wrists and ankles were of plastic and supposedly would not abrade human skin, but they served no sane purpose now, and Holt would have removed them if he could.

A stranger seeing the girl Lucinda, who sat now at Janda's side to feed him, might have supposed her to be his daughter. She was his sister, five years younger than he. She was also a girl of rare beauty, and perhaps Mical's police had motives other than mercy in sending her to Nogara's court unmarked and unbrainwashed. It was rumored that the demand for certain kinds of entertainment was strong among the courtiers, and the turnover among the entertainers high.

Holt had so far kept himself from believing such stories, largely by not thinking about them. He opened the brig now—he kept it locked only to prevent Janda's straying out and falling childlike into an accident—and went in.

When the girl Lucinda had first come aboard ship her eyes had shown helpless hatred of every Esteeler. Holt had been as gentle and as helpful as possible to her in the days since then, and there was not even dislike in the face she raised to him now—there was a hope which it seemed she had to share with someone.

She said: "I think he spoke my name a few minutes ago."

"Oh?" Holt bent to look more closely at Janda, and could see no change. The outlaw's eyes still stared glassily, the right eye now and then dripping a tear that seemed to have no connection with any kind of emotion. Janda's jaw was as slack as ever, and his whole body was awkwardly slumped.

"Maybe—" Holt didn't finish.

"What?" She was almost eager.

Gods of Space, he couldn't let himself get involved with this girl. He almost wished to see hatred in her eyes again.

"Maybe," he said gently, "it will be better for your brother if he doesn't make any recovery now. You know where he's going."

Lucinda's hope, such as it was, was shocked away by his words. She was silent, staring at her brother as if she saw something new.

Holt's wrist-intercom sounded.

"Captain here," he acknowledged.

"Sir, reported a ship detected and calling us. Bearing five o'clock level to our course. Small and normal."

The last three words were the customary reassurance that a sighted ship was not possibly a berserker's giant hull. Such Flamland outlaws as were left possessed no deep space ships, so Holt had no reason to be cautious.

He went back to the bridge and looked at the small shape on the detector screen. It was unfamiliar to him, but that was hardly surprising, as there were many shipyards orbiting many planets. Why, though, should any ship approach and hail him in deep space?

Plague?

"No, no plague," answered a radio voice, through bursts of static, when he put the question to the stranger. The video signal from the other ship was also jumpy, making it hard to see the speaker's face. "Caught a speck of dust on my last jump, and my fields are shaky. Will you take a few passengers aboard?"

"Certainly." For a ship on the brink of a C-plus jump to collide with the gravitational field of a sizable dustspeck was a rare accident, but not unheard of. And it would explain the noisy communications. There was still nothing to alarm Holt.

The stranger sent over a launch which clamped to the courier's airlock. Wearing a smile of welcome for distressed passengers, Holt opened the lock. In the next moment he and the half dozen men who made up his crew were caught helpless by an inrush of metal—a berserker's boarding party, cold and merciless as nightmare.

The machine seized the courier so swiftly and efficiently that no one could offer real resistance, but they did not immediately kill any of the humans. They tore the drive units from one of the lifeboats and herded Holt and his crew and his erstwhile prisoners into the boat.

"It wasn't a berserker on the screen, it wasn't," the Second Officer kept repeating to Holt. The humans sat side by side, jammed against one another in the small space. The machines were allowing them air and water and food, and had started to take them out one at a time for questioning.

"I know, it didn't look like one," Holt answered. "The berserkers are probably forming themselves into new shapes, building themselves new weapons. That's only logical, after the Stone Place. The only odd thing is that no one foresaw it."

A hatch clanged open, and a pair of roughly man-shaped machines entered the boat, picking their way precisely among the nine cramped humans until they reached the one they wanted.

"No, he can't talk!" Lucinda shrieked. "Don't take him!"

But the machines could not or would not hear. They pulled Janda to his feet and marched him out. The girl followed, dragging at them, trying to argue with them. Holt could only scramble uselessly after her in the narrow space, afraid that one of the machines would turn and kill her. But they only kept her from following them out of the lifeboat, pushing her back from the hatch with metal hands as gently resistless as time. Then they were gone with Janda, and the hatch was closed again. Lucinda stood gazing at it blankly. She did not move when Holt put his arm around her.

After a timeless period of waiting, the humans saw the hatch open again. The machines were back, but they did not return Janda. Instead they had come to take Holt.

Vibrations echoed through the courier's hull; the machines seemed to be rebuilding her. In a small-chamber sealed off from the rest of the shop by a new bulkhead, the berserker computer-brain had set up electronic eyes and ears and a speaker for itself, and here Holt was taken to be questioned.

The berserkers interrogated Holt at great length, and almost every question concerned Johann Karlsen. It was known that the berserkers regarded Karlsen as their chief enemy, but this one seemed to be obsessed with him—and unwilling to believe that he was really dead.

"I have captured your charts and astrogational settings," the berserker reminded Holt. "I know your course is to *Nirvana,* where supposedly the non-functioning Karlsen has been taken. Describe this *Nirvana*-ship used by the life-unit Nogara."

So long as it had asked only about a dead man, Holt had given the berserker straight answers, not wanting to be tripped up in a useless lie. But a flagship was a different matter, and now he hesitated. Still, there was little he could say about *Nirvana* if he wanted to. And he and his fellow prisoners had had no chance to agree on any plan for deceiving the berserker; certainly it must be listening to everything they said in the lifeboat.

"I've never seen the *Nirvana,*" he answered truthfully. "Logic tells me it must be a strong ship, since the highest human leaders travel on it." There was no harm in telling the machine what it could certainly deduce for itself.

A door opened suddenly, and Holt started in surprise as a strange man entered the interrogation chamber. Then he saw that it was not a man, but some creation of the berserker. Perhaps its flesh was plastic, perhaps some product of tissue culture.

"Hi, are you Captain Holt?" asked the figure. There was no gross flaw in it, but a ship camouflaged with the greatest skill looks like nothing so much as a ship that has been camouflaged.

When Holt was silent, the figure asked: "What's wrong?"

Its speech alone would have given it away, to an intelligent human who listened carefully.

"You're not a man," Holt told it.

The figure sat down and went limp.

The berserker explained: "You see I am not capable of making an imitation life-unit that will be accepted by real ones face to face. Therefore I require that you, a real life-unit, help me make certain of Karlsen's death."

Holt said nothing.

"I am a special device," the berserker said, "built by the berserkers with one prime goal, to bring about with certainty Karlsen's death. If you help me prove him dead, I will willingly free you and the other life-units I now hold. If you refuse to help, all of you will receive the most unpleasant stimuli until you change your mind."

Holt did not believe that it would ever willingly set them free. But he had nothing to lose by talking, and he might at least gain for himself and the others a death free of most unpleasant stimuli. Berserkers preferred to be efficient killers, not sadists.

"What sort of help do you want from me?" Holt asked.

"When I have finished building myself into the courier we are going on to *Nirvana*, where you will deliver your prisoners. I have read the orders. After being interviewed by the human leaders on *Nirvana*, the prisoners are to be taken on to Esteel for confinement. Is it not so?"

"It is."

The door opened again, and Janda shuffled in, bent and bemused.

"Can't you spare this man any more questioning?" Holt asked the berserker.

"He can't help you in any way."

There was only silence. Holt waited uneasily. At last, looking at Janda, he realized that something about the outlaw had changed. The tears had stopped flowing from his right eye. When Holt saw this he felt a mounting horror that he could not have explained, as if his subconscious already knew what the berserker was going to say next.

"What was bone in this life-unit is now metal," the berserker said. "Where blood flowed, now preservatives are pumped. Inside the skull I have placed a computer, and in the eyes are cameras to gather the evidence I must have on Karlsen. To match the behavior of a brainwashed man is within my capability."

"I do not hate you," Lucinda said to the berserker when it had her alone for interrogation. "You are an accident, like a planet-quake, like a pellet of dust hitting a ship near light-speed. Nogara and his people are the ones I hate. If his brother was not dead I would kill him with my own hands and willingly bring you his body."

"Courier Captain? This is Governor Mical, speaking for the High Lord Nogara. Bring your two prisoners over to *Nirvana* at once."

"At once, sir," Holt acknowledged.

After coming out of C-plus travel within sight of *Nirvana*, the assassin-machine had taken Holt and Lucinda from the lifeboat. Then it had let the boat, with Holt's crew still on it, drift out between the two ships, as if men were using it to check the courier's field. The men on the boat were to be the berserker's hostages, and its shield if it was discovered. And by leaving them there, it doubtless wanted to make more credible the prospect of their eventual release.

Holt had not known how to tell Lucinda of her brother's fate, but at last he had managed somehow. She had wept for a minute, and then she had become very calm.

Now the berserker put Holt and Lucinda into a launch for a trip to *Nirvana*. The machine that had been Lucinda's brother was aboard the launch already, waiting, slumped and broken-looking as the man had been in the last days of his life.

When she saw that figure, Lucinda stopped. Then in a clear voice she said: "Machine, I wish to thank you. You have done my brother a kindness no human would do for him. I think I would have found a way to kill him myself before his enemies could torture him any more."

The *Nirvana*'s airlock was strongly armored, and equipped with automated defenses that would have repelled a rush of boarding machines, just as *Nirvana*'s beams and missiles would have beaten off any heavy-weapons attack a courier, or a dozen couriers, could launch. The berserker had foreseen all this.

An officer welcomed Holt aboard. "This way, Captain. We're all waiting." "All?"

The officer had the well-fed, comfortable look that came with safe and easy duty. His eyes were busy appraising Lucinda. "There's a celebration underway in the Great Hall. Your prisoners' arrival has been much anticipated."

Music throbbed in the Great Hall, and dancers writhed in costumes more obscene than any nakedness. From a table running almost the length of the Hall, serving machines were clearing the remnants of a feast. In a thronelike chair behind the center of the table sat the High Lord Nogara, a rich cloak thrown over his shoulders, pale wine before him in a crystal goblet. Forty or fifty revelers flanked him at the long table, men and women and a few of whose sex Holt could not at once be sure. All were drinking and laughing, and some were donning masks and costumes, making ready for further celebration.

Heads turned at Holt's entrance, and a moment of silence was followed by a cheer. In all the eyes and faces turned now toward his prisoners, Holt could see nothing like pity.

"Welcome, Captain," said Nogara in a pleasant voice, when Holt had remembered to bow. "Is there news from Flamland?"

"None of great importance, sir."

A puffy-faced man who sat at Nogara's right hand leaned forward on the table. "No doubt there is great mourning for the late governor?"

"Of course, sir." Holt recognized Mical. "And much anticipation of the new."

Mical leaned back in his chair, smiling cynically. "I'm sure the rebellious population is eager for my arrival. Girl, were you eager to meet me? Come, pretty one, round the table, here to me." As Lucinda slowly obeyed, Mical gestured to the serving devices. "Robots, set a chair for the man—there, in the center of the floor. Captain, you may return to your ship."

Felipe Nogara was steadily regarding the manacled figure of his old enemy Janda, and what Nogara might be thinking was hard to say. But he seemed content to let Mical give what orders pleased him.

"Sir," said Holt to Mical. "I would like to see—the remains of Johann Karlsen."

That drew the attention of Nogara, who nodded. A serving machine drew back the sable draperies, revealing an alcove in one end of the Hall. In the alcove, before a huge viewport, rested the coffin.

Holt was not particularly surprised; on many planets it was the custom to feast in the presence of the dead. After bowing to Nogara he turned and saluted and walked toward the alcove. Behind him he heard the shuffle and clank of Janda's manacled movement, and held his breath. A muttering passed along the table, and then a sudden quieting in which even the throbbing music ceased. Probably Nogara had gestured permission for Janda's walk, wanting to see what the brainwashed man would do.

Holt reached the coffin and stood over it. He hardly saw the frozen face inside it, or the blur of the hypermass outside the port. He hardly heard the whispers and giggles of the revelers. The only picture clear in his mind showed the faces of his crew as they waited helpless in the grip of the berserker.

The machine clothed in Janda's flesh came shuffling up beside him, and its eyes of glass stared down into those of ice. A photograph of retinal patterns taken back to the waiting berserker for comparison with old captured records would tell it that this was really Karlsen.

A faint cry of anguish made Holt look back toward the long table, where he saw Lucinda pulling herself away from Mical's clutching arm. Mical and his friends were laughing.

"No, Captain, I am no Karlsen," Mical called down to him, seeing Holt's expression. "And do you think I regret the difference? Johann's prospects are not bright. He is rather bounded by a nutshell, and can no longer count himself king of infinite space!"

"Shakespeare!" cried a sycophant, showing appreciation of Mical's literary erudition.

"Sir." Holt took a step forward. "May I—may I now take the prisoners back to my ship?"

Mical misinterpreted Holt's anxiety. "Oh, ho! I see you appreciate some of life's finer things, Captain. But as you know, rank has its privileges. The girl stays here."

He had expected them to hold on to Lucinda, and she was better here than with the berserker.

"Sir, then if—if the man alone can come with me. In a prison hospital on Esteel he may recover—"

"Captain." Nogara's voice was not loud, but it hushed the table. "Do not *argue* here."

"No, sir."

Mical shook his head. "My thoughts are not yet of mercy to my enemies, Captain. Whether they may soon turn in that direction—well, that depends." He again reached out a leisurely arm to encircle Lucinda. "Do you know, Captain, that hatred is the true spice of love?"

Holt looked helplessly back at Nogara. Nogara's cold eye said: One more word, courier, and you find yourself in the brig. I do not give two warnings.

If Holt cried berserker now, the thing in Janda's shape might kill everyone in the Hall before it could be stopped. He knew it was listening to him, watching his movements.

"I—I am returning to my ship," he stuttered. Nogara looked away, and no one else paid him much attention. "I will . . . return here . . . in a few hours perhaps. Certainly before I drive for Esteel."

Holt's voice trailed off as he saw that a group of the revelers had surrounded Janda. They had removed the manacles from the outlaw's dead limbs, and were putting a horned helmet on his head, giving him a shield and a spear and a cloak of fur, equipage of an old Norse warrior of Earth—first to coin and bear the dread name of berserker.

"Observe, Captain," mocked Mical's voice. "At our masked ball we do not fear the fate of Prince Prospero. We willingly bring in the semblance of the terror outside!"

"Poe!" shouted the sycophant, in glee.

Prospero and Poe meant nothing to Holt, and Mical was disappointed.

"Leave us, Captain," said Nogara, making a direct order of it.

"Leave, Captain Holt," said Lucinda in a firm, clear voice. "We all know you wish to help those who stand in danger here. Lord Nogara, will Captain Holt be blamed in any way for what happens here when he has gone?"

There was a hint of puzzlement in Nogara's clear eyes. But he shook his head slightly, granting the asked-for absolution.

And there was nothing for Holt to do but go back to the berserker to argue and plead with it for his crew. If it was patient, the evidence it sought might be forthcoming. If only the revelers would have mercy on the thing they thought was Janda.

Holt went out. It had never entered his burdened mind that Karlsen was only frozen.

Mical's arm was about her hips as she stood beside his chair, and his voice purred up at her. "Why, how you tremble, pretty one . . . it moves me that such a pretty one as you should tremble at my touch, yes, it moves me deeply. Now, we are no longer enemies, are we? If we were, I should have to deal harshly with your brother."

She had given Holt time to get clear of the *Nirvana*. Now she swung her arm with all her strength. The blow turned Mical's head halfway round, and made his neat gray hair fly wildly.

There was a sudden hush in the Great Hall, and then a roar of laughter that reddened all of Mical's face to match the handprint on his cheek. A man behind Lucinda grabbed her arms and pinned them. She relaxed until she felt his grip loosen slightly, and then she grabbed up a table knife. There was another burst of laughter as Mical ducked away and the man behind Lucinda seized her again. Another man came to help him and the two of them, laughing, took away the knife and forced her to sit in a chair at Mical's side.

When the governor spoke at last his voice quavered slightly, but it was low and almost calm.

"Bring the man closer," he ordered. "Seat him there, just across the table from us."

While his order was being carried out, Mical spoke to Lucinda in a conversational tone. "It *was* my intent, of course, that your brother should be treated and allowed to recover."

"Lying piece of filth," she whispered, smiling.

Mical only smiled back. "Let us test the skill of my mind-control technicians," he suggested. "I'll wager no bonds will be needed to hold your brother in his chair, once I have done this." He made a curious gesture over the table, toward the glassy eyes that looked out of Janda's face. "So. But he will still be aware, with every nerve, of all that happens to him. You may be sure of that."

She had planned and counted on something like this happening, but now she felt as if she was exhausted from breathing evil air. She was afraid of fainting, and at the same time wished that she could.

"Our guest is bored with his costume." Mical looked up and down the table. "Who will be first to take a turn at entertaining him?"

There was a spattering of applause as a giggling effeminate arose from a nearby chair.

"Jamy is known for his inventiveness," said Mical in pleasant tones to Lucinda. "I insist you watch closely, now. Chin up!"

On the other side of Mical, Felipe Nogara was losing his air of remoteness. As if reluctantly, he was being drawn to watch. In his bearing was a rising expectancy, winning out over disgust.

Jamy came giggling, holding a small jeweled knife.

"Not the eyes," Mical cautioned. "There'll be things I want him to see, later."

"Oh, certainly!" Jamy twittered. He set the horned helmet gingerly aside, and wiped the touch of it from his fingers. "We'll just start like this on one cheek, with a bit of skin—"

Jamy's touch with the blade was gentle, but still too much for the dead flesh. At the first peeling tug, the whole lifeless mask fell red and wet from around the staring eyes, and the steel berserker-skull grinned out.

Lucinda had just time to see Jamy's body flung across the Hall by a steel-boned arm before the men holding her let go and turned to flee for their lives, and she was able to duck under the table. Screaming bedlam broke loose, and in another moment the whole table went over with a crash before the berserker's strength. The machine, finding itself discovered, thwarted in its primary function of getting away with the evidence on Karlsen, had reverted to the old berserker goal of simple slaughter. It killed efficiently. It moved through the Hall, squatting and hopping grotesquely, mowing its way with scythelike arms, harvesting howling panic into bundles of bloody stillness.

At the main door, fleeing people jammed one another into immobility, and the assassin worked methodically among them, mangling and slaying. Then it turned and came down the Hall again. It came to Lucinda, still kneeling where the table-tipping had exposed her; but the machine hesitated, recognizing her as a semipartner in its prime function. In a moment it had dashed on after another target.

It was Nogara, swaying on his feet, his right arm hanging broken. He had come up with a heavy handgun from somewhere, and now he fired left-handed as the machine charged down the other side of the overturned table toward him. The gunblasts shattered Nogara's friends and furniture but only grazed his moving target.

At last one shot hit home. The machine was wrecked, but its impetus carried it on to knock Nogara down again.

There was a shaky quiet in the Great Hall, which was wrecked as if by a bomb. Lucinda got unsteadily to her feet. The quiet began to give way to sobs and moans and gropings, everywhere, but no one else was standing.

She picked her way dazedly over to the smashed assassin machine. She felt only a numbness, looking at the rags of clothing and flesh that still clung to its metal frame. Now in her mind she could see her brother's face as it once was, strong and smiling.

Now, there was something that mattered more than the dead, if she could only recall what it was—of course, the berserker's hostages, the good kind spacemen. She could try to trade Karlsen's body for them.

The serving machines, built to face emergencies on the order of spilled wine, were dashing to and fro in the nearest thing to panic that mechanism could achieve. They impeded Lucinda's progress, but she had the heavy coffin wheeled halfway across the Hall when a weak voice stopped her. Nogara had dragged himself up to a sitting position against the overturned table.

He croaked again: "—alive."

"What?"

"Johann's alive. Healthy. See? It's a freezer."

"But we all told the berserker he was dead." She felt stupid with the impact of one shock after another. For the first time she looked down at Karlsen's face, and long seconds passed before she could tear her eyes away. "It has hostages. It wants his body."

"No." Nogara shook his head. "I see, now. But no. I won't give him to berserkers, alive." A brutal power of personality still emanated from his broken body. His gun was gone, but his power kept Lucinda from moving. There was no hatred left in her now.

She protested: "But there are seven men out there."

"Berserkers like me." Nogara bared pain-clenched teeth. "It won't let prisoners go. Here. The key . . ." He pulled it from inside his torn-open tunic.

Lucinda's eyes were drawn once again to the cold serenity of the face in the coffin. Then on impulse she ran to get the key. When she did so Nogara slumped over in relief, unconscious or nearly so.

The coffin lock was marked in several positions, and she turned it to EMERGENCY REVIVAL. Lights sprang on around the figure inside, and there was a hum of power.

By now the automated systems of the ship were reacting to the emergency. The serving machines had begun a stretcher-bearer service, Nogara being one of the first victims they carried away. Presumably a robot medic was in action somewhere. From behind Nogara's throne chair a great voice was shouting:

"This is ship defense control, requesting human orders! What is the nature of emergency?"

"Do not contact the courier ship!" Lucinda shouted back. "Watch it for an attack. But don't hit the lifeboat!"

The glass top of the coffin had become opaque.

Lucinda ran to the viewport, stumbling over the body of Mical and going on without a pause. By putting her face against the port and looking out at an angle she could just see the berserker-courier, pinkly visible in the wavering light of the hypermass, its lifeboat of hostages a small pink dot still in place before it.

How long would it wait, before it killed the hostages and fled?

When she turned away from the port, she saw that the coffin's lid was open and the man inside was sitting up. For just a moment, a moment that was to stay in Lucinda's mind, his eyes were like a child's fixed helplessly on hers. Then power began to grow behind his eyes, a power somehow completely different from his brother's and perhaps even greater.

Karlsen looked away from her, taking in the rest of his surroundings, the devastated Great Hall and the coffin. "Felipe," he whispered, as if in pain, though his half-brother was no longer in sight.

Lucinda moved toward him and started to pour out her story, from the day in the Flamland prison when she had heard that Karlsen had fallen to the plague. Once he interrupted her. "Help me out of this thing, get me space armor." His arm was hard and strong when she grasped it, but when he stood beside her he was surprisingly short. "Go on, what then?"

She hurried on with her tale, while serving machines came to arm him. "But why were you frozen?" she ended, suddenly wondering at his health and strength.

He ignored the question. "Come along to Defense Control. We must save those men out there."

He went familiarly to the nerve center of the ship and hurled himself into the combat chair of the Defense Officer, who was probably dead. The panel before Karlsen came alight and he ordered at once: "Get me in contact with that courier."

Within a few moments a flat-sounding voice from the courier answered routinely. The face that appeared on the communication screen was badly lighted; someone viewing it without advance warning would not suspect that it was anything but human.

"This is High Commander Karlsen speaking, from the *Nirvana*." He did not call himself governor or lord, but by his title of the great day of the Stone Place. "I'm coming over there. I want to talk to you men on the courier."

The shadowed face moved slightly on the screen. "Yes, sir."

Karlsen broke off the contact at once. "That'll keep its hopes up. Now, I need a launch. You, robots, load my coffin aboard the fastest one available. I'm on emergency revival drugs now and I may have to refreeze for a while."

"You're not really going over there?"

Up out of the chair again, he paused. "I know berserkers. If chasing me is that thing's prime function it won't waste a shot or a second of time on a few hostages while I'm in sight."

"You can't go," Lucinda heard herself saying. "You mean too much to all men—"

"I'm not committing suicide, I have a trick or two in mind." Karlsen's voice changed suddenly. "You say Felipe's not dead?"

"I don't think he is."

Karlsen's eyes closed while his lips moved briefly, silently. Then he looked at Lucinda and grabbed up paper and a stylus from the Defense Officer's console. "Give this to Felipe," he said, writing. "He'll set you and the captain free if I ask it. You're not dangerous to his power. Whereas I . . ."

He finished writing and handed her the paper. "I must go. God be with you."

From the Defense Officer's position, Lucinda watched Karlsen's crystalline launch leave the *Nirvana* and take a long curve that brought it near the courier at a point some distance from the lifeboat.

"You on the courier," Lucinda heard him say. "You can tell it's really me here on the launch, can't you? You can DF my transmission? Can you photograph my retinas through the screen?"

And the launch darted away with a right-angle swerve, dodging and twisting at top acceleration, as the berserker's weapons blasted the space where it had been. Karlsen had been right. The berserker spent not a moment's delay or a single shot on the lifeboat, but hurled itself instantly after Karlsen's launch.

"Hit that courier!" Lucinda screamed. "Destroy it!" A salvo of missiles left the *Nirvana*, but it was a shot at a receding target, and it missed. Perhaps it missed because the courier was already in the fringes of the distortion surrounding the hypermass.

Karlsen's launch had not been hit, but it could not get away. It was a glassy dot vanishing behind a screen of blasts from the berserker's weapons, a dot being forced into the maelstrom of the hypermass.

"Chase them!" cried Lucinda, and saw the stars tint blue ahead; but almost instantly the *Nirvana*'s autopilot countermanded her order, barking mathematical assurance that to accelerate any further in that direction would be fatal to all aboard.

The launch was now going certainly into the hypermass, gripped by a gravity that could make any engines useless. And the berserker-ship was going headlong after the launch, caring for nothing but to make sure of Karlsen.

The two specks tinted red, and redder still, racing before an enormous falling cloud of dust as if flying into a planet's sunset sky. And then the red shift of the hypermass took them into invisibility, and the universe saw them no more.

Soon after the robots had brought the men from the lifeboat safe aboard *Nirvana*, Holt found Lucinda alone in the Great Hall, gazing out the viewport.

"He gave himself to save you," she said. "And he'd never even seen you."

"I know." After a pause Holt said: "I've just been talking to the Lord Nogara. I don't know why, but you're to be freed, and I'm not to be prosecuted for bringing the damned berserker aboard. Though Nogara seems to hate both of us . . ."

She wasn't listening, she was still looking out the port.

"I want you to tell me all about him someday," Holt said, putting his arm around Lucinda. She moved slightly, ridding herself of a minor irritation that she had hardly noticed. It was Holt's arm, which dropped away.

"I see," Holt said, after a while. He went to look after his men.

REDEMPTION IN THE QUANTUM REALM

Frederik Pohl

Frederik Pohl is both a writer of the first rank and one of the most important editors in the history of the SF field. He has edited magazines such as *Galaxy* and *If*, original anthologies such as *Star Science Fiction*, and the Bantam Books publishing line. But most of the time he has been the satirical SF writer whom Kingsley Amis, in his influential book on SF, *New Maps of Hell*, called the best in the field. See the Budrys essay for more information. He published a variety of classic stories in the 1950s, and a series of famous collaborations with C. M. Kornbluth beginning with *The Space Merchants*. His second flowering as a writer began in the 1970s with "The Gold at the Starbow's End," *Man Plus*, and *Gateway*, and has never abated. As evidenced by "Redemption in the Quantum Realm," he is still at the peak of his satirical powers in the 1990s.

Transcript of interview with Arthur John Delaporte, Ph.D.

When I first met Jeremy Burskin I was Science Master at the Buckingham School in Warwick, Massachusetts. He was one of my students.

I was then twenty-nine years old and recently married. The marriage did not last—Madge divorced me a couple of years later—but at the time I felt that I needed that job. I'm sure you know of Buckingham. It's a prep school of the kind where Daddy enters your name for it the day after you're born. For most of the hundred and forty years of its existence Buck Prep had concentrated on the classics. They'd dropped Greek from the curriculum only ten years earlier and they had never had a science master before I got there. But there was a new Headmaster, Rev. John E. Abernathy, and he was a new broom determined to sweep clean.

At my final interview he explained his intentions to me. "By the time our chaps go on to their universities I want them to be fully prepared for the technological world they will live their lives in, Delaporte. I want them to be fully numerate and science-literate. Are you the man who can make them so?"

"I think so, Headmaster," I said.

He picked a pipe from the rack on his desk and began gouging it out with a tool on his keyring; it made a nasty fingernails-on-the-blackboard noise. He looked up at me in a challenging way. "I don't want you to limit yourself to the rudiments of old-fashioned classical science, levers and test tubes and all that sort of thing. I want you to take our boys right to the cutting edge. I've had this out with our new mathematics master, and he understands that his curriculum must not end with algebra and geometry. I believe he has already instilled the rudiments of calculus into our sixth formers, and by the beginning of the Easter term his classes will be dealing with fractals and chaos theory. I've seen to it that they are already provided with computers for every student."

When he paused again I thought I'd better say something. "That seems very wise, Headmaster."

"I expect no less from you. Relativity, quantum mechanics, cosmology, recombinant DNA—perhaps I should mention that I myself am a subscriber to both *Scientific American* and *Natural History*—I want every Buck grad to understand the principles that underlie all these matters. Oh, not as a specialist might, of course; they're only boys, after all. But I insist that they have at least a grounding in the basics. Enough to whet their interest, Delaporte. Enough to get them started. Thirty years from now I want to see at least one Old Buck as a Nobel laureate—along with those other graduates who will honor us as leaders of industry, heads of great universities and, very likely, among the statesmen who will lead our country. I look to you to make that possible, Delaporte. That will be your principal charge here, although you will also, of course, take your regular rota with coaching the sports teams, overseeing the dormitories, and leading morning chapel. I welcome you to Buckingham."

I don't suppose I have to say that teaching greasy teenagers was not what I had in mind when I was working toward my doctorate in physics. It was just the best I could get, once my post-doc ran out and there was no funding for a permanent position.

Buck Prep did have its advantages, though. One of the best things about the position was the little cottage that went with it. That charmed Madge, at least at first, and so I really did my best to hold the job. I think I did pretty well, as a matter of fact, though there's really no way you can teach everything the Head wanted to a bunch of seventeen-year-olds who've never had a science class before. I came close, though. I stole a couple of ideas from a Triple-A-S program designed for ghetto kids whose schools weren't any good, like doing electrophoresis with strips of wet newspaper and different colored M&Ms—I had to buy the M&Ms out of my own pocket, because there wasn't any budget for "experimental materials." I explained wave-particle duality to them. I showed them how Einstein had demonstrated that light was composed of particles by the way a photon knocked electrons loose from the right kind of metals—the basis for the photoelectric cell—and then I showed them how they could prove to themselves that it was also a wave. (The way you do that is by holding two fingers very close together an inch in front of your eyes; the vertical lines you see between your knuckles are interference fringes, which of course are only possible for waves.)

I think the boys liked me. They seemed to enjoy the class; they even did their homework. When Madge and I had them over for tea on every second Sunday—that was another of the Head's ideas; I think he'd seen *Goodbye, Mr. Chips* too many times in his youth—they charmed Madge with their good nature an fresh young high spirits. That was good, because it made it easier for me to charm her, too, at least for a while. Everything seemed to be going fine until right after the Christmas holidays, when the senior runner came up to me as the class was ending, touching his school cap and informing me that the Head would be grateful if I could step over to his study when convenient.

The Head wasn't alone. Sitting next to him in front of the fireplace was Dr. Fabian, the school chaplain, looking displeased. "Do sit down, Delaporte," the Head said heartily. "Tea? I'll be Mother. You're two lumps and no milk if I remember correctly?"

The fact that they were drinking tea meant that it was to be a discussion, not an execution, but as soon as I had my teacup balanced on my knee the Head opened up. "It's young Burskin," he said. "Dr. Fabian said he's been making atheistic remarks. Some of the other boys are taking them seriously."

"Good heavens," I said.

The chaplain was glaring at me. "He blames it on you," he said. "He says you've proved scientifically that there's no God."

"Impossible! Certainly not! I give you my word there has never been any discussion of religion in my class—"

"Of course there hasn't," the Head soothed. "If there had been I'm sure you would have made it clear that religion is a matter of inspired faith and science a question of measurable fact. They are two quite separate realms and there is no conflict between them, is there? No, we're agreed on that; but, all the same, I can't have parents coming to me with fears that Buck Prep is spreading doubt. You'd better have a word with Burskin."

Although Buck Prep was highly traditional in most ways, it did not permit caning. I sometimes regretted that. It meant that when I had to call a boy in for some fault he knew that the worst that was likely to happen to him was a hundred extra lines or, at worst, being campused on the next weekend.

When I let Burskin into the cottage his expression was serious but not intimidated. "Sir?" he said. "You wish to see me?"

I sat down but kept him standing. It was not a social occasion, and I got right to the point. "Why did you tell McIlwraith and Gorman that I've been proving that God does not exist?"

"But you have, sir, haven't you? I mean, I don't *think* I got it wrong. It was when you were telling us about Heisenberg's Uncertainty Principle. You talked about that cat of Mr. Schrödinger's; the one that was in a box? With some poison gas that might or might not kill it? Then you said that as long as the cat was in the closed box it could be either alive or dead, but the minute anyone observed it it had to be one or the other; I made a note of it at the time, you called it 'the collapse of the wave function.' Isn't that right?"

I was aware of Madge listening from the bedroom. It made me sterner than I might otherwise have been. "Don't put words in my mouth, Burskin. You know perfectly well that I said nothing at all about God."

"No, sir," he agreed, "not directly. But you said that was true of all particles.

Like an electron. You said as long as the electron looked like a wave it could be anywhere—that was what Mr. Niels Bohr said, wasn't it? I mean, I got that right, didn't I, sir? But as soon as the electron was observed it became a particle and was only in one particular place after that, because then the wave function would collapse."

"Yes?"

"But they haven't all collapsed, have they, sir?"

"Of course not."

"Well, sir, the way it looked to me, they should have. They've been observed, if what Chaplain tells us is right. I mean observed by God, sir. He's supposed to observe everything, isn't he, even the sparrow's fall? He's omniscient, that's what Chaplain says. So if there really was a God, he would have observed all those wave functions and they would have collapsed long ago, wouldn't they? Only they haven't. I only drew the logical conclusions."

Transcript of interview with Franklin R. Burskin, M.D.

The fact that I was Jerry's big brother didn't mean we were close. There was six years between us. By the time he was out of kindergarten I was already off at Buckingham Prep, and by the time he got to Buck I was in my freshman year at Harvard.

Of course I heard about the way he wised off at Buck, but I didn't pay much attention. I was in my third year of medical school by then. I did manage to get home for a weekend during the spring break while Jerry was there. Mom was doing her best to forget about the whole thing. Dad wasn't. He'd had to go up to Buck to plead with the Head and he was still sore about it. "Talk sense to your brother," he ordered me. "Take my car. Take him out for a soda or something. Get him out of my sight."

Jerry was willing enough to get out of the house. I picked up a six-pack at the 7-Eleven and we sat in Dad's car with the motor running and the air conditioner going, popping brews. "You came goddam close to being expelled," I told him. "That's pretty stupid. You know Dad's having business troubles. He doesn't need this from you."

He gave me a cocky look. "Relax, big brother. I've got it all straightened out."

"Bullshit. They don't keep atheists at Buck Prep."

"What makes you think I'm an atheist? Nobody at Buck says I am. Even old asshole Fabian took it back once I explained it to him."

"Explain it to me, then."

He popped another can and did. Or tried. I didn't know much about this quantum stuff, but when he told me about sitting down with the Chaplain and the Head and this new science geek, Delaporte, I had to admire his nerve. "I just played the Head's words back to him, Frankie. Religion's about faith, science is about observation. Then I got bright. I said God probably didn't have to peek into the atomic nucleus to see what the particles were doing—hell, He created them in the first place, right? So the observer problem didn't matter."

"They bought that?"

"The Head did. He wanted to. It fit right in with the way he was running the school."

I mulled that over. "So what you're saying is that God's kind of near-sighted?"

He stopped in the middle of lighting a cigarette; even though the air was running I'd already rolled the windows down so the smoke wouldn't stay in Dad's car. "Where did you get that idea?"

"What you said. He sees everything that happens except the really little things that He doesn't bother with."

"Well, that's one way to look at it," he said after a moment. Then he was quiet for a long time. I don't know. Do you suppose maybe I gave him the idea then?

Anyway, I figured I'd done my duty to my family and the beer was all gone. When he finished his cigarette I got ready to leave. "Eat a couple of these mints for your breath," I ordered and headed for home. I took off the next morning. It was a long drive to Florida, and I wasn't going to spend my whole spring break at home.

Well, then that fall Dad had his stroke and things got bad. Dad didn't die right away. There were all those weeks in intensive care, and then he was home with twenty-four-hour nursing for a long time. Naturally the business went to hell, too, and after the funeral it turned out the money was mostly gone.

Something had to give. We couldn't ask Mom to give up the house; I had to finish medical school, or the whole thing would have been wasted. So Jerry had to leave Buck Prep at the end of the Christmas term anyway, and then there just wasn't enough left over to pay for Harvard and law school, the way Dad had planned it out. The kid was on his own.

Mom was upset when he got himself into that little denominational school in Texas—I don't even remember what they called themselves, but of course our family had always been Episcopalians. By then I was doing my residency. Thirty-six hours on at a stretch, no sleep—there was no way I could get time off to go home and talk to her. I did my best to calm her down on the phone. "At least he's getting a college education," I told her, "and it's free. Don't worry about Jerry. He'll take care of himself."

Well, he did, didn't he? I was right about that.

I admit that I was pretty pissed off when I first heard about the Holy Church of Quantal Redemption. I'd left the HMO by then, and it could have been a real embarrassment for a brand-new proctologist just trying to get established in private practice if it got out that he had a brother running some kind of religious nut cult. Still, I have to say that, in a way, I was almost proud of the little turd.

Transcript of interview with Stacey Krebs.

At the time of my conversion I was a security guard at the Garden. That meant I patrolled the stairways and passages with my two German shepherds; I needed two because Slappy was trained to sniff for firearms and Moe for drugs. Both of the dogs were attack-trained, but I never actually had to send them after anybody. Once they started growling and showing their teeth and tugging at the leash even the drunks calmed down.

We got every kind of performance you can imagine at the Garden. I took them as they came. Of course, some events were worse than others. We never had any problem with the sports crowds, and the only headache with the circus was that the animal smells confused the dogs. Concerts were bad, with all the young girls screaming and trying to throw their panties up on the stage, and I really hated the political conventions because everybody there thought he was a VIP. And you never knew what you were going to get with the religious revival meetings, because when fifteen thousand people got the spirit of God boiling over in them they just weren't going to listen to anybody telling them what to do.

That was what I was afraid of when the Quantals took the place for a five-night stay, but they surprised me. Although the Garden was packed even the first night, it wasn't like that at all. The scalpers were getting as much as a hundred bucks a ticket outside, but the crowd inside was the most orderly I ever saw. One of the preachers would talk for a while, and they'd clap; and then they'd sing a hymn or listen to some organ music or a choir, and then there'd be some more talking. While I was patrolling the passages I couldn't hear what was going on very well, but then I stopped by the main entrance where Annie Esposito was running the checkroom. Everybody who could get in was already inside. Even the teams running the weapons scanners had ducked out for a cup of coffee, so it was quiet there. You could hear the speakers that were rigged up outside for the people who couldn't get in. Annie was listening. "How's it going, hon?" I asked her. She didn't answer, except to say, "Sssshh."

Moe crept under the counter to put his head in her lap and she scratched his ears absently while she listened. That wasn't a good thing to do to an attack dog, who was supposed to stay basically hostile to everybody but his handler, but Annie and I had a thing going. It wasn't perfect. Most of the time she cut me off before we got to bed, and when we did make it, maybe once or twice a month, she was as likely as not to start crying afterward because she'd sinned. What Annie really wanted was for us to get married. I knew that. I would have done it, too, except I still happened to have a wife, somewhere or other, and after she ran off I couldn't find her long enough to get a divorce.

What Annie was listening to didn't sound religious to me. It was more like a lecture. Some man was explaining that God had a whole universe to take care of, and He couldn't bother himself with all the details so He had to use His ministers to keep in touch. That made sense, sort of, but then he got off on a lot of talk about all the other galaxies and how many there were and how far away. I didn't see the point. Then he stopped, the crowd applauded politely, the organ struck up and the choir began to belt out *The Old Rugged Cross.*

"It'll be Reverend Burskin next," Annie said, really looking at me for the first time. "He's pretty inspiring, Stacey. He hears some of the testifying himself, you know."

I thought I knew what she was talking about, because I'd seen the little booths around the sides of the auditorium, all of them always filled, with lines waiting to get into them. I said, "So what about after the show, hon? How would you like us to have something to confess to tomorrow?"

"Don't be such a dope," she said, but it didn't sound like a real No. "Anyway, they don't have confessionals, exactly. Haven't you heard what they're saying?"

I shrugged. There'd been stuff about the Quantals in the papers, but I never get much past the sports pages.

"Well, they're going to keep some of those booths open after the public leaves. For anybody on the staff who wants to testify, I mean. I think I might try it."

"Aw, what do you want to do that for?" I began, trying to talk her out of it. Not that I cared what she might tell some preacher, but if we got out of there too late she'd claim she was too sleepy for a date. But then Slappy began to growl softly; the weapons-check crew were coming back, and that meant that the supervisor was on the prowl. So I blew her a kiss and moved on with the dogs.

But then I did try to listen. Now and then I caught a glimpse of Reverend Burskin through the open doors; he was younger than I'd expected, looking pretty imposing in his white robes. He was telling the crowd how wonderful it was going to be in Heaven, and how none of them needed to worry about Hell; all they had to do was testify for his auditors.

What the hell. When the crowd began filing out they all looked happier than any audience I'd ever seen in the Garden before. So when the cleanup crews were beginning to pick up the litter I got in line for one of the booths that had remained open. I couldn't see the person on the other side of the screen but it was a woman's voice. When I gave my name she stopped me short.

"Don't say anything else just yet, Stacey. Let me explain what's happening here first. You see, I'm an ordained minister in the Holy Church of Quantal Redemption. Think of me as a telephone line to God. He isn't going to pay any attention to what you do most of the time, but when you talk to me you're talking right to Him. So tell me exactly what you want Him to know about you, okay? Start with good deeds. Have you done anything you're proud of lately?"

"You mean"—I hesitated, trying to think of something—"you mean like giving money to the poor, like?"

"That's a good start. Or offering somebody a helping hand. Or just being a friend when somebody needs you. Don't be afraid to brag. God wants to love you, Stacey. Work with Him here, all right? Just give Him the evidence He needs to save you, that's all it takes."

"What about, well, the bad things?"

"Stacey, Stacey," she sighed, "aren't you listening to me? If you *want* God to know bad things about you, that's certainly your privilege. But what goes on God's holy record is only whatever you tell me here, so make up your own mind what you want to say."

So that's how I signed up with the Quantals.

I hadn't been getting along all that well with Father Graziano anyway, and the Quantals just made me a better offer. Annie and I began going to their church on 47th Street, and things really began to pick up between us. Matter of fact, she stopped all that crying, and two weeks later she moved in with me.

Transcript of interview with Arthur John Delaporte, Ph.D.

I want to make it perfectly clear that at no time did I ever hold any grudge against Jeremy Burskin. I had no reason to. He wasn't responsible for getting me fired from my job teaching science at Buck Prep; when the trustees finally got fed up with the Head's innovations and canned him they dumped all his appointees too. As a matter of fact, I owed Jerry a lot, although the first time he tracked me down and made his proposition I turned him down flat. At first.

"Shit, Artie," he said, reasoning with me, "what the hell have you got to lose?"

"My job?"

"Right. Your job. Your job as a substitute science teacher in public high schools where half the kids are absent and the other half carry guns."

"I never said it was great, but it pays the rent."

He didn't answer that directly, just rolled his eyes as he looked around at the studio apartment I was living in. Well, the place wasn't much. But Madge was long gone by then and I didn't need much. "What I'm offering you," he said, "is a chance to get in on the ground floor of the biggest growth industry in America. I'm talking about real money. I'm talking about *religion*."

"I haven't been inside a church since they kicked me out of Buck."

He shook his head. "No, no, Artie, you're not hearing me. I'm not talking about you joining my flock, I'm talking about you getting into *management*. I need to have a real scientist in with me. You've got the degree. I'll take care of the rest—ordaining you, for starters. How does Reverend Arthur John Dela-porte sound?"

I said, "Crazy."

"Artie," he said, sighing, "if you insist on pissing away the best offer you're ever going to have, I don't want you to think that it's going to blast all my hopes of success. There's thousands of other Ph.D.s around that need a job. I came looking for you because you're the one that got me started—even if you didn't mean to—and I don't forget my friends. Are you afraid you'd be breaking the law? Not a chance. I'm duly ordained myself—"

"From Joe Bob's Quick Service Diploma Factory of Lubbock, Texas."

"From a fully accredited religious university, recognized in every state of the union. So's my church. You call up the Secretary of State and check it out for yourself; we're legit. Tell you what. I've got a tent meeting going in Camden to-morrow night. Come along. See for yourself. You don't have to do a thing, just check it out—though, of course, if you decide you're willing to give a little talk on that wave-particle thing and the observer business I'll pay you for your time. Say a hundred bucks. Cash. Right on the spot."

Well, I couldn't pass up a hundred bucks. I went. And then I stayed.

I made out real well, too. Next to Jeremy Burskin I was just about the second highest-ranking person in the church, and Jerry hadn't lied. The money really rolled in.

The place where we really took off was when we did the Garden in New York City. We signed up twenty-three thousand communicants in five days, and what they paid, admission tickets and love offerings combined, was an average of fifty-four dollars each. If you want to see what a million dollars looks like, multiply that out for yourself.

New York was just the beginning. Within five years we had played just about every big auditorium in the country, Soldier's Field, the Hollywood Bowl—you name it. Every time we played a city we picked up another ten or twenty thousand people, and they stayed with us. We opened branch churches in every city, and we hardly ever lost a convert. Why would anybody leave? We offered the best product of any denomination in the country. When our worshippers died, we explained to them, God, or maybe one of His angels, would look in the great golden book and see what the records said, and on the basis of that they would be saved or damned. Saved was, well, heavenly. Damned was *bad*. But God couldn't be expected to follow every last single soul every minute of every day. God would go by what His ordained ministers passed on to Him. Not just us, either; we never said that. We never claimed that the Holy Church of Quantal Redemption was the only direct-line link to God. We were perfectly up-front in saying that any minister, priest, or rabbi could pass the word along Up There.

But we were the ones who encouraged the testifiers to tell us the *good* stuff. We didn't ask them about their sins. We left that up to their common sense. We never did anything like giving them lie-detector tests, either, and if some of them might have stretched the truth a little about their charitable donations or the number of aged relatives they cared for that was their business.

I have to say that many times I thought I was the luckiest man in the world, and I owed it all to Jeremy Burskin. Maybe the high spot was in the third year, when Madge found out what I was doing and turned up after services, one night in Albany, all sweet and repentant and ready to just try one more time to see if we could get back what we once had, Artie, please? I slipped her a couple of hundred bucks for old times' sake before I sent her away; I didn't believe in carrying a grudge. But I did send her away. Who wanted to be tied down to one recycled lady when there were so many fresh young ones around?

Yes, that was definitely one of the high spots, but there weren't any low ones . . . at least, there weren't until Jerry began drinking.

Transcript of interview with Elizabeth Neisman, a.k.a. Lilibet Van Nuys.

Changing my name had nothing to do with the Church. It was my agent's idea, long before I converted, right after I got the nose job and the silicone and the tooth caps. He looked me over and said I might as well go all the way and get a whole new identity if I really wanted to get into the movies.

Well, I did—invented a new name, got a new wardrobe heavy on thigh boots and sleeveless tops, made up a whole family story for background—but the movies weren't interested anyway. When Reverend Burskin's circus came to town I was working as a dancer in one of the places on Hollywood Boulevard. It didn't pay much. That was all right; I couldn't really dance much, either, and, with a little help from the guy I was seeing at the time, it paid the rent. The guy was Henny Glass. I guess he did me a good turn, because Henny was the one who took me to one of the meetings on my night off because he thought it would be kicky. The rest, like they say, is history.

History is what Henny was after that night, anyway. I went *to* the meeting with him, but the guy I left with was my booth minister, Richy Mannering. And it was Richy who came around to say good-bye when the Reverend's group finished their run in L.A., and it was Richy who said I was a good listener, had a nice personality, would do well to join the church and apply for the booth minister's course at the headquarters in Colorado.

It sounded like a good idea—better than anything else I had going for me then, anyway. So I did. They let me in on my first try, and the course was no problem. Richy was right about my being a good listener, and that was half of what the training was about. The other half was learning the patter about Heisenberg and quantum indeterminacy, but I aced that, too—I was always good at pouring a textbook into one part of my brain the night before a test and having it come out right the next day. After all, I'd turned down a scholarship to graduate school at the U of Texas in order to make my run at Hollywood. When we newly accredited booth ministers had our graduation party at the Mansion up on the top of the hill I was Number Two in the class, and would easily have been Number One if I'd wanted to push just a little harder.

So there I was, twenty-three years old and a full-fledged minister of the church, and, believe me, the living was easy. We got paid well, salary plus commissions; that's when I began to be able to put a little money away in the mutual funds. We got to see a lot of the country, too. Once or twice a month we'd all take the campaign to a new city and between times we might be sent to help out a new church somewhere. The rest of the time we spent at the Mansion in Aspen, where we didn't have anything to do but ski or swim or sunbathe or have fun. Every night was party night at the Mansion.

I don't want you to think that there were orgies going on all the time. There wasn't anything like that. People did go to bed with each other sometimes— well, fairly often, really—but what's surprising about that? We were all young and healthy, and we never did it in public and scared the horses. There was plenty to drink for anybody who wanted it, too, and it wasn't hard to find a little recreational dope now and then—well, you could say that about the dorms at the U of T, too. The Mansion was really a lot like those dorms. There were video games and tapes of every movie you ever heard of, and about a million music tapes with really fine systems to play them on; there was a library with eight thousand books and all the magazines in the world; there was the indoor pool and the outdoor pool and the fitness gym; there were horses for anybody who felt like exploring the trails around the mountain—if money could buy it, the Reverend had bought it for us. And, of course, for himself, because he believed in having a good time, too. And it was all *free.*

I don't mean just free of money. I mean free of guilt, too, because after all that was what the whole thing was all about.

See, what made the job the best I ever could imagine was that we were *helping* people. They'd come into my booth scared and worried, and I'd explain to them that God really wanted them to be saved, and I'd invite them to tell me the things about themselves that they wanted God to know, and they'd leave at the end of twenty minutes or so with their heads in the air, hopeful and happy.

That describes all of us, too. Not just the staff and the booth ministers. I mean everybody, even up to the people at the very top, the lawyers, the accountants, our science guru, Rev. Dr. Arthur John Delaporte, and the Reverend Jeremy himself. They were mostly older than the rest of us, sure, but that was the only difference. I was pretty close to a couple of them, so I know. Even Dr. Artie. He was the oldest of the lot, and sometimes a little more reserved, but that didn't matter. In fact, I thought it was good; I felt I could talk to him about more serious things. Once when we'd been skinny-dipping, late at night, and we were bundled up in towels at the edge of the indoor pool, he said something about his age, and I reassured him right away. I said, "You're young where it counts, hon. Besides, you know so much, and I have to tell you that the thing that really turns me on in a man is intelligence."

I could see that that pleased him. He pushed himself up on an elbow to pour a little more champagne and then lifted his glass to toast me. "So tell me what knowledge you want me to share with you."

"Not a thing right now," I said, yawning.

"There must be something you don't know," he insisted.

"Well—" I thought for a minute. "Well, maybe there is. Like where all the guilt goes."

"The what?"

"The guilt. The bad feelings people come to us with. When they leave the booth it's all gone, usually, but where did it go?"

That made him laugh. "Why does it have to go anywhere?"

"I don't know. I guess I was just thinking there had to be some law of conservation of guilt, you know? Like conservation of energy and all that?"

"Huh," he said. Then he said, "You know what a black hole is? Things just disappear into it, matter and energy, everything. And then they're *gone*. They never show up again."

"Do we have a black hole?"

"If we do," he said, grinning, "it's probably the Reverend Jeremy himself. Are you warm yet? Is it about time we went upstairs?"

Well, it was, and that was that. It was just date talk. It didn't mean anything. Only I'm not sure I didn't make a mistake when, a couple of nights later around the same pool, I happened to mention it to the Reverend Jeremy.

Transcript of interview with Arthur John Delaporte, Ph.D.

The week it began to look like serious trouble we were doing Phoenix, Arizona.

It was really big business there; we always did well with the retirement areas, where the rich old geezers had plenty of time to start worrying about some of the things they'd done to get rich. In spite of all that, Jerry had a lot on his mind. *Newsweek* had come out with that big smart-ass story of theirs, with his picture on the cover and the headline "Prophet of God the Inattentive?" And we'd been talking about getting into the televangelist business, and there were all these TV people trying to do deals with us. The last day we were in Phoenix we had lunch with six of them in Jerry's suite—they had a proposition about setting up a cable channel of our own—and we opened a whole bunch of bottles of wine. When we'd got rid of the television suits and I went off to take a nap before the evening session I guess Jerry just decided to finish off all the bottles that were left over. He threw up when his dresser was getting him into his robes. They had to pull out a spare set, and he stumbled and faltered through his preaching.

Well, that didn't seem to matter. Nobody noticed. Only when I finally got him to bed he looked up at me and said, "Did you ever think maybe we're calling attention to ourselves?"

"That's why we have P.R. people."

"No, I mean God's attention. To me."

Drunks say funny things, of course. I had a pretty good idea that one of the girls had been talking to him, and I was even pretty sure I knew which one—Lili. She was a nice enough kid and pretty smart, too, but smart in a rather dumb way. She was always thinking about things that really didn't have anything to do with the bottom line.

I didn't worry much about it, because the next morning he was fine. We did Oklahoma City later that month, and then Atlanta, and although I knew he was hitting the bottle he mostly saved it until after work. But when we got to New Orleans he was pissed onstage again. That was beginning to look like a trend, so afterward I took him back to the hotel and fed him black coffee until he was coherent enough to tell me what was going on. "I'm scared," he said simply.

"Come on, Jerry. Are you worrying about that Congressional committee? They're never going to touch us."

"Fuck the Congressional committee. I'm scared of God."

That set me back. We never, *ever*, talked about God except in line of duty. He saw the expression on my face and pushed the coffee cup away. "You don't see the problem, do you? What we tell the customers," he said, "is that we're God's TV cameras. He only sees what's going on through our eyes because we're His ordained ministers."

"So?"

"So He sees *us,* Artie. We're flagging His attention. We're the stations He's tuned in on. Don't you worry about what He might be seeing of you and me—especially me? Because I do, Artie. I'm going to die some day. We all are, sooner or later; and I worry a lot about what might be coming next."

And, you know, I couldn't talk him out of it.

I never saw a man go to pieces the way Jeremy Burskin did. We had to cancel Detroit. We spread the word that he was on a retreat—it was the Betty Ford Clinic, actually—but when he came out he wasn't drinking anymore, no, but he couldn't make himself get up on that stage again.

Rumors began to spread. Worse than that, our own organization was affected. We had to postpone the rest of the tour. Jerry had become a liability.

I could see only one way of salvaging the operation and I took it.

By then Jerry was holed up in his private place in Aspen, just a couple of miles from the Mansion, with guards around to keep the curious out. I joined him there. In spite of the doctor's orders I brought him a present, a bottle of thirty-year-old Scotch, and while I peeled off the cap I said, "Jerry, I've got an idea. You're frightened of God's punishment after you die, and maybe you're right. There's a way out of it, though. Suppose you never had to die, exactly, at all?"

I don't know if he would have agreed to it sober, but I didn't let him get sober again. Not that night, not on our charter flight to Los Angeles, not through all the preparations I'd arranged for him.

So business is pretty good again. Admittedly it's not the same without Jerry. Our grosses are down some, sure, but I've learned how to give the pitch myself, with the help of a couple of drama coaches, and we never fail to invoke the memory of our late leader in every session. There's a big blown-up picture of him in his robes, looking saintly, that I use for a backdrop behind the grand altar, and when I turn to ask his blessing at the end of each performance it usually brings down the house.

I think, in a way, Jerry would be proud of me—if, of course, he was in a position to have an opinion on such matters from his cryonic capsule.

It's a pity that he began to buy into his own pitch. I'm not making the same mistake.

Well, *so* far I'm not, anyway; and if it ever gets to the point where I *do*, well, maybe I'll take a turn in the freezer myself and be not any longer alive, exactly, but maybe also not quiet dead enough to have to worry about Final Judgment.

DEVIL YOU DON'T KNOW

Dean Ing

Dean Ing is an engineer-turned-writer whose SF is in the tradition of Robert A. Heinlein—tough-minded, self-reliant, hard SF. He began to publish regularly in SF in the 1970s and then in the mid-1980s focused on the popular genre of techno-thriller. His latest major SF novel was *The Big Lifters* in 1988. Some of his best work has been short fiction. Of his short story collections, *High Tension* is of particular interest.

Maffei, brushing at his cheap suit, produced his papers with confidence. They were excellent forgeries. "I dunno the patient from whozis," he said. "Will she need sedation? A jacket?"

The receptionist was your standard sanitarium model: stunning, crisp, jargony, her uniform a statement of medical competence as spurious as Maffei's authorization. "Dina Valerie Clark," she read. "I did an ops transfer profile on her. If I may see your ID, sir?" It was not really a question.

Both driver's license and psychiatric aide registration were genuine enough. Neither card hinted that this stocky aide, Christopher Maffei, was also M.D., Ph.D., and in his present capacity, SPY. To stay in character he rephrased his question while surrendering the cards. "Will the kid need restraint?"

"It doesn't say," she murmured, returning his ID. "We can sign her over to you after your exit interview."

"My interview? Lady, I'm just the taxi to some clinic in Nebraska."

"It's only a formality," she purred, fashioning him a brief bunny-nose full of sexual conspiracy.

Maffei avoided laughing. In three years of residency and five of research, he had observed enough morons to be a passable simulacrum on his own. "I never done that before," he lied. He had listened to these sales pitches only too often. "Can I use your phone? Dr. Carmichael can talk to you from Springfield . . ."

"Sign here, please, and here, and there," in ten-below tones.

Maffei smiled and signed. *You're beaten by invincible ignorance,* he thought. *Maybe we should start a club.* He straightened and looked around, realizing the receptionist had buzzed for Val Clarke.

She came toward him slowly at first down the long hallway, made smaller by her outsized luggage. It was very expensive luggage, the guilt-assuaging hardware a wealthy parent would provide for an unwanted child. Chris still chafed at what it had cost him.

As Val neared him, he saw that her hair had been shorn almost to the scalp. Lice, probably. Her height was scarcely that of a ten-year-old. The frail angular body, still too large for her head, was yet too small for its oddly misaligned and bovine eyes. She wore the same white ankle socks, slippers, and trousers she'd had when entering Nodaway Retreat two weeks before. Her smiling gaze swept up to his, then past, and she broke into a stumbling skip toward the entrance.

"You must be Valerie Clarke," Maffei said with forced gaiety, catching gently at her pipestem wrist.

The vacant smile foundered. A silent nod. No more skipping; the girl stood awaiting whatever this vast authoritarian world might dictate.

"Let's get you to an ice-cream cone," Maffei said, letting her bring the suitcases. He maintained the running patter while strapping her into his electric four-seater and stowing the luggage behind. "I bet you'd like a Frostylite, hm?"

Tucking his slight paunch under the steering wheel, Maffei whirred them toward the automatic gate. It slid aside, then back, as they emerged onto the highway. Val Clarke slumped in her seat with a lip-blubbering parody of released tension. "Oh, come on, Val, it can't be that bad," Maffei smirked.

"Not for you it can't. It isn't your screwed-up implants, pal, you try running an inside surveillance with an intermittent transceiver short sometime and I'll patronize *you*."

He glanced from the road to her, reaching out to her tiny skull and gently stroked behind her ear. "No swelling. If it were a mastoid infection you'd know it for sure."

The girl shrugged upward in her seat, barely able to see over the battery cowl ahead. "I'll survive. Well, what do you make of Nodaway Retreat?"

"Typical ultraconservative ripoff," he mused, barely audible over the hum and tire noise. "From your reports I make it one staff member per twenty patients, minimal life-support for everyone concerned except for the up-front crew; one honest-to-God R.N. and a pair of general practitioners who look in once a month from Des Moines to trade sedatives for fees."

"I've seen worse. Remember Ohio?"

Maffei nodded sagely. Val Clarke had scarcely been admitted when her transmission began to read like a bedlam litany. Rickettsia and plain starvation, a "bad ward" where three children of normal intelligence were chained, and a nightly victimization of youthful male patients by the staff. "That's what my survey is about; to change all that. It was the worst I ever saw," he admitted.

Val flicked him a quick glance, but Maffei intended no sarcasm. He had seen two staff members wearing masks of outraged innocence, and strap marks on Val's thin calves after the general warrant had been served—really more raid than service, brought on by Val's moment-to-moment account via her miniscule implanted transceiver. In the space of thirty-six hours Val had seen two compound femur fractures on a girl who had jumped from her high window, and a gang assault of one profoundly retarded child by besmocked thugs. The worst Maffei had seen in Ohio was not precisely the worst Val Clarke had seen; but then, Maffei bore no stigmata of retardation.

It was Valerie Clarke's tragedy to have been born with an autosomal dominant inheritance which was instantly diagnosed as mental retardation. The astonishing width between her eyes had a name of its own: hypertelorism. It
explained nothing except that Val's great brown orbs were set a trifle too far
apart to please a society which, paradoxically, distrusted eyes set too close together. Her lustrous roan hair normally covered a skull which, from its small
size, also had a special stigma with label attached: microcephaly. Her ears flared
a bit, particularly noticeable now that her hair was shorn, and at twenty-two, Val
Clarke passed for twelve even without her training bra.

Any competent specialist could adjust to the fact that Val's intelligence was
normal, her motivation superb—a recipe for "genius." The unadjusted expectation was something else again. Val, an early victim of maldiagnosis and
parental rejection, knew the signs of a good sanitarium from the inside because
she had experienced enough bad ones in childhood.

When Val was thirteen, a suspicious young intern named Chris Maffei taught
her basic algebra and the scatology of three foreign languages to prove his point.
After that, her schooling was more formal if not exactly conventional. Any girl
who patterned herself after Chris Maffei could junk the word "convention" at
the outset, with the obvious exception of medical conventions, where Chris read
scholarly papers and pumped for any grant money he could locate.

Now Chris was a year into a fat HEW grant to study the adequacy of private
mental homes; and if he had not actually suggested that Val volunteer for commitment in these places, he had not omitted oblique hints at the notion. Nor
turned down her offer. It was a symbiosis: Maffei had his spy, Val her spymaster.

"Hey," she said. He looked around and briefly laid his hand over the one she
offered palm up. "Thanks for reeling me in so fast."

One corner of his mouth went up. "Had to. That short was interfering with
my favorite live soap opera."

"Shmuck," she said tenderly—Maffei had never entirely managed to socialize her language. "Speaking of soap, you could introduce Nodaway to the idea."

"I'll note it when I debrief you after supper. I was in the army with a G.P.
near here. If I know Farr, he'll do an Onward Christian Soldiers when I send
him my notes on the place."

"Fine. And by the way, good guru, you just passed a Frostylite. You
p'omised," she added, expertly faking a vocal retardation slur.

"First things first. We need a battery recharge to make Joplin tonight."

Startled: "Why Joplin, of all places? That's south."

"Because I have you scheduled for a scrub-up and transceiver check there
tonight. And because after that we're going into the Deep South."

She was silent but he lip-read her response: *Oh, my God.*

After the Joplin stop, Maffei's little sedan hummed on barrel tires toward Mississippi. Val failed to concentrate on Durrell's *Clea.* The source of her unease
was not the September heat, but the fact that she had slept at the clinic in Joplin.
Chris lavished care on her as he would on a rare and exorbitant device, but she
did not delude herself on the point. Val needed a secure relationship and physical human warmth. Very well then: he shared motel rooms with her. She also
needed passionate attention, as anyone might when in constant proximity to a

beloved. Chris dutifully pleased her when, on rare occasions, she was insistent enough. The one thing Valerie Clarke could not elicit from Chris was his desire.

Durrell's velvet prose wasn't helping Val's mood. She studied her reflection in the car window. *Ms. Universe I'm not. If I expect this sex object of mine—okay, twenty pounds overweight and why shouldn't he be?—to come fawning over my Dumbo ears I'm worse than microcephalic, I'm scatocephalic.* She traced a tentative forefinger along the pink smoothness of one ear. At least she had perfect skin. "Chris, why do you put me out before making the transceiver check if you don't make an incision?"

He yawned before answering, flexing strong hands on the wheel. "We do, Val. Those antennae are so fine I can run 'em just inside the dermis, on the fossa of your helix—uh, inside your ear rim. A microscalpel does it; almost no bleeding and it heals quick as boo. But I have to keep you abso-bloody-lutely still. Same for the X-ray check on your implant circuitry. It's a whole lot bigger in area than it might be, since I wanted it spread out for easy maintenance."

"You didn't cut down to the mastoid?"

"No need to fix the resonator; I just incised a tiny slit to your circuit chip. It was a hairline circuit fracture, just right for laser repair. Total heat doesn't amount to a paramecium's hotfoot, using the miniaturized Stanford rig. See, you don't *have* to hurt the one you love." He grinned.

"I'll remind you of that after supper."

He clucked his tongue in mock dismay, still grinning. Message clear, will comply, out. She returned to Durrell as the kilometers hummed away.

The supper hush puppies in Vicksburg were a pleasant surprise, not by being in the least digestible but in their lingering aftertaste. When she and Chris vented simultaneous belches later, her fit of giggles might have caused a lesser man to make war, not love. All credit to the Maffei mystique, she decided still later, as she lazed on the motel bed and watched Chris attack his toenails. "You never told me how you got those mangled toes," she murmured. "We beautiful people are repelled by physical deformity, y'know."

He looked up, preoccupied, then grinned. "Same way I got this," he rubbed his finger over the broken nose that gave him a faintly raffish look. "Soccer. Did I ever tell you I once played against Pelé?"

She fetched him a wondering smile. "Wow; no."

Deadpan: "Well, I never did—but Lord knows what I may've told you." Dodging the flung pillow, he went on. "You'd best save your energy for tomorrow, Val. We'll be delivering you up to the graces of Gulfview Home around noon."

Retrieving the pillow, she placed it in her lap and hugged it, eyes half closed, dreaming awake. "A view of the gulf will be nice. I hope this is a clean place—and please, God, air-conditioned."

"Don't count on it. It's forty kilometers from the gulf; how's that for an auspicious start?"

She shrugged. "It figures. But why this place? We're kind of off our itinerary." She wriggled beneath the covers, hiding her thin limbs.

He put away his clipper and reached for the lightplate, waving it to a diffuse nightlight. "A tip from HealthEdWelfare," he said, swinging under the coverlet. After a long pause he added, "You'll have a contact inside: a Ms. May Endicott.

She won't know about you, but she knows something, I guess. And an insider's tip is a good place to start. Better the devil you know, and all that. I'll find out what sent her running to HEW after we commit you. Most likely a snoopy old dowager with fallen arches and clammy handshake." He grew silent, realizing that Val's response was the softest of snores. Chris Maffei fell asleep wondering if Gulfview and old Ms. Endicott would fit his preconceptions.

Gulfview Home squatted precisely in the center of its perimeter fencing; held its white clapboard siding aloof like skirts from the marauding grass. Viewing the grounds, it was hard to imagine much organized recreation for patients. Chris identified himself to the automatic gate, then rolled his window back up to escape the muggy air. In silence, they pulled up before the one-story structure.

Their expectations followed earlier studies which, since the 1950s, had always shown higher per capita need for institutional treatment in the Southeast—and lower per capita effectiveness. The region was catching up; but, in 1989, still lagged. To Chris, it was a problem in analysis. To Val, stumbling up Gulfview's steps with her luggage, the first problem was a dread akin to stage fright. It always was; and as always, she hid her fear from Chris. The air conditioning was a relief, but a new fear sidled up to Val when they found the receptionist. She was, and wasn't, old Ms. Endicott.

Chris saw that Ol' Miz Endicott had very high arches for such small feet. He stood watching as May Endicott ushered a vacant-eyed Val Clarke from the reception room. A waist he could span with two hands, but la Endicott hourglassed to very nice extremes. Rather like a pneumatic gazelle by Disney, he judged.

Endicott boasted thick brown curls. "Dye job" was Val's whispered aside as she stumbled, entirely in character, with her luggage. But Chris was not listening.

The Endicott woman returned in moments, to help Chris complete papers placing Val Clarke squarely in the hands of a private jail—or asylum, rehab home, whatever it might prove to be. "We were expectin' you, but the senior staff are busy at the moment. The child's history seems well documented," she remarked in a soft patrician drawl. "Do you think she might be a trainable?"

Chris hesitated. A trainable might have free run of the place, or might be closely watched if it were more of a prison. Suddenly he remembered that May Endicott was, after all, a potential ally. "Depends on how good you are, I guess," he said. "I'm told you're concerned for the patients."

"We try—I think," she said as if genuinely pondering.

"I mean you, personally."

A flicker of subtlety in the dark sloe eyes. "I can't imagine who . . ."

"Just a friend in the discipline," he said easily. "Henry E. Wilks. How's that for a set of initials?"

"I don't . . ." she began, and then she did. "Well," she said in a throaty whisper. It set Maffei atingle. "And what are all the Wilkses doin' these days?"

"Waiting to hear from me," he replied, enjoying the respect in her oval face. "And I'm waiting to hear from you. I don't need to meet the staff just yet."

"I'm in the book, M. A. Endicott, in town. Perhaps this evenin'?"

He nodded and continued with the forms, pointedly sliding a blank set into his disreputable attaché case. As he rose, he noted that May Endicott's hands trembled. Anticipation? Fear?

Chris made a leisurely trip into town, bought a sandwich, then found the Endicott address. It was after five P.M. when he parked. He began to study the commitment forms—the fine print could sometimes raise hackles—and he remembered the barbecue sandwich. During his third bite he remembered Val Clarke and fumbled for his comm unit. Although the major amplification and tight-band scrambling modes were built into the car, they also enhanced the signal to and from his pocket unit. Without the car, his range was perhaps two kilometers. With it, over thirty. Val, behind high fencing and well beyond the town limits, should be within range. But you never knew . . .

He thumbed the voice actuator. The cassette, as usual, was recording all transmission into the system. "Val? How'sa girl? I haven't heard a peep." *Nor thought about one,* he told himself. He waited for a moment and was about to try again.

"i gave up on you around suppertime," the speaker replied. Implant devices did not yet rival conventional transmission. Val could receive a voice with fair fidelity but could only transmit by subvocalizing. With lips parted slightly she could transmit almost silently and as well as, say, a tyro ventriloquist; but bone conduction and minute power sources had their limitations. Val Clarke's nuances of intonation and verbal style were sacrificed for the shorthand speech of covert work. In short, she sounded very like a machine. Maffei would have denied that he preferred it that way.

"I was doing errands. And it's only getting to be suppertime now," he objected.

"not when you're running a money mill," Val replied. "it's on cassette. these people use patients to serve meals—and to cook 'em, from the taste of it. yuchhh."

"If you're bitching about food, you can't have much worse on your mind."

"yeah? try thinking of me in here on an army cot, and you outside with miz handy cot."

"Endicott," he chuckled at the mike. "I'll review the tape later. What else is new?"

"i'm in isolation 'til they figure how to use me, i think. two males, a female, all young and retarded, doing chores."

He thought for a moment. "Good therapy for 'em, unless the chores include lobotomies and group gropes. Who's in charge?"

"you got me, chris. and i wish you did, this doesn't smell right, quiet as a tomb in my room with very soft wallpaper and no view at all. when i say isolated, i mean locked away. but the kids gave me a toy."

"Something educational?"

"a rubber duckie, swear to god. well, they're nice kids."

"Look; I have some reading to do, and a session with the Endicott lady so we can plan. I'll check with you later. Don't eat your duckie."

"same to you, fella," in monotonic reply. He smirked at the speaker, but no answer seemed very useful. He pocketed the comm unit and returned to his sandwich and forms.

Although commitment forms varied, they generally claimed almost total control over their wards. Chris Maffei had doctored Val's records to assure that she would not be subjected to insulin shock treatment, surgery, or unusual medication. The forms implied that Gulfview could damned well amputate her head if they chose, but there were safeguards against such treatment. For one thing, Val could transmit her plight and get help from Maffei. Or, if it came to that, she could simply admit her charade. In sixteen previous investigations, she had never blown her cover.

Maffei was munching a pickle slice when he saw the steam plume of the bus, two blocks away. It slid past him a moment later, slowing to disgorge the unmistakeable form of May Endicott. She had a very forthright stride, he decided, and admired it until she disappeared into her apartment. The pickle disposed of, Maffei crammed the forms into his attaché case and grunted, sweating, from the car. Val was right: he'd have to watch his weight.

At his knock, the door whisked open. May Endicott tugged him in by a sleeve, darting quick looks over his shoulder at her innocent shrubbery. She shut the door just as quickly and jumped at his reaction. "Gentlemen don't usually laugh at me."

"They should, if you treat 'em like jewel thieves," Maffei grinned. Beneath the makeup, he saw, she was quite young. "A poor beginning, ma'am. We really don't have anything to be furtive about, do we?"

The faintest relaxation of erect shoulders, and: "I'm not sure, Mr. Moffo."

"Maffei; Dr. Christopher Maffei, Johns Hopkins, to be insufferable about it," he said, getting the expected response. "Can we sit?"

She had a merry musical laugh of her own, waving him to a couch between stacks of periodicals. He saw several journals on abnormal psychology and special education. Idly he checked the issue numbers as they talked. His first goal was to put this latent centerfold at ease, simply done by asking her to talk about herself.

May was agreeable to the low-key interrogation. Modestly raised in Montgomery; a two-year nursing certificate with notions of an R.N. to come; parents retired; summer work in a state hospital. "I don't know if I have a callin'," she finished, "but I like to feel I'm bein' used well."

"You will be," Maffei said cryptically, and flipped back the journal he held. "Thought I might find myself here. Just a small reference," he added with exaggerated modesty.

She saw him referenced by another author and looked away. "You embarrass me, Dr. Maffei; I should've recognized your name."

"Hey, none of that," he laughed. "I'm Chris and you're May, if you don't mind it. You seemed jumpy and I wanted to reassure you, that's all. Want my full ID?"

She sat back, relaxed, strong calves crossed fetchingly as she glanced through his cards. Maffei had a rising sense that this would be one of his more pleasant investigations. "Understand, May, I hope you're wrong about your job. As you know, private homes run a long gamut from excellent to atrocious." She nodded, beginning to pour an aperitif.

"I can't survey every asylum in the country, but the HEW agreed to pick up the tab for a little"—he searched for an Endicott trigger-word—"chivalrous snooping. I have no official standing beyond what the AMA lends me, which is vague enough, God knows. But soon I'll have a fair sampling of the virtues and vices of private sanitariums. Who's mistreating patients? What staff training is most needed? Where should the gummint step in? Not exactly cloak-and-dagger

stuff, May, but not the questions your average institutional exec likes to hear."
He did not add that the book from his research might be a muckraking best-
seller.

"So you don't ask out loud," she prompted.

"Right; I try to find someone like you, and whisper in her ear."

Rising smoothly, she purred, "Well, now I know you're really a doctor. De-
velopin' your bedside manner." Maffei realized his gaffe too late and refused to
admit it was accidental. "Let's say my Freudian halfslip is showing and let it go,"
he said. "I mean, no, dammit, that's not what I meant." A pause. "Do you have
this effect on *every*body?"

She stood quietly, reaching some internal decision. Then, "It's a problem,"
she admitted, with a sunburst grin that took Maffei by frontal assault. "Physician, heal thyself."

"It may take some patchwork," he chuckled, "but bear with me."

A nod; slow and ageless.

"Professionally, I need you to check on a list of things. You reported that the
last receptionist had no specialized training, was lucky to have the job, but
seemed anxious to leave. And when she left, she did it in style. Expensive car and
so on."

"A Lotus Cellular, no less," May put in. "And I know Lana Jo Fowler's family and they couldn't support that kind of spo'ty habit."

"Maybe she had sugar-daddy support?"

"That's how she let on," Mary said, "but she wouldn't say that if it were
true. I think she was bein' paid off. I don't know what for, Lana Jo was no
dumplin', and no brain either.

"Then there's Dr. Tedder," she continued, "I mean both Drs. Tedder,
Lurene and Rhea." It did not escape Maffei that she named the woman first.
"They live on the grounds and I don't see him much, but he isn't my idea of a
doctor, more like a wino, and she—is—a—sight, a proper *sight*," she finished,
rolling her eyes melodramatically.

"You haven't mentioned the honcho."

"Dr. Merkle? Rob Merkle is unmentionable, maybe that's why. Those soft
sausage hands; but when he keeps 'em to himself he's competent. I'll say this, he
knows where every penny goes."

"No doubt. Well, I need data like where Merkle and the Tedders did their
residencies, what's the cost of boarding a patient, the sources of referrals, types
of therapy, type and dosage of drugs prescribed and by whom, dietitian's schedule . . ."

"Whew," with lips pursed in kissable fashion, Maffei thought. "That's a tall
number."

"I haven't begun," he said sadly.

"We both have," she smiled. "I smell cheap barbecue sauce on you, but
could you use a shrimp salad anyway?"

"A small one. Need help?"

"It's woman's work," she said, surprising him again by her atavism. By the
end of the evening, May had a long list of Maffei's professional needs and a
sketchy idea of his personal ones. Never once did he mention Valerie Clarke. He
could not have said exactly why.

*   *   *

Val awoke to depressingly familiar voices, muffled by the padding on her walls. It was not the timbre of a remembered person but the quasi-linguistic chanting of mentally retarded children that she recognized. Aware that the staff might be watching by monitor, Val lay on her musty bedding and played with her fingers. She reconstructed the ward's morning by inference from the subdued noises. A parrotlike male recited a holovision commercial with astonishing fidelity: *one* trainable, sure as hell. Footsteps, peals of animal glee, angry hoots in their wake: horseplay, probably unsupervised and therefore dangerous. A bucket dropped (kicked?) hard and a howl of dismay; some poor MR klutzing his cleaning chores. Every few minutes, shuffling thumps at her door. Val gave up on that one and lay back to give her fingers a rest.

Her door swung open so quickly that Val jumped. It was no trick to register a fearful MR grimace. The heavy door seemed a trifle to the dray-horse muscles of Dr. Lurene Tedder. The pale deepset eyes flanked an aquiline Tudor nose, and Val sensed great stamina in Lurene Tedder's hundred and seventy pounds. Yet the most striking feature was hair, seemingly tons of it, a cascade of blue-black tresses spilling over her shoulders, an emblem utterly female crowning the stocky woman.

A voice fortified with testosterone: "Hello, Valerie. Time for us to get up." A practiced smile fled across the face, to be replaced by a gaze that promised to miss very little. "Do we understand?"

Val waited a moment to nod assent, then stood, hands at her sides.

"Can we talk? Dr. Lurene, can we say that? Dr. Lurene," the big woman crooned.

My, but she loves the sound of that, Val thought. She nodded.

"Then *say* it, you . . . try and say it, Valerie."

Val said it in unfeigned fright. Lurene Tedder's ignorance of MR training was so blatant that Val wondered momentarily if she were being baited by a patient. "Docta Luween," she said again, dully, and again.

Lurene Tedder nodded, again treated Val to a smile; but this time it lingered. "I think we're gonna work out fine."

And the operative word is "work," Val thought. She risked a hint of a smile with eyes that begged for acceptance. Only half of it was pretense.

Lurene Tedder motioned Val from the cell, and Val, scurrying to comply, nearly collided with May Endicott. Thrusting a folder brusquely at May, the Tedder woman produced an expensive hairbrush and, sweeping it through her one glory, hurried off. "Find something therapeutic for this one," she flung over a broad shoulder.

May, placing a gentle hand on Val's arm, called, "Were you going to do an assessment?" Her tone implied that Tedder had merely forgotten.

"Oh, sure, yeah," as the big woman sailed on from the ward, her voice booming louder. "Send her to, uh, our office about three."

Thick steel-faced fiber doors swing to and fro in Lurene Tedder's wake. Val looked straight ahead, half fearing that eye contact with May Endicott would reveal too much. May aspirated a bitter sigh, then brightened as she turned to Val. "I'm goin' to introduce you to some people, Valerie," she promised. These were the first friendly words Val had heard, and almost she began to forgive May Endicott her splendor in gender.

May did not hurry, nor ask questions of Val, but maundered, talking easily, from one patient to another down the row of beds. Val noted the linolamat floor approvingly; you could fall on it without harm, yet May's virginally white, whorishly spiked heels left no indentation. *Why must the woman flaunt it so?* The floor's barely perceptible slope led to a small drainage grate in the ward center; Val thought herself petty to hope a high-style heel might catch in it. She let details register without quick eye movement, indexing data with mnemonic tricks Chris had taught her. This was Val's métier, and doing it well, she outpaced her fears for the moment.

But: *Why doesn't she slip me the high sign,* Val thought. She and Chris always chose a fresh code word for ID and a general all-is-well signal, but May Endicott had not used it.

May broke into the reverie: "Is there anything you'd like to see especially, Valerie?"

After a long pause for pseudoserious pondering: "Chitlins?"

Val privately admitted that the Endicott bimbo had a nice laugh. "Well, not today anyway. We're havin' a fortified soup"—as if to herself adding, "what else?"

Val pointed to a patient May had ignored. "Big Boy," she slurred.

May smiled again at this wholly understated description, then walked to the end bed. Val stepped near and gazed upon a mountain of flesh. It was alive, in a way.

"This is Gerald Rankine," May began. Doubtless, she did not expect Val to understand much, but persisted. Rankine was eighteen, an enormous smooth-faced cherub in cutaway pajamas. Severely retarded, he would vegetate in a clinic for as long as his body might function. May guessed his weight at four hundred pounds, and Val saw, with an old shock of recognition, that the great body was asymmetrical The limbs and even the head were distinctly larger on the right side. "He can eat when we help," May ended, "and we give him medicine so he won't hurt himself."

Hurt himself? If this great thing was subject to seizures, Val opined silently, he needed better accommodations than these. She wondered if Rankine had bedsores; and if he felt them; and if it were more ethical to maintain him or not to, under the circumstances. It was hopeless to feel assured at any answer. She was saved from further speculation by May's greeting to someone approaching from the ward kitchen. Val knew better than to turn on her own volition.

"Laura, honey," May said happily. "We have a new girl; I think she might be a help." And then May pulled Val around, and Val swept her eyes up a slender girlish form to meet—no eyes at all.

Laura Dunning was in many respects a lissome sixteen. She moved well, spoke with a charming drawl, dressed neatly, with pert nose and an enviable rosebud mouth. But the high forehead continued down to her cheeks with only faint, shallow depressions where her eyes would be in a more rational world. Val cudgeled her memory for a similar case, could find none. And somehow, inexplicably, Laura Dunning was very beautiful to look upon. Perhaps her animated speech helped; an old theorist's prescription for superb speech performance was an intelligent female with good hearing, blind from birth.

Val expected a fleeting fingertip inspection of her face, shoulders, arms, and hands by the blind Laura. Instead, she offered her hand to be shaken. Another discard from an embarrassed family, Laura was obviously no more MR than was Val herself.

As Val took the proffered hand, May seemed to shift roles and excused herself. "I'll go double-check that darlin' soup," she said in pleasant sarcasm, and Val was left with the blind girl.

Laura began taking, talking, eliciting brief answers now and then from Val, evidently deciding what chores Val might be willing and able to perform. Disturbingly, the blind girl studied every answer with satisfaction—or was it secret amusement? When Laura turned to lead Val to the ward kitchen, she did so with balletic grace. Val was no stranger to the blind—but in some way, she felt, Laura Dunning was extraordinarily sighted.

Under close supervision, Val had no chance to give a detailed response when Maffei transmitted before noon. She cut in only long enough to respond with their code word. Anxious to begin his paper chase of senior staff documentation, Chris elected to leave Val on her own. "We can count on Endicott," he assured her. "I'll leave the comm unit recorder here at the motel; you can report when you get the chance, even if I'm out of range."

Again Val muttered their code word, loudly enough that May, hovering supportively near, chuckled. Satisfied, Chris keyed out.

Lunch was passable, kitchen chores simple, her three o'clock assessment a misnomer. Val left the Tedder office at suppertime, squired by Laura Dunning and too angry at the Tedder couple to trust herself in an immediate report. Laura, her every gesture as assured as a sighted dancer's, wangled fresh bedding for Val in a ward bed next to Laura's own. Val waited a half hour, pulled her pillow over most of her head, and began to transmit.

" . . . and then i realized they never intended legit tests," she recorded, nearing the crux of her message. "assessment? i scrubbed their deleted floor! rhea tedder's stoned on something; middle-age, middle-size, middlin' scared of docta luween. he'd make a great spy, you can overlook him so easy. i expected him to float up to the ceiling when he wasn't grabbing for my goodies. no sweat, lurene handled him. but they had no motor skills hardware, no nothing for m.r. tests that i saw.

"the rankine boy could be hell on square wheels if he *is* epileptic. can't tell from laura if it's gran mal, akinetic, myoclonic, whatever. i can hear me asking!

"caught sight of merkin—see merkle's goatee and you get the connection. fifty, hefty, soft mouth, dead eyes, voice like the bottom note of a pipe organ. badliver skin, i'd say. treats lurene as peer, maybe something going there between 'em.

"drug dispensing: weird but may be okay. there's a lot of it. the blind girl— her you have to meet—does the work and i swear she's efficient. gets dosages from the staff. boy, does she empathize; a girl had a petit mal seizure tonight, laura's ears must be like tuning forks. stopped dead, turned toward the kid shuddering. lucky me, i got to help clean the beddypoo. laura says she doesn't mind, helping the helpers. some help: profound m.r. and epilepsy.

"and what's with miz bandicoot, haven't you told her i'm me? and what the hell keeps you out so long, can't you xmit? sure leaves me out on a long string, and if you infer i'm strung out, you're improving.

"i suspect merkle uses drugs as babysitters; no organized play beyond what laura fixes, they all love her. 'course, some get enough exercise working. i think they do it for laura, and i also think lurene knows it.

"nutrition: okay, i think. hell of a good modern kitchen with equipment they don't need to make soup. m.r.'s keep the stainless shiny. tons of soy flour; so what else is new? tedders and merkle set up meals after lights out, i can hear 'em in there now. merkle doesn't seem the type for menial work, but that's his voice.

"and i ache all over from charlady chores. drop me a postcard someday, i could use good news." Sleep came easily to Val after that; the lax operation at Gulfview had given Val a breadth of insight that ordinarily might take weeks. Surely, she felt, Chris would wrap this job up easily. It was a lullaby thought, a beguiling diversion that left her utterly unprepared for the morrow.

Val tried to doze through the ward's early morning chaos, failed, and feigned sleep to query Chris Maffei. Instantly this reply began in her head. She felt the elation of contact trickle away as he continued.

"Hey, Mata Hari, we're making progress," he began. "I'm transcribing now at, uh, two A.M. Got back from—uh—an interview to the comm unit late and just finished your tape. Great stuff, hon." Val needed one guess to identify his late evening interviewee.

"Nothing on the Tedders yet," he went on. "But data retrieval isn't all that good here in town, I can get to a records center in Biloxi if I'm up bright and early."

So he's already hull-down on the horizon from me this morning, Val thought.

"Keep your eyes open for indiscriminate use of phenobarb, Valium, Zarontin, all the old standby zonkers. You recall the drill: Valium's the same size pill regardless of dose, it's the color—well, you know.

"I haven't blown your cover to May . . ."—the barest of hesitations, then the surname added—"Endicott because what she doesn't know, she can't reveal. What she already knows is incriminating enough. Merkle might be tricky—or worse.

"The rundown on Robin Terence Merkle looked okay at first; bona fides from med school and AMA. But no special work with MR; he went into pharmaceutical research with a chemical company from '71 to '83. Took an enviable vacation, then until starting Gulfview in '85. On a hunch, I dropped in at the local cop shop and asked about the last receptionist before Endicott; Lana Jo Fowler, a local girl. And there's a missing-persons sheet on her. They found her nifty Lotus abandoned in a Hattiesburg parking lot and she'd been dropping school-girl hints about hitting it rich. It occurred to me that maybe something rich hit *her.*

"The desk sergeant said they'd done their number on the Fowler girl, a plain sort who got her popularity the only way she knew how. One of their many blind leads was a gentleman who'd recently paid for her visa and hovercraft fare to Cancun, down the Yucatán. A very proper professional man. Rob Merkle.

"The police aren't disposed to worry about it, but the girl's family is. Which leaves me with hunches. If any of 'em are right, Merkle knows where Lana Jo Fowler is, and she knows where something expensive is. Mexico? Ironic thing is, I'm in a better position than a small-time police department to spend time on it.

"In case you wonder. I'm not sidestepping to pursue this little mystery. I suspect the Gulfview operation should be shut down, but I don't want to pillory a guy who may be doing his half-assed best." His yaw whispered though Val's head. "If you're as tired as I am, you'll thank me for not waking you. I'll get a few hours' sleep and then head for Biloxi. 'Night."

Val struggled to avoid a sense of being discarded. Told herself that Chris had given so little new instruction because she had done so much so quickly. Took it for granted that Chris was seeing May Endicott at night, and rationalized that he had no better way to confer with the woman. Val's intuition said that Chris was lagging at his forte, the massing of inferences from paperwork. *He's floundering for once, poor love,* she told herself, then felt the gentle touch of Laura Dunning on her arm. She could arise easily enough, but must remember not to shine.

The blind girl seemed pleased that her new retarded helper wanted to accompany her everywhere—even to the bathroom, where Val affected concern that she was made to stand away from Laura's stall. Val sensed no suspicion when Laura allowed her to help dispense the morning's dosages in the ward. Again there was that rarely felt response in deeply retarded patients to a special person. Laura dispensed as much tender loving care as anything, but one oddity began to form a pattern. The more obvious the retardation in a patient, generally the less assured was Laura's deft handling of capsule or liquid suspension. The great vegetative Rankine took a Shetland pony's dose of Dilantin, the cream-yellow suspension given by syringe directly into his slack mouth. Yet Laura fumbled the simple task.

Val was congratulating herself on a complete survey of all-too-heavy ward drug dosage when: "Did we miss anyone?" Laura asked.

Val thought, *How would I know, with an IQ of forty,* and only smiled in answer, a gesture totally lost on Laura.

Laura persisted, "Did we have any medicine left?"

Perspiration began to form at Val's hairline. The questions could be innocent, but they were perfect tripwires for an unwary actress. Val chose the most equivocal response she knew, a murmuring whine that begged relief from stress without imparting any linguistic content. "Mmmmuuhummmaaaahh," she sniveled.

Laura's laugh was merry, guileless. "Well, I guess not." She straightened up from the silent mass of young Rankine, and her hand unerringly found Val's head to pat it, once. "You're a great help. Thank you," she said, and permitted Val to follow her to a holovision set at the end of the ward. Laura, Val found, could enjoy the audio even if she could not receive the images; and she enjoyed company.

Val squirmed as she watched the holo. Suspicions, caromed through her head, leaving hot sparks that would not die. It was barely possible that Laura was equipped with some incredibly effective stage makeup and could see—but that seemed wildly unlikely. It was more possible that she had been briefed by the staff to test newcomers for hidden intelligence. Or perhaps Val had somehow conveyed something to this child-woman, something that Laura's sensitivity would respond to, without knowing what that something was. It was also quite likely that Val was overly suspicious; but Valerie Clarke had learned the folly of easily accepting the comfortable answer. She began to hum a repetitious tune from a holo commercial in what she hoped was suitably MR until a male patient shushed her.

Val helped at the noon meal, serving two patients who were unable to eat by themselves. Laura kept one hand on the patient's chin, the other she laid lightly on Val's wrist, until satisfied that Val could complete the chore. The meal and its inevitable cleanup served to lessen Val's ennui while Chris Maffei chased his papers—but Val was not to be idle for long.

The afternoon quiet was punctuated by the skritch of scrub brushes on linolamat as Dr. Robin Merkle made his rounds. Val, part of the work force, entertained a faint hope that Merkle gave adequate attention to his charges. Merkle propped a clipboard on his substantial belly to make occasional notations. The inconspicuous Rhea Tedder cradled more clipboards as he followed behind. Several times the smaller man spoke—Val thought, a little diffidently. Merkle smiled, or did not smile, behind the goatee, but only shrugged in reply. Lurene Tedder stood before the great locked double doors of the ward, preening her dark tresses with her brush, watching her minions scrub. With stolid calm, scrubbing more quietly, Val crept within earshot of the men.

Tedder eased up to exchange clipboards with Merkle. "Lissen, Rob, I could really use a hit," he wheedled. Val paused, addressed a speck of detritus with a trembling fingernail. "Just a little one," Tedder insisted.

Val kept her face down, trying to be invisible, and was rewarded. "One more request," Merkle said in his quietest pleasant basso, "and you get none tonight. We want to be on top of our cycle for tonight's delivery, don't we?" Val thought, *Now I know where Docta Luween gets that "we" crap. Really grooves on Merkle.*

New hope surged in Rhea Tedder's voice. "Then after tonight, again tomorrow with supper?"

A long silence. Val could almost taste the astringent look from Merkle.

"Just checkin' on my cycle," Tedder said. "You're the expert."

An avuncular laugh from the portly Merkle. "Yes, indeed," he bubbled, "and we'll be friends then, will we not?"

Tedder joined in the laugh, a neurotic *henh, henh* that Val knew from a thousand holo stereotypes of dirty old men. Rhea Tedder was nominally harmless, she thought. *Unless you weigh eighty pounds like I do.*

A cracking slap from across the ward drew the men's attention. Val began to scrub away from them. She could hear, but not yet see, Lurene Tedder at *her* specialty: corporal punishment.

The victim was a young man perhaps twenty-five years old, a quiet one with teeth ruined from habitual gritting together. Val risked a view from her vantage point behind Laura Dunning's bed. Laura sat, knuckles pale as she gripped the coverlet, facing away from the scene.

"You act like a dog, you get treated like a dog," the Tedder woman said in derision. One hand still holding the hairbrush, Lurene Tedder clutched her other hand into the young man's tangled hair. She was plainly pleased that he struggled as she forced his face into something on the floor.

Merkle raised his voice slightly in reproof: "Lurene . . ."

She released her hold with a shrug-and-grin display, satisfied with her punishment of any patient who fouled her ward floor with his excrement. Val mused that it might actually be possible to train a patient away from such pathetic lapses, in the manner of a Lurene Tedder—but at what cost to the patient? Then she saw what the others missed: the youth-rising, arms windmilling crazily as the woman looked away. He fell on her without warning. His hands were fouled, too, and while he dealt no serious blows, Val thought his repayment apt.

It was no contest; neither of the male staff tried to help, and in a moment, repeated slaps reduced the youth to a cringing serf at Lurene Tedder's feet.

She then applied further discipline.

In all, the hairbrush hammered only a dozen times; but Val shuddered each time it fell. She realized that Lurene Tedder was not using the flat of the brush but the far more damaging bristles, a thousand dull needles seeking passage through the coarse fabric of the youth's ward smock. Seeking, and finding.

The woman paused for breath. Merkle stepped up, took her hairbrush gently, his face a study in mild pique. He ignored the sobbing wretch at their feet. Rhea Tedder, shuffling near them, was the only member of the staff to notice the real victim. He managed to get the young man to his feet and hauled him toward the distant bathroom, and Laura moved in swift silence to help.

Val followed. She paused at the bathroom entrance to survey the ward. Some patients were unaffected by the beating, but others contributed to a pulsing obbligato of fear and misery. Over it, Rob Merkle soothed his dear friend Lurene, who had now taken her brush. It was faintly stained with blood, but unheeding, she brushed away her waning fury and punctuated each stroke with curses. Merkle knew his patients; he drew Lurene out of the ward with practiced aplomb and a promise of gin.

In the bathroom, Rhea Tedder had relinquished the youth to Laura, who peeled the filthy smock from the patient with infinite care. Val remembered to make a low repetitive moan without words, though the words were dangerously close at hand. The youth's back, neck, and arms oozed bright red pinprick droplets. The physical damage was only moderate, Val saw as they bathed their charge in water hot enough to be soporific as well as cleansing. The damage to muddled psyche would be impossible to assess.

When Laura Dunning asked for synthoderm, Tedder grumbled, but he got it and applied the healing spray himself, mumbling all the while. His complaints were all variants on the "Why me, God?" theme, but he was at least willing to give minimal aid, and for this, Val was grateful.

As he left them, Tedder paused an instant and Val felt a grasp on her buttock. It was untimely, covert, somehow more prank than overture. *He's easily pleased,* she thought. Laura would have to wonder why Val chuckled.

But: "Yes, it's too much, Charles Clegg," Laura said. This was the first time Val had heard the youth's name. "She just doesn't know. But," Laura added opaquely, "she will."

Valerie Clarke puzzled over this prediction. Laura, withdrawn into herself and for once less than agile, enlisted Val's aid in getting young Clegg dried, reclothed, and back to his bed. Drugs were again dispensed to some of the patients after supper but this time Laura rejected Val's help. "Go and see the nice holo," she said in no-nonsense tones, and Val played the obedient child.

Alone for all practical purposes, Val signaled Chris Maffei while she watched the distant Laura move among the beds. As she expected, Chris was still out of range. She spoke to the remote cassette. " . . . haven't seen any of the staff since then," she said, completing her account of the ward violence. "didn't see your sweetie-pie at all. she too sleepy today?

"dental care: have i mentioned it? some m.r.'s need caps and there's caries everywhere. and something about laura has me on edge, something i can't specify. yes, i can, too; she isn't on merkle's side but maybe not on ours either. i guess she's just on her own side, and i can't blame her.

"i gave you rhea tedder's conversation with merkle verbatim, and if he's not on a drug maintenance schedule i'm an m.r. for real. and his sweet wife needs a leash; her ordinary interactions are patho, can't guess why merkel keeps either of 'em. maybe you can tell me what delivery merkle expects at night; my guess is, it ain't pepperoni pizza. i get the feeling i'm holding a basketful of cobras and no flute. how soon can you reel me in? i really can't justify a mayday, but i mean, how much do we need to learn beyond this? well, it's your show. just get back to me, okay? all i have to do is play with my fingers and hope the evening stays nice and dull."

Presently, Laura slipped into a tattered seat near Val. Fidgety at first, the blind girl soon began to relax, and Val guessed, incorrectly, that Laura's quietude was a pure effort of will. They watched the holo for hours, becalmed with the surrogate window on a trivial makebelieve world. It was quite late when Val heard the staff in the nearby kitchen, and later still when the screaming began.

Val, semientranced before the holovision set, started up violently. The ward lights had automatically cycled off at nine P.M., and only she and Laura lounged before the holo. Vainly she peered down the ward to identify the noise that had aroused her. Was there a spasmodic movement on one of the beds? Val darted a glance at Laura, whose shadowed face and inert form suggested sleep. With the barest whisper of her clothing, Val snaked out of her seat and into the ward's center aisle.

The next moment found her unable to cope. The noise ripped through the ward again: a hoarse, unsexed and dreadful mooing from the nearby ward kitchen. A bombard of metal gongs told her that something flailed among the huge kitchen metalware. She could hear Merkle shouting, and now his voice held tenor overtones. As the terrible lowing segued to a gasping scream, Val recognized the voice of Lurene Tedder, muffled by blows.

Val glanced quickly toward Laura and had the nightmare sense of duality, two places at once, cause and effect in one. At the same instant, the kitchen door emitted stark light that flooded the ward, followed by the struggling forms of Merkle and the Tedders. Rhea hung from one of Lurene's arms while Merkle pinioned the other. Lurene Tedder's prized hairbrush fell at their feet as the men steered her toward the cell where Val had spent her first night. Valerie Clarke crouched motionless in the aisle, alone and desperately vulnerable—but unseen in the tumult.

Lurene's feet seemed willing enough to follow Merkle's staggering lead, yet her arms strained convulsively for freedom. Val ducked between beds, saw Rhea Tedder lose his grip for a twinkling. Lurene's arm thrashed once, catching herself squarely on the chin. She sagged at the blow and her husband regained his purchase. The big woman subsided into breathless sobs as the men led her into the cell. The cell door remained ajar.

Val saw the vandalized kitchen through its open door. Dark ovals of blood shared spots on the floor with a scattering of white powder that Val supposed was sugar until she heard the voices in the cell.

"I can hold her," came the deep voice between labored breaths. "Get the hypospray and a cartridge of cytovar from my office. Wait: first grab her damnable security brush and toss it in here, it might help. Can you do that much?"

The brush lay two meters from Val. She sank to the floor. A pair of feet shambled near and she heard Rhea Tedder in an old monologue as he retrieved the brush. He stood erect, paused, gave a *huh?* of surprise, and Val gave herself up—too soon. Rhea Tedder strolled back toward the cell, oblivious of the struggle Val could plainly hear in the cell.

Rhea Tedder paused at the cell and tossed the brush in. He spoke calmly, detached. "What about the shipment, it's all over the floor in there. Hell of a waste . . ."

"LATER," Merkle boomed. "Or do you want to hold her?"

The smaller man hurried away from this threat, pausing only to unlock the doors at the end of the ward. The big room was awash with light, the cell door still open, a patient moving uneasily in her bed nearby, and Rob Merkle only meters away with a madwoman barely under control, when Valerie Clarke crept to the kitchen door. She held a discarded paper cup pilfered from a wastebasket, and in one scurrying pass she scooped a bit of powder from the floor. Then she was in darkness again, frenziedly duckwalking in deep shadow toward the holo area.

Val thrust the wadded cup far down into the seam of her seat as she settled down beside Laura Dunning. She opened her mouth wide to avoid puffing as she drew lungfuls of sweet air and waited for her adrenaline to be absorbed. She had no pockets, no prepared drop, no confederates—and no delusions of wellbeing if her petty theft were discovered. She bit her tongue as Laura spoke.

"I've been bad, Valerie, but so were you." The sweet voice scarcely carried between the seat. "We shouldn't be here, we'll have to sneak to bed." With that, the blind girl swirled up from her seat and in an erect glide, quickly found her bed near the kitchen-lit center of the ward. Val trailed her in double-time.

Then: "Pretend sleep," Val heard—or did she imagine it?—from Laura, who took her own advice. Valerie did not, for several minutes, recover enough presence of mind to call Chris Maffei. Instead she lay facing away from the cell where Lurene Tedder lay moaning, tended by Merkle and, at his shuffling return, Rhea. Val was certain that Rhea Tedder had neither the inclination nor the guts to attack his sturdy wife. She wondered how and why Merkle, the only other person with Lurene, had chosen to punish her. Valerie had not yet grasped a shred of the truth.

"chris, oh, god, chris, be there," Val transmitted her prayer of hope from halfway under her pillow.

The response was an intercept code promising live dialogue after a short wait. Then abruptly, with great good cheer: "Hi, Val! I'm working late, believe it or not, but I have a little time . . ."

"you have a mayday, too." Val rushed through her synopsis of the past few minutes, adding, "you wanta come get me? i don't know what's in this cup, but it's part of the shipment—and it bothers this little addict more'n his wife does.

if you hurry you might be able to figure what they're up to in the kitchen and storeroom."

After a long pause, Maffei replied, "I don't think Merkle will have time to worry about you tonight. You can slip your sample to May; I'll have her stop by and see you tomorrow."

"tomorrow?" The word was bereft of hope.

"Look, Val, these people are fumbling something; I've only just realized what it might be. You're my eyes and ears while they do it, and you could pick up something a whole lot bigger than either of us ever bargained for."

"e.g., rigor mortis . . ."

"Don't be melodramatic. I have a make on the Tedders; he's a pussycat. Dr. Tedder, all right. Doctor of divinity from a diploma factory in South Texas. The old mail-order business, he may pray you to death but he's a harmless fraud. His wife's a reject physical ed teacher from a girl's military school, with some experience in a chemical plant—curiously, the same company Merkle worked for. My guess is, they're a matched pair of technicians Merkle can count on."

"for what?"

"You ready for this? Sleet! A refrigerated cocaine derivative the feds turned up in New Orleans last year. It avoids most of the side effects of snow— ulcerated sinuses, convulsions, stuff your higher class of cocaine addict will pay to avoid. Potent and highly addictive. Sleet was concocted by somebody pretty bright; pure snow processed with a powdered enzyme and protein. You take it with food, the enzyme comes up to your body temperature, and your stomach lining lays a swell little hit on you when the three components interact."

"you think they're cutting it here?"

"I think Rob Merkle could be the capital-S source. You say soy flour's abundant there? I damn well bet it is, to keep fresh batches of enzyme going. It'd have to be slurried and centrifuged, dried—but, hell, once you had the process and the enzyme, your only problem would be keeping the secret and maybe fighting off your buyers. Merkle may have caught Miz Tedder sneaking some."

Val coded a "hold" signal and emerged slowly from beneath her pillow. She could hear Lurene Tedder speaking with the men, her enunciation mushmouthed but steady. Val employed cloze procedure to mentally fill in the words she missed and listened for several minutes, mystified. When she burrowed under the edge of the pillow again, she brought a new loose end with her. "something's not meshing, chris. merkle's asking lurene what happened and she can't tell him; doesn't blame him for anything. as if the invisible man lambasted her." It was a much closer guess than Val knew.

Maffei used her simile to press his earlier point. "It's *all* been invisible until now. You have a chance to see things I couldn't even get close to, and . . ."

" . . . and you can't see past those big boobies." The wrong moment, she knew; but there it was.

Chris answered *sotto voce*, as if to a male friend, and Val knew that May Endicott was within hailing distance of him. "If it'll make you feel better, she, ah, puts up a good front."

"i swoon with delight, you bastard; you could have the good sense to lie about it."

"My work is too important for lies between us, Val."

"but not too important for lays with miz randycu . . ."

"Val!" In dulcet reasonable tones: "A certain—relationship—can enhance motivation on the job." Too late he saw the sweep of that truth.

"don't i know it. but the job isn't a clean scholarly paper, the job is people—a boy who doesn't know the hurt is because nobody cares that his teeth are rotting—a lovely girl with smooth flesh where eyes should be, piecing her world together alone—kids that might be curable if anybody cared."

She could hear anger rising in Maffei's answers. For years she had used that as her motive for retreat. "And the first step is just what I'm doing, Val."

"my, my, do tell me all about it."

"*We're* doing! You know I include you."

"when you think about it." Her tones, she knew, were flat; her words harsh. She should be pleading, begging him to complement her love and need, but Valerie Clarke could not cling this time. "look, you have things to do and i don't need this. send—send may around."

"Right, I . . . you're transmitting oddly. Rhythm's off or something. Trouble?" He rapped out the last word.

She was glad Chris could not see the runny nose, cheeks glistening with her tears. "i'm—jumpy, i guess. forget it."

"Well—if you're sure you don't need bailout." His intonation asked, instead of offering, reassurance.

Despite her growing fear, choking back a reminder that she had clearly sent a mayday, she replied, "i'm sure. go 'way, lemme sleep—please, chris."

For a full half-minute Val lay still, commanding her small frame to stop heaving with sobs that might wake Laura. It was easier than ever, now, to empathize with children who could not expect help from Outside.

Then: "Val?"

"yeah."

"Are you really sure? I'm worried; you don't sound right."

"you want a framed affidavit? i said i was."

"I just sensed . . . as if someone had tied you up and forced you to say it. Give me the word."

"somebody did, a long time ago; and chitlins, goddamnit, chitlins!"

Then the channel was silent. For a long while, sleep evaded Valerie. Self-doubt shored her insomnia. She was both losing Chris Maffei and throwing him away; the hard facts militated against her when opponents were violent and massive; and somehow, she knew, she had been witness to more than she could absorb. Sleep came while she searched for a neglected detail. She should have analyzed them in pairs.

If Valerie Clarke awoke sluggishly, she could take comfort in the notion that the staff had managed even less sleep than she. The kitchen was spotless and Rhea Tedder, not Lurene, superintended the breakfast. When May Endicott appeared in the ward to help him, Val noted the shadows under those seductive eyes and enjoyed a nice mixture of emotions.

Twice May found Val's gaze and twice Val treated her to the briefest of enigmatic smiles. Under Laura's tutelage, Val fed two patients and there was no secret way to retrieve her problematic sample, much less pass it on. Immediately after the cleanup—always necessary with patients who fed like caged creatures—Val made her way to the holo area. May could not know Val's intent and soon followed in a manner much too bright, forthright, and amateurish.

May's greeting was tentative and too loud. Val replied in a mumble. "Beg your pardon," May said, leaning near.

"Quit calling attention to us," Val murmured calmly, "and sit down, and especially, *pipe* down,"

May sat as if felled. She was blushing as she studied the holo. "Dr. Maffei said tell you his communication set is damaged," she said finally. Two other patients, sitting near, ignored their entire exchange. "But he's getting it fixed now. And he trusted me as a courier. You do have something for me to bring him?" The naive brown eyes radiated concern.

A nod indistinguishable at any distance. "When I leave, it'll be in my seat. For God's sake, get it out of here. And get me out, too, as soon as you can. Don't delay."

A winsome glance from May. Val wished the woman weren't so likable. "We say 'dawdle' in these parts." Then after a long pause, in kaffeeklatsch camaraderie: "I had no idea he was usin' you like this."

"You're even stealing my lines," Val muttered the multiple entendre with relish. To soften its impact she continued, "That goddamn comm set! What's wrong with it?"

"I don't know, Chr—Dr. Maffei said he must've hit it with his heel."

Val examined this datum for a moment. Only the scrambler module, a recent addition, was mounted in Maffei's car where it could be struck by a foot. And then only by someone in the passenger's side by kicking upward with one's toe. But with the heel . . . ?

The heel. Right. Val turned her head with great deliberation and, despite herself, a twitch on her lips. She said nothing, only looked volumes. And saw a furious blush mount the Endicott features as May realized her gaffe to someone intimately familiar with Maffei's car. Suddenly shamed by her meanness, Val arose clumsily without a word and wandered off. She had found the bit of paper cup by blind fumbling and let it drop into the seat in plain sight.

Val adopted a shuffling gait as Lurene Tedder entered the ward doorway with a tray of medication. The big woman did not notice Val's spindly person, so intent was she on something at the far end of the ward. With prickly hot icicles at the back of her head, Val knew that Lurene was studying the holo region.

Quickly the woman stepped out to the hallway and keyed a wall intercom. "Dr. Merkle, Dr. Merkle," she said in smug parody of a hospital page, "you are wanted in the ward. Right *now*," she added with the assurance of a drill sergeant.

The intercom replied, but Val could not hear it clearly.

"No, I can't, buddy-boy, I just caught me a stasher and I ain't gonna take my eyes off her." Another faint answer. "You come and see. I'll give you a hint, lover: that makes two in a row. I could be wrong, but can you chance it?"

Lurene Tedder marched into the ward again and, without conversation, relinquished the tray to Laura Dunning. The woman never took her stare from the end of the ward, and Val, playing finger games for camouflage, studied the square Tedder face. Under the telltale gleam of synthoderm the entire face was puffy, facial planes indistinct under localized swellings. Like collodion of old, synthoderm tended to peel around the mouth; the naked skin that showed was freckled with tiny scabs.

A chill scuttled down Val's backbone; Lurene's punishment had been a terrific hiding across her face with her own hairbrush! The eyes glittered even more deeply beneath swollen brows and Val knew that Lurene Tedder was fortunate to retain her eyesight. Yet she could be civil to Merkle—who strode into the ward at the moment Laura chose to begin dispensing dosages.

Val shuddered with relief as the pair moved past her. She hurried to Laura's side to take her "instruction" in dispensing the drugs. A backward glance revealed that Merkle and Tedder, talking quickly, were converging on May Endicott. Val wondered whether May had the good sense to think of a cover activity, and guessed against it. As she saw her guess confirmed, Val began to hope that May would brazen or physically force her way out.

From the first moment, May's fear was emblazoned on her face. The dialogue rose in volume until Laura paused, her head cocked attentively. "She's the only good thing that's happened here," Laura said quietly, "and now she'll be gone."

May exchanged glares with Lurene while Merkle, much the tallest, looked down at May. For a second he craned his head to one side at May's cleavage, then thrust one hand into it in a lightning maneuver. May jerked her hands up— too late. Merkle stepped back to examine his prize and Lurene Tedder moved to intercept May's desperate grab.

While May darted anguished looks around her, Merkle studied the scrap of heavy paper and its contents. Brusquely he gave an order and fell behind as May led a procession toward Val's end of the ward. It seemed that they might pass outside until Merkle, with a silent thumb-jerk, indicated the isolation cell to Lurene Tedder. Val considered, for one instant, the possibility of a diversion. Flinging the tray; anything.

No one was prepared for Laura Dunning's reaction. Screaming, "She doesn't hurt anybody," Laura dived past Val and upset the tray as she flung herself at the sounds of combat.

Merkle spun to catch the little girl while Lurene grappled with May. He took no punishment and, with a backhand cuff, sent Laura squalling to the floor. The blind girl, hopelessly unequal to the fray, moaned as she rolled aside. She nursed her right shoulder as, still sobbing, she found her bed and lay back.

Val knelt in the spill of drugs, terrified and inert. She had never felt so vulnerable to physical violence, and almost transmitted an open "mayday" before remembering that Maffei could not receive it.

May's body was not fashioned for the rough-and-tumble of a Lurene Tedder, and after a brief struggle, May was flung into the cell. The door slammed shut, locked under Tedder's key.

Merkle ignored Val, the drugs, and faint pounding from inside the cell, patting Lurene in the manner of a coach with a favored athlete. "You were right," he grunted. They were three meters from Valerie Clarke. "Where did she get it?"

Val hefted a bottle, wondering which skull to aim for, somehow remembering to keep her jaw slack and her eyes slightly averted. An eternal moment later Lurene hazarded, "Must've hidden it down by the holo someplace. You'll have to ask her when."

"You anticipate me," Merkle said jovially, urging Lurene to the ward entrance. As he paused to lock the ward doors, Val heard him continue. "She has to sleep sometime; it'll be simple to find out then." They receded down the hall and Val heard a last fragment. "Not shortage of time, or of scop. I told you this setup would be ideal for it . . ."

A youth began to take interest in the strewn capsules and Val scooped up the mess quickly before taking it to Laura. A corner of her brain marveled that Merkle could simply stride away from an addict's array of downers, knowing that any of the patients might ingest any or all of the drugs—or simply lie down and wallow in them. She sat down heavily on the side of Laura's bed and leaped up again at Laura's quick gasp.

"Don't, oh, don't! My shoulder," Laura moaned, and Val realized that her small mass had jarred the bed. "Valerie?"

Val answered guardedly. She could call no one, trust no one; Laura might suspect, but had no proof that Val was equipped with that formidable tool, knowledge. On the other hand, May certainly knew. And if Merkle employed scopolamine on May Endicott, he would soon strip the imposture bare. Val sat on her bed, trembling.

It was clear that Laura could not dispense medication. Val judged it was half-past ten, and thinking of the chaos of a dozen interrupted medication schedules in an unsupervised MR ward, she administered the dosages she recalled. Nor was she really out of character: idiot-savant retardates had been known to demonstrate a memory far beyond that of normal people.

The docile Rankine was one of her failures. Laura had evidently stepped on the big needleless syringe which she would have used to administer his whopping dose of Dilantin suspension. Val wasted half a bottle of the stuff trying to pour it past his lips, then gave it up. Rankine was not disposed to help take the dosage by this unfamiliar method; very well, then. He would simply have to bear it with several others whose dosages Val could not recall.

Val lay back on her bed, vainly transmitting to Chris Maffei every few minutes. Interrupted by a low sobbing from Laura, she suddenly considered the remaining drugs. Surely a yellow Valium, only five milligrams, couldn't hurt. She found one in her leftover cache and laid it to Laura's lips.

Laura took it greedily with an attempted smile. "Not enough," she confided. Val stiffened, then relaxed. Even recognizing the drug by taste or shape, how could the blind Laura know a white two-milligram pill from a potent blue ten? But perhaps even ten would not be too much. If the scapula were broken, Laura's pain was surely intense. Val administered another yellow pill and lay back to narrowcast another blazing "mayday" to Chris Maffei.

Two patients scuffled briefly. Another yodeled for joy. Val studied the narrow clerestory windows, knowing that even her very small head would not fit, presuming that she could smash the glass tiles. And if she tried to signal May, only meters away in the isolation cell, the staff could easily pick it up via monitors.

Laura breathed more regularly now, the Valium taking its effect. Lying full length on her bed, Val found satisfaction in her act of loving kindness. Then, without preamble, a delicious lassitude washed through her body as through gauze. Val saw that her right hand was stroking her thigh. Eerily, it did not respond to her next command. "Stop that," she said aloud. She felt a presence not her own; it was purest intuition to reply.

Val composed another message. Deliberately unformed, not vocalized but simply broadcast thought, a cloudy montage of unease and avoidance. No effect, but her left forearm nuzzled her bud of a breast before she could stop it. On an instant surmise Val thought hard of a putrid slime, mentally smelled it, pictured it. Holding the thought, she felt something slip away. It was like a fever breaking, a fever unannounced but somehow benign, that now began reluctantly to loose its hold. Quickly Val visualized a smile; the smile she valued most, the dimpled puckish leer of Chris Maffei.

Then, despite her effort to halt it, her right hand patted her left wrist, twice. She watched her hands intently, a sham catatonic, for many seconds. Whatever it was, it had withdrawn. To where?

Across from Valerie Clarke lay the girl who was prone to mild epileptic seizures. Charles Clegg, the youth who had taken the hairbrush beating, stood near the girl, pointing, laughing. Below a certain level of socialization there is little empathy, and Clegg's amusement stemmed from the girl's loss of control. It was over now, at any rate, with no harm done.

Val told herself she had her own goose flesh to ponder, then in a fresh surge of adrenaline, mentally connected the events. Lurene Tedder did not know the source of her flogging. And Val had a lucid flash of memory during *that* event: the epileptic girl had jerked on her bed while Laura Dunning, otherwise inert before the holo, sat and pounded her hand on her chair arm. Suddenly Laura's subliminal hand movement was meaningful.

Just now, the MR girl had suffered another spasm, while some unseen presence bade Val to caress herself. Who had reason to thank Val? She rolled over, lying now on her side, and faced Laura.

"What do you need?" Laura spoke soothingly, in deep repose. Val had said nothing.

All thought of keeping her cover vanished, Val answered, "You said you'd been bad, Laura. Did *you* make that woman punish herself?"

"I'm not sorry."

Good Jesus, I'm hallucinating. This isn't real. "And you thanked me just then—a minute ago?"

"I *am* sorry for that" was the contrite reply. "You're normal, you didn't need it like that."

Another thought whirled in Val's head. "I don't even have to talk out loud, do I?"

"Better to talk. Thoughts are so fast they're confusing sometimes. And it hurts sometimes."

"You don't know your strength," Val confided. "I believe you trigger those seizures the others have."

Laura could not weep tears, but she could cry. "Sorry. Sorry. Sorry. So much pain and confusion, I try to help. I'm sorry."

"You do help," Val said. "You can help now if you can listen in on those miserable sons of bitches to see what they're up to."

A long pause, then: "Too far away. I have to take medicine to make people do things. I steal it. Can't be sure when the power will come, sometimes it doesn't. Sorry, sorry," the blind girl wept, her high forehead furrowed in grief.

Val soothed Laura, kneeling next to her, thin fingers on the girl's wrist. A rattle of keys at the ward doorway, and Val eased back into the bed. Merkle came in first, Lurene next. They held the doors open for Rhea, who wheeled a gurney into the ward. Val realized then that they did not intend May Endicott to walk out of the cell, and subvocalized a prayerful plea to Maffei. Nothing. *Kicked it with your heel, you turd*, she raged.

There was no desperate speed in the preparations. Val guessed they had simply tired of waiting for answers, and had elected to overpower May Endicott before drugging her. "Laura," she whispered, "can you help May when they open that cell door?"

"It's not coming," Laura breathed as the cell door swung open. The trio stormed the pathetic May and slammed the door.

Val flew to the cell and cursed herself for not having checked the lock mechanism earlier. No use in any case: without a key, she could not lock them in, and she went jelly-kneed at the thought of entering that cell with anything less than a riot gun. From the muffled noises Val knew that May was going under sedation. Merkle's bass resonated in the cell but wall padding strained it of content.

She ran to the ward doors. Metal-faced, securely locked, as was the kitchen. But with enough mass piled on the waiting gurney, it might just possibly be accelerated down the ward to smash the doors. And smashing the wheeled metal cot itself might slow them in getting May from the ward. Val did not need a legal opinion to conclude that, with every additional step a fresh felony, the staff of Gulfview might welcome premeditated murder. Whatever might have happened to the Fowler girl, Val did not relish seeing it repeated. She tugged at the gurney, wheeled it up the center aisle toward the holo area. Perhaps the chairs would serve, if she could pile them on, or enlist patients in her enterprise.

She could get no one to aid in her little game. Patients strolled over to watch, slack-jointed and empty-eyed, as Val managed to tip two seats up into the gurney. Whimpering with the effort, she pulled the vehicle near the ponderous holovision set, all of a meter wide and massing perhaps a hundred pounds. She reached to disconnect the wiring, but at least one patient knew what that meant. He wanted his program, and the skinny girl with frightened eyes wanted to pull its plug. He screamed, face twisted in sudden ferocity, and thrust Val away.

Val raced to the side of Laura Dunning, who seemed asleep but for the mobility of her features. "Laura, is Valium the medicine for your power? Could you make some patients help me smash those doors?"

"Dilantin's the only thing that works," came the soft reply. "I only discovered it recently. Do you have any?"

Val whirled to her cache of unused drugs beneath her pillow. They were gone. Disoriented for the moment, she looked up to see young Charles Clegg. He held capsules in one hand while trying to bite off the safety cap of the Dilantin bottle. He had seen people drink it; maybe it would taste good.

Valerie Clarke did not know she could leap so fast, with such hand-eye coordination. She flashed past Clegg in a two-handed grab and the bottle was hers. Clegg was between her and Laura, but Val thought to circle around behind beds across the ward. It was at this juncture that Dr. Robin Merkle emerged from the cell.

He scanned the ward, saw Val, and then spotted the gurney filled with furniture. He looked almost pleased. Val saw it in his face: her cover was blown.

Val held the crucial Dilantin and Merkle, the advantage. He also wielded the hypospray, which could accept pressure cartridges of anything from saline solution to curare. While he could not know Val's intention, Merkle obviously proposed to take her into custody here and now. Their eyes locked. Neither spoke. Lurene Tedder hurried to cut Val off from her narrow corridor between beds and wall.

"Easy, Rob," Lurene cautioned, and Merkle stopped to listen. Val took a step back, poised. "This li'l thing didn't get here on her own; somebody Outside will be askin'."

"If we wait, it's a sure bust," Merkle rumbled as if reasserting an old position. "On the new schedule, we can process another, oh, say eighty pounds of protein." He beamed at Valerie. "Thirty hours or so at twenty-three Celsius."

At this, even Lurene Tedder blinked. "We're gonna *process* these two?" Val first saw the flicker of revulsion in the woman's face, then realized what it meant to her, Valerie Clarke, and had to steady herself against fainting.

"For more enzyme. Matuase doesn't care what it feeds on," Merkle said, pleased at his logic. "These ladies will complete a perfect irony. Part of the operation, as it were."

Sickened with loathing, Val fanned a faint spark of hope that Lurene would rebel. The lump in Val's throat forbade her any speech; the pounding of her heart was physical pain. Then, with a great sigh, Lurene said, "Well, it's better tactics than planting 'em, like you-know-who," and closed in on Valerie Clarke.

The thought of herself as finely ground fodder in some unknown enzyme production phase nearly robbed Val of consciousness, but the approach of Lurene and Merkle was galvanic. Val spun and ran for the gurney, hoping to get it underway before they could stop her. A quasi-female laugh followed her like a promise of extinction. Val collided against an inert patient, reached the gurney, began to thrust it ahead of her down the center of the ward. Even as it began to roll, she saw that she was simply too small for the task.

Lurene danced almost playfully out into the aisle, hands spread before her to intercept the loaded gurney. Val grabbed the thing she held in her teeth and hurled it at the woman, then was aware of her mistake. Val's missile connected against Lurene Tedder's forehead, but the soft plastic bottle had little effect and Lurene diverted the gurney between two beds. Val saw Merkle stoop to retrieve the Dilantin bottle as it skittered near him. The bottle went into his pocket. She had literally hurled her last hope away, and in a stumbling panic Val fell over the huge form of Gerald Rankine looming in his bed near the holo.

Rankine stirred slightly and opened unfocused eyes. Val scrambled over the great form and into the holo area, now devoid of its two heaviest seats. Lurene Tedder bawled for Rhea, who trotted up the ward for his instructions.

As Val cowered behind the holovision, mindless with terror, Lurene waved Rhea around while she herself took a frontal approach. Merkle moved to cut off any escape behind the beds; and the very proximity of the three triggered Val as it might any small and cornered animal.

Val flung herself into Rhea Tedder as Lurene crashed against the holo set in pursuit. Rhea found himself grappling with a small demon, all thin sticks and sharp edges, that spat and clawed as he held on. Recovering, the sturdy Lurene thrust herself away from the holo, already tottering on its stand from her impact, and then Lurene tackled Val in a smothering embrace. Merkle had time to laugh once as he saw Lurene's clumsy success, but he did not see the holo as it toppled onto the silent staring young Rankine.

Lifted aloft by the big woman, Val caught a glimpse of the holo set. It leaned drunkenly on Rankine's midriff, its great window facing his eyes, its picture transmuted into bursts of flickering light by the rough handling.

Val took two fistfuls of hair and wrenched, trying to tear it from Lurene Tedder's abundant mop. Val's throat was too constricted to scream and Lurene only snarled. From down the ward, then, floated a dreamlike, ecstatic moan. "Ohhhh, it's a *lovely* one," cried Laura Dunning, borne into an orgasmic flood of silently thundering energy.

Because Merkle was most distant from the melee, he was first to catapult himself down the aisle. Val felt muscular arms relax and, kicking furiously, vacated Lurene Tedder's shoulder. Lurene staggered, nearly fell, then began to accelerate down the center of the ward after Merkle. Rhea Tedder tried to follow but tripped over Val before he began to run.

A welter of impressions clamored in Val's head. The holo, crashing to the floor as young Rankine jerked in the throes of a truly leviathan epileptic seizure. Howls of helpless terror from Merkle and the woman, bleats from Rhea, as the three found themselves sprinting harder down the ward. Laura Dunning's cooing luxuriance in a stream of almost sexual power was lower-pitched, but Val heard it. Valerie Clarke splayed hands over her ears and blanched an instant before Merkle impacted against the great double doors.

Merkle, with a hysterical falsetto shriek, never even raised his hands. He slammed the metal door-facing with a concussive report that jolted every patient, every fixture. Headfirst, arms and legs pumping, driven by two hundred and sixty pounds of his beloved protein, Dr. Robin Merkle comprised part one of Laura Dunning's battering ram.

Lurene Tedder's last scream was entirely feminine; she managed to turn her head to one side as she obliterated herself against the sheet steel.

The doors, bent under Merkle's hapless assault, flew ajar; a lock mechanism clattered into the corridor beyond as Lurene fell into the opening. Rhea Tedder, ever the rear guard, called his wife's name as he hurtled into the space. One shoulder caught a door frame with pitiless precision, hurled the door wide as the addict ricocheted into a corridor wall. Val, leaping to her feet, saw Rhea disappear down the corridor, lying on his side, still pantomiming a sprinter's gait on the floor. He did not stop for moments afterward; Val could hear the tortured wheeze of his breath, the ugly measured tattoo of his feet and arms beating against the corridor floor and baseboard.

The patients were shocked into retreat from the violence at the ward doorway, and none seemed tempted to approach it. For one thing—*two*—*the* remains of Rob Merkle and Lurene Tedder sprawled grotesquely in their way.

With all the caution of a nocturnal animal, Val rifled Merkle's lab smock. She found the hypospray intact and felt armed; then she hefted the Dilantin bottle—and in a moment's reflection, realized that she was doubly armed. As she faced her puzzle, odd pieces began to warp into place, and for the first time in many days, Valerie Clarke knew what it meant to smile in relief.

Quickly, gently Val checked for vital signs. She saw the ruined, misshapen head of Robin Merkle and knew why he had no pulse. Lurene Tedder lay dying, insensible, extremities twitching. In the hallway lay Rhea Tedder, unconscious from shock and fractures, his breathing fetid but steady. She judged that he would live. Her small joy in this judgment was proof that Val could still surprise herself. It was true that Rhea Tedder could answer crucial questions—but it was also true that he could ogle a homely girl. She made a note to tell Chris Maffei: *Blessed are the easily pleased, for theirs is the kingdom of Earth.*

The corridor intercom needed no special key. She punched Outside, idly musing at the closeness of help for anyone who could reach the corridor. In moments, a policewoman was taping her call.

Two minutes later Val reentered the ward. She opened the isolation cell with Merkle's keys, once again tense almost to the point of retching with thoughts of what she might find inside. May Endicott lay sprawled in fetching disarray on the cot, drugged to her marrow but apparently unhurt. That enviable body would decay one day, Val thought; but not today, at twenty-three degrees Celsius. She could see from a distance that Gerald Rankine had passed the tonic stage of his seizure, and was well into the clonic, his body jerking slightly as the effects of the monstrous seizure passed. She moved to Laura Dunning's side. It felt good to smile again.

Val wondered how to begin. "I have news for you, Laura," she said gently.

Laura was awake but, with the Valium, quite mellow. "I know. I did it without the medicine," the blind girl said proudly.

"Well—yes and no. It's seizures by other people that bring on the power, Laura. No wonder you couldn't tell when the power would come: *it isn't your power!*"

Confusion wrinkled Laura's nose. "But I make people do things."

"Can you ever," Val agreed, "but not alone. You're a—a modulator, I suppose. Rankine did not get his Dilantin today; and that could've brought on a seizure by itself. You see—oh, excuse me—you understand, whenever you stole a dose of Dilantin from Rankine or that young girl, the patient who needed it was in danger of an epileptic seizure. But the surest way to bring on a seizure is a strong blinking light—and that holo set zapped poor Rankine into the grand-paw of all grand mals, thank God."

"My," Laura murmured with a secret smile, "but it was good. But you mean, I never needed the medicine myself?"

"It probably impedes you. You need a carrier wave from some strong source, and you manage to modulate it into commands. You know what electroencephalography is? Anyway, a real thunderation seizure comes with the damnedest electrical brain discharge you can imagine, far more intense than any normal discharge. Of course, that same intensity raises hell with the higher centers of that same brain. Like trying to send Morse code through a flashlight, using lightning bolts." She raised her hands, then let them drop in frustration. "All I know is, you've gotta be sensitized in some way to modulate other people's brain discharges into commands. Normal brain activity just doesn't feature such power; those huge discharge spikes are characteristic of epilepsy. All this is simplistic, but I haven't time to detail it now." *Nor understand it yet,* she thought.

Laura sought Val's hand with her own. "You know something about these things? You'll stay with me?"

The idea settled over Valerie Clarke like a security blanket. "I've learned some from a man. I need to learn more." This astonishingly gifted girl needed her, Val realized. Her smile broadened as she stroked Laura Dunning's brow. "I'm going to claim Rhea Tedder went berserk and stampeded the others into that door. It's a weak story, Christ knows, but it'll accommodate the facts you can see." The ethics of her decision disturbed Val until she remembered Rhea Tedder holding her for the processing team.

A sigh from Laura: "I wish I really could see."

"Don't you? Through other people?"

As if showing a hole card, Laura said, "Kind of." Her hand gripped Val's desperately. "If I could do it better, I could help some of my friends here a lot more. Some of them are trying to climb walls in their heads, to get out to us."

It was possible, Val admitted to herself. And who would be a better tool than an honest-to-God telepath? With a machine-generated carrier wave, could Laura reinforce improved behavior patterns in a trainable MR? The possibilities were untouched, and staggering. Chris Maffei had spoken of Gulfview's problems as the devil he knew, but Val smiled at a new thought: *the devil you don't know may be an angel in disguise.*

"Who've you been talking to at night?" Val realized that Laura had, at the very least, known of the transmissions at her end.

"Dr. Christopher Maffei," Val answered. Curiously, it sounded flat. The name no longer held its familiar emotional lift. She considered this further.

"Can he help us—me?"

"Us." Val's correction was an implicit promise. "Yes, but he's a proud man, Laura. He'll want to make you famous." *Because it'll make* him *famous,* an inner voice added.

Slowly, Laura replied, "I don't think I want that."

"We may be more useful without it," Val agreed. "But I know Chris, and he has strong opinions." She grinned at a sudden unbidden thought. " 'Course, you could always run his opinions off a cliff—and I'm kidding, by the way."

After a long pause Laura asked, "Do you love him?"

Since Laura could probably sense a lie anyway, Val resolved to use utter candor. "Yes." With a starshell burst of insight Val added, "But now I don't think I need much. Does that sound harsh?"

"Your thinking isn't harsh. And Dr. Maffei: does he need you?"

Put in such blunt terms, the questions brought answers Val had never formalized. They hurt. "Yes; but you see, he's never loved me much."

"*I* love you." Laura's admission was shy, tentative. "But I don't think it's the same, is it?"

Val chuckled. " 'Fraid not. But it's enough. Was it Vonnegut who said the worst thing that can happen to you is not to get used?" A new resolve sped Val's answer. "In a few minutes a whole raft of people will be here to turn everything upside down and set it right again. You're sedated, baby, so you be goddamn good and sedate! Keep your ability to yourself, don't force any automatic behavior on anybody, don't even hint about it—until I come for you. And I will."

The hand tightened again over Val's thinner one. "You have to leave?"

"For a while. Weeks, maybe. But you and I will figure out how you tick and we don't want Chris Maffei diddling with your metronome so he can compose a best-selling ditty with it. Later, maybe. And maybe not. The trick is being used properly, isn't it, Laura?"

"You're the boss," Laura said meekly. And listening to police beepers in the distance, Valerie Clarke knew that she was, indeed, ready to assume the leaden mantel of decision-making. She wondered if Maffei's scrambler unit was repaired yet. It was the simplest of matters to find out, but Val could wait. There was plenty of time for her to put Maffei to use.

FROM THE EYE OF THE WORLD

Robert Jordan

Robert Jordan is currently the most popular fantasy writer in the world, due to his ambitious series of novels in progress, *The Wheel of Time*. Cast in the classic quest mode of the famous *Lord of the Rings* trilogy by J. R. R. Tolkien, Jordan's colossal epic runs to millions of words and will not end before the turn of the century. This excerpt was selected from the first volume of the series, *The Eye of the World*, to introduce readers to the flavor and concerns of *The Wheel of Time*, and to the type of fantasy fiction that is most popular today.

Rand sat bolt upright, gasping for breath and shivering, staring. Tam was still asleep on the bed. Slowly his breathing slowed. Half-consumed logs blazed in the fireplace with a good bed of coals built up around the fire-irons; someone had been there to tend it while he slept. A blanket lay at his feet, where it had fallen when he woke. The makeshift litter was gone, too, and his and Tam's cloaks had been hung by the door.

He wiped cold sweat from his face with a hand that was none too steady and wondered if naming the Dark One in a dream brought his attention the same way that naming him aloud did.

Twilight darkened the window; the moon was well up, round and fat, and evening stars sparkled above the Mountains of Mist. He had slept the day away. He rubbed a sore spot on his side. Apparently he had slept with the sword hilt jabbing him in the ribs. Between that and an empty stomach and the night before, it was no wonder he had had nightmares.

His belly rumbled, and he got up stiffly and made his way to the table where Mistress al'Vere had left the tray. He twitched aside the white napkin. Despite the time he had slept, the beef broth was still warm, and so was the crusty bread. Mistress al'Vere's hand was plain; the tray had been replaced. Once she decided you needed a hot meal, she did not give up till it was inside you.

He gulped down some broth, and it was all he could do to put some meat and cheese between two pieces of bread before stuffing it in his mouth. Taking big bites, he went back to the bed.

Mistress al'Vere had apparently seen to Tam, as well. Tam had been undressed, his clothes now clean and neatly folded on the bedside table, and a blanket was drawn up under his chin. When Rand touched his father's forehead, Tam opened his eyes.

"There you are, boy. Marin said you were here, but I couldn't even sit up to see. She said you were too tired for her to wake just so I could look at you. Even Bran can't get around her when she has her mind set."

Tam's voice was weak, but his gaze was clear and steady. *The Aes Sedai was right,* Rand thought. With rest he would be as good as ever.

"Can I get you something to eat? Mistress al'Vere left a tray."

"She fed me already . . . if you can call it that. Wouldn't let me have anything but broth. How can a man avoid bad dreams with nothing but broth in his . . ." Tam fumbled a hand from under the cover and touched the sword at Rand's waist. "Then it wasn't a dream. When Marin told me I was sick, I thought I had been . . . But you're all right. That is all that matters. What of the farm?"

Rand took a deep breath. "The Trollocs killed the sheep. I think they took the cow, too, and the house needs a good cleaning." He managed a weak smile. "We were luckier than some. They burned half the village."

He told Tam everything that had happened, or at least most of it. Tam listened closely, and asked sharp questions, so he found himself having to tell about returning to the farmhouse from the woods, and that brought in the Trolloc he had killed. He had to tell how Nynaeve had said Tam was dying to explain why the Aes Sedai had tended him instead of the Wisdom. Tam's eyes widened at that, an Aes Sedai in Emond's Field. But Rand could see no need to go over every step of the journey from the farm, or his fears, or the Myrddraal on the road. Certainly not his nightmares as he slept by the bed. Especially he saw no reason to mention Tam's ramblings under the fever. Not yet. Moiraine's story, though: there was no avoiding that.

"Now that's a tale to make a gleeman proud," Tam muttered when he was done. "What would Trollocs want with you boys? Or the Dark One, Light help us?"

"You think she was lying? Master al'Vere said she was telling the truth about only two farms being attacked. And about Master Luhhan's house, and Master Cauthon's."

For a moment Tam lay silent before saying, "Tell me what she said. Her exact words, mind, just as she said them."

Rand struggled. Who ever remembered the *exact* words they heard? He chewed at his lip and scratched his head, and bit by bit he brought it out, as nearly as he could remember. "I can't think of anything else," he finished. "Some of it I'm not too sure she didn't say a little differently, but it's close, anyway."

"It's good enough. It has to be, doesn't it? You see, lad, Aes Sedai are tricksome. They don't lie, not right out, but the truth an Aes Sedai tells you is not always the truth you think it is. You take care around her."

"I've heard the stories," Rand retorted. "I'm not a child."

"So you're not, so you're not." Tam sighed heavily, then shrugged in annoyance. "I should be going along with you, just the same. The world outside the Two Rivers is nothing like Emond's Field."

That was an opening to ask about Tam going outside and all the rest of it, but Rand did not take it. His mouth fell open, instead. "Just like that? I thought you would try to talk me out of it. I thought you'd have a hundred reasons I should not go." He realized he had been hoping Tam would have a hundred reasons, and good ones.

"Maybe not a hundred," Tam said with a snort, "but a few did come to mind. Only they don't count for much. If Trollocs are after you, you will be safer in Tar Valon than you could ever be here. Just remember to be wary. Aes Sedai do things for their own reasons, and those are not always the reasons you think."

"The gleeman said something like that," Rand said slowly.

"Then he knows what he's talking about. You listen sharp, think deep, and guard your tongue. That's good advice for any dealings beyond the Two Rivers, but most especially with Aes Sedai. And with Warders. Tell Lan something, and you've as good as told Moiraine. If he's a Warder, then he's bonded to her as sure as the sun rose this morning, and he won't keep many secrets from her, if any."

Rand knew little about the bonding between Aes Sedai and Warders, though it played a big part in every story about Warders he had ever heard. It was something to do with the Power, a gift to the Warder, or maybe some sort of exchange. The Warders got all sorts of benefits, according to the stories. They healed more quickly than other men, and could go longer without food or water or sleep. Supposedly they could sense Trollocs, if they were close enough, and other creatures of the Dark One, too, which explained how Lan and Moiraine had tried to warn the village before the attack. As to what the Aes Sedai got out of it, the stories were silent, but he was not about to believe they did not get something.

"I'll be careful," Rand said. "I just wish I knew why. It doesn't make any sense. Why me? Why us?"

"I wish I knew, too, boy. Blood and ashes, I wish I knew." Tam sighed heavily. "Well, no use trying to put a broken egg back in the shell, I suppose. How soon do you have to go? I'll be back on my feet in a day or two, and we can see about starting a new flock. Oren Dautry has some good stock he might be willing to part with, with the pastures all gone, and so does Jon Thane."

"Moiraine . . . the Aes Sedai said you had to stay in bed. She said weeks." Tam opened his mouth, but Rand went on. "And she talked to Mistress al'Vere."

"Oh. Well, maybe I can talk Marin around." Tam did not sound hopeful of it, though. He gave Rand a sharp look. "The way you avoided answering means you have to leave soon. Tomorrow? Or tonight?"

"Tonight," Rand said quietly, and Tam nodded sadly.

"Yes. Well, if it must be done, best not to delay. But we will see about this 'weeks' business." He plucked at his blankets with more irritation than strength. "Perhaps I'll follow in a few days anyway. Catch you up on the road. We will see if Marin can keep me in bed when I want to get up."

There was a tap at the door, and Lan stuck his head into the room. "Say your good-byes quickly, sheepherder, and come. There may be trouble."

"Trouble?" Rand said, and the Warder growled at him impatiently.

"Just hurry!"

Hastily Rand snatched up his cloak. He started to undo the sword belt, but Tam spoke up.

"Keep it. You will probably have more need of it than I, though, the Light willing, neither of us will. Take care, lad. You hear?"

Ignoring Lan's continued growls, Rand bent to grab Tam in a hug. "I will come back. I promise you that."

"Of course you will." Tam laughed. He returned the hug weakly, and ended by patting Rand on the back. "I know that. And I'll have twice as many sheep for you to tend when you return. Now go, before that fellow does himself an injury."

Rand tried to hang back, tried to find the words for the question he did not want to ask, but Lan entered the room to catch him by the arm and pull him into the hall. The Warder had donned a dull gray-green tunic of overlapping metal scales. His voice rasped with irritation.

"We have to hurry. Don't you understand the word *trouble?*"

Outside the room Mat waited, cloaked and coated and carrying his bow. A quiver hung at his waist. He was rocking anxiously on his heels, and he kept glancing off toward the stairs with what seemed to be equal parts impatience and fear. "This isn't much like the stories, Rand, is it?" he said hoarsely.

"What kind of trouble?" Rand demanded, but the Warder ran ahead of him instead of answering, taking the steps down two at a time. Mat dashed after him with quick gestures for Rand to follow.

Shrugging into his cloak, he caught up to them downstairs. Only a feeble light filled the common room; half the candles had burned out and most of the rest were guttering. It was empty except for the three of them. Mat stood next to one of the front windows, peeping out as if trying not to be seen. Lan held the door open a crack and peered into the inn yard.

Wondering what they could be watching, Rand went to join him. The Warder muttered at him to take a care, but he did open the door a trifle wider to make room for Rand to look, too.

At first he was not sure exactly what he was seeing. A crowd of village men, some three dozen or so, clustered near the burned-out husk of the peddler's wagon, night pushed back by the torches some of them carried. Moiraine faced them, her back to the inn, leaning with seeming casualness on her walking staff. Hari Coplin stood in the front of the crowd with his brother, Darl, and Bili Congar. Cenn Buie was there, as well, looking uncomfortable. Rand was startled to see Hari shake his fist at Moiraine.

"Leave Emond's Field!" the sour-faced farmer shouted. A few voices in the crowd echoed him, but hesitantly, and no one pushed forward. They might be willing to confront an Aes Sedai from within a crowd, but none of them wanted to be singled out. Not by an Aes Sedai who had every reason to take offense.

"You brought those monsters!" Darl roared. He waved a torch over his head, and there were shouts of, "You brought them!" and "It's your fault!" led by his cousin Bili.

Hari elbowed Cenn Buie, and the old thatcher pursed his lips and gave him a sidelong glare. "Those things . . . those Trollocs didn't appear until after you came," Cenn muttered, barely loud enough to be heard. He swung his head from side to side dourly as if wishing he were somewhere else and looking for a way to get there. "You're an Aes Sedai. We want none of your sort in the Two Rivers. Aes Sedai bring trouble on their backs. If you stay, you will only bring more."

His speech brought no response from the gathered villagers, and Hari scowled in frustration. Abruptly he snatched Darl's torch and shook it in her direction. "Get out!" he shouted. "Or we'll burn you out!"

Dead silence fell, except for the shuffling of a few feet as men drew back. Two Rivers folk could fight back if they were attacked, but violence was far from common, and threatening people was foreign to them, beyond the occasional shaking of a fist. Cenn Buie, Bili Congar, and the Coplins were left out front alone. Bili looked as if he wanted to back away, too.

Hari gave an uneasy start at the lack of support, but he recovered quickly. "Get out!" he shouted again, echoed by Darl and, more weakly, by Bili. Hari glared at the others. Most of the crowd failed to meet his eye.

Suddenly Bran al'Vere and Haral Luhhan moved out of the shadows, stopping apart from both the Aes Sedai and the crowd. In one hand the Mayor casually carried the big wooden maul he used to drive spigots into casks. "Did someone suggest burning my inn?" he asked softly.

The two Coplins took a step back, and Cenn Buie edged away from them. Bili Congar dived into the crowd. "Not that," Darl said quickly. "We never said that, Bran . . . ah, Mayor."

Bran nodded. "Then perhaps I heard you threatening to harm guests in my inn?"

"She's an Aes Sedai," Hari began angrily, but his words cut off as Haral Luhhan moved.

The blacksmith simply stretched, thrusting thick arms over his head, tightening massive fists until his knuckles cracked, but Hari looked at the burly man as if one of those fists had been shaken under his nose. Haral folded his arms across his chest. "Your pardon, Hari. I did not mean to cut you off. You were saying?"

But Hari, shoulders hunched as though he were trying to draw into himself and disappear, seemed to have nothing more to say.

"I'm surprised at you people," Bran rumbled. "Paet al'Caar, your boy's leg was broken last night, but I saw him walking on it today—because of her. Eward Candwin, you were lying on your belly with a gash down your back like a fish for cleaning, till she laid hands on you. Now it looks as if it happened a month ago, and unless I misdoubt there'll barely be a scar. And you, Cenn." The thatcher started to fade back into the crowd, but stopped, held uncomfortably by Bran's gaze. "I'd be shocked to see any man on the Village Council here, Cenn, but you most of all. Your arm would still be hanging useless at your side, a mass of burns and bruises, if not for her. If you have no gratitude, have you no shame?"

Cenn half lifted his right hand, then looked away from it angrily. "I cannot deny what she did," he muttered, and he did sound ashamed. "She helped me, and others," he went on in a pleading tone, "but she's an Aes Sedai, Bran. If those Trollocs didn't come because of her, why did they come? We want no part of Aes Sedai in the Two Rivers. Let them keep their troubles away from us."

A few men, safely back in the crowd, shouted then. "We want no Aes Sedai troubles!" "Send her away!" "Drive her out!" "Why did they come if not because of her?"

A scowl grew on Bran's face, but before he could speak Moiraine suddenly whirled her vine-carved staff above her head, spinning it with both hands.

Rand's gasp echoed that of the villagers, for a hissing white flame flared from each end of the staff, standing straight out like spearpoints despite the rod's whirling. Even Bran and Haral edged away from her. She snapped her arms down straight out before her, the staff parallel to the ground, but the pale fire still jetted out, brighter than the torches. Men shied away, held up hands to shield their eyes from the pain of that brilliance.

"Is this what Aemon's blood has come to?" The Aes Sedai's voice was not loud, but it overwhelmed every other sound. "Little people squabbling for the right to hide like rabbits? You have forgotten who you were, forgotten what you were, but I had hoped some small part was left, some memory in blood and bone. Some shred to steel you for the long night coming."

No one spoke. The two Coplins looked as if they never wanted to open their mouths again.

Bran said, "Forgotten who we were? We are who we always have been. Honest farmers and shepherds and craftsmen. Two Rivers folk."

"To the south," Moiraine said, "lies the river you call the White River, but far to the east of here men call it still by its rightful name. Manetherendrelle. In the Old Tongue, Waters of the Mountain Home. Sparkling waters that once coursed through a land of bravery and beauty. Two thousand years ago Manetherendrelle flowed by the walls of a mountain city so lovely to behold that Ogier stonemasons came to stare in wonder. Farms and villages covered this region, and that you call the Forest of Shadows, as well, and beyond. But all of those folk thought of themselves as the people of the Mountain Home, the people of Manetheren.

"Their King was Aemon al Caar al Thorin, Aemon son of Caar son of Thorin, and Eldrene ay Ellan ay Carlan was his Queen. Aemon, a man so fearless that the greatest compliment for courage any could give, even among his enemies, was to say a man had Aemon's heart. Eldrene, so beautiful that it was said the flowers bloomed to make her smile. Bravery and beauty and wisdom and a love that death could not sunder. Weep, if you have a heart, for the loss of them, for the loss of even their memory. Weep, for the loss of their blood."

She fell silent then, but no one spoke. Rand was as bound as the others in the spell she had created. When she spoke again, he drank it in, and so did the rest.

"For nearly two centuries the Trolloc Wars had ravaged the length and breadth of the world, and wherever battles raged, the Red Eagle banner of Manetheren was in the forefront. The men of Manetheren were a thorn to the Dark One's foot and a bramble to his hand. Sing of Manetheren, that would never bend knee to the Shadow. Sing of Manetheren, the sword that could not be broken.

"They were far away, the men of Manetheren, on the Field of Bekkar, called the Field of Blood, when news came that a Trolloc army was moving against their home. Too far to do else but wait to hear of their land's death, for the forces of the Dark One meant to make an end of them. Kill the mighty oak by hacking away its roots. Too far to do else but mourn. But they were the men of the Mountain Home.

"Without hesitation, without thought for the distance they must travel, they marched from the very field of victory, still covered in dust and sweat and blood. Day and night they marched, for they had seen the horror a Trolloc army left behind it, and no man of them could sleep while such a danger threatened Manetheren. They moved as if their feet had wings, marching further and faster than friends hoped or enemies feared they could. At any other day that march alone would have inspired songs. When the Dark One's armies swooped down upon the lands of Manetheren, the men of the Mountain Home stood before it, with their backs to the Tarendrelle."

Some villager raised a small cheer then, but Moiraine kept on as if she had not heard. "The host that faced the men of Manetheren was enough to daunt the bravest heart. Ravens blackened the sky; Trollocs blackened the land. Trollocs and their human allies. Trollocs and Darkfriends in tens of tens of thousands, and Dreadlords to command. At night their cookfires outnumbered the stars, and dawn revealed the banner of Ba'alzemon at their head. Ba'alzamon, Heart of the Dark. An ancient name for the Father of Lies. The Dark One could not have been free of his prison at Shayol Ghul, for if he had been, not all the forces of humankind together could have stood against him, but there was power there. Dreadlords, and some evil that made that light-destroying banner seem no more than right and sent a chill into the souls of the men who faced it.

"Yet, they knew what they must do. Their homeland lay just across the river. They must keep that host, and the power with it, from the Mountain Home. Aemon had sent out messengers. Aid was promised if they could hold for but three days at the Tarendrelle. Hold for three days against odds that should overwhelm them in the first hour. Yet somehow, through bloody assault and desperate defense, they held through an hour, and the second hour, and the third. For three days they fought, and though the land became a butcher's yard, no crossing of the Tarendrelle did they yield. By the third night no help had come, and no messengers, and they fought on alone. For six days. For nine. And on the tenth day Aemon knew the bitter taste of betrayal. No help was coming, and they could hold the river crossings no more."

"What did they do?" Hari demanded. Torchfires flickered in the chill night breeze, but no one made a move to draw a cloak tighter.

"Aemon crossed the Tarendrelle," Moiraine told them, "destroying the bridges behind him. And he sent word throughout his land for the people to flee, for he knew the powers with the Trolloc horde would find a way to bring it across the river. Even as the word went out, the Trolloc crossing began, and the soldiers of Manetheren took up the fight again, to buy with their lives what hours they could for their people to escape. From the city of Manetheren, Eldrene organized the flight of her people into the deepest forests and the fastness of the mountains.

"But some did not flee. First in a trickle, then a river, then a flood, men went, not to safety, but to join the army fighting for their land. Shepherds with bows, and farmers with pitchforks, and woodsmen with axes. Women went, too, shouldering what weapons they could find and marching side by side with their men. No one made that journey who did not know they would never return. But it was their land. It had been their fathers', and it would be their children's, and they went to pay the price of it. Not a step of ground was given up until it was soaked in blood, but at the last the army of Manetheren was driven back, back to here, to this place you now call Emond's Field. And here the Trolloc hordes surrounded them."

Her voice held the sound of cold tears. "Trolloc dead and the corpses of human renegades piled up in mounds, but always more scrambled over those charnel heaps in waves of death that had no end. There could be but one finish. No man or woman who had stood beneath the banner of the Red Eagle at that day's dawning still lived when night fell. The sword that could not be broken was shattered.

"In the Mountains of Mist, alone in the emptied city of Manetheren, Eldrene felt Aemon die, and her heart died with him. And where her heart had been was left only a thirst for vengeance, vengeance for her love, vengeance for her people and her land. Driven by grief she reached out to the True Source, and hurled the One Power at the Trolloc army. And there the Dreadlords died wherever they stood, whether in their secret councils or exhorting their soldiers. In the passing of a breath the Dreadlords and the generals of the Dark One's host burst into flame. Fire consumed their bodies, and terror consumed their just-victorious army.

"Now they ran like beasts before a wildfire in the forest, with no thought for anything but escape. North and south they fled. Thousands drowned attempting to cross the Tarendrelle without the aid of the Dreadlords, and at the Manetherendrelle they tore down the bridges in their fright at what might be following them. Where they found people, they slew and burned, but to flee was the need that gripped them. Until, at last, no one of them remained in the lands of Manetheren. They were dispersed like dust before the whirlwind. The final vengeance came more slowly, but it came, when they were hunted down by other peoples, by other armies in other lands. None was left alive of those who did murder at Aemon's Field.

"But the price was high for Manetheren. Eldrene had drawn to herself more of the One Power than any human could ever hope to wield unaided. As the enemy generals died, so did she die, and the fires that consumed her consumed the empty city of Manetheren, even the stones of it, down to the living rock of the mountains. Yet the people had been saved.

"Nothing was left of their farms, their villages, or their great city. Some would say there was nothing left for them, nothing but to flee to other lands, where they could begin anew. They did not say so. They had paid such a price in blood and hope for their land as had never been paid before, and now they were bound to that soil by ties stronger than steel. Other wars would wrack them in years to come, until at last their corner of the world was forgotten and at last they had forgotten wars and the ways of war. Never again did Manetheren rise. Its soaring spires and splashing fountains became as a dream that slowly faded from the minds of its people. But they, and their children, and their children's children, held the land that was theirs. They held it when the long centuries had washed the why of it from their memories. They held it until, today, there is you. Weep for Manetheren. Weep for what is lost forever."

The fires on Moiraine's staff winked out, and she lowered it to her side as if it weighed a hundred pounds. For a long moment the moan of the wind was the only sound. Then Paet al'Caar shouldered past the Coplins.

"I don't know about your story," the long-jawed farmer said. "I'm no thorn to the Dark One's foot, nor ever likely to be, neither. But my Wil is walking because of you, and for that I am ashamed to be here. I don't know if you can forgive me, but whether you will or no, I'll be going. And for me, you can stay in Emond's Field as long as you like."

With a quick duck of his head, almost a bow, he pushed back through the crowd. Others began to mutter then, offering shamefaced penitence before they, too, slipped away one by one. The Coplins, sour-mouthed and scowling once more, looked at the faces around them and vanished into the night without a word. Bili Congar had disappeared even before his cousins.

Lan pulled Rand back and shut the door. "Let's go, boy." The Warder started for the back of the inn. "Come along, both of you. Quickly!"

Rand hesitated, exchanging a wondering glance with Mat. While Moiraine had been telling the story, Master al'Vere's Dhurrans could not have dragged him away, but now something else held his feet. This was the real beginning, leaving the inn and following the Warder into the night. . . . He shook himself, and tried to firm his resolve. He had no choice but to go, but he would come back to Emond's Field, however far or long this journey was.

"What are you waiting for?" Lan asked from the door that led out of the back of the common room. With a start Mat hurried to him.

Trying to convince himself that he was beginning a grand adventure, Rand followed them through the darkened kitchen and out into the stableyard.

SPLIT LIGHT

Lisa Goldstein

Lisa Goldstein is a fantasy writer whose works include *The Red Magician, The Dream Years, Tourists,* and *Strange Devices of the Sun and Moon.* She has also written a number of short stories of SF and fantasy, collected in *Travellers in Magic.* "Split Light," from that volume, is an impressive alternate history piece that sits on the border between SF and fantasy.

> SHABBETAI ZEVI (1626–1676), the central figure
> of the largest and most momentous messianic
> movement in Jewish history subsequent to the
> destruction of the Temple . . .
> —*Encyclopedia Judaica*

He sits in a prison in Constantinople. The room is dark, his mind a perfect blank, the slate on which his visions are written. He waits.

He sees the moon. The moon spins like a coin through the blue night sky. The moon splinters and falls to earth. Its light is the shattered soul of Adam, dispersed since the fall. All over the earth the shards are falling; he sees each one, and knows where it comes to rest.

He alone can bind the shards together. He will leave this prison, become king. He will wear the circled walls of Jerusalem as a crown. All the world will be his.

His name is Shabbetai Zevi. "Shabbetai" for the Sabbath, the seventh day, the day of rest. The seventh letter in the Hebrew alphabet is zayin. In England they call the Holy Land "Zion." He is the Holy Land, the center of the world. If he is in Constantinople, then Constantinople is the center of the world.

He has never been to England, but he has seen it in his visions. He has ranged through the world in his visions, has seen the past and fragments of the future. But he does not know what will happen to him in this prison.

When he thinks of his prison the shards of light grow faint and disappear. The darkness returns. He feels the weight of the stone building above him; it is as heavy as the crown he felt a moment ago. He gives in to despair.

A year ago, he thinks, he was the most important man in the world. Although he is a Jew in a Moslem prison he gives the past year its Christian date: it was 1665. It was a date of portent; some Christians believe that 1666 will be the year of the second coming of Christ. Even among the Christians he has his supporters.

But it was to the Jews, to his own people, that he preached. As a child he had seen the evidence of God in the world, the fiery jewels hidden in gutters and trash heaps; he could not understand why no one else had noticed them, why his brother had beaten him and called him a liar. As a young man he had felt his soul kindle into light as he prayed. He had understood that he was born to heal the world, to collect the broken shards of light, to turn mourning into joy.

When he was in his twenties he began the mystical study of Kabbalah. He read, with growing excitement, about the light of God, how it had been scattered and hidden throughout the world at Adam's fall, held captive by the evil that resulted from that fall. The Jews, according to the Kabbalist Isaac Luria, had been cast across the world like sand, like sparks, and in their dispersal they symbolized the broken fate of God.

One morning while he was at prayer he saw the black letters in his prayer book dance like flame and translate themselves into the unpronounceable Name of God. He understood everything at that moment, saw the correct pronunciation of the Name, knew that he could restore all the broken parts of the world by simply saying the Name aloud.

He spoke. His followers say he rose into midair. He does not remember; he rarely remembers what he says or does in his religious trances. He knows that he was shunned in his town of Smyrna, that the people there began to think him a lunatic or a fool.

Despite their intolerance he grew to understand more and more. He saw that he was meant to bring about an end to history, and that with the coming of the end all things were to be allowed. He ate pork. He worked on the Sabbath, the day of rest, the day that he was named for or that was named for him.

Finally the townspeople could stand it no longer and banished him. He blessed them all before he went, "in the name of God who allows the forbidden."

As he left the town of his birth, though, the melancholy that had plagued him all his life came upon him again. He wandered through Greece and Thrace, and ended finally in Constantinople. In Constantinople he saw a vision of the black prison, the dungeon in which he would be immured, and in his fear the knowledge that had sustained him for so long vanished. God was lost in the world, broken into so many shards no one could discover him.

In his frantic search for God he celebrated the festivals of Passover, Shavuot, and Sukkot all in one week. He was exiled again and resumed his wandering, travelling from Constantinople to Rhodes to Cairo.

In Cairo he dreamed he was a bridegroom, about to take as his bride the holy city of Jerusalem. The next day the woman Sarah came, unattended, to Cairo.

The door to his prison opens and a guard comes in, the one named Kasim. "Stand up!" Kasim says.

Shabbetai stands. "Come with me," Kasim says.

Shabbetai follows. The guard takes him through the dungeon and out into Constantinople. It is day; the sun striking the domes and minarets of the city nearly blinds him.

Kasim leads him through the crowded streets, saying nothing. They pass covered bazaars and slave markets, coffee houses and sherbet shops. A caravan of camels forces them to stop.

When they continue on Shabbetai turns to study his guard. Suddenly he sees to the heart of the other man, understands everything. He knows that Kasim is under orders to transfer him to the fortress at Gallipoli, that the sultan himself has given him this order before leaving to fight the Venetians on Crete. "How goes the war, brother?" Shabbetai asks.

Kasim jerks as if he has been shot. He hurries on toward the wharf, saying nothing.

At the harbor Kasim hands Shabbetai to another man and goes quickly back to the city. Shabbetai is stowed in the dark hold of a ship, amid sour-smelling hides and strong spices and ripe oranges. Above him he hears someone shout, and he feels the ship creak and separate from the wharf and head out into the Sea of Marmara.

Darkness again, he thinks. He is a piece of God, hidden from sight. It is only by going down into the darkness of the fallen world that he can find the other fragments, missing since the Creation. Everything has been ordained, even this trip from Constantinople to Gallipoli.

Visions of the world around him encroach upon the darkness. He sees Pierre de Fermat, a mathematician, lying dead in France; a book is open on the table in which he has written, "I have discovered a truly remarkable proof which this margin is too small to contain." He sees Rembrandt adding a stroke of bright gold to a painting he calls "The Jewish Bride." He sees a great fire destroy London; a killing wind blows the red and orange flames down to the Thames.

He is blinded again, this time by the vast inrushing light of the world. He closes his eyes, a spark of light among many millions of others, and rocks to the motion of the ship.

Sarah's arrival in Cairo two years ago caused a great deal of consternation. No one could remember ever seeing a woman travelling by herself. She stood alone on the dock, a slight figure with long red hair tumbling from her kerchief, gazing around her as if at Adam's Eden.

Finally someone ran for the chief rabbi. He gave the order to have her brought to his house, and summoned all the elders as well.

"Who are you?" he asked. "Why are you travelling alone in such a dangerous part of the world?"

"I'm an orphan," Sarah said. "But I was raised in a great castle by a Polish nobleman. I had one servant just to pare my nails, and another to brush my hair a hundred times before I went to bed."

None of the elders answered her, but each one wore an identical expression of doubt. Why would a Polish nobleman raise a Jewish orphan? And what on earth was she doing in Cairo?

Only Shabbetai saw her true nature; only he knew that what the elders suspected was true. She had been the nobleman's mistress, passed among his circle of friends when he grew tired of her. The prophet Hosea married a prostitute, he thought. "I will be your husband," he said. "If you will have me."

He knew as he spoke that she would marry him, and his heart rejoiced.

They held the wedding at night and out of doors. The sky was dark blue silk, buttoned by a moon of old ivory. Stars without number shone.

After the ceremony the elders came to congratulate him. For Sarah's sake he pretended not to see the doubt in their eyes. "I cannot tell you how happy I am tonight," he said.

After the ceremony he brought her to his house and led her to the bedroom, not bothering to light the candles. He lay on the bed and drew her to him. Her hair was tangled; perhaps she never brushed it.

They lay together for a long time. "Shall I undress?" she asked finally. Her breath was warm on his face.

"The angels sang at my birth," he said. "I have never told anyone this. Only you."

She ran her fingers through her hair, then moved to lift her dress. He held her tightly. "We must be like the angels," he said. "Like the moon. We must be pure."

"I don't understand."

"We cannot fall into sin. If I am stained like Adam I will not be able to do the work for which I was sent here."

"The—work?"

"I was born to heal the world," he said.

The moon appeared before him in the darkened room. Its silver-white light cast everything in shadow.

The moon began to spin. No, he thought. He watched as it shattered and plummeted to earth, saw the scattered fragments hide themselves in darkness.

He cried aloud. He felt the great sadness of the world, and the doubt he had struggled with all his life returned.

"It's broken," he said. "It can never be repaired. I'll never be able to join all the pieces together."

Sarah kissed him lightly on the cheek. "Let us join together, then," she said. "Let two people stand for the entire world."

"No—"

"I heard you tell your followers that everything is permitted. Why are we not permitted to come together as husband and wife?"

"I can't," he said simply. "I have never been able to."

He expected scorn, or pity. But her expression did not change. She held him in her arms, and eventually he drifted off to sleep.

With Sarah at his side he was able to begin the mission for which he was born. Together they travelled toward Jerusalem, stopping so that he could preach along the way.

He spoke in rough huts consecrated only by the presence of ten men joined by prayer. He spoke in ancient synagogues, with lamps of twisted silver casting a wavering light on the golden letters etched into the walls. Sometimes he stood at a plain wooden table, watched by unlettered rustics who know nothing of the mysteries of Kabbalah; sometimes he preached from an altar of faded white and gold.

His message was the same wherever they went. He was the Messiah, appointed by God. He proclaimed an end to fast days; he promised women that he would set them free from the curse of Eve. He would take the crown from the Turkish sultan without war, he said, and he would make the sultan his servant.

The lost ten tribes of Israel had been found, he told the people who gathered to hear him. They were marching slowly as sleepwalkers toward the Sahara desert, uncertain of the way or of their purpose, waiting for him to unite them.

When he reached Jerusalem he circled the walls seven times on horseback, like a king. Once inside the city he won over many of the rabbis and elders. Letters were sent out to the scattered Jewish communities all over the world, to England, Holland, and Italy, proclaiming that the long time of waiting was over; the Messiah had come.

A great storm shook the world. Families sold their belongings and travelled toward Jerusalem. Others set out with nothing, trusting in God to provide for them. Letters begging for more news were sent back to Jerusalem, dated from "the first year of the renewal of the prophecy and the kingdom." Shabbetai signed the answering letters "the firstborn son of God," and even "I am the Lord your God Shabbetai Zevi," and such was the fervor of the people that very few of them were shocked.

The boat docks at Gallipoli, and Shabbetai is taken to the fortress there. Once inside he sees that he has been given a large and well-lit suite of rooms, and he understands that his followers have succeeded in bribing the officials.

The guards leave him and lock the door. However comfortable his rooms are, he is still in a prison cell. He paces for several minutes, studying the silver lamps and deep carpets and polished tables and chairs. Mosaics on the wall, fragments of red, green, and black, repeat over and over in a complex pattern.

He sits on the plump mattress and puts his head in his hands. His head throbs. With each pulse, it seems, the lamps in the room dim, grow darker, until, finally, they go out.

He is a letter of light. He is the seventh letter, the zayin. Every person alive is a letter, and together they make up the book of the world, all things past, present, and to come.

He thinks he can read the book, can know the future of the world. But as he looks on, the book's pages turn; the letters form and reshape. Futures branch off before him.

He watches as children are born, as some die, as others grow to adulthood. Some stay in their villages, farm their land, sit by their hearths with their families surrounding them. Others disperse across the world and begin new lives.

The sight disturbs him; he does not know why. A page turns and he sees ranks of soldiers riding to wars, and men and women lying dead in the streets from plague. Kingdoms fall to sword and gun and cannon.

Great wars consume the world. The letters twist and sharpen, become pointed wire. He sees millions of people herded beyond the wire, watches as they go toward their deaths.

The light grows brighter. He wants to close his eyes, to look away, but he cannot. He watches as men learn the secrets of the light, as they break it open and release the life concealed within it. A shining cloud flares above a city, and thousands more die.

No, he thinks. But the light shines out again, and this time it seems to comfort him. Here is the end of history that he has promised his followers. Here is the end of everything, the world cleansed, made anew.

The great book closes, and the light goes out.

In Jerusalem he preached to hundreds of people. They filled the synagogue, dressed in their best clothes, the men on his right hand and the women on his left. Children played and shouted in the aisles.

He spoke of rebuilding the temple, of finding the builder's stone lost since the time of Solomon. As he looked out over his audience he saw Sarah stand and leave the congregation. One of his followers left as well, a man named Aaron.

He stopped, the words he had been about to speak dying before they left his mouth. For a moment he could not go on. The people stirred in their seats.

He hurried to an end. After the service he ran quickly to the house the rabbis had given him. Sarah was already there.

"What were you doing here?" he asked.

"What do you mean?" she said. Her expression was innocent, unalarmed.

"I saw you leave with Aaron."

"With Aaron? I left to come home. I didn't feel well."

"You were a whore in Poland, weren't you?" he asked harshly. "Was there a single man in the country you didn't sleep with?"

"I was a nobleman's daughter," she said. Her voice was calm. He could not see her heart; she held as many mysteries as the Kabbalah.

"A nobleman's—" he said. "You were his mistress. And what did you do with Aaron? What did you do with all of them, all of my followers?"

"I told you—"

"Don't lie to me!"

"Listen. Listen to me. I did nothing. I have not known a man since I came to Cairo."

"Then you admit that in Poland—"

"Quiet. Yes. Yes, I was his mistress."

"And Aaron? You want him, don't you? You whore— You want them all, every man you have ever known."

"Listen," she said angrily. "You know nothing of women, nothing at all. I was his mistress in Poland, yes. But I did not enjoy it—I did it because I was an orphan, and hungry, and I needed to eat. I hated it when he came to me, but I managed to hide my feelings. I had to, or I would have starved."

"But you wanted me. On our wedding night, you said—"

"Yes. You are the only man who has ever made me feel safe."

A great pity moved him. He felt awed at the depths to which her life had driven her, the sins she had been forced to take upon herself. Could she be telling the truth? But why would she stay with him, a man of no use to her or any other woman?

"You lied to your nobleman," he said carefully. "Are you lying to me now?"

"No," she said.

He believed her. He felt free, released from the jealousy that had bound him. "You may have Aaron, you know," he said.

"What?"

"You may have Aaron, or any man you want."

"I don't— Haven't you heard me at all? I don't want Aaron."

"I understand everything now. You were a test, but through the help of God I have passed it. With the coming of the kingdom of God all things are allowed. Nothing is forbidden. You may have any man, any woman, any one of God's creatures."

"I am not a test! I am a woman, your wife! You are the only man I want!"

He did not understand why she had become angry. His own anger had gone. He left the house calmly.

From Jerusalem he travelled with his followers to Smyrna, the place where he was born. There are those who say that he was banished from Jerusalem too, that the rabbis there declared him guilty of blasphemy. He does not remember. He remembers only the sweetness of returning to his birthplace in triumph.

Thousands of men and women turned out to greet him as he rode through the city gates. Men on the walls lifted ram's horns to their lips and sounded notes of welcome. People crowded the streets, cheering and singing loudly; they raised their children to their shoulders and pointed him out as he went past.

He nodded to the right and left as he rode. A man left the assembly and stepped out in front of the procession.

Shabbetai's horse reared. "Careful, my lord!" Nathan said, hurrying to his side. Nathan was one of the many who had joined him in Jerusalem, who had heard Shabbetai's message and given up all his worldly goods.

But Shabbetai had recognized the fat, worried-looking man, and he reined in his horse. "This is my brother Joseph," he said. "A merchant."

To his surprise Joseph bowed to him. "Welcome, my lord," he said. "We hear great things of you."

Shabbetai laughed. When they were children he had told Joseph about his visions, and Joseph had beaten him for lying. Seeing his brother bent before him was more pleasing than Shabbetai could have imagined. "Rise, my friend," he said.

In the days that followed the city became one great festival. Business came to a standstill as people danced in the streets, recited psalms to one another when they met, fell into prophetic trances proclaiming the kingdom of God.

Only Sarah did not join in the city's riot. He urged her to take a lover, as so many people in the city were doing, but she refused. When he called for an end to fast days she became the only one in the city to keep the old customs.

Despite her actions he felt more strongly than ever that he was travelling down the right road, that he was close to the fulfillment of his mission. He excommunicated those who refused to believe in him. He sang love songs during prayer, and explained to the congregation the mystical meaning behind the words of the songs. He distributed the kingdoms of the earth among his followers.

His newly made kings urged him to take the crown intended for him, to announce the date of his entrance into Constantinople. He delayed, remembering the evil vision of the dark prison.

But in his euphoria he began to see another vision, one in which he took the crown from the sultan. He understood that history would be split at Constantinople, would travel down one of two diverging paths. He began to make arrangements to sail.

Two days before they were to leave Sarah came to him. "I'm not going with you," she said.

"What do you mean?" he asked. "I will be king, ruler of the world, and you will be at my side, my queen. This is what I have worked for all these years. How can you give that up?"

"I don't want to be queen."

"You don't— Why not?"

"I don't feel safe with you any longer. I don't like the things you ask me to do."

"What things?"

"What things? How can you ask me that when you tell me to lie with every one of your followers? You're like the nobleman, passing me around when you get tired of me."

"I did nothing. It was you who lusted after Aaron."

"I didn't—"

"And others too," he said, remembering the glances she had given men in the congregation. She *had* pitied him, and hated him too, just as he had always thought. "Do you think I didn't notice?"

"I've done nothing," she said. "I—"

"I won't grant you a divorce, you know."

"Of course not. If we're married you still own me, even if I'm not there. That dream you told me about, where you took Jerusalem as your bride—you want to master Jerusalem, make her bow to your will. You want to control the entire world. But have you ever thought about how you will govern once you have the sultan's crown? You want to be ruler of the earth, but what kind of ruler will you be?"

"What do you know about statecraft, about policy? I have been ordained by God to be king. And you—you have been chosen to be queen."

"No," she said. "I have not."

She turned to leave. "I excommunicate you!" he said, shouting after her. "I call upon God to witness my words—you are excommunicated!"

She continued walking as if she did not hear him.

He watched her go. Perhaps it was just as well that she was leaving. He had known for a long time that she could not grasp the vastness of the task he had been given; she had never studied Kabbalah, or had visions of the light of God. His work in the world was far more important than her private feelings, or his.

He and his followers set sail on December 30, 1665. Word of his departure had gone before him. His boat was intercepted in the Sea of Marmara, and he was brought ashore in chains.

He sits in his prison in Gallipoli and waits for the light. He has not had a vision in many days; perhaps, he thinks, they have left him. He wonders if they have been consumed by the great fires he has seen in the future.

What had gone wrong? He and his followers had been so certain; he had seen the signs, read all the portents. He was destined to be the ruler of the world.

He puts his head in his hands and laughs harshly. Ruler of the world! And instead he sits in prison, waiting to be killed or released at the whim of the Turkish sultan.

The light of God is broken, dispersed throughout the world. And like the light his own mind is broken, splitting.

There is a knock on the door, and Nathan enters. "How did you find me?" Shabbetai asks.

Nathan appears surprised. "Don't you know?" he asks.

Shabbetai says nothing.

"I bribed a great many people to get you here," Nathan says. "Are you comfortable?"

"I— Yes. Quite comfortable."

"The sultan has returned from Crete," Nathan says. "There are rumors that he will want to see you."

"When?"

"I don't know. Soon, I think. He is alarmed by the support you have among the people of Turkey." Nathan pauses and then goes on. "Some of your followers are worried. They don't believe that we can hold out against the combined armies of the sultan."

"Tell them not to fear," Shabbetai says. He is surprised at how confident he sounds. But there is no reason to worry Nathan and the others, and perhaps the visions will return. "Tell them that God watches over me."

Nathan nods, satisfied.

A few days later Shabbetai is taken by guards from Gallipoli to Adrianople. They pass through the city and come to a strong high wall. Men look down at them from the watchtowers.

Soldiers with plumed helmets stand at the wall's gate. The soldiers nod to them and motion them through. Beyond the gate is a courtyard filled with fountains and cypress trees and green plots of grass where gazelles feed.

They turn left, and come to a door guarded by soldiers. They enter through this door and are shown before the sultan and his council.

"Do you claim to be the Messiah?" a councilor asks Shabbetai.

"No," he says.

"What?" the councilor says, astonished.

"No. Perhaps I was the Messiah once. But the light has left me—I see no more and no less than other people."

The sultan moves his hand. The councilor nods to him and turns toward Shabbetai. "I see," he says. "You understand that we cannot just take your word for this. We cannot say, Very well, you may go now. Your followers outside are waiting for you—you have become a very dangerous man."

"We are prepared to offer you a choice," the sultan says. "Either convert to Islam or be put to death immediately."

The light returns, filling the room. Shabbetai gasps; he had begun to think it lost forever. The light breaks. Two paths branch off before him.

On one path he accepts death. His followers, stunned, sit in mourning for him for the required seven days. Then Nathan pronounces him a martyr, and others proclaim that he has ascended to heaven.

His following grows. Miracles are seen, and attested to by others. An army forms; they attack the Turks. A long and bloody war follows. The sultan, the man sitting so smugly before him, is killed by one of his own people, a convert to what is starting to be called Sabbatarianism.

After a decade the Turks surrender, worn out by the fighting against the Sabbatarians on one side and the Venetians on the other. Shabbetai's followers take

Constantinople; Hagia Sophia, once a church and then a mosque, is converted a third time by the victorious army.

The Sabbatarians consolidate their power, and spread across Europe and Asia. First hundreds and then thousands of heretics are put to death. Holy wars flare. Men hungry for power come to Constantinople and are given positions in the hierarchy of the new religion.

Finally, using the terrifying tools of the far future, the Sabbatarians set out to kill everyone who is not a believer. The broken light that Shabbetai saw in his vision shines across the sky as city after city is laid waste. Poisons cover the earth. At the end only a few thousand people are left alive.

Shabbetai turns his gaze away from the destruction and looks down the other path. Here he becomes a convert to Islam; he changes his name to Aziz Mehmed Effendi. The sultan, pleased at his decision, grants him a royal pension of 150 piasters a day.

His followers are shocked, but they soon invent reasons for his apostasy. Nathan explains that the conversion was necessary, that the Messiah must lose himself in darkness in order to find all the shards of God hidden in the world.

Over the years his followers begin to lose hope. Sarah dies in 1674. Two years later he himself dies. Several groups of Sabbatarians continue to meet in secret; one group even survives to the mid-twentieth century.

He turns back to the first path. Once again he is drawn to the vision of annihilation. An end to breeding and living and dying, an end to the mad ceaseless activity that covers the earth. Perhaps this is what God requires of him.

He remembers Sarah, her desire to lie with him. She thought him powerless; very well, he will show her something of power. Flame will consume her descendants, all the children he had been unable to give her.

The moon spins before him, fragments into a thousand pieces. He understands that his vision is not an allegory but real, that people will become so strong they can destroy the moon.

His head pounds. He is not powerless at all. He is the most powerful man in the world. All the people he has seen in his travels, the bakers and learned men and farmers and housewives and bandits, all of them depend for their lives on his next word.

He thinks of Sarah again, her tangled hair, her breath warm on his cheek. If he lets the world live all her children will be his, although she will not know it. Every person in the world will be his child. He can choose life, for himself and for everyone; he can do what he was chosen to do and heal the world.

The light blazes and dies. He looks up at the sultan and his men and says, calmly, "I will choose Islam."

SCIENCE FICTION & THE ADVENTURES OF THE SPHERICAL COW

Kathryn Cramer

Kathryn Cramer is an editor, critic, anthologist, and writer who is equally at home in the science fiction, fantasy, and horror genres. Her criticism has been described as "spiky and erudite." This essay is a provocative view of a basic element of science missing from SF texts: mathematics.

What does science lend to fiction that is important enough to have a genre called "science fiction"? What does science fiction do with what science gives it?

These questions also ask "What is science fiction?," restricting the definition to science fiction's relation to science. Like the city of Los Angeles, everyone knows where it is—in this case what it is—but only in the largest context, the big picture. Science fiction has no agreed-upon boundaries, no precise definition; just as Los Angeles has no commonly agreed-upon borders, but you know where you are when you're downtown, that you haven't arrived at the wrong city.

There has been a persistent view that "hard" SF is somehow the core and center of the field; that all other SF orbits around this center; and that, further-more, the characteristic of this core is a particular attitude toward science and technology.

What does science have to do with science fiction? The denomination signi-fies some relationship to science, and there have been articles and books for decades on sociology in SF, and physics in SF, and how you ought to know something about science to read it or write it, but few attempts have been made to identify the relationships between science and fiction at the genre's core since the days of John W. Campbell.

Rather than starting with science fiction and working back to science, as is the usual tack, let us start with science and work back to fiction. The usual ap-proach assumes that we know what science is, and wish only to explore science fiction. I suggest, however, that most of us do not know the side of science that lends itself to fiction as well as we might think.

Again, what does science lend to fiction?

There is a joke that experimental physicists tell about theoretical physicists that goes something like this:

A theoretical physicist loses his job at a university because of budget cuts and has to take a job as a milkman. After weeks and weeks of doing nothing but deliver milk, he cannot stand it anymore, and decides to hold a colloquium.

He assembles all the milkmen in a room, and after they have all taken their seats he walks up to the front of the room to the blackboard. Drawing a circle on the board, he says, "Consider a spherical cow of uniform density."

Primarily, the origin of the humor of this joke is that it describes the experimental physicists' view of the theoretical physicist—the theoreticians seem to exist in a world of meaningless abstraction with no bearing on the realities of experimental physics.

The other reason this joke is funny, rivalry between experimentalists and theoreticians aside, is that *all* scientific explanation is streamlined metaphor for what really is the case, partially because scientists don't know everything and partially because they throw out all small factors that muck up the mathematics. (The latter is a perfectly legitimate technique for obtaining fairly accurate results quickly.) Scientific generalizations are innately metaphorical.

Another joke—the proof that all odd numbers are prime:

The number 1 is prime, 3 is prime, 5 is prime, 7 is prime, 9 is experimental error, 11 is prime, 13 is prime, 15 is experimental error, 17 is prime, 19 is prime . . .

This misapplication of the mathematical techniques of physics to pure mathematics shows one way in which the abstraction and reality diverge. In pure math, you don't have experimental error (although there are other ways to throw non-zero terms out of an equation to simplify the calculation). The theory does not equal the fact. This is a characteristic of science that the creationists have made much of, although I don't believe that they have properly understood what it means.

Scientific generalizations are metaphors for what appears—based on mathematical relations between the data and the theory—to be the case. The difference between statements like "light is a wave" and "light is a particle" on the one hand, and "light is a rose" on the other, is not that the first two are literal facts, whereas the latter is a metaphor. All three statements are metaphoric. Rather the first two metaphors have some mathematical justification, whereas the third does not.

One presumes that, if the milkman/theoretical physicist continued with his talk, he would explain the mathematical utility of assuming, for the purpose of argument, that this particular cow is spherical and has uniform density. It is from the rules of mathematics and of formal logic (the latter considered here as a subset of mathematics) that scientific metaphors derive their apparent firm bond with reality, and hence are often mistaken for reality itself. In the complete absence of mathematics they are no more and no less meaningful than "light is a rose."

When scientific ideas and formulations are invoked in a text that does not make use of mathematics in appropriate amounts, the text relies upon the existence of other texts that do. Someone who has read only the text without the mathematics cannot fully manipulate the ideas gleaned from that text unless the reader can reconstruct them on her own. The Spherical Cow, set free to graze where she wants, becomes a creature of mythology, unbound from the fetters of mathematical convenience that kept her a creature of the mind, kept her from being a creature of the world. When cut off from mathematics, scientific theory becomes a form of folk wisdom.

However, before it can be woven into prose fiction or any other kind of prose aimed at the general reader, science must be stripped of its mathematical bones. The cow must be cut loose. This is one of the most basic constraints upon incorporating science in a work of fiction. No matter how apparently accurate the text, science must be used as mythology. It is this aspect of science that caused the Creationists to invent the term "Secular Humanism." They sensed, quite correctly, that the science in their children's text books was every bit as much a mythology as the Book of Genesis. What they failed to understand is that the textbooks exist in relation to other texts in which science is not a mythology, texts with all the mathematical underpinnings.

Except in that very stylized form called the scientific paper, readers will not tolerate more than a line or two of equations. Even then, the only equations that are acceptable are (a) highly recognizable equations that need not actually be read as mathematics, for example $E=mc^2$, and (b) simple arithmetic. This is as true of science articles in *The New York Times* as it is of science fiction. Try typing various kinds of equations on the average typewriter and you will quickly discover limits of the range of equations that the manufacturers of typewriters consider to be properly found in nonspecialized prose. Even the hardest of science fiction therefore partakes of folk wisdom.

While, in a sense, science is one of the most democratic pursuits because the experimental results establish the hierarchy of dominance, it is also one of the most elitist. Those who don't learn (formally or otherwise) the basics of calculus (or whatever branch of mathematics applies most heavily to the field in question) forever remain consumers of the body of scientific theory, and can never be its producers. Their teachers draw circles on the blackboard and say, "Today we're going to learn about the Spherical Cow," not "Consider a spherical cow." Those who don't have the math are excluded from argument over whether the cow should be spherical or circular, of uniform density or hollow in the middle; they are told to learn rather than to consider.

What science gives to science fiction is an ever-changing body of metaphor that provides at least the *illusion* of both realism and rationalism. While the realism and the rationalism of science may not correspond terribly well, the apparent belief that they do on the part of the author is what give a science fiction story the feeling we associate with hard science fiction. Science creates the character of the Spherical Cow, and the science fiction writer creates her adventures.

Given the tension that appears to exist between hard SF and the New Wave (as represented, for instance, in various anthologies edited by Judith Merril), is most surprising to discover that a number of stories in Merril's groundbreaking anthology *England Swings SF* make as much use of science as some of the "hard" SF classics like "Nightfall." Examples which come to mind are "You and Me and the Continuum" and "The Assassination of John Fitzgerald Kennedy Considered as a Downhill Motor Race & Plan for the Assassination of Jacqueline

Kennedy," both by J. G. Ballard, as well as Pamela Zoline's "The Heat Death of the Universe." None of these are, however, technophilic (a point which I will get to in a few moments), nor do they contain the kind of linear, logical-positivist extrapolation of a few isolated ideas that we associate with hard SF.

For the general reader, Isaac Asimov's "Nightfall" somehow has the trappings of hard SF, whereas the Ballard stories and the Zoline story don't. Never mind that Asimov asks us to believe in "journalists" and "closets" on a planet that is not our own, that has a number of suns, and that hasn't known night any time within recent memory. "Nightfall" has the look and feel of Real Science.

Although much effort, over the last couple of decades, has gone into pointing out the virtues of science fiction as literature, not much has gone into pointing out those virtues that science fiction derives from its unique relationship with science. The great early defenses of SF were based upon the wonder of science and the sense of that wonder aroused in the reader. At its best, science fiction tends to be about the emotional experience of discovering what is true. In "hard" SF, this experience is represented metaphorically by scientific discoveries of great consequence. This emotional experience is what "Nightfall" and "The Heat Death of the Universe" have in common.

What we habitually call "hard" SF is more precisely *technophilic* SF; as Poul Anderson put it, "Science, technology, material achievement, and the rest are basically good. In them lies a necessary if not sufficient condition for the improvement of man's lot, even his mental and spiritual lot." He also differentiates the hard SF story from other varieties of SF: "a hard science story bases itself upon real, present-day science or technology and carries these further with a minimum of imaginary forces, materials, or laws of nature."

Furthermore, a story is much more likely to be identified as "hard" SF—regardless of the amount of actual science it contains—if the narrative voice is pragmatic, deterministic, and matter-of-fact about the many high-tech artifacts among which the story takes place, and if the future (or alternate present or past) in which the protagonist lives is primarily the result of significant technological change from the here-and-now. Through repetition we have come to identify this narrative voice as "futuristic," the voices of Johnny Mnemonic and Abelard Lindsay are only its latest manifestation.

The emotional content of science is well within the literary territory of SF. In contrast, the creation of fully rounded characters is an area in which science fiction writers must compete directly with the most fashionable writers of the mainstream. For twentieth-century literature, science is like the North American continent two hundred years ago: few settlers and room for exploration. Characterization in twentieth-century literature is, in comparison, rather well understood. The continent Characterization is densely populated with aspiring writers and monolithic role models. But on the other hand, it's rather well mapped out.

Let us therefore borrow some maps from Characterization so that we may better explore Science:

Consider a spherical cow of uniform density. We'll affectionately call her Marble. Let Marble represent science in the green field of science fiction. Consider each science fiction story as a tale of some of Marble's many adventures. In some of the stories she is a major character, and in others she is not. Sometimes she even has speaking roles (otherwise known as expository lumps). But she is in all of the stories, if only as a walk-on character or as a third party, referred to in conversation, but never actually seen. If the genre under discussion is titled *Science Fiction*, give it therefore the subtitle *The Adventures of the Spherical Cow.*

THE SUN SPIDER

Lucius Shepard

Lucius Shepard is one of the most ambitious writers to enter SF in the last fifteen years. He has written only two SF novels, but has also produced a large and impressive body of short fiction, many of which are novella length. "The Sun Spider" is unusual among his works. His fiction is often set in Asia or Latin America, and often blends mainstream and genre techniques. This story, however, is set in the future, in space near the sun, and involves speculative mathematics. It is a science fictional tour de force in the manner of classic Alfred Bester, or perhaps early Samuel R. Delany: pyrotechnic, perhaps operatic, SF.

> ". . . In Africa's Namib Desert, one of the most
> hostile environments on the face of the earth, lives a
> creature known as the sun spider. Its body is furred
> pale gold, the exact color of the sand beneath which
> it burrows in search of its prey, disturbing scarcely a
> grain in its passage. It emerges from hiding only to
> snatch its prey, and were you to look directly at it
> from an inch away, you might never notice its
> presence. Nature is an efficient process, tending to
> repeat elegant solutions to the problem of survival in
> such terrible places. Thus, if—as I posit—particulate
> life exists upon the Sun, I would not be startled to
> learn it has adopted a similar form."
> —from *Alchemical Diaries*
> by Reynolds Dulambre

1
Carolyn

My husband Reynolds and I arrived on Helios Station following four years in the Namib, where he had delivered himself of the *Diaries*, including the controversial Solar Equations, and where I had become adept in the uses of boredom. We were met at the docking arm by the administrator of the Physics Section, Dr. Davis Brent, who escorted us to a reception given in Reynolds' honor, held in one of the pleasure domes that blistered the skin of the station. Even had I been unaware that Brent was one of Reynolds' chief detractors, I would have known the two of them for adversaries: in manner and physicality, they were total opposites, like cobra and mongoose. Brent was pudgy, of medium stature, with a receding hairline, and dressed in a drab standard-issue jumpsuit. Reynolds—at thirty-seven, only two years younger—might have been ten years his junior. He was tall and lean, with chestnut hair that fell to the shoulders of his cape, and possessed of that craggy nobility of feature one associates with a Shakespearean lead. Both were on their best behavior, but they could barely manage civility, and so it was quite a relief when we reached the dome and were swept away into a crowd of admiring techs and scientists.

Helios Station orbited the south pole of the Sun, and through the ports I had a view of a docking arm to which several of the boxy ships that journeyed into the coronosphere were moored. Leaving Reynolds to be lionized, I lounged beside one of the ports and gazed toward Earth, pretending I was celebrating Nation Day in Abidjan rather than enduring this gathering of particle pushers and inductive reasoners, most of whom were gawking at Reynolds, perhaps hoping he would live up to his reputation and perform a drugged collapse or start a fight. I watched him and Brent talking. Brent's body language was toadying, subservient, like that of a dog trying to curry favor; he would clasp his hands and tip his head to the side when making some point, as if begging his master not to strike him. Reynolds stood motionless, arms folded across his chest.

At one point Brent said, "I can't see what purpose you hope to achieve in beaming protons into coronal holes," and Reynolds, in his most supercilious tone, responded by saying that he was merely poking about in the weeds with a long stick.

I was unable to hear the next exchange, but then I did hear Brent say, "That may be, but I don't think you understand the openness of our community. The barriers you've erected around your research go against the spirit, the . . ."

"All my goddamned life," Reynolds cut in, broadcasting in a stagey baritone, "I've been harassed by little men. Men who've carved out some cozy academic niche by footnoting my work and then decrying it. Mousey little bastards like you. And that's why I maintain my privacy . . . to keep the mice from nesting in my papers."

He strode off toward the refreshment table, leaving Brent smiling at everyone, trying to show that he had not been affected by the insult. A slim brunette attached herself to Reynolds, engaging him in conversation. He illustrated his points with florid gestures, leaning over her, looking as if he were about to enfold her in his cape, and not long afterward they made a discreet exit.

Compared to Reynolds' usual public behavior, this was a fairly restrained display, but sufficient to make the gathering forget my presence. I sipped a drink, listening to the chatter, feeling no sense of betrayal. I was used to Reynolds' infidelities, and, indeed, I had come to thrive on them. I was grateful he had found his brunette. Though our marriage was not devoid of the sensual, most of our encounters were ritual in nature, and after four years of isolation in the desert, I needed the emotional sustenance of a lover. Helios would, I believed, provide an ample supply.

Shortly after Reynolds had gone, Brent came over to the port, and to my amazement, he attempted to pick me up. It was one of the most inept seductions to which I have ever been subject. He contrived to touch me time and again as if by accident, and complimented me several times on the largeness of my eyes. I managed to turn the conversation into harmless channels, and he got off into politics, a topic on which he considered himself expert.

"My essential political philosophy," he said, "derives from a story by one of the masters of twentieth century speculative fiction. In the story, a man sends his mind into the future and finds himself in a utopian setting, a greensward surrounded by white buildings, with handsome men and beautiful women strolling everywhere . . ."

I cannot recall how long I listened to him, to what soon became apparent as a ludicrous Libertarian fantasy, before bursting into laughter. Brent looked confused by my reaction, but then masked confusion by joining in my laughter. "Ah, Carolyn," he said. "I had you going there, didn't I? You thought I was serious!"

I took pity on him. He was only a sad little man with an inflated self-opinion; and, too, I had been told that he was in danger of losing his administrative post. I spent the best part of an hour in making him feel important; then, scraping him off, I went in search of a more suitable companion.

My first lover on Helios Station, a young particle physicist named Thom, proved overweening in his affections. The sound of my name seemed to transport him; often he would lift his head and say, "Carolyn, Carolyn," as if by doing this he might capture my essence. I found him absurd, but I was starved for attention, and though I could not reciprocate in kind, I was delighted in being the object of his single-mindedness. We would meet each day in one of the pleasure domes, dance to drift, and drink paradisiacs—I developed quite a fondness for Amouristes—and then retire to a private chamber, there to make love and watch the sunships return from their fiery journeys. It was Thom's dream to be assigned someday to a sunship, and he would rhapsodize on the glories attendant upon swooping down through layers of burning gases. His fixation with the scientific adventure eventually caused me to break off the affair. Years of exposure to Reynolds' work had armored me against any good opinion of science, and further I did not want to be reminded of my proximity to the Sun: sometimes I imagined I could hear it hissing, roaring, and feel its flames tonguing the metal walls, preparing to do us to a crisp with a single lick.

By detailing my infidelity, I am not trying to characterize my marriage as loveless. I loved Reynolds, though my affections had waned somewhat. And he loved me in his own way. Prior to our wedding, he had announced that he intended our union to be "a marriage of souls." But this was no passionate outcry, rather a statement of scientific intent. He believed in souls, believed they were the absolute expression of a life, a quality that pervaded every particle of matter and gave rise to the lesser expressions of personality and physicality. His search for particulate life upon the Sun was essentially an attempt to isolate and communicate with the anima, and the "marriage of souls" was for him the logical goal of twenty-first century physics. It occurs to me now that this search may have been his sole means of voicing his deepest emotions, and it was our core problem that I thought he would someday love me in a way that would satisfy me, whereas he felt my satisfaction could be guaranteed by the application of scientific method.

To further define our relationship, I should mention that he once wrote me that the "impassive, vaguely oriental beauty" of my face reminded him of "those serene countenances used to depict the solar disc on ancient sailing charts." Again, this was not the imagery of passion: he considered this likeness a talisman, a lucky charm. He was a magical thinker, perceiving himself as more akin to the alchemists than to his peers, and like the alchemists, he gave credence to the power of similarities. Whenever he made love to me, he was therefore making love to the Sun. To the great detriment of our marriage, every beautiful woman became for him the Sun, and thus a potential tool for use in his rituals. Given his enormous ego, it would have been out of character for him to have been faithful, and had he not utilized sex as a concentrative ritual, I am certain he would have invented another excuse for infidelity. And, I suppose, I would have had to contrive some other justification for my own.

During those first months I was indiscriminate in my choice of lovers, entering into affairs with both techs and a number of Reynolds' colleagues. Reynolds himself was no more discriminating, and our lives took separate paths. Rarely did I spend a night in our apartment, and I paid no attention whatsoever to Reynolds' work. But then one afternoon as I lay with my latest lover in the private chamber of a pleasure dome, the door slid open and in walked Reynolds. My lover—a tech whose name eludes me—leaped up and began struggling into his clothes, apologizing all the while. I shouted at Reynolds, railed at him. What right did he have to humiliate me this way? I had never burst in on him and his whores, had I? Imperturbable, he stared at me, and after the tech had scurried out, he continued to stare, letting me exhaust my anger. At last, breathless, I sat glaring at him, still angry, yet also feeling a measure of guilt . . . not relating to my affair, but to the fact that I had become pregnant as a result of my last encounter with Reynolds. We had tried for years to have a child, and despite knowing how important a child would be to him, I had put off the announcement. I was no longer confident of his capacity for fatherhood.

"I'm sorry about this." He waved at the bed. "It was urgent I see you, and I didn't think."

The apology was uncharacteristic, and my surprise at it drained away the dregs of anger. "What is it?" I asked.

Contrary emotions played over his face. "I've got him," he said.

I knew what he was referring to: he always personified the object of his search, although before too long he began calling it "the Spider." I was happy for his success, but for some reason it had made me a little afraid, and I was at a loss for words.

"Do you want to see him?" He sat beside me. "He's imaged in one of the tanks."

I nodded.

I was sure he was going to embrace me. I could see in his face the desire to break down the barriers we had erected, and I imagined now his work was done, we would be as close as we had once hoped, that honesty and love would finally have their day. But the moment passed, and his face hardened. He stood and paced the length of the chamber. Then he whirled around, hammered a fist into his palm, and with all the passion he had been unable to direct toward me, he said, "I've got him!"

"I had been watching him for over a week without knowing it: a large low-temperature area shifting about in a coronal hole. It was only by chance that I recognized him; I inadvertently nudged the color controls of a holo tank, and brought part of the low-temperature area into focus, revealing a many-armed ovoid of constantly changing primary hues, the arms attenuating and vanishing: I have observed some of these arms reach ten thousand miles in length, and I have no idea what limits apply to their size. He consists essentially of an inner complex of ultracold neutrons enclosed by an intense magnetic field. Lately it has occurred to me that certain of the coronal holes may be no more than the attitude of his movements. Aside from these few facts and guesses, he remains a mystery, and I have begun to suspect that no matter how many elements of his nature are disclosed, he will always remain so."

—from *Collected Notes*
by Reynolds Dulambre

2
Reynolds

Brent's face faded in on the screen, his features composed into one of those fawning smiles. "Ah, Reynolds," he said. "Glad I caught you."

"I'm busy," I snapped, reaching for the off switch.

"Reynolds!"

His desperate tone caught my attention.

"I need to talk to you," he said. "A matter of some importance."

I gave an amused sniff. "I doubt that."

"Oh, but it is . . . to both of us."

An oily note had crept into his voice, and I lost patience. "I'm going to switch off, Brent. Do you want to say good-bye, or should I just cut you off in mid-sentence?"

"I'm warning you, Reynolds!"

"Warning me? I'm all aflutter, Brent. Are you planning to assault me?"

His face grew flushed. "I'm sick of your arrogance!" he shouted. "Who the hell are you to talk down to me? At least I'm productive . . . you haven't done any work for weeks!"

I started to ask how he knew that, but then realized he could have monitored my energy usage via the station computers.

"You think . . ." he began, but at that point I did cut him off and turned back to the image of the Spider floating in the holo tank, its arms weaving a slow dance. I had never believed he was more than dreams, vague magical images, the grandfather wizard trapped in flame, in golden light, in the heart of power. I'd hoped, I'd wanted to believe. But I hadn't been able to accept his reality until I came to Helios, and the dreams grew stronger. Even now I wondered if belief was merely an extension of madness. I have never doubted the efficacy of madness: it is my constant, my referent in chaos.

The first dream had come when I was . . . what? Eleven, twelve? No older. My father had been chasing me, and I had sought refuge in a cave of golden light, a mist of pulsing, shifting light that contained a voice I could not quite hear: it was too vast to hear. I was merely a word upon its tongue, and there had been other words aligned around me, words I needed to understand or else I would be cast out from the light. The Solar Equations—which seemed to have been visited upon me rather than a product of reason—embodied the shiftings, the mysterious principles I had sensed in the golden light, hinted at the arcane processes, the potential for union and dissolution that I had apprehended in every dream. Each time I looked at them, I felt tremors in my flesh, my spirit, as if signaling the onset of a profound change, and . . .

The beeper sounded again, doubtless another call from Brent, and I ignored it. I turned to the readout from the particle traps monitored by the station computers. When I had discovered that the proton bursts being emitted from the Spider's coronal hole were patterned—coded, I'm tempted to say—I had been elated, especially considering that a study of these bursts inspired me to create several addenda to the Equations. They had still been fragmentary, however, and I'd had the notion that I would have to get closer to the Spider in order to complete them . . . perhaps join one of the flights into the coronosphere. My next reaction had been fear. I had realized it was possible the Spider's control was such that these bursts were living artifacts, structural components that maintained a tenuous connection with the rest of his body. If so, then the computers, the entire station, might be under his scrutiny . . . if not his control. Efforts to prove the truth of this had proved inconclusive, but this inconclusiveness was in itself an affirmative answer: the computers were not capable of evasion, and it had been obvious that evasiveness was at work here.

The beeper broke off, and I began to ask myself questions. I had been laboring under the assumption that the Spider had in some way summoned me, but now an alternate scenario presented itself. Could I have stirred him to life? I had beamed protons into the coronal holes, hadn't I? Could I have educated some dumb thing . . . or perhaps brought him to life? Were all my dreams a delusionary system of unparalleled complexity and influence, or was I merely a madman who happened to be right?

These considerations might have seemed irrelevant to my colleagues, but when I related them to my urge to approach the Spider more closely, they took on extreme personal importance. How could I trust such an urge? I stared at the Spider, at its arms waving in their thousand-mile-long dance, their slow changes in configuration redolent of Kali's dance, of myths even more obscure. There were no remedies left for my fear. I had stopped work, drugged myself to prevent dreams, and yet I could do nothing to remove my chief concern: that the Spider would use its control over the computers (if, indeed, it did control them) to manipulate me.

I turned off the holo tank and headed out into the corridor, thinking I would have a few drinks. I hadn't gone fifty feet when Brent accosted me; I brushed past him, but he fell into step beside me. He exuded a false heartiness that was even more grating than his usual obsequiousness.

"Production," he said. "That's our keynote here, Reynolds."

"We can't afford to have dead wood lying around," he went on. "Now if you're having a problem, perhaps you need a fresh eye. I'd be glad to take a look . . ."

I gave him a push, sending him wobbling, but it didn't dent his mood.

"Even the best of us run up against stone walls," he said. "And in your case, well, how long has it been since your last major work. Eight years? Ten? You can only ride the wind of your youthful successes for so . . ."

My anxiety flared into rage. I drove my fist into his stomach, and he dropped, gasping like a fish out of water. I was about to kick him, when I was grabbed from behind by the black-clad arms of a security guard. Two more guards intervened as I wrenched free, cursing at Brent. One of the guards helped Brent up and asked what should be done with me.

"Let him go," he said, rubbing his gut. "The man's not responsible."

I lunged at him, but was shoved back. "Bastard!" I shouted. "You smarmy little shit, I'll swear I'll kill you if . . ."

A guard gave me another shove.

"Please, Reynolds," Brent said in a placating tone. "Don't worry . . . I'll make sure you receive due credit."

I had no idea what he meant, and was too angry to wonder at it. I launched more insults as the guards escorted him away.

No longer in the mood for a public place, I returned to the apartment and sat scribbling meaningless notes, gazing at an image of the Spider that played across one entire wall. I was so distracted that I didn't notice Carolyn had entered until she was standing close beside me. The Spider's colors flickered across her, making her into an incandescent silhouette.

"What are you doing?" she asked, sitting on the floor.

"Nothing." I tossed my notepad aside.

"Something's wrong."

"Not at all . . . I'm just tired."

She regarded me expressionlessly. "It's the Spider, isn't it?"

I told her that, Yes, the work was giving me trouble, but it wasn't serious. I'm not sure if I wanted her as much as it seemed I did, or if I was using sex to ward off more questions. Whatever the case, I lowered myself beside her, kissed her, touched her breasts, and soon we were in that heated secret place where— I thought—not even the Spider's eyes could pry. I told her I loved her in that rushed breathless way that is less an intimate disclosure than a form of gasping, of shaping breath to accommodate movement. That was the only way I have ever been able to tell her the best of my feeling, and it was because I was shamed by this that we did not make love more often.

Afterward I could see she wanted to say something important: it was working in her face. But I didn't want to hear it, to be trapped into some new level of intimacy. I turned from her, marshalling words that would signal my need for privacy, and my eyes fell on the wall where the image of the Spider still danced . . . danced in a way I had never before witnessed. His colors were shifting through a spectrum of reds and violets, and his arms writhed in a rhythm that brought to mind the rhythms of sex, the slow beginning, the furious rush to completion, as if he had been watching us and was now mimicking the act.

Carolyn spoke my name, but I was transfixed by the sight and could not answer. She drew in a sharp breath, and seconds later I heard her cross the room and make her exit. The Spider ceased his dance, lapsing into one of his normal patterns. I scrambled up, went to the controls and flicked the display switch to off. But the image did not fade. Instead, the Spider's colors grew brighter, washing from fiery red to gold and at last to a white so brilliant, I had to shield my eyes. I could almost feel his heat on my skin, hear the sibilant kiss of his molten voice. I was certain he was in the room, I knew I was going to burn, to be swallowed in that singing heat, and I cried out for Carolyn, not wanting to leave unsaid all those things I had withheld from her. Then my fear reached such proportions that I collapsed and sank into a dream, not a nightmare as one might expect, but a dream of an immense city, where I experienced a multitude of adventures and met with a serene fate.

". . . To understand Dulambre, his relationship with his father must be examined closely. Alex Dulambre was a musician and poet, regarded to be one of the progenitors of drift: a popular dance form involving the use of improvised lyrics. He was flamboyant, handsome, amoral, and these qualities, allied with a talent for seduction, led him on a twenty-five-year fling through the boudoirs of the powerful, from the corporate towers of Abidjan to the Gardens of Novo Sibersk, and lastly to a beach on Mozambique, where at the age of forty-four he died horribly, a victim of a neural poison that purportedly had been designed for him by the noted chemist Virginia Holland. It was Virginia who was reputed to be Reynolds' mother, but no tests were ever conducted to substantiate the rumor. All we know for certain is that one morning Alex received a crate containing an artificial womb and the embryo of his son. An attached folder provided proof of his paternity and a note stating that the mother wanted no keepsake to remind her of an error in judgment.

"Alex felt no responsibility for the child, but liked having a relative to add to his coterie. Thus it was that Reynolds spent his first fourteen years globe-trotting, sleeping on floors, breakfasting off the remains of the previous night's party, and generally being ignored, if not rejected. As a defense against both this rejection and his father's charisma, Reynolds learned to mimick Alex's flamboyance and developed similar verbal skills. By the age of eleven he was performing regularly with his father's band, creating a popular sequence of drifts that detailed the feats of an all-powerful wizard and the trials of those who warred against him. Alex took pride in these performances; he saw himself as less father than elder brother, and he insisted on teaching Reynolds a brother's portion of the world. To this end he had one of his lovers seduce the boy on his twelfth birthday, and from then on Reynolds also mimicked his father's omnivorous sexuality. They did, indeed, seem brothers, and to watch Alex drape an arm over the boy's shoulders, the casual observer might have supposed them to be even closer. But there was no strong bond between them, only a history of abuse. This is not to say that Reynolds was unaffected by his father's death, an event to which he was witness. The sight of Alex's agony left him severely traumatized and with a fear of death bordering on the morbid. When we consider this fear in alliance with his difficulty in expressing love—a legacy of his father's rejections—we have gone far in comprehending both his marital problems and his obsession with immortality, with immortality in any form, even that of a child . . ."

—from *The Last Alchemist*
by Russell E. Barrett

3
Carolyn

Six months after the implantation of Reynolds' daughter in an artificial womb, I ran into Davis Brent at a pleasure dome where I had taken to spending my afternoons, enjoying the music, writing a memoir of my days with Reynolds, but refraining from infidelity. The child and my concern for Reynolds' mental state had acted to make me conservative: there were important decisions to be made, disturbing events afoot, and I wanted no distractions.

This particular dome was quite small, its walls Maxfield Parrish holographs—alabaster columns and scrolled archways that opened onto rugged mountains drenched in the colors of a pastel sunset; the patrons sat at marble tables, their drab jumpsuits at odds with the decadence of the decor. Sitting there, writing, I felt like some sad and damaged lady of a forgotten age, brought to the sorry pass of autobiography by a disappointment at love.

Without announcing himself, Brent dropped onto the bench opposite me and stared. A smile nicked the corners of his mouth. I waited for him to speak, and finally asked what he wanted.

"Merely to offer my congratulations," he said.

"On what occasion?" I asked.

"The occasion of your daughter."

The implantation had been done under a seal of privacy, and I was outraged that he had discovered my secret.

Before I could speak, he favored me with an unctuous smile and said, "As administrator, little that goes on here escapes me." From the pocket of his jumpsuit he pulled a leather case of the sort used to carry holographs. "I have a daughter myself, a lovely child. I sent her back to Earth some months back." He opened the case, studied the contents, and continued, his words freighted with an odd tension. "I had the computer do a portrait of how she'll look in a few years. Care to see it?"

I took the case and was struck numb. The girl depicted was seven or eight, and was the spitting image of myself at her age.

"I never should have sent her back," said Brent. "It appears the womb has been misshipped, and I may not be able to find her. Even the records have been misplaced. And the tech who performed the implantation, he returned on the ship with the womb and has dropped out of sight."

I came to my feet, but he grabbed my arm and sat me back down. "Check on it if you wish," he said. "But it's the truth. If you want to help find her, you'd be best served by listening."

"Where is she?" A sick chill spread through me, and my heart felt as if it were not beating but trembling.

"Who knows? Sao Paolo, Paris. Perhaps one of the Urban Reserves."

"Please," I said, a catch in my voice. "Bring her back."

"If we work together, I'm certain we can find her."

"What do you want, what could you possibly want from me?"

He smiled again. "To begin with, I want copies of your husband's deep files. I need to know what he's working on."

I had no compunction against telling him; all my concern was for the child. "He's been investigating the possibility of life on the Sun."

The answer dismayed him. "That's ridiculous."

"It's true, he's found it!"

He gaped at me.

"He calls it the Sun Spider. It's huge . . . and made of some kind of plasma."

Brent smacked his forehead as to punish himself for an oversight. "Of course! That section in the *Diaries*." He shook his head in wonderment. "All that metaphysical gabble about particulate life . . . I can't believe that has any basis in fact."

"I'll help you," I said. "But please bring her back!"

He reached across the table and caressed my cheek. I stiffened but did not draw away. "The last thing I want to do is hurt you, Carolyn. Take my word, it's all under control."

Under control.

Now it seems to me that he was right, and that the controlling agency was no man or creature, but a coincidence of possibility and wish such as may have been responsible for the spark that first set fire to the stars.

Over the next two weeks I met several times with Brent, on each occasion delivering various of Reynolds' files; only one remained to be secured, and I assured Brent I would soon have it. How I hated him! And yet we were complicitors. Each time we met in his lab, a place of bare metal walls and computer banks, we would discuss means of distracting Reynolds in order to perform my thefts, and during one occasion I asked why he had chosen Reynolds' work to pirate, since he had never been an admirer.

"Oh, but I am an admirer," he said. "Naturally I despise his personal style, the passing off of drugs and satyrism as scientific method. But I've never doubted his genius. Why, I was the one who approved his residency grant."

Disbelief must have showed on my face, for he went on to say, "It's true. Many of the board were inclined to reject him, thinking he was no longer capable of important work. But when I saw the Solar Equations, I knew he was still a force to reckon with. Have you looked at them?"

"I don't understand the mathematics."

"Fragmentary as they are, they're astounding, elegant. There's something almost mystical about their structure. You get the idea there's no need to study them, that if you keep staring at them they'll crawl into your brain and work some change." He made a church-and-steeple of his fingers. "I hoped he'd finish them here but . . . well, maybe that last file."

We went back to planning Reynolds' distraction. He rarely left the apartment anymore, and Brent and I decided that the time to act would be during his birthday party the next week. He would doubtless be heavily drugged, and I would be able to slip into the back room and access his computer. The discussion concluded, Brent stepped to the door that led to his apartment, keyed it open and invited me for a drink. I declined, but he insisted and I preceded him inside.

The apartment was decorated in appallingly bad taste. His furniture was of a translucent material that glowed a sickly bluish-green, providing the only illumination. Matted under glass on one wall was a twentieth century poster of a poem entitled "Desiderata," whose verses were the height of mawkish romanticism. The other walls were hung with what appeared to be ancient tapestries, but which on close inspection proved to be pornographic counterfeits, depicting subjects such as women mating with stags. Considering these appointments, I found hypocritical Brent's condemnation of Reynolds' private life. He poured wine from a decanter and made banal small talk, touching me now and then as he had during our first meeting. I forced an occasional smile, and at last, thinking I had humored him long enough, I told him I had to leave.

"Oh, no," he said, encircling my waist with an arm. "We're not through."

I pried his arm loose: he was not very strong.

"Very well." He touched a wall control, and a door to the corridor slid open. "Go."

The harsh white light shining through the door transformed him into a shadowy figure and made his pronouncement seem a threat.

"Go on." He drained his wine. "I've got no hold on you."

God, he thought he was clever! And he was . . . more clever than I, perhaps more so than Reynolds. And though he was to learn that cleverness has its limits, particularly when confronted by the genius of fate, it was sufficient to the moment.

"I'll stay," I said.

". . . In the dance of the Spider, in his patterned changes in color, the rhythmic waving of his fiery arms, was a kind of language, the language that the Equations sought to clarify, the language of my dreams. I sat for hours watching him; I recorded several sequences on pocket holographs and carried them about in hopes that this propinquity would illuminate the missing portions of the Equations. I made some progress, but I had concluded that a journey sunwards was the sort of propinquity I needed—I doubted I had the courage to achieve it. However, legislating against my lack of courage was the beauty I had begun to perceive in the Spider's dance, the hypnotic grace: like that of a Balinese dancer, possessing a similar allure. I came to believe that those movements were signaling all knowledge, infinite possibility. My dreams began to be figured with creatures that I would have previously considered impossible— dragons, imps, men with glowing hands or whose entire forms were glowing, all a ghostly, grainy white; now these creatures came to seem not only possible but likely inhabitants of a world that was coming more and more into focus, a world to which I was greatly attracted. Sometimes I would lie in bed all day, hoping for more dreams of that world, of the wizard who controlled it. It may be that I was using the dreams to escape confronting a difficult and frightening choice. But in truth I have lately doubted that it is even mine to make."

—from *Collected Notes*
by Reynolds Dulambre

4
Reynolds

I remember little of the party, mostly dazed glimpses of breasts and thighs, sweaty bodies, lidded eyes. I remember the drift, which was performed by a group of techs. They played Alex's music as an *hommage,* and I was taken back to my years with the old bastard-maker, to memories of beatings, of walking in on him and his lovers, of listening to him pontificate. And, of course, I recalled that night in Mozambique when I watched him claw at his eyes, his face. Spitting missiles of blood, unable to scream, having bitten off his tongue. Sobered, I got to my feet and staggered into the bedroom, where it was less crowded, but still too crowded for my mood. I grabbed a robe, belted it on and keyed my study door.

As I entered, Carolyn leaped up from my computer. On the screen was displayed what looked to be a page from my deep files. She tried to switch off the screen, but I caught her arm and checked the page: I had not been mistaken. "What are you doing?" I shouted, yanking her away from the computer.

"I was just curious." She tried to jerk free.

Then I spotted the microcube barnacled to the computer: she had been recording. "What's that?" I asked, forcing her to look at it. "What's that? Who the hell are you working for?"

She began to cry, but I wasn't moved. We had betrayed each other a thousand times, but never to this degree.

"Damn you!" I slapped her. "Who is it?"

She poured out the story of Brent's plan, his demands on her. "I'm sorry," she said, sobbing. "I'm sorry."

I felt so much then, I couldn't characterize it as fear or anger or any specific emotion. In my mind's eye I saw the child, that scrap of my soul, disappearing down some earthly sewer. I threw off my robe, stepped into a jumpsuit.

"Where are you going?" Carolyn asked, wiping away tears.

I zipped up the jumpsuit.

"Don't!" Carolyn tried to haul me back from the door. "You don't understand!"

I shoved her down, locked the door behind me, and went storming out through the party and into the corridor. Rage flooded me. I needed to hurt Brent. My reason was so obscured that when I reached his apartment, I saw nothing suspicious in the fact that the door was open . . . though I later realized he must have had a spy at the party to warn him of anything untoward. Inside, Brent was lounging in one of those ridiculous glowing chairs, a self-satisfied look on his face, and it was that look more than anything, more than the faint scraping at my rear, that alerted me to danger. I spun around to see a security guard bringing his laser to bear on me. I dove at him, feeling a discharge of heat next to my ear, and we went down together. He tried to gouge my eyes, but I twisted away, latched both hands in his hair and smashed his head against the wall. The third time his head impacted, it made a softer sound than it had the previous two, and I could feel the skull shifting beneath the skin like pieces of broken tile in a sack. I rolled off the guard, horrified, yet no less enraged. And when I saw that Brent's chair was empty, when I heard him shouting in the corridor, even though I knew his shouts would bring more guards, my anger grew so great that I cared nothing for myself, I only wanted him dead.

By the time I emerged from the apartment, he was sprinting around a curve in the corridor. My laser scored the metal wall behind him the instant before he went out of sight. I ran after him. Several of the doorways along the corridor slid open, heads popped out, and on seeing me, ducked back in. I rounded the curve, spotted Brent, and fired again . . . too high by inches. Before I could correct my aim, half-a-dozen guards boiled out of a side corridor and dragged him into cover. Their beams drew smouldering lines in the metal by my hip, at my feet, and I retreated, firing as I did, pounding on the doors, thinking that I would barricade myself in one of the rooms and try to debunk Brent's lies, to reveal his deceit over the intercom. But none of the doors opened, their occupants having apparently been frightened by my weapon.

Two guards poked their heads around the curve, fired, and one of the beams came so near that it torched the fabric of my jumpsuit at the knee. I beat out the flames and ran full tilt. Shouts behind me, beams of ruby light skewering the air above my head. Ahead, I made out a red door that led to a docking arm, and having no choice, I keyed it open and raced along the narrow passageway. The first three moorings were empty, but the fourth had a blue light glowing beside the entrance hatch, signaling the presence of a ship. I slipped inside, latched it, and moved along the tunnel into the airlock; I bolted that shut, then went quickly along the mesh-walled catwalk toward the control room, toward the radio. I was on the point of entering the room, when I felt a shudder go all through the ship and knew it had cast loose, that it was headed sunwards.

Panicked, I burst into the control room. The chairs fronting the instrument panel were empty, the panel itself aflicker with lights; the ship was being run by computer. I sat at the board, trying to override, but no tactic had any effect. Then Brent's voice came over the speakers. "You've bought yourself a little time, Reynolds," he said. "That's all. When the ship returns, we'll have you."

I laughed.

It had been my hope that he had initiated the ship's flight, but his comments made clear that I was now headed toward the confrontation I had for so long sought to avoid, brought to this pass by a computer under the control of the creature for whom I had searched my entire life, a creature of fire and dreams, the stuff of souls. I knew I would not survive it. But though I had always dreaded the thought of death, now that death was hard upon me, I was possessed of a strange confidence and calm . . . calm enough to send this transmission, to explore the confines of this my coffin, even to read the manuals that explain its operation. I had never attempted to understand the workings of the sunships, and I was interested to read of the principles that underlie each flight. As the ship approaches the Sun, it will monitor the magnetic field direction and determine if the Archimedean spiral of the solar wind is oriented outward.

If all is as it should be, it will descend to within one A.U. and will skip off the open-diverging magnetic field of a coronal hole. It will be traveling at such a tremendous speed, its actions will be rather like those of a charged particle caught in a magnetic field, and as the field opens out, it will be flung upward, back toward Helios . . . that is, it will be flung up and out if a creature who survives by stripping particles of their charge does not inhabit the coronal hole in question. But there is little chance of that.

I wonder how it will feel to have my charge stripped. I would not care to suffer the agonies of my father.

The closer I come to the Sun, the more calm I become. My mortal imperfections seem to be flaking away. I feel clean and minimal, and I have the notion that I will soon be even simpler, the essential splinter of a man. I have so little desire left that only one further thing occurs to me to say.

Carolyn, I . . .

". . . A man walking in a field of golden grass under a bright sky, walking steadfastly, though with no apparent destination, for the grasslands spread to the horizon, and his thoughts are crystal-clear, and his heart, too, is clear, for his past has become an element of his present, and his future—visible as a sweep of golden grass carpeting the distant hills, beyond which lies a city sparkling like a glint of possibility—is as fluent and clear as his thought, and he knows his future will be shaped by his walking, by his thought and the power in his hands, especially by that power, and of all this he wishes now to speak to a woman whose love he denied, whose flesh had the purity of the clear bright sky and the golden grasses who was always the heart of his life even in the country of lies, and here in the heartland of the country of truth is truly loved at last . . ."

—from *The Resolute Lover*
part of The White Dragon Cycle

5
Carolyn

After Reynolds had stolen the sunship—this, I was informed, had been the case—Brent confined me to my apartment and accused me of conspiring with Reynolds to kill him. I learned of Reynolds' death from the security guard who brought me supper that first night; he told me that a prominence (I pictured it to be a fiery fishing lure) had flung itself out from the Sun and incinerated the ship. I wept uncontrollably. Even after the computers began to translate the coded particle bursts emanating from the Spider's coronal hole, even when these provided to be the completed Solar Equations, embodied not only in mathematics but in forms comprehensible to a layman, still I wept. I was too overwhelmed by grief to realize what they might portend.

I was able to view the translations on Reynolds' computer, and when the stories of The White Dragon Cycle came into view, I understood that whoever or whatever had produced them had something in particular to say to me. It was *The Resolute Lover,* the first of the cycle, with its numerous references to a wronged beautiful woman, that convinced me of this. I read the story over and over, and in so doing I recalled Brent's description of the feelings he had had while studying the equations. I felt in the focus of some magical lens, I felt a shimmering in my flesh, confusion in my thoughts . . . not a confusion of motive but of thoughts running in new patterns, colliding with each other like atoms bred by a runaway reactor. I lost track of time, I lived in a sweep of golden grasses, in an exotic city where the concepts of unity and the divisible were not opposed, where villains and heroes and beasts enacted ritual passions, where love was the ordering pulse of existence.

One day Brent paid me a visit. He was plumped with self-importance, with triumph. But though I hated him, emotion seemed incidental to my goal—a goal his visit helped to solidify—and I reacted to him mildly, watching as he moved about the room, watching me and smiling.

"You're calmer than I expected," he said.

I had no words for him, only calm. In my head the Resolute Lover gazed into a crystal of Knowledge, awaiting the advent of Power. I believe that I, too, smiled.

"Well," he said. "Things don't always work out as we plan. But I'm pleased with the result. The Spider will be Reynolds' great victory . . . no way around that. Still, I've managed to land the role of Sancho Panza to his Don Quixote, the rationalist who guided the madman on his course."

My smile was a razor, a knife, a flame.

"Quite sufficient," he went on, "to secure my post . . . and perhaps even my immortality."

I spoke to him in an inaudible voice that said Death.

His manner grew more agitated; he twitched about the room, touching things. "What will I do with you?" he said. "I'd hate to send you to your judgment. Our nights together . . . well, suffice it to say I would be most happy if you'd stay with me. What do you think? Shall I testify on your behalf, or would you prefer a term on the Urban Reserves?"

Brent, Brent, Brent. His name was a kind of choice.

"Perhaps you'd like time to consider?" he said.

I wished my breath was poison.

He edged toward the door. "When you reach a decision, just tell the guard outside. You've two months till the next ship. I'm betting you'll choose survival."

My eyes sent him a black kiss.

"Really, Carolyn," he said. "You were never a faithful wife. Don't you think this pose of mourning somewhat out of character?"

Then he was gone, and I returned to my reading.

Love.

What part did it play in my desire for vengeance, my furious calm? Sorrow may have had more a part, but love was certainly a factor. Love as practiced by the Resolute Lover. This story communicated this rigorous emotion, and my heartsickness translated it to vengeful form. My sense of unreality, of tremulous being, increased day by day, and I barely touched my meals.

I am not sure when the Equations embodied by the story began to take hold, when the seeded knowledge became power. I believe it was nearly two weeks after Brent's visit. But though I felt my potential, my strength, I did not act immediately. In truth, I was not certain I could act or that action was to be my course. I was mad in the same way Reynolds had been: a madness of self-absorption, a concentration of such intensity that nothing less intense had the least relevance.

One night I left off reading, went into my bedroom and put on a sheer robe, then wrapped myself in a cowled cloak. I had no idea why I was doing this. The seductive rhythms of the story were coiling through my head and preventing thought. I walked into the front room and stood facing the door. Violent tremors shook my body. I felt frail, insubstantial, yet at the same time possessed of fantastic power: I knew that nothing could resist me . . . not steel or flesh or fire. Inspired by this confidence, I reached out my right hand to the door. The hand was glowing a pale white, its form flickering, the fingers lengthening and attenuating, appearing to ripple as in a graceful dance. I did not wonder at this. Everything was as it should be. And when my hand slid into the door, into the metal, neither did I consider that remarkable. I could feel the mechanisms of the lock; I—or rather my ghostly fingers—seemed to know the exact function of every metal bit, and after a moment the door hissed open.

The guard peered in, startled, and I hid the hand behind me. I backed away, letting the halves of my cloak fall apart. He stared, glanced left and right in the corridor, and entered. "How'd you do the lock?" he asked.

I said nothing.

He keyed the door, testing it, and slid it shut, leaving the two of us alone in the room. "Huh," he said. "Must have been a computer foul-up."

I came close beside him, my head tipped back as if to receive a kiss, and he smiled, he held me around the waist. His lips mashed against mine, and my right hand, seeming almost to be acting on its own, slipped into his side and touched something that beat wildly for a few seconds, and then spasmed. He pushed me away, clutching his chest, his face purpling, and fell to the floor. Emotionless, I stepped over him and went out into the corridor, walking at an unhurried pace, hiding my hand beneath the cloak.

On reaching Brent's apartment, I pressed the bell, and a moment later the door opened and he peered forth, looking sleepy and surprised. "Carolyn!" he said. "How did you get out?"

"I told the guard I planned to stay with you," I said, and as I had done with the guard, I parted the halves of my cloak.

His eyes dropped to my breasts. "Come in," he said, his voice blurred.

Once inside, I shed the cloak, concealing my hand behind me. I was so full of hate, my mind was heavy and blank like a stone. Brent poured some wine, but I refused the glass. My voice sounded dead, and he shot me a searching look and asked if I felt well. "I'm fine," I told him.

He set down the wine and came toward me, but I moved away.

"First," I said, "I want to know about my daughter."

That brought him up short. "You have no daughter," he said after a pause. "It was all a hoax."

"I don't believe you."

"I swear it's true," he said. "When you went for an exam, I had the tech inform you of a pregnancy. But you weren't pregnant. And when you came for the implantation procedure, he anesthetized you and simply stood by until you woke up."

It would have been in character, I realized, for him to have done this. Yet he also might have been clever enough to make up the story, and thus keep a hold on me, one he could inform me of should I prove recalcitrant

"But you can have a child," he said, sidling toward me. "Our child, Carolyn. I'd like that, I'd like it very much." He seemed to be having some difficulty in getting the next words out, but finally they came: "I love you."

What twisted shape, I wondered, did love take in his brain?

"Do you?" I said.

"I know it must be hard to believe," he said. "You can't possibly understand the pressure I've been under, the demands that forced my actions. But I swear to you, Carolyn, I've always cared for you. I knew how oppressed you were by Reynolds. Don't you see? To an extent I was acting on your behalf. I wanted to free you."

He said all this in a whining tone, edging close, so close I could smell his bitter breath. He put a hand on my breast, lifted it. . . . Perhaps he did love me in his way, for it seemed a treasuring touch. But mine was not. I laid my palely glowing hand on the back of his neck. He screamed, went rigid, and oh, how that scream made me feel! It was like music, his pain. He stumbled backward, toppled over one of the luminous chairs, and lay writhing, clawing his neck.

"Where is she?" I asked, kneeling beside him.

Spittle leaked between his gritted teeth. "I'll . . . find her, bring her . . . oh!"

I saw I could never trust him. Desperate, he would say anything. He might bring me someone else's child. I touched his stomach, penetrating the flesh to the first joint of my fingers, then wiggling them. Again he screamed. Blood mapped the front of his jumpsuit.

"Where is she?" I no longer was thinking about the child: she was lost, and I was only tormenting him.

His speech was incoherent, he tried to hump away. I showed him my hand, how it glowed, and his eyes bugged.

"Do you still love me?" I asked, touching his groin, hooking my fingers and pulling at some fiber.

Agony bubbled in his throat, and he curled up around his pain, clutching himself.

I could not stop touching him. I orchestrated his screams, producing short ones, long ones, ones that held a strained hoarse chord. My hatred was a distant emotion. I felt no fury, no glee. I was merely a craftsman, working to prolong his death. Pink films occluded the whites of his eyes, his teeth were stained to crimson, and at last he lay still.

I sat beside him for what seemed a long time. Then I donned my cloak and walked back to my apartment. After making sure no one was in the corridor, I dragged the dead guard out of the front room and propped him against the corridor wall. I reset the lock, stepped inside, and the door slid shut behind me. I felt nothing. I took up *The Resolute Lover*, but even my interest in it had waned. I gazed at the walls, growing thoughtless, remembering only that I had been somewhere, done some violence; I was perplexed by my glowing hand. But soon I fell asleep, and when I was waked by the guards unlocking the door, I found that the hand had returned to normal.

"Did you hear anything outside?" asked one of the guards.

"No," I said. "What happened?"

He told me the gory details, about the dead guard and Brent. Like everyone else on Helios Station, he seemed more confounded by these incomprehensible deaths than by the fantastic birth that had preceded them.

"The walls of the station have been plated with gold, the corridors are thronged with tourists, with students come to study the disciplines implicit in the Equations, disciplines that go far beyond the miraculous transformation of my hand. Souvenir shops sell holos of the Spider, recordings of The White Dragon Cycle (now used to acclimate children to the basics of the equations), and authorized histories of the sad events surrounding the Spider's emergence. The pleasure domes reverberate with Alex Dulambre's drifts, and in an auditorium constructed for this purpose, Reynolds' clone delivers daily lectures on the convoluted circumstances of his death and triumph. The place is half amusement park, half shrine. Yet the greatest memorial to Reynolds' work is not here; it lies beyond the orbit of Pluto and consists of a vast shifting structure of golden light wherein dwell those students who have mastered the disciplines and overcome the bonds of corporeality. They are engaged, it is said, in an unfathomable work that may have taken its inspiration from Reynolds' metaphysical flights of fancy, or—and many hold to this opinion—may reflect the Spider's design, his desire to rid himself of the human nuisance by setting us upon a new evolutionary course. After Brent's death I thought to join in this work. But my mind was not suited to the disciplines; I had displayed all the mastery of which I was capable in dispensing with Brent.

"I have determined to continue the search for my daughter. It may be—as Brent claimed—that she does not exist, but it is all that is left to me, and I have made my resolve accordingly. Still, I have not managed to leave the station, because I am drawn to Reynolds' clone. Again and again I find myself in the rear of the auditorium, where I watch him pace the dias, declaiming in his most excited manner. I yearn to approach him, to learn how like Reynolds he truly is. I am certain he has spotted me on several occasions, and I wonder what he is thinking, how it would be to speak to him, touch him. Perhaps this is perverse of me, but I cannot help wondering . . ."

—from *Days In The Sun*
by Carolyn Dulambre

6
Carolyn/Reynolds

I had been wanting to talk with her since . . . well, since this peculiar life began. Why? I loved her, for one thing. But there seemed to be a far more compelling reason, one I could not verbalize. I suppressed the urge for a time, not wanting to hurt her; but seeing that she had begun to appear at the lectures, I finally decided to make an approach.

She had taken to frequenting a pleasure dome named Spider's. Its walls were holographic representations of the Spider, and these were strung together with golden webs that looked molten against the black backdrop, like seams of unearthly fire. In this golden dimness the faces of the patrons glowed like spirits, and the glow seemed to be accentuated by the violence of the music. It was not a place to my taste, nor—I suspect—to hers. Perhaps her patronage was a form of courage, of facing down the creature who had caused her so much pain.

I found her seated in a rear corner, drinking an Amouriste, and when I moved up beside her table, she paid me no mind. No one ever approached her; she was as much a memorial as the station itself, and though she was still a beautiful woman, she was treated like the wife of a saint. Doubtless she thought I was merely pausing by the table, looking for someone. But when I sat opposite her, she glanced up and her jaw dropped.

"Don't be afraid," I said.

"Why should I be afraid?"

"I thought my presence might . . . discomfort you."

She met my eyes unflinchingly. "I suppose I thought that, too."

"But . . ?"

"It doesn't matter."

A silence built between us.

She wore a robe of golden silk, cut to expose the upper swells of her breasts, and her hair was pulled back from her face, laying bare the smooth serene lines of her beauty, a beauty that had once fired me, that did so even now.

"Look," I said. "For some reason I was drawn to talk to you, I feel I have . . ."

"I feel the same." She said this with a strong degree of urgency, but then tried to disguise the fact. "What shall we talk about?"

"I'm not sure."

She tapped a finger on her glass. "Why don't we walk?"

Everyone watched as we left, and several people followed us into the corridor, a circumstance that led me to suggest that we talk in my apartment. She hesitated, then signalled agreement with the briefest of nods. We moved quickly through the crowds, managing to elude our pursuers, and settled into a leisurely pace. Now and again I caught her staring at me, and asked if anything was wrong.

"Wrong?" She seemed to be tasting the word, trying it out. "No," she said. "No more than usual."

I had thought that when I did talk to him I would find he was merely a counterfeit, that he would be nothing like Reynolds, except in the most superficial way. But this was not the case. Walking along that golden corridor, mixing with the revelers who poured between the shops and bars, I felt toward him as I had on the day we had met in the streets of Abidjan: powerfully attracted, vulnerable, and excited. And yet I did perceive a difference in him. Whereas Reynolds' presence had been commanding and intense, there had been a brittleness to that intensity, a sense that his diamond glitter might easily be fractured. With this Reynolds, however, there was no such inconstancy. His presence—while potent—was smooth, natural, and unflawed.

Everywhere we walked we encountered the fruits of the Equations: matter transmitters; rebirth parlors, where one could experience a transformation of both body and soul; and the omnipresent students, some of them half-gone into a transcorporeal state, cloaked to hide this fact, but their condition evident by their inward-looking eyes. With Reynolds beside me, all this seemed comprehensible, not—as before—a carnival of meaningless improbabilities. I asked what he felt on seeing the results of his work, and he said, "I'm really not concerned with it."

"What are you concerned with?"

"With you, Carolyn," he said.

The answer both pleased me and made me wary. "Surely you must have more pressing concerns," I said.

"Everything I've done was for you." A puzzled expression crossed his face.

"Don't pretend with me!" I snapped, growing angry. "This isn't a show; this isn't the auditorium."

He opened his mouth, but bit back whatever he had been intending to say, and we walked on.

"Forgive me," I said, realizing the confusion that must be his. "I . . ."

"No need for forgiveness," he said. "All our failures are behind us now."

I didn't know from where these words were coming. They were my words, yet they also seemed spoken from a place deep inside myself, one whose existence had been hidden until now, and it was all I could do to hold them back. We passed into the upper levels of the station, where the permanent staff was quartered, and as we rounded a curve, we nearly ran into a student standing motionless, gazing at the wall: a pale young man with black hair, a thin mouth, and a gray cape. His eyes were dead-looking, and his voice sepulchral. "It awaits," he said.

They are so lost in self-contemplation, these students, that they are likely to say anything. Some fancy them oracles, but not I: their words struck me as being random, sparks from a frayed wire.

"What awaits?" I asked, amused.

"Life . . . the city."

"Ah," I said. "And how do I get there?"

"You . . ." He lapsed into an open-mouthed stare.

Carolyn pulled at me, and we set off again. I started to make a joke about the encounter, but seeing her troubled expression, I restrained myself.

When we entered my apartment, she stopped in the center of the living room, transfixed by the walls. I had set them to display the environment of the beginning of *The Resolute Lover:* an endless sweep of golden grasses, with a sparkling on the horizon that might have been the winking of some bright tower.

"Does this bother you?" I asked, gesturing at the walls.

"No, they startled me, that's all." She strolled along, peering at the grasses, as if hoping to catch sight of someone. Then she turned, and I spoke again from that deep hidden place, a place that now—responding to the sight of her against those golden fields—was spreading all through me.

"Carolyn, I love you," I said . . . and this time I knew who it was that spoke.

He had removed his cloak, and his body was shimmering, embedded in that pale glow that once had made a weapon of my right hand. I backed away, terrified. Yet even in the midst of fear, it struck me that I was not as terrified as I should have been, that I was not at the point of screaming, of fleeing.

"It's me, Carolyn," he said.

"No," I said, backing further away.

"I don't know why you should believe me." He looked at his flickering hand. "I didn't understand it myself until now."

"Who are you?" I asked, gauging the distance to the door.

"You know," he said. "The Spider . . . he's all through the station. In the computer, the labs, even in the tanks from which my cells were grown. He's brought us together again."

He tried to touch me, and I darted to the side.

"I won't hurt you," he said.

"I've seen what a touch can do."

"Not my touch, Carolyn."

I doubted I could make it to the door, but readied myself for a try.

"Listen to me, Carolyn," he said. "Everything we wanted in the beginning, all the dreams and fictions of love, they can be ours."

"I never wanted that," I said. "You did! I only wanted normalcy, not some . . ."

"All lovers want the same thing," he said. "Disillusionment leads them to pretend they want less." He stretched out his hands to me. "Everything awaits us, everything is prepared. How this came to be, I can't explain. Except that it makes a funny kind of sense for the ultimate result of science to be an incomprehensible magic."

I was still afraid, but my fear was dwindling, lulled by the rhythms of his words, and though I perceived him to be death, I also saw clearly that he was Reynolds, Reynolds made whole.

"This was inevitable," he said. "We both knew something miraculous could happen . . . that's why we stayed together, despite everything. Don't be afraid. I could never hurt you more than I have."

"What's inevitable?" I asked. He was too close for me to think of running, and I thought I could delay him, put him off with questions.

"Can't you feel it?" He was so close, now, I could feel his heat. "I can't tell you what it is, Carolyn, only that it is, that it's life . . . a new life."

"The Spider," I said. "I don't understand, I . . ."

"No more questions," he said, and slipped the robe from my shoulders.

His touch was warmer than natural, making my eyelids droop, but causing no pain. He pulled me down to the floor, and in a moment he was inside me, we were heart to heart, moving together, enveloped in that pale flickering glow; and amidst the pleasure I felt, there was pain, but so little it did not matter . . .

. . . and I, too, was afraid, afraid I was not who I thought, that flames and nothingness would obliterate us, but in having her once again, in the consummation of my long wish, my doubts lessened . . .

. . . and I could no longer tell whether my eyes were open or closed, because sometimes when I thought them closed, I could see him, his face slack with pleasure, head flung back . . .

. . . and when I thought they were open I would have a glimpse of another place wherein she stood beside me, glimpses at first too brief for me to fix them in mind . . .

. . . and everything was whirling, changing, my body, my spirit, all in flux, and death—if this was death—was a long decline, a sweep of golden radiance, and behind me I could see the past reduced to a plain and hills carpeted with golden grasses . . .

. . . and around me golden towers, shimmering, growing more stable and settling into form moment by moment, and people shrouded in golden mist who were also becoming more real, acquiring scars and rags and fine robes, carrying baskets and sacks . . .

. . . and this was no heaven, no peaceful heaven, for as we moved beneath those crumbling towers of yellow stone, I saw soldiers with oddly shaped spears on the battlements, and the crowds around us were made up of hardbitten men and women wearing belted daggers, and old crones bent double under the weight of sacks of produce, and younger women with the look of ill-usage about them, who leaned from the doors and windows of smoke-darkened houses and cried out their price . . .

. . . and the sun overhead seemed to shift, putting forth prominences that rippled and undulated as in a dance, and shone down a ray of light to illuminate the tallest tower, the one we had sought for all these years, the one whose mystery we must unravel . . .

. . . and the opaque image of an old man in a yellow robe was floating above the crowd, his pupils appearing to shift, to put forth fiery threads as did the sun, and he was haranguing us, daring us all to penetrate his tower, to negotiate his webs and steal the secrets of time . . .

. . . and after wandering all day, we found a room in an inn not half a mile from the wizard's tower, a mean place with grimy walls and scuttlings in the corners and a straw mattress that crackled when we lay on it. But it was so much more than we'd had in a long, long time, we were delighted, and when night had fallen, with moonlight streaming in and the wizard's tower visible through a window against the deep blue of the sky, the room seemed palatial. We made love until well past midnight, love as we had never practiced it: trusting, unfettered by inhibition. And afterward, still joined, listening to the cries and music of the city, I suddenly remembered my life in that other world, the Spider, Helios Station, everything, and from the tense look on Carolyn's face, from her next words, I knew that she, too, had remembered.

"Back at Helios," she said, "we were making love, lying exactly like this, and . . ." She broke off, a worry line creasing her brow. "What if this is all a dream, a moment between dying and death?"

"Why should you think that?"

"The Spider . . . I don't know. I just felt it was true."

"It's more reasonable to assume that everything is a form of transition between the apartment and this room. Besides, why would the Spider want you to to die?"

"Why has he done any of this? We don't even know what he is . . . a demon, a god."

"Or something of mine," I said.

"Yes, that . . . or death."

I stroked her hair, and her eyelids fluttered down.

"I'm afraid to go to sleep," she said.

"Don't worry," I said. "I think there's more to this than death."

"How do you know?"

"Because of how we are."

"That's why I think it *is* death," she said. "Because it's too good to last."

"Even if it is death," I told her, "in this place death might last longer than our old lives."

Of course I was certain of very little myself, but I managed to soothe her, and soon she was asleep. Out the window, the wizard's tower—if, indeed, that's what it was—glowed and rippled, alive with power, menacing in its brilliance. But I was past being afraid. Even in the face of something as unfathomable as a creature who has appropriated the dream of a man who may have dreamed it into existence and fashioned thereof either a life or a death, even in a world of unanswerable questions, when love is certain—love, the only question that is its own answer—everything becomes quite simple, and, in the end, a matter of acceptance.

We live in an old chaos of the sun.

—Wallace Stevens

SCIENCE FICTION AND "LITERATURE"—OR, THE CONSCIENCE OF THE KING

Delivered at Minicon, 1979

Samuel R. Delany

Samuel R. Delany is one of the great living SF writers, with a reputation extending far beyond the SF field for his literary criticism (he has written a book on Wagner and Artaud, and influential pieces on gay writers and on black writers—he himself is black and gay). His SF includes the controversial novel *Dhalgren, Babel 17, The Einstein Intersection,* and his fantasy *Neveryon* series. He won a Hugo Award as well for his volume of autobiography, *The Motion of Light in Water.* In this piece, he considers one of the central issues of the SF field, the relationship of the genre of science fiction to the main body of literature.

At Oxford in 1892 the French poet Mallarmé delivered a lecture that began with the now-famous line, *"On à touché au vers"*: someone has been tampering with poetry. Today, some eighty years later, I had thought of beginning, "Someone has been tampering with science fiction." But if I did, I would have to make some distinctions between 1892 and 1979 right off. For one thing, in 1892 the person who was doing (by far!) the most tampering was Mallarmé himself—along with a few poets who were comparatively closely associated with him (they came for coffee every Tuesday evening).

The tampering I'm talking of is not coming from within science fiction. When I read writers who are just my juniors, in length of time published if not in age (John Varley, James Tiptree, Jr., Michael Bishop, Vonda McIntyre, Jean Mark Gawron, Suzy McKee Charnas, or Joseph Haldeman, to name the most random few), though of course I see local disagreements, a whole variety of different approaches to the world between them and me, between each of them and each other, I don't sense any violent rupture between these newer writers and those writers who are my immediate contemporaries (Disch, Le Guin, Niven, Russ, Zelazny, to name another random few). Also, though most of us within the field no doubt feel the New Wave controversy of a decade or so ago is far too frequently exhumed, there's at least one point about it that is all too seldom made and might well vanish if someone doesn't record it. Again, there were obviously a variety of local differences. But even the term *New Wave* (first used for science fiction in 1966), which was applied to me often enough by 1968, gained its currency mainly in the mouths of a number of writers who apparently took a great deal of pleasure in standing up on platforms and saying, "Well, I guess I'm an Old Wave writer." I can honestly say I never seriously referred to myself as a "New Wave writer" and the number of times I did jokingly could be counted on one hand; and I think the same would probably go for the other writers who, from time to time, got lumbered with the term. Consider: The writer whom I personally heard say, most often and from the most platforms, "Well I guess I'm an Old Wave writer," was Frederik Pohl, who was back then my most supportive editor at the now-defunct magazines *If* and *Worlds of Tomorrow*. Today he is my most supportive editor at Bantam Books. Does this allow for differences? Yes. But it doesn't speak of rupture.

The tampering I'm talking about does produce a sense of rupture. Though there is much disagreement among writers of all generations about whether this rupture is a good or a bad thing, we all sense it. It is the tampering that comes from academia, from critics who have become "interested" in science fiction.

Mallarmé came from Paris to Oxford to defend his own tampering and that of his fellow poets. I have barely recovered from a term as research fellow at the Center for Twentieth Century Studies at the University of Wisconsin (research topic: contemporary science fiction) and have limped back to the fold here . . . to *defend* academic tampering.

"*On à touché au vers?*" Well, to paraphrase Yale critic Paul de Man, "*On à touché au critique.*" People have also been tampering with academic criticism recently. Myself, I've been tampering with SF criticism for all I'm worth. But the only way to launch a good defense of anything is first to separate out what's definitely bad; when something doesn't work and leads nowhere, covering it up doesn't do anyone any good. We have to locate why this tampering is experienced as rupture and as encounter—and I don't mean simple xenophobia. Having had a chance to teach science fiction at two universities in the last few years, as well as a chance to write my share of criticism and survey the present academic response to science fiction, I'm in a particularly good position to experience the rupture aspect—and yes, it *is* an experience!

In 1975, when I was organizing a scholarly symposium on science fiction at the University of Buffalo, SUNY, I was extremely excited to have in attendance an exemplary Joyce scholar and literary theoretician who was about to publish a book on science fiction with a polysyllabic title from a highly respected university press. The day the symposium began, advance copies of the book arrived. I made a breakfast appointment with this very affable gentleman to discuss his book with him the next day—and stayed up till four o'clock in the morning reading the book twice and filling the margins with notes and comments. Over scrambled eggs and toast, I gave him my notes: they ranged from proofreading errors to corrections of dates to respectful deferences on matters of opinion. But at one point I referred to something he had said about the use of matter transmission in science fiction, using Niven's *Ringworld* for his example. His idea had to do with "matter transmission as a metaphor for telekinesis" and what he felt telekinesis meant to people. "I'm just curious," I said, "why, if you wanted to make a point about telekinesis, you didn't refer, say, to Alfred Bester's *The Stars My Destination*, where the idea is dealt with directly and in very much the manner that you outline. Do you think, perhaps, the book has received too much attention? Or perhaps it's not as good as people are always going on as if it were?"

And this gentleman, who had been writing so eloquently about Le Guin's themes and Sturgeon's prose, looked at me with perfect ingenuousness and asked: "Bester? *The Stars My Destination*? Is this a book or an author I should have heard of before?"

This is totally disorienting; it throws the whole discussion onto the level of surrealism. Someone who writes a book on a topic, about whom you can say "They don't know the field," is usually someone who gets dates wrong, forgets small facts, comes to wrongheaded opinions. Perhaps there are a number of important works they haven't read recently enough or closely enough and therefore are relying too heavily on what another writer had to say about them. But imagine asking someone who has just written a book on twentieth-century poetry why T. S. Eliot or *The Waste Land* weren't mentioned, only to get the perfectly serious answer, "T. S. Eliot? *The Waste Land*? Is this a poem or a poet I should have heard of before?"

This is rupture.

And it is a rupture that a graduate degree generally precludes from the field of literary studies.

This particular critic, I'm happy to report, over the following two years did a lot of homework and wrote a much better book on science fiction with a much less polysyllabic title, which was published by a different university press.

But the experience of rupture remains.

Then there was the academic critic who had discovered Michael Moorcock's delightful *Warlord of the Air* and claimed, in a chapter on science fiction in his book on the fantastic, that Mr. Moorcock had, out of sheer original genius, invented an entirely new subgenre of science fiction, which he dubbed "the historical alternative story." He went on to say that, although he suspected there would be a lot of argument among regular SF fans about whether Moorcock's brand-new SF twist should be accepted or not, he felt this new form really should be included in the overall genre of science fiction . . . just as if Dick's *The Man in the High Castle* had never been written, nor been presented its much deserved Hugo Award for best SF novel of its year—not to mention his complete ignorance of all the other parallel-world stories ("historical alternative" indeed!) from Ward Moore's *Bring the Jubilee* to Hilary Bailey's "The Fall of Frenchy Steiner" and Joanna Russ's *The Female Man*! This same academic, comparing the reader response to Sturgeon's *More Than Human* and Clarke's *Childhood's End* (two novels published in 1953), though noting that both books were good felt Sturgeon's was the better; he then went on to locate internal reasons in both novels to explain why the Clarke had outsold the Sturgeon! Does anyone remember that about ten years ago there was a very successful movie called *2001: A Space Odyssey*, which catapulted Clarke into a multimillion-dollar ad campaign, from which time the numerous reprints of all his books by and large date? If you compare the first fourteen years of both books, you find that both were reprinted six times; and according to people who were then at Ballantine Books, the paperback publisher of both novels, the Sturgeon marginally outsold the Clarke! So much for internal reasons.

Perhaps the most awkward ignorance I've encountered in an academic concerned what academics themselves have done in science fiction: on the organizing end of another SF symposium, I recently received an abstract of a paper to be presented that opened with the blanket statement that nobody ever took science fiction seriously before 1973! The first time I was ever invited to address the Modern Language Association on science fiction was in 1967. But the Continuing Seminar on Science Fiction of the Modern Language Association was founded in 1958—indeed, it is the second-oldest continuing seminar in that august organization that includes thousands of college professors!

I experience all of these as rupture. They represent simple ignorance. They are bad criticism. The healthiest response I can think of to start with is a good, hearty laugh. But we can't stop with laughter, because there is so much ignorance. One of the things laughter allows us to do is get back far enough to see that there *is* a pattern of it. The rupture we experience—that I experience—is not a rupture that comes from the critics' abuse of specific texts. After all, I've been reading SF book reviews in the magazines for going on twenty-five years, and I've certainly developed enough calluses to badly thought-out appraisals of individual SF books by now.

The rupture I experience is a rupture with my own knowledge of the history of SF writing. The working assumption of most academic critics (an assumption that certainly, yes, distorts what they have to say of specific texts) is that somehow the history of science fiction began precisely at the moment they began to read it—or, as frequently, in the nebulous yesterday of sixteenth- and seventeenth-century utopias. For both notions accomplish the same thing: they obviate the real lives, the real development, and finally the real productions of real SF writers, a goodly number of whom are still alive, if not kicking. This is why the best histories of science fiction remain the commentaries of Merril and Asimov in their various anthologies, the collected reviews of Knight in *In Search of Wonder,* of Blish in *The Issue at Hand* and *More Issues at Hand,* and of the Panshins in *SF in Dimension*; for the rest one must go digging through back issues of old SF magazines for reviews by Merril, Budrys, del Rey, and Miller. Frequently wrong, frequently brilliant, wrong or right they were *responding* to what was happening in the field; and their criticism, in conjunction with the texts, is the only way to *find* what was happening, whether as ambiance or as dates and occurrences. And this is equally why something like Aldiss' *Billion Year Spree,* entertaining as parts of it are, is basically useless as a history of science fiction—for it covers desultory writing from Mary Shelley's *Frankenstein* to the first use of the term *science fiction* in 1929, then careens through all that legitimately bears the SF label itself in a handful of pages that, once it passes the Second World War, becomes mere listing.

Then what do we do with this debacle of historical ignorance; what do we do with the rupture?

I'll start by telling you the very first time I sensed it—because, oddly, back then it did *not* come from an academic. It came from directly within the SF precincts. In 1966 I attended my first World Science Fiction Convention (the twenty-fourth annual), the Tricon, with somewhat over three thousand attendees, held over Labor Day weekend in Cleveland. All the talk among the professional writers that year was of one New York editor at a major publishing house who had just upped his company's output of hardcover science fiction from two novels a year, which it had been for the last ten years, to twenty-four (!) novels a year (which, incidentally, it has been for the last twelve years). All we pros, young and old, talked of this man in reverent tones as a great gentleman, practically a scholar, seriously committed to the field and deeply concerned with the development of the genre. That weekend Roger Zelazny's *This Immortal* tied with Frank Herbert's *Dune* for the Hugo. Indeed, that weekend was the first time I met Zelazny in person. (Back then, because our last names shared five letters, we were frequently mistaken for one another by readers.) Over dinner with Roger and his wife in the hotel's rather ornate restaurant—it had a transparent plastic bridge over a luminous fishpond—he mentioned that *This Immortal* had, months ago, been submitted to this fabled editor, who'd bounced it. Well, certainly there was nothing remarkable there. But back in New York, a week later, the will of the gods conspired so that this very editor called up and invited *me* to lunch! And that is how it came to pass, during a lull in the conversation after the first very dry martini and before the fillet of sole, that I casually remarked: "I was just in Cleveland last week, and Zelazny's *This Immortal* tied with *Dune* for the Hugo. You may have missed out on something there: Zelazny tells me he submitted it to you and you bounced it."

And the great man, shining hope of the genre, committed to and concerned about the development of the field, looked at me across the rim of his martini glass and, with a slight frown, inquired: "The Hugo award? Now what's that?"

This was my first encounter with that complete dissociation with what I had taken to be the real world: the SF editor of a major publishing house, who himself edited twenty-four SF novels a year, did not in 1966 know what the Hugo award was! It was precisely this feeling that returned, only a few years later, when I began to encounter what, with only a little overpoliteness, one might call "certain academic blind spots."

The point, of course, is that such rupture as we experience it at the hands of academics is not new. We've experienced it before in the hands of editors and publishers who really *do* have their hands on our economic jugular veins. And we've survived it, survived it very well! In 1951 there were some fifteen texts published that could reasonably be called SF novels—including the serials in magazines and the first volume of Isaac Asimov's *Foundation* series, a compilation of stories written since 1942. Last year over 14 percent of *all* original fiction published in the United States was science fiction. (That's just shy of five hundred books.) And so my anecdote about my 1966 editor is finally just curve-fixing to show how sharply the slope has been rising. No, the imposition of a rupture with our own history is not new to us.

You simply cannot break off one history from a phenomenon, however, without replacing it by another—even if you replace it with nothing more than the equally historical assumption that the phenomenon you have just stripped of its past *has* no significant history. We've talked a lot about rupture and only in passing about encounter. The encounter, of course, is between the new history that has been stuck on the original phenomenon and the phenomenon itself—in this case science fiction. Now here's a little leap. But follow it carefully, because it tells a lot about where we're shortly going to go. To say that a phenomenon has *no* significant history at all is a way of allowing yourself to treat it *as if* its history were exactly the same as that of some other phenomenon you are already acquainted with. I don't mean the same in its dates and occurrences, but rather the same in its values, processes, ways of understanding it and responding to it. To say that a phenomenon *does* have a significant history is to say that its history is *different* from the history of something else: that's what makes it significant. To assume that something—like science fiction—has no *significant* history in the past is to assume that its history-to-come will be no different from the last phenomenon whose history you've been studying. (Again, I don't mean identical dates and happenings, but in values and responses to ways the phenomenon can be meaningful.) And the historical phenomenon most literary critics have been studying hardest is, of course, literature.

After we have passed the sense of rupture, here is where we locate the sense of encounter. And it's the growing number of feet of shelf space in bookstores, the growing number of readers who turn to science fiction, the growing number of hours that readers are devoting to science fiction, and the growing number of courses given on science fiction in the country's high schools and universities (over five hundred at last count) that give this encounter its interest and urgency.

What we have to remember, before all our images of growing amounts of shelf space, growing numbers of readers, all with their economic implications and insinuations, is that the battle is *not* between texts.

If I hold a copy of, say, Clement's *Mission of Gravity* in one hand and Salinger's *Catcher in the Rye* in the other, there's no encounter. Even if I read one right after the other, there still is no real encounter between the stories themselves. The encounter comes after both texts are read, in the whole space of values, judgments, ways of response: which responses (and reading itself is basically a *response* to a text) are more pleasurable, which are more useful; and it's only when we reach the question "Which text is more available?" that the whole economic situation which lurks behind our initial set of images for this encounter intrudes on and contours this encounter—rather than being (according to the capitalist ideal anyway) simply an economic response to the encounter itself.

For the purposes of the rest of this essay (and the rest of this book), then, we must think of literature and science fiction not as two different sets of labeled texts, but as two different sets of values, two different ways of response, two different ways of making texts make sense, two different ways of reading—or what one academic tradition would call two different discourses (and the meaning of *discourse* here is not simply explanation, but rather a range of understanding that involves certain characteristic utterances: the larger process that allows explanations to be and be a part of). The encounter, then, is between two discourses, science fiction and literature, and it is won or lost through pleasure and use. The encounter could be hugely influenced by economic availability; but since availability of both discourses seems assured (the one, literature, wide; the other, science fiction, growing), we can discount that for the present.

A number of times I have written extensively about the way the discourse (the way of understanding, the way of responding, the way of reading) called science fiction differs from the discourse called literature, particularly that bulk of literature we SF readers call mundane fiction (from *mundus,* meaning the world; stories that take place on the Earth in the present or past. Any other connotations? Well, turnabout is fair play). There are clear and sharp differences right down to the way we read individual sentences.

Then her world exploded.

If such a string of words appeared in a mundane fiction text, more than likely we would respond to it as an emotionally muzzy metaphor about the inner aspects of some incident in a female character's life. In an SF text, however, we must retain the margin to read these words as meaning that a planet, belonging to a woman, blew up.

He turned on his left side.

The discourse of mundane fiction more or less constrains us to read such a string of words as referring to some kind of masculine, insomniac tossings. SF discourse retains the greater margin to read such words as meaning that a male threw a switch activating the circuitry of his sinistral flank.

And there are many other sentences with a perfectly clear and literal meaning in science fiction that if written within the discourse of mundane fiction (e.g., *The door dilated,* from Heinlein's novel *Beyond This Horizon* [1948]) would simply be meaningless or, at best, extremely awkward.

Consider: There is no sentence I can think of that could theoretically appear in a text of mundane fiction that could not also be worked into some text of science fiction—whereas there are many, many sentences in science fiction that would be hard or impossible to work into a text of mundane fiction. SF discourse gives many sentences clear and literal meanings, sentences that in mundane fiction would be meaningless or at any rate very muzzily metaphorical. Just at the level of lucid and literal sentences, then, which is the larger way of response, the wider range of understanding? Which offers the greater range of readings for possible sentences? The point should be made here, lest I be misunderstood, that greater statistical range does not necessarily mean higher aesthetic accomplishment. Within the precincts of literature, Racine's plays use only about three thousand different words while Shakespeare's use approximately ten thousand—and Joyce's novel *Ulysses* uses over thirty thousand. The relative number of words available and, by extension, the relative number of sentences only suggest why writers of varying temperaments might be attracted to one field or the other.

More recently I have been exploring the way we actually organize the information from SF texts, exploring the organization principles of SF discourse. Because in the discourse of mundane fiction the world is a given, we use each sentence in a mundane fiction text as part of a sort of hunt-and-peck game: All right, what part of the world must I summon up in my imagination to pay attention to (and, equally, what other parts—especially as sentences build up—had I best not pay attention to at all) if I want this story to hang together? In science fiction the world of the story is not a given, but rather a construct that changes from story to story. To read an SF text, we have to indulge a much more fluid and speculative kind of game. With each sentence we have to ask what in the world of the tale would have to be different from our world for such a sentence to be uttered—and thus, as the sentences build up, we build up a world in specific dialogue, in a specific tension, with our present concept of the real.

Again, to take a string of words that, alone, might lend itself to either discourse, here is a sentence from Pohl and Kornbluth's *The Space Merchants:* "I rubbed depilatory soap over my face and rinsed it with the trickle from the fresh water tap."

If this were mundane fiction, because the world in mundane fiction is a given world, we would read the adjective "fresh" (in the real world, of course, the vast majority of water faucets are fresh water faucets) as either an unnecessary writerly redundancy (and therefore an auctorial failing) or some comment on the consciousness of the character: perhaps he is abnormally aware of the water's freshness for some subjective reason. Similarly, the trickle we would read either as support for, or contrast with, this particular subjective state. But though hints of this reading are of course there, in the SF text where it actually occurs this sentence is telling us much, much more. In the world of *The Space Merchants,* because of the overpopulation, apartments have both fresh water *and* salt water taps—and the second half of this sentence is one of the more important phrases from which we learn this. The trickle tells us specifically that the fresh water supply in this particular building is low, even though it's a luxury apartment complex. Yes, states of mind are suggested about the character by this sentence in context; but in SF discourse we must retain the margin to take such information and build a world specifically different from, and in dialogue with, our own.

With readers who have difficulty negotiating the specific rhetoric of the SF text, I've found that their problems center on the numberless rhetorical figures SF writers use to suggest, imply, or sometimes vividly draw the differences between the stories' world and ours. Unless the nature of the world of the story is completely spelled out for them in solid, expository paragraphs, they simply can't take the hints, the suggestions, the little throwaways with which inventive SF writers get this dialogue going in the minds of those readers comfortable with the discourse. They can't form these hints and throwaways into any vision of a different world. But then, where would they have had the opportunity to learn? Certainly not in contemporary mundane fiction. And yes, with practice most of them got a *lot* better at it.

I find science fiction's literalization of the language and its wealth of clear and lucid sentences simply and sensually pleasurable. I find the dialogue it sets up with the real world (a dialogue that mundane fiction simply cannot indulge) both pleasurable and useful—if only because it keeps the possibility of dialogue alive. But if we really want to explore the encounter between values that, finally, *is* the encounter between literature and science fiction, we have to go into the values of literature as well.

The French scholar Michel Foucault is one of the most radical and fascinating thinkers to tackle this problem. In an essay called "What Is an Author?" he notes that many of the values of literary discourse are tied up in the very concept of the "author" of a work. The author (or, as he sometimes calls it, the "author-function") becomes the focus for some of literature's most central values. In this essay he writes:

> It seems . . . that the manner in which literary criticism once defined the author—or rather constructed the author, beginning with existing texts and discourses—is directly derived from the manner in which Christian tradition authenticated (or rejected) the [religious] texts at its disposal. In order to "rediscover" an author in a work, modern literary criticism uses ways similar to those that Christian religious commentary employed when trying to prove the values of a text by its author's saintliness. In *De Viribus illustribus,* Saint Jerome explains that bearing the same name is

not sufficient to identify legitimately authors of more than one work: different individuals could have had the same name, or one man could have, illegitimately, borrowed another's patronymic. . . . How then can one attribute several discourses to one and the same author? How can one use the author-function to determine if one is dealing with one or several individuals? Saint Jerome proposes four criteria: (1) if among several books attributed to an author one is inferior to the others, it must be withdrawn from the list of the author's works (the author is therefore defined as a unified level of value); (2) the same should be done if certain texts contradict the doctrine expounded in the author's other works (the author is then defined as a field of conceptual or theoretical unity); (3) one must also exclude works that are written in a different style, containing words and expressions not ordinarily found in the writer's production (the author is here conceived of as a stylistic unity); (4) finally, one must consider as interpolated those texts which quote people or mention events subsequent to the author's death (the author is here seen as a historical unity and the crossroads of a limited number of events).

Modern literary criticism, even when—as is now customary—it does not concern itself with authentification, still defines the author no differently . . . (using the author's biography, the determination of his individual perspective, the analysis of his social position, and the revelation of his basic design): the author is . . . the principle of a certain unity of writing—all differences having to be resolved, at least in part, by the principles of evolution, maturation, or influence.

This is from a revised version of the lecture *What Is an Author,* given in 1969 at the Société Française de Philosophie, which will soon appear in an anthology *Textual Strategies* (Cornell University Press; Ithaca, 1979), edited by Josúe Y. Harari. (I have very modestly revised the translation at a few points. The unrevised version of this lecture may be found in *Language, Counter-Memory, Practice,* by Michel Foucault, edited by Donald F. Bouchard, Ithaca, New York, Cornell University Press, 1977.)

Clustered around the literary concept of "author," then, we find this quartet of literary values: unity of value, theoretical unity, stylistic unity, historical unity. It is a little sobering to consider that a discipline like literary criticism fell out of the dogmatic religious enterprise. But these values are certainly among its controlling parameters. One of the last major battles in the history of the English novel was the furor over whether or not D. H. Lawrence was to be accepted as a Great Author or consigned to the category of interesting crackpot. The critic R. F. Leavis, in his book on Lawrence that pretty much settled the question (*D. H. Lawrence: Novelist* [1955]), sets out to prove Lawrence's greatness, right in chapter one, by showing the "unity" of Lawrence's works.

And I have seen at least one master's thesis written about my own science fiction that set out to show me an author worthy of serious consideration, by demonstrating the "unity" in my own works.

At this point we have to ask: Are these unities part of SF discourse? Should they be applied to science fiction?

I've already talked about the way, sentence by sentence, science fiction can differ from mundane fiction. I've talked as well about the way science fiction organizes this sentential information—not only into a story but also into a world—differently from the way mundane fiction organizes its information. I also feel that if we look for this quartet of literary unities—valuative, theoretical, stylistic, and historical—in SF discourse, whether clustered around the "author" or not, we will find absolutely diametric values.

Working backwards through them:

One must consider as unauthentic "those texts that quote people or mention events subsequent to the author's death." Well, that certainly lets science fiction out of the historical-unity game! Science fiction's very commitment to its future vision means that the SF writer is always quoting people and mentioning events subsequent to the writer's death! So this basic image of historical unity is denied at the outset. But it's not the image we are concerned with so much as the value as an operative function—and the historical value science fiction seems to operate by, more than any other, is one of historical plurality, a value diametric to the unitary value of literature. This is reflected not only in the diverging historical views within the production of a single writer (nothing stops me from writing three SF stories, all set in New York City in 2001, one in an overpopulated world, one in a depopulated world, and one in a world whose population has managed to stabilize at, say, two and a half billion: they would simply be three different "historical" extrapolations), but also the parallel universe tales set in the pasts that so astonished the academic about whom I wrote earlier.

This is possibly the place to point out that the author, or author-function, simply plays a very different role in SF discourse from the one it plays in the discourse of literature. I doubt I have ever called myself an "SF author"; the term would simply feel too uncomfortable in my mouth. When someone asks me my profession, I say I'm an SF writer. Again, I think most other SF writers feel the same. By and large SF readers tend to be much more concerned with stories than with writers. But this leads us to the next value, the value of unity of style.

Science fiction's origins in the pulps and its persistence as a generally popular writing category simply mitigate against the sort of stylistic unity that literature privileges both in the productions of single writers and, certainly, in the production of the whole field. SF writers are always adopting different styles for different stories; and evolution, maturation, or even influence are just not operative factors: the stories, and the various levels of the readers, demand them. For a good long time now science fiction has been responding to readers of all levels: someone who loves the simplistic thrust of a Perry Rhodan book is probably not going to love the technosocial recomplications of a John Varley or the logicolinguistic invention of a Jean Mark Gawron (although I know of at least one mathematics professor who reads all three avidly). The point, however, is that all three are science fiction. But because of the range of markets, the range of readers, there is simply very little chance of stylistic unity as we find it in the literary concept of author-function. If anything, there seems to be a highly valued ideal of stylistic plurality—especially since the science fiction of the '60s.

And what about theoretical unity? The other side of science fiction's commitment to historical plurality is an equal commitment to theoretical plurality. What has most confounded the folks searching for definitions of science fiction relating to scientific subject matter is the number of SF stories that clearly contradict known science—all the stories with faster-than-light travel, for example. Then, of course, there are all the undeniably SF stories about magic (e.g.,

Cogswell's "Wall Around the World," Blish's *Black Easter*). To say, "Well, in these tales magic is treated in a 'scientific way,'" only confuses the question: currently the existence of magic runs counter to scientific theory, and that's all there is to it. Then there are all the stories about ESP, which, if not exactly contradicted by prevailing theory, are certainly rendered highly dubious by it. Mumbling about "exceptions that prove the rule," whatever that means, simply doesn't cover the case. The concept of theoretical plurality, as an operative value, does. For there to be such a value, science fiction, across its range, *must* deal with conflicting theories. This value does not have to fix itself to the "author" function in science fiction: not every writer feels it necessary to choose opposing theoretical constructs from tale to tale—although many of the best have. I would venture, however, that every SF writer aware that her/his own work is theoretically consistent with itself is also aware of one or more SF writers with whom that theory conflicts, whether the theory be political, sociological, or scientific. And there's your value of theoretical plurality.

Finally there is unity of value itself. As history and theory, whether unitary or plural, form two sides of a single coin, so style and value, whether unitary or plural, form two sides of another (and here, of course, style means a little more than merely the way one uses words: there are styles of thinking, styles of perception). The same factors that ensure that science fiction will not exhibit any unity of style in the literary sense, but rather a plurality of styles both within the production of single writers and throughout the field's range, also ensure that science fiction actively strives for a plurality of value (i.e., worth). Once a text is adjudged "literature," we can say it partakes of a certain (admittedly vague and almost impossible to define) value, a value that, however vague, consists of a juxtaposition of theoretical, stylistic, and historical elements. This value—the text's literary value—mitigates for the text's preservation, its study, its reproduction. But once more, this is *not* the case with science fiction. Having adjudged a text science fiction, we have made no unitary statement, however vague or at whatever level of suggestion or implication, about its value. I suspect this is because, again, innate to the discourse of science fiction is the concept of value plurality.

It may be well to point out here exactly what I have done so that no one is tempted to overvalue *this* exploration. I have simply taken the list of values Foucault has recovered from the literary concept of "author" and let them guide me through a range of science fiction—whereupon I found some values that pretty much oppose the literary ones. I have not necessarily discovered the *most* important values of science fiction. *They* may lie completely elsewhere. The ones I've found are highlighted only when held up against the literary.

So . . . do I feel that science fiction will, or should, be taken over by literature in the current encounter? I sincerely hope it is not. And the only way I feel it can be taken over is for very bad academic criticism—the kind that strips science fiction of its history; that ignores it as a discourse, as a particular way of reading and responding to texts; and that obscures its values of historical, theoretical, stylistic, and valuative plurality—to swamp what I feel is a responsible academic approach, of which I offer my own preceding argument as a modest example.

This brings us to what may well be the most important battlefield in the encounter. Around every text there is a space for interpretation. There is no way to abolish the interpretive space from around the text: it comes into existence as soon as we recognize that words have meanings, most more than one each. Most of us who have a strong sense of that space have it through the interpretive use it has been put to in literary criticism.

Take a sentence from a very entertaining book by the poet John Ciardi, *How Does a Poem Mean*: "A poem is a machine for making choices." Does this mean a poem is a machine to decide between A and B? Or does it mean a poem is a machine for generating situations in which some choice is involved? In other words, is *making choices* to be taken idiomatically (make a choice: choose A or B) or literally (make—that is, create—a choice situation). Having unpacked these two possible meanings from our text, there are several possible ways to relate them, and which one we choose depends on whether our basic discursive values are unitary or plural.

I can say: Let it mean either *one* you want; choose which *one* you prefer. (Liberal as it is, it's still unitary.)

Or I can say: Logically, you can't decide between A and B *until* you've generated the choice situation. Therefore, it must mean generate a choice situation first, then make it. (Here, we've made a logical hierarchy out of the two meanings, which is tantamount to reducing it to a single argument. We're still unitary here.)

If I'm feeling very inventive I can say: first one must choose whether or not to interpret the poetic text, and only after one has made this choice is there the possibility of the text generating a choice situation; so it must mean first choose, then generate. (I've just reversed the hierarchy, but it's still unitary.)

And the other thing I can say is: To read the sentence "A poem is a machine for making choices," we have to read it first one way *or* the other. But the moment we have, the suggestion of the other meaning rises up to obliterate the former in our minds, and the meaning plays back and forth between the two; so that the joy, the wit, the delight of the text comes from that play between *both* meanings, which prevents it from totalizing into any unitary or hierarchical form.

Here we have followed plural values, in an attempt to capture something of the experience of reading the line in the first place—the same experience that got us started on our various unitary interpretations.

Locating the play in the interpretive space, rather than positing a unitary or hierarchical explanation, is something that some of the most intriguing academics have been working with. Some names? Jacques Derrida, Shoshana Felman, Paul de Man, Barbara Johnson. It can be done in a number of ways: In the song from Shakespeare's play *Cymbeline* we find the lines

> *Golden lads and girls all must*
> *As chimney sweepers come to dust.*

It seems a clear (if double) statement about the inevitable death of (or the necessity of work for) even the young and beautiful as well as the dirty and grubby. Some time in the '30s, however, a scholar traveling in Warwickshire, the county of Shakespeare's birth, discovered that the local term for the flowers we call dandelions was *golden boys,* and that when the pale fuzz was blown off the dandelions' heads the farmers then called them *chimney sweepers.* Apparently, these local terms are several hundred years old. Read the two lines again. They haven't *lost* any of their meaning. But a range of play has been introduced with the recovery of the local Warwickshire dialect. If one wants to be "literary" about things, one can hierarchize *all* the meanings into a logical, unitary order to turn them into a single, coherent essay. Indeed, as we have seen before, we can turn them into several different coherent essays and then (if you want) begin all over again, hierarchizing *them*. I would hazard that Shakespeare's delight in the line, as well as the delight of his audience, was in the simple play of plural meanings that we now have, knowing both the literal and dialectal interpretation of the terms.

What does this little diversion have to do with science fiction? Well, when Roger Zelazny, in *This Immortal,* writes of a biologist breeding poisonous fleas (called *slishi*) to kill off an invasion of spiderbats on the Monterey coast, "When the spiderbats return to Capistrano, the slishi will be waiting," he is basically initiating the same sort of play as Shakespeare. But to perceive the play one must know that there was once an extremely sentimental old lyric, "When the Swallows Return to Capistrano." Zelazny's line puts that sentiment in play with the grim literalness, and the result is amusing and entertaining; and, though highly suggestive, it does not really lend itself to a unitary, single interpretation.

(If we may add play to play: it seems that the play's the thing . . . !)

Here's another way that historical awareness can indicate the play in both a "literary" writer like Shakespeare and an SF writer like . . . Isaac Asimov!

We know from historical research that Shakespeare's plays were performed with elaborate costumes—and *no* scenery at all (if you don't believe me, check Asimov's two-volume *Asimov's Guide to Shakespeare*). This is why the characters spend so much time describing where they are in ways that, if a cowboy in your latest Western movie did it, ("Well, here I am in this dark wood full of elms and sycamore, as the light dims and the pinecones cast long shadows over the dead leaves around my boots"), would make the audience howl. To know this today allows us to read these parts of the dramas in a context that lets them do their jobs again; it lets us respond to the many subtle ways descriptions of locations are worked in—rather like the little throwaway bits that give you the world of an SF story—even in the midst of dialogue. They no longer seem gray, awkward, and superfluous. We are no longer left giggling at best, or simply scratching our heads at worst. I think a good giggle may be the better way to start because it is a *response* to the text. And the person who can't giggle at all is simply unresponsive to *our* current movie and theater conventions of realistic scenery; that's a little less forgivable than not knowing Shakespeare's theatrical conventions. Moreover, without the giggle, you miss out on the historical play that time has overlaid on Shakespeare's texts.

Where did Asimov go in all this?

Here's a bit of history that time and again I've found helpful in teaching people the "Foundation" stories. The first story we read today in *Foundation* (the last actually written) was written in 1951; it begins in a spaceport. Most of the students at the class where I taught the stories had come to the college by plane. One of the facts I found helpful for the students in trying to visualize the story is this:

In 1951 air travel was much less a part of people's lives than today. There was *no* commercial jet travel. Asimov had never ridden on a plane at this time, nor probably visited an airport more than a time or two at most. If you want to visualize Asimov's spaceport, don't start with your own experience at Kennedy, O'Hare, or L.A. International. Instead, just before you read the story, go back and visualize a major train station. Grand Central Station in New York City, Union Station in Los Angeles, Victoria Station in London, or Gare de l'oest in Paris. Does this mean Asimov's spaceport *is* a train station? Of course not! But if you use a train station as your basic imaginative material, the whole story will be more vivid, things will seem to make more sense, and you will see much more in your mind's eye when you read it. (And for what it's worth, well after I started using this little pedagogic prod, Dr. A. heard about it and complimented me on my insight.)

Notice that all this information, when written into the interpretive space around the text (whether it is Shakespeare's text, Asimov's, or Zelazny's), results in the text's becoming more vivid. *More* things can go on in the text. The information is not used to constrain the text to a single, unified meaning. Rather, in each case it releases meanings that then come into the play of meanings that is the text. (Think of *play* not so much as children's fun or adult competition, but as the give in a gear or a steering wheel that has play in its movement; although all those other meanings represent points about which the play—in the word *play*—moves, as does the idea of theatrical play as well.) Notice this is *not* the same as saying "The text can mean anything you want," with its implication, "Choose whichever *one* you prefer," which gets us back to the unitary.

This seems to me to be, with both literary texts *and* SF texts, the proper use of the interpretive space that lies about them both. An awful lot of SF readers, however, confuse the existence of that interpretive space with the values the interpretations most often written into that space have, most often, supported: those literary values that are unitary or authoritarian. The response of these readers (frequently our older readers), no doubt impelled by the best of intentions and a suspicion that unitary values are inappropriate to a writing field so clearly a pluralistic enterprise, is simply to deny all existence to the interpretive space around the SF text. The usual way of accomplishing this is for these readers to assume a conscientiously philistine approach—which is what they intuitively feel is opposed to a "literary" approach. "First of all," they say, "science fiction is merely entertainment." But can't you hear, lurking behind this statement, an appeal not to the notion of a plurality of values but to a single value, "entertainment value," meant to totalize the whole field? This is simply the mirror image of the statement "Literary texts have literary value." The good ones presumably have more of it, the bad ones less, but all literary texts have some. This, presumably, is why they are literature in the first place. "SF texts have entertainment value." The good ones, again, have more, the bad ones less.

The values are different, but both are unitary.

Whenever I encounter that particular phrase, "Science fiction is entertainment," I like to insert a little verbal play into the interpretive space around it. *Entertain* has two meanings in English: one can entertain friends, an audience, oneself. But one can also entertain ideas (trivial or profound), notions (pleasant or sad), and fancies (pretty or ugly).

If science fiction is "entertainment" in both senses, then its values must generate from the play between them.

But of course the significance of "Science fiction is merely entertainment" is

not just as a single pronouncement that ends there. It is part of a whole philistine reader-view, and is associated with a whole galaxy of pronouncements. Anyone who has been around science fiction for any length of time will recognize
that they all go together:

"I like an SF story that's told in good, simple language with none of your
fancy writing or experimentation, with a nice, clear beginning, middle, and
end."

But haven't we encountered, on the level of values, something very like this?
Of course. It's nothing but an appeal for a unity of style.

"I like an SF story that sticks to good, hard science that we can all understand if we just know our general physics and chemistry."

But on the value level, we should recognize this one too: it's the call for theoretical unity, loud and clear.

"I guess I just wish they would write SF stories the way they did back in the
sixties/fifties/forties. . . ." (You can choose your decade; there're adherents to
all of them today.) You guessed it: it's the cry for historical unity.

Paradoxically, it is just this most philistine of reader reactions that, despite its
good intentions, most strongly encourages the appropriation of science fiction
by literature—because it writes in that space an interpretation of science fiction
(and the philistine interpretation of science fiction is no *less* an interpretation of
science fiction than the notion of science fiction with no significant history is a
historical notion) that, through a process finally not too far from bad academic
criticism, has very little awareness of the structure of SF discourse, either as a
historically sensitive process (although the philistine may be aware of the history
and able to spot academic bloopers with the best) or as a present reality, in
which each contemporary writer is inserting her or his play into the plurality—
valuative, theoretical, stylistic, and historical—around which our SF discourse is
organized. For we are not talking about complexity, or even quality, of interpretation, but about the values a whole range of interpretations, good and bad,
simple and complex, reinforce. And the philistine view is right there, with all its
authoritarian vigor, at the center of the literary enterprise—even though it may
well be the play of pluralities that the person expressing that view is actually responding to in any given SF text that delights.

What this essay has been on the verge of proposing, as some of you by now
no doubt have suspected, is nothing less than the appropriation of literature by
science fiction. This has been suggested, with varying degrees of play, by various
writers at various times in the past. But it is just what gives the phenomenon its
aspect of encounter that also, today, makes that a possible outcome. Again, I
must remind you, I do not mean an economically encouraged encounter between texts—texts labeled "science fiction" driving texts labeled "literature" off
the shelves of the stores and out of the hands of the readers. Even the rise of science fiction from practically zero percent to fifteen percent of American fiction
production in twenty-five years or the rise from zero to about five hundred SF
classes does not seriously threaten the production of texts of the sort we call
mundane fiction or poetry. There are too many other economic pressures, pressures from universities and journalistic pressures, that would bring the process
to a grinding halt at fifty/fifty if not well before. I am still talking about the encounter between discourses, between responses, between ways of reading texts,
ways of using the interpretive space around them.

There are many people who read only literature.

There are many people who read only science fiction.

But there are also people who have moved from one to the other. The label "silly kid's stuff," so long applied to science fiction, was there to suggest that the natural and healthy movement over the period of maturation was from science fiction *to* literature, with its concomitant suggestion that any movement in the other direction implies mental softening. But of course there *are* many people who have recently moved in the other direction—another expression of the encounter.

I talked to one such man not long ago. A historian specializing in the beginnings of the nineteenth century, he had been a great reader of literature, but had found, over a period of five or six years, that he was reading more and more science fiction until, for the last two years, other than his journals and nonfiction he read nothing else. "I was really afraid to go back and read a 'serious' novel," he told me. "I didn't know what would happen. Finally, in fear and trembling, I picked up Jane Austen's *Pride and Prejudice*, always one of my favorites, just to see what happened when I did. . . . Do you know something? I thoroughly enjoyed it, more than I ever had before. But I realized something. Before, I used to read novels to tell me how the world really was at the time they were written. This time, I read the book asking myself what kind of world would have had to exist for Austen's story to have taken place—which, incidentally, is completely different from the world as it actually was back then. I know. It's my period."

As far as I can tell, this man has started to read Austen as if her novels were science fiction. There had been an encounter. And on some very deep level, part of the discourse of science fiction has triumphed over the discourse of literature—without, I suspect, any significant rupture for literature.

I think I have made it fairly clear by now: I believe that reading science fiction as if it were literature is a waste of time. I suspect that reading literature as if it were "literature" is also pretty much a waste of time. The discourse of science fiction gives us a way to construct worlds in clear and consistent dialogue with the world that is, alas, the case. Literature's unitary priorities do not. And in a world where an "alas" must be inserted into such a description of it, the dialectical freedom of science fiction has to be privileged.

It is possible that, on the level of values, reading literature as if it were science fiction may be the only hope for literature—if, while we're doing it, we don't commit the same sort of historical ruptures that we in science fiction have already suffered at the hands of both editors and uninformed academics. And we must read—and write—science fiction as if it were *really* science fiction, and not just a philistine hack job purveying the same unitary values as literature but in their most debased form.

SOULS

Joanna Russ

Joanna Russ (see also the note on Russ's essay) has published little fiction in recent years, having turned for the most part to criticism. This is one of the last major pieces to appear before she fell nearly silent. It is her homage to James Tiptree, Jr. (for more information, see the note on Tiptree), a re-imagining of "Beam Us Home" and "The Women Men Don't See," two of Tiptree's finest pieces.

Deprived of other Banquet
I entertained Myself—
—Emily Dickinson

This is the tale of the Abbess Radegunde and what happened when the Norse-men came. I tell it not as it was told to me but as I saw it, for I was a child then and the Abbess had made a pet and errand-boy of me, although the stern old Wardress, Cunigunt, who had outlived the previous Abbess, said I was more in the Abbey than out of it and a scandal. But the Abbess would only say mildly, "Dear Cunigunt, a scandal at the age of seven?" which was turning it off with a joke, for she knew how harsh and disliking my new stepmother was to me and my father did not care and I with no sisters or brothers. You must understand that joking and calling people "dear" and "my dear" was only her manner; she was in every way an unusual woman. The previous Abbess, Herrade, had found that Radegunde, who had been given to her to be fostered, had great gifts and so sent the child south to be taught, and that has never happened here before. The story has it that the Abbess Herrade found Radegunde seeming to read the great illuminated book in the Abbess's study; the child had somehow pulled it off its stand and was sitting on the floor with the volume in her lap, sucking her thumb and turning the pages with her other hand just as if she were reading.

"Little two-years," said the Abbess Herrade, who was a kind woman, "what are you doing?" She thought it amusing, I suppose, that Radegunde should pre-tend to read this great book, the largest and finest in the Abbey, which had many, many books, more than any other nunnery or monastery I have ever heard of: a full forty then, as I remember. And then little Radegunde was doing the book no harm.

"Reading, Mother," said the little girl.

"Oh, reading?" said the Abbess, smiling; "Then tell me what are you read-ing," and she pointed to the page.

"This," said Radegunde, "is a great *D* with flowers and other beautiful things about it, which is to show that *Dominus,* our Lord God, is the greatest thing and the most beautiful and makes everything to grow and be beautiful, and then it goes on to say *Domine nobis pacem,* which means *Give peace to us, O Lord.*"

Then the Abbess began to be frightened but she said only, "Who showed you this?" thinking that Radegunde had heard someone read and tell the words or had been pestering the nuns on the sly.

"No one," said the child; "Shall I go on?" and she read page after page of the Latin, in each case telling what the words meant.

There is more to the story, but I will say only that after many prayers the Abbess Herrade sent her foster-daughter far southwards, even to Poitiers, where Saint Radegunde had ruled an Abbey before, and some say even to Rome, and in these places Radegunde was taught all learning, for all the learning there is in the world remains in these places. Radegunde came back a grown woman and nursed the Abbess through her last illness and then became Abbess in her turn. They say that the great folk of the Church down there in the south wanted to keep her because she was such a prodigy of female piety and learning, there where life is safe and comfortable and less rude than it is here, but she said that the gray skies and flooding winters of her birthplace called to her very soul. She often told me the story when I was a child: how headstrong she had been and how defiant, and how she had sickened so desperately for her native land that they had sent her back, deciding that a rude life in the mud of a northern village would be a good cure for such a rebellious soul as hers.

"And so it was," she would say, patting my cheek or tweaking my ear; "See how humble I am now?" for you understand, all this about her rebellious girl-hood, twenty years back, was a kind of joke between us. "Don't you do it," she would tell me and we would laugh together, I so heartily at the very idea of my being a pious monk full of learning that I would hold my sides and be unable to speak.

She was kind to everyone. She knew all the languages, not only ours, but the Irish too and the tongues folks speak to the north and south, and Latin and Greek also, and all the other languages in the world, both to read and write. She knew how to cure sickness, both the old women's way with herbs or leeches and out of books also. And never was there a more pious woman! Some speak ill of her now she's gone and say she was too merry to be a good Abbess, but she would say, "Merriment is God's flowers," and when the winter wind blew her headdress awry and showed the gray hair—which happened once; I was there and saw the shocked faces of the Sisters with her—she merely tapped the band back into place, smiling and saying, "Impudent wind! Thou showest thou hast power which is more than our silly human power, for it is from God"—and this quite satisfied the girls with her.

No one ever saw her angry. She was impatient sometimes, but in a kindly way, as if her mind were elsewhere. It was in Heaven, I used to think, for I have seen her pray for hours or sink to her knees—right in the marsh!—to see the wild duck fly south, her hands clasped and a kind of wild joy on her face, only to rise a moment later, looking at the mud on her habit and crying half-ruefully, half in laughter, "Oh, what will Sister Laundress say to me? I am hopeless! Dear child, tell no one; I will say I fell," and then she would clap her hand to her mouth, turning red and laughing even harder, saying, "I *am* hopeless, telling lies!"

The town thought her a saint, of course. We were all happy then, or so it seems to me now, and all lucky and well, with this happiness of having her amongst us burning and blooming in our midst like a great fire around which we could all warm ourselves, even those who didn't know why life seemed so good. There was less illness; the food was better; the very weather stayed mild; and people did not quarrel as they had before her time and do again now. Nor do I think, considering what happened at the end, that all this was nothing but the fancy of a boy who's found his mother, for that's what she was to me; I brought her all the gossip and ran errands when I could and she called me Boy News in Latin; I was happier than I have ever been.

And then one day those terrible beaked prows appeared in our river.

I was with her when the warning came, in the main room of the Abbey tower just after the first fire of the year had been lit in the great hearth; we thought ourselves safe, for they had never been seen so far south and it was too late in the year for any sensible shipman to be in our waters. The Abbey was host to three Irish priests, who turned pale when young Sister Sibihd burst in with the news, crying and wringing her hands; one of the brothers exclaimed a thing in Latin which means "God protect us!" for they had been telling us stories of the terrible sack of the monastery of Saint Columbanus and how everyone had run away with the precious manuscripts or had hidden in the woods, and that was how Father Cairbre and the two others had decided to go "walk the world," for this (the Abbess had been telling it all to me for I had no Latin) is what the Irish say when they leave their native land to travel elsewhere.

"God protects our souls, not our bodies," said the Abbess Radegunde briskly. She had been talking with the priests in their own language or in the Latin, but this she said in ours so even the women workers from the village would understand. Then she said, "Father Cairbre, take your friends and the younger Sisters to the underground passages; Sister Diemud, open the gates to the villagers; half of them will be trying to get behind the Abbey walls and the others will be fleeing to the marsh. You, Boy News, down to the cellars with the girls." But I did not go and she never saw it; she was up and looking out one of the window slits instantly. So was I. I had always thought the Norsemen's big ships came right up on land—on legs, I supposed—and was disappointed to see that after they came up our river they stayed in the water like other ships and the men were coming ashore by wading in the water, just as if they had been like all other folk. Then the Abbess repeated her order—"Quickly! Quickly!"—and before anyone knew what had happened she was gone from the room. I watched from the tower window; in the turmoil nobody bothered about me. Below, the Abbey grounds and gardens were packed with folk, all stepping on the herb plots and the Abbess's paestum roses, and great logs were being dragged to bar the door set in the stone walls round the Abbey, not high walls, to tell truth, and Radegunde was going quickly through the crowd, crying, Do this! Do that! Stay, thou! Go, thou! and like things.

Then she reached the door and motioned Sister Oddha, the doorkeeper, aside—the old Sister actually fell to her knees in entreaty—and all this, you must understand, was wonderfully pleasant to me. I had no more idea of danger than a puppy. There was some tumult by the door—I think the men with the logs were trying to get in her way—and Abbess Radegunde took out from the neck of her habit her silver crucifix, brought all the way from Rome, and shook it impatiently at those who would keep her in. So of course they let her through at once.

I settled into my corner of the window, waiting for the Abbess's crucifix to bring down God's lightning on those tall, fair men who defied Our Savior and the law and were supposed to wear animal horns on their heads, though these did not (and I found out later that's just a story; that is not what the Norse do). I did hope that the Abbess or Our Lord would wait just a little while before destroying them, for I wanted to get a good look at them before they all died, you understand. I was somewhat disappointed, as they seemed to be wearing breeches with leggings under them and tunics on top, like ordinary folk, and cloaks also, though some did carry swords and axes and there were round shields piled on the beach at one place. But the long hair they had was fine, and the bright colors of their clothes, and the monsters growing out of the heads of the ships were splendid and very frightening, even though one could see that they were only painted, like the pictures in the Abbess's books.

I decided that God had provided me with enough edification and could now strike down the impious strangers.

But He did not.

Instead the Abbess walked alone towards these fierce men, over the stony river bank, as calmly as if she were on a picnic with her girls. She was singing a little song, a pretty tune that I repeated many years later, and a well-traveled man said it was a Norse cradle-song. I didn't know that then, but only that the terrible, fair men, who had looked up in surprise at seeing one lone woman come out of the Abbey (which was barred behind her; I could see that), now began a sort of whispering astonishment among themselves. I saw the Abbess's gaze go quickly from one to the other—we often said that she could tell what was hidden in the soul from one look at the face—and then she picked the skirt of her habit up with one hand and daintily went among the rocks to one of the men—one older than the others, as it proved later, though I could not see so well at the time—and said to him, in his own language:

"Welcome, Thorvald Einarsson, and what do you, good farmer, so far from your own place, with the harvest ripe and the great autumn storms coming on over the sea?" (You may wonder how I knew what she said when I had no Norse; the truth is that Father Cairbre, who had not gone to the cellars after all, was looking out the top of the window while I was barely able to peep out the bottom, and he repeated everything that was said for the folk in the room, who all kept very quiet.)

Now you could see that the pirates were dumbfounded to hear her speak their own language and even more so that she called one by his name; some stepped backwards and made strange signs in the air and others unsheathed axes or swords and came running towards the Abbess. But this Thorvald Einarsson put up his hand for them to stop and laughed heartily.

"Think!" he said; "There's no magic here, only cleverness—what pair of ears could miss my name with the lot of you bawling out 'Thorvald Einarsson, help

me with this oar'; 'Thorvald Einarsson, my leggings are wet to the knees';
'Thorvald Einarsson, this stream is as cold as a Fimbulwinter!'"

The Abbess Radegunde nodded and smiled. Then she sat down plump on
the river bank. She scratched behind one ear, as I had often seen her do when
she was deep in thought. Then she said (and I am sure that this talk was carried
on in a loud voice so that we in the Abbey could hear it):

"Good friend Thorvald, you are as clever as the tale I heard of you from your
sister's son, Ranulf, from whom I learnt the Norse when I was in Rome, and to
show you it was he, he always swore by his gray horse, Lamefoot, and he had a
difficulty in his speech; he could not say the sounds as we do and so spoke of you
always as 'Torvald.' Is not that so?"

I did not realize it then, being only a child, but the Abbess was—by this
speech—claiming hospitality from the man, and had also picked by chance or inspiration the cleverest among these thieves and robbers, for his next words were:

"I am not the leader. There are no leaders here."

He was warning her that they were not his men to control, you see. So she
scratched behind ear again and got up. Then she began to wander, as if she
did not know what to do, from one to the other of these uneasy folk—for some
backed off and made signs at her still, and some took out their knives—singing
her little tune again and walking slowly, more bent over and older and infirm-
looking than we had ever seen her, one helpless little woman in black before all
those fierce men. One wild young pirate snatched the headdress from her as she
passed, leaving her short gray hair bare to the wind; the others laughed and he
that had done it cried out:

"Grandmother, are you not ashamed?"

"Why, good friend, of what?" said she mildly.

"Thou art married to thy Christ," he said, holding the headdress covering
behind his back, "but this bridegroom of thine cannot even defend thee against
the shame of having thy head uncovered! Now if thou wert married to me—"

There was much laughter. The Abbess Radegunde waited until it was over.
Then she scratched her bare head and made as if to turn away, but suddenly she
turned back upon him with the age and infirmity dropping from her as if they
had been a cloak, seeming taller and very grand, as if lit from within by some
great fire. She looked directly into his face. This thing she did was something we
had all seen, of course, but they had not, nor had they heard that great, grand
voice with which she sometimes read the Scriptures to us or talked with us of the
wrath of God. I think the young man was frightened, for all his daring. And I
know now what I did not then: that the Norse admire courage above all things
and that—to be blunt—everyone likes a good story, especially if it happens right
in front of your eyes.

"Grandson!"—and her voice tolled like the great bell of God; I think folk
must have heard her all the way to the marsh!—"Little grandchild, thinkest thou
that the Creator of the World who made the stars and the moon and the sun and
our bodies, too, and the change of the seasons and the very earth we stand on—
yea, even unto the shit in thy belly!—thinkest thou that such a being has a big
house in the sky where he keeps his wives and goes in to fuck them as thou
wouldst thyself or like the King of Turkey? Do not dishonor the wit of the
mother who bore thee! We are the servants of God, not his wives, and if we tell
our silly girls they are married to the Christ it is to make them understand that

they must not run off and marry Otto Farmer or Ekkehard Blacksmith, but stick to their work, as they promised. If I told them they were married to an Idea they would not understand me, and neither dost thou."

(Here Father Cairbre, above me in the window, muttered in a protesting way about something.)

Then the Abbess snatched the silver cross from around her neck and put it into the boy's hand, saying: "Give this to thy mother with my pity. She must pull out her hair over such a child."

But he let it fall to the ground. He was red in the face and breathing hard.

"Take it up," she said more kindly, "take it up, boy; it will not hurt thee and there's no magic in it. It's only pure silver and good workmanship; it will make thee rich." When she saw that he would not—his hand went to his knife—she *tched* to herself in a motherly way (or I believe she did, for she waved one hand back and forth as she always did when she made that sound) and got down on her knees—with more difficulty than was truth, I think—saying loudly, "I will stoop, then; I will stoop," and got up, holding it out to him, saying, "Take. Two sticks tied with a cord would serve me as well."

The boy cried, his voice breaking, "My mother is dead and thou art a witch!" and in an instant he had one arm around the Abbess's neck and with the other his knife at her throat. The man Thorvald Einarsson roared "Thorfinn!" but the Abbess only said clearly, "Let him be. I have shamed this man but did not mean to. He is right to be angry."

The boy released her and turned his back. I remember wondering if these strangers could weep. Later I heard—and I swear that the Abbess must have somehow known this or felt it, for although she was no witch, she could probe at a man until she found the sore places in him and that very quickly—that this boy's mother had been known for an adulteress and that no man would own him as a son. It is one thing among those people for a man to have what the Abbess called a concubine and they do not hold the children of such in scorn as we do, but it is a different thing when a married woman has more than one man. Such was Thorfinn's case; I suppose that was what had sent him *viking*. But all this came later; what I saw then—with my nose barely above the window-slit—was that the Abbess slipped her crucifix over the hilt of the boy's sword—she really wished him to have it, you see—and then walked to a place near the walls of the Abbey but far from the Norsemen. I think she meant them to come to her. I saw her pick up her skirts like a peasant woman, sit down with legs crossed, and say in a loud voice:

"Come! Who will bargain with me?"

A few strolled over, laughing, and sat down with her.

"All!" she said, gesturing them closer.

"And why should we all come?" said one who was farthest away.

"Because you will miss a bargain," said the Abbess.

"Why should we bargain when we can take?" said another.

"Because you will only get half," said the Abbess. "The rest you will not find."

"We will ransack the Abbey," said a third.

"Half the treasure is not in the Abbey," said she.

"And where is it then?" said yet another.

She tapped her forehead. They were drifting over by twos and threes. I have

heard since that the Norse love riddles and this was a sort of riddle; she was giving them good fun.

"If it is in your head," said the man Thorvald, who was standing behind the
others, arms crossed, "we can get it out, can we not?" And he tapped the hilt of
his knife.

"If you frighten me, I shall become confused and remember nothing," said
the Abbess calmly. "Besides, do you wish to play that old game? You saw how
well it worked the last time. I am surprised at you, Ranulf's mother's-brother."

"I will bargain then," said the man Thorvald, smiling.

"And the rest of you?" said Radegunde. "It must be all or none; decide for
yourselves whether you wish to save yourselves trouble and danger and be rich,"
and she deliberately turned her back on them. The men moved down to the
river's edge and began to talk among themselves, dropping their voices so that
we could not hear them anymore. Father Cairbre, who was old and short-
sighted, cried, "I cannot hear them. What are they doing?" and I cleverly said,
"I have good eyes, Father Cairbre," and he held me up to see, so it was just at
the time that the Abbess Radegunde was facing the Abbey tower that I appeared
in the window. She clapped one hand across her mouth. Then she walked to the
gate and called (in a voice I had learned not to disregard; it had often got me a
smacked bottom), "Boy News, down! Come down to me here *at once!* And
bring Father Cairbre with you."

I was overjoyed. I had no idea that she might want to protect me if anything
went wrong. My only thought was that I was going to see it all from wonderfully close by, so I wormed my way, half-suffocated, through the folk in the
tower room, stepping on feet and skirts, and having to say every few seconds,
"But I *have* to! The Abbess wants me," and meanwhile she was calling outside
like an Empress, "Let that boy through! Make a place for that boy! Let the Irish
priest through!" until I crept and pushed and complained my way to the very
wall itself—no one was going to open the gate for us, of course—and there was
a great fuss and finally someone brought a ladder. I was over at once, but the old
priest took a longer time, although it was a low wall, as I've said, the builders
having been somewhat of two minds about making the Abbey into a true
fortress.

Once outside it was lovely, away from all that crowd, and I ran, gloriously
pleased, to the Abbess, who said only, "Stay by me, whatever happens," and immediately turned her attention away from me. It had taken so long to get Father
Cairbre outside the walls that the tall foreign men had finished their talking and
were coming back—all twenty or thirty of them—towards the Abbey and the
Abbess Radegunde, and most especially of all, me. I could see Father Cairbre
tremble. They did look grim, close by, with their long, wild hair and the brightness of their strange clothes. I remember that they smelled different from us,
but cannot remember how after all these years. Then the Abbess spoke to them
in that outlandish language of theirs, so strangely light and lilting to hear from
their bearded lips, and then she said something in Latin to Father Cairbre, and
he said to us, with a shake in his voice:

"This is the priest, Father Cairbre, who will say our bargains aloud in our
own tongue so that my people may hear. I cannot deal behind their backs. And
this is my foster-baby, who is very dear to me and who is now having his curios-

ity rather too much satisfied, I think." (I was trying to stand tall like a man but had one hand secretly holding on to her skirt; so that was what the foreign men had chuckled at!) The talk went on, but I will tell it as if I had understood the Norse, for to repeat everything twice would be tedious.

The Abbess Radegunde said, "Will you bargain?"

There was a general nodding of heads, with a look of: After all, why not?

"And who will speak for you?" said she.

A man stepped forward; I recognized Thorvald Einarsson.

"Ah yes," said the Abbess dryly. "The company that has no leaders. Is this leaderless company agreed? Will it abide by its word? I want no treachery-planners, no Breakwords here!"

There was a great mutter at this. The Thorvald man (he *was* big, close up!) said mildly, "I sail with none such. Let's begin."

We all sat down.

"Now," said Thorvald Einarsson, raising his eyebrows, "according to my knowledge of this thing, you begin. And according to my knowledge you will begin by saying that you are very poor."

"But no," said the Abbess, "we are rich." Father Cairbre groaned. A groan answered him from behind the Abbey walls. Only the Abbess and Thorvald Einarsson seemed unmoved; it was as if these two were joking in some way that no one else understood. The Abbess went on, saying, "We are very rich. Within is much silver, much gold, many pearls, and much embroidered cloth, much fine-woven cloth, much carved and painted wood, and many books with gold upon their pages and jewels set into their covers. All this is yours. But we have more and better: herbs and medicines, ways to keep food from spoiling, the knowledge of how to cure the sick; all this is yours. And we have more and better even than this; we have the knowledge of Christ and the perfect understanding of the soul, which is yours, too, any time you wish; you have only to accept it."

Thorvald Einarsson held up his hand. "We will stop with the first," he said, "and perhaps a little of the second. That is more practical."

"And foolish," said the Abbess politely, "in the usual way." And again I had the odd feeling that these two were sharing a joke no one else even saw. She added, "There is one thing you may not have, and that is the most precious of all."

Thorvald Einarsson looked inquiring.

"*My people.* Their safety is dearer to me than myself. They are not to be touched, not a hair on their heads, not for any reason. Think: you can fight your way into the Abbey easily enough, but the folk in there are very frightened of you and some of the men are armed. Even a good fighter is cumbered in a crowd. You will slip and fall upon each other without meaning to or knowing that you do so. Heed my counsel. Why play butcher when you can have treasure poured into your laps like kings, without work? And after that there will be as much again, when I lead you to the hidden place. An earl's mountain of treasure. Think of it! And to give all this up for slaves, half of whom will get sick and die before you get them home—and will need to be fed if they are to be any good. Shame on you for bad advice-takers! Imagine what you will say to your wives and families: Here are a few miserable bolts of cloth with blood spots that won't come out, here are some pearls and jewels smashed to powder in the fighting, here is a torn piece of embroidery which was whole until someone stepped on it in the battle, and I had slaves but they died of illness and I fucked a pretty young nun and meant to bring her back, but she leapt into the sea. And oh yes, there was twice as much again and all of it whole but we decided not to take that. Too much trouble, you see."

This was a lively story and the Norsemen enjoyed it. Radegunde held up her hand.

"People!" she called in German, adding, "Sea-rovers, hear what I say; I will repeat it for you in your tongue" (and so she did): *"People, if the Norsemen fight us, do not defend yourselves but smash everything! Wives, take your cooking knives and shred the valuable cloth to pieces! Men, with your axes and hammers hew the altars and the carved wood to fragments! All, grind the pearls and smash the jewels against the stone floors! Break the bottles of wine! Pound the gold and silver to shapelessness! Tear to pieces the illuminated books! Tear down the hangings and burn them!*

"But" (she added, her voice suddenly mild) "if these wise men will accept our gifts, let us heap untouched and spotless at their feet all that we have and hold nothing back, so that their kinsfolk will marvel and wonder at the shining and glistering of the wealth they bring back, though it leave us nothing but our bare stone walls."

If anyone had ever doubted that the Abbess Radegunde was inspired by God, their doubts must have vanished away, for who could resist the fiery vigor of her first speech or the beneficent unction of her second? The Norsemen sat there with their mouths open. I saw tears on Father Cairbre's cheeks. Then Thorvald Einarsson said, "Abbess—"

He stopped. He tried again but again stopped. Then he shook himself, as a man who has been under a spell, and said:

"Abbess, my men have been without women for a long time."

Radegunde looked surprised. She looked as if she could not believe what she had heard. She looked the pirate up and down, as if puzzled, and then walked around him as if taking his measure. She did this several times, looking at every part of his big body as if she were summing him up while he got redder and redder. Then she backed off and surveyed him again, and with her arms akimbo like a peasant, announced very loudly in both Norse and German:

"What! Have they lost the use of their hands?"

It was irresistible, in its way. The Norse laughed. Our people laughed. Even Thorvald laughed. I did too, though I was not sure what everyone was laughing about. The laughter would die down and then begin again behind the Abbey walls, helplessly, and again die down and again begin. The Abbess waited until the Norsemen had stopped laughing and then called for silence in German until there were only a few snickers here and there. She then said:

"These good men—Father Cairbre, tell the people—these good men will forgive my silly joke. I meant no scandal, truly, and no harm, but laughter is good; it settles the body's waters, as the physicians say. And my people know that I am not always as solemn and good as I ought to be. Indeed I am a very great sinner and scandal-maker. Thorvald Einarsson, do we do business?"

The big man—who had not been so pleased as the others, I can tell you!—

looked at his men and seemed to see what he needed to know. He said: "I go in with five men to see what you have. Then we let the poor folk on the grounds go, but not those inside the Abbey. Then we search again. The gate will be locked and guarded by the rest of us; if there's any treachery, the bargain's off."

"Then I will go with you," said Radegunde. "That is very just and my presence will calm the people. To see us together will assure them that no harm is meant. You are a good man, Torvald—forgive me; I call you as your nephew did so often. Come, Boy News, hold on to me.

"Open the gate!" she called then; "All is safe!" and with the five men (one of whom was that young Thorfinn who had hated her so) we waited while the great logs were pulled back. There was little space within, but the people shrank back at the sight of those fierce warriors and opened a place for us.

I looked back and the Norsemen had come in and were standing just inside the walls, on either side the gate, with their swords out and their shields up. The crowd parted for us more slowly as we reached the main tower, with the Abbess repeating constantly, "Be calm, people, be calm. All is well," and deftly speaking by name to this one or that. It was much harder when the people gasped upon hearing the big logs pushed shut with a noise like thunder, and it was very close on the stairs; I heard her say something like an apology in the queer foreign tongue, something that probably meant, "I'm sorry that we must wait." It seemed an age until the stairs were even partly clear and I saw what the Abbess had meant by the cumbering of a crowd; a man might swing a weapon in the press of people but not very far and it was more likely he would simply fall over someone and crack his head. We gained the great room with the big crucifix of painted wood and the little one of pearls and gold, and the scarlet hangings worked in gold thread that I had played robbers behind so often before I learned what real robbers were: these tall, frightening men whose eyes glistened with greed at what I had fancied every village had. Most of the Sisters had stayed in the great room, but somehow it was not so crowded, as the folk had huddled back against the walls when the Norsemen came in. The youngest girls were all in a corner, terrified—one could smell it, as one can in people—and when that young Thorfinn went for the little gold-and-pearl cross, Sister Sibihd cried in a high, cracked voice, "It is the body of our Christ!" and leapt up, snatching it from the wall before he could get to it.

"Sibihd!" exclaimed the Abbess, in as sharp a voice as I had ever heard her use; "Put that back or you will feel the weight of my hand, I tell you!"

Now it is odd, is it not, that a young woman desperate enough not to care about death at the hands of a Norse pirate should nonetheless be frightened away at the threat of getting a few slaps from her Abbess? But folk are like that. Sister Sibihd returned the cross to its place (from whence young Thorfinn took it) and fell back among the nuns, sobbing, "He desecrates Our Lord God!"

"Foolish girl!" snapped the Abbess. "God only can consecrate or desecrate; man cannot. That is a piece of metal."

Thorvald said something sharp to Thorfinn, who slowly put the cross back on its hook with a sulky look which said, plainer than words: Nobody gives me what I want. Nothing else went wrong in the big room or the Abbess's study or the storerooms, or out in the kitchens. The Norsemen were silent and kept their hands on their swords but the Abbess kept talking in a calm way in both tongues; to our folk she said, "See? It is all right but everyone must keep still. God will protect us." Her face was steady and clear and I believed her a saint, for she had saved Sister Sibihd and the rest of us.

But this peacefulness did not last, of course. Something had to go wrong in all that press of people; to this day I do not know what. We were in a corner of the long refectory, which is the place where the Sisters or Brothers eat in an Abbey, when something pushed me into the wall and I fell, almost suffocated by the Abbess's lying on top of me. My head was ringing and on all sides there was a terrible roaring sound with curses and screams, a dreadful tumult as if the walls had come apart and were falling on everyone. I could hear the Abbess whispering something in Latin over and over in my ear. There were dull, ripe sounds, worse than the rest, which I know now to have been the noise steel makes when it is thrust into bodies. This all seemed to go on forever and then it seemed to me that the floor was wet. Then all became quiet. I felt the Abbess Radegunde get off me. She said:

"So this is how you wash your floors up north." When I lifted my head from the wet rushes and saw what she meant, I was very sick into the corner. Then she picked me up in her arms and held my face against her bosom so that I would not see but it was no use; I had already seen: all the people lying about sprawled on the floor with their bellies coming out, like heaps of dead fish, old Walafrid with an axe-handle standing out of his chest—he was sitting up with his eyes shut in a press of bodies that gave him no room to lie down—and the young beekeeper, Uta, from the village, who had been so merry, lying on her back with her long braids and her gown all dabbled in red dye and a great stain of it on her belly. She was breathing fast and her eyes were wide open. As we passed her, the noise of her breathing ceased.

The Abbess said mildly, "Thy people are thorough housekeepers, Earl Split-gut."

Thorvald Einarsson roared something at us and the Abbess replied softly, "Forgive me, good friend. You protected me and the boy and I am grateful. But nothing betrays a man's knowledge of the German like a word that bites, is it not so? And I had to be sure."

It came to me then that she had called him "Torvald" and reminded him of his sister's son so that he would feel he must protect us if anything went wrong. But now she would make him angry, I thought, and I shut my eyes tight. Instead he laughed and said in odd, light German, "I did no housekeeping but to stand over you and your pet. Are you not grateful?"

"Oh very, thank you," said the Abbess with such warmth as she might show to a Sister who had brought her a rose from the garden, or another who copied her work well, or when I told her news, or if Ita the cook made a good soup. But he did not know that the warmth was for everyone and so seemed satisfied. By now we were in the garden and the air was less foul; she put me down, although my limbs were shaking, and I clung to her gown, crumpled, stiff, and blood-reeking though it was. She said, "Oh, my God, what a deal of washing hast Thou given us!" She started to walk towards the gate and Thorvald Einarsson took a step towards her. She said, without turning round: "Do not insist, Thorvald, there is no reason to lock me up. I am forty years old and not likely to be running away into the swamp what with my rheumatism and the pain in my knees and the folk needing me as they do."

There was a moment's silence. I could see something odd come into the big man's face. He said quietly:

"I did not speak, Abbess."

She turned, surprised. "But you did. I heard you."

He said strangely, "I did not."

Children can guess sometimes what is wrong and what to do about it without knowing how; I remember saying, very quickly, "Oh, she does that sometimes. My stepmother says old age has addled her wits," and then, "Abbess, may I go to my stepmother and my father?"

"Yes, of course," she said, "run along, Boy News—" and then stopped, looking into the air as if seeing in it something we could not. Then she said very gently, "No, my dear, you had better stay here with me," and I knew, as surely as if I had seen it with my own eyes, that I was not to go to my stepmother or my father because both were dead.

She did things like that, too, sometimes.

For a while it seemed that everyone was dead. I did not feel grieved or frightened in the least, but I think I must have been, for I had only one idea in my head: that if I let the Abbess out of my sight, I would die. So I followed her everywhere. She was let to move about and comfort people, especially the mad Sibihd, who would do nothing but rock and wail, but towards nightfall, when the Abbey had been stripped of its treasures, Thorvald Einarsson put her and me in her study, now bare of its grand furniture, on a straw pallet on the floor, and bolted the door on the outside. She said:

"Boy News, would you like to go to Constantinople, where the Emperor is and the domes of gold and all the splendid pagans? For that is where this man will take me to sell me."

"Oh yes!" said I, and then, "But will he take me, too?"

"Of course," said the Abbess, and so it was settled. Then in came Thorvald Einarsson, saying:

"Thorfinn is asking for you." I found out later that they were waiting for him to die; none other of the Norse had been wounded but a farmer had crushed Thorfinn's chest with an axe and he was expected to die before morning. The Abbess said:

"Is that a good reason to go?" She added, "I mean that he hates me; will not his anger at my presence make him worse?"

Thorvald said slowly, "The folk here say you can sit by the sick and heal them. Can you do that?"

"To my knowledge, not at all," said the Abbess Radegunde, "but if they believe so, perhaps that calms them and makes them better. Christians are quite as foolish as other people, you know. I will come if you want," and though I saw that she was pale with tiredness, she got to her feet. I should say that she was in a plain brown gown taken from one of the peasant women because her own was being washed clean, but to me she had the same majesty as always. And for him too, I think.

Thorvald said, "Will you pray for him or damn him?"

She said, "I do not pray, Thorvald, and I never damn anybody; I merely sit." She added, "Oh let him; he'll scream your ears off if you don't," and this meant me for I was ready to yell for my life if they tried to keep me from her.

They had put Thorfinn in the chapel, a little stone room with nothing left in it now but a plain wooden cross, not worth carrying off. He was lying, his eyes closed, on the stone altar with furs under him, and his face was gray. Every time he breathed there was a bubbling sound, a little, thin, reedy sound, and as I crept closer I saw why, for in the young man's chest was a great red hole with pink things sticking out of it, all crushed, and in the hole one could see something jump and fall, jump and fall, over and over again. It was his heart beating. Blood kept coming from his lips in a froth. I do not know, of course, what either said, for they spoke in the Norse, but I saw what they did and heard much of it talked of between the Abbess and Thorvald Einarsson later, so I will tell it as if I knew.

The first thing the Abbess did was to stop suddenly on the threshold and raise both hands to her mouth as if in horror. Then she cried furiously to the two guards:

"Do you wish to kill your comrade with the cold and damp? Is this how you treat one another? Get fire in here and some woollen cloth to put over him! No, not more skins, you idiots, *wool* to mold to his body and take up the wet. Run now!"

One said sullenly, "We don't take orders from you, Grandma."

"Oh no?" said she. "Then I shall strip this wool dress from my old body and put it over that boy and then sit here all night in my flabby naked skin! What will this child's soul say to God when it departs this flesh? That his friends would not give up a little of their booty so that he might fight for life? Is this your fellowship? Do it, or I will strip myself and shame you both for the rest of your lives!"

"Well, take it from his share," said the one in a low voice, and the other ran out. Soon there was a fire on the hearth and russet-colored woollen cloth— "From my own share," said one of them loudly, though it was a color the least costly, not like blue or red—and the Abbess laid it loosely over the boy, carefully putting it close to his sides but not moving him. He did not look to be in any pain, but his color got no better. But then he opened his eyes and said in such a little voice as a ghost might have, a whisper as thin and reedy and bubbling as his breath:

"You . . . old witch. But I beat you . . . in the end."

"Did you, my dear?" said the Abbess. "How?"

"Treasure," he said, "for my kinfolk. And I lived as a man at last. Fought . . . and had a woman . . . the one here with the big breasts, Sibihd. . . . Whether she liked it or not. That was good."

"Yes, Sibihd," said the Abbess mildly. "Sibihd has gone mad. She hears no one and speaks to no one. She only sits and rocks and moans and soils herself and will not feed herself, although if one puts food in her mouth with a spoon, she will swallow."

The boy tried to frown. "Stupid," he said at last. "Stupid nuns. The beasts do it."

"Do they?" said the Abbess, as if this were a new idea to her. "Now that is very odd. For never yet heard I of a gander that blacked the goose's eye or hit her over the head with a stone or stuck a knife in her entrails when he was through. When God puts it into their hearts to desire one another, she squats and he comes running. And a bitch in heat will jump through the window if you lock the door. Poor fools! Why didn't you camp three hours' downriver and wait? In a week half the young married women in the village would have been slipping away at night to see what the foreigners were like. Yes, and some un-married ones, and some of my own girls, too. But you couldn't wait, could you?"

"No," said the boy, with the ghost of a brag. "Better . . . this way."

"This way," said she. "Oh yes, my dear, old granny knows about *this* way! Pleasure for the count of three or four and the rest of it as much joy as rolling a stone uphill."

He smiled a ghostly smile. "You're a whore, grandma."

She began to stroke his forehead. "No, grandbaby," she said, "but all Latin is not the Church Fathers, you know, great as they are. One can find a great deal in those strange books written by the ones who died centuries before Our Lord was born. Listen," and she leaned closer to him and said quietly:

> *"Syrian dancing girl, how subtly you sway*
> *those sensuous limbs,*
> *Half-drunk in the smoky tavern, lascivious*
> *and wanton,*
> *Your long hair bound back in the Greek way,*
> *clashing the castanets in your hands—"*

The boy was too weak to do anything but look astonished. Then she said this:

> "I love you so that anyone permitted to sit near you and talk to you seems to me like a god; when I am near you my spirit is broken, my heart shakes, my voice dies, and I can't even speak. Under my skin I flame up all over and I can't see; there's thunder in my ears and I break out in a sweat, as if from fever; I turn paler than cut grass and feel that I am ut-terly changed; I feel that Death has come near me."

He said, as if frightened, "Nobody feels like that."

"They do," she said.

He said, in feeble alarm, "You're trying to kill me!"

She said, "No, my dear. I simply don't want you to die a virgin."

It was odd, his saying those things and yet holding on to her hand where he had got at it through the woollen cloth; she stroked his head and he whispered, "Save me, old witch."

"I'll do my best," she said. "You shall do your best by not talking and I by not tormenting you any more, and we'll both try to sleep."

"Pray," said the boy.

"Very well," said she, "but I'll need a chair," and the guards—seeing, I sup-pose, that he was holding her hand—brought in one of the great wooden chairs from the Abbey, which were too plain and heavy to carry off, I think. Then the Abbess Radegunde sat in the chair and closed her eyes. Thorfinn seemed to fall asleep. I crept nearer her on the floor and must have fallen asleep myself almost at once, for the next thing I knew a gray light filled the chapel, the fire had gone out, and someone was shaking Radegunde, who still slept in her chair, her head leaning to one side. It was Thorvald Einarsson and he was shouting with excitement in his strange German, "Woman, how did you do it! How did you do it!"

"Do what?" said the Abbess thickly. "Is he dead?"

"Dead?" exclaimed the Norseman. "He is healed! Healed! The lung is whole and all is closed up about the heart and the shattered pieces of the ribs are grown together! Even the muscles of the chest are beginning to heal!"

"That's good," said the Abbess, still half asleep. "Let me be."

Thorvald shook her again. She said again, "Oh, let me sleep." This time he hauled her to her feet and she shrieked, "My back, my back! Oh, the saints, my rheumatism!" and at the same time a sick voice from under the blue woollens— a sick voice but a man's voice, not ghost's—said something in Norse.

"Yes, I hear you," said the Abbess; "you must become a follower of the White Christ right away, this very minute. But *Dominus noster*, please do You put it into these brawny heads that I must have a tub of hot water with pennyroyal in it? I am too old to sleep all night in a chair and I am one ache from head to foot."

Thorfinn got louder.

"Tell him," said the Abbess Radegunde to Thorvald in German, "that I will not baptize him and I will not shrive him until he is a different man. All that child wants is someone more powerful than your Odin god or your Thor god to pull him out of the next scrape he gets into. Ask him: Will he adopt Sibihd as his sister? Will he clean her when she soils herself and feed her and sit with his arm about her, talking to her gently and lovingly until she is well again? The Christ does not wipe out our sins only to have us commit them all over again and that is what he wants and what you all want, a God that gives and gives and gives, but God does not give; He takes and takes and takes. He takes away everything that is not God until there is nothing left but God, and none of you will understand that! There is no remission of sins; there is only change and Thorfinn must change before God will have him."

"Abbess, you are eloquent," said Thorvald, smiling, "but why do you not tell him all this yourself?"

"Because I ache so!" said Radegunde. "Oh, do get me into some hot water!" and Thorvald half led and half supported her as she hobbled out. That morning, after she had had her soak—when I cried, they let me stay just outside the door—she undertook to cure Sibihd, first by rocking her in her arms and talking to her, telling her she was safe now, and promising that the Northmen would go soon, and then when Sibihd became quieter, leading her out into the woods with Thorvald as a bodyguard to see that we did not run away, and little dark Sister Hedwic, who had stayed with Sibihd and cared for her. The Abbess would walk for a while in the mild autumn sunshine and then she would direct Sibihd's face upwards by touching her gently under the chin and say, "See? There is God's sky still," and then, "Look, there are God's trees; they have not changed," and telling her that the world was just the same and God still kindly to folk, only a few more souls had joined the Blessed and were happier waiting for us in Heaven than we could ever be, or even imagine being, on the poor earth. Sister Hedwic kept hold of Sibihd's hand. No one paid more attention to me than if I had been a dog, but every time poor Sister Sibihd saw Thorvald she would shrink away and you could see that Hedwic could not bear to look at him at all; every time he came in her sight she turned her face aside, shut her eyes hard, and bit her lower lip. It was a quiet, almost warm day, as autumn can be sometimes, and the Abbess found a few little blue late flowers growing in a sheltered place against a log and put them into Sibihd's hand, speaking of how beautifully and cunningly God had made all things. Sister Sibihd had enough wit to hold on to the flowers, but her eyes stared and she would have stumbled and fallen if Hedwic had not led her.

Sister Hedwic said timidly, "Perhaps she suffers because she has been defiled, Abbess," and then looked ashamed. For a moment the Abbess looked shrewdly at young Sister Hedwic and then at the mad Sibihd. Then she said:

"Dear daughter Sibihd and dear daughter Hedwic, I am now going to tell you something about myself that I have never told to a single living soul but my confessor. Do you know that as a young woman I studied at Avignon and from there was sent to Rome, so that I might gather much learning? Well, in Avignon I read mightily our Christian Fathers but also in the pagan poets, for as it has been said by Ermenrich of Ellwangen: As dung spread upon a field enriches it to good harvest, thus one cannot produce divine eloquence without the filthy writings of the pagan poets. This is true but perilous; only I thought not so, for I was very proud and fancied that if the pagan poems of love left me unmoved that was because I had the gift of chastity right from God Himself and I scorned sensual pleasures and those tempted by them. I had forgotten, you see, that chastity is not given once and for all like a wedding ring that is put on never to be taken off, but is a garden which each day must be weeded, watered, and trimmed anew, or soon there will be only brambles and wilderness.

"As I have said, the words of the poets did not tempt me, for words are only marks on the page with no life save what we give them. But in Rome there were not only the old books, daughters, but something much worse.

"There were statues. Now you must understand that these are not such as you can imagine from our books, like Saint John or the Virgin; the ancients wrought so cunningly in stone that it is like magic; one stands before the marble holding one's breath, waiting for it to move and speak. They are not statues at all but beautiful naked men and women. It is a city of sea-gods pouring water, daughter Sibihd and daughter Hedwic, of athletes about to throw the discus, and runners and wrestlers and young emperors, and the favorites of kings, but they do not walk the streets like real men, for they are all of stone.

"There was one Apollo, all naked, which I knew I should not look on but which I always made some excuse to my companions to pass by, and this statue, although three miles distant from my dwelling, drew me as if by magic. Oh, he was fair to look on! Fairer than any youth alive now in Germany, or in the world, I think. And then all the old loves of the pagan poets came back to me: Dido and Aeneas, the taking of Venus and Mars, the love of the moon, Diana, for the shepherd boy—and I thought that if my statue could only come to life, he would utter honeyed love-words from the old poets and would be wise and brave, too, and what woman could resist him?"

Here she stopped and looked at Sister Sibihd but Sibihd only stared on, holding the little blue flowers. It was Sister Hedwic who cried, one hand pressed to her heart:

"Did you pray, Abbess?"

"I did," said Radegunde solemnly, "and yet my prayers kept becoming something else. I would pray to be delivered from the temptation that was in the statue and then, of course, I would have to think of the statue itself, and then I would tell myself that I must run, like the nymph Daphne, to be armored and sheltered within a laurel tree, but my feet seemed to be already rooted to the ground, and then at the last minute I would flee and be back at my prayers again. But it grew harder each time and at last the day came when I did not flee."

"Abbess, *you?*" cried Hedwic with a gasp. Thorvald, keeping his watch a little way from us, looked surprised. I was very pleased—I loved to see the Abbess astonish people; it was one of her gifts—and at seven I had no knowledge of lust except that my little thing felt good sometimes when I handled it to make water, and what had that to do with statues coming to life or women turning into laurel trees? I was more interested in mad Sibihd, the way children are; I did not know what she might do, or if I should be afraid of her, or, if I should go mad myself, what it would be like. But the Abbess was laughing gently at Hedwic's amazement.

"Why not me?" said the Abbess. "I was young and healthy and had no special grace from God any more than the hens or the cows do! Indeed I burned so with desire for that handsome young hero—for so I had made him in my mind, as a woman might do with a man she has seen a few times on the street—that thoughts of him tormented me waking and sleeping. It seemed to me that because of my vows I could not give myself to this Apollo of my own free will, so I would dream that he took me against my will, and oh, what an exquisite pleasure that was!"

Here Hedwic's blood came all to her face and she covered it with her hands. I could see Thorvald grinning, back where he watched us.

"And then," said the Abbess, as if she had not seen either of them, "a terrible fear came to my heart that God might punish me by sending a ravisher who would use me unlawfully, as I had dreamed my Apollo did, and that I would not even wish to resist him, and would feel the pleasures of a base lust, and would know myself a whore and a false nun forever after. This fear both tormented and drew me. I began to steal looks at young men in the streets, not letting the other Sisters see me do it, thinking: Will it be he? Or he? Or he?

"And then it happened. I had lingered behind the others at a melon-seller's, thinking of no Apollos or handsome heroes but only of the convent's dinner, when I saw my companions disappearing round a corner. I hastened to catch up with them—and made a wrong turning—and was suddenly lost in a narrow street—and at that very moment a young fellow took hold of my habit and threw me to the ground! You may wonder why he should do such a mad thing, but as I found out afterwards, there are prostitutes in Rome who affect our way of dress to please the appetites of certain men who are depraved enough to— Well, really, I do not know how to say it! Seeing me alone, he had thought I was one of them and would be glad of a customer and a bit of play. So there was a reason for it.

"Well, there I was on my back with this young fellow, sent as a vengeance by God, as I thought, trying to do exactly what I had dreamed, night after night, my statue should do. And do you know, it was nothing in the least like my dream! The stones at my back hurt me, for one thing. And instead of melting with delight, I was screaming my head off in terror and kicking at him as he tried to pull up my skirts, and praying to God that this insane man might not break any of my bones in his rage!

"My screams brought a crowd of people and he went running, so I got off with nothing worse than a bruised back and a sprained knee. But the strangest thing of all was that, while I was cured forever of lusting after my Apollo, instead I began to be tormented by a new fear—that I had lusted after *him*, that foolish young man with the foul breath and the one tooth missing!—and I felt strange creepings and crawlings over my body that were half like desire and half like fear and half like disgust and shame with all sorts of other things mixed in—I know that is too many halves, but it is how I felt—and nothing at all like the burning desire I had felt for my Apollo. I went to see the statue once more before I left Rome and it seemed to look at me sadly, as if to say: Don't blame me, poor girl; I'm only a piece of stone. And that was the last time I was so proud as to believe that God had singled me out for a special gift, like chastity—or a special sin, either—or that being thrown down on the ground and hurt had anything to do with any sin of mine, no matter how I mixed the two together in my mind. I dare say you did not find it a great pleasure yesterday, did you?"

Hedwic shook her head. She was crying quietly. She said, "Thank you, Abbess," and the Abbess embraced her. They both seemed happier, but then all of a sudden Sibihd muttered something, so low that one could not hear her.

"The—" she whispered and then she brought it out but still in a whisper: "The blood."

"What, dear, your blood?" said Radegunde.

"No mother," said Sibihd, beginning to tremble, "the blood. All over us. Walafrid and—and Uta—and Sister Hildegarde—and everyone broken and spilled out like a dish! And none of us had done anything but I could smell it all over me and the children screaming because they were being trampled down, and those demons come up from Hell though we had done nothing and—and—I understand, mother, about the rest, but I will never, ever forget it, oh Christ, it is all around me now, oh mother, the *blood!*"

Then Sister Sibihd dropped to her knees on the fallen leaves and began to scream, not covering her face as Sister Hedwic had done, but staring ahead with her wide eyes as if she were blind or could see something we could not. The Abbess knelt down and embraced her, rocking her back and forth, saying, "Yes, yes, dear, but we are here; we are here now; that is gone now," but Sibihd continued to scream, covering her ears as if the scream were someone else's and she could hide herself from it.

Thorvald said, looking, I thought, a little uncomfortable, "Cannot your Christ cure this?"

"No," said the Abbess. "Only by undoing the past. And that is the one thing He never does, it seems. She is in Hell now and must go back there many times before she can forget."

"She would make a bad slave," said the Norseman, with a glance at Sister Sibihd, who had fallen silent and was staring ahead of her again; "You need not fear that anyone will want her."

"God," said the Abbess Radegunde calmly, "is merciful."

Thorvald Einarsson said, "Abbess, I am not a bad man."

"For a good man," said the Abbess Radegunde, "you keep surprisingly bad company."

He said angrily, "I did not choose my shipmates. I have had bad luck!"

"Ours has," said the Abbess, "been worse, I think."

"Luck is luck," said Thorvald, clenching his fists. "It comes to some folk and not to others."

"As you came to us," said the Abbess mildly. "Yes, yes, I see, Thorvald Einarsson; one may say that luck is Thor's doing or Odin's doing, but you must know that our bad luck is your own doing and not some god's. You are our bad luck, Thorvald Einarsson. It's true that you're not as wicked as your friends, for they kill for pleasure and you do it without feeling, as a business, the way one hews down grain. Perhaps you have seen today some of the grain you have cut. If you had a man's soul, you would not have gone *viking*, luck or no luck, and if your soul were bigger still, you would have tried to stop your shipmates, just as I talk honestly to you now, despite your anger, and just as Christ Himself told the truth and was nailed on the cross. If you were a beast, you could not break God's law and if you were a man you would not, but you are neither and that makes you a kind of monster that spoils everything it touches and never knows the reason, and that is why I will never forgive you until you become a man, a true man with a true soul. As for your friends—"

Here Thorvald Einarsson struck the Abbess on the face with his open hand and knocked her down. I heard Sister Hedwic gasp in horror, and behind us Sister Sibihd began to moan. But the Abbess only sat there, rubbing her jaw and smiling a little. Then she said:

"Oh, dear, have I been at it again? I am ashamed of myself. You are quite right to be angry, Thorvald; no one can stand me when I go on in that way, least of all myself; it is such a bore. Still, I cannot seem to stop it; I am too used to being the Abbess Radegunde, that is clear. I promise never to torment you again, but you, Thorvald, must never strike me again, because you will be very sorry if you do."

He took a step forward.

"No, no, my dear man," the Abbess said merrily, "I mean no threat—how could I threaten you?—I mean only that I will never tell you any jokes, my spirits will droop, and I will become as dull as any other woman. Confess it now: I am the most interesting thing that has happened to you in years and I have entertained you better, sharp tongue and all, than all the *skalds* at the Court of Norway. And I know more tales and stories than they do—more than anyone in the whole world—for I make new ones when the old ones wear out.

"Shall I tell you a story now?"

"About your Christ?" said he, the anger still in his face.

"No," said she, "about living men and women. Tell me, Thorvald, what do you men want from us women?"

"To be talked to death," said he, and I could see there was some anger in him still, but he was turning it to play also.

The Abbess laughed in delight. "Very witty!" she said, springing to her feet and brushing the leaves off her skirt. "You are a very clever man, Thorvald. I beg your pardon, Thorvald. I keep forgetting. But as to what men want from women, if you asked the young men, they would only wink and dig one another in the ribs, but that is only how they deceive themselves. That is only body calling to body. They themselves want something quite different and they want it so much that it frightens them. So they pretend it is anything and everything else: pleasure, comfort, a servant in the home. Do you know what it is that they want?"

"What?" said Thorvald.

"The mother," said Radegunde, "as women do, too; we all want the mother. When I walked before you on the riverbank yesterday, I was playing the mother. Now you did nothing, for you are no young fool, but I knew that sooner or later one of you, so tormented by his longing that he would hate me for it, would reveal himself. And so he did: Thorfinn, with his thoughts all mixed up between witches and grannies and whatnot. I knew I could frighten him, and through him, most of you. That was the beginning of my bargaining. You Norse have too much of the father in your country and not enough mother, with all your honoring of your women; that is why you die so well and kill other folk so well—and live so very, very badly."

"You are doing it again," said Thorvald, but I think he wanted to listen all the same.

"Your pardon, friend," said the Abbess. "You are brave men; I don't deny it. But I know your *sagas* and they are all about fighting and dying and afterwards not Heavenly happiness but the end of the world: everything, even the gods, eaten by the Fenris-wolf and the Midgard snake! What a pity, to die bravely only because life is not worth living! The Irish knew better. The pagan Irish were heroes, with their Queens leading them to battle as often as not, and Father Cairbre, God rest his soul, was complaining only two days ago that the common Irish folk were blasphemously making a goddess out of God's mother, for do they build shrines to Christ or Our Lord or pray to them? No! It is Our Lady of the Rocks and Our Lady of the Sea and Our Lady of the Grove and Our Lady of this or that from one end of the land to the other. And even here it is only the Abbey folk who speak of God the Father and of Christ. In the village if one is sick or another in trouble it is: Holy Mother, save me! and: *Mariam Virginem,* intercede for me, and: Blessed Virgin, blind my husband's eyes! and: Our Lady, preserve my crops, and so on, men and women both. We all need the mother."

"You, too?"

"More than most," said the Abbess.

"And I?"

"Oh no," said the Abbess, stopping suddenly, for we had all been walking slowly back towards the village as she spoke. "No, and that is what drew me to you at once. I saw it in you and knew you were the leader. It is followers who make leaders, you know, and your shipmates have made you leader, whether you know it or not. What you want is—how shall I say it? You are a clever man, Thorvald, perhaps the cleverest man I have ever met, more even than the scholars I knew in my youth. But your cleverness has had no food. It is a cleverness of the world and not of books. You want to travel and know about folk and their customs, and what strange places are like, and what has happened to men and women in the past. If you take me to Constantinople, it will not be to get a price for me but merely to go there; you went seafaring because this longing itched at you until you could bear it not a year more; I know that."

"Then you are a witch," said he, and he was not smiling.

"No, I only saw what was in your face when you spoke of that city," said she.

"Also there is gossip that you spent much time in Göteborg as a young man, idling and dreaming and marveling at the ships and markets when you should have been at your farm."

She said, "Thorvald, I can feed that cleverness. I am the wisest woman in the world. I know everything—everything! I know more than my teachers; I make it up or it comes to me, I don't know how, but it is real—real!—and I know more than anyone. Take me from here, as your slave if you wish but as your friend also, and let us go to Constantinople and see the domes of gold, and the walls all inlaid with gold, and the people so wealthy you cannot imagine it, and the whole city so gilded it seems to be on fire, and pictures as high as a wall, set right in the wall and all made of jewels so there is nothing else like them, redder than the reddest rose, greener than the grass, and with a blue that makes the sky pale!"

"You are indeed a witch," said he, "and not the Abbess Radegunde."

She said slowly, "I think I am forgetting how to be the Abbess Radegunde."

"Then you will not care about them anymore," said he and pointed to Sister Hedwic, who was still leading the stumbling Sister Sibihd.

The Abbess's face was still and mild. She said, "I care. Do not strike me, Thorvald, not ever again, and I will be a good friend to you. Try to control the worst of your men and leave as many of my people free as you can—I know them and will tell you which can be taken away with the least hurt to themselves or others—and I will feed that curiosity and cleverness of yours until you will not recognize this old world anymore for the sheer wonder and awe of it; I swear this on my life."

"Done," said he, adding, "but with my luck, your life is somewhere else, locked in a box on top of a mountain, like the troll's in the story, or you will die of old age while we are still at sea."

"Nonsense," she said. "I am a healthy mortal woman with all my teeth, and I mean to gather many wrinkles yet."

He put his hand out and she took it; then he said, shaking his head in wonder, "If I sold you in Constantinople, within a year you would become Queen of the place!"

The Abbess laughed merrily and I cried in fear, "Me, too! Take me too!" and she said, "Oh yes, we must not forget little Boy News," and lifted me into her arms. The frightening tall man, with his face close to mine, said in his strange sing-song German:

"Boy, would you like to see the whales leaping in the open sea and the seals barking on the rocks? And cliffs so high that a giant could stretch his arms up and not reach their tops? And the sun shining at midnight?"

"Yes!" said I.

"But you will be a slave," he said, "and may be ill-treated and will always have to do as you are bid. Would you like that?"

"No!" I cried lustily, from the safety of the Abbess's arms; "I'll fight!"

He laughed a mighty, roaring laugh and tousled my head—rather too hard, I thought—and said, "I will not be a bad master, for I am named for Thor Redbeard and he is strong and quick to fight but good-natured, too, and so am I," and the Abbess put me down and so we walked back to the village, Thorvald and the Abbess Radegunde talking of the glories of this world and Sister Hedwic saying softly, "She is a saint, our Abbess, a saint, to sacrifice herself for the good of the people," and all the time behind us, like a memory, came the low, witless sobbing of Sister Sibihd, who was in Hell.

When we got back we found that Thorfinn was better and the Norsemen were to leave in the morning. Thorvald had a second pallet brought into the Abbess's study and slept on the floor with us that night. You might think his men would laugh at this, for the Abbess was an old woman, but I think he had been with one of the young ones before he came to us. He had that look about him. There was no bedding for the Abbess but an old brown cloak with holes in it, and she and I were wrapped in it when he came in and threw himself down, whistling, on the other pallet. Then he said:

"Tomorrow, before we sail, you will show me the old Abbess's treasure."

"No," said she. "That agreement was broken."

He had been playing with his knife and now ran his thumb along the edge of it. "I can make you do it."

"No," said she patiently, "and now I am going to sleep."

"So you make light of death?" he said. "Good! That is what a brave woman should do, as the *skalds* sing, and not move, even when the keen sword cuts off her eyelashes. But what if I put this knife here not to your throat but to your little boy's? You would tell me then quick enough!"

The Abbess turned away from him, yawning and saying, "No, Thorvald, because you would not. And if you did, I would despise you for a cowardly oath-breaker and not tell you for that reason. Good night."

He laughed and whistled again for a bit. Then he said:

"Was all that true?"

"All what?" said the Abbess. "Oh, about the statue. Yes, but there was no ravisher. I put him in the tale for poor Sister Hedwic."

Thorvald snorted, as if in disappointment. "Tale? You tell lies, Abbess!"

The Abbess drew the old brown cloak over her head and closed her eyes. "It helped her."

Then there was a silence, but the big Norseman did not seem able to lie still. He shifted this way and that, stared at the ceiling, turned over, shifted his body again as if the straw bothered him, and again turned over. He finally burst out, "But what happened!"

She sat up. Then she shut her eyes. She said, "Maybe it does not come into your man's thoughts that an old woman gets tired and that the work of dealing with folk is hard work, or even that it is work at all. Well!

"Nothing 'happened,' Thorvald. Must something happen only if this one fucks that one or one bangs in another's head? I desired my statue to the point of such foolishness that I determined to find a real, human lover, but when I raised my eyes from my fancies to the real, human men of Rome and unstopped my ears to listen to their talk, I realized that the thing was completely and eternally impossible. Oh, those younger sons with their skulking, jealous hatred of the rich, and the rich ones with their noses in the air because they thought themselves of such great consequence because of their silly money, and the timidity of the priests to their superiors, and their superiors' pride, and the artisans' hatred of the peasants, and the peasants being worked like animals from morning until night, and half the men I saw beating their wives and the other half out to cheat some poor girl of her money or her virginity or both—this was enough to put out any fire! And the women doing less harm only because they had less power to do harm, or so it seemed to me then. So I put all away, as one does with any disappointment. Men are not such bad folk when one stops expecting them to be gods, but they are not for me. If that state is chastity, then a weak stomach is temperance, I think. But whatever it is, I have it, and that's the end of the matter."

"*All* men?" said Thorvald Einarsson with his head to one side, and it came to me that he had been drinking, though he seemed sober.

"Thorvald," said the Abbess, "what you want with this middle-aged wreck of a body I cannot imagine, but if you lust after my wrinkles and flabby breasts and lean, withered flanks, do whatever you want quickly and then for Heaven's sake, let me sleep. I am tired to death."

He said in a low voice, "I need to have power over you."

She spread her hands in a helpless gesture. "Oh Thorvald, Thorvald, I am a weak little woman over forty years old! Where is the power? All I can do is talk!"

He said, "That's it. That's how you do it. You talk and talk and talk and everyone does just as you please; I have seen it!"

The Abbess said, looking sharply at him, "Very well. If you must. *But if I were you, Norseman, I would as soon bed my own mother.* Remember that as you pull my skirts up."

That stopped him. He swore under his breath, turning over on his side, away from us. Then he thrust his knife into the edge of his pallet, time after time. Then he put the knife under the rolled-up cloth he was using as a pillow. We had no pillow so I tried to make mine out of the edge of the cloak and failed. Then I thought that the Norseman was afraid of God working in Radegunde, and then I thought of Sister Hedwic's changing color and wondered why. And then I thought of the leaping whales and the seals, which must be like great dogs because of the barking, and then the seals jumped on land and ran to my pallet and lapped at me with great icy tongues of water so that I shivered and jumped and then I woke up.

The Abbess Radegunde had left the pallet—it was her warmth I had missed—and was walking about the room. She would step and pause, her skirts making a small noise as she did so. She was careful not to touch the sleeping Thorvald. There was a dim light in the room from the embers that still glowed under the ashes in the hearth, but no light came from between the shutters of the study window, now shut against the cold. I saw the Abbess kneel under the plain wooden cross which hung on the study wall and heard her say a few words in Latin; I thought she was praying. But then she said in a low voice:

"'Do not call upon Apollo and the Muses, for they are deaf things and vain.' But so are you, Pierced Man, deaf and vain."

Then she got up and began to pace again. Thinking of it now frightens me, for it was the middle of the night and no one to hear her—except me, but she thought I was asleep—and yet she went on and on in that low, even voice as if it were broad day and she were explaining something to someone, as if things that had been in her thoughts for years must finally come out. But I did not find anything alarming in it then, for I thought that perhaps all Abbesses had to do such things, and besides she did not seem angry or hurried or afraid; she sounded as calm as if she were discussing the profits from the Abbey's bee-keeping—which

I had heard her do—or the accounts for the wine cellars—which I had also heard—and there was nothing alarming in that. So I listened as she continued walking about the room in the dark. She said:

"Talk, talk, talk, and always to myself. But one can't abandon the kittens and puppies; that would be cruel. And being the Abbess Radegunde at least gives one something to do. But I am so sick of the good Abbess Radegunde; I have put on Radegunde every morning of my life as easily as I put on my smock, and then I have had to hear the stupid creature praised all day!—sainted Radegunde, just Radegunde who is never angry or greedy or jealous, kindly Radegunde who sacrifices herself for others and always the talk, talk, talk, bubbling and boiling in my head with no one to hear or understand, and no one to answer. No, not even in the south, only a line here or a line there, and all written by the dead. Did they feel as I do? That the world is a giant nursery full of squabbles over toys and the babes thinking me some kind of goddess because I'm not greedy for their dolls or bits of straw or their horses made of tied-together sticks?

"Poor people, if only they knew! It's so easy to be temperate when one enjoys nothing, so easy to be kind when one loves nothing, so easy to be fearless when one's life is no better than one's death. And so easy to scheme when the success or failure of the scheme doesn't matter.

"Would they be surprised, I wonder, to find out what my real thoughts were when Thorfinn's knife was at my throat? Curiosity! But he would not do it, of course; he does everything for show. And they would think I was twice holy, not to care about death.

"Then why not kill yourself, impious Sister Radegunde? Is it your religion which stops you? Oh, you mean the holy wells, and the holy trees, and the blessed saints with their blessed relics, and the stupidity that shamed Sister Hedwic and the promises of safety that drove poor Sibihd mad when the blessed body of her Lord did not protect her and the blessed love of the blessed Mary turned away the sharp point of not one knife? Trash! Idle leaves and sticks, reeds and rushes, filth we sweep off our floors when it grows too thick. As if holiness had anything to do with all of that. As if every place were not as holy as every other and every thing as holy as every other, from the shit in Thorfinn's bowels to the rocks on the ground. As if all places and things were not clouds placed in front of our weak eyes, to keep us from being blinded by that glory, that eternal shining, that blazing all about us, that torrent of light that is everything and is in everything! That is what keeps me from the river, but it never speaks to me or tells me what to do, and to it good and evil are the same—no, it is something else than good or evil; it *is*, only—so it is not God. That I know.

"So, people, is your Radegunde a witch or a demon? Is she full of pride or is Radegunde abject? Perhaps she is a witch. Once, long ago, I confessed to Old Gerbertus that I could see things that were far away merely by closing my eyes, and I proved it to him, too, and he wept over me and gave me much penance, crying, 'If it come of itself it may be a gift of God, daughter, but it is more likely the work of a demon, so do not do it!' And then we prayed and I told him the power had left me, to make the poor old puppy less troubled in its mind, but that was not true, of course. I could still see Turkey as easily as I could see him, and places far beyond: the squat wild men of the plains on their ponies, and the strange tall people beyond that with their great cities and odd eyes, as if one pulled one's eyelid up on a slant, and then the seas with the great wild lands and the cities more full of gold than Constantinople, and then the water again until one comes back home, for the world's a ball, as the ancients said.

"But I did stop somehow, over the years. Radegunde never had time, I suppose. Besides, when I opened that door it was only pictures, as in a book, and all to no purpose, and after a while I had seen them all and no longer cared for them. It is the other door that draws me, when it opens itself but a crack and strange things peep through, like Ranulf sister's-son and the name of his horse. That door is good but very heavy; it always swings back after a little. I shall have to be on my deathbed to open it all the way, I think.

"The fox is asleep. He is the cleverest yet; there is something in him so that at times one can almost talk to him. But still a fox, for the most part. Perhaps in time . . .

"But let me see; yes, he is asleep. And the Sibihd puppy is asleep, though it will be having a bad dream soon, I think, and the Thorfinn kitten is asleep, as full of fright as when it wakes, with its claws going in and out, in and out, lest something strangle it in its sleep."

Then the Abbess fell silent and moved to the shuttered window as if she were looking out, so I thought that she was indeed looking out—but not with her eyes—at all the sleeping folk, and this was something she had done every night of her life to see if they were safe and sound. But would she not know that *I* was awake? Should I not try very hard to get to sleep before she caught me? Then it seemed to me that she smiled in the dark, although I could not see it. She said in that same low, even voice: "Sleep or wake, Boy News; it is all one to me. Thou hast heard nothing of any importance, only the silly Abbess talking to herself, only Radegunde saying good-bye to Radegunde, only Radegunde going away— don't cry, Boy News; I am still here—but there: Radegunde has gone. This Norseman and I are alike in one way: our minds are like great houses with many of the rooms locked shut. We crowd in a miserable huddled few, like poor folk, when we might move freely among them all, as gracious as princes. It is fate that locked away so much of the Norseman from the Norseman—see, Boy News, I do not say his name, not even softly, for that wakes folks—but I wonder if the one who bolted me in was not Radegunde herself, she and Old Gerbertus— whom I partly believed—they and the years and years of having to be Radegunde and do the things Radegunde did and pretend to have the thoughts Radegunde had and the endless, endless lies Radegunde must tell everyone, and Radegunde's utter and unbearable loneliness."

She fell silent again. I wondered at the Abbess's talk this time: saying she was not there when she was, and about living locked up in small rooms—for surely the Abbey was the most splendid house in all the world and the biggest—and how could she be lonely when all the folk loved her? But then she said in a voice so low that I could hardly hear it:

"Poor Radegunde! So weary of the lies she tells and the fooling of men and women with the collars round their necks and bribes of food for good behavior and a careful twitch of the leash that they do not even see or feel. And with the Norseman it will be all the same: lies and flattery and all of it work that never ends and no one ever even sees, so that finally Radegunde will lie down like an ape in a cage, weak and sick from hunger, and will never get up.

"Let her die now. There: Radegunde is dead. Radegunde is gone. Perhaps the door was heavy only because she was on the other side of it, pushing against me. Perhaps it will open all the way now. I have looked in all directions: to the east, to the north and south, and to the west, but there is one place I have never looked and now I will: away from the ball, straight up. Let us see—"

She stopped speaking all of a sudden. I had been falling asleep, but this silence woke me. Then I heard the Abbess gasp terribly, like one mortally stricken, and then she said in a whisper so keen and thrilling that it made the hair stand up on my head: *Where art thou?* The next moment she had torn the shutters open and was crying out with all her voice: *Help me! Find me! Oh come, come, come, or I die!*

This waked Thorvald. With some Norse oath he stumbled up and flung on his sword-belt, and then put his hand to his dagger; I had noticed this thing with the dagger was a thing Norsemen liked to do. The Abbess was silent. He let out his breath in an oof! and went to light the tallow dip at the live embers under the hearth-ashes; when the dip had smoked up, he put it on its shelf on the wall.

He said in German, "What the devil, woman! What has happened?"

She turned round. She looked as if she could not see us, as if she had been dazed by a joy too big to hold, like one who has looked into the sun and is still dazzled by it so that everything seems changed, and the world seems all God's and everything in it like Heaven. She said softly, with her arms around herself, hugging herself: "My people. The real people."

"What are you talking of!" said he.

She seemed to see him then, but only as Sibihd had beheld us; I do not mean in horror as Sibihd had, but beholding through something else, like someone who comes from a vision of bliss which still lingers about her. She said in the same soft voice, "They are coming for me, Thorvald. Is it not wonderful? I knew all this year that something would happen, but I did not know it would be the one thing I wanted in all the world."

He grasped his hair. "*Who* is coming?"

"My people," she said, laughing softly. "Do you not feel them? I do. We must wait three days, for they come from very far away. But then—oh, you will see!"

He said, "You've been dreaming. We sail tomorrow."

"Oh no," said the Abbess simply. "You cannot do that for it would not be right. They told me to wait; they said if I went away, they might not find me."

He said slowly, "You've gone mad. Or it's a trick."

"Oh no, Thorvald," said she. "How could I trick you? I am your friend. And you will wait these three days, will you not, because you are my friend also."

"You're mad," he said, and started for the door of the study, but she stepped in front of him and threw herself on her knees. All her cunning seemed to have deserted her, or perhaps it was Radegunde who had been the cunning one. This one was like a child. She clasped her hands and tears came out of her eyes; she begged him, saying:

"Such a little thing, Thorvald, only three days! And if they do not come, why then we will go anywhere you like, but if they do come you will not regret it, I promise you; they are not like the folk here and that place is like nothing here. It is what the soul craves, Thorvald!"

He said, "Get up, woman, for your God's sake!"

She said, smiling in a sly, frightened way through her blubbered face, "If you let me stay, I will show you the old Abbess's buried treasure, Thorvald."

He stepped back, the anger clear in him. "So this is the brave old witch who cares nothing for death!" he said. Then he made for the door, but she was up again, as quick as a snake, and had flung herself across it.

She said, still with that strange innocence, "Do not strike me. Do not push me. I am your friend!"

He said, "You mean that you lead me by a string round the neck, like a goose. Well, I am tired of that!"

"But I cannot do that anymore," said the Abbess breathlessly, "not since the door opened. I am not able now." He raised his arm to strike her and she cowered, wailing, "Do not strike me! Do not push me! Do not, Thorvald!"

He said, "Out of my way then, old witch!"

She began to cry in sobs and gulps. She said, "One is here but another will come! One is buried but another will rise! She will come, Thorvald!" and then in a low, quick voice, "Do not push open this last door. There is one behind it who is evil and I am afraid"—but one could see that he was angry and disappointed and would not listen. He struck her for a second time and again she fell, but with a desperate cry, covering her face with her hands. He unbolted the door and stepped over her and I heard his footsteps go down the corridor. I could see the Abbess clearly—at that time I did not wonder how this could be, with the shadows from the tallow dip half hiding everything in their drunken dance—but I saw every line in her face as if it had been full day and in that light I saw Radegunde go away from us at last.

Have you ever been at some great King's court or some Earl's and heard the story-tellers? There are those so skilled in the art that they not only speak for you what the person in the tale said and did, but they also make an action with their faces and bodies as if they truly were that man or woman, so that it is a great surprise to you when the tale ceases, for you almost believe that you have seen the tale happen in front of your very eyes and it is as if a real man or woman had suddenly ceased to exist, for you forget that all this was only a teller and a tale.

So it was with the woman who had been Radegunde. She did not change; it was still Radegunde's gray hairs and wrinkled face and old body in the peasant woman's brown dress, and yet at the same time it was a stranger who stepped out of the Abbess Radegunde as out of a gown dropped to the floor. This stranger was without feeling, though Radegunde's tears still stood on her cheeks, and there was no kindness or joy in her. She got up without taking care of her dress where the dirty rushes stuck to it; it was as if the dress were an accident and did not concern her. She said in a voice I had never heard before, one with no feeling in it, as if I did not concern her or Thorvald Einarsson either, as if neither of us were worth a second glance:

"Thorvald, turn around."

Far up in the hall something stirred.

"Now come back. This way."

There were footsteps, coming closer. Then the big Norseman walked clumsily into the room—jerk! jerk! jerk! at every step as if he were being pulled by a rope. Sweat beaded his face. He said, "You—how?"

"By my nature," she said. "Put up the right arm, fox. Now the left. Now both down. Good."

"You—troll!" he said.

"That is so," she said. "Now listen to me, you. There's a man inside you but he's not worth getting at; I tried moments ago when I was new-hatched and he's buried too deep, but now I have grown beak and claws and care nothing for him. It's almost dawn and your boys are stirring; you will go out and tell them that we must stay here another three days. You are weatherwise; make up some story they will believe. And don't try to tell anyone what happened here tonight; you will find that you cannot."

"Folk—come," said he, trying to turn his head, but the effort only made him sweat.

She raised her eyebrows. "Why should they? No one has heard anything. Nothing has happened. You will go out and be as you always are and I will play Radegunde. For three days only. Then you are free."

He did not move. One could see that to remain still was very hard for him; the sweat poured and he strained until every muscle stood out. She said:

"Fox, don't hurt yourself. And don't push me; I am not fond of you. My hand is light upon you only because you still seem to me a little less unhuman than the rest; do not force me to make it heavier. To be plain: I have just broken Thorfinn's neck, for I find that the change improves him. Do not make me do the same to you."

"No worse . . . than death," Thorvald brought out.

"Ah no?" said she, and in a moment he was screaming and clawing at his eyes. She said, "Open them, open them; your sight is back," and then, "I do not wish to bother myself thinking up worse things, like worms in your guts. Or do you wish dead sons and a dead wife? Now go.

"*As you always do,*" she added sharply, and the big man turned and walked out. One could not have told from looking at him that anything was wrong.

I had not been sorry to see such a bad man punished, one whose friends had killed our folk and would have taken them for slaves—yet I was sorry, too, in a way, because of the seals barking and the whales—and he *was* splendid, after a fashion—and yet truly I forgot all about that the moment he was gone, for I was terrified of this strange person or demon or whatever it was, for I knew that whoever was in the room with me was not the Abbess Radegunde. I knew also that it could tell where I was and what I was doing, even if I made no sound, and was in a terrible riddle as to what I ought to do when soft fingers touched my face. It was the demon, reaching swiftly and silently behind her.

And do you know, all of a sudden everything was all right! I don't mean that she was the Abbess again—I still had very serious suspicions about that—but all at once I felt light as air and nothing seemed to matter very much because my stomach was full of bubbles of happiness, just as if I had been drunk, only nicer. If the Abbess Radegunde were really a demon, what a joke that was on her people! And she did not, now that I came to think of it, seem a bad sort of demon, more the frightening kind than the killing kind, except for Thorfinn, of course, but then Thorfinn had been a very wicked man. And did not the angels of the Lord smite down the wicked? So perhaps the Abbess was an angel of the Lord and not a demon, but if she were truly an angel, why had she not smitten the

Norsemen down when they first came and so saved all our folk? And then I thought that, whether angel or demon, she was no longer the Abbess and would love me no longer, and if I had not been so full of the silly happiness which kept tickling about inside me, this thought would have made me weep.

I said, "Will the bad Thorvald get free, demon?"

"No," she said. "Not even if I sleep."

I thought: *But she does not love me.*

"I love thee," said the strange voice, but it was not the Abbess Radegunde's and so was without meaning, but again those soft fingers touched me and there was some kindness in them, even if it was a stranger's kindness.

Sleep, they said.

So I did.

The next three days I had much secret mirth to see the folk bow down to the demon and kiss its hands and weep over it because it had sold itself to ransom them. That is what Sister Hedwic told them. Young Thorfinn had gone out in the night to piss and had fallen over a stone in the dark and broken his neck, which secretly rejoiced our folk, and his comrades did not seem to mind much either, save for one young fellow who had been Thorfinn's friend, I think, and so went about with a long face. Thorvald locked me up in the Abbess's study with the demon every night and went out—or so folk said—to one of the young women, but on those nights the demon was silent and I lay there with the secret tickle of merriment in my stomach, caring about nothing.

On the third morning I woke sober. The demon—or the Abbess—for in the day she was so like the Abbess Radegunde that I wondered—took my hand and walked us up to Thorvald, who was out picking the people to go aboard the Norsemen's boats at the riverbank to be slaves. Folk were standing about weeping and wringing their hands; I thought this strange, because of the Abbess's promise to pick those whose going would hurt least, but I know now that least is not none. The weather was bad, cold rain out of mist, and some of Thorvald's companions were speaking sourly to him in the Norse, but he talked them down—bluff and hearty—as if making light of the weather. The demon stood by him and said, in German, in a low voice so that none might hear: "You will say we go to find the Abbess's treasure and then you will go with us into the woods."

He spoke to his fellows in Norse and they frowned; but the end of it was that two must come with us, for the demon said it was such a treasure as three might carry. The demon had the voice and manner of the Abbess Radegunde, all smiles, so they were fooled. Thus we started out into the trees behind the village, with the rain worse and the ground beginning to soften underfoot. As soon as the village was out of sight the two Norsemen fell behind, but Thorvald did not seem to notice this; I looked back and saw the first man standing in the mud with one foot up, like a goose, and the second with his head lifted and his mouth open so that the rain fell in it. We walked on, the earth sucking at our shoes and all of us getting wet: Thorvald's hair stuck fast against his face and the demon's old brown cloak clinging to its body. Then suddenly the demon began to breathe harshly and it put its hand to its side with a cry. Its cloak fell off and it stumbled before us between the wet trees, not weeping but breathing hard. Then I saw, ahead of us through the pelting rain, a kind of shining among the bare treetrunks, and as we came nearer the shining became more clear until it was very plain to see, not a blazing thing like a fire at night but a mild and even brightness as though the sunlight were coming through the clouds pleasantly but without strength, as it often does at the beginning of the year.

And then there were folk inside the brightness, both men and women, all dressed in white, and they held out their arms to us and the demon ran to them, crying out loudly and weeping, but paying no mind to the tree branches, which struck it across the face and body. Sometimes it fell but it quickly got up again. When it reached the strange folk they embraced it and I thought that the filth and mud of its gown would stain their white clothing, but the foulness dropped off and would not cling to those clean garments. None of the strange folk spoke a word, nor did the Abbess—I knew then that she was no demon, whatever she was—but I felt them talk to one another, as if in my mind, although I know not how this could be nor the sense of what they said. An odd thing was that as I came closer I could see they were not standing on the ground, as in the way of nature, but higher up, inside the shining, and that their white robes were nothing at all like ours, for they clung to the body so that one might see the people's legs all the way up to the place where the legs joined, even the women's. And some of the folk were like us, but most had a darker color and some looked as if they had been smeared with soot—there are such persons in the far parts of the world, you know, as I found out later; it is their own natural color—and there were some with the odd eyes the Abbess had spoken of—but the oddest thing of all I will not tell you now. When the Abbess had embraced and kissed them all and all had wept, she turned and looked down upon us: Thorvald standing there as if held by a rope and I, who had lost my fear and had crept close in pure awe, for there was such a joy about these people, like the light about them, mild as spring light and yet as strong as in a spring where the winter has gone forever.

"Come to me, Thorvald," said the Abbess, and one could not see from her face if she loved or hated him. He moved closer—jerk! jerk!—and she reached down and touched his forehead with her fingertips, at which one side of his lip lifted, as a dog's does when it snarls.

"As thou knowest," said the Abbess quietly, "I hate thee and would be revenged upon thee. Thus I swore to myself three days ago, and such vows are not lightly broken."

I saw him snarl again and he turned his eyes from her.

"I must go soon," said the Abbess, unmoved, "for I could stay here long years only as Radegunde and Radegunde is no more; none of us can remain here long as our proper selves or even in our true bodies, for if we do we go mad like Sibihd or walk into the river and drown or stop our own hearts, so miserable, wicked, and brutish does your world seem to us. Nor may we come in large companies, for we are few and our strength is not great and we have much to learn and study of thy folk so that we may teach and help without marring all in our ignorance. And ignorant or wise, we can do naught except thy folk aid us.

"Here is my revenge," said the Abbess, and he seemed to writhe under the touch of her fingers, for all they were so light; "Henceforth be not Thorvald Farmer nor yet Thorvald Seafarer but Thorvald Peacemaker, Thorvald Warhater, put into anguish by bloodshed and agonized at cruelty. I cannot make long thy life—that gift is beyond me—but I give thee this: to the end of thy days, long or short, thou wilt know that it is neither good nor evil, as I do, and this knowing will trouble and frighten thee always, as it does me, and so about this one thing, as about many another, Thorvald Peacemaker will never have peace.

"Now, Thorvald, go back to the village and tell thy comrades I was assumed into the company of the saints, straight up to Heaven. Thou mayst believe it, if thou wilt. That is all my revenge."

Then she took away her hand and he turned and walked from us like a man in a dream, holding out his hands as if to feel the rain and stumbling now and again, as one who wakes from a vision.

Then I began to grieve, for I knew she would be going away with the strange people and it was to me as if all the love and care and light in the world were leaving me. I crept close to her, meaning to spring secretly onto the shining place and so go away with them, but she spied me and said, "Silly Radulphus, you cannot," and that *you* hurt me more than anything else, so that I began to bawl.

"Child," said the Abbess, "come to me," and loudly weeping I leaned against her knees. I felt the shining around me, all bright and good and warm, that wiped away all grief, and then the Abbess's touch on my hair.

She said, "Remember me. And be . . . content."

I nodded, wishing I dared to look up at her face, but when I did, she had already gone with her friends. Not up into the sky, you understand, but as if they moved very swiftly backwards among the trees—although the trees were still behind them somehow—and as they moved, the shining and the people faded away into the rain until there was nothing left.

Then there was no rain. I do not mean that the clouds parted or the sun came out; I mean that one moment it was raining and cold and the next the sky was clear blue from side to side and it was splendid, sunny, breezy, bright, sailing weather. I had the oddest thought that the strange folk were not agreed about doing such a big miracle—and it was hard for them, too—but they had decided that no one would believe this more than all the other miracles folk speak of, I suppose. And it would surely make Thorvald's lot easier when he came back with wild words about saints and Heaven, as indeed it did, later.

Well, that is the tale, really. She said to me "Be content" and so I am; they call me Radulf the Happy now. I have had my share of trouble and sickness but always somewhere in me there is a little spot of warmth and joy to make it all easier, like a traveler's fire burning out in the wilderness on a cold night. When I am in real sorrow or distress I remember her fingers touching my hair and that takes part of the pain away, somehow. So perhaps I got the best gift, after all. And she said also, "Remember me," and thus I have, every little thing, although it all happened when I was the age my own grandson is now, and that is how I can tell you this tale today.

And the rest? Three days after the Norsemen left, Sibihd got back her wits and no one knew how, though I think I do! And as for Thorvald Einarsson, I have heard that after his wife died in Norway he went to England and ended his days there as a monk, but whether this story be true or not I do not know.

I know this: they may call me Happy Radulf all they like, but there is much that troubles me. Was the Abbess Radegunde a demon, as the new priest says? I cannot believe this, although he called half her sayings nonsense and the other half blasphemy when I asked him. Father Cairbre, before the Norse killed him, told us stories about the Sidhe, that is the Irish fairy people, who leave changelings in human cradles, and for a while it seemed to me that Radegunde must be a woman of the Sidhe when I remembered that she could read Latin at the age of two and was such a marvel of learning when so young, for the changelings the fairies leave are not their own children, you understand, but one of the fairy-folk themselves, who are hundreds upon hundreds of years old, and the other fairy-folk always come back for their own in the end. And yet this could not have been, for Father Cairbre said also that the Sidhe are wanton and cruel and without souls, and neither the Abbess Radegunde nor the people who came for her were one blessed bit like that, although she did break Thorfinn's neck—but then it may be that Thorfinn broke his own neck by chance, just as we all thought at the time, and she told this to Thorvald afterwards, as if she had done it herself, only to frighten him. She had more of a soul with a soul's griefs and joys than most of us, no matter what the new priest says. He never saw her or felt her sorrow and lonesomeness, or heard her talk of the blazing light all around us—and what can that be but God Himself? Even though she did call the crucifix a deaf thing and vain, she must have meant not Christ, you see, but only the piece of wood itself, for she was always telling the Sisters that Christ was in Heaven and not on the wall. And if she said the light was not good or evil, well, there is a traveling Irish scholar who told me of a holy Christian monk named Augustinus who tells us that all which is, is good, and evil is only a lack of the good, like an empty place not filled up. And if the Abbess truly said there was no God, I say it was the sin of despair, and even saints may sin, if only they repent, which I believe she did at the end.

So I tell myself and yet I know the Abbess Radegunde was no saint, for are the saints few and weak, as she said? Surely not! And then there is a thing I held back in my telling, a small thing and it will make you laugh and perhaps means nothing one way or the other but it is this:

Are the saints bald?

These folk in white had young faces but they were like eggs; there was not a stitch of hair on their domes! Well, God may shave His saints if He pleases, I suppose.

But I know she was no saint. And then I believe that she did kill Thorfinn and the light was not God and she not even a Christian or maybe even human and I remember how Radegunde was to her only a gown to step out of at will, and how she truly hated and scorned Thorvald until she was happy and safe with her own people. Or perhaps it was like her talk about living in a house with the rooms shut up; when she stopped being Radegunde first one part of her came back and then the other—the joyful part that could not lie or plan and then the angry part—and then they were all together when she was back among her own folk. And then I give up trying to weigh this matter and go back to warm my soul at the little fire she lit in me, that one warm, bright place in the wide and windy dark.

But something troubles me even there, and will not be put to rest by the memory of the Abbess's touch on my hair. As I grow older it troubles me more and more. It was the very last thing she said to me, which I have not told you but will now. When she had given me the gift of contentment, I became so happy that I said, "Abbess, you said you would be revenged on Thorvald, but all you did was change him into a good man. That is no revenge!"

What this saying did to her astonished me, for all the color went out of her face and left it gray. She looked suddenly old, like a death's head, even standing there among her own true folk with love and joy coming from them so strongly that I myself might feel it. She said, "I did not change him. I lent him my eyes; that is all." Then she looked beyond me, as if at our village, at the Norsemen loading their boats with weeping slaves, at all the villages of Germany and England and France where the poor folk sweat from dawn to dark so that the great lords may do battle with one another, at castles under siege with the starving folk within eating mice and rats and sometimes each other, at the women carried off or raped or beaten, at the mothers wailing for their little ones, and beyond this at the great wide world itself with all its battles which I had used to think so grand, and the misery and greediness and fear and jealousy and hatred of folk one for the other, save—perhaps—for a few small bands of savages, but they were so far from us that one could scarcely see them. She said: *No revenge? Thinkest thou so, boy?* And then she said as one who believes absolutely, as one who has seen all the folk at their living and dying, not for one year but for many, not in one place but in all places, as one who knows it all over the whole wide earth:

Think again. . . .

OVERDRAWN AT THE MEMORY BANK

John Varley

John Varley exploded into SF in the mid-1970s with a number of impressive long stories that made him a reputation as the most significant new SF writer of the decade. He continued to produce fine work throughout the 1980s, a few novels and stories, but his continuing impact comes from the stories from his first flowering, collected in *The Persistence of Vision* and *The Barbie Murders*. This is from the former.

It was schoolday at the Kenya disneyland. Five nine-year-olds were being shown around the medico section where Fingal lay on the recording table, the top of his skull removed, looking up into a mirror. Fingal was in a bad mood (hence the trip to the disneyland) and could have done without the children. Their teacher was doing his best, but who can control five nine-year-olds?

"What's the big green wire do, teacher?" asked a little girl, reaching out one grubby hand and touching Fingal's brain where the main recording wire clamped to the built-in terminal.

"Lupus, I told you you weren't to touch anything. And look at you, you didn't wash your hands." The teacher took the child's hand and pulled it away.

"But what does it matter? You told us yesterday that the reason no one cares about dirt like they used to is dirt isn't dirty anymore."

"I'm sure I didn't tell you exactly *that*. What I said was that when humans were forced off Earth, we took the golden opportunity to wipe out all harmful germs. When there were only three thousand people alive on the moon after the Occupation it was easy for us to sterilize everything. So the medico doesn't need to wear gloves like surgeons used to, or even wash her hands. There's no danger of infection. But it isn't polite. We don't want this man to think we're being impolite to him, just because his nervous system is disconnected and he can't do anything about it, do we?"

"No, teacher."

"What's a surgeon?"

"What's 'infection'?"

Fingal wished the little perishers had chosen another day for their lessons, but as the teacher had said, there was very little he could do. The medico had turned his motor control over to the computer while she took the reading. He was paralyzed. He eyed the little boy carrying the carved stick, and hoped he didn't get a notion to poke him in the cerebrum with it. Fingal was insured, but who needs the trouble?

"All of you stand back a little so the medico can do her work. That's better. Now, who can tell me what the big green wire is? Destry?"

Destry allowed as how he didn't know, didn't care, and wished he could get out of here and play spat ball. The teacher dismissed him and went on with the others.

"The green wire is the main sounding electrode," the teacher said. "It's attached to a series of very fine wires in the man's head, like the ones you have, which are implanted at birth. Can anyone tell me how the recording is made?"

The little girl with the dirty hands spoke up.

"By tying knots in string."

The teacher laughed, but the medico didn't. She had heard it all before. So had the teacher, of course, but that was why he was a teacher. He had the patience to deal with children, a rare quality now that there were so few of them.

"No, that was just an analogy. Can you all say analogy?"

"Analogy," they chorused.

"Fine. What I told you is that the chains of FPNA are very much *like* strings with knots tied in them. If you make up a code with every millimeter and every knot having a meaning, you could write words in string by tying knots in it. That's what the machine does with the FPNA. Now . . . can anyone tell me what FPNA stands for?"

"Ferro-Photo-Nucleic Acid," said the girl, who seemed to be the star pupil.

"That's right, Lupus. It's a variant on DNA, and it can be knotted by magnetic fields and light, and made to go through chemical changes. What the medico is doing now is threading long strings of FPNA into the tiny tubes that are in the man's brain. When she's done, she'll switch on the machine and the current will start tying knots. And what happens then?"

"All his memories go into the memory cube," said Lupus.

"That's right. But it's a little more complicated than that. You remember what I told you about a divided cipher? The kind that has two parts, neither of which is any good without the other? Imagine two of the strings, each with a lot of knots in them. Well, you try to read one of them with your decoder, and you find out that it doesn't make sense. That's because whoever wrote it used two strings, with knots tied in different places. They only make sense when you put them side by side and read them that way. That's how this decoder works, but the medico uses twenty-five strings. When they're all knotted the right way and put into the right openings in that cube over there," he pointed to the pink cube on the medico's bench, "they'll contain all this man's memories and personality. In a way, he'll be in the cube, but he won't know it, because he's going to be an African lion today."

This excited the children, who would much rather be stalking the Kenya savanna than listening to how a multi-holo was taken. When they quieted down the teacher went on, using analogies that got more strained by the minute.

"When the strings are in . . . class, pay attention. When they're in the cube, a current sets them in place. What we have then is a multi-holo. Can anyone tell me why we can't just take a tape recording of what's going on in this man's brain, and use that?"

One of the boys answered, for once.

"Because memory isn't . . . what's that word?"

"Sequential?"

"Yeah, that's it. His memories are stashed all over his brain and there's no way to sort them out. So this recorder takes a picture of the whole thing at once, like a hologram. Does that mean you can cut the cube in half and have two people?"

"No, but that's a good question. This isn't that sort of hologram. This is something like . . . like when you press your hand into clay, but in four dimensions. If you chip off a part of the clay after it's dried, you lose part of the information, right? Well, this is sort of like that. You can't see the imprint because it's too small, but everything the man ever did and saw and heard and thought will be in the cube."

"Would you move back a little?" asked the medico. The children in the mirror over Fingal's head shuffled back and became more than just heads with shoulders sticking out. The medico adjusted the last strand of FPNA suspended in Fingal's cortex to the close tolerances specified by the computer.

"I'd like to be a medico when I grow up," said one boy.

"I thought you wanted to go to college and study to be a scientist."

"Well, maybe. But my friend is teaching me to be a medico. It looks a lot easier."

"You should stay in school, Destry. I'm sure your parents will want you to make something of yourself." The medico fumed silently. She knew better than to speak up—education was a serious business and interference with the duties of a teacher carried a stiff fine. But she was obviously pleased when the class thanked her and went out the door, leaving dirty footprints behind them.

She viciously flipped a switch, and Fingal found he could breathe and move the muscles in his head.

"Lousy conceited college graduate," she said. "What the hell's wrong with getting your hands dirty, I ask you?" She wiped the blood from her hands onto her blue smock.

"Teachers are the worst," Fingal said.

"Ain't it the truth? Well, being a medico is nothing to be ashamed of. So I didn't go to college, so what? I can do my job, and I can see what I've done when I'm through. I always did like working with my hands. Did you know that being a medico used to be one of the most respected professions there was?"

"Really?"

"Fact. They had to go to college for years and years, and they made a hell of a lot of money, let me tell you."

Fingal said nothing, thinking she must be exaggerating. What was so tough about medicine? Just a little mechanical sense and a steady hand, that was all you needed. Fingal did a lot of maintenance on his body himself, going to the shop only for major work. And a good thing, at the prices they charged. It was not the sort of thing one discussed while lying helpless on the table, however.

"Okay, that's done." She pulled out the modules that contained the invisible FPNA and set them in the developing solution. She fastened Fingal's skull back on and tightened the recessed screws set into the bone. She turned his motor control back over to him while she sealed his scalp back into place. He stretched and yawned. He always grew sleepy in the medico's shop; he didn't know why.

"Will that be all for today, sir? We've got a special on blood changes, and since you'll just be lying there while you're out doppling in the park, you might as well—"

"No, thanks. I had it changed a year ago. Didn't you read my history?"

She picked up the card and glanced at it. "So you did. Fine. You can get up now, Mr. Fingal." She made a note on the card and set it down on the table. The door opened and a small face peered in.

"I left my stick," said the boy. He came in and started looking under things, to the annoyance of the medico. She attempted to ignore the boy as she took down the rest of the information she needed.

"And are you going to experience this holiday now, or wait until your double has finished and play it back then?"

"Huh? Oh, you mean . . . yes, I see. No, I'll go right into the animal. My psychist advised me to come out here for my nerves, so it wouldn't do me much good to wait it out, would it?"

"No, I suppose it wouldn't. So you'll be sleeping here while you dopple in the park. Hey!" She turned to confront the little boy, who was poking his nose into things he should stay away from. She grabbed him and pulled him away.

"You either find what you're looking for in one minute or you get out of here, you see?" He went back to his search, giggling behind his hand and looking for more interesting things to fool around with.

The medico made a check on the card, glanced at the glowing numbers on her thumbnail and discovered her shift was almost over. She connected the memory cube through a machine to a terminal in the back of Fingal's head.

"You've never done this before, right? We do this to avoid blank spots, which can be confusing sometimes. The cube is almost set, but now I'll add the last ten minutes to the record at the same time I put you to sleep. That way you'll experience no disorientation, you'll move through a dream state to full awareness of being in the body of a lion. Your body will be removed and taken to one of our slumber rooms while you're gone. There's nothing to worry about."

Fingal wasn't worried, just tired and tense. He wished she would go on and do it and stop talking about it. And he wished the little boy would stop pounding his stick against the table leg. He wondered if his headache would be transferred to the lion.

She turned him off.

They hauled his body away and took his memory cube to the installation room. The medico chased the boy into the corridor and hosed down the recording room. Then she was off to a date she was already late for.

The employees of Kenya disneyland installed the cube into a metal box set into the skull of a full-grown African lioness. The social structure of lions being what it was, the proprietors charged a premium for the use of a male body, but Fingal didn't care one way or the other.

A short ride in an underground railroad with the sedated body of the Fingal-lioness, and he was deposited beneath the blazing sun of the Kenya savanna. He awoke, sniffed the air, and felt better immediately.

The Kenya disneyland was a total environment buried twenty kilometers beneath Mare Moscoviense on the far side of Luna. It was roughly circular, with a radius of two hundred kilometers. From the ground to the "sky" was two kilometers except over the full-sized replica of Kilimanjaro, where it bulged to allow clouds to form in a realistic manner over the snowcap.

The illusion was flawless. The curve of the ground was consistent with the curvature of the Earth, so that the horizon was much more distant than anything Fingal was used to. The trees were real, and so were all the animals. At night an astronomer would have needed a spectroscope to distinguish the stars from the real thing.

Fingal certainly couldn't spot anything wrong. Not that he wanted to. The colors were strange but that was from the limitations of feline optics. Sounds were much more vivid, as were smells. If he'd thought about it, he would have realized the gravity was much too weak for Kenya. But he wasn't thinking; he'd come here to avoid that.

It was hot and glorious. The dry grass made no sound as he walked over it on broad pads. He smelled antelope, wildebeest, and . . . was that baboon? He felt pangs of hunger but he really didn't want to hunt. But he found the lioness body starting on a stalk anyway.

Fingal was in an odd position. He was in control of the lioness, but only more or less. He could guide her where he wanted to go, but he had no say at all over instinctive behaviors. He was as much a pawn to these as the lioness was. In one sense, he *was* the lioness; when he wished to raise a paw or turn around, he simply did it. The motor control was complete. It felt great to walk on all fours, and it came as easily as breathing. But the scent of the antelope went on a direct route from the nostrils to the lower brain, made a connection with the rumblings of hunger, and started him on the stalk.

The guidebook said to surrender to it. Fighting it wouldn't do anyone any good, and could frustrate you. If you were paying to be a lion, read the chapter on "Things to Do," you might as well *be* one, not just wear the body and see the sights.

Fingal wasn't sure he liked this as he came downwind of the antelope and crouched behind a withered clump of scrub. He pondered it while he sized up the dozen or so animals grazing just a few meters from him, picking out the small, the weak, and the young with a predator's eye. Maybe he should back out now and go on his way. These beautiful creatures were not harming him. The Fingal part of him wished mostly to admire them, not eat them.

Before he quite knew what had happened, he was standing triumphant over the bloody body of a small antelope. The others were just dusty trails in the distance.

It had been incredible!

The lioness was fast, but might as well have been moving in slow motion compared to the antelope. Her only advantage lay in surprise, confusion, and quick, all-out attack. There had been the lifting of a head; ears had flicked toward the bush he was hiding in, and he had exploded. Ten seconds of furious exertion and he bit down on a soft throat, felt the blood gush and the dying kicks of the hind legs under his paws. He was breathing hard and the blood coursed through his veins. There was only one way to release the tension.

He threw his head back and roared his bloodlust.

*   *   *

He'd had it with lions at the end of the weekend. It wasn't worth it for the few minutes of exhilaration at the kill. It was a life of endless stalking, countless failures, then a pitiful struggle to get a few bites for yourself from the kill you had made. He found to his chagrin that his lioness was very low in the dominance order. When he got his kill back to the pride—he didn't know why he had dragged it back but the lioness seemed to know—it was promptly stolen from him. He/she sat back helplessly and watched the dominant male take his share, followed by the rest of the pride. He was left with a dried haunch four hours later, and had to contest even that with vultures and hyenas. He saw what the premium payment was for. That male had it *easy*.

But he had to admit that it had been worth it. He felt better; his psychist had been right. It did one good to leave the insatiable computers at his office for a weekend of simple living. There were no complicated choices to be made out here. If he was in doubt, he listened to his instincts. It was just that the next time, he'd go as an elephant. He'd been watching them. All the other animals pretty much left them alone, and he could see why. To be a solitary bull, free to wander where he wished with food as close as the nearest tree branch . . .

He was still thinking about it when the collection crew came for him.

He awoke with the vague feeling that something was wrong. He sat up in bed and looked around him. Nothing seemed to be out of place. There was no one in the room with him. He shook his head to clear it.

It didn't do any good. There was still something wrong. He tried to remember how he had gotten there, and laughed at himself. His own bedroom! What was so remarkable about that?

But hadn't there been a vacation, a weekend trip? He remembered being a lion, eating raw antelope meat, being pushed around within the pride, fighting it out with the other females and losing and retiring to rumble to him/herself.

Certainly he should have come back to human consciousness in the disneyland medical section. He couldn't remember it. He reached for his phone, not knowing who he wished to call. His psychist, perhaps, or the Kenya office.

"I'm sorry, Mr. Fingal," the phone told him. "This line is no longer available for outgoing calls. If you'll—"

"Why not?" he asked, irritated and confused. "I paid my bill."

"That is of no concern to this department, Mr. Fingal. And please do not interrupt. It's hard enough to reach you. I'm fading, but the message will be continued if you look to your right." The voice and the power hum behind it faded. The phone was dead.

Fingal looked to his right and jerked in surprise. There was a hand, a woman's hand, writing on his wall. The hand faded out at the wrist.

"Mene, Mene . . ." it wrote, in thin letters of fire. Then the hand waved in irritation and erased that with its thumb. The wall was smudged with soot where the words had been.

"You're projecting, Mr. Fingal," the hand wrote, quickly etching out the words with a manicured nail. "That's what you expected to see." The hand underlined the word "expected" three times. "Please cooperate, clear your mind, and see what is *there*, or we're not going to get anywhere. Damn, I've about exhausted this medium."

And indeed it had. The writing had filled the wall and the hand was now down near the floor. The apparition wrote smaller and smaller in an effort to get it all in. Fingal had an excellent grasp on reality, according to his psychist. He held tightly onto that evaluation like a talisman as he leaned closer to the wall to read the last sentence.

"Look on your bookshelf," the hand wrote. "The title is *Orientation in your Fantasy World.*"

Fingal knew he had no such book, but could think of nothing better to do.

His phone didn't work, and if he was going through a psychotic episode he didn't think it wise to enter the public corridor until he had some idea of what was going on. The hand faded out, but the writing continued to smolder.

He found the book easily enough. It was a pamphlet, actually, with a gaudy cover. It was the sort of thing he had seen in the outer offices of the Kenya disneyland, a promotional booklet. At the bottom it said, "Published under the auspices of the Kenya computer; A. Joachim, operator." He opened it and began to read.

CHAPTER ONE
"Where Am I?"

You're probably wondering by now where you are. This is an entirely healthy and normal reaction, Mr. Fingal. Anyone would wonder, when beset by what seem to be paranormal manifestations, if his grasp on reality had weakened. Or, in simple language, "Am I nuts, or what?"

No, Mr. Fingal, you are not nuts. But you are not, as you probably think, sitting on your bed, reading a book. It's all in your mind. You are still in the Kenya disneyland. More specifically, you are contained in the memory cube we took of you before your weekend on the savanna. You see, there's been a big goof-up.

CHAPTER TWO
"What Happened?"

We'd like to know that, too, Mr. Fingal. But here's what we do know. Your body has been misplaced. Now, there's nothing to worry about, we're doing all we can to locate it and find out how it happened, but it will take some time. Maybe it's small consolation, but this has never happened before in the seventy-five years we've been operating, and as soon as we find out how it happened this time, you can be sure we'll be careful not to let it happen again. We're pursuing several leads at this time, and you can rest easy that your body will be returned to you intact just as soon as we locate it.

You are awake and aware right now because we have incorporated your memory cube into the workings of our H-210 computer, one of the finest holo-memory systems available to modern business. You see, there are a few problems.

CHAPTER THREE
"*What* Problems?"

It's kind of hard to put in terms you'd understand, but let's take a crack at it, shall we?

The medium we use to record your memories isn't the one you've probably used yourself as insurance against accidental death. As you must know, that system will store your memories for up to twenty years with no degradation or loss of information, and is quite expensive. The system we use is a temporary one, good for two, five, fourteen, or twenty-eight days, depending on the length of your stay. Your memories are put in the cube, where you might expect them to remain static and unchanging, as they do in your insurance recording. If you thought that, you would be wrong, Mr. Fingal. Think about it. If you die, your bank will immediately start a clone from the plasm you stored along with the memory cube. In six months, your memories would be played back into the clone and you would awaken, missing the memories that were accumulated in your body from the time of your last recording. Perhaps this has happened to you. If it has, you know the shock of awakening from the recording process to be told that it is three or four years later, and that you had died in that time.

In any case, the process we use is an *ongoing* one, or it would be worthless to you. The cube we install in the African animal of your choice is capable of adding the memories of your stay in Kenya to the memory cube. When your visit is over, these memories are played back into your brain and you leave the disneyland with the exciting, educational, and refreshing experiences you had as an animal, though your body never left our slumber room. This is known as "doppling," from the German *doppelganger.*

Now, to the problems we talked about. Thought we'd *never* get around to them, didn't you?

First, since you registered for a weekend stay, the medico naturally used one of the two-day cubes as part of our budget-excursion fare. These cubes have a safety factor, but aren't much good beyond three days at best. At the end of that time the cube would start to deteriorate. Of course, we fully expect to have you installed in your own body before then. Additionally, there is the problem of storage. Since these ongoing memory cubes are intended to be in use all the time your memories are stored in them, it presents certain problems when we find ourselves in the spot we are now in. Are you following me, Mr. Fingal? While the cube has already passed its potency for use in coexisting with a live host, like the lioness you just left, it *must* be kept in constant activation at all times or loss of information results. I'm sure you wouldn't want that to happen, would you? Of course not. So what we have done is to "plug you in" to our computer, which will keep you aware and healthy and guard against the randomizing of your memory nexi. I won't go into that; let it stand that randomizing is not the sort of thing you'd like to have happen to you.

CHAPTER FOUR
"So What Gives, Huh?"

I'm glad you asked that. (Because you *did* ask that, Mr. Fingal. This booklet is part of the analogizing process that I'll explain further down the page.)

Life in a computer is not the sort of thing you could just jump into and hope to retain the world-picture compatibility so necessary for sane functioning in this complex society. This has been tried, so take our word for it. Or rather, my word. Did I introduce myself? I'm Apollonia Joachim, First Class Operative for the DataSafe computer trouble-shooting firm. You've probably never heard of us, even though you do work with computers.

Since you can't just become aware in the baffling, on-and-off world that passes for reality in a data system, your mind, in cooperation with an analogizing program I've given the computer, interprets things in ways that seem safe and comfortable to it. The world you see around you is a figment of your imagination. Of course, it looks real to you because it comes from the same part of the mind that you normally use to interpret reality. If we wanted to get philosophical about it, we could probably argue all day about what constitutes reality and why the one you are perceiving now is any less real than the one you are used to. But let's not get into that, all right?

The world will likely continue to function in ways you are accustomed for it to function. It won't be exactly the same. Nightmares, for instance. Mr. Fingal, I hope you aren't the nervous type, because your nightmares can come to life where you are. They'll seem quite real. You should avoid them if you can, because they can do you real harm. I'll say more about this later if I need to. For now, there's no need to worry.

CHAPTER FIVE
"What Do I Do Now?"

I'd advise you to continue with your normal activities. Don't be alarmed at anything unusual. For one thing, I can only communicate with you by means of paranormal phenomena. You see, when a message from me is fed into the computer, it reaches you in a way your brain is not capable of dealing with. Naturally, your brain classifies this as an unusual event and fleshes the communication out in unusual fashion. Most of the weird things you see, if you stay calm and don't let your own fears out of the closet to persecute you, will be me. Otherwise, I anticipate that your world should look, feel, taste, sound, and smell pretty normal. I've talked to your psychist. He assures me that your world-grasp is strong. So sit tight. We'll be working hard to get you out of there.

CHAPTER SIX
"Help!"

Yes, we'll help you. This is a truly unfortunate thing to have happened, and of course we will refund all your money promptly. In addition, the lawyer for Kenya wants me to ask you if a lump sum settlement against all future damages is a topic worthy of discussion. You can think about it; there's no hurry.

In the meantime, I'll find ways to answer your questions. It might become unwieldy the harder your mind struggles to normalize my communications into things you are familiar with. That is both your greatest strength—the ability of your mind to bend the computer world it doesn't wish to see into media you are familiar with—and my biggest handicap. Look for me in tea leaves, on billboards, on holovision; anywhere! It could be exciting if you get into it.

Meanwhile, if you have received this message you can talk to me by filling in the attached coupon and dropping it in the mailtube. Your reply will probably be waiting for you at the office. Good luck!

Yes! I received your message and am interested in the exciting opportunities in the field of *computer living!* Please send me, without cost or obligation, your exciting catalog telling me how I can *move up* to the big, wonderful world outside!

NAME..
ADDRESS ....
I.D...

Fingal fought the urge to pinch himself. If what this booklet said was true—and he might as well believe it—it would hurt and he would *not* wake up. He pinched himself anyway. It hurt.

If he understood this right, everything around him was the product of his imagination. Somewhere, a woman was sitting at a computer input and talking to him in normal language, which came to his brain in the form of electron pulses it could not cope with and so edited into forms he was conversant with. He was analogizing like mad. He wondered if he had caught it from the teacher, if analogies were contagious.

"What the hell's wrong with a simple voice from the air?" he wondered aloud. He got no response, and was rather glad. He'd had enough mysteriousness for now. And on second thought, a voice from the air would probably scare the pants off him.

He decided his brain must know what it was doing. After all, the hand startled him but he hadn't panicked. He could *see* it, and he trusted his visual sense more than he did voices from the air, a classical sign of insanity if ever there was one.

He got up and went to the wall. The letters of fire were gone, but the black smudge of the erasure was still there. He sniffed it: carbon. He fingered the rough paper of the pamphlet, tore off a corner, put it in his mouth and chewed it. It tasted like paper.

He sat down and filled out the coupon and tossed it to the mailtube.

Fingal didn't get angry about it until he was at the office. He was an easygoing person, slow to boil. But he finally reached a point where he had to say something.

Everything had been so normal he wanted to laugh. All his friends and acquaintances were there, doing exactly what he would have expected them to be doing. What amazed and bemused him was the number and variety of spear carriers, minor players in this internal soap opera. The extras that his mind had cooked up to people the crowded corridors, like the man he didn't know who had bumped into him on the tube to work, apologized, and disappeared, presumably back into the bowels of his imagination.

There was nothing he could do to vent his anger but test the whole absurd setup. There was doubt lingering in his mind that the whole morning had been a fugue, a temporary lapse into dreamland. Maybe he'd never gone to Kenya, after all, and his mind was playing tricks on him. To get him there, or keep him away? He didn't know, but he could worry about that if the test failed.

He stood up at his desk terminal, which was in the third column of the fifteenth row of other identical desks, each with its diligent worker. He held up his hands and whistled. Everyone looked up.

"I don't believe in you," he screeched. He picked up a stack of tapes on his desk and hurled them at Felicia Nahum at the desk next to his. Felicia was a good friend of his, and she registered the proper shock until the tapes hit her. Then she melted. He looked around the room and saw that everything had stopped like a freeze-frame in a motion picture.

He sat down and drummed his fingers on his desk top. His heart was pounding and his face was flushed. For an awful moment he had thought he was wrong. He began to calm down, glancing up every few seconds to be sure the world really *had* stopped.

In three minutes he was in a cold sweat. What the hell had he *proved?* That this morning had been real, or that he really was crazy? It dawned on him that he would never be able to test the assumptions under which he lived.

A line of print flashed across his terminal.

"But when could you ever do so, Mr. Fingal?"

"Ms. Joachim?" he shouted, looking around him. "Where are you? I'm afraid."

"You mustn't be," the terminal printed. "Calm yourself. You have a strong sense of reality, remember? Think about this: even before today, how could you be sure the world you saw was not the result of catatonic delusions? Do you see what I mean? The question 'What is reality?' is, in the end, unanswerable. We all must accept at some point what we see and are told, and live by a set of untested and untestable assumptions. I ask you to accept the set I gave you this morning because, sitting here in the computer room where you cannot see me, my world picture tells me that they are the true set. On the other hand, you could believe that I'm deluding myself, that there's nothing in the pink cube I see and that you're a spear carrier in *my* dream. Does that make you more comfortable?"

"No," he mumbled, ashamed of himself. "I see what you mean. Even if I am crazy, it would be more comfortable to go along with it than to keep fighting it."

"Perfect, Mr. Fingal. If you need further illustrations you could imagine yourself locked in a straitjacket. Perhaps there are technicians laboring right now to correct your condition, and they are putting you through this psychodrama as a first step. Is that any more attractive?"

"No, I guess it isn't."

"The point is that it's as reasonable an assumption as the set of facts I gave you this morning. But the main point is that you should behave the same whichever set is true. Do you see? To fight it in the one case will only cause you trouble, and in the other, would impede the treatment. I realize I'm asking you to accept me on faith. And that's all I can give you."

"I believe in you," he said. "Now, can you start everything going again?"

"I told you I'm not in control of your world. In fact, it's a considerable obstacle to me, seeing as I have to talk to you in these awkward ways. But things should get going on their own as soon as you let them. Look up."

He did, and saw the normal hum and bustle of the office. Felicia was there at her desk, as though nothing had happened. Nothing had. Yes, something had, after all. The tapes were scattered on the floor near his desk, where they had fallen. They had unreeled in an unruly mess.

He started to pick them up, then saw they weren't as messy as he had thought. They spelled out a message in coils of tape.

"You're back on the track," it said.

For three weeks Fingal was a very good boy. His co-workers, had they been real people, might have noticed a certain standoffishness in him, and his social life at home was drastically curtailed. Otherwise, he behaved exactly as if everything around him were real.

But his patience had limits. This had already dragged on for longer than he had expected. He began to fidget at his desk, let his mind wander. Feeding information into a computer can be frustrating, unrewarding, and eventually stultifying. He had been feeling it even before his trip to Kenya; it had been the *cause* of his trip to Kenya. He was sixty-eight years old, with centuries ahead of him, and stuck in a ferro-magnetic rut. Longlife could be a mixed blessing when you felt boredom creeping up on you.

What was getting to him was the growing disgust with his job. It was bad enough when he merely sat in a real office with two hundred real people, shoveling slightly unreal data into a much-less-than-real-to-his-senses computer. How much worse now, when he knew that the data he handled had no meaning to anyone but himself, was nothing but occupational therapy created by his mind and a computer program to keep him busy while Joachim searched for his body.

For the first time in his life he began punching some buttons for himself. Under slightly less stress he would have gone to see his psychist, the approved and perfectly normal thing to do. Here, he knew he would only be talking to himself. He failed to perceive the advantages of such an idealized psychoanalytic process; he'd never really believed that a psychist did little but listen in the first place.

He began to change his own life when he became irritated with his boss. She pointed out to him that his error index was on the rise, and suggested that he shape up or begin looking for another source of employment.

This enraged him. He'd been a good worker for twenty-five years. Why should she take that attitude when he was just not feeling himself for a week or two?

Then he was angrier than ever when he thought about her being merely a projection of his own mind. Why should he let *her* push him around?

"I don't want to hear it," he said. "Leave me alone. Better yet, give me a raise in salary."

"Fingal," she said promptly, "you've been a credit to your section these last weeks. I'm going to give you a raise."

"Thank you. Go away." She did, by dissolving into thin air. This really made his day. He leaned back in his chair and thought about his situation for the first time since he was young.

He didn't like what he saw.

In the middle of his ruminations, his computer screen lit up again.

"Watch it, Fingal," it read. "That way lies catatonia."

He took the warning seriously, but didn't intend to abuse the newfound power. He didn't see why judicious use of it now and then would hurt anything. He stretched, and yawned broadly. He looked around, suddenly hating the office with its rows of workers indistinguishable from their desks. Why not take the day off?

On impulse, he got up and walked the few steps to Felicia's desk.

"Why don't we go to my house and make love?" he asked her.

She looked at him in astonishment, and he grinned. She was almost as surprised as when he had hurled the tapes at her.

"Is this a joke? In the middle of the day? You have a job to do, you know. You want to get us fired?"

He shook his head slowly. "That's not an acceptable answer."

She stopped, and rewound from that point. He heard her repeat her last sentences backwards, then she smiled.

"Sure, why not?" she said.

Felicia left afterwards in the same slightly disconcerting way his boss had left earlier, by melting into the air. Fingal sat quietly in his bed, wondering what to do with himself. He felt he was getting off to a bad start if he intended to edit his world with care.

His telephone rang.

"You're damn right," said a woman's voice, obviously irritated with him. He sat up straight.

"Apollonia?"

"Ms. Joachim to you, Fingal. I can't talk long; this is quite a strain on me. But listen to me, and listen hard. Your navel is very deep, Fingal. From where you're standing, it's a pit I can't even see the bottom of. If you fall into it I can't guarantee to pull you out."

"But do I have to take *everything* as it is? Aren't I allowed some self-improvement?"

"Don't kid yourself. That wasn't self-improvement. That was sheer laziness. It was nothing but masturbation, and while there's nothing wrong with that, if you do it to the exclusion of all else, your mind will grow in on itself. You're in grave danger of excluding the external universe from your reality."

"But I thought there was no external universe for me here."

"Almost right. But I'm feeding you external stimuli to keep you going. Besides, it's the attitude that counts. You've never had trouble finding sexual partners; why do you feel compelled to alter the odds now?"

"I don't know," he admitted. "Like you said, laziness, I guess."

"That's right. If you want to quit your job, feel free. If you're serious about self-improvement, there are opportunities available to you there. Search them out. Look around you, explore. But don't try to meddle in things you don't understand. I've got to go now. I'll write you a letter if I can, and explain more."

"Wait! What about my body? Have they made any progress?"

"Yes, they've found out how it happened. It seems . . ." Her voice faded out, and he switched off the phone.

The next day he received a letter explaining what was known so far. It seemed that the mix-up had resulted from the visit of the teacher to the medico section on the day of his recording. More specifically, the return of the little boy after the others had left. They were sure now that he had tampered with the routing card that told the attendants what to do with Fingal's body. Instead of moving it to the slumber room, which was a green card, they had sent it somewhere—no one knew where yet—for a sex change, which was a blue card. The medico, in her haste to get home for her date, had not noticed the switch. Now the body could be in any of several thousand medico shops in Luna. They were looking for it, and for the boy.

Fingal put the letter down and did some hard thinking.

Joachim had said there were opportunities for him in the memory banks. She had also said that not everything he saw was his own projections. He was receiving, was capable of receiving, external stimuli. Why was that? Because he would tend to randomize without them, or some other reason? He wished the letter had gone into that.

In the meantime, what did he do?

Suddenly he had it. He wanted to learn about computers. He wanted to know what made them tick, to feel a sense of power over them. It was particularly strong when he thought about being a virtual prisoner inside one. He was like a worker on an assembly line. All day long he labors, taking small parts off a moving belt and installing them on larger assemblies. One day, he happens to wonder who puts the parts on the belt. Where do they come from? How are they made? What happens after he installs them?

He wondered why he hadn't thought of it before.

The admissions office of the Lunar People's Technical School was crowded. He was handed a form and told to fill it out. It looked bleak. The spaces for "previous experience" and "aptitude scores" were almost blank when he was through with them. All in all, not a very promising application. He went to the desk and handed the form to the man sitting at the terminal.

The man fed it into the computer, which promptly decided Fingal had no talent for being a computer repairperson. He started to turn away when his eye was caught by a large poster behind the man. It had been there on the wall when he came in, but he hadn't read it.

LUNA NEEDS
COMPUTER TECHNICIANS.
THIS MEANS YOU,
MR. FINGAL!

Are you dissatisfied with your present employment? Do you feel you were cut out for better things? Then today may be your lucky day. You've come to the right place, and if you grasp this golden opportunity you will find doors opening that were closed to you.

Act, Mr. Fingal. This is the time. Who's to check up on you? Just take that stylus and fill in the application any old way you want. Be grandiose, be daring! The fix is in, and you're on your way to

BIG MONEY!

The secretary saw nothing unusual in Fingal's coming to the desk a second time, and didn't even blink when the computer decided he was eligible for the accelerated course.

It wasn't easy at first. He really did have little aptitude for electronics, but aptitude is a slippery thing. His personality matrix was as flexible now as it would ever be. A little effort at the right time would go a long way toward self-improvement. What he kept telling himself was that everything that made him what he was, was etched in that tiny cube wired in to the computer, and if he was careful he could edit it.

Not radically, Joachim told him in a long, helpful letter later in the week. That way led to complete disruption of the FPNA matrix and catatonia, which in this case would be distinguishable from death only to a hair splitter.

He thought a lot about death as he dug into the books. He was in a strange position. The being known as Fingal would not die in any conceivable outcome of this adventure. For one thing, his body was going toward a sex change and it was hard to imagine what could happen to it that would kill it. Whoever had custody of it now would be taking care of it just as well as the medicos in the slumber room would have. If Joachim was unsuccessful in her attempt to keep him aware and sane in the memory bank, he would merely awake and remember nothing from the time he fell asleep on the table.

If, by some compounded unlikelihood, his body *was* allowed to die, he had an insurance recording safe in the vault of his bank. The recording was three years old. He would awaken in the newly grown clone body knowing nothing of the last three years, and would have a fantastic story to listen to as he was brought up to date.

But none of that mattered to *him*. Humans are a time-binding species, existing in an eternal *now*. The future flows through them and becomes the past, but it is always the present that counts. The Fingal of three years ago was *not* the Fingal in the memory bank. The simple fact about immortality by memory recording was that it was a poor solution. The three-dimensional cross section that was the Fingal of now must always behave as if his life depended on his actions, for he would feel the pain of death if it happened to him. It was small consolation to a dying man to know that he would go on, several years younger and less wise. If Fingal lost out here, he would *die*, because with memory recording he was three people: the one who lived now, the one lost somewhere on Luna, and the one potential person in the bank vault. They were really no more than close relatives.

Everyone knew this, but it was so much better than the alternative that few people rejected it. They tried not to think about it and were generally successful. They had recordings made as often as they could afford them. They heaved a sigh of relief as they got onto the table to have another recording taken, knowing that another chunk of their lives was safe for all time. But they awaited the awakening nervously, dreading being told that it was now twenty years later because they had died sometime after the recording and had to start all over. A lot can happen in twenty years. The person in the new clone body might have to cope with a child he or she had never seen, a new spouse, or the shattering news that his or her employment was now the function of a machine.

So Fingal took Joachim's warnings seriously. Death was death, and though he could cheat it, death still had the last laugh. Instead of taking your whole life from you, death now only claimed a percentage, but in many ways it was the most important percentage.

He enrolled in classes. Whenever possible, he took the ones that were available over the phone lines so he needn't stir from his room. He ordered his food and supplies by phone and paid his bills by looking at them and willing them out of existence. It could have been intensely boring, or it could have been wildly interesting. After all, it was a dream world, and who doesn't think of retiring into fantasy from time to time? Fingal certainly did, but firmly suppressed the idea when it came. He intended to get out of this dream.

For one thing, he missed the company of other people. He waited for the weekly letters from Apollonia (she now allowed him to call her by her first name) with a consuming passion and devoured every word. His file of such letters bulged. At lonely moments he would pull one out at random and read it again and again.

On her advice, he left the apartment regularly and stirred around more or less at random. During these outings he had wild adventures. Literally. Apollonia hurled the external stimuli at him during these times and they could be anything from The Mummy's Curse to Custer's Last Stand with the original cast. It beat hell out of the movies. He would just walk down the public corridors and open a door at random. Behind it might be King Solomon's mines or the sultan's harem. He endured them all stoically. He was unable to get any pleasure from sex. He knew it was a one-handed exercise, and it took all the excitement away.

His only pleasure came in his studies. He read everything he could about computer science and came to stand at the head of his class. And as he learned, it began to occur to him to apply his knowledge to his own situation.

He began seeing things around him that had been veiled before. Patterns. The reality was starting to seep through his illusions. Every so often he would look up and see the faintest shadow of the real world of electron flow and fluttering circuits he inhabited. It scared him at first. He asked Apollonia about it on one of his dream journeys, this time to Coney Island in the mid-twentieth century. He liked it there. He could lie on the sand and talk to the surf. Overhead, a skywriter's plane spelled out the answers to his questions. He studiously ignored the brontosaurus rampaging through the roller coaster off to his right.

"What does it mean, O Goddess of Transistoria, when I begin to see circuit diagrams on the walls of my apartment? Overwork?"

"It means the illusion is beginning to wear thin," the plane spelled out over the next half hour. "You're adapting to the reality you have been denying. It could be trouble, but we're hot on the trail of your body. We should have it soon and get you out of there." This had been too much for the plane. The sun was down now, the brontosaurus vanquished and the plane out of gas. It spiraled into the ocean and the crowds surged closer to the water to watch the rescue. Fingal got up and went back to the boardwalk.

There was a huge billboard. He laced his fingers behind his back and read it.

"Sorry for the delay. As I was saying, we're almost there. Give us another few months. One of our agents thinks he will be at the right medico shop in about one week's time. From there it should go quickly. For now, avoid those places where you see the circuits showing through. They're no good for you, take my word for it."

Fingal avoided the circuits as long as he could. He finished his first courses in computer science and enrolled in the intermediate section. Six months rolled by.

His studies got easier and easier. His reading speed was increasing phenomenally. He found that it was more advantageous for him to see the library as composed of books instead of tapes. He could take a book from the shelf, flip through it rapidly, and know everything that was in it. He knew enough now to realize that he was acquiring a facility to interface directly with the stored knowledge in the computer, bypassing his senses entirely. The books he held in his hands were merely the sensual analogs of the proper terminals to touch. Apollonia was nervous about it, but let him go on. He breezed through the intermediate and graduated into the advanced classes.

But he was surrounded by wires. Everywhere he turned, in the patterns of veins beneath the surface of a man's face, in a plate of French fries he ordered for lunch, in his palmprints, overlaying the apparent disorder of a head of blonde hair on the pillow beside him.

The wires were analogs of analogs. There was little in a modern computer that consisted of wiring. Most of it was made of molecular circuits that were either embedded in a crystal lattice or photographically reproduced on a chip of silicon. Visually, they were hard to imagine, so his mind was making up these complex circuit diagrams that served the same purpose but could be experienced directly.

One day he could resist it no longer. He was in the bathroom, on the traditional place for the pondering of the imponderable. His mind wandered, speculating on the necessity of moving his bowels, wondering if he might safely eliminate the need to eliminate. His toe idly traced out the pathways of a circuit board incorporated in the pattern of tiles on the floor.

The toilet began to overflow, not with water, but with coins. Bells were ringing happily. He jumped up and watched in bemusement as his bathroom filled with money.

He became aware of a subtle alteration in the tone of the bells. They changed from the merry clang of jackpot to the tolling of a death knell. He hastily looked around for a manifestation. He knew that Apollonia would be angry.

She was. Her hand appeared and began to write on the wall. This time the writing was in his blood. It dripped menacingly from the words.

"What are you doing?" the hand wrote, and having writ, moved on. "I told you to leave the wires alone. Do you know what you've done? You may have wiped the financial records for Kenya. It could take *months* to straighten them out."

"Well, what do I care?" he exploded. "What have they done for me lately? It's *incredible* that they haven't located my body by now. It's been a full *year.*"

The hand bunched up in a fist. Then it grabbed him around the throat and squeezed hard enough to make his eyes bulge out. It slowly relaxed. When Fingal could see straight, he backed warily away from it.

The hand fidgeted nervously, drummed its fingers on the floor. It went to the wall again.

"Sorry," it wrote, "I guess I'm getting tired. Hold on."

He waited, more shaken than he remembered being since his odyssey began. There's nothing like a dose of pain, he reflected, to make you realize that it *can* happen to you.

The wall with the words of blood slowly dissolved into a heavenly panorama. As he watched, clouds streamed by his vantage point and mixed beautifully with golden rays of sunshine. He heard organ music from pipes the size of sequoias.

He wanted to applaud. It was so overdone, and yet so convincing. In the center of the whirling mass of white mist an angel faded in. She had wings and a halo, but lacked the traditional white robe. She was nude, and hair floated around her as if she were under water.

She levitated to him, walking on the billowing clouds, and handed him two stone tablets. He tore his eyes away from the apparition and glanced down at the tablets:

> *Thou shalt not screw around with*
> *things thou dost not understand.*

"All right, I promise I won't," he told the angel. "Apollonia, is that you? Really you, I mean?"

"Read the Commandments, Fingal. This is hard on me."

He looked back at the tablets.

> Thou shalt not meddle in the hardware systems of the Kenya Corporation, for Kenya shall not hold him indemnifiable who taketh freedoms with its property.
> Thou shalt not explore the limits of thy prison. Trust in the Kenya Corporation to extract thee.
> Thou shalt not program.
> Thou shalt not worry about the location of thy body, for it has been located, help is on the way, the cavalry has arrived, and all is in hand.
> Thou shalt meet a tall, handsome stranger who will guide thee from thy current plight.
> Thou shalt stay tuned for further developments.

He looked up and was happy to see that the angel was still there.

"I won't, I promise. But where is my body, and why has it taken so long to find it? Can you—"

"Know thou that appearing like this is a great taxation upon me, Mr. Fingal. I am undergoing strains the nature of which I have not time to reveal to thee. Hold thy horses, wait it out, and thou shalt soon see the light at the end of the tunnel."

"Wait, don't go." She was already starting to fade out.

"I cannot tarry."

"But . . . Apollonia, this is charming, but why do you appear to me in these crazy ways? Why all the pomp and circumstance? What's wrong with letters?" She looked around her at the clouds, the sunbeams, the tablets in his hand, and at her body, as if seeing them for the first time. She threw her head back and laughed like a symphony orchestra. It was almost too beautiful for Fingal to bear.

"Me?" she said, dropping the angelic bearing. "Me? I don't pick 'em, Fingal. I told you, it's *your* head, and I'm just passing through." She arched her eyebrows at him. "And really, sir, I had no idea you felt this way about me. Is it puppy love?" And she was gone, except for the grin.

The grin haunted him for days. He was disgusted with himself about it. He hated to see a metaphor overworked so. He decided his mind was just an inept analogizer.

But everything had its purpose. The grin forced himself to look at his feelings. He was in love, hopelessly, ridiculously, just like a teenager. He got out all his old letters from her and read through them again, searching for the magic words that could have inflicted this on him. Because it was *silly*. He'd never met her except under highly figurative circumstances. The one time he had seen her, most of what he saw was the product of his own mind.

There were no clues in the letters. Most of them were as impersonal as a textbook, though they tended to be rather chatty. Friendly, yes; but intimate, poetic, insightful, revealing? No. He failed utterly to put them together in any way that should add up to love, or even a teenage crush.

He attacked his studies with renewed vigor, awaiting the next communication. Weeks dragged by with no word. He called the post office several times, placed personal advertisements in every periodical he could think of, took to scrawling messages on public buildings, sealed notes in bottles and flushed them down the disposal, rented billboards, bought television time. He screamed at the empty walls of his apartment, buttonholed strangers, tapped Morse Code on the water pipes, started rumors in skid-row taprooms, had leaflets published and distributed all over the solar system. He tried every medium he could think of, and could not contact her. He was alone.

He considered the possibility that he had died. In his present situation, it might be hard to tell for sure. He abandoned it as untestable. That line was hazy enough already without his efforts to determine which side of the life/death dichotomy he inhabited. Besides, the more he thought about existing as nothing more than kinks in a set of macromolecules plugged into a data system, the more it frightened him. He'd survived this long by avoiding such thoughts.

His nightmares moved in on him, set up housekeeping in his apartment. They were a severe disappointment, and confirmed his conclusion that his imagination was not as vivid as it might be. They were infantile boogeymen, the sort that might scare him when glimpsed hazily through the fog of a nightmare, but were almost laughable when exposed to the full light of consciousness. There was a large, talkative snake that was crudely put together, fashioned from the incomplete picture a child might have of a serpent. A toy company could have done a better job. There was a werewolf whose chief claim to dread was a tendency to shed all over Fingal's rugs. There was a woman who consisted mostly of breasts and genitals, left over from his adolescence, he suspected. He groaned in embarrassment every time he looked at her. If he had ever been that infantile he would rather have left the dirty traces of it buried forever.

He kept booting them into the corridor but they drifted in at night like poor relations. They talked incessantly, and always about him. The things they knew! They seemed to have a very low opinion of him. The snake often expressed the opinion that Fingal would never amount to anything because he had so docilely accepted the results of the aptitude tests he took as a child. That hurt, but the best salve for the wound was further study.

Finally a letter came. He winced as soon as he got it open. The salutation was enough to tell him he wasn't going to like it.

Dear Mr. Fingal,

I won't apologize for the delay this time. It seems that most of my manifestations have included an apology and I feel I deserved a rest this time. I can't be always on call. I have a life of my own.

I understand that you have behaved in an exemplary manner since I last talked with you. You have ignored the inner workings of the computer just as I told you to do. I haven't been completely frank with you, and I will explain my reasons.

The hook-up between you and the computer is, and always has been, two-way. Our greatest fear at this end had been that you would begin interfering with the workings of the computer, to the great discomfort of everyone. Or that you would go mad and run amok, perhaps wrecking the entire data system. We installed you in the computer as a humane necessity, because you would have died if we had not done so, though it would have cost you only two days of memories. But Kenya is in the business of selling memories, and holds them to be a sacred trust. It was a mix-up on the part of the Kenya Corporation that got you here in the first place, so we decided we should do everything we could for you.

But it was at great hazard to our operations at this end.

Once, about six months ago, you got tangled in the weather-control sector of the computer and set off a storm over Kilimanjaro that is still not fully under control. Several animals were lost.

I have had to fight the Board of Directors to keep you on-line, and several times the program was almost terminated. You know what that means.

Now, I've leveled with you. I wanted to from the start, but the people who own things around here were worried that you might start fooling around out of a spirit of vindictiveness if you knew these facts, so they were kept from you. You could still do a great deal of damage before we could shut you off. I'm laying it on the line now, with directors chewing their nails over my shoulder. *Please* stay out of trouble.

On to the other matter.

I was afraid from the outset that what has happened might happen. For over a year I've been your only contact with the world outside. I've been the only other person in your universe. I would have to be an extremely cold, hateful, awful person—which I am not—for you *not* to feel affection for me under those circumstances. You are suffering from intense sensory deprivation, and it's well known that someone in that state becomes pliable, suggestible, and lonely. You've attached your feelings to me as the only thing around worth caring for.

I've tried to avoid intimacy with you for that reason, to keep things firmly on a last-name basis. But I relented during one of your periods of despair. And you read into my letters some things that were not there. Remember, even in the printed medium it is your mind that controls what you see. Your censor has let through what it wanted to see and maybe even added some things of its own. I'm at your mercy. For all I know, you may be reading this letter as a passionate affirmation of love. I've added every reinforcement I know of to make sure the message comes through on a priority channel and is not garbled. I'm sorry to hear that you love me. I do not, repeat not, love you in return. You'll understand why, at least in part, when we get you out of there.

It will never work, Mr. Fingal. Give it up.

Apollonia Joachim

Fingal graduated first in his class. He had finished the required courses for his degree during the last long week after his letter from Apollonia. It was a bitter victory for him, marching up to the stage to accept the sheepskin, but he clutched it to him fiercely. At least he had made the most of his situation, at least he had not meekly let the wheels of the machine chew him up like a good worker.

He reached out to grasp the hand of the college president and saw it transformed. He looked up and saw the bearded, robed figure flow and writhe and become a tall, uniformed woman. With a surge of joy, he knew who it was. Then the joy became ashes in his mouth, which he hurriedly spit out.

"I always knew you'd choke on a figure of speech," she said, laughing tiredly.

"You're here," he said. He could not quite believe it. He stared dully at her, grasping her hand and the diploma with equal tenacity. She was tall, as the prophecy had said, and handsome. Her hair was cropped short over a capable face, and the body beneath the uniform was muscular. The uniform was open at the throat, and wrinkled. There were circles under her eyes, and the eyes were bloodshot. She swayed slightly on her feet.

"I'm here, all right. Are you ready to go back?" She turned to the assembled students. "How about it, gang? Do you think he deserves to go back?"

The crowd went wild, cheering and tossing mortarboards into the air. Fingal turned dazedly to look at them, with a dawning realization. He looked down at the diploma.

"I don't know," he said. "I don't know. Back to work at the data room?"

She clapped him on the back.

"No. I promise you that."

"But how could it be different? I've come to think of this piece of paper as something . . . real. Real! How could I have deluded myself like that? Why did I accept it?"

"I helped you along," she said. "But it wasn't all a game. You really did learn all the things you learned. It won't go away when you return. That thing in your hand is imaginary, for sure, but who do you think prints the real ones? You're registered where it counts—in the computer—as having passed all the courses. You'll get a real diploma when you return."

Fingal wavered. There was a tempting vision in his head. He'd been here for over a year and had never really exploited the nature of the place. Maybe that business about dying in the memory bank was all a shuck, another lie invented to keep him in his place. In that case, he could remain here and satisfy his wildest desires, become king of the universe with no opposition, wallow in pleasure no emperor ever imagined. Anything he wanted here he could have, anything at all.

And he really felt he might pull it off. He'd noticed many things about this place, and now had the knowledge of computer technology to back him up. He could squirm around and evade their attempts to erase him, even survive if they removed his cube by programming himself into other parts of the computer. He could do it.

With a sudden insight he realized that he had no desires wild enough to keep him here in his navel. He had only one major desire right now, and she was slowly fading out. A lap dissolve was replacing her with the old college president.

"Coming?" she asked.

"Yes." It was as simple as that. The stage, president, students, and auditorium faded out and the computer room at Kenya faded in. Only Apollonia remained constant. He held onto her hand until everything stabilized.

"Whew," she said, and reached around behind her head. She pulled out a wire from her occipital plug and collapsed into a chair. Someone pulled a similar wire from Fingal's head, and he was finally free of the computer.

Apollonia reached out for a steaming cup of coffee on a table littered with empty cups.

"You were a tough nut," she said. "For a minute I thought you'd stay. It happened once. You're not the first to have this happen to you, but you're no more than the twentieth. It's an unexplored area. Dangerous."

"Really?" he said. "You weren't just saying that?"

"No," she laughed. "Now the truth can be told. It *is* dangerous. No one had ever survived more than three hours in that kind of cube, hooked into a computer. You went for six. You *do* have a strong world picture."

She was watching him to see how he reacted to this. She was not surprised to see him accept it readily.

"I should have known that," he said. "I should have thought of it. It was only six hours out here, and more than a year for me. Computers think faster. Why didn't I see that?"

"I helped you not see it," she admitted. "Like the push I gave you not to question why you were studying so hard. Those two orders worked a lot better than some of the orders I gave you."

She yawned again, and it seemed to go on forever.

"See, it was pretty hard for me to interface with you for six hours straight. No one's ever done it before; it can get to be quite a strain. So we've both got something to be proud of."

She smiled at him but it faded when he did not return it.

"Don't look so hurt, Fingal. What *is* your first name? I knew it, but erased it early in the game."

"Does it matter?"

"I don't know. Surely you must see why I haven't fallen in love with you, though you may be a perfectly lovable person. I haven't had *time*. It's been a very long six hours, but it was still only six hours. What can I do?"

Fingal's face was going through awkward changes as he absorbed that. Things were not so bleak after all.

"You could go to dinner with me."

"I'm already emotionally involved with someone else, I should warn you of that."

"You could still go to dinner. You haven't been exposed to my new determination. I'm going to really make a case."

She laughed warmly and got up. She took his hand.

"You know, it's possible that you might succeed. Just don't put wings on me again, all right? You'll never get anywhere like that."

"I promise. I'm through with visions—for the rest of my life."

THE GIRL WHO WAS PLUGGED IN

James Tiptree, Jr.

James Tiptree, Jr., was the SF pseudonym of Alice B. Sheldon, who burst into flower in SF in the early 1970s and remained a central figure until her death by suicide in the late 1980s. The discovery in the late seventies that he was a she was a social earthquake in the SF field. There is now a James Tiptree, Jr., Award given annually to a work or works of "gender-bending" SF. Her two novels, *Up the Walls of the World* and *Brightness Falls from the Air*, are significant SF works, but her major impact was through her short fiction, which showed an extraordinary range and intensity. "The Girl Who Was Plugged In" is her precursor to the cyberpunk fiction of the 1980s.

Listen, zombie. Believe me. What I could tell you—you with your silly hands leaking sweat on your growth-stocks portfolio. One-ten lousy hacks of AT&T on twenty-percent margin and you think you're Evel Knievel. AT&T . . . You doubleknit dummy, how I'd love to show you something.

Look, dead daddy, I'd say. See for instance that rotten girl?

In the crowd over there, that one gaping at her gods. One rotten girl in the city of the future. (That's what I said.) Watch.

She's jammed among bodies, craning and peering with her soul yearning out of her eyeballs. Love! Oo-ooh, love them! Her gods are coming out of a store called Body East. Three youngbloods, larking along loverly. Dressed like simple streetpeople but . . . smashing. See their great eyes swivel above their nose-filters, their hands lift shyly, their inhumanly tender lips melt? The crowd moans. Love! This whole boiling megacity, this whole fun future world loves its gods.

You don't believe gods, dad? Wait. Whatever turns you on, there's a god in the future for you, custom-made. Listen to this mob. "I touched his foot! Ow-oow, I TOUCHED Him!"

Even the people in the GTX tower up there love the gods—in their own way and for their own reasons.

The funky girl on the street, she just loves. Grooving on their beautiful lives, their mysterioso problems. No one ever told her about mortals who love a god and end up as a tree or a sighing sound. In a million years it'd never occur to her that her gods might love her back.

She's squashed against the wall now as the godlings come by. They move in a clear space. A holocam bobs above but its shadow never falls on them. The store display screens are magically clear of bodies as the gods glance in and a beggar underfoot is suddenly alone. They give him a token. "Aaaaah!" goes the crowd.

Now one of them flashes some wild new kind of timer and they all trot to catch a shuttle, just like people. The shuttle stops for them—more magic. The crowd sighs, closing back. The gods are gone.

(In a room far from—but not unconnected to—the GTX tower a molecular flipflop closes too, and three account tapes spin.)

Our girl is still stuck by the wall while guards and holocam equipment pull away. The adoration's fading from her face. That's good, because now you can see she's the ugly of the world. A tall monument to pituitary dystrophy. No surgeon would touch her. When she smiles, her jaw—it's half purple—almost bites her left eye out. She's also quite young, but who could care?

The crowd is pushing her along now, treating you to glimpses of her jumbled torso, her mismatched legs. At the corner she strains to send one last fond spasm after the godlings' shuttle. Then her face reverts to its usual expression of dim pain and she lurches onto the moving walkway, stumbling into people. The walkway junctions with another. She crosses, trips and collides with the casualty rail. Finally she comes out into a little place called a park. The sportshow is working, a basketball game in 3-di is going on right overhead. But all she does is squeeze onto a bench and huddle there while a ghostly free-throw goes by her ear.

After that nothing at all happens except a few furtive hand-mouth gestures which don't even interest her benchmates.

But you're curious about the city? So ordinary after all, in the FUTURE?

Ah, there's plenty to swing with here—and it's not all that *far* in the future, dad. But pass up the sci-fi stuff for now, like for instance the holovision technology that's put TV and radio in museums. Or the worldwide carrier field bouncing down from satellites, controlling communication and transport systems all over the globe. That was a spin-off from asteroid mining, pass it by. We're watching that girl.

I'll give you just one goodie. Maybe you noticed on the sportshow or the streets? No commercials. No ads.

That's right. NO ADS. An eyeballer for you.

Look around. Not a billboard, sign, slogan, jingle, skywrite, blurb, sublim-flash in this whole fun world. Brand names? Only in those ticky little peep-screens on the stores and you could hardly call that advertising. How does that finger you?

Think about it. That girl is still sitting there.

She's parked right under the base of the GTX tower as a matter of fact. Look up and you can see the sparkles from the bubble on top, up there among the domes of godland. Inside that bubble is a boardroom. Neat bronze shield on the door: Global Transmissions Corporation—not that that means anything.

I happen to know there's six people in that room. Five of them technically male, and the sixth isn't easily thought of as a mother. *They are absolutely unremarkable.* Those faces were seen once at their nuptials and will show again in their obituaries and impress nobody either time. If you're looking for the secret

Big Blue Meanies of the world, forget it. I know. Zen, do I know! Flesh? Power? Glory? You'd horrify them.

What they do like up there is to have things orderly, especially their communications. You could say they've dedicated their lives to that, to freeing the world from garble. Their nightmares are about hemorrhages of information: channels screwed up, plans misimplemented, garble creeping in. Their vast wealth only worries them, it keeps opening new vistas of disorder. Luxury? They wear what their tailors put on them, eat what their cooks serve them. See that old boy there—his name is Isham—he's sipping water and frowning as he listens to a databall. The water was prescribed by his medistaff. It tastes awful. The databall also contains a disquieting message about his son, Paul.

But it's time to go back down, far below to our girl. Look!

She's toppled over sprawling on the ground.

A tepid commotion ensues among the bystanders. The consensus is she's dead, which she disproves by bubbling a little. And presently she's taken away by one of the superb ambulances of the future, which are a real improvement over ours when one happens to be around.

At the local bellevue the usual things are done by the usual team of clowns aided by a saintly mop-pusher. Our girl revives enough to answer the questionnaire without which you can't die, even in the future. Finally she's cast up, a pumped-out hulk on a cot in the long, dim ward.

Again nothing happens for a while except that her eyes leak a little from the understandable disappointment of finding herself still alive.

But somewhere one GTX computer has been tickling another, and toward midnight something does happen. First comes an attendant who pulls screens around her. Then a man in a business doublet comes daintily down the ward. He motions the attendant to strip off the sheet and go.

The groggy girl-brute heaves up, big hands clutching at bodyparts you'd pay not to see.

"Burke? P. Burke, is that your name?"

"Y-yes." Croak. "Are you . . . policeman?"

"No. They'll be along shortly, I expect. Public suicide's a felony."

" . . . I'm sorry."

He has a 'corder in his hand. "No family, right?"

"No."

"You're seventeen. One year city college. What did you study?"

"La—languages."

"H'm. Say something."

Unintelligible rasp.

He studies her. Seen close, he's not so elegant. Errand-boy type.

"Why did you try to kill yourself?"

She stares at him with dead-rat dignity, hauling up the gray sheet. Give him a point, he doesn't ask twice.

"Tell me, did you see Breath this afternoon?"

Dead as she nearly is, that ghastly love-look wells up. Breath is the three young gods, a loser's cult. Give the man another point, he interprets her expression.

"How would you like to meet them?"

The girl's eyes bug out unequally.

"I have a job for someone like you. It's hard work. If you did well you'd be meeting Breath and stars like that all the time."

Is he insane? She's deciding she really did die.

"But it means you never see anybody you know again. Never, *ever.* You will be legally dead. Even the police won't know. Do you want to try?"

It all has to be repeated while her great jaw slowly sets. *Show me the fire I walk through.* Finally P. Burke's prints are in his 'corder, the man holding up the rancid girl-body without a sign of distaste. It makes you wonder what else he does.

And then—THE MAGIC. Sudden silent trot of litterbearers tucking P. Burke into something quite different from a bellevue stretcher, the oiled slide into the daddy of all luxury ambulances—real flowers in that holder!—and the long jarless rush to nowhere. Nowhere is warm and gleaming and kind with nurses. (Where did you hear that money can't buy genuine kindness?) And clean clouds folding P. Burke into bewildered sleep.

. . . Sleep which merges into feedings and washings and more sleeps, into drowsy moments of afternoon where midnight should be, and gentle businesslike voices and friendly (but very few) faces, and endless painless hyposprays and peculiar numbnesses . . . and later comes the steadying rhythm of days and nights, and a quickening which P. Burke doesn't identify as health, but only knows that the fungus place in her armpit is gone . . . and then she's up and following those few new faces with growing trust, first tottering, then walking strongly, all better now—clumping down the short hall to the tests, tests, tests, and the other things.

And here is our girl, looking—

If possible, worse than before. (You thought this was Cinderella transistorized?)

The disimprovement in her looks comes from the electrode jacks peeping out of her sparse hair, and there are other meldings of flesh and metal. On the other hand, that collar and spinal plate are really an asset; you won't miss seeing that neck.

P. Burke is ready for training in her new job.

The training takes place in her suite, and is exactly what you'd call a charm course. How to walk, sit, eat, speak, blow her nose, how to stumble, to urinate, to hiccup—DELICIOUSLY. How to make each nose-blow or shrug delightfully, subtly different from any ever spooled before. As the man said, it's hard work.

But P. Burke proves apt. Somewhere in that horrible body is a gazelle, a houri who would have been buried forever without this crazy chance. See the ugly duckling go!

Only it isn't precisely P. Burke who's stepping, laughing, shaking out her shining hair. How could it be? P. Burke is doing it all right, but she's doing it through something. The something is to all appearances a live girl. (You were warned, this is the FUTURE.)

When they first open the big cryocase and show her her new body she says just one word. Staring, gulping, "How?"

Simple, really. Watch P. Burke in her sack and scuffs stump down the hall beside Joe, the man who supervises the technical part of her training. Joe doesn't mind P. Burke's looks, he hasn't noticed them. To Joe system matrices are beautiful.

They go into a dim room containing a huge cabinet like a one-man sauna and a console for Joe. The room has a glass wall that's all dark now. And just for your information, the whole shebang is five hundred feet underground near what used to be Carbondale, Pa.

Joe opens the sauna-cabinet like a big clamshell standing on end with a lot of funny business inside. Our girl shucks her shift and walks into it bare, totally unembarrassed. *Eager.* She settles in face-forward, butting jacks into sockets. Joe closes it carefully onto her humpback. Clunk. She can't see in there or hear or move. She hates this minute. But how she loves what comes next!

Joe's at his console and the lights on the other side of the glass wall come up. A room is on the other side, all fluff and kicky bits, a girly bedroom. In the bed is a small mound of silk with a rope of yellow hair hanging out.

The sheet stirs and gets whammed back flat.

Sitting up in the bed is the darlingest girl child you've EVER seen. She quivers—porno for angels. She sticks both her little arms straight up, flips her hair, looks around full of sleepy pazazz. Then she can't resist rubbing her hands down over her minibreasts and belly. Because, you see, it's the godawful P. Burke who is sitting there hugging her perfect girl-body, looking at you out of delighted eyes.

Then the kitten hops out of bed and crashes flat on the floor.

From the sauna in the dim room comes a strangled noise. P. Burke, trying to rub her wired-up elbow, is suddenly smothered in *two* bodies, electrodes jerking in her flesh. Joe juggles inputs, crooning into his mike. The flurry passes; it's all right.

In the lighted room the elf gets up, casts a cute glare at the glass wall and goes into a transparent cubicle. A bathroom, what else? She's a live girl, and live girls have to go to the bathroom after a night's sleep even if their brains are in a sauna cabinet in the next room. And P. Burke isn't in that cabinet, she's in the bathroom. Perfectly simple, if you have the glue for that closed training circuit that's letting her run her neural system by remote control.

Now let's get one thing clear. P. Burke does not *feel* her brain is in the next room, she feels it's in that sweet little body. When you wash your hands, do you feel the water is running on your brain? Of course not. You feel the water on your hand, although the "feeling" is actually a potential-pattern flickering over the electrochemical jelly between your ears. And it's delivered there via the long circuits from your hands. Just so, P. Burke's brain in the cabinet feels the water on her hands in the bathroom. The fact that the signals have jumped across space on the way in makes no difference at all. If you want the jargon, it's known as eccentric projection or sensory reference and you've done it all your life. Clear?

Time to leave the honey-pot to her toilet training—she's made a booboo with the toothbrush, because P. Burke can't get used to what she sees in the mirror—

But wait, you say. Where did that girl-body come from?

P. Burke asks that too, dragging out the words.

"They grow 'em," Joe tells her. He couldn't care less about the flesh department. "PDs. Placental decanters. Modified embryos, see? Fit the control implants in later. Without a Remote Operator it's just a vegetable. Look at the feet—no callus at all." (He knows because they told him.)

"Oh . . . oh, she's incredible . . ."

"Yeah, a neat job. Want to try walking-talking mode today? You're coming on fast."

And she is. Joe's reports and the reports from the nurse and the doctor and style man go to a bushy man upstairs who is some kind of medical cybertech but mostly a project administrator. His reports in turn go—to the GTX boardroom? Certainly not, did you think this is a *big* thing? His reports just go up. The point is, they're green, very green. P. Burke promises well.

So the bushy man—Doctor Tesla—has procedures to initiate. The little kitten's dossier in the Central Data Bank, for instance. Purely routine. And the phase-in schedule which will put her on the scene. This is simple: a small exposure in an off-network holoshow.

Next he has to line out the event which will fund and target her. That takes budget meetings, clearances, coordinations. The Burke project begins to recruit and grow. And there's the messy business of the name, which always gives Doctor Tesla an acute pain in the bush.

The name comes out weird, when it's suddenly discovered that Burke's "P." stands for *Philadelphia*. Philadelphia? The astrologer grooves on it. Joe thinks it would help identification. The semantics girl references *brotherly love, Liberty-Bell, main-line, low teratogenesis,* blah-blah. Nicknames—Philly? Pala? Pooty? Delphi? Is it good, bad? Finally *Delphi* is gingerly declared goodo. ("Burke" is replaced by something nobody remembers.)

Coming along now. We're at the official checkout down in the underground suite, which is as far as the training circuits reach. The bushy Doctor Tesla is there, braced by two budgetary types and a quiet fatherly man whom he handles like hot plasma.

Joe swings the door wide and she steps shyly in.

Their little Delphi, fifteen and flawless.

Tesla introduces her around. She's child-solemn, a beautiful baby to whom something so wonderful has happened you can feel the tingles. She doesn't smile, she . . . brims. That brimming joy is all that shows of P. Burke, the forgotten hulk in the sauna next door. But P. Burke doesn't know she's alive—it's Delphi who lives, every warm inch of her.

One of the budget types lets go a libidinous snuffle and freezes. The fatherly man, whose name is Mr. Cantle, clears his throat.

"Well, young lady, are you ready to go to work?"

"Yes sir," gravely from the elf.

"We'll see. Has anybody told you what you're going to do for us?"

"No, sir." Joe and Tesla exhale quietly.

"Good." He eyes her, probing for the blind brain in the room next door. "Do you know what *advertising* is?"

He's talking dirty, hitting to shock. Delphi's eyes widen and her little chin goes up. Joe is in ecstasy at the complex expressions P. Burke is getting through. Mr. Cantle waits.

"It's, well, it's when they used to tell people to buy things." She swallows. "It's not allowed."

"That's right." Mr. Cantle leans back, grave. "Advertising as it used to be is against the law. *A display other than the legitimate use of the product, intended to promote its sale.* In former times every manufacturer was free to tout his wares any way, place, or time he could afford. All the media and most of the landscape was taken up with extravagant competing displays. The thing became uneconomic. The public rebelled. Since the so-called Huckster Act, sellers have been restrained to, I quote, 'displays in or on the product itself, visible during its legitimate use or in on-premise sales.'" Mr. Cantle leans forward. "Now tell me, Delphi, why do people buy one product rather than another?"

"Well . . ." Enchanting puzzlement from Delphi. "They, um, they see them and like them, or they hear about them from somebody?" (Touch of P. Burke there; she didn't say, from a friend.)

"Partly. Why did *you* buy your particular body-lift?"

"I never had a body-lift, sir."

Mr. Cantle frowns; what gutters did they drag for these Remotes?

"Well, what brand of water do you drink?"

"Just what was in the faucet, sir," says Delphi humbly. "I—I did try to boil it—"

"Good God." He scowls; Tesla stiffens. "Well, what did you boil it in? A cooker?"

The shining yellow head nods.

"What *brand* of cooker did you buy?"

"I didn't buy it, sir," says frightened P. Burke through Delphi's lips. "But— I know the best kind! Ananga has a Burnbabi, I saw the name when she—"

"Exactly!" Cantle's fatherly beam comes back strong; the Burnbabi account is a strong one, too. "You saw Ananga using one so you thought it must be good, eh? And it is good or a great human being like Ananga wouldn't be using it. Absolutely right. And now, Delphi, you know what you're going to be doing for us. You're going to show some products. Doesn't sound very hard, does it?"

"Oh, no, sir . . ." Baffled child's stare; Joe gloats.

"And you must never, *never* tell anyone what you're doing." Cantle's eyes bore for the brain behind this seductive child.

"You're wondering why we ask you to do this, naturally. There's a very serious reason. All those products people use, foods and health aids and cookers and cleaners and clothes and car—they're all made by *people.* Somebody put in years of hard work designing and making them. A man comes up with a fine new idea for a better product. He has to get a factory and machinery, and hire workmen. Now. What happens if people have no way of hearing about his product? Word-of-mouth is far too slow and unreliable. Nobody might ever stumble onto his new product or find out how good it was, right? And then he and all the people who worked for him—they'd go bankrupt, right? So, Delphi, there has to be *some way* that large numbers of people can get a look at a good new product, right? How? By letting people see you using it. You're *giving that man a chance.*"

Delphi's little head is nodding in happy relief.

"Yes, sir, I do see now—but sir, it seems so sensible, why don't they let you—"

Cantle smiles sadly.

"It's an overreaction, my dear. History goes by swings. People overreact and pass harsh unrealistic laws which attempt to stamp out an essential social process. When this happens, the people who understand have to carry on as best they can until the pendulum swings back. He sighs. "The Huckster Laws are bad, inhuman laws, Delphi, despite their good intent. If they were strictly observed they would wreak havoc. Our economy, our society would be cruelly destroyed. We'd be back in caves!" (His inner fire is showing; if the Huckster Laws were strictly enforced he'd be back punching a databank.)

"It's our duty, Delphi. Our solemn social duty. Nor are we breaking the law. You will be using the product. But people wouldn't understand, if they knew. They would become upset, just as you did. So you must be very, very careful not to mention any of this to anybody."

(And somebody will be very, very carefully monitoring Delphi's speech circuits.)

"Now we're all straight, aren't we? Little Delphi here"—he is speaking to the invisible creature next door—"Little Delphi is going to live a wonderful, exciting life. She's going to be a girl people watch. And she's going to be using fine products people will be glad to know about and helping the good people who make them. Yours will be a genuine social contribution." He keys up his pitch; the creature in there must be older.

Delphi digests this with ravishing gravity.

"But sir, how do I—?"

"Don't worry about a thing. You'll have people behind you whose job it is to select the most worthy products for you to use. Your job is just to do as they say. They'll show you what outfits to wear to parties, what suncars and viewers to buy and so on. That's all you have to do."

Parties—clothes—suncars! Delphi's pink mouth opens. In P. Burke's starved seventeen-year-old head the ethics of product sponsorship float far away.

"Now tell me in your own words what your job is, Delphi."

"Yes sir. I—I'm to go to parties and buy things and use them as they tell me, to help the people who work in factories."

"And what did I say was so important?"

"Oh—I shouldn't let anybody know, about the things."

"Right." Mr. Cantle has another paragraph he uses when the subject shows, well, immaturity. But he can sense only eagerness here. Good. He doesn't really enjoy the other speech.

"It's a lucky girl! who can have all the fun she wants while doing good for others, isn't it?" He beams around. There's a prompt shuffling of chairs. Clearly this one is go.

Joe leads her out, grinning. The poor fool thinks they're admiring her coordination.

It's out into the world for Delphi now, and at this point the up-channels get used. On the administrative side account schedules are opened, subprojects activated. On the technical side the reserved bandwidth is cleared. (That carrier field, remember?) A new name is waiting for Delphi, a name she'll never hear. It's a long string of binaries which have been quietly cycling in a GTX tank ever since a certain Beautiful Person didn't wake up.

The name winks out of cycle, dances from pulses into modulations of modulations, whizzes through phasing, and shoots into a giga-band beam racing up to a synchronous satellite poised over Guatemala. From there the beam pours twenty thousand miles back to earth again, forming an all-pervasive field of structured energics supplying tuned demand-points all over the CanAm quadrant.

With that field, if you have the right credit rating you can sit at a GTX console and operate a tuned ore-extractor in Brazil. Or—if you have some simple credentials like being able to walk on water—you could shoot a spool into the network holocam shows running day and night in every home and dorm. *Or* you could create a continentwide traffic jam. Is it any wonder GTX guards those inputs like a sacred trust?

Delphi's "name" appears as a tiny analyzable nonredundancy in the flux, and she'd be very proud if she knew about it. It would strike P. Burke as magic; P. Burke never even understood robotcars. But Delphi is in no sense a robot. Call her a waldo if you must. The fact is she's just a girl, a real live girl with her brain in an unusual place. A simple real-time on-line system with plenty of bit-rate— even as you and you.

The point of all this hardware, which isn't very much hardware in this society, is so Delphi can walk out of that underground suite, a mobile demand-point draining an omnipresent fieldform. And she does—eighty-nine pounds of tender girl flesh and blood with a few metallic components, stepping out into the sunlight to be taken to her new life. A girl with everything going for her including a meditech escort. Walking lovely, stopping to widen her eyes at the big antennae system overhead.

The mere fact that something called P. Burke is left behind down underground has no bearing at all. P. Burke is totally un-self-aware and happy as a clam in its shell. (Her bed has been moved into the waldo cabinet room now.) And P. Burke isn't in the cabinet; P. Burke is climbing out of an airvan in a fabulous Colorado beef preserve and her name is Delphi. Delphi is looking at live Charlais steers and live cottonwoods and aspens gold against the blue smog and stepping over live grass to be welcomed by the reserve super's wife.

The super's wife is looking forward to a visit from Delphi and her friends and by a happy coincidence there's a holocam outfit here doing a piece for the nature nuts.

You could write the script yourself now while Delphi learns a few rules about structural interferences and how to handle the tiny time lag which results from the new forty-thousand-mile parenthesis in her nervous system. That's right— the people with the leased holocam rig naturally find the gold aspen shadows look a lot better on Delphi's flank than they do on a steer. And Delphi's face improves the mountains too, when you can see them. But the nature freaks aren't quite as joyful as you'd expect.

"See you in Barcelona, kitten," the head man says sourly as they pack up.

"Barcelona?" echoes Delphi with that charming little subliminal lag. She sees where his hand is and steps back.

"Cool, it's not her fault," another man says wearily. He knocks back his grizzled hair. "Maybe they'll leave in some of the gut."

Delphi watches them go off to load the spools on the GTX transport for processing. Her hand roves over the breast the man had touched. Back under Carbondale, P. Burke has discovered something new about her Delphi-body.

About the difference between Delphi and her own grim carcass.

She's always known Delphi has almost no sense of taste or smell. They explained about that: Only so much bandwidth. You don't have to taste a suncar, do you? And the slight overall dimness of Delphi's sense of touch—she's familiar with that, too. Fabrics that would prickle P. Burke's own hide feel like a cool plastic film to Delphi.

But the blank spots. It took her a while to notice them. Delphi doesn't have much privacy; investments of her size don't. So she's slow about discovering there's certain definite places where her beastly P. Burke body *feels* things that Delphi's dainty flesh does not. H'mm! Channel space again, she thinks—and forgets it in the pure bliss of being Delphi.

You ask how a girl could forget a thing like that? Look. P. Burke is about as far as you can get from the concept *girl*. She's a female, yes—but for her, sex is a four-letter word spelled P-A-I-N. She isn't quite a virgin; you don't want the details. She'd been about twelve and the freak-lovers were bombed blind. When they came down they threw her out with a small hole in her anatomy and a mortal one elsewhere. She dragged off to buy her first and last shot and she can still hear the clerk's incredulous guffaws.

Do you see why Delphi grins, stretching her delicious little numb body in the sun she faintly feels? Beams, saying, "Please, I'm ready now."

Ready for what? For Barcelona like the sour man said, where his nature-thing is now making it strong in the amateur section of the Festival. A winner! Like he also said, a lot of strip-mines and dead fish have been scrubbed but who cares with Delphi's darling face so visible?

So it's time for Delphi's face and her other delectabilities to show on Barcelona's Playa Neuva. Which means switching her channel to the EurAf synchsat.

They ship her at night so the nanosecond transfer isn't even noticed by that insignificant part of Delphi that lives five hundred feet under Carbondale, so excited the nurse has to make sure she eats. The circuit switches while Delphi "sleeps," that is while P. Burke is out of the waldo cabinet. The next time she plugs in to open Delphi's eyes it's no different—do you notice which relay boards your calls go through?

And now for the event that turns the sugarcube from Colorado into the PRINCESS.

Literally true, he's a prince, or rather an Infante of an old Spanish line that got shined up in the Neomonarchy. He's also eighty-one, with a passion for birds—the kind you see in zoos. Now it suddenly turns out that he isn't poor at all. Quite the reverse; his old sister laughs in their tax lawyer's face and starts restoring the family hacienda while the Infante totters out to court Delphi. And little Delphi begins to live the life of the gods.

What do gods do? Well, everything beautiful. But (remember Mr. Cantle?) the main point is Things. Ever see a god empty-handed? You can't be a god without at least a magic girdle or an eight-legged horse. But in the old days some stone tablets or winged sandals or a chariot drawn by virgins would do a god for life. No more! Gods make it on novelty now. By Delphi's time the hunt for new god-gear is turning the earth and seas inside-out and sending frantic fingers to the stars. And what gods have, mortals desire.

So Delphi starts on a Euromarket shopping spree squired by her old Infante, thereby doing her bit to stave off social collapse.

Social what? Didn't you get it, when Mr. Cantle talked about a world where advertising is banned and fifteen billion consumers are glued to their holocam shows? One capricious self-powered god can wreck you.

Take the nose-filter massacre. Years, the industry worked years to achieve an almost invisible enzymatic filter. So a couple of pop-gods show up wearing nose-filters like *big purple bats*. By the end of the week the world market is screaming for purple bats. Then it switched to bird-heads and skulls. By the time the industry retooled the crazies had dropped bird-heads and gone to injection globes. Blood!

Multiply that by every consumer industry and you can see why it's economic to have a few controllable gods. Especially with the beautiful hunk of space R&D the Peace Department laid out for, and which the taxpayers are only too glad to have taken off their hands by an outfit like GTX which everybody knows is almost a public trust.

And so you—or rather, GTX—find a creature like P. Burke and give her Delphi. And Delphi helps keep things *orderly*, she does what you tell her to. Why? . . . That's right, Mr. Cantle never finished his speech.

But here come the tests of Delphi's button-nose twinkling in the torrent of news and entertainment. And she's noticed. The feedback shows a flock of viewers turning up the amps when this country baby gets tangled in her new colloidal body-jewels. She registers at a couple of major scenes, too, and when the Infante gives her a suncar, little Delphi trying out suncars is a tiger. There's a solid response in high-credit country. Mr. Cantle is humming his happy tune as he cancels a Benelux subnet option to guest her on a nude cook-show called Wok Venus.

And now for the superposh old-world wedding! The hacienda has Moorish baths and six-foot silver candelabras and real black horses and the Spanish Vatican blesses them. The final event is a grand gaucho ball with the old prince and his little Infante on a bowered balcony. She's a spectacular doll of silver lace, wildly launching toy doves at her new friends whirling by below.

The Infante beams, twitches his old nose to the scent of her sweet excitement. His doctor has been very helpful. Surely now, after he has been so patient with the suncars and all the nonsense—

The child looks up at him, saying something incomprehensible about "breath." He makes out that she's complaining about the three singers she had begged for.

"They've changed!" she marvels. "Haven't they changed? They're so dreary. I'm so happy now!"

And Delphi falls fainting against a gothic vargueno.

Her American duenna rushes up, calls help. Delphi's eyes are open, but Delphi isn't there. The duenna pokes among Delphi's hair, slaps her. The old prince grimaces. He has no idea what she is beyond an excellent solution to his tax problems, but he had been a falconer in his youth. There comes to his mind the small pinioned birds which were flung up to stimulate the hawks. He pockets the veined claw to which he had promised certain indulgences and departs to design his new aviary.

And Delphi also departs with her retinue to the Infante's newly discovered yacht. The trouble isn't serious. It's only that five thousand miles away and five hundred feet down P. Burke has been doing it too well.

They've always known she has terrific aptitude. Joe says he never saw a Remote take over so fast. No disorientations, no rejections. The psychomed talks about self-alienation. She's going into Delphi like a salmon to the sea.

She isn't eating or sleeping, they can't keep her out of the body-cabinet to get her blood moving, there are necroses under her grisly sit-down. Crisis!

So Delphi gets a long "sleep" on the yacht and P. Burke gets it pounded through her perforated head that she's endangering Delphi. (Nurse Fleming thinks of that, thus alienating the psychomed.)

They rig a pool down there (Nurse Fleming again) and chase P. Burke back and forth. And she loves it. So naturally when they let her plug in again Delphi loves it too. Every noon beside the yacht's hydrofoils darling Delphi clips along in the blue sea they've warned her not to drink. And every night around the shoulder of the world an ill-shaped thing in a dark barrow beats its way across a sterile pool.

So presently the yacht stands up on its foils and carries Delphi to the program Mr. Cantle has waiting. It's long-range; she's scheduled for at least two decades' product life. Phase One calls for her to connect with a flock of young ultra-riches who are romping loose between Brioni and Djakarta where a competitor named PEV could pick them off.

A routine luxgear op see; no politics, no policy angles, and the main budget items are the title and the yacht, which was idle anyway. The storyline is that Delphi goes to accept some rare birds for her prince—who cares? The *point* is that the Haiti area is no longer radioactive and look!—the gods are there. And so are several new Carib West Happy Isles which can afford GTX rates, in fact two of them are GTX subsids.

But you don't want to get the idea that all these newsworthy people are wired-up robbies, for pity's sake. You don't need many if they're placed right. Delphi asks Joe about that when he comes down to Baranquilla to check her over. (P. Burke's own mouth hasn't said much for a while.)

"Are there many like me?"

"Nobody's like you, buttons. Look, are you still getting that Van Allen warble?"

"I mean, like Davy. Is he a Remote?"

(Davy is the lad who is helping her collect the birds. A sincere redhead who needs a little more exposure.)

"Davy? He's one of Matt's boys. Some psychojob. They haven't any channel."

"What about the real ones? Djuma van O, or Ali, or Jim Ten?"

"Djuma was born with a pile of GTX basic where her brain should be, she's nothing but a pain. Jimsy does what his astrologer tells him. Look, peanut, where do you get the idea you aren't real? You're the realest. Aren't you having joy?"

"Oh, Joe!" Flinging her little arms around him and his analyzer grids. "Oh, *me gusto mucho, muchissimo!*"

"Hey, hey." He pets her yellow head, folding the analyzer.

Four thousand miles north and five hundred feet down a forgotten hulk in a body-waldo glows.

And is she having joy. To waken out of the nightmare of being P. Burke and find herself a peri, a star-girl? On a yacht in paradise with no more to do than adorn herself and play with toys and attend revels and greet her friends—her, P. Burke, having friends!—and turn the right way for the holocams? Joy!

And it shows. One look at Delphi and the viewers know: DREAMS CAN COME TRUE.

Look at her riding pillion on Davy's sea-bike, carrying an apoplectic macaw in a silver hoop. *Oh, Morton, let's go there this winter!* Or learning the Japanese chinchona from that Kobe group, in a dress that looks like a blowtorch rising from one knee, and which should sell big in Texas. *Morton, is that real fire?* Happy, happy little girl!

And Davy. He's her pet and her baby and she loves to help him fix his red-gold hair. (P. Burke marveling, running Delphi's fingers through the curls.) Of course Davy is one of Matt's boys—not impotent exactly, but very *very* low drive. (Nobody knows exactly what Matt does with his bitty budget but the boys are useful and one or two have made names.) He's perfect for Delphi; in fact the psychomed lets her take him to bed like two kittens in a basket. Davy doesn't mind the fact that Delphi "sleeps" like the dead. That's when P. Burke is out of the body-waldo up at Carbondale, attending to her own depressing needs.

A funny thing about that. Most of her sleepy-time Delphi's just a gently ticking lush little vegetable waiting for P. Burke to get back on the controls. But now and again Delphi all by herself smiles a bit or stirs in her "sleep." Once she breathed a sound: "Yes."

Under Carbondale P. Burke knows nothing. She's asleep too, dreaming of Delphi, what else? But if the bushy Dr. Tesla had heard that single syllable his bush would have turned snow-white. Because Delphi is TURNED OFF.

He doesn't. Davy is too dim to notice and Delphi's staff boss, Hopkins, wasn't monitoring.

And they've all got something else to think about now, because the cold-fire dress sells half a million copies, and not only in Texas. The GTX computers already know it. When they correlate a minor demand for macaws in Alaska the problem comes to human attention: Delphi is something special.

It's a problem, see, because Delphi is targeted on a limited consumer bracket. Now it turns out she has mass-pop potential—those macaws in *Fairbanks,* man!—it's like trying to shoot mice with an ABM. A whole new ball game. Dr. Tesla and the fatherly Mr. Cantle start going around in headquarters circles and buddy-lunching together when they can get away from a seventh-level weasel boy who scares them both.

In the end it's decided to ship Delphi down to the GTX holocam enclave in Chili to try a spot on one of the mainstream shows. (Never mind why an Infante takes up acting.) The holocam complex occupies a couple of mountains where an observatory once used the clear air. Holocam total-environment shells are very expensive and electronically super-stable. Inside them actors can move freely without going off-register and the whole scene or any selected part will show up in the viewer's home in complete 3-di, so real you can look up their noses and much denser than you get from mobile rigs. You can blow a tit ten feet tall when there's no molecular skiffle around.

The enclave looks—well, take everything you know about Hollywood-

Burbank and throw it away. What Delphi sees coming down is a neat giant mushroom-farm, domes of all sizes up to monsters for the big games and stuff. It's orderly. The idea that art thrives on creative flamboyance has long been torpedoed by proof that what art needs is computers. Because this showbiz has something TV and Hollywood never had—*automated inbuilt viewer feedback*. Samples, ratings, critics, polls? Forget it. With that carrier field you can get realtime response-sensor from every receiver in the world, served up at your console. That started as a thingie to give the public more influence on content.

Yes.

Try it, man. You're at the console. Slice to the sex-age-educ-econ-ethnocetera audience of your choice and start. You can't miss. Where the feedback warms up, give 'em more of that. Warm—warmer—*hot!* You've hit it—the secret itch under those hides, the dream in those hearts. You don't need to know its name. With your hand controlling all the input and your eye reading all the response you can make them a god . . . and somebody'll do the same for you.

But Delphi just sees rainbows, when she gets through the degaussing ports and the field relay and takes her first look at the insides of those shells. The next thing she sees is a team of shapers and technicians descending on her, and millisecond timers everywhere. The tropical leisure is finished. She's in gigabuck mainstream now, at the funnel maw of the unceasing hose that's pumping the sight and sound and flesh and blood and sobs and laughs and dreams of *reality* into the world's happy head. Little Delphi is going plonk into a zillion homes in prime time and nothing is left to chance. Work!

And again Delphi proves apt. Of course it's really P. Burke down under Carbondale who's doing it, but who remembers that carcass? Certainly not P. Burke, she hasn't spoken through her own mouth for months. Delphi doesn't even recall dreaming of her when she wakes up.

As for the show itself, don't bother. It's gone on so long no living soul could unscramble the plotline. Delphi's trial spot has something to do with a widow and her dead husband's brother's amnesia.

The bother comes after Delphi's spots begin to flash out along the worldhose and the feedback appears. You've guessed it, of course. Sensational! As you'd say, they IDENTIFY.

The report actually says something like InskinEmp with a string of percentages meaning that Delphi not only has it for anybody with a y-chromosome, but also for women and every thing in between. It's the sweet supernatural jackpot, the million-to-one.

Remember your Harlow? A sexpot, sure. But why did bitter hausfraus in Gary and Memphis know that the vanilla-ice-cream goddess with the white hair and crazy eyebrows was *their baby girl?* And write loving letters to Jean warning her that their husbands weren't good enough for her? Why? The GTX analysts don't know either, but they know what to do with it when it happens.

(Back in his bird sanctuary the old Infante spots it without benefit of computers and gazes thoughtfully at his bride in widow's weeds. It might, he feels, be well to accelerate the completion of his studies.)

The excitement reaches down to the burrow under Carbondale where P. Burke gets two medical exams in a week and a chronically inflamed electrode is replaced. Nurse Fleming also gets an assistant who doesn't do much nursing but is very interested in access doors and identity tabs.

And in Chile little Delphi is promoted to a new home up among the stars' residential spreads and a private jitney to carry her to work. For Hopkins there's a new computer terminal and a full-time schedule man. What is the schedule crowded with?

Things.

And here begins the trouble. You probably saw that coming too.

"What does she think she is, a goddam *consumer rep?*" Mr. Cantle's fatherly face in Carbondale contorts.

"The girl's upset," Miss Fleming says stubbornly. "She *believes* that, what you told her about helping people and good new products."

"They are good products," Mr. Cantle snaps automatically, but his anger is under control. He hasn't got where he is by irrelevant reactions.

"She says the plastic gave her a rash and the glo-pills made her dizzy."

"Good god, she shouldn't swallow them," Doctor Tesla puts in agitatedly.

"You told her she'd use them," persists Miss Fleming. Mr. Cantle is busy figuring how to ease this problem to the weasel-faced young man. What, was it a goose that lays golden eggs?

Whatever he says to level Seven, down in Chile the offending products vanish. And a symbol goes into Delphi's tank matrix, one that means roughly *Balance unit resistance against PR index*. This means that Delphi's complaints will be endured as long as her Pop Response stays above a certain level. (What happens when it sinks need not concern us.) And to compensate, the price of her exposure-time rises again. She's a regular on the show now and response is still climbing.

See her under the sizzling lasers, in a holocam shell set up as a walkway accident. (The show is guesting an acupuncture school expert.)

"I don't think this new body-lift is safe," Delphi's saying. "It's made a funny blue spot on me—look, Mr. Vere."

She wiggles to show where the mini-grav pak that imparts a delicious sense of weightlessness is attached.

"So don't leave it *on*, Dee. With your meat—watch that deck-spot, it's starting to synch."

"But if I don't wear it, it isn't honest. They should insulate it more or something, don't you see?"

The show's beloved old father, who is the casualty, gives a senile snigger.

"I'll tell them," Mr. Vere mutters. "Look now, as you step back bend like this so it just shows, see? And hold two beats."

Obediently Delphi turns, and through the dazzle her eyes connect with a pair of strange dark ones. She squints. A quite young man is lounging alone by the port, apparently waiting to use the chamber.

Delphi's used by now to young men looking at her with many peculiar expressions, but she isn't used to what she gets here. A jolt of something somber and knowing. *Secrets.*

"Eyes! Eyes, Dee!"

She moves through the routine, stealing peeks at the stranger. He stares back. He knows something.

When they let her go she comes shyly to him.

"Living wild, kitten." Cool voice, hot underneath.

"What do you mean?"

"Dumping on the product. You trying to get dead?"

"But it isn't right," she tells him. "They don't know, but I do, I've been wearing it."

His cool is jolted.

"You're out of your head."

"Oh, they'll see I'm right when they check it," she explains. "They're just so busy. When I tell them—"

He is staring down at little flower-face. His mouth opens, closes. "What are you doing in this sewer anyway? Who are you?"

Bewilderedly she says, "I'm Delphi."

"Holy Zen."

"What's wrong? Who are you, please?"

Her people are moving her out now, nodding at him.

"Sorry we ran over, Mister Uhunh," the script girl says.

He mutters something, but it's lost as her convoy bustles her toward the flower-decked jitney.

(Hear the click of an invisible ignition-train being armed?)

"Who was he?" Delphi asks her hair man.

The hair man is bending up and down from his knees as he works.

"Paul. Isham. Three," he says and puts a comb in his mouth.

"Who's that? I can't see."

He mumbles around the comb, meaning "Are you jiving?" Because she has to be, in the middle of the GTX enclave.

Next day there's a darkly smoldering face under a turban-towel when Delphi and the show's paraplegic go to use the carbonated pool.

She looks.

He looks.

And the next day, too.

(Hear that automatic sequencer cutting in? The system couples, the fuels begin to travel.)

Poor old Isham senior. You have to feel sorry for a man who values order: when he begets young, genetic information is still transmitted in the old ape way. One minute it's a happy midget with a rubber duck—look around and here's this huge healthy stranger, opaquely emotional, running with God knows who. Questions are heard where there's nothing to question, and eruptions claiming to be moral outrage. When this is called to Papa's attention—it may take time, in that boardroom—Papa does what he can, but without immortality-juice the problem is worrisome.

And young Paul Isham is a bear. He's bright and articulate and tender-souled and incessantly active and he and his friends are choking with appallment at the world their fathers made. And it hasn't taken Paul long to discover that *his* father's house has many mansions and even the GTX computers can't relate everything to everything else. He noses out a decaying project which adds up to something like Sponsoring Marginal Creativity (the freelance team that "discovered" Delphi was one such grantee). And from there it turns out that an agile lad named Isham can get his hands on a viable packet of GTX holocam facilities.

So here he is with his little band, way down the mushroom-farm mountain, busily spooling a show which has no relation to Delphi's. It's built on bizarre techniques and unsettling distortions pregnant with social protest. An *underground* expression to you.

All this isn't unknown to his father, of course, but so far it has done nothing more than deepen Isham senior's apprehensive frown.

Until Paul connects with Delphi.

And by the time Papa learns this, those invisible hypergolics have exploded, the energy-shells are rushing out. For Paul, you see, is the genuine article. He's serious. He dreams. He even reads—for example, *Green Mansions*—and he wept fiercely when those fiends burned Rima alive.

When he hears that some new GTX pussy is making it big he sneers and forgets it. He's busy. He never connects the name with this little girl making her idiotic, doomed protest in the holocam chamber. This strangely simple little girl.

And she comes and looks up at him and he sees Rima, lost Rima the enchanted bird girl, and his unwired human heart goes twang.

And Rima turns out to be Delphi.

Do you need a map? The angry puzzlement. The rejection of the dissonance Rima-hustling-for-GTX-My-Father. Garbage, cannot be. The loitering around the pool to confirm the swindle . . . dark eyes hitting on blue wonder, jerky words exchanged in a peculiar stillness . . . the dreadful reorganization of the image into Rima-Delphi *in My Father's tentacles*—

You don't need a map.

Nor for Delphi either, the girl who loved her gods. She's seen their divine flesh close now, heard their unamplified voices call her name. She's played their god-games, worn their garlands. She's even become a goddess herself, though she doesn't believe it. She's not disenchanted, don't think that. She's still full of love. It's just that some crazy kind of *hope* isn't—

Really you can skip all this, when the loving little girl on the yellow-brick road meets a Man. A real human male burning with angry compassion and grandly concerned with human justice, who reaches for her with real male arms and—boom! She loves him back with all her heart.

A happy trip, see?

Except.

Except that it's really P. Burke four thousand miles away who loves Paul. P. Burke the monster, down in a dungeon smelling of electrode-paste. A caricature of a woman burning, melting, obsessed with true love. Trying over twenty-double-thousand miles of hard vacuum to reach her beloved through girl-flesh numbed by an invisible film. Feeling his arms around the body he thinks is hers, fighting through shadows to give herself to him. Trying to taste and smell him through beautiful dead nostrils, to love him back with a body that goes dead in the heart of the fire.

Perhaps you get P. Burke's state of mind?

She has phases. The trying, first. And the shame. The SHAME. *I am not what thou lovest.* And the fiercer trying. And the realization that there is no, no way, none. Never. *Never.* . . . A bit delayed, isn't it, her understanding that the bargain she made was forever? P. Burke should have noticed those stories about mortals who end up as grasshoppers.

You see the outcome—the funneling of all this agony into one dumb protoplasmic drive to fuse with Delphi. To leave, to close out the beast she is chained to. *To become Delphi.*

Of course it's impossible.

However her torments have an effect on Paul. Delphi-as-Rima is a potent enough love object, and liberating Delphi's mind requires hours of deeply satisfying instruction in the rottenness of it all. Add in Delphi's body worshipping his flesh, burning in the fire of P. Burke's savage heart—do you wonder Paul is involved?

That's not all.

By now they're spending every spare moment together and some that aren't so spare.

"Mister Isham, would you mind staying out of this sports sequence? The script calls for Davy here."

(Davy's still around, the exposure did him good.)

"What's the difference?" Paul yawns. "It's just an ad. I'm not blocking that thing."

Shocked silence at his two-letter word. The script girl swallows bravely.

"I'm sorry, sir, our directive is to do the *social sequence* exactly as scripted. We're having to respool the segments we did last week, Mister Hopkins is very angry with me."

"Who the hell is Hopkins? Where is he?"

"Oh, please, Paul. *Please.*"

Paul unwraps himself, saunters back. The holocam crew nervously check their angles. The GTX boardroom has a foible about having things *pointed* at them and theirs. Cold shivers, when the image of an Isham nearly went onto the world beam beside that Dialadinner.

Worse yet. Paul has no respect for the sacred schedules which are now a full-time job for ferret boy up at headquarters. Paul keeps forgetting to bring her back on time and poor Hopkins can't cope.

So pretty soon the boardroom data-ball has an urgent personal action-tab for Mr. Isham senior. They do it the gentle way, at first.

"I can't today, Paul."

"Why not?"

"They say I have to, it's *very* important."

He strokes the faint gold down on her narrow back. Under Carbondale, Pa., a blind mole-woman shivers.

"Important. Their importance. Making more gold. Can't you see? To them you're just a thing to get scratch with. A *huckster.* Are you going to let them screw you, Dee? Are you?"

"Oh, Paul—"

He doesn't know it but he's seeing a weirdie; Remotes aren't hooked up to make much tears.

"Just say no, Dee. No. Integrity. You have to."

"But they say it's my job—"

"Don't you believe I can take care of you, Dee? Baby, baby, you're letting them rip us. You have to choose. Tell them, no."

"Paul . . . I w-will . . ."

And she does. Brave little Delphi (insane P. Burke). Saying "No, please, I promised, Paul."

They try some more, still gently.

"Paul, Mr. Hopkins told me the reason they don't want us to be together so much. It's because of who you are, your father."

She thinks his father is like Mr. Cantle, maybe.

"Oh great. Hopkins. I'll fix him. Listen, I can't think about Hopkins now. Ken came back today, he found out something."

They are lying on the high Andes meadow watching his friends dive their singing kites.

"Would you believe, on the coast the police have *electrodes in their heads?*"

She stiffens in his arms.

"Yeah, weird. I thought they only used PPs on criminals and the army. Don't you see, Dee—something has to be going on. Some movement. Maybe somebody's organizing. How can we find out?" He pounds the ground behind her. "We should make *contact!* If we could only find anything."

"The, the news . . . ?" she asks distractedly.

"The news." He laughs. "There's nothing in the news except what they want people to know. Half the country could burn up and nobody would know it if they didn't want. Dee, can't you take what I'm explaining to you? They've got the whole world programmed! Total control of communication. They've got everybody's minds wired in to think what they show them and want what they give them and they give them what they're programmed to want—you can't break in or out of it, you can't *get hold* of it anywhere. I don't think they even have a plan except to keep things going round and round—and God knows what's happening to the people or the earth or the other planets, maybe. One great big vortex of lies and garbage pouring round and round getting bigger and bigger and nothing can ever change. If people don't wake up soon we're through!"

He pounds her stomach softly.

"*You* have to break out, Dee."

"I'll try, Paul, I will—"

"You're mine. They can't have you."

And he goes to see Hopkins, who is indeed cowed.

But that night up under Carbondale the fatherly Mr. Cantle goes to see P. Burke.

P. Burke? On a cot in a utility robe like a dead camel in a tent, she cannot at first comprehend that he is telling *her* to break it off with Paul. P. Burke has never seen Paul. *Delphi* sees Paul. The fact is, P. Burke can no longer clearly recall that she exists apart from Delphi.

Mr. Cantle can scarely believe it either but he tries.

He points out the futility, the potential embarrassment for Paul. That gets a dim stare from the bulk on the bed. Then he goes into her duty to GTX, her job, isn't she grateful for the opportunity, etcetera. He's very persuasive.

The cobwebby mouth of P. Burke opens and croaks.

"No."

Nothing more seems to be forthcoming.

Mr. Cantle isn't dense, he knows an immovable obstacle when he bumps one. He also knows an irresistible force: GTX. The simple solution is to lock the waldo-cabinet until Paul gets tired of waiting for Delphi to wake up. But the cost, the schedules! And there's something odd here . . . he eyes the corporate asset hulking on the bed and his hunch-sense prickles.

You see, Remotes don't love. They don't have real sex, the circuits designed that out from the start. So it's been assumed that it's *Paul* who is diverting himself or something with the pretty little body in Chile. P. Burke can only be doing what comes natural to any ambitious gutter-meat. It hasn't occurred to anyone that they're dealing with the real hairy thing whose shadow is blasting out of every holoshow on earth.

Love?

Mr. Cantle frowns. The idea is grotesque. But his instinct for the fuzzy line is strong; he will recommend flexibility.

And so, in Chile:

"Darling, I don't have to work tonight! And Friday too—isn't that right, Mr. Hopkins?"

"Oh, great. When does she come up for parole?"

"Mr. Isham, please be reasonable. Our schedule—surely your own production people must be needing you?"

This happens to be true. Paul goes away. Hopkins stares after him wondering distastefully why an Isham wants to ball a waldo. (How sound are those boardroom belly-fears—garble creeps, creeps in!) It never occurs to Hopkins that an Isham might not know what Delphi is.

Especially with Davy crying because Paul has kicked him out of Delphi's bed.

Delphi's bed is under a real window.

"Stars," Paul says sleepily. He rolls over, pulling Delphi on top. "Are you aware that this is one of the last places on earth where people can see the stars? Tibet, too, maybe . . ."

"Paul . . ."

"Go to sleep. I want to see you sleep."

"Paul, I . . . I sleep so *hard,* I mean, it's a joke how hard I am to wake up. Do you mind?"

"Yes."

But finally, fearfully, she must let go. So that four thousand miles north a crazy spent creature can crawl out to gulp concentrates and fall on her cot. But not for long. It's pink dawn when Delphi's eyes open to find Paul's arms around her, his voice saying rude, tender things. He's been kept awake. The nerveless little statue that was her Delphi-body nuzzled him in the night.

Insane hope rises, is fed a couple of nights later when he tells her she called his name in her sleep.

And that day Paul's arms keep her from work and Hopkins' wails go up to headquarters where the sharp-faced lad is working his sharp tailbone off packing Delphi's program. Mr. Cantle defuses that one. But next week it happens again, to a major client. And ferret-face has connections on the technical side.

Now you can see that when you have a field of complexly heterodyned energy modulations tuned to a demand-point like Delphi there are many problems of standwaves and lashback and skiffle of all sorts which are normally balanced out with ease by the technology of the future. By the same token they can be delicately unbalanced too, in ways that feed back into the waldo operator with striking results.

"Darling—what the hell! What's wrong? DELPHI!"

Helpless shrieks, writhings. Then the Rima-bird is lying wet and limp in his arms, her eyes enormous.

"I . . . I wasn't supposed to . . ." she gasps faintly. "They told me not to . . ."

"Oh my god . . . *Delphi.*"

And his hard fingers are digging in her thick yellow hair. Electronically knowledgeable fingers. They freeze.

"You're a *doll!* You're one of those. PP implants. They control you. I should have known. Oh God, I should have known."

"No, Paul," she's sobbing. "No, no, no—"

"Damn them. Damn them, what they've done—you're not *you*—"

He's shaking her, crouching over her in the bed and jerking her back and forth, glaring at the pitiful beauty.

"No!" She pleads (it's not true, that dark bad dream back there). "I'm Delphi!"

"My father. Filth, pigs—damn them, damn them, damn them."

"No, no," she babbles. "They were good to me—" P. Burke underground mouthing, "They were good to me—AAH-AAAAH!"

Another agony skewers her. Up north the sharp young man wants to make sure this so-tiny interference works. Paul can scarcely hang onto her, he's crying too. "I'll kill them."

His Delphi, a wired-up slave! Spikes in her brain, electronic shackles in his bird's heart. Remember when those savages burned Rima alive?

"I'll *kill* the man that's doing this to you."

He's still saying it afterward but she doesn't hear. She's sure he hates her now, all she wants is to die. When she finally understands that the fierceness is tenderness she thinks it's a miracle. *He knows—and he still loves!*

How can she guess that he's got it a little bit wrong?

You can't blame Paul—give him credit that he's even heard about pleasure-pain implants and snoops, which by their nature aren't mentioned much by those who know them most intimately. That's what he thinks is being used on Delphi, something to *control* her. And to listen—he burns at the unknown ears in their bed.

Of waldo-bodies and objects like P. Burke he has heard nothing.

So it never crosses his mind as he looks down at his violated bird, sick with fury and love, that he isn't holding *all* of her. Do you need to be told the mad resolve jelling in him now?

To free Delphi.

How? Well, he is after all Paul Isham III. And he even has an idea where the GTX neurolab is. In Carbondale.

But first things have to be done for Delphi, and for his own stomach. So he gives her back to Hopkins and departs in a restrained and discreet way. And the Chile staff is grateful and do not understand that his teeth don't normally show so much.

And a week passes in which Delphi is a very good, docile little ghost. They let her have the load of wildflowers Paul sends and the bland loving notes. (He's playing it coony.) And up in headquarters weasel boy feels that *his* destiny has clicked a notch onward floats the word up that he's handy with little problems.

And no one knows what P. Burke thinks in any way whatever, except that

Miss Fleming catches her flushing her food down the can and next night she faints in the pool. They haul her out and stick her with IVs. Miss Fleming frets, she's seen expressions like that before. But she wasn't around when crazies who called themselves Followers of the Fish looked through flames to life everlasting. P. Burke is seeing Heaven on the far side of death too. Heaven is spelled P-a-u-l, but the idea's the same. *I will die and be born again in Delphi.*

Garbage, electronically speaking. No way.

Another week and Paul's madness has become a plan. (Remember, he does have friends.) He smolders, watching his love paraded by her masters. He turns out a scorching sequence for his own show. And finally, politely, he requests from Hopkins a morsel of his bird's free time, which duly arrives.

"—I thought you didn't want me anymore," she's repeating as they wing over mountain flanks in Paul's suncar. "Now you know—"

"Look at me!"

His hand covers her mouth and he's showing her a lettered card.

DON'T TALK THEY CAN HEAR EVERYTHING WE SAY.

I'M TAKING YOU AWAY NOW.

She kisses his hand. He nods urgency, flipping the card.

DON'T BE AFRAID. I CAN STOP THE PAIN IF THEY TRY TO HURT YOU.

With his free hand he shakes out a silvery scrambler-mesh on a power pack. She is dumfounded.

THIS WILL CUT THE SIGNALS AND PROTECT YOU DARLING.

She's staring at him, her head going vaguely from side to side, No.

"Yes!" He grins triumphantly. "Yes!"

For a moment she . . . wonders. That powered mesh will cut off the field, all right. It will also cut off Delphi. But he is *Paul.* Paul is kissing her, she can only seek him hungrily as he sweeps the suncar through a pass.

Ahead is an old jet ramp with a shiny bullet waiting to go. (Paul also has credits and a Name.) The little GTX patrol courier is built for nothing but speed. Paul and Delphi wedge in behind the pilot's extra fuel tank and there's no more talking when the torches start to scream.

They're screaming high over Quito before Hopkins starts to worry. He wastes another hour tracking the beeper on Paul's suncar. The suncar is sailing a pattern out to sea. By the time they're sure it's empty and Hopkins gets on the hot flue to headquarters the fugitives are a sourceless howl above Carib West.

Up at headquarters weasel boy gets the squeal. His first impulse is to repeat his previous play but then his brain snaps to. This one is too hot. Because, see, although in the long run they can make P. Burke do anything at all except maybe *live,* instant emergencies can be tricky. And—Paul Isham III.

"Can't you order her back?"

They're all in the GTX tower monitor station, Mr. Cantle and ferret-face and Joe and a very neat man who is Mr. Isham senior's personal eyes and ears.

"No sir," Joe says doggedly. "We can read channels, particularly speech, but we can't interpolate organized pattern. It takes the waldo op to send one-to-one—"

"What are they saying?"

"Nothing at the moment, sir." The console jockey's eyes are closed. "I believe they are, ah, embracing."

"They're not answering," a traffic monitor says. "Still heading zero zero three zero—due north, sir."

"You're certain Kennedy is alerted not to fire on them?" the neat man asks anxiously.

"Yes sir."

"Can't you just turn her off?" The sharp-faced lad is angry. "Pull that beast out of the controls!"

"If you cut the transmission cold you'll kill the Remote," Joe explains for the third time. "Withdrawal has to be phased right, you have to fade over to the Remote's own autonomics. Heart, breathing, cerebellum would go blooey. If you pull Burke out you'll probably finish her too. It's a fantastic cybersystem, you don't want to do that."

"The investment." Mr. Cantle shudders.

Weasel boy puts his hand on the console jock's shoulder; it's the contact who arranged the No-no effect for him.

"We can at least give them a warning signal, sir." He licks his lips, gives the neat man his sweet ferret smile. "We know that does no damage."

Joe frowns, Mr. Cantle sighs. The neat man is murmuring into his wrist. He looks up. "I am authorized," he says reverently, "I am authorized to, ah, direct a signal. If this is the only course. But minimal, minimal."

Sharp-face squeezes his man's shoulder.

In the silver bullet shrieking over Charleston Paul feels Delphi arch in his arms. He reaches for the mesh, hot for action. She thrashes, pushing at his hands, her eyes roll. She's afraid of that mesh despite the agony. (And she's right.) Frantically Paul fights her in the cramped space, gets it over her head. As he turns the power up she burrows free under his arm and the spasm fades.

"They're calling you again, Mister Isham!" the pilot yells.

"Don't answer. Darling, keep this over your head damn it how can I—"

An AX90 barrels over their nose, there's a flash.

"Mister Isham! Those are Air Force jets!"

"Forget it," Paul shouts back. "They won't fire. Darling, don't be afraid."

Another AX90 rocks them.

"Would you mind pointing your pistol at my head where they can see it, sir?" the pilot howls.

Paul does so. The AX90s take up escort formation around them. The pilot goes back to figuring how he can collect from GTX, too, and after Goldsboro AB the escort peels away.

"Holding the same course," Traffic is reporting to the group around the monitor. "Apparently they've taken on enough fuel to bring them to towerport here."

"In that case it's just a question of waiting for them to dock." Mr. Cantle's fatherly manner revives a bit.

"Why can't they cut off that damn freak's life-support?" the sharp young man fumes. "It's ridiculous."

"They're working on it," Cantle assures him.

What they're doing, down under Carbondale, is arguing.

Miss Fleming's watchdog has summoned the bushy man to the waldo room.

"Miss Fleming, you will obey orders."

"You'll kill her if you try that, sir. I can't believe you meant it, that's why I didn't. We've already fed her enough sedative to affect heart action; if you cut any more oxygen she'll die in there."

The bushy man grimaces. "Get Doctor Quine here fast."

They wait, staring at the cabinet in which a drugged, ugly madwoman fights for consciousness, fights to hold Delphi's eyes open.

High over Richmond the silver pod starts a turn. Delphi is sagged into Paul's arm, her eyes swim up to him.

"Starting down now, baby. It'll be over soon, all you have to do is stay alive, Dee."

" . . . Stay alive . . ."

The traffic monitor has caught them. "Sir! They've turned off for Carbondale—Control has contact—"

"Let's go."

But the headquarters posse is too late to intercept the courier wailing into Carbondale. And Paul's friends have come through again. The fugitives are out through the freight dock and into the neurolab admin port before the guard gets organized. At the elevator Paul's face plus his handgun get them in.

"I want Doctor—what's his name, Dee? Dee!"

" . . . Tesla . . ." She's reeling on her feet.

"Doctor Tesla. Take me down to Tesla, fast."

Intercoms are squalling around them as they whoosh down, Paul's pistol in the guard's back. When the door slides open the bushy man is there.

"I'm Tesla."

"I'm Paul Isham. *Isham*. You're going to take your flaming implants out of this girl—now. Move!"

"What?"

"You heard me. Where's your operating room? Go!"

"But—"

"Move! Do I have to burn somebody?"

Paul waves the weapon at Dr. Quine, who has just appeared.

"No, no," says Tesla hurriedly. "But I can't, you know. It's impossible, there'll be nothing left."

"You screaming well can, right now. You mess up and I'll kill you," says Paul murderously. "Where is it, there? And wipe the creep that's on her circuits now."

He's backing them down the hall, Delphi heavy on his arm.

"Is this the place, baby? Where they did it to you?"

"Yes," she whispers, blinking at a door. "Yes . . ."

Because it is, see. Behind that door is the very suite where she was born.

Paul herds them through it into a gleaming hall. An inner door opens and a nurse and a gray man rush out. And freeze.

Paul sees there's something special about that inner door. He crowds them past it and pushes it open and looks in.

Inside is a big mean-looking cabinet with its front door panels ajar.

And inside that cabinet is a poisoned carcass to whom something wonderful, unspeakable, is happening. Inside is P. Burke the real living woman who knows that HE is there, coming closer—Paul whom she had fought to reach through forty thousand miles of ice!—PAUL is here!—is yanking at the waldo doors—

The doors tear open and a monster rises up.

"Paul darling!" croaks the voice of love and the arms of love reach for him. And he responds.

Wouldn't you, if a gaunt she-golem flab-naked and spouting wires and blood came at you—clawing you with metal-studded paws—

"Get away!" He knocks wires.

It doesn't much matter which wires, P. Burke has so to speak her nervous system hanging out. Imagine somebody jerking a handful of your medulla—

She crashes onto the floor at his feet, flopping and roaring *PAUL-PAUL-PAUL* in rictus.

It's doubtful he recognizes his name or sees her life coming out of her eyes at him. And at the last it doesn't go to him. The eyes find Delphi, fainting by the doorway, and die.

Now of course Delphi is dead, too.

There's total silence as Paul steps away from the thing by his foot.

"You killed her," Tesla says. "That was her."

"Your control." Paul is furious, the thought of that monster fastened into little Delphi's brain nauseates him. He sees her crumpling and holds out his arms. Not knowing she is dead.

And Delphi comes to him.

One foot before the other, not moving very well—but moving. Her darling face turns up. Paul is distracted by the terrible quiet, and when he looks down he sees only her tender little neck.

"Now you get the implants out," he warns them. Nobody moves.

"But, but she's dead," Miss Fleming whispers wildly.

Paul feels Delphi's life under his hand, they're talking about their monster. He aims his pistol at the gray man.

"You. If we aren't in your surgery when I count three I'm burning off this man's leg."

"Mr. Isham," Tesla says desperately, "you have just killed the person who animated the body you call Delphi. Delphi herself is dead. If you release your arm you'll see what I say is true."

The tone gets through. Slowly Paul opens his arm, looks down.

"Delphi?"

She totters, sways, stays upright. Her face comes slowly up.

"Paul . . ." Tiny voice.

"Your crotty tricks," Paul snarls at them. "Move!"

"Look at her eyes," Dr. Quine croaks.

They look. One of Delphi's pupils fills the iris, her lips writhe weirdly.

"Shock." Paul grabs her to him. "Fix her!" He yells at them, aiming at Tesla.

"For God's sake . . . bring it in the lab." Tesla quavers.

"Good-bye-bye," says Delphi clearly. They lurch down the hall, Paul carrying her, and meet a wave of people.

Headquarters has arrived.

Joe takes one look and dives for the waldo room, running into Paul's gun. "Oh no, you don't."

Everybody is yelling. The little thing in his arm stirs, says plaintively, "I'm Delphi."

And all through the ensuing jabber and ranting she hangs on, keeps it up, the ghost of P. Burke or whatever whispering crazily "Paul . . . Paul . . . Please, I'm Delphi . . . Paul?"

"I'm here, darling, I'm here." He's holding her in the nursing bed. Tesla talks, talks, talks unheard.

"Paul . . . don't sleep . . ." the ghost-voice whispers. Paul is in agony, he will not accept, WILL NOT believe. Tesla runs down.

And then near midnight Delphi says roughly, "Ag-ag-ag—" and slips onto the floor, making a rough noise like a seal.

Paul screams. There's more of the *ag-ag* business and more gruesome convulsive disintegrations, until by two in the morning Delphi is nothing but a warm little bundle of vegetative functions hitched to some expensive hardware—the same that sustained her before her life began. Joe finally persuades Paul to let him at the waldo-cabinet. Paul stays by her long enough to see her face change in a dreadfully alien and coldly convincing way, and then he stumbles out bleakly through the group in Tesla's office.

Behind him Joe is working wet-faced, sweating to reintegrate the fantastic complex of circulation, respiration, endocrines, midbrain homeostasis, the patterned flux that was a human being—it's like saving an orchestra abandoned in midair. Joe is also crying a little; he alone had truly loved P. Burke. P. Burke, now a dead pile on a table, was the greatest cybersystem he has ever known, and he never forgets her.

The end, really.

You're curious? Sure, Delphi lives again. Next year she's back on the yacht getting sympathy for her tragic breakdown. But there's a different chick in Chile, because while Delphi's new operator is competent, you don't get two P. Burkes in a row—for which GTX is duly grateful.

The real belly-bomb of course is Paul. He was *young*, see. Fighting abstract wrong. Now life has clawed into him and he goes through gut rage and grief and grows in human wisdom and resolve. So much so that you won't be surprised, some time later, to find him—where?

In the GTX boardroom, dummy. Using the advantage of his birth to radicalize the system. You'd call it "boring from within."

That's how he put it, and his friends couldn't agree more. It gives them a warm, confident feeling to know that Paul is up there. Sometimes one of them that is still around runs into him and gets a big hello.

And the sharp-faced lad?

Oh, he matures too. He learns fast, believe it. For instance, he's the first to learn that an obscure GTX research unit is actually getting something with their loopy temporal anomalizer project. True, he doesn't have a physics background, and he's bugged quite a few people. But he doesn't really learn about that until the day he stands where somebody points him during a test run—

—and wakes up lying on a newspaper headlined NIXON UNVEILS PHASE TWO.

Lucky he's a fast learner.

Believe it, zombie. When I say *growth* I mean growth. Capital appreciation. You can stop sweating. There's a great future there.

BURNING CHROME

William Gibson

William Gibson published occasional SF stories for nearly a decade and then, in 1984, the novel *Neuromancer*, later followed by two sequels, *Count Zero* and *Mona Lisa Overdrive*. *Neuromancer*, and to a certain extent some of the short stories collected in *Burning Chrome* ("Johnny Mnemonic" and the title story, particularly), became the central texts of a new movement, the hot, hip thing in 1980s SF, cyberpunk, and Gibson himself became a pop-culture hero. He had invented *cyberspace*, the word for the idea of that place you inhabit when you are on your computer connected by a modem to the larger computer communications universe. Hackers worshipped him; everyone read him.

It was hot, the night we burned Chrome. Out in the malls and plazas, moths were batting themselves to death against the neon, but in Bobby's loft the only light came from a monitor screen and the green and red LEDs on the face of the matrix simulator. I knew every chip in Bobby's simulator by heart; it looked like your workaday Ono-Sendai VII, the "Cyberspace Seven," but I'd rebuilt it so many times that you'd have had a hard time finding a square millimeter of factory circuitry in all that silicon.

We waited side by side in front of the simulator console, watching the time display in the screen's lower left corner.

"Go for it," I said, when it was time, but Bobby was already there, leaning forward to drive the Russian program into its slot with the heel of his hand. He did it with the tight grace of a kid slamming change into an arcade game, sure of winning and ready to pull down a string of free games.

A silver tide of phosphenes boiled across my field of vision as the matrix began to unfold in my head, a 3-D chessboard, infinite and perfectly transparent. The Russian program seemed to lurch as we entered the grid. If anyone else had been jacked into that part of the matrix, he might have seen a surf of flickering shadow roll out of the little yellow pyramid that represented our computer. The program was a mimetic weapon, designed to absorb local color and present itself as a crash-priority override in whatever context it encountered.

"Congratulations," I heard Bobby say. "We just became an Eastern Seaboard Fission Authority inspection probe. . . .” That meant we were clearing fiberoptic lines with the cybernetic equivalent of a fire siren, but in the simulation matrix we seemed to rush straight for Chrome’s database. I couldn’t see it yet, but I already knew those walls were waiting. Walls of shadow, walls of ice.

Chrome: her pretty childface smooth as steel, with eyes that would have been at home on the bottom of some deep Atlantic trench, cold gray eyes that lived under terrible pressure. They said she cooked her own cancers for people who crossed her, rococo custom variations that took years to kill you. They said a lot of things about Chrome, none of them at all reassuring.

So I blotted her out with a picture of Rikki. Rikki kneeling in a shaft of dusty sunlight that slanted into the loft through a grid of steel and glass: her faded camouflage fatigues, her translucent rose sandals, the good line of her bare back as she rummaged through a nylon gear bag. She looks up, and a half-blond curl falls to tickle her nose. Smiling, buttoning an old shirt of Bobby’s, frayed khaki cotton drawn across her breasts.

She smiles.

“Son of a bitch,” said Bobby, “we just told Chrome we’re an IRS audit and three Supreme Court subpoenas. . . . Hang on to your ass. Jack . . .”

So long, Rikki. Maybe now I see you never.

And dark, so dark, in the halls of Chrome’s ice.

Bobby was a cowboy, and ice was the nature of his game, *ice* from ICE, Intrusion Countermeasures Electronics. The matrix is an abstract representation of the relationships between data systems. Legitimate programmers jack into their employers’ sector of the matrix and find themselves surrounded by bright geometries representing the corporate data.

Towers and fields of it ranged in the colorless nonspace of the simulation matrix, the electronic consensus-hallucination that facilitates the handling and exchange of massive quantities of data. Legitimate programmers never see the walls of ice they work behind, the walls of shadow that screen their operations from others, from industrial-espionage artists and hustlers like Bobby Quine.

Bobby was a cowboy. Bobby was a cracksman, a burglar, casing mankind’s extended electronic nervous system, rustling data and credit in the crowded matrix, monochrome nonspace where the only stars are dense concentrations of information, and high above it all burn corporate galaxies and the cold spiral arms of military systems.

Bobby was another one of those young-old faces you see drinking in the Gentleman Loser, the chic bar for computer cowboys, rustlers, cybernetic second-story men. We were partners.

Bobby Quine and Automatic Jack. Bobby’s the thin, pale dude with the dark glasses, and Jack’s the mean-looking guy with the myoelectric arm. Bobby’s software and Jack’s hard; Bobby punches console and Jack runs down all the little things that can give you an edge. Or, anyway, that’s what the scene watchers in the Gentleman Loser would’ve told you, before Bobby decided to burn Chrome. But they also might’ve told you that Bobby was losing his edge, slowing down. He was twenty-eight, Bobby, and that’s old for a console cowboy.

Both of us were good at what we did, but somehow that one big score just wouldn’t come down for us. I knew where to go for the right gear, and Bobby had all his licks down pat. He’d sit back with a white terry sweatband across his forehead and whip moves on those keyboards faster than you could follow, punching his way through some of the fanciest ice in the business, but that was when something happened that managed to get him totally wired, and that didn't happen often. Not highly motivated, Bobby, and I was the kind of guy who's happy to have the rent covered and a clean shirt to wear.

But Bobby had this thing for girls, like they were his private tarot or something, the way he'd get himself moving. We never talked about it, but when it started to look like he was losing his touch that summer, he started to spend more time in the Gentleman Loser. He'd sit at a table by the open doors and watch the crowd slide by, nights when the bugs were at the neon and the air smelled of perfume and fast food. You could see his sunglasses scanning those faces as they passed, and he must have decided that Rikki's was the one he was waiting for, the wild card and the luck changer. The new one.

I went to New York to check out the market, to see what was available in hot software.

The Finn's place has a defective hologram in the window; METRO HOLO-GRAFIX, over a display of dead flies wearing fur coats of gray dust. The scrap's waist-high, inside, drifts of it rising to meet walls that are barely visible behind nameless junk, behind sagging pressboard shelves stacked with old skin magazines and yellow-spined years of *National Geographic*.

"You need a gun," said the Finn. He looks like a recombo DNA project aimed at tailoring people for high-speed burrowing. "You're in luck. I got the new Smith and Wesson, the four-oh-eight Tactical. Got this xenon projector slung under the barrel, see, batteries in the grip, throw you a twelve-inch high-noon circle in the pitch dark at fifty yards. The light source is so narrow, it's almost impossible to spot. It's just like voodoo in a nightfight."

I let my arm clunk down on the table and started the fingers drumming; the servos in the hand began whining like overworked mosquitoes. I knew that the Finn really hated the sound.

"You looking to pawn that?" He prodded the Duralumin wrist joint with the chewed shaft of a felt-tip pen. "Maybe get yourself something a little quieter?"

I kept it up. "I don't need any guns, Finn."

"Okay," he said, "okay," and I quit drumming. "I only got this one item, and I don't even know what it is." He looked unhappy. "I got it off these bridge-and-tunnel kids from Jersey last week."

"So when'd you ever buy anything you didn't know what it was, Finn?"

"Wise ass." And he passed me a transparent mailer with something in it that looked like an audio cassette through the bubble padding. "They had a passport," he said. "They had credit cards and a watch. And that."

"They had the contents of somebody's pockets, you mean."

He nodded. "The passport was Belgian. It was also bogus, looked to me, so I put it in the furnace. Put the cards in with it. The watch was okay, a Porsche, nice watch."

It was obviously some kind of plug-in military program. Out of the mailer, it looked like the magazine of a small assault rifle, coated with nonreflective black plastic. The edges and corners showed bright metal; it had been knocking around for a while.

"I'll give you a bargain on it, Jack. For old times' sake."

I had to smile at that. Getting a bargain from the Finn was like God repeal-ing the law of gravity when you have to carry a heavy suitcase down ten blocks of airport corridor.

"Looks Russian to me," I said. "Probably the emergency sewage controls for some Leningrad suburb. Just what I need."

"You know," said the Finn, "I got a pair of shoes older than you are. Some-times I think you got about as much class as those yahoos from Jersey. What do you want me to tell you, it's the keys to the Kremlin? You figure out what the goddamn thing is. Me, I just sell the stuff."

I bought it.

Bodiless, we swerve into Chrome's castle of ice. And we're fast, fast. It feels like we're surfing the crest of the invading program, hanging ten above the seething glitch systems as they mutate. We're sentient patches of oil swept along down corridors of shadow.

Somewhere we have bodies, very far away, in a crowded loft roofed with steel and glass. Somewhere we have microseconds, maybe time left to pull out.

We've crashed her gates disguised as an audit and three subpoenas, but her defenses are specifically geared to cope with that kind of official intrusion. Her most sophisticated ice is structured to fend off warrants, writs, subpoenas. When we breached the first gate, the bulk of her data vanished behind core-command ice, these walls we see as leagues of corridor, mazes of shadow. Five separate landlines spurted May Day signals to law firms, but the virus had already taken over the parameter ice. The glitch systems gobble the distress calls as our mimetic subprograms scan anything that hasn't been blanked by core com-mand.

The Russian program lifts a Tokyo number from the unscreened data, choos-ing it for frequency of calls, average length of calls, the speed with which Chrome returned those calls.

"Okay," says Bobby, "we're an incoming scrambler call from a pal of hers in Japan. That should help."

Ride 'em, cowboy.

Bobby read his future in women; his girls were omens, changes in the weather, and he'd sit all night in the Gentleman Loser, waiting for the season to lay a new face down in front of him like a card.

I was working late in the loft one night, shaving down a chip, my arm off and the little waldo jacked straight into the stump.

Bobby came in with a girl I hadn't seen before, and usually I feel a little funny if a stranger sees me working that way, with those leads clipped to the hard carbon studs that stick out of my stump. She came right over and looked at the magnified image on the screen, then saw the waldo moving under its vacuum-sealed dust cover. She didn't say anything, just watched. Right away I had a good feeling about her; it's like that sometimes.

"Automatic Jack, Rikki. My associate."

He laughed, put his arm around her waist, something in his tone letting me know that I'd be spending the night in a dingy room in a hotel.

"Hi," she said. Tall, nineteen or maybe twenty, and she definitely had the goods. With just those few freckles across the bridge of her nose, and eyes somewhere between dark amber and French coffee. Tight black jeans rolled to mid-calf and a narrow plastic belt that matched the rose-colored sandals.

But now when I see her sometimes when I'm trying to sleep, I see her somewhere out on the edge of all this sprawl of cities and smoke, and it's like she's a hologram stuck behind my eyes, in a bright dress she must've worn once, when I knew her, something that doesn't quite reach her knees. Bare legs long and straight. Brown hair, streaked with blond, hoods her face, blown in a wind from somewhere, and I see her wave good-bye.

Bobby was making a show of rooting through a stack of audio cassettes. "I'm on my way, cowboy," I said, unclipping the waldo. She watched attentively as I put my arm back on.

"Can you fix things?" she asked.

"Anything, anything you want, Automatic Jack'll fix it." I snapped my Duralumin fingers for her.

She took a little simstim deck from her belt and showed me the broken hinge on the cassette cover.

"Tomorrow," I said, "no problem."

And my oh my, I said to myself, sleep pulling me down the six flights to the street, *what'll Bobby's luck be like with a fortune cookie like that? If his system worked, we'd be striking it rich any night now.* In the street I grinned and yawned and waved for a cab.

Chrome's castle is dissolving, sheets of ice shadow flickering and fading, eaten by the glitch systems that spin out from the Russian program, tumbling away from our central logic thrust and infecting the fabric of the ice itself. The glitch systems are cybernetic virus analogs, self-replicating and voracious. They mutate constantly, in unison, subverting and absorbing Chrome's defenses.

Have we already paralyzed her, or is a bell ringing somewhere, a red light blinking? Does she know?

Rikki Wildside, Bobby called her, and for those first few weeks it must have seemed to her that she had it all, the whole teeming show spread out for her, sharp and bright under the neon. She was new to the scene, and she had all the miles of malls and plazas to prowl, all the shops and clubs, and Bobby to explain the wild side, the tricky wiring on the dark underside of things, all the players and their names and their games. He made her feel at home.

"What happened to your arm?" she asked me one night in the Gentleman Loser, the three of us drinking at a small table in a corner.

"Hang-gliding," I said, "accident."

"Hang-gliding over a wheatfield," said Bobby, "place called Kiev. Our Jack's just hanging there in the dark, under a Nightwing parafoil, with fifty kilos of radar jammer between his legs, and some Russian asshole accidentally burns his arm off with a laser."

I don't remember how I changed the subject, but I did.

I was still telling myself that it wasn't Rikki who was getting to me, but what Bobby was doing with her. I'd known him for a long time, since the end of the war, and I knew he used women as counters in a game, Bobby Quine versus fortune, versus time and the night of cities. And Rikki had turned up just when he needed something to get him going, something to aim for. So he'd set her up as a symbol for everything he wanted and couldn't have, everything he'd had and couldn't keep.

I didn't like having to listen to him tell me how much he loved her, and knowing he believed it only made it worse. He was a past master at the hard fall and the rapid recovery, and I'd seen it happen a dozen times before. He might as well have had NEXT printed across his sunglasses in green Day-Glo capitals, ready to flash out at the first interesting face that flowed past the tables in the Gentleman Loser.

I knew what he did to them. He turned them into emblems, sigils on the map of his hustler's life, navigation beacons he could follow through a sea of bars and neon. What else did he have to steer by? He didn't love money, in and of itself, not enough to follow its lights. He wouldn't work for power over other people; he hated the responsibility it brings. He had some basic pride in his skill, but that was never enough to keep him pushing.

So he made do with women.

When Rikki showed up, he needed one in the worst way. He was fading fast, and smart money was already whispering that the edge was off his game. He needed that one big score, and soon, because he didn't know any other kind of life, and all his clocks were set for hustler's time, calibrated in risk and adrenaline and that supernal dawn calm that comes when every move's proved right and a sweet lump of someone else's credit clicks into your own account.

It was time for him to make his bundle and get out; so Rikki got set up higher and further away than any of the others ever had, even though—and I felt like screaming it at him—she was right there, alive, totally real, human, hungry, resilient, bored, beautiful, excited, all the things she was. . . .

Then he went out one afternoon, about a week before I made the trip to New York to see the Finn. Went out and left us there in the loft, waiting for a thunderstorm. Half the skylight was shadowed by a dome they'd never finished, and the other half showed sky, black and blue with clouds. I was standing by the bench, looking up at that sky, stupid with the hot afternoon, the humidity, and she touched me, touched my shoulder, the half-inch border of taut pink scar that the arm doesn't cover. Anybody else ever touched me there, they went on to the shoulder, the neck. . . .

But she didn't do that. Her nails were lacquered black, not pointed, but tapered oblongs, the lacquer only a shade darker than the carbon-fiber laminate that sheathes my arm. And her hand went down the arm, black nails tracing a weld in the laminate, down to the black anodized elbow joint, out to the wrist, her hand soft-knuckled as a child's, fingers spreading to lock over mine, her palm against the perforated Duralumin.

Her other palm came up to brush across the feedback pads, and it rained all afternoon, raindrops drumming on the steel and soot-stained glass above Bobby's bed.

Ice walls flick away like supersonic butterflies made of shade. Beyond them, the matrix's illusion of infinite space. It's like watching a tape of a prefab building going up; only the tape's reversed and run at high speed, and these walls are torn wings.

Trying to remind myself that this place and the gulfs beyond are only representations, that we aren't "in" Chrome's computer, but interfaced with it, while the matrix simulator in Bobby's loft generates this illusion . . . The core data begin to emerge, exposed, vulnerable. . . . This is the far side of ice, the view of the matrix I've never seen before, the view that fifteen million legitimate console operators see daily and take for granted.

The core data tower around us like vertical freight trains, color-coded for access. Bright primaries, impossibly bright in that transparent void, linked by countless horizontals in nursery blues and pinks.

But ice still shadows something at the center of it all: the heart of all Chrome's expensive darkness, the very heart . . .

It was late afternoon when I got back from my shopping expedition to New York. Not much sun through the skylight, but an ice pattern glowed on Bobby's monitor screen, a 2-D graphic representation of someone's computer defenses, lines of neon woven like an Art Deco prayer rug. I turned the console off, and the screen went completely dark.

Rikki's things were spread across my workbench, nylon bags spilling clothes and makeup, a pair of bright red cowboy boots, audio cassettes, glossy Japanese magazines about simstim stars. I stacked it all under the bench and then took my arm off, forgetting that the program I'd bought from the Finn was in the right-hand pocket of my jacket, so that I had to fumble it out left-handed and then get it into the padded jaws of the jeweller's vise.

The waldo looks like an old audio turntable, the kind that played disc records, with the vise set up under a transparent dust cover. The arm itself is just over a centimeter long, swinging out on what would've been the tone arm on one of those turntables. But I don't look at that when I've clipped the leads to my stump; I look at the scope, because that's my arm there in black and white, magnification 40×.

I ran a tool check and picked up the laser. It felt a little heavy; so I scaled my weight-sensor input down to a quarter-kilo per gram and got to work. At 40× the side of the program looked like a trailer truck.

It took eight hours to crack: three hours with the waldo and the laser and four dozen taps, two hours on the phone to a contact in Colorado, and three hours to run down a lexicon disc that could translate eight-year-old technical Russian.

Then Cyrillic alphanumerics started reeling down the monitor, twisting themselves into English halfway down. There were a lot of gaps, where the lexicon ran up against specialized military acronyms in the readout I'd bought from my man in Colorado, but it did give me some idea of what I'd bought from the Finn.

I felt like a punk who'd gone out to buy a switchblade and come home with a small neutron bomb.

Screwed again, I thought. *What good's a neutron bomb in a streetfight?* The thing under the dust cover was right out of my league. I didn't even know where to unload it, where to look for a buyer. Someone had, but he was dead, someone with a Porsche watch and a fake Belgian passport, but I'd never tried to move in those circles. The Finn's muggers from the 'burbs had knocked over someone who had some highly arcane connections.

The program in the jeweller's vise was a Russian military icebreaker, a killer-virus program.

It was dawn when Bobby came in alone. I'd fallen asleep with a bag of take-out sandwiches in my lap.

"You want to eat?" I asked him, not really awake, holding out my sandwiches. I'd been dreaming of the program, of its waves of hungry glitch systems and mimetic subprograms; in the dream it was an animal of some kind, shapeless and flowing.

He brushed the bag aside on his way to the console, punched a function key. The screen lit with the intricate pattern I'd seen there that afternoon. I rubbed sleep from my eyes with my left hand, one thing I can't do with my right. I'd fallen asleep trying to decide whether to tell him about the program. Maybe I should try to sell it alone, keep the money, go somewhere new, ask Rikki to go with me.

"Whose is it?" I asked.

He stood there in a black cotton jumpsuit, an old leather jacket thrown over his shoulders like a cape. He hadn't shaved for a few days, and his face looked thinner than usual.

"It's Chrome's," he said.

My arm convulsed, started clicking, fear translated to the myoelectrics through the carbon studs. I spilled the sandwiches; limp sprouts, and bright yellow dairy-produce slices on the unswept wooden floor.

"You're stone crazy," I said.

"No," he said, "you think she rumbled it? No way. We'd be dead already. I locked on to her through a triple-blind rental system in Mombasa and an Algerian comsat. She knew somebody was having a look-see, but she couldn't trace it."

If Chrome had traced the pass Bobby had made at her ice, we were good as dead. But he was probably right, or she'd have had me blown away on my way back from New York. "Why her, Bobby? Just give me one reason. . . ."

Chrome: I'd seen her maybe half a dozen times in the Gentleman Loser. Maybe she was slumming, or checking out the human condition, a condition she didn't exactly aspire to. A sweet little heart-shaped face framing the nastiest pair of eyes you ever saw. She'd looked fourteen for as long as anyone could remember, hyped out of anything like a normal metabolism on some massive program of serums and hormones. She was as ugly a customer as the street ever produced, but she didn't belong to the street anymore. She was one of the Boys, Chrome, a member in good standing of the local Mob subsidiary. Word was, she'd gotten started as a dealer, back when synthetic pituitary hormones were still proscribed. But she hadn't had to move hormones for a long time. Now she owned the House of Blue Lights.

"You're flat-out crazy, Quine. You give me one sane reason for having that stuff on your screen. You ought to dump it, and I mean *now*. . . ."

"Talk in the Loser," he said, shrugging out of the leather jacket. "Black Myron and Crow Jane. Jane, she's up on all the sex lines, claims she knows where the money goes. So she's arguing with Myron that Chrome's the controlling interest in the Blue Lights, not just some figurehead for the Boys."

" 'The Boys,' Bobby," I said. "That's the operative word there. You still capable of seeing that? We don't mess with the Boys, remember? That's why we're still walking around."

"That's why we're still poor, partner." He settled back into the swivel chair in front of the console, unzipped his jumpsuit, and scratched his skinny white chest. "But maybe not for much longer."

"I think maybe this partnership just got itself permanently dissolved."

Then he grinned at me. That grin was truly crazy, feral and focused, and I knew that right then he really didn't give a shit about dying.

"Look," I said, "I've got some money left, you know? Why don't you take it and get the tube to Miami, catch a hopper to Montego Bay. You need a rest, man. You've got to get your act together."

"My act, Jack," he said, punching something on the keyboard, "never has been this together before." The neon prayer rug on the screen shivered and woke as an animation program cut in, ice lines weaving with hypnotic frequency, a living mandala. Bobby kept punching, and the movement slowed; the pattern resolved itself, grew slightly less complex, became an alternation between two distant configurations. A first-class piece of work, and I hadn't thought he was still that good. "Now," he said, "there, see it? Wait. There. There again. And there. Easy to miss. That's it. Cuts in every hour and twenty minutes with a squirt transmission to their comsat. We could live for a year on what she pays them weekly in negative interest."

"Whose comsat?"

"Zürich. Her bankers. That's her bankbook, Jack. That's where the money goes. Crow Jane was right."

I stood there. My arm forgot to click.

"So how'd you do in New York, partner? You get anything that'll help me cut ice? We're going to need whatever we can get."

I kept my eyes on his, forced myself not to look in the direction of the waldo, the jeweller's vise. The Russian program was there, under the dust cover.

Wild cards, luck changers.

"Where's Rikki?" I asked him, crossing to the console, pretending to study the alternating patterns on the screen.

"Friends of hers," he shrugged, "kids, they're all into simstim." He smiled absently. "I'm going to do it for her, man."

"I'm going out to think about this, Bobby. You want me to come back, you keep your hands off the board."

"I'm doing it for her," he said as the door closed behind me. "You know I am."

And down now, down, the program a roller coaster through this fraying maze of shadow walls, gray cathedral spaces between the bright towers. Headlong speed.

Black ice. Don't think about it. Black ice.

Too many stories in the Gentleman Loser; black ice is a part of the mythology. Ice that kills. Illegal, but then aren't we all? Some kind of neural-feedback weapon, and you connect with it only once. Like some hideous Word that eats the mind from the inside out. Like an epileptic spasm that goes on and on until there's nothing left at all . . .

And we're diving for the floor of Chrome's shadow castle.

Trying to brace myself for the sudden stopping of breath, a sickness and final slackening of the nerves. Fear of that cold Word waiting, down there in the dark.

*   *   *

I went out and looked for Rikki, found her in a café with a boy with Sendai eyes, half-healed suture lines radiating from his bruised sockets. She had a glossy brochure spread open on the table, Tally Isham smiling up from a dozen photographs, the Girl with the Zeiss Ikon Eyes.

Her little simstim deck was one of the things I'd stacked under my bench the night before, the one I'd fixed for her the day after I'd first seen her. She spent hours jacked into that unit, the contact band across her forehead like a gray plastic tiara. Tally Isham was her favorite, and with the contact band on, she was gone, off somewhere in the recorded sensorium of simstim's biggest star. Simulated stimuli: the world—all the interesting parts, anyway—as perceived by Tally Isham. Tally raced a black Fokker ground-effect plane across Arizona mesa tops. Tally dived the Truk Island preserves. Tally partied with the super-rich on private Greek islands, heartbreaking purity of those tiny white seaports at dawn.

Actually she looked a lot like Tally, same coloring and cheekbones. I thought Rikki's mouth was stronger. More sass. She didn't want to *be* Tally Isham, but she coveted the job. That was her ambition, to be in simstim. Bobby just laughed it off. She talked to me about it, though. "How'd I look with a pair of these?" she'd ask, holding a full-page headshot, Tally Isham's blue Zeiss Ikons lined up with her own amber-brown. She'd had her corneas done twice, but she still wasn't twenty-twenty; so she wanted Ikons. Brand of the stars. Very expensive.

"You still window-shopping for eyes?" I asked as I sat down.

"Tiger just got some," she said. She looked tired, I thought.

Tiger was so pleased with his Sendais that he couldn't help smiling, but I doubted whether he'd have smiled otherwise. He had the kind of uniform good looks you get after your seventh trip to the surgical boutique; he'd probably spend the rest of his life looking vaguely like each new season's media front-runner; not too obvious a copy, but nothing too original, either.

"Sendai, right?" I smiled back.

He nodded. I watched as he tried to take me in with his idea of a professional simstim glance. He was pretending that he was recording. I thought he spent too long on my arm. "They'll be great on peripherals when the muscles heal," he said, and I saw how carefully he reached for his double espresso. Sendai eyes are notorious for depth-perception defects and warranty hassles, among other things.

"Tiger's leaving for Hollywood tomorrow."

"Then maybe Chiba City, right?" I smiled at him. He didn't smile back. "Got an offer, Tiger? Know an agent?"

"Just checking it out," he said quietly. Then he got up and left. He said a quick good-bye to Rikki, but not to me.

"That kid's optic nerves may start to deteriorate inside six months. You know that, Rikki? Those Sendais are illegal in England, Denmark, lots of places. You can't replace nerves."

"Hey, Jack, no lectures." She stole one of my croissants and nibbled at the tip of one of its horns.

"I thought I was your adviser, kid."

"Yeah. Well, Tiger's not too swift, but everybody knows about Sendais. They're all he can afford. So he's taking a chance. If he gets work, he can replace them."

"With these?" I tapped the Zeiss Ikon brochure. "Lot of money, Rikki. You know better than to take a gamble like that."

She nodded. "I want Ikons."

"If you're going up to Bobby's, tell him to sit tight until he hears from me."

"Sure. It's business?"

"Business," I said. But it was craziness.

I drank my coffee, and she ate both my croissants. Then I walked her down to Bobby's. I made fifteen calls, each one from a different pay phone.

Business. Bad craziness.

All in all, it took us six weeks to set the burn up, six weeks of Bobby telling me how much he loved her. I worked even harder, trying to get away from that.

Most of it was phone calls. My fifteen initial and very oblique enquiries each seemed to breed fifteen more. I was looking for a certain service Bobby and I both imagined as a requisite part of the world's clandestine economy, but which probably never had more than five customers at a time. It would be one that never advertised.

We were looking for the world's heaviest fence, for a non-aligned money laundry capable of dry-cleaning a megabuck on-line cash transfer and then forgetting about it.

All those calls were a waste, finally, because it was the Finn who put me on to what we needed. I'd gone up to New York to buy a new blackbox rig, because we were going broke paying for all those calls.

I put the problem to him as hypothetically as possible.

"Macao," he said.

"Macao?"

"The Long Hum family. Stockbrokers."

He even had the number. You want a fence, ask another fence.

The Long Hum people were so oblique that they made my idea of a subtle approach look like a tactical nuke-out. Bobby had to make two shuttle runs to Hong Kong to get the deal straight. We were running out of capital, and fast. I still don't know why I decided to go along with it in the first place; I was scared of Chrome, and I'd never been all that hot to get rich.

I tried telling myself that it was a good idea to burn the House of Blue Lights because the place was a creep joint, but I just couldn't buy it. I didn't like the Blue Lights, because I'd spent a supremely depressing evening there once, but that was no excuse for going after Chrome. Actually I halfway assumed we were going to die in the attempt. Even with that killer program, the odds weren't exactly in our favor.

Bobby was lost in writing the set of commands we were going to plug into the dead center of Chrome's computer. That was going to be my job, because Bobby was going to have his hands full trying to keep the Russian program from going straight for the kill. It was too complex for us to rewrite, and so he was going to try to hold it back for the two seconds I needed.

I made a deal with a streetfighter named Miles. He was going to follow Rikki the night of the burn, keep her in sight, and phone me at a certain time. If I wasn't there, or didn't answer in just a certain way, I'd told him to grab her and put her on the first tube out. I gave him an envelope to give her, money and a note.

Bobby really hadn't thought about that, much, how things would go for her if we blew it. He just kept telling me he loved her, where they were going to go together, how they'd spend the money.

"Buy her a pair of Ikons first, man. That's what she wants. She's serious about that simstim scene."

"Hey," he said, looking up from the keyboard, "she won't need to work. We're going to make it, Jack. She's my luck. She won't ever have to work again."

"Your luck," I said. I wasn't happy. I couldn't remember when I had been happy. "You seen your luck around lately?"

He hadn't, but neither had I. We'd both been too busy.

I missed her. Missing her reminded me of my one night in the House of Blue Lights, because I'd gone there out of missing someone else. I'd gotten drunk to begin with, then I'd started hitting Vasopressin inhalers. If your main squeeze has just decided to walk out on you, booze and Vasopressin are the ultimate in masochistic pharmacology; the juice makes you maudlin and the Vasopressin makes you remember, I mean really remember. Clinically they use the stuff to counter senile amnesia, but the street finds its own uses for things. So I'd bought myself an ultra-intense replay of a bad affair; trouble is, you get the bad with the good. Go gunning for transports of animal ecstasy and you get what you said, too, and what she said to that, how she walked away and never looked back.

I don't remember deciding to go to the Blue Lights, or how I got there, hushed corridors and this really tacky decorative waterfall trickling somewhere, or maybe just a hologram of one. I had a lot of money that night; somebody had given Bobby a big roll for opening a three-second window in someone else's ice.

I don't think the crew on the door liked my looks, but I guess my money was okay.

I had more to drink there when I'd done what I went there for. Then I made some crack to the barman about closet necrophiliacs, and that didn't go down too well. Then this very large character insisted on calling me War Hero, which I didn't like. I think I showed him some tricks with the arm, before the lights went out, and I woke up two days later in a basic sleeping module somewhere else. A cheap place, not even room to hang yourself. And I sat there on that narrow foam slab and cried.

Some things are worse than being alone. But the thing they sell in the House of Blue Lights is so popular that it's almost legal.

At the heart of darkness, the still center, the glitch systems shred the dark with whirlwinds of light, translucent razors spinning away from us; we hang in the center of a silent slow-motion explosion, ice fragments falling away forever, and Bobby's voice comes in across light-years of electronic void illusion—

"Burn the bitch down. I can't hold the thing back—"

The Russian program, rising through towers of data, blotting out the playroom colors. And I plug Bobby's homemade command package into the center of Chrome's cold heart. The squirt transmission cuts in, a pulse of condensed information that shoots straight up, past the thickening tower of darkness, the Russian program, while Bobby struggles to control that crucial second. An unformed arm of shadow twitches from the towering dark, too late.

We've done it.

The matrix folds itself around me like an origami trick.
And the loft smells of sweat and burning circuitry.
I thought I heard Chrome scream, a raw metal sound, but I couldn't have.

Bobby was laughing, tears in his eyes. The elapsed-time figure in the corner of the monitor read 07:24:05. The burn had taken a little under eight minutes. And I saw that the Russian program had melted in its slot.

We'd given the bulk of Chrome's Zürich account to a dozen world charities. There was too much there to move, and we knew we had to break her, burn her straight down, or she might come after us. We took less than ten percent for ourselves and shot it through the Long Hum set-up in Macao. They took sixty percent of that for themselves and kicked what was left back to us through the most convoluted sector of the Hong Kong exchange. It took an hour before our money started to reach the two accounts we'd opened in Zürich.

I watched zeros pile up behind a meaningless figure on the monitor. I was rich.

Then the phone rang. It was Miles. I almost blew the code phrase.

"Hey, Jack, man, I dunno—what's it all about, with this girl of yours? Kinda funny thing here . . ."

"What? Tell me."

"I been on her, like you said, tight but out of sight. She goes to the Loser, hangs out, then she gets a tube. Goes to the House of Blue Lights—"

"She what?"

"Side door. *Employees* only. No way I could get past their security."

"Is she there now?"

"No, man, I just lost her. It's insane down here, like the Blue Lights just shut down, looks like for good, seven kinds of alarms going off, everybody running, the heat out in riot gear. . . . Now there's all this stuff going on, insurance guys, real-estate types, vans with municipal plates. . . ."

"Miles, where'd she go?"

"Lost her, Jack."

"Look, Miles, you keep the money in the envelope, right?"

"You serious? Hey, I'm real sorry. I—"

I hung up.

"Wait'll we tell her," Bobby was saying, rubbing a towel across his bare chest.

"You tell her yourself, cowboy. I'm going for a walk."

So I went out into the night and the neon and let the crowd pull me along, walking blind, willing myself to be just a segment of that mass organism, just one more drifting chip of consciousness under the geodesics. I didn't think, just put one foot in front of another, but after a while I did think, and it all made sense. She'd needed the money.

I thought about Chrome, too. That we'd killed her, murdered her, as surely as if we'd slit her throat. The night that carried me along through the malls and plazas would be hunting her now, and she had nowhere to go. How many enemies would she have in this crowd alone? How many would move, now they weren't held back by fear of her money? We'd taken her for everything she had. She was back on the street again. I doubted she'd live till dawn.

Finally I remembered the café, the one where I'd met Tiger.

Her sunglasses told the whole story, huge black shades with a telltale smudge of fleshtone paintstick in the corner of one lens. "Hi, Rikki," I said, and I was ready when she took them off.

Blue. Tally Isham blue. The clear trademark blue they're famous for, ZEISS IKON ringing each iris in tiny capitals, the letters suspended there like flecks of gold.

"They're beautiful," I said. Paintstick covered the bruising. No scars with work that good. "You made some money."

"Yeah, I did." Then she shivered. "But I won't make any more, not that way."

"I think that place is out of business."

"Oh." Nothing moved in her face then. The new blue eyes were still and very deep.

"It doesn't matter. Bobby's waiting for you. We just pulled down a big score."

"No. I've got to go. I guess he won't understand, but I've got to go."

I nodded, watching the arm swing up to take her hand; it didn't seem to be part of me at all, but she held on to it like it was.

"I've got a one-way ticket to Hollywood. Tiger knows some people I can stay with. Maybe I'll even get to Chiba City."

She was right about Bobby. I went back with her. He didn't understand. But she'd already served her purpose, for Bobby, and I wanted to tell her not to hurt for him, because I could see that she did. He wouldn't even come out into the hallway after she had packed her bags. I put the bags down and kissed her and messed up the paintstick, and something came up inside me the way the killer program had risen above Chrome's data. A sudden stopping of the breath, in a place where no word is. But she had a plane to catch.

Bobby was slumped in the swivel chair in front of his monitor, looking at his string of zeros. He had his shades on, and I knew he'd be in the Gentleman Loser by nightfall, checking out the weather, anxious for a sign, someone to tell him what his new life would be like. I couldn't see it being very different. More comfortable, but he'd always be waiting for that next card to fall.

I tried not to imagine her in the House of Blue Lights, working three-hour shifts in an approximation of REM sleep, while her body and a bundle of conditioned reflexes took care of business. The customers never got to complain that she was faking it, because those were real orgasms. But she felt them, if she felt them at all, as faint silver flares somewhere out on the edge of sleep. Yeah, it's so popular, it's almost legal. The customers are torn between needing someone and wanting to be alone at the same time, which has probably always been the name of that particular game, even before we had the neuroelectronics to enable them to have it both ways.

I picked up the phone and punched the number for her airline. I gave them her real name, her flight number. "She's changing that," I said, "to Chiba City. That's right. Japan." I thumbed my credit card into the slot and punched my ID code. "First class." Distant hum as they scanned my credit records. "Make that a return ticket."

But I guess she cashed the return fare, or else she didn't need it, because she hasn't come back. And sometimes late at night I'll pass a window with posters of simstim stars, all those beautiful, identical eyes staring back at me out of faces that are nearly as identical, and sometimes the eyes are hers, but none of the faces are, none of them ever are, and I see her far out on the edge of all this sprawl of night and cities, and then she waves good-bye.

TOWARDS AN AESTHETIC OF SCIENCE FICTION

Joanna Russ

What makes a science fiction story good SF? How does a science fiction story differ in aesthetic goals from a story in another genre? For decades Joanna Russ has been the leading feminist SF writer and critic. Her fiction includes the classic *The Female Man*, and her criticism the classic *How to Suppress Women's Writing*, as well as the recent collection *To Write Like a Woman*, which reprints many of her important essays on SF (including this one).

Is science fiction literature?

Yes.

Can it be judged by the usual literary criteria?

No.

Such a statement requires not only justification but considerable elaboration. Written science fiction is, of course, literature, although science fiction in other media (films, drama, perhaps even painting or sculpture) must be judged by standards other than those applied to the written word.* Concentrating on science fiction as literature, primarily as prose fiction, this paper will attempt to indicate some of the limitations critics encounter in trying to apply traditional literary criticism to science fiction. To be brief, the access of academic interest in science fiction that has occurred during the last few years has led to considerable difficulty. Not only do academic critics find themselves imprisoned by habitual (and unreflecting) condescension in dealing with this particular genre; quite often their critical tools, however finely honed, are simply not applicable to a body of work that—despite its superficial resemblance to realistic or naturalistic twentieth-century fiction—is fundamentally a drastically different form of literary art.

---

*"Environments" and similar examples of contemporary art seem to lend themselves to science fiction. For example, as of this writing, an "archeological" exhibit of the fictional Civilization of Llhuros is visiting our local museum. Strictly speaking, the exhibit is fantasy and not science fiction, since the creator (Professor Norman Daly of Cornell University) makes no attempt to place this imaginary country in either a known, a future, or an extraterrene history.

Fine beginnings have been made in the typology of science fiction by Darko Suvin* of McGill University, who builds on the parameters prescribed for the genre by the Polish writer and critic, Stanislaw Lem.** Samuel Delany, a science-fiction writer and theorist, has dealt with the same matters in a recent paper concerned largely with problems of definition.†

One very important point which emerges in the work of all three critics is that standards of plausibility—as one may apply them to science fiction—must be derived not only from the observation of life as it is or has been lived, but also, rigorously and systematically, from science. And in this context "science" must include disciplines ranging from mathematics (which is formally empty) through the "hard" sciences (physics, astronomy, chemistry) through the "soft" sciences (ethology, psychology, sociology) all the way to disciplines which as yet exist only in the descriptive or speculative state (history, for example, or political theory).

Science fiction is not fantasy, for the standards of plausibility of fantasy derive not from science, but from the observation of life as it is—inner life, perhaps, in this case. Mistakes in scientific possibility do not turn science fiction into fantasy. They are merely mistakes. Nor does the outdating of scientific theory transform the science fiction of the past into fantasy.‡ Error-free science fiction is an ideal as impossible of achievement as the nineteenth-century ideal of an "objective," realistic novel. Not that in either case the author can be excused for not trying; unreachability is, after all, what ideals are for. But only God can know enough to write either kind of book perfectly.

For the purposes of the aesthetics of science fiction, a remark of Professor Suvin's made casually at the 1968 annual meeting of the Modern Language Association seems to me extremely fruitful. Science fiction, said Suvin, is "quasi-medieval." Professor Suvin has not elaborated on this insight, as he seems at the moment more concerned with the nature of science fiction's cognitive relation to what he calls the "zero world" of "empirically verifiable properties around the author."§ To me the phrase "quasi-medieval" suggests considerable insight, particularly into the reasons why critical tools developed with an entirely different literature in mind often do not work when applied to science fiction. I should like to propose the following:

That science fiction, like much medieval literature, is *didactic*.

That, despite superficial similarities to naturalistic (or other) modern fiction, the protagonists of science fiction are always collective, never individual persons (although individuals often appear as exemplary or representative figures).

That science fiction's emphasis is always on *phenomena*—to the point where reviewers and critics can commonly use such phrases as "the idea as hero."

That science fiction is not only didactic, but very often awed, worshipful, and *religious* in tone. Damon Knight's famous phrase for this is "the sense of

---

*See particularly "On the Poetics of the Science Fiction Genre," *College English* 34 (1972): 372–82.
**For example, "On the Structural Analysis of Science Fiction," SFS 1(1973): 26–33.
†"About Five Thousand One Hundred and Seventy-Five Words," *Extrapolation* 10(1969): 52–66.
‡At least not immediately. Major changes in scientific theory may lead to major reevaluation of the fiction, but most science fiction hasn't been around long enough for that. I would agree with George Bernard Shaw that didactic literature does (at least in part) wear out with time, but most science fiction can still rest on the Scottish verdict of "not proven."
§Suvin (note 2), p. 377.

wonder."* To substantiate this last, one needs only a headcount of Messiahs in recent science fiction novels, the abrupt changes of scale (either spatial or temporal) used to induce cosmic awe in such works as Olaf Stapledon's *Last and First Men,* James Blish's *Surface Tension,* stories like Isaac Asimov's "Nightfall" and "The Last Question," Arthur C. Clarke's "Nine Billion Names of God," and the change of tone at the end of Clarke's *Childhood's End* or Philip José Farmer's story "Sail On! Sail On!" (The film *2001* is another case in point.)

The emphasis on phenomena, often at the complete expense of human character, needs no citation; it is apparent to anyone who has any acquaintance with the field. Even in pulp science fiction populated by grim-jawed heroes, the human protagonist, if not Everyman, is a glamorized version of Super-everyman. That science fiction is didactic hardly needs proof, either. The pleasure science fiction writers take in explaining physics, thirtieth-century jurisprudence, the mechanics of teleportation, patent law, four-dimensional geometry, or whatever happens to be on the tapis, lies open in any book that has not degenerated into outright adventure story with science-fiction frills.† Science fiction even has its favorite piece of theology. Just as contemporary psychoanalytic writers cannot seem to write anything without explaining the Oedipus complex at least once, so science fiction writers dwell lovingly on the time dilation consequent to travel at near light-speed. Science is to science fiction (by analogy) what medieval Christianity was to deliberately didactic medieval fiction.

I would like to propose that contemporary literary criticism (not having been developed to handle such material) is not the ideal tool for dealing with fiction that is explicitly, deliberately, and baldly *didactic.* (Modern criticism appears to experience the same difficulty in handling the eighteenth-century *contes philosophiques* Professor Suvin cites as among the precursors of science fiction.) Certainly if one is to analyze didactic literature, one must first know what system of beliefs or ideas constitutes the substance of the didacticism. A modern critic attempting to understand science fiction without understanding modern science is in the position of a medievalist attempting to read *Piers Plowman* without any but the haziest ideas about medieval Catholicism. (Or, possibly, like a modern critic attempting to understand Bertolt Brecht without any knowledge of Marxist economic analysis beyond a vague and uninformed distrust.)

An eminent critic (who knows better now) once asked me during a discussion of a novel of Kurt Vonnegut's, "But when you get to the science, don't you just make it up?" The answer, of course, is no. Science fiction must not offend against what is known. Only in areas where nothing is known—or knowledge is uncertain—is it permissible to just "make it up." (Even then, what is made up must be systematic, plausible, rigorously logical, and must avoid offending against what is known to be known.)

Of course, didactic fiction does not always tell people something new; often it tells them what they already know, and the retelling becomes a reverent ritual, very gratifying to all concerned. There is some of this in science fiction, although (unlike the situation obtaining in medieval Christianity) this state of affairs is considered neither necessary nor desirable by many readers. There is

---

*Damon Knight, *In Search of Wonder* (2d ed., 1967). The phrase is used throughout.
†From time to time what might even be called quasi-essays appear, e.g., Larry Niven, "The Theory and Practice of Teleportation," *Galaxy,* March 1969.

science fiction that concentrates on the very edges of what is known. There is even science fiction that ignores what is known. The latter is bad science fiction."*

How can a criticism developed to treat a post-medieval literature of individual destinies, secular concerns, and the representation of what is (rather than what might be) illuminate science fiction?

Science fiction presents an eerie echo of the attitudes and interests of a pre-industrial, pre-Renaissance, pre-secular, pre-individualistic culture. It has been my experience that medievalists take easily and kindly to science fiction, that they are often attracted to it, that its didacticism presents them with no problems, and that they enjoy this literature much more than do students of later literary periods.† So, in fact, do city planners, architects, archaeologists, engineers, rock musicians, anthropologists, and nearly everybody except most English professors.

Without knowledge of or appreciation of the "theology" of science fiction—that is, science—what kind of criticism will be practiced on particular science fiction works?

Often critics may use their knowledge of the recurrent and important themes of Western culture to misperceive what is actually in a science-fiction story. For example, recognizable themes or patterns of imagery can be insisted on far beyond their actual importance in the work simply because they are familiar to the critic. Or the symbolic importance of certain material can be misread because the significance of the material in the cultural tradition that science fiction comes from (which is overwhelmingly that of science, not literature) is simply not known to the critic. Sometimes material may be ignored because it is not part of the critic's cognitive universe.

For example, in H. G. Wells's magnificent novella, *The Time Machine,* a trip into the eight-thousandth century presents us with a world that appears to be directly reminiscent of Eden, a "weedless garden" full of warm sunlight, untended but beautiful flowers, and effortless innocence. Wells even has his Time Traveler call the happy inhabitants of this garden "Eloi" (from the Hebrew "Elohim"). Certainly the derivation of these details is obvious. Nor can one mistake the counter-world populated by bleached monsters. But the critic may make too much of all this. For example, Bernard Bergonzi (I suspect his behavior would be fairly typical) overweights Wells's heavenly/demonic imagery.§ Certainly *The Time Machine*'s pastoral future does echo a great deal of material important in the Western literary tradition, but it is a mistake to think of these (very obtrusive) clusters of Edenic-pastoral/hellish imagery as the "hidden" meaning of Wells's Social Darwinism. On the contrary, it is the worlds of Eloi and the Morlocks that are put in the employ of the Social Darwinism, which is itself only an example of mindless evolution, of the cruelty of material determinism, and of the tragic mindlessness of all physical process. The real center of Wells's story is not even in his ironic reversal of the doctrine of the fortunate fall

---

*A dictum attributed to Theodore Sturgeon, science-fiction writer, is that 90 percent of anything is bad.

†As of this writing, SUNY Binghamton is presenting a summer course in science fiction taught by a graduate student who is—a medievalist.

§Bernard Bergonzi, *The Early H. G. Wells* (Manchester, 1961), p. 52ff.

(evolution, in Wells's view in *The Time Machine,* inevitably produces what one might call the unfortunate rise—the very production of intelligence, of mind, is what must, sooner or later, destroy mind). Even the human devolution pictured in the story is only a special case of the iron physical law that constitutes the true center of the book and the true agony of Wells's vision. This vision is easy to overlook, not because it is subtle, indirect, or hidden, but because it is so blatantly hammered home in all the Time Traveler's speculations about evolution and—above all—in a chapter explicitly entitled "The Farther Vision." As Eric Bentley once remarked, "clarity is the first requisite of didacticism."* Didactic art must, so to speak, wear its meaning on its sleeve. *The Time Machine* is not about a lost Eden; it is—passionately and tragically—about the Three Laws of Thermodynamics, especially the second. The slow cooling of the sun in "The Farther Vision" foreshadows the heat-death (as exemplified by Weena's presumed death and the threat to the Time Traveler himself from the Morlocks) is bad enough; the "wilderness of rotting paper" in the Palace of Green Porcelain, an abandoned museum, is perhaps worse; the complete disappearance of mind in humanity's remote descendents (the kangaroo-like animals) is horrible; but the death of absolutely everything, the physical degradation of the entire universe, is a Gotterdämmerung earlier views of the nature of the universe could hardly conceive—*let alone prove.* As the Time Traveler says after leaving "that remote and awful twilight," "I'm sorry to have brought you out here in the cold."

Unless a critic can bring to *The Time Machine* not only a knowledge of the science that stands behind it, but the passionate belief that such knowledge is real and that it matters, the critic had better stay away from science fiction. Persons to whom the findings of science seem only bizarre, fanciful, or irrelevant to everyday life, have no business with science fiction—or with science for that matter—although they may deal perfectly well with fiction that ignores both science and the scientific view of reality.

For example, a short story by Ursula K. Le Guin, "The Masters" (in *Fantastic,* Feb. 1963), has as its emotional center the rediscovery of the duodecimal system. To criticize this story properly one must know about three things: the Arabic invention of the zero, the astounding importance of this invention for mathematics (and hence the sciences), and the fact that one may count with any base. In fact, the duodecimal system, with its base of 12, is far superior for some uses to our decimal system with its base of 10.

A third example of ways science fiction can be misread can be provided by Hal Clement's novel, *Close to Critical.* The story treats of an alien species inhabiting a planet much like Jupiter. Some psychoanalytic critic, whose name I have unfortunately forgotten, once treated material like this (the story was, I think, Milton Rothman's "Heavy Planet") as psychoneurotic, i.e., the projection of repressed infantile fears. And certainly a Jovian or Jovian-like landscape would be extremely bizarre. Clement's invented world, with its atmosphere three thousand times as dense as ours, its gravity three times ours, its total darkness, its pinecone-shaped inhabitants, its hundred-foot-wide "raindrops" that condense at night and evaporate each morning, can easily be perceived by the scientifically ignorant as a series of grotesque morbidities. In such a view, *Close*

---

*Eric Bentley, *The Playwright as Thinker* (New York, 1967), p. 224.

to Critical is merely nightmarish. But to decide this is to ignore the evidence. Clement's gas-giant is neither nightmarish nor grotesque, but merely accurate. In fact, Mr. Clement is the soberest of science fiction writers, and his characters are always rational, humane, and highly likeable. The final effect of the novel is exactly the opposite of nightmare; it is affectionate familiarity. The Jovian-like world is a real world. One understands and appreciates it. It is, to its inhabitants, no worse and no better than our own. It is, finally, beautiful—in the same way and for the same reasons that Earth is beautiful. *Close to Critical* evokes Knight's "sense of wonder" because it describes a genuinely possible place, indeed a place that is highly likely according to what we know of the universe. The probability of the setting is what makes the book elegant—in the mathematical sense, that is: aesthetically satisfying. If there is anything grotesque in Clement's work, it is in the strain caused by the split between idea-as-hero (which is superbly handled) and the human protagonists, who are neither interesting, probable, nor necessary, and whose appearance in the book at all is undoubtedly due to the American pulp tradition out of which American science fiction arose after World War I. The book suffers from serious confusion of form.

Science fiction, like medieval painting, addresses itself to the mind, not the eye. We are not presented with a representation of what we know to be true through direct experience; rather, we are given what we know to be true through other means—or in the case of science fiction, what we know to be at least possible. Thus the science-fiction writer can portray Jupiter as easily as the medieval painter can portray Heaven; neither of them has been there, but that doesn't matter. To turn from other modern fiction to science fiction is oddly like turning from Renaissance painting, with all that flesh and foreshortening, to the clarity and luminousness of painters who paint ideas. For this reason, science fiction, like much medieval art, can deal with transcendental events. Hence the tendency of science fiction towards wonder, awe, and a religious or quasi-religious attitude towards the universe.

Persons who consider science untrue, or irrelevant to what really matters, or inimical to humane values, can hardly be expected to be interested in science fiction. Nor can one study science fiction as some medievalists (presumably) might study their material—that is, by finding equivalents for a system of beliefs they cannot accept in literal form. To treat medieval Catholicism as irrelevant to medieval literature is bad scholarship; to treat it as somebody else's silly but interesting superstitions is likewise extremely damaging to any consideration of the literature itself. But nonscientific equivalents for the Second Law of Thermodynamics or the intricacies of genetics—or whatever a particular science fiction story is about—will not do, either. Science bears too heavily on all our lives for that. All of us—willy-nilly—must live as if we believed the body of modern science to be true. Moreover, science itself contains methods for determining what about it is true—not metaphorically true, or metaphysically true, or emotionally true, but simply, plainly, physically, literally true.

If the critic believes that scientific truth is unreal, or irrelevant to his (the critic's) business, then science fiction becomes only a series of very odd metaphors for "the human condition" (which is taken to be different from or unconnected to any scientific truths about the universe). Why should an artist draw metaphors from such a peculiar and totally extra-literary source? Especially when there are so many more intelligent (and intelligible) statements of the human condition that already exist—in our (non-science-fiction) literary tradition? Are writers of science fiction merely kinky? Or perverse? Or stubborn? One can imagine what C. P. Snow would have to say about this split between the two cultures.

One thing he might say is that science fiction bridges the two cultures. It draws its beliefs, its material, its great organizing metaphors, its very attitudes from a culture that could not exist before the industrial revolution, before science became both an autonomous activity and a way of looking at the world. In short, science fiction is *not* derived from traditional Western literary culture, and critics of traditional Western literature have good reason to regard science fiction as a changeling in the literary cradle.

Perhaps science fiction is one symptom of a change in sensibility (and culture) as profound as that of the Renaissance. Despite its ultra-American, individualistic muscle-flexing, science fiction (largely American in origins and influence)* is collective in outlook, didactic, materialist, and, paradoxically, often intensely religious or mystical. Such a cluster of traits reminds one not only of medieval culture, but, possibly, of tendencies in our own, post-industrial culture. It may be no accident that elaborate modern statements of the aesthetic of the *didactic* are to be found in places like Brecht's "A Short Organum for the Theatre."** Of course, didactic art does not necessarily mean propaganda or political Leftism. But there are similarities between Samuel Delany's insistence that modern literature must be concerned not with passion, but with perception,† Suvin's definition of science fiction as a literature of "cognitive estrangement,"‡ George Bernard Shaw's insistence on art as didactic, Brecht's definition of art as a kind of experiment, and descriptions of science fiction as "thought experiments."§ It is as if literary and dramatic art were being asked to perform tasks of analysis and teaching as a means of dealing with some drastic change in the conditions of human life.

Science fiction is the only modern literature to take work as its central and characteristic concern.

Except for some modern fantasy (e.g., the novels of Charles Williams), science fiction is the only kind of modern narrative literature to deal directly (often awkwardly) with religion as process, not as doctrine, i.e., the ground of feeling and experience from which religion springs.

Like much "post-modern" literature (Nabokov, Borges), science fiction deals commonly, typically, and often insistently with epistemology.

It is unlikely that science fiction will ever become a major form of literature. Life-as-it-is (however glamorized or falsified) is more interesting to most people than the science-fictional life-as-it-might-be. Moreover, the second depends on an understanding and appreciation of the first. In a sense, science fiction includes (or is parasitic on, depending on your point of view) non-science fiction.

However, there is one realm in which science fiction will remain extremely

---

*Kingsley Amis emphasizes that twentieth-century science fiction is predominantly an American phenomenon: *New Maps of Hell* (New York, 1960), p. 17 (or Ballantine Books ed., p. 17), q.v.
**In *Brecht on Theatre*, trans. John Willett (New York, 1962), pp. 179–205.
†In a talk given at the MLA seminar on science fiction, December 1968, in New York.
‡Suvin (note 2), p. 372.
§This phrase has been used so widely in the field that original attribution is impossible.

important. It is the only modern literature that attempts to assimilate imaginatively scientific knowledge about reality and the scientific method, as distinct from the merely practical changes science has made in our lives. The latter are important and sometimes overwhelming, but they can be dealt with imaginatively in exactly the same way a Londoner could have dealt with the Great Plague of 1665 ("Life is full of troubles") or the way we characteristically deal with our failures in social organization ("Man is alienated"). Science fiction is also the only modern literary from (with the possible exception of the detective puzzle) that embodies in its basic assumptions the conviction that finding out, or knowing about something—however impractical the knowledge—is itself a crucial good. Science fiction is a positive response to the post-industrial world, not always in its content (there is plenty of nostalgia for the past and dislike of change in science fiction), but in its very assumptions, its very form.

Criticism of science fiction cannot possibly look like the criticism we are used to. It will—perforce—employ an aesthetic in which the elegance, rigorousness, and systematic coherence of explicit ideas is of great importance.* It will therefore appear to stray into all sorts of extraliterary fields: metaphysics, politics, philosophy, physics, biology, psychology, topology, mathematics, history, and so on. The relations of foreground and background that we are so used to after a century and a half of realism will not obtain. Indeed, they may be reversed. Science-fiction criticism will discover themes and structures (like those of Olaf Stapledon's *Last and First Men)* that may seem recondite, extra-literary, or plain ridiculous. Themes we customarily regard as emotionally neutral will be charged with emotion. Traditionally "human" concerns will be absent; protagonists may be all but unrecognizable as such. What in other fiction would be marvelous will here be merely accurate or plain; what in other fiction would be ordinary or mundane will here be astonishing, complex, wonderful. (For example, allusions to the death of God will be trivial jokes, while metaphors involving the differences between telephone switchboards and radio stations will be poignantly tragic. Stories ostensibly about persons will really be about topology. Erotics will be intracranial, mechanical [literally], and moving.)†

Science fiction is, of course, about human concerns. It is written and read by human beings. But the culture from which it comes—the experiences, attitudes, knowledge, and learning that one must bring to it—these are not at all what we are used to as proper to literature. They may, however, be increasingly proper to human life. According to Professor Suvin, the last century has seen a sharp rise in the popularity of science fiction in all the leading industrial nations of the world.§ There will, in all probability, be more and more science fiction written and, therefore, more and more of a need for its explication and criticism.

Such criticism will not be easy. The task of a modern critic of science fiction might be compared to the difficulties of studying Shakespeare's works armed

---

*Suvin (note 2), p. 381, as follows: "The consistency of extrapolation, precision of analogy, and width of reference in such a cognitive discussion turn into aesthetic factors . . . a cognitive—*in most cases strictly scientific—element becomes a measure of aesthetic quality.*"
†In turn, James Blish's *Black Easter* (which I take to be about Manicheanism), Stapledon's *Last and First Men* (the Martian invasion), A. J. Deutsch's "A Subway Named Moebius" (frequently anthologized), and George Zebrowski's "Starcrossed" (in *Eros in Orbit,* ed. Joseph Elder, 1973).
§Suvin (note 2), p. 372.

only with a vast, miscellaneous mass of Elizabethan and Jacobean plays, a few remarks of Ben Jonson's, some scattered eulogies on Richard Burbage, Rowe's
comments on *Othello,* and a set of literary standards derived exclusively from the
Greek and Latin classics—which, somehow, do not quite fit.

Some beginnings have been made in outlining an aesthetics of science fiction, particularly in the work of Lem and Suvin, but much remains to be done.
Perhaps the very first task lies in discovering that we are indeed dealing with a
new and different literature. Applying the standards and methods one is used to
can have only three results: the dismissal of all science fiction as non-literature,
a preference for certain narrow kinds of science fiction (because they can be understood at least partly in the usual way), or a misconceiving and misperception
of the very texts one is trying to understand. The first reaction seems to be the
most common. In the second category one might place the odd phenomenon
that critics inexperienced in the field seem to find two kinds of fiction easy to
deal with: seventeenth-century flights to the moon and dystopias. Thus *Brave
New World* and *1984* have received much more critical attention than, say,
Shaw's late plays or Stapledon's work. The third category has hitherto been rare
because academic consideration of science fiction has been rare, but it could become all too common if the increasing popularity of college courses in the subject is not accompanied by criticism proper to the subject. Futurologists,
physicists, and sociologists may use science fiction in extra-literary ways, but
they are not literary critics. If the literary critics misperceive or misconceive their
material, the results will be to discourage readers, discourage science-fiction
writers (who are as serious about their work as any other writers), destroy the
academic importance of the subject itself, and thus impoverish the whole realm
of literature, of which science fiction is a new—but a vigorous and growing—
province.

IDENTIFYING THE OBJECT

Gwyneth Jones

Gwyneth Jones was the harbinger of the 1980s and '90s renaissance now in full swing in British SF. Her novel *Divine Endurance* appeared the same year as Gibson's *Neuromancer*, 1984, and its impact is still growing. She has become one of the leading feminist critics of SF, in the tradition of Joanna Russ and Ursula K. Le Guin. Her masterpiece to date, *White Queen*, is the first of a trilogy that includes *North Wind* and a forthcoming novel about aliens who arrive to settle Earth and exploit it. "Identifying the Object" is a short story featuring the central characters of *White Queen*, Johnny and Braemar.

Tunguska: In June, 1908, there was an extraordinary explosion somewhere in or over Siberia. That night in London you could read a newspaper by the light of the fireball. There were no consequences. The location of the crater was not even determined until twenty years later, after the intervention of a World War and a revolution. But in our time we are ready for Tunguska. It can happen to us immediately. We have the technology. We have the anticipation: what they call in my country the longing, the *hiraeth*. I am a freelance journalist. My name is Anna Jones Morgan Davis. I begged, argued, lied, pleaded for two days and nights solid, after I found out about the expedition to the site. I left home possessed by one iron determination: to be there when the object was identified.

The transit lounge of the desert airport was a breeze block garage with glass doors and a sand-scoured wooden floor. Johnny Guglioli and I were pursued there by a skinny and very dark little man in a khaki uniform too heavy for the climate. Whenever he managed to catch Johnny's eye he hissed softly and made a wistful, obscene gesture: rubbing his thumb against two fingers. A broken digital clock hung as if half strangled from an exposed cable above the shuttered coffee bar. A single monitor screen, fixed to one of the concrete roof beams, showed the quivering green word "departures": and nothing more. Parties of Africans sat about the floor. I hadn't had a chance to change into protective disguise, so the men reacted instantly to my appearance.

In one of the rows of seats a lone white woman traveler lay sleeping, stretched over her battered flight bag along three black plastic spoon-shapes. A cracked panama had slipped from her sun-browned face.

Johnny and I were in trouble. Johnny was American, but had come back from somewhere to London for the trip. For our separate reasons we'd missed the first leg of the official journey. We had expected to join the expedition here, for a special charter to the capital of the country that lay to the south. Our destination was in there somewhere, beyond the desert and the great river. But we had missed the plane. Perhaps we had missed the plane. . . . The real trouble was that Johnny would not bribe, because bribery and corruption were the root causes of so much of Africa's misery.

The hall was devoid of information sources. The little man, whose hissing and hovering was making Johnny look like a girl alone at a late-night bus stop, had already told us what he was going to tell.

"I'll ask one of the women," I said.

But she spoke no French or English or didn't want to get involved. Faces around her gazed stonily out of the archipelago of dark robes and peeping finery. A woman made an unintelligible comment in a tone of deep contempt: the natives were hostile.

We tried to remain calm.

Johnny stretched and pressed his hands behind his head, raising the fan of eel-brown hair that was overheating his neck. He looked, momentarily, like a hostage getting ready to be shot.

"Embarkation for Planet X: colonist class. Isn't it weird how these places always manage to make you believe there's no air outside. That's futurism for you, comes from the cultural phase our world was in when the standard concept of 'airport' was laid down. I mean, look at those chairs—"

"I suppose they might be more comfortable in a lower gravity."

I had bumped into Johnny by chance at Gatwick. Our paths had crossed several times before, in our small world; and we'd always enjoyed each other's company. Johnny Guglioli was a young American (USA citizen I mean) of a highly recognizable type: shrewd, naive, well informed and passionate about the world's ills and the possibility of curing them. His writing had a strangeness that worried people a little, even after it had been toned down by his editors, and his selfless arrogance infuriated many. But I respected Johnny. He could be absurdly didactic. But loud or brash, his eyes never lost the uneasiness of those children of Utopia, good Americans, who have woken up and found themselves—well, *here*, where the rest of us live.

For that bruised puzzlement in the face of what people call normality I could forgive him a good deal. I could forgive him—almost—this disaster.

In any more hopeful location I'd have walked out of the airport and found myself a bus. But there was nothing outside the dusty glass doors, in the place where Johnny said we couldn't breathe: only a few dead thornbushes, the red track from the airport building and an endless waste of sand.

Aircon fans roared in a mind-deadening way and without any noticeable effect on the heat. I wondered how many of the Africans here had been awake that night. I wished I knew how the hell to deal with Johnny, whose button black eyes had gone blank with stubborn virtue . . . though it would break his heart to miss this gig. I was tortured by the suspicion that somewhere close there was a VIP lounge where the rest of the expedition were sipping cold drinks.

"Shall we try the Virgin desk again?"

The lone white woman sat up, yawned, and said, "Oh, hallo Anna. So you're in this too? How are the kids?"

She smiled dazzlingly. "I suppose you're another Snark hunter?"

I hadn't recognized her. Awake her face shed years, its expert makeup lighting up like magic.

"Johnny Guglioli," I said. "Braemar Wilson." And took a mental step backwards. The smile was clearly meant for Johnny alone.

I'd known Brae for a long time, known her before she adopted that *nomme de guerre*. The last time I'd seen her in an airport her heels had been three inches high. Her dewy complexion had never seen the sun, and apart from the essential smart briefcase her luggage was none of her business. But she was equally immaculate in this role. Wherever did she get those shorts? They were perfect.

"Braemar Wilson as in the pop-soc vids?"

"The same. Though I'm almost ashamed to admit it, in such company. I've read your work, Johnny. If I told you how much I admire you, I'd sound like a groupie."

It was the name, she'd once told me, on the gate of the miserable little house she'd been renting after her divorce. Some redundant housewives start up phone-a-birthday-cake businesses. Mrs. Wilson had become, in a very few years, a household name in the burgeoning "infotainment" market. Her girlish deprecation irritated me. She had no reason to defer to young Johnny. The ground she covered was hack, but not the treatment.

"Hell no!" cried Johnny. "I want to be the groupie. That 'Death and the Human Family' thing! It was terrific!"

There was a break for mutually appraising laughter—in which Brae warned me, by withholding eye contact, not to presume on our long acquaintance in any way. I wouldn't have dreamed of it.

"Maybe you can tell us what's going on." Johnny affected a casual tone. "Did we really miss our ride, or are these guys just teasing?"

"Oh, it's gone all right. A late change: I feel less paranoid now I know you two didn't get the news either."

She examined us.

"What's the problem? You transferred to the scheduled flight, didn't you? Or what are you doing in here?"

Johnny's lightly tan-screened face turned brick color.

"The flight's full. We're fucking grounded."

Braemar looked at our little man, who was still making his obscene gesture. She enveloped the whole situation in a smile so tender and so knowing that Johnny had to ignore it.

"What's my reward, Johnny, if I get you back on stream?"

Having ignored the smile he was able to laugh: to groan with theatrical sincerity. "Name it! My life is yours to command!"

So that's how it's done, I thought.

She never asked us for money, then or later. She simply took our coupons away, and brought them back turned into boarding passes. I have no idea how Johnny imagined that this was achieved, or if he was just plain faking too.

*   *   *

The hotel was a huge tower, a landmark of the French-planned city center. The taxidriver had called it "L'Iceberg": it looked as far out of place and as rotten as might be expected at this latitude. We could see from the outside whole swathes of yellow-stained decay, sinister great fissures in the white slabs, broken windows.

There was no phone and no drinking water in my room so I had to come down again. I found the coffee shop and bought a bottle of local beer. There was no one about. Brae and Johnny were maybe sleeping, maybe (I surmised grumpily) improving their acquaintance somewhere. The rest of our gang was on a sightseeing tour and there seemed to be no other guests. Miraculously, I got through to Wales on a cardphone in the lobby. Unfortunately it wasn't my husband or my wife who picked up the handset. It was Jacko, Sybil's child but my darling.

"Is Daddy there, Jacky? Or your Mummy? Go and fetch someone, sweetheart—"

"Mummyanna—" He sighed heavily, and broke the connection. I couldn't get through again.

Outside in the desolate boulevard young women sat selling vegetables. In front of one of them three tiny aubergines lay in the dust, another had a withered pimento and a bunch of weeds. There were no customers. Africa looked like a dead insect, a carcass sucked dry and blown away by the wind. It was too late. No one would ever know what city might have stood here: alien to me, efficient, rich in the storied culture of a bloody and complex past.

People come to my country to see the castles.

In my business I am always dealing with the forward-echo, that phenomenon which is supposedly forbidden in our continuum. But things do affect the world before they happen, I know it. I'm always piecing together footage which is significant because of some event further down the line. I was caught in one of those moments now. Because I couldn't talk to my family it seemed as if the world was about to end. I wished Johnny and I had stayed back in the desert, trying to do right.

There was a banquet that night in the Leonid Breshnev suite: a bowl of tinned grapefruit segments with a cherry at every place. One of my neighbors was another journalist, a silly Japanese woman. On the other I found a Major Derek Whynton, military observer for NATO: a chiseled-profile, blue-eyed, very British type. I was foolish enough to remark—between the grapefruit and the fried grasscutter—that I'd thought the evidence was conclusively against the kind of activity he'd be interested in. I triggered an interminable lecture, and worse. Some men will take absolutely anything for a sexual invitation—and of course this was Africa, where you can't be too careful. In the middle of the monitoring-industry PR he smiled archly, laid a hand on my knee and asked me if I was married.

"Yes, twice."

He angled himself so he could count my rings, and blanched visibly.

"Two husbands?" He sounded seriously alarmed.

"One husband, two wives."

The major was relieved, but mildly disgusted. "Polygamy, eh? That's a remarkable regression. I don't mean to be offensive, but it seems odd that any modern young woman can accept that arrangement."

"If that was the arrangement, I wouldn't accept it."

There was a big darn at my place. I studied it, intensely bored. A clean white tablecloth is a lovely thing. But when a thing gets to be more trouble than it is worth you throw it out. Or put it in a museum. There is no human artifact so sacred it deserves to stay in circulation forever.

At least I'd got rid of the hand. Major Derek marked me down as emergency rations, only slightly less dodgy than the local whores. He discovered he had to hurry away somewhere, between the ice cream and the speeches.

Spiky electric candelabra hung low over the crowd, like spiders in ambush. Some bulbs were brilliant, some dark; making a broken pattern that was repeated as if continuously by the glass doors to the roof terrace. It looked as if something out there was eating up the stars in random mouthfuls.

Johnny was at the bar, with Brae. She wore a pricey little khaki number, Islamically modest. Johnny probably thought it was her old school uniform. She was regaling him with bad-taste stories about the African notables. Johnny didn't mind this too much. They were only politicians.

"What about that guy Obofun Ade—in the white with the kind of hippie embroidery?"

Nigerian pharmaceuticals billionaire, vocal backer of the West Africa Federation Initiative. The African contingent at this gathering was alarming: almost as if something really important had happened.

"A lot of what Ade says makes sense . . ."

"True enough. But you know where the money comes from?"

"Cheap neuro-drugs, undercutting the fat-cat multinationals—"

"They say his family's plant is based on kidnapping streetkids."

"Aaah—"

"Rows of them. Kept alive in vats . . ."

"Aaah, *Brae* . . ."

I was listening before they saw me, they were being loud.

"I don't want to hear any more of your dirty jokes. You'll get us thrown out—"

"Jokes?" said Brae. Her eyes slid contemptuously around the colorful gathering, her fingers tightened around her glass. I could see the indigo shade in her unpolished nails: a sign that Johnny was unlikely to read. "Who's joking? They were always like it. 'As we neared the city we passed several human sacrifices, live women slaves gagged and pegged on their backs to the ground, the abdominal wall being cut in the form of a cross and the uninjured gut hanging out. These poor women were allowed to die like this in the sun. . . . Sacrificed human beings were lying in the path and bush—even in the King's compound the sight and stench of them was awful. Dead and mutilated bodies seemed to be everywhere—by God! may I never see such sights again! . . .' Benin, 1897. I memorize a lot of stuff. It's handy to have it on tap when I'm recording. That's from *The Diary of a Surgeon with the Benin Punitive Expedition*. The Benin were losing a war of worlds at the time and I suppose they still are: in which situation these people seem to think that anything goes."

I suppose I looked unhappy. Brae smiled at me serenely, with a warning in her eyes. Johnny decided to ignore this last weird assault on his liberal conscience.

"Hi Anna. Having fun?"

I was annoyed over his defection, especially since I had the impression, even more clearly than at the desert airport, that Brae was wishing that I would vanish. So I just shrugged.

Braemar took out a cigarette and lit it. Johnny was *astonished*. I don't suppose he'd ever seen a lady smoking before. She smelled of something as unsophisticated as a chocolate bar, most unlike the taste of the Brae I knew. The sweetness and the tomboy plain frock made a stunning combination. Braemar was pushing middle-age, and too clever to lie about it overtly. But she'd done an expert job on confusing the issue tonight. Poor Johnny! In her way, Brae was as much an armaments expert as Major Whynton.

She turned, drawing stagily on the cigarette, to survey the room. "Isn't this place wonderful? I feel like Bette Davis on a liner. Or like Marlene Dietrich in a saloon. I think this must be the restaurant at the end of the universe."

Something was chewing up the stars outside. Johnny laughed.

"Ah, c'mon, Brae. Life will go on. Let's face it, the overwhelming majority of human beings couldn't give a shit even suppose—which I doubt—that we find the real thing lurking up in them there swamps . . . Hell, some of them work here. We might as well be dentists as far as he's concerned."

The barman grinned.

"But we need the aliens, Johnny. And we need them to be out of reach. The futuristic encounter with otherness has been our afterlife for as long as our culture can remember. What else can it be—the other world, of spiritually etiolated lifestyles, reduced surfaces: cleanliness, order, protein pills for food? Where did the first crude practitioners of the SF genre conceive these images of white garbed citizens thronging the shining corridors? There is only one other world, Johnny, one theater of eternal mysteries and unreachable solutions. We go there when we die. What we're doing here is enacting one of those stories where some champion unwisely takes on Death as an opponent. If the meeting that belongs on, that essentially *is*, for us, the other side of things: if that event invades the world of experiences—then what can happen next?"

Johnny smiled indulgently: but it was time to show some muscle. In conversations of this kind he expected to be the one spinning out wild skeins of logorrhea.

"Crap," he said. "You know as well as I do there's nothing going on here. It's just a good gig: plane tickets, free drinks, and some kind of copy. I'm planning to write it up for the *National Enquirer.*"

Braemar grinned slyly.

"I have heard," she remarked, "that ufology is the nearest thing the USA has developed to an ethnic religion. You know, like Hinduism or Islam. The poor kill animals and wear posies. The intellectuals pretend that's all crap. But you still catch them making *puja* sometimes."

The brown river was huge, it looked vast as a continent. A river like that impresses on you sharply the scale of Africa. There were market stalls along the waterfront, customs booths, warehouses and a long open shed through which I could see the boat pier. Two black limos and a Jeep were pulled up beside our shiny bus. A man in a sober white man's suit—it was the Minister for Culture, I had spoken to him briefly at the banquet—was talking heatedly to a group of river policemen. His aides hung back, hands dangling by their sides. The inevitable bodyguard (there was a war somewhere about: there always is, in Africa) stood at attention, rifle butts along their trouser seams.

Our state-visitors' cruiser had dematerialized. There was only the regular riverboat. It was standing at the pier now, stuffed with people. I hadn't let them put anything of mine in the baggage compartment (I've played this game before). I shouldered my bags and quietly got down. I bought myself a cold Coke, the bottle decanted over a fistful of ice into a small plastic bag with a straw. Soon Johnny and Brae drifted up.

"You reckon that ice is okay?"

"No," I said, my belly instantly beginning to gripe.

So he bought a drink and stood grimly sucking: as if he was showing some kind of solidarity by courting diarrhea. Braemar declined.

"I think we've entered the Zone," she said.

Johnny brightened a little.

"Yeah, the situation's hopeless. Pods all around us. Don't you think that guy in the suit has a kind of pod-ish look too?"

We sat on a decaying wooden bench by the entrance to the pier. The bus slowly emptied: our gang prowled uneasily. What happened next was perhaps inevitable. An English journalist lost his head and tried to shove his way through to the boat. The soldiers hurried over . . .

Johnny jumped up on the bench, waving his plastic of ice and cola. "The aliens are among us!" he yelled. "They've taken over these peoples' minds! Are you gonna let them get you too? Come on, you guys! Where's your journalistic integrity? This is the greatest story ever told!"

I don't believe he realized that people might get killed. I did, and it didn't slow me down. The pack surged. A mindless mediaperson greed possessed me. I burrowed, kicked, shoved, elbowed . . . until a shot was fired, and everything went quiet.

Someone got hold of my arm. It was one of the soldiers. My bowels turned to water. I saw them going after another figure: couldn't see who. Everyone else was being rifle-prodded back through the shed.

"*Vous devez payer,* madame—"

In the back of the neck, the death of all my nightmares . . .

"Pay for your fare!" repeated the soldier, thrusting me further up the gangway. "First-class aircon!"

The Minister for Culture didn't speak to the arbitrarily chosen few. Presumably the gesture alone satisfied, proving that his government had done its best and the debacle was our fault. Dazed with gratitude, I turned to see who had shared my luck. First come, first served: Johnny was through, and Brae. So was Major Derek Whynton.

On the fabled state cruiser there would have been a satellite dish and a powerful radio link. On the riverboat there was a primitive radio room, available only for emergencies. We were lost in space. But we were still in the game.

At sunset the four of us stood in a line at the first-class rail. A vast swathe of brown water had opened between us and the shore. The red ball of the sun was sliding down behind a row of smokestacks on the bare horizon.

"We call this the post-holocaust," said Brae, "not because of something that won't happen: it might still, just a different ideology's finger on the button. But because of what's happened already. That famous clichéd scenario is all here.

The poisoned land, mutated weather systems, birth defects and famines. The cities weirdly transformed into festering sores. Global nuclear conflict, it's obvious now, was a schizophrenic's coded warning of the disaster we were in the process of inflicting on ourselves."

Johnny gave her a long look, which said he understood that this small-talk was customized for his benefit. Silence lengthened, the chant of insects receding as we entered deep water.

"These Thirdworlders are all crazy," said Johnny after a while, perhaps by way of apology for his stunt at the pier. "Their minds are fixed on prestige and not being seen to fuck up. Sometimes you have to cut through it."

"I expect the others are pods by now," sighed Brae. "Poor things. I wonder will any of us survive to the end."

Major Derek was gazing ashore with a soldierlike air designed to convey that he was thinking about something very important. I almost sympathized: I felt a little *de trop* myself.

On Braemar's bare forearm, which rested on the rail, I noticed what appeared to be a tattoo, though that seemed unlikely. It was new to me, whatever it was. It said CAVEAT EMPTOR.

Johnny looked down, and grinned.

"Braemar, is that a real tattoo? Or did you just write that there with blue ballpoint in the toilet at L'Iceberg?"

She looked up at him—she's not a particularly small woman, but Braemar always manages to look up.

"Well, Johnny. You know what they say . . ."

Johnny leaned down and thoughtfully applied the test to Braemar's tanned and downy flesh. Suck it and see . . .

[*In her cabin, Braemar stowed away certain supplies with finicky care, and disposed a few items on display. Expensive and immoral swiss cosmetics; a handful of delicate underwear tossed over a box of compact books by her bunk. "All that can be said, can be said clearly," she murmured, studying the effect. "What cannot be said must be passed over in silence."*

She started to eat fried plantain from a newspaper package: removing the square of banana leaf in the bottom she read a report of demonstrations in Washington, D.C. The police are joining the blacks in protest against corruption and . . .

"How touching—"

Her fingertips gently brushed the blurred faces.

She licked her fingers and stripped off her shirt and shorts. If you look down with your back straight and you can't see your navel, you are in bikini trim. Braemar put her heels together and looked down. Fine. But the mirror, lit by a brutal fluorescent tube, pulled out her bones and gave her the face of a famine victim, a toothless, flat-dugged grandmother in a ragged sari. She gazed at the naked death's head for a sad moment—everything vanishes. She made corrections.]

Braemar had to have a victim. I suppose she'd have made Derek over into a pacifist for the duration, if he'd been the one. Maybe she'd have preferred the clean-cut soldier, but he was impervious. Bit of an old boiler, one saw him thinking. And been around . . . You couldn't distract Major Derek from the main point by any intellectual fancywork. So Johnny learned to laugh at her dirty jokes, and appreciate her olde-worlde coquetries; while the poor gazed at us across pipe-clayed hawsers, and the river oozed by. After a day or two she shucked off the tomboy and took to tiny plastique sunsuits that made her look like Doris Day on Mars. I thought that was a big mistake, but Brae knew better. She had Johnny jumping. Once he caught her in low company, tête-à-tête with an African down by the lifeboats. The black man fled. I heard racist assumption, and that awful note of *ownership* in my poor friend's voice.

"Hey! How come you suddenly speak their lingo?"

Brae gave me one of her swift and deadly glances: and swooped like a mother hen on the loose cuff of his shirt.

"Is that a fashion point, Johnny? You might catch that on something and hurt yourself."

He melted like ice cream.

"Aaah—sorry mama."

"Well, well. Leave it around somewhere in the saloon, and we'll see what the button fairy can do."

The button fairy! Oh, Johnny.

He cornered me on the twilit deck after dinner, demanding information. I told him nothing, of course. He was very suspicious. He hated her makeup. What was the point in painting herself like that, here in the middle of nowhere?

I was in no mood for his intimate confessions.

"Johnny," I said. "You know exactly what the point is."

He grinned, he blushed. He'd never had anyone daub herself in the blood of tortured animals for his sake before.

He loved it.

There were no longer tin-roofed markets at the piers, or smokestacks along the horizon. Tall trees began to emerge, back where the swamp became solid ground. The mosquitoes, not much of a threat while the river was wide, became as horrible as the stagnant heat.

At every halt Johnny and I would disembark, I to record my forward echoes and Johnny to smell the air. What did you see in the sky that night? What have you heard? It felt like the progress of the Magi. My French barely penetrated the local patois: maybe that was why we never got anything but blank stares. We returned with parcels of fruit and strange sticky food, sheepish under the cat calls of the boat's whores, who leaned out from the second-class saloon and shouted for us to film them and make them famous.

Braemar didn't interfere with these trips. But by staying on board, taking no pictures, doing no work of her own, she managed to devalue them.

I wasn't feeling well. The boat food was horrible. Travel and stress had messed up my menstrual cycle, leaving me with a heaviness that lay on my mind like unfocused guilt or grief. Johnny and Braemar baited Major Derek and played their "death of science fiction" game. Telepathy quizzes, impenetrable allusions. How would we four survive under the tentacled master-race? Derek they had down as a collaborator, I was to join the resistance . . . I just became more depressed. She couldn't even leave our fantasy quest alone. Any wild-eyed hope of friendly aliens seemed ludicrous, in competition with the brutal realism of what she was doing to Johnny.

Our cabin showers had ceased to function. I was queuing at the only working ladies' washroom, down in the teeming hold. The women were friendly enough, but as I reached the door a crewman appeared and grabbed me. "Madame, *douche, douche privee:* le cap'tan wants . . ."

The cabin was tiny, and hot as an oven. A huge woman sat in the curtained bunk, robed in green and indigo with an intricate indigo headcloth. Her full lips looked not painted but naturally, deeply red. She gestured towards the shower. The bunk curtains twitched: did she have someone hidden there? I stepped into the stall, dropped my sarong and began to wash, the relief of cool water on my skin so intense I didn't care who was watching. When the water stopped, somebody pulled open the door.

"Haoi, Haoi—" shouted the little man, as I grabbed my wrap.

He wore an immaculate white shirt and trousers, his plum-dark face was bloomed and fissured with age. The woman held something bright that moved: a toy of some kind. The captain was brandishing a bag of shrimp crackers.

Oh, *Hanoi*—

"You were in Vietnam?"

"Oue, Oue, Hanoi. Saigon. Long time ago."

I wanted to rush away and get my gear. A retired foreign legionnaire: this was wonderful—

The captain beamed, satisfied that he had established credentials. "English— *moi, non.*" He gesticulated further. I gathered that the woman was his interpreter. I was about to launch into French, but she spoke first.

"You must not ask," said the indigo woman sleepily. "All this asking questions, that makes problems."

She lifted the thing in her hands. As the captain pushed me out of the door, soaking wet with an armful of wet belongings, I glimpsed again the fluid, metallic movement.

I reached my cabin just in time to throw up. It crossed my mind that David's vasectomy had failed and I was pregnant. It must be a boy this time, the little alien inside fighting with my inimical chemistry.

The boat anchored at dawn out in mid-channel, just below a muddy confluence. The halt was for our benefit: it was time for us to leave the great river. Several hours later a small boat came chugging out of the emptiness. Johnny and Brae were in the saloon, studying the garbled "Briefing" we'd all been handed back at the capital. I was on deck with the major.

Derek jumped up and was at the rail as a vision of military splendor arose: polished capbrim well down over the eyes.

"Good morning, my name is Simon Krua. I'm looking for the International Expedition to Lake Gerard?"

My heart sank. The major grew visibly larger as he stuck out his hand.

"Derek Whynton, Lieutenant Krua. Major, actually. Well, you've found us. Let me introduce—ah—Mrs. Anna Jones: a British lady journalist." The major gave his barking laugh. "There are two of them, I'm afraid. Two ladies, and a young American chap. The media, you know. Don't worry, I'll keep them out of your hair."

The riverboat was silent as we left it. Not a single whore stuck her head out to scream good-bye. We crossed a borderline trimmed with sticks and small branches, from gruel-color to muddy umber, and swept around into the narrower stream. A tiny, ancient steamer was waiting for us, a kind of caelocanth of the swamps. I don't know what would have happened if the whole party had got this far. It was hard to see how even we four were going to be stowed.

Johnny cackled. "I think I'm on the wrong trip. Did I book for the dinosaur hunt? I didn't mean to do that. No wait, is this the fabled Hollywood retro-world? Bogart and Hepburn androids are about to come swanning out of the mangroves."

Nobody laughed, particularly not Simon Krua.

The Major had a lot of heavy black boxes. While they were being stowed by Krua's soldiers, he turned on us—in the cramped and cluttered after deck that was to be our territory. His blue eyes gleamed in triumph.

"Now listen."

We had no choice, there was nowhere to go.

"There has been a serious infringement of the London Peace Accord, and I surely don't need to tell you what that means. I'm sorry, but whatever wild ideas you may have had that's the whole story. My mission is to investigate, and to keep my findings quiet pending a full international inquiry. You've been allowed to come along so far because circumstances dictated it: but I'm going to have to confiscate all recordings, and take charge of your equipment."

There was a deafening silence.

"From now on, the ladies will not go on shore at all. This is dangerous country, guerrilla forces are active. Johnny, may I ask you to use some common-sense . . . ? Please pack up and itemize your professional effects. Receipts will be issued, naturally."

He disappeared into the deckhouse, shutting the door.

Johnny whistled, on a slow note of sour amazement. "The Empire Strikes Back. Now we'll be sorry for the way we teased the miserable jerk."

Braemar stared bleakly at a pile of divers' airbottles, stacked in the stern—for once completely silenced.

I was shaking with rage. I found a roll of tape and began to seal my forward echoes. There is never any way out when you run up against the bastard military. They have no *respect*. What seems to us utterly inviolable, like consecrated communion bread in old christendom, they'll take and swing and smash its brains out against a wall. . . .

It must have been Major Whynton who told the captain of the riverboat to give me that warning. Maybe it was the powers behind him who had canceled the cruiser. I would have shared these thoughts with Johnny and Brae, but it would only have made Johnny quite unmanageably provocative. And I still meant to *be there,* at the end of this trail.

[*What's your real name, Brae?"*

"Alice in Wonderland. Kali. Jael. James Bond, 007, licensed to kill. I'm in deep cover."

"You won't tell me, will you? It's childish."

"I haven't a real name, Johnny. I've never been identified."

The moon had risen, the night was immaculately black and white. The African Queen (the boat didn't seem to have any other name) was tied up so close to the bank that they'd been able to clamber into the mud-stalking branches and sneak on shore. A tree had fallen: they were sitting on its trunk above the water. They passed a joint of the grass that Braemar had bought on the big boat. When it was done Brae took out her cigarettes and lit one.

Johnny removed it from her fingers and snuffed it out. "Destroy yourself on your own time. I don't want to catch your cancer."

Braemar laughed. She loved to be bullied.

In her cabin on the boat he had moved a small heap of underwear to find out what books she was reading. Like bruised leaves the scraps of silk released a tender perfume: vanilla and roses, the scent of her flesh. He was assaulted by a mad impulse to steal something, to wear it. Something strange was happening to his libido, to be traced no doubt to the combination of poor nourishment, little sleep, and excellent East African blow. He was in a state of quiet sexual frenzy: thoughts of fucking Brae with Anna and the whole first class looking on, of all three of them setting on Major Derek and forcing gross pleasures on him.

But to be doing it with this corrupt middle-aged woman was a perverse orgy in itself. Who was the real Braemar? How did one get to meet her? That was a canard. The invocation, by means of all the masks, of an essential mystery forever out of reach, was only another routine in the ancient cabaret.

Which he at once loved and hated: a sickeningly pleasant combination. Is this normality? he wondered. My God. Is this how it feels to be a regular guy?

"Actually, I couldn't care less. You're Brae to me, and no other label would get me closer to the inside of that box that doesn't occupy any normal space. All I want is somewhere where I can fuck you without being at the same time ravaged by foot-long poisonous centipedes, or overheard by Major Derek."

"We could try the dinghy."

"The guy who drove us over from the big boat sleeps in there. And the cookboy sleeps in the rowing boat."

Irritably, Johnny threw the stuffed cigarette into the water.

"Shit—"

He scrambled out to retrieve it.

"Johnny, you're crazy. What are you? A New Age Hasidim? Don't you know it is impossible for anyone to keep the whole of the law?"

He shoved the wet cigarette into his shirt pocket. She was right, the new Torah was as ridiculous as any other set of rules. As if one less cigarette end in the wilderness would save a poisoned Planet.

"Do you feel weird, Brae? Do you have a strange feeling like a kind of psychic travel sickness: brainstem nausea, and it is getting stronger by the day?"

"I don't feel anything that isn't perfectly normal."

"I just wondered."

"Johnny."

She took his hand, still cool and wet from the river, and laid it along her groin.

"That's otherness. That's where you meet the alien. If you could always have a breast to suck and an accommodating cunt to hold you, you'd never miss the rest of the world, with or without flying saucers. You are everything that matters, Johnny. And I'm the place where you belong."

He looked at her, the cool moonlight mysteriously altering his young face, cutting time's shadows in its rounded outline: and withdrew his hand.

"Talking dirty again," he said. "I think I'll throw you in the river."

"You really want them, don't you?"

He shrugged his shoulders.

"I'm curious. There are UFOs every day. There's never before been an official snark-hunt like this one. I just want to know—"

Countless insects chanted. Something much larger suddenly howled out a long dying fall of sound. Johnny was instantly distracted.

"Hey! A wild animal! I didn't know there were any of those left."

He dropped to the path and hurried along it, heedless of centipedes. Brae followed, until he suddenly stopped dead. There were points of gold in the blackness ahead: a cloud of sentient fireflies, the outline of a mind.

"What is that—?" he breathed, awed.

"It's a village, Johnny."

"Huh." He scowled, annoyed at himself. "Those pods are fucking sneaky. It's probably only pretending to be a village."

But the lights in the darkness held him. "When you see that," he murmured. "Raw, as the cave-people saw it—you know why the stars in the sky had to be people, why stories were made up about them. What else could those steady little fires in the night possibly mean?"

Braemar touched his arm, turned him to face her.

"Johnny, supposing I told you the truth? Supposing I told you: I'm a member of a secret international organization, on a vital undercover mission. And I need your help."

"My God," said Johnny, at last. "You're not joking, are you?"

She shook her head.

He felt a new rush of gloriously mingled lust and disorientation. It was another game, more fun. It might even be the truth: why not? Braemar could be anyone.

"You're after the Major? Yeah. I worked it out for myself. He wants some dirt: Reds in the swamp. And I reckon our friend Krua's already made sure he won't be disappointed. The bastards, they'd take us all to hell with them if they got the chance. What are we going to do about it?"

Her smile was mocking.

"Oh, no Johnny. The truth is better than that."]

The lake was kidney-shaped, about a kilo across and five long, the long axis aligned roughly north-south under a natural plateau in the surrounding hills. The landing site was supposed to be somewhere around here. The local warzone was up beyond, cutting off air and road access. The water was completely opaque. It stank. The soldiers had investigated its depths and found nothing: I didn't envy them the experience.

There was a well-established camp on shore, out of bounds to us. Derek and Krua vanished into the jungle every day with a line of laden, sweating squaddies. We were left behind, supposedly under guard. But the soldiers were friendly and venal. There was the dinghy with its outboard, and the old rowing boat, Other Ranks, For The Use Of. Taxi rates were soon established.

I tramped up the winding path, Sackey, the civilian cook, agreeably silent beside me.

I was thinking about Braemar, the way she was when I was teaching a welfare course in media technology, to help pay my way through college. She was years older than me, but so young: so abject, with her constant childcare hassles and her meanly obstructive husband. I became her confidante. She told me about her childhood in East Africa: Asian mother, white daddy. Things had gone sour when the family came back to England, the usual bloody mess of domestic violence. Brae had escaped—but then, casebook style, married a carbon copy of the father. Those two beauties had left her with a bitter shame about her "mixed blood," which came out in twisted ways. How embarrassing it would be if Johnny guessed her secret—after he'd learned to grin at her dirty jokes. Of course I wasn't going to give her away. I'm on Brae's side, I really am. I just hate what the world has made of her.

We climbed through open woodland to the plateau. The day was hot but not sweltering, the country very beautiful. From above Lake Gerard was peacock green, like a piece of glass stamped down by a hard heel into the plushy treetops. The African Queen was a dozing waterbeetle. I was worried. Braemar had always used her feminine wiles with ruthless skill (and thought I was a fool to have dumped my "natural" armaments). But now she'd become doubly artificial: ultrafemininity as a conscious construct. The way she made him laugh at her racist jokes. The way she seemed to watch with satisfaction while my good American experimented with the vicious old games. It scared me, the cold way she set herself up to be at once despised and enjoyed.

"It's down here, Mrs. Anna—"

I clambered after Sackey into the dry bed of a stream. It had dried out very quickly. Crusts of stiffened algae clung to the smooth rocks. The banks were coated, in a narrow swathe on either side, with scum and debris. I saw something shining and picked up what seemed to be half a crumpled can. The metal was a brilliant translucent blue. I rubbed the bright bloom, it didn't come off. I put it down. Sackey came up and looked: he delved the pockets of his tattered cut-offs.

"Look, I found these. You want to buy?" He laughed. "No, only joking. We are selling, both of us. Did you pay your airfare?"

"No, I didn't."

"Good, excellent. All sheer profit for you."

I didn't get a good look at the things Sackey held out. He stowed them away quickly.

Then we came to it. The bed of the boiled off stream ran into an open depression, wide as a motorway junction and roughly oval. It was bare red and yellow clay, it had sides about two meters high. There was no sign of burning, nothing charred or withered. Above the rim all around flattened trees and bushes were masked in a veil of dried mud.

"Monsieur Sackey, why would nobody downriver talk to us about what happened?"

He shrugged. "Jealousy," he suggested.

"Where are the aliens now?"

"Hiding." He looked sly. "Sightings may be rare."

I walked into the center. Sackey stayed where he was. I suppose he thought he'd see enough of the place when the tourists started pouring in. I felt a prickling of adrenaline in my uneasy belly. Supposing, after all, something awesome was about to happen to me: a conversion experience? This was the brink. No sane person had ever crossed it.

I saw a small figure hunkered down and poking at the ground. It was Johnny. He smiled as I came up, a wide stretching mouth made meaningless by the black lenses above. He removed his sunglasses and looked at me quizzically.

"Hi. It's Johnny. Johnny Guglioli, remember?"

"I'm sorry, Johnny. I was—"

"Impressed. Mmm." He rubbed yellow earth between his fingers. "What d'you reckon, Anna? Roadworks?"

I remembered Major Derek's version.

"Have you a geiger counter on you?"

"Don't be ridiculous."

Suddenly I felt very sick. I squatted, my head in my hands.

"Anna, what's wrong?"

"I think I'm pregnant."

"Oh, shit. The snip didn't take, you mean?" He looked embarrassed. "Um, sorry. Unwarrantable assumption, and none of my business. What are you going to do?"

I knew what I'd promised. One each is what we'd agreed. There are simply too many people. Why should the Bangladeshis give up their children if we wouldn't?

"I suppose I'll have to face up to my marriage vows."

The nausea passed. I heaved a sigh.

"We don't believe in this thing, do we Johnny?"

"Not me. You know, it probably is roadworks. If we carry on over the hill we'll find a big corral of Jap civil engineering plant. We've stumbled upon an illicit hardwood logging operation. We'll probably all get shot and dumped in the swamp."

"And what people saw in the sky?"

"Aurora." He put the glasses back on, and smiled without his eyes again. "We have no neighbors, Anna. No one here but us chickens. Maybe we'll set off one day in a relative way and come back and visit ourselves. That's the only hope."

His manner was very odd, I couldn't make it out.

"Let's get back. It makes sense to get home before the Major. Those tantrums aren't good for the poor guy."

[*At dead of night, Johnny sneaked into the deckhouse. He found the box that Braemar had marked without difficulty, his pencil of light picking out the smudge of Murasaki Rose on a white MOD Supplies docket. She'd had one of the soldiers identify it—by making him want to frighten her, she said. Dangerous little kitten! He suckered a tiny processor that he called his "skeleton key" beside the lock—in a few seconds it had the combination.*

Such are the legitimate tools of investigative journalism: for the people have a right to know. Tough luck on the Major if he didn't understand the rules.

All was quiet. Giggling silently, Johnny opened Major Derek's smart briefcase with his skeleton, raised the sliver of a screen and loaded a disc that was helpfully labeled (when will they ever learn) with the dates of the snark hunt. He glanced at some of the files: the maps and notes, and shook his head over them a little. Then did things to the disc that were not good for its long-term memory. He checked the rest of the contents of the case. But Braemar had assured him there was no hard copy, not yet. No paper written notes. And she seemed to know her business.

How wonderful to be Johnny Guglioli, rightful heir of the greatest civilization the world has ever known. How wonderful to enjoy all the old adventures, with all the new virtues intact.

Out on deck again he stood by the rail and stared, at his own hands which were actually shaking. But only his body was afraid and excited. Johnny's mind rode above, perfectly cool.

He gazed into Africa, in no hurry to get out of sight (I couldn't sleep—): planning the rest of the coup, while tremors of some emotion that his mind did not care to name ran through and through his limbs.]

We were in the kitchen at home. David was trying to get Directory Inquiries to give him the number of some chicken expert. (Oh, those tiresome birds and their diseases.) The woman on the phone explained that she couldn't because of the attack. "What 'attack'?" asked David. WHAM. The kitchen windows went white with a blinding, blinding, silent flash.

Then it was afterwards. There was a big room in which people were huddled in little family groups. People kept doing stupid things: wanting to open the door, to uncover the windows. I was running around trying to stop them, I was making Jacko hide under some cardboard. I was amazed at myself. I'd always been sure that only an idiot would try to survive the end of the world.

All the while, dreaming, I knew that "Nuclear War" was only a label, only the mask of some different catastrophe.

I opened my eyes. Braemar knelt beside me, but she'd turned into a glistening creature with gills and goggle eyes. I sat up and pushed aside my net. We all slept on deck, it was only luck that Johnny or the Major hadn't woken too. The glistening stuff was wetwear: the bulbous head a mask and some kind of soft baglike air supply.

"Brae? What are you doing?"

The bag pumped. She pulled off her mask.

"The Creature From The Black Lagoon. I'm sorry, Anna. Don't be scared. I turn out to be a kind of goodie in the last reel."

She looked, as they say, as if she'd seen a ghost.

"Do you believe in the law, Anna?"

She sounded drunk. Maybe that was the explanation. She'd stolen some fancy diving gear from Derek's boxes, swum ashore and located a disco somewhere.

"I suppose I do. Not anything more than you could put in two sentences: but the law, yes, I do."

"Thou shalt not kill, and so forth? So do I." She shuddered. "But there's the *agrapta nomima*. That's what Antigone said to Creon in the play: Sophocles. She could disobey the king's edicts because the unwritten law, *agrapta nomima*, was greater."

"Braemar! You haven't been chucking Major Derek's stuff into the lake?"

She shook her head. She looked awfully strange. I almost demanded *what have you done with the real Braemar?* But I'd have felt such a fool.

"I was horrified when I saw you at the airport. You knew me well Anna: and you'll wonder, and you'll suspect. But I think I can trust you. In the end, I think you'll understand."

I lay there trying to read these omens until another dream engulfed me.

Black water parted under the swampy trees. Figures rose to their feet. Standing waist-high they seemed human as shadows, or spirits: smooth, ungendered bodies. They looked out at the empty lake and mugged relief and excitement. One of them lifted cupped hands with reverence and solemn delight. As the drops fell a voice whispered in my mind.

Water of life—

They all made the same gesture, bowed their faces and drank as if taking a sacrament. Shipwrecked but undismayed they stood triumphant in Eldorado.

We have come home.

Next morning Johnny had vanished. Apparently he'd swum for it, because both boats were where they should be. Of course I remembered my dream, but I said nothing. Derek was absolutely livid. He sent out a search party. He stamped around glowering like an outraged father. *I will be master in my own house!* It says something for the effectiveness of the military regime, that while the row was going on Brae and I didn't speak. We didn't risk exchanging so much as a glance.

About an hour before noon something came roaring out of the trees on the lake shore. It was a motorbike. Johnny jumped off the back, and hailed us cheerfully.

"Ahoy, African Queen! Anyone want a cold beer?"

He'd been to town. Walked out to the trail and hitched a ride to the local cosmopolis. He had brought back a sack of bottled beer and a lump of ice wrapped up in sodden straw. He was inordinately pleased with himself.

Major Derek recalled the search party and, controlling himself violently, announced that he could no longer be responsible for us. He had radioed for assistance. We'd be leaving as soon as our transport arrived.

The heat settled. Major Derek sulked in the deckhouse. Johnny wavered along the African Queen's rail clutching a beer bottle, in shorts and a singlet: right foot in a wetwear ankleboot, left foot bare. This improved his balance, he claimed.

"A trick I learned on the ratridden wharves of New Byzantium."

My dreams had dissipated. It was only Johnny and Brae, up to their eyes in some stupid scheme of revenge. And I was sick as a dog. I didn't want to vomit, only to die. I crawled under my net and let the voices fade.

Johnny shook me gently awake. I felt as if I'd been asleep for days, but was aware that only an hour or two had passed.

I sat up.

"Where—?"

The African Queen was eerily silent. Johnny's backpack and camera bag were standing on the deck beside him, all strapped up. My kit was there too.

"What's happened?"

"Major Whynton and Lieutenant Krua have been called away."

"Where's Brae?"

"She'll join us."

Sackey rowed us to the shore. We took a different path from the one that went up to the plateau, and soon stood on a red dirt road. A couple of other people joined us, and then a Jeep with an open back full of passengers came rattling along.

Johnny paid our fares. A teenage girl's personal stereo buzzed by my ear. A very weary young boy swayed opposite me, hugging an assault rifle as if it was a teddy bear. After an hour or so little bungalows in swept, bare yards began to line the road.

"What about the war?" I asked, bemused.

Johnny shrugged. "Oh, wars. People learn to live with them."

We sat outside a cafe in the marketplace of the small town. Johnny explained everything. Simon Krua and Major Derek had been planting evidence of illicit weapons testing. Johnny and Brae had found out, and had been secretly undoing the evil work. This morning was the climax. When Johnny sneaked into town he had suborned the staff of the local radio station—not hard, the man hadn't been paid for months—and consequently Major Derek had learned of an exciting development in the local war. He and the soldiers had rushed off to join in. By the time they discovered there was no excitement, their plans here would be in ruins and the three of us would have got clean away.

The story was a little garbled: and I felt like a child left out of secrets. But mostly it went right past me. I just wanted to be at home, safe with Syb and David and the kids.

"Where's Brae?" I asked again.

"She's tying up a few loose ends."

The marketplace was surrounded by crude breezeblock buildings with red iron roofs. A few women, one or two men, listlessly guarded the pitiful goods: children's nylon underwear, little blackened corpses of smoked monkey, piles of ancient French magazines. Johnny had ordered beer for us. It came warm, with tumblers full of dirty ice.

"Pity there's no story."

"No chance," he agreed. "In war-mongering, even to expose a fake amounts to an ugly rumor." He frowned, staring towards the road we'd come in by. "I hope she's okay back there. . . . Well, she ought to be. She's an African, after all."

I started. "You knew that?"

Johnny shrugged. "Yeah, well. I read up some bios when I got the passenger list, before we left London."

He sounded a little ashamed of himself, as well he might. I got the feeling that this small confession signaled some kind of breakdown between them, and I was glad. I wanted to welcome him back into our haven of shared assumptions. But I felt too ill, and his mood seemed bleaker by the moment.

"Johnny, don't fall in love with her. It'll be bad for both of you. She hates men, you know."

"I know," he said. "I know she does."

Above the cinema a hand-painted poster featured a giant, snarling white woman in a bikini. Our getaway car, a big old Mercedes, was hunkered by the storm drain below. Children in grimy clothes were playing (what riches!) with a bright plastic toy. I felt very low. I couldn't think of anything to say to Johnny. I was glad when he got up and went to talk to our driver.

So there were no aliens. I drank beer, and let myself acknowledge the disappointment, for the first time. How sad. To have hiked out into the desert, to the burning bush, knees knocking, ready to meet God: and found there was nothing but the sun on an old plastic bag. Of course that was why Johnny seemed so

odd, and Braemer too. The embarrassment of having almost been believers . . .
It was going to take us three days to drive to Maiduguri and the airport, right
through this war that "people had got used to." (My blood ran cold—to think
of my Johnny expressing such a hard and commonplace opinion.) I would pull
myself together. I would record the trip. That and the river journey should make
a saleable item.

The toy that the children were playing with caught my eye. I tried to look
away: but found that I could not. I called to the children in French: "May I see
that thing?"

A little boy came over, put it on the table. It was like a kind of—millipede?
It was the same blue as the metal I had found. I couldn't for the life of me tell
whether it was alive, or a machine. I reached out to touch. He giggled, and
grabbed it. In a moment the group of children had scampered out of sight.

A cold prickling of excitement burst out like sweat. . . . With a sudden dire
premonition, I grabbed my camera bag.

I use the simplest stock and hardware. I want to be able to edit my own
work, cheaply. I don't have the might of a big company behind me. The cassettes looked all right. When I took the seals off, they fell apart. It was gone,
every scrap of my forward echoes.

Johnny came back. He stood looking at the wreckage with his blacked-out
eyes.

I stared up at him, having the most ridiculous nightmares.

"Johnny, *what's going on?* Where's Braemer?"

"She's blowing up a kind of plane," he said, with the air of someone abandoning all pretense. He took off his glasses. He was Johnny Guglioli still. It was
everything else that had changed.

I said, "They're here, aren't they? The UFO was real."

Johnny nodded warily.

"What is Braemar doing?"

"What I told you. She's blowing up an abandoned aircraft. Okay, a spacecraft. I'm sorry Anna. But you must see, we couldn't tell you. They have to stay
in hiding for now. Or the Major Dereks of this world will fuck up everything."

His smug grin affronted me. I felt for a moment that I was still reacting like
a sulky child. But I had my forward echoes: their occult message, no good at the
end of this quest. The certainty that there was nothing benign hiding behind
Braemar's charade. The sickness in my belly. I could not tell him why, but he was
wrong: *he was wrong.*

"I'm going back to the lake!"

I didn't wait to see what he would do. I ran for the car, and he came pelting
after.

[*Braemar was on the deck of the African Queen. She studied her face in a small
mirror. The tomboy nudity that Johnny so approved, she had captured it exactly today: good. She stowed the mirror in her flightbag. Her hands were sweating. Braemar had none of Johnny's confidence. Such power as she possessed over the world's
gadgetry was stolen goods, liable to betray her at any moment like the giant's purse
in the story.*

*She thought of the horror of what she was doing. She thought of the innocent vir-
gin whom she had seduced, and ruined. She straightened her shoulders and half un-*

consciously began to sing as she waited for the seconds to tick away: lost voice of a small girl in scratchy uniform. She had loved that brown serge from far away very dearly, though it was so hot and ugly.

"—land of our birth our faith our pride
for who's dear sake our fathers died—"

The naive sentiment of words and music comforted her.]

We came over the rail. Braemar turned around. Out of the corner of my eye I saw Sackey, who had rowed us out, mugging abject apology. Her people were everywhere—confederation of the dispossessed, the colonized.

How strange that I had seen her as acting the role of her self. What I had seen was Braemar undercover, recreating her old effects for a new purpose. Did she really need an accomplice? She could probably have managed alone: but Braemar couldn't change that far. It couldn't be the Major either. His response might be the same in the end. But Braemar wasn't going to wait for his kind to find specious justification for their reflexes.

"Where are they?" I cried frantically. "Are they alive?"

"I think so," said Braemar, without so much as blinking. "I was still getting readings of warm things moving around inside the lifepod, when I placed the charges."

Johnny's stunned silence made her furious.

"Don't you judge me, Johnny!" she shouted. "Or judge me if you like, I don't care. I know I'm right. This is self-defense. Oh, I know they won't mean any harm, not at first at any rate. But you, you and I and our whole world and history, we will still be worse than dead: *meaningless.*"

"They could be ordinary," said Johnny. In the voice of a child at Christmas, dreaming of walking snowmen, talking animals. "They could be our friends."

"If they're so ordinary, how come they're here? You need to lie to yourself, Johnny. I don't. That's the only difference between us. I can call them human, call them innocent: and still do what has to be done."

I began to move in, carefully. The talking was a good sign.

"Where's the detonator, Brae? Please, come on, tell—"

I risked a glance at Johnny, signaling him (I hoped) to grab her while I lunged for that bag. His face was blood-drained.

"Braemar, you can't be serious," he whispered. "You know I never meant this—"

She began to sob.

I lunged. Johnny grabbed me. . . .

Across the water the shore rose into a low red cliff, crowned with trees. As I fell headlong, I saw the bottle glass surface under this cliff burst open. Water leapt into the air. Trees shook, ran like liquid: tons of earth and greenery began to topple. Everything was shaking. I lay on the deck with my hands clasped over my head.

The soldiers were waiting for us. Strange meeting—it's difficult to recall the details of that aftermath. None of us said a word about aliens. We were escorted to the trail, put into an army Jeep. Our personal baggage, which had been left in the Mercedes, came back to us minus the recording equipment. Eventually Major Derek appeared, got in beside the driver and we drove away.

Later, we had a debriefing. The military had found nothing: no aliens. No crashed nuclear fighter. The "landslide" had been a natural occurrence. There was no story at all.

Braemar recanted the lifepod. She returned to the military hoax story. She was a secret agent for peace: the rest, she said, had been a "smokescreen." Her eyes, while she explained this, were supremely cynical, the eyes of a clever coquette who knows no one can untangle *all* her lies. She walked out of the hotel in Maiduguri and disappeared into the African crowd. I suppose I will meet her again in a year or two—pale-skinned, immaculately feminine. She will expect me to have forgotten everything, I will know this without asking.

After she'd gone, Johnny told me the other version. The secret network of the faithful, who knew that the aliens had already arrived and went around protecting them from the authorities. He had played along—"suspending disbelief," he said. It had seemed like another of her games. And now neither of us knew what to believe. Was there actually a secret organization, devoted to stamping out alien intelligence wherever it appeared? It was just too farfetched, we agreed. Already, like the military, we had resigned ourselves. Already we began to suppress and deny our own memories (so that now, as I write, I *do not know* what really happened). My tapes are gone. They would have shown nothing anyway, nothing but a certain atmosphere . . .

But as we traveled home together I could barely bring myself to speak to Johnny Guglioli. I still remembered that he had grabbed for me, not Braemar. . . . Maybe the aliens were never real, but that moment of choice was. He would never admit it but she'd recruited him all right. Without even trying, she'd shown him exactly what happens to the colonized. Her cheating ways, her sly subservience: habitual, automatic self-contempt. When he was actually faced with it, Johnny was ready to kill the innocent strangers. Because he didn't want to be a nigger. He didn't want to be a *woman* for the rest of his life.

I sat staring out of the plane window. At least I didn't feel pregnant anymore. But Johnny and Braemar haunted me: that doomed encounter between self and otherness. I saw my face in the glass, looking solemnly in from the empty air. And I wished that I could darken every window in the world. So that every clear, hard barrier would become a mirror, and no one who looked through would be able to see anything out there—but their own face, looking back.

THE MOUNTAIN TO MOHAMMED

Nancy Kress

Nancy Kress entered the field as a fantasy novelist at the end of the 1970s, but was publishing SF short stories at the same time, many of which were highly regarded enough to support the publication of an SF collection, *Trinity and Other Stories*, in 1985. After three novels, she moved entirely to SF in the late 1980s. She has come fully into her powers as a novelist in the 1990s with the *Beggars* trilogy *(Beggars in Spain, Beggars and Choosers, Beggars Ride)*. Her SF (and her non-SF thriller, *Oaths and Miracles*) has always been concerned with biological science and medicine, as in this story.

> *A person gives money to the physician.*
> *Maybe he will be healed.*
> *Maybe he will not be healed.*
> —The Talmud

When the security buzzer sounded, Dr. Jesse Randall was playing *go* against his computer. Haruo Kaneko, his roommate at Downstate Medical, had taught him the game. So far nineteen shiny black and white stones lay on the grid under the scanner field. Jesse frowned; the computer had a clear shot at surrounding an empty space in two moves, and he couldn't see how to stop it. The buzzer made him jump.

Anne? But she was on duty at the hospital until one. Or maybe he remembered her rotation wrong. . . .

Eagerly he crossed the small living room to the security screen. It wasn't Anne. Three stories below a man stood on the street, staring into the monitor. He was slight and fair, dressed in jeans and frayed jacket with a knit cap pulled low on his head. The bottoms of his ears were red with cold.

"Yes?" Jesse said.

"Dr. Randall?" The voice was low and rough.

"Yes."

"Could you come down here a minute to talk to me?"

"About what?"

"Something that needs talkin' about. It's personal. Mike sent me."

A thrill ran through Jesse. This was it, then. He kept his voice neutral. "I'll be right down."

He turned off the monitor system, removed the memory disk, and carried it into the bedroom, where he passed it several times over a magnet. In a gym bag he packed his medical equipment: antiseptics, antibiotics, sutures, clamps, syringes, electromed scanner, as much equipment as would fit. Once, shoving it all in, he laughed. He dressed in a warm pea coat bought second-hand at the Army-Navy store and put the gun, also bought second-hand, in the coat pocket. Although of course the other man would be carrying. But Jesse liked the feel of it, a slightly heavy drag on his right side. He replaced the disk in the security system and locked the door. The computer was still pretending to consider its move for *go,* although of course it had near-instantaneous decision capacity.

"Where to?"

The slight man didn't answer. He strode purposefully away from the building, and Jesse realized he shouldn't have said anything. He followed the man down the street, carrying the gym bag in his left hand.

Fog had drifted in from the harbor. Boston smelled wet and gray, of rotting piers and dead fish and garbage. Even here, in the Morningside Security Enclave, where that part of the apartment maintenance fees left over from security went to keep the streets clean. Yellow lights gleamed through the gloom, stacked twelve stories high but crammed close together; even insurables couldn't afford to heat much space.

Where they were going there wouldn't be any heat at all.

Jesse followed the slight man down the subway steps. The guy paid for both of them, a piece of quixotic dignity that made Jesse smile. Under the lights he got a better look: The man was older than he'd thought, with webbed lines around the eyes and long, thin lips over very bad teeth. Probably hadn't ever had dental coverage in his life. What had been in his genescan? God, what a system.

"What do I call you?" he said as they waited on the platform. He kept his voice low, just in case.

"Kenny."

"All right, Kenny," Jesse said, and smiled. Kenny didn't smile back. Jesse told himself it was ridiculous to feel hurt; this wasn't a social visit. He stared at the tracks until the subway came.

At this hour the only other riders were three hard-looking men, two black and one white, and an even harder-looking Hispanic girl in a low-cut red dress. After a minute Jesse realized she was under the control of one of the black men sitting at the other end of the car. Jesse was careful not to look at her again. He couldn't help being curious, though. She looked healthy. All four of them looked healthy, as did Kenny, except for his teeth. Maybe none of them were uninsurable; maybe they just couldn't find a job. Or didn't want one. It wasn't his place to judge.

That was the whole point of doing this, wasn't it?

The other two times had gone as easy as Mike said they would. A deltoid suture on a young girl wounded in a knife fight, and burn treatment for a baby scalded by a pot of boiling water knocked off a stove. Both times the families had been so grateful, so respectful. They knew the risk Jesse was taking. After he'd treated the baby and left antibiotics and analgesics on the pathetic excuse for a kitchen counter, a board laid across the non-functional radiator, the young Hispanic mother had grabbed his hand and covered it with kisses. Embarrassed, he'd turned to smile at her husband, wanting to say something, wanting to make clear he wasn't just another sporadic do-gooder who happened to have a medical degree.

"I think the system stinks. The insurance companies should never have been allowed to deny health coverage on the basis of genescans for potential disease, and employers should never have been allowed to keep costs down by health-based hiring. If this were a civilized country, we'd have national health care by now!"

The Hispanic had stared back at him, blank-faced.

"Some of us are trying to do better," Jesse said.

It was the same thing Mike—Dr. Michael Cassidy—had said to Jesse and Anne at the end of a long drunken evening celebrating the halfway point in all their residencies. Although, in retrospect, it seemed to Jesse that Mike hadn't drunk very much. Nor had he actually said very much outright. It was all implication, probing masked as casual philosophy. But Anne had understood, and refused instantly. "God, Mike, you could be dismissed from the hospital! The regulations forbid residents from exposing the hospital to the threat of an uninsured malpractice suit. There's no money."

Mike had smiled and twirled his glasses between fingers as long as a pianist's. "Doctors are free to treat whomever they wish, at their own risk, even uninsurables. *Carter v. Sunderland.*"

"Not while a hospital is paying their malpractice insurance as residents, if the hospital exercises its right to so forbid. *Janisson v. Lechchevko.*"

Mike laughed easily. "Then forget it, both of you. It's just conversation."

Anne said, "But do you personally risk—"

"It's not right," Jesse cut in—couldn't she see that Mike wouldn't want to incriminate himself on a thing like this?—"that so much of the population can't get insurance. Every year they add more genescan pre-tendency barriers, and the poor slobs haven't even got the diseases yet!"

His voice had risen. Anne glanced nervously around the bar. Her profile was lovely, a serene curving line that reminded Jesse of those Korean screens in the expensive shops on Commonwealth Avenue. And she had lovely legs, lovely breasts, lovely everything. Maybe, he'd thought, now that they were neighbors in the Morningside Enclave . . .

"Another round," Mike had answered.

Unlike the father of the burned baby, who never had answered Jesse at all. To cover his slight embarrassment—the mother had been so effusive—Jesse gazed around the cramped apartment. On the wall were photographs in cheap plastic frames of people with masses of black hair, all lying in bed. Jesse had read about this: It was a sort of mute, powerless protest. The subjects had all been photographed on their death beds. One of them was a beautiful girl, her eyes closed and her hand flung lightly over her head, as if asleep. The Hispanic followed Jesse's gaze and lowered his eyes.

"Nice," Jesse said. "Good photos. I didn't know you people were so good with a camera."

Still nothing.

Later, it occurred to Jesse that maybe the guy hadn't understood English.

* * *

The subway stopped with a long screech of equipment too old, too poorly maintained. There was no money. Boston, like the rest of the country, was broke. For a second Jesse thought the brakes weren't going to catch at all and his heart skipped, but Kenny showed no emotion and so Jesse tried not to, either. The car finally stopped. Kenny rose and Jesse followed him.

They were somewhere in Dorchester. Three men walked quickly toward them and Jesse's right hand crept toward his pocket. "This him?" one said to Kenny.

"Yeah," Kenny said. "Dr. Randall," and Jesse relaxed.

It made sense, really. Two men walking through this neighborhood probably wasn't a good idea. Five was better. Mike's organization must know what it was doing.

The men walked quickly. The neighborhood was better than Jesse had imagined: small row houses, every third or fourth one with a bit of frozen lawn in the front. A few even had flowerboxes. But the windows were barred, and over all hung the gray fog, the dank cold, the pervasive smell of garbage.

The house they entered had no flowerbox. The steel front door, triple-locked, opened directly into a living room furnished with a sagging sofa, a TV, and an ancient daybed whose foamcast headboard flaked like dandruff. On the daybed lay a child, her eyes bright with fever.

Sofa, TV, headboard vanished. Jesse felt his professional self take over, a sensation as clean and fresh as plunging into cool water. He knelt by the bed and smiled. The girl, who looked about nine or ten, didn't smile back. She had a long, sallow, sullen face, but the long brown hair on the pillow was beautiful: clean, lustrous, and well-tended.

"It's her belly," said one of the men who had met them at the subway. Jesse glanced up at the note in his voice, and realized that he must be the child's father. The man's hand trembled as he pulled the sheet from the girl's lower body. Her abdomen was swollen and tender.

"How long has she been this way?"

"Since yesterday," Kenny said, when the father didn't answer.

"Nausea? Vomiting?"

"Yeah. She can't keep nothing down."

Jesse's hands palpated gently. The girl screamed.

Appendicitis. He just hoped to hell peritonitis hadn't set in. He didn't want to deal with peritonitis. Not here.

"Bring in all the lamps you have, with the brightest watt bulbs. Boil water—" He looked up. The room was very cold. "Does the stove work?"

The father nodded. He looked pale. Jesse smiled and said, "I don't think it's anything we can't cure, with a little luck here." The man didn't answer.

Jesse opened his bag, his mind racing. Laser knife, sterile clamps, scaramine—he could do it even without nursing assistance provided there was no peritonitis. But only if . . . the girl moaned and turned her face away. There were tears in her eyes. Jesse looked at the man with the same long, sallow face and brown hair. "You her father?"

The man nodded.

"I need to see her genescan."

The man clenched both fists at his side. Oh, God, if he didn't *have* the official printout . . . sometimes, Jesse had read, uninsurables burned them. One woman, furious at the paper that would forever keep her out of the middle class, had mailed hers, smeared with feces, and packaged with a plasticine explosive, to the president. There had been headlines, columns, petitions . . . and nothing had changed. A country fighting for its very economic survival didn't hesitate to expend front-line troops. If there was no genescan for this child, Jesse couldn't use scaramine, that miracle immune-system booster, to which about 15 percent of the population had a fatal reaction. Without scaramine, under these operating conditions, the chances of post-operative infection were considerably higher. If she couldn't take scaramine . . .

The father handed Jesse the laminated printout, with the deeply embossed seal in the upper corner. Jesse scanned it quickly. The necessary RB antioncogene on the eleventh chromosome was present. The girl was not potentially allergic to scaramine. Her name was Rosamund.

"Okay, Rose," Jesse said gently. "I'm going to help you. In just a little while you're going to feel so much better. . . ." He slipped the needle with anesthetic into her arm. She jumped and screamed, but within a minute she was out.

Jesse stripped away the bedclothes, despite the cold, and told the men how to boil them. He spread Betadine over her distended abdomen and poised the laser knife to cut.

The hallmark of his parents' life had been caution. *Don't fall, now! Drive carefully! Don't talk to strangers!* Born during the Depression—the other one—they invested only in Treasury bonds and their own one-sixth acre of suburban real estate. When the marching in Selma and Washington had turned to killing in Detroit and Kent State, they shook their heads sagely: *See? We said so. No good comes of getting involved in things that don't concern you.* Jesse's father had held the same job for thirty years; his mother considered it immoral to buy anything not on sale. They waited until she was over forty to have Jesse, their only child.

At sixteen, Jesse had despised them; at twenty-four, pitied them; at twenty-eight, his present age, loved them with a despairing gratitude not completely free of contempt. They had missed so much, dared so little. They lived now in Florida, retired and happy and smug. "The pension"—they called it that, as if it were a famous diamond or a well-loved estate—was inflated by Collapse prices into providing a one-bedroom bungalow with beige carpets and a pool. In the pool's placid, artificially blue waters, the Randalls beheld chlorined visions of triumph. "Even after we retired," Jesse's mother told him proudly, "we didn't have to go backward."

"That's what comes from thrift, son," his father always added. "And hard work. No reason these deadbeats today couldn't do the same thing."

Jesse looked around their tiny yard at the plastic ducks lined up like headstones, the fanatically trimmed hedge, the blue-and-white striped awning, and his arms made curious beating motions, as if they were lashed to his side. "Nice, Mom. Nice."

"You know it," she said, and winked roguishly. Jesse had looked away before she could see his embarrassment. Boston had loomed large in his mind, compelling and vivid and hectic as an exotic disease.

There was no peritonitis. Jesse sliced free the spoiled bit of tissue that had been Rosamund's appendix. As he closed with quick, sure movements, he heard a click. A camera. He couldn't look away, but out of a sudden rush of euphoria he said to whoever was taking the picture, "Not one for the gallery this time. This one's going to *live.*"

When the incision was closed, Jesse administered a massive dose of scaramine. Carefully he instructed Kenny and the girl's father about the medication, the little girl's diet, the procedures to maintain asepsis which, since they were bound to be inadequate, made the scaramine so necessary. "I'm on duty the next thirty-six hours at the hospital. I'll return Wednesday night, you'll either have to come get me or give me the address, I'll take a taxi and—"

The father drew in a quick, shaky breath like a sob. Jesse turned to him. "She's got a strong fighting chance, this procedure isn't—" A woman exploded from a back room, shrieking.

"No, no, noooooo . . ." She tried to throw herself on the patient. Jesse lunged for her, but Kenny was quicker. He grabbed her around the waist, pinning her arms to her sides. She fought him, wailing and screaming, as he dragged her back through the door. "Murderer, baby killer, nooooooo—"

"My wife," the father finally said. "She doesn't . . . doesn't understand."

Probably doctors were devils to her, Jesse thought. Gods who denied people the healing they could have offered. Poor bastards. He felt a surge of quiet pride that he could teach them different.

The father went on looking at Rosamund, now sleeping peacefully. Jesse couldn't see the other man's eyes.

Back home at the apartment, he popped open a beer. He felt fine. Was it too late to call Anne?

It was—the computer clock said 2:00 A.M. She'd already be sacked out. In seven more hours his own thirty-six-hour rotation started, but he couldn't sleep.

He sat down at the computer. The machine hadn't moved to surround his empty square after all. It must have something else in mind. Smiling, sipping at his beer, Jesse sat down to match wits with the Korean computer in the ancient Japanese game in the waning Boston night.

Two days later, he went back to check on Rosamund. The rowhouse was deserted, boards nailed diagonally across the window. Jesse's heart began to pound. He was afraid to ask information of the neighbors; men in dark clothes kept going in and out of the house next door, their eyes cold. Jesse went back to the hospital and waited. He couldn't think what else to do.

Four rotations later the deputy sheriff waited for him outside the building, unable to pass the security monitors until Jesse came home.

COMMONWEALTH OF MASSACHUSETTS
SUFFOLK COUNTY   SUPERIOR COURT

To *Jesse Robert Randall* of *Morningside Security Enclave, Building 16, Apartment 3C, Boston,* within our county of Suffolk. Whereas *Steven & Rose Gocek* of Boston within our County of Suffolk have begun an action of Tort against you returnable in the Superior Court holden at Boston within our County of Suffolk on *October 18, 2004,* in which action damages are claimed in the sum of *$2,000,000* as follows:

TORT AND/OR CONTRACT FOR MALPRACTICE

as will more fully appear from the declaration to be filed in said Court when and if said action is entered therein:

WE COMMAND YOU, if you intend to make any defense of said action, that on said date or within such further time as the law allows you cause your written appearance to be entered and your written answer or other lawful pleadings to be filed in the office of the Clerk of the Court to which said writ is returnable, and that you defend against said action according to law.

Hereof fail not at your peril, as otherwise said judgment may be entered against you in said action without further notice.

Witness, *Lawrence F. Monastersky, Esquire*, at *Boston*, the *fourth* day of *March* in the year of our Lord two thousand *four*.

Alice P. McCarren

Clerk

Jesse looked up from the paper. The deputy sheriff, a soft-bodied man with small, light eyes, looked steadily back.

"But what . . . what happened?"

The deputy looked out over Jesse's left shoulder, a gesture meaning he wasn't officially saying what he was saying. "The kid died. The one they say you treated."

"Died? Of what? But I went back . . ." He stopped, filled with sudden sickening uncertainty about how much he was admitting.

The deputy went on staring over his shoulder. "You want my advice, Doc? Get yourself a lawyer."

Doctor, lawyer, Indian chief, Jesse thought suddenly, inanely. The inanity somehow brought it all home. He was being sued. For malpractice. By an uninsurable. Now. Here. Him, Jesse Randall. Who had been only trying to help.

"Cold for this time of year," the deputy remarked. "They're dying of cold and malnutrition down there, in Roxbury and Dorchester and Southie. Even the goddamn weather can't give us a break."

Jesse couldn't answer. A wind off the harbor fluttered the paper in his hand.

"These are the facts," the lawyer said. He looked tired, a small man in a dusty office lined with second-hand law books. "The hospital purchased malpractice coverage for its staff, including residents. In doing so, it entered into a contract with certain obligations and exclusions for each side. If a specific incident falls under these exclusions, the contract is not in force with regard to that incident. One such exclusion is that residents will not be covered if they treat uninsured persons unless such treatment occurs within the hospital setting or the resident has reasonable grounds to assume that such a person is insured. Those are not the circumstances you described to me."

"No," Jesse said. He had the sensation that the law books were falling off the top shelves, slowly but inexorably, like small green and brown glaciers. Outside, he had the same sensation about the tops of buildings.

"Therefore, you are not covered by any malpractice insurance. Another set of facts: Over the last five years jury decisions in malpractice cases have averaged 85 percent in favor of plaintiffs. Insurance companies and legislatures are made up of insurables, Dr. Randall. However, juries are still drawn by lot from the general citizenry. Most of the educated general citizenry finds ways to get out of jury duty. They always did. Juries are likely to be 65 percent or more uninsurables. It's the last place the havenots still wield much real power, and they use it."

"You're saying I'm dead," Jesse said numbly. "They'll find me guilty."

The little lawyer looked pained. "Not 'dead,' Doctor. Convicted—most probably. But conviction isn't death. Not even professional death. The hospital may or may not dismiss you—they have that right—but you can still finish your training elsewhere. And malpractice suits, however they go, are not of themselves grounds for denial of a medical license. You can still be a doctor."

"Treating who?" Jesse cried. He threw up his hands. The books fell slightly faster. "If I'm convicted I'll have to declare bankruptcy—there's no way I could pay a jury settlement like that! And even if I found another residency at some third-rate hospital in Podunk, no decent practitioner would ever accept me as a partner. I'd have to practice alone, without money to set up more than a hole-in-the-corner office among God-knows-*who* . . . and even that's assuming I can find a hospital that will let me finish. All because I wanted to help people who are getting shit on!"

The lawyer took off his glasses and rubbed the lenses thoughtfully with a tissue. "Maybe," he said, "they're shitting back."

"What?"

"You haven't asked about the specific charges, Doctor."

"Malpractice! The brat died!"

The lawyer said, "Of massive scaramine allergic reaction."

The anger leeched out of Jesse. He went very quiet.

"She was allergic to scaramine," the lawyer said. "You failed to ascertain that. A basic medical question."

"I—" The words wouldn't come out. He saw again the laminated genescan chart, the detailed analysis of chromosome 11. A camera clicking, recording that he was there. The hysterical woman, the mother, exploding from the back room: *nooooooooooo. . . .* The father standing frozen, his eyes downcast.

It wasn't possible.

Nobody would kill their own child. Not to discredit one of the fortunate ones, the haves, the insurables, the employables . . . No one would do that.

The lawyer was watching him carefully, glasses in hand.

Jesse said, "Dr. Michael Cassidy—" and stopped.

"Dr. Cassidy what?" the lawyer said.

But all Jesse could see, suddenly, was the row of plastic ducks in his parents' Florida yard, lined up as precisely as headstones, garish hideous yellow as they marched undeviatingly wherever it was they were going.

"No," Mike Cassidy said. "I didn't send him."

They stood in the hospital parking lot. Snow blew from the east. Cassidy wrapped both arms around himself and rocked back and forth. "He didn't come from us."

"He said he did!"

"I know. But he didn't. His group must have heard we were helping illegally, gotten your name from somebody—"

"But why?" Jesse shouted. "Why frame me? Why kill a child just to frame *me*? I'm nothing!"

Cassidy's face spasmed. Jesse saw that his horror at Jesse's position was real, his sympathy genuine, and both useless. There was nothing Cassidy could do.

"I don't know," Cassidy whispered. And then, "Are you going to name me at your malpractice trial?"

Jesse turned away without answering, into the wind.

Chief of Surgery Jonathan Eberhart called him into his office just before Jesse started his rotation. Before, not after. That was enough to tell him everything. He was getting very good at discovering the whole from a single clue.

"Sit down, Doctor," Eberhart said. His voice, normally austere, held unwilling compassion. Jesse heard it, and forced himself not to shudder.

"I'll stand."

"This is very difficult," Eberhart said, "but I think you already see our position. It's not one any of us would have chosen, but it's what we have. This hospital operates at a staggering deficit. Most patients cannot begin to cover the costs of modern technological health care. State and federal governments are both strapped with enormous debt. Without insurance companies and the private philanthropical support of a few rich families, we would not be able to open our doors to anyone at all. If we lose our insurance rating we—"

"I'm out on my ass," Jesse said. "Right?"

Eberhart looked out the window. It was snowing. Once Jesse, driving through Oceanview Security Enclave to pick up a date, had seen Eberhart building a snowman with two small children, probably his grandchildren. Even rolling lopsided globes of cold, Eberhart had had dignity.

"Yes, Doctor. I'm sorry. As I understand it, the facts of your case are not in legal dispute. Your residency here is terminated."

"Thank you," Jesse said, an odd formality suddenly replacing his crudeness. "For everything."

Eberhart neither answered nor turned around. His shoulders, framed in the gray window, slumped forward. He might, Jesse thought, have had a sudden advanced case of osteoporosis. For which, of course, he would be fully insured.

He packed the computer last, fitting each piece carefully into its original packing. Maybe that would raise the price that Second Thoughts was willing to give him: *Look, almost new, still in the original box.* At the last minute he decided to keep the playing pieces for *go*, shoving them into the suitcase with his clothes and medical equipment. Only this suitcase would go with him.

When the packing was done, he walked up two flights and rang Anne's bell. Her rotation ended a half hour ago. Maybe she wouldn't be asleep yet.

She answered the door in a loose blue robe, toothbrush in hand. "Jesse, hi, I'm afraid I'm really beat—"

He no longer believed in indirection. "Would you have dinner with me to-morrow night?"

"Oh, I'm sorry, I can't," Anne said. She shifted her weight so one bare foot stood on top of the other, a gesture so childish it had to be embarrassment. Her toenails were shiny and smooth.

"After your next rotation?" Jesse said. He didn't smile.

"I don't know when I—"

"The one after that?"

Anne was silent. She looked down at her toothbrush. A thin pristine line of toothpaste snaked over the bristles.

"Okay," Jesse said, without expression. "I just wanted to be sure."

"Jesse—" Anne called after him, but he didn't turn around. He could already tell from her voice that she didn't really have anything more to say. If he had turned it would have been only for the sake of a last look at her toes, polished and shiny as *go* stones, and there really didn't seem to be any point in looking.

He moved into a cheap hotel on Boylston Street, into a room the size of a supply closet with triple locks on the door and bars on the window, where his money would go far. Every morning he took the subway to the Copley Square library, rented a computer cubicle, and wrote letters to hospitals across the country. He also answered classified ads in the *New England Journal of Medicine,* those that offered practice out-of-country where a license was not crucial, or low-paying medical research positions not too many people might want, or supervised assistantships. In the afternoons he walked the grubby streets of Dorchester, looking for Kenny. The lawyer representing Mr. and Mrs. Steven Gocek, parents of the dead Rosamund, would give him no addresses. Neither would his own lawyer, he of the collapsing books and desperate clientele, in whom Jesse had already lost all faith.

He never saw Kenny on the cold streets.

The last week of March, an unseasonable warm wind blew from the south, and kept up. Crocuses and daffodils pushed up between the sagging buildings. Children appeared, chasing each other across the garbage-laden streets, crying raucously. Rejections came from hospitals, employers. Jesse had still not told his parents what had happened. Twice in April he picked up a public phone, and twice he saw again the plastic ducks marching across the artificial lawn, and something inside him slammed shut so hard not even the phone number could escape.

One sunny day in May he walked in the Public Garden. The city still maintained it fairly well; foreign tourist traffic made it profitable. Jesse counted the number of well-dressed foreigners versus the number of ragged street Bostonians The ratio equaled the survival rate for uninsured diabetics.

"Hey, mister, help me! Please!"

A terrified boy, ten or eleven, grabbed Jesse's hand and pointed. At the bottom of a grassy knoll an elderly man lay crumpled on the ground, his face twisted.

"My grandpa! He just grabbed his chest and fell down! Do something! Please!"

Jesse could smell the boy's fear, a stink like rich loam. He walked over to the old man. Breathing stopped, no pulse, color still pink . . .

No.

This man was an uninsured. Like Kenny, like Steven Gocek. Like Rosamund.

"Grandpa!" the child wailed. "Grandpa!"

Jesse knelt. He started mouth-to-mouth. The old man smelled of sweat, of old flesh. No blood moved through the body. "Breathe, dammit, breathe," Jesse heard someone say, and then realized it was him. *"Breathe,* you old fart, you uninsured deadbeat, you stinking ingrate, breathe—"

The old man breathed.

He sent the boy for more adults. The child took off at a dead run, returning twenty minutes later with uncles, father, cousins, aunts, most of whom spoke some language Jesse couldn't identify. In that twenty minutes none of the well-dressed tourists in the Garden approached Jesse, standing guard beside the old man, who breathed carefully and moaned softly, stretched full-length on the grass. The tourists glanced at him and then away, their faces tightening.

The tribe of family carried the old man away on a homemade stretcher. Jesse put his hand on the arm of one of the young men. "Insurance? Hospital?"

The man spat onto the grass.

Jesse walked beside the stretcher, monitoring the old man until he was in his own bed. He told the child what to do for him, since no one else seemed to understand. Later that day he went back, carrying his medical bag, and gave them the last of his hospital supply of nitroglycerin. The oldest woman, who had been too busy issuing orders about the stretcher to pay Jesse any attention before, stopped dead and jabbered in her own tongue.

"You a doctor?" the child translated. The tip of his ear, Jesse noticed, was missing. Congenital? Accident? Ritual mutilation? The ear had healed clean.

"Yeah," Jesse said. "A doctor."

The old woman chattered some more and disappeared behind a door. Jesse gazed at the walls. There were no deathbed photos. As he was leaving, the woman returned with ten incredibly dirty dollar bills.

"Doctor," she said, her accent harsh, and when she smiled Jesse saw that all her top teeth and most of her bottom ones were missing, the gum swollen with what might have been early signs of scurvy.

"Doctor," she said again.

He moved out of the hotel just as the last of his money ran out. The old man's wife, Androula Malakassas, found him a room in somebody else's rambling, dilapidated boardinghouse. The house was noisy at all hours, but the room was clean and large. Androula's cousin brought home an old, multi-positional dentist chair, probably stolen, and Jesse used that for both examining and operating table. Medical substances—antibiotics, chemotherapy, IV drugs—which he had thought of as the hardest need to fill outside of controlled channels, turned out to be the easiest. On reflection, he realized this shouldn't have surprised him.

In July he delivered his first breech birth, a primapara whose labor was so long and painful and bloody he thought at one point he'd lose both mother and baby. He lost neither, although the new mother cursed him in Spanish and spit at him. She was too weak for the saliva to go far. Holding the warm-assed, nine-pound baby boy, Jesse had heard a camera click. He cursed too, but feebly; the sharp thrill of pleasure that pierced from throat to bowels was too strong.

In August he lost three patients in a row, all to conditions that would have needed elaborate, costly equipment and procedures: renal failure, aortic aneurysm, narcotic overdose. He went to all three funerals. At each one the family and friends cleared a little space for him, in which he stood surrounded by respect and resentment. When a knife fight broke out at the funeral of the aneurysm, the family hustled Jesse away from the danger, but not so far away that he couldn't treat the loser.

In September a Chinese family, recent immigrants, moved into Androula's sprawling boardinghouse. The woman wept all day. The man roamed Boston, looking for work. There was a grandfather who spoke a little English, having learned it in Peking during the brief period of American industrial expansion into the Pacific Rim before the Chinese government convulsed and the American economy collapsed. The grandfather played *go*. On evenings when no one wanted Jesse, he sat with Lin Shujen and moved the polished white and black stones over the grid, seeking to enclose empty spaces without losing any pieces. Mr. Lin took a long time to consider each move.

In October, a week before Jesse's trial, his mother died. Jesse's father sent him money to fly home for the funeral, the first money Jesse had accepted from his family since he'd finally told them he had left the hospital. After the funeral Jesse sat in the living room of his father's Florida house and listened to the elderly mourners recall their youths in the vanished prosperity of the fifties and sixties.

"Plenty of jobs then for people who're willing to work."

"Still plenty of jobs. Just nobody's willing anymore."

"Want everything handed to them. If you ask me, this collapse'll prove to be a good thing in the long run. Weed out the weaklings and the lazy."

"It was the sixties we got off on the wrong track, with Lyndon Johnson and all the welfare programs—"

They didn't look at Jesse. He had no idea what his father had said to them about him.

Back in Boston, stinking under Indian summer heat, people thronged his room. Fractures, cancers, allergies, pregnancies, punctures, deficiencies, imbalances. They were resentful that he'd gone away for five days. He should be here; they needed him. He was the doctor.

The first day of his trial, Jesse saw Kenny standing on the courthouse steps. Kenny wore a cheap blue suit with loafers and white socks. Jesse stood very still, then walked over to the other man. Kenny tensed.

"I'm not going to hit you," Jesse said.

Kenny watched him, chin lowered, slight body balanced on the balls of his feet. A fighter's stance.

"I want to ask something," Jesse said. "It won't affect the trial. I just want to know. Why'd you do it? Why did *they*? I know the little girl's true genescan showed 98 percent risk of leukemia death within three years, but even so—how could you."

Kenny scrutinized him carefully. Jesse saw that Kenny thought Jesse might be wired. Even before Kenny answered, Jesse knew what he'd hear. "I don't know what you're talking about, man."

"You couldn't get inside the system. Any of you. So you brought me out. If Mohammed won't go to the mountain—"

"You don't make no sense," Kenny said.

"Was it worth it? To you? To them? Was it?"

Kenny walked away, up the courthouse steps. At the top waited the Goceks, who were suing Jesse for two million dollars he didn't have and wasn't insured for, and that they knew damn well they wouldn't collect. On the wall of their house, wherever it was, probably hung Rosamund's deathbed picture, a little girl with a plain, sallow face and beautiful hair.

Jesse saw his lawyer trudge up the courthouse steps, carrying his briefcase. Another lawyer, with an equally shabby briefcase, climbed in parallel several feet away. Between the two men the courthouse steps made a white empty space.

Jesse climbed, too, hoping to hell this wouldn't take too long. He had an infected compound femoral fracture, a birth with potential erythroblastosis fetalis, and an elderly phlebitis, all waiting. He was especially concerned about the infected fracture, which needed careful monitoring because the man's genescan showed a tendency toward weak T-cell production. The guy was a day laborer, foul-mouthed and ignorant and brave, with a wife and two kids. He'd broken his leg working illegal construction. Jesse was determined to give him at least a fighting chance.

WALL, STONE, CRAFT

Walter Jon Williams

Walter Jon Williams is the author of many fine SF novels and stories, including *Aristoi* and *Metropolitan*, and historical fiction as well. In his landmark critical history of SF, *Billion Year Spree*, Brian Aldiss proposed Mary Shelley as the first important SF writer, and this idea has gained wide acceptance. The famous events leading to the composition of her compelling novel *Frankenstein* have exerted a powerful fascination on many writers. Here Williams considers those events and people in a work of SF.

1

She awoke, there in the common room of the inn, from a brief dream of roses and death. Once Mary came awake she recalled there were wild roses on her mother's grave, and wondered if her mother's spirit had visited her.

On her mother's grave, Mary's lover had first proposed their elopement. It was there the two of them had first made love.

Now she believed she was pregnant. Her lover was of the opinion that she was mistaken. That was about where it stood.

Mary concluded that it was best not to think about it. And so, blinking sleep from her eyes, she sat in the common room of the inn at Le Caillou and resolved to study her Italian grammar by candlelight.

Plurals. *La nascita, le nascite. La madre, le madri. Un bambino, i bambini . . .*

Interruption: stampings, snortings, the rattle of harness, the barking of dogs. Four young Englishmen entered the inn, one in scarlet uniform coat, the others in fine traveling clothes. Raindrops dazzled on their shoulders. The innkeeper bustled out from the kitchen, smiled, proffered the register.

Mary, unimpressed by anything English, concentrated on the grammar.

"Let me sign, George," the redcoat said. "My hand needs the practice."

Mary glanced up at the comment.

"I say, George, here's a fellow signed in Greek!" The Englishman peered at yellowed pages of the inn's register, trying to make out the words in the dim light of the innkeeper's lamp. Mary smiled at the English officer's efforts.

"Perseus, I believe the name is. Perseus Busseus—d'ye suppose he means

Bishop?—Kselleius. And he gives his occupation as 'te anthropou philou'—that would make him a friendly fellow, eh?—" The officer looked over his shoulder and grinned, then returned to the register. " 'Kai atheos.' " The officer scowled, then straightened. "Does that mean what I think it does, George?"

George—the pretty auburn-haired man in byrons—shook rain off his short cape, stepped to the register, examined the text. "Not 'friendly fellow,' " he said. "That would be 'anehr philos.' 'Anthropos' is mankind, not man." There was the faintest touch of Scotland in his speech.

"So it is," said the officer. "It comes back now."

George bent at his slim waist and looked carefully at the register. "What the fellow says is, 'Both friend of man and—' " He frowned, then looked at his friend. "You were right about the 'atheist,' I'm afraid."

The officer was indignant. "Ain't funny, George," he said.

George gave a cynical little half-smile. His voice changed, turned comical and fussy, became that of a high-pitched English schoolmaster. "Let us try to make out the name of this famous atheist." He bent over the register again. "Perseus—you had that right, Somerset. Busseus—how *very* irregular. Kselleius—Kelly? Shelley?" He smiled at his friend. His voice became very Irish. "Kelly, I imagine. An atheistical upstart Irish schoolmaster with a little Greek. But what the Busseus might be eludes me, unless his middle name is Omnibus."

Somerset chuckled. Mary rose from her place and walked quietly toward the pair. "The gentleman's name is Bysshe, sir," she said. "Percy Bysshe Shelley."

The two men turned in surprise. The officer—Somerset—bowed as he perceived a lady. Mary saw for the first time that he had one empty sleeve pinned across his tunic, which would account for the comment about the hand. The other—George, the man in byrons—swept off his hat and gave Mary a flourishing bow, one far too theatrical to be taken seriously. When he straightened, he gave Mary a little frown.

"Bysshe Shelley?" he said. "Any relation to Sir Bysshe, the baronet?"

"His grandson."

"Sir Bysshe is a protegé of old Norfolk." This an aside to his friends. Radical Whiggery was afoot, or so the tone implied. George returned his attention to Mary as the other Englishmen gathered about her. "An interesting family, no doubt," he said, and smiled at her. Mary wanted to flinch from the compelling way he looked at her, gazed upward, intently, from beneath his brows. "And are you of his party?"

"I am."

"And you are, I take it, Mrs. Shelley?"

Mary straightened and gazed defiantly into George's eyes. "Mrs. Shelley resides in England. My name is Godwin."

George's eyes widened, flickered a little. Low English murmurs came to Mary's ears. George bowed again. "Charmed to meet you, Miss Godwin."

George pointed to each of his companions with his hat. "Lord Fitzroy Somerset." The armless man bowed again. "Captain Harry Smith. Captain Austen of the Navy. Pásmány, my fencing master." Most of the party, Mary thought, were young, and all were handsome, George most of all. George turned to Mary again, a little smile of anticipation curling his lips. His burning look was almost insolent. "My name is Newstead."

Mortal embarrassment clutched at Mary's heart. She knew her cheeks were burning, but still she held George's eyes as she bobbed a curtsey.

George had not been Marquess Newstead for more than a few months. He had been famous for years both as an intimate of the Prince Regent and the most dashing of Wellington's cavalry officers, but it was his exploits on the field of Waterloo and his capture of Napoleon on the bridge at Genappe that had made him immortal. He was the talk of England and the Continent, though he had achieved his fame under another name.

Before the Prince Regent had given him the title of Newstead, auburn-haired, insolent-eyed George had been known as George Gordon Noël, the sixth Lord Byron.

Mary decided she was not going to be impressed by either his titles or his manner. She decided she would think of him as George.

"Pleased to meet you, my lord," Mary said. Pride steeled her as she realized her voice hadn't trembled.

She was spared further embarrassment when the door burst open and a servant entered followed by a pack of muddy dogs—whippets—who showered them all with water, then howled and bounded about George, their master. Standing tall, his strong, well-formed legs in the famous side-laced boots that he had invented to show off his calf and ankle, George laughed as the dogs jumped up on his chest and bayed for attention. His lordship barked back at them and wrestled with them for a moment—not very lordlike, Mary thought—and then he told his dogs to be still. At first they ignored him, but eventually he got them down and silenced.

He looked up at Mary. "I can discipline men, Miss Godwin," he said, "but I'm afraid I'm not very good with animals."

"That shows you have a kind heart, I'm sure," Mary said.

The others laughed a bit at this—apparently kindheartedness was not one of George's better-known qualities—but George smiled indulgently.

"Have you and your companion supped, Miss Godwin? I would welcome the company of fellow English in this tiresome land of Brabant."

Mary was unable to resist an impertinence. "Even if one of them is an atheistical upstart Irish schoolmaster?"

"Miss Godwin, I would dine with Wolfe Tone himself." Still with that intent, under-eyed look, as if he was dissecting her.

Mary was relieved to turn away from George's gaze and look toward the back of the inn, in the direction of the kitchen. "Bysshe is in the kitchen giving instructions to the cook. I believe my sister is with him."

"Are there more in your party?"

"Only the three of us. And one rather elderly carriage horse."

"Forgive us if we do not invite the horse to table."

"Your ape, George," Somerset said dolefully, "will be quite enough."

Mary would have pursued this interesting remark, but at that moment Bysshe and Claire appeared from out of the kitchen passage. Both were laughing, as if at a shared secret, and Claire's black eyes glittered. Mary repressed a spasm of annoyance.

"Mary!" Bysshe said. "The cook told us a ghost story!" He was about to go on, but paused as he saw the visitors.

"We have an invitation to dinner," Mary said. "Lord Newstead has been kind enough—"

"Newstead!" said Claire. "*The* Lord Newstead?"

George turned his searching gaze on Claire. "I'm the only Newstead I know."

Mary felt a chill of alarm, for a moment seeing Claire as George doubtless saw her: black-haired, black-eyed, fatally indiscreet, and all of sixteen.

Sometimes the year's difference in age between Mary and Claire seemed a century.

"Lord Newstead!" Claire babbled. "I recognize you now! How exciting to meet you!"

Mary resigned herself to fate. "My lord," she said, "may I present my sister, Miss Jane—Claire, rather, Claire Clairmont, and Mr. Shelley."

"Overwhelmed and charmed, Miss Clairmont. Mr. Perseus Omnibus Kselleius, *tí kánete?*"

Bysshe blinked for a second or two, then grinned. *"Thanmásia eùxaristô,"* returning politeness, *"kaí eseís?"*

For a moment Mary gloried in Bysshe, in his big frame in his shabby clothes, his fair, disordered hair, his freckles, his large hands—and his absolute disinclination to be impressed by one of the most famous men on Earth.

George searched his mind for a moment. *"Polú kalá, eùxaristô. Thá éthela ná—"* He groped for words, then gave a laugh. "Hang the Greek!" he said. "It's been far too many years since Trinity. May I present my friend Somerset?"

Somerset gave the atheist a cold Christian eye. "How d'ye do?"

George finished his introductions. There was the snapping of coach whips outside, and the sound of more stamping horses. The dogs began barking again. At least two more coaches had arrived. George led the party into the dining room. Mary found herself sitting next to George, with Claire and Bysshe across the table.

"Damme, I quite forgot to register," Somerset said, rising from his bench. "What bed will you settle for, George?"

"Nothing less than Bonaparte's."

Somerset signed. "I thought not," he said.

"Did Bonaparte sleep here in Le Caillou?" Claire asked.

"The night before Waterloo."

"How exciting! Is Waterloo nearby?" She looked at Bysshe. "Had we known, we could have asked for his room."

"Which we then would have had to surrender to my lord Newstead," Bysshe said tolerantly. "He has greater claim, after all, than we."

George gave Mary his intent look again. His voice was pitched low. "I would not deprive two lovely ladies of their bed for all the Bonapartes in Europe."

But rather join us in it, Mary thought. That look was clear enough.

The rest of George's party—servants, aides-de-camp, clerks, one black man in full Mameluke fig, turned-up slippers, ostrich plumes, scarlet turban and all—carried George's equipage from his carriages. In addition to an endless series of trunks and a large miscellany of weaponry there were more animals. Not only the promised ape—actually a large monkey, which seated itself on George's shoulder—but brightly colored parrots in cages, a pair of greyhounds, some hooded hunting hawks, songbirds, two forlorn-looking kit foxes in cages, which set all the dogs howling and jumping in eagerness to get at them, and a half-grown panther in a jewelled collar, which the dogs knew better than to bark at. The innkeeper was loud in his complaint as he attempted to sort them all out and stay outside of the range of beaks, claws, and fangs.

Bysshe watched with bright eyes, enjoying the spectacle. George's friends looked as if they were weary of it.

"I hope we will sleep tonight," Mary said.

"If you sleep not," said George, playing with the monkey, "we shall contrive to keep you entertained."

How gracious to include your friends in the orgy, Mary thought. But once again kept silent.

Bysshe was still enjoying the parade of frolicking animals. He glanced at Mary. "Don't you think, Maie, this is the very image of philosophical anarchism?"

"You are welcome to it, sir," said Somerset, returning from the register. "George, your mastiff has injured the ostler's dog. He is loud in his complaint."

"I'll have Ferrante pay him off."

"See that you do. And have him pistol the brains out of that mastiff while he's at it."

"Injure poor Picton?" George was offended. "I'll have none of it."

"Poor Picton will have his fangs in the ostler next."

"He must have been teasing the poor beast."

"Picton will kill us all one day." Grudgingly.

"Forgive us, Somerset-laddie." Mary watched as George reached over to Somerset and tweaked his ear. Somerset reddened but seemed pleased.

"Mr. Shelley," said Captain Austen. "I wonder if you know what surprises the kitchen has in store for us."

Austen was a well-built man in a plain black coat, older than the others, with a lined and weathered naval face and a reserved manner unique in this company.

"Board 'em in the smoke! That's the Navy for you!" George said. "Straight to the business of eating, never mind the other nonsense."

"If you ate wormy biscuit for twenty years of war," said Harry Smith, "you'd care about the food as well."

Bysshe gave Austen a smile. "The provisions seem adequate enough for a country inn," he said. "And the rooms are clean, unlike most in this country. Claire and the Maie and I do not eat meat, so I had to tell the cook how to prepare our dinner. But if your taste runs to fowl or something in the cutlet line I daresay the cook can set you up."

"No meat!" George seemed enthralled by the concept. "Disciples of J. F. Newton, as I take it?"

"Among others," said Mary.

"But are you well? Do you not feel an enervation? Are you not feverish with lack of a proper diet?" George leaned very close and touched Mary's forehead with the back of one cool hand while he reached to find her pulse with the other. The monkey grimaced at her from his shoulder. Mary disengaged and placed her hands on the table.

"I'm quite well, I assure you," she said.

"The Maie's health is far better than when I met her," Bysshe said.

"Mine too," said Claire.

"I believe most diseases can be conquered by proper diet," said Bysshe. And then he added,

"He slays the lamb that looks him in the face,
And horribly devours his mangled flesh."

"Let's have some mangled flesh tonight, George," said Somerset gaily.

"Do let's," added Smith.

George's hand remained on Mary's forehead. His voice was very soft. "If eating flesh offend thee," he said, "I will eat but only greens."

Mary could feel her hackles rise. "Order what you please," she said. "I don't care one way or another."

"Brava, Miss Godwin!" said Smith thankfully. "Let it be mangled flesh for us all, and to perdition with all those little Low Country cabbages!"

"I don't like them, either," said Claire.

George removed his hand from Mary's forehead and tried to signal the innkeeper, who was still struggling to corral the dogs. George failed, frowned, and lowered his hand.

"I'm cheered to know you're familiar with the works of Newton," Bysshe said.

"I wouldn't say *familiar*," said George. He was still trying to signal the innkeeper. "I haven't read his books. But I know he wants me not to eat meat, and that's all I need to know."

Bysshe folded his big hands on the table. "Oh, there's much more than that. Abstaining from meat implies an entire new moral order, in which mankind is placed on an equal level with the animals."

"George in particular should appreciate that," said Harry Smith, and made a face at the monkey.

"I think I prefer being ranked above the animals," George said. "And above most people, too." He looked up at Bysshe. "Shall we avoid talk of food matters before we eat? My stomach's rumbling louder than a battery of Napoleon's daughters." He looked down at the monkey and assumed a high-pitched Scots dowager's voice. "An' sae is Jerome Bonaparte's, annit nae, Jerome?"

George finally succeeded in attracting the innkeeper's attention and the company ordered food and wine. Bread, cheese, and pickles were brought to tide them over in the meantime. Jerome Bonaparte was permitted off his master's lap to roam free along the table and eat what he wished.

George watched as Bysshe carved a piece of cheese for himself. "In addition to Newton, you would also be a follower of William Godwin?"

Bysshe gave Mary a glance, then nodded. "Ay. Godwin also."

"I thought I recognized that 'philosophical anarchism' of yours. Godwin was the rage when I was at Harrow. But not so much thought of now, eh? Excepting of course his lovely namesake." Turning his gaze to Mary.

Mary gave him a cold look. "Truth is ever in fashion, my lord," she said.

"Did you say *ever* or *never*?" Playfully. Mary said nothing, and George gave a shrug. "Truthful Master Godwin, then. And who else?"

"Ovid," Mary said. The officers looked a little serious at this. She smiled. "Come now—he's not as scandalous as he's been made out. Merely playful."

This did not reassure her audience. Bysshe offered Mary a private smile. "We've also been reading Mary Wollstonecraft."

"Ah!" George said. "Heaven save us from intellectual women!"

"Mary Wollstonecraft," said Somerset thoughtfully. "She was a harlot in France, was she not?"

"I prefer to think of my mother," said Mary carefully, "as a political thinker and authoress."

There was sudden silence as Somerset turned white with mortification. Then George threw back his head and laughed.

"Sunburn me!" he said. "That answers as you deserve!"

Somerset visibly made an effort to collect his wits. "I am most sorry, Miss—" he began.

George laughed again. "By heaven, we'll watch our words hereafter!"

Claire tittered. "I was in suspense, wondering if there would be a mishap. And there was, there *was!*"

George turned to Mary and managed to compose his face into an attitude of solemnity, though the amusement that danced in his eyes denied it.

"I sincerely apologize on behalf of us all, Miss Godwin. We are soldiers and are accustomed to speaking rough among ourselves, and have been abroad and are doubtless ignorant of the true worth of any individual"—he searched his mind for a moment, trying to work out a graceful way to conclude—"outside of our own little circle," he finished.

"Well said," said Mary, "and accepted." She had chosen more interesting ground on which to make her stand.

"Oh yes!" said Claire. "Well said indeed!"

"My mother is not much understood by the public," Mary continued. "But intellectual women, it would seem, are not much understood by *you.*"

George leaned away from Mary and scanned her with cold eyes. "On the contrary," he said. "I am married to an intellectual woman."

"And she, I imagine . . ." Mary let the pause hang in the air for a moment, like a rapier before it strikes home. ". . . resides in England?"

George scowled. "She does."

"I'm sure she has her books to keep her company."

"And Francis Bacon," George said, his voice sour. "Annabella is an authority on Francis Bacon. And she is welcome to reform *him*, if she likes."

Mary smiled at him. "Who keeps *you* company, my lord?"

There was a stir among his friends. He gave her that insolent, under-eyed look again.

"I am not often lonely," he said.

"Tonight you will rest with the ghost of Napoleon," she said. "Which of you has better claim to that bed?"

George gave a cold little laugh. "I believe that was decided at Waterloo."

"The Duke's victory, or so I've heard."

George's friends were giving each other alarmed looks. Mary decided she had drawn enough Byron blood. She took a piece of cheese.

"Tell us about Waterloo!" Claire insisted. "Is it far from here?"

"The field is a mile or so north," said Somerset. He seemed relieved to turn to the subject of battles. "I had thought perhaps you were English tourists come to visit the site."

"Our arrival is coincidence," Bysshe said. He was looking at Mary narrow-eyed, as if he was trying to work something out. "I'm somewhat embarrassed for funds, and I'm in hope of finding a letter at Brussels from my—" He began to say "wife," but change the word to "family."

"We're on our way to Vienna," Smith said.

"The long way 'round," said Somerset. "It's grown unsafe in Paris—too many old Bonapartists lurking with guns and bombs, and of course George is the laddie they hate most. So we're off to join the Duke as diplomats, but we plan to meet with his highness of Orange along the way. In Brussels, in two days' time."

"Good old Slender Billy!" said Smith. "I haven't seen him since the battle."

"The battle!" said Claire. "You said you would tell us!"

George gave her an irritated look. "Please, Miss Clairmont, I beg you. No battles before dinner." His stomach rumbled audibly.

"Bysshe," said Mary, "didn't you say the cook had told you a ghost story?"

"A good one, too," said Bysshe. "It happened in the house across the road, the one with the tile roof. A pair of old witches used to live there. Sisters." He looked up at George. "We may have ghosts before dinner, may we not?"

"For all of me, you may."

"They dealt in charms and curses and so on, and made a living supplying the, ah, the supernatural needs of the district. It so happened that two different men had fallen in love with the same girl, and each man applied to one of the weird sisters for a love charm—each to a different sister, you see. One of them used his spell first and won the heart of the maiden, and this drove the other suitor into a rage. So he went to the witch who had sold him his charm, and demanded she change the young lady's mind. When the witch insisted it was impossible, he drew his pistol and shot her dead."

"How very un-Belgian of him," drawled Smith.

Bysshe continued unperturbed. "So quick as a wink," he said, "the dead witch's sister seized a heavy kitchen cleaver and cut off the young man's head with a single stroke. The head fell to the floor and bounced out the porch steps. And ever since that night"—he leaned across the table toward Mary, his voice dropping dramatically—"people in the house have sometimes heard a thumping noise, and seen the *suitor's head, dripping gore, bouncing down the steps!*"

Mary and Bysshe shared a delicious shiver. George gave Bysshe a thoughtful look.

"D'ye credit this sort of thing, Mr. Omnibus?"

Bysshe looked up. "Oh yes. I have a great belief in things supernatural."

George gave an insolent smile, and Mary's heart quickened as she recognized a trap.

"Then how can you be an atheist?" George asked.

Bysshe was startled. No one had ever asked him this question before. He gave a nervous laugh. "I am not so much opposed to God," he said, "as I am a worshipper of Galileo and Newton. And of course an enemy of the established Church."

"I see."

A little smile drifted across Bysshe's lips.

> *"Yes!" he said, "I have seen God's worshippers unsheathe*
> *The sword of his revenge, when grace descended,*
> *Confirming all unnatural impulses,*
> *To satisfy their desolating deeds;*
> *And frantic priests waved the ill-omened cross*
> *O'er the unhappy earth; then shone the sun*
> *On showers of gore from the upflashing steel*
> *Of safe assassin—"*

"And *have* you seen such?" George's look was piercing.

Bysshe blinked at him. "Beg pardon?"

"I asked if you *had* seen showers of gore, upflashing steel, all that sort of thing."

"Ah. No." He offered George a half-apologetic smile. "I do not hold warfare consonant with my principles."

"Yes." George's stomach rumbled once more. "It's rather more in my line than yours. So I think I am probably better qualified to judge it . . ." His lip twisted. ". . . *and* your principles."

Mary felt her hackles rise. "Surely you don't dispute that warfare is a great evil," she said. "And that the church blesses war and its outcome."

"The church—" He waved a hand. "The chaplains we had with us in Spain were fine men and did good work, from what I could see. Though we had damn few of them, as for the most part they preferred to judge war from their comfortable beds at home. And as for war—ay, it's evil. Yes. Among other things."

"*Among other things!*" Mary was outraged. "What other things?"

George looked at each of the officers in turn, then at Mary. "War is an abomination, I think we can all agree. But it is also an occasion for all that is great in mankind. Courage, comradeship, sacrifice. Heroism and nobility beyond the scope of imagination."

"Glory," said one-armed Somerset helpfully.

"Death!" snapped Mary. "Hideous, lingering death! Disease. Mutilation!" She realized she had stepped a little far, and bobbed her head toward Somerset, silently begging his pardon for bringing up his disfigurement. "Endless suffering among the starving widows and orphans," she went on. "Early this year Bysshe and Jane and I walked across the part of France that the armies had marched over. It was a desert, my lord. Whole villages without a single soul. Women, children, and cripples in rags. Many without a roof over their head."

"Ay," said Harry Smith. "We saw it in Spain, all of us."

"Miss Godwin," said George, "those poor French people have my sympathy as well as yours. But if a nation is going to murder its rightful king, elect a tyrant, and attack every other nation in the world, then it can but expect to receive that which it giveth. I reserve far greater sympathy for the poor orphans and widows of Spain, Portugal, and the Low Countries."

"And England," said Captain Austen.

"Ay," said George, "and England."

"I did not say that England has not suffered," said Mary. "Anyone with eyes can see the victims of the war. And the victims of the Corn Bill as well."

"Enough." George threw up his hands. "I heard enough debate on the Corn Bill in the House of Lords—I beg you, not here."

"People are starving, my lord," Mary said quietly.

"But thanks to Waterloo," George said, "they at least starve in peace."

"Here's our flesh!" said a relieved Harry Smith. Napkins flourished, silverware rattled, the dinner was laid down. Bysshe took a bite of his cheese pie, then sampled one of the little Brabant cabbages and gave a freckled smile—he had not, as had Mary, grown tired of them. Smith, Somerset, and George chatted about various Army acquaintances, and the others ate in silence. Somerset, Mary noticed, had come equipped with a combinations knife-and-fork and managed his cutlet efficiently.

George, she noted, ate only a little, despite the grumblings of his stomach.

"Is it not to your taste, my lord?" she asked.

"My appetite is off." Shortly.

"That light cavalry figure don't come without sacrifice," said Smith. "I'm an infantryman, though," brandishing knife and fork, "and can tuck in to my vittles."

George gave him an irritated glance and sipped at his hock. "Cavalry, infantry, Senior Service, staff," he said, pointing at himself, Smith, Austen, and Somerset with his fork. The fork swung to Bysshe. "Do you, sir, have an occupation? Besides being atheistical, I mean."

Bysshe put down his knife and fork and answered deliberately. "I have been a scientist, and a reformer, and a sort of an engineer. I have now taken up poetry."

"I didn't know it was something to be *taken up*," said George.

"Captain Austen's sister does something in the literary line, I believe," Harry Smith said.

Austen gave a little shake of his head. "Please, Harry. Not here."

"I know she publishes anonymously, but—"

"She doesn't want it known," firmly, "and I prefer her wishes be respected."

Smith gave Austen an apologetic look. "Sorry, Frank."

Mary watched Austen's distress with amusement. Austen had a spinster sister, she supposed—she could just imagine the type—who probably wrote ripe horrid Gothic novels, all terror and dark battlements and cloaked sensuality, all to the constant mortification of the family.

Well, Mary thought. She should be charitable. Perhaps they were good.

She and Bysshe liked a good gothic, when they were in the mood. Bysshe had even written a couple, when he was fifteen or so.

George turned to Bysshe. "That was your own verse you quoted?"

"Yes."

"I thought perhaps it was, as I hadn't recognized it."

"Queen Mab," said Claire. "It's *very* good." She gave Bysshe a look of adoration that sent a weary despairing cry through Mary's nerves. "It's got all Bysshe's ideas in it," she said.

"And the publisher?"

"I published it myself," Bysshe said, "in an edition of seventy copies."

George raised an eyebrow. "A self-published phenomenon, forsooth. But why so few?"

"The poem is a political statement in accordance with Mr. Godwin's *Political Justice.* Were it widely circulated, the government might act to suppress it, and to prosecute the publisher." He gave a shudder. "With people like Lord Ellenborough in office, I think it best to take no chances."

"Lord Ellenborough is a great man," said Captain Austen firmly. Mary was surprised at his emphatic tone. "He led for Mr. Warren Hastings, do you know, during his trial, and that trial lasted seven years or more and ended in acquittal. Governor Hastings did me many a good turn in India—he was the making of me. I'm sure I owe Lord Ellenborough my purest gratitude."

Bysshe gave Austen a serious look. "Lord Ellenborough sent Daniel Eaton to prison for publishing Thomas Paine," he said. "And he sent Leigh Hunt to prison for publishing the truth about the Prince Regent."

"One an atheist," Austen scowled, "the other a pamphleteer."

"Why, so am I both," said Bysshe sweetly, and, smiling, sipped his spring water. Mary wanted to clap aloud.

"It is the duty of the Lord Chief Justice to guard the realm from subversion," said Somerset. "We were at war, you know."

"We are no longer at war," said Bysshe, "and Lord Ellenborough still sends good folk to prison."

"At least," said Mary, "he can no longer accuse reformers of being Jacobins. Not with France under the Bourbons again."

"Of course he can," Bysshe said. "Reform is an idea, and Jacobinism is an idea, and Ellenborough conceives them the same."

"But are they not?" George said.

Mary's temper flared. "Are you serious? Comparing those who seek to correct injustice with those who—"

"Who cut the heads off everyone with whom they disagreed?" George interrupted. "I'm perfectly serious. Robespierre was the very type of reformer—virtuous, sober, sedate, educated, a spotless private life. And how many thousands did he murder?" He jabbed his fork at Bysshe again, and Mary restrained the impulse to slap it out of his hand. "You may not like Ellenborough's sentencing, but a few hours in the pillory or a few months in prison ain't the same as beheading. And that's what reform in England would come to in the end—mobs and demagogues heaping up death, and then a dictator like Cromwell, or worse luck Bonaparte, to end liberty for a whole generation."

"I do not look to the French for a model," said Bysshe, "but rather to America."

"So did the French," said George, "and look what *they* got."

"If France had not desperately needed reform," Bysshe said, "there would have been nothing so violent as their revolution. If England reforms itself, there need be no violence."

"Ah. So if the government simply resigns, and frame-breakers and agitators and democratic philosophers and wandering poets take their place, then things shall be well in England."

"Things will be better in any case," Bysshe said quietly, "than they are now."

"Exactly!" Claire said.

George gave his companions a knowing look. *See how I humor this vagabond?* Mary read. Loathing stirred her heart.

Bysshe could read a look as well as Mary. His face darkened. "Please understand me," he said. "I do not look for immediate change, nor do I preach violent revolution. Mr. Godwin has corrected that error in my thought. There will be little amendment for years to come. But Ellenborough is old, and the King is old and mad, and the Regent and his loathsome brothers are not young . . ." He smiled. "I will outlive them, will I not?"

George looked at him. "Will you outlive me, sir? I am not yet thirty."

"I am three-and-twenty." Mildly. "I believe the odds favor me."

Bysshe and the others laughed, while George looked cynical and dyspeptic. *Used to being the young cavalier,* Mary thought. *He's not so young any longer— how much longer will that pretty face last?*

"And of course advance of science may turn this debate irrelevant," Bysshe went on. "Mr. Godwin calculates that with the use of mechanical aids, people may reduce their daily labor to an hour or two, to the general benefit of all."

"But you oppose such machines, don't ye?" George said. "You support the Luddites, I assume?"

"Ay, but—"

"And the frame-breakers are destroying the machines that have taken their livelihood, aren't they? So where is your general benefit, then?"

Mary couldn't hold it in any longer. She slapped her hand down on the table, and George and Bysshe started. "The riots occur because the profits of the looms were not used to benefit the weavers, but to enrich the mill owners! Were the owners to share their profits with the weavers, there would have been no disorder."

George gave her a civil bow. "Your view of human nature is generous," he said, "if you expect a mill owner to support the families of those who are not even his employees."

"It would be for the good of all, wouldn't it?" Bysshe said. "If he does not want his mills threatened and frames broken."

"It sounds like extortion wrapped in pretty philosophy."

"The mill owners will pay one way or another," Mary pointed out. "They can pay taxes to the government to suppress the Luddites with militia and dragoons, or they can have the goodwill of the people, and let the swords and muskets rust."

"They will buy the swords every time," George said. "They are useful in ways other than suppressing disorder, such as securing trade routes and the safety of the nation." He put on a benevolent face. "You must forgive me, but your view of humanity is too benign. You do not account for the violence and passion that are in the very heart of man, and which institutions such as law and religion are intended to help control. And when science serves the passions, only tragedy can result—when I think of science, I think of the science of Dr. Guillotin."

"We are fallen," said Captain Austen. "Eden will never be within our grasp."

"The passions are a problem, but I think they can be turned to good," said Bysshe. "That is—" He gave an apologetic smile. "That is the aim of my current work. To use the means of poetry to channel the passions to a humane and beneficent aim."

"I offer you my very best wishes," condescendingly, "but I fear mankind will disappoint you. Passions are—" George gave Mary an insolent, knowing smile. "—are the downfall of many a fine young virtue."

Mary considered hitting him in the face. Bysshe seemed not to have noticed George's look, nor Mary's reaction. "Mr. Godwin ventured the thought that dreams are the source of many irrational passions," he mused. "He believes that should we ever find a way of doing without sleep, the passions would fall away."

"Ay!" barked George. "Through enervation, if nothing else."

The others laughed. Mary decided she had had enough, and rose.

"I shall withdraw," she said. "The journey has been fatiguing."

The gentlemen, Bysshe excepted, rose to their feet. "Good night, Maie," he said. "I will stay for a while, I think."

"As you like, Bysshe." Mary looked at her sister. "Jane? I mean Claire? Will you come with me?"

"Oh, no." Quickly. "I'm not at all tired."

Annoyance stiffened Mary's spine. "As you like," she said.

George bowed toward her, picked a candle off the table, and offered her an arm. "May I light you up the stair? I should like to apologize for my temerity in contradicting such a charming lady." He offered his brightest smile. "I think *my* poor virtue will extend that far, yes?"

She looked at him coldly—she couldn't think it customary, even in George's circles, to escort a woman to her bedroom.

Damn it anyway. "My lord," she said, and put her arm through his.

Jerome Bonaparte made a flying leap from the table and landed on George's shoulder. It clung to his long auburn hair, screamed, and made a face, and the others laughed. Mary considered the thought of being escorted up to bed by a lord and a monkey, and it improved her humor.

"Goodnight, gentlemen," Mary said. "Claire."

The gentlemen reseated themselves and George took Mary up the stairs. They were so narrow and steep that they couldn't go up abreast; George, with the candle, went first, and Mary, holding his hand, came up behind. Her door was the first up the stairs; she put her hand on the wooden door handle and turned to face her escort. The monkey leered at her from his shoulder.

"I thank you for your company, my lord," she said. "I fear your journey was a little short."

"I wished a word with you," softly, "a little apart from the others."

Mary stiffened. To her annoyance her heart gave a lurch. "What word is that?" she asked.

His expression was all affability. "I am sensible to the difficulties that you and your sister must be having. Without money in a foreign country, and with your only protector a man—" He hesitated. Jerome Bonaparte, jealous for his attention, tugged at his hair. "A charming man of noble ideals, surely, but without money."

"I thank you for your concern, but it is misplaced," Mary said. "Claire and I are perfectly well."

"Your health ain't my worry," he said. Was he deliberately misunderstanding? Mary wondered in fury. "I worry for your future—you are on an adventure with a man who cannot support you, cannot see you safe home, cannot marry you."

"Bysshe and I do not wish to marry." The words caught at her heart. "We are free."

"And the damage to your reputation in society—" he began, and came up short when she burst into laughter. He looked severe, while the monkey mocked him from his shoulder. "You may laugh now, Miss Godwin, but there are those who will use this adventure against you. Political enemies of your father at the very least."

"That isn't why I was laughing. I am the daughter of William Godwin and Mary Wollstonecraft—I *have* no reputation! It's like being the natural daughter of Lucifer and the Scarlet Woman of Babylon. Nothing is expected of us, nothing at all. Society has given us license to do as we please. We were dead to them from birth."

He gave her a narrow look. "But you have at least a little concern for the proprieties—why else travel pseudonymously?"

Mary looked at him in surprise. "What d'you mean?"

He smiled. "Give me a little credit, Miss Godwin. When you call your sister *Jane* half the time, and your protector calls you *May . . .* "

Mary laughed again. "*The* Maie—Maie for short—is one of Bysshe's pet names for me. The other is Pecksie."

"Oh."

"And Jane is my sister's given name, which she has always hated. Last year she decided to call herself Clara or Claire—this week it is Claire."

Jerome Bonaparte began to yank at George's ear, and George made a face, pulled the monkey from his shoulder, and shook it with mock ferocity. Again he spoke in the cracked Scots dowager's voice. "Are ye sae donsie wicked, creeture? Tae Elba w'ye!"

Mary burst into laughter. George gave her a careless grin, then returned the monkey to his shoulder. It sat and regarded Mary with bright, wise eyes.

"Miss Godwin, I am truly concerned for you, believe else of me what you will."

Mary's laughter died away. She took the candle from his hand. "Please, my lord. My sister and I are perfectly safe in Mr. Shelley's company."

"You will not accept my protection? I will freely give it."

"We do not need it. I thank you."

"Will you not take a loan, then? To see you safe across the Channel? Mr. Shelley may pay me back if he is ever in funds."

Mary shook her head.

A little of the old insolence returned to George's expression. "Well. I have done what I could."

"Good night, Lord Newstead."

"Good night."

Mary readied herself for bed and climbed atop the soft mattress. She tried to read her Italian grammar, but the sounds coming up the stairway were a distraction. There was loud conversation, and singing, and then Claire's fine voice, unaccompanied, rising clear and sweet up the narrow stair.

Torcere, Mary thought, looking fiercely at her book, *attorcere, rattorcere, scontorcere, torcere.*

Twist. Twist, twist, twist, twist.

Claire finished, and there was loud applause. Bysshe came in shortly afterwards. His eyes sparkled and his color was high. "We were singing," he said.

"I heard."

"I hope we didn't disturb you." He began to undress.

Mary frowned at her book. "You did."

"And I argued some more with Byron." He looked at her and smiled. "Imagine it—if we could convert Byron! Bring one of the most famous men in the world to our views."

She gave him a look. "I can think of nothing more disastrous to our cause than to have him lead it."

"Byron's famous. And he's a splendid man." He looked at her with a self-conscious grin. "I have a pair of byrons, you know, back home. I think I have a good turn of ankle, but the things are the very devil to lace. You really need servants for it."

"He's Newstead now. Not Byron. I wonder if they'll have to change the name of the boot?"

"Why would he change his name, d'you suppose? After he'd become famous with it."

"Wellington became famous as Wellesley."

"Wellington *had* to change his name. His brother was *already* Lord Wellesley." He approached the bed and smiled down at her. "He likes you."

"He likes any woman who crosses his path. Or so I understand."

Bysshe crawled into the bed and put his arm around her, the hand resting warmly on her belly. He smelled of the tobacco he'd been smoking with George. She put her hand atop his, feeling on the third finger the gold wedding ring he still wore. Dissatisfaction crackled through her. "You are free, you know." He spoke softly into her ear. "You can be with Byron if you wish."

Mary gave him an irritated look. "I don't *wish* to be with Byron. I want to be with you."

"But you *may*," whispering, the hand stroking her belly, "be with Byron if you want."

Temper flared through Mary. "I don't *want* Byron!" she said. "And I don't want Mr. Thomas Jefferson Hogg, or any of your other friends!"

He seemed a little hurt. "Hogg's a splendid fellow."

"Hogg tried to seduce your wife, and he's tried to seduce me. And I don't understand how he remains your best friend."

"Because we agree on everything, and I hold him no malice where his intent was not malicious." Bysshe gave her a searching look. "I only want you to be free. If we're not free, our love is chained, chained absolutely, and all ruined. I can't live that way—I found that out with Harriet."

She sighed, put her arm around him, drew her fingers through his tangled hair. He rested his head on her shoulder and looked up into her eyes. "I want to be *free* to be with you," Mary told him. "Why will that not suit?"

"It suits." He kissed her cheek. "It suits very well." He looked up at her happily. "And if Harriet joins us in Brussels, with a little money, then all shall be perfect."

Mary gazed at him, utterly unable to understand how he could think his wife would join them, or why, for that matter, he thought it a good idea.

He misses his little boy, she thought. *He wants to be with him.*

The thought rang hollow in her mind.

He kissed her again, his hand moving along her belly, touching her lightly. "My golden-haired Maie." The hand cupped her breast. Her breath hissed inward.

"Careful," she said. "I'm very tender there."

"I will be nothing but tenderness." The kisses reached her lips. "I desire nothing but tenderness for you."

She turned to him, let his lips brush against hers, then press more firmly. Sensation, a little painful, flushed her breast. His tongue touched hers. Desire rose and she put her arms around him.

The door opened and Claire came in, chattering of George while she undressed. Mood broken, tenderness broken, there was nothing to do but sleep.

"Come and look," Mary said, "here's a cat eating roses; she'll turn into a woman, when beasts eat these roses they turn into men and women." But there was no one in the cottage, only the sound of the wind.

Fear touched her, cold on the back of her neck.

She stepped into the cottage, and suddenly there was something blocking the sun that came through the windows, an enormous figure, monstrous and black and hungry . . .

Nausea and the sounds of swordplay woke her. A dog was barking maniacally. Mary rose from the bed swiftly and wrapped her shawl around herself. The room was hot and stuffy, and her gorge rose. She stepped to the window, trying not to vomit, and opened the pane to bring in fresh air.

Coolness touched her cheeks. Below in the courtyard of the inn was Pásmány, the fencing teacher, slashing madly at his pupil, Byron. Newstead. *George,* she reminded herself, she would remember he was *George.*

And serve him right.

She dragged welcome morning air into her lungs as the two battled below her. George was in his shirt, planted firmly on his strong, muscular legs, his pretty face set in an expression of intent calculation. Pásmány flung himself at the man, darting in and out, his sword almost fluid in its movement. They were using straight heavy sabers, dangerous even if unsharpened, and no protective equipment at all. A huge black dog, tied to the vermilion wheel of a big dark-blue barouche, barked at the both of them without cease.

Nausea swam over Mary; she closed her eyes and clutched the windowsill. The ringing of the swords suddenly seemed very far away.

"Are they fighting?" Claire's fingers clutched her shoulder. "Is it a duel? Oh, it's *Byron!*"

Mary abandoned the window and groped her way to the bed. Sweat beaded on her forehead. Bysshe blinked muzzily at her from his pillow.

"I must go down and watch," said Claire. She reached for her clothing and, hopping, managed to dress without missing a second of the action outside. She grabbed a hairbrush on her way out the door and was arranging her hair on the run even before the door slammed behind her.

"Whatever is happening?" Bysshe murmured. She reached blindly for his hand and clutched it.

"Bysshe," she gasped. "I am with child. I must be."

"I shouldn't think so." Calmly. "We've been using every precaution." He touched her cheek. His hand was cool. "It's the travel and excitement. Perhaps a bad egg."

Nausea blackened her vision and bent her double. Sweat fell in stately rhythm from her forehead to the floor. "This can't be a bad egg," she said. "Not day after day."

"Poor Maie." He nestled behind her, stroked her back and shoulders. "Perhaps there is a flaw in the theory," he said. "Time will tell."

No turning back, Mary thought. She had *wanted* there to be no turning back, to burn every bridge behind her, commit herself totally, as her mother had, to her beliefs. And now she'd succeeded—she and Bysshe were linked forever, linked by the child in her womb. Even if they parted, if—free, as they both wished to be—he abandoned this union, there would still be that link, those bridges burnt, her mother's defiant inheritance fulfilled . . .

Perhaps there is a flaw in the theory. She wanted to laugh and cry at once.

Bysshe stroked her, his thoughts his own, and outside the martial clangor went on and on.

It was some time before she could dress and go down to the common rooms. The sabre practice had ended, and Bysshe and Claire were already breaking their fast with Somerset, Smith, and Captain Austen. The thought of breakfast made Mary ill, so she wandered outside into the courtyard, where the two breathless swordsmen, towels draped around their necks, were sitting on a bench drinking water, with a tin dipper, from an old wooden bucket. The huge black dog barked, foaming, as she stepped out of the inn, and the two men, seeing her, rose.

"Please sit, gentlemen," she said, waving them back to their bench; she walked across the courtyard to the big open gate and stepped outside. She leaned against the whitewashed stone wall and took deep breaths of the country air. Sweet-smelling wildflowers grew in the verges of the highway. Prosperous-looking villagers nodded pleasantly as they passed about their errands.

"Looking for your haunted house, Miss Godwin?"

George's inevitable voice grated on her ears. She looked at him over her shoulder. "My intention was simply to enjoy the morning."

"I hope I'm not spoiling it."

Reluctant courtesy rescued him from her own riposting tongue. "How was the Emperor's bed?" she said finally.

He stepped out into the road. "I believe I slept better than he did, and longer." He smiled at her. "No ghosts walked."

"But you still fought a battle after your sleep."

"A far, far better one. Waterloo was not something I would care to experience more than once."

"I shouldn't care to experience it even the first time."

"Well. You're female, of course." All offhand, unaware of her rising hackles. He looked up and down the highway.

"D'ye know, this is the first time I've seen this road in peace. I first rode it north during the retreat from Quatre Bras, a miserable rainy night, and then there was the chase south after Boney the night of Waterloo, then later the advance with the army to Paris . . ." He shook his head. "It's a pleasant road, ain't it? Much better without the armies."

"Yes."

"We went along there." His hand sketched a line across the opposite horizon. "This road was choked with retreating French, so we went around them. With two squadrons of Vandeleur's lads, the twelfth, the Prince of Wales's Own, all I could find once the French gave way. I knew Boney would be running, and I knew it had to be along this road. I had to find him, make certain he would never trouble our peace. Find him for England." He dropped right fist into left palm.

"Boney'd left two battalions of the Guard to hold us, but I went around them. I knew the Prussians would be after him, too, and their mounts were fresher. So we drove on through the night, jumping fences, breaking down hedges, galloping like madmen, and then we found him at Genappe. The bridge was so crammed with refugees that he couldn't get his barouche across."

Mary watched carefully as George, uninvited, told the story that he must, by now, have told a hundred times, and wondered why he was telling it now to someone with such a clear distaste for things military. His color was high, and he was still breathing hard from his exercise; sweat gleamed on his immaculate forehead and matted his shirt; she could see the pulse throbbing in his throat. Perhaps the swordplay and sight of the road had brought the memory back; perhaps he was merely, after all, trying to impress her.

A female, of course. Damn the man.

"They'd brought a white Arab up for him to ride away," George went on. "His Chasseurs of the Guard were close around. I told each trooper to mark his enemy as we rode up—we came up at a slow trot, in silence, our weapons sheathed. In the dark the enemy took us for French—our uniforms were similar enough. I gave the signal—we drew pistols and carbines—half the French saddles were emptied in an instant. Some poor lad of a cornet tried to get in my way, and I cut him up through the teeth. Then there he was—the Emperor. With one foot in the stirrup, and Roustam the Mameluke ready to boost him into the saddle."

A tigerish, triumphant smile spread across George's face. His eyes were focused down the road, not seeing her at all. "I put my dripping point in his face, and for the life of me I couldn't think of any French to say except to tell him to sit down. *'Asseyez-vous!'* I ordered, and he gave me a sullen look and sat down, right down in the muddy roadway, with the carbines still cracking around us and bullets flying through the air. And I thought, He's finished. He's done. There's nothing left of him now. We finished off his bodyguard—they hadn't a chance after our first volley. The French soldiers around us thought we were the Prussian advance guard, and they were running as fast as their legs could carry them. Either they didn't know we had their Emperor or they didn't care. So we dragged Boney's barouche off the road, and dragged Boney with it, and ten minutes later the Prussians galloped up—the Death's Head Hussars under Gneisenau, all in black and silver, riding like devils. But the devils had lost the prize."

Looking at the wild glow in George's eyes Mary realized that she'd been wrong—the story was not for her at all, but for *him*. For George. He needed it somehow, this affirmation of himself, the enunciated remembrance of his moment of triumph.

But why? Why did he need it?

She realized his eyes were on her. "Would you like to see the coach, Miss Godwin?" he asked. The question surprised her.

"It's here?"

"I kept it." He laughed. "Why not? It was mine. What Captain Austen would call a fair prize of war." He offered her his arm. She took it, curious about what else she might discover.

The black mastiff began slavering at her the second she set foot inside the courtyard. Its howls filled the air. "Hush, Picton," George said, and walked straight to the big gold-trimmed blue coach with vermilion wheels. The door had the Byron arms and the Latin motto CREDE BYRON.

Should she believe him? Mary wondered. And if so, how much?

"This is Bonaparte's?" she said.

"Was, Miss Godwin. Till June sixteenth last. *Down,* Picton!" The dog lunged at him, and he wrestled with it, laughing, until it calmed down and began to fawn on him.

George stepped to the door and opened it. "The Imperial symbols are still on the lining, as you see." The door and couch were lined with rich purple, with golden bees and the letter N worked in heavy gold embroidery. "Fine Italian leatherwork," he said. "Drop-down secretaries so that the great man could write or dictate on the march. Holsters for pistols." He knocked on the coach's polished side. "Bulletproof. There are steel panels built in, just in case any of the Great Man's subjects decided to imitate Marcus Brutus." He smiled. "I was glad for that steel in Paris, I assure you, with Bonapartist assassins lurking under every tree." A mischievous gleam entered his eye. "And last, the best thing of all." He opened a compartment under one of the seats and withdrew a solid silver chamber pot. "You'll notice it still bears the imperial *N.*"

"Vanity in silver."

"Possibly. Or perhaps he was afraid one of his soldiers would steal it if he didn't mark it for his own."

Mary looked at the preposterous object and found herself laughing. George looked pleased and stowed the chamber pot in its little cabinet. He looked at her with his head cocked to one side. "You will not reconsider my offer?"

"No." Mary stiffened. "Please don't mention it again."

The mastiff Picton began to howl again, and George seized its collar and told it to behave itself. Mary turned to see Claire walking toward them.

"Won't you be joining us for breakfast, my lord?"

George straightened. "Perhaps a crust or two. I'm not much for breakfast."

Still fasting, Mary thought. "It would make such sense for you to give up meat, you know," she said. "Since you deprive yourself of food anyway."

"I prefer not to deny myself pleasure, even if the quantities are necessarily restricted."

"Your swordplay was magnificent."

"Thank you. Cavalry style, you know—all slash and dash. But I *am* good, for a' that."

"I know you're busy, but—" Claire bit her lip. "Will you take us to Waterloo?"

"Claire!" cried Mary.

Claire gave a nervous laugh. "Truly," she said. "I'm absolutely with child to see Waterloo."

George looked at her, his eyes intent. "Very well," he said. "We'll be driving through it in any case. And Captain Austen has expressed an interest."

Fury rose in Mary's heart. "Claire, how *dare* you impose—"

"Ha' ye nae pity for the puir lassie?" The Scots voice was mock-severe. "Ye shallnae keep her fra' her Waterloo."

Claire's Waterloo, Mary thought, was exactly what she wanted to keep her from.

George offered them his exaggerated, flourishing bow. "If you'll excuse me, ladies, I must give the necessary orders."

He strode through the door. Pásmány followed, the swords tucked under his arm. Claire gave a little joyous jump, her shoes scraping on cobbles. "I can hardly believe it," she said. "Byron showing us Waterloo!"

"I can't believe it either," Mary said. She sighed wearily and headed for the dining room.

Perhaps she would dare to sip a little milk.

They rode out in Napoleon's six-horse barouche, Claire, Mary, and Bysshe inside with George, and Smith, Somerset, and Captain Austen sharing the outside rear seat. The leather top with its bulletproof steel inserts had been folded away and the inside passengers could all enjoy the open air. The barouche wasn't driven by a coachman up top, but by three postboys who rode the right-hand horses, so there was nothing in front to interrupt the view. Bysshe's mule and little carriage, filled with bags and books, ate dust behind along with the officers' baggage coaches, all driven by George's servants.

The men talked of war and Claire listened to them with shining eyes. Mary concentrated on enjoying the shape of the low hills with their whitewashed farmhouses and red tile roofs, the cut fields of golden rye stubble, the smell of wildflowers and the sound of birdsong. It was only when the carriage passed a walled farm, its whitewash marred by bullets and cannon shot, that her reverie was marred by the thought of what had happened here.

"La Haie Sainte," George remarked. "The King's German Legion held it throughout the battle, even after they'd run out of ammunition. I sent Mercer's horse guns to keep the French from the walls, else Lord knows what would have happened." He stood in the carriage, looked left and right, frowned. "These roads we're about to pass were sunken—an obstacle to both sides, but mainly to the French. They're filled in now. Mass graves."

"The French were cut down in heaps during their cavalry attack," Somerset added. "The piles were eight feet tall, men and horses."

"How gruesome!" laughed Claire.

"Turn right, Swinson," said George.

Homemade souvenir stands had been set up at the crossroads. Prosperous-looking rustics hawked torn uniforms, breastplates, swords, muskets, bayonets. Somerset scowled at them. "They must have made a fortune looting the dead."

"And the living," said Smith. "Some of our poor wounded weren't brought in till two days after the battle. Many had been stripped naked by the peasants."

A young man ran up alongside the coach, shouting in French. He explained he had been in the battle, a guide to the great Englishman Lord Byron, and would guide them over the field for a few guilders.

"Never heard of you," drawled George, and dismissed him. "Hey! Swinson! Pull up here."

The postboys pulled up their teams. George opened the door of the coach and strolled to one of the souvenir stands. When he returned it was with a

French breastplate and helmet. Streaks of rust dribbled down the breastplate, and the helmet's horsehair plume smelled of mildew.

"I thought we could take a few shots at it," George said. "I'd like to see whether armor provides any protection at all against bullets—I suspect not. There's a movement afoot at Whitehall to give breastplates to the Household Brigade, and I suspect they ain't worth the weight. If I can shoot a few holes in this with my Mantons, I may be able to prove my point."

They drove down a rutted road of soft earth. It was lined with thorn hedges, but most of them had been broken down during the battle and there were long vistas of rye stubble, the gentle sloping ground, the pattern of plow and harvest. Occasionally the coach wheels grated on something, and Mary remembered they were moving along a mass grave, over the decaying flesh and whitening bones of hundreds of horses and men. A cloud passed across the sun, and she shivered.

"Can ye pull through the hedge, Swinson?" George asked. "I think the ground is firm enough to support us—no rain for a few days at least." The lead postboy studied the hedge with a practiced eye, then guided the lead team through a gap in it.

The barouche rocked over exposed roots and broken limbs, then ground onto a rutted sward of green grass, knee-high, that led gently down into the valley they'd just crossed. George stood again, his eyes scanning the ground. "Pull up over there," he said, pointing, and the coachman complied.

"Here you can see where the battle was won," George said. He tossed his clanging armor out onto the grass, opened the coach door and stepped out himself. The others followed, Mary reluctantly. George pointed with one elegant hand at the ridge running along the opposite end of the valley from their own, a half mile opposite.

"Napoleon's grand battery," he said. "Eighty guns, many of them twelve-pounders—Boney called them his daughters. He was an artillerist, you know, and he always prepared his attacks with a massed bombardment. The guns fired for an hour and put our poor fellows through hell. Bylandt's Dutchmen were standing in the open, right where we are now, and the guns broke 'em entirely.

"Then the main attack came, about two o'clock. Count d'Erlon's corps, sixteen thousand strong, arrayed twenty-five men deep with heavy cavalry on the wings. They captured La Haye and Papelotte, those farms over there on the left, and rolled up this ridge with drums beating the *pas de charge* . . ."

George turned. There was a smile on his face. Mary watched him closely—the pulse was beating like d'Erlon's drums in his throat, and his color was high. He was loving every second of this.

He went on, describing the action, and against her will Mary found herself seeing it, Picton's division lying in wait, prone on the reverse slope, George bringing the heavy cavalry up, the cannons banging away. Picton's men rising, firing their volleys, following with the bayonet. The Highlanders screaming in Gaelic, their plumes nodding as they drew their long broadswords and plunged into the fight, the pipers playing "Johnnie Cope" amid all the screams and clatter. George leading the Household and Union Brigades against the enemy cavalry, the huge grain-fed English hunters driving back the chargers from Normandy. And then George falling on d'Erlon's flanks, driving the French in a frightened mob all the way back across the valley while the British horsemen slashed at their backs. The French gunners of the grand battery unable to fire for fear of hitting their own men, and then dying themselves under the British sabres.

Mary could sense as well the things George left out. The sound of steel grating on bone. Wails and moans of the wounded, the horrid challenging roars of the horses. And in the end, a valley filled with stillness, a carpet of bodies and pierced flesh . . .

George gave a long sigh. "Our cavalry are brave, you know, far too brave for their own good. And the officers get their early training in steeplechases and the hunt, and their instinct is to ride straight at the objective at full gallop, which is absolutely the worst thing cavalry can ever do. After Slade led his command to disaster back in the Year Twelve, the Duke realized he could only commit cavalry at his peril. In Spain we finally trained the horse to maneuver and to make careful charges, but the Union and Household troops hadn't been in the Peninsula, and didn't know the drill. . . . I drove myself mad in the weeks before the battle, trying to beat the recall orders into them." He laughed self-consciously. "My heart was in my mouth during the whole charge, I confess, less with fear of the enemy than with terror my own men would run mad. But they answered the trumpets, all but the Inniskillings, who wouldnae listen—the Irish blood was up—and while they ran off into the valley, the rest of us stayed in the grand battery. Sabred the gunners, drove off the limbers with the ready ammunition—and where we could we took the wheels off the guns, and rolled 'em back to our lines like boys with hoops. And the Inniskillings—" He shook his head. "They ran wild into the enemy lines, and Boney loosed his lancers at 'em, and they died almost to a man. I had to watch from the middle of the battery, with my officers begging to be let slip again and rescue their comrades, and I had to forbid it."

There were absolute tears in George's eyes. Mary watched in fascination and wondered if this was a part of the performance, or whether he was genuinely affected—but then she saw that Bysshe's eyes had misted over and Somerset was wiping his eyes with his one good sleeve. So, she thought, she *could* believe Byron, at least a little.

"Well." George cleared his throat, trying to control himself. "Well. We came back across the valley herding thousands of prisoners—and that charge proved the winning stroke. Boney attacked later, of course—all his heavy cavalry came knee-to-knee up the middle, between La Haie Sainte and Hougoumont," gesturing to the left with one arm, "we had great guns and squares of infantry to hold them, and my heavies to counterattack. The Prussians were pressing the French at Plancenoit and Papelotte. Boney's last throw of the dice sent the Old Guard across the valley after sunset, but our Guards under Maitland held them, and Colborne's Fifty-second and the Belgian Chasseurs got round their flanks, and after they broke I let the Household and Union troopers have their head— we swept 'em away. Sabred and trampled Boney's finest troops right in front of his eyes, all in revenge for the brave, mad Inniskillings—the only time his Guard ever failed in attack, and it marked the end of his reign. We were blown by the end of it, but Boney had nothing left to counterattack with. I knew he would flee. So I had a fresh horse brought up and went after him."

"So you won the battle of Waterloo!" said Claire.

George gave her a modest look that, to Mary, seemed false as the very devil. "I was privileged to have a decisive part. But 'twas the Duke that won the battle. We all fought at his direction."

"But you captured Napoleon and ended the Empire!"

He smiled. "That I did do, lassie, ay."

"Bravo!" Claire clapped her hands.

Harry Smith glanced up with bright eyes. "D'ye know, George," he said, "pleased as I am to hear this modest recitation of your accomplishments, I find precious little mention in your discourse of the *infantry*. I seem to remember fighting a few Frenchies myself, down Hougoumont way, with Reille's whole corps marching down on us, and I believe I can recollect in my dim footsoldier's mind that I stood all day under cannonshot and bursting mortar bombs, and that Kellerman's heavy cavalry came wave after wave all afternoon, with the Old Guard afterward as a lagniappe . . ."

"I am pleased that you had some little part," George said, and bowed from his slim cavalry waist.

"Your lordship's condescension does you more credit than I can possibly express." Returning the bow.

George reached out and gave Smith's ear an affectionate tweak. "May I continue my tale? And then we may travel to Captain Harry's part of the battlefield, and he will remind us of whatever small role it was the footsoldiers played."

George went through the story of Napoleon's capture again. It was the same, sentiment for sentiment, almost word for word. Mary wandered away, the fat moist grass turning the hem of her skirt green. Skylarks danced through the air, trilling as they went. She wandered by the old broken thorn hedge and saw wild roses blossoming in it, and she remembered the wild roses planted on her mother's grave.

She thought of George Gordon Noël with tears in his eyes, and the way the others had wanted to weep—even Bysshe, who hadn't been there—and all for the loss of some Irishmen who, had they been crippled or out of uniform or begging for food or employment, these fine English officers would probably have turned into the street to starve . . .

She looked up at the sound of footsteps. Harry Smith walked up and nodded pleasantly. "I believe I have heard George give this speech," he said.

"So have I. Does he give it often?"

"Oh yes." His voice dropped, imitated George's limpid dramatics. *"He's finished. He's done. There's nothing left of him now."* Mary covered amusement with her hand. "Though the tale has improved somewhat since the first time," Smith added. "In this poor infantryman's opinion."

Mary gave him a careful look. "Is he all he seems to think he is?"

Smith gave a thin smile. "Oh, ay. The greatest cavalryman of our time, to be sure. Without doubt a genius. *Chevalier sans peur et*—well, I won't say *sans reproche*. Not quite." His brow contracted as he gave careful thought to his next words. "He purchased his way up to colonel—that would be with Lady Newstead's money—but since then he's earned his spurs."

"He truly is talented, then."

"Truly. But of course he's lucky, too. If Le Marchant hadn't died at Salamanca, George wouldn't have been able to get his heavy brigade, and if poor General Cotton hadn't been shot by our own sentry George wouldn't have got all the cavalry in time for Vitoria, and of course if Uxbridge hadn't run off with Wellington's sister-in-law then George might not have got command at Waterloo. . . . Young and without political influence as he is, he wouldn't have *kept* all those commands for long if he hadn't spent his every leave getting soused with that unspeakable hound, the Prince of Wales. Ay, there's been luck involved. But who won't wish for luck in his life, eh?"

"What if his runs out?"

Smith gave this notion the same careful consideration. "I don't know," he said finally. "He's fortune's laddie, but that don't mean he's without character."

"You surprise me, speaking of him so frankly."

"We've been friends since Spain. And nothing I say will matter in any case." He smiled. "Besides, hardly anyone ever asks for *my* opinion."

The sound of Claire's laughter and applause carried across the sward. Smith cocked an eye at the other party. "Boney's at sword's point, if I'm not mistaken."

"Your turn for glory."

"Ay. If anyone will listen after George's already won the battle." He held out his arm and Mary took it. "You should meet my wife. Juanita—I met her in Spain at the storming of Badajoz. The troops were carrying away the loot, but I carried her away instead." He looked at her thoughtfully. "You have a certain spirit in common."

Mary felt flattered. "Thank you, Captain Smith. I'm honored by the comparison."

They moved to another part of the battlefield. There was a picnic overlooking the château of Hougoumont that lay red-roofed in its valley next to a well-tended orchard. Part of the château had been destroyed in the battle, Smith reported, but it had been rebuilt since.

Rebuilt, Mary thought, by owners enriched by battlefield loot.

George called for his pistols and moved the cuirass a distance away, propping it up on a small slope with the helmet sitting on top. A servant brought the Mantons and loaded them, and while the others stood and watched, George aimed and fired. Claire clapped her hands and laughed, though there was no discernible effect. White gunsmoke drifted on the morning breeze. George presented his second pistol, paused to aim, fired again. There was a whining sound and a scar appeared on the shoulder of the cuirass. The other men laughed.

"That cuirassier's got you for sure!" Harry Smith said.

"May I venture a shot?" Bysshe asked. George assented.

One of George's servants reloaded the pistols while George gave Bysshe instruction in shooting. "Hold the arm out straight and use the bead to aim."

"I like keeping the elbow bent a little," Bysshe said. "Not tucked in like a duellist, but not locked, either."

Bysshe took effortless aim—Mary's heart leaped at the grace of his movement—then Bysshe paused an instant and fired. There was a thunking sound and a hole appeared in the French breastplate, directly over the heart.

"Luck!" George said.

"Yes!" Claire said. "Purest luck!"

"Not so," Bysshe said easily. "Observe the plume holder." He presented the other pistol, took briefest aim, fired. With a little whine the helmet's metal plume holder took flight and whipped spinning through the air. Claire applauded and gave a cheer.

Mary smelled powder on the gentle morning wind.

Bysshe returned the pistols to George. "Fine weapons," he said, "though I prefer an octagonal barrel, as you can sight along the top."

George smiled thinly and said nothing.

"Mr. Shelley," said Somerset, "you have the makings of a soldier."

"I've always enjoyed a good shoot," Bysshe said, "though of course I won't fire at an animal. And as for soldiering, who knows what I might have been were I not exposed to Mr. Godwin's political thought?"

There was silence at this. Bysshe smiled at George. "You shouldn't lock the elbow out," he said. "That fashion, every little motion of the body transmits itself to the weapon. If you keep the elbow bent a bit, it forms a sort of a spring to absorb involuntary muscle tremors and you'll have better control." He looked at the others gaily. "It's not for nothing I was an engineer!"

George handed the pistols to his servant for loading. "We'll fire another volley," he said. His voice was curt.

Mary watched George as the Mantons were loaded, as he presented each pistol—straight-armed—and fired again. One knocked the helmet off its perch, the other struck the breastplate at an angle and bounced off. The others laughed, and Mary could see a little muscle twitching in George's cheek.

"My turn, George," said Harry Smith, and the pistols were recharged. His first shot threw up turf, but the second punched a hole in the cuirass. "There," Smith said, "that should satisfy the Horse Guards that armor ain't worth the weight."

Somerset took his turn, firing awkwardly with his one hand, and missed both shots.

"Another volley," George said.

"We have an appointment in Brussels, George."

There was something unpleasant in his tone, and the others took hushed notice. The pistols were reloaded. George presented the first pistol at the target, and Mary could see how he was vibrating with passion, so taut his knuckles were white on the pistol-grip. His shots missed clean.

"Bad luck, George," Somerset said. His voice was calming. "Probably the bullets were deformed and didn't fly right."

"Another volley," said George."

"We have an appointment in Brussels, George."

"It can wait."

The others drew aside and clustered together while George insisted on firing several more times. "What a troublesome fellow he is," Smith muttered. Eventually George put some holes in the cuirass, collected it, and stalked to the coach, where he had the servants strap it to the rear so that he could have it sent to the Prince of Wales.

Mary sat as far away from George as possible. George's air of defiant petulance hung over the company as they started north on the Brussels road. But then Bysshe asked Claire to sing, and Claire's high, sweet voice rose above the green countryside of Brabant, and by the end of the song everyone was smiling. Mary flashed Bysshe a look of gratitude.

The talk turned to war again, battles and sieges and the dead, a long line of uniformed shadows, young, brave men who fell to the French, to accident, to camp fever. Mary had little to say on the subject that she hadn't already offered, but she listened carefully, felt the soldiers' sadness at the death of comrades, the rejoicing at victory, the satisfaction of a deadly, intricate job done well. The feelings expressed seemed fine, passionate, even a little exalted. Bysshe listened and spoke little, but gradually Mary began to feel that he was somehow included in this circle of men and that she was not—perhaps his expert pistol shooting had made him a part of this company.

A female, of course. War was a fraternity only, though the suffering it caused made no distinction as to sex.

"May I offer an observation?" Mary said.

"Of course," said Captain Austen.

"I am struck by the passion you show when speaking of your comrades and your—shall I call it your craft?"

"Please, Miss Godwin," George said. "The enlisted men may have a *craft*, if you like. We are gentlemen, and have a *profession.*"

"I intended no offense. But still—I couldn't help but observe the fine feelings you show towards your comrades, and the attention you give to the details of your . . . profession."

George seemed pleased. "Ay. Didn't I speak last night of war being full of its own kind of greatness?"

"Greatness perhaps the greater," Bysshe said, "by existing in contrast to war's wretchedness."

"Precisely," said George.

"Ay," Mary said, "but what struck me most was that you gentlemen showed such elevated passion when discussing war, such sensibility, high feeling, and utter conviction—more than I am accustomed to seeing from any . . . respectable males." Harry Smith gave an uncomfortable laugh at this characterization.

"Perhaps you gentlemen practice war," Mary went on, "because it allows free play to your passions. You are free to feel, to exist at the highest pitch of emotion. Society does not normally permit this to its members—perhaps it *must* in order to make war attractive."

Bysshe listened to her in admiration. "Brava!" he cried. "War as the sole refuge of the passions—I think you have struck the thing exactly."

Smith and Somerset frowned, working through the notion. It was impossible to read Austen's weathered countenance. But George shook his head wearily.

"Mere stuff, I'm afraid," he said. "Your analysis shows an admirable ingenuity, Miss Godwin, but I'm afraid there's no more place for passion on the battlefield than anywhere else. The poor Inniskillings had passion, but look what became of *them.*" He paused, shook his head again. "No, it's drill and cold logic and a good eye for ground that wins the battles. In my line it's not only my own sensibility that must be mastered, but those of hundreds of men and horses."

"Drill is meant to master the passions," said Captain Austen. "For in a battle, the impulse, the overwhelming passion, is to run away. This impulse must be subdued."

Mary was incredulous. "You claim not to experience these elevated passions which you display so plainly?"

George gave her the insolent, under-eyed look again. "All passions have their place, Miss Godwin. I reserve mine for the appropriate time."

Resentment snarled up Mary's spine. "Weren't those tears I saw standing in your eyes when you described the death of the Inniskillings? Do you claim that's part of your drill?"

George's color brightened. "I didn't shed those tears during the battle. At the time I was too busy damning those cursed Irishmen for the wild fools they were, and wishing I'd flogged more of them when I'd the chance."

"But wasn't Bonaparte's great success on account of his ability to inspire his soldiers and his nation?" Bysshe asked. "To raise their passions to a great pitch and conquer the world?"

"And it was the uninspired, roguey English with their drill and discipline who put him back in his place," George said. "Bonaparte should have saved the speeches and put his faith in the drill-square."

Somerset gave an amused laugh. "This conversation begins to sound like one of Mrs. West's novels of Sense and Sensibility that were so popular in the Nineties," he said. "I suppose you're too young to recall them. *A Gossip's Story*, and *The Advantages of Education*. My governess made me read them both."

Harry Smith looked at Captain Austen with glittering eyes. "In *fact*—" he began.

Captain Austen interrupted. "One is not blind to the world of feeling," he said, "but surely Reason must rule the passions, else even a good heart can be led astray."

"I can't agree," Bysshe said. "Surely it is Reason that has led us to the world of law, and property, and equity, and kingship—and all the hypocrisy that comes with upholding these artificial formations, and denying our true nature, all that deprives us of life, of true and natural goodness."

"Absolutely!" said Claire.

"It is Reason," Mary said, "which makes you deny the evidence of my senses. I *saw* your emotion, gentlemen, when you discussed your dead comrades. And I applaud it."

"It does you credit," Bysshe added.

"Do you claim not to feel anything in battle?" Mary demanded. "Nothing at all?"

George paused a moment, then answered seriously. "My concentration is very great. It is an elevated sort of apprehension, very intent. I must be aware of so much, you see—I can't afford to miss a thing. My analytical faculty is always in play."

"And that's all?" cried Mary.

That condescending half-smile returned. "There isnae time for else, lass."

"At the height of a charge? In the midst of an engagement?"

"Then especially. An instant's break in my concentration and all could be lost."

"Lord Newstead," Mary said, "I cannot credit this."

George only maintained his slight smile, knowing and superior. Mary wanted to wipe it from his face, and considered reminding him of his fractious conduct over the pistols. *How's that for control and discipline,* she thought.

But no, she decided, it would be a long, unpleasant ride to Brussels if she upset George again.

Against her inclinations, she concluded to be English, and hypocritical, and say nothing.

Bysshe found neither wife nor money in Brussels, and George arranged lodgings for them that they couldn't afford. The only option Mary could think of was to make their way to a channel port, then somehow try to talk their way to England with promise of payment once Bysshe had access to funds in London.

It was something for which she held little hope.

They couldn't afford any local diversions, and so spent their days in a graveyard, companionably reading.

And then, one morning two days after their arrival in Brussels, as Mary lay ill in their bed, Bysshe returned from an errand with money, coins clanking in a bag. "We're saved!" he said, and emptied the bag into her lap.

Mary looked at the silver lying on the comforter and felt her anxiety ease. They were old Spanish coins with the head of George III stamped over their original design, but they were real for all that. "A draft from Har . . . from your wife?" she said.

"No." Bysshe sat on the bed, frowned. "It's a loan from Byron—Lord Newstead, I mean."

"Bysshe!" Mary sat up and set bedclothes and silver flying. "You took money from that man? Why?"

He put a paternal hand on hers. "Lord Newstead convinced me it would be in your interest, and Claire's. To see you safely to England."

"We'll do well enough without his money! It's not even his to give away, it's his wife's."

Bysshe seemed hurt. "It's a loan," he said. "I'll pay it back once I'm in London." He gave a little laugh. "I'm certain he doesn't expect repayment. He thinks we're vagabonds."

"He thinks worse of us than that." A wave of nausea took her and she doubled up with a little cry. She rolled away from him. Coins rang on the floor. Bysshe put a hand on her shoulder, stroked her back.

"Poor Pecksie," he said. "Some English cooking will do you good."

"Why don't you believe me?" Tears welled in her eyes. "I'm with child, Bysshe!"

He stroked her. "Perhaps. In a week or two we'll know for certain." His tone lightened. "He invited us to a ball tonight."

"Who?"

"Newstead. The ball's in his honor, he can invite whomever he pleases. The Prince of Orange will be there, and the English ambassador."

Mary had no inclination to be the subject of one of George's freaks. "We have no clothes fit for a ball," she said, "and I don't wish to go in any case."

"We have money now. We can buy clothes." He smiled. "And Lord Newstead said he would loan you and Claire some jewels."

"Lady Newstead's jewels," Mary reminded.

"All those powerful people! Imagine it! Perhaps we can affect a conversion."

Mary glared at him over her shoulder. "That money is for our passage to England. George wants only to display us, his tame Radicals, like his tame monkey or his tame panther. We're just a caprice of his—he doesn't take either us or our arguments seriously."

"That doesn't invalidate our arguments. We can still make them." Cheerfully. "Claire and I will go, then. She's quite set on it, and I hate to disappoint her."

"I think it will do us no good to be in his company for an instant longer. I think he is . . ." She reached behind her back, took his hand, touched it. "Perhaps he is a little mad," she said.

"Byron? Really? He's *wrong*, of course, but . . ."

Nausea twisted her insides. Mary spoke rapidly, desperate to convince Bysshe of her opinions. "He so craves glory and fame, Bysshe. The war gave expression to his passions, gave him the achievement he desired—but now the war's over and he can't have the worship he needs. That's why he's taken up with us—he wants even *our* admiration. There's no future for him now—he could follow Wellington into politics but he'd be in Wellington's shadow forever that way. He's got nowhere to go."

There was a moment's silence. "I see you've been giving him much thought," Bysshe said finally.

"His marriage is a failure—he can't go back to England. His relations with women will be irregular, and—"

"*Our* relations are irregular, Maie. And it's the better for it."

"I didn't mean that. I meant he cannot love. It's worship he wants, not love. And those pretty young men he travels with—there's something peculiar in that. Something unhealthy."

"Captain Austen is neither pretty nor young."

"He's along only by accident. Another of George's freaks."

"And if you think he's a paederast, well—we should be tolerant. Plato believed it a virtue. And George always asks after *you.*"

"I do not wish to be in his thoughts."

"He is in yours." His voice was gentle. "And that is all right. You are free."

Mary's heart sank. "It is *your* child I have, Bysshe," she said.

Bysshe didn't answer. *Torcere*, she thought. *Attorcere, rattorcere.*

Claire's face glowed as she modelled her new ball gown, circling on the parlor carpet of the lodgings George had acquired for Bysshe's party. Lady Newstead's jewels glittered from Claire's fingers and throat. Bysshe, in a new coat, boots, and pantaloons, smiled approvingly from the corner.

"Very lovely, Miss Clairmont," George approved.

George was in full uniform, scarlet coat, blue facings, gold braid, and byrons laced tight. His cocked hat was laid carelessly on the mantel. George's eyes turned to Mary.

"I'm sorry you are ill, Miss Godwin," he said. "I wish you were able to accompany us."

Bysshe, Mary presumed, had told him this. Mary found no reason why she should support the lie.

"I'm not ill," she said mildly. "I simply do not wish to go—I have some pages I wish to finish. A story called *Hate.*"

George and Bysshe flushed alike. Mary, smiling, approached Claire, took her hand, admired gown and gems. She was surprised by the affect: the jewels, designed for an older woman, gave Claire a surprisingly mature look, older and more experienced than her sixteen years. Mary found herself growing uneasy.

"The seamstress was shocked when she was told I needed it tonight," Claire said. "She had to call in extra help to finish in time." She laughed. "But money mended everything!"

"For which we may thank Lord Newstead," Mary said, "and Lady Newstead to thank for the jewels." She looked up at George, who was still smouldering from her earlier shot. "I'm surprised, my lord, that she allows them to travel without her."

"Annabella has her own jewels," George said. "These are mine. I travel often without her, and as I move in the highest circles, I want to make certain that any lady who finds herself in my company can glitter with the best of them."

"How chivalrous." George cocked his head, trying to decide whether or not this was irony. Mary decided to let him wonder. She folded her hands and smiled sweetly.

"I believe it's time to leave," she said. "You don't want to keep his highness of Orange waiting."

Cloaks and hats were snatched; good-byes were said. Mary managed to whisper to Claire as she helped with her cloak.

"Be careful, Jane," she said.

Resentment glittered in Claire's black eyes. "*You* have a man," she said.

Mary looked at her. "So does Lady Newstead."

Claire glared hatred and swept out, fastening bonnet-strings. Bysshe kissed Mary's lips, George her hand. Mary prepared to settle by the fire with pen and manuscript, but before she could sit, there was a knock on the door and George rushed in.

"Forgot me hat," he said. But instead of taking it from the mantel, he walked to where Mary stood by her chair and simply looked at her. Mary's heart lurched at the intensity of his gaze.

"Your hat awaits you, my lord," she said.

"I hope you will reconsider," said George.

Mary merely looked at him, forced him to state his business. He took her hand in both of his, and she clenched her fist as his fingers touched hers.

"I ask you, Miss Godwin, to reconsider my offer to take you under my protection," George said.

Mary clenched her teeth. Her heart hammered. "I am perfectly safe with Mr. Shelley," she said.

"Perhaps not as safe as you think." She glared at him. George's eyes bored into hers. "I gave him money," he said, "and he told me you were free. Is that the act of a protector?"

Rage flamed through Mary. She snatched her hand back and came within an inch of slapping George's face.

"Do you think he's sold me to you?" she cried.

"I can conceive no other explanation," George said.

"You are mistaken and a fool." She turned away, trembling in anger, and leaned against the wall.

"I understand this may be a shock. To have trusted such a man, and then discovered—"

The wallpaper had little bees on it, Napoleon's emblem. "Can't you understand that Bysshe was perfectly literal!" she shouted. "I am free, he is free, Claire is free—free to go, or free to stay." She straightened her back, clenched her fists. "I will stay. Good-bye, Lord Newstead."

"I fear for you."

"Go away," she said, speaking to the wallpaper; and after a moment's silence she heard George turn, and take his hat from the mantel, and leave the building.

Mary collapsed into her chair. The only thing she could think was, *Poor Claire.*

2

Mary was pregnant again. She folded her hands over her belly, stood on the end of the dock, and gazed up at the Alps.

Clouds sat low on the mountains, growling. The passes were closed with avalanche and unseasonal snow, the *vaudaire* storm wind tore white from the steep waves of the gray lake, and *Ariel* pitched madly at its buoy by the waterfront, its mast-tip tracing wild figures against the sky.

The *vaudaire* had caused a "seiche"—the whole mass of the lake had shifted toward Montreux, and water levels had gone up six feet. The strange freshwater tide had cast up a line of dead fish and dead birds along the stony waterfront, all staring at Mary with brittle glass eyes.

"It doesn't look as if we'll be leaving tomorrow," Bysshe said. He and Mary stood by the waterfront, cloaked and sheltered by an umbrella. Water broke on the shore, leaped through the air, reaching for her, for Bysshe. . . . It spattered at her feet.

She thought of Harriet, Bysshe's wife, hair drifting, clothes floating like seaweed. Staring eyes like dark glass. Her hands reaching for her husband from the water.

She had been missing for weeks before her drowned body was finally found.

The *vaudaire* was supposed to be a warm wind from Italy, but its warmth was lost on Mary. It felt like the burning touch of a glacier.

"Let's go back to the hotel," Mary said. "I'm feeling a little weak."

She would deliver around the New Year unless the baby was again premature.

A distant boom reached her, was echoed, again and again, by mountains. Another avalanche. She hoped it hadn't fallen on any of the brave Swiss who were trying to clear the roads.

She and Bysshe returned to the hotel through darkening streets. It was a fine place, rather expensive, though they could afford it now. Their circumstances had improved in the last year, though at cost.

Old Sir Bysshe had died, and left Bysshe a thousand pounds per year. Harriet Shelley had drowned, bricks in her pockets. Mary had given birth to a premature daughter who had lived only two weeks. She wondered about the child she carried—she had an intuition all was not well. Death, perhaps, was stalking her baby, was stalking them all.

In payment for what? Mary wondered. What sin had they committed?

She walked through Montreux's wet streets and thought of dead glass eyes, and grasping hands, and hair streaming like seaweed. Her daughter dying alone in her cradle at night, convulsing, twitching, eyes open and tiny red face torn with mortal terror.

When Mary had come to the cradle later to nurse the baby, she had thought it in an unusually deep sleep. She hadn't realized that death had come until after dawn, when the little corpse turned cold.

Death. She and Bysshe had kissed and coupled on her mother's grave, had shivered together at the gothic delights of *Vathek*, had whispered ghost stories to one another in the dead of night till Claire screamed with hysteria. Somehow death had not really touched her before. She and Bysshe had crossed war-scarred France two years ago, sleeping in homes abandoned for fear of Cossacks, and somehow death had not intruded into their lives.

"Winter is coming," Bysshe said. "Do we wish to spend it in Geneva? I'd rather push on to Italy and be a happy salamander in the sun."

"I've had another letter from Mrs. Godwin."

Bysshe sighed. "England, then."

She sought his hand and squeezed it. Bysshe wanted the sun of Italy, but Bysshe was her sun, the blaze that kept her warm, kept her from despair. Death had not touched *him*. He flamed with life, with joy, with optimism.

She tried to stay in his radiance. Where his light banished the creeping shadows that followed her.

As they entered their hotel room they heard the wailing of an infant and found Claire trying to comfort her daughter Alba. "Where have you been?" Claire demanded. There were tears on her cheeks. "I fell asleep and dreamed you'd abandoned me! And then I cried out and woke the baby."

Bysshe moved to comfort her. Mary settled herself heavily onto a sofa.

In the small room in Montreux, with dark shadows creeping in the corners and the *vaudaire* driving against the shutters, Mary put her arms around her unborn child and willed the shade of death to keep away.

Bysshe stopped short in the midst of his afternoon promenade. "Great heavens," he said. His tone implied only mild surprise—he was so filled with life and certitude that he took most of life shocks purely in stride.

When Mary looked up, she gasped and her heart gave a crash.

It was a barouche—*the* barouche. Vermilion wheels, liveried postboys wearing muddy slickers, armorial bearings on the door, the bulletproof top raised to keep out the storm. Baggage piled on platforms fore and aft.

Rolling past as Mary and Bysshe stood on the tidy Swiss sidewalk and stared. CREDE BYRON, Mary thought viciously. As soon credit Lucifer.

The gray sky lowered as they watched the barouche grind past, steel-rimmed wheels thundering on the cobbles. And then a window dropped on its leather strap, and someone shouted something to the postboys. The words were lost in the *vaudaire*, but the postboys pulled the horses to a stop. The door opened and George appeared, jamming a round hat down over his auburn hair. His jacket was a little tight, and he appeared to have gained a stone or more since Mary had last seen him. He walked toward Bysshe and Mary, and Mary tried not to stiffen with fury at the sight of him.

"Mr. Omnibus! *Ti kánete?*"

"Very well, thank you."

"Miss Godwin." George bowed, clasped Mary's hand. She closed her fist, reminded herself that she hated him.

"I'm Mrs. Shelley now."

"My felicitations," George said.

George turned to Bysshe. "Are the roads clear to the west?" he asked. "I and my companion must push on to Geneva on a matter of urgency."

"The roads have been closed for three days," Bysshe said. "There have been both rockslides and avalanches near Chexbres."

"That's what they told me in Vevey. There was no lodging there, so I came here, even though it's out of our way." George pressed his lips together, a pale line. He looked over his shoulder at the coach, at the mountainside, at the dangerous weather. "We'll have to try to force our way through tomorrow," he said. "Though it will be damned hard."

"It shouldn't," Bysshe said. "Not in a heavy coach like that."

George looked grim. "It was unaccountably dangerous just getting here," he said.

"Stay till the weather is better," Bysshe said, smiling. "You can't be blamed if the weather holds you up."

Mary hated Bysshe for that smile, even though she knew he had reasons to be obliging.

Just as she had reasons for hating.

"Nay." George shook his head, and a little Scots fell out. "I cannae bide."

"You might make it on a mule."

"I have a lady with me." Shortly. "Mules are out of the question."

"A boat . . . ?"

"Perhaps if the lady is superfluous," Mary interrupted, "you could leave her behind, and carry out your errand on a mule, alone."

The picture was certainly an enjoyable one.

George looked at her, visibly mastered his unspoken reply, then shook his head.

"She must come."

"Lord Newstead," Mary went on, "would you like to see your daughter? She is not superfluous either, and she is here."

George glanced nervously at the coach, then back. "Is Claire here as well?"

"Yes."

George looked grim. "This is not . . . a good time."

Bysshe summoned an unaccustomed gravity. "I think, my lord," Bysshe said, "there may never be a better time. You have not been within five hundred miles of your daughter since her birth. You are on an urgent errand and may not tarry—very well. But you must spend a night here, and can't press on till morning. There will never be a better moment."

George looked at him stony-eyed, then nodded. "What hotel?"

"La Royale."

He smiled. "Royal, eh? A pretty sentiment for the Genevan Republic."

"We're in Vaud, not Geneva."

"Still not over the border?" George gave another nervous glance over his shoulder. "I need to set a faster pace."

His long hair streamed in the wind as he stalked back to the coach. Mary could barely see a blond head gazing cautiously from the window. She half-expected that the coach would drive on and she would never see George again, but instead the postboys turned the horses from the waterfront road into the town, toward the hotel.

Bysshe smiled purposefully and began to stride to the hotel. Mary followed, walking fast across the wet cobbles to keep up with him. "I can't but think that good will come of this," he said.

"I pray you're right."

Much pain, Mary thought, *however it turned out.*

*   *   *

George's new female was tall and blond and pink-faced, though she walked hunched over as if embarrassed by her height, and took small, shy steps. She was perhaps in her middle twenties.

They met, embarrassingly, on the hotel's wide stair, Mary with Claire, Alba in Claire's arms. The tall blond, lower lip outthrust haughtily, walked past them on the way to her room, her gaze passing blankly over them. Perhaps she hadn't been told who Alba's father was.

She had a maid with her and a pair of George's men, both of whom had pistols stuffed in their belts. For a wild moment Mary wondered if George had abducted her.

No, she decided, this was only George's theatricality. He didn't have his menagerie with him this time, no leopards or monkeys, so he dressed his postboys as bandits.

The woman passed. Mary felt Claire stiffen. "She looks like *you,*" Claire hissed.

Mary looked at the woman in astonishment. "She doesn't. Not at all."

"She does! Tall, blond, fair eyes . . ." Claire's own eyes filled with tears. "Why can't she be dark, like me?"

"Don't be absurd!" Mary seized her sister's hand, pulled her down the stairs. "Save the tears for later. They may be needed."

In the lobby Mary saw more of George's men carrying in luggage. Pásmány, the fencing master, had slung a carbine over one shoulder. Mary's mind whirled—perhaps this was an abduction after all.

Or perhaps the blond's family—or husband—was in pursuit.

"This way." Bysshe's voice. He led them into one of the hotel's candlelit drawing rooms, closed the crystal-knobbed door behind them. A huge porcelain stove loomed over them.

George stood uncertain in the candlelight, elegant clothing over muddy boots. He looked at Claire and Alba stonily, then advanced, peered at the tiny form that Claire offered him.

"Your daughter Alba," Bysshe said, hovering at his shoulder.

George watched the child for a long, doubtful moment, his auburn hair hanging down his forehead. Then he straightened. "My offer rests, Miss Clairmont, on its previous terms."

Claire drew back, rested Alba on her shoulder. "Never," she said. She licked her lips. "It is too monstrous."

"Come, my lord," Bysshe said. He ventured to put a hand on George's shoulder. "Surely your demands are unreasonable."

"I offered to provide the child with means," George said, "to see that she is raised in a fine home, free from want, and among good people—friends of mine, who will offer her every advantage. I would take her myself but," hesitating, "my domestic conditions would not permit it."

Mary's heart flamed. "But at the cost of forbidding her the sight of her mother!" she said. "That is too cruel."

"The child's future will already be impaired by her irregular connections," George said. "Prolonging those connections could only do her further harm." His eyes flicked up to Claire. "Her mother can only lower her station, not raise it. She is best off with a proper family who can raise her with their own."

Claire's eyes flooded with tears. She turned away, clutching Alba to her. "I won't give her up!" she said. The child began to cry.

George folded his arms. "That settles matters. If you won't accept my offer, then there's an end." The baby's wails filled the air.

"Alba cries for her father," Bysshe said. "Can you not let her into your heart?"

A half-smile twitched across George's lips. "I have no absolute certainty that I *am* this child's father."

A keening sound came from Claire. For a wild, raging moment Mary looked for a weapon to plunge into George's breast. "Unnatural man!" she cried. "Can't you acknowledge the consequences of your own behavior?"

"On the contrary, I am willing to ignore the questionable situation in which I found Miss Clairmont and to care for the child completely. But only on my terms."

"I don't trust his promises!" Claire said. "He abandoned me in Munich without a penny!"

"We agreed to part," George said.

"If it hadn't been for Captain Austen's kindness, I would have starved." She leaned on the door jamb for support, and Mary joined her and buoyed her with an arm around her waist.

"You ran out into the night," George said. "You wouldn't take money."

"I'll tell her!" Claire drew away from Mary, dragged at the door, hauled it open. "I'll tell your new woman!"

Fear leaped into George's eyes. "Claire!" He rushed to the door, seized her arm as she tried to pass; Claire wrenched herself free and staggered into the hotel lobby. Alba wailed in her arms. George's servants were long gone, but hotel guests stared as if in tableaux, hats and walking-sticks half-raised. Fully aware of the spectacle they were making, Mary, clumsy in pregnancy, inserted herself between George and Claire. Claire broke for the stair, while George danced around Mary like an awkward footballer. Mary rejoiced in the fact that her pregnancy seemed only to make her more difficult to get around.

Bysshe put an end to it. He seized George's wrist in a firm grip. "You can't stop us all, my lord," he said.

George glared at him, his look all fury and ice. "What d'ye want, then?"

Claire, panting and flushed, paused halfway up the stair. Alba's alarmed shrieks echoed up the grand staircase.

Bysshe's answer was quick. "A competence for your daughter. Nothing more."

"A thousand a year," George said flatly. "No more than that."

Mary's heart leaped at the figure that doubled the family's income.

Bysshe nodded. "That will do, my lord."

"I want nothing more to do with the girl than that. Nothing whatever."

"Call for pen and paper. And we can bring this to an end."

Two copies were made, and George signed and sealed them with his signet before bidding them all a frigid good-night. The first payment was made that night, one of George's men coming to the door carrying a valise that clanked with gold. Mary gazed at it in amazement—why was George carrying so much?

"Have we done the right thing?" Bysshe wondered, looking at the valise as Claire stuffed it under the bed. "This violence, this extortion?"

"We offered love," Mary said, "and he returned only finance. How else could we deal with him?" She sighed. "And Alba will thank us."

Claire straightened and looked down at the bed. "I only wanted him to pay," said Claire. "Any other considerations can go to the devil."

The *vaudaire* blew on, scarcely fainter than before. The water level was still high. Dead fish still floated in the freshwater tide. "I would venture it," Bysshe said, frowning as he watched the dancing *Ariel*, "but not with the children."

Children. Mary's smile was inward as she realized how real her new baby was to Bysshe. "We can afford to stay at the hotel a little longer," she said.

"Still—a reef in the mains'l would make it safe enough."

Mary paused a moment, perhaps to hear the cold summons of Harriet Shelley from beneath the water. There was no sound, but she shivered anyway. "No harm to wait another day."

Bysshe smiled at her hopefully. "Very well. Perhaps we'll have a chance to speak to George again."

"Bysshe, sometimes your optimism is . . ." She shook her head. "Let us finish our walk."

They walked on through windswept morning streets. The bright sun glared off the white snow and deadly black ice that covered the surrounding high peaks. Soon the snow and ice would melt and threaten avalanche once more. "I am growing weary with this town," Bysshe said.

"Let's go back to our room and read *Chamouni*," Mary suggested. Mr. Coleridge had been a guest of her father's, and his poem about the Alps a favorite of theirs now they were lodged in Switzerland.

Bysshe was working on writing another descriptive poem on the Vale of Chamouni—unlike Coleridge, he and Mary had actually seen the place—and as an homage to Coleridge, Bysshe was including some reworked lines from *Kubla Khan.*

The everlasting universe of things, she recited to herself, *flows through the mind.* Lovely stuff. Bysshe's best by far.

On their return to the hotel they found one of George's servants waiting for them. "Lord Newstead would like to see you."

Ah, Mary thought. *He wants his gold back.*

Let him try to take it.

George waited in the same drawing room in which he'd made his previous night's concession. Despite the bright daylight the room was still lit by lamps— the heavy dark curtains were drawn against the *vaudaire*. George was standing straight as a whip in the center of the room, a dangerous light in his eyes. Mary wondered if this was how he looked in battle.

"Mr. Shelley," George said, and bowed, "I would like to hire your boat to take my party to Geneva."

Bysshe blinked. "I—" he began, then, "*Ariel* is small, only twenty-five feet. Your party is very large and—"

"The local commissaire visited me this morning," George interrupted. "He has forbidden me to depart Montreux. As it is vital for me to leave at once, I must find other means. And I am prepared to pay well for them."

Bysshe looked at Mary, then at George. Hesitated again. "I suppose it would be possible . . ."

"Why is it," Mary demanded, "that you are forbidden to leave?"

George folded his arms, looked down at her. "I have broken no law. It is a ridiculous political matter."

Bysshe offered a smile. "If that's all, then . . ."

Mary interrupted. "If Mr. Shelley and I end up in jail as a result of this, I wonder how ridiculous it will seem."

Bysshe looked at her, shocked. "Mary!"

Mary kept her eyes on George. "Why should we help you?"

"Because . . ." He paused, ran a nervous hand through his hair. Not used, Mary thought, to justifying himself.

"Because," he said finally, "I am assisting someone who is fleeing oppression."

"Fleeing a husband?"

"Husband?" George looked startled. "No—her husband is abroad and cannot protect her." He stepped forward, his color high, his nostrils flared like those of a warhorse. "She is fleeing the attentions of a seducer—a powerful man who has callously used her to gain wealth and influence. I intend to aid her in escaping his power."

Bysshe's eyes blazed. "Of *course* I will aid you!"

Mary watched this display of chivalry with a sinking heart. The masculine confraternity had excluded her, had lost her within its own rituals and condescension.

"I will pay you a further hundred—" George began.

"Please, my lord. I and my little boat are entirely at your service in this noble cause."

George stepped forward, clasped his hand. "Mr. Omnibus, I am in your debt."

The *vaudaire* wailed at the window. Mary wondered if it was Harriet's call, and her hands clenched into fists. She would resist the cry if she could.

Bysshe turned to Mary. "We must prepare." Heavy in her pregnancy, she followed him from the drawing room, up the stairs, toward their own rooms. "I will deliver Lord Newstead and his lady to Geneva, and you and Claire can join me there when the roads are cleared. Or if weather is suitable I will return for you."

"I will go with you," Mary said. "Of course."

Bysshe seemed surprised that she would accompany him on this piece of masculine knight-errantry. "It may not be entirely safe on the lake," he said.

"I'll make it safer—you'll take fewer chances with me aboard. And if I'm with you, George is less likely to inspire you to run off to South America on some noble mission or other."

"I wouldn't do that." Mildly. "And I think you are being a little severe."

"What has George done for us that we should risk anything for him?"

"I do not serve him, but his lady."

"Of whom he has told you nothing. You don't even know her name. And in any case, you seem perfectly willing to risk *her* life on this venture."

Alba's cries sounded through the door of their room. Bysshe paused a moment, resignation plain in his eyes, then opened the door. "It's for Alba, really," he said. "The more contact between George and our little family, the better it may be for her. The better chance we will have to melt his heart."

He opened the door. Claire was holding her colicky child. Tears filled her black eyes. "Where have you been for so long? I was afraid you were gone forever!"

"You know better than that." Mary took the baby from her, the gesture so natural that sadness took a moment to come—the memory that she had held her own lost child this way, held it to her breast and felt the touch of its cold lips.

"And what is this about George?" Claire demanded.

"He wants me to take him down the lake," Bysshe said. "And Mary wishes to join us. You and Alba can remain here until the roads are clear."

Claire's voice rose to a shriek. *"No! Never!"* She lunged for Alba and snatched the girl from Mary's astonished arms. "You're going to abandon me—just like George! You're all going to Geneva to laugh at me!"

"Of course not," Bysshe said reasonably.

Mary stared at her sister, tried to speak, but Claire's cries trampled over her intentions.

"You're abandoning me! I'm useless to you—worthless! You'll soon have your own baby!"

Mary tried to comfort Claire, but it was hopeless. Claire screamed and shuddered and wept, convinced that she would be left forever in Montreux. In the end there was no choice but to take her along. Mary received mean satisfaction in watching Bysshe as he absorbed this reality, as his chivalrous, noble-minded expedition alongside the hero of Waterloo turned into a low family comedy, George and his old lover, his new lover, and his wailing bastard.

And ghosts. Harriet, lurking under the water. And their dead baby calling.

Ariel bucked like a horse on the white-topped waves as the *vaudaire* keened in the rigging. Frigid spray flew in Mary's face and her feet slid on slippery planking. Her heart thrashed into her throat. The boat seemed half-full of water. She gave a despairing look over her shoulder at the retreating rowboat they'd hired to bring them from the jetty to their craft.

"Bysshe!" she said. "This is hopeless."

"Better once we're under way. See that the cuddy will be comfortable for Claire and Alba."

"This is madness."

Bysshe licked joyfully at the freshwater spray that ran down his lips. "We'll be fine, I'm sure."

He was a much better sailor than she: she had to trust him. She opened the sliding hatch to the cuddy, the little cabin forward, and saw several inches of water sloshing in the bottom. The cushions on the little seats were soaked. Wearily, she looked up at Bysshe.

"We'll have to bail."

"Very well."

It took a quarter hour to bail out the boat, during which time Claire paced back and forth on the little jetty, Alba in her arms. She looked like a specter with her pale face peering out from her dark shawl.

Bysshe cast off the gaskets that reefed the mainsail to the boom, then jumped forward to the halyards and raised the sail on its gaff. The wind tore at the canvas with a sound like a cannonade, open-hand slaps against Mary's ears.

The shrouds were taut as bowstrings. Bysshe reefed the sail down, hauled the halyards and topping life again till the canvas was taut, lowered the leeboards, then asked Mary to take the tiller while he cast *Ariel* off from its buoy.

Bysshe braced himself against the gunwale as he hauled on the mooring line, drawing *Ariel* up against the wind. When Bysshe cast off from the buoy the boat paid instantly off the wind and the sail filled with a rolling boom. Water surged under the boat's counter and suddenly, before Mary knew it, *Ariel* was flying fast. Fear closed a fist around her windpipe as the little boat heeled and the tiller almost yanked her arms from their sockets. She could hear Harriet's wails in the windsong. Mary dug her heels into the planks and hauled the tiller up to her chest, keeping *Ariel* up into the wind. Frigid water boiled up over the lee counter, pouring into the boat like a waterfall.

Bysshe leapt gracefully aft and released the mainsheet. The sail boomed out with a crash that rattled Mary's bones and the boat righted itself. Bysshe took the tiller from Mary, sheeted in, leaned out into the wind as the boat picked up speed. There was a grin on his face.

"Sorry!" he said. "I should have let the sheet go before we set out."

Bysshe tacked and brought *Ariel* into the wind near the jetty. The sail boomed like thunder as it spilled wind. Waves slammed the boat into the jetty. The mast swayed wildly. The stone jetty was at least four feet taller than the boat's deck. Mary helped Claire with the luggage—gold clanked heavily in one bag—then took Alba while Bysshe assisted Claire into the boat.

"It's *wet,*" Claire said when she saw the cuddy.

"Take your heavy cloak out of your bags and sit on it," Mary said.

"This is *terrible,*" Claire said, and lowered herself carefully into the cuddy.

"Go forrard," Bysshe said to Mary, "and push off from the jetty as hard as you can."

Forrard. Bysshe so enjoyed being nautical. Clumsy in skirts and pregnancy, Mary climbed atop the cuddy and did as she was asked. The booming sail filled, Mary snatched at the shrouds for balance, and *Ariel* leaped from the jetty like a stone from a child's catapult. Mary made her way across the tilting deck to the cockpit. Bysshe was leaning out to weather, his big hands controlling the tiller easily, his long fair hair streaming in the wind.

"I won't ask you to do that again," he said. "George should help from this point."

George and his lady would join the boat at another jetty—there was less chance that the authorities would intervene if they weren't seen where another Englishman was readying his boat.

Ariel raced across the waterfront, foam boiling under its counter. The second jetty—a wooden one—approached swiftly, with cloaked figures upon it. Bysshe rounded into the wind, canvas thundering, and brought *Ariel* neatly to the dock. George's men seized shrouds and a mooring line and held the boat in its place.

George's round hat was jammed down over his brows and the collar of his cloak was turned up, but any attempt at anonymity was wrecked by his famous laced boots. He seized a shroud and leaped easily into the boat, then turned to help his lady.

She had stepped back, frightened by the gunshot cracks of the luffing sail, the wild swings of the boom. Dressed in a blue silk dress, broad-brimmed bonnet, and heavy cloak, she frowned with her haughty lower lip, looking disdainfully at the little boat and its odd collection of passengers.

George reassured his companion. He and one of his men, the swordmaster Pásmány, helped her into the boat, held her arm as she ducked under the boom.

George grabbed the brim of his hat to keep the wind from carrying it away and performed hasty introductions. "Mr. and Mrs. Shelley. The Comtesse Laufenburg."

Mary strained her memory, trying to remember if she'd ever heard the name before. The comtesse smiled a superior smile and tried to be pleasant. "Enchanted to make cognizance of you," she said in French.

A baby wailed over the sound of flogging canvas. George straightened, his eyes a little wild.

"Claire is here?" he asked.

"She did not desire to be abandoned in Montreux," Mary said, trying to stress the word *abandoned.*

"My God!" George said. "I wish you had greater consideration of the . . . realities."

"Claire is free and may do as she wishes," Mary said.

George clenched his teeth. He took the comtesse by her arm and drew her toward the cuddy.

"The boat will be better balanced," Bysshe called after, "if the comtesse will sit on the weather side." *And perhaps,* Mary thought, *we won't capsize.*

George gave Bysshe a blank look. "The larboard side," Bysshe said helpfully. Another blank look.

"Hang it! The left."

"Very well."

George and the comtesse ducked down the hatchway. Mary would have liked to have eavesdropped on the comtesse's introduction to Claire, but the furious rattling sail obscured the phrases, if any. George came up, looking grim, and Pásmány began tossing luggage toward him. Other than a pair of valises, most of it was military: a familiar-looking pistol case, a pair of sabers, a brace of carbines. George stowed it all in the cuddy. Then Pásmány himself leaped into the boat, and George signaled all was ready. Bysshe placed George by the weather rail, and Pásmány squatted on the weather foredeck.

"If you gentlemen would push us off?" Bysshe said.

The sail filled and *Ariel* began to move fast, rising at each wave and thudding into the troughs. Spray rose at each impact. Bysshe trimmed the sail, the luff trembling just a little, the rest full and taut, then cleated the mainsheet down.

"A long reach down the length of the lake," Bysshe said with a smile. "Easy enough sailing, if a little hard on the ladies."

George peered out over the cuddy, his eyes searching the bank. The old castle of Chillon bulked ominously on the shore, just south of Montreux.

"When do we cross the border into Geneva?" George asked.

"Why does it matter?" Bysshe said. "Geneva joined the Swiss Confederation last year."

"But the administrations are not yet united. And the more jurisdictions that lie between the comtesse and her pursuers, the happier I will be."

George cast an uncomfortable look astern. With spray dotting his cloak, his hat clamped down on his head, his body disposed awkwardly on the weather side of the boat, George seemed thoroughly miserable—and in an overwhelming flood of sudden understanding, Mary suddenly knew why. It was over for him. His noble birth, his fame, his entire life to this point—all was as naught. Passion had claimed him for its own. His career had ended: there was no place for him in the army, in diplomatic circles, even in polite society. He'd thrown it all away in this mad impulse of passion.

He was an exile now, and the only people whom he could expect to associate with him were other exiles.

Like the exiles aboard *Ariel*.

Perhaps, Mary thought, he was only now realizing it. Poor George. She actually felt sorry for him.

The castle of Chillon fell astern, like a grand symbol of George's hopes, a world of possibility not realized.

"Beg pardon, my lord," she said, "but where do you intend to go?"

George frowned. "France, perhaps," he said. "The comtesse has . . . some friends . . . in France. England, if France won't suit, but we won't be able to stay there long. America, if necessary."

"Can the Prince Regent intervene on your behalf?"

George's smile was grim. "If he wishes. But he's subject to strange fits of morality, particularly if the sins in question remind him of his own. Prinny will *not* wish to be reminded of Mrs. Fitzherbert and Lady Hertford. He *does* wish to look upright in the eyes of the nation. And he has no loyalty to his friends, none at all." He gave a poised, slow-motion shrug. "Perhaps he will help, if the fit is on him. But I think not." He reached inside his greatcoat, patted an inside pocket. "Do you think I can light a cigar in this wind? If so, I hope it will not discomfort you, Mrs. Shelley."

He managed a spark in his strike-a-light, puffed madly till the tinder caught, then ignited his cigar and turned to Bysshe. "I found your poems, Mr. Omnibus. Your *Queen Mab* and *Alastor*. The latter of which I liked better, though I liked both well enough."

Bysshe looked at him in surprise. Wind whistled through the shrouds. "How did you find *Mab*? There were only seventy copies, and I'm certain I can account for each one."

George seemed pleased with himself. "There are few doors closed to me." Darkness clouded his face. "Or rather, *were*." With a sigh. He wiped spray from his ear with the back of his hand.

"I'm surprised that you liked *Mab* at all," Bysshe said quickly, "as its ideas are so contrary to your own."

"You expressed them well enough. As a verse treatise of Mr. Godwin's political thought, I believed it done soundly—as soundly as such a thing *can* be done. And I think you can have it published properly now—it's hardly a threat to public order, Godwin's thought being so out of fashion even among radicals." He drew deliberately on his cigar, then waved it. The wind tore the cigar smoke from his mouth in little wisps. "*Alastor*, though better poetry, seemed in contrast to have little thought behind it. I never understood what that fellow was *doing* on the boat—was it a metaphor for life? I kept waiting for something to *happen*."

Mary bristled at George's condescension. What are *you* doing on this little boat? she wanted to ask.

Bysshe, however, looked apologetic. "I'm writing better things now."

"He's writing *wonderful* things now," Mary said. "An ode to Mont Blanc. An essay on Christianity. A hymn to intellectual beauty."

George gave her an amused look. "Mrs. Shelley's tone implies that, to me, intellectual beauty is entirely a stranger, but she misunderstands my point. I found it remarkable that the same pen could produce both *Queen Mab* and *Alastor,* and have no doubt that so various a talent will produce very good work in the poetry line—provided," nodding to Bysshe, "that Mr. Shelley continues in it, and doesn't take up engineering again, or chemistry." He grinned. "Or become a sea captain."

"He is and remains a poet," Mary said firmly. She used a corner of her shawl to wipe spray from her cheek.

"Who else do you like, my lord?" Bysshe asked.

"Poets, you mean? Scott, above all. Shakespeare, who is sound on political matters as well as having a magnificent . . . shall I call it a *stride?* Burns, the great poet of my country. And our Laureate."

"Mr. Southey was kind to me when we met," Bysshe said. "And Mrs. Southey made wonderful tea-cakes. But I wish I admired his work more." He looked up. "What do you think of Milton? The Maie and I read him constantly."

George shrugged. "Dour Puritan fellow. I'm surprised you can stand him at all."

"His verse is glorious. And he wasn't a Puritan, but an Independent, like Cromwell—his philosophy was quite unorthodox. He believed, for example, in plural marriage."

George's eyes glittered. "Did he now."

"Ay. And his Satan is a magnificent creation, far more interesting than any of his angels or his simpering pedantic Christ. That long, raging fall from grace, into darkness visible."

George's brows knit. Perhaps he was contemplating his own long fall from the Heaven of polite society. His eyes turned to Mary.

"And how is the originator of Mr. Shelley's political thought? How does your father, Mrs. Shelley?"

"He is working on a novel. An important work."

"I am pleased to hear it. Does he progress?"

Mary was going to answer simply "Very well," but Bysshe's answer came first. "Plagued by lack of money," he said. "We will be going to England to succor him after this, ah, errand is completed."

"Your generosity does you credit," George said, and then resentment entered his eyes and his lip curled. "Of course, you will be able to better afford it, now."

Bysshe's answer was mild. "Mr. Godwin lives partly with our support, but he will not speak to us since I eloped with his daughter. You will not acknowledge Alba, but at least you've been . . . persuaded . . . to do well by her."

George preferred not to rise to this, settled instead for clarification. "You support a man who won't acknowledge you?"

"It is not my father-in-law I support, but rather the author of *Political Justice.*"

"A nice discernment," George observed. "Perhaps over-nice."

"One does what goodness one can. And one hopes people will respond." Looking at George, who smiled cynically around his cigar.

"Your charity speaks well for you. But perhaps Mr. Godwin would have greater cause to finish his book if poverty were not being made so convenient for him."

Mary felt herself flushing red. But Bysshe's reply again was mild. "It isn't that simple. Mr. Godwin has dependents, and the public that once celebrated his thought has, alas, forgotten him. His novel may retrieve matters. But a fine thing such as this work cannot be rushed—not if it is to have the impact it deserves."

"I will bow to your expertise in matters of literary production. But still . . . to support someone who will not even speak to you—that is charity indeed. And it does not speak well for Mr. Godwin's gratitude."

"My father is a great man!" Mary knew she was speaking hotly, and she bit back on her anger. "But he judges by a . . . a very high standard of morality. He will accept support from a sincere admirer, but he has not yet understood the depth of sentiment between Bysshe and myself, and believes that Bysshe has done my reputation harm—not," flaring again, "that I would care if he had."

Ariel thudded into a wave trough, and George winced at the impact. He adjusted his seat on the rail and nodded. "Mr. Godwin will accept money from an admirer, but not letters from an in-law. And Mr. Shelley will support the author of *Political Justice,* but not *his* in-laws."

"And *you*," Mary said, "will support a blackmailer, but not a daughter."

George's eyes turned to stone. Mary realized she had gone too far for this small boat and close company.

"Gentlemen, it's cold," she announced. "I will withdraw."

She made her way carefully into the cuddy. The tall comtesse was disposed uncomfortably, on wet cushions, by the hatch, the overhead planking brushing the top of her bonnet. Her gaze was mild, but her lip was haughty. There was a careful three inches between her and Claire, who was nursing Alba and, clearly enough, a grudge.

Mary walked past them to the peak, sat carefully on a wet cushion near Claire. Their knees collided every time *Ariel* fell down a wave. The cuddy smelled of wet stuffing and stale water. There was still water sluicing about on the bottom.

Mary looked at Claire's baby and felt sadness like an ache in her breast.

Claire regarded her resentfully. "The French bitch hates us," she whispered urgently. "Look at her expression."

Mary wished Claire had kept her voice down. Mary leaned out to look at the comtesse, managed a smile. *"Vous parlez anglais?"* she asked.

"Non. Je regrette. Parles-tu français?" The comtesse had a peculiar accent. As, with a name like Laufenburg, one might expect.

Pleasant of her, though, to use the intimate *tu. "Je comprends un peu."* Claire's French was much better than hers, but Claire clearly had no interest in conversation.

The comtesse looked at the nursing baby. A shadow flitted across her face. "My own child," in French, "I was forced to leave behind."

"I'm sorry." For a moment Mary hated the comtesse for having a child to leave, that and for the abandonment itself.

No. Bysshe, she remembered, had left his own children. It did not make one unnatural. Sometimes there were circumstances.

Speech languished after this unpromising beginning. Mary leaned her head against the planking and tried to sleep, sadly aware of the cold seep of water up her skirts. The boat's movement was too violent to be restful, but she composed herself deliberately for sleep. Images floated through her mind: the great crumbling keep of Chillon, standing above the surging gray water like the setting of one of "Monk" Lewis's novels; a gray cat eating a blushing rose; a figure, massive and threatening, somehow both George and her father Godwin, flinging back the bed-curtains to reveal, in the bright light of morning, the comtesse Laufenburg's placid blond face with its outthrust, Habsburg lip.

Habsburg. Mary sat up with a cry and banged her skull on the deckhead.

She cast a wild look at Claire and the comtesse, saw them both drowsing, Alba asleep in Claire's lap. The boat was rolling madly in a freshening breeze: there were ominous, threatening little shrieks of wind in the rigging. The cuddy stank badly.

Mary made her way out of the cuddy, clinging to the sides of the hatch as the boat sought to pitch her out. Bysshe was holding grimly to the tiller with one big hand, controlling the sheet with the other while spray soaked his coat; George and Pásmány were hanging to the shrouds to keep from sliding down the tilted deck.

Astern was Lausanne, north of the lake, and the Cornettes to the south; and Mont Billiat, looming over the valley of the Dranse to the south, was right abeam; they were smack in the middle of the lake, with the *vaudaire* wind funneling down the valley, stronger than ever with the mountain boundary out of the way.

Mary seized the rail, hauled herself up the tilting deck toward George. "I know your secret," she said. "I know who your woman is."

George's face ran with spray; his auburn hair was plastered to the back of his neck. He fixed her with eyes colder than the glaciers of Mont Blanc. "Indeed," he said.

"Marie-Louise of the house of Habsburg." Hot anger pulsed through her, burned against the cold spindrift on her face. "Former Empress of the French!"

Restlessly, George turned his eyes away. "Indeed," he said again.

Mary seized a shroud and dragged herself to the rail next to him. Bysshe watched in shock as Mary shouted into the wind. "Her husband abroad! Abroad, forsooth—all the way to St. Helena! Forced to leave her child behind, because her father would never let Napoleon's son out of his control for an instant. Even a Habsburg lip—my God!"

"Very clever, Miss Godwin. But I believe you have divined my sentiments on the subject of clever women." George gazed ahead, toward Geneva. "Now you see why I wish to be away."

"I see only vanity!" Mary raged. "Colossal vanity! You can't stop fighting Napoleon even now! Even when the battlefield is only a bed!"

George glared at her. "Is it my damned fault that Napoleon could never keep his women?"

"It's your damned fault that *you* keep her!"

George opened his mouth to spit out a reply and then the *vaudaire*, like a giant hand, took *Ariel*'s mast in its grasp and slammed the frail boat over. Bysshe cried out and hauled the tiller to his chest and let the mainsheet go, all far too late. The deck pitched out from under Mary's heels and she clung to the shroud for dear life. Pásmány shouted in Hungarian. There was a roar as the sail hit the water. The lake foamed over the lee rail and the wind tore Mary's breath away. There were screams from the cuddy as water poured into the little cabin.

"Halyards and topping lift!" Bysshe gasped. He was clinging to the weather rail: a breaker exploded in his face and he gasped for air. "Let 'em go!"

If the sail filled with water all was lost. Mary let go of the shroud and palmed her way across the vertical deck. Freezing lakewater clutched at her ankles. Harriet Shelley shrieked her triumph in Mary's ears like the wind. Mary lurched forward to the mast, flung the halyard and topping lift off their cleats. The sail sagged free, empty of everything but the water that poured onto its canvas surface, turning it into a giant weight that would drag the boat over. Too late.

"Save the ladies, George!" Bysshe called. His face was dead-white but his voice was calm. "I can't swim!"

Water boiled up Mary's skirts. She could feel the dead weight dragging her down as she clutched at George's leg and hauled herself up the deck. She screamed as her unborn child protested, a gouging pain deep in her belly.

George raged wildly. "Damn it, Shelley, what can I *do?*" He had a leg over one of the shrouds; the other was Mary's support. The wind had taken his hat and his cloak rattled around him like wind-filled canvas.

"Cut the mast free!"

George turned to Mary. "My sword! Get it from the cabin!"

Mary looked down and into the terrified black eyes of Claire, half-out of the cuddy. She held a wailing Alba in her arms. "Take the baby!" she shrieked.

"Give me a sword!" Mary said. A wave broke over the boat, soaking them all in icy rain. Mary thought of Harriet smiling, her hair trailing like seaweed.

"Save my baby!"

"The *sword!* Byron's *sword! Give it!*" Mary clung to George's leg with one hand and thrust the crying babe away with the other.

"*I hate you!*" Claire shrieked, but she turned and fumbled for George's sword. She held it up out of the hatch, and Mary took the cut steel hilt in her hand and drew it rasping from the scabbard. She held it blindly above her head and felt George's firm hand close over hers and take the sabre away. The pain in her belly was like a knife. Through the boat and her spine she felt the thudding blows as George hacked at the shrouds, and then there was a rending as the mast splintered and *Ariel,* relieved of its top-hamper, swung suddenly upright.

Half the lake seemed to splash into the boat as it came off its beam-ends. George pitched over backwards as *Ariel* righted itself, but Mary clung to his leg and kept him from going into the lake while he dragged himself to safety over the rail.

Another wave crashed over them. Mary clutched at her belly and moaned. The pain was ebbing. The boat pirouetted on the lake as the wind took it, and then *Ariel* jerked to a halt. The wreckage of the mast was acting as a sea-anchor, moderating the wave action, keeping the boat stable. Alba's screams floated high above *Ariel's* remains.

Wood floats, Mary remembered dully. And *Ariel* was wood, no matter how much water slopped about in her bottom.

Shelley staggered to his feet, shin-deep in lake water. "By God, George," he gasped. "You've saved us."

"By God," George answered, "so I have." Mary looked up from the deck to see George with the devil's light in his eyes, his color high and his sabre in his hand. So, she reckoned, he must have seemed to Napoleon at Genappe. George bent and peered into the cuddy.

"Are the ladies all right?"

"Je suis bien, merci." From the Austrian princess.

"Damn you to hell, George!" Claire cried. George only grinned.

"I see we are well," he said.

And then Mary felt the warm blood running down the insides of her legs, and knew that George was wrong.

Mary lay on a bed in the farmhouse sipping warm brandy. Reddening cloths were packed between her legs. The hemorrhage had not stopped, though at least there was no pain. Mary could feel the child moving within her, as if struggling in its terror. Over the click of knitting needles, she could hear the voices of the men in the kitchen, and smell George's cigar.

The large farm, sitting below its pastures that stretched up the Noirmont, was owned by a white-mustached old man named Fleury, a man who seemed incapable of surprise or confusion even when armed men arrived at his doorstep, carrying between them a bleeding woman and a sack filled with gold. He turned Mary over to his wife, hitched up his trousers, put his hat on, and went to St. Prex to find a doctor.

Madame Fleury, a large woman unflappable as her husband, tended Mary and made her drink a brandy toddy while she sat by Mary and did her knitting.

When Fleury returned, his news wasn't good. The local surgeon had gone up the road to set the bones of some workmen caught in an avalanche—perhaps there would be amputations—but he would return as soon as he could. The road west to Geneva was still blocked by the slide; the road east to Lausanne had been cleared. George seemed thoughtful at the news. His voice echoed in from the kitchen. "Perhaps the chase will simply go past," he said in English.

"What sort of pursuit do you anticipate?" Bysshe asked. "Surely you don't expect the Austrian Emperor to send his troops into Switzerland."

"Stranger things have happened," George said. "And it may not be the Emperor's own people after us—it might be Neipperg, acting on his own."

Mary knew she'd heard the name before, and tried to recall it. But Bysshe said, "The general? Why would he be concerned?"

There was cynical amusement in George's voice. "Because he's her highness's former lover! I don't imagine he'd like to see his fortune run away."

"Do you credit him with so base a motive?"

George laughed. "In order to prevent Marie-Louise from joining Bonaparte, Prince Metternich *ordered* von Neipperg to leave his wife and to seduce her highness—and that one-eyed scoundrel was only too happy to comply. His reward was to be the co-rulership of Parma, of which her highness was to be Duchess."

"Are you certain of this?"

"Metternich told me at his dinner table over a pipe of tobacco. And Neipperg *boasted* to me, sir!" A sigh, almost a snarl, came from George. "My heart wrung at his words, Mr. Shelley. For I had already met her highness and—"

Words failed him for a moment. "I determined to rescue her from Neipperg's clutches, though all the Hungarian Grenadiers of the Empire stood in the way!"

"That was most admirable, my lord," Bysshe said quietly.

Claire's voice piped up. "Who is this Neipperg?"

"Adam von Neipperg is a cavalry officer who defeated Murat," Bysshe said. "That's all I know of him."

George's voice was thoughtful. "He's the best the Austrians have. Quite the *beau sabreur,* and a diplomat as well. He persuaded Crown Prince Bernadotte to switch sides before the battle of Leipzig. And yes, he defeated Murat on the field of Tolentino, a few weeks before Waterloo. Command of the Austrian army was another of Prince Metternich's rewards for his . . . services."

Murat, Mary knew, was Napoleon's great cavalry general. Neipperg, the best Austrian cavalryman, had defeated Murat, and now Britain's greatest horseman had defeated Napoleon *and* Neipperg, one on the battlefield and both in bed.

Such a competitive little company of cavaliers, she thought. Madame Fleury's knitting needles clacked out a complicated pattern.

"You think he's going to come after you?" Bysshe asked.

"I would," simply. "And neither he nor I would care what the Swiss think about it. And he'll find enough officers who will want to fight for the, ah, *honor* of their royal family. And he certainly has scouts or agents among the Swiss looking for me—surely one of them visited the commissaire of Montreux."

"I see." Mary heard the sound of Bysshe rising from his seat. "I must see to Mary."

He stepped into the bedroom, sat on the edge of the bed, took her hand. Madame Fleury barely looked up from her knitting.

"Are you better, Pecksie?"

"Nothing has changed." *I'm still dying,* she thought.

Bysshe sighed. "I'm sorry," he said, "to have exposed you to such danger. And now I don't know what to do."

"And all for so little."

Bysshe was thoughtful. "Do you think liberty is so little? And Byron—the voice of monarchy and reaction—fighting for freedom! Think of it!"

My life is bleeding away, Mary thought incredulously, *and his child with it.* There was poison in her voice when she answered.

"This isn't about the freedom of a woman, it's about the freedom of one man to do what he wants."

Bysshe frowned at her.

"He can't love," Mary insisted. "He felt no love for his wife, or for Claire." Bysshe tried to hush her—her voice was probably perfectly audible in the kitchen. But it was pleasing for her not to give a damn.

"It's not love he feels for that poor woman in the cellar," she said. "His passions are entirely concerned with himself—and now that he can't exorcise them on the battlefield, he's got to find other means."

"Are you certain?"

"He's a mad whirlwind of destruction! Look what he did to Claire. And now he's wrecked *Ariel,* and he may yet involve us all in a battle—with Austrian cavalry, forsooth! He'll destroy us all if we let him."

"Perhaps it will not come to that."

George appeared in the door. He was wrapped in a blanket and carried a carbine, and if he was embarrassed by what he'd heard, he failed to display it. "With your permission, Mr. Shelley, I'm going to try to sink your boat. It sits on a rock just below our location, a pistol pointed at our head."

Bysshe looked at Mary. "Do as you wish."

"I'll give you privacy, then." And pointedly closed the door.

Mary heard his bootsteps march out, the outside door open and close. She put her hand on Bysshe's arm. *I am bleeding to death,* she thought. "Promise me you will take no part in anything," she said. "George will try to talk you into defending the princess—he knows you're a good shot."

"But what of Marie-Louise? To be dragged back to Austria by force of arms—what a prospect! An outrage, inhuman and degrading."

I am bleeding to death, Mary thought. But she composed a civil reply. "Her condition saddens me. But she was born a pawn and has lived a pawn her entire life. However this turns out, she will be a pawn either of George or of Metternich, and we cannot change that. It is the evil of monarchy and tyranny that has made her so. We may be thankful we were not born among her class."

There were tears in Bysshe's eyes. "Very well. If you think it best, I will not lift a hand in this."

Mary put her arms around him, held herself close to his warmth. She clenched trembling hands behind his back.

Soon, she thought, *I will lack the strength to do even this. And then I will die.*

There was a warm and spreading lake between her legs. She felt very drowsy as she held Bysshe, the effects of the brandy, and she closed her eyes and tried to rest. Bysshe stroked her cheek and hair. Mary, for a moment, dreamed.

She dreamed of pursuit, a towering, shrouded figure stalking her over the lake—but the lake was frozen, and as Mary fled across the ice she found other people standing there, people to whom she ran for help only to discover them all dead, frozen in their places and covered with frost. Terrified, she ran among them, seeing to her further horror that she knew them all: her mother and namesake; and Mr. Godwin; and George, looking at her insolently with eyes of black ice; and lastly the figure of Harriet Shelley, a woman she had never met in life but who Mary knew at once. Harriet stood rooted to a patch of ice and held in her arms the frost-swathed figure of a child. And despite the rime that covered the tiny face, Mary knew at once, and with agonized despair, just whose child Harriet carried so triumphantly in her arms.

She woke, terror pounding in her heart. There was a gunshot from outside. She felt Bysshe stiffen. Another shot. And then the sound of pounding feet.

"They're here, damn it!" George called. "And my shot missed!"

Gunfire and the sound of hammering swirled through Mary's perceptions. Furniture was shifted, doors barricaded, weapons laid ready. The shutters had already been closed against the *vaudaire*, so no one had to risk himself securing the windows. Claire and Alba came into Mary's room, the both of them screaming; and Mary, not giving a damn any longer, sent them both out. George put them in the cellar with the Austrian princess—Mary was amused that they seemed doomed to share quarters together. Bysshe, throughout, only sat on the bed and held Mary in his arms. He seemed calm, but his heart pounded against her ear. M. Fleury appeared, loading an old Charleville musket as he offhand-edly explained that he had served in one of Louis XVI's mercenary Swiss regi-ments. His wife put down her knitting needles, poured buckshot into her apron pockets, and went off with him to serve as his loader. Afterwards Mary won-dered if that particular episode, that vision of the old man with his gun and pow-der horn, had been a dream—but no, Madame Fleury was gone, her pockets filled with lead.

Eventually the noise died away. George came in with his Mantons stuffed in his belt, looking pleased with himself. "I think we stand well," he said. "This place is fine as a fort. At Waterloo we held Hougoumont and La Haye Sainte against worse—and Neipperg will have no artillery. The odds aren't bad—I counted only eight of them." He looked at Bysshe. "Unless you are willing to join us, Mr. Shelley, in defense of her highness's liberty."

Bysshe sat up. "I wish no man's blood on my hands." Mary rejoiced at the firmness in his voice.

"I will not argue against your conscience, but if you won't fight, then per-haps you can load for me?"

"What of Mary?" Bysshe asked.

Indeed, Mary thought. *What of me?*

"Can we arrange for her, and for Claire and Alba, to leave this house?"

George shook his head. "They don't dare risk letting you go—you'd just in-form the Swiss authorities. I could negotiate a cease-fire to allow you to become their prisoners, but then you'd be living in the barn or the outdoors instead of more comfortably in here." He looked down at Mary. "I do not think we should move your lady in any case. Here in the house it is safe enough."

"But what if there's a battle? My God—there's already been shooting!"

"No one was hurt, you'll note—though if I'd had a Baker or a jäger rifle in-stead of my puisny little carbine, I daresay I'd have dropped one of them. No—what will happen now is that they'll either try an assault, which will take a while to organize, because they're all scattered out watching the house, and which will cost them dearly in the end . . . or they'll wait. They don't know how many peo-ple we have in here, and they'll be cautious on that account. We're inside, with plenty of food and fuel and ammunition, and they're in the outdoors facing un-seasonably cold weather. And the longer they wait, the more likely it will be that our local Swiss yeomen will discover them, and then . . ." He gave a low laugh. "Austrian soldiers have never fared well in Switzerland, not since the days of William Tell. Our Austrian friends will be arrested and imprisoned."

"But the surgeon? Will they not let the surgeon pass?"

"I can't say."

Bysshe stared. "My God! Can't you speak to them?"

"I will ask if you like. But I don't know what a surgeon can do that we can-not."

Bysshe looked desperate. "There must be something that will stop the bleeding!"

Yes, Mary thought. *Death. Harriet has won.*

George gazed down at Mary with thoughtful eyes. "A Scotch midwife would sit her in a tub of icewater."

Bysshe stiffened like a dog on point. "Is there ice? Is there an ice cellar?" He rushed out of the room. Mary could hear him stammering out frantic questions in French, then Fleury's offhand reply. When Bysshe came back he looked stricken. "There is an icehouse, but it's out behind the barn."

"And in enemy hands." George sighed. "Well, I will ask if they will permit Madame Fleury to bring ice into the house, and pass the surgeon through when he comes."

George left the room and commenced a shouted conversation in French with someone outside. Mary winced at the volume of George's voice. The voice outside spoke French with a harsh accent.

No, she understood. They would not permit ice or a surgeon to enter the house.

"They suspect a plot, I suppose," George reported. He stood wearily in the doorway. "Or they think one of my men is wounded."

"They want to make you watch someone die," Mary said. "And hope it will make you surrender."

George looked at her. "Yes, you comprehend their intent," he said. "That is precisely what they want." Bysshe looked horrified.

George's look turned intent. "And what does Mistress Mary want?"

Mary closed her eyes. "Mistress Mary wants to live, and to hell with you all."

George laughed, a low and misanthropic chuckle. "Very well. Live you shall—and I believe I know the way."

He returned to the other room, and Mary heard his raised voice again. He was asking, in French, what the intruders wanted, and in passing comparing their actions to Napoleon's abduction of the Duc d'Enghien, justly abhorred by all nations.

"A telling hit," Mary said. "Good old George." She wrapped her two small pale hands around one of Bysshe's big ones.

The same voice answered, demanding that Her Highness the Duchess of Parma be surrendered. George returned that her highness was here of her own free will, and that she commanded that they withdraw to their own borders and trouble her no more. The emissary said his party was acting for the honor of Austria and the House of Habsburg. George announced that he felt free to doubt that their shameful actions were in any way honorable, and he was prepared to prove it, *corps-à-corps,* if *Feldmarschall-leutnant* von Neipperg was willing to oblige him.

"My God!" Bysshe said. "He's calling the blackguard out!"

Mary could only laugh. A duel, fought for an Austrian princess and Mary's bleeding womb.

The other asked for time to consider. George gave it.

"This neatly solves our dilemma, don't it?" he said after he returned. "If I beat Neipperg, the rest of those German puppies won't have direction—they'd be on the road back to Austria. Her royal highness and I will be able to make our way to a friendly country. No magistrates, no awkward questions, and a long head start." He smiled. "And all the ice in the world for Mistress Mary."

"And if you lose?" Bysshe asked.

"It ain't to be thought of. I'm a master of the sabre, I practice with Pásmány almost daily, and whatever Neipperg's other virtues I doubt he can compare with me in the art of the sword. The only question," he turned thoughtful, "is whether we can trust his offer. If there's treachery . . ."

"Or if he insists on pistols!" Mary found she couldn't resist pointing this out. "You didn't precisely cover yourself with glory the last time I saw you shoot."

George only seemed amused. "Neipperg only has one eye—I doubt he's much of a shot, either. My second would have to insist on a sabre fight," and here he smiled, *"pour l'honneur de la cavalerie."*

Somehow Mary found this satisfying. "Go fight, George. I know you love your legend more than you ever loved that Austrian girl—and this will make a nice end to it."

George only chuckled again, while Bysshe looked shocked. "Truthful Mistress Mary," George said. "Never without your sting."

"I see no point in politeness from this position."

"You would have made a good soldier, Mrs. Shelley."

Longing fell upon Mary. "I would have made a better mother," she said, and felt tears sting her eyes.

"God, Maie!" Bysshe cried. "What I would not give!" He bent over her and began to weep.

It was, Mary considered, about time, and then reflected that death had made her satirical.

George watched for a long moment, then withdrew. Mary could hear his boots pacing back and forth in the kitchen, and then a different, younger voice called from outside.

The *Feldmarschall-leutnant* had agreed to the encounter. He, the new voice, was prepared to present himself as von Neipperg's second.

"A soldier all right," George commented. "Civilian clothes, but he's got that sprig of greenery that Austrian troops wear in their hats." His voice lifted. "That's far enough, laddie!" He switched to French and said that his second would be out shortly. Then his bootsteps returned to Mary's room and put a hand on Bysshe's shoulder.

"Mr. Shelley," he said, "I regret this intrusion, but I must ask—will you do me the honor of standing my second in this affaire?"

"Bysshe!" Mary cried. "Of course not!"

Bysshe blinked tear-dazzled eyes but managed to speak clearly enough. "I'm totally opposed to the practice. It's vicious and wasteful and utterly without moral foundation. It reeks of death and the dark ages and ruling-class affection."

George's voice was gentle. "There are no other gentlemen here," he said. "Pásmány is a servant, and I can't see sending our worthy M. Fleury out to negotiate with those little noblemen. And—" He looked at Mary. "Your lady must have her ice and her surgeon."

Bysshe looked stricken. "I know nothing of how to manage these encounters," he said. "I would not do well by you. If you were to fall as a result of my bungling, I should never forgive myself."

"I will tell you what to say, and if he doesn't agree, then bring negotiations to a close."

"Bysshe," Mary reminded, "you said you would have nothing to do with this."

Bysshe wiped tears from his eyes and looked thoughtful.

"Don't you see this is theater?" Mary demanded. "George is adding this scene to his legend—he doesn't give a damn for anyone here!"

George only seemed amused. "You are far from death, madam, I think, to show such spirit," he said. "Come, Mr. Shelley! Despite what Mary thinks, a fight with Neipperg is the only way we can escape without risking the ladies."

"No," Mary said.

Bysshe looked thoroughly unhappy. "Very well," he said. "For Mary's sake, I'll do as you ask, provided I do no violence myself. But I should say that I resent being placed in this . . . *extraordinary* position in the first place."

Mary settled for glaring at Bysshe.

More negotiations were conducted through the window, and then Bysshe, after receiving a thorough briefing, straightened and brushed his jacket, brushed his knees, put on his hat, and said good-bye to Mary. He was very pale under his freckles.

"Don't forget to point out," George said, "that if von Neipperg attempts treachery, he will be instantly shot dead by my men firing from this house."

"Quite."

He left Mary in her bed. George went with him, to pull away the furniture barricade at the front door.

Mary realized she wasn't about to lie in bed while Bysshe was outside risking his neck. She threw off the covers and went to the window. Unbarred the shutter, pushed it open slightly.

Wet coursed down her legs.

Bysshe was holding a conversation with a stiff young man in an overcoat. After a few moments, Bysshe returned and reported to George. Mary, feeling like a guilty child, returned to her bed.

"Baron von Strickow—that's Neipperg's second—was taken with your notion of the swordfight *pour la cavalerie,* but insists the fight should be on horseback." He frowned. "They know, of course, that you haven't a horse with you."

"No doubt they'd offer me some nag or other." George thought for a moment. "Very well. I find the notion of a fight on horseback too piquant quite to ignore—tell them that if they insist on such a fight, they must bring forward six saddled horses, and that I will pick mine first, and Neipperg second."

"Very well."

Bysshe returned to the negotiations, and reported back that all had been settled. "With ill grace, as regards your last condition. But he conceded it was fair." Bysshe returned to Mary's room, speaking to George over his shoulder. "Just as well you're doing this on horseback. The yard is wet and slippery—poor footing for sword work."

"I'll try not to do any quick turns on horseback, either." George stepped into the room, gave Mary a glance, then looked at Bysshe. "Your appreciation of our opponents?"

"The Baron was tired and mud-covered. He's been riding hard. I don't imagine the rest of them are any fresher." Bysshe sat by Mary and took her hand. "He wouldn't shake my hand until he found out my father was a baronet. And then I wouldn't shake his."

"Good fellow!"

Bysshe gave a self-congratulatory look. "I believe it put him out of countenance."

George was amused. "These kraut-eaters make me look positively democratic." He left to give Pásmány his carbine and pistols—"the better to keep Neipperg honest."

"What of the princess?" Mary wondered. "Do you suppose he will bother to tell her of these efforts on her behalf?"

Shortly thereafter came the sound of the kitchen trap being thrown open, and George's bootheels descending to the cellar. Distant French tones, the sound of female protest, George's calm insistence. Claire's furious shrieks. George's abrupt reply, and then his return to the kitchen.

George appeared in the door, clanking in spurs and with a sword in his hand. Marie-Louise, looking pale, hovered behind him.

Mary looked up at Bysshe. "You won't have to participate in this any longer, will you?"

George answered for him. "I'd be obliged if Mr. Shelley would help me select my horse. Then you can withdraw to the porch—but if there's treachery, be prepared to barricade the door again."

Bysshe nodded. "Very well." He rose and looked out the window. "The horses are coming, along with the Baron and a one-eyed man."

George gave a cursory look out the window. "That's the fellow. He lost the eye at Neerwinden—French sabre cut." His voice turned inward. "I'll try to attack from his blind side—perhaps he'll be weaker there."

Bysshe was more interested in the animals. "There are three white horses. What are they?"

"Lipizzaners of the royal stud," George said. "The Roman Caesars rode 'em, or so the Austrians claim. Small horses by the standard of our English hunters, but strong and very sturdy. Bred and trained for war." He flashed a smile. "They'll do for me, I think."

He stripped off his coat and began to walk toward the door, but recollected, at the last second, the cause of the fight and returned to Marie-Louise. He put his arms around her, murmured something, and kissed her cheek. Then, with a smile, he walked into the other room. Bysshe, deeply unhappy, followed. And then Mary, ignoring the questioning eyes of the Austrian princess, worked her way out of bed and went to the window.

From the window Mary watched as George took his time with the horses, examining each minutely, discoursing on their virtues with Bysshe, checking their shoes and eyes as if he were buying them. The Austrians looked stiff and disapproving. Neipperg was a tall, bull-chested man, handsome despite the eye-patch, with a well-tended halo of hair.

Perhaps George dragged the business out in order to nettle his opponent.

George mounted one of the white horses and trotted it round the yard for a brief while, then repeated the experiment with a second Lipizzaner. Then he went back to the first and declared himself satisfied.

Neipperg, seeming even more rigid than before, took the second horse, the one George had rejected. Perhaps it was his own, Mary thought.

Bysshe retreated to the front porch of the farmhouse, Strickow to the barn, and the two horsemen to opposite ends of the yard. Both handled their horses expertly. Bysshe asked each if he were ready, and received a curt nod.

Mary's legs trembled. She hoped she wouldn't fall. She had to see it. *"Un,"* Strickow called out in a loud voice. *"Deux. Trois!"* Mary had expected the combatants to dash at each other, but they were too cautious, too professional—instead each goaded his beast into a slow trot and held his sabre with the hilt high, the blade dropping across the body, carefully on guard. Mary noticed that George was approaching on his opponent's blind right side. As they came together there were sudden flashes of silver, too fast for the eye to follow, and the sound of ringing steel.

Then they were past. But Neipperg, as he spurred on, delivered a vicious blind swipe at George's back. Mary cried out, but there was another clang—George had dropped his point behind his back to guard against just that attack.

"Foul blow!" Bysshe cried, from the porch, then clapped his hands. "Good work, George!"

George turned with an intent smile on his face, as if he had the measure of his opponent. There was a cry from elsewhere in the farmhouse, and Claire came running, terror in her eyes. "Are they fighting?" she wailed, and pushed past Mary to get to the window.

Mary tried to pull her back and failed. Her head swam. "You don't want to watch this," she said.

Alba began to cry from the cellar. Claire pushed the shutters wide and thrust her head out.

"Kill him, George!" she shouted. "Kill him!"

George gave no sign of having heard—he and Neipperg were trotting at each other again, and George was crouched down over his horse's neck, his attention wholly on his opponent.

Mary watched over Claire's shoulder as the two approached, as blades flashed and clanged—once, twice—and then George thrust to Neipperg's throat and Mary gasped, not just at the pitilessness of it, but at its strange physical consummation, at the way horse and rider and arm and sword, the dart of the blade and momentum of the horse and rider, merged for an instant in an awesome moment of perfection . . .

Neipperg rode on for a few seconds while blood poured like a tide down his white shirtfront, and then he slumped and fell off his animal like a sack. Mary shivered, knowing she'd just seen a man killed, killed with absolute forethought and deliberation. And George, that intent look still on his face as he watched Neipperg over his shoulder, lowered his scarlet-tipped sword and gave a careless tug of the reins to turn his horse around . . .

Too careless. The horse balked, then turned too suddenly. Its hind legs slid out from under it on the slick grass, George's arms windmilled as he tried to regain his balance, and the horse, with an almost-human cry, fell heavily on George's right leg.

Claire and Mary cried out. The Lipizzaner's legs flailed in the air as he rolled over on George. Bysshe launched himself off the porch in a run. George began to scream, a sound that raised the hair on Mary's neck.

And, while Adam von Neipperg twitched away his life on the grass, Marie-Louise of Austria, France, and Parma, hearing George's cries of agony, bolted hysterically for the door and ran out onto the yard and into the arms of her countryman.

"No!" George insisted. "No surgeons!"

Not a word, Mary noted, for the lost Marie-Louise. She watched from the doorway as his friends carried him in and laid him on the kitchen table. The impassive M. Fleury cut the boot away with a pair of shears and tore the leather away with a suddenness that made George gasp. Bysshe peeled away the bloody stocking, and bit his lip at the sight of protruding bone.

"We *must* show this to the surgeon, George," Bysshe said. "The foot and ankle are shattered."

"No!" Sweat beaded on George's forehead. "I've seen surgeons at their work. My God—" There was horror in his eyes. "I'll be a *cripple!*"

M. Fleury said nothing, only looked down at the shattered ankle with his knowing veteran's eyes. He hitched up his trousers, took a bucket from under the cutting board, and left to get ice for Mary.

The Austrians were long gone, ridden off with their blond trophy. Their fallen paladin was still in the yard—he'd only slow down their escape.

George was pale and his skin was clammy. Claire choked back tears as she looked down at him. "Does it hurt very much?"

"Yes," George confessed, "it does. Perhaps Madame Fleury would oblige me with a glass of brandy."

Madame Fleury fetched the jug and some glasses. Pásmány stood in the corner exuding dark Hungarian gloom. George looked up at Mary, seemed surprised to find her out of bed.

"I seem to be unlucky for your little family," he said. "I hope you will forgive me."

"If I can," said Mary.

George smiled. "Truthful Miss Mary. How fine you are." A spasm of pain took him and he gasped. Madame Fleury put some brandy in his hand and he gulped it.

"Mary!" Bysshe rushed to her. "You should not be seeing this. Go back to your bed."

"What difference does it make?" Mary said, feeling the blood streaking her legs; but she allowed herself to be put to bed.

Soon the tub of icewater was ready. It was too big to get through the door into Mary's room, so she had to join George in the kitchen after all. She sat in the cold wet, and Bysshe propped her back with pillows, and they both watched as the water turned red.

George was pale, gulping brandy from the bottle. He looked at Bysshe.

"Perhaps you could take our mind off things," he said. "Perhaps you could tell me one of your ghost stories."

Bysshe could not speak. Tears were running down his face. So to calm him, and to occupy her time when dying, Mary began to tell a story. It was about an empty man, a Swiss baron who was a genius but who lacked any quality of soul. His name, in English, meant the Franked Stone—the stone whose noble birth had paid its way, but which was still a stone, and being a stone unable to know love.

And the baron had a wasting disease, one that caused his limbs to wither and die. And he knew he would soon be a cripple.

Being a genius the baron thought he knew the answer. Out of protoplasm and electricity and parts stolen from the graveyard he built another man. He called this man a monster, and held him prisoner. And every time one of the baron's limbs began to wither, he'd arrange for his assistants to cut off one of the monster's limbs, and use it to replace the baron's withered part. The monster's own limb was replaced by one from the graveyard. And the monster went through enormous pain, one hideous surgical procedure after another, but the baron didn't care, because he was whole again and the monster was only a monster, a thing he had created.

But then the monster escaped. He educated himself and grew in understanding and apprehension and he spied on the baron and his family. In revenge the monster killed everyone the baron knew, and the baron was angered not because he loved his family but because the killings were an offense to his pride. So the baron swore revenge on the monster and began to pursue him.

The pursuit took the baron all over the world, but it never ended. At the end the baron pursued the monster to the arctic, and disappeared forever into the ice and mist, into the heart of the white desert of the Pole.

Mary meant the monster to be Soul, of course, and the baron Reason. Because unless the two could unite in sympathy, all was lost in ice and desolation.

It took Mary a long time to tell her story, and she couldn't tell whether George understood her meaning or not. By the time she finished the day was almost over, and her own bleeding had stopped. George had drunk himself nearly insensible, and a diffident notary had arrived from St. Prex to take everyone's testimony.

Mary went back to bed, clean sheets and warmth and the arms of her lover. She and her child would live.

The surgeon came with them, took one look at George's foot, and announced it had to come off.

The surgery was performed on the kitchen table, and George's screams rang for a long time in Mary's dreams.

In a few days Mary had largely recovered. She and Bysshe thanked the Fleurys and sailed to Geneva on a beautiful autumn day in their hired boat. George and Claire—for Claire was George's again—remained behind to sort out George's legal problems. Mary didn't think their friendship would last beyond George's immediate recovery, and she hoped that Claire would not return to England heavy with another child.

After another week's recovery in Geneva, Bysshe and Mary headed for England and the financial rescue of Mr. Godwin. Mary had bought a pocketbook and was already filling its pages with her story of the Franked Stone. Bysshe knew any number of publishers, and assured her it would find a home with one of them.

Frankenstein was an immediate success. At one point there were over twenty stage productions going on at once. Though she received no money from the stage adaptations, the book proved a very good seller, and was never out of print. The royalties proved useful in supporting Bysshe and Mary and Claire— once she returned to them, once more with child—during years of wandering, chiefly in Switzerland and Italy.

George's promised thousand pounds a year never materialized.

And the monster, the poor abused charnel creature that was Mary's settlement with death, now stalked through the hearts of all the world.

George went to South America to sell his sword to the revolutionary cause.

Mary and Bysshe, reading of his exploits in tattered newspapers sent from England, found it somehow satisfying that he was, at last and however reluctantly, fighting for liberty.

They never saw him again, but Mary thought of him often—the great, famed figure, limping painfully through battle after battle, crippled, ever-restless, and in his breast the arctic waste of the soul, the franked and steely creator with his heart of stone.

BOOBS

Suzy McKee Charnas

Suzy McKee Charnas is a tough-minded and highly accomplished writer of feminist science fiction (for instance, *Motherlines* and *The Furies*) and fantasy *(The Vampire Tapestry)*. Her occasional forays into short fiction have not to date been collected except in small-press chapbooks. "Boobs" is a Hugo-winning story, a witty feminist fantasy of empowerment, about growing up and turning into a monster—and liking it a lot.

The thing is, it's like your brain wants to go on thinking about the miserable history mid-term you have to take tomorrow, but your body takes over. And what a body! You can see in the dark and run like the wind and leap parked cars in a single bound.

Of course you pay for it next morning (but it's worth it). I always wake up stiff and sore, with dirty hands and feet and face, and I have to jump in the shower fast so Hilda won't see me like that.

Not that she would know what it was about, but why take chances? So I pretend it's the other thing that's bothering me. So she goes, "Come on, sweetie, everybody gets cramps, that's no reason to go around moaning and groaning. What are you doing, trying to get out of school just because you've got your period?"

If I didn't like Hilda, which I do even though she is only a stepmother instead of my real mother, I would show her something that would keep me out of school forever, and it's not fake, either.

But there are plenty of people I'd rather show that to.

I already showed that dork Billy Linden.

"Hey, Boobs!" he goes, in the hall right outside Homeroom. A lot of kids laughed, naturally, though Rita Frye called him an asshole.

Billy is the one that started it, sort of, because he always started everything, him with his big mouth. At the beginning of term, he came barreling down on me hollering, "Hey, look at Bornstein, something musta happened to her over the summer! What happened, Bornstein? Hey, everybody, look at Boobs Bornstein!"

He made a grab at my chest, and I socked him in the shoulder, and he punched me in the face, which made me dizzy and shocked and made me cry, too, in front of everybody.

I mean, I always used to wrestle and fight with the boys, being that I was strong for a girl. All of a sudden it was different. He hit me hard, to really hurt, and the shock sort of got me in the pit of my stomach and made me feel nauseous, too, as well as mad and embarrassed to death.

I had to go home with a bloody nose and lie with my head back and ice wrapped in a towel on my face and dripping down into my hair.

Hilda sat on the couch next to me and patted me. She goes, "I'm sorry about this, honey, but really, you have to learn it sometime. You're all growing up and the boys are getting stronger than you'll ever be. If you fight with boys, you're bound to get hurt. You have to find other ways to handle them."

To make things worse, the next morning I started to bleed down there, which Hilda had explained carefully to me a couple of times, so at least I knew what was going on. Hilda really tried extra hard without being icky about it, but I hated when she talked about how it was all part of these exciting changes in my body that are so important and how terrific it is to "become a young woman."

Sure. The whole thing was so messy and disgusting, worse than she had said, worse than I could imagine, with these black clots of gunk coming out in a smear of pink blood—I thought I would throw up. That's just the lining of your uterus, Hilda said. Big deal. It was still gross.

And plus, the *smell*.

Hilda tried to make me feel better, she really did. She said we should "mark the occasion" like primitive people do, so it's something special, not just a nasty thing that just sort of falls on you.

So we decided to put poor old Pinkie away, my stuffed dog that I've slept with since I was three. Pinkie is bald and sort of hard and lumpy, since he got put in the washing machine by mistake, and you would never know he was all soft plush when he was new, or even that he was pink.

Last time my friend Gerry-Anne came over, before the summer, she saw Pinky laying on my pillow and though she didn't say anything, I could tell she was thinking that was kind of babyish. So I'd been thinking about not keeping Pinky around anymore.

Hilda and I made him this nice box lined with pretty scraps from her quilting class, and I thanked him out loud for being my friend for so many years, and we put him up in the closet, on the top shelf.

I felt terrible, but if Gerry-Anne decided I was too babyish to be friends with anymore, I could end up with no friends at all. When you have never been popular since the time you were skinny and fast and everybody wanted you on their team, you have that kind of thing on your mind.

Hilda and Dad made me go to school the next morning so nobody would think I was scared of Billy Linden (which I was) or that I would let him keep me away just by being such a dork.

Everybody kept sneaking funny looks at me and whispering, and I was sure it was because I couldn't help walking funny with the pad between my legs and because they could smell what was happening, which as far as I knew hadn't happened to anybody else in Eight A yet. Just like nobody else in the whole grade had anything real in their stupid training bras except me, thanks a lot.

Anyway I stayed away from everybody as much as I could and wouldn't talk to Gerry-Anne, even, because I was scared she would ask me why I walked funny and smelled bad.

Billy Linden avoided me just like everybody else, except one of his stupid buddies purposely bumped into me so I stumbled into Billy on the lunch-line. Billy turns around and he goes, real loud, "Hey, Boobs, when did you start wearing black and blue makeup?"

I didn't give him the satisfaction of knowing that he had actually broken my nose, which the doctor said. Good thing they don't have to bandage you up for that. Billy would be hollering up a storm about how I had my nose in a sling as well as my boobs.

That night I got up after I was supposed to be asleep and took off my underpants and T-shirt that I sleep in and stood looking at myself in the mirror. I didn't need to turn a light on. The moon was full and it was shining right into my bedroom through the big dormer window.

I crossed my arms and pinched myself hard to sort of punish my body for what it was doing to me.

As if that could make it stop.

No wonder Edie Siler had starved herself to death in the tenth grade! I understood her perfectly. She was trying to keep her body down, keep it normal-looking, thin and strong, like I was too, back when I looked like a person, not a cartoon that somebody would call "Boobs."

And then something warm trickled in a little line down the inside of my leg, and I knew it was blood and I couldn't stand it anymore. I pressed my thighs together and shut my eyes hard, and I did something.

I mean I felt it happening. I felt myself shrink down to a hard core of sort of cold fire inside my bones, and all the flesh part, the muscles and the squishy insides and the skin, went sort of glowing and free-floating, all shining with moonlight, and I felt a sort of shifting and balance-changing going on.

I thought I was fainting on account of my stupid period. So I turned around and threw myself on my bed, only by the time I hit it, I knew something was seriously wrong.

For one thing, my nose and my head were crammed with these crazy, rich sensations that it took me a second to even figure out were smells, they were so much stronger than any smells I'd ever smelled. And they were—I don't know—*interesting* instead of just stinky, even the rotten ones.

I opened my mouth to get the smells a little better, and heard myself panting in a funny way as if I'd been running, which I hadn't, and then there was this long part of my face sticking out and something moving there—my tongue.

I was licking my chops.

Well, there was this moment of complete and utter panic. I tore around the room whining and panting and hearing my toenails clicking on the floorboards, and then I huddled down and crouched in the corner because I was scared Dad and Hilda would hear me and come to find out what was making all this racket.

Because I could hear them. I could hear their bed creak when one of them turned over, and Dad's breath whistling a little in an almost snore, and I could smell them too, each one with a perfectly clear bunch of smells, kind of like those desserts of mixed ice cream they call a medley.

My body was twitching and jumping with fear and energy, and my room—it's a converted attic-space, wide but with a ceiling that's low in places—my room felt like a jail. And plus, I was terrified of catching a glimpse of myself in the mirror. I had a pretty good idea of what I would see, and I didn't want to see it.

Besides, I had to pee, and I couldn't face trying to deal with the toilet in the state I was in.

So I eased the bedroom door open with my shoulder and nearly fell down the stairs trying to work them with four legs and thinking about it, instead of letting my body just do it. I put my hands on the front door to open it, but my hands weren't hands, they were paws with long knobby toes covered with fur, and the toes had thick black claws sticking out of the ends of them.

The pit of my stomach sort of exploded with horror, and I yelled. It came out this wavery "wooo" noise that echoed eerily in my skullbones. Upstairs, Hilda goes, "Jack, what was that?" I bolted for the basement as I heard Dad hit the floor of their bedroom.

The basement door slips its latch all the time, so I just shoved it open and down I went, doing better on the stairs this time because I was too scared to think. I spent the rest of the night down there, moaning to myself (which meant whining through my nose, really) and trotting around rubbing against the walls trying to rub off this crazy shape I had, or just moving around because I couldn't sit still. The place was thick with stinks and these slow-swirling currents of hot and cold air. I couldn't handle all the input.

As for having to pee, in the end I managed to sort of hike my butt up over the edge of the slop-sink by Dad's workbench and let go in there. The only problem was that I couldn't turn the taps on to rinse out the smell because of my paws.

Then about three A.M. I woke up from a doze curled up in a bare place on the floor where the spiders weren't so likely to walk, and I couldn't see a thing or smell anything either, so I knew I was okay again even before I checked and found fingers on my hands again instead of claws.

I zipped upstairs and stood under the shower so long that Hilda yelled at me for using up the hot water when she had a load of wash to do that morning. I was only trying to steam some of the stiffness out of my muscles, but I couldn't tell her that.

It was real weird to just dress and go to school after a night like that. One good thing, I had stopped bleeding after only one day, which Hilda said wasn't so strange for the first time. So it had to be the huge greenish bruise on my face from Billy's punch that everybody was staring at.

That and the usual thing, of course. Well, why not? *They* didn't know I'd spent the night as a wolf.

So Fat Joey grabbed my book bag in the hallway outside science class and tossed it to some kid from Eight B. I had to run after them to get it back, which of course was set up so the boys could cheer the jouncing of my boobs under my shirt.

I was so mad I almost caught Fat Joey, except I was afraid if I grabbed him, maybe he would sock me like Billy had.

Dad had told me, Don't let it get you, kid, all boys are jerks at that age.

Hilda had been saying all summer, Look, it doesn't do any good to walk around all hunched up with your arms crossed, you should just throw your shoulders back and walk like a proud person who's pleased that she's growing up. You're just a little early, that's all, and I bet the other girls are secretly envious of you, with their cute little training bras, for Chrissake, as if there was something that needed to be *trained*.

It's okay for her, she's not in school, she doesn't remember what it's like.

So I quit running and walked after Joey until the bell rang, and then I got my book bag back from the bushes outside where he threw it. I was crying a little, and I ducked into the girls' room.

Stacey Buhl was in there doing her lipstick like usual and wouldn't talk to me like usual, but Rita came bustling in and said somebody should off that dumb dork Joey, except of course it was really Billy that put him up to it. Like usual.

Rita is okay except she's an outsider herself, being that her kid brother has AIDS, and lots of kids' parents don't think she should even be in the school. So I don't hang around with her a lot. I've got enough trouble, and anyway I was late for Math.

I had to talk to somebody, though. After school I told Gerry-Anne, who's been my best friend on and off since fourth grade. She was off at the moment, but I found her in the library and I told her I'd had a weird dream about being a wolf. She wants to be a psychiatrist like her mother, so of course she listened.

She told me I was nuts. That was a big help.

That night I made sure the back door wasn't exactly closed, and then I got in bed with no clothes on—imagine turning into a wolf in your underpants and T-shirt—and just shivered, waiting for something to happen.

The moon came up and shone in my window, and I changed again, just like before, which is not one bit like how it is in the movies—all struggling and screaming and bones snapping out with horrible cracking and tearing noises, just the way I guess you would imagine it to be, if you knew it had to be done by building special machines to do that for the camera and make it look real: if you were a special effects man, instead of a werewolf.

For me, it didn't have to look real, it was real. It was this melting and drifting thing, which I got sort of excited by it this time. I mean it felt—interesting. Like something I was doing, instead of just another dumb body-mess happening to me because some brainless hormones said so.

I must have made a noise. Hilda came upstairs to the door of my bedroom, but luckily she didn't come in. She's tall, and my ceiling is low for her, so she often talks to me from the landing.

Anyway I'd heard her coming, so I was in my bed with my whole head shoved under my pillow, praying frantically that nothing showed.

I could smell her, it was the wildest thing—her own smell, sort of sweaty but sweet, and then on top of it her perfume, like an ice-pick stuck in my nose. I didn't actually hear a word she said, I was too scared, and also I had this ripply shaking feeling inside me, a high that was only partly terror.

See, I realized all of a sudden, with this big blossom of surprise, that I didn't have to be scared of Hilda, or anybody. I was strong, my wolf-body was strong, and anyhow one clear look at me and she would drop dead.

What a relief, though, when she went away. I was dying to get out from under the weight of the covers, and besides I had to sneeze. Also I recognized that part of the energy roaring around inside me was hunger.

They went to bed—I heard their voices even in their bedroom, though not exactly what they said, which was fine. The words weren't important anymore, I could tell more from the tone of what they were saying.

Like I knew they were going to do it, and I was right. I could hear them messing around right through the walls, which was also something new, and I have never been so embarrassed in my life. I couldn't even put my hands over my ears, because my hands were paws.

So while I was waiting for them to go to sleep, I looked myself over in the big mirror on my closet door.

There was this big wolf head with a long slim muzzle and a thick ruff around my neck. The ruff stood up as I growled and backed up a little.

Which was silly of course, there was no wolf in the bedroom but me. But I was all strung out, I guess, and one wolf, me in my wolf body, was as much as I could handle the idea of, let alone two wolves, me and my reflection.

After that first shock, it was great. I kept turning one way and another for different views.

I was thin, with these long, slender legs but strong, you could see the muscles, and feet a little bigger than I would have picked. But I'll take four big feet over two big boobs any day.

My face was terrific, with jaggedy white ripsaw teeth and eyes that were small and clear and gleaming in the moonlight. The tail was a little bizarre, but I got used to it, and actually it had a nice plumy shape. My shoulders were big and covered with long, glossy-looking fur, and I had this neat coloring, dark on the back and a sort of melting silver on my front and underparts.

The thing was, though, my tongue, hanging out. I had a lot of trouble with that, it looked gross and silly at the same time. I mean, that was *my tongue,* about a foot long and neatly draped over the points of my bottom canines. That was when I realized that I didn't have a whole lot of expressions to use, not with that face, which was more like a mask.

But it was alive, it was my face, those were my own long black lips that my tongue licked.

No doubt about it, this was *me.* I was a werewolf, like in the movies they showed over Halloween weekend. But it wasn't anything like your ugly movie werewolf that's just some guy loaded up with pounds and pounds of makeup. I was *gorgeous.*

I didn't want to just hang around admiring myself in the mirror, though. I couldn't stand being cooped up in that stuffy, smell-crowded room.

When everything settled down and I could hear Dad and Hilda breathing the way they do when they're sleeping, I snuck out.

The dark wasn't very dark to me, and the cold felt sharp like vinegar, but not in a hurting way. Everyplace I went, there were these currents like waves in the air, and I could draw them in through my long wolf nose and roll the smell of them over the back of my tongue. It was like a whole different world, with bright sounds everywhere and rich, strong smells.

And I could run.

I started running because a car came by while I was sniffing at the garbage bags on the curb, and I was really scared of being seen in the headlights. So I took off down the dirt alley between our house and the Morrisons' next door, and holy cow, I could tear along with hardly a sound, I could jump their picket fence without even thinking about it. My back legs were like steel springs and I came down solid and square on four legs with almost no shock at all, let alone worrying about losing my balance or twisting an ankle.

Man, I could run through that chilly air all thick and moisty with smells, I could almost fly. It was like last year, when I didn't have boobs bouncing and yanking in front even when I'm only walking fast.

Just two rows of neat little bumps down the curve of my belly. I sat down and looked.

I tore open garbage bags to find out about the smells in them, but I didn't eat anything from them. I wasn't about to chow down on other people's stale hotdog-ends and pizza crusts and fat and bones scraped off their plates and all mixed in with mashed potatoes and stuff.

When I found places where dogs had stopped and made their mark, I squatted down and pissed there too, right on top, I just wiped them *out*.

I bounded across that enormous lawn around the Wanscombe place, where nobody but the Oriental gardener ever sets foot, and walked up the back and over the top of their BMW, leaving big fat pawprints all over it. Nobody saw me, nobody heard me, I was a shadow.

Well, except for the dogs, of course.

There was a lot of barking when I went by, real hysterics, which at first I was really scared about. But then I popped out of an alley up on Ridge Road, where the big houses are, right in front of about six dogs that run together. Their owners let them out all night and don't care if they get hit by a car.

They'd been trotting along with the wind behind them, checking out all the garbage bags set out for pickup the next morning. When they saw me, one of them let out a yelp of surprise, and they all skidded to a stop.

Six of them. I was scared. I growled.

The dogs turned fast, banging into each other in their hurry, and trotted away.

I don't know what they would have done if they met a real wolf, but I was something special, I guess.

I followed them.

They scattered and ran.

Well, I ran too, and this was a different kind of running. I mean, I stretched, and I raced, and there was this joy. I chased one of them.

Zig, zag, this little terrier-kind of dog tried to cut left and dive under the gate of somebody's front walk, all without a sound—he was running too hard to yell, and I was happy running quiet.

Just before he could ooze under the gate, I caught up with him and without thinking I grabbed the back of his neck and pulled him off his feet and gave him a shake as hard as I could, from side to side.

I felt his neck crack, the sound vibrated through all the bones of my face.

I picked him up in my mouth, and it was like he hardly weighed a thing. I trotted away holding him up off the ground, and under a bush in Baker's Park I held him down with my paws and I bit into his belly, which was still warm and quivering.

Like I said, I was hungry.

The blood gave me this rush like you wouldn't believe. I stood there a minute looking around and licking my lips, just sort of panting and tasting the taste because I was stunned by it, it was like eating honey or the best chocolate malted you ever had.

So I put my head down and chomped that little dog, like shoving your face into a pizza and inhaling it. God, I was *starved*, so I didn't mind that the meat was tough and rank-tasting after that first wonderful bite. I even licked blood off the ground after, never mind the grit mixed in.

I ate two more dogs that night, one that was tied up on a clothesline in a cruddy yard full of rusted-out car parts down on the South side, and one fat old yellow dog out snuffling around on his own and way too slow. He tasted pretty bad, and by then I was feeling full, so I left a lot.

I strolled around the park, shoving the swings with my big black wolf nose, and I found the bench where Mr. Granby sits and feeds the pigeons every day, never mind that nobody else wants the dirty birds around crapping on their cars. I took a dump there, right where he sits.

Then I gave the setting moon a goodnight, which came out quavery and wild, "Loo-loo-loo!" And I loped toward home, springing off the thick pads of my paws and letting my tongue loll out and feeling generally super.

I slipped inside and trotted upstairs, and in my room I stopped to look at myself in the mirror.

As gorgeous as before, and only a few dabs of blood on me, which I took time to lick off. I did get a little worried—I mean, suppose that was it, suppose having killed and eaten what I'd killed in my wolf shape, I was stuck in this shape forever? Like, if you wander into a fairy castle and eat or drink anything, that's it, you can't ever leave. Suppose when the morning came I didn't change back?

Well, there wasn't much I could do about that one way or the other, and to tell the truth, I felt like I wouldn't mind; it had been worth it.

When I was nice and clean, including licking off my own bottom which seemed like a perfectly normal and nice thing to do at the time, I jumped up on the bed, curled up, and corked right off. When I woke up with the sun in my eyes, there I was, my own self again.

It was very strange, grabbing breakfast and wearing my old sweatshirt that wallowed all over me so I didn't stick out so much, while Hilda yawned and shuffled around in her robe and slippers and acted like her and Dad hadn't been doing it last night, which I knew different.

And plus, it was perfectly clear that she didn't have a clue about what *I* had been doing, which gave me a strange feeling.

One of the things about growing up which they're careful not to tell you is, you start having more things you don't talk to your parents about. And I had a doozie.

Hilda goes, "What's the matter, are you off Sugar Pops now? Honestly, Kelsey, I can't keep up with you! And why can't you wear something nicer than that old shirt to school? Oh, I get it: disguise, right?"

She sighed and looked at me kind of sad but smiling, her hands on her hips. "Kelsey, Kelsey," she goes, "if only I'd had half of what you've got when *I* was a girl—I was flat as an ironing board, and it made me so miserable, I can't tell you."

She's still real thin and neat-looking, so what does she know about it? But she meant well, and anyhow I was feeling so good I didn't argue.

I didn't change my shirt, though.

That night I didn't turn into a wolf. I laid there waiting, but though the moon came up, nothing happened no matter how hard I tried, and after a while I went and looked out the window and realized that the moon wasn't really full anymore, it was getting smaller.

I wasn't so much relieved as sorry. I bought a calendar at the school book sale two weeks later, and I checked the full moon nights coming up and waited anxiously to see what would happen.

Meantime, things rolled along as usual. I got a rash of zits on my chin. I would look in the mirror and think about my wolf-face that had beautiful sleek fur instead of zits.

Zits and all I went to Angela Durkin's party, and next day Billy Linden told everybody that I went in one of the bedrooms at Angela's and made out with him, which I did not. But since no grown-ups were home and Fat Joey brought grass to the party, most of the kids were stoned and didn't know who did what or where anyhow.

As a matter of fact, Billy once actually did get a girl in Seven B high one time out in his parents' garage, and him and two of his friends did it to her while she was zonked out of her mind, or anyway they said they did, and she was too embarrassed to say anything one way or the other, and a little while later she changed schools.

How I know about it is the same way everybody else does, which is because Billy was the biggest boaster in the whole school, and you could never tell if he was lying or not.

So I guess it wasn't so surprising that some people believed what Billy said about me. Gerry-Anne quit talking to me after that. Meantime Hilda got pregnant.

This turned into a huge discussion about how Hilda had been worried about her biological clock so she and Dad had decided to have a kid, and I shouldn't mind, it would be fun for me and good preparation for being a mother myself later on, when I found some nice guy and got married.

Sure. Great preparation. Like Mary O'Hare in my class, who gets to change her youngest baby sister's diapers all the time, yick. She jokes about it, but you can tell she really hates it. Now it looked like it was my turn coming up, as usual.

The only thing that made life bearable was my secret.

"You're laid back today," Devon Brown said to me in the lunchroom one day after Billy had been specially obnoxious, trying to flick rolled-up pieces of bread from his table so they would land on my chest. Devon was sitting with me because he was bad at French, my only good subject, and I was helping him out with some verbs. I guess he wanted to know why I wasn't upset because of Billy picking on me. He goes, "How come?"

"That's a secret," I said, thinking about what Devon would say if he knew a werewolf was helping him with his French: *loup. Manger.*

He goes, "What secret?" Devon has freckles and is actually kind of cute-looking.

"A secret," I go, "so I can't tell you, dummy."

He looks real superior and he goes, "Well, it can't be much of a secret, because girls can't keep secrets, everybody knows that."

Sure, like that kid Sara in Eight B who it turned out her own father had been molesting her for years, but she never told anybody until some psychologist caught on from some tests we all had to take in seventh grade. Up till then, Sara kept her secret fine.

And I kept mine, marking off the days on the calendar. The only part I didn't look forward to was having a period again, which last time came right before the change.

When the time came, I got crampy and more zits popped out on my face, but I didn't have a period.

I changed, though.

The next morning they were talking in school about a couple of prize miniature Schnauzers at the Wanscombes that had been hauled out of their yard by somebody and killed, and almost nothing left of them.

Well, my stomach turned a little when I heard some kids describing what Mr. Wanscombe had found over in Baker's Park, "the remains," as people said. I felt a little guilty, too, because Mrs. Wanscombe had really loved those little dogs, which somehow I didn't think about at all when I was a wolf the night before, trotting around hungry in the moonlight.

I knew those Schnauzers personally, so I was sorry, even if they were irritating little mutts that made a lot of noise.

But heck, the Wanscombes shouldn't have left them out all night in the cold. Anyhow, they were rich, they could buy new ones if they wanted.

Still and all, though. I mean, dogs are just dumb animals. If they're mean, it's because they're wired that way or somebody made them mean, they can't help it. They can't just decide to be nice, like a person can. And plus, they don't taste so great, I think because they put so much junk in commercial dogfoods—anti-worm medicine and ashes and ground-up fish, stuff like that. Ick.

In fact after the second Schnauzer I had felt sort of sick and I didn't sleep real well that night. So I was not in a great mood to start with; and that was the day that my new brassiere disappeared while I was in gym. Later on I got passed a note telling me where to find it: stapled to the bulletin board outside the Principal's office, where everybody could see that I was trying a bra with an underwire.

Naturally, it had to be Stacey Buhl that grabbed my bra while I was changing for gym and my back was turned, since she was now hanging out with Billy and his friends.

Billy went around all day making bets at the top of his lungs on how soon I would be wearing a D-cup.

Stacey didn't matter, she was just a jerk. Billy mattered. He had wrecked me in that school forever, with his nasty mind and his big, fat mouth. I was past crying or fighting and getting punched out. I was boiling, I had had enough crap from him, and I had an idea.

I followed Billy home and waited on his porch until his mom came home and she made him come down and talk to me. He stood in the doorway and talked through the screen door, eating a banana and lounging around like he didn't have a care in the world.

So he goes, "Whatcha want, Boobs?"

I stammered a lot, being I was so nervous about telling such big lies, but that probably made me sound more believable.

I told him that I would make a deal with him: I would meet him that night in Baker's Park, late, and take off my shirt and bra and let him do whatever he wanted with my boobs if that would satisfy his curiosity and he would find somebody else to pick on and leave me alone.

"What?" he said, staring at my chest with his mouth open. His voice squeaked and he was practically drooling on the floor. He couldn't believe his good luck.

I said the same thing over again.

He almost came out onto the porch to try it right then and there. "Well, shit," he goes, lowering his voice a lot, "why didn't you say something before? You really mean it?"

I go, "Sure," though I couldn't look at him.

After a minute he goes, "Okay, it's a deal. Listen, Kelsey, if you like it, can we, uh, do it again, you know?"

I go, "Sure. But Billy, one thing: this is a secret, between just you and me. If you tell anybody, if there's one other person hanging around out there to-night—"

"Oh no," he goes, real fast, "I won't say a thing to anybody, honest. Not a word, I promise!"

Not until afterward, of course, was what he meant, which if there was one thing Billy Linden couldn't do, it was to keep quiet if he knew something bad about another person.

"You're gonna like it, I know you are," he goes, speaking strictly for himself as usual. "Jeez. I can't believe this!"

But he did, the dork.

I couldn't eat much for dinner that night, I was too excited, and I went up-stairs early to do homework, I told Dad and Hilda.

Then I waited for the moon, and when it came, I changed.

Billy was in the park. I caught a whiff of him, very sweaty and excited, but I stayed cool. I snuck around for a while, as quiet as I could—which was real quiet—making sure none of his stupid friends were lurking around. I mean, I wouldn't have trusted just his promise for a million dollars.

I passed up half a hamburger lying in the gutter where somebody had parked for lunch next to Baker's Park. My mouth watered, but I didn't want to spoil my appetite. I was hungry and happy, sort of singing inside my own head, "Shoo, fly, pie, and an apple-pan-dowdie . . ."

Without any sound, of course.

Billy had been sitting on a bench, his hands in his pockets, twisting around to look this way and that way, watching for me—for my human self—to come join him. He had a jacket on, being it was very chilly out.

Which he didn't stop to think that maybe a sane person wouldn't be crazy enough to sit out there and take off her top leaving her naked skin bare to the breeze. But that was Billy all right, totally fixed on his own greedy self and with-out a single thought for somebody else. I bet all he could think about was what a great scam this was, to feel up old Boobs in the park and then crow about it all over school.

Now he was walking around the park, kicking at the sprinkler-heads and glancing up every once in a while, frowning and looking sulky.

I could see he was starting to think that I might stand him up. Maybe he even suspected that old Boobs was lurking around watching him and laughing to herself because he had fallen for a trick. Maybe old Boobs had even brought some kids from school with her to see what a jerk he was.

Actually that would have been pretty good, except Billy probably would have broken my nose for me again, or worse, if I'd tried it.

"Kelsey?" he goes, sounding mad.

I didn't want him stomping off home in a huff. I moved up closer, and I let the bushes swish a little around my shoulders.

He goes, "Hey, Kelse, it's late, where've you been?"

I listened to the words, but mostly I listened to the little thread of worry flickering in his voice, low and high, high and low, as he tried to figure out what was going on.

I let out the whisper of a growl.

He stood real still, staring at the bushes, and he goes, "That you, Kelse? Answer me."

I was wild inside. I couldn't wait another second. I tore through the bushes and leaped for him, flying.

He stumbled backward with a squawk—"What!"—jerking his hands up in front of his face, and he was just sucking in a big breath to yell with when I hit him like a demo-derby truck.

I jammed my nose past his feeble claws and chomped down hard on his face.

No sound came out of him except this wet, thick gurgle, which I could more taste than hear because the sound came right into my mouth with the gush of his blood and the hot mess of meat and skin that I tore away and swallowed.

He thrashed around, hitting at me, but I hardly felt anything through my fur. I mean, he wasn't so big and strong laying there on the ground with me straddling him all lean and wiry with wolf-muscle. And plus, he was in shock. I got a strong whiff from below as he let go of everything right into his pants.

Dogs were barking, but so many people around Baker's Park have dogs to keep out burglars, and the dogs make such a racket all the time that nobody pays any attention. I wasn't worried. Anyway, I was too busy to care.

I nosed in under what was left of Billy's jaw and I bit his throat out.

Now let him go around telling lies about people.

His clothes were a lot of trouble and I really missed having hands. I managed to drag his shirt out of his belt with my teeth, though, and it was easy to tear his belly open. Pretty messy, but once I got in there, it was better than Thanksgiving dinner. Who would think that somebody as horrible as Billy Linden could taste so *good*?

He was barely moving by then, and I quit thinking about him as Billy Linden anymore. I quit thinking at all, I just pushed my head in and pulled out delicious steaming chunks and ate until I was picking at tidbits, and everything was getting cold.

On the way home I saw a police car cruising the neighborhood the way they do sometimes. I hid in the shadows and of course they never saw me.

There was a lot of washing up to do in the morning, and when Hilda saw my sheets she shook her head and she goes, "You should be more careful about keeping track of your period so as not to get caught by surprise."

Everybody in school knew something had happened to Billy Linden, but it wasn't until the day after that that they got the word. Kids stood around in little huddles trading rumors about how some wild animal had chewed Billy up. I would walk up and listen in and add a really gross remark or two, like part of the game of thrilling each other green and nauseous with made-up details to see who would upchuck first.

Not me, that's for sure. I mean, when somebody went on about how Billy's whole head was gnawed down to the skull and they didn't even know who he was except from the bus pass in his wallet, I got a little urpy. It's amazing the things people will dream up. But when I thought about what I had actually done to Billy, I had to smile.

It felt totally wonderful to walk through the halls without having anybody yelling, "Hey, Boobs!"

There are people who just plain do not deserve to live. And the same goes for Fat Joey, if he doesn't quit crowding me in science lab, trying to get a feel.

One funny thing, though, I don't get periods at all anymore. I get a little crampy, and my breasts get sore, and I break out more than usual—and then instead of bleeding, I change.

Which is fine with me, though I take a lot more care now about how I hunt on my wolf nights. I stay away from Baker's Park. The suburbs go on for miles and miles, and there are lots of places I can hunt and still get home by morning. A running wolf can cover a lot of ground.

And I make sure I make my kills where I can eat in private, so no cop car can catch me unawares, which could easily have happened that night when I killed Billy, I was so deep into the eating thing that first time. I look around a lot more now when I'm eating a kill, I keep watch.

Good thing it's only once a month that this happens, and only a couple of nights. "The Full Moon Killer" has the whole state up in arms and terrified as it is.

Eventually I guess I'll have to go somewhere else, which I'm not looking forward to at all. If I can just last until I can have a car of my own, life will get a lot easier.

Meantime, some wolf nights I don't even feel like hunting. Mostly I'm not as hungry as I was those first times. I think I must have been storing up my appetite for a long time. Sometimes I just prowl around and I run, boy do I run.

If I am hungry, sometimes I eat from the garbage instead of killing somebody. It's no fun, but you do get a taste for it. I don't mind garbage as long as once in a while I can have the real thing fresh-killed, nice and wet. People can be awfully nasty, but they sure taste sweet.

I do pick and choose, though. I look for people sneaking around in the middle of the night, like Billy, waiting in the park that time. I figure they've got to be out looking for trouble at that hour, so whose fault is it if they find it? I have done a lot more for the burglary problem around Baker's Park than a hundred dumb "watchdogs," believe me.

Gerry-Anne is not only talking to me again, she has invited me to go on a double-date with her. Some guy she met at a party invited her, and he has a friend. They're both from Fawcett Junior High across town, which will be a change. I was nervous, but finally I said yes. We're going to the movies next weekend. My first real date! I am still pretty nervous, to tell the truth.

For New Year's, I have made two solemn vows.

One is that on this date I will not worry about my chest, I will not be self-conscious, even if the guy stares.

The other is, I'll never eat another dog.

TO BRING IN FINE THINGS: THE SIGNIFICANCE OF SCIENCE FICTION PLOTS

Brian Stableford

Brian Stableford is a leading writer of SF, fantasy, and horror fiction, and one of the most influential critics of the literature. Although his doctorate is in sociology, his literary scholarship is legendary. In recent years, he has published a number of essays on "practical theory," of which this is one. At a time when the virtues of characterization are perhaps overdiscussed, Stableford's consideration of plot is a much-needed corrective.

My title is borrowed from a satirical play, *The Rehearsal,* written in 1671 by George Villiers, the second Duke of Buckingham. In this comedy the absurdly opinionated playwright Mr. Bayes explains to two observers the thinking behind his dramatic entertainment currently in rehearsal, which seems to them to be a farrago of nonsense compounded from plagiarized themes and absurd posturings. One of the hapless onlookers complains at one point that while some melodramatic trumpery is paraded upon the stage the plot is standing still. Bayes scornfully puts him in his place by exclaiming: "Why, what the devil is a plot for, but to bring in fine things?" In bowdlerized versions of the play the line is rendered: "What is the significance of a plot but to bring in fine things?"

It is the same Mr. Bayes who has given to the world the memorable and oft-quoted phrase: "the plot thickens." Samuel R. Delany has done Mr. Bayes the favor of taking that remark seriously in his essay on the construction of SF narratives, "Thickening the Plot,"* and I hope that I may be forgiven for doing likewise and arguing that this intended figure of fun might have a point after all, and that there may be some justice in suggesting that the significance of a plot *is* that it brings in fine things.

It is necessary to begin with matters of definition, and the deceptively simple question of what aspect of a story actually is "the plot." One possible answer is to regard a plot as a kind of synoptic description so that—for example—the plot of "The Time Machine" might be rendered as follows: a man who has invented

---

*Delany, Samuel R. "Thickening the Plot" in *The Jewel-Hinged Jaw,* Berkley, 1978, pp. 147–154.

a machine which travels through time tells a group of his friends what he has discovered about the ultimate future of the human species.

In this view, it is the contents of the plot which determines whether a story belongs to a particular genre; "The Time Machine" is science fiction because it deploys science-fictional ideas.

There is, however, another way of defining plot which has strikingly different implications. An example can be found in an essay on science fiction writing by Robert A. Heinlein,* which informs us that three basic plots are functional to *all* kinds of story-telling. They are, says Heinlein, Boy Meets Girl; The Little Tailor; and The Man Who Learned Better. This assurance has stuck in my mind ever since I first read it, exerting such a mesmeric fascination that when I first contemplated writing this paper I was tempted to entitle it "Boy Meets Text; The Little Tale-Teller; and The Reader Who Learned Better," but refrained on the grounds that it was too convoluted.

In this way of looking at things, a plot is regarded as something which operates at a more fundamental level than a mere synopsis of events. The voyage which the time-traveler undertakes in "The Time Machine" here becomes simply one more item in the great and multifarious tradition of stories of People Who Learned Better. Very many SF stories are, in fact, stories of People Who Learn Better, though the characters in question sometimes achieve more prestigious status in so doing, like the little tailor after whom Heinlein named his second basic plot, and if they are boys they very often meet a girl as well (or, of course, *vice versa*). Many science fiction stories, therefore, have all three of Heinlein's basic plots lurking inside them—and so do many stories from other genres.

This definitive shift can be metaphorically expressed by saying that while the descriptive-synopsis account of what a plot is refers to the narrative flesh of the story, the Heinleinian account refers to a deeper, more skeletal structure. Damon Knight[†] has written about a time when he worked (alongside other science fiction writers) for the Scott Meredith Literary Agency, where he was required to educate would-be writers in the use of a "Plot Skeleton" which was allegedly essential to the construction of saleable fiction. This Plot Skeleton began with the establishment of a sympathetic lead character in confrontation with an urgent problem of some kind, proceeded by showing how his initial attempts to solve the problem are frustrated, and concluded by showing how his efforts eventually prevail in bringing about a solution.

If we analyze them in terms of this Plot Skeleton we see immediately that Heinlein's three basic plots are in fact different variations on the same theme. Stories, according to the Plot Skeleton, are accounts of people led by desire or necessity to break through frustrating circumstances to achieve success; Heinlein's basic plots simply point to different kinds of success: romantic, social, and educational.

People who have written about the Meredith Plot Skeleton have usually done so in uncomplimentary terms. It is held up as testimony to the fact that

*Heinlein, Robert A. "On the Writing of Speculative Fiction" in *Of Worlds Beyond,* ed. Lloyd Arthur Eschbach, Advent, 1964, p. 14.
†Knight, Damon. "Knight Piece" in *Hell's Cartographers,* ed. Brian Aldiss and Harry Harrison, Weidenfeld & Nicolson, 1975, p. 122.

working for the pulps was a sad and tawdry business, confining writers within a straitjacket of crassly formularized expectations. It is true, of course, that many short stories have been written which do not appear to have even the ghost of the Plot Skeleton within them, but I would like to propose that it is, nevertheless, an analytical tool of some significance, which does bear a close relationship to the fundamental nature and utility of fiction.

It is worth noting that although it has no parallel alternatives after the fashion of Heinlein's supposedly basic plots, the Plot Skeleton is capable of one significant mutation, into which might be called an "anti-plot" or "tragic variant." This removes the successful conclusion, by substituting failure or by preserving frustration.

It is worth noting that this is not so much a simple *inversion* of the plot as a *perversion* of it. The anti-plot is entirely parasitic upon the plot, and would not have the effect upon the reader which it does if it were not for the fact that the reader has an expectation of some sort that success is the preferred outcome of a plot. It is the fact that the reader hopes that the plot will come out right which, if it does not, produces that special feeling of disappointment which we call "tragedy." We would not weep when we arrive at a downbeat ending were we not aware that in some sense, stories ought to end happily. Tragedy occurs, if you will forgive the hypogram, when a plot *sickens*.

This observation leads to an interesting general question. Why do the events in stories matter to their readers? Why does it make us joyful when an imaginary character in an imaginary story achieves his heart's desire, and why do we experience such a sharp sensation of tragedy when, instead, the unfolding logic of events within the story brings him inexorably to destruction?

We must remember, though, that the Plot Skeleton calls for a sympathetic lead character. We only care about *some* imaginary characters in such a way that we can rejoice in their successes and weep over their frustrations and failures. There are other characters—villains—whose successes cause us pain and whose ultimate destruction makes us exultant.

What is it about characters which makes them sympathetic? It is not that they are like us—at least, not in any simple sense—as anyone will readily understand who has sat in an audience watching the film *E.T.* or the play *Peter Pan.* In either case we may see large numbers of people reduced to tears by the plight of imaginary characters who bear very little resemblance to us—so little, in fact, that the part of E.T. is played by a plastic doll and the part of Tinkerbell by a spotlight!

The reason why we have such considerable sympathy for these non-human characters, while we righteously loathe the all-too-human foes who threaten them, has nothing to do with biological similarity and everything to do with moral compatibility. The simple fact is that we love the good guys, whoever and whatever they may be, and we hate the bad guys. This makes it perfectly clear that the nature and utility of fiction is intricately bound up with the notion of moral order.

The universe in which we live does not distribute its rewards and punishments according to any discernible moral order. As St. Matthew and everyone else has observed, the rain falls on the just and the unjust alike. The wicked are no more likely than the good to be struck by lightning or devoured by chance, and the virtuous are in no way protected by their innocence from suffering and misfortune. This is a prospect so intrinsically horrific that one of the principal occupations of the human imagination throughout history has been to support the pretense that this is mere appearance and not reality, that there is a good God—albeit one who moves in mysterious ways—and that there will be another life after death where the moral account-book will belatedly be balanced and we will all get what we really deserve.

This occupation of the human imagination is really only a special, and arguably rather silly, subcategory of a wider and generally more sensible occupation: making up stories.

The world of fiction is intrinsically and necessarily different from the world in which we find ourselves. The virtuous and the wicked characters are creations of an author, who is in sole charge of what happens to them, and who can distribute rewards and punishments as he wishes.

If, in a story, the virtuous suffer and the wicked flourish, it is no mere accident of happenstance—it is because the author has determined that things should turn out that way: it is not an absence of moral order, but a *refusal*, a calculated sickening of the plot. There is no way that an author can avoid moral responsibility for his fictional world and its characters. He may decide to throw dice to decide what happens next, and to whom, but that too is a refusal—a deliberate abandonment of moral prerogative. This is why the reader of a story can and does expect that the movement of the plot will be towards success, and thus knows that when success is refused a calculated violation of moral order has been committed. That is the essence of tragedy.

These observations can help us to understand certain features of reading behavior which might otherwise seem puzzling—for instance, that most people would rather read upbeat stories than downbeat stories. We can now see why so many readers like to read the same kind of book repeatedly, even though the same items of narrative flesh are repeated along with the same basic skeleton; what these readers are doing is participating in a ritual of moral affirmation whose force depends on repetition, and which is akin to other kinds of affirmative rituals maintained in our society and others, variously dubbed "religious," "legal," and "magical." We perceive, too, that when an audience rises to its collective feet and cheers wildly when the villain in a story goes bloodily to his destruction, it is not because its members are latent sadists but because they recognize a ritual propriety in what is happening. This fact is unfortunately overlooked in most discussions about the role and effects of violence in the media, which is why most of those discussions are futile.

At a more fundamental level, these observations about the relationship of fiction to moral order help us to see why stories exist at all, and how vital they are to life in human communities. Stories were the first, and remain one of the most important, tools which people have for exploring the question of how we ought to exercise such power as we have to make our lives and our world better. They are all the more important if we are prepared to recognize, as we ought to be, that there is no moral order already laid down for us as if engraved on stone by a careful creator; moral order is something which must itself be created and continually refined. People who believe otherwise are, of course, hostile to story-tellers.

It may appear that the skeletal definition of a plot rules out the possibility of distinguishing literary genres from one another at the level of plot. It suggests that all kinds of fiction are similar in that they share the same essential structure and dynamic. However, the similarity which genres have to one another is more a matter of homology than resemblance.

The homology of actual vertebrate skeletons consists in the fact that they are all variations on one basic theme, so that the arm of a man, the wing of a bird, and the flipper of a dolphin all contain structures which are specific functional adaptations of the same basic set of bones. We can look at genres of fiction in much the same way, so that a genre can have unique qualities because of the way it adapts the elementary skeleton of plot to different particular functions. Genres of fiction cannot avoid fundamental engagements with questions of moral order, but different genres of fiction—by virtues of the apparatus of ideas, characters, and settings which they deploy—can and do engage different questions of moral order, and engage them in different ways. Science fiction is no exception.

If we examine the particular kinds of moral question which science fiction is uniquely fitted to raise and explore, it seems to me to become obvious that science fiction is a very important kind of fiction, which does not at all deserve the contempt in which it is held by many literary critics. Science fiction is important, in this view, because it is capable of getting forthrightly to grips with certain problems in moral philosophy which other kinds of fiction can confront only with difficulty, if at all.

One of the most fundamental questions of moral philosophy is how a moral community ought to be defined. To which other entities do we owe moral consideration, and why? In their involvement with this question most stories are hamstrung by their attachment to mundane circumstance. Mundane fiction can ask whether animals have rights and it can present case studies relating to the welfare of the unborn, but it cannot do what moral philosophers have increasingly found themselves forced to do, which is to move beyond mundane examples and ask questions about hypothetical cases. If we are properly to pose the question of what it is which determines whether another entity should or should not belong to our moral community, and if we are properly to explore the feelings which we could and might have towards potential candidates for membership in our moral fiction, then we cannot do without science fiction. I do not say simply that science fiction is useful in this regard, I say that it is *necessary*.

Less fundamental to moral philosophy, but of considerable importance in political philosophy, is the question of what we can or ought to mean by the word "progress." Proper consideration of this issue necessitates backtracking, because it is necessary to refer to another fairly fundamental aspect of fiction, which I have so far left unmentioned; the role played by heroes.

The Meredith Plot Skeleton does not refer to heroes; it speaks only of a "sympathetic lead character." This is not simply coyness, because a sympathetic central character is not necessarily a hero. A protagonist becomes a hero when the problem with which he is faced is not merely his own, but that of a larger group. A hero operates on behalf of others; his projects have moral weight for the whole community. In the days of the first stories, a hero operated on behalf of his family or his tribe; more recent heroes may act on behalf of their religion or their nation. The change of state which a hero attempts to bring about is collective rather than individual, and a successful change of state is one to which we can legitimately attach the label of "progress." One can speak of "progress" in respect of the individual, the tribe, or the nation, but nowadays progress usually means the project of mankind taken as a whole.

Just as those philosophers who have tried to determine what it is that entitles an entity to inclusion in a moral community have been inexorably drawn to the construction of hypothetical entities, so political philosophers who have tried to determine what projects the human species ought to undertake for its collective betterment have been inexorably drawn to the construction of hypothetical societies—to the imagery of Utopia.

The hypothetical societies of the future are by definition unreachable by mundane fiction; only science fiction can properly confront the moral questions implicit in the political task of steering the human world into a future replete with threats and opportunities—questions which have become desperately urgent in recent times because of the accelerating pace of technological development. What the heroes of science fiction do, whether their project is to save or to destroy, or merely to survive within the hypothetical societies in which they move, has implications for the collective decisions real people must make about how to use the technologies which are emerging and evolving around them. Again, I do not say simply that science fiction is useful in this respect; I say that it is *necessary*.

It may be well to pause here in order to make clear exactly what role it is that I suppose fiction to be capable of playing in these moral debates—and, for that matter, what role moral philosophy itself can and does play. As I have said, I do not believe that there is any moral order already built into the universe, whether it be one which has already been revealed to us by one of those persons who have claimed to be favored with divine revelations or one which still remains to be revealed. The bounds of our moral community and the proper direction of progress are *decisions* which we have to make, not discoveries; stories and exercises in moral philosophy are necessary to explore the logical and emotional consequences which would flow from different directions. Clearly, this is not a religious point of view; it is, in fact, a straightforwardly anti-religious point of view—but as a devout atheist I believe, sincerely and passionately, that the worst catastrophe in human history has been the hijacking of moral philosophy by religion. Attempts to justify notions of good and evil by attaching them to commandments of imaginary gods have, in my estimation, engendered suffering on a scale so frightful that it hardly bears contemplation.

Not all fiction, of course, is anti-religious, but fiction, by virtue of its nature, does stand in a problematic relationship to religion. Science fiction stands in a more problematic relationship than other genres, not so much because individual science fiction stories posit a secularized view of the universe—that ambition is frequently compromised—but because when it is viewed *as a genre* it cannot help but deny and defy the disease of faith. No matter how many individual science fiction writers may fall prey to that disease—becoming would-be prophets instead of speculators—science fiction taken as a whole will always declare that there is a multitude of possible futures, and that the past of actual history is one of a multitude of alternative histories.

By virtue of its multifariousness, science fiction is fundamentally antithetical to the kind of blind, closed, and savage thinking which is enshrined in religious fundamentalism. The moral order of science fiction as a genre is therefore logically incompatible with the kind of thinking which declares that there is only one virtuous path for the individual and for mankind, and that adherents of other ways are blasphemers who should be put to death.

If we are to come to a proper understanding of the kind of universe we live in, and our place within it, and what opportunities we may have for shaping our place within it, we cannot do so without appropriate fictions. Many of those appropriate fictions do and will belong to the genre of science fiction. Again, I do not say simply that science fiction is useful; I say that it is *necessary*.

In conclusion I must, of course, return to my starting point, and to the comic recklessness of Mr. Bayes. Can we not, in the light of what we have found out about what plots are and what they are for, put a kinder construction on what he said when he took umbrage at the suggestion that his plot had paused in its movement through frustration to success? What finer things are there, after all, in the world of human thought than questions of how human life ought to be lived, and how it might be lived better—and what the devil *is* a plot for, but to bring on those fine things?

SPIDER SILK

Andre Norton

Andre Norton is the grandest of the grand dames of SF. She has been writing since the 1930s and has been a popular figure in SF since the 1950s. Her fantasy and SF novels for young adults have introduced generations of readers to the pleasures of the field. Her most famous works have been set in the Witch World, a science fantasy setting that has become the paradigm for hundreds of other works. This is a story of Witch World.

1

The Big Storm in the Year of the Kobold came late, long past the month when such fury was to be expected. This was all part of that evil which the Guardians had drawn upon Estcarp when they summoned up their greatest power to blast and twist the mountain lands, seal off passes through which had come the invasion from Karsten.

Rannock lay open to that storm. Only the warning dream-sending to the Wise Woman, Ingvarna, drew a portion of the women and children to the higher lands, there to watch with fear and trembling the sea's fierce assault upon the coast. So high dashed those waves that water covered and boiled about the Serpent Teeth of the upper ledges. Only here, in pockets among the Tor rocks, could a fugitive crouch in almost mindless terror, awaiting the end.

Of the fishing fleet which had set out yesterday morn, who had any hopes now of its return save perhaps a scattering of wreckage, playthings of the storm waves?

There was left only a handful of old men and boys, and one or two such as Herdrek, the Twist-Leg, the village smith. For Rannock was as poor in men as it was in all else since the war years had ravaged Estcarp. To the north perched Alizon, a hawk ready to be unleashed upon its neighbor; from the south Karsten boiled and bubbled, if aught was still left alive beyond the wrecked mountain passages.

Men who had marched with the Borderers under Lord Simon Tregarth or served beneath the Banners of the Witch Women of Es—where were they? Long since, their kin had given up any hope of their return. There had been no true peace in this land since old Nabor (who could count his years at more than a hundred) had been in his green youth.

It was Nabor now who battled the strength of the wind to the Tor, dragged himself up to stand, hunched shoulder to shoulder, with Ingvarna. As she, he looked to the sea uneasily. That she expected still their own fleet, he could not believe, foresighted as all knew her to be.

Waves mounted, to pound giant fists against the rock. Nabor caught sight of a ship rising and falling near the Serpent's dread fangs. Then a huge swell whirled it over those sharp threats into the comparative calm beyond. Nabor sighed with the relief of a seaman who had witnessed a miracle, life won from the very teeth of rock death. Also, Rannock had the right of storm wrack. If that ship survived so far, its cargo was forfeit now to any who could bring it to shore. He half-turned to seek the shelter of the Tor hollows, rouse Herdrek, the others, with this promise of fortune.

However, Ingvarna turned her head. Through the drifts of rain her eyes held his. There was a warning in her steady gaze. "One comes—" He saw her lips shape the words rather than voice them above the roar of wind and wave.

At the same moment, there was such a crash as equaled the drum of thunder, the lash of lightning. The strange ship might have beaten the menace of the reef's fangs, but now had been driven halfway up the beach, where it was fast breaking up under the hammer blows of the surf.

Herdrek stumped out to join them. "It is a raider," he commented during a lull of the wind. "Perhaps one of the Sea Wolves of Alizon." He spat at the wreck below.

Ingvarna was already scrambling over the rocks towards the shore, as if what lay there were of vast importance. Herdrek shouted after her a warning, but she did not even turn her head. With a curse at the folly of females, which a second later he devoutly hoped the Wise Woman had not been able to pick out of the air, the smith followed her, two of the lads venturing in his wake.

At least when they reached the shore level, the worst of the storm was spent. Waves drew a torn seaweed veil around the broken vessel. Herdrek made fast a rope about his waist, gave dire warnings to his followers to keep a tight hold upon it. Then he ventured into the surf, using that cordage from wind-rent sails, hanging in loops down the shattered sides, to climb aboard.

There was a hatch well tamped down, roped shut. He drew belt knife to slash the fastening.

"Ho!" His voice rolled hollowly into the dark beneath him. "Anyone below?"

A thin cry answered, one which might issue from the throat of a seabird such as already coasted over the subsiding surface of the sea on hunt for the bounty of the storm. Yet he thought not. Gingerly, favoring his stiff leg, the smith lowered himself into the stinking hold. What he found there made him retch, and then heated in him dull anger against those who had mastered this vessel. She had been a slaver, such as Rannock's men had heard tell of—dealing in live cargo.

But of that cargo, only one survived. Her, Herdrek carried gently from the horror of that prison. A little maid, her small arms no more than skin slipped glovelike on bones, her eyes great, gray, and blankly open. Ingvarna took the strange child from the smith as one who had the authority of clan and home hearth, wrapping the little one's thin, shivering body in her own warm cloak.

From whence Dairine came, those of Rannock never learned. That slavers raided far was no secret. Also, the villagers soon discovered the child was blind. Ingvarna, though she was a Wise One, greatly learned in herbs and spells, the setting of bones, the curing of wounds, shook her head sadly over that discovery, saying that the child's blindness came from no hurt of body. Rather, she must have looked upon some things so horrible that thereafter her mind closed and refused all sight.

Though she must have been six or seven winters old, yet also speech seemed riven from her, and only fear was left to be her portion. Although the women of Rannock would have tried to comfort her, yet secretly in their hearts they were willing that she bide with Ingvarna, who treated her oddly, they thought. For the Wise Woman did not strive to make life easier in any way for the child. Rather, from the first, Ingvarna treated the sea waif not as one maimed in body, and perhaps in mind, but rather as she might some daughter of the village whom she had chosen to be her apprentice in the harsh school of her own learning.

These years were bleak for Rannock. Full half the fleet did not return from out of the maw of that storm. Nor did any of the coastwise traders come. The following winter was a lean one. But in those dark days, Dairine showed first her skill. Though her eyes might not see what her fingers wrought, yet she could mend fishing nets with such cleverness that even the experienced women marveled.

And in the following spring, when the villagers husked the loquth balls to free their seeds for new plantings, Dairine busied herself with the silken inner fibers, twisting and turning those. Ingvarna had Herdrek make a small spindle, and showed the child how this tool might be best put to work.

Good use did Dairine make of it, too. Her small, birdclaw fingers drew out finer thread than any had achieved before, freer from knotting than any the villagers had seen. Yet never seemed she satisfied, but strove ever to make her spinning yet finer, more smooth.

The Wise Woman continued her fosterling's education in other ways, teaching her to use her fingers, her nose, in the herb garden. Dairine learnt easily the spelling which was part of a Wise Woman's knowledge. She absorbed such very quickly, yet always there was about her an impatience. When she made mistakes, then her anger against herself was great. The greatest when she tried to explain some tool or need which she seemed unable to describe but for which she evinced a need.

Ingvarna spoke to Herdrek (who was now village elder), saying that perhaps the craft of the Wise Woman might aid in regaining a portion of Dairine's lost memory. When he demanded why she had not voiced such a matter before, Ingvarna answered gravely:

"This child is not blood of our blood, and she was captive to the sea wolves. Have we the right to recall to her past horrors? Perhaps Gunnore, who watches over all womankind, has taken away her memory of the past in pity. If so—"

He bit his thumb, watching Dairine as she paced back and forth before the loom which he had caused to be set up for her, now and then halting to slap her hand upon the frame in frustration. It seemed as if she longed to force the heavy wood into another pattern which would serve her better.

"I think that she grows more and more unhappy," he agreed slowly. "At first she seemed content. Now there are times when she acts as a snow cat encaged against her will. I do not like to see her so."

The Wise Woman nodded. "Well enough. In my mind, this is a right choice."

Ingvarna went to the girl, taking both her hands, drawing her around so that she might look directly into those blind eyes. At Ingvarna's touch, Dairine stood still. "Leave us!" the Wise Woman commanded the smith.

Early that evening as Herdrek stood at his forge, Dairine walked into the light of his fire. She came to him unhesitatingly. So acute was her hearing that she often startled the villagers by her recognition of another presence. Now she held out her hands to him as she might to a father she loved. And he knew all was well.

By midsummer, when the loquths had flowered and their blossoms dropped, Dairine went often into the fields, fingering the swelling bolls. Sometimes she sang, queer, foreign-tongued words, as if the plants were children (now knee height, and then shoulder height) who must be amused and cherished.

Herdrek had changed her loom as the girl suggested might be done. From Ingvarna, she learned the mysteries of dyes, experimenting on her own. She had no real friend among the few children of the dying village. Firstly, because she did not range much afield, save with Ingvarna, of whom most were in awe. Secondly, because her actions were strange and she seemed serious and more adult than the years they believed to be hers.

In the sixth year after her coming, a Sulcar ship put in at Rannock, the first strange vessel they had sighted since the wreck of the slaver. Its captain brought news that the long war was at last over.

The defeat of the Karsten invaders, who so drained the powers of the rulers of Estcarp, had been complete. Koris of Gorm was now Commander of Estcarp, since so many of the Guardians had perished when they turned the full extent of their power upon the enemy. Yet the land was hardly at peace. The sea wolves of the coast had been augmented by ships of the broken and defeated navy of Karsten. And as in times of chaos, other wolfheads, without any true lands or allegiance, now ravaged the land wherever they might. Though the forces under Captain General Koris sought to protect the boundaries, yet to clearly defeat such hit-and-run raids was yet well beyond the ability of any defending force.

The Sulcar Captain was impressed by the latest length of Dairine's weaving, offering for it, when he bargained with Ingvarna, a much better price than he had thought to pay out in this forgotten village. He was much interested also in the girl, speaking to her slowly in several tongues. However, she answered him only in the language of Estcarp, saying she knew no other.

Still, he remarked privately to Ingvarna that somewhere in the past he had seen those like unto her, though where and when during his travels he could not bring to mind. Still, he thought that she was not of common stock.

It was a year later that the Wise Woman wrought the best she could for her sea-gift foundling.

No one knew how old Ingvarna was, for the Wise Woman showed no advance of age, as did those less learned in the many uses of herbs and medicants. But it was true that she walked more slowly, and that she no longer went alone when she sought out certain places of Power, taking Dairine ever with her. What the two did there no one knew, for who would spy on any woman with the Witch Talent?

On this day, the few fishing boats had taken to sea before dawn. At moonrise the night before, the Wise Woman and her fosterling had gone inland to visit a certain very ancient place. There Ingvarna kindled a fire which burned not naturally red, but rather blue. Into those flames, she tossed small, tightly bound bundles of dried herbs so that the smoke which arose was heavily scented. But she watched not that fire. Rather, a slab of stone set behind its flowering. That stone had a surface like unto glass, the color of a fine sword blade.

Dairine stood a little behind the Wise Woman. Though Ingvarna had taught her so much over the years, to make her other senses serve her in place of her missing sight, so that her fingers were ten eyes, her nostrils, her ears could catch scent and sound to an extent far outreaching the skill of ordinary mankind; yet at moments such as this, the longing to be as others awoke in her a sense of loss so dire that to her eyes came tears, flowing silently down her cheeks. Much Ingvarna had given her. Still, she was not as the others of Rannock. And ofttimes loneliness settled upon her as a burdensome cloak. Now the girl sensed that Ingvarna planned for her some change. But that it would make her see as others saw—that she could not hope for.

She heard clearly the chanting of the Wise Woman. The odor of the burning herbs filled her nose, now and then made her gasp for a less heavy lungful of air. Then came a command, not given in words, nor by some light touch against her arm and shoulder. But into her mind burst an order and Dairine walked ahead, her hands outstretched, until her ten fingers flattened against a throbbing surface. Warm it was, near to a point which would sear her flesh, while its throb was in twin beat to her own heart. Still, Dairine stood firm, while the chant of the Wise Woman came more faintly, as if the girl had been shifted from farther away in space from her foster mother.

Then she felt an inward flow from the surface she touched, a warmth which spread along her hands, her wrists, up her arms. Fainter still came the voice of Ingvarna petitioning on her behalf, strange and half-forgotten powers.

Slowly the warmth receded. But how long Dairine had stood so wedded to that surface she could not see, the girl never knew. Except that there came a moment when her hands fell, as if too heavily burdened for her to raise.

"What is done, is done." Ingvarna's voice at the girl's left sounded as weighted as Dairine's hands felt. "All I have to give, this I have freely shared with you. Though being blind as men see blindness, yet you have sight such as few can own to. Use it well, my fosterling."

From that day it became known that Dairine did indeed have strange powers of "seeing"—through her hands. She could take up a thing which had been made and tell you of the maker, of how long since it had been wrought. A shred of fleece from one of the thin-flanked hill sheep put into her fingers would enable her to guide an anxious owner to where the lost flock member had strayed.

There was one foretelling which she would not do, after she came upon its secret by chance only. For she had taken the hand of little Hulde during the Harvest Homing dance. Straightway thereafter, Dairine dropped her grasp upon the child's small fingers, crying out and shrinking away from the villagers, to seek out Ingvarna's house and therein hide herself. Within the month, Hulde had died of a fever. Thereafter, the girl used her new sight sparingly, and always with a fear plain to be seen haunting her.

In the Year of the Weldworm, when Dairine passed into young womanhood, Ingvarna died, swiftly. As if foreseeing another possible end, she summoned death as one summons a servant to do one's bidding.

Though Dairine was no true Wise Woman, yet thereafter she took on many of the duties of her foster mother. Within a month after the Wise Woman's burial, the Sulcar ship returned.

As the Captain told the forgotten village the news of the greater world, his eyes turned ever to Dairine, her hands busy with thread she spun as she listened. Among those of the village, she was indeed one apart, with her strange silver-fair hair, silver-light eyes.

Sibbald Ortis, Sibbald the Wrong-Handed—thus they had named him after a sea battle had lopped off his hand, and a smith in another land had made him one of metal—was that captain. He was new come to command and young—though he had lived near all his life at sea after the manner of his people.

Peace, after a fashion, he told them, had encompassed the land at least. For Koris of Gorm now ruled Estcarp with a steady hand. Alizon had been defeated in some invasion that nation had attempted overseas. And Karsten was in chaos, one prince or lord always rising against another. While the sea wolves were being hunted down, one after another, to a merciless end.

Having made clear that he was in Rannock on lawful business, the Captain now turned briskly to the subject of trade. What had they, if anything, which would be worth stowage in his own ship?

Herdrek was loathe to spread their poverty before these strangers. Also, he wanted, with a desire he could hardly conceal, some of the tools and weapons he had seen in casual use among them. Yet what had Rannock? Fish dried to take them through a lean winter, some woven lengths of wool.

The villagers would be hard put even to give these visitors guest-right, with the feast they were entitled to. And to fail in that was to deny their own heritage.

Dairine, listening to the Captain, had wished she dared touch his hand, and thus learn what manner of a man he was who had journeyed so far and seen so much. A longing was born in her to be free of the narrow, well-known ways of Rannock, to see what lay beyond in the world. Her fingers steadily twirled her thread, but her thoughts were elsewhere.

Then she lifted her head a little, for she knew someone was now standing at her side. There was the tang of sea-salted leather, and other odors. This was a stranger, one of the Sulcar men.

"You work that thread with skill, maid."

She recognized the Captain's voice. "It is my skill, Lord Captain."

"They tell me that fate has served you harshly," he spoke bluntly then. But she liked him the better for that bluntness.

"Not so, Lord Captain. These of Rannock have been ever kind. And I was fosterling to their Wise Woman. Also, my hands serve well, if my eyes are closed upon this world. Come, you, and see!" She spoke with pride as she arose from her stool, thrusting her spindle into her girdle.

Thus Dairine brought him to the cottage which was hers, sweet within for all its scents of herbs. She gestured to where stood the loom Herdrek had made her.

"As you see, Lord Captain, I am not idle, even though I may be blind."

For she knew that there, in the half-done web, there was no mistake.

Ortis was silent for a moment. Then she heard the hiss of his breath expelled in wonder.

"But this is weaving of the finest! There is no fault in color or pattern. . . . How can this be done?"

"With one's two hands, Lord Captain!" She laughed. "Here, give me a possession of yours that I may show you better how fingers can be eyes."

Within her there was a new excitement, for something told her that this was a moment of importance in her life. She heard then a faint swish as if some bit of woven stuff were being shaken free. A clinging length was pressed into the hand she held out.

"Tell me," he commanded, "from whence came this, and how was it wrought?"

Back and forth between her fingers, the girl slipped the ribband of silken stuff.

Woven—yes. But her "seeing" hands built no mind picture of human fingers at the business. No, strangely ill-formed were those members engaged in the weaving. And so swift were they also that they seemed to blur. No woman, as Dairine knew women, had fashioned this. But female—strongly, almost fiercely female.

"Spider silk—" She was not aware that she had spoken aloud until she heard the sound of her own words. "Yet not quite spider. A woman weaving—still, not a woman. . . ."

She raised the ribband to her cheek. There was a wonder in such weaving which brought to life in her a fierce longing to know more and more.

"You are right." The Captain's voice broke her preoccupation with that need to learn. "This comes from Usturt. And had a man but two full bolts of it within his cargo, he could count triple profits from such a voyage alone."

"Where lies Usturt?" Dairine demanded. If she could go there—learn what could be learned. "And who are the weavers? I do not see them as beings like unto our own people."

She heard his breath hiss again. "To see the weavers," he said in a low voice, "is death. They hate all mankind—"

"Not so, Lord Captain!" Dairine answered him then. "It is not mankind that they hate—it is all males." For from the strip between her fingers came that knowledge.

For a moment she was silent. Did he doubt her?

"At least no man sails willingly to Usturt," he replied. "I had that length from one who escaped with his bare life. He died upon our deck shortly after we fished him from a waterlogged raft."

"Captain," she stroked the silk, "you have said that this weaving is a true treasure. My people are very poor and grow poorer. If one were to learn the secret of such weaving, might not good come of it?"

With a sharp jerk he took the ribband from her.

"There is no such way."

"But there is!" Her words came in an eager tumble, one upon the other. "Women—or female things—wove this. They might treat with a woman—one who was already a weaver."

Great, calloused hands closed upon her shoulders.

"Girl, not for all the gold in Karsten would I send any woman into Usturt! You know not of what you speak. It is true that you have gifts of the Talent. But you are no confirmed Guardian, and you are blind. What you suggest is such a folly— Aye, Vidruth, what is it now?"

Dairine had already sensed that someone had approached.

"The tide rises. For better mooring, Captain, we need move beyond the rocks."

"Aye. Well, girl, may the Right Hand of Lraken be your shield. When a ship calls, no captain lingers."

Before she could even wish him well, he was gone. Retreating, she sat down on her hard bench by the loom. Her hands trembled, and from her eyes the tears seeped. She felt bereft, as if she had had for a space a treasure and it had been torn from her. For she was certain that her instinct had been right, that if any could have learned the secret of Usturt, she was that one.

Now, when she put a hand out to finger her own weaving, the web on the loom seemed coarse, utterly ugly. In her mind, she held queer vision of a deeply forested place in which great, sparkling webs ran in even strands from tree to tree.

Through the open door puffed a wind from the sea. Dairine lifted her face to it as it tugged at her hair.

"Maid!"

She was startled. Even with her keen ears, she had not heard anyone approach so loud was the wind-song.

"Who are you?" she asked quickly.

"I am Vidruth, maid, mate to Captain Ortis."

She arose swiftly. "He has thought more upon my plan?" For she could see no other reason for the seaman to seek her out in this fashion.

"That is so, maid. He awaits us now. Give me your hand—so . . ."

Fingers grasped hers tightly. She strove to free her hand. This man—there was that in him which was—wrong— Then out of nowhere, came a great, smothering cloak, folded about her so tightly she could not struggle. There were unclean smells to affront her nostrils, but the worst was that this Vidruth had swung her up across his shoulder so that she could have been no more than a bundle of trade goods.

2

So was she brought aboard what was certainly a ship, for in spite of the muffling of the cloak, Dairine used her rears, her nose. However, in her mind, she could not sort out her thoughts. Why had Captain Ortis so vehemently, and truthfully (for she had read that truth in his touch), refused to bring her? Then this man of his had come to capture her as he might steal a woman during some shore raid?

The Sulcarmen were not slave traders, that was well known. Then why?

Hands pulled away the folds of the cloak at last. The air she drew thankfully into her lungs was not fresh, rather tainted with stinks which made her feel unclean even to sniff. She thought that her prison must lie deep within the belly of the ship.

"Why have you done this?" Dairine asked of the man she could hear breathing heavily near her.

"Captain's orders," he answered, leaning so close she not only smelt his uncleanly body, but gathered with that a sensation of heat. "He has eyes in his head, has the Captain. You be a smooth-skinned, likely wench—"

"Let her be, Wak!" That was Vidruth.

"Aye, Captain," the other answered with a slur of sly contempt. "Here she be, safe and sound—"

"And here she stays, Wak, safe from your kind. Get out!"

There was a growl from Wak, as if he were close to questioning the other's right to so order him. Then Dairine's ears caught a sound which might have been that of a panel door sliding into place.

"You are not the Captain," she spoke into the silence between them.

"There has been a change of command," he returned. "The Captain, he has not brought us much luck in months agone. When we learned that he would not try to better his fortune—he was—"

"Killed!"

"Not so. Think you we want a blood feud with all his clan? The Sulcarmen take not lightly to those who let the red life out of someone of their stock."

"I do not understand. You are all Sulcar—"

"That we are not, girl. The world has changed since those ruled the waves about the oceans. They were fighters and fighting men get killed. The Kolder they fought, and they blew up Sulcarkeep in that fighting, taking the enemy—but also too many of their own—on into the Great Secret. Karsten they fought, and they were at the taking of Gorm, aye. Then they have patrolled against the sea wolves of Alizon. Men they have lost, many men. Now if they take a ship out of harbor, they do it with others than just their kin to raise sails and set the course. No, we do not kill Sibbald Ortis, we may need him later. But he is safe laid.

"Now let us to the business between us, girl. I heard the words you spoke with Ortis. Also did I learn much about you from those starvelings who live in Rannock. You have some of the Talents of the Wise Women, if you cannot call upon the full Power, blind as you are. You yourself said it—if any can treat with those devil females of Usturt, it must be one such as you.

"Think on that spider silk, girl. You held that rag that Ortis has. And you can do mighty things, unless all those at Rannock are crazed in their wits. Which I do not believe. This is a chance which a man may have offered to him but once in a lifetime."

She heard the greed in his voice. And perhaps that greed would be her protection. Vidruth would take good care to keep her safe. Just as he held somewhere Sibbald Ortis for a like reason.

"Why did you take me so, if your intentions are good? If you heard my words to the Captain, you know I would have gone willingly."

He laughed. "Do you think those shore-side halflingmen would have let you go? With three-quarters of the Guardians dead, their own Wise Woman laid also in her grave shaft, would they willingly have surrendered to us even your small Talent? The whole land is hard pressed now for any who hold even a scrap of the Power.

"No matter. They will welcome you back soon enough after you have learned the secret of Usturt. If it then still be in your mind to go to them."

"But how do you know that in Usturt I shall work for you?"

"Because you will not want the Captain to be given over to them. They do not have a pleasant way with captives."

There was fear behind his words, a fear born of horror, which he fought to control.

"Also, if you do not do as we wish, we can merely sail and leave you on Usturt for the rest of your life. No ship goes there willingly. A long life for you perhaps, girl, alone with none of your own kind—think of that."

He was silent for a moment before he added, "It is a bargain, girl, one we swear to keep. You deal with the weavers, we take you back to Rannock, or anywhere else you name. The Captain, he can be set ashore with you even. No more harm done. And a portion of the silk for your own. Why, you can buy all of Rannock and make yourself a Keep lady!"

"There is one thing—" She was remembering Wak. "I am not such a one as any of your men can take at his will. Know you not what happens then to any Talent I may possess?"

When Vidruth answered her, there was a deep note of menace in his voice, though it was not aimed at her.

"All men know well that the Talent departs from a woman who lies with a man. None shall trouble you."

"So be it," she returned, with an outward calm it was hard for her to assume. "Have you the bit of silk? Let me learn from it what I can."

She heard him move away the grate of whatever door kept snug her prison. As that sound ceased, she put out her hands to explore. The cubby was small, there was a shelflike bunk against the wall, a stool which seemed bolted to the deck, nought else. Did they have Captain Ortis pent in such a hole also? And how had this Vidruth managed so well the takeover of the Captain's command? What she had read of Sibbald Ortis during their brief meeting had not been such as to lead her to think he was one easily overcome by an enemy.

But she was sitting quietly on the stool when Vidruth returned to drop the length of ribband across her quiet hands.

"Learn all you can," he urged her. "We have two days of sail if this wind continues to favor us, then we shall raise Usturt. Food, water, what you wish shall be brought to you, and there is a guard without so that you need not be troubled."

With the silk between her hands, Dairine concentrated upon what it could tell her. She had no illusions concerning Vidruth. To him and the others, she was only a tool to their hands. Because she was sightless, he might undervalue her, for all his talk of Talent and Power. She had discovered many times in the past that such was so.

Deliberately, Dairine closed out the world about her, shut her ears to creak of timber, wash of wave, her nose to the many smells which offended it. Once more her "sight" turned inward. She could "see" the blur of those hands (which were not quite hands) engaged in weaving. Colors she had no words to describe were clear and bright. For the material she saw so was not one straight length of color, but shimmered from one shade to another.

Dairine tried now to probe beyond that shift of color to the loom from which it had come. She had an impression of tall, dark shafts. Those were not of well-planed and smooth wood; no, they had the crooked surface of—trees— standing trees!

The hands—concentrate now upon the moving hands of the weaver.

But the girl had only reached that point of recognition when there was a knock to distract her concentration. Exasperated, she turned her head to the door of the cubby.

"Come!"

Again the squeak of hinge, the sound of boots, the smell of sea-wet leather and man-skin. The newcomer cleared his throat as if ill at ease.

"Lady, here is food."

She swirled the ribband about her wrist, put out her hands, for suddenly she was hungry and athirst.

"By your leave, lady," he fitted the handle of a mug into her right hand, placed a bowl on the palm of the other. "There is a spoon. It is only ship's ale, lady, and stew."

"My thanks," she said in return. "And what name do you go by, ship's man?"

"Rothar, lady. I am a blank shield and no real seaman. But since I know no trade but war, one venture is nigh as good as another."

"Yet of this venture you have some doubts." She had set the mug on the deck, kept upright between her worn sandals. Now she seized his hand, held it to read. For it seemed to Dairine that she must not let this opportunity of learning more of Vidruth's followers go, and she sensed that this Rothar was not of the same ilk as Wak.

"Lady"—his voice was very low and swift—"they say that you have knowledge of herb craft. Why then has Vidruth not taken you to the Captain that you may learn what strange, swift illness struck him down?"

There was youth in the hand Dairine held and not, she believed, any desire to deceive.

"Where lies the Captain?" she asked in as low a voice.

"In his cabin. He is fevered and raves. It is as if he has come under some en-sorcelment and—"

"Rothar!" From the door, another voice sharp as an order. The hand she held jerked free from hers. But not before she had felt the spring of fear.

"I promised no man shall trouble you. Has this cub been at such tricks?" Vidruth demanded.

"Not so." Dairine was surprised her voice remained so steady. "He has been most kind in bringing me food and drink, both of which I needed."

"And having done so—out!" Vidruth commanded. "Now"—she heard the door close behind the other—"what have you learned, girl, from this piece of silk?"

"I have had but a little time, lord. Give me more. I must study it."

"See that you do" was his order as he also departed.

He did not come again, nor did Rothar ever once more bring her food. She thought, though, of what the young man had said concerning the Captain. Vidruth's tale made her believe that the whole ship's company had been behind the mate's scheme to take command and sail to Usturt. There were herbs which, put in a man's food or drink, could plunge him into the depths of fever. If she could only reach the Captain, she would know. But there was no faring forth from this cubby.

Now and again Vidruth would suddenly appear to demand what more she had learned from the ribband. There was such an avid greediness in his questions that sometimes rising uneasiness nearly broke through her control. At last she answered with what she believed to be the truth.

"Have you never heard, Captain, that the Talent cannot be forced? I have tried to read from this all which I might. But this scrap was not fashioned by a race such as ours. An alien nature cannot be so easily discovered. For all my attempts, I cannot build a mind picture of these people. What I see clearly is only the weaving."

When he made no answer, Dairine continued:

"This is a thing not of the body, but the mind. Along such a road one creeps as a babe, one does not race as one full grown."

"You have less than a day now. Before sundown, Usturt shall rise before us. I know only what I have heard tell of witch powers, and that may well be changed by the telling and retelling. Remember, girl, your life can well ride on your 'seeing'!"

She heard him go. The ribband no longer felt so light and soft. Rather, it had taken on the heaviness of a slave chain binding her to his will. She ate ship's biscuits from the plate he had brought her. It was true time was passing, and she had done nothing of importance.

Oh, she could now firmly visualize the loom and see the silk come into being beneath the flying fingers. But the body behind those hands, that she could not see. Nor did any of the personality of the weavers who had made that which she held come clear to her, for all her striving.

Captain Ortis—he came in the reading, for he had held this. And Vidruth also. There was a third who was more distant, lying hid under a black cloud of fear. Was this day or night? She had lost track of time. That the ship still ran before the wind, she sensed.

Then—she was not alone in the cubby! Yet she had not heard the warning creak of the door. Fear kept her tense, hunched upon the stool, listening with all her might.

"Lady?"

Rothar! But how had he come?

"Why are you here?" Dairine had to wet her lips with her tongue before she could shape those words.

"They move now to put you ashore on Usturt, lady! Captain Ortis, he came up leaning on Vidruth's arm, his body all atremble. He gives no orders, only Vidruth. Lady, there is some great wrong here—for we are at Usturt. And Vidruth commands. Such is not right."

"I knew that I must go to Usturt," she returned. "Rothar, if you have any allegiance to your captain, know he is a prisoner to Vidruth in some manner, even as I have been. And if I do not do as Vidruth says, there will be greater trouble—death—"

"You do not understand." His voice was very husky. "There are monsters on this land. To see them even, they say, makes a man go mad!"

"But I shall not see them," Dairine reminded him. "How long do I have?"

"Some moments yet."

"Where am I and how did you get here?"

"You are in the treasure hold, below the Captain's own cabin. I have used the secret opening to reach you as this is the first time Vidruth and the Captain have been out of it. Now they must watch carefully for the entrance to the inner reef."

"Can you get me into the Captain's cabin?" If, in those moments, she might discover what hold Vidruth had over Captain Ortis, she perhaps would be able to help a man she trusted.

"Give me your hands, then, lady. I fear we have very little time."

She reached out, and her wrists were instantly caught in a hold tight enough to be painful, but she made no sound of complaint. Then she found herself pulled upward with a vast heave as if Rothar must do this all in a single effort. When he set her on her feet once more, she sensed she was in a much larger space. And there was the fresh air from the sea blowing in as if through some open port.

But the air was not enough to hide from her that telltale scent—a scent of evil.

"Let me go, touch me not now," she told Rothar. "I seek that which must be found, and your slightest touch will confuse my course."

Slowly she turned away from the wind, facing to her right.

"What lies before me?"

"The Captain's bed, lady."

Step by step she approached in that direction. The sniff of evil was stronger. What it might be she had no idea, for though Ingvarna had taught her to distinguish that which was of the shadow, she knew little more. The fetid odor of some black sorcery was rank.

"The bed," she ordered now, "do you strip off its coverings. If you find aught which is strange, be sure you do not touch it with your hand. Rather, use something of iron, if you can, to pluck it forth. And then throw it quickly into the sea."

He asked no questions, but she could hear his hurried movements. And then—

"There is a—a root, most misshapen. It lies under the pillow, lady."

"Wait!" Perhaps the whole of that bed place was now impregnated by what evil had been introduced. To destroy its source might not be enough. "Bundle all—pillow, coverings—give them to the sea!" she ordered. "Let me back then into the treasure cubby, and if there be time, make the bed anew. I do not know what manner of ensorcelment has been wrought here. But it is of the Shadow, not of the Power. Take care that you keep yourself also from contact with it."

"That will I do of a certainty, lady!" His answer was fervent. "Stand well back, I will get rid of this."

She retreated, hearing the click of his sea boots on the planking as he passed her toward the source of the sea wind.

"Now"—he was back at her side—"I shall see you safe, lady. Or as safe as you can be until the Captain comes to his mind once more and Vidruth be removed from command."

His hands closed upon her, lowered her back down into the cubby. She listened intently. But if he closed that trap door, and she was sure that he had, it had fallen into place without a sound.

3

She had not long to wait, for the opening on the floor level of the cubby was opened and she recognized Vidruth's step.

"Listen well, girl," he commanded. "Usturt is an island, one of a string of islands, reaching from the shore. At one time, they may all have been a part of the coast. But now some are only bare rock with such a wash of sea around them as no man can pass. So think not that you have any way of leaving save by our favor. We shall set you ashore and keep down-sea thereafter. But when you have learned what we wish, then return to the shore and there leave three stones piled one upon another. . . ."

To Dairine, his arrangements seemed to be not well thought out. But she questioned nothing. What small hopes she had she could only pin on Rothar and the Captain. Vidruth's hand tightened about her arm. He drew her to a ladder, set her hands upon its rungs.

"Climb, girl. And you had better play well your part. There are those among us who fear witchcraft and say there is only one certain way to disarm a witch. That, you have heard. . . ."

She shivered. Yes, there was a way to destroy a witch—by enjoying the woman. All men were well versed in that outrage.

"Rothar shall set you ashore," Vidruth continued. "And we shall watch your going. Think not to talk him out of his orders, for there is no place elsewhere. . . ."

Dairine was on the deck now, heard the murmur of voices. Where stood Captain Ortis? Vidruth gave her no time to try to sort out the sounds. Under his compelling, the girl came up against the rail. Then Vidruth caught her up as if she were a small child and lowered her until other hands steadied her, easing her down upon a plank seat.

Around her was the close murmur of the sea, and she could hear the grate of oars within their locks.

"Do you believe me witch, Rothar?" she asked.

"Lady, I do not know what you are. But that you are in danger with Vidruth, that I can swear to. If the Captain comes into his own mind again—"

He broke off and then continued. "Through the war, I have come to hate any act which makes man or woman unwillingly serve another. There is no future before me, for I am wastage of war, having no trade save that of killing. Therefore, I will do what I may to help you and the Captain."

"You are young to speak so, of being without a future."

"I am old in killing," he told her bleakly. "And of such men as Vidruth leads, I have seen amany. Lady, we are near the shore. And those on the ship watch us well. When I set you on the beach, take forth carefully what you find in my belt, hide it from all. It is a knife made of the best star-steel, fashioned by the hand of Hamraker himself. Not mine in truth, but the Captain's."

Dairine did as he ordered when he carried her from the sand-smoothing waves to the drier reach beyond. Memory stirred in her. Once there had been such a knife and—firelight had glinted on it—

"No!" she cried aloud to deny memory. Yet her fingers remained curled about that hilt.

"Yes!" He might not understand her inner turmoil, but his hold on her tightened. "You must keep it.

"Walk straight ahead," he told her. "Those on the ship have the great dart caster trained on you. There are trees ahead—within those, there the spiders are said to be. But, lady, though I dare not move openly in your aid now, for that would bring me quick death to no purpose, yet what I can do, that I shall."

Uncertainty held Dairine. She felt naked in this open which she did not know. Yet she must not appear concerned to those now watching her. She had the ribband of silk looped about her wrist. And within the folds of her skirt, she held also the knife. Turning her head slightly from one side to another, she listened with full concentration, walking slowly forward against the drag of the sand.

Coolness ahead—she must be entering the shade of the trees. She put out her hand, felt rough bark, slid around it, setting the trunk as a barrier between that dart thrower of which Rothar had warned, and her back.

Then she knew, as well as if her eyes could tell her, that it was not alone the ship's company who watched. She was moving under observation of someone—or something—else. Dairine used her sense of perception, groping as she did physically with her hands, seeking what that might be.

A moment later she gasped with shock. A strong mental force burst through the mind door she had opened. She felt as if she had been caught in a giant hand, raised to the level of huge eyes which surveyed her outwardly and inwardly.

Dairine swayed, shaken by that nonphysical touch, search. It was nonhuman. Yet she realized, as she fought to recover her calm, it was not inimical—yet.

"Why come you here, female?"

In Dairine's mind, the word shaped clearly. Still, she could build up no mental picture of her questioner. She faced a little to the right, held out the hand about which she had bound the ribband.

"I seek those able to weave such beauty," she replied aloud, wondering if they could hear, or understand, her words.

Again that sensation of being examined, weighed. But this time she stood quiet, unshaken under it.

"You think this thing beautiful?" Again the mind question.

"Yes."

"But you have not eyes to see it." Harshly that came, as if to deny her claim.

"I have not eyes, that is the truth. But my fingers have been taught to serve me in their place. I, too, weave, but only after the manner of my own people."

Silence, then a touch on the back of her hand, so light and fleeting Dairine was not even sure she had really felt it. The girl waited, for she understood this was a place with its own manner of barriers, and she might continue only if those here allowed it.

Again a touch on her hand, but this time it lingered. Dairine made no attempt to grasp, though she tried to read through that contact. And saw only bright whirls.

"Female, you may play with threads after the crude fashion of your kind. But call yourself not a weaver!" There was arrogance in that.

"Can one such as I learn the craft as your people know it?"

"With hands as clumsy as this?" There came a hard rap across her knuckles. "Not possible. Still, you may come, see with your fingers what you cannot hope to equal."

The touch slid across her hand, became a sinewy band about her wrist as tight as the cuff of a slave chain. Dairine knew now there was no escape. She was being drawn forward. Oddly, though she could not read the nature of the creature who guided her, there flowed from its contact a sharp mental picture of the way ahead.

This was a twisted path. Sometimes she brushed against the trunks of trees; again she sensed they crossed clear areas—until she was no longer sure in what direction the beach now lay.

At last they came into an open space where there was some protection other than branches and leaves overhead to ward off the sun. Her ears picked up small, scuttling sounds.

"Put out your hand!" commanded her guide. "Describe what you find before you."

Dairine obeyed, moving slowly and with caution. Her fingers found a solid substance, not unlike the barked tree trunk. Only, looped about it, warp lines of thread were stretched taut. She transferred her touch to those lines, tracing them to another bar. Then she knelt, fingering the length of cloth. This was smooth as the ribband. A single thread led away—that must be fastened to the shuttle of the weaver.

"So beautiful!"

For the first time since Ingvarna had trained her, Dairine longed for actual sight. The need to *see* burned in her. Color—somehow as she touched the woven strip, the fact of color came to her. Yet all she could "read" of the weaver was a blur of narrow, nonhuman hands.

"Can you do such, you who claim to be a weaver?"

"Not this fine." Dairine answered with the truth. "This is beyond anything I have ever touched."

"Hold out your hands!" This time Dairine sensed that the order had not come from her guide, but another.

The girl spread out her fingers, palms up. There followed a feather-light tracing on her skin along each finger, gliding across her palm.

"It is true. You are a weaver—after a fashion. Why do you come to us, female?"

"Because I would learn." Dairine drew a deep breath. What did Vidruth's idea of trade matter now? This was of greater importance. "I would learn from those who can do this."

She continued to kneel, waiting. There was communication going on about her, but none she could catch and hold with either eye or mind. If these weavers would shelter her, what need had she to return to Vidruth? Rothar's plans? Those were too uncertain. If she won the good will of these, she had shelter against the evil of her own kind.

"Your hands are clumsy, you have no eyes." That was like a whiplash. "Let us see what you *can* do, female."

A shuttle was thrust into her hand. She examined it carefully by touch. Its shape was slightly different from those she had always known, but she could use it. Then she surveyed, the same way, the web on the loom. The threads of both warp and woof were very fine, but she concentrated until she could indeed "see" what hung there. Slowly she began to weave, but it took a long time and what she produced in her half inch of fabric was noticeably unlike that of the beginning.

Her hands shaking, the girl sat back on her heels, frustrated. All her pride in her past work was wiped out. Before these, she was a child beginning a first ragged attempt to create cloth.

Yet when she had relaxed from concentrating on her task and was aware once more of those about her, she did not meet the contempt she had expected. Rather, a sensation of surprise.

"You are one perhaps who can be taught, female," came that mind voice of authority. "If you wish."

Dairine turned her face eagerly in the direction from which she believed that message had come. "I do wish, Great One!"

"So be it. But you will begin even as our hatchlings, for you are not yet a weaver."

"That I agree." The girl ran her fingers ruefully across the fabric before her.

If Vidruth expected her return into his power now—she shrugged. And let Rothar concentrate upon the Captain and his own plight. What seemed of greatest importance to her was that she must be able to satisfy these weavers.

They seemed to have no real dwelling except this area about their looms. Nor were there any furnishings save the looms themselves. And those stood in no regular pattern. Dairine moved cautiously about, memorizing her surroundings by touch.

Though she sensed a number of beings around her, none touched her, mind or body. And she made no advances in turn, somehow knowing such would be useless.

Food they did bring her, fresh fruit. And there were some finger-lengths of what she deemed dried meat. Perhaps it was better she did not know the origin of that.

She slept when she tired on a pile of woven stuff, not quite as silky as that on the looms, yet so tightly fashioned she thought it might pass the legendary test of carrying water within its folds. Her sleep was dreamless. And when she awoke, she found it harder to remember the men or the ship, even Rothar or the Captain. Rather, they were like some persons she had known once in distant childhood, for the place of the weavers was more and more hers. And she *must* learn. To do that was a fever burning in her.

There was a scuttling sound and then a single order:

"Eat!"

Dairine groped before her, found more of the fruit. Even before she was quite finished, there came a twitch on her skirt.

"This ugly thing covering your body, you cannot wear it for thread gathering."

Thread gathering? She did not know the meaning of that. But it was true that her skirt, if she moved out of the open space about the looms, caught on branches. She arose and unfastened her girdle, the lacings of her bodice, allowed the dress to slip away into a puddle about her feet. Wearing only her brief chemise, Dairine felt oddly free. But she sought out her girdle again, wrapped it around her slim waist, putting there within the knife.

There came one of those light touches, and she faced about.

"Thread hangs between the trees"—her guide gave a small tug—"touch it with care. Shaken, it will become a trap. Prove that you have the lightness of fingers to be able to learn from us."

No more instructions came. Dairine realized they must be again testing her. She must prove she was able to gather this thread. Gather it how? Just as she questioned that, something was pushed into her hand. She discovered she held a smooth rod, the length of her lower arm. This must be a winder for the thread.

Now there was a grasp again on her wrist, drawing her away from the looms, on under the trees. Even as her left hand brushed a tree trunk came the order: "Thread!"

There would be no profit in blind rushing. She must concentrate all her well-trained perceptive sense to aid her to find thread here.

Into her mind slid a very dim picture. Perhaps that came from the very far past which she never tried to remember. A green field lay open under the morning sun and on it were webs pearled with dew. Was what she sought allied to the material of such webs?

Who could possibly harvest the fine threads of such webs? A dark depression weighed upon Dairine. She wanted to hurl the collecting rod from her, to cry aloud that no one could do such a thing.

Then she had a vision of Ingvarna standing there. That lack of self-pity, that belief in herself which the Wise Woman had fostered, revived. To say that one could not do a thing before one ever tried was folly.

In the past her sense of perception had only located for her things more solid than a tree-hung thread. But now it must serve her better.

Under her bare feet, for she had left her sandals with her dress, lay a soft mass of long-fallen leaves. Around here there appeared to be no ground growth—only the trees.

Dairine paused, advancing her hand until her fingertips rested on bark. With caution, she slid that touch up and around the trunk. A faint impression was growing in her. Here was what she sought.

Then—she found the end of a thread. The rest of it was stretched out and away from the tree. With infinite care, Dairine broke the thread, putting the freed end to the rod. To her vast relief, it adhered there as truly as it had to the tree trunk. Now . . . she did not try to touch the thread, but she wound slowly, with great care, moving to keep the strand taut before her, evenly spread on the rod.

Round and round—then her hand scraped another tree trunk. Dairine gave a sigh of relief, hardly daring to believe she had been successful in harvesting her first thread. But one was little enough, and she must not grow overconfident. Think only of the thread! She found another end and, with the same slow care, began once more to wind.

To those without sight, day is as night, night is as day. Dairine no longer lived within the time measure of her own kind. She went forth between intervals of sleep and food to search for the tree-looped thread, wondering if she so collected something manufactured by the weavers themselves or a product of some other species.

Twice she made the error she had been warned against, had moved too hastily, with overconfidence, shaken the thread. Thus she found herself entrapped in a sticky liquid which flowed along the line, remaining fast caught until freed by a weaver.

Though she was never scolded, each time her rescuer projected an aura of such disdain for this clumsiness that Dairine cringed inwardly.

The girl had early learned that the weavers were all female. What they did with the cloth they loomed, she had not yet discovered. They certainly did not use it all, neither had she any hint that they traded it elsewhere. Perhaps the very fact of creation satisfied some need rampant in them.

Those who, like her, hunted threads were the youngest of this nonhuman community. Yet she was able to establish no closer communication with them than she did with the senior weavers.

Once or twice there was an uneasy hint of entrapment about her life in the loom place. Why did everything which had happened before she arrived now seem so distant and of such negligible account?

If the weavers did not speak to her save through mind speech—and that rarely—they were not devoid of voices, for those at the looms hummed. Though the weird melody they so evoked bore little resemblance to human song, it became a part of one. Even Dairine's hand moved to its measure and by it her thoughts were lulled. In all the world, there were only the looms, the thread to be sought for them—only this was of any importance.

There came a day when they gave her an empty loom and left her to thread it. Even in the days of her life in the village, this had been a matter which required her greatest dexterity and concentration. Now, as she worked with unfamiliar bars, it was even worse. She threaded until her fingertips were sore, her head aching from such single-minded using of perception, while all about her the humming of the weavers urged her on and on.

When fatigue closed in upon her, she slept. And she paused to eat only because she knew that her body must have fuel. At last she knew that she had finished, for good or ill.

Now her fingers, as she rubbed her aching head, were stiff. It was difficult to flex them. Still, the hum set her body swaying in answer to its odd rhythm.

To Dairine's surprise, no weaver came to inspect her work, to say whether it was adequately or poorly done. When she had rested so that she could once more control her fingers, she began to weave. As she did so, she discovered that she too hummed, echoing the soft sound about her.

As she worked, there was a renewal of energy within her. Maybe her hands did not move as swiftly as the blur of elongated fingers she had seen in her mind, but they followed the rhythm of the hum and they seemed sure and knowing, not as if her own will but some other force controlled them. She was weaving—well or ill she did not know or care. It was enough that she kept to the beat of the quiet song.

Only when she reached the end of her thread supply, and sat with an empty shuttle in her hand, did Dairine rouse, as one from a dream. Her whole body ached, her hand fell limply on her knee. In her was the sharpness of hunger. There was no longer to be heard the hum of the others.

The girl arose stiffly, stumbled to her sleeping place. There was food which she mouthed before she lay down on the cloth, her face turned up to whatever roof was between her and the sky, feeling drained, exhausted—all energy gone from her body, as was logical thought from her mind.

4

Dairine awoke into fear, her hands were clenched, long shivers shook her body. The dream which had driven her into consciousness abruptly faded, leaving only a sense of terror behind. However, it had broken the spell of the weavers, her memory was once more sharp and clear.

How long had she been here? What had happened when she had not returned to the shore? Had the ship under Vidruth's control left, thinking her lost? And Rothar? the Captain?

Slowly she turned her head from side to side, aware of something else. Though she could not see them, she knew that the looms ringing her in were vacant, the weavers were gone!

Now Dairine believed she must have been caught in some invisible web, and had only this moment broken free. Why had she chosen to come here? Why had she remained? The ribband of stuff was gone from her wrist—had that set some ensorcelment upon her?

Fool! She could not see as the rest of the world saw. Now it appeared that even her carefully fostered sense of perception had, in some manner, deceived her. As Dairine arose, her hand brushed the loom where she had labored for so long. Curiosity made her stoop to finger the width her efforts had created. Not quite as smooth as the ribband, but far, far better than her first attempt.

Only—where were the weavers? The shadow of terror lingering from her dream sent her moving purposefully about the clearing. Each loom was empty, the woven cloth gone. She kicked against something—groped to find it. A collecting rod for thread.

"Where—where are you?" she dared to call aloud. The quiet seemed so menacing she longed to set her back to some tree, to raise a defense. Against whom—or what?

Dairine did not believe that Vidruth and his men would dare to penetrate the wood. But did the weavers have other enemies, and had fled those, not taking the trouble to warn her?

Breathing faster, she set hand on the hilt of the knife at her girdle. Where *were* they? Her call had echoed so oddly that she dared not try again. Only her fear grew as she tried to listen.

There was the rustle of tree leaves. Nothing else. Nor could she pick up by mind touch any suggestion of another life form nearby. Should she believe that the cloth missing from each loom meant her co-workers had left for an ordered purpose, not in flight? Would she be able to track them?

Never before had she put to such a use that sense Ingvarna had trained in her. Also, that the weavers had their own guards, Dairine was well aware. She was not sure that she herself mattered enough in their eyes for them to set any defense against her seeking their company. Suppose, with a collecting rod in her hand, she was to leave the loom place as if on the regular mission of hunting thread?

First she must have food. That she located, by scent, in two bins. The fruit was too soft, overripe, and there was none of the dried sticks left. But she ate all she could.

Then, rod conspicuously in hand, the girl ventured into the woods. All the nearby threads must have been harvested, her questing fingers could find none as she played out her game for any who might watch.

And there *were* watchers! Not the weavers, for the impression these gave her was totally different—more feeble sparks as compared to a well-set fire. As she moved, so did they, hovering near, yet making no attempt to come in contact with her.

She discovered a thread on a tree. Skillfully, she wound it on her rod, took so a second and third. However, at the next, she flinched away. Any thread anchored here must have been disturbed, for she smelled the acrid odor of the sticky coating.

The next two trees supported similarly gummed threads. Did that mean these had been prepared to keep her prisoner? Dairine turned a little. Already, she was out of familiar territory. Thus she expected to meet at any moment opposition, either from the threads or those watchers.

Next was a tree free of thread. Trusting to her sense of smell, she sought another opening, hoping that the unthreaded trees would mark a trail. Though she moved a little faster, she kept to her pretense of seeking threads from each tree she encountered. The watchers had not left her, though she picked up no betraying sound, only knew they were there.

Another free tree—this path was a zigzag puzzle. And she had to go so slowly. One more free tree, and then, from her left, a sound at last—a faint moaning.

It was human, that sound, enough to feed her fear. This—somehow this all seemed a shadow out of her now-forgotten dream. In her dream she had known the sufferer—

Dairine halted. The watchers were drawing in. She could tell they had amassed between her and the direction from which the moan came. Thus she had a choice—to ignore the sound or to try to circle around.

No sign, make no sign that she heard. Keep on hunting for threads—strive to deceive the watchers. All her nature rebelled against abandoning one who might be in trouble, even if he were one of Vidruth's men.

She put out her hand as if searching for thread, more than half expecting to touch a sticky web. From those watchers she believed she picked up an answering sensation of uncertainty. This might be her only chance.

Her fingers closed about a thick band of woven stuff. That led in turn downward to a bag, the flap of the top turned over and stuck to the fabric so tightly she could not open it. The bag was very large, pulling down the branch from which it was suspended. And within it—something had been imprisoned!

Dairine jerked back. She did not know if she had cried out. What was sealed within that bag, her perception told her, had been alive, was now only newly dead. She forced herself to run fingers once more along the surface of the dangling thing. Too small—surely too small to be a man!

Now that the girl knew no human was so encased, she wanted no greater knowledge of the contents. As she stepped away, her shoulder grazed a second bag. She realized that she moved among a collection of them, and all they held was death.

Only, she could still hear that moaning. And it was human. Also, at last the watchers had dropped behind. As if this place were one they dared not enter.

Those bags—Dairine hated to brush against them. Some seemed far lighter than others and twirled about dizzily as she inadvertently touched them. Others dipped heavily with their burdens.

The moans—

The girl made herself seek what hung before her now. Her collecting rod was in her girdle. In its place, she held the knife. When she touched this last bag, feeble movement answered. There was a muffled cry which Dairine was sure was one for help.

She ripped at the silk with knife point. The tightly woven fabric gave reluctantly, this was no easily torn material. She hacked and pulled until she heard a half-stifled cry!

"For Sul's sake—"

Dairine dragged away the slashed silk. There was indeed a man ensnared. However, about him now was sticky web, for its acrid scent was heavy on the air. Against that, her knife was of no avail. To touch such would only make her prisoner, too.

She gathered up the folds of the torn bag and, using pieces to shield her fingers, tore and worried at the web. To her relief, she was succeeding. She could feel that his own struggles to throw off his bonds were more successful.

Also, she knew whom she fought to free—Rothar! It was as if he had been a part of that dream she could not remember.

Dairine spoke his name, asking him if he were near free.

"Yes. Though I still hang. But that now is a small matter—"

Dairine heard a threshing movement, then the sound of his weight touching the ground. His breath hissed heavily in and out.

"Lady, in nowise could you have come at a better time." His hand closed about her arm. She felt him sway and then recover balance.

"You are hurt?"

"Not so. Hungry and needful of a drink. I do not know how long I have hung in that larder. The Captain—he will think us both dead."

"Larder!" That one grim word struck her like a blow.

"Did you not know? Yes, this is the spider females' larder, where they preserve their males—"

Dairine fought rising nausea. Those bags of silk, the beautifully woven silk! And to be used so.

"There is someone—something—out there," he said.

The watchers, her protective sense, alerted her. They were now moving in again.

"Can you see them?" Dairine asked.

"Not clearly." Then he changed that to "Yes!"

"They have throwing cords of web, such as they used on me before. No blade can cut those—"

"The bag!"

"What do you mean?"

Covered with the bag's rent material, she had been able to pull loose his bindings. Those sticky cords could not find purchase against the woven silk. As she explained that, her knife was wrenched from her hold and she heard sounds of ripping.

The watchers—as Rothar worked to empty other bags, Dairine strove to perceive them by mind. They had neared, but once more had halted, as if this were a place which they feared to enter even if ordered to do so to hold the humans captive.

"They spin their lines now," Rothar told her. "They plan to wall us in."

"Let them believe us helpless," she commanded.

"But you think we are not?"

"With the bags, perhaps not."

If she could only *see!* Dairine could have cried aloud in her frustration. Who were the watchers? She was sure they were not the weavers themselves. Perhaps these were the ones who supplied the thread she had harvested so carefully in the past.

Rothar once more was back at her side, a bundle of silk from plundered bags. The girl dared not let herself remember *what* had been in those bags.

"Tell me," she said, "what is the nature of those spinning out there?"

She could sense his deep aversion, revulsion. "Spiders. Giant spiders. They are furred and the size of hounds."

"What are they doing?"

"They are enwebbing an opening. Beyond that on either side are already nets. Now they are disappearing. Only one is left, hanging in the center of the fresh web."

Through her grasp on his wrist, Dairine could read his thoughts, his mind picture, even more clearly, to add to the scene his words had built for her.

"Those others may have gone to summon the weavers"—she made an alarming guess. "So for the present, we have only that one guard to deal with."

"And the web—"

She loosed her hold upon him, clutched a length of the raggedly cut silk. "This we must bind about our bodies. Do not touch the web save with this between your flesh and it."

"I understand."

Dairine moved forward. "I must loose the web," she told him. "The guard will be your matter. Lead me to a tree where the web is anchored."

His hand was on her shoulders. Under his gentle urging, she was guided to the left, was moved forward step by cautious step.

"The tree is directly before you now, lady. Have no fear of the guard." His promise was grim.

"Remember, let nothing of the web touch your flesh."

"Be sure I am well shielded," he assured her.

She fingered rough bark, around her hand and arm the silk was well and tightly anchored. There—she had discovered the end of an anchoring thread. But this was far stronger and thicker than any she had harvested before.

"Ha!" Rothar gave a cry—was no longer beside her.

Dairine found a second thread, felt vibrations along it. The guard must be making ready to defend its web. However, she must concentrate on the finding of each thread, of breaking such loose from the tree.

There was no way for her to know how many threads she must snap so. From her right came the sound of scuffling, heavy breathing.

"Ah!" Rothar's voice fiercely triumphant. "The thing is safely dead, lady. You are right, the cords it threw at me were well warded by the cloth."

"Keep watch. Those which were with it may still return," she warned.

"That I know!" he agreed.

The girl moved as swiftly as she could, discovering thread ends, snapping them. Not only might the spiders return, but the weavers. And them she feared even more.

"The web is down," he told her.

However, she felt little relief at what might be a small victory.

"Lady, now it would be well to wrap our feet and legs with this silk, they could well lay ground webs for our undoing."

"Yes!" She had not thought of that, only of the threading cords from tree to tree.

"Let me get more silk."

Dairine stood waiting, her whole body tense as she strained to use ears and inner senses to assess what might lie in wait beyond. Then he was back and, with no by-your-leave, busied himself wrapping her feet and legs with lengths of silk, tying the strips tightly in places.

While she, who had once so loved the ribband Captain Ortis had shown her, wanted to shrink from any touch of that stuff. Save now it might be their salvation.

"That is the best I can do." He released her foot after tying a last knot about her ankle. "Do you hear aught, lady?"

"Not yet. But they will come."

"Who—what are the weavers?" he asked.

"I know not. But they do not hold our kind high in esteem."

He laughed shortly. "How well do I know that! Yet they did you no harm."

"Because, I think, I am without sight, and also a female who knows a little of their own trade. They are proud of their skill and wished to impress me."

"Shall we go then?"

"We must watch for trees bare of threads."

"Those I can see, lady. Perhaps trusting in my kind of sight, we can go the quicker. There has been much happened. The Captain, though he is still weak, again commands his ship. Vidruth is—dead. But the Captain could not get that scum which his mate has signed to come ashore. And only he can hold them in control."

"Thus you alone are here?"

He did not answer her directly. "Set your hand to my belt. And I shall take heed in my going, I promise," was all he said.

Such a journey was humiliating for Dairine. So long had it been since she must turn to one of her kind as a guide. But she knew that he was right.

So Captain Ortis, released from the evil spell, had taken command. She wondered briefly how Vidruth had died, there had been a queer little hesitancy in Rothar's telling of that. For now she must put her mind on what lay immediately before them. That the weavers would allow them to escape easily she did not believe.

A moment later she knew she was right. They were once more under observation, she sensed. This new, stronger contact was not that of the watchers.

"They come!" she warned.

"We must reach the shore! It is among the trees that they set their traps. And I have a signal fire built there, ready to be lighted, which will bring in the *Sea Raven*."

"Can you see any such traps?"

She could feel his impatience and doubt in the slight contact of her fingers against his body where they were hooked about his belt.

"No. But there are no straight trails among the trees. Webs hang here and there; one can only dodge back and forth between those."

Dairine was given no warning, had no time to loose her hold. Rothar suddenly fell forward and down, bearing her with him. Her side scraped painfully against a broken end of branch. It was as if the very earth under them had opened.

5

The smell of freshly turned soil was thick in her nostrils. She lay against Rothar and he was moving. In spite of her bruises, the jarring shock of that fall, Dairine sat up. Where they had landed she did not know, but she guessed they were now under the surface of the ground.

"Are you hurt?" asked her companion.

"No. And you?"

"My arm caught under me when I landed. I hope it is only a bad bruising and no break. We are in one of their traps. They had it coated over." There was a note of self-disgust bleak in his voice.

Dairine was glad he had told her the bald truth. Rising to her feet, the girl put out her hands to explore the pit. Freshly dug, the earth of its sides was moist and sticky. Here and there a bit of root projected. Could they use such to pull themselves out? Before she could ask that of Rothar, words shot harshly into her mind.

"Female, why have you stolen this meat from us?"

Dairine turned her head toward the opening which must be above. So close that voice, she could believe that a head bobbed there, eyes watched them gloatingly.

"I know not your meaning," she returned with all the spirit she could summon. "*This* is a man of my people, one who came seeking me because he felt concern."

"That with you is our meat!"

Cold menace in that message brought not fear, but a growing anger to Dairine. She would not accept that any man was—*meat*. These weavers—she had considered them creatures greater than herself because of the beauty they created, because of their skill. She had accepted their arrogance because she also accepted that she was inferior in that skill.

Yet to what purpose did they put their fine creations? Degrading and loathsome usage by her own belief. With a flash of true understanding, she was now certain that she had not been free here, never so until she had awakened in the deserted loom place. They had woven about her thoughts a web of ensorcelment which had bound her to them and their ways, just as at this moment they had entrapped her body.

"No man is your meat," she returned.

What answered her then was no mind words, rather a blast of uncontrolled fury. She swayed under that mental blow, but she did not fall. Rothar called out her name, his arm was about her, holding her steady.

"Do not fear for me," she said and tried to loosen her grip. This was her battle. Her foot slipped in the soft earth of the pit and she stumbled. She flung out her arms to keep herself off the wall. There was a sharp pain just above her eyes, and then only blackness in which she was totally lost.

Heat—heat of blazing fire. And through it screaming—terrible screaming—which tortured her ears. There was no safety left in the world. She had curled herself into a small space of blessed dark, hiding. But she could still see—see with her *eyes!* No, she would not look, she dared not look—at the swords in the firelight—at the thing streaming with blood which hung whimpering from two knives driven like hooks into the wall to hold it upright. She willed herself fiercely *not* to see.

"Dairine! Lady!"

"No—" She screamed her denial. "I will not look!"

"Lady!"

"I will not—"

There were flashes of color about her. No mind pictures these—the fire, the blood, the swords—

"Dairine!"

A face, wavery, as if she saw it mirrored in troubled water, a man's face. His sword—he would lift the sword and then—

"No!" she screamed again.

A sharp blow rocked her head from side to side. Oddly enough, that steadied her sight. A man's face near hers, yes, but no fire, no sword dripping blood, no wall against which a thing hung whimpering.

He held her gently, his eyes searching hers.

They—they were not—not in the Keep of Trin. Dairine shuddered; memory clung about her as a foul cloak. Trin was long, long ago. There had been the sea, and then Ingvarna and Rannock. And now—now they were on Usturt. She was not sure what had happened.

But she *saw.*

Had Ingvarna believed that some day this sight would return to her? Not sight totally destroyed, but sight denied by a child who had been forced to look upon such horrors that she would not let herself face the true world openly again.

Her sight had returned. But that was not what the weavers had intended. No, their burst of mind fury had been sent to cut her down. Not death had they given her, but new life.

Then *she,* who had sent that thrust of mind power, looked over and down upon the prey.

Dairine battled her fear. No retreat this time. She must make herself face this new horror. Ingvarna's teachings went deep, had strengthened her for this very moment of her life, as if the Wise Woman had been enabled to trace the years ahead and know what would aid her fosterling.

The girl did not raise her hand but she struck back, her newfound sight centering upon that horror of a countenance. Human it was in dreadful part, arachnoid in another, such as to send one witless with terror. And the thought strength of the weaver was gathering to blast Dairine.

Those large, many-faceted eyes blinked. Dairine's did not.

"Be ready," the girl said to Rothar, "they are preparing to take us."

Down into the pit whirled sticky web lines hurled by the weaver's spider servants. Those caught and clung to root ends and then fell upon the two.

"Let them think for this moment," Dairine said, "that we are helpless."

He did not question her as more and more of the lines dropped upon them, lying over their arms, legs. Dull gray was the cloth which they had wound about them. That had none of the shimmering quality her mind had given to it. Perhaps the evil use to which this had been put had killed that opalescence.

While the cords fell, the girl did not shift her gaze, but met straightly the huge, alien eyes, those cold and deadly eyes, of the weaver. In and in, Dairine aimed her power, that power Ingvarna had fostered in her, boring deep to reach the brain behind the eyes. Untrained in most of the Wise Woman's skills, she intuitively knew that this was her only form of attack, an attack which must also serve as defense.

Were those giant eyes dulling a little? The girl could not be sure, she could not depend upon her newly restored sight.

About them, the web lengths had ceased to fall. But there was new movement around the lip of the pit above.

Now! Gathering all her strength, pulling on every reserve she believed she might have, Dairine launched a direct thought blow at the weaver. That weird figure writhed, uttered a cry which held no note of human in it. For a moment, it hunched so. Then that misshapen, nightmare body fell back, out of Dairine's range of sight. She was aware of no more mental pressure. No, instead came a weak panic, a fear which wiped away all the weaver's strength.

"They—they are going!" Rothar cried out.

"For a while perhaps." Dairine still held the creatures of the loom in wary respect. They had not thought her a worthy foe, so perhaps they had not unleashed against her all that they might. But while the weavers were still bewildered, shaken, at least she and Rothar had gained time.

The young man beside her was already shaking off the cords. Those curled limply away from his fabric-covered body, just as they fell from hers as he jerked at them. She blinked. Now that the necessity for focusing her eyes on the weaver was past, Dairine found it hard to see. It was a distinct effort for her to fasten on any one object, bring that into clear shape. This was something she must learn, even as she had learned to make her fingers see for her.

Though he winced as he tried to use his left arm, Rothar won out of the pit by drawing on the root ends embedded in the soil. Then he unbuckled his belt and lowered it for her aid.

Out of the earth prison, Dairine stood still for a long moment, turning her head right and left. She could not see them in the dusky shadows among the trees, yet they were there, weavers, spinners, both. But she sensed also that they were still shaken, as if all their strength of purpose had lain only in the will of the one she had temporarily bested.

All were that weaver's own brood—the arachnoid-human, the arachnoid complete. They were subject to the Great One's will, her thoughts controlled them, and they were her tools, the projections of herself. Until the Great Weaver regained her own balance, these would be no menace. But how long could such a respite last for those she would make her prey?

Dairine saw mistily a brighter patch ahead, sunlight fighting the dusk of this now-sinister wood.

"Come!" Rothar reached for her hand, clasped it tight. "The shore must lie there!"

The girl allowed him to draw her forward, away from the leaderless ones.

"The signal fire," he was saying. "But let me give light to that and the Captain will bring in the ship."

"Why did you come—alone from that ship?" Dairine asked suddenly, as they broke out of the shade of the forest into a hard brilliance of the sun upon the sand. So hurting was that light that she must shelter her eyes with her hand.

Peering between her fingers, Dairine saw him shrug. "What does it matter how a man who is already dead dies? There was a chance to reach you. The Captain could not take it, for that rogue's spell left him too weak, though he raged against it. None other could he trust—"

"Except you. You speak of yourself as a man already dead, yet you are not. I was blind—now I see. I think Usturt has given us both that which we dare not throw lightly away."

His somber face, in which his eyes were far too old and shadowed, became a little lighter as he smiled.

"Lady, well do they speak of your powers. You are of the breed who may make a man believe in anything, even perhaps himself. And there lies our signal waiting."

He gestured to a tall heap of driftwood. In spite of the slippage of the sand under his enwrapped feet, he left her side and ran toward it.

Dairine followed at a slower pace. There was the Captain and there was this Rothar who risked his life, even though he professed to find that of little matter. Perhaps now there would be others to touch upon her life, mayhap even her heart in years to come. She had these years to weave, and she must do so with care, matching each strand to another in brightness, as all had heretofore been wrought in darkness. The past was behind her. There was no need to glance back over her shoulder unto the dusk of the woods. Rather must she search out seaward whence would come the next strand to add to her pattern of weaving.

A BRAVER THING

Charles Sheffield

Charles Sheffield is a physicist and writer who began publishing SF at the end of the 1970s and quickly gained a reputation as a new star of hard SF in the tradition of Arthur C. Clarke. He in fact writes SF of all descriptions, but always with a positive view of scientific knowledge as a tool for solving problems.

The palace banquet is predictably dull, but while the formal speeches roll on with their obligatory nods to the memory of Alfred Nobel and his famous bequest, it is not considered good manners to leave or to chat with one's neighbors. I have the time and opportunity to think about yesterday; and, at last, to decide on the speech that I will give tomorrow.

A Nobel Prize in physics means different things to different people. If it is awarded late in life, it is often viewed by the recipient as the capstone on a career of accomplishment. Awarded early (Lawrence Bragg was a Nobel Laureate at twenty-five) it often defines the winner's future; an early Prize may also announce to the world at large the arrival of a new titan of science (Paul Dirac was a Nobel Laureate at thirty-one).

To read the names of the Nobel prize winners in physics is almost to recapitulate the history of twentieth-century physics, so much so that the choice of winners often seems self-evident. No one can imagine a list without Planck, the Curies, Einstein, Bohr, Schrödinger, Dirac, Fermi, Yukawa, Bardeen, Feynman, Weinberg, or the several Wilson's (though Rutherford is, bizarrely, missing from the Physics roster, having been awarded his Nobel Prize in Chemistry).

And yet the decision-making process is far from simple. A Nobel Prize is awarded not for a lifetime's work, but explicitly for a particular achievement. It is given only to living persons, and as Alfred Nobel specified in his will, the prize goes to "the person who shall have made the most important discovery or invention within the field of physics."

It is those constraints that make the task of the Royal Swedish Academy of Sciences so difficult. Consider these questions:

- What should one do when an individual is regarded by his peers as one of the leading intellectual forces of his generation, but no single accomplishment offers the clear basis for an award? John Archibald Wheeler is not a Nobel Laureate; yet he is a "physicist's physicist," a man who has been a creative force in half a dozen different fields.

- How does one weight a candidate's *age*? In principle, not at all. It is not a variable for consideration; but in practice every committee member knows when time is running out for older candidates, while the young competition will have opportunities for many years to come.
- How soon after a theory or discovery is it appropriate to make an award? Certainly, one should wait long enough to be sure that the accomplishment is "most important," as Nobel's will stipulates; but if one waits too long, the opportunity may vanish with the candidate. Max Born was seventy-two years old when he received the Nobel Prize in 1954—for work done almost thirty years earlier on the probabilistic interpretation of the quantum mechanical wave function. Had George Gamow lived as long as Born, surely he would have shared with Penzias and Wilson the 1978 prize, for the discovery of the cosmic background radiation. Einstein was awarded the Nobel Prize in 1921, at the age of forty-two. But it cited his work on the photoelectric effect, rather than the theory of relativity, which was still considered open to question. And if his life had been no longer than that of Henry Moseley or Heinrich Hertz, Einstein would have died unhonored by the Nobel Committee.

So much for logical choices. I conclude that the Nobel rules allow blind Atropos to play no less a part than Athene in the award process.

My musings can afford to be quite detached. I know how the voting must have gone in my own case, since although the work for which my award is now being given was published only four years ago, already it has stimulated an unprecedented flood of other papers. Scores more are appearing every week, in every language. The popular press might seem oblivious to the fundamental new view of nature implied by the theory associated with my name, but they are very aware of its monstrous practical potential. A small test unit in orbit around Neptune is already returning data, and in the tabloids I have been dubbed Giles "Starman" Turnbull. To quote *The New York Times*: "The situation is unprecedented in modern physics. Not even the madcap run from the 1986 work of Müller and Bednorz to today's room-temperature superconductors can compete with the rapid acceptance of Giles Turnbull's theories, and the stampede to apply them. The story is scarcely begun, but already we can say this, with confidence: Professor Turnbull has given us the stars."

The world desperately needs heroes. Today, it seems, I am a hero. Tomorrow? We shall see.

In a taped television interview last week, I was asked how long my ideas had been gestating before I wrote out the first version of the Turnbull Concession Theory. And can you recall a moment or an event, asked the reporter, which you would pinpoint as seminal?

My answer must have been too vague to be satisfactory, since it did not appear in the final television clip. But in fact I could have provided a very precise location in space-time, at the start of the road that led me to Stockholm, to this dinner, and to my first (and, I will guarantee, my last) meeting with Swedish royalty.

Eighteen years ago, it began. In late June, I was playing in a public park two miles from my home when I found a leather satchel sitting underneath a bench. It was nine o'clock at night, and nearly dark. I took the satchel home with me.

My father's ideas of honesty and proper behavior were and are precise to a fault. He would allow me to examine the satchel long enough to determine its owner, but not enough to explore the contents. Thus it was, sitting in the kitchen of our semi-detached council house, that I first encountered the name of Arthur Sandford Shaw, penned in careful red ink on the soft beige leather interior of the satchel. Below his name was an address on the other side of town, as far from the park as we were but in the opposite direction.

Should we telephone Arthur Sandford Shaw's house, tell him that we had his satchel, and advise him where he could collect it?

No, said my father gruffly. Tomorrow is Saturday. You cycle over in the morning and return it.

To a fifteen-year-old, even one without specific plans, a Saturday morning in June is precious. I hated my father then, for his unswerving, blinkered attitude, as I hated him for the next seventeen years. Only recently have I realized that "hate" is a word with a thousand meanings.

I rode over the next morning. Twice I had to stop and ask my way. The Shaw house was in the Garden Village part of the town, an area that I seldom visited. The weather was preposterously hot, and at my father's insistence I was wearing a jacket and tie. By the time that I dismounted in front of the yellow brick house with its steep red-tile roof and diamond glazed windows, sweat was trickling down my face and neck. I leaned my bike against a privet hedge that was studded with sweet-smelling and tiny white flowers, lifted the satchel out of my saddlebag, and rubbed my sleeve across my forehead.

I peered through the double gates. They led to an oval driveway, enclosing a bed of well-kept annuals.

I saw pansies, love-in-a-mist, delphiniums, phlox, and snapdragons. I know their names now, but of course I did not know them *then*.

And if you ask me, do I truly remember this so clearly, I must say, of course I do; and will, until my last goodnight. I have that sort of memory. Lev Landau once said, "I am not a genius. Einstein and Bohr are geniuses. But I am very talented." To my mind, Landau (1962 Nobel Laureate, and the premier Soviet physicist of his generation) was certainly a genius. But I will echo him, and say that while I am not a genius, I am certainly very talented. My memory in particular has always been unusually precise and complete.

The sides of the drive curved symmetrically around to meet at a brown-and-white painted front door. I followed the edge of the gravel as far as the front step, and there I hesitated.

For my age, I was not lacking in self-confidence. I had surveyed the students in my school, and seen nothing there to produce discomfort. It was clear to me that I was mentally far superior to all of them, and the uneasy attitude of my teachers was evidence—to me, at any rate—that they agreed with my assessment.

But this place overwhelmed me. And not just with the size of the house, though that was six times as big as the one that I lived in. I had seen other big houses; far more disconcerting were the trained climbing roses and espaliered fruit trees, the weed-free lawn, the bird-feeders, and the height, texture, and improbable but right color balance within the flower beds. The garden was so carefully structured that it seemed a logical extension of the building at its center. For the first time, I realized that a garden could comprise more than a hodgepodge of grass and straggly flowers.

So I hesitated. And before I could summon my resolve and lift the brass knocker, the door opened.

A woman stood there. At five-feet-five, she matched my height exactly. She smiled at me, eye to eye.

Did I say that the road to Stockholm began when I found the satchel? I was wrong. It began with that smile.

"Yes? Can I help you?"

The voice was one that I still thought of as "posh," high-pitched and musical, with clear vowels. The woman was smiling again, straight white teeth and a broad mouth in a high-cheekboned face framed by curly, ash-blond hair. I can see that face before me now, and I know intellectually that she was thirty-five years old. But on that day I could not guess her age to within fifteen years. She could have been twenty, or thirty, or fifty, and it would have made no difference. She was wearing a pale-blue blouse with full sleeves, secured at the top with a mother-of-pearl brooch and tucked into a gray wool skirt that descended to mid-calf. On her feet she wore low-heeled tan shoes, and no stockings.

I found my voice.

"I've brought this back." I held out the satchel, my defense against witchcraft.

"So I see." She took it from me. "Drat that boy, I doubt he even knows he lost it. I'm Marion Shaw. Come in."

It was an order. I closed the door behind me and found myself following her along a hall that passed another open door on the left. As we approached, a piano started playing rapid staccato triplets, and I saw a red-haired girl crouched over the keyboard of a baby grand.

My guide paused and stuck her head in for a moment. "Not so fast, Meg. You'll never keep up that pace for the whole song." And then to me, as we walked on, "Poor old Schubert, 'Impatience' is right; it's what he'd feel if he heard that. Do you play?"

"We don't have a piano."

"Mm. I sometimes wonder why we do."

We had reached an airy room that faced the back garden of the house. My guide went in before me, peered behind the door, and clucked in annoyance.

"Arthur's gone again. Well, he can't be far. I know for a fact that he was here five minutes ago." She turned to me. "Make yourself at home, Giles. I'll find him."

Giles. I have been terribly self-conscious about my first name since I was nine years old. By the time that I was twenty I had learned how to use it to my advantage, to suggest a lineage that I never had. But at fifteen it was the bane of my life. In a class full of Tom's and Ron's and Brian's and Bill's, it did not fit. I cursed my fate, to be stuck with a "funny" name, just because one of my long-dead uncles had suffered with it.

But there was stronger witchcraft at work here. I had arrived unheralded on her doorstep.

"How do you know my name?"

That earned another smile. "From your father. He called me early this morning, to make sure someone would be home. He didn't want you to bike all this way for nothing."

She went out, and left me in the room of my dreams.

It was about twelve feet square, with an uncarpeted floor of polished hardwood. All across the far wall was a window that began at waist height, ran to the ceiling, and looked south to a vegetable garden. The windowsill was a long work bench, two feet deep, and on it stood a dozen projects that I could identify. In the center was a compound microscope, with slides scattered all around. I found tiny objects on them as various as a fly's leg, a single strand of hair, and two or three iron filings. The mess on the left-hand side of the bench was a half-ground telescope lens, covered with its layer of hardened pitch and with the grinding surface sitting next to it. The right side, just as disorderly, was a partially assembled model airplane, radio-controlled and with a two c.c. diesel engine. Next to that stood an electronic balance, designed to weigh anything from a milligram to a couple of kilos, and on the other side was a blood-type testing kit. The only discordant note to my squeamish taste was a dead puppy, carefully dissected, laid out, and pinned organ by organ on a two-foot square of thick hardboard. But that hint of a possible future was overwhelmed by the most important thing of all: everywhere, in among the experiments and on the floor and by the two free-standing aquariums and next to the flat plastic box behind the door with its half-inch of water and its four black-backed, fawn-bellied newts, there were *books*.

Books and books and books. The other three walls of the room were shelved and loaded from floor to ceiling, and the volumes that scattered the work bench were no more than a small sample that had been taken out and not replaced. I had never seen so many hardcover books outside a public library or the town's one and only technical bookstore.

When Marion Shaw returned with Arthur Sandford Shaw in tow I was standing in the middle of the room like Buridan's Ass, unable to decide what I wanted to look at the most. I was in no position to see my own eyes, but if I had been able to do so I have no doubt that the pupils would have been twice their normal size. I was suffering from sensory overload, first from the house and garden, then from Marion Shaw, and finally from that paradise of a study. Thus my initial impressions of someone whose life so powerfully influenced and finally directed my own are not as clear in my mind as they ought to be. I also honestly believe that I never did see Arthur clearly, if his mother were in the room.

Some things I can be sure of. Arthur Shaw made his height early, and although I eventually grew to within an inch of him, at our first meeting he towered over me by seven or eight inches. His coordination had not kept pace with his growth, and he had a gawky and awkward manner of moving that would never completely disappear. I know also that he was holding in his right hand a live frog that he had brought in from the garden, because he had to pop that in an aquarium before he could, at his mother's insistence, shake hands with me.

For the rest, his expression was surely the half-amused, half-bemused smile that seldom left his face. His hair, neatly enough cut, never looked it. Some stray spike on top always managed to elude brush and comb, and his habit of running his hands up past his temples swept his hair untidily off his forehead.

"I'm pleased to meet you," he said. "Thank you for bringing it back."

He was, I think, neither pleased nor displeased to meet me. It was nice to have his satchel back (as Marion Shaw had predicted, he did not know he had left it behind in the park), but the thought of what might have happened had he lost it, with its cargo of schoolbooks, did not disturb him as it would have disturbed me.

His mother had been following my eyes.

"Why don't you show Giles your things," she said. "I'll bet that he's interested in science, too."

It was an implied question. I nodded.

"And why don't I call your mother," she said, "and see if it's all right for you to stay to lunch?"

"My mother's dead." I wanted to stay to lunch, desperately. "And my dad will be at work 'til late."

She raised her eyebrows, but all she said was, "So that's settled, then." She held out her hand. "Let me take your jacket, you don't need that while you're indoors."

Mrs. Shaw left to organize lunch. We played, though Arthur Shaw and I would both have been outraged to hear such a verb applied to our efforts. We were engaging in serious experiments of chemistry and physics, and reviewing the notebooks in which he recorded all his earlier results. Even in our first meeting he struck me as a bit strange, but that slight negative was swamped by a dozen positive reactions. The orbit in which I had traveled all my life contained no one whose interests in any way resembled my own. It was doubly shocking to meet a person who was as interested in science as I was, and who had on the shelves of his own study more reference sources than I dreamed existed.

Lunch was an unwelcome distraction. Mrs. Shaw studied me as openly as my inspection of her was covert, Arthur sat in thoughtful silence, and the table conversation was dominated by the precocious Megan, who at twelve years old apparently loved horses and boats, hated anything to do with science, school-work, or playing the piano, and talked incessantly when I badly wanted to hear from the other two. (I know her still; my present opinion is that I was a little harsh in the assessment of eighteen years ago—but not much.) Large quantities of superior food and the beatific presence of Marion Shaw saved lunch from being a disaster, and finally Arthur and I could escape back to his room.

At five o'clock I felt obliged to leave and cycle home. I had to make dinner for my father. The jacket that was returned to me was newly stitched at the elbow where a leather patch had been working loose, and a missing black button on the cuff had been replaced. It was Marion Shaw rather than Arthur who handed me my coat and invited me to come to the house again the following week, but knowing her as I do now I feel sure that the matter was discussed with him before the offer was made. I mention as proof of my theory that as I was pulling my bike free of the privet hedge, Arthur pushed into my hand a copy of E. T. Bell's *Men of Mathematics*. "It's pretty old," he said offhandedly. "And it doesn't give enough details. But it's a classic. It think it's terrific—and so does Mother."

I rode home through the middle of town. When I arrived there, my own house felt as alien and inhospitable to me as the far side of the moon.

*   *   *

It was Tristram Shandy who set out to write the story of his life, and never progressed much beyond the day of his birth.

If I am to avoid a similar problem, I must move rapidly in covering the next few years. And yet at the same time it is vital to define the relationship between the Shaw family and me, if the preposterous request that Marion Shaw would make of me thirteen years later, and my instant aquiescence to it, are to be of value in defining the road to Stockholm.

For the next twenty-seven months I enjoyed a double existence. "Enjoyed" is precisely right, since I found both lives intensely pleasurable. In one world I was Giles Turnbull, the son of a heel-man at Hendry's Shoe Factory, as well as Giles Turnbull, student extraordinary, over whom the teachers at my school nodded their heads and for whom they predicted a golden scholastic future. In that life, I moved through a thrilling but in retrospect unremarkable sequence of heterosexual relationships, with Angela, Louise, and finally with Jennie.

At the same time, I became a regular weekend visitor to the Shaw household. Roland Shaw, whom my own father described with grudging respect after two meetings as "sharp as a tack," had a peripheral effect on me, but he was a seldom-seen figure absorbed in his job, family, and garden. It was Marion and Arthur who changed me and shaped me. From him I learned concentration, tenacity, and total attack on a single scientific problem (the school in my other life rewarded facility and speed, not depth). I learned that there were many right approaches, since he and I seldom used the same attack on a problem. I also learned—surprisingly—that there might be more than one right answer. One day he casually asked me, "What's the average length of a chord in a unit circle?" When I had worked out an answer, he pointed out with glee that it was a trick question. There are at least three "right" answers, depending on the mechanical definition you use for "average."

Arthur taught me thoroughness and subtlety. From Marion Shaw I learned everything else. She introduced me to Mozart, to the Chopin waltzes and études, to the Beethoven symphonies, and to the first great Schubert song cycle, while steering me clear of Bach fugues, the *Ring of the Nibelung*, Beethoven's late string quartets and *Winterreise*. "There's a place for those, later in life," she said, "and it's a wonderful place. But until you're twenty you'll get more out of *Die Schöne Müllerin* and Beethoven's Seventh." Over the dinner table, I learned why sane people might actually read Wordsworth and Milton, to whom an exposure at school had generated an instant and strong distaste. ("Boring old farts," I called them, though never to Marion Shaw.)

And although nothing could ever give me a personal appreciation for art and sculpture, I learned a more important lesson: that there were people who could tell the good from the bad, and the ugly from the beautiful, as quickly and as naturally as Arthur and I could separate a rigorous mathematical proof from a flawed one, or a beautiful theory from an ugly one.

The Shaw household also taught me, certainly with no intention to do so, how to fake it. Soon I could talk a plausible line on music, literature, or architecture, and with subtle hints from Marion I mastered that most difficult technique, when to shut up. From certain loathed guests at her dinner table I learned to turn on (and off) a high-flown, euphuistic manner of speech that most of the world confuses with brain-power. And finally, walking around the garden with Marion for the sheer pleasure of her company, I picked up as a bonus a conversational knowledge of flowers, insects, and horticulture, subjects which interested me as little as the sequence of Chinese dynasties.

It's obvious, is it not, that I was in love with her? But it was a pure, asexual love that bore no relationship to the explorations, thrills, and physical urgencies of Angela, Louise, and Jennie. And if I describe a paragon who sat somewhere between Saint and Superwoman, it is only because I saw her that way when I was sixteen years old, and I have never quite lost the illusion. I know very well, today, that Marion was a creature of her environment, as much as I was shaped by mine. She had been born to money, and she had never had to worry about it. It was inevitable that what she *thought* she was teaching me would become transformed when I took it to a house without books and servants, and to a way of life where the battle for creature comforts and self-esteem was fought daily.

I looked upon the world of Marion Shaw, and wanted it and her. Desperately. But I knew no way to possess them.

"It were all one that I should love a bright particular star, and think to wed it, he is so above me," Marion quoted to me one day, for no reason I cold understand. That's how I, mute and inglorious, felt about her.

And by a curious symmetry, Megan Shaw trailed lovelorn after me, just as I trailed after her mother. One day, to my unspeakable embarrassment, Megan cornered me in the music room and told me that she loved me. She took the initiative, and tried to kiss me. At fourteen she was becoming a beauty, but I, who readily took the part of eager sexual aggressor with my girlfriends, could no more have touched her than I could have played the Chopin polonaise with which she had been struggling. I muttered, mumbled, ducked my head, and ran.

Despite such isolated moments of awkwardness, that period was still my personal Nirvana, a delight in the sun that is young once only. But even at sixteen and seventeen I sensed that, like any perfection, this one could not endure.

The end came after two years, when Arthur went off to the university. He and I were separated in age by only six months, but we went to different schools and we were, more important, on opposite sides of the Great Divide of the school year.

He had taken the Cambridge scholarship entrance exam the previous January and been accepted at King's College, without covering himself with glory. If his failure to gain a scholarship or exhibition upset his teachers, it surprised me not at all. And when I say that I knew Arthur better than anyone, while still not knowing him, that makes sense to me if to no one else.

Success in the Cambridge scholarship entrance examinations in mathematics calls for a good deal of ingenuity and algebraic technique, but the road to success is much smoother if you also know certain tricks. Only a finite number of questions can be asked, and certain problems appear again and again. A bright student, without being in any way outstanding, can do rather well by practicing on the papers set in previous years.

And this, of course, was what Arthur absolutely refused to do. He had that rare independence of spirit, which disdained to walk the well-trod paths. He would not practice examination technique. That made the exams immeasurably harder. A result which, with the help of a clever choice of coordinate system or transformation, dropped out in half a dozen lines, would take several pages of laborious algebra by a direct approach. Genius would find that trick of technique in real time, but to do so consistently, over several days, was too much to ask of any student. Given Arthur's fondness for approaching a problem *ab ovo*, without reference to previous results, and adding to it a certain obscurity of presentation that even I, who knew him well, had found disturbing, it was a wonder that he had done as well as he had.

I had observed what happened. It took no great intellect to resolve that I would not make the same mistake. I worked with Arthur, until his departure for Cambridge in early October, on new fields of study (I had long passed the limits of my teachers at school). Then I changed my focus, and concentrated on the specifics of knowledge and technique needed to do well in the entrance examinations.

Tests of any kind always produce in me a pleasurable high of adrenaline. In early December I went off to Cambridge, buoyed by a good-luck kiss (my first) from Marion Shaw, and a terse, "Do your best, lad," from my father. I stayed in Trinity College, took the exams without major trauma, saw a good deal of Arthur, and generally had a wonderful time. I already knew something of the town, from a visit to Arthur halfway through Michaelmas Term.

The results came just before Christmas. I had won a major scholarship to Trinity. I went up the following October.

And at that point, to my surprise, my course and Arthur's began to move apart. We were of course in different colleges, and of different years, and I began to make new friends. But more important, back in our home town the bond between us had seemed unique: he was the single person in my world who was interested in the arcana of physics and mathematics. Now I had been transported to an intellectual heaven, where conversations once possible only with Arthur were the daily discourse of hundreds.

I recognized those changes of setting, and I used them to explain to Marion Shaw why Arthur and I no longer saw much of each other. I also, for my own reasons, minimized to her the degree of our estrangement; for if I were never to see Arthur during college breaks, I would also not see Marion.

There were deeper reasons, though, for the divergence, facts which I could not mention to her. While the university atmosphere, with its undergraduate enthusiasms and overflowing intellectual energy, opened me and made me more gregarious, so that I formed dozens of new friendships with both men and women, college life had exactly the opposite effect on Arthur. As an adolescent he had tended to emotional coolness and intellectual solitude. At Cambridge those traits became more pronounced. He attended few lectures, worked only in his rooms or in the library, and sought no friends. He became somewhat nocturnal, and his manner was increasingly brusque and tactless.

That sounds enough to end close acquaintance; but there was a deeper reason still, one harder to put my finger on. The only thing I can say is that Arthur now made me highly *uncomfortable*. There was a look in his eyes, of obsession and secret worry, that kept me on the edge of my seat. I wondered if he had become homosexual, and was enduring the rite of passage that implied. There had been no evidence of such tendencies during the years I had known him, except that he had shown no interest in girls.

A quiet check with a couple of my gay friends disposed of that theory. Both the grapevine and their personal observations of Arthur indicated that if he was not attracted to women, neither was he interested in men. That was a vast relief. I had seen myself being asked to explain the inexplicable to Marion Shaw.

I accepted the realities: Arthur did not want to be with me, and I was uncomfortable with him. So be it. I would go on with my studies.

And in those studies our new and more distant relationship had anther effect, one that ultimately proved far more important than personal likes and dislikes. For I could no longer *compare* myself with Arthur.

In our first two years of acquaintance, he had been my calibration point. As someone a little older than me, and a full year ahead in a better school, he served as my pacer. My desire was to know what Arthur knew, to be able to solve the problems that he could solve. And on the infrequent occasions when I found myself ahead of him, I was disproportionately pleased.

Now my pace-setting hare had gone. The divergence that I mentioned was intellectual as well as personal. And because Arthur had always been my standard of comparison, it took me three or four years to form a conclusion that others at the university had drawn long before.

His lack of interest in attending lectures, coupled with his insistence on doing things his own way, led to as many problems in the Tripos examinations as it had in scholarship entrance. His supervision partner found him "goofy," while their supervisor didn't seem to understand what he was talking about. Arthur was always going off, said his partner, in irrelevant *digressions.* By contrast, my old approach of focusing on what was needed to do well in exams, while making friends with both students and faculty, worked as well as ever.

In sum, my star was ascendant. I did splendidly, was secretly delighted, and publicly remained nonchalant and modest.

And yet I knew, somewhere deep inside, that Arthur was more creative than I. He generated ideas and insights that I would never have. Surely that would weigh most heavily, in the great balance of academic affairs?

Apparently not. To my surprise, it was I alone who at the end of undergraduate and graduate studies was elected to a Fellowship, and stayed on at Cambridge. Arthur would have to leave, and fend for himself. After considering a number of teaching positions at other universities both in Britain and abroad, he turned his back on academia. He accepted a position as a research physicist with A.N.F. Gesellschaft, a European hi-tech conglomerate headquartered in Bonn.

In August he departed Cambridge to take up his new duties. I would remain, living in college and continuing my research. When we had dinner together a few days before he left he seemed withdrawn, but no more than usual. I mentioned that I was becoming more and more interested in the problem of space-time quantization, and proposed to work on it intensely. He came to life then, and said that in his opinion I was referring to the most important open question of physics. I was delighted by that reaction, and told him so. At that point his moodiness returned and remained for the rest of the evening.

When we parted at midnight there was no formality or sense of finality in our leave-taking. And yet for several years I believed that on that evening the divergence of our worldliness became complete. Only later did I learn that from a scientific point of view they had separated, only to run parallel to each other.

And both roads led to Stockholm.

*   *   *

When one sets forth on an unknown intellectual trail it is easy to lose track of time, place, and people. For the next four years the sharp realities of my world were variational principles, Lie algebra, and field theory. Food and drink, concerts, vacations, friends, social events, and even lovers still had their place, but they stood on the periphery of my attention, slightly misty and out of focus.

I saw Arthur a total of five times in those four years, and each was in a dinner-party setting at his parents' house. In retrospect I can recognize an increasing remoteness in his manner, but at the time he seemed like the same old Arthur, ignoring any discussion or guest that didn't interest him. No opportunity existed for deep conversation between us; neither of us sought one. He never said a word about his work, or what he thought of life in Bonn. I never talked about what I was trying to do in Cambridge.

It was the shock of my life to be sitting at tea in the Senate House, one gloomy November afternoon, and be asked by a topologist colleague from Churchill College, "You used to hang around with Arthur Shaw, didn't you, when he was here?"

At my nod, he tapped the paper he was holding. "Did you see this, Turnbull," he said, "on page ten? He's dead."

And when I looked at him, stupefied: "You didn't know? Committed suicide. In Germany. His obituary's here."

He said more, I'm sure, and so did I. But my mind was far away as I took the newspaper from him. It was a discreet two inches of newsprint. Arthur Sandford Shaw, aged twenty-eight. Graduate of King's College, Cambridge, son of etc. Coroner's report, recent behavior seriously disturbed . . . no details.

I went back to my rooms in Trinity and telephoned the Shaw house. While it was ringing, I realized that no matter who answered I had no idea what to say. I put the phone back on its stand and paced up and down my study for the next hour, feeling more and more sick. Finally I made the call and it was picked up by Marion.

I stumbled through an expression of regret. She hardly gave me time to finish before she said, "Giles, I was going to call you tonight. I'd like to come to Cambridge. I must talk to you."

The next day I had scheduled appointments for late morning and afternoon, two with research students, one with the college director of studies on the subject of forthcoming entrance interviews, and one with a visiting professor from Columbia. I could have handled them and still met with Marion. I canceled every one, and went to meet her at the station.

The only thing I could think of when I saw her step off the train was that she had changed hardly at all since that June morning, thirteen years ago, when we first met. It took close inspection to see that the ash-blond hair showed wisps of gray at the temples, and that a network of fine lines had appeared at the outer corners of her eyes.

Neither of us had anything to say. I put my arms around her and gave her an embarrassed hug, and she leaned her head for a moment on my shoulder. In the taxi back to college we talked the talk of strangers, about the American election results, new compact disk recordings, and the town's worsening traffic problems.

We did not go to my rooms, but set out at once to walk on the near-deserted paths of the College Backs. The gloom of the previous afternoon had intensified. It was perfect weather for *weltschmerz*, cloudy and dark, with a thin drizzle falling. We stared at the crestfallen ducks on the Cam and the near-leafless oaks, while I waited for her to begin. I sensed that she was winding herself up to say something unpleasant. I tried to prepare myself for anything.

It came with a sigh, and a murmured, "He didn't kill himself, you know. That's what the report said, but it's wrong. He was murdered."

I was not prepared for anything. The hair rose on the back of my neck.

"It sounds insane," she went on. "But I'm sure of it. You see, when Arthur was home in June, he did something that he'd never done before. He talked to me about his work. I didn't understand half of it"—she smiled, a tremulous, tentative smile; I noticed that her eyes were slightly bloodshot from weeping—"you'd probably say not even a tenth of it. But I could tell that he was terrifically excited, and at the same time terribly worried and depressed."

"But what was he doing? Wasn't he working for that German company?" I was ashamed to admit it, but in my preoccupation with my own research I had not given a moment's thought in four years to Arthur's doings, or to A.N.F. Gesellschaft.

"He was still there. He was in his office the morning of the day that he died. And what he was doing was terribly important."

"You talked to them?"

"They talked to us. The chief man involved with Arthur's work is called Otto Braun, and he flew over two days ago specially to talk to me and Roland. He said he wanted to be sure we would hear about Arthur's death directly, rather than just being officially notified. Braun admitted that Arthur had done very important work for them."

"But if that's true, it makes no sense at all for anyone to think of killing him. They'd do all they could to keep him alive."

"Not if he'd found something they were desperate to keep secret. They're a commercial operation. Suppose that he found something hugely valuable? And suppose that he told them that it was too important for one company to own, and he was going to let everyone in on it."

It sounded to me like a form of paranoia that I would never have expected in Marion Shaw. Arthur would certainly have been obliged to sign a nondisclosure agreement with the company he worked for, and there were many legal ways to assure his silence. In any case, to a hi-tech firm Arthur and people like him were the golden goose. Companies didn't murder their most valuable employees.

We were walking slowly across the Bridge of Sighs, our footsteps echoing from the stony arch. Neither of us spoke until we had strolled all the way through the first three courts of St. John's College, and turned right onto Trinity Street.

"I know you think I'm making all this up," said Marion at last, "just because I'm so upset. You're just humoring me. You're so logical and clear-headed, Giles, you never let yourself go overboard about anything."

There is a special hell for those who feel but cannot tell. I started to protest, half-heartedly.

"That's all right," she said. "You don't have to be polite to me. We've known each other too long. You don't think I understand anything about science, and maybe I don't. But you'll admit that I know a fair bit about people.

And I can tell you one thing, Otto Braun was keeping something from us. Something important."

"How do you know?"

"I could read it in his eyes."

That was an unarguable statement, but it was not persuasive. The drizzle was slowly turning into a persistent rain, and I steered us away from Kings Parade and towards a coffee shop. As we passed through the doorway she took my arm.

"Giles, do you remember Arthur's notebooks?"

It was a rhetorical question. Anyone who knew Arthur knew his notebooks. Maintaining them was his closest approach to a religious ritual. He had started the first one when he was twelve years old. A combination of personal diary, scientific workbook, and clippings album, they recorded everything in his life that he believed to be significant.

"He still kept them when he went to Germany," Marion continued. "He even mentioned them, the last time he was home, because he wanted me to send him the same sort of book that he always used, and he had trouble getting them there. I sent him a shipment in August. I asked Otto Braun to send them back to me, with Arthur's personal things. He told me there were no notebooks. There were only the work journals that every employee of ANF was obliged to keep."

I stared at her across the little table, with its red-and-white checkered cloth. At last, Marion was offering evidence for her case. I moved the salt and pepper shakers around on the table. Arthur may have changed in the past four years, but he couldn't have changed that much. Habits were habits.

She leaned forward, and put her hands over mine. "I know. I said to Braun just what you're thinking. Arthur always kept notebooks. They had to exist, and after his death they belonged to me. I wanted them back. He wriggled and sweated, and said there was nothing. But if I want to know what Arthur left, he said, I can get someone I trust who'll understand Arthur's work, and have them go over to Bonn. Otto Braun will let them see everything there is."

She gazed at me with troubled gray eyes.

I picked up my coffee cup and took an unwanted sip. Some requests for help were simply too much. The next two weeks were going to be chaotic. I had a horrendous schedule, with three promised papers to complete, two London meetings to attend, half a dozen important seminars, and four out-of-town visitors. I had to explain to her somehow that there was no way for me to postpone any part of it.

But first I had to explain matters to someone else. I *had* been in love with Marion Shaw, I told myself, there was no use denying it. Hopelessly, and desperately, and mutely. She had been at one time my *inamorata,* my goddess, the central current of my being; but that was ten years ago. First love's impassioned blindness had long since passed away in colder light.

I opened my mouth to say that I could not help.

Except that this was still my Maid Marion, and she needed me.

The next morning I was on my way to Bonn.

Otto Braun was a tall, heavily built man in his mid-thirties, with a fleshy face, a high forehead, and swept-back dark hair. He had the imposing and slightly doltish look of a Wagnerian *heldentenor*—an appearance that I soon learned was totally deceptive. Otto Braun had the brains of a dozen Siegfrieds, and his command of idiomatic English was so good that his slight German accent seemed like an affectation.

"We made use of certain ancient principles in designing our research facility," he said, as we zipped along the Autobahn in his Peugeot. "Don't be misled by its appearance."

He had insisted on meeting me at Wahn Airport, and driving me (at eighty-five miles an hour) to the company's plant. I studied him, while to my relief he kept his eyes on the road ahead and the other traffic. I could not detect in him any of the shiftiness that Marion Shaw had described. What I did sense was a forced cheerfulness. Otto Braun was uneasy.

"The monasteries of northern Europe were designed to encourage deep meditation," he went on. "Small noise-proof cells, hours of solitary confinement, speech only at certain times and places. Well, deep meditation is what we're after. Of course, we've added a few modern comforts—heat, light, coffee, computers, and a decent cafeteria." He smiled. "So don't worry about your accommodation. Our guest quarters at the lab receive high ratings from visitors. You can see the place now, coming into view over on the left."

I had been instructed not to judge by appearances. Otherwise, I would have taken the research facility of ANF Gesellschaft to be the largest concrete prison blockhouse I had ever seen. Windowless, and surrounded by smooth lawns that ended in a tall fence, it stood fifty feet high and several hundred long. All it needed were guard dogs and machine-gun towers.

Otto Braun drove us through the heavy, automatically opening gates and parked by a side entrance.

"No security?" I said.

He grinned, his first sign of genuine amusement. "Try getting out without the right credentials, Herr Doktor Professor Turnbull."

We traversed a deserted entrance hall to a quiet, carpeted corridor, went up in a noiseless elevator, and walked along to an office about three meters square. It contained a computer, a terminal, a desk, two chairs, a blackboard, a filing cabinet, and a bookcase.

"Notice anything unusual about this room?" he said.

I had, in the first second. "No telephone."

"Very perceptive. The devil's device. Do you know, in eleven years of operation, no one has ever complained about its absence? Every office, including my own, is the same size and shape and has the same equipment in it. We have conference rooms for the larger meetings. This was Dr. Shaw's office and it is, in all essentials, exactly as he left it."

I stared around me with increased interest. He gestured to one of the chairs, and didn't take his eyes off me.

"Mrs. Shaw told me you were his best friend," he said. It was midway between a question and a statement.

"I knew him since we were both teenagers," I replied. And then, since that was not quite enough, "I was probably as close a friend as he had. But Arthur did not encourage close acquaintances."

He nodded. "That makes perfect sense to me. Dr. Shaw was perhaps the most talented and valuable employee we have ever had. His work on quantized Hall effect devices was unique, and made many millions of marks for the company. We rewarded him well and esteemed his work highly. Yet he was not some-one who was easy to know." His eyes were dark and alert, half-hidden in that pudgy face. They focused on me with a higher intensity level. "And Mrs. Shaw. Do you know her well?"

"As well as I know anyone."

"And you have a high regard for each other?"

"She has been like a mother to me."

"Then did she confide in you her worry—that her son Arthur did not die by his own hand, and his death was in some way connected with our company?"

"Yes, she did." My opinion of Otto Braun was changing. He had something to hide, as Marion had said, but he was less and less the likely villain. "Did she tell *you* that?"

"No. I was forced to infer it, from her questions about what he was doing for us. Hmph." Braun rubbed at his jowls. "Herr Turnbull, I find myself in a most difficult situation. I want to be as honest with you as I can, just as I wanted to be honest with Mr. and Mrs. Shaw. But there were things I could not tell them. I am forced to ask again: is your concern for Mrs. Shaw sufficient that you are willing to withhold certain facts from her? Please understand, I am not sug-gesting any form of criminal behavior. I am concerned only to minimize sor-row."

"I can't answer that question unless I know what the facts are. But I think the world of Marion Shaw. I'll do anything I can to make the loss of her son eas-ier for her."

"Very well." He sighed. "I will begin with something that you could find out for yourself, from official sources. Mrs. Shaw thinks there was some sort of foul play in Arthur Shaw's death. I assure you that he took his own life, and the proof of that is provided by the curious manner of his death. Do you know how he died?"

"Only that it was in his apartment."

"It was. But he chose to leave this world in a way that I have never before encountered. Dr. Shaw removed from the lab a large plastic storage bag, big enough to hold a mattress. It is equipped with a zipper along the outside, and when that zipper is closed, such a bag is quite airtight." He paused. Otto Braun was no machine. This explanation was giving him trouble. "Dr. Shaw took it to his apartment. At about six o'clock at night he turned the bag inside out and placed it on top of his bed. Then he changed to his pajamas, climbed into the bag, and zipped it from the inside. Sometime during that evening he died, of as-phyxiation." He looked at me unhappily. "I am no expert in 'locked room' mys-teries, Professor Turnbull, but the police made a thorough investigation. They are quite sure that no one could have closed that bag from the outside. Dr. Shaw took his own life, in a unique and perverse way."

"I see why you didn't want Mr. and Mrs. Shaw to know this. Let me assure you that they won't learn it from me." I felt nauseated. Now that I knew how Arthur had died, I would have rather remained ignorant.

He raised dark eyebrows. "But they *do* know, Professor Turnbull. Naturally, they insisted on seeing the coroner's report on the manner of his death, and I was in no position to keep such information from them. Mrs. Shaw's suspicion of me arose from a quite different incident. It came when she asked me to re-turn Dr. Shaw's journals to her."

"And you refused."

"Not exactly. I denied their existence. Maybe that was a mistake, but I do not pretend to be infallible. If you judge after examination that the books should be released to Dr. Shaw's parents, I will permit it to happen." Otto Braun stood up and went across to the gray metal file cabinet. He patted the side of it. "These contain Arthur Shaw's complete journals. On the day of his death, he took them all and placed them in one of the red trash containers in the corridor, from which they would go to the shredder and incinerator. I should explain that at ANF we have many commercial secrets, and we are careful not to allow our competitors to benefit from our garbage. Dr. Shaw surely believed that his notebooks would be destroyed that night."

He pulled open a file drawer, and I saw the familiar spiral twelve-by-sixteen ledgers that Arthur had favored since childhood.

"As you see, they were not burned or shredded," Braun went on. "In the past we've had occasional accidents, in which valuable papers were placed by oversight into the red containers. So our cleaning staff—all trusted employees— are instructed to check with me if they see anything that looks like a mistake. An alert employee retrieved all these notebooks and brought them to my office, asking approval to destroy them."

It seemed to me that Marion Shaw had been right on at least one thing. For if after examining Arthur's ledgers, Otto Braun had *not* let them be destroyed, they must contain material of value to ANF.

I said this to him, and he shook his head. "The notebooks had to be kept, in case they were needed as evidence for the investigation of death by suicide. They were, in fact, one of the reasons why I am convinced that Dr. Shaw took his own life. Otherwise I would have burned them. Every piece of work that Dr. Shaw did relevant to ANF activities was separately recorded in our ANF work logs. His own notebooks . . ." He paused. "Beyond that, I should not go. You will draw your own conclusions."

He moved away from the cabinet, and steered me with him towards the door. "It is six o'clock, Professor, and I must attend our weekly staff meeting. With your permission, I will show you to your room and then leave you. We can meet tomorrow morning. Let me warn you. You were his friend; be prepared for a shock."

He would make no other comment as we walked to the well-furnished suite that had been prepared for me, other than to say again, as he was leaving, "It is better if you draw your own conclusions. Be ready for a disturbing evening."

The next morning I was still studying Arthur's notebooks.

It is astonishing how, even after five years, my mind reaches for that thought. When I relive my three days in Bonn I feel recollection rushing on, faster and faster, until I reach the point where Otto Braun left me alone in my room. And then memory leaps out towards the next morning, trying to clear the dark chasm of that night.

I cannot permit that luxury now.

It took about three minutes to settle my things in the guest suite at the ANF laboratory. Then I went to the cafeteria, gulped down a sandwich and two cups of tea, and hurried back to Arthur's office. The gray file cabinet held twenty-seven ledgers; many more than I expected, since Arthur normally filled only two or three a year.

In front of the ledgers was a heavy packet wrapped in white plastic. I opened that first, and almost laughed aloud at the incongruity of the contents, side-by-side with Arthur's work records. He had enjoyed experimental science, but the idea of car or bicycle repair was totally repugnant to him. This packet held an array of screwdrivers, heavy steel wire, and needle-nosed and broad-nosed pliers, all shiny and brand-new.

I replaced the gleaming tool kit and turned to the ledgers. If they were equally out of character . . .

It was tempting to begin with the records from the last few days of his life. I resisted that urge. One of the lessons that he had taught me in adolescence was an organized approach to problems, and now I could not afford to miss anything even marginally significant to his death. The ledgers were neatly numbered in red ink on the top right-hand corner of the stiff cover, twenty-two through forty-eight. It was about six-thirty in the evening when I picked up Volume Twenty-two and opened it to the first page.

That gave me my first surprise. I had expected to see only the notebooks for the four years that Arthur had been employed by ANF Gesellschaft. Instead, the date at the head of the first entry was early April, seven and a half years ago. This was a notebook from Arthur's final undergraduate year at Cambridge. Why had he brought with him such old ledgers, rather than leaving them at his parents' house?

The opening entry was unremarkable, and even familiar. At that time, as I well remembered, Arthur's obsession had been quantized theories of gravity. He was still coming to grips with the problem, and his note said nothing profound. I skimmed it and read on. Successive entries were strictly chronological. Mixed in with mathematics, physics, and science references was everything else that had caught his fancy—scraps of quoted poetry (he was in a world-weary Housman phase), newspaper clippings, comments on the weather, lecture notes, cricket scores, and philosophical questions.

It was hard to read at my usual speed. For one thing I had forgotten the near-illegible nature of Arthur's personal notes. I could follow everything, after so many years of practice, but Otto Braun must have had a terrible time. Despite his command of English, some of the terse technical notes and equations would be unintelligible to one of his background. Otto was an engineer. It would be astonishing if his knowledge extended to modern theoretical physics.

And yet in some ways Otto Braun would have found the material easier going than I did. I *could* not make myself read fast, for the words of those old notebooks whispered in my brain like a strange echo of false memory. Arthur and I had been in the same place at the same time, experiencing similar events, and many of the things that he felt worth recording had made an equal impression on me. We had discussed many of them. This was my own Cambridge years, my own life, seen from a different vantage point and through a lens that imposed a subtle distortion on shapes and colors.

And then it changed. The final divergence began.

It was in December, eight days before Christmas, that I caught a first hint of something different and repugnant. Immediately following a note on quantized red shifts came a small newspaper clipping. It appeared without comment, and it reported the arrest of a Manchester man for the torture, murder, and dismemberment of his own twin daughters. He had told the police that the six-year-olds had "deserved all they got."

That was the first evidence of a dark obsession. In successive months and years, Arthur Shaw's ledgers told of his increasing preoccupation with death; and it was never the natural, near-friendly death of old age and a long, fulfilled life, but always the savage deaths of small children. Death unnatural, murder most foul. The clippings spoke of starvation, beating, mutilation, and torture. In every case Arthur had defined the source, without providing any other comment. He must have combed the newspapers in his search, for I, reading those same papers in those same editions, had not noticed the articles.

It got worse. Nine years ago it had been one clipping every few pages. By the time he went to live in Bonn the stories of brutal death occupied more than half the journals, and his sources of material had become worldwide.

And yet the Arthur that I knew still existed. It was bewildering and frightening to recognize the cool, analytical voice of Arthur Shaw, interspersed with the bloody deeds of human monsters. The poetry quotes and the comments on the weather and current events were still there, but now they shared space with a catalog of unspeakable acts.

Four years ago, just before he came to Bonn, another change occurred. It was as though the author of the written entries had suddenly become *aware* of the thing that was making the newspaper clippings. When Arthur discovered that the other side of him was there, he began to comment on the horror of the events that he was recording. He was shocked, revolted, and terrified by them.

And yet the clippings continued, along with the lecture notes, the concerts attended, the careful record of letters written; and there were the first hints of something else, something that made me quiver.

I read on, to midnight and beyond until the night sky paled. Now at last I am permitted the statement denied to me earlier: The next morning I was still studying Arthur's notebooks.

Otto Braun came into the office, looked at me, and nodded grimly.

"I am sorry, Professor Turnbull. It seemed to me that nothing I could say would be the same as allowing you to read for yourself." He came across to the desk. "The security officer says you were up all night. Have you eaten breakfast?"

I shook my head.

"I thought not." He looked at my hands, which were perceptibly shaking. "You must have rest."

"I can't sleep."

"You will. But first you need food. Come with me. I have arranged for us to have a private dining-room."

On the way to the guest quarters I went to the bathroom. I saw myself in the mirror there. No wonder Otto Braun was worried. I looked terrible, pale and unshaven, with purple-black rings under my eyes.

In the cafeteria Braun loaded a tray with scrambled eggs, *speckwurst*, croissants, and hot coffee, and led me to a nook off the main room. He watched like a worried parent to make sure that I was eating, before he would pour coffee for himself.

"Let me begin with the most important question," he said. "Are you convinced that Arthur Shaw took his own life?"

"I feel sure of it. He could not live with what one part of him was becoming. The final entry in his journal says as much. And it explains the way he chose to die."

Enough is enough, Arthur had written. *I can't escape from myself. "To cease upon the midnight with no pain." Better to return to the womb, and never be born . . .*

"He wanted peace, and to hide away from everything," I went on. "When you know that, the black plastic bag makes more sense."

"And you agree with my decision?" Braun's chubby face was anxious. "To keep the notebooks away from his parents."

"It was what he would have wanted. They were supposed to be destroyed, and one of his final entries proves it. He said, 'I have done one braver thing.' "

His brow wrinkled, and he put down his cup. "I saw that. But I did not understand it. He did not say what he had done."

"That's because it's part of a quotation, from a poem by John Donne. 'I have done one braver thing, Than all the worthies did, And yet a braver thence doth spring, And that, to keep it hid.' He *wanted* what he had been doing to remain secret. It was enormously important to him."

"That is a great relief. I hoped that it was so, but I could not be sure. Do you agree with me, we can now destroy those notebooks?"

I paused. "Maybe that is not the best answer. It will leave questions in the mind of Marion Shaw, because she is quite sure that the books must exist. Suppose that you turn them over to my custody? If I tell Marion that I have them, and want to keep them as something of Arthur's, I'm sure she will approve. And of course I will never let her see them."

"Ah." Braun gave a gusty sigh of satisfaction. "That is a most excellent suggestion. Even now, I would feel uneasy about destroying them. I must admit, Professor Turnbull, that I had doubts as to my own wisdom when I agreed to allow you to come here and examine Dr. Shaw's writings. But everything has turned out for the best, has it not? If you are not proposing to eat those eggs . . ."

Everything for the best, thought Otto Braun, and probably in the best of all possible worlds.

We had made the decision. The rest was details. Over the next twelve hours, he and I wrote the script.

I would handle Marion and Roland Shaw. I was to confirm that Arthur's death had been suicide, while his mind was unbalanced by overwork. If they talked to Braun again about his earlier discomfort in talking to them, it was because he felt he had failed them. He had not done enough to help, he would say, when Arthur so obviously needed him. (No lie there; that's exactly how Otto felt.)

And the journals? I would tell the Shaws of Arthur's final wish, that they be destroyed. Again, no lie; and I would assure them that I would honor that intent.

I went home. I did it, exactly as we had planned. The only intolerable moment came when Marion Shaw put her arms around me, and actually *thanked* me for what I had done.

Because, of course, neither she nor Otto Braun nor anyone else in the world knew what I *had* done.

When I read the journals and saw Arthur's mind fluttering towards insanity, I was horrified. But it was not only the revelation of madness that left me the next morning white-faced and quivering. It was excitement derived from the *other* content of the ledgers, material interwoven with the cool comments on personal affairs and the blood-obsessed newspaper clippings.

Otto Braun, in his relief at seeing his own problems disappear, had grabbed at my explanation of Arthur's final journal entries, without seeing that it was wholly illogical. "I have done one braver thing," quoted Arthur. But that was surely not referring to the newspaper clippings and his own squalid obsessions. He was appalled by them, and said so. What was the "brave thing" that he had done?

I knew. It was in the notebooks.

For four years, since Arthur's departure from Cambridge, I had concentrated on the single problem of a unified theory of quantized space-time. I made everything else in my life of secondary importance, working myself harder than ever before, to the absolute limit of my powers. At the back of my mind was always Arthur's comment: this was the most important problem in modern physics.

It was the best work I had ever done. I suspect that it is easily the best work that I will ever do.

What I had not known, or even vaguely suspected, was that Arthur Shaw had begun to work on the same problem after he went to Bonn.

I found that out as I went through his work ledgers. How can I describe the feeling, when in the middle of the night in Arthur's old office I came across scribbled thoughts and conjectures that I had believed to belong in my head alone? They were mixed in hodge-podge with everything else, side-by-side with the soccer scores, the day's high temperature, and the horror stories of child molestation, mutilation, and murder. To Otto Braun or anyone else, those marginal scribbles would have been random nonsensical jottings. But I recognized that integral, and that flux quantization condition, and that invariant.

How can I describe the feeling?

I cannot. But I am not the first to suffer it. Thomas Kydd and Ben Jonson must have been filled with the same awe in the 1590s, when Shakespeare carried the English language to undreamed-of heights. *Hofkapellmeister* Salieri knew it, to his despair, when Mozart and his God-touched work came on the scene at the court of Vienna. Edmund Halley surely felt it, sitting in Newton's rooms at Trinity College in 1684, and learning that the immortal Isaac had discovered laws and invented techniques that would make the whole System of the World *calculable;* and old Legendre was overwhelmed by it, when the *Disquisitiones* came into his hands and he marveled at the supernatural mathematical powers of the young Gauss.

When half-gods go, the gods arrive. I had struggled with the problem of space-time quantization, as I said, with every working neuron of my brain. Arthur Shaw went so far beyond me that it took all my intellect to mark his path. "It were all one that I should love a bright particular star, and think to wed it, he is so above me." But I could see what he was doing, and I recognized what

I had long suspected. Arthur was something that I would never be. He was a true genius.

I am not a genius, but I am very talented. I could follow where I could not lead. From the hints, scribbled theorems, and conjectures in Arthur Shaw's notebooks I assembled the whole; not perhaps as the gorgeous tapestry of thought that Arthur had woven in his mind, but enough to make a complete theory with profound practical implications.

That grand design was the "braver thing" that he knew he had done, an intellectual feat that placed him with the immortals.

It was also, paradoxically, the cause of his death.

Some scientific developments are "in the air" at a particular moment; if one person does not propose them, another will. But other creative acts lie so far outside the mainstream of thought that they seem destined for a single individual. If Einstein had not created the theory of general relativity, it is quite likely that it would not exist today. Arthur Shaw knew what he had wrought. His approach was totally novel, and he was convinced that without his work an adequate theory might be centuries in the future.

I did not believe that; but I might have, if I had not been stumbling purblind along the same road. The important point, however, is that Arthur *did* believe it.

What should he do? He had made a wonderful discovery. But when he looked inside himself, he saw in that interior mirror only the glassy essence of the angry ape. He had in his grasp the wondrous spell that would send humanity to the stars—but he regarded us as a bloody-handed, bloody-minded humanity, raging out of control through the universe.

His duty as he saw it was clear. He must do the braver thing, and destroy both his ideas and himself.

What did I do?

I think it is obvious.

Arthur's work had always been marred by obscurity. Or rather, to be fair to him, in his mind the important thing was that he understand an idea, not that he be required to explain it to someone of lesser ability.

It took months of effort on my part to convert Arthur's awkward notation and sketchy proofs to a form that could withstand rigorous scrutiny. At that point the work felt like my own; the re-creation of his half-stated thoughts was often indistinguishable from painful invention.

Finally I was ready to publish. By that time Arthur's ledgers had been, true to my promise, long-since destroyed, for whatever else happened in the world I did not want Marion Shaw to see those notebooks or suspect anything of their contents.

I published. I could have submitted the work as the posthumous papers of Arthur Sandford Shaw . . . except that someone would certainly have asked to see the original material.

I published. I could have assigned joint authorship, as Shaw and Turnbull . . . except that Arthur had never presented a line on the subject, and the historians would have probed and probed to learn what his contribution had been.

I published—as Giles Turnbull. Three papers expounded what the world now knows as the Turnbull Concession Theory. Arthur Shaw was not mentioned. It is not easy to justify that, even to myself. I clung to one thought: Arthur had wanted his ideas suppressed, but that was a consequence of his own state of mind. It was surely better to give the ideas to the world, and risk their abuse in human hands. *That,* I said to myself, was the braver thing.

I published. And because there were already eight earlier papers of mine in the literature, exploring the same problem, acceptance of the new theory was quick, and my role in it was never in doubt.

Or almost never. In the past four years, at scattered meetings around the world, I have seen in perhaps half a dozen glances the cloaked hint of a question. The world of physics holds a handful of living giants. They see each other clearly, towering above the rest of us, and when someone whom they have assessed as one of the pygmies shoots up to stand tall, not at their height but even well above them, there is at least a suspicion . . .

There is a braver thing.

Last night I telephoned my father. He listened quietly to everything that I had to tell him, then he replied, "Of course I won't say a word about that to Marion Shaw. And neither will you." And at the end he said what he had not said when the Nobel announcement was made: "I'm proud of you, Giles."

At the cocktail party before tonight's dinner, one of the members of the Royal Swedish Academy of Sciences was tactless enough to tell me that he and his colleagues found the speeches delivered by the Nobel laureates uniformly boring. It's always the same, he said, all they ever do is recapitulate the reason that the award had been made to them in the first place.

I'm sure he is right. But perhaps tomorrow I can be an exception to that rule.

This is a birthday present for Bob Porter.
—Charles Sheffield, February 27, 1989.

GETTING REAL

Susan Shwartz

Susan Shwartz is a fantasy and science fiction writer and anthologist. She has done a number of books in collaboration with Andre Norton and edited an anthology in honor of Norton. By day, she dons a suit and works in New York City in a large firm in the financial district that does things with money. She has in the past worked as a temp.

Someone had scrawled the usual dirty joke on the Temp Fugit Employment Agency sign, I noticed as I dodged the dawn trucking shift down Fulton Street. And dirty puns are bad for business, so I smeared off the graffiti with the front page of the *New York Post*. The sign's edge slashed open the sketch a police artist had made of the Subway Slasher, who scared commuters to death—when he didn't stab them.

In the ladies', I reached for the pink tubes of Realité. Once I got my fresh ID assignment, I'd fine-tune, but I could apply the base coats right now. I started spraying and painting and injecting Realité—think of it as a sort of psychic steroid that lets temps register on the eyes of Real employers and coworkers.

Up front, Temp Fugit looks a whole lot like any other mid-range temp agency: Cosmopolitan, Apple, Irene Cohen—anywhere they sell word-processing staff. The lobby has machine-tooled chairs, assembly-line artwork, and AMA publications and self-help mags up our hypothetical wazoos.

If Reals do stumble into the office, they sit around tapping their manicures till they get disgusted when no receptionists or counselors may-I-help them. Then they stamp out. So they never see the dressing rooms where we become the people in our ID envelopes.

One of the other temps had a *New York Daily News* with a sketch of the Subway Slasher and photos of his victims on it, but no one really looked at that or one another. Temps aren't likely to be mugged. And we really don't like one another much.

You thought it was just actors who temped, didn't you? Actors do work temp between gigs, but there's all the difference in the world between people who work temporary jobs and temporary people.

New York's cruddy with us. Employers use us for the scut work. After all, do you think anyone cares what a goddamned temp feels? You'd walk into us on the street if we didn't dodge you; you try to take the seats we're already in; and you only really talk to us in the instant you pick up more work and go "Wouldja mind . . ." If you're being very formal, you go, "Hey, wouldja mind."

Mostly, we temps forget our real names and families. Fair enough: they forgot us long ago. Check it out, if you don't believe me. Get any nice, big family in the burbs to show you its scrapbook. Make sure you pick a big one; there's never enough life in big families to go around.

Just you look. There's always one kid, a little scrawny, a little pale, a little shadowy even then, usually half cut off by bad camera angles or glare. Once you know how to look, you can always tell who's going to turn temp once it hits puberty. School makes it even easier. Usually, the temp doesn't have a photo in the yearbook. Even if it does, there's no nice list of college-impressing clubs and activities under the photo, either. College simply means anonymous B-minus, C-plus in the big lecture courses where the teachers and TAs don't look at anyone. Mostly, temps mark time, years of never understanding why they're not called on, why people damned near walk through them on the street, why what they say just doesn't seem to register.

Don't ask me what temps do who can't make it to New York. This city needs us. It's got all sorts of jobs that people only do if they've halfway fallen through the cracks already. Temps fit right in; and since no one notices us, we can live safe from the mob, muggers, crackheads, and homeboys gone wilding.

Sure, it's tough. But it's tough for the Reals too. Much we care about them. All we care about is getting and keeping enough life to keep on dreaming, pretending that one day we'll figure it out and we'll be real too.

Because New York's the most alive place there is, with its electrifying street dance of cars and horses and bikers dodging, and walkers doing that broken-field walk, rising on their toes to dodge someone, swearing ("Hey ouddatowna, moveit why doncha!"), or turning to "checkitout," whatever *it* is, never breaking stride.

Shoppers prowl like hunters in sneaks and walking shoes. The men stalk ahead, clearing unnecessary room for the women who even dress like predators in black leather or long, long black fur. They walk heads up, their eyes glazed, and they don't see anything but the perfection of their grooming in the windows as they strut past.

Simple Reaganomics. This city's so damned alive that some of that life's got to trickle down even to us.

Mostly, we live on the street. It's kind of hard to bribe supers and Realtors when they can't see the hand that holds the cash. You learn after one or two tries—out of sight, out of mind. The bastards pocket the bribes and rent the place to someone else.

I've moved up (or underground) in the world. Got a place in one of the caves off the E-train terminus at the World Trade Center. There's always a crowd there, and you can usually find papers and boxes and food in the garbage from the stores and restaurants. There've been lots of papers lately. Mostly about this slasher.

Sure, you have to share papers with the crazies, but there's so much stuff thrown out, there's enough to go around. I had to learn to share with the Reals who make their homes among the urine-smelling blue posts of the E-train terminus. At first, I just used to take what I wanted till Tink called me on it.

"You mustn't think we don't see you," she told me in that voice of hers. Once it was soft and careful; now it's cracked from screaming and her last run-in with pneumonia, or maybe it's TB. "You have to share," she told me, wagging an index finger, and I got to see the children's librarian under the rags, the caked makeup, and the sores.

Tink used to be a children's librarian till budget cuts closed her school and finished the job of driving her around the bend that kids, parents, and school boards started. For a while, she read her books aloud to herself in Bellevue, Thorazined to the max, but budget cuts—Reaganomics again, see?—made them stop warehousing crazies. They call it mainstreaming. What it means is that they turn crazies loose on the streets.

Mostly crazies and temps don't get along much. They're real—so what? We're sane, but who gives a shit? Crazies like Tink, that's who. It's short for Tinkerbell. Sometimes she hasn't got change for Thunderbird, but she always manages to curl her hair, and it's still a rusty blond. Usually, she wears a straw hat with flowers on it, and she carries her stuff in a neat wire cart. The transies and rentacops don't chase her off the benches, and all the winos know her.

Tink even has a cat, a black-and-white thing we call Rabbit on account of he's so skinny his ears look too big for his head. Tink runs this stop. Not even the kids who sleep in the trains bully her. Tink's the one who made the other crazies like Sailor fall in line. I pay back by bringing back things from places that crazies can't get into: food, sometimes; pills; books for Tink when I can.

I glanced around Temp Fugit. Anything there that Tink might like? I glanced at the self-help books on the table. Never mind them. Besides, Tink had a new book some kid must have dropped and boohooed about all last night. Something about a velveteen rabbit. She was muttering to herself as she read it, folding each page back real careful, and her smile really made her look like Tinkerbell. She looked up as I passed, and I'll swear that part of that smile was even for me.

"This is going to be a good day," I muttered at the roomful of temps, who sat flexing their fingers. Real computer operators and typists are klutzy; sixty-five wpm and they're good, they think. Most of us go over one hundred without kicking into second gear.

My sense that today would be the day I'd get a really choice assignment grew. It wasn't just that Tink had smiled at me. Today, the Apostle to the E train had been playing by the turnstiles; and it's always a good day when he's there.

Now I know you've seen the Apostle. He's not temp or crazy; he's real, and he's a celebrity—he's even been on the *Tonight* show. Went to Juilliard; I've heard that he's played in Carnegie Hall. Sometimes, he finishes a concert and heads straight to the E train, where he does an instant replay of his program. When the trains howl in, he stops and chats, and always wows the out-of-towners with flashy sweeps of his bow and tosses of his little Dutch-boy haircut. His cards say he's James Graseck, but Tink calls him the Apostle, and the name's stuck.

Anyhow, the Apostle was playing as I walked by, and I could almost swear he winked at me. I wanted to ask him, but a woman walked by in her little Reeboks and sox with the cuff stripe to match her coat and suit, and tipped him a buck.

He bowed like an old-style cavalier and launched into Vivaldi's *Four Seasons*. A regular. I liked the look of her and followed her up Fulton on my way to Temp Fugit. Pretending I was her, had a job and an apartment, and all.

Nice dreams, I thought as I waited for my turn at the tape machine. Temp Fugit keeps its tapes in the booths that other agencies use for typing tests. Like *Mission Impossible*. If caught, Temp Fugit will deny all knowledge of your existence.

Tape told me I'd hit the jackpot this time, all right. Long-term temp assignment at Seaport Securities, the big firm by the East River. Even now after the Crash—which was a real-person event that really registered with the temps; brokerages cut way back on hiring when the market went China Syndrome—Wall Street is happy hunting ground for temps. The yups want their work done like *now*, and they treat clericals like Handi Wipes. Well, temps are used to that shit.

And there's always the chance that even a temp might get lucky and get a full-time job. Once you're in the pipeline, New York rules apply: climb, get your Series Seven, make enough money, and you get to be real.

Believe me, there's a lot of people in this city who'd be temps if they didn't have money.

My assignment ID told me I was Debbie Goldman. The capsule bio said she was staying with people while she looked for an apartment; she'd majored in Bus. Admin. Most secretarial and computer-ops types major in "something practical" while they keyboard through school and dream of being Melanie Griffith in *Working Girl*.

I looked at the picture again. By the time I applied Realité-based mascara, I'd polished a characterization of Ms. Goldman—me as I'd be when I headed to Seaport. Good sills—which I had; corporate dresser—thank you, Temp Fugit, for your nice wardrobe.

I walked down Fulton to the harbor, a real nice place with tall ships at anchor and the kind of expensive stores that temps shouldn't even dream of. After you've bounced from assignment to assignment for a few years, it gets so you can tell how a place is going to be the instant you walk into it. Seaport Securities has its own building, glossy red stone, aluminum, and lots of glass. Point one for Seaport.

The lobby rated another point. It had fresh flowers that looked like they're changed every week whether they need to be or not. And mega-corporate art: Frank Stella, I thought, expensive arcs and rainbows high overhead. The elevators were another plus: shiny paint, no graffiti or scratches, and fresh carpeting. I used the glossy walls to check my persona. The door purred open and I faced the final test: staff.

"M'elpyou," said the receptionist, her gold earrings jangling as she set down the phone. "I mean," she corrected herself, "may I help you?"

"I'm Debbie Goldman," I told her. "I was told to report to Lisa Black, she's your—" I didn't want to say office manager or head secretary; corporate women get really defensive of their titles.

"Administrative VP," the receptionist supplied. "She's real nice. But she's in a meeting. You just sit here and read the paper, and when she comes down, I'll tell her you're here."

Under cover of the *Wall Street Journal,* I checked the place out. More corporate art. Flowers even up here, and I didn't think that this floor was where the real senior people were—too many cubicles and not enough offices with doors. I liked the way that people came off the elevators, walking in groups, men and women, veterans and kids together. That's a good sign, that people get along when they talk like that. I checked my clothes against what the other women were wearing. The others wore nice coats and sneakers, with their sox matching the coats, trimlike.

Someone came out to relieve the receptionist. "New girl here, Debbie," said the receptionist who was going off-shift. "She's here to see Lisa."

Not "Ms. Black." Friendly place.

"Where is she?"

"Breakfast with the research director. They must be crying about the way the analysts go through secretaries again."

The first receptionist snorted and eyed me for longevity value. So, this might be a test? Assign me to an analyst and see if I could take the pressure before trying me on a real job? Temps pray, and I prayed really hard right then.

The elevator purred open. "There's Lisa now. Lisa, Debbie Goldman's here to see you."

It was the woman from the subway, the one who'd tipped the Apostle and whose look I'd liked. She'd traded her Reeboks for pumps and she looked even better than she had on the street. Nice suit, and a silk blouse with a soft bow rather than a shirt with a severe neckline. That's always good; the hard-tailored ones can be a real bitch to work for.

Laying the paper aside—neatly, Debbie, dammit!—I stood up politely and came forward, waiting for her handshake. Mine, thanks to the Realité, would be nice and warm, too.

"Am I glad to see you, Debbie," she said. "One of our gals just left, and there's an analyst who's got a report that has to get out. I'm always glad to deal with Temp Fugit; it always tests its people on Lotus and WordPerfect, which is just what we need."

"I'll do my best, Ms. Black," I said. Always a good thing to say, and it keeps you from asking the other questions, like What're the people I'll be working with like, where's lunch, are the regular secretaries friendly, and Please, will you keep me? I glanced around, a shall-I-get-started look that I've been told makes me seem eager to work hard.

"People call me Lisa," said Lisa. "We're all on first names here. Of course, if the president comes down from thirty-six, that's different." She laughed, and I laughed dutifully back to show I understood the decencies of chain of command. "Would you like to use the ladies' room before I take you in?"

She glanced over at the off-shift receptionist, who had lingered by the desk. "Daniella, want to do me a big favor?" she asked. "Debbie's going to be working with Rick Grimaldi."

Daniella grinned real fast, then wiped it before Lisa Black had to shake her head. After all, you don't tell outsiders who's a real bastard to work with. "Now, Rick's going to want to get to work right away. I'll bet that Debbie here hasn't had any coffee yet this morning, and if I know Rick, she won't have any chance to get any, either."

Lisa fished in her handbag and came up with a pretty wallet. Mark Cross, no less. Hmm. Seaport paid well, then. She pulled out a dollar.

"How you take it?" Daniella asked me.

"Regular," I said.

When I came out of the ladies' (I'd done a good job on my makeup), Lisa Black led me over to a workstation where a cup of coffee steamed.

"We call Rick 'the Prince,'" she told me, and waited for me to get the joke.

"Because he's named Grimaldi, like the Prince of Monaco? Any relation?" I wouldn't have been surprised if she'd said yes, but she laughed.

"No. Because he's very demanding. But you can handle that, can't you?"

Two women passing her grinned and shook their heads.

"I hope so," I said. At that point, he could have had horns, a tail, and a whip, and I'd have tried my damnedest.

Instead, he had a fast handshake, a this-is-the-best-you-could-do glare at Lisa, and what looked like half the papers and disks in the office. Which promptly got dumped perilously close to the coffee, and I rescued them. "Let's see you enter these numbers," he demanded, and stood over me while I worked. The woman at the next workstation grimaced. If I were real, I suppose I'd have a right to have a fit. As it was, I was there to type, and I typed.

Thanks to Realité, my fingers didn't chill and cramp as he stared at them, tapping his foot and lamenting that nobody, nobody at all cared whether his work got done and how sharper than a serpent's tooth it was to have a thankless secretary, typical boss ratshit; and I typed while my coffee got cold. Finally, he humphed and dumped more paper right on my keyboard. I managed not to sigh as I disentangled myself. This wad included a take-out menu.

"Want me to order in for you?" I asked. Now, look, I know real secretaries don't have to get coffee and sandwiches anymore. I know that. I also know that execs—male and female MBA created them—are just dying for someone who isn't wise to the fact that times have changed. It's not that they actually need the goddamned sandwiches and coffee; they just like giving orders and being served. Besides, sandwiches in the Seaport area are a good four dollars each, plus coffee and cole slaw or whatever. He might say, "Order for yourself, too."

He did. Bingo. Hey, if I worked late, maybe he'd tell me to order dinner, too.

When I left for the day, half-wobbling from exhaustion, I walked by Lisa Black's desk, and she flashed thumbs-up at me. She looked relieved, and I wondered how many temps Prince Grimaldi had gone through.

I had half a sandwich and a piece of carrot cake for Tink, who let me feed Rabbit some scraps of smoked turkey. Rabbit purred and licked my hand.

Grimaldi's quarterly report dragged on. Gradually, the secretaries smiled and called me Debbie. After all, there's no use in wasting friendliness on someone who might be fired an hour from now. But for the long-term temp who looks like she's working out—her, you say "good morning" to. Her, you smile at in the mirror in the ladies' room. All those Kimberlys and Theresas and Carols and Heathers, fussing with their moussed hair and their nails, chirping at one another; and they talked to me, too, including me in the babble of What He Did, What I Said About It, and How I Fixed That Bitch.

It was hard to pretend I cared about Challenge, Career Opportunities, Learning Experiences, and all the other upwardly mobile jargon that staff chants to reassure itself. It was hard to contribute to the discussions of the best way to climb the ladder when all I wanted to do was survive. And it was hard to believe that that was all the Reals seemed to want to do either. Funny, if I were real, I probably wouldn't do it any different.

Unlike me, the Reals were scared of the slasher. So I had to act scared, too.

"Make the Prince send you home in a cab," Carol told me, the day that the *Daily News* ran a think-piece about the slasher. "You're entitled if you work after seven P.M."

I decided I'd wait till Grimaldi offered. Days passed, and the slasher managed to sneak past the cops and chalk up more victims; still, Grimaldi never thought to ask if I wanted help getting home. Again, typical. Execs know the Rules, just as well as us temps, but they just love getting something for nothing—an extra hour or so of work or maybe just the petty thrill of watching someone get off the phone just because they walk up. Or not having to put car service on expense account.

I knew I was fitting in after a couple of weeks when Heather asked me to contribute to Carvel cake and champagne for Kimberly. I know they just did it because they needed extra money, but all the same, I was pleased.

The next day, the transit cops found another one in the Canal Street subway tunnel—dead, this time, and cut bad. Kimberly was there when they took it out. I found her in the ladies', gurgling and sobbing, holding a piece of paper towel to the careful lines she had painted under her eyes so they wouldn't smudge as she wept. She was surrounded by the usual throng, patting her shoulder and crooning as she shuddered.

I was washing my hands alone at the other sink when Lisa Black came in. "The analysts are complaining that no one's picking up the phones," she announced as she entered. Then, seeing Kimberly, "What's wrong?"

"I . . . I saw . . . My boyfriend wants me to quit and find a job in Brooklyn, and we need the money . . ." She burst into tears, ruining her eyeliner and her precautions, and the light winked off the tiny diamond on her shaking left hand.

"That tears it," Lisa declared. "I'm calling car service to take you all home tonight. Are any of you afraid to go by yourselves? I can poll the guys and see who's going where."

Headshakes and sheepish laughs. I dried my hands.

"This means you, too," she told me. "Where do you live, Debbie?"

"I'm staying with friends for now," I said. "I get on at World Trade; it's pretty safe there if I stay in the center of the platform."

Lisa nodded. "That's my stop, too. All the same, if it gets late, you take a cab home, you hear?"

Sure, I'd take a cab home to the E train. Sure. The one time I'd been put into a taxi, the man took off down the street, shaking his head as if he couldn't understand why his signal light was off. Three blocks later, he picked up a fare, and I slipped out. Never saw me.

I nodded obedience. "What're you going to do?" I asked.

"Me?" Lisa said. "I'm not worried. Stories say that the slasher picks on young girls. I'm too old."

She was about my age, maybe younger, I thought, if you allow for the fact that temps seem to age more slowly than Reals—the result, probably, of less connection to the world. But her comment brought protests from the women she supervised, even a reluctant gurgle of a laugh from Kimberly.

I ducked past as the women trooped out, heading for the phones and the analysts and the piled-up work. Lisa must have thought I'd left too, or she wouldn't have done what she did then. Leaning forward, she stared at herself in the mirror, one hand stroking the soft skin beneath her eyes as if she were brushing dry ashes from her face with her ringless left hand. She stroked the corners of her eyes where a few wrinkles were starting. For all that, though, her face was surprisingly youthful.

"Old," she whispered, her voice hollow and almost breaking. "So old." With that, she fumbled in her bag, pulled out a pillbox, and grimaced as she swallowed something and washed it down with water from the tap.

She must not have seen me. I applied more Realité at lunch.

Prince Grimaldi let me out at five that day. I huddled near Tink on the bench right by the stairs and wiped the makeup from my face as she read her book at me: the story of a velveteen toy that a child loved and cherished, but that knew it was never real and would never be real, unless someone loved it enough to make it real.

No one would ever, no one had ever loved me that much, I thought, and felt a whimper in my throat. "Old, so old," I remembered Lisa saying. At least, people could see her.

"What good is it?" I scoffed at Tink, who scowled at me, the upper layers of her makeup cracking as she scowled.

"What else is there?" she asked. This must have been one of her good days, when her thoughts were clear and she could talk without spitting and swearing. "You want to live, you have to be real. But real's more 'n sitting clean and pretty. You want to be real, someone has to give you life. Someone has to care. And then you have to believe you're real, real enough to care about."

When I tried to ask questions, Tink picked up the book again, humming. Shortly afterward, she nodded off. When I covered her with warm, dry papers, Rabbit leapt up and didn't even hiss at me for once. Must have been all the leftovers I'd been feeding him.

"Stop chirping," one of the temps snapped in the dressing room at Temp Fugit the next day. "Can't you just put on your Realité and leave me alone? You talk talk talk. Like you think you're real. Like you're really fooling yourself."

That was a longer speech than I'd gotten out of anyone in all the years I'd worked out of Temp Fugit, and the anger in it startled me. Of course, I talked in the ladies'. You always had to talk in the ladies' at Seaport. That was where you heard the news, where you got the company Rules explained.

I finished up my sprays and paints real fast and left, to a mutter of "Thinks she's people, just because she's got a long-term job."

Later that morning, Grimaldi called me in and told me he had a full-time secretary starting Monday. "I wish I'd seen you when I was interviewing," he said.

So this was good-bye. Well, I couldn't say it was nice knowing him, but there were people here I'd miss.

"You've worked well for me," he told me. (News to me.) "And that's rare these days. So I've recommended you to Whittington. His secretary's going on maternity leave and might not come back. By that time, if you work out, who knows? Let me have your résumé, will you?"

I printed him a copy, gave it to him, and he grunted approval at the math minor. Sure, I was good at math. You don't need to be real to do equations. "I've spoken to Lisa Black," he told me before he headed off to a company meeting. "She'll get your paperwork from personnel. Go talk to her when you finish pasting up the tables, will you?"

I nodded, thanked him, and headed out.

"You want to remember that lots of your junior analysts start as secretaries," he told me. "Think about it."

I never had an order I liked better. Even Lisa looked pleased. Politics said it was because her decision had paid off and now Grimaldi owed her, but I thought part of her satisfaction was for me. If I played my cards right . . . I could see myself angling for sponsorship to take the Series Seven for broker right now.

And was that the best thing I could think of to do with being real? Would I walk through people, not seeing them, real or temp, except as things to do what I needed them to? Would I run scared? Was it better to be someone like Grimaldi, who used people, or Tink, who'd been used up?

"I saw you in World Trade Center," Lisa Black told me. "You were talking to one of the street people, the woman who wears those hats, you know who I mean?"

"Tink?" The name slipped out before I could stop myself.

"That's her name?"

"What they call her."

"James"—she meant the Apostle—"warned me that some of these people can turn on you. You want to watch them," Lisa warned me. "Is this some sort of volunteer work for your church or something? Wouldn't Meals on Wheels be a safer bet?"

I hated to lie to her, so I muttered something.

Lisa reached for her purse and hauled out a twenty. "I noticed that her legs are pretty badly ulcerated. This would buy some mercurochrome and bandages, maybe some vitamins. Do you accept donations from outsiders?"

I started to shake my head no, but she insisted, and I took the money.

After Tink finished bandaging her legs, she presided over a feast of junk food. I'd told her she needed gloves, but potato chips and rotgut it was.

I left halfway through and went to sleep. A cold nose woke me hours later. It was Rabbit. I didn't know we were on that good of terms.

"What is it, cat?" I asked.

Rabbit meowed, almost a howl.

So I got up and had a look. God, I wished I hadn't. Now I was glad that Tink had had her party. It was the last one she'd ever have. Some time during the night, the Subway Slasher had got her. Blood from the grin under her chin had drenched her tatty parka and splashed down onto the bandages, which were still clean where the blood hadn't soaked them. She'd been too drunk to run or scream. Please God, she'd been too drunk to know what hit her.

I screamed, but nothing answered: no voices, no footsteps, no whistle. I'd have been glad of anyone, but Sailor was God-knows-where and even the men who sleep on cardboard by the token booths seemed to have vanished. So I sat there for what had to be hours, Rabbit with me. After a while, I put my arms about my shoulders, remembering dimly that when I was a child, before I'd temped out, hugs had helped. Rabbit crawled up next to me and scrambled onto my lap. To my surprise, he licked my face; to my greater surprise, I had been crying.

"Sweet Jesus," came a new voice. Rabbit yowled and beat it. I looked up, and it was James the Apostle, just standing there, clutching his violin case and music stand. No point taking Tink's pulse, he saw that straight off. Instead, he covered her face with Bach and ran to call 911.

When he came back, he circled Tink gingerly. His foot hit something, and he rescued it from a puddle I didn't want to look at. Tink's last book, *The Velveteen Rabbit.* Shaking his head, the Apostle tucked it into his music.

"They'll be here soon," he remarked. He was an artist, and with his mission to the subways, he had to be slightly mad himself. I thought he really could see me. "Did Tink tell you about the book, about being real? I read it to my son. This is what I think. It takes life to be real. And if there's been a death, stands to reason that there's space for another real live person. Tink had a lot of heart. And I think she cared about you. Why not take the chance? Be real."

He gestured, and I suddenly knew that all I had to do was uncover her face, touch it, and believe, just like Tink and the Apostle said, and I'd be real. "Lord, I believe," they say in church. "Help Thou mine unbelief."

To be real. To care. To be cared about. To hurt the way I'd hurt when I saw that slash in Tink's wrinkled throat. To see Sailor lurking in the shadows, still afraid to come out, though Tink had been his buddy, tears pouring from ganja-reddened eyes, but afraid to come near the cops. Did he run? Was that why he looks so sad?

Courage, like danger and grief, was not a temp's concern; we were safe from that kind of pain. Why let myself in for it if I didn't have to? I was being smart, practical, I told myself.

What a damned liar.

I didn't have the guts. Or anything else.

The Apostle watched the space where I was—all right, let's say he watched me—until he realized I wasn't going to try. "Too frightened?" he asked. "What a shame."

The cops arrived in a blare of whistles and a clatter of heavy, important shoes and walkie-talkies. Two of them almost ran right through where I stood. I headed back to my little cache of treasures—clothes of my own, Reeboks just like Lisa's, nail polish the color of Kimberly's—I'd collected since starting at Seaport. My eyes burned as if Realité had spilled into them or I'd poked myself with a mascara wand, and my shoulders shook.

At Temp Fugit, it took twice the usual dose of Realité to get me looking human. I had a sink to myself, and none of the temps spoke to me. They flicked glances at me, but I found it easy to read the expressions in their eyes. Go away.

By the time I got to Seaport, I had the shakes, good and proper. But I managed to hide them until I made the morning trip to the ladies'. Lisa was there, listening as two of the girls whispered about the slasher's latest.

"The violinist found her," Heather said. "You know him."

"I saw James," Lisa said. "He's really upset. I told him to go home, but he just stood there crying and playing something Hebrew and wailing that made the violin cry too. Then some more cops came to talk with him."

She must have seen my face because she gestured them to shut up, a down slash of her hand, real haughty and not at all like her. "You're white as a sheet," she told me. "Debbie, what's . . . Oh, Debbie," she breathed as it sank in. (Smart woman, our Lisa.) "Did you know the woman they're talking about? Was that—"

"Tink," I said, and my voice husked. From someplace in my eyes I didn't know I had, tears burst out, smearing my eyeliner and smudging the Realité I'd applied that morning. I put my hands over my face and just sobbed. For the first time in my life, I was the center of a comforting circle. Hands patted my shoulders (the comfort I'd sought in wrapping arms about myself), and voices crooned sorrow as Lisa explained that I'd done volunteer work in the World Trade Center and I knew the woman who'd been killed.

"Just last night," I said, "I bought her bandages and mercurochrome, and then gave her the rest of your money. She used it . . ." I gasped because it hurt to get the words out. "She said she'd use it to buy booze and potato chips for the other people there. One last party . . ."

I swear, I wasn't the only one crying by then.

Tears rolled down Lisa's face, but she ignored them. "I'm glad she did that. I'm glad she had that. Maybe this won't be wasted. Maybe she'll give the police some more clues. But you, Debbie, what do we do with you? If you go home, will there be anyone there to take care of you?"

Home was the E train. Home used to be Tink. It was better to be here. I shook my head. A wet towel patted my face. It would wash away the Realité and no one would see me. I jerked away.

"Easy there. It's just water. Debbie, you're dead-white. Do you feel dizzy? I'm taking you to the nurse. The rest of you, scoot. Back to work."

As she led me to the elevator, I got a glimpse of myself in the big mirrors. Tears and that towel had washed off all the Realité. Yet Lisa and the other women could see me. The nurse who let me lie down on a real mattress could see me too.

To my shock, when Lisa led me to a cab and shut the door on me with "You go to bed early and call me if you need anything," the driver glanced into the back seat. "Where to, miss?"

Miss. Not "hey wouldja." But I wasn't real. I'd denied the gift. I tucked the scrap of paper with Lisa's phone number on it away. I'd keep it, but I'd never use it.

"World Trade," I said.

The cab drove me straight there. When I paid, the driver even thanked me for his tip.

Rush hour was over by the time I reached the E train. Casual, too-clean loungers hung out by Papillon Boutique and the newsstand at the entrance; others held newspaper props: no chance I'd get my hands on those papers, was there? They knit their brows as I passed, as if something troubled them. Not me, surely.

I could hear the Apostle playing in a far corner of the station. Funny, I'd have thought he'd clear out. I gave him a wide berth and wished I didn't have to be here either.

The bench where I'd found Tink bore a WET PAINT sign, and the cement floor had been scrubbed even of the chalk marks cops draw around a body. Someone had already left a crumpled pizza box on the bench. I whistled under my breath, then called softly, "Here, Rabbit. Nice kitty."

Sailor emerged, not a black-and-white cat. For a miracle, his gray eyes were clear of grass fumes, though they were still reddened.

"You, girl. You come'ere. I wants to talk to you," he said.

Passersby swerved to avoid the street person in dirty clothes and dreadlocks, his feet bare, talking to himself in the subway. If they'd seen me, they'd done more than swerve. They'd have run so they wouldn't get involved.

"You get yo'self out of heah," he told me.

"Tink said I could stay," I protested. I felt my eyes get hot again and saw tears well up in Sailor's.

"Tink . . . ain't heah no more! I says you cain't stay. This ain' no place for you now, Tink bein' gone and all dat. You different, girl. You be live now, you be young lady. You go with yo' kind now, not talk to old Sailor 'cept'n he ax you fo' any change."

"But I don't have any place—"

"You get!"

"But I'm tired."

"Hokay, then," Sailor grudged me, a vast concession. "But tomorra, fo' sure!"

It had been stupid even to try to argue with Sailor. After all these years of smoking and rotten living, he didn't have enough logic left to appeal to. I'd have to move. Maybe Temp Fugit would let me store my things in the wardrobe? The way temps there had been glaring at me, I didn't like that idea at all, but it was the best I could come up with right now.

I headed toward the tunnels where I'd stashed my stuff. A rustling ahead of me . . . My head came up. "Rabbit? C'mere, kitty."

I hadn't brought Rabbit anything. Poor cat must be starving unless someone had dropped a Big Mac.

"Rabbit," I coaxed. More rustling, as if he'd burrowed into the papers of my bed. "Rabbit, it's O.K. I'll get you something. You just wait, kitty."

I half-turned to go back into the light.

Hands grabbed me, slammed across my chest, across my chin and mouth. My eyes bulged as light from the never-to-be-reached corridor glanced off a thin knife, held right at throat level. I planted my feet and tried to scream, but the knife pressed in and I felt warmth trickle down my collar. Damn, that thing would have to be cleaned.

Words in three languages, one of them sewer, hissed and gurgled in my ears. What he was going to do to me. Slut. *Puta*. Piece of meat. Like the old witch. Thought I was so great.

I was a goddamned temp! Why'd the slasher pick on me?

From far off, I could hear the Apostle's violin. And voices. If I could get free, just a little, I could scream. Why would anyone hear a temp?

Same reason that the slasher had picked one as a victim. He was a crazy; he could see temps. Maybe he hadn't seen a temp, though. Maybe he'd seen a damned fool suicidal out-of-town woman, checking out the tunnels. Someone as real as she was real stupid.

All it took, Tink and the Apostle had said, was belief. Belief and life. And mine was in danger now.

Mine. My life. But I was a temp. I didn't have a life, I reminded myself.

Then why'd my body tense? Why'd I worry that people in the office would hate it if I got killed? Why'd I draw the deepest breath I'd ever drawn in my miserable excuse for a life—and why'd my voice die in my throat?

I tried to tear free of the grip that was dragging me back into the darkness of the tunnels, darkness he knew better than the cops, even.

His arm tightened around me, fingers groping, and I tried to break away. The cut on my neck deepened, and I flinched. My mouth bumped against the slasher's hand—more suggestions there—and I bit as hard as I could. God, I hoped he didn't have AIDS, but I had to do something.

"Stop it," he hissed, but the knife fell for a moment.

I stomped where I hoped his instep might be, just as the girls in the ladies' said you should. He howled and his grip dropped for just a minute. I was out of that tunnel so fast . . . But he ran after me, grabbed my arm, and whirled me around.

After seeing him, I don't know why anyone would want to see horror films, either. He had eyes and breath like a werewolf or something.

His hand was bleeding. I had marked him. I could register on someone.

He was stronger than I, he could drag me back into the tunnel, and once I was back there . . . I hadn't hurt him bad enough. You either fight to kill or not at all, they say in the ladies'; because if you fight just hard enough to make them mad, you won't come out of it.

Now I heard voices coming after me, and I screamed again, trying to jerk free. A yowling hiss came from the tunnel, and Rabbit launched himself at the slasher's face, claws out and switchblading. He yelled like someone splashed a vampire with holy water, and slammed the cat off him and into the concrete wall.

"Rabbit!" The cat's pain freed my voice. Real weird thing to yell, isn't it, Debbie, when you're fighting for your life. Even then, I realized I'd called myself my ID name. Guess I'd be stuck with it if I lived.

"Stop that! Cops! Help!" A voice I remembered panted as the Apostle ran toward me. The slasher had me off-balance; in a minute, he'd slam my head against a wall. If I was real lucky, I'd never feel what would happen next.

"Fire," some woman shrieked. People always do something about fire.

The Apostle put on a burst of speed. His right hand grasped his violin by the delicate neck, like a baseball bat he was going to slam down on the slasher's head.

Not the violin. Not the music. Tink had loved the music. Lisa loved it. And so, I realized, did I. As much as anything else, it had called me to life.

I summoned all my strength and threw my weight against the slasher. My legs tangled up and I went down.

But so did he. As he stumbled, my adrenaline spiked up, and I heaved him off me, almost into the air. He saw where he was falling, and he had time to scream once before he hit the third, the electrified rail, and bounced, stiffening, fingers spasming, as a smell of singed hair, burning, dirty clothes, and something like rotted food made me gag.

If there's been a death, stands to reason there's space for another real live person.

I didn't want life if it meant dealing with the Subway Slasher.

Oh, no? Then why'd you fight, dummy? You had to fight. He was so horrible, he made you see that even your life was worth something.

The temps don't want you around anymore, and neither does Sailor. Lisa saw you. The girls saw you. The nurse saw you. Even the taxi driver and James . . . and the slasher.

You damned well bet you're alive, girl. I felt the life in the air, rising from the tracks, the concrete, the people around me—even from myself. And I grabbed it and made it mine. Made it me.

It burned like hell, and I thought I'd never felt or tasted anything so fine.

James the violinist hugged me. "Did he hurt you?" he asked. Man was better at playing than talking, that was for sure. From the corner of my eye, I saw Rabbit sit, lick a paw, then limp away.

"I couldn't let you break your violin," I whimpered. "Not for me."

"You're people," said the Apostle. "What else could I have done?" Then I cried like a baby when the doctor spanks it. Cried all the way to the precinct, where a female cop took charge of me, stayed in the room while a doctor patched up my neck. Then she called Lisa to come and get me.

Here's the miracle. She did.

Somehow—Sailor, maybe? he'd had brains once, before he scrambled them—my stuff turned up at Seaport. So did I, and they had cake and champagne and a senior vice president to shake my hand and say that Seaport was proud of me. So I never went back to Temp Fugit, after all. Lisa said that personnel would handle the agency fee, now that I was going full-time. I spent part of my first morning back at Seaport checking the bulletin board for roommates.

Lucky for me that Heather's roommate moved in with her boyfriend about then. Heather's another one like Lisa and James the violinist. Not just real, but real people. And she likes cats.

So I'm down here in the E train again with this stupid basket and some roast beef from the corner deli. I saw James and tried to give him a dollar, but he waved it away with a sweep of his bow. "First time's on the house," he said. Someone else framed the front page of an old *Post*. "Hero Subway Violinist Foils Slasher." He pretends to wince when he sees it, but he props it against his music stand.

A cat with a bad paw, a cat that knows my voice—how hard can it be to catch?

An old man in dreadlocks, his eyes red, points. "You lookin' for a little cat, miss?"

My God, it's Sailor, and I never noticed. But he winks at me, holds out his hand for a buck (I give him ten), and I know he understands.

Here, Rabbit. Nice Rabbit. Look what I've got for you. Come on out, Rabbit.

Woman in a suit, calling to a cat on the subway platform—I must look as crazy as Sailor.

Rabbit. Come on, cat.

There you are, kitty. Into the basket.

Rabbit's going to have a real home now. Just like me.

TRUE NAMES

Vernor Vinge

Vernor Vinge is one of the masters of hard science fiction who has moved to the forefront of the field in recent years. He is also, of all hard SF writers, the one who has been often concerned over the years with computers and advances in computer technology. In contrast to William Gibson, who invented an image so popular and potent that it has been imposed on the real world of computers, Vinge is the writer who understands the technology and most accurately forecast and described in his SF the world of personal computer communication. "True Names" is perhaps his most important story.

In the once-upon-a-time days of the First Age of Magic, the prudent sorcerer regarded his own true name as his most valued possession but also the greatest threat to his continued good health, for—the stories go—once an enemy, even a weak unskilled enemy, learned the sorcerer's true name, then routine and widely known spells could destroy or enslave even the most powerful. As times passed, and we graduated to the Age of Reason and thence to the first and second industrial revolutions, such notions were discredited. Now it seems that the Wheel has turned full circle (even if there never really was a First Age) and we are back to worrying about true names again:

The first hint Mr. Slippery had that his own True Name might be known—and, for that matter, known to the Great Enemy—came with the appearance of two black Lincolns humming up the long dirt driveway that stretched through the dripping pine forest down to Road 29. Roger Pollack was in his garden weeding, had been there nearly the whole morning, enjoying the barely perceptible drizzle and the overcast, and trying to find the initiative to go inside and do work that actually makes money. He looked up the moment the intruders turned, wheels squealing, into his driveway. Thirty seconds passed, the cars came out of the third-generation forest to pull up beside and behind Pollack's Honda. Four heavy-set men and a hard-looking female piled out, started purposefully across his well-tended cabbage patch, crushing tender young plants with a disregard which told Roger that this was no social call.

Pollack looked wildly around, considered making a break for the woods, but the others had spread out and he was grabbed and frog-marched back to his house. (Fortunately the door had been left unlocked. Roger had the feeling that they might have knocked it down rather than ask him for the key.) He was shoved abruptly into a chair. Two of the heaviest and least collegiate-looking of his visitors stood on either side of him. Pollack's protests—now just being voiced—brought no response. The woman and an older man poked around among his sets. "Hey, I remember this, Al: It's the script for *1965*. See?" The woman spoke as she flipped through the holo-scenes that decorated the interior wall.

The older man nodded. "I told you. He's written more popular games than any three men and even more than some agencies. Roger Pollack is something of a genius."

They're novels, damn you, not games! Old irritation flashed unbidden into Roger's mind. Aloud: "Yeah, but most of my fans aren't as persistent as you all."

"Most of your fans don't know that you are a criminal, Mr. Pollack."

"Criminal? I'm no criminal—but I do know my rights. You FBI types must identify yourselves, give me a phone call, and—"

The woman smiled for the first time. It was not a nice smile. She was about thirty-five, hatchet-faced, her hair drawn back in the single braid favored by military types. Even so it could have been a nicer smile. Pollack felt a chill start up his spine. "Perhaps that would be true, if we *were* the FBI or if you were *not* the scum you are. But this is a Welfare Department bust, Pollack, and you are suspected—putting it kindly—of interference with the instrumentalities of National and individual survival."

She sounded like something out of one of those asinine scripts he occasionally had to work on for government contracts. Only now there was nothing to laugh about, and the cold between his shoulder blades spread. Outside the drizzle had become a misty rain sweeping across the Northern California forests. Normally he found that rain a comfort, but now it just added to the gloom. Still, if there was any chance he could wriggle out of this, it would be worth the effort. "Okay, so you have license to hassle innocents, but sooner or later you're going to discover that I *am* innocent and then you'll find out what hostile media coverage can really be like." *And thank God I backed up my files last night. With luck, all they'll find is some out-of-date stockmarket schemes.*

"You're no innocent, Pollack. An *honest* citizen is content with an ordinary data set like yours there." She pointed across the living room at the forty-by-fifty-centimeter data set. It was the great-grandchild of the old CRT's. With color and twenty-line-per-millimeter resolution, it was the standard of government offices and the more conservative industries. There was a visible layer of dust on Pollack's model. The femcop moved quickly across the living room and poked into the drawers under the picture window. Her maroon business suit revealed a thin and angular figure. "An *honest* citizen would settle for a standard processor and a few thousand megabytes of fast storage." With some superior intuition she pulled open the center drawer—right under the marijuana plants—to reveal at least five hundred cubic centimeters of optical memory, neatly racked and threaded through to the next drawer which held correspondingly powerful CPUs. Even so, it was nothing compared to the gear he had buried under the house.

She drifted out into the kitchen and was back in a moment. The house was a typical airdropped bungalow, small and easy to search. Pollack had spent most of his money on the land and his . . . hobbies. "And finally," she said, a note of

triumph in her voice, "an *honest* citizen does not need one of these!" She had finally spotted the Other World gate. She waved the electrodes in Pollack's face.

"Look, in spite of what you may want, all this is still legal. In fact, that gadget is scarcely more powerful than an ordinary games interface." That should be
a good explanation, considering that he was a novelist.

The older man spoke almost apologetically, "I'm afraid Virginia has a tendency to play cat and mouse, Mr. Pollack. You see, we know that in the Other
World you are Mr. Slippery."

"Oh."

There was a long silence. Even "Virginia" kept her mouth shut. This had
been, of course, Roger Pollack's great fear. They had discovered Mr. Slippery's
True Name and it was Roger Andrew Pollack TIN/SSAN 0959-34-2861, and
no amount of evasion, tricky programming, or robot sources could ever again
protect him from them. "How did you find out?"

A third cop, a technician type, spoke up. "It wasn't easy. We wanted to get
our hands on someone who was really good, not a trivial vandal—what your
Coven would call a lesser warlock." The younger man seemed to know the jargon, but you could pick that up just by watching the daily paper. "For the last
three months, DoW has been trying to find the identity of someone of the cal-
iber of yourself or Robin Hood, or Erythrina, or the Slimey Limey. We were
having no luck at all until we turned the problem around and began watching
artists and novelists. We figured at least a fraction of them must be attracted to
vandal activities. And they would have the talent to be good at it. Your participation novels are the best in the world." There was genuine admiration in his
voice. *One meets fans in the oddest places.* "So you were one of the first people we
looked at. Once we suspected you, it was just a matter of time before we had the
evidence."

It was what he had always worried about. A successful warlock cannot afford
to be successful in the real world. He had been greedy; he loved both realms too
much.

The older cop continued the technician's almost diffident approach. "In any
case, Mr. Pollack, I think you realize that if the Federal government wants to
concentrate all its resources on the apprehension of a single vandal, we can do
it. The vandals' power comes from their numbers rather than their power as individuals."

Pollack repressed a smile. That was a common belief—or faith—within government. He had snooped on enough secret memos to realize that the Feds really believed it, but it was very far from true. He was not nearly as clever as
someone like Erythrina. He could only devote fifteen or twenty hours a week to
SIG activities. Some of the others must be on welfare, so complete was their
presence on the Other Plane. The cops had nailed him simply because he was a
relatively easy catch.

"So you have something besides jail planned for me?"

"Mr. Pollack, have you ever heard of the Mailman?"

"You mean on the Other Plane?"

"Certainly. He has had no notoriety in the, uh, real world as yet."

For the moment there was no use lying. They must know that no member
of a SIG or coven would ever give his True Name to another member. There
was no way he could betray any of the others—*he hoped.*

"Yeah, he's the weirdest of the werebots."

"Werebots?"

"Were-robots, like werewolves—get it? They don't really mesh with coven imagery. They want some new mythos, and this notion that they are humans who can turn into machines seems to suit them. It's too dry for me. This Mailman, for instance, never uses real-time communication. If you want anything from him, you usually have to wait a day or two for each response—just like the old-time hardcopy mail service."

"That's the fellow. How impressed are you by him?"

"Oh, we've been aware of him for a couple years, but he's so slow that for a long time we thought he was some clown on a simple data set. Lately, though, he's pulled some really—" Pollack stopped short, remembering just who he was gossiping with.

"—some really tuppin stunts, eh, Pollack?" The femcop "Virginia" was back in the conversation. She pulled up one of the roller chairs, till her knees were almost touching his, and stabbed a finger at his chest. "You may not know just how tuppin. You vandals have caused Social Security Records enormous problems, and Robin Hood cut IRS revenues by three percent last year. You and your friends are a greater threat than any foreign enemy. Yet you're nothing compared to this Mailman."

Pollack was rocked back. It must be that he had seen only a small fraction of the Mailman's japes. "You're actually scared of him," he said mildly.

Virginia's face began to take on the color of her suit. Before she could reply, the older cop spoke. "Yes, we are scared. We can scarcely cope with the Robin Hoods and the Mr. Slipperys of the world. Fortunately, most vandals are interested in personal gain or in proving their cleverness. They realize that if they cause too much trouble, they could no doubt be identified. I suspect that tens of thousands of cases of Welfare and Tax fraud are undetected, committed by little people with simple equipment who succeed because they don't steal much—perhaps just their own income tax liability—and don't wish the notoriety which you, uh, warlocks go after. If it weren't for their petty individualism, they would be a greater threat than the nuclear terrorists.

"But the Mailman is different; he appears to be ideologically motivated. He is *very* knowledgeable, *very* powerful. Vandalism is not enough for him; he wants control . . ." The Feds had no idea how long it had been going on, at least a year. It never would have been discovered but for a few departments in the Federal Screw Standards Commission which kept their principal copy records on paper. Discrepancies showed up between those records and the decisions rendered in the name of the FSSC. Inquiries were made; computer records were found at variance with the hardcopy. More inquiries. By luck more than anything else, the investigators discovered that decision modules as well as data were different from the hardcopy backups. For thirty years government had depended on automated central planning, shifting more and more from legal descriptions of decision algorithms to program representations that could work directly with data bases to allocate resources, suggest legislation, outline military strategy.

The takeover had been subtle, and its extent was unknown. That was the horror of it. It was not even clear just what groups within the Nation (or without) were benefitting from the changed interpretations of Federal law and resource allocation. Only the decision modules in the older departments could be directly checked, and some thirty percent of them showed tampering. ". . . and that percentage scares us as much as anything, Mr. Pollack. It would take a large team of technicians and lawyers *months* to successfully make just the changes that we have detected."

"What about the military?" Pollack thought of the Finger of God installations and the thousands of missiles pointed at virtually every country on Earth. If Mr. Slippery had ever desired to take over the world, that is what he would have gone for. To hell with pussy-footing around with Social Security checks.

"No. No penetration there. In fact, it was his attempt to infiltrate"— the older cop glanced hesitantly at Virginia, and Pollack realized who was the boss of this operation —"NSA that revealed the culprit to be the Mailman. Before that it was anonymous, totally without the ego-flaunting we see in big-time vandals. But the military and NSA have their own systems. Impractical though that is, it paid off this time." Pollack nodded. The SIG steered clear of the military, and especially of NSA.

"But if he was about to slide through DoW and Department of Justice defenses so easy, you really don't know how much a matter of luck it was that he didn't also succeed with his first try on NSA. . . . I think I understand now. You need help. You hope to get some member of the Coven to work on this from the inside."

"It's not a *hope*, Pollack," said Virginia. "It's a certainty. Forget about going to jail. Oh, we could put you away forever on the basis of some of Mr. Slippery's pranks. But even if we don't do that, we can take away your license to operate. You know what that means."

It was not a question, but Pollack knew the answer nevertheless: ninety-eight percent of the jobs in modern society involved some use of a data set. Without a license, he was virtually unemployable—and that left Welfare, the prospect of sitting in some urbapt counting flowers on the wall. Virginia must have seen the defeat in his eyes. "Frankly, I am not as confident as Ray that you are all that sharp. But you are the best we could catch. NSA thinks we have a chance of finding the Mailman's true identity if we can get an agent into your coven. We want you to continue to attend coven meetings, but now your chief goal is not mischief but the gathering of information about the Mailman. You are to recruit any help you can without revealing that you are working for the government—you might even make up the story that you suspect the Mailman of being a government plot. (I'm sure you see he has some of the characteristics of a Federal agent working off a conventional data set.) Above all, you are to remain alert to contact from us, and give us your instant cooperation in anything we require of you. Is all this perfectly clear, Mr. Pollack?"

He found it difficult to meet her gaze. He had never really been exposed to extortion before. There was something . . . dehumanizing about being used so. "Yeah," he finally said.

"Good." She stood up, and so did the others. "If you behave, this is the last time you'll see us in person."

Pollack stood too. "And afterward, if you're . . . satisfied with my performance?"

Virginia grinned, and he knew he wasn't going to like her answer. "Afterward, we can come back to considering *your* crimes. If you do a good job, I would have no objection to your retaining a standard data set, maybe some of your interactive graphics. But I'll tell you, if it weren't for the Mailman, nabbing Mr. Slippery would make my month. There is no way I'd risk your continuing to abuse the System."

Three minutes later, their sinister black Lincolns were halfway down the drive, disappearing into the pines. Pollack stood in the drizzle watching till long after their sound had faded to nothing. He was barely aware of the cold wet across his shoulders and down his back. He looked up suddenly, feeling the rain in his face, wondering if the Feds were so clever that they had taken the day into account: the military's recon satellites could no doubt monitor their cars, but the civilian satellites the SIG had access to could not penetrate these clouds. Even if some other member of the SIG did know Mr. Slippery's True Name, they would not know that the Feds had paid him a visit.

Pollack looked across the yard at his garden. *What a difference an hour can make.*

By late afternoon, the overcast was gone. Sunlight glinted off millions of water-drop jewels in the trees. Pollack waited till the sun was behind the tree line, till all that was left of its passage was a gold band across the taller trees to the east of his bungalow. Then he sat down before his equipment and prepared to ascend to the Other Plane. What he was undertaking was trickier than anything he had tried before, and he wanted to take as much time as the Feds would tolerate. A week of thought and research would have suited him more, but Virginia and her pals were clearly too impatient for that.

He powered up his processors, settled back in his favorite chair, and carefully attached the Portal's five sucker electrodes to his scalp. For long minutes nothing happened: a certain amount of self-denial—or at least self-hypnosis—was necessary to make the ascent. Some experts recommended drugs or sensory isolation to heighten the user's sensitivity to the faint, ambiguous signals that could be read from the Portal. Pollack, who was certainly more experienced than any of the pop experts, had found that he could make it simply by staring out into the trees and listening to the wind-surf that swept through their upper branches.

And just as a daydreamer forgets his actual surroundings and sees other realities, so Pollack drifted, detached, his subconscious interpreting the status of the West Coast communication and data services as a vague thicket for his conscious mind to inspect, interrogate for the safest path to an intermediate haven. Like most exurb data-commuters, Pollack rented the standard optical links: Bell, Boeing, Nippon Electric. Those, together with the local West Coast data companies, gave him more than enough paths to proceed with little chance of detection to any accepting processor on Earth. In minutes, he had traced through three changes of carrier and found a place to do his intermediate computing. The comsats rented processor time almost as cheaply as ground stations, and an automatic payment transaction (through several dummy accounts set up over the last several years) gave him sole control of a large data space within milliseconds of his request. The whole process was almost at a subconscious level—the proper functioning of numerous routines he and others had devised over the last four years. Mr. Slippery (the other name was avoided now, even in his thoughts) had achieved the fringes of the Other Plane. He took a quick peek through the eyes of a low-resolution weather satellite, saw the North American continent spread out below, the terminator sweeping through the West, most of the plains clouded over. One never knew when some apparently irrelevant information might help—and though it could all be done automatically through subconscious access, Mr. Slippery had always been a romantic about spaceflight.

He rested for a few moments, checking that his indirect communication links were working and that the encryption routines appeared healthy, untampered with. (Like most folks, honest citizens or warlocks, he had no trust for the government standard encryption routines, but preferred the schemes that had leaked out of academia—over NSA's petulant objections—during the last fifteen years.) Protected now against traceback, Mr. Slippery set out for the Coven itself. He quickly picked up the trail, but this was never an easy trip, for the SIG members had no interest in being bothered by the unskilled.

In particular, the traveler must be able to take advantage of subtle sensory indications, and see in them the environment originally imagined by the SIG. The correct path had the aspect of a narrow row of stones cutting through a gray-greenish swamp. The air was cold but very moist. Weird, towering plants dripped audibly onto the faintly iridescent water and the broad lilies. The subconscious knew what the stones represented, handled the chaining of routines from one information net to another, but it was the conscious mind of the skilled traveler that must make the decisions that could lead to the gates of the Coven, or to the symbolic "death" of a dump back to the real world. The basic game was a distant relative of the ancient Adventure that had been played on computer systems for more than forty years, and a nearer relative of the participation novels that are still widely sold. There were two great differences, though. This game was more serious, and was played at a level of complexity impossible without the use of the EEG input/output that the warlocks and the popular data bases called Portals.

There was much misinformation and misunderstanding about the Portals. Oh, responsible data bases like the *LA Times* and the *CBS News* made it clear that there was nothing supernatural about them or about the Other Plane, that the magical jargon was at best a romantic convenience and at worst obscurantism. But even so, their articles often missed the point and were both too conservative and too extravagant. You might think that to convey the full sense imagery of the swamp, some immense bandwidth would be necessary. In fact, that was not so (and if it were, the Feds would have quickly been able to spot warlock and werebot operations). A typical Portal link was around fifty thousand baud, far narrower than even a flat video channel. Mr. Slippery could feel the damp seeping through his leather boots, could feel the sweat starting on his skin even in the cold air, but this was the response of Mr. Slippery's imagination and subconscious to the cues that were actually being presented through the Portal's electrodes. The interpretation could not be arbitrary or he would be dumped back to reality and would never find the Coven; to the traveler on the Other Plane, the detail was there as long as the cues were there. And there is nothing new about this situation. Even a poor writer—if he has a sympathetic reader and an engaging plot—can evoke complete internal imagery with a few dozen words of description. The difference now is that the imagery has interactive significance, just as sensations in the real world do. Ultimately, the magic jargon was perhaps the closest fit in the vocabulary of millennium Man.

The stones were spaced more widely now, and it took all Mr. Slippery's skill to avoid falling into the noisome waters that surrounded him. Fortunately, after another hundred meters or so, the trail rose out of the water, and he was walking on shallow mud. The trees and brush grew in close around him, and large spider webs glistened across the trail and between some of the trees along the side.

Like a yo-yo from some branch high above him, a red-banded spider the size of a man's fist descended into the space right before the traveler's face. "Beware, beware," the tiny voice issued from dripping mandibles. "Beware, beware," the words were repeated, and the creature swung back and forth, nearer and farther from Mr. Slippery's face. He looked carefully at the spider's banded abdomen. There were many species of deathspider here, and each required a different response if a traveler was to survive. Finally he raised the back of his hand and held it level so that the spider could crawl onto it. The creature raced up the damp fabric of his jacket to the open neck. There it whispered something very quietly.

Mr. Slippery listened, then grabbed the animal before it could repeat the message and threw it to the left, at the same time racing off into the tangle of webs and branches on the other side of the trail. Something heavy and wet slapped into the space where he had been, but he was already gone—racing at top speed up the incline that suddenly appeared before him.

He stopped when he reached the crest of the hill. Beyond it, he could see the solemn, massive fortress that was the Coven's haven. It was not more than five hundred meters away, illuminated as the swamp had been by a vague and indistinct light that came only partly from the sky. The trail leading down to it was much more open than the swamp had been, but the traveler proceeded as slowly as before: the sprites the warlocks set to keep guard here had the nasty—though preprogrammed—habit of changing the rules in deadly ways.

The trail descended, then began a rocky, winding climb toward the stone and iron gates of the castle. The ground was drier here, the vegetation sparse. Leathery snapping of wings sounded above him, but Mr. Slippery knew better than to look up. Thirty meters from the moat, the heat became more than uncomfortable. He could hear the lava popping and hissing, could see occasional dollops of fire splatter up from the liquid to scorch what vegetation still lived. A pair of glowing eyes set in coal-black head rose briefly from the moat. A second later, the rest of the creature came surging into view, cascading sparks and lava down upon the traveler. Mr. Slippery raised his hand just so, and the lethal spray separated over his head to land harmlessly on either side of him. He watched with apparent calm as the creature descended ancient stone steps to confront him.

Alan—that was the elemental's favorite name—peered nearsightedly, his head weaving faintly from side to side as he tried to recognize the traveler. "Ah, I do believe we are honored with the presence of Mr. Slippery, is it not so?" he finally said. He smiled, an open grin revealing the glowing interior of his mouth. His breath did not show flame but did have the penetrating heat of an open kiln. He rubbed his clawed hands against his asbestos T-shirt as though anxious to be proved wrong. Away from his magna moat, the dead black of his flesh lightened, trying to contain his body heat. Now he looked almost reptilian.

"Indeed it is. And come to bring my favorite little gifts." Mr. Slippery threw a leaden slug into the air and watched the elemental grab it with his mouth, his eyes slitted with pleasure—melt-in-your-mouth pleasure. They traded conversation, spells, and counterspells for several minutes. Alan's principal job was to determine that the visitor was a known member of the Coven, and he ordinarily did this with little tests of skill (the magma bath he had tried to give Mr. Slippery) and by asking the visitor questions about previous activities within the castle. Alan was a personality simulator, of course. Mr. Slippery was sure that there had never been a living operator behind that toothless, glowing smile. But he was certainly one of the best, probably the product of many hundreds of blocks of psylisp programming, and certainly superior to the little "companionship" programs you can buy nowadays, which generally become repetitive after a few hours of conversation, which don't grow, and which are unable to counter weird responses. Alan had been with the Coven and the castle since before Mr. Slippery had become a member, and no one would admit to his creation (though Wiley J. was suspected). He hadn't even had a name until this year, when Erythrina had given him that asbestos Alan Turing T-shirt.

Mr. Slippery played the game with good humor, but care. To "die" at the hands of Alan would be a painful experience that would probably wipe a lot of unbacked memory he could ill afford to lose. Such death had claimed many petitioners at this gate, folk who would not soon be seen on this plane again.

Satisfied, Alan waved a clawed fist at the watchers in the tower, and the gate—ceramic bound in wolfram clasps—was rapidly lowered for the visitor. Mr. Slippery walked quickly across, trying to ignore the spitting and bubbling that he heard below him. Alan—now all respectful—waited till he was in the castle courtyard before doing an immense belly-flop back into his magma swimming hole.

Most of the others, with the notable exception of Erythrina, had already arrived. Robin Hood, dressed in green and looking like Errol Flynn, sat across the hall in very close conversation with a remarkably good-looking female (but then they could all be remarkably good-looking here) who seemed unsure whether to project blonde or brunette. By the fireplace, Wiley J. Bastard, the Slimey Limey, and DON.MAC were in animated discussion over a pile of maps. And in the corner, shaded from the fireplace and apparently unused, sat a classic remote printing terminal. Mr. Slippery tried to ignore that teleprinter as he crossed the hall.

"Ah, it's Slip." DON.MAC looked up from the maps and gestured him closer. "Take a look here at what the Limey has been up to."

"Hmm?" Mr. Slippery nodded at the others, then leaned over to study the top map. The margins of the paper were aging vellum, but the "map" itself hung in three dimensions, half sunk into the paper. It was a typical banking defense and cash-flow plot—that is, typical for the SIG. Most banks had no such clever ways of visualizing the automated protection of their assets. (For that matter, Mr. Slippery suspected that most banks still looked wistfully back to the days of credit cards and COBOL.) This was the sort of thing Robin Hood had developed, and it was surprising to see the Limey involved in it. He looked up questioningly. "What's the jape?"

"It's a reg'lar double-slam, Slip. Look at this careful, an' you'll see it's no ord'n'ry protection map. Seems like what you blokes call the Mafia has taken over this banking net in the Maritime states. They must be usin' Portals to do it so slick. Took me a devil of a time to figure out it was them as done it. *Ha ha!* but now that I have . . . look here, you'll see how they've been launderin' funds, embezzlin' from straight accounts.

"They're ever so clever, but not so clever as to know about Slimey." He poked a finger into the map and a trace gleamed red through the maze. "If they're lucky, they'll discover this tap next autumn, when they find themselves maybe three billion dollars short, and not a single sign of where it all disappeared to."

The others nodded. There were many covens and SIGs throughout this plane. Theirs, The Coven, was widely known, had pulled off some of the most publicized pranks of the century. Many of the others were scarcely more than social clubs. But some were old-style criminal organizations which used this plane for their own purely pragmatic and opportunistic reasons. Usually such groups weren't too difficult for the warlocks to victimize, but it was the Slimey Limey who seemed to specialize in doing so.

"But, geez, Slimey, these guys play rough, even rougher than the Great Enemy." That is, the Feds. "If they ever figure out who you really are, you'll die the True Death for sure."

"I may be slimy, but I ain't crazy. There's no way I could absorb three billion dollars—or even three million—without being discovered. But I played it like Robin over there: the money got spread around three million ordinary accounts here and in Europe, one of which just happens to be mine."

Mr. Slippery's ears perked up. "Three million accounts, you say? Each with a sudden little surplus? I'll bet I could come close to finding your True Name from that much, Slimey."

The Limey made a faffling gesture. "It's actually a wee bit more complicated. Face it, chums, none of you has ever come close to sightin' me, an' you know more than any Mafia."

That was true. They all spent a good deal of their time in this plane trying to determine the others' True Names. It was not an empty game, for the knowledge of another's True Name effectively made him your slave—as Mr. Slippery had already discovered in an unpleasantly firsthand way. So the warlocks constantly probed one another, devised immense programs to sieve government-personnel records for the idiosyncrasies that they detected in each other. At first glance, the Limey should have been one of the easiest to discover: he had plenty of mannerisms. His Brit accent was dated and broke down every so often into North American. Of all the warlocks, he was the only one neither handsome nor grotesque. His face was, in fact, so ordinary and real that Mr. Slippery had suspected that it might be his true appearance and had spent several months devising a scheme that searched U.S. and common Europe photo files for just that appearance. It had been for nothing, and they had all eventually reached the conclusion that the Limey must be doubly or triply deceptive.

Wiley J. Bastard grinned, not too impressed. "It's nice enough, and I agree that the risks are probably small, Slimey. But what do you really get? An ego boost and a little money. But we," he gestured inclusively, "are worth more than that. With a little cooperation, we could be the most powerful people in the real world. Right, DON?"

DON.MAC nodded, smirking. His face was really the only part of him that looked human or had much flexibility of expression—and even it was steely gray.

The rest of DON's body was modeled after the standard Plessey-Mercedes all-weather robot.

Mr. Slippery recognized the reference. "So you're working with the Mailman now, too, Wiley?" He glanced briefly at the teleprinter.

"Yup."

"And you still won't give us any clue what it's all about?"

Wiley shook his head. "Not unless you're serious about throwing in with us. But you all know this: DON was the first to work with the Mailman, and he's richer than Croesus now."

DON.MAC nodded again, that silly smile still on his face.

"Hmmm." It was easy to get rich. In principle, the Limey could have made three billion dollars off the Mob in his latest caper. The problem was to become that rich and avoid detection and retribution. Even Robin Hood hadn't mastered that trick—but apparently DON and Wiley thought the Mailman had done that and more. After his chat with Virginia, he was willing to believe it. Mr. Slippery turned to look more closely at the teleprinter. It was humming faintly, and as usual it had a good supply of paper. The paper was torn neatly off at the top, so that the only message visible was the Mailman's asterisk prompt. It was the only way they ever communicated with this most mysterious of their members: type a message on the device, and in an hour or a week the machine would rattle and beat, and a response of up to several thousand words would appear. In the beginning, it had not been very popular—the idea was cute, but the delays made conversation just too damn dull. He could remember seeing meters of Mailman output lying sloppily on the stone floor, mostly unread. But now, every one of the Mailman's golden words was eagerly sopped up by his new apprentices, who very carefully removed every piece of output, leaving no clues for the rest of them to work with.

"Ery!" He looked toward the broad stone stairs that led down from the courtyard. It was Erythrina, the Red Witch. She swept down the stairs, her costume shimmering, now revealing, now obscuring. She had a spectacular figure and an excellent sense of design, but of course that was not what was remarkable about her. Erythrina was the sort of person who knew much more than she ever said, even though she always seemed easy to talk to. Some of her adventures—though unadvertised—were in a class with Robin Hood's. Mr. Slippery had known her well for a year; she was certainly the most interesting personality on this plane. She made him wish that all the secrets were unnecessary, that True Names could be traded as openly as phone numbers. What was she really?

Erythrina nodded to Robin Hood, then proceeded down the hall to DON.MAC, who had originally shouted greetings and now continued, "We've just been trying to convince Slimey and Slip that they are wasting their time on pranks when they could have real power and real wealth."

She glanced sharply at Wiley, who seemed strangely irritated that she had been drawn into the conversation. "'We' meaning you and Wiley and the Mailman?"

Wiley nodded. "I just started working with them last week, Ery," as if to say, *and you can't stop me.*

"You may have something, DON. We all started out as amateurs, doing our best to make the System just a little bit uncomfortable for its bureaucratic masters. But we are experts now. We probably understand the System better than anyone on Earth. That should equate to power." It was the same thing the other two had been saying, but she could make it much more persuasive. Before his encounter with the Feds, he might have bought it (even though he always knew that the day he got serious about Coven activities and went after real gain would also be the day it ceased to be an enjoyable game and became an all-consuming job that would suck time away from the projects that made life entertaining).

Erythrina looked from Mr. Slippery to the Limey and then back. The Limey was an easygoing sort, but just now he was a bit miffed at the way his own pet project had been dismissed. "Not for me, thanky," he said shortly and began to gather up his maps.

She turned her green, faintly oriental eyes upon Mr. Slippery. "How about you, Slip? Have you signed up with the Mailman?"

He hesitated. *Maybe I should.* It seemed clear that the Mailman's confeder-ates were being let in on at least part of his schemes. In a few hours, he might be able to learn enough to get Virginia off his back. And perhaps destroy his friends to boot; it was a hell of a bargain. *God in Heaven, why did they have to get mixed up in this? Don't they realize what the Government will do to them, if they really try to take over, if they ever try to play at being more than vandals?* "Not . . . not yet," he said finally. "I'm awfully tempted, though."

She grinned, regular white teeth flashing against her dark, faintly green face. "I, too. What do you say we talk it over, just the two of us?" She reached out a slim, dark hand to grasp his elbow. "Excuse us, gentlemen; hopefully, when we get back, you'll have a couple of new allies." And Mr. Slippery felt himself gen-tly propelled toward the dark and musty stairs that led to Erythrina's private haunts.

Her torch burned and glowed, but there was no smoke. The flickering yellow lit their path for scant meters ahead. The stairs were steep and gently curving. He had the feeling that they must do a complete circle every few hundred steps: this was an immense spiral cut deep into the heart of the living rock. And it was alive. As the smell of mildew and rot increased, as the dripping from the ceiling grew subtly louder and the puddles in the worn steps deeper, the walls high above their heads took on shapes, and those shapes changed and flowed to follow them. Erythrina protected her part of the castle as thoroughly as the castle itself was guarded against the outside world. Mr. Slippery had no doubt that if she wished, she could trap him permanently here, along with the lizards and the rock sprites. (Of course he could always "escape" simply by falling back into the real world, but until she relented or he saw through her spells, he would not be able to access any other portion of the castle.) Working on some of their pro-jects, he had visited her underground halls, but never anything this deep.

He watched her shapely form preceding him down, down, down. Of all the Coven (with the possible exception of Robin Hood, and of course the Mail-man), she was the most powerful. He suspected that she was one of the original founders. If only there were some way of convincing her (without revealing the source of his knowledge) that the Mailman was a threat. If only there was some way of getting her cooperation in nailing down the Mailman's True Name.

Erythrina stopped and he bumped pleasantly into her. Over her shoulder, a high door ended the passage. She moved her hand in a pattern hidden from Mr.

Slippery and muttered some unlocking spell. The door split horizontally, its halves pulling apart with oiled and massive precision. Beyond, he had the impression of spots and lines of red breaking a further darkness.

"Mind your step," she said and hopped over a murky puddle that stood before the high sill of the doorway.

As the door slid shut behind them, Erythrina changed the torch to a single searing spot of white light, like some old-time incandescent bulb. The room was bright-lit now. Comfortable black leather chairs sat on black tile. Red engraving, faintly glowing, was worked into the tile and the obsidian of the walls. In contrast to the stairway, the air was fresh and clean—though still.

She waved him to a chair that faced away from the light, then sat on the edge of a broad desk. The point light glinted off her eyes, making them unreadable. Erythrina's face was slim and fine-boned, almost Asian except for the pointed ears. But the skin was dark, and her long hair had the reddish tones unique to some North American blacks. She was barely smiling now, and Mr. Slippery wished again he had some way of getting her help.

"Slip, I'm scared," she said finally, the smile gone.

You're scared! For a moment, he couldn't quite believe his ears. "The Mailman?" he asked, hoping.

She nodded. "This is the first time in my life I've felt outgunned. I need help. Robin Hood may be the most competent, but he's basically a narcissist; I don't think I could interest him in anything beyond his immediate gratifications. That leaves you and the Limey. And I think there's something special about you. We've done a couple things together," she couldn't help herself, and grinned remembering. "They weren't real impressive, but somehow I have a feeling about you: I think you understand what things up here are silly games and what things are really important. If you think something is really important, you can be trusted to stick with it even if the going gets a little . . . bloody."

Coming from someone like Ery, the words had special meaning. It was strange, to feel both flattered and frightened. Mr. Slippery stuttered for a moment, inarticulate. "What about Wiley J? Seems to me you have special . . . influence over him."

"You knew . . . ?"

"Suspected."

"Yes, he's my thrall. Has been for almost six months. Poor Wiley turns out to be a life-insurance salesman from Peoria. Like a lot of warlocks, he's rather a Thurberesque fellow in real life: timid, always dreaming of heroic adventures and grandiose thefts. Only nowadays people like that can realize their dreams. . . . Anyway, he doesn't have the background, or the time, or the skill that I do, and I found his True Name. I enjoy the chase more than the extortion, so I haven't leaned on him too hard; now I wish I had. Since he's taken up with the Mailman, he's been giving me the finger. Somehow Wiley thinks that what they have planned will keep him safe even if I give his True Name to the cops!"

"So the Mailman actually has some scheme for winning political power in the real world?"

She smiled. "That's what Wiley thinks. You see, poor Wiley doesn't know that there are more uses for True Names than simple blackmail. I know everything he sends over the data links, everything he has been told by the Mailman."

"So what are they up to?" It was hard to conceal his eagerness. *Perhaps this will be enough to satisfy Virginia and her goons.*

Erythrina seemed frozen for a moment, and he realized that she too must be using the low-altitude satellite net for preliminary processing: her task had just been handed off from one comsat to a nearer bird. Ordinarily it was easy to disguise the hesitation. She must be truly upset.

And when she finally replied, it wasn't really with an answer. "You know what convinced Wiley that the Mailman could deliver on his promises? It was DON.MAC—and the revolution in Venezuela. Apparently DON and the Mailman had been working on that for several months before Wiley joined them. It was to be the Mailman's first demonstration that controlling data and information services could be used to take permanent political control of a state. And Venezuela, they claimed, was perfect: it has enormous data-processing facilities—all just a bit obsolete, since they were bought when the country was at the peak of its boom time."

"But that was clearly an internal coup. The present leaders are local—"

"Nevertheless, DON is supposedly down there now, the real *Jefe,* for the first time in his life able to live in the physical world the way we do in this plane. If you have your own country, you are no longer small fry that must guard his True Name. You don't have to settle for crumbs."

"You said 'supposedly.'"

"Slip, have you noticed anything strange about DON lately?"

Mr. Slippery thought back. DON.MAC had always been the most extreme of the werebots—after the Mailman. He was not an especially talented fellow, but he did go to great lengths to sustain the image that he was both machine and human. His persona was always present in this plane, though at least part of the time it was a simulator—like Alan out in the magma moat. The simulation was fairly good, but no one had yet produced a program that could really pass the Turing test: that is, fool a real human for any extended time. Mr. Slippery remembered the silly smile that seemed pasted on DON's face and the faintly repetitive tone of his lobbying for the Mailman. "You think the real person behind DON is gone, that we have a zombie up there?"

"Slip, I think the real DON is *dead,* and I mean the True Death."

"Maybe he just found the real world more delightful than this, now that he owns such a big hunk of it?"

"I don't think he owns anything. It's just barely possible that the Mailman had something to do with that coup; there are a number of coincidences between what they told Wiley beforehand and what actually happened. But I've spent a lot of time floating through the Venezuelan data bases, and I think I'd know if an outsider were on the scene, directing the new order.

"I think the Mailman is taking us on one at a time, starting with the weakest, drawing us in far enough to learn our True Names—and then destroying us. So far he has only done it to one of us. I've been watching DON.MAC both directly and automatically since the coup, and there has never been a real person behind that facade, not once in two thousand hours. Wiley is next. The poor slob hasn't even been told yet what country his kingdom is to be—evidence that the Mailman doesn't really have the power he claims—but even so, he's ready to do practically anything for the Mailman, and against us.

"Slip, we have *got* to identify this *thing,* this Mailman, before he can get us."

She was even more upset than Virginia and the Feds. And she was right. For the first time, he felt more afraid of the Mailman than the government agents. He held up his hands. "I'm convinced. But what should we do? You've got the best angle in Wiley. The Mailman doesn't know you've got a tap through him, does he?"

She shook her head. "Wiley is too chicken to tell him, and doesn't realize that I can do this with his True Name. But I'm already doing everything I can with that. I want to pool information, guesses, with you. Between us maybe we can see something new."

"Well for starters, it's obvious that the Mailman's queer communication style—those long time delays—is a ploy. I know that fellow is listening all the time to what's going on in the Coven meeting hall. And he commands a number of sprites in real time." Mr. Slippery remembered the day the Mailman—or at least his teleprinter—had arrived. The image of an American Van Lines truck had pulled up at the edge of the moat, nearly intimidating Alan. The driver and loader were simulators, though good ones. They had answered all of Alan's questions correctly, then hauled the shipping crate down to the meeting hall. They hadn't left till the warlocks signed for the shipment and promised to "wire a wall outlet" for the device. This enemy definitely knew how to arouse the curiosity of his victims. Whoever controlled that printer seemed perfectly capable of normal behavior. *Perhaps it's someone we already know, like in the mysteries where the murderer masquerades as one of the victims. Robin Hood?*

"I know. In fact, he can do many things faster than I. He must control some powerful processors. But you're partly wrong: the living part of him that's behind it all really does operate with at least a one-hour turnaround time. All the quick stuff is programmed."

Mr. Slippery started to protest, then realized that she could be right. "My God, what could that mean? Why would he deliberately saddle himself with that disadvantage?"

Erythrina smiled with some satisfaction. "I'm convinced that if we knew that, we'd have this guy sighted. I agree it's too great a disadvantage to be a simple red herring. I think he must have some time-delay problem to begin with, and—"

"—and he has exaggerated it?" But even if the Mailman were an Australian, the low satellite net made delays so short that he would probably be indistinguishable from a European or a Japanese. There was no place on Earth where . . . *but there are places off Earth!* The mass-transit satellites were in synchronous orbit 120 milliseconds out. There were about two hundred people there. And further out, at L5, there were at least another four hundred. Some were near-permanent residents. A strange idea, but still a possibility.

"*I* don't think he has exaggerated. Slip, I think the Mailman—not his processors and simulators, you understand—is at least a half-hour out from Earth, probably in the asteroid belt."

She smiled suddenly, and Mr. Slippery realized that his jaw must be resting on his chest. Except for the Joint Mars Recon, no human had been anywhere near that far out. *No human.* Mr. Slippery felt his ordinary, everyday world disintegrating into sheer science fiction. This was ridiculous.

"I know you don't believe; it took me a while to. He's not so obvious that he doesn't add in some time delay to disguise the cyclic variation in our relative positions. But it *is* a consistent explanation for the delay. These last few weeks I've been sniffing around the classified reports on our asteroid probes; there are definitely some mysterious things out there."

"Okay. It's consistent. But you're talking about an interstellar *invasion*. Even if NASA had the funding, it would take them decades to put the smallest interstellar probe together—and decades more for the flight. Trying to invade anyone with those logistics would be impossible. And if these aliens have a decent stardrive, why do they bother with deception? They could just move in and brush us aside."

"Ah, that's the point, Slip. The invasion I'm thinking of doesn't need any 'stardrive,' and it works fine against any race at exactly our point of development. Right: most likely interstellar war is a fantastically expensive business, with decade lead times. What better policy for an imperialistic, highly technological race than to lie doggo listening for evidence of younger civilizations? When they detect such, they send only one ship. When it arrives in the victims' solar system, the Computer Age is in full bloom there. We in the Coven know how fragile the present system is; it is only fear of exposure that prevents some warlocks from trying to take over. Just think how appealing our naïveté must be to an older civilization that has thousands of years of experience at managing data systems. Their small crew of agents moves in as close as local military surveillance permits and gradually insinuates itself into the victims' system. They eliminate what sharp individuals they detect in that system—people like us—and then they go after the bureaucracies and the military. In ten or twenty years, another fiefdom is ready for the arrival of the master race."

She lapsed into silence, and for a long moment they stared at each other. It did all hang together with a weird sort of logic. "What can we do, then?"

"That's the question." She shook her head sadly, came across the room to sit beside him. Now that she had said her piece, the fire had gone out of her. For the first time since he had known her, Erythrina looked depressed. "We could just forsake this plane and stay in the real world. The Mailman might still be able to track us down, but we'd be of no more interest to him than anyone else. If we were lucky, we might have years before he takes over." She straightened. "I'll tell you this: if we want to live as warlocks, we have to stop him soon—within days at most. After he gets Wiley, he may drop the con tactics for something more direct.

"If I'm right about the Mailman, then our best bet would be to discover his communication link. That would be his Achilles' heel; there's no way you can hide in the crowd when you're beaming from that far away. We've got to take some real chances now, do things we'd never risk before. I figure that if we work together, maybe we can lessen the risk that either of us is identified."

He nodded. Ordinarily a prudent warlock used only limited bandwidth and so was confined to a kind of linear, personal perception. If they grabbed a few hundred megahertz of comm space, and a bigger share of rented processors, they could manipulate and search files in a way that would boggle Virginia the femcop. Of course, they would be much more easily identifiable. With two of them, though, they might be able to keep it up safely for a brief time, confusing the government and the Mailman with a multiplicity of clues. "Frankly, I don't buy the alien part. But the rest of what you say makes sense, and that's what counts. Like you say, we're going to have to take some chances."

"Right!" She smiled and reached behind his neck to draw his face to hers. She was a very good kisser. (Not everyone was. It was one thing just to look gorgeous, and another to project and respond to the many sensory cues in something as interactive as kissing.) He was just warming to this exercise of their mutual abilities when she broke off. "And the best time to start is right now. The others think we're sealed away down here. If strange things happen during the next few hours, it's less likely the Mailman will suspect *us*." She reached up to catch the light point in her hand. For an instant, blades of harsh white slipped out from between her fingers; then all was dark. He felt faint air motion as her hands moved through another spell. There were words, distorted and unidentifiable. Then the light was back, but as a torch again, and a door—a second door—had opened in the far wall.

He followed her up the passage that stretched straight and gently rising as far as the torchlight shone. They were walking a path that could not be—or at least that no one in the Coven could have believed. The castle was basically a logical structure "fleshed" out with the sensory cues that allowed warlocks to move about it as one would a physical structure. Its moats and walls were part of that logical structure, and though they had no physical reality outside of the varying potentials in whatever processors were running the program, they were proof against the movement of the equally "unreal" perceptions of the inhabitants of the plane. Erythrina and Mr. Slippery could have escaped the deep room simply by falling back into the real world, but in doing so, they would have left a chain of unclosed processor links. Their departure would have been detected by every Coven member, even by Alan, even by the sprites. An orderly departure scheme, such as represented by this tunnel, could only mean that Erythrina was far too clever to need his help, or that she had been one of the original builders of the castle some four years earlier (lost in the Mists of Time, as the Limey put it).

They were wild dogs now, large enough so as not likely to be bothered, small enough to be mistaken for the amateur users that are seen more and more in the Other Plane as the price of Portals declines and the skill of the public increases. Mr. Slippery followed Erythrina down narrow paths, deeper and deeper into the swamp that represented commercial and government data space. Occasionally he was aware of sprites or simulators watching them with hostile eyes from nests off to the sides of the trail. These were idle creations in many cases—program units designed to infuriate or amuse later visitors to the plane. But many of them guarded information caches, or peepholes into other folks' affairs, or meeting places of other SIGs. The Coven might be the most sophisticated group of users on this plane, but they were far from being alone.

The brush got taller, bending over the trail to drip on their backs. But the water was clear here, spread in quiet ponds on either side of their path. Light came from the water itself, a pearly luminescence that shone upward on the trunks of the waterbound trees and sparkled faintly in the droplets of water in their moss and leaves. That light was the representation of the really huge data bases run by the government and the largest companies. It did not correspond to a specific geographical location, but rather to the main East/West net that stretches through selected installations from Honolulu to Oxford, taking advantage of the time zones to spread the user load.

"Just a little bit farther," Erythrina said over her shoulder, speaking in the beast language (encipherment) that they had chosen with their forms.

Minutes later, they shrank into the brush, out of the way of two armored hackers that proceeded implacably up the trail. The pair drove in single file, the impossibly large eight-cylinder engines on their bikes belching fire and smoke and noise. The one bringing up the rear carried an old-style recoilless rifle decorated with swastikas and chrome. Dim fires glowed through their blackened face plates. The two dogs eyed the bikers timidly, as befitted their present disguise, but Mr. Slippery had the feeling he was looking at a couple of amateurs who were imaging beyond their station in life: the bikes' tires didn't always touch the ground, and the tracks they left didn't quite match the texture of the muck. Anyone could put on a heroic image in this plane, or appear as some dreadful monster. The problem was that there were always skilled users who were willing to cut such pretenders down to size—perhaps even to destroy their access. It befitted the less experienced to appear small and inconspicuous, and to stay out of others' way.

(Mr. Slippery had often speculated just how the simple notion of using high-resolution EEGs as input/output devices had caused the development of the "magical world" representation of data space. The Limey and Erythrina argued that sprites, reincarnation, spells, and castles were the natural tools here, more natural than the atomistic twentieth-century notions of data structures, programs, files, and communications protocols. It was, they argued, just more convenient for the mind to use the global ideas of magic as the tokens to manipulate this new environment. They had a point; in fact, it was likely that the governments of the world hadn't caught up to the skills of the better warlocks simply because they refused to indulge in the foolish imaginings of fantasy. Mr. Slippery looked down at the reflection in the pool beside him and saw the huge canine face and lolling tongue looking up at him; he winked at the image. He knew that despite all his friends' high intellectual arguments, there was another reason for the present state of affairs, a reason that went back to the Moon Lander and Adventure games at the "dawn of time": it was simply a hell of a lot of fun to live in a world as malleable as the human imagination.)

Once the riders were out of sight, Erythrina moved back across the path to the edge of the pond and peered long and hard down between the lilies, into the limpid depths. "Okay, let's do some cross-correlation. You take the JPL data base, and I'll take the Harvard Multispectral Patrol. Start with data coming off space probes out to ten AUs. I have a suspicion the easiest way for the Mailman to disguise his transmissions is to play trojan horse with data from a NASA spacecraft."

Mr. Slippery nodded. One way or another, they should resolve her alien invasion theory first.

"It should take me about half an hour to get in place. After that, we can set up for the correlation. Hmmm . . . if something goes wrong, let's agree to meet as Mass Transmit Three," and she gave a password scheme. Clearly that would be an emergency situation. If they weren't back in the castle within three or four hours, the others would certainly guess the existence of her secret exit.

Erythrina tensed, then dived into the water. There was a small splash, and the lilies bobbed gently in the expanding ring waves. Mr. Slippery looked deep, but as expected, there was no further sign of her. He padded around the side of the pool, trying to identify the special glow of the JPL data base.

There was thrashing near one of the larger lilies, one that he recognized as obscuring the NSA connections with the East/West net. A large bullfrog scrambled out of the water onto the pad and turned to look at him. "Aha! Gotcha, you sonofabitch!"

It was Virginia; the voice was the same, even if the body was different. "*Shhhhhh!*" said Mr. Slippery, and looked wildly about for signs of eavesdroppers. There were none, but that did not mean they were safe. He spread his best privacy spell over her and crawled to the point closest to the lily. They sat glaring at each other like some characters out of La Fontaine: The Tale of the Frog and Dog. How dearly he would love to leap across the water and bite off that fat little head. Unfortunately the victory would be a bit temporary. "How did you find me?" Mr. Slippery growled. If people as inexperienced as the Feds could trace him down in his disguise, he was hardly safe from the Mailman.

"You forget," the frog puffed smugly. "We know your Name. It's simple to monitor your home processor and follow your every move."

Mr. Slippery whined deep in his throat. *In thrall to a frog. Even Wiley has done better than that.* "Okay, so you found me. Now what do you want?"

"To let you know that we want results, and to get a progress report."

He lowered his muzzle till his eyes were even with Virginia's. "Heh heh. I'll give you a progress report, but you're not going to like it." And he proceeded to explain Erythrina's theory that the Mailman was an alien invasion.

"Rubbish," spoke the frog afterward. "Sheer fantasy! You're going to have to do better than that, Pol—er, Mister."

He shuddered. She had almost spoken his Name. Was that a calculated threat or was she simply as stupid as she seemed? Nevertheless, he persisted. "Well then, what about Venezuela?" He related the evidence Ery had that the coup in that country was the Mailman's work.

This time the frog did not reply. Its eyes glazed over with apparent shock, and he realized that Virginia must be consulting people at the other end. Almost fifteen minutes passed. When the frog's eyes cleared, it was much more subdued. "We'll check on that one. What you say is possible. Just barely possible. If true . . . well, if it's true, this is the biggest threat we've had to face this century."

And you see that I am perhaps the only one who can bail you out. Mr. Slippery relaxed slightly. If they only realized it, they were thralled to him as much as the reverse—at least for the moment. Then he remembered Erythrina's plan to grab as much power as they could for a brief time and try to use that advantage to flush the Mailman out. With the Feds on their side, they could do more than Ery had ever imagined. He said as much to Virginia.

The frog croaked, "*You* . . . want . . . *us* . . . to give you carte blanche in the Federal data system? Maybe you'd like to be President and Chair of the JCS, to boot?"

"Hey, that's not what I said. I know it's an extraordinary suggestion, but this is an extraordinary situation. And in any case, you know my Name. There's no way I can get around that."

The frog went glassy-eyed again, but this time for only a couple of minutes. "We'll get back to you on that. We've got a lot of checking to do on the rest of your theories before we commit ourselves to anything. Till further notice, though, you're grounded."

"Wait!" What would Ery do when he didn't show? If he wasn't back in the castle in three or four hours, the others would surely know about the secret exit.

The frog was implacable. "I said, you're grounded, Mister. We want you back in the real world immediately. And you'll stay grounded till you hear from us. Got it?"

The dog slumped. "Yeah."

"Okay." The frog clambered heavily to the edge of the sagging lily and dumped itself ungracefully into the water. After a few seconds, Mr. Slippery followed.

Coming back was much like waking from a deep daydream; only here it was the middle of the night.

Roger Pollack stood, stretching, trying to get the kinks out of his muscles. Almost four hours he had been gone, longer than ever before. Normally his concentration began to fail after two or three hours. Since he didn't like the thought of drugging up, this put a definite limit on his endurance in the Other Plane.

Beyond the bungalow's picture window, the pines stood silhouetted against the Milky Way. He cranked open a pane and listened to the night birds trilling in the trees. It was near the end of spring; he liked to imagine he could see dim polar twilight to the north. More likely it was just Crescent City. Pollack leaned close to the window and looked high into the sky, where Mars sat close to Jupiter. It was hard to think of a threat to his own life from as far away as that.

Pollack backed up the spells acquired during this last session, powered down his system, and stumbled off to bed.

The following morning and afternoon seemed the longest of Roger Pollack's life. How would they get in touch with him? Another visit of goons and black Lincolns? What had Erythrina done when he didn't make contact? Was she all right?

And there was just no way of checking. He paced back and forth across his tiny living room, the novel-plots that were his normal work forgotten. *Ah, but there is a way.* He looked at his old data set with dawning recognition. Virginia had said to stay out of the Other Plane. But how could they object to his using a simple data set, no more efficient than millions used by office workers all over the world?

He sat down at the set, scraped the dust from the handpads and screen. He awkwardly entered long-unused call symbols and watched the flow of news across the screen. A few queries and he discovered that no great disasters had occurred overnight, that the insurgency in Indonesia seemed temporarily abated. (Wiley J. was not to be king just yet.) There were no reports of big-time data vandals biting the dust.

Pollack grunted. He had forgotten how tedious it was to see the world through a data set, even with audio entry. In the Other Plane, he could pick up this sort of information in seconds, as casually as an ordinary mortal might glance out the window to see if it is raining. He dumped the last twenty-four hours of the world bulletin board into his home memory space and began checking through it. The bulletin board was ideal for untraceable reception of messages: anyone on Earth could leave a message—indexed by subject, target audience, and source. If a user copied the entire board, and *then* searched it, there was no outside record of exactly what information he was interested in. There were also simple ways to make nearly untraceable entries on the board.

As usual, there were about a dozen messages for Mr. Slippery. Most of them were from fans; the Coven had greater notoriety than any other vandal SIG. A few were for other Mr. Slipperys. With five billion people in the world, that wasn't surprising.

And one of the memos was from the Mailman; that's what it said in the source field. Pollack punched the message up on the screen. It was in caps, with no color or sound. Like all messages directly from the Mailman, it looked as if it came off some incredibly ancient I/O device:

YOU COULD HAVE BEEN RICH. YOU COULD HAVE RULED. INSTEAD YOU CONSPIRED AGAINST ME. I KNOW ABOUT THE SECRET EXIT. I KNOW ABOUT YOUR DOGGY DEPAR-TURE. YOU AND THE RED ONE ARE DEAD NOW. IF YOU EVER SNEAK BACK ONTO THIS PLANE, IT WILL BE THE TRUE DEATH—I AM THAT CLOSE TO KNOWING YOUR NAMES. *****WATCH FOR ME IN THE NEWS, SUCKER*********

Bluff, thought Roger. *He wouldn't be sending out warnings if he has that kind of power.* Still, there was a dropping sensation in his stomach. The Mailman shouldn't have known about the dog disguise. Was he onto Mr. Slippery's connection with the Feds? If so, he might really be able to find Slippery's True Name. And what sort of danger was Ery in? What had she done when he missed the rendezvous at Mass Transmit 3?

A quick search showed no messages from Erythrina. Either she was looking for him in the Other Plane, or she was as thoroughly grounded as he.

He was still stewing on this when the phone rang. He said, "Accept, no video send." His data set cleared to an even gray: the caller was not sending video either.

"You're still there? Good." It was Virginia. Her voice sounded a bit odd, subdued and tense. Perhaps it was just the effect of the scrambling algorithms. He prayed she would not trust that scrambling. He had never bothered to make his phone any more secure than average. (And he had seen the schemes Wiley J. and Robin Hood had devised to decrypt thousands of commercial phone messages in real-time and monitor for key phrases, signaling them when anything interesting was detected. They couldn't use the technique very effectively, since it took an enormous amount of processor space, but the Mailman was probably not so limited.)

Virginia continued, "No names, okay? We checked out what you told us and . . . it looks like you're right. We can't be sure about your theory about *his* origin, but what you said about the international situation was verified." So the Venezuela coup had been an outside takeover. "Furthermore, we think *he* has infiltrated us much more than we thought. It may be that the evidence we had of unsuccessful meddling was just a red herring." Pollack recognized the fear in her voice now. Apparently the Feds saw that they were up against something catastrophic. They were caught with their countermeasures down, and their only hope lay with unreliables like Pollack.

"Anyway, we're going ahead with what you suggested. We'll provide you two with the resources you requested. We want you in the Other . . . place as soon as possible. We can talk more there."

"I'm on my way. I'll check with my friend and get back to you there." He cut the connection without waiting for a reply. Pollack sat back, trying to savor this triumph and the near-pleading in the cop's voice. Somehow, he couldn't. He knew what a hard case she was; anything that could make her crawl was more hellish than anything he wanted to face.

His first stop was Mass Transmit 3. Physically, MT3 was a two-thousand-tonne satellite in synchronous orbit over the Indian Ocean. The Mass Transmits handled most of the planet's noninteractive communications (and in fact that included a lot of transmission that most people regarded as interactive—such as human/human and the simpler human/computer conversations). Bandwidth and processor space was cheaper on the Mass Transmits because of the 240- to 900-millisecond time delays that were involved.

As such, it was a nice out-of-the-way meeting place, and in the Other Plane it was represented as a five-meter-wide ledge near the top of a mountain that rose from the forests and swamps that stood for the lower satellite layer and the ground-based nets. In the distance were two similar peaks, clear in pale sky.

Mr. Slippery leaned out into the chill breeze that swept the face of the mountain and looked down past the timberline, past the evergreen forests. Through the unnatural mists that blanketed those realms, he thought he could see the Coven's castle.

Perhaps he should go there, or down to the swamps. There was no sign of Erythrina. Only sprites in the forms of bats and tiny griffins were to be seen here. They sailed back and forth over him, sometimes soaring far higher, toward the uttermost peak itself.

Mr. Slippery himself was in an extravagant winged man form, one that subtly projected amateurism, one that he hoped would pass the inspection of the enemy's eyes and ears. He fluttered clumsily across the ledge toward a small cave that provided some shelter from the whistling wind. Fine, wind-dropped snow lay in a small bank before the entrance. The insects he found in the cave were no more than what they seemed—amateur transponders.

He turned and started back toward the drop-off; he was going to have to face this alone. But as he passed the snowbank, the wind swirled it up and tiny crystals stung his face and hands and nose. *Trap!* He jumped backward, his fastest escape spell coming to his lips, at the same time cursing himself for not establishing the spell before. The time delay was just too long; the trap lived here at MT3 and could react faster than he. The little snow-devil dragged the crystals up into a swirling column of singing motes that chimed in near-unison, "W-w-wait-t-t!"

The sound matched deep-set recognition patterns; this was Erythrina's work. Three hundred milliseconds passed, and the wind suddenly picked up the rest of the snow and whirled into a more substantial, taller column. Mr. Slippery realized that the trap had been more of an alarm, set to bring Ery if he should be recognized here. But her arrival was so quick that she must already have been at work somewhere in this plane.

"Where have you been-n-n!" The snow-devil's chime was a combination of rage and concern.

Mr. Slippery threw a second spell over the one he recognized she had cast. There was no help for it: he would have to tell her that the Feds had his Name. And with that news, Virginia's confirmation about Venezuela and the Feds' offer to help.

Erythrina didn't respond immediately—and only part of the delay was light lag. Then the swirling snow flecks that represented her gusted up around him. "So you lose no matter how this comes out, eh? I'm sorry, Slip."

Mr. Slippery's wings drooped. "Yeah. But I'm beginning to believe it will be the True Death for us all if we don't stop the Mailman. He really means to take over . . . everything. Can you imagine what it would be like if all the governments' wee megalomaniacs got replaced by one big one?"

The usual pause. The snow-devil seemed to shudder in on itself. "You're right; we've got to stop him even if it means working for Sammy Sugar and the entire DoW." She chuckled, a near-inaudible chiming. "Even if it means that *they* have to work for *us*." She could laugh; the Feds didn't know her Name. "How did your Federal Friends say we could plug into their system?" Her form was changing again—to a solid, winged form, an albino eagle. The only red she allowed herself was in the eyes, which gleamed with inner light.

"At the Laurel end of the old arpa net. We'll get something near carte blanche on that and on the DoJ domestic intelligence files, but we have to enter through one physical location and with just the password scheme they specify." He and Erythrina would have more power than any vandals in history, but they would be on a short leash, nevertheless.

His wings beat briefly, and he rose into the air. After the usual pause, the eagle followed. They flew almost to the mountain's peak, then began the long, slow glide toward the marshes below, the chill air whistling around them. In principle, they could have made the transfer to the Laurel terminus virtually instantaneously. But it was not mere romanticism that made them move so cautiously—as many a novice had discovered the hard way. What appeared to the conscious mind as a search for air currents and clear lanes through the scattered clouds was a manifestation of the almost-subconscious working of programs that gradually transferred processing from rented space on MT3 to low satellite and ground-based stations. The game was tricky and time-consuming, but it made it virtually impossible for others to trace their origin. The greatest danger of detection would probably occur at Laurel, where they would be forced to access the system through a single input device.

The sky glowed momentarily; seconds passed, and an airborne fist slammed into them from behind. The shock wave sent them tumbling tail over wing toward the forests below. Mr. Slippery straightened his chaotic flailing into a headfirst dive. Looking back—which was easy to do in his present attitude—he saw the peak that had been MT3 glowing red, steam rising over descending avalanches of lava. Even at this distance, he could see tiny motes swirling above the inferno. (Attackers looking for the prey that had fled?) Had it come just a few seconds earlier, they would have had most of their processing still locked into MT3 and the disaster—whatever it really was—would have knocked them out of this plane. It wouldn't have been the True Death, but it might well have grounded them for days.

On his right, he glimpsed the white eagle in a controlled dive; they had had just enough communications established off MT3 to survive. As they fell deeper into the humid air of the lowlands, Mr. Slippery dipped into the news channels: word was already coming over the *LA Times* of the fluke accident in which the Hokkaido aerospace launching laser had somehow shone on MT3's optics. The laser had shone for microseconds and at reduced power; the damage had been nothing like a Finger of God, say. No one had been hurt, but wideband communications would be down for some time, and several hundred million dollars of information traffic was stalled. There would be investigations and a lot of very irate customers.

It had been no accident, Mr. Slippery was sure. The Mailman was showing his teeth, revealing infiltration no one had suspected. He must guess what his opponents were up to.

They leveled out a dozen meters above the pine forest that bordered the swamps. The air around them was thick and humid, and the faraway mountains were almost invisible. Clouds had moved in, and a storm was on the way. They were now securely locked into the low-level satellite net, but thousands of new users were clamoring for entry, too. The loss of MT3 would make the Other Plane a turbulent place for several weeks, as heavy users tried to shift their traffic here.

He swooped low over the swamp, searching for the one particular pond with the one particularly large water lily that marked the only entrance Virginia would permit them. There! He banked off to the side, Erythrina following, and looked for signs of the Mailman or his friends in the mucky clearings that surrounded the pond.

But there was little purpose in further caution. Flying about like this, they would be clearly visible to any ambushers waiting by the pond. *Better to move fast now that we're committed.* He signaled the red-eyed eagle, and they dived toward the placid water. That surface marked the symbolic transition to observation mode. No longer was he aware of a winged form or of water coming up and around him. Now he was interacting directly with the I/O protocols of a computing center in the vicinity of Laurel, Maryland. He sensed Ery poking around on her own. This wasn't the arpa entrance. He slipped "sideways" into an old-fashioned government office complex. The "feel" of the 1990-style data sets was unmistakable. He was fleetingly aware of memos written and edited, reports hauled in and out of storage. One of the vandals' favorite sports—and one that even the moderately skilled could indulge in—was to infiltrate one of these office complexes and simulate higher level input to make absurd and impossible demands on the local staff.

This was not the time for such games, and this was still not the entrance. He pulled away from the office complex and searched through some old directories. Arpa went back more than half a century, the first of the serious data nets, now (figuratively) gathering dust. The number was still there, though. He signaled Erythrina, and the two of them presented themselves at the log-in point and provided just the codes that Virginia had given him.

. . . and they were in. They eagerly soaked in the megabytes of password keys and access data that Virginia's people had left there. At the same time, they were aware that this activity was being monitored. The Feds were taking an immense chance leaving this material here, and they were going to do their best to keep a rein on their temporary vandal allies.

In fifteen seconds, they had learned more about the inner workings of the Justice Department and DoW than the Coven had in fifteen months. Mr. Slippery guessed that Erythrina must be busy plotting what she would do with all that data later on. For him, of course, there was no future in it. They drifted out of the arpa "vault" into the larger data spaces that were the Department of Justice files. He could see that there was nothing hidden from them; random archive retrievals were all being honored and with a speed that would have made deception impossible. They had subpoena power and clearances and more.

"Let's go get 'im, Slip." Erythrina's voice seemed hollow and inhuman in this underimaged realm. (How long would it be before the Feds started to make their data perceivable analogically, as on the Other Plane? It might be a little undignified, but it would revolutionize their operation—which, from the Coven's standpoint, might be quite a bad thing.)

Mr. Slippery "nodded." Now they had more than enough power to undertake the sort of work they had planned. In seconds, they had searched all the locally available files on off-planet transmissions. Then they dove out of the DoJ net, Mr. Slippery to Pasadena and the JPL planetary probe archives, Erythrina to Cambridge and the Harvard Multispectral Patrol.

It should take several hours to survey these records, to determine just what transmissions might be cover for the alien invasion that both the Feds and Erythrina were guessing had begun. But Mr. Slippery had barely started when he noticed that there were dozens of processors within reach that he could just grab with his new Federal powers. He checked carefully to make sure he wasn't upsetting air traffic control or hospital life support, then quietly stole the computing resources of several hundred unknowing users, whose data sets automatically switched to other resources. Now he had more power than he ever would have risked taking in the past. On the other side of the continent, he was aware that Erythrina had done something similar.

In three minutes, they had sifted through five years' transmissions far more thoroughly than they had originally planned.

"No sign of him," he sighed and "looked" at Erythrina. They had found plenty of irregular sources at Harvard, but there was no orbital fit. All transmissions from the NASA probes checked out legitimately.

"Yes." Her face, with its dark skin and slanting eyes, seemed to hover beside him. Apparently with her new power, she could image even here. "But you know, we haven't really done much more than the Feds could—given a couple months of data set work. . . . I know, it's more than we had planned to do. But we've barely used the resources they've opened to us."

It was true. He looked around, feeling suddenly like a small boy let loose in a candy shop: he sensed enormous data bases and the power that would let him use them. Perhaps the cops had not intended them to take advantage of this, but it was obvious that with these powers, they could do a search no enemy could evade. "Okay," he said finally, "let's pig it."

Ery laughed and made a loud snuffling sound. Carefully, quickly, they grabbed noncritical data-processing facilities along all the East/West nets. In seconds, they were the biggest users in North America. The drain would be clear to anyone monitoring the System, though a casual user might notice only increased delays in turnaround. Modern nets are at least as resilient as old-time power nets—but like power nets, they have their elastic limit and their breaking point. So far, at least, he and Erythrina were far short of those.

—but they were experiencing what no human had ever known before, a sensory bandwidth thousands of times normal. For seconds that seemed without end, their minds were filled with a jumble verging on pain, data that was not information and information that was not knowledge. To hear ten million simultaneous phone conversations, to see the continent's entire video output, should have been a white noise. Instead it was a tidal wave of detail rammed through the tiny aperture of their minds. The pain increased, and Mr. Slippery panicked. This could be the True Death, some kind of sensory burnout—

Erythrina's voice was faint against the roar, *"Use everything, not just the inputs!"* And he had just enough sense left to see what she meant. He controlled more than raw data now; if he could master them, the continent's computers could process this avalanche, much the way parts of the human brain preprocess their input. More seconds passed, but now with a sense of time, as he struggled to distribute his very consciousness through the System.

Then it was over, and he had control once more. But things would never be the same: the human that had been Mr. Slippery was an insect wandering in the cathedral his mind had become. There simply was more there than before. No sparrow could fall without his knowledge, via air traffic control; no check could be cashed without his noticing over the bank communication net. More than three hundred million lives swept before what his senses had become.

Around and through him, he felt the other occupant—Erythrina, now equally grown. They looked at each other for an unending fraction of a second, their communication more kinesthetic than verbal. Finally she smiled, the old smile now deep with meanings she could never image before. "Pity the poor Mailman now!"

Again they searched, but now it was through all the civil data bases, a search that could only be dreamed of by mortals. The signs were there, a near invisible system of manipulations hidden among more routine crimes and vandalisms. Someone had been at work within the Venezuelan system, at least at the North American end. The trail was tricky to follow—their enemy seemed to have at least some of their own powers—but they saw it lead back into the labyrinths of the Federal bureaucracy: resources diverted, individuals promoted or transferred, not quite according to the automatic regulations that should govern. These were changes so small they were never guessed at by ordinary employees and only just sensed by the cops. But over the months, they added up to an instability that neither of the two searchers could quite understand except to know that it was planned and that it did the status quo no good.

"He's still too sharp for us, Slip. We're all over the civil nets and we haven't seen any living sign of him; yet we know he does heavy processing on Earth or in low orbit."

"So he's either off North America, or else he has penetrated the . . . military."

"I bet it's a little of both. The point is, we're going to have to follow him."

And that meant taking over at least part of the U.S. military system. Even if that was possible, it certainly went far beyond what Virginia and her friends had intended. As far as the cops were concerned, it would mean that the threat against the government was tripled. So far he hadn't detected any objections to their searching, but he was aware of Virginia and her superiors deep in some kind of bunker at Langley, intently watching a whole wall full of monitors, trying to figure out just what he was up to and if it was time to pull the plug on him.

Erythrina was aware of his objections almost as fast as he could bring them to mind. "We don't have any choice, Slip. We have to take control. The Feds aren't the only thing watching us. If we don't get the Mailman on this try, he is sure as hell going to get us."

That was easy for her to say. None of her enemies yet knew her True Name. Mr. Slippery had somehow to survive *two* enemies. On the other hand, he suspected that the deadlier of those enemies was the Mailman. "Only one way to go and that's up, huh? Okay, I'll play."

They settled into a game that was familiar now, grabbing more and more computing facilities, but now from common Europe and Asia. At the same time, they attacked the harder problem—infiltrating the various North American military nets. Both projects were beyond normal humans or any group of normal humans, but by now their powers were greater than any single civil entity in the world.

The foreign data centers yielded easily, scarcely more than minutes' work. The military was a different story. The Feds had spent many years and hundreds of billions of dollars to make the military command and control system secure. But they had not counted on the attack from all directions that they faced now; in moments more, the two searchers found themselves on the inside of the NSA control system—

—and under attack! Impressions of a dozen sleek, deadly forms converging on them, and sudden loss of control over many of the processors he depended on. He and Erythrina flailed out wildly, clumsy giants hacking at fast-moving hawks. There was imagery here, as detailed as on the Other Plane. They were fighting people with some of the skills the warlocks had developed—and a lot more power. But it was still an uneven contest. He and Erythrina had too much experience and too much sheer processing mass behind them. One by one, the fighters flashed into incandescent destruction.

He realized almost instantly that these were not the Mailman's tools. They were powerful, but they fought only as moderately skilled warlocks might. In fact, they had encountered the most secret defense the government had for its military command and control. The civilian bureaucracies had stuck with obsolete data sets and old-fashioned dp languages, but the cutting edge of the military is always more willing to experiment. They had developed something like the warlocks' system. Perhaps they didn't use magical jargon to describe their computer/human symbiosis, but the techniques and the attitudes were the same. These swift-moving fighters flew against a background imagery that was like an olive-drab Other Plane.

Compared to his present power, they were nothing. Even as he and Erythrina swept the defenders out of the "sky," he could feel his consciousness expanding further as more and more of the military system was absorbed into their pattern. Every piece of space junk out to one million kilometers floated in crystal detail before his attention; in a fraction of a second he sorted through it all, searching for some evidence of alien intelligence. No sign of the Mailman.

The military and diplomatic communications of the preceding fifty years showed before the light of their minds. At the same time as they surveyed the satellite data, Mr. Slippery and Erythrina swept through these bureaucratic communications, looking carefully but with flickering speed at every requisition for toilet paper, every "declaration" of secret war, every travel voucher, every one of the trillions of pieces of "paper" that made it possible for the machinery of state to creak forward. And here the signs were much clearer: large sections were subtly changed, giving the same feeling the eye's blind spot gives, the feeling that nothing is really obscured but that some things are simply gone. Some of the distortions were immense. Under their microscopic yet global scrutiny, it was obvious that all of Venezuela, large parts of Alaska, and most of the economic base for the low satellite net were all controlled by some single interest that had little connection with the proper owners. Who their enemy was was still a mystery, but his works loomed larger and larger around them.

In a distant corner of what his mind had become, tiny insects buzzed with homicidal fury, tiny insects who knew Mr. Slippery's True Name. They knew what he and Erythrina had done, and right now they were more scared of the two warlocks than they had ever been of the Mailman. As he and Ery continued their search, he listened to the signals coming from the Langley command post, followed the helicopter gunships that were dispatched toward a single rural bungalow in Northern California—and changed their encrypted commands so that the sortie dumped its load of death on an uninhabited stretch of the Pacific.

Still with a tiny fraction of his attention, Mr. Slippery noticed that Virginia—actually her superiors, who had long since taken over the operation—knew of this defense. They were still receiving real-time pictures from military satellites.

He signaled a pause to Erythrina. For a few seconds, she would work alone while he dealt with these persistent antagonists. He felt like a man attacked by several puppies: they were annoying and could cause substantial damage unless he took more trouble than they were worth. They had to be stopped without causing themselves injury.

He should freeze the West Coast military and any launch complexes that could reach his body. Beyond that, it would be a good idea to block recon satellite transmission of the California area. And of course, he'd better deal with the Finger of God installations that were above the California horizon. Already he felt one of those heavy lasers, sweeping along in its ten-thousand-kilometer orbit, go into aiming mode and begin charging. He still had plenty of time—at least two or three seconds—before the weapons laser reached its lowest discharge threshold. Still, this was the most immediate threat. Mr. Slippery sent a tendril of consciousness into the tiny processor aboard the Finger of God satellite—

—and withdrew, bloodied. *Someone was already there.* Not Erythrina and not the little military warlocks. *Someone* too great for even him to overpower.

"*Ery!* I've found him!" It came out a scream. The laser's bore was centered on a spot thousands of kilometers below, a tiny house that in less than a second would become an expanding ball of plasma at the end of a columnar explosion descending through the atmosphere.

Over and over in that last second, Mr. Slippery threw himself against the barrier he felt around the tiny military processor—with no success. He traced its control to the lower satellite net, to bigger processors that were equally shielded. Now he had a feel for the nature of his opponent. It was not the direct imagery he was used to on the Other Plane; this was more like fighting blindfolded. He could sense the other's style. The enemy was not revealing any more of himself than was necessary to keep control of the Finger of God for another few hundred milliseconds.

Mr. Slippery slashed, trying to cut the enemy's communications. But his opponent was strong, much stronger—he now realized—than himself. He was vaguely aware of the other's connections to the computing power in those blind-spot areas he and Erythrina had discovered. But for all that power, he was almost the enemy's equal. There was something missing from the other, some critical element of imagination or originality. If Erythrina would only come, they might be able to stop him. Milliseconds separated him from the True Death. He looked desperately around. *Where is she?*

Military Status announced the discharge of an Orbital Weapons Laser. He cowered even as his quickened perceptions counted the microseconds that remained till his certain destruction, even as he noticed a ball of glowing plasma expanding about what had been a Finger of God—*the Finger that had been aimed at him!*

He could see now what had happened. While he and the other had been fighting, Erythrina had commandeered another of the weapons satellites, one already very near discharge threshold, and destroyed the threat to him.

Even as he realized this, the enemy was on him again, this time attacking conventionally, trying to destroy Mr. Slippery's communications and processing space. But now that enemy had to fight both Erythrina and Mr. Slippery. The other's lack of imagination and creativity was beginning to tell, and even with his greater strength, they could feel him slowly, slowly losing resources to his weaker opponents. There was something familiar about this enemy, something Mr. Slippery was sure he could see, given time.

Abruptly the enemy pulled away. For a long moment, they held each other's sole attention, like cats waiting for the smallest sign of weakness to launch back into combat—only here the new attack could come from any of ten thousand different directions, from any of the communications nodes that formed their bodies and their minds.

From beside him, he felt Erythrina move forward, as though to lock the other in her green-eyed gaze. "You know who we have here, Slip?" He could tell that all her concentration was on this enemy, that she almost vibrated with the effort. "This is our old friend DON.MAC grown up to super size, and doing his best to disguise himself."

The other seemed to tense and move even further in upon himself. But after a moment, he began imaging. There stood DON.MAC, his face and Plessey-Mercedes body the same as ever. DON.MAC, the first of the Mailman's converts, the one Erythrina was sure had been killed and replaced with a simulator. "And all the time he's been the Mailman. The last person we would suspect, the Mailman's first victim."

DON rolled forward half a meter, his motors keening, his hydraulic fists raised. But he did not deny what Mr. Slippery said. After a moment he seemed to relax. "You are very . . . clever. But then, you two have had help; I never thought you and the cops would cooperate. That was the one combination that had any chance against the 'Mailman.' " He smiled, a familiar automatic twitch. "But don't you see? It's a combination with lethal genes. We three have much more in common than you and the government.

"Look around you. If we were warlocks before, we are gods now. Look!" Without letting the center of their attention wander, the two followed his gaze. As before, the myriad aspects of the lives of billions spread out before them. But now, many things were changed. In their struggle, the three had usurped virtually all of the connected processing power of the human race. Video and phone communications were frozen. The public data bases had lasted long enough to notice that something had gone terribly, terribly wrong. Their last headlines, generated a second before the climax of the battle, were huge banners announcing GREATEST DATA OUTAGE OF ALL TIME. Nearly a billion people watched blank data sets, feeling more panicked than any simple power blackout could ever make them. Already the accumulation of lost data and work time would cause a major recession.

"They are lucky the old arms race is over, or else independent military units would probably have already started a war. Even if we hand back control this instant, it would take them more than a year to get their affairs in order." DON.MAC smirked, the same expression they had seen the day before when he was bragging to the Limey. "There have been few deaths yet. Hospitals and aircraft have some stand-alone capability."

Even so . . . Mr. Slippery could see thousands of aircraft stacked up over major airports from London to Christchurch. Local computing could never coordinate the safe landing of them all before some ran out of fuel.

" *We* caused all that—with just the fallout of our battle," continued DON. "If we chose to do them harm, I have no doubt we could exterminate the human race." He detonated three warheads in their silos in Utah just to emphasize his point. With dozens of video eyes, in orbit and on the ground, Mr. Slippery and Erythrina watched the destruction sweep across the launch sites. "Consider: how are we different from the gods of myth? And like the gods of myth, we can rule and prosper, just so long as we don't fight among ourselves." He looked expectantly from Mr. Slippery to Erythrina. There was a frown on the Red One's dark face; she seemed to be concentrating on their opponent just as fiercely as ever.

DON.MAC turned back to Mr. Slippery. "Slip, you especially should see that we have no choice but to cooperate. *They know your True Name.* Of the three of us, your life is the most fragile, depending on protecting your body from a government that now considers you a traitor. You would have died a dozen times over during the last thousand seconds if you hadn't used your new powers.

"And you can't go back. Even if you play Boy Scout, destroy me, and return all obedient—even then they will kill you. They know how dangerous you are, perhaps even more dangerous than I. They can't afford to let you exist."

And megalomania aside, that made perfect and chilling sense. As they were talking, a fraction of Mr. Slippery's attention was devoted to confusing and obstructing the small infantry group that had been air-dropped into the Arcata region just before the government lost all control. Their superiors had realized how easily he could countermand their orders, and so the troops were instructed to ignore all outside direction until they had destroyed a certain Roger Pollack. Fortunately they were depending on city directories and orbit-fed street maps, and he had been keeping them going in circles for some time now. It was a nuisance, and sooner or later he would have to decide on a more permanent solution.

But what was a simple nuisance in his present state would be near-instant death if he returned to his normal self. He looked at Erythrina. Was there any way around DON's arguments?

Her eyes were almost shut, and the frown had deepened. He sensed that more and more of her resources were involved in some pattern analysis. He wondered if she had even heard what DON.MAC said. But after a moment her eyes came open, and she looked at the two of them. There was triumph in that look. "You know, Slip, I don't think I have ever been fooled by a personality simulator, at least not for more than a few minutes."

Mr. Slippery nodded, puzzled by this sudden change in topic. "Sure. If you talk to a simulator long enough, you eventually begin to notice little inflexibilities. I don't think we'll ever be able to write a program that could pass the Turing test."

"Yes, little inflexibilities, a certain lack of imagination. It always seems to be the tipoff. Of course DON here has always pretended to be a program, so it was hard to tell. But I was sure that for the last few months there has been no living being behind his mask . . .

". . . and furthermore, I don't think there is anybody there even now." Mr. Slippery's attention snapped back to DON.MAC. The other smirked at the accusation. Somehow it was not the right reaction. Mr. Slippery remembered the strange, artificial flavor of DON's combat style. In this short an encounter, there could be no really hard evidence for her theory. She was using her intuition and whatever deep analysis she had been doing these last few seconds.

"But that means we still haven't found the Mailman."

"Right. This is just his best tool. I'll bet the Mailman simply used the pattern he stole from the murdered DON.MAC as the basis for this automatic defense system we've been fighting. The Mailman's time lag is a very real thing, not a red herring at all. Somehow it is the whole secret of who he really is.

"In any case, it makes our present situation a lot easier." She smiled at DON.MAC as though he were a real person. Usually it was easier to behave that way toward simulators; in this case, there was a good deal of triumph in her smile. "You almost won for your master, DON. You almost had us convinced. But now that we know what we are dealing with, it will be easy to—"

Her image flicked out of existence, and Mr. Slippery felt DON grab for the resources Ery controlled. All through near-Earth space, they fought for the weapon systems she had held till an instant before.

And alone, Mr. Slippery could not win. Slowly, slowly, he felt himself bending before the other's force, like some wrestler whose bones were breaking one by one under a murderous opponent. It was all he could do to prevent the DON construct from blasting his home; and to do that, he had to give up progressively more computing power.

Erythrina was gone, gone as though she had never been. Or was she? He gave a sliver of his attention to a search, a sliver that was still many times more powerful than any mere warlock. That tiny piece of consciousness quickly noticed a power failure in southern Rhode Island. Many power failures had developed during the last few minutes, consequent to the data failure. But this one was strange. In addition to power, comm lines were down and even his intervention could not bring them to life. It was about as thoroughly blacked out as a place could be. This could scarcely be an accident.

. . . and there was a voice, barely telephone quality and almost lost in the mass of other data he was processing. *Erythrina!* She had, via some incredibly tortuous detour, retained a communication path to the outside.

His gaze swept the blacked-out Providence suburb. It consisted of new urbapts, perhaps one hundred thousand units in all. Somewhere in there lived the human that was Erythrina. While she had been concentrating on DON.MAC, he must have been working equally hard to find her True Name. Even now, DON did not know precisely who she was, only enough to black out the area she lived in.

It was getting hard to think; DON.MAC was systematically dismantling him. The lethal intent was clear: as soon as Mr. Slippery was sufficiently reduced, the Orbital Lasers would be turned on his body, and then on Erythrina's. And then the Mailman's faithful servant would have a planetary kingdom to turn over to his mysterious master.

He listened to the tiny voice that still leaked out of Providence. It didn't make too much sense. She sounded hysterical, panicked. He was surprised that she could speak at all; she had just suffered—in losing all her computer connections—something roughly analogous to a massive stroke. To her, the world was now seen through a keyhole, incomplete, unknown, and dark.

"There is a chance; we still have a chance," the voice went on, hurried and slurred. "An old military communication tower north of here. Damn. I don't know the number or grid, but I can see it from where I'm sitting. With it you could punch through to the roof antenna . . . has plenty of bandwidth, and I've got some battery power here . . . but *hurry.*"

She didn't have to tell him that; he was the guy who was being eaten alive. He was almost immobilized now, the other's attack squeezing and stifling where it could not cut and tear. He spasmed against DON's strength and briefly contacted the comm towers north of Providence. Only one of them was in line of sight with the blacked-out area. Its steerable antenna was very, very narrow beam.

"Ery, I'm going to need your house number, maybe even your antenna id."

A second passed, two—a hellish eon for Mr. Slippery. In effect, he had asked her for her True Name—he who was already known to the Feds. Once he returned to the real world, there would be no way he could mask this information from them. He could imagine her thoughts: never again to be free. In her place, he would have paused too, but—

"*Ery!* It's the True Death for both of us if you don't. He's got me!"

This time she barely hesitated. "D-Debby Charteris, four thousand four hundred forty-eight Grosvenor Row. Cut off like this, I don't know the antenna id. Is my name and house enough?"

"Yes. Get ready!"

Even before he spoke, he had already matched the name with an antenna rental and aligned the military antenna on it. Return contact came as he turned his attention back to DON.MAC. With luck, the enemy was not aware of their conversation. Now he must be distracted.

Mr. Slippery surged against the other, breaking communications nodes that served them both. DON shuddered, reorganizing around the resources that were left, then moved in on Mr. Slippery again. Since DON had greater strength to begin with, the maneuver had cost Mr. Slippery proportionately more. The enemy had been momentarily thrown off balance, but now the end would come very quickly.

The spaces around him, once so rich with detail and colors beyond color, were fading now, replaced by the sensations of his true body straining with animal fear in its little house in California. Contact with the greater world was almost gone. He was scarcely aware of it when DON turned the Finger of God back upon him—

Consciousness, the superhuman consciousness of before, returned almost unsensed, unrecognized till awareness brought surprise. Like a strangling victim back from oblivion, Mr. Slippery looked around dazedly, not quite realizing that the struggle continued.

But now the roles were reversed. DON.MAC had been caught by surprise, in the act of finishing off what he thought was his only remaining enemy. Erythrina had used that surprise to good advantage, coming in upon her opponent from a Japanese data center, destroying much of DON's higher reasoning centers before the other was even aware of her. Large, unclaimed processing units lay all about, and as DON and Erythrina continued their struggle, Mr. Slippery quietly absorbed everything in reach.

Even now, DON could have won against either one of them alone, but when Mr. Slippery threw himself back into the battle, they had the advantage. DON.MAC sensed this too, and with a brazenness that was either mindless or genius, returned to his original appeal. "There is still time! The Mailman will still forgive you."

Mr. Slippery and Erythrina ripped at their enemy from both sides, disconnecting vast blocks of communications, processing and data resources. They denied the Mass Transmits to him, and one by one put the low-level satellites out of synch with his data accesses. DON was confined to land lines, tied into a single military net that stretched from Washington to Denver. He was flailing, randomly using whatever instruments of destruction were still available. All across the midsection of the US, silo missiles detonated, ABM lasers swept back and forth across the sky. The world had been stopped short by the beginning of their struggle, but the ending could tear it to pieces.

The damage to Mr. Slippery and Erythrina was slight, the risk that the random strokes would seriously damage them small. They ignored occasional slashing losses and concentrated single-mindedly on dismantling DON.MAC. They discovered the object code for the simulator that was DON, and zeroed it. DON—or his creator—was clever and had planted many copies, and a new one awakened every time they destroyed the running copy. But as the minutes passed, the simulator found itself with less and less to work with. Now it was barely more than it had been back in the Coven.

"*Fools!* The Mailman is your natural ally. The Feds will *kill* you! Don't you underst—"

The voice stopped in midshriek, as Erythrina zeroed the currently running simulator. No other took up the task. There was a silence, an . . . absence . . . throughout. Erythrina glanced at Mr. Slippery, and the two continued their search through the enemy's territory. This data space was big, and there could be many more copies of DON hidden in it. But without the resources they presently held, the simulator could have no power. It was clear to both of them that no effective ambush could be hidden in these unmoving ruins.

And they had complete copies of DON.MAC to study. It was easy to trace the exact extent of his infection of the system. The two moved systematically, changing what they found so that it would behave as its original programmers had intended. Their work was so thorough that the Feds might never realize just how extensively the Mailman and his henchman had infiltrated them, just how close he had come to total control.

Most of the areas they searched were only slightly altered and required only small changes. But deep within the military net, there were hundreds of trillions of bytes of program that seemed to have no intelligible function yet were clearly connected with DON's activities. It was apparently object code, but it was so huge and so ill organized that even they couldn't decide if it was more than hash now. There was no possibility that it had any legitimate function; after a few moments' consideration, they randomized it.

At last it was over. Mr. Slippery and Erythrina stood alone. They controlled all connected processing facilities in near-Earth space. There was no place within that volume that any further enemies could be lurking. And there was no evidence that there had ever been interference from beyond.

It was the first time since they had reached this level that they had been able to survey the world without fear. (He scarcely noticed the continuing, pitiful attempts of the American military to kill his real body.) Mr. Slippery looked around him, using all his millions of perceptors. The Earth floated serene. Viewed in the visible, it looked like a thousand pictures he had seen as a human. But in the ultraviolet, he could follow its hydrogen aura out many thousands of kilometers. And the high-energy detectors on satellites at all levels perceived the radiation belts in thousands of energy levels, oscillating in the solar wind. Across the oceans of the world, he could feel the warmth of the currents, see just how fast they were moving. And all the while, he monitored the millions of tiny voices that were now coming back to life as he and Erythrina carefully set the human race's communication system back on its feet and gently prodded it into function. Every ship in the seas, every aircraft now making for safe landing, every one of the loans, the payments, the meals of an entire race registered clearly on some part of his consciousness. With perception came power; almost everything he saw, he could alter, destroy, or enhance. By the analogical rules of the covens, there was only one valid word for themselves in their present state: they were gods.

". . . we could rule," Erythrina's voice was hushed, self-frightened. "It might be tricky at first, assuring our bodies protection, but we could rule."

"There's still the Mailman—"

She seemed to wave a hand, dismissingly. "Maybe, maybe not. It's true we still are no closer to knowing who he is, but we do know that we have destroyed all his processing power. We would have plenty of warning if he ever tries to reinsinuate himself into the System." She stared at him intently, and it wasn't until some time later that he recognized the faint clues in her behavior and realized that she was holding something back.

What she said was all so clearly true; for as long as their bodies lived, they could rule. And what DON.MAC had said seemed true: they were the greatest threat the "forces of law and order" had ever faced, and that included the Mailman. How could the Feds afford to let them be free, how could they even afford to let them *live*, if the two of them gave up the power they had now? But— "A lot of people would have to die if we took over. There are enough independent military entities left on Earth that we'd have to use a good deal of nuclear blackmail, at least at first."

"Yeah," her voice was even smaller than before, and the image of her face was downcast. "During the last few seconds I've done some simulating on that. We'd have to take out four, maybe six, major cities. If there are any command centers hidden from us, it could be a lot worse than that. And we'd have to develop our own human secret-police forces as folks began to operate outside our system. . . . Damn. We'd end up being worse than the human-based government."

She saw the same conclusion in his face and grinned lopsidedly. "You can't do it and neither can I. So the State wins again."

He nodded, "reached" out to touch her briefly. They took one last glorious minute to soak in the higher reality. Then, silently, they parted, each to seek his own way downward.

It was not an instantaneous descent to ordinary humanity. Mr. Slippery was careful to prepare a safe exit. He created a complex set of misdirections for the army unit that was trying to close in on his physical body; it would take them several hours to find him, far longer than necessary for the government to call them off. He set up preliminary negotiations with the Federal programs that had been doing their best to knock him out of power, telling them of his determination to surrender if granted safe passage and safety for his body. In a matter of seconds he would be talking to humans again, perhaps even Virginia, but by then a lot of the basic ground rules would be automatically in operation.

As per their temporary agreements, he closed off first one and then another of the capabilities that he had so recently acquired. It was like stopping one's ears, then blinding one's eyes, but somehow much worse since his very ability to think was being deliberately given up. He was like some lobotomy patient (victim) who only vaguely realizes now what he has lost. Behind him the Federal forces were doing their best to close off the areas he had left, to protect themselves from any change of heart he might have.

Far away now, he could sense Erythrina going through a similar procedure, but more slowly. That was strange; he couldn't be sure with his present faculties, but somehow it seemed that she was deliberately lagging behind and doing something more complicated than was strictly necessary to return safely to normal humanity. And then he remembered that strange look she had given him while saying that they had not figured out who the Mailman was.

One could rule as easily as two!

The panic was sudden and overwhelming, all the more terrible for the feeling of being betrayed by one so trusted. He struck out against the barriers he had so recently allowed to close in about him, but it was too late. He was already weaker than the Feds. Mr. Slippery looked helplessly back into the gathering dimness, and saw . . .

. . . Ery coming down toward the real world with him, giving up the advantage she had held all alone. Whatever problems had slowed her must have had nothing to do with treachery. And somehow his feeling of relief went beyond the mere fact of death avoided—Ery was still what he had always thought her.

He was seeing a lot of Virginia lately, though of course not socially. Her crew had set up offices in Arcata, and twice a week she and one of her goons would come up to the house. No doubt it was one of the few government operations carried out face-to-face. She or her superiors seemed to realize that anything done over the phone might be subject to trickery. (Which was true, of course. Given several weeks to himself, Pollack could have put together a robot phone connection and—using false ids and priority permits—been on a plane to Djakarta.)

There were a lot of superficial similarities between these meetings and that first encounter the previous spring:

Pollack stepped to the door and watched the black Lincoln pulling up the drive. As always, the vehicle came right into the carport. As always, the driver got out quickly, eyes flickering coldly across Pollack. As always, Virginia moved with military precision (in fact, he had discovered, she had been promoted out of the Army to her present job in DoW intelligence). The two walked purposefully toward the bungalow, ignoring the summer sunlight and the deep wet green of the lawn and pines. He held the door open for them, and they entered with silent arrogance. As always.

He smiled to himself. In one sense nothing had changed. They still had the power of life and death over him. They could still cut him off from everything he loved. But in another sense . . .

"Got an easy one for you today, Pollack," she said as she put her briefcase on the coffee table and enabled its data set. "But I don't think you're going to like it."

"Oh?" He sat down and watched her expectantly.

"The last couple of months, we've had you destroying what remains of the Mailman and getting the National program and data bases back in operation."

Behind everything, there still stood the threat of the Mailman. Ten weeks after the battle—the War, as Virginia called it—the public didn't know any more than that there had been a massive vandalism of the System. Like most major wars, this had left ruination in everyone's camp. The U.S. government and the economy of the entire world had slid far toward chaos in the months after that battle. (In fact, without his work and Erythrina's, he doubted if the U.S. bureaucracies could have survived the Mailman War. He didn't know whether this made them the saviors or the betrayers of America.) But what of the enemy? His power was almost certainly destroyed. In the last three weeks Mr. Slippery had found only one copy of the program kernel that had been DON.MAC, and that had been in nonexecutable form. But the man—or the beings—behind the Mailman was just as anonymous as ever. In that, Virginia, the government, and Pollack were just as ignorant as the general public.

"Now," Virginia continued, "we've got some smaller problems—mopping-up action, you might call it. For nearly two decades, we've had to live with the tuppin vandalism of irresponsible individuals who put their petty self-interest ahead of the public's. Now that we've got you, we intend to put a stop to that:

"We want the True Names of all abusers currently on the System, in particular the members of this so-called coven you used to be a part of."

He had known that the demand would eventually come, but the knowledge made this moment no less unpleasant. "I'm sorry, I can't."

"Can't? Or won't? See here, Pollack, the price of your freedom is that you play things our way. You've broken enough laws to justify putting you away forever. And we both know that you are so dangerous that you *ought* to be put away. There are people who feel even more strongly than that, Pollack, people who are not as soft in the head as I am. They simply want you and your girlfriend in Providence safely dead." The speech was delivered with characteristic flat bluntness, but she didn't quite meet his eyes as she spoke. Ever since he had returned from the battle, there had been a faint diffidence behind her bluster.

She covered it well, but it was clear to Pollack that she didn't know if she should fear him or respect him—or both. In any case, she seemed to recognize a basic mystery in him; she had more imagination than he had originally thought. It was a bit amusing, for there was very little special about Roger Pollack, the man. He went from day to day feeling a husk of what he had once been and trying to imagine what he could barely remember.

Roger smiled almost sympathetically. "I can't *and* I won't, Virginia. And I don't think you will harm me for it— Let me finish. The only thing that frightens your bosses more than Erythrina and me is the possibility that there may be other unknown persons—maybe even the Mailman, back from wherever he has disappeared to—who might be equally powerful. She and I are your only real experts on this type of subversion. I bet that even if they could, your people wouldn't train their own clean-cut, braided types as replacements for us. The more paranoid a security organization is, the less likely it is to trust anyone with this sort of power. Mr. Slippery and Erythrina are the known factors, the experts who turned back from the brink. Our restraint was the only thing that stood between the Powers That Be and the Powers That Would Be."

Virginia was speechless for a moment, and Pollack could see that this was the crux of her changed attitude toward him. All her life she had been taught that the individual is corrupted by power: she boggled at the notion that he had been offered mastery of all mankind—and had refused it.

Finally she smiled, a quick smile that was gone almost before he noticed it. "Okay. I'll pass on what you say. You may be right. The vandals are a long-range threat to our basic American freedoms, but day to day, they are a mere annoyance. My superiors—the Department of Welfare—are probably willing to fight them as we have in the past. They'll tolerate your, uh, disobedience *in this single matter* as long as you and Erythrina loyally protect us against the superhuman threats."

Pollack felt a great sense of relief. He had been so afraid DoW would be willing to destroy him for this refusal. But since the Feds would never be free of their fear of the Mailman, he and Debby Charteris—Erythrina—would never be forced to betray their friends.

"But," continued the cop, "that doesn't mean you get to ignore the covens.

The most likely place for superhuman threats to resurface is from within them. The vandals are the people with the most real experience on the System— even the Army is beginning to see that. And if a superhuman type originates outside the covens, we figure his ego will still make him show off to them, just as with the Mailman.

"In addition to your other jobs, we want you to spend a couple of hours a week with each of the major covens. You'll be one of the 'boys'—only now you're under responsible control, watching for any sign of Mailman-type influence."

"I'll get to see Ery again!"

"No. That rule still stands. And you should be grateful. I don't think we could tolerate your existence if there weren't two of you. With only one in the Other Plane at a time, we'll always have a weapon in reserve. And as long as we can keep you from meeting there, we can keep you from scheming against us. This is serious, Roger: if we catch you two or your surrogates playing around in the Other Plane, it will be the end."

"Hmm."

She looked hard at him for a moment, then appeared to take that for acquiescence. The next half hour was devoted to the details of this week's assignments. (It would have been easier to feed him all this when he was in the Other Plane, but Virginia—or at least DoW—seemed wedded to the past.) He was to continue the work on Social Security Records and the surveillance of the South American data nets. There was an enormous amount of work to be done, at least with the limited powers the Feds were willing to give him. It would likely be October before the welfare machinery was working properly again. But that would be in time for the elections.

Then, late in the week, they wanted him to visit the Coven. Roger knew he would count the hours; it had been so long.

Virginia was her usual self, intense and all business, until she and her driver were ready to leave. Standing in the carport, she said almost shyly, "I ran your *Anne Boleyn* last week. . . . It's really very good."

"You sound surprised."

"No. I mean yes, maybe I was. Actually I've run it several times, usually with the viewpoint character set to Anne. There seems to be a lot more depth to it than other participation games I've read. I've got the feeling that if I am clever enough, someday I'll stop Henry and keep my head!"

Pollack grinned. He could imagine Virginia, the hard-eyed cop, reading *Anne* to study the psychology of her client-prisoner—then gradually getting caught up in the action of the novel. "It is possible."

In fact, it was possible she might turn into a rather nice human being someday.

But by the time Pollack was starting back up the walk to his house, Virginia was no longer on his mind. He was going back to the Coven!

A chill mist that was almost rain blew across the hillside and obscured the far distance in shifting patches. But even from here, on the ridge above the swamp, the castle looked different: heavier, stronger, darker.

Mr. Slippery started down the familiar slope. The frog on his shoulder seemed to sense his unease and its clawlets bit tighter into the leather of his jacket. Its beady yellow eyes turned this way and that, recording everything. (Altogether, that frog was much improved—almost out of amateur status nowadays.)

The traps were different. In just the ten weeks since the War, the Coven had changed them more than in the previous two years. Every so often, he shook the gathering droplets of water from his face and peered more closely at a bush or boulder by the side of the path. His advance was slow, circuitous, and interrupted by invocations of voice and hand.

Finally he stood before the towers. A figure of black and glowing red climbed out of the magma moat to meet him. Even Alan had changed: he no longer had his asbestos T-shirt, and there was no humor in his sparring with the visitor. Mr. Slippery had to stare upward to look directly at his massive head. The elemental splashed molten rock down on them, and the frog scampered between his neck and collar, its skin cold and slimy against his own. The passwords were different, the questioning more hostile, but Mr. Slippery was a match for the tests and in a matter of minutes Alan retreated sullenly to his steaming pool, and the drawbridge was lowered for their entrance.

The hall was almost the same as before: perhaps a bit drier, more brightly lit. There were certainly more people. And they were all looking at him as he stood in the entranceway. Mr. Slippery gave his traveling jacket and hat to a liveried servant and started down the steps, trying to recognize the faces, trying to understand the tension and hostility that hung in the air.

"Slimey!" The Limey stepped forward from the crowd, a familiar grin splitting his bearded face.

"Slip! Is that really you?" (Not entirely a rhetorical question, under the circumstances.)

Mr. Slippery nodded, and after a moment, the other did, too. The Limey almost ran across the space that separated them, stuck out his hand, and clapped the other on the shoulder. "Come on, come on! We have rather a lot to talk about!"

As if on cue, the others turned back to their conversations and ignored the two friends as they walked to one of the sitting rooms that opened off the main hall. Mr. Slippery felt like a man returning to his old school ten years after graduation. Almost all the faces were different, and he had the feeling that he could never belong here again. But this was only ten weeks, not ten years.

The Slimey Limey shut the heavy door, and the sounds from the main room were muted. He waved Slip to a chair and made a show of mixing them some drinks.

"They're all simulators, aren't they?" Slip said quietly.

"Uh?" The Limey broke off his stream of chatter and shook his head glumly. "Not all. I've recruited four or five apprentices. They do their best to make the place look thriving and occupied. You may have noticed various improvements in our security."

"It looks stronger, but it's more appearance than fact."

Slimey shrugged. "I really didn't expect it to fool the likes of you."

Mr. Slippery leaned forward. "Who's left from the old group, Slimey?"

"DON's gone. The Mailman is gone. Wiley J. Bastard shows up a couple of times a month, but he's not much fun anymore. I think Erythrina's still on the System, but she hasn't come by. I thought you were gone until today."

"What about Robin Hood?"

"Gone."

That accounted for all the top talents. Virginia the Frog hadn't been giving away all that much when she excused him from betraying the Coven. Slip wondered if there was any hint of smugness in the frog's fixed and lipless smile.

"What happened?"

The other sighed. "There's a depression on down in the real world, in case you hadn't noticed; and it's being blamed on us vandals.

"—I know, that could scarcely explain Robin's disappearance, only the lesser ones. Slip, I think most of our old friends are either dead—Truly Dead—or very frightened that if they come back into this Plane, they will become Truly Dead."

This felt very much like history repeating itself. "How do you mean?"

The Limey leaned forward. "Slip, it's quite obvious the government's feeding us lies about what caused the depression. They say it was a combination of programming errors and the work of 'vandals.' We know that can't be true. No ordinary vandals could cause that sort of damage. Right after the crash, I looked at what was left of the Feds' data bases. Whatever ripped things up was more powerful than any vandal. . . . And I've spoken with—p'raps I should say interrogated—Wiley. I think what we see in the real world and on this plane is in fact the wreckage of a bloody major war."

"Between?"

"Creatures as far above me as I am above a chimp. The names we know them by are the Mailman, Erythrina . . . and just possibly Mr. Slippery."

"Me?" Slip tensed and sent out probes along the communications links which he perceived had created the image before him. Even though on a leash, Mr. Slippery was far more powerful than any normal warlock, and it should have been easy to measure the power of this potential opponent. But the Limey was a diffuse, almost nebulous presence. Slip couldn't tell if he were facing an opponent in the same class as himself; in fact, he had no clear idea of the other's strength, which was even more ominous.

The Limey didn't seem to notice. "That's what I thought. Now I doubt it. I wager you were used—like Wiley and possibly DON—by the other combatants. And I see that now you're in *someone's* thrall." His finger stabbed at the yellow-eyed frog on Mr. Slippery's shoulder, and a sparkle of whiskey flew into the creature's face. Virginia—or whoever was controlling the beast—didn't know what to do, and the frog froze momentarily, then recovered its wits and emitted a pale burst of flame.

The Limey laughed. "But it's no one very competent. The Feds is my guess. What happened? Did they sight your True Name, or did you just sell out?"

"The creature's my familiar, Slimey. We all have our apprentices. If you really believe we're the Feds, why did you let us in?"

The other shrugged. "Because there are enemies and enemies, Slip. Beforetime, we called the government the Great Enemy. Now I'd say they are just one in a pantheon of nasties. Those of us who survived the crash are a lot tougher, a lot less frivolous. We don't think of this as all a wry game anymore. And we're teaching our apprentices a lot more systematically. It's not near so much fun.

Now when we talk of traitors in the Coven, we mean real, life-and-death treachery.

"But it's necessary. When it comes to it, if we little people don't protect ourselves, we're going to be eaten up by the government or . . . certain other creatures I fear even more."

The frog shifted restively on Mr. Slippery's shoulder, and he could imagine Virginia getting ready to deliver some speech on the virtue of obeying the laws of society in order to reap its protection. He reached across to pat its cold and pimply back; now was not the time for such debate.

"You had one of the straightest heads around here, Slip. Even if you aren't one of us anymore, I don't reckon you're an absolute enemy. You and your . . . friend may have certain interests in common with us. There are things you should know about—if you don't already. An' p'raps there'll be times you'll help us similarly."

Slip felt the Federal tether loosen. Virginia must have convinced her superiors that there was actually help to be had here. "Okay. You're right. There was a war. The Mailman was the enemy. He lost and now we're trying to put things back together."

"Ah, that's just it, old man. *I don't think the war is over.* True, all that remains of the Mailman's constructs are 'craterfields' spread through the government's program space. But something like him is still very much alive." He saw the disbelief in Mr. Slippery's face. "I know, you an' your friends are more powerful than any of us. But there are many of us—not just in the Coven—and we have learned a lot these past ten weeks. There are signs, so light an' fickle you might call 'em atmosphere, that tell us something like the Mailman is still alive. It doesn't quite have the texture of the Mailman, but it's there."

Mr. Slippery nodded. He didn't need any special explanations of the feeling. *Damn! If I weren't on a leash, I would have seen all this weeks ago, instead of finding it out secondhand.* He thought back to those last minutes of their descent from godhood and felt a chill. He knew what he must ask now, and he had a bad feeling about what the answer might be. Somehow he had to prevent Virginia from hearing that answer. It would be a great risk, but he still had a few tricks he didn't think DoW knew of. He probed back along the links that went to Arcata and D.C., feeling the interconnections and the redundancy checks. If he was lucky, he would not have to alter more than a few hundred bits of the information that would flow down to them in the next few seconds. "So who do you think is behind it?"

"For a while, I thought it might be you. Now I've seen you and, uh, done some tests, I know you're more powerful than in the old days and probably more powerful than I am now, but you're no superman."

"Maybe I'm in disguise."

"Maybe, but I doubt it." The Limey was coming closer to the critical words that must be disguised. Slip began to alter the redundancy bits transmitted through the construct of the frog. He would have to fake the record both before and after those words if the deception was to escape detection completely. "No, there's a certain style to this presence. A style that reminds me of our old friend, REorbyitnh rHionoad." The name he said, and the name Mr. Slippery heard, was "Erythrina." The name blended imperceptibly in its place, the name the frog heard, and reported, was "Robin Hood."

"Hmm, possible. He always seemed to be power hungry." The Limey's eyebrows went up fractionally at the pronoun "he." Besides, Robin had been a fantastically clever vandal, not a power grabber. Slimey's eyes flickered toward the frog, and Mr. Slippery prayed that he would play along. "Do you really think this is as great a threat as the Mailman?"

"Who knows? The presence isn't as widespread as the Mailman's, and since the crash no more of us have disappeared. Also, I'm not sure that . . . he . . . is the only such creature left. Perhaps the original Mailman is still around."

And you can't decide who it is that I'm really trying to fool, can you?

The discussion continued for another half hour, a weird three-way fencing match with just two active players. On the one hand, he and the Limey were trying to communicate past the frog, and on the other, the Slimey Limey was trying to decide if perhaps Slip was the real enemy and the frog a potential ally. The hell of it was, Mr. Slippery wasn't sure himself of the answer to that puzzle.

Slimey walked him out to the drawbridge. For a few moments, they stood on the graven ceramic plating and spoke. Below them, Alan paddled back and forth, looking up at them uneasily. The mist was a light rain now, and a constant sizzling came from the molten rock.

Finally Slip said, "You're right in a way, Slimey. I am someone's thrall. But I will look for Robin Hood. If you're right, you've got a couple of new allies. If he's too strong for us, this might be the last you see of me."

The Slimey Limey nodded, and Slip hoped he had gotten the real message: He would take on Ery all by himself.

"Well then, let's hope this ain't good-bye, old man."

Slip walked back down into the valley, aware of the Limey's not unsympathetic gaze on his back.

How to find her, how to speak with her? And survive the experience, that is. Virginia had forbidden him—literally on pain of death—from meeting with Ery on this plane. Even if he could do so, it would be a deadly risk for other reasons. What had Ery been doing in those minutes she dallied, when she had fooled him into descending back to the human plane before her? At the time, he had feared it was a betrayal. Yet he had lived and had forgotten the mystery. Now he wondered again. It was impossible for him to understand the complexity of those minutes. Perhaps she had weakened herself at the beginning to gull him into starting the descent, and perhaps then she hadn't been quite strong enough to take over. Was that possible? And now she was slowly, secretly building back her powers, just as the Mailman had done? He didn't want to believe it, and he knew if Virginia heard his suspicions, the Feds would kill her immediately. There would be no trial, no deep investigation.

Somehow he must get past Virginia and confront Ery—confront her in such a way that he could destroy her if she were a new Mailman. *And there is a way!* He almost laughed: it was absurd and absurdly simple, and it was the only thing that might work. All eyes were on this plane, where magic and power flowed easily to the participants. He would attack from beneath, from the lowly magic-less real world!

But there was one final act of magic he must slip past Virginia, something absolutely necessary for a real world confrontation with Erythrina.

He had reached the far ridge and was starting down the hillside that led to the swamps. Even preoccupied, he had given the right signs flawlessly. The guardian sprites were not nearly so vigilant towards constructs moving away from the castle. As the wet brush closed in about them, the familiar red and black spider—or its cousin—swung down from above.

"Beware, beware," came the tiny voice. From the flecks of gold across its abdomen, he knew the right response: left hand up and flick the spider away. Instead Slip raised his right hand and struck at the creature.

The spider hoisted itself upward, screeching faintly, then dropped toward Slip's neck—to land squarely on the frog. A free-for-all erupted as the two scrambled across the back of his neck, pale flame jousting against venom. Even as he moved to save the frog, Mr. Slippery melted part of his attention into a data line that fed a sporting good store in Montreal. An order was placed and later that day a certain very special package would be in the mail to the Boston International Rail Terminal.

Slip made a great show of dispatching the spider, and as the frog settled back on his shoulder, he saw that he had probably fooled Virginia. That he had expected. Fooling Ery would be much the deadlier, chancier thing.

If this afternoon were typical, then July in Providence must be a close approximation to Hell. Roger Pollack left the tube as it passed the urbapt block and had to walk nearly four hundred meters to get to the tower he sought. His shirt was soaked with sweat from just below the belt line right up to his neck. The contents of the package he had picked up at the airport train station sat heavily in his right coat pocket, tapping against his hip with every step, reminding him that this was high noon in more ways than one.

Pollack quickly crossed the blazing concrete plaza and walked along the edge of the shadow that was all the tower cast in the noonday sun. All around him the locals swarmed, all ages, seemingly unfazed by the still, moist, hot air. Apparently you could get used to practically anything.

Even an urbapt in summer in Providence. Pollack had expected the buildings to be more depressing. Workers who had any resources became data commuters and lived outside the cities. Of course, some of the people here were data-set users too and so could be characterized as data commuters. Many of them worked as far away from home as any exurb dweller. The difference was that they made so little money (when they had a job at all) that they were forced to take advantage of the economies of scale the urbapts provided.

Pollack saw the elevator ahead but had to detour around a number of children playing stickball in the plaza. The elevator was only half-full, so a wave from him was all it took to keep it grounded till he could get aboard.

No one followed him on, and the faces around him were disinterested and entirely ordinary. Pollack was not fooled. He hadn't violated the letter of Virginia's law; he wasn't trying to see Erythrina on the data net. But he was going to see Debby Charteris, which came close to being the same thing. He imagined the Feds debating with themselves, finally deciding it would be safe to let the two godlings get together if it were on this plane where the *State* was still the ultimate, all-knowing god. He and Debby would be observed. Even so, he would somehow discover if she were the threat the Limey saw. If not, the Feds would never know of his suspicions. But if Ery had betrayed them all and meant to set herself up in place of—or in league with—the Mailman, then in the next few minutes one of them would die.

*   *   *

The express slid to a stop with a deceptive gentleness that barely gave a feeling of lightness. Pollack paid and got off.

Floor 25 was mainly shopping mall. He would have to find the stairs to the residential apts between Floors 25 and 35. Pollack drifted through the mall. He was beginning to feel better about the whole thing. *I'm still alive, aren't I?* If Ery had really become what the Limey and Slip feared, then he probably would have had a little "accident" before now. All the way across the continent he sat with his guts frozen, thinking how easy it would be for someone with the Mailman's power to destroy an air transport, even without resorting to the military's lasers. A tiny change in navigation or traffic-control directions, and any number of fatal incidents could be arranged. But nothing had happened, which meant that either Ery was innocent or that she hadn't noticed him. (And that second possibility was unlikely if she were a new Mailman. One impression that remained stronger than any other from his short time as godling was the omniscience of it all.)

It turned out the stairs were on the other side of the mall, marked by a battered sign reminiscent of old-time highway markers: FOOTS > 26–30. The place wasn't really too bad, he supposed, eyeing the stained but durable carpet that covered the stairs. And the hallways coming off each landing reminded him of the motels he had known as a child, before the turn of the century. There was very little trash visible, the people moving around him weren't poorly dressed, and there was only the faintest spice of disinfectant in the air. Apt module 28355, where Debbie Charteris lived, might be high-class. It did have an exterior view, he knew that. Maybe Erythrina—Debbie—*liked* living with all these other people. Surely, now that the government was so interested in her, she could move anywhere she wished.

But when he reached it, he found Floor 28 no different from the others he had seen: carpeted hallway stretching away forever beneath dim lights that showed identical module doorways dwindling in perspective. What was Debbie/Erythrina like that she would choose to live here?

"Hold it." Three teenagers stepped from behind the slant of the stairs. Pollack's hand edged toward his coat pocket. He had heard of the gangs. These three looked like heavies, but they were well and conservatively dressed, and the small one actually had his hair in a braid. They wanted very much to be thought part of the establishment.

The short one flashed something silver at him. "Building Police." And Pollack remembered the news stories about Federal Urban Support paying youngsters for urbapt security: "A project that saves money and staff, while at the same time giving our urban youth an opportunity for responsible citizenship."

Pollack swallowed. Best to treat them like real cops. He showed them his id. "I'm from out of state. I'm just visiting."

The other two closed in, and the short one laughed. "That's sure. Fact, Mr. Pollack, Sammy's little gadget says you're in violation of Building Ordinance." The one on Pollack's left waved a faintly buzzing cylinder across Pollack's jacket, then pushed a hand into the jacket and withdrew Pollack's pistol, a lightweight ceramic slug-gun perfect for hunting hikes—and which should have been perfect for getting past a building's weapon detectors.

Sammy smiled down at the weapon, and the short one continued, "Thing you didn't know, Mr. Pollack, is Federal law requires a metal tag in the butt of these cram guns. Makes 'em easy to detect." Until the tag was removed. Pollack suspected that somehow this incident might never be reported.

The three stepped back, leaving the way clear for Pollack. "That's all? I can go?"

The young cop grinned. "Sure. You're out-of-towner. How could you know?"

Pollack continued down the hall. The others did not follow. Pollack was fleetingly surprised: maybe the FUS project actually worked. Before the turn of the century, goons like those three would have at least robbed him. Instead they behaved something like real cops.

Or maybe—and he almost stumbled at this new thought—*they all work for Ery now.* That might be the first symptom of conquest: the new god would simply become the government. And he—the last threat to the new order—was being granted one last audience with the victor.

Pollack straightened and walked on more quickly. There was no turning back now, and he was damned if he would show any more fear. Besides, he thought with a sudden surge of relief, it was out of his control now. If Ery was a monster, there was nothing he could do about it; he would not have to try to kill her. If she were not, then his own survival would be proof, and he need think of no complicated tests of her innocence.

He was almost hurrying now. He had always wanted to know what the human being beyond Erythrina was like; sooner or later he would have had to do this anyway. Weeks ago he had looked through all the official directories for the state of Rhode Island, but there wasn't much to find: Linda and Deborah Charteris lived at 28355 Place on 4448 Grosvenor Row. The public directory didn't even show their "interests and occupations."

28313, 315, 317 . . .

His mind had gone in circles, generating all the things Debby Charteris might turn out to be. She would not be the exotic beauty she projected in the Other Plane. That was too much to hope for; but the other possibilities vied in his mind. He had lived with each, trying to believe that he could accept whatever turned out to be the case:

Most likely, she was a perfectly ordinary looking person who lived in an urbapt to save enough money to buy high-quality processing equipment and rent dense comm lines. Maybe she wasn't good-looking, and that was why the directory listing was relatively secretive.

Almost as likely, she was massively handicapped. He had seen that fairly often among the warlocks whose True Names he knew. They had extra medical welfare and used all their free money for equipment that worked around whatever their problem might be—paraplegia, quadriplegia, multiple sense loss. As such, they were perfectly competitive on the job market, yet old prejudices often kept them out of normal society. Many of these types retreated into the Other Plane, where one could completely control one's appearance.

And then, since the beginning of time, there had been the people who simply did not like reality, who wanted another world, and if given half a chance would live there forever. Pollack suspected that some of the best warlocks might be of this type. Such people were content to live in an urbapt, to spend all their money on processing and life-support equipment, to spend days at a time in the

Other Plane, never moving, never exercising their real world bodies. They grew more and more adept, more and more knowledgeable—while their bodies slowly wasted. Pollack could imagine such a person becoming an evil thing and taking over the Mailman's role. It would be like a spider sitting in its web, its victims all humanity. He remembered Ery's contemptuous attitude on learning he never used drugs to maintain concentration and so stay longer in the Other Plane. He shuddered.

And there, finally, and yet too soon, the numbers 28355 stood on the wall before him, the faint hall light glistening off their bronze finish. For a long moment, he balanced between the fear and the wish. Finally he reached forward and tapped the door buzzer.

Fifteen seconds passed. There was no one nearby in the hall. From the corner of his eye, he could see the "cops" lounging by the stairs. About a hundred meters the other way, an argument was going on. The contenders rounded the faraway corner and their voices quieted, leaving him in near silence.

There was a click, and a small section of the door became transparent, a window (more likely a holo) on the interior of the apt. And the person beyond that view would be either Deborah or Linda Charteris.

"Yes?" The voice was faint, cracking with age. Pollack saw a woman barely tall enough to come up to the pickup on the other side. Her hair was white, visibly thin on top, especially from the angle he was viewing.

"I'm . . . I'm looking for Deborah Charteris."

"My granddaughter. She's out shopping. Downstairs in the mall, I think." The head bobbed, a faintly distracted nod.

"Oh. Can you tell me—" *Deborah, Debby.* It suddenly struck him what an old-fashioned name that was, more the name of a grandmother than a granddaughter. He took a quick step to the door and looked down through the pane so that he could see most of the other's body. The woman wore an old-fashioned skirt and blouse combination of some brilliant red material.

Pollack pushed his hand against the immovable plastic of the door. "Ery, please. Let me in."

The pane blanked as he spoke, but after a moment the door slowly opened. "Okay." Her voice was tired, defeated. Not the voice of a god boasting victory.

The interior was decorated cheaply and with what might have been good taste except for the garish excesses of red on red. Pollack remembered reading somewhere that as you age, color sensitivity decreases. This room might seem only mildly bright to the person Erythrina had turned out to be.

The woman walked slowly across the tiny apt and gestured for him to sit. She was frail, her back curved in a permanent stoop, her every step considered yet tremulous. Under the apt's window, he noticed an elaborate GE processor system. Pollack sat and found himself looking slightly upward into her face.

"Slip—or maybe I should call you Roger here—you always were a bit of a romantic fool." She paused for breath, or perhaps her mind wandered. "I was beginning to think you had more sense than to come out here, that you could leave well enough alone."

"You . . . you mean, you didn't know I was coming?" The knowledge was a great loosening in his chest.

"Not until you were in the building." She turned and sat carefully upon the sofa.

"I had to see who you really are," and that was certainly the truth. "After this spring, there is no one the likes of us in the whole world."

Her face cracked in a little smile. "And now you see how different we are. I had hoped you never would and that someday they would let us back together on the Other Plane. . . . But in the end, it doesn't really matter." She paused, brushed at her temple, and frowned as though forgetting something, or remembering something else.

"I never did look much like the Erythrina you know. I was never tall, of course, and my hair was never red. But I didn't spend my whole life selling life insurance in Peoria, like poor Wiley."

"You . . . you must go all the way back to the beginning of computing."

She smiled again, and nodded just so, a mannerism Pollack had often seen on the Other Plane. "Almost, almost. Out of high school, I was a keypunch operator. You know what a keypunch is?"

He nodded hesitantly, visions of some sort of machine press in his mind.

"It was a dead-end job, and in those days they'd keep you in it forever if you didn't get out under your own power. I got out of it and into college quick as I could, but at least I can say I was in the business during the stone age. After college, I never looked back; there was always so much happening. In the Nasty Nineties, I was on the design of the ABM and FoG control programs. The whole team, the whole of DoD for that matter, was trying to program the thing with procedural languages; it would take 'em a thousand years and a couple of wars to do it that way, and they were beginning to realize as much. I was responsible for getting them away from CRTs, for getting into really interactive EEG programming—what they call portal programming nowadays. Sometimes . . . sometimes when my ego needs a little help, I like to think that if I had never been born, hundreds of millions more would have died back then, and our cities would be glassy ponds today.

". . . And along the way there was a marriage . . ." her voice trailed off again, and she sat smiling at memories Pollack could not see.

He looked around the apt. Except for the processor and a fairly complete kitchenette, there was no special luxury. What money she had must go into her equipment, and perhaps in getting a room with a real exterior view. Beyond the rising towers of the Grosvenor complex, he could see the nest of comm towers that had been their last-second salvation that spring. When he looked back at her, he saw that she was watching him with an intent and faintly amused expression that was very familiar.

"I'll bet you wonder how anyone so daydreamy could be the Erythrina you knew in the Other Plane."

"Why, no," he lied. "You seem perfectly lucid to me."

"Lucid, yes. I am still that, thank God. But I know—and no one has to tell me—that I can't support a train of thought like I could before. These last two or three years, I've found that my mind can wander, can drop into reminiscence, at the most inconvenient times. I've had one stroke, and about all 'the miracles of modern medicine' can do for me is predict that it will not be the last one.

"But in the Other Plane, I can compensate. It's easy for the EEG to detect failure of attention. I've written a package that keeps a thirty-second backup; when distraction is detected, it forces attention and reloads my short-term memory. Most of the time, this gives me better concentration than I've ever had in my life. And when there is a really serious wandering of attention, the package can interpolate for a number of seconds. You may have noticed that, though perhaps you mistook it for poor communications coordination."

She reached a thin, blue-veined hand toward him. He took it in his own. It felt so light and dry, but it returned his squeeze. "It really is me—Ery—inside, Slip."

He nodded, feeling a lump in his throat.

"When I was a kid, there was this song, something about us all being aging children. And it's so very, very true. Inside I still feel like a youngster. But on this plane, no one else can see . . ."

"But I know, Ery. We knew each other on the Other Plane, and I know what you truly are. Both of us are so much more there than we could ever be here." This was all true: even with the restrictions they put on him now, he had a hard time understanding all he did on the Other Plane. What he had become since the spring was a fuzzy dream to him when he was down in the physical world. Sometimes he felt like a fish trying to imagine what a man in an airplane might be feeling. He never spoke of it like this to Virginia and her friends: they would be sure he had finally gone crazy. It was far beyond what he had known as a warlock. And what they had been those brief minutes last spring had been equally far beyond that.

"Yes, I think you do know me, Slip. And we'll be . . . friends as long as this body lasts. And when I'm gone—"

"I'll remember; I'll always remember you, Ery."

She smiled and squeezed his hand again. "Thanks. But that's not what I was getting at. . . ." Her gaze drifted off again. "I figured out who the Mailman was and I wanted to tell you."

Pollack could imagine Virginia and the other DoW eavesdroppers hunkering down to their spy equipment. "I hoped you knew something." He went on to tell her about the Slimey Limey's detection of Mailman-like operations still on the System. He spoke carefully, knowing that he had two audiences.

Ery—even now he couldn't think of her as Debby—nodded. "I've been watching the Coven. They've grown, these last months. I think they take themselves more seriously now. In the old days, they never would have noticed what the Limey warned you about. But it's not the Mailman he saw, Slip."

"How can you be sure, Ery? We never killed more than his service programs and his simulators—like DON.MAC. We never found his True Name. We don't even know if he's human or some science-fictional alien."

"You're wrong, Slip. I know what the Limey saw, and I know who the Mailman is—or was," she spoke quietly, but with certainty. "It turns out the Mailman was the greatest cliché of the Computer Age, maybe of the entire Age of Science."

"Huh?"

"You've seen plenty of personality simulators in the Other Plane. DON.MAC—at least as he was rewritten by the Mailman—was good enough to fool normal warlocks. Even Alan, the Coven's elemental, shows plenty of human emotion and cunning." Pollack thought of the new Alan, so ferocious and intimidating. The Turing T-shirt was beneath his dignity now. "Even so, Slip, I don't think you've ever believed you could be permanently fooled by a simulation, have you?"

"Wait. Are you trying to tell me that the Mailman was just another simulator? That the time lag was just to obscure the fact that he was a simulator? That's ridiculous. You know his powers were more than human, almost as great as ours became."

"But do you think you could ever be fooled?"

"Frankly, no. If you talk to one of those things long enough, they display a repetitiveness, an inflexibility that's a giveaway. I don't know; maybe someday there'll be programs that can pass the Turing test. But whatever it is that makes a person a person is terribly complicated. Simulation is the wrong way to get at it, because being a person is more than symptoms. A program that was a person would use enormous data bases, and if the processors running it were the sort we have now, you certainly couldn't expect real-time interaction with the outside world." And Pollack suddenly had a glimmer of what she was thinking.

"That's the critical point. Slip: *if you want real-time interaction.* But the Mailman—the sentient, conversational part—never did operate real time. We thought the lag was a communications delay that showed the operator was off-planet, but really he was here all the time. It just took him hours of processing time to sustain seconds of self-awareness."

Pollack opened his mouth, but nothing came out. It went against all his intuition, almost against what religion he had, but it might just barely be possible. The Mailman had controlled immense resources. All his quick time reactions could have been the work of ordinary programs and simulators like DON.MAC. The only evidence they had for his humanity were those teleprinter conversations where his responses were spread over hours.

"Okay, for the sake of argument, let's say it's possible. Someone, somewhere had to write the original Mailman. Who was that?"

"Who would you guess? The government, of course. About ten years ago. It was an NSA team trying to automate system protection. Some brilliant people, but they could never really get it off the ground. They wrote a developmental kernel that by itself was not especially effective or aware. It was designed to live within larger systems and gradually grow in power and awareness, *independent* of what policies or mistakes the operators of the system might make.

"The program managers saw the Frankenstein analogy—or at least they saw a threat to their personal power—and quashed the project. In any case, it was very expensive. The program executed slowly and gobbled incredible data space."

"And you're saying that someone conveniently left a copy running all unknown?"

She seemed to miss the sarcasm. "It's not that unlikely. Research types are fairly careless—outside of their immediate focus. When I was in FoG, we lost thousands of megabytes 'between the cracks' of our data bases. And back then, that was a lot of memory. The development kernel is not very large. My guess is a copy was left in the system. Remember, the kernel was designed to live untended if it ever started executing. Over the years it slowly grew—both because of its natural tendencies and because of the increased power of the nets it lived in."

Pollack sat back on the sofa. Her voice was tiny and frail, so unlike the warm, rich tones he remembered from the Other Plane. But she spoke with the same authority.

Debby's—Erythrina's—pale eyes stared off beyond the walls of the apt, dreaming. "You know, they are right to be afraid," she said finally. "Their world is ending. Even without us, there would still be the Limey, the Coven—and someday most of the human race."

Damn. Pollack was momentarily tongue-tied, trying desperately to think of something to mollify the threat implicit in Ery's words. *Doesn't she understand that DoW would never let us talk unbugged? Doesn't she know how trigger-happy scared the top Feds must be by now?*

But before he could say anything, Ery glanced at him, saw the consternation in his face, and smiled. The tiny hand patted his. "Don't worry, Slip. The Feds are listening, but what they're hearing is tearful chitchat—you overcome to find me what I am, and me trying to console the both of us. They will never know what I really tell you here. They will never know about the gun the local boys took off you."

"What?"

"You see, I lied a little. I know why you really came. I know you thought that *I* might be the new monster. But I don't want to lie to you anymore. You risked your life to find out the truth, when you could have just told the Feds what you guessed." She went on, taking advantage of his stupefied silence. "Did you ever wonder what I did in those last minutes this spring, after we surrendered—when I lagged behind you in the Other Plane?

"It's true, we really did destroy the Mailman; that's what all that unintelligible data space we plowed up was. I'm sure there are copies of the kernel hidden here and there, like cancers in the System, but we can control them one by one as they appear.

"I guessed what had happened when I saw all that space, and I had plenty of time to study what was left, even to trace back to the original research project. Poor little Mailman, like the monsters of fiction—he was only doing what he had been designed to do. He was taking over the System, protecting it from everyone—even its owners. I suspect he would have announced himself in the end and used some sort of nuclear blackmail to bring the rest of the world into line. But even though his programs had been running for several years, he had only had fifteen or twenty hours of human type self-awareness when we did him in. His personality programs were that slow. He never attained the level of consciousness you and I had on the System.

"But he really was self-aware, and that was the triumph of it all. And in those few minutes, I figured out how I could adapt the basic kernel to accept any input personality. . . . That is what I really wanted to tell you."

"Then what the Limey saw was—"

She nodded. "Me . . ."

She was grinning now, an open though conspiratorial grin that was very familiar. "When Bertrand Russell was very old, and probably as dotty as I am now, he talked of spreading his interests and attention out to the greater world and away from his own body, so that when that body died he would scarcely notice it, his whole consciousness would be so diluted through the outside world.

"For him, it was wishful thinking, of course. But not for me. My kernel is out here in the System. Every time I'm there, I transfer a little more of myself.

The kernel is growing into a true Erythrina, who is also truly me. When this body dies," she squeezed his hand with hers, "when this body dies, *I* will still be, and you can still talk to me."

"Like the Mailman?"

"Slow like the Mailman. At least till I design faster processors. . . .

". . . So in a way, I am everything you and the Limey were afraid of. *You* could probably still stop me, Slip." And he sensed that she was awaiting his judgment, the last judgment any human would ever be allowed to levy upon her.

Slip shook his head and smiled at her, thinking of the slow-moving guardian angel that she would become. *Every race must arrive at this point in its history,* he suddenly realized. A few years or decades in which its future slavery or greatness rests on the goodwill of one or two persons. It could have been the Mailman. Thank God it was Ery instead.

And beyond those years or decades . . . for an instant, Pollack came near to understanding things that had once been obvious. Processors kept getting faster, memories larger. What now took a planet's resources would someday be possessed by everyone. Including himself.

Beyond those years or decades . . . were millennia. And Ery.

SCIENCE FICTION:
A SELECTIVE GUIDE TO SCHOLARSHIP

Gary K. Wolfe

Given the considerable number of books and journals now available, it may seem surprising that formal academic scholarship came rather late to the science fiction field. Before the 1970s, the majority of reference works in the field were the work of dedicated fans, and the most astute criticism came from professional writers seeking to establish a serious dialogue about the nature and potential of what they were coming to view as a genuine literary form, and not merely a pop fiction market. The tradition of the writer-critic, established in the 1950s by James Blish, Damon Knight, James Gunn, and a few others, has been a consistent and important part of science fiction scholarship, carried on after the 1950s by Algis Budrys, Norman Spinrad, Alexei Panshin, Samuel R. Delany, and most recently Damien Broderick—all of whom are represented in this bibliography, but who by no means exhaust the list of SF writers who have produced significant criticism (for example, Kim Stanley Robinson's perceptive study of Philip K. Dick is omitted along with all other single-author studies).

For the most part, the work of these writer-critics appeared originally in magazines and later in book form from specialty or commercial publishers. In the 1970s, academic and university presses—perhaps in response to a growing interest in science fiction in the college classroom, perhaps in recognition of a younger generation of literary scholars who were not ashamed of their own interest in the field—began producing substantial numbers of titles which often brought the tools of contemporary literary theory to bear on the genre, adding a whole new set of voices to those of the fans and the professionals—and generating a whole new set of debates. This new interest from the academy also made it apparent that traditional library reference books were of little use to the student of science fiction, and by the end of the 1970s several new reference titles—devoted entirely to the genre and to correcting the lacunae of standard literary references—had also begun to appear (some of these are listed in Section I below).

Scholarly journals devoted to the field had appeared as early as 1959 (with *Extrapolation,* then little more than a newsletter), but blossomed in the 1970s, with the British *Foundation* (1972) and the Canadian-American *Science-Fiction Studies* (1973). Later journals with substantial content involving science fiction include *The Journal of the Fantastic in the Arts* (1988) and *Para•doxa* (1995). Most academic and critical journals, while providing scholarship and criticism that ranges from the brilliant to the impenetrable, are of little use as a guide to the current—or even very recent—state of the field, however. For this, scholars as well as fans must rely on the review columns of the major fiction magazines— *Asimov's, The Magazine of Fantasy and Science Fiction, Analog*—and on the short reviews of fanzines such as *Science Fiction Chronicle* and the Science Fiction Research Association's own *SFRA Review*. In recent years, the *SFRA Review* has sought to publish a few more in-depth articles in an effort to bridge the gap between commercial review media and academic journals. Currently, the best candidates for such a science fiction–oriented "literary magazine" are *Locus,* which began as a fanzine in 1968 and now combines news, reviews, and occasional literary essays; and *The New York Review of Science Fiction* (1988), which emphasizes long reviews and essays rather than news.

The selective list below includes general reference works and broad-based historical or theoretical studies of science fiction. It omits individual author studies; studies focusing on film, television, or art; essay anthologies and conference proceedings; works of a highly specialized nature; teaching and writing guides likely to be unavailable; and works emphasizing allied genres such as utopian fiction or fantasy. For a far more thorough bibliography that does cover many of these areas—annotating over five hundred titles of works about SF— consult Neil Barron's *Anatomy of Wonder,* 4th edition.

I. Major Reference Works

Barron, Neil, ed. *Anatomy of Wonder 4: A Critical Guide to Science Fiction.* Bowker, 1995. The fourth edition of what has become a standard annotated bibliographical guide to fiction as well as nonfiction, research and teaching aids, and library collections of science fiction. Especially valuable for libraries.

Clute, John, and Peter Nicholls, ed. *The Encyclopedia of Science Fiction.* St. Martin's, 1993. With over 4,300 entries and 1.2 million words, easily the most indispensable single reference volume in the field. A 1995 trade paperback corrected errata from the original, and a CD-ROM was also released in 1995.

Pringle, David. *The Ultimate Guide to Science Fiction: An A–Z of Science Fiction Books by Title.* 2nd edition. Scolar Press, 1995. An alphabetical listing of over 3,500 science fiction books by title, complete with brief critical comments and star ratings.

St. James Guide to Science Fiction Writers. 4th edition. St. James Press, 1995. The most recent edition of a reference formerly titled *Twentieth-Century Science Fiction Writers.* Entries include biographical summaries, brief critical essays, and bibliographies.

Survey of Science Fiction Literature. Salem Press, 1979. A five-volume collection of 2,000-word essays on 500 key science fiction works by title. Although quality varies, the treatment of each title is more extensive than in most reference works.

II. Critical and Historical Studies

Aldiss, Brian W., and David Wingrove. *Trillion Year Spree: The History of Science Fiction.* Atheneum, 1986. A revision and expansion of Aldiss's earlier *Billion Year Spree* (1973), and a comprehensive survey of the evolution of science fiction as a literary form, beginning with Mary Shelley's *Frankenstein.* The definitive single-volume history of the field, written with grace and wit and a distinctively personal viewpoint. A good sampling of Aldiss's more personal essays on the field is *The Detached Retina: Aspects of SF and Fantasy* (1995).

Alkon, Paul K. *Origins of Futuristic Fiction.* University of Georgia Press, 1987. A scholarly analysis of the early history of literature set in the future, from 1659 to the early nineteenth century, principally in England and France.

Amis, Kingsley. *New Maps of Hell: A Survey of Science Fiction*. Harcourt, 1960. The first serious discussion of science fiction by a recognized literary figure, this series of lectures was a landmark in gaining wider recognition for the genre.

Bailey, J(ames) O(sler). *Pilgrims Through Space and Time: Trends and Patterns in Scientific and Utopian Fiction*. Argus, 1947. Bailey's adaptation of his 1934 doctoral dissertation was the first scholarly exploration of science fiction's roots, and inspired the name for the Science Fiction Research Association's annual Pilgrim Award, given to distinguished scholars in the field. Much of the work is superseded by later scholarship, however.

Barr, Marleen S. *Feminist Fabulation: Space/Postmodern Fiction*. University of Iowa Press, 1992. An impassioned and personal argument in defense of speculative feminist fiction which "unmasks patriarchal master narratives" and includes works by Lynn Abbey, Marion Zimmer Bradley, Octavia Butler, Isak Dinesen, Gail Godwin, Carol Hill, Doris Lessing, Marge Piercy, Pamela Sargent, and Christa Wolf.

Bartter, Martha A. *The Way to Ground Zero: The Atomic Bomb in American Science Fiction*. Greenwood, 1988. One of the most meticulous studies of a single theme in American science fiction discusses works ranging from pre–World War I "superweapon" stories through to the 1980s, with coverage strongest in the 1940s and 1950s.

Bleiler, Everett M. *Science Fiction: The Early Years*. Kent State University Press, 1991. An ambitious attempt to describe more than 3,000 stories and novels (as well as influential works of nonfiction) which define the prehistory of science fiction from ancient Greece through the 1930s. This is a landmark of SF scholarship, both definitive and indispensable for students of the field's history.

Blish, James (as William Atheling, Jr.). *The Issue at Hand: Studies in Contemporary Magazine Science Fiction*. Advent, 1964. Together with Damon Knight, Blish was a pioneer in establishing critical standards for science fiction during the 1950s. His essays and occasional speeches are collected here and in two additional volumes: *More Issues at Hand* (1970) and *The Tale That Wags the God* (edited by Cy Chauvin, 1987). "William Atheling" is a pseudonym borrowed from Ezra Pound.

Brians, Paul. *Nuclear Holocausts: Atomic War in Fiction, 1895–1984*. Kent State University Press, 1987. A long essay on nuclear war in fiction is followed by a near-definitive (through the early 1980s) annotated bibliography of more than 800 stories and novels, together with a chronology, checklists, and detailed title and subject indexes. An indispensable source for exploring this major theme.

Broderick, Damien. *Reading by Starlight: Postmodern Science Fiction*. Routledge, 1995. As much an exploration of science fiction theory as of science fiction itself, this group of essays offers useful insights concerning the definitions and characteristics of the field, with commentary on works by Delany, Aldiss, and others.

Budrys, Algis. *Benchmarks: Galaxy Bookshelf*. Southern Illinois University Press, 1985. Following Knight and Blish, Budrys was perhaps the field's most significant and controversial writer-critic of the 1960s and 1970s. This volume collects reviews from *Galaxy* magazine in the late 1960s covering some 161 books.

Bukatman, Scott. *Terminal Identity: The Virtual Subject in Postmodern Science Fiction*. Duke University Press, 1993. An ambitious and sometimes densely theoretical attempt to trace the disappearance of the traditional narrative "subject" in works by major recent science fiction writers—although Bukatman actually pays as much attention to various "postmodern" media as to fiction.

Carter, Paul A. *The Creation of Tomorrow: Fifty Years of Magazine Science Fiction*. Columbia University Press, 1977. A knowledgeable and entertaining survey of the major preoccupations revealed by magazine science fiction from 1919 through the 1950s, and one which provides an essential counterpoint to the more novel-based histories of the field. Carter's treatment of the World War II era is especially informative.

Clareson, Thomas D. *Some Kind of Paradise: The Emergence of American Science Fiction.* Greenwood Press, 1985. A comprehensive history of American science fiction from 1870–1930, and a companion piece to Clareson's bibliography *Science Fiction in America, 1870s–1930s.*

Clarke, I. F. *The Pattern of Expectation: 1644–2001.* Basic Books, 1979. A study of future speculation from the eighteenth century to modern science fiction, tracing the shift from technological and scientific optimism to more dystopian visions. Clarke's *Tale of the Future From the Beginning to the Present Day* (1978) is a useful companion bibliography.

Clarke, I. F. *Voices Prophesying War: Future Wars, 1763–3749.* Oxford University Press, 1992. A revision of a classic 1966 study, and the standard history of future war literature, although Clarke's coverage of more recent material is relatively inconsistent.

Clute, John. *Strokes: Essays and Reviews, 1966–1986.* Serconia Press, 1988. Clute is England's leading science fiction critic, and his strong opinions and vivid prose make his reviews worth reading. A later collection, *Look at the Evidence* (1996) contains more recent material, while Clute's bestselling *SF: The Illustrated Encyclopedia* (1995) is of greater interest as a visual companion to the field than as a critical or reference work.

del Rey, Lester. *The World of Science Fiction, 1926–1976: The History of a Subculture.* Ballantine, 1979. An opinionated informal survey, primarily of interest as a major writer's sometimes rather insular view of the field's development.

Delany, Samuel R. *The American Shore: Meditations on a Tale of Science Fiction by Thomas M. Disch.* Angouleme. Dragon Press, 1978. Delany was the first of the writer-critics to combine the professional writer's perspective with that of major postmodernist theoreticians, and this book is the most detailed deconstruction of a single SF text to date. More accessible approaches to Delany's criticism are *The Jewel-Hinged Jaw: Notes on the Language of Science Fiction* (1977), which contains fourteen essays; *Starboard Wine: More Notes on the Language of Science Fiction* (1984), which contains ten, covering such topics as the role of language in science fiction and the ideal science fiction class syllabus; and *Silent Interviews* (1994), a collection of interviews with Delany conducted in writing rather than orally.

Foote, Bud. *The Connecticut Yankee in the Twentieth Century: Travel to the Past in Science Fiction.* Greenwood, 1990. Arguing that Twain's classic established a paradigm for a whole subgenre of science fiction, Foote discusses a wide variety of works in a well-focused thematic study.

Franklin, H. Bruce. *War Stars: The Superweapon and the American Imagination.* Oxford University Press, 1988. Franklin is one of the scholars most astute at treating science fiction themes in sociopolitical perspective, and this cultural history of superweapon ideology covers not only fiction but the role of science fiction in envisioning public policy such as Reagan's "Star Wars" campaign. Franklin's *Future Perfect* (1966; revised 1995) is the standard anthology of nineteenth-century American science fiction, with extensive critical commentary.

Greenland, Colin. *The Entropy Exhibition: Michael Moorcock and the British "New Wave" in Science Fiction.* Routledge, 1983. A history of science fiction's most famous *avant-garde* movement, the "New Wave" of the 1960s in England. Greenland focuses not only on Moorcock, but on Brian Aldiss and J. G. Ballard, as well as sex in SF, "anti-space" and "inner space" fiction, and the theorizing behind the movement.

Gunn, James E. *Alternate Worlds: The Illustrated History of Science Fiction.* Prentice-Hall, 1975. One of the first popular histories of the field, reflecting a kind of consensus view held by many writers and critics of the postwar period. Gunn's essays are in part collected in *Inside Science Fiction: Essays on Fantastic Literature* (1992). Gunn is the only person who has served as president of both the Science Fiction Writers of America and the Science Fiction Research Association, and this dual perspective is reflected in his critical work.

Hartwell, David G. *Age of Wonders: Exploring the World of Science Fiction.* Walker, 1984. An informal general guidebook to the field, combining an editor's perspective with an academic's critical judgments. The 1985 paperback adds reading lists and suggestions for developing a course in SF. A newly revised edition was published in 1996 by Tor Books.

Hillegas, Mark R. *The Future as Nightmare: H. G. Wells and the Anti-Utopians.* Oxford, 1967. An early classic of science fiction criticism, significant for having defined the anti-utopian tradition and its connections to the field. In addition to Wells, Forster, Capek, Zamiatin, Huxley, Orwell, and Lewis, Hillegas discusses Bradbury, Pohl and Kornbluth, Clarke, and Vonnegut.

Hume, Kathryn. *Fantasy and Mimesis: Responses to Reality in Western Literature.* Methuen, 1984. Hume argues that the fantastic—including science fiction—has historically served as a "counter-tradition" to literature's more realistic mimetic tradition, rather than as merely a genre or backwater of literature.

Huntington, John. *Rationalizing Genius: Ideological Strategies in the Classic American Science Fiction Short Story.* Rutgers University Press, 1989. Huntington seeks to reveal the underlying ideologies of three decades of American SF by analyzing the stories in a single anthology—Volume I of *The Science Fiction Hall of Fame.* His intelligent and perceptive readings are very useful to anyone teaching the stories—which often reflect values they do not openly express.

Jakubowski, Maxim, and Edward James. *The Profession of Science Fiction: SF Writers on Their Craft and Ideas.* Macmillan (UK), 1992. A collection of sixteen essays from the English journal *Foundation,* which regularly invites authors to discuss their own work.

James, Edward. *Science Fiction in the 20th Century.* Oxford (UK), 1994. A congenial overview of English and American science fiction from 1895 to the early 1990s, with some theoretical material on reading science fiction and the significance of community to the field. Brief enough to consider as a supplemental historical text in the classroom.

Ketterer, David. *New Worlds for Old: The Apocalyptic Imagination, Science Fiction, and American Literature.* Indiana University Press, 1974. An early attempt to establish a theoretical context for science fiction in American literary history, outlining a tradition that includes Poe, Melville, Twain, and modern writers like Le Guin, Lem, and Vonnegut.

Knight, Damon. *In Search of Wonder: Essays on Modern Science Fiction.* Advent, 1967. A collection of twenty-seven essays from 1951–1960. Along with James Blish, Knight was among the first writer-critics to work toward coherent critical standards, and the emerging aesthetic that one sees in these essays is still provocative today.

Lefanu, Sarah. *In the Chinks of the World Machine: Feminism and Science Fiction.* (Published in the U.S. as *Feminism and Science Fiction.*) The Women's Press, 1988. The most cogent of a considerable number of feminist studies of science fiction demonstrates both awareness of feminist theory and a broad familiarity with both U.S. and European SF by women. Theoretical chapters are followed by discussions of Tiptree, Le Guin, Charnas, Russ, and others.

Le Guin, Ursula K. *The Language of the Night: Essays on Fantasy and Science Fiction,* edited by Susan Wood. Revised edition, HarperCollins, 1992. Originally published in 1979, this collection of essays, speeches, and introductions contains some of the most widely influential critical pieces by a modern science fiction writer. A more broadranging collection is *Dancing at the Edge of the World: Thoughts on Words, Women,*

Places (1989), with thirty-two essays and speeches and seventeen book reviews, few of which focus on science fiction directly.

Lem, Stanislaw. *Microworlds: Writings on Science Fiction and Fantasy,* edited by Franz Rottensteiner. Harcourt, 1985. Ten essays by Poland's leading science fiction writer include an autobiographical piece, discussions of authors, and themes and structures.

McCaffery, Larry. *Storming the Reality Studio: A Casebook of Cyberpunk and Postmodern Science Fiction.* Duke University Press, 1992. A collection of twenty-nine fictional selections and twenty critical essays, designed to provide a theoretical, cultural, and historical context for the "cyberpunk" movement of the 1980s.

Malmgren, Carl. *Worlds Apart: Narratology of Science Fiction.* Indiana University Press, 1991. Malmgren contends that science fiction is more clearly defined by the worlds it creates than by its narrative conventions, and offers a provocative typology of modes and subtypes of the genre.

Malzberg, Barry. *The Engines of the Night: Science Fiction in the Eighties.* Doubleday, 1982. None of these thirty-six essays by science fiction's most famous depressive have to do with science fiction in the 1980s, but the range of topics and the brilliance with which Malzberg portrays the plight of the writer in a commercial genre make this among the more valuable collections of author essays.

Manlove, Colin. *Science Fiction: Ten Explorations.* Kent State, 1986. Manlove is a Scottish fantasy scholar who sees in science fiction a desire for "more life," and explores this through readings of ten representative texts by Asimov, Herbert, Clarke, Farmer, Wolfe, and others.

Meyers, Walter E. *Aliens and Linguists: Language Study and Science Fiction.* University of Georgia Press, 1980. A witty and informed study of languages and linguistic evolution as portrayed in science fiction and fantasy, showing the crucial importance of communication to many SF narratives.

Moylan, Tom. *Demand the Impossible: Science Fiction and the Utopian Imagination.* Methuen, 1986. What Moylan calls the "critical utopia" emerged in the 1970s in works by Russ, Le Guin, Piercy, and Delany, which question both the utopian tradition and their own assumptions. A provocative attempt to link modern science fiction to the utopian tradition.

Nicholls, Peter, David Langford, and Brian Stableford. *The Science in Science Fiction.* Knopf, 1983. An exploration of scientific principles and concepts underlying such topics as space travel, aliens, time travel, future wars, computers and robots, and mental powers, along with a discussion of common SF errors.

Nicolson, Marjorie Hope. *Voyages to the Moon.* Macmillan, 1948. An influential and somewhat dated early study of seventeenth- and eighteenth-century fictional moon trips, with a final chapter touching on Poe, Verne, Wells, and Lewis.

Panshin, Alexei and Cory. *The World Beyond the Hill: Science Fiction and the Quest for Transcendence.* Jeremy P. Tarcher, 1989. An ambitious attempt at an intellectual history of science fiction, valuable mainly for its detailed story-by-story analysis of the development of the "Golden Age" through 1945, mostly in *Astounding Science Fiction.*

Parrinder, Patrick. *Science Fiction: Its Criticism and Teaching.* Methuen, 1980. A brief introduction to the field for students and teachers, including an outline for a possible science fiction course; Parrinder's insights on canon-formation are especially astute. An excellent text, with notes and annotated bibliography, for the beginning student or teacher.

Philmus, Robert. *Into the Unknown: The Evolution of Science Fiction from Francis Godwin to H. G. Wells.* University of California Press, 1970. A literary history of English precursors of science fiction from Godwin and Swift to Verne and Wells. An introduction added to the 1983 paperback notes the growth of scholarship since 1970.

Pierce, John J. *Foundations of Science Fiction: A Study in Imagination and Evolution.* Greenwood, 1987. Pierce originally intended this lengthy study of SF to be published in one volume titled *Imagination and Evolution,* which now provides the subtitle for all four volumes (the second is *Great Themes of Science Fiction,* 1987; the third *When World Views Collide,* 1989; the fourth *Odd Genre,* 1994). An ambitious attempt to write a popular but well-documented history of the genre organized along thematic rather than strictly chronological lines, and viewing science fiction as an evolving fictional portrayal of the scientific world-view. *Odd Genre* is really a separate study of science fiction's relationship to other literature.

Pringle, David. *Science Fiction: The 100 Best Novels—An English-Language Selection, 1949–1984.* Xanadu, 1985. A series of mini-essays on works the author regards as canonical, from Orwell's *1984* to Gibson's *Neuromancer.* Meant to be provocative, the guide is useful for libraries and those new to the field. A companion volume is *Modern Fantasy: The Hundred Best Novels, an English-Language Selection, 1946–1987* (1988).

Rabkin, Eric S. *The Fantastic in Literature.* Princeton University Press, 1976. A clearly presented theory of the fantastic that aligns science fiction and other genres along a continuum according to the degree to which basic "ground rules" are reversed in the fictional world.

Rose, Mark. *Alien Encounters: Anatomy of Science Fiction.* Harvard University Press, 1981. A short but insightful theoretical work that argues that the human-nonhuman encounter is the central paradigm of science fiction.

Ruddick, Nicholas. *Ultimate Island: On the Nature of British Science Fiction.* Greenwood, 1993. Ruddick tries to outline the unique characteristics of British science fiction, arguing that it is neither an offshoot of the American tradition nor an extension of the older "scientific romance."

Russ, Joanna. *To Write Like a Woman: Essays in Feminism and Science Fiction.* Indiana University Press, 1995. Fourteen essays, including some very influential pieces from the early 1970s, by one of the field's most prominent feminist writers and one of its most provocative theorists.

Scholes, Robert. *Structural Fabulation: An Essay on Fiction of the Future.* University of Notre Dame Press, 1975. A brief series of four lectures delivered in 1974, and one of the first analyses of science fiction by a prominent structuralist critic. Scholes sees the field as related to a nonrealistic mode of storytelling he first described in his 1967 study *The Fabulators.*

Scholes, Robert, and Eric S. Rabkin. *Science Fiction: History/Science/Vision.* Oxford, 1977. This introductory text for the general reader begins with a brief history, followed by sections on science, discussions of major SF themes, and short analyses of ten representative novels.

Spinrad, Norman. *Science Fiction in the Real World.* Southern Illinois University Press, 1990. Fourteen essays by a major SF novelist, mostly taken from a book review column, show far more coherence than most such collections, and explore the field's relation to the mainstream, its various modes and power fantasies, and individual writers.

Stableford, Brian M. *Scientific Romance in Britain, 1890–1950.* Fourth Estate, 1985. A major study of a British tradition that Stableford regards as independent of American models and even different from science fiction itself (although Stableford sees the traditions merging by the 1950s). As a sociologist as well as novelist, Stableford not only discusses a great many works with insight, but outlines the changing publishing and market conditions as well.

Suvin, Darko. *Metamorphoses of Science Fiction: On the Poetics and History of a Literary Genre.* Yale University Press, 1979. One of the most influential theoretical studies of science fiction to date, although many find the style dense and abstract. Suvin's idea of "cognitive estrangement," the "novum," and the differences between and utopian literature and science fiction are widely cited. Suvin's ideas are further developed in the detailed bibliographical study *Victorian Science Fiction in the UK: The Discourses of Knowledge and of Power* (1983) and *Positions and Presuppositions in Science Fiction* (1988), a collection of essays.

Wagar, W. Warren. *Terminal Visions: The Literature of Last Things.* Indiana University Press, 1982. A literary and cultural history of secular end-of-the-world fictions from Mary Shelley through the work of Ballard, and the most comprehensive analysis of this major SF theme.

Warner, Harry. *All Our Yesterdays: An Informal History of Science Fiction in the Forties.* Advent, 1969. A rambling anecdotal history of science fiction fandom, mostly of the 1930s and 1940s, and possibly the most complete compilation of information anywhere about the field's organized readership during this period; useful as background on this aspect of science fiction culture.

Warrick, Patricia S. *The Cybernetic Imagination in Science Fiction.* MIT Press, 1980. A survey of human-machine relations in science fiction, based on 225 stories and novels published between 1930 and 1977, all dealing with some aspect of intelligent machines. The broad coverage alone makes this a significant study of its topic.

Wolfe, Gary K. *The Known and the Unknown: The Iconography of Science Fiction.* Kent State University Press, 1979. An examination of recurrent images or "icons" common to science fiction—spaceships, cities, robots, wastelands, monsters—arguing that such icons represent juxtapositions of the known and the unknown, separated by real or symbolic barriers.

Wollheim, Donald A. *The Universe Makers: Science Fiction Today.* Harper, 1971. An opinionated brief survey by an influential editor, notable for its outline of a "consensus cosmogony" of future history drawn from the works of "Golden Age" writers.

Wolmark, Jenny. *Aliens and Others: Science Fiction, Feminism, and Postmodernism.* University of Iowa Press, 1994. A good overview of feminist theory and science fiction, and an effective argument on how feminist writers have altered or subverted traditional gender and power roles in the field.